The tantalizing paranormal romance that la

The Elemental Mysteries

A phone call from an old friend sets Dr. Giovanni Vecchio back on the path of a mysterious manuscript he's hunted for over five hundred years. He never expected a young student librarian could be the key to unlock its secrets, nor could he have predicted the danger she would attract.

Now he and Beatrice De Novo follow a twisted maze that leads from the archives of a university library, though the fires of Renaissance Florence, and toward a confrontation hundreds of years in the making.

History and the paranormal collide in the *Elemental Mysteries*, a paranormal mystery and romance series by *USA Today* bestselling author, Elizabeth Hunter.

PRAISE FOR ELIZABETH HUNTER

Elizabeth Hunter's books are delicious and addicting, like the best kind of chocolate. She hooked me from the first page, and her stories just keep getting better and better. Paranormal romance fans won't want to miss this exciting author!

— THEA HARRISON, NYT BESTSELLING AUTHOR OF THE ELDER RACES

A Hidden Fire is saturated with mystery, intrigue, and romance...this book will make my paranormal romance top ten list of 2011.

— BETTER READ THAN DEAD

Elemental Mysteries turned into one of the best paranormal series I've read this year. It's sharp, elegant, clever, evenly paced without dragging its feet and at the same time emotionally intense.

— NOCTURNAL BOOK REVIEWS

THE ELEMENTAL MYSTERIES

Complete Series Edition

ELIZABETH HUNTER

Copyright © 2013 by Elizabeth Hunter
ISBN: 978-1-941674-33-8
All rights reserved.

All rights reserved. Except as permitted under the US Copyright Act of 1976, no part of this publication may be reproduced, distributed, or transmitted in any form or by any means, or stored in a database or retrieval system, without the prior written permission of the author.

Cover Design: Damonza.com
Edited by: Amy Eye
Formatted by: Elizabeth Hunter

This is a work of fiction. Names, characters, places, and incidents are the products of the author's imagination, or are used fictitiously. Any resemblance to actual persons, living or dead, business establishments, events, or locales is entirely coincidental.

If you're reading this book and did not purchase it or it was not purchased for your use only, please delete it and purchase your own copy from an authorized retailer. Thank you for respecting the hard work of this author.

Recurve Press LLC
PO Box 4034
Visalia, California 93278
USA

For more information about Elizabeth Hunter, please visit: ElizabethHunterWrites.com

*This special edition is dedicated
to the many readers
who have made this fictional world
something far more than I ever imagined.
Thank you.*

A HIDDEN FIRE

*But the queen cherished the wound in her veins...
and was consumed by the hidden fire.*

—Virgil, *Aeneid*, Book IV

PROLOGUE

The man stole down the hallway, his footsteps echoing in the dimly lit basement of the library. He made his way quietly, brushing aside the dark hair that fell into his eyes as he looked down. The security guard turned the corner and approached, his eyes drawn to the tall figure that glided toward him.

"Sir?"

The guard cocked his head, trying to see past the hair covering the man's eyes as he neared him in the flickering service lights.

"Sir, are you looking for the lobby? You're really not supposed to be down here."

He did not speak but continued walking directly toward the portly security guard. As he passed the guard, he held out his hand, silently brushing his finger tips along the guard's forearm before he continued down the hall, around the corner, and up the nearest staircase, never halting in his steady pace.

The guard stilled for a moment before shaking his head. He looked around the passage and wondered why he was in the hallway leading toward the old storage rooms. Checking his watch to see if his break was over, he noticed the second hand seemed to have stopped. He shook his wrist slightly before taking it off and putting it in his pocket.

"Stupid, cheap thing…" he muttered as he turned and headed back toward the break room. In the distance, he thought he heard a door in the stairwell click close.

. . .

Waiting in the deserted stacks near the bank of computer terminals on Friday evening, the man read a periodical while he observed the student-study area. His eyes scanned to the left, suddenly alert to the plain, blond girl who took a seat on the edge of the bank of computers. He observed her pull out an economics textbook and sneak a quick sip of her diet soda before she put it back in her bag. The corner of his mouth lifted, pleased by how little attention the girl had drawn from the librarian at the desk and the surrounding students.

He approached, shifting his leather messenger bag so he could sit down at the computer next to her. Taking out his own drink, he smiled politely when the girl glanced at him. He saw her cheeks fill with color as she took in his pale skin, startling green eyes, and dark curls.

"Hello," he whispered, angling his shoulders toward the student.

"Hi," she whispered back.

"Are the librarians here strict about having a drink out? I'm new at the university." He leaned toward her and noticed the scent of her fruity shampoo. He twitched his nose but remained angled toward the young woman as she responded.

"Um...not really near the stacks, but they're kind of strict by the computers," she said, her hands twisting in her lap.

When he smiled, she blushed and looked back to her economics textbook which still lay closed on the desk in front of her. She fumbled it open and glanced at his bag, which lay near his feet.

"Thanks," he said.

"Are you a student here?"

He smiled and whispered back, "I just started some research work at the university."

"Oh, that's cool. I'm Hannah. I'm a sophomore...economics."

"That's a fascinating subject, Hannah." He tried to meet her eyes, but she was still looking down at her textbook as she leafed through it.

"Oh," she laughed. "You don't have to be nice. I know most people aren't really that interested in economics."

"I'm interested in everything," he said, willing her to look up. When she did, he set his elbow next to her economics textbook and reached over with his right hand, lightly touching her forearm as he spoke. "Are you a good student, Hannah?"

She gazed into his eyes, rapt with attention and unaware of the small hairs all over her body as they lifted, drawn toward the man sitting next to her.

"Yes, I get excellent grades."

"Why are you here on a Friday night?"

"I don't have a lot of friends, and boys never ask me out," she said. "I like to come here so I'm not alone in my dorm room."

"Do you have time to help me?"

"Yes. I don't really have any school work I need to finish."

"Excellent." The man leaned toward her and murmured in the young woman's ear. She turned on the computer as he spoke, opening a search engine and typing in the phrases he murmured. He hooked his ankle with hers under the table, letting his pale skin maintain contact as he took notes in a small brown book he drew from his messenger bag. Every now and then he would lean over and whisper further instructions in the girl's ear.

A little over two hours later, he leaned back in his chair, frowning as he surveyed his notes. He looked at the large clock on the wall opposite him and at his unwitting assistant before he closed his notebook, put it back in his leather bag, and scooted away from Hannah. Keeping one hand on her shoulder and letting his fingers stroke her neck, he whispered in her ear one more time before he straightened and walked swiftly away from the computer terminals.

He kept his head down, striding toward the darkened glass of the lobby and the pressing heat of the September evening. Once he reached the doors, he looked up, and his gaze briefly met a black-haired girl's before he pushed out into the humid night and left behind the harsh fluorescent lights of Houston University's main campus library.

He walked down the concrete steps and through the alley of darkened oak trees, taking out his keys as he neared a charcoal grey, vintage Mustang. He unlocked the car, got in, and started the engine, listening with pleasure to the rhythm of the perfectly tuned engine.

Backing out, he flicked the radio knob to the local campus station and rolled the window down as he enjoyed the lick of warm, humid air along his skin.

He sped toward the lights of downtown, bypassing the tall buildings and speeding along Buffalo Bayou as he drove toward the gates of his secluded home. He turned into the short drive before the gate and tapped in the entry code with the end of a stainless steel pen he drew from the chain around his neck.

The Mustang drove forward, winding its way through the dimly lit property. He pulled his car into the brick garage behind his home and walked through the small courtyard between the outbuilding and the main house. He stopped, listening to the burbling fountain and admiring the honeysuckle vine that trailed up the garage wall and suffused the small courtyard with fragrance.

All the lights were on in the kitchen when he entered the house, and he immediately grabbed a pencil on the counter to dim them. He walked up the back stairs to his dark bedroom, disrobing and hanging his clothes in the large closet before he walked down the main stairwell, wrapped only in a large, finely spun towel. As he passed the second floor landing, he was stopped by an accented voice coming from the library.

"Back so soon?"

He turned to look at the older gentleman who was reading in front of the lit fireplace.

"A fire, Caspar?"

The older man shrugged. "I turned the air-conditioning down so it at least felt like fall."

He chuckled. "Whatever you prefer. And the library was a bit disappointing."

"Trouble finding an assistant?"

"No, I found a rather good one, in fact. I might meet her again. No, the Lincoln documents were not what I'd hoped."

"Unfortunate."

The man shrugged his shoulders. "The client isn't going anywhere."

"Off for your swim then?"

He nodded and started to move down the stairs again.

"Will you be needing anything tonight?"

He walked up the stairs and back toward the library. "Nothing, thank you."

"Enjoy the pool. It's a beautiful night."

"Enjoy your air-conditioning... and your fire," he said with a minute smile ghosting his lips.

He heard Caspar laugh as he continued down the stairs. The man walked through the sitting room and past the breakfast area where Caspar ate in the morning to the French doors leading onto the brick patio.

He folded his towel on the back of a pool chaise and quickly dove into the water, cutting through the green-lit pool with effortless efficiency.

He swam up and down the mirrored rectangle for hours, enjoying the stretch of his lean muscles and the calming buoyancy of the salt water that filled the pool.

When the lights of the secluded yard switched off automatically at two in the morning, he floated on the surface. He hung there for a few minutes, enjoying the feeling of the warm, humid air on his face as his body was supported by the water at his back. Then he dove down, sitting on the bottom of the pool for another hour, looking up as he watched the moon track across the night sky.

CHAPTER 1

Houston, Texas
September 2003

Giovanni Vecchio woke, the infrequent dream seeming to echo off the narrow walls of the small room where he rested. He sat up and stared at the photograph of Florence which hung on the opposite wall, and the sun-seared shops of the old bridge mocked him.

"Where is your home?"
"Ubi bene ibi patria. Where I prosper is my home."
"Do not forget: nothing endures, save us and the elements."

Rising, he unlocked his reinforced door and stepped into the large walk-in closet where he dressed in a white oxford shirt and a pair of slim, black slacks. He spied the grey cat from the corner of his eye.

"Good evening, Doyle."

The cat turned his copper-eyed stare toward the tall man who spoke to him.

"What did Caspar bribe you with tonight, hmm? Salmon? Fresh anchovies? Caviar?"

The cat gave a small chirp and walked out to the luxurious bedroom beyond the closet to settle on the king-sized bed there. Giovanni's thoughts still brushed at the dark dream and a faint memory teased the back of his mind.

"Tell me about death."

"The philosopher said death, which men fear as the greatest evil, may instead be the greatest good."

"But we do not fear death, do we?"

Despite the hours he had rested, he felt weary. He reached for his favorite grey jacket and walked out of the room.

"Caspar," he called as he entered the kitchen, still straightening his collar. "I want you to drive me to the library tonight."

The older man raised a curious eyebrow but put down the newspaper he had been reading.

"Of course, I'll get the car."

Giovanni gathered his messenger bag and followed Caspar out the kitchen door. They walked through the small courtyard where the dim light of the early evening still illuminated the burbling fountain, and the air was rich with the fragrance of the honeysuckle vine.

"Balance! Temperance! Find it, my son, or you will die."

He paused for a moment and watched the flow of water as it trickled over and around the rocks in the base of the fountain. Just then, a sharp breeze lifted the spray and it arched toward him, dusting his face with the cold drops. He let the heat rise to his skin and the vapor met the humid night air.

"OH WOW, CHAR WASN'T LYING."

Giovanni brushed the hair out of his eyes and glanced up from his notebook looking around for the quiet female voice as he paused in the entry to the Special Collections reading room at the Houston University library.

"Pardon me?" he asked in confusion to the girl in the corner.

The black-haired girl behind the counter smiled. He noticed a slight blush coloring her fair skin.

"Nothing," she said with a quick smile. "Nothing at all. Welcome to the Special Collections reading room. You must be Dr. Vecchio."

Giovanni frowned as he tucked his notebook into a leather messenger bag. "I am. Is Mrs. Martin unavailable this evening?" He scanned the young woman sitting behind the reference desk on the fifth floor of the library. Since the department had opened their once-weekly evening hours a year ago, the bookish Charlotte Martin had been the only employee he'd seen behind the desk of the small, windowless room that housed the rare books, manuscripts, and archives.

"She's not able to do evening shifts anymore. Family reasons, I think. Something about her kids. I'm B, her assistant." Her voice lacked the twang typical of most Texans, though the flat intonation with only a hint of accent was fairly common among native Houstonians, especially those of younger generations. "She left me notes about what you've been working on, so I'm perfectly able to assist you in your research."

Despite her rather common accent, the girl's voice held a faint quality which told him at least one of her parents was a native Spanish speaker. Her thick, black hair was pulled into a low ponytail at the nape of her neck, and she was dressed in a black button-down shirt and slim skirt. He smiled when he saw the tops of her tall Doc Marten boots almost touching her knees.

"Are you a student?" he asked.

Her chin jutted out in a barely perceptible movement which matched the quick flash of intelligence in her eyes. "I've worked here for almost three years. I'm sure doing a quick computer search or fetching a document is well within my abilities, Dr. Vecchio."

He could feel the smile crawl across his face. "I meant no disrespect...I'm sorry, what was your name?"

"Just call me B," she said, glancing down at some handwritten notes.

From where he was standing, Giovanni could see the familiar scrawl of Mrs. Martin's handwriting.

"*B?* As in the second letter of the Latin alphabet?" he asked, walking closer to the desk.

"No, the Etruscan. I'm wild like that," she muttered and glanced up. "She also put a small note here at the bottom of her instructions regarding you."

"Yes?" He waited, curious what the librarian thought bore mention to her replacement.

"Hmm, it just reads, 'He comes in every week. You're welcome.'" The girl's eyes ran from his handmade shoes, up his tall figure, finally meeting his startling, blue-green eyes. "Thanks indeed, Char," she said with a smile.

He was amused by her obvious look of approval, noting the small ruby piercing in her nose that caught the florescent lights of the reading room. Her eyes were lined in black, her skin was fair, and though she did not have classically beautiful features, he thought her dramatic looks would be eye-catching even from a distance.

"I saw you Friday night!" she blurted. "I was coming in to meet a friend after her shift. I saw you heading out."

Glancing away from her toward the door, he brushed at the dark curls that had fallen into his eyes again. "That's possible," he noted. "I like working in the evenings here."

She shrugged. "Well, obviously."

"Why?" he asked. "Why obviously?"

She raised her eyebrows. "Because you're here now? Instead of the middle of the day?"

He blinked. "Of course."

"So what do you do?"

"Me?"

The girl snorted and looked around the otherwise empty room. "Yeah."

He opened his mouth and almost considered telling her the truth, just to see what the unusual girl might say.

"I do...research."

She stood, as if waiting for him to continue. When he didn't, she smiled politely and held out a hand. "Well, it's very nice to meet you."

He paused for a moment then held out his own hand to shake hers.

"Nice to meet you as well..." He frowned a little. "What's your *real* name?"

"Why?"

"I..." Giovanni had no idea why he wanted to know, except perhaps, because she didn't seem to want to tell him. So he flashed her his most charming smile and cheered internally when he heard her heart speed up.

She rolled her eyes. "My 'real' name is Beatrice. But I hate it, so please just call me B. Everyone does, even Dr. Christiansen," she added, referencing the very formal Director of Special Collections for the library.

"Of course," he said with a small smile. "I was simply curious. For the record, however, I think Beatrice is a lovely name." He made sure to pronounce her name with the softer Italian accent it deserved.

She rolled her eyes again and tried to keep from smiling. "Well, thanks. What can I get for you this evening, Dr. Vecchio?"

"The Tibetan manuscript, please."

"Of course." She handed over a small paper slip so he could fill out the formal request for the item. Then she reached into the desk drawer to hand him a pair of silk gloves necessary for handing any of the ancient documents in the collection.

He took a seat at one of the tables in the windowless room, laying out his notebooks, a box of pencils, and a set of notes for Tenzin written in Mandarin. After a few minutes, Beatrice walked through the door from the stacks. Carefully placing the grey paper box containing the fifteenth century Tibetan book on the counter, she turned back to make sure the door to the air-controlled room was closed and locked before she walked around the desk and toward Giovanni.

> "*There is a book you need to copy for me,*" *Tenzin had asked.*
>
> "*Why do you need it copied? Isn't there a translation available somewhere?*"
>
> "*No, I want this one. It's in Houston. Didn't you just move there?*"
>
> *He frowned.* "*I didn't move here so I could copy books for you, bird girl.*"
>
> "*How do you know? Maybe that's exactly why you moved there.*"
>
> "*Ten—*"

"I have to fly. Be a good scribe and copy it. Use the...what do you call it when you send me things?"

"The fax machine."

"Yes, use that. I'm going into the mountains for a while. Have Caspar send them to Nima for me when you're done."

"I'm busy right—"

She had already hung up.

He noted again how well-preserved the manuscript was as the girl opened the acid-free paper box. The manuscript was a series of square, painted panels that contained spells purportedly used by goddesses for healing. The carved wooden covers and gold and black ink were startling in their clarity, and though it held the musty odor typical of old documents, he noted with satisfaction very little scent of mold or mildew clung to it.

"Please wear your gloves at all times and handle the pages as little as possible. Please keep all manuscript materials inside the box as you examine them. If you need further assistance in examining the document, please..."

Listening absently to the rote instructions the girl offered, his mind had already moved ahead to his task for the evening. He'd copied the first third of the small volume over the summer. He estimated careful transcription of the manuscript would take another four to five months at the rate he was working. Fortunately, time was not an issue for him on this project.

He settled down to take advantage of the two hours he had left to work on the transcription. He hoped to finish the second of the six sections by the end of the week so he could have Caspar fax it to Nima with his notes.

"Dr. Vecchio?"

"Hmm?" He bit his lip, lost in his own thoughts.

"Did you have any questions?"

He flashed her a smile before turning his face back to his work.

"No, I'm fine. Thank you, Beatrice," he said, his concentration already shifted to the manuscript in front of him. He heard the young woman quietly return to her seat behind the computer.

They worked for the next two hours, both occupied in their own projects. Every now and then, she would glance at him, but he barely noticed, engrossed in his careful transcription. The soughing of the air-conditioner provided background noise to the turning paper, the scratching of his pencil, and the quiet click of the young woman's keyboard as she typed.

Shortly before nine o'clock, she closed her books and walked to his table. He looked up at her, dazed from concentration. He saw her take note of his precise transcription of the characters. They were a nearly exact copy of the original, down to the thickness of the brush strokes he recreated with the tip of his pencil, over and over again.

"Dr. Vecchio, I have to ask for the manuscript now. The reading room is closing in fifteen minutes."

He blinked. "Oh... yes, if I could finish this last character set?"

"Of course." She waited for him, and Giovanni smiled politely as he closed the manuscript, repacked it, and put the lid on the box.

The girl took the book back to the locked stacks to put it away in the dim room where it was housed. As she locked up the stacks room, she turned back to see Giovanni putting his pencils and notes away in his leather messenger bag.

"Well—"

"Why don't you like the name Beatrice?" he asked, looking down as he fastened the brass buckle of his bag.

"Excuse me?"

He looked up at her, dark hair falling into his eyes again.

"It's a lovely name. Why do you prefer to be called by your initial?"

"It's...old. My name—it sounds like an old woman to me."

He smiled enigmatically. "Yet, you work around old things all the time."

"I guess I do."

He leaned his hip against the sturdy wooden table.

"She was Dante's muse, you know."

"Of course I know. That's why I have the stupid name to begin with. My dad was a Dante scholar." Beatrice looked down to straighten her own papers on the desk. "Kind of a fanatic, really."

He cocked his head and studied her. "Oh? Does he teach here?"

She paused and shook her head. "No, he died ten years ago. In Italy."

His eyes darted back to the table, and he pulled the strap of his bag over his head as some faint memory tickled the back of his mind.

"I'm sorry. It's none of my business. Forgive my curiosity."

She frowned. "I'm not going to start weeping or anything, if you're worried about that. It was a long time ago."

"Nevertheless, I apologize. Good evening, Beatrice." He exited the room, taking care to make as little noise as possible as he slipped down the dark hallway.

He entered the musty stairwell, taking a deep breath of the humid air to gauge who else was present. Satisfied he was alone, he rapidly descended to the first floor and made his way through the still crowded student-study area. As he approached the glass entrance, he caught a glimpse of Beatrice in the dark reflection as she stood near the elevator in the lobby, her mouth gaping as she stared at him. Not turning for even a moment, he pushed his way into the dark night and strolled toward the parking lot adjacent to the library.

When he reached it, he saw the slight flare of the cigarette as Caspar leaned against the black Mercedes sedan.

"A good evening, Gio?"

Giovanni frowned at his old friend, flicking the cigarette out of Caspar's mouth as he approached the door. He stood in front of the man, looking down on him as he spoke.

"I don't like the cigarettes. I thought you had given them up."

Caspar looked up with a mischievous grin. "If I'm only living for eighty years or so, I'm going to enjoy them."

Giovanni opened his mouth as if to say something but then shook his head and slid into the dark interior of the late-model sedan. Reaching into his messenger bag, he slid on a pair of leather gloves and crossed his arms while his friend got behind the wheel.

"Any requests?" Caspar fiddled with the stereo as Giovanni's eyes scanned the dark parking lot.

"Are the Bach fugues still in the changer?"

"Indeed they are."

Caspar switched the CD player on. In a few moments, the sedan was filled with the alternately lively and melancholy notes of the piano. Giovanni sat motionless, listening with pleasure to the modern recording of one of his favorite pieces of music.

"Mrs. Martin was not in the library this evening," Giovanni said, his voice low and bearing more than its usual light accent.

"Oh? Everything all right?"

He shrugged. "Look into it tomorrow. Call and find out why she's changed her hours. If it is simply a family issue, then it is no concern of ours."

"Of course."

The car was silent as it turned toward Buffalo Bayou.

"Inform me if it is anything other than that."

"I'll take care of it."

A few moments later, they pulled up to the gate, and the wrought iron swung aside at their approach. Giovanni pulled out his pen and used it to push down the button for the automatic window, enjoying the smooth rush of air into the vehicle as it made its way toward the house. The grounds were suffused with the scent of clematis and roses that night, and the air smelled strongly of cut grass.

"The gardeners came early," he noted.

Caspar nodded. "They did. We're supposed to get rain tonight."

"There is a new employee at the desk."

"Is that so?" Caspar stopped the car near the rear courtyard, shifting the car into park so his employer could exit the vehicle before he put it in the garage behind the house.

"A girl. A student. Beatrice De Novo. Check on her, as well."

"Of course. Anything in particular you want to know?"

He opened the door, reaching down for his leather bag before he stepped out. "There's something about the father. He was killed ten years ago in Italy. Let me know if anything jumps out at you."

"I'll take care of it."

Giovanni climbed out of the car, resting his hand lightly on the door frame. Leaning down, he spoke again to his friend.

"I'm swimming for a bit, and then I'll be in the music room for the rest of the night. I won't need anything. Good night."

And with that, he stood up, nudged the car door closed, made his way across the courtyard with the bubbling fountain, and strode into the dark house.

Caspar drove the car back to the garage, parked it, and sat in the driver's seat, petting the steering wheel lightly.

"He's getting better, darling. Only one little short on the door panel this time. Not that he noticed, of course."

Chuckling, he exited the vehicle, locked the garage, and made his way into the house, flipping on all the lights in the kitchen. He thumbed through the mail again, separating the household bills from the extensive correspondence of his employer, before he shut all but one of the lights off again and made his way to the library on the second floor.

Pouring himself a brandy, Caspar settled down with the first edition of *A Study in Scarlet* that Giovanni had given him for his sixtieth birthday. Forgoing a fire, he opened the window facing the front garden and enjoyed the closeness of the night air, which smelled of the grass clippings the gardeners had raked that afternoon.

An hour or so later, he paused when he heard the door to the music room close as Giovanni shut himself in. Caspar wondered which instrument would catch his attention, praying it wasn't one of the louder brasses. He breathed out a sigh when he heard the first notes of the piano struck. From Giovanni's thoughtful mood earlier in the evening, he expected to hear Bach, so he was surprised to hear the strange Satie melody drift up from the first floor.

"There's something about the father. He was killed ten years ago in Italy."

Caspar frowned as he remembered the familiar light he'd seen in Giovanni's eyes. He hadn't seen that light for almost five years. Part of him had hoped to never see it again.

"What are you up to, Gio?" he muttered as he stared out the open window.

The gentle dissonance of the piano was unexpectedly disturbing to the man as he sat in his favorite chair. A breeze came through the window, carrying the earthy smell of coming rain to his nose. Caspar stood, walked to the window, and shut it just before fat drops began to fall.

CHAPTER 2

"Grandma! I'm going to be late for class."

"One more shot, *Mariposa*, just let me...there. All done. The light was exactly right on that one."

Isadora Alvarez De Novo set down the camera and smiled. Beatrice stood up from the small table near the windows and plucked her bag from the floor.

"Are you painting this afternoon?" she asked as she bent to kiss her grandmother's wrinkled cheek.

"Yes, yes. I'll be in the studio all day. Will you be home for dinner?"

"Nope. Wednesday, remember? Night hours."

"Oh, of course, handsome professor day!"

"He's not a professor, Grandma. He just has a doctorate and does research at the library. I'm not sure what he is, to be honest."

"Besides tall, dark, and handsome?"

Beatrice rolled her eyes. "You mean fastidious, formal, and silent?"

"Oh, you say that, but he's probably just shy. Maybe it's because he's European."

Beatrice shook her head before she filled her travel mug from the small coffee press her grandmother had prepared for her. "I don't know. He is mysterious, that's for sure."

"He never talks to you?"

The young woman shrugged. "Sure, a little. He's always polite. I've tried making conversation, but he's very...focused. He always looks absorbed in his work. But, I could swear I've felt him watching me more than once."

Her grandmother smiled. "You're a beautiful girl, Beatrice. He would have to be blind not to notice."

Beatrice chuckled. "I really don't think it's like that. No, it's not like he's checking me out, more like he's…observing."

The old woman's eyes widened. "Could he be gay? Oh, what a disappointment. Though, maybe I could introduce him to Marta's boy then—"

"Grandma!" she laughed. "I have no idea. It's none of my business. I should be embarrassed gossiping about patrons like this. And I really have to go."

"Fine, but you need to find some nice boy to have fun with. The last one was so boring."

Beatrice walked out the door. "I'll see what I can do," she called out. "Bye!"

She sped out the door and down the steps of the small house near Rice University where she had grown up with her grandparents. Passing the oak tree that shaded the driveway, her eyes caught the dark, twisted grooves cut into the trunk close to forty years before.

S.D.

Stephen De Novo. She climbed into her small car. Despite what she had claimed to the curious Dr. Vecchio, the hollow pang of his loss still marked her life. Despite his busy schedule, she and her father had been very close. With the passing of her grandfather, Beatrice and Isadora were all that was left of the tight-knit De Novo family.

She pulled into the university parking lot and grabbed the first spot she found, running to her first class as soon as her feet hit the ground.

In fact, Beatrice felt like she ran all day, and by the time she got to the library at four o'clock, she was ready to collapse. She took the cantankerous elevator up to the fifth floor and put her books in the small office she shared with her supervisor.

"B?" she heard Charlotte call from the copy and photography room.

"Yeah, Char, I'm here. I'm sorry I'm late, it's seems like—"

"Oh, don't worry about it," Charlotte Martin said as she walked toward the reference desk. The young woman switched on the computer at the desk and logged into the library's system. "It's Wednesday today," Charlotte said with a grin.

"Yes, it is."

"Wednesday means night hours for you."

"No!" Beatrice gasped. "I'd totally forgotten about that."

"Liar." Charlotte paused for effect. "So, have you had any luck with the mysterious Dr. Vecchio?"

"What? Why is everyone asking about him today? Did you and my grandma have a meeting?"

Charlotte laughed. "No! I'm just curious. You've seen him for what—three weeks now? I'm curious what you think. He's quite the mystery around the library, you know."

"Librarians have vivid imaginations and far too much time on their hands. I think he's just a historian or something."

"A really hot, *Italian* historian with a cute—but not indecipherable—accent," Charlotte said as she wiggled her eyebrows. "And you're a gorgeous, single almost-librarian. I see possibilities."

"You and my grandmother are far too interested in my love life, or lack thereof. But thanks for calling me 'gorgeous.'"

"You are," Charlotte sighed. "You have the most perfect skin. I kind of hate you."

"And you have the perfect husband and two perfect children, so I think you win. Is Jeff enjoying having you home every night?"

Charlotte smiled and nodded. "Yes, all joking aside, thanks for taking the evening hours. It makes a huge difference with the boys involved in so many activities now."

"No problem. I can always use the cash."

"Speaking of cash, did I tell you someone very wealthy and very generous just donated a couple of letters from the Italian Renaissance to the library? We should be getting them in the next couple of weeks."

"Letters? What are they?"

Charlotte shrugged. "Not sure. I haven't seen them. I guess they're a couple letters from some Florentine poet to a friend who was a philosopher. Late fifteenth century, supposedly very well-preserved. I should remember the names, but I don't. They were in some private collection, from what I hear. Honestly, I have no idea why the university is getting them."

"Huh." Beatrice frowned. "We have hardly anything from that period. Most of the Italian stuff we have is late medieval."

"I know," Charlotte shrugged again, "but they were donated, so no one's going to complain."

"When do they get here?"

"A few weeks, maybe closer to a month or so." Charlotte laughed. "I thought Christiansen was going to piss his pants, he was so excited when he told me."

"And thank you for that mental image," she snorted. "I'm going to go to check the dehumidifiers in the stacks. I'll see you in a bit."

Beatrice was still shaking her head when she entered the manuscript room, chuckling at her playful supervisor. Charlotte Martin's enthusiasm for books and information was one of the reasons the young woman had decided to pursue a master's degree in library science. Far from stuffy, Beatrice had discovered that most libraries were small hotbeds of gossip and personal intrigue. Intrigue that she enjoyed observing but also tried to avoid by hiding in her own small department.

She checked the moisture readings in the stacks, tracking and resetting the meter for the next twenty-four hours. She walked to the center of the room to empty the plastic container from the dehumidifier that pulled excess water from the thick, South Texas air, so it wouldn't damage the delicate residents of the manuscript room.

After completing her duties in back, she pulled one of her favorite books from the shelves and opened it, poring over the vivid medieval illuminations in a German devotional. After a few minutes, she tore herself away to go help Charlotte with some filing before she settled at the reference desk for the evening and began to work on a paper for one of her classes.

At five-thirty, Charlotte waved good-bye, and by seven o'clock, Beatrice heard the familiar steps of Dr. Giovanni Vecchio—mysterious Ph.D., translator of Tibetan texts, and all around hot-piece-of-gossip-inducing-ass—enter the reading room.

"Good evening, Miss De Novo. How are you tonight?"

She heard his soft accent as he approached and saved the file she was working on before she looked up with a smile. He was wearing a pair of dark-rimmed glasses and a grey jacket that evening. His face was angular, handsome in a way that reminded her of one of the photographs in her art history textbook. His dark, curly hair and green eyes were set off by a pale complexion that seemed out of place on someone with a Mediterranean background.

Beatrice decided that no one should be that good looking—especially if they were smart. It simply put the rest of the population at a disadvantage.

"Fine, thanks. I'm fine." She sighed almost imperceptibly, and straightened her black skirt as she stood. "The Tibetan manuscript again?"

He flashed a smile and nodded. "Yes, thank you."

Beatrice went back to retrieve what she had begun to think of as "his" manuscript and walked out to Giovanni's table in the far corner of the small room. Setting it down, she noticed he already had his pencils, notebooks, and notes from the week before laid out on the table. He was nothing, if not organized and well-prepared.

"Do you need the spiel?" she asked as she handed him his silk gloves.

He smiled. "Not unless you are required to give it every time I'm here."

"I've seen you here a few weeks now. If you won't tell, I won't."

"Your flagrant disregard of protocol will be our secret, Beatrice," he said with a wink that set her heart racing. She hated her name, but maybe she didn't hate it quite as much when it rolled off his tongue with that sexy accent.

She just smiled and tried to breathe normally. "I'll be at the desk if you need anything."

"Thank you." He nodded and slipped on the gloves to pick up the book. As always, she noticed the seemingly incongruent features which only added to the mystery he presented.

His fingers were long and graceful, reminding her more of an artist than a scholar, but the body beneath his casually professional wardrobe looked like that of a trained athlete. He appeared fastidious in his appearance, but his hair always seemed just a bit too long. No matter how he was dressed, she always smiled when she saw his expression, his concentrated frown and preoccupied gaze were one hundred percent academic.

Suppressing a snicker, she went back to writing her paper.

They both worked quietly for another hour. When she finished her homework, she looked in her bag and realized she had forgotten the paperback she was reading that morning.

"Damn," she whispered.

He looked up from his work. "What?"

She frowned and looked up, surprised he had heard. "Oh, I'm sorry. It's nothing. Just forgot my book at home."

She thought she heard him laugh a little.

"What?"

He couldn't contain the smile. "You're in a *library*."

"What?" She couldn't help but smile, too. "Oh, I know, but I was reading that one. Besides, I can't exactly go wander around in the fiction section looking for a new book. I'm working."

"True."

"Unless you want to finish up early so I can go do that."

He frowned and looked at the clock on the wall. "Do you really need me to?"

Beatrice laughed out loud. "No! Of course not, I'm just teasing. I don't expect you to cut your research time short for me." She smiled as she turned to the computer to check her e-mail and look at her stock report online. She took careful note of a few investments she had left from her father's estate and emailed herself a reminder to move one of them when she got back home.

She glanced at the man copying the Tibetan book and realized he almost looked annoyed. She cleared her throat. "Thanks, though…for offering. That was nice."

He cocked one eyebrow at her. "Far be it from me to keep a woman from her book. That could become dangerous."

She shook her head a little. Giovanni smiled and returned to his transcription. They both worked in silence for a while longer before she heard him put down his pencil.

"What was it?"

"What?" Beatrice tore her eyes from the computer monitor.

"The book. The one you forgot?"

She frowned. "Oh…uh, *Bonfire of the Vanities*. Tom Wolfe."

His lips twitched when he heard the title. "Oh."

"Have you read it?"

His smile almost looked rueful as he turned back to his work. "No."

"It's good. It's set in New York. I've never been, have you?"

He nodded as he took out a blank sheet of paper and started a new page of careful notes. "I have. It's very...fast."

"Fast?"

"Yes, I prefer the pace of Southern cities."

"I can see that."

"Can you?"

She looked up to see Giovanni staring, his blue-green eyes almost burning her with the intensity of their focus.

"I—I think so," she said, glancing down to avoid his gaze.

He stared for another minute before she noticed him look back to his notes.

Beatrice let out a breath, oddly disturbed by their conversation. After another half an hour, he stood and began to pack up his materials to leave.

She watched him in amusement, his deliberate movements somehow reminding her of her late grandfather when he came home from work for the day. She flashed for a moment to the image of her Grandpa Hector emptying his pockets and setting his old-fashioned pocket watch on the dresser in her grandparents' room.

Beatrice walked over to collect the manuscript and return it to the locked stacks. By the time she came back, she caught only a glimpse of Giovanni as he rushed out the door with a quick, "Goodnight, Beatrice," called over his shoulder.

She watched him walk out the door with an admiring look, reminded again that there was nothing haphazard about the way Dr. Giovanni Vecchio moved. He walked with a fluid and silent grace that seemed as effortless as it was swift.

Beatrice exited the room a few moments after him, locking up behind her and making sure all the lights were off. She no longer expected to see him waiting for the slow elevator, and she thought she heard the click of the stairwell door as it closed down the darkened hall.

"Five flights of stairs?" she wondered quietly. "No wonder he has such a great ass." The elevator dinged just as she pushed the button to go down.

CHAPTER 3

"Going out this evening?"

Giovanni looked up from buttoning his shirt to see Caspar standing at the door to his large suite of rooms on the third floor of the house. The heavy drapes were still drawn to protect the room from the setting sun, but Giovanni was feeling uncharacteristically light as he finished his evening preparations.

"Yes." His voice was clipped, but cheerful, as he answered. "Daylight savings time, Caspar."

Though most of his existence without sunlight did not bother him, Giovanni did envy the mortal freedom of movement during daylight hours. Thus, the short days of winter and the early dark was always something he considered cause for celebration.

Caspar chuckled at the boyish excitement on his friend's face. He went to hang the dry cleaning in the large walk-in closet at the back of the room.

"It's the most wonderful time of the year," he sang, while instinctively dodging the balled up socks Giovanni threw at him. A large grey cat sitting quietly in the corner of the bed unfolded itself and went to investigate the socks.

"Still a smart ass," Giovanni said.

"Still a dark and twisted demon of the night," Caspar retorted as he hung the pressed shirts on the racks.

He grinned. "Don't tell the priest."

Caspar looked over in surprise. "Is Carwyn coming to town?"

Giovanni nodded and bent to tie his charcoal grey shoes. "December, most likely. He said he'll make a proper visit and stay for a few months."

"Excellent," Caspar replied. "I'll make sure his rooms are ready for him."

"I think he's bringing one of his beasts, as well."

The cat curled around Caspar's legs and chirped until he reached down to stroke its thick grey fur.

"Sorry, Doyle. I guess you'll have to sleep inside for a bit while the wolfhound is in town."

Doyle made his displeasure known by lifting his tail and leaping back onto the bed.

Giovanni glanced at the cat as it tiptoed across his pillows. "Make sure the gardeners check the fences, as well. I know his dogs are well-trained, but I'd hate to have one wander off like last year. Also, prepare them for the massacre that will no doubt ensue in the flower beds."

"Of course." Caspar paused, quietly observing his friend's evening preparations and looking at his watch to check the time. "It will be pleasant to see him for a longer visit this time. More like the old days."

"Yes, it will." He trailed off, his mind already darting to his agenda for the evening.

Caspar noted his friend straightening the collar of his white shirt. "You shouldn't wear white, you know. It washes you out, and you're already pale as a corpse."

Giovanni frowned and turned to him. "Funny. You've been watching the English women again, the ones with the clothing show, haven't you?" He shook his head in mock sorrow *tsk*'ing his friend as he looked in the mirror, trying to tame his hair.

Caspar sighed. "I can't help it. Their sardonic British humor and impeccable fashion sense lures me in every time. I do love an ironic woman."

Giovanni snorted and turned, grabbing his black coat from the chair by the dressing table and checking it for cat hair. "When was the last time you had a date with a woman who wasn't on the television?"

"Six months. When was the last time you did?"

"Last week." Giovanni shrugged on his jacket, satisfied it was free of grey fur.

Caspar scowled. "That doesn't count and you know it."

Giovanni walked toward the door, chuckling. "That didn't seem to be her opinion, or at least, she wasn't complaining."

Caspar listened to his steps recede down the hallway and turned to Doyle. He looked into the cat's thoughtful copper-colored eyes. "It doesn't count if they can't remember, Doyle."

Doyle looked at Caspar critically, curled into a ball, and began purring on Giovanni's pillow.

"Last week?" Caspar muttered as he left the room, turning out the lights behind him. "More like thirty years."

. . .

GIOVANNI WALKED DOWN THE STAIRS, PAUSING TO GRAB HIS CAR KEYS FROM A drawer in the kitchen before he walked into the dim light of the evening. Unwilling to waste the dark, he sped over surface streets, hoping to reach his destination before closing.

When he pulled the Mustang into the parking spot near the University of St. Thomas, he looked at the clock on the dashboard of his car. He only had fifteen minutes left before the chapel closed, so he strode across the green lawn and headed toward the octagonal brick building which housed Mark Rothko's black canvases.

As he entered the deserted chapel he had not been able to visit in months, he nodded at the docent, bypassed the various books of worship near the door, and took a seat on one of the plain wooden benches. He quieted his mind and allowed his senses to reach outward as he stared at the seemingly static paintings that lined the white walls.

His skin prickled in awareness of the lone human by the door. He allowed himself to concentrate on the solid beat of the man's heart as his ears filtered the myriad noises flowing in and around the small building.

Giovanni's eyes rested on the black canvas in front of him. The longer he stared, the more the texture and subtle swirls of paint leapt out from its depths. No longer merely black, the paintings whirled and grew, taking on dimension never noticed by the casual observer.

He sat completely still and let his soul rest in the simplicity of the quiet room. Too soon, he heard the guard's heartbeat approaching. He stood and turned, not willing to have his peace interrupted by the words of the docent asking him to leave.

As he exited the chapel, he saw the cover of the Holy Bible sitting on the shelf by the door. He was reminded of his phone call that afternoon with one of his oldest friends.

"I'm coming for a visit. A proper one."

"Are you out of whiskey or deer?"

"Neither, Sparky. You're getting in one of your moods again, I can tell." Carwyn's Welsh accent tripped across the phone line.

"Oh, you can tell from across an ocean? You must be old," Giovanni quipped in the library as he spoke on the old rotary phone. "I don't need last rites yet, Father."

"No, but you do need a bit of fun. That's why I'm interrupting my very busy drinking and eating regimen to come for a visit."

"Has Caspar been tattling on me again? Irritating child. And I'm not getting in a mood."

"Just the way your voice sounds right now tells me you're already in one," Carwyn lectured him all the way from his remote home in Northern Wales. "I'm coming for a visit, and I'm bringing one of the dogs. Lock your demon cat up."

"I have a project going right now." He attempted to distract his friend as he stared at the

flickering candle on his desk, repeatedly passing his fingers through its flame. The fire leaned toward him, dancing in the still air of the library. "And Caspar's cat is not a demon."

"The cat is yours; and you know it's far more demonic than we are. I'll not have it sleeping on my head again."

"It's not like you can suffocate."

"No, but I can get cat hair up my nose, which is not a pleasant way to wake up. What's your project?"

"Do you remember the job I did for that London banker about five years ago?" Giovanni lifted his fingers, pinching the air and drawing the candle flame upward.

"Not really, you know I find most of that dreadfully boring."

"It was a Dante thing."

"Oh yes, the Dante thing. Not much, I remember you mentioning it, that's all."

"Mmmhmm. There was an expert I heard rumors about—one of us. He was young but sounded like he was worth tracking down. In the end, I couldn't find him. Didn't need him anyway, but a mutual acquaintance mentioned a Boccaccio manuscript he had." Giovanni let the flame grow to a foot tall before he began manipulating it to curve and twist before his eyes.

"How very fascin—"

"It was a rare copy. Florentine."

"Why is this interesting to me?"

"Because I think it was one of mine."

There was a long pause on the other end of the line.

"From your library?"

"Yes."

"Who was he?"

"An American, turned in Italy around ten years ago while he was there working. I looked for him, but he vanished quite admirably."

"What does this have to do with your project?"

"I think I may have met the Dante expert's daughter at the library where I've been doing that transcription for Tenzin."

He would have laughed at the sudden silence on the phone, but he was distracted by the perfect circle the flame formed. It reminded him of the ancient symbol of a snake eating its tail. It bent to his will, turning continuously in front of his eyes as he waited for Carwyn's response.

"That's quite a coincidence."

"It would be, if either of us believed in coincidence," he murmured as he let the flame unfurl and return to its home at the tip of the candle, shrinking until it was no larger than his fingertip.

"How would anyone newly sired have access to your library? The rumors have swirled for years, but there's been no actual proof."

"Yet I am in Houston. And if I'm correct, I met the daughter of an immortal who was rumored to have a book I haven't seen for over five hundred years."

"What do you think—"

"I don't know what to think right now, Father. I need more information. I've already sent a letter to Livia. As for the girl? I'm proceeding as if it's of no consequence at the moment. She's...interesting."

"'Interesting'? I can't remember the last time—"

"Did you know daylight savings time started this week? I'll be able to visit the museum again."

"Your phone manners are abysmal, Gio. It's not polite to interrupt someone, you know, even if you're not in the same room."

Giovanni smiled into the darkened room. "I knew what you were going to say, and I didn't want to talk about it. They're hosting a lecture next week at the museum about Dali, I—"

"What a fascinating subject change. We're going to forget about the daughter?"

He smiled at the priest's interruption. "For now, yes. I see her every week at the library. I even saw her last night. So far, nothing leads me to believe she knows anything about our kind, which means her father, if he is the immortal I want, hasn't been in contact. So, there's nothing to be done at the moment. I need to investigate more."

"Fine. Let me know when the pieces move."

Giovanni paused, staring into the turning flame in front of him. "Maybe they won't. Maybe it is just a coincidence."

Carwyn's voice was soft when he replied, "Do you really believe that?"

"No."

"Dr. Vecchio?" a familiar voice asked. "What are you doing here?"

He turned, surprised to see Beatrice De Novo standing in front of a Leger painting in one of the contemporary rooms; an older woman standing next to her. The young student's typical uniform of black was broken by the deep red shirt she wore and demure black flats replaced her combat boots, as he thought of them.

"Beatrice? How unexpected to see you here." He wasn't sure why seeing her at the museum caught him off guard. It was a popular destination for students, and he tried to convince himself it was purely serendipitous she was here on the evening after he had been speaking about her. "A pleasant surprise, of course."

The older woman looking at the Leger painting turned, and he saw the history of Beatrice's slight accent in front of him as he examined the older woman. Spanish blood seemed dominant in her handsome features, and he looked into a pair of clear green eyes. She smiled and took Beatrice's arm.

"¿Es el profesor guapo, Beatriz?"

Her accent, he noted, was educated, and from the Guadalajara region of Mexico.

Beatrice laughed nervously at her grandmother's question. He smiled, happy that the girl had referred to him as 'the handsome professor.' Blushing, she smiled at Giovanni. "Dr. Vecchio, this is my grandmother, Isadora."

Giovanni bowed his head toward the older woman, charmed by the graceful formality she seemed to exude.

"Mucho gusto, Señora. Me llamo Giovanni Vecchio. Your granddaughter has been a great help to me at the library."

"And of course he speaks Spanish," he heard Beatrice mumble.

"Beatrice, manners please," Isadora chided. "Dr. Vecchio, it's a pleasure to meet you. Are you a lover of contemporary art?"

He smiled and nodded, tucking his hands carefully in his pockets. "I am. I was just visiting the Rothko Chapel before it closed and thought I would take a walk through the main collection before I left. Are you a fan of Leger?"

"I am. Though I love the surrealist collection here as well. We live near Rice, so I'm able to visit quite frequently. You are doing research at the university?"

He nodded. "Yes, though really more as a favor to a friend who studies Tibetan religious history. She lives in China and I'm transcribing a document for her."

"A lot of work for a favor." She paused, but he did not explain further, so she asked, "Are you a professor?"

Giovanni caught the curious angle of the girl's head as she listened for his response. He knew he was the focus of some speculation at the library, though he also knew even the best researcher would find nothing about him that he didn't want found.

"I am not. My family is in rare books, Señora De Novo. I work mostly in that area."

"Oh? How interesting! Are you a collector yourself? Of books? Or art?" Beatrice's grandmother nodded toward the modern portrait on the wall next to them.

He smiled enigmatically. "I have my own book collection, of course. One my family has added to for many years. I enjoy art, but I don't have a collection, per se."

"My grandmother is a very talented painter, Dr. Vecchio."

Giovanni turned to Beatrice, who had been standing, listening to their conversation. "It must be a pleasure visiting the collection with an artist."

She smiled and took the elderly woman's arm. "It is."

"Would you like to join us?" Isadora asked.

He looked at Beatrice and smiled. He decided it was a perfect opportunity to gather more information.

"Of course, it would be my pleasure."

He felt lighter as he strolled with the two women. He felt his expression— the intense concentration his friends often needled him about—soften, and

Giovanni could even feel his posture relax they walked. Like her granddaughter, Isadora was charming and very intelligent.

He glanced at Beatrice as they walked through the Menil Collection. He noticed the affectionate and familiar way the two women spoke to each other and recalled a few of the major points in Caspar's report on the girl.

Beatrice De Novo, born July 2, 1980, in Houston, Texas.

Daughter of Stephen De Novo, deceased, and Holly Cranson, whereabouts unknown.

Adopted at twelve by her paternal grandparents, Hector De Novo and Isadora Alvarez, plumber and homemaker/artist.

Senior at Houston University in the English Literature department. Accepted to the graduate program in Information Studies at the University of California, Los Angeles.

According to Caspar's sources, Beatrice had been working in the Special Collections and Archives department of the university library since her sophomore year. Apparently, she had called the department weekly for three months asking if any position had become open since her last phone call. The young woman so impressed the staid director, Dr. Christiansen, he eventually created a position for her as a reward for her persistence.

"Do you enjoy folk art, Dr. Vecchio?" he heard Isadora ask.

He turned his attention back to her. "I do."

"You should join us for the art center's *Dia de los Muertos* celebration tomorrow night, then."

"Grandma—" Beatrice tried to break in, but Isadora shot her a look. No doubt, she had not missed Giovanni's quiet examination of her granddaughter.

"I would love to, Señora." He smiled at Beatrice's shocked expression and slight blush. "But I don't want to intrude on a family outing."

"Nonsense!" Her small hand fluttered like a butterfly in dismissal of his objections. "It's like a fair. Everyone is welcome. It's been too long since I've had a handsome escort who enjoys art as much as I do." Her eyes twinkled at him and he smiled.

"Well then," he replied, "how can I refuse? But I insist you call me Giovanni, Señora De Novo." He was pleased the opportunity for further research had presented itself so conveniently. "If I'm going to escort you for the evening, that is."

"You must call me Isadora, then."

"Oh brother," Giovanni heard Beatrice mutter, as she shook her head.

"Are you from Houston originally?" Isadora asked.

He glanced with a smile from Beatrice to a Warhol painting on his left. "I grew up primarily in Northern Italy, though my father traveled frequently for his work and I often went with him. I moved to Houston three years ago," he replied, turning to meet Isadora's keen gaze. They measured each other for a few moments in the bright light of the gallery.

"Grandma," Beatrice broke in. "We'll be late for dinner if we don't leave soon."

Isadora's gaze finally left Giovanni's, and she smiled at her granddaughter. "Of course. It was such a pleasure meeting you. The art center on Main Street tomorrow? We'll be there around seven o'clock."

"I'll look forward to it. Such a pleasure to meet you, and to see you, Beatrice." He nodded at them and allowed his eyes to meet Beatrice's dark brown ones. They were narrowed in annoyance or amusement, he couldn't quite tell, but he winked at her before she turned and led her grandmother toward the lobby.

He stayed at the museum until closing, planning his objectives for the following night. He suspected Beatrice's grandmother thought she was playing matchmaker between Beatrice and the handsome book-dealer. He was more than happy to play along, as a grandmother would readily give information to a polite young man interested in her attractive granddaughter.

She was also more likely to have information on her son and what he had been working on in Italy. Beatrice had only been a child when her father was killed, but Isadora had not.

As he swam laps that evening, he thought about the girl. She was far too young for him, even if he appeared to be in his late twenties or early thirties. Her behavior was a curious mix of innocence and wariness, and he wondered how much experience she had with men. She kept to herself, but he had the distinct impression she was no wallflower.

Beatrice De Novo was intriguing, and he found her humor and intelligence far more compelling than the average college student. He knew from her physical response to him that she found him attractive, and he was comfortable using that as he determined what she knew and how it could be of use in his own search.

"Caspar?" he called out when he returned to the house after his swim.

"Yes?" he replied from the library.

Giovanni walked upstairs and stood in the doorway. Caspar had started another fire, and the familiar smell tickled his nose. Doyle was curled up in his favorite chair; the cat looked up, blinked at Giovanni, and closed his eyes again.

"Any word back from Rome?"

Caspar looked up from his book and shook his head. "You know how slow Livia can be. Added to that, she refuses electronic correspondence, even for her day staff. I suspect we might see some sort of response by the new year."

Giovanni scowled in frustration but knew his friend was probably correct.

"So you really think the girl's father was turned?" Caspar asked.

He nudged the cat off his chair.

"How many American Dante scholars were killed under mysterious circumstances in northern Italy in 1992? It's far too coincidental. If the rumors about the book are true..."

"But why are you interested in the girl?"

"Don't fret, Caspar. She's perfectly safe. And you know how nostalgic the young ones can be. He was rumored to have access to books that are rightfully mine. Now I have access to his human daughter. If I can use the connection to trade for information...or more, I will."

"But do you really think he knows about your books?"

Giovanni stared into the flames as the heat began to lift the water from his skin and dry his towel. "If it's him, and he has what was rumored, then yes. It sounded genuine. Livia will know, and she'll know who sired him. No one turns a human in that part of Europe without her knowing about it, even if it's against their will."

"And whoever sired him—"

"No one stumbles across a library that ancient and that valuable when they're that young. The sire is who I'm looking for."

"So we wait."

"Well," he mused, "we might be able to do more than that. I'm meeting with the girl and her grandmother tomorrow night."

"What? On a Friday?"

"I'm going out later." He shrugged. "Don't fret, old man."

Caspar raised his eyebrows. "A divergence from routine, Gio? What is the world coming to?"

Shaking his head, he rose and walked toward the door.

"See if you can prod some of Livia's day people tomorrow over the phone."

"Of course." Caspar paused for a moment. "Is it worth it, Gio? The books? This obsession? All these years?"

"What do you hold in your hands, my son?"

"A book."

"No, you hold knowledge. Knowledge sought for centuries. Knowledge that some have died for. Knowledge that some have killed for."

"Why would anyone kill for a book?"

"It is not a book." The slap rung in his ears. *"What is it?"*

"Knowledge."

"And knowledge is power. Do you understand?"

"Yes, Father."

Giovanni paused in the doorway, letting his wet hair drip in his eyes as he pushed back the memory, the driving need to discover pulsing in his quiet veins. "You ask me that every time I find something new."

"And you never really answer me."

"Yes, I do," he murmured. "You just don't like the answer."

He slept late the next day, not rising until the sun was low in the sky. Though he preferred more pleasant and leisurely meals, the oblivious human woman he had fed from the night before had sated his physical hungers for the week and allowed him to retain the genteel manners he had carefully cultivated for the previous three hundred years.

Giovanni dressed thoughtfully, choosing casual clothing that was more likely to set the De Novo women at ease and detract from his inhuman complexion. Though the slight current that ran under his skin allowed him to adjust its surface temperature, nothing could diminish the almost luminescent paleness.

"Ah," Caspar exclaimed when he walked into the kitchen. "The grey is a good choice. Makes you look much less demon-of-the-night."

"Please, Caspar," he implored. "A date with a live woman. Soon."

Caspar smiled and looked up from the newspaper. "I'm meeting a friend tonight, as a matter of fact. I was just looking at what movies are opening this weekend. I'm looking for something horribly gory."

"I'll never understand your affinity for those pictures."

"And I'll never understand your affinity for professional wrestling, so we're even."

Giovanni rolled his eyes. "Goodnight, Caspar."

The lights of downtown twinkled, and he could see streams of children already weaving through the neighborhood in their costumes. It was Halloween night, and with Dia de los Muertos falling on Sunday, the whole weekend would be devoted to the macabre, grotesque and mysterious. He drove through the streets, amused by the teenagers and students in their elaborate costumes, enjoying the sense of revelry in the crowded bars and clubs of the Montrose district.

He pulled into the parking lot across from the art center and immediately heard the music of mariachis fill the air. Houston's Mexican-American community was an integral part of the cultural scene, and he was happy to have an excuse to participate in the odd festival celebrating the dead. He saw children with elaborate face painting and a few adults, as well. The smells of earthy spices and sugar filled the air, and he scanned the crowd for Beatrice and her grandmother.

"Giovanni!" Isadora's clear voice called from a nearby booth selling tamales. He walked over to the older woman but his eyes were drawn to Beatrice standing behind her, holding a drink and a small paper plate with two tamales on it.

"Dr. Vecchio, how are you tonight?" It was the first time he had seen her with her hair down. It fell long and perfectly straight down her back, with a few errant pieces slipping over her ear. He held himself back from touching it; though he could admit to himself he wanted to.

"B, I'm sure you can call him Giovanni. You're not at work, after all."

He turned to Isadora. "Ladies, you're both looking lovely this evening." He smiled at Isadora, who was wearing a vivid green dress. "And of course, Beatrice, feel free to call me Giovanni."

She was dressed in black again, but this time, she wore a wide collared shirt that showed off her graceful neck and collar bones and another trim skirt that fell to her knees. He was strangely pleased to see that her combat boots were back, and she had switched her ruby piercing out for a tiny silver stud.

"Giovanni, huh? No nickname?" Beatrice asked. She frowned a little before she continued. "That must have been quite a chore to spell in kindergarten."

He smiled and watched her offer her grandmother the drink, but she made no move to unwrap the tamales she had bought.

"Oh, I've been called many things over the years, but all the men in my family are named Giovanni."

"Really? Is that traditional?"

"What is your name?"
　"Whatever I want it to be."
　"Why?"
　"Because I am superior to mortals."

He blinked to clear the unexpected flash, wondering why the memories of his father had been so near in his mind in the past few weeks. "For us, yes."

Beatrice gestured to the line of food vendors. "I'm sorry we didn't wait for you. We ate earlier, but there are plenty of things to choose from. Please help yourself; we can wait."

He shook his head, "No, I've eaten as well, thank you. Shall we go to look at the art?"

"*Ofrendas*, Mariposa. Ofrendas first," Isadora said with a smile as she took Giovanni's arm and steered them toward a small building.

"Do you know much about Dia de los Muertos?" Beatrice asked as they walked.

He shook his head. "Not much. I haven't spent a great deal of time in Latin America." He knew plenty, of course, but he preferred to hear her explanation.

"It's not usually celebrated until November second, but the art center hosts a family fair on Halloween so parents have an option other than trick-or-treating for the kids." Beatrice smiled at a pair of small children in skeleton costumes with flowers in their hair as they rushed past on the way to the carnival games.

He observed their small, retreating forms. "It certainly seems popular."

"It is. It used to be just Mexican families, but now a lot of people like the tradition."

"And the ofrendas?"

Beatrice smiled. "Just little offerings for the dead. Things they liked during their life, you know?"

They walked inside the small building to see a makeshift altar set up and decorated with marigolds, crosses, and cheerful skeletons. Small candles flickered among them. Sugar skulls were mixed with small toys and placed in front of children's pictures; bottles of tequila, mugs of chocolate, and small plates of food were propped in front of the pictures of adults.

The small room was decorated elaborately, and the walls were lined with pieces of art celebrating the holiday. The flickering lights of saint candles lit the room as they sputtered in their brightly painted votives, and he could smell incense burning.

"The art is a mix of professional and student," Beatrice murmured, withdrawing two framed photographs from the messenger bag that hung on her arm, along with a small bottle of expensive tequila.

Isadora had left them to chat with some women at the end of the altar but soon walked back to Beatrice with a smile.

"*Las photos, Beatrice?*"

"*Si, abuelita,*" she said, and handed Isadora the two small frames. They walked to the end of the altar where a few other families were setting up pictures and ofrendas.

Isadora placed the two pictures on the altar and touched their frames. Giovanni spied an older man who must have been the grandfather in one picture. The younger man in the other photograph so closely resembled Beatrice, he had little doubt it was her father. Stephen De Novo stared out of the photograph with the same dark eyes that the young woman had.

Giovanni wondered whether Stephen's eyes had changed color when he turned, as sometimes happened. Oddly enough, he found himself hoping they hadn't.

He tried to examine Beatrice's expression as she unwrapped the tamales and placed them on small plates in front of the two pictures, but her dark hair curtained her face and obscured her features. She placed the bottle of tequila between the two pictures, tilting them as if they could keep each other company on the crowded altar.

The women stepped back to examine the effect, whispering to each other in Spanish but smiling and laughing as well. He cocked his head and looked around the room.

Though it was filled with symbols and depictions of the dead, there was no fear and very little sorrow. It was unusual to find such celebration in the name of loss, and he found himself touched by the demeanor of the partygoers.

Beatrice was smiling when she turned, and he saw Isadora wander toward a group of older women, nodding at him as she walked away.

"Do you want to walk outside? There's some music playing," she asked. "I imagine she'll chat with her buddies for a while, then come join us. I have to get out of the incense." She waved her hand in front of her nose and laughed.

He had hardly noticed the heavy smell until she mentioned it. He was so accustomed to filtering out the various and sundry smells of life around him that he did it automatically. He realized he probably hadn't been breathing at all in the close environment of the crowded room.

"Of course," he said, gesturing to the doors. He placed his hand on the small of her back to lead her through the people streaming into the building. When they exited, he stepped away, suddenly aware of her body from the press of the crowd.

"Was that your father and grandfather?"

She nodded. "My grandparents raised me after my father was killed. We all lived together anyway. My mom's MIA. Dad worked a lot and traveled, so my grandparents took care of me."

"When did your grandfather pass away?" he asked, careful to keep up the ruse of an unknowing companion.

"Two years ago." She smiled wistfully. "He had heart problems."

"What happened to your father?" He paused for effect. "Unless that's too personal, of course. I don't mean to intrude."

They lingered in front of a guitarist who was playing a children's song for a small group. Beatrice shook her head, frowning a little.

"It's fine," she said quietly. "Random violence happens everywhere, I guess, even picturesque Italian cities. He was in Florence for a lecture series and was robbed. His car was taken and he was killed. I'm sure they didn't want him to identify them. And he would have. He had an almost photographic memory."

Yes, I imagine it's even better now.

"I'm sorry for your loss, Beatrice."

She turned to him, amusement evident in her face. "Why do you insist on using my name like that?"

He stepped closer. "Like what?"

She flushed, but didn't back away from him. He noticed her body was already reacting to his proximity. The hairs on her arms were drawn toward his energy and goose-bumps pricked her skin. He wondered what would happen if he reached out ran a hand along the smooth skin of her forearm. He could almost imagine the soft feel of it under his fingertips.

"You know...with the accent." Her eyebrows drew together. "And the old-fashioned manners. And what's with the grandmother-charming?" She glanced at him before looking back toward the guitarist. "Are you trying to charm me, too?"

A slow smile spread across his face. "Are you charmed, Beatrice?" he asked, letting her name roll off his tongue. "I don't think you are."

Ignoring his own reaction and reminding himself of his objective, he took a deliberate step back and slipped his hands in his pockets, nodding toward another musician at the end of the parking lot.

"Shall we?"

She followed where his eyes led and they stepped back into the flow of people.

"Your personality is too large for one letter, *Beatrice*. And, for the record, I don't think anyone charms your grandmother. She does all the charming necessary."

She laughed, her head falling back as her eyes lit in amusement.

Giovanni stopped for a second, entranced by the clear, joyful sound. He stared at her, drawn to her dark eyes. He stepped toward her a fraction too quickly, but the girl was lost in her own amusement and didn't notice.

"Yeah, Gio. My grandmother got all the charm in the De Novo family. She's got it in spades, my grandfather used to say," she replied, still chuckling.

Not all of it.

"Gio?" he asked, amused she had chosen the name only his closest friends called him.

"Well," she shrugged, "you don't look like a 'Gianni' to me, so…yeah, 'Gio.' If you're going to call me Beatrice, I'm going to call you Gio."

He stopped in the middle of the crowd, staring at her until she halted and turned back to look at him.

"What?" she asked, and her forehead wrinkled in confusion.

The people flowed around her, the seemingly endless, monotonous stream of humanity he had lived among for five hundred years. But she stood, dressed in black, her fair skin flushed with life and her brown eyes lit with a kind of intelligence, curiosity, and humor that set her apart. For a moment, he allowed himself to forget his interest in her father and enjoy the unexpected pleasure of her company.

She was bold and shy, formal and friendly. She was young, he realized, and innocent in a way he could hardly remember, yet her short life seemed to have been shaped by loss and abandonment. She was, surprisingly, rather fascinating.

"Inexplicable," he muttered under his breath, and walked toward her in the crowd.

He hadn't realized she heard him, but her eyebrows lifted in amusement.

"Nothing's inexplicable. Just not explained *yet*." She smiled at him in the noisy mass of people, and he let his green eyes linger on her face for a brief moment before they kept walking through the fair.

"Perhaps, Beatrice. Perhaps you may be right."

CHAPTER 4

"Why do you dye your hair black?"

Beatrice looked up from the computer screen to see Giovanni staring at her again from his seat in the reading room.

"What?"

"It must be dark brown anyway; why do you dye it black?" he asked again, his eyes narrowed intently on her face.

She wanted to laugh at his confused expression but kept a straight face as she answered, "Because it's almost black, but not quite."

"I don't understand."

She looked at him over the reference desk, a small smile flirting at the corner of her mouth. "I just felt like it hadn't really committed to a color, Gio. I don't do things half-assed. I don't want my hair to, either."

He set his pencil down and leaned back in his chair. "So, you're saying you dye your hair because you think it's...lazy?"

He cocked his head in amusement.

She shrugged. "Not lazy, more indecisive."

He smiled. "You realize that makes no sense, of course. Your hair color is determined by your genetic make-up and has no reflection on your personality or work ethic."

She glared at Giovanni playfully before sticking her tongue out at him.

He looked at her in astonishment for a moment before he burst into laughter. She was startled by the unfamiliar, but not unwelcome, sound and joined him before she looked at the clock on the wall. It was already ten to nine.

Still chuckling, she said, "All right, hand over the book. I've got to lock up."

He smiled at her and began to pack the manuscript for storage. She walked over, picked it up, and began her nightly closing ritual.

In the weeks since he'd joined her and her grandmother at the festival, Giovanni had become surprisingly friendly. She found him lingering around the student union on random nights of the week, holding cups of coffee he never drank and wandering through the student-study area in the library. He made a point of chatting with her, but she found his intentions as puzzling as his profession.

She had searched his name online, and though she found a myriad of rare books and antiquities dealers, his name never appeared. She found a copy of his business card with Charlotte Martin's notes, but the only contact information on it was a phone number she was reluctant to call, though she did program it into her phone.

When she asked her grandmother about the intriguing bookseller, she was shrugged off.

"It's like he's from another planet, Grandma."

"He's old-fashioned. And European. Maybe he just doesn't advertise online. There's nothing wrong with that."

"But not even a public telephone listing for his business? Not a single mention? It just seems odd." She sat at the breakfast table, drinking coffee and watching her grandmother start the chili verde for dinner that night.

"Do you feel unsafe with him?" Isadora turned to her, a look of concern evident on her face. "You're alone with him in that reading room for hours every week. I won't have you feeling unsafe."

Beatrice shook her head. "No, it's not that. There's just something..."

Isadora turned back to the stove. "You're creating a mystery where there is none, Mariposa. I think he's a nice man. Just old-fashioned." Her grandmother fell silent, and from her expression, Beatrice could tell she was reliving some of the dark times that had marked her granddaughter's teenage years. Not wanting her grandmother to worry about her strange fascination, Beatrice attempted to lighten the mood.

"Do you know he doesn't even have a mobile phone? Can you imagine?"

"Really?" Isadora may have not been as fond of technology as her granddaughter was, but she'd jumped at the chance to have a mobile phone when she realized she could talk with her circle of friends almost nonstop.

"Nope. I've never seen him with one. Come to think of it, he doesn't have a laptop, either." She frowned again. "And what researcher doesn't have a laptop these days? It's just odd."

Her grandmother laughed. "Maybe he's allergic to technology, mija."

In the weeks that followed, Dr. Giovanni Vecchio became a small obsession to her.

He was rich, she determined, after noticing a silver-haired man hold open the back door of a Mercedes sedan for him on more than one occasion when they left the library. Giovanni had taken to walking her to her small, hand-me-down Civic some evenings when she got off of work, most often to continue a conversation they were in the middle of. He'd also tried to convince her that a brisk walk down five flights of stairs was the key to good health. She sometimes joined him and sometimes simply waited near the elevators. He was an unusually fast walker.

She also determined he was in his early thirties. He looked younger but had casually mentioned too many foreign universities for her to think he had seen them all in less than that.

What bothered her the most was that something about his appearance stirred memories of a time in her life she had tried very hard to forget, and reminded her of a face she had relegated to the back of her mind. She'd tried for years to put that dark chapter of her teenage years behind her, but the more time she spent with the mysterious book dealer, the more thoughts and memories began to surface.

He stood before her now, his soft smile and beautiful eyes the very picture of politeness. He was wearing a moss-green sweater that evening which made his eyes look both green and grey at once.

"Can I walk you to your car?"

She paused, and he must have been confused by the odd look on her face because he stepped away.

"I...sorry, kind of lost in thought." She smiled. "You know, thinking about my indecisive hair." She closed her eyes and shook her head, embarrassed that she'd used thinking about her hair as an excuse for her quizzical expression.

He frowned. "Did you want—"

"Sure," she continued. "I'd like the company. Just let me shut the computers down. Can you get the lights by the door?"

He paused almost imperceptibly but turned to walk toward the doorway. As she waited to log out of the library's system, she glanced at him from the corner of her eye. He slipped his hand into his messenger bag and pulled out a pencil to flick the lights off before he tucked it back in his bag. His movements were smooth and practiced, and if she hadn't been observing him, she realized she never would have noticed.

She forced herself to look back at the computer and stood up straight when she heard the electronic sigh that indicated the machine was off. Gathering her bag, Beatrice plastered a smile on her face and walked toward the doorway to meet him.

"Join me on the stairs tonight?" he asked.

"I don't think so. My feet are killing me. Join me in the elevator?"

He looked at her for a second, surprised by her question. She'd never asked him to join her before and was curious how he would respond.

"No, thank you. You know me—I like the exercise."

She chuckled a little and smiled. "Right."

"I'll meet you downstairs."

He turned and loped toward the stairwell, his quick feet almost noiseless in the dim corridor. She muttered under her breath as she watched him.

"Right...sure I know you."

SHE RAN INTO HIM AGAIN TWO NIGHTS LATER WHILE SHE WAS WORKING ON A paper for her Medieval Literature class. She'd just finished her paper on the role of illuminations in devotional manuscripts when she saw him watching her from the archway by the coffee shop. She caught a glimpse of his pale face and was immediately thrown back to a memory from the summer she turned fifteen.

"Grandpa, I think I saw him again tonight, by the movie theater."

Her grandfather sat at his workbench in the garage, working on a small carving of a butterfly for his wife. He set his knife down and brushed off his gnarled hands, holding one out to her. She took it and came to stand next to him, her purple shirt brushing against the bench and picking up small shavings of wood she flicked away with pink-tinted nails.

"Mariposa," he squeezed her hand, "my butterfly girl, I see him too. I still see him sitting at the kitchen table in the mornings, or tinkering with me in the garage. The memories, they're natural, mija. It's normal to remember him that way."

She frowned and shook her head, unable or unwilling to share her growing fears with her down-to-earth grandfather. The dreams were getting worse, and it was becoming more difficult to spend time with her friends who only seemed to want to talk about boys, clothes, or the latest music. She looked up into her grandfather's loving and concerned face.

Hector de Nova had handled the loss of his son as well as could be expected, flying to Italy to return with a coffin he had been warned not to open. His deep sorrow had been subsumed by the need to care for his grief-stricken wife and granddaughter.

"But he—he doesn't look the same when I see him. He's too thin, and his skin ... it's not the way I remember." She felt her heart begin to race. "Am I going crazy?"

He pulled her into a fierce hug. "No, you're not crazy. Do you hear me? You're one of the most levelheaded people I know, but you need to stop thinking about him so much. It's not healthy, mija. Get out with your friends more. Have some fun."

She whispered into his collar, "Okay, Grandpa."

"And you don't tell Grandma, okay? She'll just get upset."

"I know."

"When things start to bother you, just come talk to me."

He pulled away to look into dark eyes that matched his own, the same eyes her father had. "We'll be okay, B. We'll get past this."

Her hands clenched. "Sometimes, I wish I could just forget him, Grandpa. I know that's horrible."

He kissed her forehead. "It's okay, Beatrice. It's going to be okay..."

"Beatrice?" Giovanni stood before her, wearing a grey tweed jacket and holding two cups of steaming coffee. "May I join you?"

Shaking her head slightly to clear her mind, she motioned to the red-cushioned seat across from her. "Of course. What are you doing here?"

Working out your glorious backside by walking the ten-storied staircase of the architecture building?

Stealing secret documents for the Russians? Plotting to assassinate my U.S. Foreign Policy professor? Please let it be that. Stalking me for some completely mind-boggling and inexplicable reason?

"Just meeting a friend for coffee."

"Oh really? What time are you supposed to meet him?" She looked at her watch as he frowned.

"Oh," she said in sudden realization. "Oh, me?"

He smiled and sat across from her. "I was doing some research in the stacks and I saw you leave. I thought I might take a break."

"What are you working on?"

He looked at her for a moment, as if judging whether she was worth confiding in. She raised her eyebrow when he remained silent, shrugged, and returned to typing on her laptop.

"Researching some documents for a client."

She looked up, surprised he had spoken. "That sounds interesting. What kind of documents?"

His slightly pained expression had her waving a hand.

"Never mind," she added. "None of my business."

"It's not that I don't think you're trustworthy," he said quickly. "This collector is very private. I haven't even shared the specifics with Caspar."

"Caspar?"

"Oh," he paused. "Caspar is my ..."

"Is he the guy that picks you up from the library sometimes?"

"Yes, he's my butler, I guess you could say. He works for me, but runs my house, as well. He also helps me in my work."

She raised her eyebrows and nodded. "I have never met anyone with a butler before."

"Well," he shrugged. "I suppose you have now."

"Tell the truth, Giovanni Vecchio." A mischievous look came to her eye. "You have a butler, a cool car, and I've only ever seen you at night..."

He froze, tension suddenly evident in the set of his shoulders. Beatrice leaned closer and whispered, "You're Batman, aren't you?"

His mouth dropped open in surprise before the grin overtook his face.

She smiled back at him, chuckling until he joined in. Soon, they were both laughing.

"You looked so serious for a second! What did you think I was going to say? A spy? Vampire? Hired killer?"

He shook his head in amusement. "You're confounding. No, I was just surprised you guessed. I am, in fact, Batman. I would appreciate your discretion."

She nodded with a slight smile, and took another sip of the coffee he'd brought her. It had just a touch of cream, exactly the way she liked it. "Sure you are. I'm a skeptic until I see the rubber suit. You're not fooling me."

He looked at her, smiling mischievously. "You really want to see me in a rubber suit?"

His seductive grin brought her to a halt. "What?" She blushed. "No, I was just—joking, Gio. Sheesh."

He laughed at her uncomfortable expression. Giovanni blew on his coffee, holding it in his hands and smiling at her over the edge.

"What are you working on?" he asked, setting down his drink.

She shrugged. "Medieval Lit paper."

"Dante, by any chance?"

She cocked her head. "Not my area."

"Sorry."

They looked at each other for a few moments before she relaxed again. "It's fine. Valid question, I guess. A lot of people thought I would follow in my dad's footsteps."

"But you chose not to."

She shrugged at him. "I like the library. Information science is...kind of like solving mysteries."

"So you're a detective?" he asked with a smile. "Do you like mysteries?"

She rolled her eyes. "I have no illusions of grandeur. People need information. I find out what they need to know and help them find it. It's satisfying."

"That's somewhat like your father. Isn't that what he was doing in Italy? Solving mysteries?"

Her eyes narrowed. "Maybe. You're awfully interested in ten-year-old research."

"I'm quite fond of Dante. I am Italian, after all."

"That's true." She paused. "I don't know what he was looking for." She took another sip of her coffee and couldn't help but notice the avid interest he was trying hard *not* to show. "He told my grandfather he thought he had a line on some previously unknown letters connected with the Alighieri family. Some missing collection of correspondence. You know how they used to take a collection of letters and bind them in correspondence books? I think he was looking for some of those."

"What? From Dante himself?"

Beatrice looked down at her computer. "Maybe. He wasn't specific. No one in the family was really as interested in literature as he was. I mean, I am *now*, but at the time..." She smiled as she remembered the last call her father had made to her from Italy. He had run into an old friend from school and was bubbling with excitement.

"You were twelve when he died?" Giovanni asked.

She looked up sharply. "How do you know how old I am?"

"I just assumed," he said. "You mentioned you were a senior."

She didn't know why, but she felt like he wanted something from her. She had an uneasy feeling prickling at the back of her neck and a strange energy suddenly seemed to buzz around her. She didn't feel unsafe, just like there was some piece of a puzzle she was missing, an angle to him she couldn't quite see. She looked at the pale hands he had folded across his chest and a headache began to grow behind her eyes.

"Of course," she said. Pausing for a moment, she took another drink of her coffee, noting his cup still remained untouched on the table. "Don't like your coffee?"

He shifted slightly. "It's just not the way I ordered it."

"So take it back," she said quietly. "Not that you'll drink that one, either."

He stared at her. "Why do you say that?"

She felt the hairs on the back of her neck stand on end. A slight vibration filled the air and he looked down, seemingly fascinated by the back of her laptop as his eyebrows furrowed together.

She felt a strange pressure around her, like the air right before an electrical storm. "You just don't seem to like coffee all that much."

"I don't," he said in a low voice, still staring at her computer.

"So why do you always order it?"

He looked up at her, his green eyes seemed darker the longer she stared into them. Beatrice saw his arms unfold and a hand began to creep across the table toward hers. The hairs on her wrist rose.

"Gio?" she whispered, confused by his odd behavior.

He sat back suddenly, as if shaking himself out of a trance. "I like the way it smells—coffee, I mean. I just don't like the taste." He stood, grabbing his messenger bag from the floor. "I should be going."

"Oh?" she asked, still confused by the strange exchange and the sudden clearing of the air. She felt her ears pop as when she spoke to him.

"Yes, I need to speak with Caspar. I forgot."

"Well," she cleared her throat, attempting to lighten the mood, "have fun at the bat cave."

"Excuse me?" he asked, frowning.

She shook her head. "Never mind."

"Oh yes, the bat cave." He chuckled. "I'll be sure to tell Alfred you said hello."

"Yeah, you do that."

He paused as if he had something else to say before he smiled crookedly.

"Good night, Beatrice."

They stared at each other for a few more moments before he turned to leave.

"Good night, Batman," she called. Beatrice heard him laugh as he walked through the doorway, but she sat there, drinking her coffee and staring in the direction he had gone, disturbed by something she couldn't quite grasp.

She dreamed that night: dark, twisted dreams haunted by the pale moon face of her father. Unlike her dreams as a teenager, in these she wasn't alone; Giovanni stood next to her, and soft blue flames licked along his skin.

He wasn't in the library the next week; in fact, she didn't see him at all until two weeks later when he came into the reading room for his regular evening hours. He set his messenger bag down, silently filled out the call slip, and sat patiently waiting for her to bring the Tibetan manuscript to him at the dark wood table.

She went to fetch it, her eyes flashing in annoyance at his calm demeanor. Beatrice knew it wasn't rational, but she felt as if she'd been stood up when he hadn't come to the library the previous Wednesday at his usual time. She'd wanted to see him after their odd conversation at the student union, but she hadn't.

Her vivid imagination kept tying him to her dead father so their faces overlapped in her dreams. She recalled memories she had tried to forget: a pale face glimpsed in the background at her high school graduation, strange phone calls from foreign numbers that only ended in silence and a click, and a prickling feeling along the back of her neck every time she tried to remember more from that dark period of her youth.

For some reason, she linked this mental turmoil to Dr. Giovanni Vecchio's appearance in her life, and she felt a strange resentment begin to swell toward the quiet man. They worked in silence for the next two hours, and a dull headache began to pound behind her eyes.

He walked over to her at quarter to nine, handing over the manuscript and tucking his notes away in his bag. He left ten minutes early which made her unaccountably angry. Beatrice bit her lip, smothering a frustrated scream as she waited at the reference desk for nine o'clock to come.

She walked into the hallway after her shift ended, turning to lock the reading room behind her.

"Beatrice."

She gasped when she heard Giovanni speak her name and turned to see him standing, still as a statue, in the hallway leading to the stairwell. He had dressed from head to toe in black that night, and his fair skin and strange eyes almost glowed in the dim light of the fifth floor.

"Good," she muttered. "I wanted to talk to you."

She pressed the button to call the elevator, waiting for him to join her.

"Will you walk downstairs with me?" he asked, nodding toward the stairs.

"I don't think so."

He paused. "I really don't like elevators."

"Well, I really don't like friends who have odd conversations with me, then disappear for two weeks without a word. So I'm not feeling very inclined to walk down five flights of stairs with you. If you want to talk to me, you can take the elevator like a normal person."

He tensed but didn't leave, not even when the elevator chimed and the doors opened revealing an empty compartment. She walked in, turning to look at him in challenge. Finally, he tucked his hands in his pockets and walked into the elevator, standing in the exact center of the car and staring at the doors as they closed.

Rolling her eyes, she reached forward from the back corner and pushed the button for the first floor.

"Why are you angry with me?" he asked quietly.

"You're the one that vanished for two weeks. And I'm not angry with you."

"I disagree."

"Why were you asking about my father?"

"I was curious."

"I disagree."

He remained silent as the elevator slid down to the first floor. Suddenly, the elevator jerked harshly and he threw out his left hand to steady himself. He reached for the wooden rail that ran around the compartment, but his pale hand brushed near the control panel and she saw a current arc from his finger to the metal panel. There was a bright blue flash, a small crack, and Beatrice felt a surge of electricity go through the compartment as her hair lifted. The lights went out, and the elevator came to an abrupt halt.

"What just happened?" Beatrice asked nervously. "What the hell was that? Is your hand okay? Why are we stopped?"

"I think the elevator shorted out."

"Push the alarm. Isn't there an alarm?" She leaned forward, reaching for the panel blindly, but her hands only touched his tense arm as he braced himself against the side of the elevator.

"Beatrice—"

"Isn't there supposed to be a light or something?" She scowled, irritated at being stuck in a dark elevator with him.

"I don't think—"

"Shit! How long is it going to take to get out of here? My grandma's going to be worried sick. She hates it when I get home late on Wednesdays. Oh, wait …" She began rummaging through her bag, searching blindly for her mobile phone. Reception was sketchy at best in this part of the library, but at least she could use it as a flashlight so she didn't stumble into him in the darkened car.

"I don't think your phone will work."

"Well, I won't get reception, but—"

"No, I highly doubt it will even turn on with that surge. Did you leave your laptop in your car tonight?"

She frowned at his odd question. "Yes, but—"

"Good, at least you won't lose that. I'll just buy you a new phone."

"A new phone? What the—"

"Now to figure out how to get out of here—"

"Giovanni!" she finally yelled. She felt blind, and she was starting to panic. "What the hell is going on? Why won't my phone work? And what was that flash that stopped the elevator?"

She stood in the pitch black, waiting for him to speak—for him to do anything. She couldn't even hear him breathing. He was so still, she almost thought she was imagining his presence in the elevator earlier. Beatrice was halfway convinced if she threw her arm out, she would meet nothing but dead air. The charged air in the elevator seemed to press against her, and she heart began to pound.

Finally, she heard a pop, as if someone had plugged an old lamp into a socket. A small blue light shone across from her and her eyes were drawn to it immediately.

It grew until it was the size of a lighter flame, then it got bigger, and rounder, its soft blue-green light illuminating the large hand it hovered over. She couldn't look away as it swirled and grew, slowly becoming the size of a glowing softball, held hovering over the palm of Giovanni's pale hand.

She finally dragged her eyes away from the ball of blue-green flame that now resembled the color of his unusual eyes. Her gaze tracked up his arm, the buttons of his black shirt, the still, white column of his neck, and over his grim mouth. Finally, she met his intense stare in the low light of the broken elevator.

Beatrice held her breath and stared in astonishment as the terrifying fire in his hand pulsed and swirled. She could only manage a hoarse whisper.

"What are you?"

CHAPTER 5

Giovanni's gaze was steady and his voice soothing as he looked at her in the pulsing blue light.

"Remember, Beatrice—remember when you told me at the fair that nothing was inexplicable, just not explained *yet?*"

She nodded, wondering if he could hear the race of her pulse. Her eyes darted around the compartment, instinctively looking for an escape from the strange, fire-wielding...whatever he was standing across from her. But there was no way out of the steel box, and she had no idea when anyone would notice the notoriously defective elevator wasn't running if there was no alarm.

"I'm not asking you to believe in magic, Beatrice. I'm asking you to believe that there are things in this world you don't understand yet. Things that none of us do."

Beatrice stared back at the strange blue fire and asked again, "What are you?"

"Many human myths are created as an attempt to explain the inexplicable."

Beatrice shrank into the corner of the elevator, glaring at him as he spoke. She felt her legs begin to shake, so she slid to the ground and folded them under her. Giovanni followed, sitting slowly so as not to upset the flaming blue orb still hovering over his hand.

"Thor, the Norse god of thunder," he said. "Pele, the fire god who created the Hawaiian volcanoes."

She was shaking her head in disbelief, glancing between his face and the ball of blue fire he held. Panic seemed to well up in her throat, choking her. She tried to take deep, calming breaths, but she wasn't very successful.

He spoke more quickly, "Dinosaur skeletons led to myths about dragons. Prehistoric basalt formations became the Giant's Causeway."

"*What are you?*" she asked in a stronger voice, her hands clenched into fists at her sides.

He fell silent, his eyes left hers as he stared down at the blue fire in his hand. "What do you think I am?" he asked in low voice. "Think."

"I don't remember any particular myths about pyrokinetic book dealers!"

He flicked his fingers and the flaming orb spun to the top of the compartment where it hung and twisted, still illuminating the small space. Giovanni pulled his long legs toward his body and rested his arms on his knees, his long graceful fingers loosely knit together in front of him.

"Forget the fire for a moment," he said in what she thought of as his "professor voice." She normally found it annoying but, at that moment, it was oddly comforting. "There are other myths. Other stories. *What do you think I am?*"

She remembered the first night they had met, and his inhuman speed that beat her elevator to the lobby.

"You—you're fast."

He nodded. "I'm very fast. And very strong."

She thought back to his pale face glowing on Dia de los Muertos.

"Your skin...it's pale. Really pale. And I've never seen you during the day."

"And you never will," he murmured in the pulsing blue light.

Her breathing picked up as a growing suspicion began to take shape. Her voice wavered a little as she continued, "I've never seen you eat or drink...anything."

Her heart pounded when he looked at her through the dark hair that had fallen into his eyes. "I can eat, a little, but I don't need food to survive."

"Because," she swallowed, "you drink...I mean, you're a..."

Giovanni slowly parted his lips and the tip of his tongue peeked out as he ran it slowly along his top teeth, two of which were now noticeably elongated into very sharp, white fangs.

"You're a vampire," she whispered.

He nodded slowly, and they sat across from each other in the small compartment, both seeming to gauge the other's reaction.

"You're afraid," he said.

"Yeah, well...duh."

He smiled a little at her exclamation, and it revealed his long canines even more clearly.

She leaned forward and rested her forehead on her hands. "I'm dreaming. Or crazy. I'm probably crazy, right?"

"You know you're not."

She looked up and barked out a sharp laugh. "Oh, you really have no idea." She stared at him, then back to the blue orb hovering above them. Then she looked down at the scuffed messenger bag he always carried, and the dark hair he brushed out of his face as he stared at her with inscrutable eyes.

"Are you going to kill me?"

His eyebrows furrowed together, and he almost looked offended. "No, of course not."

"Why 'of course not'? How do I know? Don't you drink human blood?"

"Not unless you're offering, but I'm really not all that hungry. And I wouldn't kill you if I did. I'm not young and I don't have to drink much."

"Well, that's...comforting."

"It should be."

She eyed his chest for a moment, and then her eyes darted to the wooden bar that ran around the elevator. She heard him snicker.

"On the off chance you were able to break that railing, and make a stake, *and* drive it into my chest—which is harder than it looks, trust me—it wouldn't do anything more than give me a rather nasty chest wound and ruin one of my favorite shirts. Relax, I have no interest in hurting you."

Her eyes met his and she could feel the blush coloring her face. She suddenly felt embarrassed that she'd thought about killing him when she'd been in his company for weeks and he'd never so much as said a rude word.

"What if I don't believe you? What if I run screaming to the security guard when we get out of here and tell him you're a vampire?"

He chuckled a little, and then he stretched his feet across the elevator and crossed his ankles. "Feel free. After all, who would believe a crazy story like that, Beatrice?"

"Right," she frowned. "Right. No one would believe me because vampires aren't real."

He smiled. "*Everyone* knows that."

She swallowed audibly and nodded. "Of course they do."

"Besides." There was a blur in the elevator, and she gasped as he seemed to materialize sitting beside her.

"How—how did you—"

"*Shhhh.*"

Beatrice could feel his whisper like a caress along her skin and her entire body reacted to him. Her heart raced. Her skin prickled. As she sucked in a breath, she realized even the air around her felt charged. He leaned in and his hand reached up to trace her cheek. It felt as if an electrical current ran along her skin when his fingertip touched it, and she shivered.

"All it would take is a few moments," he murmured, "and you wouldn't remember a thing about me."

She felt a tingle at the nape of her neck, and she realized it felt like something was vibrating *under* her skin. She gasped again and scrambled a foot away from him, shoving his hand away.

"What was that?"

"*Amnis,*" his accent was strong as the word curled from his lips.

"Uh…" Her forehead wrinkled in concentration. "Is that Latin? It's been a while, I don't remember—"

"Current. I call it 'amnis.' Some immortals who believe in magic call it 'glamour' or 'thrall,' but it's not magic. It's simply energy manipulated by the current that runs under our skin."

His logical voice spurred her natural curiosity. "Really? That's…weird, and kind of fascinating. So really? You can just make me forget all this? Because I can tell you, that's not sounding real likely at the moment."

Giovanni smiled. "Yes, I can tap into your cerebral cortex and manipulate your memories, your senses, even the words that come out of your mouth."

For some reason, the thought of him messing with her brain suddenly scared her far more than the idea of him getting hungry.

"Have you done that to me before?" she whispered. "Did you make me trust you?" A thought occurred to her and her temper flared. "Did you use that on my grandma?"

"No, Beatrice," he spoke calmly. "Trust is an emotion, and I can't manipulate emotion. Those are centered in the limbic system, and amnis doesn't seem to affect that. That's also why some long-term memories are harder to erase or change."

She stared at him as he sat next to her with the same academic expression he wore when transcribing documents. "You're talking about all this like it's some kind of science experiment."

"I'm not a scientist. Though, I suppose it is a kind of science experiment," he mused quietly. "One I've been working on for many years."

He shrugged as he settled into the corner next to her, and that familiar gesture did more than anything else to set her at ease. Her logical brain told her he probably wouldn't bother explaining any of this if he was planning to kill her and drink her blood. Besides that, she couldn't really imagine Dr. Giovanni Vecchio doing anything quite that rude.

The blue flame continued to swirl above them without any apparent effort on his part, though she knew from its inception he must be manipulating it. It was the same way he had shorted out the elevator, killed her phone, and made the hair on her body stand at attention when he got too close. He controlled this electric current, this…"amnis."

"So you don't think it's magic? It seems like magic." She frowned. "And I always thought of vampires as magic." She suddenly sat up in excitement. "Are there other creatures? Werewolves? Demons? Fairies?"

He snorted at her and looked down his nose a little. "Fairies?"

She was a little pissed off he seemed so dismissive. "Hey, you're the one with the glowing blue fire and suddenly pointy teeth, mister. Don't give me that look. Doesn't seem that far-fetched to me."

He raised a single eyebrow. "My teeth are stimulated by a certain set of physical triggers related to blood flow, Beatrice. It's perfectly natural."

"Natural for *you*," she muttered.

"Yes. Besides," he picked up her phone where it had fallen on the floor of the elevator and tossed it to her. She fumbled a little but picked it up. "What do you think humanity would have called *this* two or three hundred years ago? You don't think they would have thought mobile phones were magic? What about laser surgery? Basic medicines?" He shook his head and said something in Latin.

"How old are you?"

He cocked his head but remained silent.

"I'm sorry, is that a rude question? My grandmother would probably say it was."

His face softened into a smile. "It's not something we talk about. We guard our origins carefully." He paused before he continued. "I'm over five hundred years old."

"Renaissance? Wow...I was almost wondering if you were born during the late middle ages because of the Dante interest."

He shifted and cleared his throat. "No, Dante wasn't fashionable in my day. Too coarse. Too *medieval*. My father was all about the classics."

"So why all the questions about my dad? I gotta tell you, that was kinda..."

The smile dropped from her face. She put her head between her knees as a thought nudged the back of her mind.

"Why were you asking about my father, Gio?" Beatrice asked quietly.

"What do you mean?"

She looked up at him, no longer afraid and wanting answers from the pale man whose face haunted her dreams.

Just like another face she'd tried so hard to forget.

"Why were you asking about my father? Did you...know him? Before he died?" A sudden thought struck her. "Do you know who killed him? Was he killed by a—a vampire?"

He didn't say anything, but continued to stare at her as her heart rate rose.

"Why aren't you saying anything?" She gulped and tears came to her eyes. "Did *you*...you didn't...I mean—"

"I didn't kill your father, Beatrice. I wouldn't do that."

"Then why were you..."

As she trailed off, she closed her eyes and it was as if puzzle pieces began to fall in the darkness. A quiet gasp left her throat.

Giovanni's pale face in her dreams.

A familiar tingle along her spine.

A throbbing began to take root at the base of her skull, but she pushed through it and a quiet and familiar voice whispered in her mind.

"Just forget, Mariposa. I'm so sorry. I love you. I'm sorry..."

She swallowed the lump in her throat as the tears trailed down her cheeks. "Oh...*oh*," she whispered. "My father's like you, isn't he? My father's a vampire."

Giovanni remained still and silent as the rest of the puzzle took shape.

Her confusing dreams the summer she turned fifteen. Followed by an inexplicable depression that seemed to drag her under despite the loving support of her grandparents. Her withdrawal. The strange and inexplicable moods.

She heard Giovanni murmur from across the compartment, "You are an extraordinarily perceptive girl, Beatrice De Novo."

A memory from a night in her grandfather's garage pushed its way to the front of her mind.

"Sometimes, I wish I could just forget him, Grandpa."

Tears fell hot on her cheeks. "Oh, he is... and he tried to make me forget him," she said, wiping her eyes with the back of her hand.

She saw him lean forward, suddenly alert. "What do you—"

"The summer I was fifteen, I saw my father. He was sitting on a bench in a park across from the library where I had a summer job. It was just a flash," she whispered and snapped her fingers. "Like that. I thought I was going crazy. He didn't look how I remembered him. He was too thin, and his face...that pale face, just like yours."

He leaned back and reached into his bag to hand her a linen handkerchief. "If you were fifteen, it would have been about three years after he was sired. He would have been in control of his senses and his bloodlust by then. So it's entirely possible, yes. Many newly sired vampires make the mistake of trying to contact their family."

"I kept seeing him for months." She looked as she took the handkerchief and held it in twisted fingers. "I really thought I was going crazy. I stopped going out with my friends. I stopped...everything. My grandparents didn't know what was going on. I thought I was losing it. And there were these crazy dreams."

She frowned, dabbing her eyes and trying to access memories she now suspected had been tampered with. She kept feeling the strange itch at the nape of her neck every time she tried to recall more, and the headache began to pound.

"He might have tried to talk to you, and you didn't react well. If he did, it's possible he tried to wipe the memories from your mind." He didn't try to comfort her, but his presence was soothing nonetheless.

"But he was my father."

He nodded. "Exactly. Your memories of him would be very firmly entrenched. You would have noticed if he manipulated them. Not consciously... not at the time, anyway. You may have been depressed, withdrawn, and you wouldn't have understood why."

"I *was* depressed," she whispered. "My grandparents had no idea what was wrong with me. I had handled his death as well as could be expected and this happened years later. I went to counselors, therapists...no one could figure it out. Why would he do that?"

He shook his head. "He was young, Beatrice. He probably had no idea how it could affect you."

She remained silent for a few minutes, sitting still in the blue light of the broken elevator.

"Why are you telling me all this?" she finally asked.

He paused and she tried to read his expression in the dim light.

"I don't know. I shouldn't be telling you any of this."

"That's not true. You should tell me if it's about my father. Why were you asking about—"

He glanced away, but not before she noticed the sudden light in his green eyes.

"You *want* something. You want something from me."

He looked back, this time wearing a carefully blank expression.

"I don't know what you mean."

She shook her head. "No, not me. You want something from *him*. From my father. That's why you were asking about him."

Giovanni's stillness made him seem even more inhuman than his fangs, which had slipped behind his lips and out of sight.

"You want what he was looking for in Italy, don't you? You're a book dealer. Do you want what he was after?"

She knew she was correct when she saw a minute flicker in his eyes. She laughed ruefully. "Why in the world do you think I can help you with *that*?"

"Would you like to see your father again, Beatrice? I know he'd like to see you."

She narrowed her eyes. "Do you know where he is? He's in Europe, isn't he? There were phone calls—"

"I don't know. Not exactly. And I wouldn't go knocking on his door if I did. That's not how it's done."

She frowned. "Then how is it done? I want to see him."

He rolled his eyes, whispering some sort of foreign curse before he looked at her again. "Vampires are private. Secretive. Otherwise we don't last very long."

She raised an eyebrow at him. "You don't seem all that private and secretive to me."

"Yes, and I'm sure Caspar will have something very clever to say about that," he muttered.

"Your butler knows?"

"Caspar's been with me since he was a boy. He knows everything."

"How—"

"That's his story to tell."

They sat in silence for a few more minutes, the blue fire still rotating above them. She clutched the linen handkerchief he had given her and tried to calm the swirl of emotions threatening her stomach. Pushing past the shock of revelation, she was relieved to know her father was alive, in some way, and had tried to contact her.

Even though he'd apparently messed up her cerebral cortex in the process.

"Giovanni?"

"Yes?"

"Now that I know all your superhero secrets, can you maybe get us out of here?"

His eyebrows lifted. "Oh, of course. No reason not to, I suppose."

More quickly than she could imagine, he stood, jumped up, knocked the center panel away from the ceiling and, with a flick of his hand, sent the blue fire out the top of the elevator compartment.

"Oh...wow," she murmured.

"Do you have all your things?" he asked, not even a little out of breath as he stood before her.

She quickly gathered her useless phone and made sure all her belongings were tucked securely into her shoulder bag. She stood before him, suddenly much more aware of how tall he was.

"Okay. Got it."

"All right. Put your arms around my waist and hold on tightly. Squeeze in, the panel is somewhat narrow."

"Okay."

She wrapped her arms around Giovanni's waist and tucked her body into his. She still felt the strange energy that seemed to radiate from him, and she tried to calm her reaction. She also tried not to think about the muscular torso she could feel beneath his clothes or the grip of his large hand at her waist.

"And Beatrice?"

"Yeah?" She looked up to see him wearing a playful grin.

"You'll never know *all* my superhero secrets."

And in what felt like a quick hop, she was jerked along with him as he leapt from the floor of the elevator to the top of the steel box which hung from thick cables in the dark shaft.

"Hang on."

"Planning on it," she gasped.

The blue flame still hovered over them as he swung her onto his back and, using only his hands, climbed the walls of the elevator shaft back up to the fifth floor. She held on to his neck, suddenly grateful he didn't need to breathe.

Actually, she realized, she wasn't sure about that.

"Do you need to breathe?"

He made a somewhat strangled noise that sounded negative, so she just kept holding tight. Using one hand to hang onto the service ladder, he pried open the elevator doors with the other, opening them enough to swing her onto the landing. She watched him disappear back down the elevator shaft, only to return a moment later holding his belongings. He flicked his finger, and the blue flame returned to his palm before he spread his hand gracefully, and the flames appeared to soak into his skin.

"And that," he commented as if he was making a remark about the weather, "is why I prefer the stairs."

She laughed nervously and smiled at him, still speechless from his clearly inhuman show of strength. He turned back to the doors, and slid them closed with the palms of his hands before he turned back to her.

"Care to join me?" A smile twitched the corner of his mouth.

"Yeah, stairs sound good."

He opened the door to the stairwell and held up a hand as he appeared to listen for a moment. Seemingly satisfied, he motioned her toward the open door.

Her mind started to compile a list of reasons she should *not* enter an empty stairwell with a vampire, but she shoved them aside, reminding herself he'd just rescued her from an even more confined space.

"I'm doing pretty well with the not-freaking-out-thing, right?"

"Very well." He nodded. "Quite impressive."

They walked in silence the rest of the way, both of them sneaking measuring glances at each other as they descended. When they reached the first floor, he held the door open for her again. She hesitated, knowing somehow when she walked through the doors, she would be different—fundamentally changed by the knowledge she now possessed.

She took a deep breath and walked through the door. Giovanni put a hand on the small of her back in a gesture she normally would have found too personal but, considering the circumstances, she didn't mind. They walked quickly out the front doors and into the dark night together.

"I'll drive you home," he said.

"That's really not necessary."

He rolled his eyes. "Beatrice, I've just told you that mythological creatures exist, and that your father—who you thought was killed—is probably one of them. Please, allow me to drive you home so I don't have to worry about you crashing your car into a guardrail."

She paused, but couldn't think of a comeback.

"Good point."

"Thank you."

"You'd worry?"

His eyes darted to the side, but he continued walking. "I'll have Caspar pick you up in the morning in time for your first class. I promise you won't be late."

She realized she would rather have time to think on the drive home anyway. Plus, she decided she might have one or two questions for Batman's butler.

"Fine, you can drive me home."

"That's my car over there." Giovanni nodded toward the grey Mustang near the rear of the parking lot.

"Nice."

A small smile lifted the corner of his mouth. "I like it."

"I do, too." Her eyes raked over the sleek lines of the vintage car. "How can you drive this if you can't even ride in an elevator?"

"Good question." He shrugged. "Older cars don't seem to be bothered by me, though I always wear gloves when I drive. New cars, however..." He shook his head. "Far too many electronics. I can hardly ride in one without breaking it. Caspar makes me sit in the back seat of his car now."

"That's got to be really inconvenient."

"Let's just say, sometimes, I really miss horses."

Beatrice smiled as she sat back in the burnished leather seat of the Mustang, and she examined his face in the sporadic light of the street lamps as he started the car and backed out. His car smelled like leather and smoke, and she realized the odd scent she often caught from him was the same as the air after an electrical storm, which suddenly made much more sense.

"Gio?" she asked after they had merged on the highway.

"Hmm?" He had returned to his more taciturn demeanor since entering the car.

"Do all vampires do the fire thing?"

He glanced at her before turning his face back to the road. "No, we all have some sort of affinity for one of the elements, though. No one seems to know why."

"Elements? Not like chemistry, though, right?"

He shook his head. "The classical elements: fire, earth, wind, and water."

"And you can make fire?"

"Not precisely. I can *manipulate* fire. I use my amnis to make a spark from static electricity, and then I can make that spark grow into whatever shape or type of fire I want."

She responded dryly. "So you can make fire."

He shrugged. "Basically, yes."

"That seems kind of dangerous."

He nodded as he took the exit off the freeway headed to her grandmother's small house. "It is. It's quite hard to control. Not many fire immortals grow to be as old as me."

"Why not?"

He sighed as if explaining something to a small child. "Well, when you are young and clumsy, it's rather easy to set yourself on fire."

A quick laugh escaped her, and she slapped a hand over her mouth before she looked at him, embarrassed by her amusement. Giovanni did not look amused.

She cleared her throat. "Sorry. It's not funny. I mean, it kind of is, but not really."

"It's really not."

"Of course not," she replied seriously.

"Fire is one of the few ways we can die."

"Sorry."

They drove silently for a few more minutes.

"So I guess that would make you kind of a bad-ass."

He nodded. "Yes, that would be another reason not many of us grow as old as me. We tend to be targeted by those who feel threatened."

"Have you been targeted?"

He looked at her as the car was stopped at a red light. "Not in a long time."

She stared at him for a few more minutes before she faced forward again.

"Good."

They continued driving down Greenbriar Street, and she realized she hadn't given him a single direction.

"Gio?"

"Yes?"

"You know exactly where my grandmother lives, don't you?"

He hesitated for a moment. "Yes."

She chewed on her lip a little, trying to calmly absorb this new knowledge.

"You know when my birthday is, too, don't you?"

"Yes."

They continued down the dark streets.

"Childhood pet?"

He cleared his throat in what she guessed was a purely habitual gesture.

"I've never understood the appeal of Chihuahuas, to be honest."

She nodded, trying to brush aside the flutter of panic that started to well up. "Well, it was a long-haired one. They're kind of cute. And Frito was really more my grandma's dog anyway."

The awkward silence stretched on as she continued to wonder just how extensively he had pried into her background. She felt like, if she asked, he might just know the contents of her refrigerator.

"I have a cat," he blurted out. "A chartreux. They chirp instead of meow. His name is Doyle."

"Oh." She was strangely relieved by his odd, personal confession. "I don't know anything about cats. Is that a breed?"

"Yes, technically the cat is Caspar's, but Doyle likes me best," he said this proudly, as if it was a personal distinction.

"Well...cool."

They were turning onto her grandmother's street, and she began to wonder how this strange, but illuminating, night would end.

"Gio?"

"Yes?" He pulled up in front of the house, and waited with the engine idling.

"We're still kind of friends, right?"

She saw the corner of his mouth turn up in a smile. "I'd like to think so. I hope so."

"You're not going to break into my room and mess with my memories tonight, are you?"

He paused before answering softly, "No, Beatrice. I won't do that."

She hesitated. "Will you ever?"

He wore an unreadable expression when he answered.

"I don't know."

She felt a catch in her throat. "I don't understand this, not really. Part of me is still wondering whether I'm going to wake up and realize it was all a weird nightmare."

He frowned for a moment before leaning toward her, and she felt the strange buzz of energy again. He lifted a hand and tucked a piece of hair behind her ear.

"We'll talk tomorrow night."

Beatrice felt a sudden, overwhelming swell of panic, but she nodded before she slipped from the car. As she stood on the path, the dark night seemed to close around her and formerly familiar shadows grew ominous. She almost ran toward the front door, locking it behind her as she heard the Mustang pull away.

CHAPTER 6

Giovanni straightened when he heard the door to the kitchen open. He had stayed up to wait for Caspar's return to the house after he delivered Beatrice to her first class of the morning.

He heard the older man moving through the house and lingering in the kitchen.

"Caspar!" he called from the shelter of the dim living room.

"Oh," the older man called as he walked into the room. "I didn't realize you would still be awake, I—"

"I'm exhausted. How was it?"

Caspar shrugged. "Fine, very little traffic this morning. We made it to the university with plenty of time before her first class. Parking on that campus is absolutely hideous first thing in the morning."

"So?"

"She's lovely, by the way. Surveillance photos never really do a woman justice. She has the most lovely skin, and that hair—"

"Caspar, you know what I'm asking, please don't make me kill you."

A frown settled onto Caspar's face and he cleared his throat.

"She was a bit...discomfited. I suppose it's understandable. She asked that I give you a message."

Giovanni scowled. He'd thought she had taken the news better than most.

"What was the message?"

"'Don't call me, I'll call you.'"

Giovanni looked down, his book suddenly forgotten. He closed it and set it carefully on the low coffee table before he stood.

"Thank you for driving her to campus. I'm retiring for the day."

He was halfway up the stairs when he heard his friend mutter quietly, "Damn."

HE DIDN'T CALL HER, BUT AFTER TWO WEEKS AND A CURT PHONE CALL FROM Tenzin in China, Giovanni did go back to the reading room at the library to continue his transcription of the Tibetan book.

His eyes immediately sought her out when he entered the small, windowless room. She glanced up from the computer, paused, but then continued typing as he spread out his work materials at the table nearest her desk. He ignored her racing heart and neither one of them spoke. He saw her fill out the call slip herself and dart back to the stacks to grab the manuscript.

He jotted a quick note that he put on her desk before he sat down. He was careful not to examine her too closely when she returned, but smiled a little when he noticed she was wearing her combat boots with her slim black skirt.

"Thank you, Beatrice," he murmured as she set down the grey box. She paused for a moment, as if she had something to say, but then he heard a small sigh.

"You're welcome, Dr. Vecchio. Please let me know if there are any other library materials you need."

He gritted his teeth when he heard her address him formally, but remained silent and began his careful work. He heard Beatrice sit down at her desk again and pick up the small note he had left near the keyboard. He glanced at her from the corner of his eye and saw her fold the note and slip it in her bag. He hid a small smile and went back to writing.

For the next two weeks, they continued their near silent interaction, each week she brought him the document he requested, paused as if she wanted to tell him something, and then returned to her desk without speaking. Each week he worked on transcribing the ancient characters, took careful stock of her appearance and left afterward with scarcely a word exchanged with the stubborn girl.

He was trying to be patient, but he'd heard nothing about Stephen De Novo from Livia's people in Rome and was beginning to feel as if the first lead he'd had in five years was dangling just out of his grasp.

It was a Friday night, and Giovanni was preparing to go out for the evening when he heard the buzz from the phone in the kitchen, signaling a car was at the gate. He frowned and walked quickly down the stairs just in time to hear Caspar hit the intercom.

"Yes?"

"It's Beatrice De Novo."

Caspar immediately buzzed her in before turning to look at Giovanni.

"It's Friday. Will you be all right?"

Giovanni shrugged and walked upstairs to hang up his jacket. He paused to check his appearance in the mirror, wishing he wasn't wearing black as it accentuated his pale skin, but also feeling a perverse pleasure that he had no need to hide his true nature any longer.

He'd never doubted she was trustworthy. Maybe it was her careful handling of the rare texts that contained so much elusive knowledge, or maybe it was the guarded expression in the girl's dark eyes, but he knew Beatrice was someone who could keep secrets, including her own.

He walked downstairs to hear Caspar opening the door for her.

"Miss De Novo, what a pleasure to see you again."

"Thanks, Caspar. How've you been?"

"Very well, thank you. I was able to catch that showing of *Night of the Living Dead* you told me about. It was wonderful."

"Cool! Glad you saw it. I never got out to the theater. No one does zombies like Romero."

Giovanni turned the corner and paused in the doorway of the kitchen.

She was wearing black, of course, but nothing about it made her seem inhuman. Her smooth skin practically pulsed with life, and his eyes were drawn to the graceful column of her neck. Her long hair was pulled back, and his fingers itched to release it from the band at the nape of her neck.

She saw him, and for the first time since the night in the elevator, she called him by his name.

"Hi, Gio."

"Hello."

Caspar interjected, "Beatrice, can I get you something to drink?"

She turned to the older man. "A Coke? Do you have...Coke?"

Giovanni chuckled. "Yes, we have Coke. Caspar's quite fond of it."

She blushed. "Just that, thanks."

"And I'll fix myself a drink in the living room, Caspar." He looked at Beatrice. "If you'll join me?"

She nodded and allowed him to usher her into the brightly lit living room, filled with comfortable furniture and a large flat screen television which hung on the wall.

"Oh, wow. That T.V. is huge," Beatrice mused as she walked over to observe the large screen. "The picture's probably really good, right?"

"Caspar couldn't very well watch bad special effects from old horror movies on a small, low-resolution screen, could he?"

Beatrice glanced over her shoulder with a smile on her face. "Of course not."

He just smiled at her, unexpectedly pleased to see her wander around his house and examine his belongings. He was tempted to show her his library but decided to wait and see why she had come to his home before he offered.

Caspar came in a few moments later as he was pouring himself a whiskey at the sideboard.

"Please let me know if there is anything else you need, Beatrice."

"Call me B, Caspar. Only Mr. Formal over there insists on calling me Beatrice." Giovanni grinned with his back to the room, more determined than ever to call her by her given name at every opportunity.

"Of course, B."

"Thanks."

Giovanni finished pouring his drink and turned back to face the room. Beatrice was sitting in one of the leather armchairs—the one he usually used—so he sat to her left on the sofa.

"Will there be anything else?"

He shook his head, and Caspar left them alone. Giovanni sat silently, sipping the whiskey Carwyn had brought him from Ireland the year before and waiting to see why she had come. He felt a small surge of triumph when she unfolded the note he'd left for her weeks ago and set it on her lap.

"So the job you mentioned, what kind of job is it?" she asked.

"A research position. Primarily computer work."

"Why me?" she asked, her eyes still carrying a shade of suspicion as she looked at him.

So I can find out more about your father and his habits. So I have something to offer him in exchange when I do find him—which I will. Also, you smell like honeysuckle.

He blinked at the last thought but shrugged nonchalantly. "You have more than the necessary skill set. Most of the information I need to search for is online now. Obviously, you can imagine why that is problematic. Caspar can help, but he's neither as technologically savvy as you are, nor does he have your background in information sciences." He paused before he continued. "Though he does make an excellent cocktail, and that shouldn't be overlooked."

"Thank you!" he heard his friend call from the kitchen. Giovanni and Beatrice exchanged a smile before she remembered she was being suspicious. She frowned a little and asked another question.

"I'm sure there are plenty of people you could hire. Why me?"

He stared at her challenging expression before he set his drink down and leaned back into the plush couch. "Well, you seemed to have handled the whole 'blood sucking demon of the night' thing fairly well, so I thought I'd take a stab at not having to meddle with the brains of every assistant I use."

Her expression was carefully blank as she absorbed his words. He leaned forward and sipped his drink, noticing her watching him carefully.

"Go ahead," he offered quietly.

"What?"

"I can see a million questions swirling around that brain of yours. Just ask them."

She squirmed in her seat. "I didn't want to be rude."

He sat back again and stretched a long arm along the back of the sofa. Though he was usually a secretive creature, he found himself curious what she would ask.

"Go ahead," he murmured as he watched her examine him.

"You drink whiskey."

"Yes."

"So, do you eat? Do you need to?"

"I have to drink blood to survive. Human is the most nutritionally satisfying and tastes the best, of course—"

"Of course," she interjected and he smiled.

"But I can also survive on animal blood if I need to, and many immortals choose to do that. They just have to feed more often."

"How often?"

"Drinking human blood? About once a week."

She perked up. "Oh, well that's not so bad. Oh, unless—"

"No, I don't have to 'drain' a blood donor, Beatrice. I don't have to kill to survive."

She paused, a small smile ghosting her lips. "Unlike us, who kill animals all the time."

He shrugged. "I wasn't going to mention that if you weren't."

She met his eyes, a tentative warmth creeping into her expression. "So, you don't need to, but you do eat a little."

He leaned forward and took another sip of whiskey. "Our bodies are very... slow. Well, the processes are, anyway. My hair grows, just very slowly. My fingernails will as well. We digest normally, but again, very slowly. So I can eat and drink, but I don't need to, though it becomes uncomfortable if I go too long without anything in my stomach."

"So the coffee thing?"

He shrugged. "I really just like the way it smells. I think it tastes absolutely vile, though. I don't know how you drink so much of it."

She grinned, finally looking relaxed as she sat in his chair. "I like it. You drink blood. *That* smells and tastes vile, if you ask me."

"Touché."

"Thank you."

She paused again before asking, "So, the wooden stake through the heart thing is apparently a myth, but you can be killed by fire. Anything else?"

"Should I be concerned that one of your first questions is how to kill me?"

Her jaw dropped. "What? No! I didn't mean...I was just curious."

He snorted. "Well, you can remain so."

"What about the sun?" she asked. "Extra toasty?"

"I'm not going to burst into flames, but I avoid tanning beds."

"Silver?"

"Some of my favorite cufflinks."

"Garlic?"

"Please," he sneered. "I'm Italian."

She was wearing an almost adorable scowl as he ruined all of her movie stereotypes of his kind. He was usually bored by human reactions, but found himself enjoying hers. For his part, Giovanni hoped she would take the job as his research assistant. Besides the valuable connection she provided to her father, she was extremely bright, and he found it relaxing not to have to hide around her.

He could also monitor any other vampire who became aware of her. Houston's immortal population was small, and most tended to mind their own business—which was why he had chosen the humid city in the south of Texas—but if he had discovered her, her father's sire could, as well.

Beatrice was still sipping her drink and sneaking looks at him when she thought he wasn't looking.

"So, if I take this job, where would you want to work? At the university?"

"No, here. I have top of the line equipment upstairs and extensive firewalls to keep my research private, along with numerous electronic editions of reference texts and a large library. I just can't use any of the computers."

"That has *got* to be frustrating."

"Very. Because of my nature and affinity toward fire, I'm even less able to use modern technology than most vampires. It has become more and more complicated as the years go by."

"Good thing you have Caspar."

"Yes, it is. He's very useful, despite the fact that he's a horrible eavesdropper."

"I heard that!" Caspar called from the kitchen. Giovanni cocked his eyebrow at Beatrice, who stifled a laugh.

"So, if I take this job—*if* I take it—what kind of hours are we talking about? And what do you actually do? Can I ask?"

He nodded and took another sip of whiskey as Caspar came into the living room to refill Beatrice's drink and set a small plate of cheese and olives on the coffee table.

"Of course. I only work when I want to, so it would be part-time. Evenings, of course, but I'm flexible as to which ones. Fridays are not usually available. I don't have to work, but immortality is dreadfully boring for the idle rich, so I try to keep myself occupied. I'm a hunter by nature, so I hunt rare documents and books for private clients, along with some antiquities. Collectibles, art, that sort of thing, though antiquities are not particularly interesting to me."

"So, do you work mostly for other—other vampires?"

"Mostly yes, though not exclusively. I don't advertise, and since clients find me through referral, I tend to take work from those who have worked with me in the past. Most of those people are immortal."

She sat quietly, staring into her drink before she spoke again. "Wow."

He frowned. "What? Why? Why 'wow?'"

"You're like a—a book detective. That's really cool."

He couldn't suppress his smile. "I think so, yes."

"And you want to pay me to help you find books and antiques?"

"That's the idea."

She paused for a moment, biting her lip before she asked, "Will you help me find my father?"

The blood began to rush in his veins and he smothered a low growl of satisfaction when he heard her. It was perfect. She wanted exactly the same thing he did, though probably for very different reasons.

"Yes," he said with a smile he hoped didn't show his extended fangs. "I'll find him."

Beatrice smiled. "Then I'll take it, I don't even care if you're an asshole when you're working. Besides, what you do is a book lover's dream job."

He shrugged. "Well, if you're going to be pursuing a career for eternity, it might as well be something you enjoy."

"I'll say so."

He tried to suppress the smile that wanted to take over his face. "So you agree to work for me? I confess, I've never had an assistant other than Caspar. I might very well be an asshole when I'm working."

"You are!" Caspar shouted from the kitchen.

Beatrice laughed outright when she heard him, and Giovanni couldn't help but join her. His mind began to race with thoughts of finding his books, and he couldn't deny that the girl's amusing presence was an added bonus.

He saw a grey streak dart down the stairs from the corner of his eye then Doyle was there, curling himself around Beatrice's combat boots and looking longingly at Giovanni with copper colored eyes.

"Oh, hi. Hi, Cat." Beatrice seemed more than a bit taken aback by the large feline investigating her. Doyle sniffed her boots for a few moments before he jumped on the couch next to Giovanni.

"You're not getting any cheese from me, Doyle. I'm told it's not good for you."

"That is a very large cat."

"He is." Doyle chirped and shoved his head under Giovanni's hand. Beatrice grinned at them both. "He's very smart. But spoiled. That is Caspar's doing, I'm afraid. He keeps trying to buy his love through extravagant meals."

"It's going to work one of these days," Caspar muttered as he came in to lift Doyle from Giovanni's lap. "Come now, Doyle. I have some lovely tuna for you in the kitchen."

Caspar tucked the cat under his arm and walked back to the kitchen, winking at Beatrice as he left the room.

"So when can I see your library?" She was practically bouncing in her seat.

Giovanni smothered a smile. "So forward, Beatrice. Just jump right in and ask to see a vampire's library, why don't you? Not even dinner first?"

Her mouth dropped open and she flushed bright red. "What? That's not part of the job, is it?"

He could not stop the laughter that burst out. "No! I was teasing you. I don't expect—no, definitely not. That's not part of—no. No."

She curled her lip. "Well, now I'm almost offended. I can't smell *that* bad."

His gaze suddenly focused on her neck and the slight flush that lingered there. He felt the raw hunger in his throat, and he knew he had waited too long. He needed to feed. And soon.

"No," he said hoarsely. The tender skin on her neck began to pulse slightly as her heart rate picked up. "You smell..."

She must have felt the energy that suddenly charged the room, because she stiffened in her chair, staring at him. He heard her heart race, and the scent of adrenaline began to perfume the air.

"Gio," Caspar called as he walked briskly into the living room. "Do you and B need a refreshment on your drinks?" The older man came to stand between Giovanni and the girl, breaking his concentration and snapping him out of the sudden bloodlust that had taken him by surprise.

"No." Giovanni cleared his throat. "Beatrice was just leaving." He stood and went to offer Beatrice a hand as she rose from her chair. She eyed him cautiously, glancing between him and Caspar as she stood.

"I apologize. I do need to go out this evening. We'll have to see the library another time," he spoke quietly, hoping she couldn't detect the fangs lengthening in his mouth as he approached.

From the way she stared at his lips, he suspected they were not as hidden as he hoped.

"Sure," she said. "I need to get home, anyway. My grandmother is probably waiting up."

"Of course."

Caspar took Beatrice by the arm and walked her toward the kitchen door. She glanced over her shoulder, and Giovanni tried to temper his hungry stare as she walked away. From the sound of her heart, and the scent of her blood, he wasn't very successful.

Still, she did not look away.

He took a deep breath, his nostrils flaring at the deliciously rich scent of her blood slowly dissipated in the air around him. He walked over to the chair where she sat, bending down to run his face along the back much as the cat had scented her legs earlier.

His eyes narrowed and his throat burned. He quickly walked upstairs to grab his coat before the hunger overtook him. Taking a deep breath as he stepped outside, feeling his skin burn as he wrestled down the instincts he had battled for five hundred years.

"Why is she here?"

"For you. My blood is gone from your system and you need sustenance."

"I don't want—"

"You will not drain her. That only exhibits a lack of control. Though you are young, you must never be without self-control, do you understand me?"

"Yes, Father."

"Now feed."

After he was sure his control was intact, he headed for the nightclubs which would already be packed on Friday night.

Brushing against the bouncer at the door to one of his favorite clubs, he quickly found a table only occupied by a few college boys. He held out his hand to introduce himself and, with a quick use of amnis, convinced them he was an acquaintance they had invited out for the evening. As the night progressed, college girls passed by drawn to his looks, but put off by his manner when he brushed them aside. Finally, he spotted a pair of women who appeared to be in their late twenties eyeing him from across the club.

He observed them for a few minutes, noting their provocative clothing and the body language indicating they were looking for sex. Abandoning his oblivious companions at the table, he approached the women, leaning down and trying to ignore the stale scent of fruit body wash and forget the smell of honeysuckle.

"Hi, I'm John," he said with a flat American accent, holding out his hand to shake first one, then the other's hand. Their minds were weak and would be easy to manipulate. And though the prospect of sex with the two women surprisingly distasteful to him that evening, he sensed both of them were in good health and would not suffer any ill effects when he took their blood. He could easily manipulate them into thinking they'd had a very enjoyable time.

The blonde batted her lashes. "You're hot."

He smiled and held out a hand to her before he leaned over and let his lips feather across the neck of the slightly less crass brunette. He inhaled her scent, ignoring the smell of cheap alcohol that tainted her blood.

He would drink deeply that night.

CHAPTER 7

"Oh, wow."

"What do you think?"

"I tried to imagine, but—I mean...it's so much more—"

"Think it's large enough to keep you satisfied for a while?"

"It's so much bigger than I expected."

He backed away, leaving Beatrice to gaze in wonder at the library that took up half of the second floor.

"I think I'll just leave you two alone for a bit," he said.

"Okay," she said.

"Would you like a fire?"

"Okay." She wandered toward the map case, peering into it with awe.

"How about something to drink? Should I have Caspar bring something up?"

"Sure."

"Mind if I just take a quick sip from your carotid before I go?"

"Yeah, that's fine," she murmured as she stared at a sixteenth century map of South America.

"Right then," he cleared his throat and ignored the low, hungry burn. "I'll be back later. Enjoy."

"Okay. Gio?"

"Hmm?"

A small smile quirked her lips. "I heard the carotid thing. No."

"No harm in asking."

"But yes to the fire. It's cold in here."

He smiled, walking over to the small fireplace with the grouping of chairs surrounding it. Leaning down, he turned on the gas valve and snapped his fingers, quickly tossing a blue flame toward the vents which filled the grate with a warm glow. He saw Beatrice watching him. He looked at her as he stood, and she grinned.

"Still very cool, Batman."

He winked. "Well, I have a library to compete with now."

She sighed and looked at him sympathetically. "Cool flame tricks aside, there's no competition."

He lifted his eyebrow. "Library wins?"

"Every single time."

He laughed and walked toward the doorway. "Feel free to wander around. There's only one locked case, which is of no importance to your work. Everything else is made to be read. Familiarize yourself with the computers tonight. Caspar has created an account for you with your first name as the login identification and last name as the password. Keep it that way."

"You got it. Your computers, your rules."

He gave a curt nod. "I'll be downstairs in my study making some phone calls."

She was already engrossed in a first edition Austen he had purchased in London in the late 1800s. He smiled and left her with his books.

Giovanni walked downstairs, and asked Caspar to bring Beatrice a drink in the library. Since they were working from his home, he could start soon after he rose and had no need to wait for sunset to leave the house. He was surprised how much the idea of having a competent assistant invigorated him. He'd spent the previous fifteen years watching the slow transfer of information from paper to electronic medium with dread, knowing that eventually, much of the information vital to his work would be out of his grasp. Her agreement to work with him, knowing who and what he was, lifted an unanticipated weight off his shoulders.

Beatrice had agreed to work from five-thirty to nine o'clock, Mondays and Thursdays, leaving Tuesday free for some activity she did with her grandmother, and Wednesday for her regular library hours.

He was satisfied with the arrangement and found himself pleased with the prospect of seeing her three nights a week. He knew he could hardly ask for more and was confident his research would go much faster than it had in the past.

He picked up the phone and dialed Carwyn's number.

"Jesus, Mary, and Joseph," the priest said. "Why are you calling me again? You're like a child waiting for Father Christmas. This girl can't be that interesting."

Giovanni chuckled and ignored his friend's question. "I thought you liked hearing my voice."

"And you said she was interesting, not irresistible."

"Stop making assumptions."

"Oh? So you're not 'interested' in her *that* way?"

He frowned, and his mind flashed to the image of Beatrice in his library, browsing the books with a small smile and laughing eyes. Then he remembered the feel of her soft body pressed against his as they jumped out of the broken elevator.

"She's a student, an assistant. A contact, in a manner of speaking."

"Because you always take this kind of interest in students and assistants and contacts," his friend said sarcastically. "Just remember that I'm available for confession should the need arise."

"Amusing. I'll keep that in mind," he muttered, eager to change the subject. "I was calling to let you know we're having an unexpected cold spell, so you might need a sweater."

"Your 'cold spells' are balmy spring weather compared to my mountains. I'm packing my loudest Hawaiian shirts."

He winced. "Please no."

"I just ordered a new one. Had it shipped to your place. Lots of pink flowers on it. Should clash nicely with my hair."

"Do you know what looks good with your demon hair? Ecclesiastical black."

"Boring. I'm only wearing the uniform now when I celebrate mass."

"Hmm, and how is your congregation?"

"Small, but faithful as always."

He sipped his drink. "I'm glad you're staying longer, Carwyn. Something's going to happen. I don't know what, but too many pieces are moving at once for this to be ignored. This girl. Her father. I'm not sure whether to smile or shore up my defenses."

The silence stretched over the line before the Welshman spoke again in his tripping accent, "Have you talked to Tenzin?"

He shook his head though there was no one to see. "Caspar talked to Nima… well, e-mailed her anyway. Apparently they're both being silent lately."

"She usually only does that when she's meditating."

"Yes, I know."

The silence stretched again. "Well, if there's something to know—"

"She'll send word."

"Yes."

Both were silent on the line again as they gathered their thoughts.

"I'm glad I'm coming, too, if for no other reason than to eat Caspar's food. He's a much better cook than Sister Maggie."

"Be careful how loud you say that, Father. Gruel for a month if she hears you."

"She's happy to get rid of me for a while. She's going to visit her sister's family in Kerry while I'm gone."

"We're looking forward to seeing you. Doyle especially."

"And on that note, I'm hanging up. Don't call me again unless there's an emergency. I'll be there in two weeks, for heaven's sake. Oh, have you ordered the match already?"

"Of course. It's on the night after you get here."

"Excellent. Goodbye."

"I'll see you next week."

Giovanni hung up the phone and picked up the printouts Caspar had made of his e-mails from the previous day. Looking through them, he noticed they were still being put off by Livia's people in Rome, and his client for the Lincoln documents was making a fuss again. He was bored by the whole matter and wondered whether he should just return the rude human's retainer and move on to something more interesting.

Then again, he realized, the case might be a good one to give to Beatrice. It was sure to keep her busy. The client was human, so the consequences of missing something or failing to find the requested document were negligible. Yes, he thought, it might be a good first project for the persistent Miss De Novo.

He almost overlooked the last email in the stack. It was short, cryptic, and had clearly come from an immortal, as it was sent to the e-mail address he gave only to vampire clients. The message was brief, and the sender used an obviously false address.

They'll be there soon, and there's more where they came from.
You're welcome.
L

He looked at the date and time the e-mail was received and stared at the final initial. Giovanni opened the locked drawer on the top right-hand side of his desk and slid the paper inside. Then he leaned back, sipped his whiskey, and let his thoughts wander to the past.

"IT'S THERE SOMEWHERE."

"I've looked, Gio. It's not."

"Yes, Beatrice, it is. The client has been waiting for this document for months now. It is your job to find it. We know it was sold at auction in 1993. We know it's in a private collection somewhere on the Eastern seaboard," he lectured her as he pored over one of his journals he had taken from his locked cabinet. "Put the pieces together. There are only so many auction houses that deal with that kind of document on the East coast, and most of them keep old catalogues online now."

"From ten years ago?"

He shrugged as he sat at the dark oak table in the middle of the room. "Well, that's what I hired you for. I tracked it to the auction. The rest is the easy part. Look at the list I gave you."

He had put her on the trail of the boring Lincoln document earlier that night while he looked over some of his past clients, trying to ascertain who, exactly, the mysterious 'L' might be who had sent the cryptic e-mail. He wasn't wasting energy on speculating what he or she might have sent, as there wasn't enough information yet. Whoever it was, he was certain it was related to Stephen De Novo and his lost books.

"This is going to take forever."

"Forever is a very relative term when you're talking to me. It's going to take more time than you've spent on previous projects your insipid professors at the university have assigned you. Not forever."

"Old man," she muttered under her breath.

"Warned you, B," Caspar called from the doorway.

"I should have listened; his looks are deceiving," she grumbled as she turned her eyes away from him to blink at the glowing monitor.

He ignored them both and took out one of his journals from the period before he was turned, when Savonarola's bonfires tore through the city of his birth.

Caspar walked over and set a mug of hot tea in front of Beatrice before taking a whiskey to Giovanni. The butler set the tray down on the coffee table and picked up his own book to read in his favorite chair by the fire. It was Beatrice's third week working at the house, and the three of them had already fallen into a comfortable rhythm.

Giovanni darted around the library, often moving so quickly he startled Beatrice as she sat behind the computer, clicking the keys as she stared at the monitor, searching the vast digital territory he could not access. Giovanni would call out search terms as he worked, and she shooed him away if he got too close to the electronic equipment.

Caspar joined them to read halfway through the evening, often bantering about favorite horror films with Beatrice or needling Giovanni in various languages.

Doyle moved almost as quickly as the vampire, jumping from lap to lap and looking for any imminent treats to be dropped or sneaked behind Giovanni's back.

"Seriously, Gio. I see *one* of these houses you list with catalogues online, the rest—"

The kitchen door slammed, and they all started at the sound. Giovanni held up a hand for silence, but didn't hear any additional noise. Caspar walked swiftly to Beatrice's desk and stood next to her, looking far more dangerous than one might expect from a sixty-seven-year-old butler.

Giovanni, on the other hand, let out a low growl and slipped out the door in the blink of an eye.

He paused on the stairs, sniffed the air, and relaxed.

"You can hide, Carwyn, but your wet wolfhound cannot. I have company. Stop scaring the guest."

All of a sudden, something pounced on his back, and Giovanni and the silent intruder tumbled down the stairs in a blur. They rolled toward the entry way, knocking over a green vase that stood in the exquisitely appointed room. A pale white hand shot out, catching the vase before it hit the ground and tossing it toward the plush sofa.

"That is turn of the century Bien Hoa. If you break *it*, I will break *you*," Giovanni gasped out as his friend put him in a choke hold.

"Oh, it's fine, Gio! You're such a prissy bastard sometimes." Carwyn twisted around, trying to capture his friend's leg in a lock, but failed. Carwyn had never been faster than him. His only advantage lay in his broad shoulders, heavily muscled arms, and the element of surprise, which he had lost.

Giovanni twisted around, finally getting out of the choke-hold and flipping backward over Carwyn's head to leap on his back. In no time, the Welshman was flat on his face with one arm twisted behind him, and a long leg bent his knees at angles that would have broken a mortal man.

Giovanni decided to shock him, just for good measure. Carwyn hissed when he felt the sharp sizzle course through his body.

"Damn it, Sparky!" he yelped. "Not fair."

"Yield?"

"Of course, you bloody Italian, I yield. Now let me up."

Giovanni stood with a grin, holding his hand out to his old friend who scowled at him and grabbed it in a harder grip than strictly necessary. Carwyn walked over to the couch to retrieve the vase.

"See? Not a scratch. I was an expert archer, you know." He pulled back an arm as if aiming an arrow and sighted Giovanni with one blue eye. "Sired in my prime."

"Archery does not translate to tossing Vietnamese ceramics, you idiot," Giovanni scowled and dusted off the vase before setting on its stand. "And where is your dog? It better not be digging anything up."

Carwyn shrugged his broad shoulders. "I'm sure he is. So, where's the new blood?"

Giovanni nodded to the top of the stairs.

Carwyn looked to the top of the landing where Caspar stood, looking on in amusement. Beatrice peeked out from behind him, her dark eyes taking in the clearly immortal being now standing in the entryway.

The new vampire almost tripped up the landing, his wild auburn hair flying and a grin overtaking his face as he peeked at Beatrice, who was still hiding behind Caspar.

"Now, Cas, tell her I won't bite, will you?" Carwyn grinned and shot a wink at her. Beatrice stepped out from Caspar's shadow to examine Giovanni's friend more carefully.

Carwyn stuck out a hand. "Father Carwyn ap Bryn, my dear."

Beatrice shook it tentatively, her small hand dwarfed by the mountain of a man in front of her. "Father?" she asked skeptically.

He winked at her before bending to press a kiss her delicate fingers. "Indeed." Carwyn brought her hand up, suddenly twisting it to sniff her wrist. "No wonder you wanted to hire her, Gio." Carwyn smiled. "She smells delectable."

Giovanni caught Beatrice's quick gasp as he climbed the stairs. Caspar was chuckling and trying to shove Carwyn toward the library, and Beatrice hung back, her face flushed with embarrassment and her hand still caught in the Welshman's grip.

"Give her hand back, old man," Giovanni muttered in a voice only an immortal would hear.

Carwyn growled a little and shot him a look, but let Beatrice's hand drop and walked into the library with Caspar. Giovanni stepped onto the landing, observing Beatrice's reaction carefully. Her heart rate was rapid, but there was no smell of adrenaline in the air, so he knew she wasn't afraid. Nevertheless, he approached her cautiously.

"He's harmless, really. Far more harmless than me."

She glanced at the entryway. "Really? Tell that to your vase."

Reassured of her mood, he placed a hand on the small of her back to lead her into the library where Caspar was pouring a drink from a crystal decanter, and Doyle was hissing at the large Welshman who shoved him out of his favorite chair.

"It's raining out there, Gio. I come to your place to escape the rain, for heaven's sake. I get enough of this at home."

Giovanni was curious what Beatrice would make of one of his oldest friends. Though Carwyn was a priest, he rarely wore any kind of uniform, preferring to dress himself more like a surfer than a man of the cloth when he visited the United States.

He removed his soggy coat and hung it on the back of his chair, revealing a garish shirt with scantily clad hula girls dancing across the back. He must have caught Beatrice's stare, because he only smiled again and sat down, reaching for the drink Caspar held out to him.

A HIDDEN FIRE

"Thanks, Cas. We don't *have* to wear black, you know." He nodded toward Giovanni, who had shown Beatrice to the small couch in front of the fire and sat down next to her. "This one does it because he thinks it makes him look dashing, or he really is that boring. Haven't figured that one out."

"I vote boring," Caspar quipped. "God knows I've tried to break him out of his shell."

"Though," Carwyn shrugged. "Look at the girl, Cas. Perhaps he's met his match in the black wardrobe department."

"Thanks," Beatrice finally piped in.

He winked at her. "Great boots, my dear. Do you ride motorcycles? And if not, would you like to?"

Giovanni leaned into the back of the couch, stretching his arm casually behind Beatrice, unable to completely turn off his territorial instincts around another vampire, even his old and trusted friend.

"You're early, Father. Everything all right in Wales?" he asked nonchalantly.

The sharp glint in the Welshman's eye told him they would be having a more private discussion once the humans left, and tension made the blood begin to move in his veins. He instinctively moved closer to Beatrice, who was listening to a story Carwyn had begun relating about one of their more outrageous exploits in London in the late 1960s when Caspar had been much younger.

The three friends took turns making the girl laugh with their wild tales and quick, needling humor, and Giovanni took a strange kind of delight in the amused expression that lit Beatrice's face every time Caspar or Carwyn told a story that proved to be embarrassing to him. He simply shrugged and took another sip of his whiskey.

After a couple of hours, he noticed Beatrice's eyes begin to droop, and she nestled a little more into his side on the small sofa. He pushed aside the urge to reach down and run a hand along her hair. "Caspar," he asked quietly, "could you drive Beatrice home, please?"

She sat up, as if surprised by Giovanni's question. She glanced at her watch, not realizing it had been pressed into his leg and was now dead.

She shook it for a second then glared at him in annoyance.

He shrugged. "I'll buy you a new one tomorrow."

"Yes, you will. I'd appreciate a ride home, Cas, it must be late."

"I'd be happy to drive you. Let these two old men catch up on their secret vampire business without us."

She chuckled, having no idea how true the statement was. "I'm surprised my grandma hasn't called already." She yawned and stretched as she stood, treating Giovanni to a glimpse of the smooth skin at her waist. He shifted slightly, looking away as she stepped over his long legs.

Gathering her bags from the desk she used, she quickly followed Caspar out of the library.

"Good night, everyone. I'll see you on Wednesday, Gio. Carwyn," she smiled, "very interesting meeting you."

"Likewise, B. I'm sure I'll be seeing you around." The Welshman stretched his long legs in front of him and batted away the cat as they listened to Caspar and Beatrice walk down the stairs. Only when they had both heard the kitchen door slam shut did Carwyn turn to Giovanni with a grim look on his face.

"Heard from your son lately?"

CHAPTER 8

Beatrice and Charlotte stared at the letters Dr. Christiansen spread out on the table like a proud father.

"This could be the start of a very exciting new collection, ladies."

"I have to confess, even though they're thematic orphans in our collection, they are so damn cool," Charlotte murmured as she examined the old parchment.

"How old are they?" Beatrice asked.

The grey-haired director set the letters down on the table in the reading room and pulled out a sheaf of notes from his briefcase. "They've been dated to 1484. A very important year in the Italian Renaissance—really, what some would consider Florence's golden age. It was before Savonarola, and there was a blossoming of art, philosophy, classical studies—"

"James, we know what the Italian Renaissance is," Charlotte remarked.

"Well..." The academic blushed a little. "It's a very exciting pair of letters. The translation was done at the University of Ferrara, and the letters were authenticated there as well."

"Is Renaissance Italian much different from modern Italian?" Beatrice asked, wishing, as she often did, that her father were still around to see some of the treasures she came across in her work.

"Somewhat, but we don't have to worry about that. Professor Scalia is practically chomping at the bit to take a look at them, and he's an expert in the language. I suspect the whole of the history department, classics department, and the philosophy department will be our very eager visitors for quite some time."

"Philosophy department?" Beatrice asked, still examining the well-preserved letters on the table. She couldn't help but admire how clean the edges of the parchment were. They look like they had been preserved by a professional archivist when they were first written.

"Oh yes, the letters are written from Count Giovanni Pico della Mirandola, a notable philosopher, to his friend, Angelo Poliziano, who was a scholar and poet in Florence. The two men had quite a correspondence and were known to be part of a close group of friends, all great thinkers and some quite controversial. Indeed, one of their circle was Savonarola himself."

"The crazy priest that burned all the books?" Beatrice asked.

Charlotte said, "There was a lot more to him than that. He was a fascinating individual, despite the bonfires." She looked over at Dr. Christiansen. "Do the letters mention Savonarola?"

"Only briefly. Feel free to take a look at the translations. They're mainly personal letters. Pico spends some of the first letter talking about an orphan—or an illegitimate child of some sort, either is likely—that Poliziano had found in Florence; Pico had taken the child into his house. The count had no children of his own. The first letter is mostly discussing the boy's education, but there is some mention of Poliziano introducing Pico to Lorenzo de Medici for the first time, and that is very significant."

Beatrice stared at the document, examining the curl of the ancient script and the old, yellowing parchment.

"FIRENZE, 1484
  Caro Giovanni..."

1484, SHE THOUGHT. WAS IT A COINCIDENCE? COUNT GIOVANNI PICO DELLA MIRANDOLA. She shook her head. It was ridiculous to think he would have kept the same name for over 500 years.

A faint memory of their meeting at the museum stirred in the back of her mind.

"All the men in my family are named Giovanni."

"Well, ladies, much to do today! We'll have to enjoy these treasures later. Charlotte, how are the preparations for the History of Physics exhibit coming?"

Charlotte and Dr. Christiansen began discussing the exhibit the department was helping curate the following month, and Beatrice packed away the recently acquired documents and wandered back to the stacks to set the Florentine letters in the spot Dr. Christiansen had mentioned to her earlier. He seemed to think that more of the historical correspondence might be given to the university in the future.

Beatrice wondered again who the generous anonymous donor could be, and why exactly he had chosen a relatively obscure state university in Texas to be the recipient of such a generous gift. Thinking about the strange turn her life had taken in the previous two months, she wondered where to draw the line between coincidence and calculation.

She went about her duties preoccupied with the mysterious letters, finally escaping to the stacks that afternoon to examine them and look over the translation of the first letter.

Most of it detailed the new addition to the Pico household, a boy of seven named Jacopo, who the Count adopted and intended to educate. It sounded like he was the illegitimate child of one of the Pico brothers, though the letter didn't say which.

One passage seemed to leap from the page:

"LORENZO HAS MENTIONED YOU SEVERAL TIMES SINCE YOUR VISIT WITH HIM. *He was amused by your sometimes outrageous statements; and I believe, were you to find yourself back in Florence anytime soon, he would be most delighted to continue your acquaintance.*"

WOW, SHE THOUGHT, LORENZO DE MEDICI. LORENZO THE MAGNIFICENT. Could Giovanni have met him? If he was really over five hundred years old, it was possible.

There was mention of city gossip: a strange man named Niccolo Andros, something about Lorenzo's children, and finally, a mention of some sort of scandal Pico was involved in with a married woman.

That brought a flush to her cheeks, and she set the notes down. It was hard not to imagine a woman being attracted to Giovanni. Despite his brusque demeanor, she still couldn't seem to help the growing attraction she had to the vampire.

She read the letter four times, making notes and jotting down names and dates. She examined the second letter, but decided to do some research on the two men before reading it. She had little background in the Italian Renaissance, and the person she knew was most knowledgeable was the one person she couldn't ask. She snorted as she imagined how the conversation would go:

"*Oh, hey, Gio. Do you happen to be a fifteenth century philosopher named Giovanni Pico? Oh, and what does all this have to do with my father, by the way?*"

"*Please go back to searching through endlessly boring auction catalogues, Beatrice. I'm far smarter than you are and too stuck-up to answer your questions. Also, I'm very good-looking and can get away with being an asshole.*"

Beatrice sighed and slipped the notes into her messenger bag. She would have time to go online at home after she took her grandmother to dinner with her friends that night.

"Beatrice, you must get a picture of Giovanni for the girls!"

She scowled at her grandmother's voice from the kitchen as she finished putting on her make-up for their night out. Isadora and her closest friends had kept a long-standing dinner engagement every Tuesday night for as long as she could remember. It used to be the time that Beatrice and her grandfather would spend in his workshop or watching old horror movies together, but since his death she had joined her grandmother for the weekly outings.

At first, it was simply so she wouldn't feel the aching loss of her grandfather, but now she enjoyed the evenings with the interesting group of women.

"Grandma, I'm not going to ask my boss for a picture to show your friends. It's embarrassing."

"But he's so handsome! Maybe with your phone camera?"

"No! That's creepy. I don't think he likes getting his picture taken anyway."

Probably not a good idea when you've been around for over 500 years, she thought as she lined her eyes in black.

"Well, it's very exciting. You must tell everyone about the thrilling book mysteries you're helping to solve now."

Beatrice laughed. "I've been searching online auction catalogues for a single document for almost a month, Grandma. It's not as glamorous as it sounds."

"Still," Isadora smiled as she walked into the bathroom to check her hair in the mirror. "The library sounds beautiful. Can you imagine how jealous your father would be? He'd be so proud of you."

Beatrice fell silent as she thought about her father. She'd been reluctant to bring him up to Giovanni since the night she agreed to work for him, still unsure of what the vampire really wanted with her. Though she'd been reassured by meeting Caspar, she still had the uneasy feeling that there was a lot about Giovanni Vecchio she didn't know.

And maybe a lot she didn't *want* to know.

"Always be grateful for unexpected opportunities, Mariposa. You never know where a job like this might lead." Isadora turned and patted her granddaughter's cheek. "Imagine what exciting things might be in your future!"

Beatrice sighed. "It's just a research job, Grandma. But it's a good one, and I have no complaints about my boss. He's demanding, but it's not anything I didn't sign up for."

"You said he has an interesting friend visiting from overseas? Who is he? Is he a book dealer as well?"

She grinned when she thought of Carwyn. Since their meeting, the unusual priest had charmed her, although she didn't know what to make of him at first.

He looked like he had been turned in his thirties, but had the personality and humor of a teenager. He wore the ugliest Hawaiian shirts she had ever seen, but still seemed to attract more than his share of female attention when he and Giovanni had visited the library together.

He was as boisterous as Giovanni was taciturn, yet the friendly affection between them was obvious and she had started to see a slightly softer side to the aloof vampire.

"No, Carwyn's not a book dealer; he's a priest of some sort. He's Welsh, I think. I guess he usually comes out this time of year. I think they're working on a project together."

"Well, that sounds lovely. It's so nice to have friends with the same interests."

Like drinking blood, avoiding electronic equipment, and staying out of sunlight so you don't burn to a crisp, she mused silently as she pulled her long hair into a low ponytail.

She grabbed her purse and helped Isadora to the car. Her grandmother immediately began texting her friends that they were on their way and Beatrice took advantage of the silence to think about the past week.

The two vampires had been working on something they didn't want anyone to know about; she was sure of it. Carwyn had come to the library with Giovanni the previous Wednesday, but they spent more time speaking in furtive whispers than they had transcribing characters for the mysterious Tenzin. When she went to the house on Thursday the odd mood had continued.

Even Caspar seemed out of the loop, and she had no idea what they would hide from someone they seemed to trust so much. Giovanni had been secretive before, and Carwyn's appearance seemed to have done nothing but intensified his mood.

Their veiled references to their friend in China also caught her attention. She knew Tenzin was another immortal that had been friends with them for presumably hundreds of years, but anytime her name was mentioned an odd sense of foreboding fell over the two men.

"Oh, Beatrice, there it is!"

She brushed her concerns away when she spotted the small restaurant where her grandmother's three closest friends were waiting outside. As she pulled into the parking lot, her grandmother waved like a school girl and Beatrice smiled, wondering for the thousandth time why she couldn't be more like her grandmother when it came to making friends.

Beatrice hadn't always been antisocial. When she was younger, she'd had lots of friends. Even after her father died, she'd been a happy child, wrapped in the comfort of her grandparents' home. It wasn't until the summer she had seen her father again that her social life began to collapse. It had never really recovered.

She tried to shove back the bitterness that reared its head when she thought about the cause of her depression. The self-destructive choices she'd made still haunted her at times. During that dark period, she mostly found solace in books. Never an avid reader before, she pulled herself out of depression by escaping into the other worlds books offered.

She realized it probably wasn't the healthiest way to cope, but between the library and her grandfather, she had managed to make it through high school. After that, she had buried herself in her college studies, and it wasn't until she'd begun working at the university library that she felt like she found her niche.

"B, honey, you just look more gorgeous every time I see you!" she heard her grandmother's friend, Sally Devereaux, call across the parking lot. Sally was the epitome of a Texas matriarch, complete with the requisite giant hair, heavy twang, and big personality. The others in the group, Marta Voorhies and Laura Gambetti, were quieter.

"How is your wonderful new job, B?" Marta asked.

"Yes, Isadora says you're working for an Italian gentleman," Laura added with wink. "Italian men are, of course, the most handsome on the planet."

Beatrice laughed at the women's curiosity. She had a feeling that knowing her employer was a five hundred-year-old vampire would do nothing to put them off. They would probably just ask to see his fangs.

"Hey, everyone. Yeah, it's pretty cool. I'll tell you all about it during dinner, okay?"

"If we don't get in there, we aren't going to be dining, girls!" Sally boomed. "Let's go inside, we'll talk while we eat."

"Yes," Isadora added, "and you can try to persuade her to get a picture of him."

"Grandma—"

"Oh, B, you must!"

"Is he really that handsome?"

"More importantly, is he single?"

"I'd like to hear more about his work; it sounds fascinating!"

Beatrice sighed deeply, enveloped in their familiar chatter and followed the four women inside.

Hours later, after she had tentatively agreed to take a picture of her boss and set her grandmother up on a blind date with Caspar at Sally's insistence, she drove back to their small house.

"Beatrice, did you remember to pick up those art books for me from the library?" Isadora asked. "I need them to teach my class tomorrow."

"Oh shoot. I got them, and then left them at Gio's last night when I was working. I'm sorry."

"It's no problem, dear. I did want them soon so I could show the young man in my class about the brush technique I was trying to explain. When do you go back?"

She frowned. "You know, I'll run by and get them. Otherwise I won't be back until Thursday night."

"Oh, it's too late. I don't want to wake anyone for some silly books."

"Trust me, they'll be awake."

"Well, if you're sure..."

"I'm sure it'll be fine." Beatrice reasoned that even if Giovanni was out with Carwyn, Caspar was likely to be home. Plus, the vampire's house in River Oaks wasn't all that far from her grandmother's place.

She dropped Isadora off and made the short drive to Giovanni's home. As she pulled up to the gate, she could just see Carwyn's huge Irish wolfhound peek his head over the low wall.

She pushed the button to call the house.

"Yes?"

"It's B, Caspar. I forgot some books here last night. Do you mind if I come in quick and grab them?"

She heard the gate buzz and the butler's amused voice could be heard as she pulled forward. "Of course not, and—may I add—what wonderful timing you have, my dear!"

Narrowing her eyes at the odd statement, she pulled through the gate, keeping her window down as Bran, Carwyn's grey dog, trotted alongside her car.

"How's it going tonight, Bran?" The huge dog huffed as he escorted her up the driveway.

"Dig up any more roses?" Beatrice grinned, remembering the amusing rant Giovanni had gone on last Thursday after a particularly muddy set of footprints found their way into the living room. "Manage to find Doyle yet?"

At the mention of the cat's name, the wolfhound abruptly halted, looked across the yard as if remembering something and let out a bellow before he shot across the lawn.

Laughing at the amusing and very friendly dog, Beatrice finally pulled behind the garage where she usually parked her small car. She walked to the kitchen door and knocked, pleased to see Caspar's smiling face through the glass panels.

"Ah! B, I'm so glad you're here. No one ever believes me, but now you'll know the truth."

She frowned in confusion. "Uh...Cas, what are you talking about, and does it involve bodily injury? Because I kind of like this blouse, and I'm not wearing my boots."

Caspar smiled. "No, but he always comes across as so dignified, doesn't he? Now, my dear," the grey-haired butler winked, "you'll know the real Giovanni."

And with that mysterious statement, he practically pulled her into the kitchen. She looked around in confusion for a moment before she heard the loud yells coming from the living room.

"Bloody bastard, I did not see that coming!"

"Use the folding chair! It's sitting in the corner for a reason!"

Beatrice's eyes widened when she heard the two men yelling. The sound of applause filled the living room and the surround sound poured into the kitchen.

"That's not—" Beatrice started.

"Oh yes." Caspar nodded. "It's exactly what you think."

"Well, I'll be damned," she muttered. "Cas, you have made my year."

Beatrice walked silently into the living room, suddenly happy to be wearing her soft ballet flats. She approached the two vampires watching the television, who had well over a thousand years of life between them, careful to keep her distance so they didn't smell her.

Giovanni had donned his usual grey sweater and black slacks for the evening, but Carwyn appeared to be wearing a garish t-shirt with an ugly masked face on it. They were totally absorbed with the spectacle on the television screen. Just then, the crowd went wild and both vampires jumped up shouting.

"Tap out, you buggering idiot!"

"Use the damn folding chair!"

Beatrice couldn't believe the ammunition she had just been given.

"Hey, guys."

They both spun around when they heard her quiet voice from the back of the living room. Carwyn grinned at her.

"Hello, B! Grab a beer, you're just in time. The main event's on right after this match."

Giovanni, if possible, looked even paler than normal. "Beatrice, this is—were you scheduled to work tonight?" He scratched at the back of his neck in obvious discomfort.

"Nope. Just came by to pick up a couple of books I forgot from the library." She smiled as he squirmed. This mental picture was priceless.

He continued to stare at her, speechless and obviously embarrassed, until he heard the roar from the crowd and Carwyn shouted again. Giovanni spun around to see what was happening on the television.

"Finally! Damn it, Gio. They always go for the folding chair."

"Of course they do. Folding chairs are always there for a reason. They're never just stage props."

Shaking her head, she walked closer to the back of the couch. Both men were staring at the television again, completely engrossed in the professional wrestling match on screen.

"Seriously, guys? Professional wrestling? I might have suspected archery or fencing. Hell, even soccer—"

"Football!" they shouted simultaneously.

"—wouldn't have been that big a surprise, but this?"

Barely clothed women walked around the ring, and flashing lights filled the screen. The announcers shouted about the final match-up of the night, which was on just after the previously taped profiles of the two participants.

"This is the most bloody brilliant sport ever invented," Carwyn almost whispered in awe as he stared at the screen.

"It's not a sport!"

Both turned to look at her in disgust.

"That's not the point!" Carwyn shouted.

"You see, Beatrice," Giovanni started, while the priest turned the volume down just low enough so they could be heard. "Professional wrestling is simply the most modern interpretation of an ancient tradition of stylized verbal battles between enemies. From the time that Homer recorded the Iliad, the emergence of what Scottish scholars call 'flyting'—"

"That would be a verbal battle preceding a physical one, but considered equally as important to the overall outcome," Carwyn interjected.

"Exactly. Throughout world myth, warriors have engaged in a verbal struggle that is as symbolically important as the battle itself. You can see examples in early Anglo-Saxon literature—"

"You've read *Beowulf*, haven't you, English major?"

Giovanni glanced at the priest, but continued in his most academic voice. "Beowulf is only one example, of course. The concept is also prevalent in various Nordic, Celtic, and Germanic epic traditions. Even Japanese and Arabic literature are rife with examples."

"Exactly." Carwyn nodded along. "See, modern professional wrestling is following in a grand epic tradition. Doesn't matter if it's staged, and it doesn't matter who wins, really—"

"Well, I don't know about—"

"What matters," Carwyn shot his friend a look before he continued, "is that the warriors impress the audience as much with their verbal acuity as their physical prowess."

Giovanni nodded. "It's really very fitting within classical Western tradition."

Beatrice stared at them and began to snicker.

"Did you two just come up with some really academic, smart-sounding rationalization for why you're watching professional wrestling on pay-per-view?"

Carwyn said, "Are you kidding? It took us years to come up with that. Grab a beer and sit down."

Still snickering, she walked into the kitchen, where Caspar was holding an open long-neck for her. "Do you—"

He shook his head. "Oh no, this is their own crass amusement. I'll have nothing to do with it, no matter how many times they cite *Beowulf*."

Beatrice chuckled and took the beer. "I guess I can hang out for a while. After all," she smiled, "the main event is just ahead!"

Caspar smiled and went back to his crossword puzzle on the counter. She walked back into the living room and sat in the open spot between the two vampires. Carwyn was already shouting at the screen on her left, but Giovanni sat back, slightly more subdued as he stretched his left arm across the back of the couch and looked at her.

Beatrice said, "It's kind of cute, to be honest."

"Really?"

"You're usually so dignified," she raised her beer to take a drink, and Giovanni leaned in slightly with a small smile on his lips. "It's kind of nice—"

Just then, he grabbed the beer out of her hand and jerked her arm toward his body. His nostrils flared and his eyes glowed as he pulled her hand to his face and inhaled deeply. Her heart rate shot up when she heard the growl rip from his throat, and his left arm coiled around her waist.

"Gio—"

"Where is he?" he hissed.

CHAPTER 9

"Giovanni, let her go."

He was lost in instinct, trapped in the scent of the unexpected enemy on a human his nature had claimed, even if his mind had not. His fangs descended, spurred by the sudden rush of blood in his veins and the unseen threat. He wanted to sink his teeth into her, marking her as his own so no other would dare to touch her.

"Giovanni!" He heard the priest's voice as if he was calling from far away.

"Gio," she whispered; her pulse pounded in his ears, and the scent of her panic rolled off her in seductive waves. "Please, don't—I don't understand—"

His head inched toward her neck, the ancient, territorial compulsion roaring through him to drink and claim her blood as his own. He felt the current in his fingertips crawl across the girl's skin as the amnis began to run through him and into her.

"Giovanni di Spada!"

He stared, hypnotized by the pulsing heartbeat that sped faster the closer he held her. His own heart began to thump faster and he bared his fangs.

"I will end you if you harm the innocent!" Carwyn roared in Italian, the language of his youth finally breaking through the haze that clouded Giovanni's rational mind.

His hooded eyes flew open, and the vampire leapt away from the girl, staring at her in horror when he saw the tears coursing down her face. He stopped breathing and took another step back, pushing down the snarl that threatened to erupt when Carwyn stepped between him and Beatrice.

"Outside. Now!"

He tried to look around Carwyn. "Beatrice—"

"Now, before I throw you out!" he yelled as Caspar stood gaping in the doorway.

Giovanni threw open the terrace doors and stalked outside. Caspar met him pacing near the pool a few minutes later with a bag of blood from the refrigerator. Biting directly into the bag, Giovanni ignored the stale taste as he sucked it dry. He felt the volatile energy licking along his skin, so he stripped off his clothes, and dove to the bottom of the pool where he sat in utter stillness, gradually slowing the beat of his normally silent heart.

He watched the moon through the dark water, disgusted with his actions in the living room and furious with himself for losing control of his base nature after hundreds of years of strict discipline.

> *"What is our first lesson from Plato?"*
> *"'For a man to conquer himself is the first and noblest of all victories.'"*
> *"You must always be stronger than your nature. Do you understand?"*
> *"Yes, Father."*
> *"It is the key to your survival in any circumstance. You more than any other."*

He didn't know how long he sat at the bottom of the pool, but eventually his ears alerted him to the faint splash near the shallow end as something broke the still surface.

He shot up, shocked to see Beatrice sitting near the steps with her shoes off, and her feet dangling near the steps.

"Hey."

He didn't speak, but scanned the surrounding area, spotting Carwyn who sat, glaring at him from one of the chaises on the terrace. Giovanni nodded toward his old friend, his eyes communicating his careful control, and he saw the priest relax. He looked back to the solemn young woman who met his gaze without flinching.

"I would offer an apology, Beatrice De Novo."

The girl had no idea how rare an occasion it was for Giovanni to admit wrongdoing, so she only narrowed her eyes. "Is it going to happen again?"

He paused, wanting to answer honestly. "I had underestimated how territorial I felt toward you. I won't make the mistake again."

"Why do you feel territorial about me?" she asked quietly.

He treaded water, still keeping his distance. "You are under my *aegis*, whether you accept it or not." Giovanni ignored the sudden tension he sensed from Carwyn on the patio, choosing to lock his gaze on the girl at the end of the pool.

"What does that mean?" She looked at him, confusion evident in her features.

There was no need for her to know the full extent of his aegis, or that by claiming her, he had every right to drink from her as he wished. He decided the simplest explanation was best.

"It means I have taken responsibility for you in my world. Part of that responsibility is to protect you, and I failed in that tonight."

"You stopped."

He couldn't speak, afraid that honesty would send her running. If Carwyn had not been there, he wouldn't have stopped.

She must have seen the truth in his eyes. "Would you have killed me?"

Most definitely not. "No ... but I would have marked you. Without your permission."

She frowned and looked at him curiously. "Do humans—do they *ever* give you their permission?"

He avoided the question, diving and surfacing a few feet from her. She looked away, flustered by his presence, so he retreated a few feet.

"Wh—who is Giovanni di Spada?" she asked.

"Who?"

"Carwyn, he called you that when you were...you know."

Giovanni frowned a little, faintly remembering the priest calling the name of his more violent past. "Giovanni de Spada is the name I was using when Carwyn and I met. I went by that name for almost two hundred years. He still forgets and calls me that occasionally."

"So you changed the last name, but you kept Giovanni?"

He nodded, baffled by her questions, but willing to entertain them if it regained some of the trust he had broken. "It seemed easier to keep the given name. If I ever traveled back to the same place or the same business and someone happened to remember me, it was easy enough to claim I was a relative. And, of course, there were no photographs until recently."

"Oh," she nodded, "that makes sense."

"It wasn't difficult to change your identity for most of history."

"And now?"

He shrugged. "Now it is harder, but not impossible."

She paused and finally met his eyes. He could see her start to relax and wished he had not agreed to avoid using his amnis on her. It would make questioning her far more straightforward.

"Who did you meet today?" he asked quietly, slowly moving closer to her at the edge of the pool.

"Who did I—what? I met..." she cleared her throat, suddenly flustered again, "lots of people, Gio. What does that—"

"You met someone new. A stranger. You had the scent of another immortal on you," he said, keeping his voice carefully neutral.

She scowled at him. "I did not! I had a completely normal day. I didn't meet any vampires. I think I'd know what to look for at this point, don't you?" He could hear her pulse pick up, but he sensed it was from anger, not fear.

He glanced at Carwyn, who moved slightly closer to the pool, his hands in his pockets as he sauntered toward them.

"I smelled it too, B. It was faint, but it was there. It's on your hands. Gio's nose has always been sharper. Did you shake hands with anyone? Go anywhere new?"

She rolled her eyes and huffed in frustration. "I went to school and work. I went to dinner with my grandma and her friends. I went to a new Thai restaurant where none of the waiters looked any paler than usual, Carwyn. I didn't meet a vampire!"

"Something," Giovanni muttered, swimming over to the edge of the pool and lifting himself up. "There has to be something." He strode over the patio, dripping cold water as he walked. He only remembered his nudity when he heard Beatrice gasp a little from the steps.

Carwyn rolled his eyes and tossed Giovanni a towel from the end of the chaise. "Cover yourself up. We all know she'd rather see *me* naked."

He glanced over his shoulder toward Beatrice, who was blushing and staring at his feet. He smiled when he realized why her heart had been racing.

It didn't appear to be anger.

He slung the towel around his waist and walked back toward her, holding a hand out to help her up. She was still looking anywhere but at him.

"Beatrice," he said, trying to smother the smile. "I apologize. My behavior in the living room was unconscionable. It won't happen again." She still refused to look at him. He sighed and dropped his hand.

"It's fine, Gio," she said, bright red in the face. "Just don't scare me like that again."

"I'll try not to." He held out his hand again; this time she took it and allowed him to help her stand.

"And don't think I didn't feel the current thing when you grabbed me. Do *not* mess with my brain."

He allowed her to see the edge of his smile. "Understood."

She nodded, resolve clear in her eyes. "I'm going to go call my grandmother so she doesn't worry. I'll be up in the library when I'm done."

"Thank you."

"You're welcome. Now go put some clothes on. Because if you want me to concentrate, you can't dangle that much naked man in front of me. Vampire or not."

Giovanni stifled a grin as he walked into the house, punching a laughing Carwyn as he walked by.

"Ow," the priest pouted, back to his normally gregarious nature.

"Liar."

"I'm practicing for wrestling!"

Giovanni couldn't stop the grin that spread across his face or the sense of satisfaction as he ran upstairs to get dressed.

She still hadn't run.

He met them all in the library, where Carwyn started a fire and Caspar had already brought drinks for everyone. The butler sat next to the girl on the couch, leaving the two end chairs for the vampires to perch.

Neither vampire sat; Carwyn leaned a shoulder into the mantle and watched the room, while Giovanni roamed the length of the library. His mind was shuffling information, moving clues like a puzzle. Now that he could think more rationally, the pieces were beginning to fall into place. The anger, however, was only beginning to grow.

"Carwyn," he heard Beatrice ask as he walked toward his locked cabinet, "why can you use the stereo and the remotes when Gio can't? You've got the same current under your skin, right?"

Giovanni's eyes shot to his friend's, who simply shrugged a little before he answered.

"Well," he winked at Beatrice. "Let's just say I'm better grounded than Sparky over there."

"Better groun—oh, elements! Fire. Earth. Air. Water. Are you an earth vampire, or something?"

He nodded and stared at her in the flickering light from the hearth. "Such a clever girl," he murmured. "I wonder what else we can figure out together, hmm?" He glanced back to Giovanni, who only nodded silently at the back of the library.

"Beatrice," the priest continued, "may I smell your hand, dear girl? Just once more. I promise not to get all fangy."

Beatrice smiled and glanced over her shoulder at Giovanni.

"Sure." She held out her hand. "But I'm pretty positive I didn't meet a vampire today. My day was completely boring. The only exciting thing about it was a couple of new documents at work. And that's..." She trailed off and Giovanni could see her make the connection. "I mean...the documents—"

She broke off abruptly when she saw the gleam in Carwyn's eyes. He bent over her hand as if he was going to kiss it, but just like the night they met, he inhaled a deep, almost predatory, breath over her fingertips.

"Carwyn?" Giovanni asked with growing certainty.

"Parchment," he muttered into her hand. His blue eyes shot up. "The new documents at the library—I need to know what they were. Where were they from? Were they bought? Donated? I need to know everything you can tell me about them."

Giovanni felt electricity begin to charge the air as he moved closer to the couch, but the priest held up a hand as Beatrice's eyes began to dart nervously around the room. Caspar reached over and patted the girl's arm.

"Everyone take a step back," the butler said soothingly. "I'm sure Beatrice is already an expert, gentlemen. Let her speak."

She glanced gratefully at him, and Caspar smiled in encouragement.

"It's—it was donated anonymously. It's a letter. There are two of them. From the Italian Renaissance. Two friends, a philosopher and a—a poet. They were authenticated at the University of Ferrara. Dated 1484. From Florence."

Giovanni was drawn to her voice, walking silently over to stand by the fire as she spoke. Her eyes lifted and met his.

Carwyn's eyes darted between him and the young woman. "Who were the letters addressed to, B?"

"Giovanni..." she began, staring with her warm brown eyes. "Count Giovanni Pico della Mirandola. That's who the letters were for."

He looked away, hoping she had not seen the flicker of recognition at the old name. He ignored the burning in his chest as he walked back to the library table and collected himself. He glanced over to see Carwyn smiling at her.

"Anything else you can remember? It really would be helpful."

She shook her head. "It sounded like they were mostly personal. I only read the translation on one. They were talking about a new servant, or squire, or—or something like that, and his education. There was something about meeting Lorenzo de Medici." She blushed slightly and glanced back at him; his eyes were glued to her as she spoke. "Something about a scandal. I can't—I can't remember all of it. I'm sorry."

"Oh, I think you've remembered plenty," Caspar broke in. "I'm sure that's what they needed to know."

She looked for him in the back of the library. "Did a vampire donate those letters, Gio?"

He still didn't speak but nodded as he stared into the fire.

Carwyn finally answered her. "I think that's where you picked up the scent. He must have handled them before they were donated."

Giovanni was careful to keep strict control of his features as his mind flew in a thousand directions, finally settling onto one inescapable conclusion.

He had been deceived.

"Gio?"

He heard her voice and knew what she wanted to ask.

"Giovanni?" she almost whispered.

"Do not ask questions you know I will not answer, Beatrice," he bit out.

"But—"

"It's not—" he broke off for a moment, "not for you."

She stood to face him. Giovanni could see the angry confusion in her eyes, and he could not blame her. She squared her shoulders and turned to Carwyn.

"I'm going home. I guess I'll see you at the library tomorrow."

Caspar stood with her. "I'll see you out." The butler escorted the young woman out of the library, but not before she shot him a pointed glare.

Carwyn rushed over to Giovanni as soon as the two humans were out of the room and began speaking in rushed Latin.

"The letters—"

"'They'll be there soon, and there's more where they came from,'" Giovanni muttered, quoting the mysterious e-mail from weeks before they had both been baffled by. "'You're welcome.'"

"Lorenzo sent the letters, Gio. It's the only explanation. He must have slept with them on his pillow for the scent to be that strong."

"Those letters were bound in a correspondence book. If he has those two, he has all of them. If he has the correspondence books..."

"He has all your books."

Giovanni leaned his hip against the table, still staring into the fire as the memory of other fires haunted him. "We don't know that he has them all."

"But the rumors—"

"Are rumors, nothing more. It is possible...many things are possible. What we do know is he has the correspondence books and he sent the letters." Giovanni cursed. "And if his note is correct, there will be more."

"He was never one to bluff," Carwyn growled. "Why? Why now?"

"Why didn't I know he had them?" Giovanni asked, pushing away from the table and pacing the length of the library with deliberate strides. "After five *hundred* years? Or why is he sending them now?"

"You tell me. You know him far better than I ever will. What's his game?"

Giovanni stalked the room, mentally shifting the pieces, and trying to make sense of everything they had learned that night. One disturbing thought kept circling his mind until it was all he could think about.

"You're missing his boldest move, Carwyn," he muttered to the priest as he halted, leaning against the oak table and staring at the empty desk in the corner of the room. "He didn't send them to me." He nodded toward the desk. "He sent them to her."

Carwyn's eyes widened as he turned to stare at the girl's desk and heard Giovanni murmur, "He sent them to Beatrice."

CHAPTER 10

He had gone to prison for love.
She couldn't tear her eyes away from the translation of the second letter of Angelo Poliziano to Giovanni Pico as she huddled in the stacks, avoiding the packed reading room on Wednesday afternoon. Pico had been imprisoned for his affair with a married woman and only escaped because of his connection to Lorenzo de Medici.

> "I hope this letter finds you well, and free from the imprisonment which shocked us all. By this time, Signore Andros should have arrived in Arezzo with the letter from Lorenzo. Do not feel the need to thank me for my intervention, for the Medici was eager to take your part in the matter and needed little convincing, from either myself or the odd Greek."

He had gone to stay with Signore Niccolo Andros in Perugia, presumably to study Andros's library of mystic texts and recover from his imprisonment.

What happened to the little boy? Beatrice wondered as she skimmed over the notes from the second letter. The letter mentioned their mutual friends, even Savonarola himself, but Beatrice was more enthralled by the hints of scandal than she was about the more historical significance of the translation.

She read it twice, adding to her notes on the first which she then tucked carefully in her bag. Though both letters had been under the intense scrutiny Dr. Christiansen had predicted throughout the day, she had managed early in her shift to get her hands on them for a few minutes to make a copy of the notes. There was little doubt in her mind that Giovanni and Carwyn knew exactly who the letters had come from. She scratched down a reminder to herself to tell them that Dr. Christiansen mentioned more letters would be arriving.

"B?" Charlotte called. She shoved her copy of the translation and her notes into her messenger bag and stood up, pretending to examine a stack of photographs that needed to be catalogued.

"Hey, I know you're as sick of the philosophers as I am," Charlotte sighed, "but could you come take care of the reading room for a bit?"

"Sure."

"I know you're going to be here all night, but if I don't get a break from the chatter, I'm going to end up throwing old reference books at them."

Beatrice smiled and held in a laugh. The reading room was unusually packed that afternoon, as the philosophy department took a look at the documents. The history department had already come and gone for the day, and the Italian studies department was due that evening. Apparently they had all worked out some tentative custody agreement for the Pico letters.

"Are they scheduled to stay through the evening hours?" she asked, conscious of the two guests she had no doubt would be showing up when it was dark enough.

Charlotte nodded. "Yeah, I guess philosophy's leaving at five, and then the Italian chair is showing up to take a look at them. Have you met Dr. Scalia?"

She shook her head.

"He's a hoot. He's got these enormous glasses and looks like an owl, but he's sweet man and not too chatty. He'll be here most of the evening, so between him and Dr. Handsome, you should have a pretty quiet room."

Beatrice sighed, wondering whether poor Dr. Scalia was going to shake hands with Dr. Vecchio and forget about the letters he was supposed to be examining. She had a feeling Giovanni would be more than happy if the Italian professor suddenly remembered he needed to pick up his dry-cleaning. She might have to lay some ground rules about playing with cerebral cortexes while in the library.

Reminding herself that Carwyn would also be in attendance, she decided there would definitely need to be ground rules.

Every now and then, she had wondered why she had so easily accepted her strange new reality. The more she thought about it, the more Beatrice decided that the idea of vampires just didn't seem that far-fetched.

She could accept there were things in the world that science didn't understand yet, and who was to say that some of those things didn't have fangs and need to survive by drinking human blood?

As she sat at the reference desk, listening to philosophers quietly argue the meaning of this, or the implication of that, she thought about how much had changed since Giovanni had lived as a human. If Dr. Giovanni Vecchio was, indeed, the Italian count the letters were addressed to, that meant that he was

540 years old, and even at age twenty-three had been considered one of the most progressive humanist philosophers of the Renaissance.

He hadn't answered her questions, but it was too coincidental that the two mysterious letters had been donated by a vampire to the very library where Giovanni had chosen to do his research and she worked. They had to be connected.

Not long after six o'clock, a small man with a shock of silver-grey hair walked through the double doors.

"Dr. Scalia?" she asked of the man, who did remind her of an owl with his large round glasses and tiny nose.

He smiled eagerly. "Yes, yes! And you are?"

"I'm Beatrice De Novo. It's a pleasure to meet you. You have an appointment for the Pico letters, is that correct?"

"Yes, thank you."

As she listened to another academic wax eloquent on the importance of the two Italian letters, Giovanni and Carwyn silently entered the reading room. She quickly settled Dr. Scalia at the table with the Pico letters and walked over to the two vampires.

"Okay," she whispered in her sternest librarian voice, "he's a sweet, old man, and I don't want you two to mess with his brain. He's a professor. He needs it."

Giovanni frowned. "Really, Beatrice, how clumsy do you think we are? He would never realize—"

"Don't care. It's *his* brain. Stay out and wait your turn."

She saw Giovanni's nostrils flare a little in annoyance, or maybe he had simply caught the scent of the old parchment at the other table. Carwyn, she thought, looked like he might break into laughter at any minute and kept glancing between his friend and Beatrice.

"Fine. If I could have the Tibetan manuscript then, Miss De Novo."

She rolled her eyes at his tone, but turned and walked back to the stacks to get the manuscript for him as he chose a table near the small professor who was already busy taking notes.

By the time she got back, she noticed that Giovanni had assumed his usual position at the table, though he was watching Dr. Scalia with an almost predatory stare. She set the book down in front of him and grabbed a pencil and a piece of paper from the stack he had sitting on the table. With a quick scribble and a fold, she wrote a small note and propped it in front of the 500 year old vampire.

No biting. No altering cerebral cortexes. Have a nice day.

He couldn't keep the smile from sneaking across his face. He looked up at her, winked, and bent his head to his notes.

Wearing her own smile, she walked back to the reference desk to find Carwyn had pulled a chair over and was reading the paperback she had started that morning. As always, he was eye-catching in a loud Hawaiian shirt that clashed with his red hair and made his blue eyes seem to pop out.

He glanced up from the book. "Do you—"

"Shhh!" She glared and put her finger to her lips.

"Such a librarian. You need wee glasses sitting on the tip of your nose when you do that," he whispered loudly. She heard Giovanni shift at his table and she looked over her shoulder to see him glaring at Carwyn. Snickering, the mischievous vampire reached into her book bag and pulled out the notebook that she'd been using to take notes on the mysterious Pico and his letters.

She could see when Carwyn discovered the notes, but he didn't look angry. On the contrary, he looked inordinately pleased and immediately flipped to the back of the notebook and began to write.

You're a curious thing, B.

Flipping the notebook to her, she read and took a moment to respond.

I've had some curious things happen to me this fall. Also, I feel like we're passing notes in study hall.

We are, he wrote back. *So, what do you want to know that Professor Chatty won't tell you?*

She couldn't hold in the snort when she wrote, *Everything.*

Carwyn just smiled and took a few moments to write back.

I can't tell you his story. One, I don't know all of it. I don't think anyone does. Two, what I do know is not mine to tell. But you're welcome to ask me anything about my life that you'd like.

She cocked an eyebrow at him. *Anything?*

Other than what color pants I'm wearing (red, by the way) I'm an open book.

She held back the giggle. *Always try to match your hair and your underwear. It's just a good rule of thumb. How old are you?*

He smiled and wrote back. *I'm around thirty-five...plus a thousand years. Approximately.*

Beatrice gaped for a moment, trying to reconcile a thousand years with the relatively young man before her. She tried to imagine the things Carwyn must have seen and how much the world had changed since he was human. She couldn't begin to imagine.

Where were you born?

Gwynedd. Northern part of Wales.

And you're still there?

For the most part, I always have been. I'm quite the homebody, unlike our Gio.

She narrowed her eyes and wrote, *Are you really a priest?*

He chuckled quietly. *Yes, you don't have to be an old man, you know. And my father was a priest. And my grandfather. And one of my sons became abbott of our community after I was gone.*

She frowned. *Kinda lax on that whole celibacy thing, huh?*

Carwyn grinned. *Not uncommon in the Welsh church. And it was before Gregory. (Look it up.) Many Welsh priests married. Rome had a hard time conquering Wales. Militarily and ecclesiastically.* He winked as he finished the sentence.

So you were married?

He just nodded and smiled. "Efa," he whispered.

She paused for a moment. *What happened to your wife? Your children?*

Carwyn offered a wistful smile. *My wife went to our God before I was turned. She died quite young from a fever. Our children were taken in by our community when I disappeared. I went back years later. Those that survived had good lives.*

She looked at him, and for a moment, she could see the hundreds of years in his eyes, but they quickly lit again in joy.

There is a time for sorrow and a time for joy, he wrote. *I have a new family now.*

Beatrice raised her eyebrows in question and he continued writing with a smile.

You'll come to Wales someday and meet them. I have eleven children. Most of them have stayed fairly close to home. We keep the British deer population under control.

She mouthed 'wow,' but only wrote, *So none of you bite people?*

He grinned. *Not usually. Just if they smell really good, like you. Joking.*

She rolled her eyes. *Never married again? Do vampires even get married? That seems kind of normal for the mystical undead creatures of the night.*

Some do. He smiled. *It's not uncommon. One of my sons has been married for four hundred years now. I haven't ever wanted to again.*

Her eyes bugged out. *How do you stay married to someone for 400 years?*

He frowned seriously before he wrote back. *Separate vacations.*

She couldn't contain the small laugh that escaped her. She glanced up, and Dr. Scalia was still raptly studying the Pico letters, but Giovanni was glaring at her and Carwyn in annoyance. She rolled her eyes and mouthed, 'Get back to work.'

Giovanni smiled and shook his head a little.

She caught Carwyn watching them out of the corner of his eye. He began to scribble on the notebook again.

He's never married.

She paused for a moment and Carwyn continued writing. He handed the notebook to her.

Don't pretend you weren't curious.

She glared at him. *I can't even imagine Professor Frosty dating,* she wrote quickly and tossed the notebook at him.

Then it was Carwyn who couldn't hold in the snort. He wrote something in bold letters and underlined it twice.

Opposite. Of. Frosty.

She shook her head but couldn't think of anything to write back, so she busied herself checking her e-mail as Carwyn scribbled. After a while, she leaned back in her chair and he handed her the book again, a mischievous grin on his face.

Do you like Gio? Check yes or no. He had sketched two small boxes underneath the question with a large arrow pointing to the "yes" box.

She rolled her eyes and wrote back. *How can you be this childish after a thousand years?*

He raised his eyebrows and jotted down. *That's not a yes or no.*

Screwing her mouth up in annoyance, she wrote back. *Once upon a time, B made some very bad choices about boys. Then she went to college and continued making bad choices about men. Then B got smart and decided to take a break. The End.*

Carwyn smiled and winked at her before writing on the notebook. *Well, obviously, you need to be dating a vampire.*

At that statement, Beatrice grabbed the notebook and snapped it closed, handed Carwyn a romance novel Charlotte had stashed in the bottom drawer of the desk, and opened her own book to read.

"Don't be a coward, B," he said in a sing-song voice as he opened the book that looked like it had a shirtless pirate on the front. "Ooh," he whispered. "The thrilling tale of Don Fernando and the beautiful Sophie. Been meaning to read this one."

And with that, Carwyn wiggled his eyebrows and began reading. Beatrice tried to pay attention to her book, but her gaze continued to drift up to the dark-haired man seated at the table in front of her. All of a sudden, she had a memory of him rising out of the water the night before—the most perfect man she had ever seen—without a stitch of clothing on, and she couldn't help the flush that rose to her cheeks. She had gotten more than an eyeful before she forced herself to look away.

"Hmm, I've never had that reaction to Cormac McCarthy myself, but then, everyone's different," Carwyn whispered as a smile teased the corner of his mouth.

She saw Giovanni raise his head, no doubt hearing his friend's comment and possibly wondering why Beatrice's heartbeat had picked up so suddenly.

"Stupid vampires with their stupid preternatural senses," she muttered, but she knew Carwyn could hear her because his shoulders began shaking with silent laughter.

It was almost nine o'clock when Dr. Scalia finally started packing up his things and made his way over to the reference desk.

"Miss De Novo, please give Dr. Christiansen my regards. Such a wonderful acquisition. I'm informed that we will probably be receiving more in the next months, is that correct? Do you know if they are from the same correspondents?"

She could feel the charge as two sets of eye narrowed in on her as she answered the small professor.

"I don't know the details of all that. I've heard rumors from Dr. Christiansen, but you'd really have to ask him," she said in a small voice, well aware that both Carwyn and Giovanni could hear the rapid beating of her heart.

"Well, I'm sure I'll be seeing you again."

"Have a good night," she answered as he left the room. The door was scarcely closed before Giovanni rushed over to her with no attempt to hide his speed.

"More? When? When did you hear this? Are they from the same donor? When are they coming? Have they already been authenticated?"

"Holy unanswered questions, Batman! Back off, okay?" Beatrice huffed a little and saw Carwyn smother another smile. "Dr. Christiansen mentioned that there *might* be more letters to me and Char, but as far as I know it's just a rumor. Nothing official."

"Oh, there'll be more," Carwyn muttered.

Giovanni shot him a glance. "Shut up."

"Hey, don't tell him to shut up, Gio. At least he doesn't treat me like an idiot who doesn't understand anything."

He frowned. "I don't—I mean…I don't think you're an idiot in any way, Beatrice." She thought he almost looked offended.

"Yeah? Well, it sure feels that way sometimes." He was looking at her with that blank expression he wore when he didn't want to tell her something. It made her want to throw something at him.

"Listen," she said. "I'm not an idiot. I know you guys know *who* the letters are from and I suspect you know why he's sending them." She swallowed hard and expressed the fear she'd had last night. "I'm also guessing that this has something to do with my father, because otherwise all this just seems *way* too coincidental. And I don't really believe in coincidences."

Carwyn was smiling at her with a proud gleam in his eye. "Clever girl, B. Such a clever girl."

"Carwyn," Giovanni said sharply. "Don't—"

"She figured out a good portion on her own without all the background we have. You may as well tell her the rest." Then Carwyn spit out something in Latin that Beatrice couldn't understand, but it made Giovanni seem to growl. He looked at Carwyn with a glare that almost reminded her of the mood that had overtaken him the previous night.

"What's going on?" she asked tentatively.

Carwyn shook his head and Giovanni seemed to gather himself again.

"Carwyn and I have a disagreement on some things, Beatrice. But he is correct. There's a large part of this that does relate to your father, and we should inform you of that."

"These letters," Giovanni walked over to the table and sat in front of the two yellowed pieces of parchment before he continued quietly. "These are my letters. And by that, I mean they are part of a collection I had at one time. It was taken from me and I've been searching for it."

He looked at Beatrice, and she again had the feeling of seeing each long year of his existence stretch out in the depth of his gaze.

"I've been searching for almost four hundred years. I was told it had been destroyed. Many years later, I discovered parts of it had been saved, but scattered. Now, however," he leaned back and crossed his arms as he gazed at the two letters, "I think it is intact. And I know who took it, who the donor is."

He turned to look at her. "I'm not going to tell you how I know, so don't ask. He's dangerous, that's all you need to know and if you ever see another immortal that I don't introduce you to, I want you to tell me or Carwyn immediately."

"Bossy," she muttered.

"Mortal," he threw back, and Carwyn laughed. "I'm not joking about this, Beatrice. Our world isn't ruled by laws, or even convention. The strongest, smartest, and wealthiest have the most power. And power is the only law. This vampire has brains, strength, and wealth in abundance. I manage to live the way I do because I stay off the radar—"

"That, and he likes his enemies toasted *extra* crispy!" Carwyn spouted.

"—but this one," he glared at the priest, "has sought me out. I don't know for certain why now, but," he paused, letting his eyes rake over her, "I have my suspicions."

He fell silent and continued examining the documents, taking special note of the left side of the parchment where it appeared a cut had been carefully made. Beatrice watched him, going over all the cryptic pieces of information she had gleaned in the weeks since she had learned the truth about Giovanni and her father.

"Is it because of me? Because we met? What does this have to do with my father?"

Giovanni halted his perusal to stare at her, and the flicker she saw for a brief moment spurred her on.

"I mean...you've been looking for these books. My dad was looking for something in Italy." Suddenly, all the pieces fell together in her mind. "It was *this*, wasn't it? What my dad was looking for? It was *your* books. Your letters. Or something related to it, right? That's why you agreed to help me find my father." She stepped closer to him, challenging the powerful immortal who watched her silently. "I'm right, aren't I?"

She saw Carwyn and Giovanni exchange loaded looks.

"Told you," Carwyn muttered.

Giovanni said something to him in Latin that sounded like a curse, but then he turned back to Beatrice. She could see the war in his eyes, but he finally gave a slight nod. "Yes, you're partially correct."

She was speechless for a moment, amazed he had actually told her anything. "So...okay, this guy that stole your books or letters or whatever he has—what does he want now?"

She saw Carwyn and Giovanni exchange another glance.

"We think he might be looking for your father," Carwyn said quietly. "We're not sure why, but that's probably why he sent the letters here."

"Okay, so my dad knows something...all right. And this guy's dangerous, right? Does he make fire like Gio?"

Carwyn said, "No, he—"

"You don't need to know—"

She glared at Giovanni. "I want to know who he is!"

"How very unfortunate for you." He continued to examine the letters, looking over the second one and handling it as if it was made of finely spun glass.

"You arrogant ass—"

"Lorenzo," he said. "He goes by Lorenzo now."

Beatrice's mouth fell open, "He's not—"

"No," Carwyn said. "No, not the one you're thinking of."

Giovanni brought the letters up to his face to finally examine them more closely. "He likes to give people the impression that he's one of the Medici's bastards," he murmured as he searched the old parchment. "He's not, but some think he is, and it adds to the mystique, I suppose. He likes notoriety." He inhaled deeply, closing his eyes, and Beatrice could see them dart behind his closed lids as if he was searching his memory for some piece that had escaped.

"You see, B," Carwyn spoke in an even tone, "some in our world choose to seek power. Power over land, humans, riches. And he wants something from Giovanni, otherwise, he wouldn't be doing this. There is something he thinks he can gain."

"Or someone," Giovanni mused quietly, and the already quiet room fell completely silent.

"Someone?" Beatrice finally asked, her eyes nervous and looking toward the door as if a threat could walk through at any time. "Not—not me, right?"

Neither of them spoke, only looked at her with those infuriatingly blank expressions. Even Carwyn was wearing one, and it made her want to scream.

"Not *me*! I don't know anything. I wouldn't know anything about anything if Giovanni hadn't clued me in. I mean—" she suddenly turned to Giovanni. "Why did you tell me this shit?" she practically yelled, her fear palpable.

"You asked, and you figured most of it out on your own," Carwyn said softly. "Could we have kept it from you? Even if we tried? Would you rather have us make you forget? It wouldn't matter now."

Beatrice watched Giovanni stand and walk toward her; it was almost as if each step in her direction forced her farther and farther away from the safe, unremarkable life she had known. She had the simultaneous urge to run away from the approaching menace and run toward him and hold on for dear life. The problem, she realized, was that she had no idea whether he would catch her either way.

"I don't know anything," she said hoarsely, "He can't want me. I don't—why does he want me?"

For a fleeting moment, she saw pity touch his eyes. "Because your father does."

CHAPTER 11

He looked over the translation of the letter, reading words his eyes hadn't touched for five hundred years. Even years later, Poliziano's warm humor shone through the pages. He frowned when he found the paragraph he had been looking for.

These texts you speak of promise much hermetic knowledge, if they are what you believe them to be. In the celebration of our classical fathers, we too often neglect the older ideas of the East. I am glad that such rare treasures have found their way to your discerning hands, and I have no doubt you will find much wisdom from their examination.

"Yes!"

Giovanni's head shot up when he heard her. Beatrice's triumphant shout echoed across his home library and he watched as she jumped from her desk and began to do some sort of victory dance across the room.

"Anything you want to tell me?" he asked dryly.

"Only that I am," she said with a huge smile, "the most awesome and amazing assistant in the entire world." She continued to dance, wiggling in no particular rhythm toward the center of the room as he looked on in amusement. He tried to keep a straight face but was soon chuckling and shaking his head.

"Not that I'm doubting your...awesomeness, but is there a particular reason it should be celebrated at the moment?" he asked with a reluctant smile.

She continued to dance, and he had an increasingly difficult time not staring at her lithe form as it moved closer to him. His eyes were drawn to her swaying hips and graceful waist, and he felt his blood begin to stir. She danced and hummed a wordless tune, a smile lighting her face and her dark eyes reflecting the gold lamp light as she leaned down toward him at the table.

"Guess who found the Lincoln speech?" she asked with a playful grin, her elbows leaning on the table and her hands cupping her chin.

He allowed a slow smile to spread across his face when he saw her delight. She had found it more quickly than he thought she would. In the midst of his current predicament, the successful completion of her task was a pleasant surprise.

"Well done, Beatrice," he said quietly.

She narrowed her eyes at his decidedly muted response, but softened them after a moment and sat down across from him at the table. He could almost see the energy vibrating off her.

"It's such a rush! Do you get this way after you find something?"

He nodded. "Though my dance skills obviously need work after seeing yours."

She stuck her tongue out at him, and he had the almost irresistible urge to lean across the table and bite it. He shoved down the impulse and tried to focus on what she was saying.

"—surprised you haven't asked me yet."

"Hmm?"

She looked shocked. "Were you actually not listening? As in distracted? As in—"

"I was reading the letters, Beatrice. How did you find the speech? Please enlighten me, oh awesome assistant."

She smiled and settled in her chair to relate her brilliance to him. As she recounted the steps she had taken to find, first, the auction house where it had been sold, and then the collector who had made the winning bid, he watched her, pleased to hear her methodical approach that so closely matched his own.

Despite her success, a small frown settled between her eyebrows.

"Gio?"

"What's bothering you?"

"Why did he spend so much money? Our client? The final bid for the speech notes wasn't nearly as much as what it must have cost him to find the documents. Why was he willing to spend so much?"

Giovanni shrugged a little and looked down at the pictures of the five hundred-year-old letter in front of him.

"What do you pay for sentiment, Beatrice? What do you pay for the memory of what an object or a book or a document evokes?"

She looked down at the pictures he held. "Is that why the letters are so important to you? Is that why you've looked for your books for so long?"

He paused for a moment, deliberating how much he would tell her. "The collection I seek was extensive and contained valuable texts, many of them original or unique. It has existed far longer than me—far longer. When I thought it was lost...many of the books and manuscripts contain valuable ancient knowledge, Beatrice. There is far more than my own sentiment involved."

She looked at him skeptically.

"But," he continued, "they hold some sentimental value as well." He shuffled the papers in front of him. "That, of course, is secondary."

He glanced at her, noting the thoughtful expression that had clouded her earlier glee.

"Grab your jacket," he said as he stood and put the photographs and notes in his locked cabinet.

"What?"

"It's your first big find. I am like your boss—"

"You *are* my boss, unless you've decided to stop paying me."

He smiled. "Fine, then I'm taking you out for a drink. Something other than Coke."

Giovanni saw a faint flush stain her cheeks. "Gio, you don't have to—"

"Get your coat, Beatrice."

She paused for a moment then stood and went to turn off the computers. She joined him at the door of the library and they walked downstairs together.

"Where's Carwyn tonight?"

"Out hunting. It's one of the reasons he likes visiting Texas. He's very fond of deer."

"He may have mentioned that once or twice. So, how does he..."

"Take down a deer?"

She frowned, but shrugged, obviously curious about his friend. Giovanni chuckled.

"I don't think he'd mind me saying. He has a friend he hunts with, Carwyn is social like that, and...have you ever seen a group of wolves stalk an animal?"

"You mean he—"

"Mmmhmm. It is a group activity."

"Have you ever gone with him?" She paused on the stairs, her eyes lit with interest.

He only smiled. "I'm not as fond of deer as he is."

She nodded silently and began walking again. "So now that I've found the speech notes, what do you do? What's the next step?"

They waved at Caspar, who was working on his laptop in the kitchen. Giovanni wondered whether he was reading the daily surveillance report on Beatrice and her grandmother he'd commissioned.

He had been having both of them watched since he realized the girl was Lorenzo's target. She wasn't the end game for his old enemy, but she was undoubtedly a step to get what he wanted.

Stephen De Novo, he decided, must have taken something quite valuable from the vampire.

"Gio? So what's the next step? I mean, you can't just go take the document." A sudden thought must have occurred to her. "Wait—you could, couldn't you? Shit, am I an accomplice now?" Her eyes were wide and she had come to a standstill in the small courtyard by the garage.

He smiled and pulled her arm to get her moving again. "I'm not a thief, Beatrice. I would scarcely need to be, would I?" He cocked an eyebrow at her playfully.

She gasped. "Gio, you cannot use your mind voodoo to make people give you manuscripts!"

"Why not?" he asked innocently.

"Because it's wrong! It's completely unethical. Because—"

"I don't use amnis to get documents, Beatrice."

"Oh," she said, slightly deflated. "Well...good."

He couldn't erase the smile on his face as he opened the door to the Mustang for her. Suddenly feeling playful, he leaned down as she got in the car and whispered in her ear, "Most of the time, anyway."

He shut the door before she could start speaking again, still laughing as he walked around the car. She was glaring at him when he got in and started it.

"What?"

She scowled. "I don't know whether to believe you or not."

"That's probably a wise choice."

"You're so reassuring."

"I'm not a thief." He smiled. "I'll let the client know I've found what he's looking for and ask him how much he is willing to offer. Then, I will approach the owner of the documents and negotiate a price."

They drove through the dark streets toward a small pub tucked into a quiet corner of Rice Village.

"What if they don't want to sell? And where are we going?"

"We're going to a pub. And I rarely fail to procure an item."

She glanced at him from the corner of her eye before she looked back at the road. "What if it's not for sale?"

His lip curled almost instinctively. "Don't be naive. For the right price, everything is for sale."

The car was silent for a few minutes, and Giovanni almost wished that she would turn on the radio for him. He finally heard her take a deep breath.

"That's kind of depressing," she murmured.

He shrugged as he pulled into the small parking lot behind the building. "That's human nature. Much changes in the world, but not that."

"No?"

He parked the car and looked at her in the shadows of the street lights. "Five hundred years says no."

Giovanni hated the sadness he saw in her eyes, but knew that life would teach her the same lesson, whether he placated her in that moment or not.

"So it is important to learn that which helps us to cope with the cruel vagaries of life and the persistent ebb and rise of the human situation."

She raised a skeptical eyebrow as he reached across to unclip her seatbelt. He passed deliberately close to her and felt her warm breath catch. Leaning back, he smiled, just a little.

"Oh yeah?" she asked, clearing her throat. "What's that?"

He smiled when he heard her heartbeat pick up.

"Whiskey."

THEY WALKED INTO THE DARK PUB, AND GIOVANNI NODDED AT THE PALE man sitting in the corner of the room on a low couch. The vampire nodded back in the shadows and, to Giovanni's chagrin, gestured toward the chairs across from him. He put a hand on the small of Beatrice's back and led her toward the dark corner, though he stood casually instead of taking a seat.

"Giovanni," the man said in greeting. "To what do I owe the pleasure tonight?"

Though the vampire spoke to Giovanni in English, Gavin Wallace's strong brogue must have been difficult to understand, because he felt Beatrice lean forward slightly.

He could tell she was taking in every detail of the man's appearance, from his sandy-brown hair and deceptively human brown eyes, to the stylishly rumpled jacket which complemented his easy good looks. Gavin must have been turned in his early thirties, but his wardrobe reflected his more youthful clientele. At least, Giovanni thought, the human clientele.

"Just out with a friend, Gavin. How are the college kids?" He hoped the slight pressure he put on Beatrice's back would let her know to let him do the talking. As always, her perception paid off and she remained silent and watchful at his side.

"Very thirsty, thank you. You have a lovely companion tonight," the blond vampire smiled, looking Beatrice over carefully. "Did you want a chaser? That redhead you seemed to like last month is in the back room, I believe."

He shrugged. "Not necessary, but thank you." Giovanni couldn't help but notice the stiffness in Beatrice's shoulders that accompanied Gavin's frank perusal of the girl's neck. He suddenly realized he had never been specific about how and where he fed with her, and he wondered what questions he would face once they were alone. He deliberately put an arm around her shoulders and drew her slightly closer, making sure the other vampire caught the possessive gleam in his eye.

"Ah, is that how it is? Well," Gavin raised an eyebrow and smirked, "I suppose I *can* still be surprised."

"Gavin, did you want company tonight?" Giovanni asked out of politeness, hoping the vampire would answer in the negative.

"Oh, I don't want to intrude on your evening with a friend," he replied, "but don't be a stranger. I think it would be beneficial for us to catch up soon."

Nodding at the subtle message, Giovanni took Beatrice's hand and led them to an empty couch near the fireplace. They both sat down and he leaned over to murmur in her ear.

"He'll be able to hear everything we say in a normal voice, Beatrice. Just so you know."

"Yeah," she said softly. Her heart was now beating far more rapidly than he would have liked. "I kind of figured. Does he think we're..."

"That's the impression I want him to have. If he thinks I drink from you, he won't touch you. Nor will anyone else in the bar out of courtesy."

They both fell silent and he could almost see the rush of questions racing through her mind.

"A chaser, huh?"

He shrugged. "Not necessary, but a polite offer."

She looked down at her lap and whispered. "So—what, he keeps humans around as refreshments? What kind of bar is this?"

"It's a popular one for a certain crowd, and one where people do not ask questions. One where they keep certain things to themselves."

"Even the humans?"

"*Especially* the humans." He paused, trying to decipher the expression on her face. She was frowning, but he sensed more worry than anger. "No one lures them here, Beatrice, if that's what you're wondering. No one has to."

"So what? They like it? They like being...bitten?"

He only raised an eyebrow and gave her a cocky look.

"Well, that is certainly interesting," she said, still speaking in a low voice. "Can I ask why you brought me here? Warning? Field trip? Or do you just have the munchies?"

He put an arm around the back of the sofa, leaning close enough that his claim couldn't be doubted by the rest of the room, but not so close that he would make her uncomfortable. Her heartbeat had yet to slow down.

"I brought us here for two reasons, Beatrice. One, if certain people decide to make their appearance in the city, it would be beneficial for them to think of you as 'my human,' and yes—" he anticipated her response, "I know how insulting that sounds to you, but that's not the way he thinks."

"The way who thinks? Gavin or Lorenzo?"

"Either. Both. Gavin's a good sort, mostly, but that's the most common way of viewing humans in our world."

"As property? Food?"

"Neither, precisely. Or maybe a little bit of both. But in a fond sort of way."

"Like a pet?" she whispered scornfully.

He smiled again. "I most certainly do not think of you as a pet, Beatrice."

She narrowed her eyes. "You better not. What's the second reason?"

He leaned to the side and reached for a small bar menu on the coffee table in front of them. "The second and most important reason is, this place has the best selection of whiskey in the city."

Her lip curled. "I don't like whiskey."

"You have probably only had horrible whiskey that bars serve because it's cheap. These whiskeys," he held up the menu, "are not that kind."

A server slid silently toward him, and Giovanni held up two fingers as he spoke.

"Two of the scotch tastings, please. And a small glass of water."

"The premium board, Dr. Vecchio?"

He gave a slight nod. "Yes."

Beatrice just looked at him in amusement.

"The name's Vecchio. Giovanni Vecchio," she said with a horrendously bad Scottish accent.

"But are you the good Bond girl, or the bad one?"

Beatrice winked at him and said, "Wouldn't you like to know?"

He just shook his head, enjoying her audacity as she looked around the pub. It was atmospheric, to say the least, though not fussy.

Gavin Wallace had a distinct dislike for the sentimental or stuffy. The Night Hawk pub had clean, white-washed walls that showed off the old woodwork around the windows and made the large stone fireplace in the center of the room the focal point. It had little decoration and even less in the way of food.

The reason people, including most of the small immortal community of Houston, came to Gavin's pub was because he served the finest and most extensive collection of whiskeys and bourbons in the city and probably the state.

"Do you mostly drink whiskey?" she asked. "It's the only thing I've ever seen you drink."

He shrugged. "If I don't drink much, I'm going to drink what I like. And I like whiskey."

"Shaken, not stirred?"

He laughed lightly and looked into her eyes, still surprised by how amusing he found her, and how easy her company continued to be.

"Neither. Good whiskey should be served neat, that is, with no accompaniment or mixers, with a slight bit of good water to open up the scent and flavor."

"Wow, you really know how to show a girl a good time," she said dryly. "You're making this sound like ten tons of fun."

He shook his head at her. "It *is* fun. You'll like it."

"How do you know? I don't even drink that much. I have a beer now and then on the rare occasions I hang out with friends. Or watch pro-wrestling, but that's a recent thing."

"You know, that's really more Car—"

"'Get the folding chair!'" she said in an odd voice.

He frowned. "Was that supposed to be me?"

"I never said accents were a strength, Dr. Vecchio."

Giovanni watched her laughing at him, amused that she could be both humorous and alluring at the same time. In the months they had spent together, he had expected his curiosity and interest in her to wane. He was surprised when it had not. In fact, he enjoyed her company more as they spent time together, but he was reluctant to examine the reasons too closely.

"No," he murmured quietly. "I believe your strengths lie elsewhere, Beatrice."

She stared at him, an unreadable expression blanketing her normally open face. "Giovanni, what—what are we...I mean—"

"Just enjoying a drink." He tried to lighten his voice, but he couldn't stop staring at her mouth, even as the server set two trays in front of them, five small glasses on each tray.

"Just a drink, huh?"

He nodded and his hand lifted to tuck a piece of hair behind her ear. He rubbed it between his fingers for just a moment before he pulled away and moved forward on the couch to pick up a glass. He could hear Beatrice's heart race, but he took a deep breath and tried to calm his own blood as it began to churn.

After pouring half an inch of water into two glasses of the light gold liquid, he handed one to her. She took it, and stared into the glass, looking at it against the light of the fireplace.

"The color is pretty. It's warm." She peered at him from the corner of her eye.

"It is. These are all single malt whiskeys, which means they haven't been blended with other types. They're all scotch—little nod to our host." Giovanni nodded toward Gavin, who was glancing at them in the corner. "So it's whisky without the 'e.' Generally, the lighter the color," he held up his glass and touched the edge to hers, "the lighter the flavor. The water opens up the scent."

"So," she asked quietly, "I should smell it now?"

He nodded. "Go ahead, but not too deeply. I'm curious what you'll detect."

"Is there something I'm looking for?"

Giovanni shook his head. "Not necessarily. Everyone's nose is different. I'm just curious."

He watched as she bent her head to inhale the aroma of the whisky.

"Swirl it in the glass, just a little."

"What?"

"Swirl it," he said, covering her hand with his own as he rotated the glass in a small circle. "Just a little." He could already smell the scent of the gold scotch rising from her hand.

"Oh," she said quietly before lifting the tulip-shaped glass to her nose. He watched as she inhaled, and a flush rose to her skin as the aroma of the whisky rose from the glass. "It's sweet. It smells a little bit like oranges and flowers. But...kind of earthy, too. Does that make sense?"

He nodded as she brought the glass to her lips and sipped. She immediately wrinkled her face and he smiled.

"It's strong," she said with a laugh.

"Taste it again. Another sip. You're just tasting the alcohol. If you roll it in your mouth a bit, you'll taste more."

"Okay."

She took another small sip of the light whisky and nodded. "I think...I like it. I don't think I could drink much, though. It's very intense."

"Intense is a good word for it."

"Which one is your favorite?"

He frowned, looking at the selection in front of him. Any one of the five would make a good drink, but as he thought about it, there was one he knew he would pick over the others. He pointed the second glass, light amber in color.

"Of these? This one."

Beatrice smiled and reached for the small pitcher of water, adding just as much as he had to the first glasses. She lifted it to her nose and smelled again.

"Sweet again, but not quite as much. And...it almost seems clearer. Do you know what I mean?"

He nodded. "The flavors in this one are very straightforward. Have a taste now."

He sipped it and watched her reaction as she tried the second glass.

"It's good. It's still strong, simpler, like the way it smells. But..." she took a second taste, letting the whiskey linger a little longer in her mouth, "it kind of grows, doesn't it? It's more complicated than it seems at first."

"Perceptive as always, Beatrice," he said softly. He stared at her as she examined the glasses in front of her, finishing the drink she held in her hand. She set the glass down on the table and looked at him eagerly.

"Okay, which one next?"

"So you like it?" he asked with a smile.

Beatrice nodded. "Yeah, I do. It's kind of cool, you know? Do they all taste so different? And, of course, scotch is a way cooler than beer."

"Is it?"

She winked at him. "Of course it is. Don't tell Carwyn, though."

"I'm sure both he and Caspar would argue their drink preferences. Caspar is a huge wine snob."

She shrugged. "So far, I'm liking the scotch, Gio."

He leaned forward and continued to tell her bits about each one as she tasted them. She was surprisingly receptive to the complex flavors, and he found himself inordinately pleased. Finally, they reached the last glass, a heavier, gold whisky aged seventeen years. He handed it to her and felt her fingers brush his own.

"So this one—"

"No lectures this time. Just let me taste it."

He grinned. "Fair enough, my awesome assistant. Tell me what you think."

"Oh, I will," she said a little loudly.

"Beatrice?"

"What?

Giovanni chuckled. "You don't drink much, do you?"

She grinned back and leaned into his shoulder. "Nope."

Still chuckling, he watched her as she tasted the last scotch, but the laughter died when he saw her close her eyes. She licked her lips, and he could see the flush stain her cheeks.

"*This* one," she murmured. "This one's my favorite."

He could see the slow pulse in her neck, and he watched as her tongue darted out again to taste.

"Oh?" he asked in a low voice.

She nodded. "Sweet and smoky. It almost—it tingles in my mouth." Her eyes opened and he realized he had leaned toward her without thinking, her hypnotic tone drawing him in.

He fought the rush of blood in his veins until he realized they were being watched from the corner and her face was tilted toward his as if she was asking her lover for a kiss.

Placing an arm around her waist, he pulled her toward him and leaned down to cover her mouth with his own. He meant for it to be simple, a light kiss to cover the deception of his claim on her, but he tasted the gold whisky on her lips as they moved under his own.

She was kissing him back.

And he couldn't stop his hand from stroking the gentle curve of her back or his mouth from opening to hers. His tongue reached out, sampling the sweet taste that lingered on her lips as she opened her own mouth to taste his. A soft sigh left her as they kissed, and the scent of her breath mirrored the taste of the whisky.

She moved closer, and his other hand reached up to her neck, pulling her more deeply into their kiss. He could feel his thumb linger over the pulse point under her chin, stroking lightly as it raced. He lost track of time; all he could think of was the soft feel of her body as she leaned into him, the scent of her breath, and her taste as it overwhelmed his senses.

It was clear and sweet, and the faint human memory of drinking cool water on a hot day flickered in the back of his mind. He wanted more.

Much more.

He pulled her closer and felt the delicate press of her breasts against his chest. A low kind of growl began to rise from him when he felt her heart beat against him. His fangs descended and her roaming tongue found them, but instead of recoiling, a soft moan came from her throat and her hand lifted to stroke his cheek.

It was the moment when he felt the urge to lay her down on the couch, brush her long hair aside, and drink deeply from her neck that he began to back off. The sudden realization of where they were and who she was began to take hold, and he loosened his grip, trying to regain his rigid control.

Giovanni didn't want to create suspicion, so he let his lips trail to her ear. She was still breathing rapidly, and her other arm had reached around his back.

"They're watching," he whispered hoarsely in her ear, letting his lips brush against the soft skin there.

Beatrice panted a little, and he could still feel the blood rushing through her veins.

"What?" she asked in confusion.

"Gavin and a few others." He swallowed, ignoring the low burn in his throat. "They're watching us." He closed his eyes, continuing his deceit. "They think we're together, remember? We should leave now, but make sure we don't give ourselves away."

"Don't give—oh," she let out a sharp breath. "Right. They think...right." She swallowed and he tried to ignore the acid note in her voice. "Wouldn't want to give them the wrong impression, would we?"

He hesitated before answering, "No."

He lingered at her ear as she calmed her breathing, brushing a kiss across her flushed cheek before he drew away from her.

Giovanni avoided her eyes as he pulled out his wallet, leaving more than enough to cover the drinks on the coffee table. He stood, holding out his hand to help Beatrice up. She took it and he could feel the stiffness in her fingers. Nonetheless, he pulled her to him, tucking her under his arm as they made their way out of the building.

He felt her stiffen as he nodded toward Gavin in the corner, and he hoped that her expression didn't give them away. He couldn't risk a glance. She tried to pull away from him when they got out the door, but he still held her close.

"Watching," he said. "Someone is still watching."

Giovanni held her small body under his for as long as he could, feeling the fleeting comfort of the contact he knew would soon be denied. He opened the car door slowly, finally releasing her as she got in. He walked to the driver's side, anticipating her sharp rebuke as soon as they were alone, but she was silent as they pulled onto the main road. After a few moments, her silence bothered him more than her anger.

"We're not far from my grandmother's house. Could you just drop me off there?" she asked with careful nonchalance. "I'll drop by the house tomorrow and get my things."

"Beatrice—"

"I'm sure my grandmother's wondering where I am. I'm usually not out this late, even on nights I work."

His mind raced, trying to find something to say that would break through the coldness in the air, but he couldn't. Taking their kiss too far had been his mistake.

"Of course," he said quietly. "I'll let Caspar know to expect you sometime tomorrow."

She was silent again when he glanced at her profile. Her face was impassive, and her eyes were shadowed as she stared into the night.

"The notes about the Lincoln documents are on the desk. Since I found them, I'm going to take some time off. I need to help my grandmother with some things."

He pushed back the protest that sprang to his lips and gritted his teeth. "Of course. How many days do you need?"

She shrugged. "I'll let Caspar know."

As they pulled up to her grandmother's house, he saw her gather her purse and release her seatbelt. She opened the car door and exited the Mustang as soon as it had stopped. He looked over at her, but she wouldn't meet his eyes.

"Beatrice..." he began, trying to forget the feel of her lips against his.

She paused, bending down to meet his eyes, as if daring him to protest.

He opened his mouth, but words escaped him when he met her dark stare.

"Good night, Dr. Vecchio."

She shut the door firmly. He watched her walk to the small house and go inside then glanced down the street, looking for the surveillance vehicle that was supposed to be watching. Noting the license plate of the unobtrusive minivan parked down the block, he leaned his head back and sighed.

He couldn't stop thinking about the feel of her lips against his and her sweet taste. Her body fit against his perfectly; he indulged himself in the memory of her small breasts pressed against his chest and the feel of her hands stroking his jaw. While he enjoyed sex with the women he usually fed from, he never pursued any sort of personal connection with them farther than a shared, fleeting pleasure.

With Beatrice, he realized the lines were beginning to blur. Reminding himself of his purpose in pursuing the girl, he shoved down the more tender feelings that threatened to surface.

Giving one last glance to the light that filled the room on the second floor, he revved the engine to a low growl and pulled away.

CHAPTER 12

"You're sulking."
"Am not."
"Yes, you are."
Her grandmother eyed her from across the kitchen table. Isadora set down her book and looked at her granddaughter with a raised eyebrow.

Beatrice looked down at her toast. "How was your date with Caspar?"

Isadora smiled. "It was wonderful. It would have been much more pleasant if we hadn't spent half the night talking about you and Giovanni sulking in your respective corners."

"Hmm," she hummed. She couldn't suppress the satisfaction she felt hearing that Caspar said Giovanni was sulking, too.

She hadn't seen him for two weeks. Not since the night she was forced to face the hard truth that Giovanni, polite and cultured as he seemed, sucked on strange women's necks for sustenance and probably did a lot of other things she didn't want to think about. The night she had been informed that she was viewed as a kind of property or pet in his world, no matter how he tried to sugarcoat that fact.

The night he'd kissed her. And she'd kissed him back.

And what a kiss it was, she thought with a sigh.

Remembering it was enough to raise her temperature. The way his lips had moved against hers, and the barely perceptible shiver she'd felt from him when her tongue touched his fangs. His arms. The heat. His hands on her back ...she shook her head and tried to push back the memory, but she could feel herself blushing as she sat at the table with her grandmother.

She cleared her throat. "I doubt Giovanni is sulking. Caspar just likes to pester him."

"How long as he worked for Gio? Caspar talks about him like he's known him his whole life."

She didn't know the whole of Caspar's story, but she knew Giovanni said they'd been together since Caspar was a boy.

"You'd have to ask him. I think he may have worked for Gio's family." There, that was vague enough. She'd let Caspar fill in whatever details he wanted.

While her initial promise to set Caspar and her grandmother up on a blind date had been in jest, the more Beatrice had thought about it, the more it made sense. When she'd asked Caspar about it, he'd been enthusiastic at her attempt at matchmaking. They'd gone out the night before and Isadora was glowing.

"Well, he's lovely. And has such a wonderful sense of humor."

"Unlike his boss," she muttered as she drank her coffee. She may have said it, but she knew it wasn't true. Though he had a dry, acerbic wit, Giovanni's humor was one of the things she liked most about him.

And she couldn't deny she liked him. Though she had been attracted to him from the beginning, the more she learned, the more she was drawn to him. He could be so aloof, but she was beginning to see the "opposite of frosty" side Carwyn had told her about weeks ago.

That kiss, she thought again as her grandmother chattered on about her date.

"Beatrice, you should go back to work. You're avoiding him. Does this have anything to do with feelings you may have developed—"

"Nope," she lied, cutting her grandmother off. "No feelings. He's my boss. I'm just taking some time off. I have some projects that need my attention, Grandma. And I don't want you and Caspar gossiping, okay? I'm just...taking some time off. That's all."

She gulped down the rest of her coffee, ignoring the almost laser-like stare she knew her grandmother was giving her.

"Well, aren't you full of shit! Also, Caspar and I will gossip about anything we please." She smiled sweetly at Beatrice, who finished up her toast and stood to leave. "Working tonight? It's—"

"Wednesday. Yeah, night hours." She had taken the previous Wednesday night off like a coward but refused to avoid it any more. She'd just suck it up and ignore her conflicting feelings for the man...vampire...whatever. After all, she was a professional.

"Have a nice day, Mariposa. I'll see you tomorrow. I have a date with Caspar tonight."

"Cool. Have fun. Don't do anything...you know what? I don't even want to know or imagine. Bye!" She kissed her grandmother on the cheek and walked to the door.

She spotted the minivan parked down the street as she backed out of the driveway. It followed her down the street, always keeping that careful distance she'd become accustomed to. At first the ever-present family car had freaked her out, but when she noticed Giovanni giving them a satisfied glance when he saw them one night, she knew it had been his doing.

First, it had pissed her off. Then, it had freaked her out. But the more she thought about how many things had changed in her world, and the danger that Giovanni and Carwyn had hinted at, the more the thought she could get used to having someone keeping an eye on her safety.

She glanced in her rear view mirror as she took the exit for the university. *Yep,* she thought, *still there.*

She wasn't dumb; she'd known Giovanni had an ulterior motive for hiring her, but she was also willing to put up with it if he could really find her father. It wasn't until the letters had arrived that the gravity of the danger she was in began to sink in.

If her father had been killed because of something he found out about these books, who was to say her life wasn't in danger, too?

"What the hell kind of mess did you get me into, Dad?" she wondered for the thousandth time as she pulled into one of the crowded lots. She wondered if her father even knew he had put her in danger. She wondered if he thought about her at all.

Every time she asked about her father, Giovanni simply said he was still waiting to hear. From who or what, she didn't know.

By the time she walked to the library for her shift, she had successfully managed to shove all thoughts of Dr. Giovanni Vecchio from her brain. This was immediately ruined when she got up to the fifth floor and saw Dr. Christiansen and Charlotte bent over a now familiar shipping box she knew would have a return address from the University of Ferrara in Italy.

Dr. Christiansen looked up with a smile. "Another letter arrived!"

"Of course it did," she muttered.

She set her bag down behind the reference desk and walked over to look. She glanced at the parchment, but quickly grabbed the notes that accompanied them.

"I'll go make a couple of copies for the next flood of professors," Beatrice said as she took the notes—which she knew would include a translation—back to the copy and imaging room.

Hours later she sat in the empty reading room, perusing the translation of the fourth Pico letter. Word of the new document hadn't spread yet, so the reading room was deserted as she looked over her notes. It was another letter from the scholar, Angelo Poliziano. He talked more about the mystical books in

Signore Andros's library, some trip to Paris Pico was taking, and asked after the little boy, but it was the third section which caught her attention.

> *I will not linger in this letter, but hope to hear a response from you soon regarding the matter of G. Do not think that your unsigned correspondence has gone unnoticed. Your sonnets have been read in the very rooms of Lorenzo's home. While they are beautiful work—some of your best—I beg of you to be more discreet in your admiration. You are fortunate so many ladies share the fair skin and dark hair of your muse, as their generality may yet prevent you from becoming embroiled in another scandal.*

She shook her head, scribbling nonsense in the margins of her notebook.

Was this truly Giovanni? she asked herself as she finished the letter. Friend of Lorenzo de Medici? Philosopher at age twenty-three and contemporary of some of the greatest minds of the Italian Renaissance? A poet who longed for another man's wife?

The man who seemed so cold and yet kissed her with such passion?

She closed her eyes and forced herself to think with her brain instead of her hormones.

When Beatrice had gone through her darkest teenage years, she had turned to almost anyone who seemed to offer a little warmth. Now, she shuddered to think how foolish she had been and how self-destructive. She had forced herself to take a break from the opposite sex since she decided that dark and destructive weren't nearly as attractive as she had thought they were at seventeen.

But she didn't like being alone, and she had the same desires that most twenty-two-year-old women had. A part of her thrilled at the idea of her interest in Giovanni being returned, but the other part of her had the cold realization that a relationship with a five hundred-year-old vampire, who probably wanted to drink her blood more than he wanted to cuddle, was the textbook definition of unhealthy.

On second thought, she was pretty sure most textbooks didn't cover that one.

She heard the door to the reading room open, tucked the notes in her bag, and braced herself before she looked up.

And Carwyn stood in front of her.

"Surprise!"

She glanced at the smiling vampire before her eyes darted to the doors he had just walked through.

"Oh, Count Stuffy della Prissypants is not with me. He had to venture to the fair city of New York to negotiate purchase on a certain prize his awesome assistant found." Carwyn clucked his tongue at her and winked. "And you didn't even tell me. I would have taken you to a horror movie, a really bad one."

She mustered up a smile. "It's good to see you. I wasn't expecting—"

"No, I expect you weren't from the sad, little look on your face. But cheer up!" He pulled a chair over and sat next to the desk. "I'm all yours for the night. And I won't even pretend to transcribe an old book so I can stare at you longingly from the corner of my eye." He kicked his feet up on the desk. "Thank God none of the boring professors are here."

"Carwyn," she said with a smile. "Have I told you lately that you're kind of awesome?"

He winked. "No, but I'm always game to hear it. Forget the Italian, darling Beatrice. Run away with me. We'll go to Hawaii."

"Oh yeah?"

"I'll make us a cave by the sea where the sun won't touch me and we'll spend every night swimming naked and drinking fruity drinks while we make the fishes blush."

She giggled and shook her head at his mischievous grin. "You...are something else."

His grin suddenly turned sweet as he looked at her.

"As are you, darling girl. As are you."

He opened his mouth again, as if to say something, and she felt a faint stirring in the air, but finally, his grin returned and the tension seemed to scatter.

"Could you really make a cave?"

"What?" He looked surprised by her question. "Oh, yes. Of course. Volcanic rock is very soft."

She shook her head. "That's so crazy. I wish Gio would tell me about that stuff."

"What do you want to know? No one here but vampires and crazy people."

"Well," she smiled, "what can all the different vampires do? There's four kinds, right? Like the four elements? You can make caves, Gio can make fire—"

"Well, strictly speaking—"

"Yeah, yeah," she waved a hand, "static electricity, manipulation of the elements, got that part. So, it's probably the same with all of them then." She frowned. "How do you know what element you'll be? Do you get to pick? Is it something that happens right away when you get..."

"Sired? Or turned. Those are the proper terms in our world." Carwyn sighed and leaned back in his chair. "With my children—"

"Your children?"

"Yes, I call them sons and daughters. It depends on the sire, but immortal families can be very much like human families. We just tend to look a bit closer in age," he said with a laugh.

"How do you—I mean how do you become..." She paused, unsure of how to phrase her question.

"Most of the common myths are true about that," Carwyn said. "When I sire a child, almost all of their blood is drained, either by me or someone else. The important thing is that the majority of the blood is replaced with my own. That is what creates the connection."

"And what *is* the connection? Do you...control them or something?"

"Sadly, no," he laughed. "I can't compel them to do my bidding." Carwyn paused for a moment and a wistful look came to his eyes.

"It's very much the way I remember feeling about my human children, to be honest. Only much more...intense, as everything is. It's not an easy decision, choosing to make a child, and it has such long-term consequences. If nothing violent happens to myself or my children, we will be a family for eternity. It's a very strong commitment to make to another being and, as a consequence, I do have quite a lot of influence over my children. We're very close."

"What about your sire? Is he—"

"She, actually. And my sire is no longer living."

She could sense from the look in his eyes that it wasn't something the normally open vampire wanted to talk about, so she changed the subject.

"Did you ever, I mean, do vampires ever turn people that they love? Like, if your wife had been living—"

"I wouldn't have turned her myself," he said quickly. "Well, not if I knew the consequences of it. It's *not* a romantic connection, Beatrice. The feelings really are more paternal, so it's not an ideal situation if a vampire falls in love with a human and they're turned."

"Why not?"

"If the human does choose to become immortal, they would have to be turned by a vampire other than their lover, and then that other vampire would have a very strong connection and influence over the one turned. Your feelings toward your sire run very deep, positive or negative. It could become quite complicated."

She looked down at the desk. "Right. I guess that makes sense," she said quietly. She opened her e-mail and busied herself checking the news online. Carwyn was silent, but she could still feel him watching her.

"You know," he said suddenly. "All my children are earth vampires. It runs in families that way."

"Oh really?" she said as she typed.

"Yes, it's almost unheard of for a vampire to sire out of their element. Water from water. Earth from earth. Wind from wind, and so forth."

"Huh, that's interesting. So it's kind of genetic, I guess."

"Except for *fire*." Her eyes darted up to find Carwyn watching her.

"Oh really?"

"Yes, they tend to just pop up like the bastard redhead every now and then. Anyone can sire them. Water, Air, Earth. Very unpredictable. Bit of a shame, of course."

A HIDDEN FIRE

She leaned back, curious to see where the clever priest was going with his train of thought. "And why is it a shame?"

"Let's just say I'm glad I'm not a fire vamp." His voice dropped. "Glad to never have sired one, either."

She swallowed the lump in her throat, almost afraid to ask her next question. "And why is that?"

He put his feet down and rested his arms on the desk. She watched him, transfixed by his vivid blue eyes as the air around her became charged. When he finally spoke, his voice had a low, hypnotic quality to it.

"You see, Beatrice, it's a dangerous thing to wield fire. Dangerous for yourself, and dangerous for those around you. More than one sire—even a good one—will *kill* a son or daughter that shows the affinity toward fire almost immediately."

"Why—"

"And if the sire doesn't kill them, the young vampire will often kill himself—purely by accident—and they'll likely take a few others with them. Very, *very* volatile, those fire vamps."

"But," she stuttered, "Gio—"

"Those that do live are usually very gifted, and *very* strong," he continued. "And their sires will take advantage of that. Because if you control a fire vampire, Beatrice, you control a very, *very* powerful weapon."

Her chest was constricted as she absorbed the implication of what Carwyn was saying. "Did Gio's sire—"

"Now, *I* would never want that life for a child of mine. I'd never abuse my influence like *some* would; but even without my interference, to live in peace, my son or daughter would have to develop almost inhuman self-control."

Like him, she thought, suddenly gaining new perspective on Giovanni's dispassionate demeanor.

"And you'd have to be very careful how you used your power. Ironically...you'd probably seem a little cold to most people."

She flashed back to the heat that poured off Giovanni when he held her. What would have happened if he'd lost control? What had Carwyn written to her?

'Opposite. Of. Frosty.'

"No, I wouldn't want to be a fire vampire, because if I managed to live—and wasn't manipulated as a powerful weapon by the one who made me—I'd most likely live a very lonely life," Carwyn said quietly. "Do you understand what I'm saying?"

She nodded and cleared her throat a little. "I understand."

The now solemn vampire leaned back to relax in his chair. "I knew you were a clever girl."

"So," she swallowed the lump in her throat. "If you ever had a fire vampire for a child, do you think...they'd always be alone?"

He shrugged and smiled a little. "I think that all things are possible for him who believes."

She smiled. "Oh yeah?"

"And I also believe that love can work miracles."

"Love?" She cocked an eyebrow at him. "What about friendship? Can that work miracles, too?"

Carwyn rolled his eyes. "Silly B, love *is* friendship...just with less clothes, which makes it far more brilliant."

She burst into laughter, glad he had finally broken the tension that hovered between them. "You are the most ridiculous man I have ever met. And maybe the worst priest."

"Or the *best*," he said with a wink, as he reached for the romance novel in the bottom drawer. "Think carefully about that one."

She snorted. "I'll take it into consideration." She turned back to her computer and opened a paper she was supposed to be working on. Carwyn opened the book and began to read, still sneaking glances at her until she finally sighed in frustration.

"What now? I really should get some work done."

"Come back to work. He's far more of a pain in the ass since you've been gone. He pretends nothing's wrong, but he's all mopey and has no sense of humor. I think he might hurt my dog if you don't."

"Nice blackmail, Father."

He shrugged and only looked at her with hopeful eyes.

She finally smiled. "I wasn't going to stay away forever, you know."

"Will you tell me why you left?"

She shook her head firmly. "No."

"I tell you all sorts of things," he muttered.

"You have got to be the most immature thousand year old I've ever met."

He folded his arms and scowled. "I'm not even going to offer the most obvious retort to that."

She smiled as she watched him but realized, if there was one person she instinctively trusted in this whole messy world she had found herself in, it was Carwyn. As far as she could tell, he had no ulterior motive to tell her anything, and he always answered her questions.

"Bad choices about men, remember?" she finally said, referring to their last conversation in the reading room. "Trying to make better choices in life, Carwyn. When it comes to... you know."

He stared at her for a moment before he nodded. "Understood."

"And don't say a word to—"

"Count Prissypants tells me nothing. Therefore, I tell him nothing."

She sighed. "I was actually going to say Caspar. I think he and my grandma are thick as thieves now."

His eyes lit up. "Oooh, let's gossip about them, shall we?"

Beatrice smiled, gave up, and shut down her computer.

CHAPTER 13

The first thing Giovanni smelled when he walked into the house at three in the morning early Friday was the *coq au vin* Caspar must have cooked for dinner the night before. The second thing he smelled was Beatrice.

A smile tugged at the corner of his mouth. He had hoped she would come back to work before he needed to leave for New York. In the back of his mind, he entertained a fanciful notion of taking her with him and showing her the lights of Manhattan, taking her to a play, or walking through the Met.

"You're back."

He turned when he heard Caspar at the kitchen door.

"I am. Why are you still awake? And is there anything I need to know?" Giovanni busied himself emptying his pockets on the counter and looking through the mail Caspar had set out.

"I'm awake because I wanted to talk to you. I'm sure you've realized B is back at work. She and her grandmother had dinner here earlier in the evening. Also, I am completely smitten with Isadora."

"I don't blame you one bit. She's a charming woman," he mumbled as he looked through the file of e-mails Caspar had printed out.

"I find myself irritated that I've been living in this city for years and had no idea she existed."

He looked up at Caspar, disarmed by the sincerity in the man's voice. He cocked his head. "I'm glad for you, Caspar. You deserve to find someone like that. You've been alone too long."

"So have you."

A HIDDEN FIRE

Considering Caspar's sentimental nature, he knew where his old friend was going, but it still gave Giovanni pause. "Caspar—"

"I want to talk to you about B."

Giovanni shrugged. "There's nothing to talk about. The girl—"

"Don't be so damn dismissive." His eyes shot up, surprised by Caspar's angry tone.

"I'm not dismissing you." He frowned and set the papers down on the counter.

"*Her*, Gio, you're dismissive of her."

He sighed and stuffed his hands in his pockets, examining the older man. "I have no idea what you're talking about, Caspar. How am I—"

"You talk about her like she's a child. Maybe a bright and entertaining child, but a child nonetheless."

Giovanni rolled his eyes and walked toward the living room, but Caspar only followed him. He stopped to pour himself a drink at the sideboard. When he turned, Caspar was still looking at him with an impatient expression.

"She *is* a child."

"She's not."

He shook his head. "She's only twenty-two—"

"She's not as naive as you think, old man."

Giovanni's glass crashed down to the table and he looked up, suddenly angry at his friend.

"I am an old man," he quietly bit out. "A very old man, Caspar. I was an old man 450 years ago. Do you forget that? Do you forget that I was already an old man when I took you in as a child? Do you forget that I will remain an old man long after you leave this world? Do you have any concept of how many human friends I have seen grow old and die?"

"I know she's young, and I know you want her to help search for your books, but I also realize—"

"You realize? Do you? She's twenty-two. Do you remember what that is?" He shook his head. "I confess, I don't remember being twenty-two. It's been too long. But I remember you at twenty-two."

"Do you?"

He swallowed his emotions and tried to smile. "Of course I do. I remember... everything." He looked at the old man he had watched over for sixty-four years, and the memories flooded over him. "I remember the first time you played a piano when you were six, and how your eyes lit up. The first time you drove a car, which terrified me, but you were so excited. The first time you ran away from home, and how sorry you were when you came back four hours later. The first time you were drunk, and how bloody arrogant you were at eighteen."

Caspar only frowned and shook his head. "What—"

"I remember you at twenty-two, Caspar. And you were so damn bold. You were fearless. Do you remember? The first time you fell in love was when you were twenty-two."

Caspar smiled wistfully. "Claire."

"Beautiful Claire Lipton! The darling of your young heart. Do you remember? The only woman you would ever love. Wasn't that what you said? She was incandescent in your eyes."

"Gio—"

"Where is she now? Where is beautiful Claire? When did you stop loving her? When was the last time you even thought of her?"

Caspar paused, finally nodding in understanding before he went to pour himself a drink; then he sat down on the sofa and stared into the cold fireplace. Giovanni picked up his scotch and settled into his chair. He noticed that Beatrice's scent lingered in it, and he wondered whether she had sat there that evening.

His eyes softened as he looked at the man he had watched grow up, mature, and eventually grow old. He knew he would someday face Caspar's death, and that day grew closer with every sunset.

"Caspar," he said. "Beloved son of my friend, David. You have been my child, my friend, my confidante, my ally in this world. And I will be here long after you have left me. What are you asking of me? Do you even realize?"

Caspar glared at him. "Do you think I want you to be alone when I'm gone? Do you think I don't know? Don't pretend she is only part of your search. I can tell you have feelings for her. I know you want her."

Giovanni set down his drink, gripping the arms of the chair as he followed Caspar's eyes to the cold grate.

"If I had feelings for her...they are inappropriate. I need her—"

"*You* need—"

"*I need her,*" he glared at Caspar, "to trust me. I need to keep her safe from my own mistake, and I need her to find her father."

"To find out what he knows."

"Yes, and to find out why Lorenzo wants him so badly."

"So you'll keep her safe so you can use her to find her father."

"Yes," he said, his face carefully blank.

"And that's the only reason you're keeping her around?"

Giovanni sat stiffly in his chair. "That's the main reason, yes."

Caspar's eyes narrowed. "You're such a liar sometimes."

"And you're melodramatic."

He stood and walked to the fireplace to light it. The nights were starting to carry the soft warmth of springtime, but they were still cool enough that he knew a fire wouldn't be unwelcome to the old man on the sofa. He snapped his fingers to ignite the kindling in the grate and carefully added a few pieces of wood.

"You act like you're so cold," Caspar said. "But you're not, and don't pretend that her father is the only reason you're interested in her."

He crouched down at the grate and willed the small fire to grow. "I will find her father. I will find my collection. I will take care of Lorenzo, and then Beatrice De Novo can go on to live a relatively normal life."

"Oh? Is that so? Do you plan to wipe her memory, too?"

He paused, the thought of wiping himself from the girl's memory more painful than he wanted to admit. But, he rationalized, there was no need for it.

"Of course not. She's obviously trustworthy, and after the Lorenzo problem is gone, there is no reason she couldn't have a relationship with her father. She deserves that."

"She deserves a relationship with her father?"

Giovanni stared into the growing flames. "Of course. I wouldn't deny her that. Not if I could help it."

"But you'd deny her yourself."

He felt a flare of anger, but he tamped it down and stood up to turn back to Caspar, his posture deliberately casual. "I'm not going to discuss this."

"Why not?" Caspar asked. "Don't you think she has feelings for you? Do you see the way she looks at you? Carwyn and I both see it. As surprising as it might be to you, the two of you fit together like—"

"Do you think I haven't thought of it, Caspar?" His temper snapped and he could feel the flames jump in the grate behind him. "Do you think I haven't thought about keeping her?"

"Then why don't you—"

"The nights we've spent poring over this book or that map? The way she makes everything lighter? The way I find myself having to hold back from telling her everything—everything? Like she would even want to know?"

"How do you know she doesn't want to know, you stubborn old fool?"

"You think I haven't fantasized about taking her?" he bit out. "About having her in my life? Do you think I haven't thought about it?"

Caspar stood stiffly to walk closer to the fire. "So what's stopping you? She'll still help you find her father. She wants it as much as you do. Do you think she's not smart enough to understand the consequences? You won't even give her a chance, you idiot! Or are you just afraid that she'll say no?"

A sharp longing rose in his chest, but it was smothered by bitterness. "She's a child. She doesn't know what she wants at this age. At twenty-two you wanted to marry Claire Lipton and run away together to join the theater. Three years after that, you wanted to become an airline pilot. And after that—"

"You know, I already know I have a short attention span, you obnoxious git. You don't have to rub it in."

Giovanni took a deep breath, and laid a hand on Caspar's shoulder. "The point is, she's at an impulsive age, and if she has feelings for me, they are…infatuation. It wouldn't be fair to take advantage of that."

"But you'll use her to find her father, won't you? No problem taking advantage of that."

He stiffened and pulled away. "You said yourself, she wants to find him, too."

Tears pricked Caspar's eyes when he looked at him.

"You're a good man, Giovanni Vecchio. Don't forget that in this mad search."

Caspar turned and walked back to the sofa, sitting and picking up his drink. He stared into the fire and Giovanni watched the calm settle over him.

"You know, I don't remember much from my life before you. I was so young when you took me in. I remember hiding in that attic in Rotterdam with my father. I remember how hot it was, how stifling. I remember the smell of dust and old paper from the books my father saved."

"You were such a quiet child."

"I remember seeing you for the first time," he continued, "and my father holding me and telling me I could trust you because you were an old friend. That you weren't one of the bad men, even though you were a stranger. That you would take care of me."

Giovanni sat down in his chair and took a sip of scotch.

"Were you scared? When I took you to England? When you had to be locked up during the day in the house when you were little? I tried to explain it the best way I could, but you were only four or five, you must have been confused."

Caspar shrugged. "Children are so adaptable. I don't remember being afraid. I remember being a little older and realizing that most children didn't sleep during the day and that most went to school, but by then I understood what you were. And then, there were all our adventures."

Giovanni had taken Caspar on many trips as the boy had grown older and more useful. He had always been a wonderful companion. At first, he had called him his son, then his nephew, then eventually his brother as their appearances became more similar and Caspar aged.

In his long life, the boy he had rescued remained the human Giovanni had loved the most, and it had broken his heart when Caspar told him in his forties he had decided he didn't want to be turned. He was the first human the vampire had truly wanted to sire.

He looked at the old man. "Has it been a good life with me, Caspar? Do you regret never marrying or having children? Did I keep you from that?"

Caspar shook his head. "I never felt like, had I wanted a family, they would have been unwelcome to you. And I know how fond you are of children. No, I just never found the right woman, I suppose."

"Isadora?" Giovanni asked with a smile.

He shook his head, a smile creeping across his face. "She's one of a kind, Gio.

My lord, she's so bloody adorable. I want to steal her away and monopolize her every moment."

"You are smitten, old friend."

"Completely. You've met her, can you blame me?"

Giovanni smiled thinking of Isadora and Beatrice. He thought about the two women, grey hair against black, with their heads together, smiling on Dia de los Muertos. He thought of the way they laughed and teased each other, and the ease and love between them. In his mind, he saw Beatrice as she aged, her dramatic features slowly taking on the handsome dignity of her grandmother and her eyes exhibiting the unique wisdom that was only evident from a life well lived.

"No, I certainly can't blame you, Caspar. They're stunning."

Caspar gave him a pointed look, but Giovanni continued. "If things get dangerous in the city, take Isadora to the house in Kerrville. You'll both be out of the way there. I don't want to have to worry about you."

"What about B?"

"No, she stays here. I'll need her."

"What do you mean?"

He shrugged. "Don't worry. Nothing will happen to her."

"Because you need her?"

He glanced at Casper in the flickering light. The fire had started to die down, and he could feel the dawn beginning to tug at him after his long journey.

"You need her," Caspar repeated, "so you'll keep her safe?"

"Of course."

Caspar nodded and finished his drink, setting it down on the coffee table and standing up from the sofa. "Of course."

The old man walked upstairs, his step slightly slower than the year before as he climbed to the second floor. The next year would be slower still, until it would be necessary to move his old friend to one of the rooms on the ground floor. Though he knew Caspar was in excellent health, he also knew that the passing of time carried inevitability and with that would come loss.

He spent another hour staring into the fire before he finally banked it and climbed the stairs. He entered his walk-in closet, took off his old watch and put it on the dresser before he stripped out of his clothes and placed them in the laundry basket for Caspar to tend in the morning. He punched in the code to his sleeping chamber and walked through the reinforced door.

As he entered, he looked around at the spartan furniture that decorated the space. There was only a small bed; despite his tall frame, his body would hardly move while in its day rest, a desk where he kept some writing paper, the older fountain pens he still preferred, and a rotary phone. The one piece of decoration was the photograph of the Arno River that flowed through the heart of Florence and the arches of the Ponte Vecchio that spanned it. The picture had been taken in the middle of the day, and the shops along the bridge glowed vividly in the searing Italian sun.

On the wall opposite the framed photograph, there was a large bookcase filled with his collection of journals. In them were the collected memories of five hundred years; no one had ever read them besides himself. As he lay in bed and waited for the pull of day, he tried to imagine Beatrice in this small, confined room.

He could not.

Giovanni heard her before he scented her, and he scented her when she walked in the house. He forced himself to sit at the table in his library and examine the fifth letter as Beatrice chatted with Caspar in the kitchen. It was a lighthearted letter; with Poliziano teasing about the debates in Rome and warning his friend to not speak publicly about the mystic texts Andros had given him.

> "I do hope you keep in mind the rather stringent positions our Holy Father has taken regarding anything of a mystical nature. I know you are enamored of your Eastern texts and your thoughts of philosophical harmony, but I do not wish for you to fall under his scrutiny. I have no doubt the result would be to no one's liking."

The debates, he remembered, had not been successful, and the Pope had only been angered. He smiled when he saw the closing paragraph.

> "On a more pleasant note, I was pleased to read Jacopo's letter, and gratified he recalls his time in Benevieni's household so fondly. Indeed, my friend, along with your philosophical work, I believe what you have accomplished with his education will be one of your finest achievements."

He paused in his examination when he heard Beatrice climb the stairs. He couldn't help but notice her step did not have its usual exuberance.

"Hey."

He looked up to meet her dark eyes, immediately tempted to throw away every stern admonition he had given himself when he saw her form-fitting black shirt and slim burgundy skirt. He glanced at her feet and smiled when he saw she was wearing her combat boots again, but he forced himself to stay seated.

"Hello, Beatrice."

"So I heard you got it. The Lincoln speech. Was the buyer happy?"

He nodded slowly. "Yes. Happy parties on both sides, and a good commission for me."

"Great. That's great."

A HIDDEN FIRE

She sauntered into the library, eventually making her way back to the desk where her computer had rested silently during her absence. She turned it on, and Giovanni searched his mind, trying to find a way to bypass the wall that had risen between them.

He had an idea. "I have another project for you."

She frowned a little as she concentrated on the computer screen. "Oh, really?" she said. "What's up?"

"It's related to the Pico letters."

Her eyes met his, obviously surprised. "The letters? You mean—that's...you trust me to find stuff about the letters?"

He frowned, "Of course I do. Why do you think I wouldn't trust you?"

She just stared at him for a few minutes before a sharp laugh escaped her, and she shook her head. "Do I think...I don't—Giovanni, I don't know what to think about you. About anything. I just—I should just stop trying to figure you out, honestly."

Giovanni took a deep breath and stood, perching his hip on the corner of the large table before he answered. "Beatrice, that night at the pub—"

"Did you mean it?" Her voice was barely above a whisper. "That kiss?"

Yes, he thought, but remained silent as she stood and walked toward him.

She looked at him, frowning as she bit her lip. "Because at first I thought you did—I mean, it felt real to me—and then you implied that you were acting."

I wasn't, he thought again. *I wanted to sink my fangs into you, drink your blood, strip your clothes off and—*

"But then, I thought about it more."

He felt his fangs drop and his skin begin to heat as she drew closer, and he forced his body to remain still instead of rushing to meet her.

"I thought about it more, and realized there are some things a man can't fake. And the way you kissed me..." Her lips were full and flush from when she had bit them nervously. He crossed his arms on his chest so he couldn't touch her as she continued in a low voice, "The way it felt, Gio, I don't think it was fake at all."

She stood in front of him, her eyes bold as she met his hungry stare, and all Giovanni would have had to do was take one step and he could have wrapped his body around hers, laid his mouth on her soft neck, and swallowed the thick blood that called to him. He swallowed slowly, and ignored the burn in his throat and the smell of honeysuckle and lemon that filled the air.

"I'm not going to deny that I'm attracted to you, Beatrice. Denying that would be foolish and insulting to us both."

"But you're not going to kiss me again, are you?"

"No."

"Did you want to bite me?"

He searched her eyes, trying to determine what answer she wanted, but though he had observed humanity for five hundred years, her enigmatic eyes were still a mystery to him.

"Yes."

"But you won't do that, either?"

His body yearned to say yes, but his mind rebelled at the consequences of that kind of intimacy.

"No. I won't bite you," he said, hoping he was strong enough not to break his word.

"Why not? You could. I'm not strong enough to stop you."

He straightened his shoulders and tore his eyes from her to look toward the fireplace.

"It wouldn't be a prudent decision, Beatrice. For either of us."

He saw her swallow out of the corner of his eye and detected the thin edge of regret in her eyes before she turned and walked to her desk. He knew his answer had pleased neither of them, but she was too valuable to be anything more than a human under his protection.

They sat in silence for a few minutes, neither of them looking at the other, as the fire crackled in the grate. Eventually, he heard her open a desk drawer. She pulled something out and walked over to him where he stood at the table, his arms still crossed and his hands clenched. She was carrying a notepad and a black ball-point pen.

"So, what do you want me to find, boss?"

CHAPTER 14

"Just taste it," a playful voice implored.
"I'm telling you, I don't like lamb!"
"But, darling, you have never tried *my* lamb before."

The sound of Caspar and Isadora's voices drifted out from the kitchen, interspersed with the occasional chuckle or tinkling laugh. Beatrice saw Giovanni frowning toward the door from his seat at the dining room table, and she had to stifle a laugh.

"Caspar!" her grandmother shouted before breaking into a fit of what could only be described as giggles. Now Beatrice was the one frowning, and she glanced over at Giovanni to find him watching her with an eyebrow cocked in amusement.

"Do you wonder?" he asked.

She shook her head. "Absolutely not. I don't even want to speculate."

He smiled and continued sorting through the catalogue printouts she had made for him.

They had finally fallen back into a comfortable work rhythm after the kiss in January, eventually finding a way to work with each other while giving each other space. Ironically, it was even more evident to Beatrice that she had developed serious feelings for Giovanni the longer they worked together. It didn't help that they were now pursuing the same project and had even more time to interact.

Following his hunch, Giovanni and Beatrice searched for other documents he thought might have been sold or donated from his original collection of books, manuscripts and letters. He speculated that Lorenzo was attempting to draw her father out of hiding, and if Lorenzo had given some documents away, he might have given or sold others, as well. If Giovanni knew *why* Lorenzo was so determined to find her dad, he wasn't telling her.

She'd discovered a cache of documents donated to the University of Leeds that Giovanni thought might have been the original Dante correspondence Stephen De Novo mentioned to his father, and Giovanni unearthed another set of letters between Girolamo Benevieni and Giovanni Pico that had been bought by a private collection in Perugia.

"This is odd," he muttered as he looked at the details from another auction in Rome. "There's something...Beatrice, call Carwyn, will you?"

"Sure, he's outside with Bran?"

"Probably trying to cover up another horticultural disaster that beast has inflicted on my gardens."

"Aw, Gio, you'll miss him when he's gone."

"Carwyn, yes. The dog, no." Just then, Doyle jumped on his lap and shoved his fuzzy grey head under Giovanni's hand. Beatrice had to smile that neither seemed to notice the cat's hair standing on end every time Giovanni touched him.

"No, no one will miss the wolfhound, will they, Doyle?" he murmured, continuing to stroke the cat's back as he read. Watching the vampire read at the table with his dark hair falling into his eyes, a frown furrowing his brow and his lips pursed as he tickled under the cat's chin gave Beatrice the irrational desire to crawl into his lap and curl up, just to see if she might get the same treatment.

"Beatrice?"

"Hmm?" she asked in a dazed voice as she stared at the cat.

She finally looked up to see him watching her, his eyes hooded and his hand still on Doyle's back. "Were you going to—" He cleared his throat and looked out the dark window.

"Carwyn. Right. I'll just...I'll call—you know, I'll just walk outside and find him. I could use a...walk."

She got up and quickly exited the room, just as another burst of laughter rang out from the kitchen. Beatrice winced and walked quickly through the French doors and across the brick patio by the pool.

She didn't mind her grandmother and Caspar dating. In fact, she was ridiculously happy that they got along so well; it was just somewhat cruel that her sixty-eight-year-old grandmother had a more exciting love life than she did.

A boy from Beatrice's art history class had taken her to dinner the weekend before, and she had enjoyed it. His name was Jeff, and he was polite and funny. She even laughed a little when he related stories about the drama in the office where he was interning and would probably work in the fall. He took her back to her grandmother's house and gave her a really nice kiss.

She had absolutely no desire to see him again.

Beatrice cursed Giovanni's superior kissing skills and intriguing personality as she walked through the grounds. Summer had almost settled on Houston, and the air hung heavy with leftover warmth from the day and the smell of honeysuckle. The roses were blooming and, as she rounded the corner near the small gazebo, she heard Carwyn muttering to his dog again.

"—not going to let you come back next year if you keep this up, Bran. And honestly, I don't understand your fascination with rose roots. Is it just to annoy him?"

She heard the dog snuffle and half-expected him to respond. After all, vampires existed, so why not talking wolfhounds? She heard additional words that sounded a lot like curses, but she was pretty sure they were in Welsh, and couldn't understand them.

"Carwyn?" she called across the lawn. The vampire turned to her with a guilty expression, and she watched in fascination as the numerous piles of dirt in Caspar's prized rose garden started crawling across the lawn and back toward the holes the dog had dug them from. The dark earth didn't float, exactly, but appeared to simply move by its own volition when Carwyn flicked his fingers at it. It was almost as if the dirt had become a living thing, and small piles chased each other across the dark grass.

"B! No need to tell the professor about Bran's indiscretion now, is there?"

She just stared at the self-moving dirt.

"That is so freaking cool. How do you—I mean, I know you—that is just so...cool."

"Thanks. This? This is no big deal. Try fixing the mess that six or seven of these monsters make in a vegetable garden before a scary nun finds them. Now that's a challenge."

"Really?" She frowned as she continued to watch the small piles of dirt gradually disappear into the earth. Even the grass seemed to knit itself together where the dog had dug it up.

"No, not really. I'm joking. Moving boulders is a slight workout. Or causing an earthquake, manipulating faults, things like that. Gardening isn't really much of a challenge anymore."

"You can cause earthquakes?"

He sighed, a playful look in his eyes. "There's such a delicious joke there, but I'm going to be good and hold back. With the amount of sexual tension permeating these grounds, even a bad 'rock your world' line is liable to ignite something."

"Very funny." She rolled her eyes and tried to remember why she came to find him. "Gio's got a question for you, I think. Something about a private collection in Central Italy? Or maybe it's the auction he's curious about, I'm not sure."

Carwyn immediately ran to the house at vampire speed, leaving Beatrice and Bran in the garden. She looked at the dog, who seemed to smile playfully before he loped off in the direction of the hydrangeas.

"Slowest thing here," she muttered. "Why do I always have to be the slowest thing here?"

When she reached the French doors, she heard Carwyn speaking in quick Italian into the rotary phone by the small desk in the living room.

Italian and Spanish had enough similarity that she could understand snatches of what she heard. She knew he mentioned books, and she heard the Italian words for "Vatican" and "library" pop up more than once.

He finally put down the phone and Giovanni started in with the questions, this time, at least, they were in English. He kept his voice low, mindful of Caspar and Isadora in the kitchen.

"So? What did the he say?"

Carwyn shook his head and spoke quietly. "Not one of theirs. He says that sounds close to one of the fronts they'll use in private auctions sometimes—enough that someone who was bidding more casually wouldn't suspect—but it's definitely not them. And he doesn't know about any new Savonarola correspondence, though he sounded like he was practically drooling at the thought."

Giovanni frowned. "So if it *is* Lorenzo, and he's not using these to draw De Novo out—because these would hold no interest for a Dante scholar—why was he selling correspondence books from the fifteenth century, and buying them from himself?"

Carwyn had been leaning against the wall, looking out the dark windows with a finger tapping his chin. Suddenly, he smiled wickedly. "Oh, Giovanni. Virgil himself would be impressed with your virtue. He's doing it because he's a clever, clever boy. And clever boys who want to clean money might just use a private auction to do it."

Giovanni let loose a string of Italian curses and slapped a hand on the table, scaring the cat, who jumped off his lap and ran upstairs.

"What does he do?" Beatrice asked.

They both looked at her as if they'd forgotten she was there.

"I mean...that's laundering money, right? That's what you're talking about? Don't drug dealers do that kind of thing? Is he a drug dealer?"

Carwyn shrugged. "He's got his hands in any number of fairly dirty pots. Smuggling mostly, and other types of clandestine shipping. Not all of it necessarily illegal, but most of it...questionable. I wouldn't be surprised if he has his fingers in drugs or anything else. The question is – why does he need some of his funds clean at this point?"

"He won't need it to find her father. He has other channels for that. He's planning something," Giovanni muttered, frowning again and biting a lip in concentration as he studied the printouts in front of him. "In the human world? Something legitimate?"

Carwyn was still tapping his chin. "Whatever it is, it has something to do with the books."

"Why?" she asked.

Giovanni was sitting silently at the table, shaking his head. "Too much coincidence. To many pieces moving at once," he muttered. "Her father. My books. The letters. Now the money..." He kept muttering to himself as suspicion grew in her mind.

Her father. Giovanni's books. Lorenzo stole the books and wanted her father. A connection started to tickle the back of her brain, but she shoved it to the side for the moment and turned to Carwyn.

"Isn't it easier to do that stuff electronically? Laundering money? Why is he doing it through auctions?"

Carwyn chuckled. "I'm sure it is, and someone with half a fool's worth of knowledge in electronic markets could do it better than he could. But he's not all that up on digital technology, I'm betting."

"He's not, though I'm sure he thinks he is. Lorenzo was always overconfident. He was never very good at adaptation. Many immortals aren't," Giovanni said. "I know some vampires who took fifty years or so to even start driving a car."

Beatrice rolled her eyes. "You crazy international men of mystery, you."

Giovanni looked at her. "You think *we're* backward, you should meet—"

"Tenzin!" the priest yelled then lowered his voice, looking over his shoulder at the kitchen door, as if suddenly remembering the humans in the house. "Oh, she's the worst, isn't she? Has she ever been in a car? I've never seen it. And I can't even imagine her getting in a plane."

Giovanni snorted. "I got her in a carriage once in India, and she nearly kicked the door down getting out so fast."

Beatrice just listened to them talk about their friend, intensely curious about the woman who seemed to inspire such simultaneous awe and affection.

"How does she get around if she doesn't drive or fly? Does she walk everywhere?" she asked.

They both stopped chuckling and looked at her. Carwyn winked. "Who says she doesn't fly?"

Her jaw dropped. "No freaking way!"

"'Like a bird,'" the priest sung under his breath. "So bloody convenient controlling air, isn't it?"

"Carwyn," Giovanni muttered in warning. "Not your place."

"Oh, B won't say anything when she meets her, will you? Besides, I imagine Tenzin's already seen her in a dream or two anyway. She probably knows Beatrice better than she knows herself."

Giovanni huffed and began putting his documents away. "Ignore him. It's getting late. You should probably get your grandmother home."

She rolled her eyes. "That's right. Don't want to get the kids in bed too late, do we? Besides, if we get in too late, our friendly neighborhood surveillance guys might start sweating in their minivan." She had begun teasing Giovanni about their guards after her initial discomfort about them wore off. Now, she liked knowing they were there.

"Well, B. This is goodbye for now," Carwyn walked over to embrace her. "But not goodbye forever, you must promise."

She let herself be enveloped by the mountain of a man who had become a trusted friend and confidante over the last four months. She had known he was leaving the next night—though she had no idea how any of them traveled—and Beatrice struggled to hold in the tears that wanted to escape as she hugged him.

"Now, now, darling girl. Just let me know when I need to come and rescue you from boredom, all right?" She laughed against his chest and felt him squeeze her just a little tighter. "I'm only a phone call away."

"I'm going to miss you so much," she whispered. "You'll be back?"

"Of course!" He stepped back and dabbed at her eyes with the edge of his flowered shirt. "There now. And you'll be back to Houston for Christmas, will you not?"

She nodded and sniffed. "Yep, and let's face it, the weather in L.A.'s got to be better than this, right? And your shirts will totally fit in. You have to come visit me."

He winked and chucked Beatrice under her chin as she composed herself. "And see all the California girls? Count on it."

Gathering her things, she gave one last look to the smiling man in front of her then glanced toward Giovanni. "I'll see you on Wednesday?"

He nodded and winked. "Count on it."

The next Wednesday, Giovanni and Beatrice chatted quietly about her end-of-term projects and finals, taking advantage of the empty reading room before Dr. Scalia arrived for his seven-thirty appointment. There was also a new professor coming at eight o'clock to see the Pico letters.

"When do you think you'll move?"

"I want to be there by the middle of August. That should give me enough time to find my way around before classes start."

She knew they weren't mentioning it, but the prospect of the Lorenzo problem continuing unresolved into the fall was something that hung heavy over her plans for the future.

"That's a good idea. I want you to know," he paused and looked around the empty room. "I just want you to know that you don't have to worry about your grandmother. Whatever happens. Please don't let that trouble you. I will make sure...nothing will happen to her."

She nodded, touched by his concern for her grandmother, which was no doubt partly the result of Caspar's growing affection, but also—she hoped—at least partially out of concern for her, as well.

"Thanks. That does—" She broke off when the small Italian professor stepped through the door of the reading room.

"Ah!" he said. "How are you young people today? Dr. Vecchio, a pleasure as always. How goes your transcription?"

Giovanni glanced at the open scroll which sat lonely on his table near the desk and smiled at the twinkling eyes of the cheerful academic.

"Slow, at the moment, since I am pestering Miss De Novo with questions. I'd better get back to work and let her get your letter."

"Oh, don't mind me...well, actually do! I'm very excited to get a look at this new document."

Beatrice smiled at both of them, filled out the call slip and went back to the stacks to grab Dr. Scalia's letter, and the letter the professor with the eight o'clock appointment requested to save her a trip back. Walking out the door, she tripped a little, and one of the document boxes slid out of her grasp.

"Oh!" she said, but before it could hit the ground, Giovanni darted over and caught it with almost inhuman speed. He glanced over his shoulder at Dr. Scalia, who already had his back to them getting out his notebooks.

Beatrice shook her head a little, and mouthed, "Close one."

He whispered, "I forget myself around you, Beatrice."

Suddenly, his proximity caused her to blush, and she quickly spun and set the document box on the counter, trying to distract herself and wishing he couldn't hear the sudden rush of her pulse.

"Beatrice," she heard him whisper. She took a deep breath and turned around, meeting his eyes. They burned with the strange intensity she often noticed when the energy crackled around him. She didn't know what mechanism of his immortality caused his eyes to change the way they did, but at that moment, they were an almost swirling blue-green, the color she'd seen in pictures of the sun-washed Mediterranean Sea.

His fingers brushed hers when he handed her the box containing the precious new letter, but she pulled away from his gaze and walked over to take the document to Dr. Scalia's table. She saw Giovanni walk back to his own table and begin work, so she sat down at the reference desk, pulling out her own translation of the Pico letter.

He was in prison again. This time, it was Paris and his friends didn't have as much influence.

We are working to see to your speedy release, and I hope you will retain good spirits in the meantime. I have been most disheartened to hear of your poor treatment, and I hope, by this time, you have been given better access to your books and to Jacopo, though your man assured me he was being well taken care of.

She had finished reading the letter for the third time, taking notes in her quickly expanding notebook when she heard the door push open. Beatrice looked up, immediately aware of the hiss of energy that filled the room. She glanced toward the door to see an attractive man in his mid-thirties approach the reference desk with a smile on his face.

Something about him gave her pause and as he approached the desk, she knew what it was.

This was definitely another vampire.

A distinct tremor ran down her spine. He was more than handsome, with his pale curling hair, soft blue eyes, and almost feminine features. He reminded Beatrice of a Botticelli painting she had seen during her recent research on the Italian Renaissance. However, the light behind his smiling eyes was cold, and she looked at Giovanni to reassure herself.

Unfortunately, Giovanni's expression was anything but reassuring. His nostrils were flared, and he looked as inhumanly fierce as she had ever seen him. She immediately glanced at Dr. Scalia to see if he had noticed anything. Luckily the cheerful academic was happily immersed in his research and took no notice of anything else.

Giovanni rose and walked to the desk, passing Dr. Scalia on the way and placing his hand on the academic. The small professor immediately rose, packed up his things, and without a word, walked out the door and down the hall. The three of them, Beatrice, Giovanni, and the new vampire who had walked through the doors, waited until the click of the stairwell door echoed down the hall.

She could barely catch the movement as Giovanni shoved the blond vampire up against the wall, where he dangled as he was held by the throat. Blue fire licked along Giovanni's hands, and the cuffs of his oxford shirt began to smoke. As the flames grew, she noticed they were almost immediately quenched as the moisture in the room was drawn to the nameless man who wore a twisted smile.

What do you know? she thought. *Water quenches fire.*

Giovanni stood there, completely still with his fangs bared at the intruder and a low growl emanated from his chest, as the vampires' elements fought their silent battle. Beatrice looked on in horror, completely unsure of what she should say or do.

As if reading her mind, Giovanni growled, "Beatrice, stay back. Take both the letters and lock yourself in the stacks."

"Oh, why shouldn't she stay, Giovanni?" the blond man mocked in an eerily melodic voice. "After all, this concerns her, too. Plus, she smells as delicious as her father." The vampire's eyes strayed to hers, and she found herself baring her own useless teeth. He only laughed. "I wonder if she tastes as good as he did!"

"Shut up, Lorenzo."

"But, Papà, I do so love telling secrets!"

CHAPTER 15

"Papà? As in—what the hell?"
Giovanni ignored Beatrice, keeping his eyes and his hands on his son, who was still hanging a foot off the ground and laughing at him. *Insolent boy*, he thought. Siring Lorenzo, while it had seemed the most honorable thing at the time, remained Giovanni's biggest regret in five hundred years.

"Papà, don't you want to introduce me to your little toy?" Lorenzo sniffed the air. "She smells delicious when she's afraid. Her father was, too, you know. Such a perceptive human he was. Clever, clever man. Is she clever, too?"

"Stay quiet and stay still," Giovanni growled. He had always been stronger than Lorenzo; even when they were human, the boy could never have bested him. With their comparative elements and the strength of their blood now, it was still no contest.

"Hey, vampires," he heard Beatrice say. "Just letting you know that the library is still open. Granted, this isn't the most hopping place on the fifth floor, but there are people who could just walk in."

The two vampires continued to stare at each other, and small flames burst out periodically over Giovanni's hands and were quickly extinguished by Lorenzo as he manipulated the moisture in the air.

"She's lovely, too. Is she good in bed? She's American, I bet she is."

Giovanni tightened his grip on the other man's throat as he held him up, but Lorenzo only let out a rasping laugh. "They can be so feisty. But she's young! I can't imagine she knows what she's doing yet," he choked out.

He snarled at the laughing man, part of him wishing he could simply tear his son's head of and be rid of the problem. Until he had his books, however, it wasn't something he wanted to risk.

"Seriously," Beatrice spoke again. He could hear her voice shaking. "I think I heard the elevator ding just now. So either kill him quick, Gio, or let him down so no one calls security."

Her words finally registered, and he lowered Lorenzo to the ground, but didn't release him from his grip.

"By the way, 'Dad,' can I just say, thanks a bunch for living in this lovely humid climate?" Lorenzo affected a flat Middle American accent. "Makes it so much easier for me to put out the little love sparks you throw off. Whatever you do, don't move to the desert, it would just throw me off."

Giovanni angled himself so he was between the delicate blond man and Beatrice and the letters. "Why are you here?"

"Can't I just come for a visit? It's been—what? One hundred years or so? Time just flies when you're building a business empire. Sorry I forgot to send Christmas cards."

"He's really your son?" he heard Beatrice ask.

"In a manner of speaking," Giovanni muttered, glaring at the mocking vampire.

"That hurts, Dad. Really, it does."

"Shut up."

Lorenzo peeked over Giovanni's shoulder and winked at Beatrice. "He can just be so cross about sharing, you know? Hello, by the way. I'm Lorenzo. You must be the lovely Beatrice. I've heard so much about you, my dear."

"You killed my father, didn't you?" Beatrice whispered.

Giovanni wondered when she had figured it out. He was betting that Lorenzo's words tonight had only confirmed her suspicions. He had suspected that his son was Stephen's sire months ago, but hadn't wanted to say anything to her.

"Kill is such a harsh term. And not really all that accurate; after all, I sired him as well. He's alive and well...I think. Naughty boy, that Stephen, running away from me like that."

Though his tone was teasing, Giovanni recognized the cold light in Lorenzo's eyes that had only grown stronger in the last hundred years.

"I want to know why you're in Houston. I'm assuming you sent the letters, didn't you?"

"Oh," Lorenzo's eyes lit up, "are we telling old stories? Does she know all about us? Did you tell her our little secret? Does she know about old Nic?" He grinned slowly when he saw the slow burn in Giovanni's eyes. "Oh, I just bet she doesn't, does she?"

"Why are you here?" he roared in Italian. Blue flames flared on his arms, and he felt the scraps of his sleeves turn to ash and drift to the ground. "Is this some sick game to you? Tell me your purpose, boy, and leave!"

Lorenzo looked as if he had won a prize. "Oh, she's wonderful...or is it your books? What has finally caused Niccolo's perfect boy to lose his temper? It's too beautiful for words." A sick, dulcet laugh burbled from his throat.

"Gio?"

He tensed when he heard the tremor in Beatrice's voice. He could tell she was terrified and trying to hide it. He wished he could reach out and calm the race of her pulse. Its frantic beat was starting to distract even him, and he knew that if he could feel the delicious burn in his throat, then Lorenzo must have been aching to feed from her.

He took an unnecessary breath, hoping the habitual action would calm him, and slowly the blue flames were absorbed by his skin. Lorenzo also took a deep breath, and his nostrils flared as he scented the air. A slow smile grew on his son's face, and his eyes closed in satisfaction.

"She does smell like her father," he purred. "You would have loved his taste, Giovanni. So pure—like a cool drink of water on a hot day. Do you remember that? So refreshing. But again, I spend too much time reminiscing."

Lorenzo opened his eyes and attempted to straighten his charred jacket. "I do believe I have an appointment at seven o'clock. If you could allow Beatrice to get my document for me, there's no need for you to linger."

"Go to hell," Giovanni said in a calm voice. "Why are you here? I obviously know you have my books, you lying bastard. So what else do you want?"

"The girl, of course. I need her to get her father; he's become quite the problem child." Lorenzo clucked his tongue and shook his head. "So typical for adolescents, I'm afraid. You were lucky with me, Giovanni. I waited almost fifty years before I began to give you headaches."

Lorenzo looked over his shoulder again and winked at the terrified girl. "It's just a phase, my dear. No need to worry about your father. I'll have him back into the fold in no time."

Giovanni stepped away from Lorenzo and went to position himself closer to Beatrice, who stood guarding the letters on the table like a mother hen. "The girl is mine. Leave."

"Is she?" Lorenzo cocked his head. "Is she really, Giovanni? That would be something, wouldn't it? Quite out of character for you, keeping a human. Whatever could be the attraction?" The vampire eyed Beatrice with new interest, and another feral growl issued from Giovanni's throat.

Lorenzo looked at him hopefully. "I'll pay you, of course. Especially if she's that much fun. I'm not expecting something for nothing. I'd even be willing to trade."

Giovanni's eyes narrowed. "Not expecting something for nothing? Now that's out of character for you, Lorenzo."

The blond vampire rolled his eyes. "Now, really, you act as if you got nothing out of the deal, Papà. And we both know that's not true. What are a few old books and letters between father and son, hmm?" Then he slipped closer to them, twisting his neck around to peer at Beatrice before he looked up at Giovanni again. "Then again, maybe they're worth more than I thought."

Lorenzo brushed the blond curls from his forehead and flicked a bit of ash from his sleeve. Giovanni could see the outline of the burns his hands left on his throat already healing, but he wouldn't be able to wear his jacket again. He stood in front of his son, fuming silently.

"Well, Giovanni, talkative as ever, I see." Lorenzo sighed. "I suppose I'll just have to make an appointment for another time. Maybe one of my associates can come take a look during the day when it's more convenient."

He winked at Beatrice. "Either way, I'll see my letters again. It was really more of a loan to pique your curiosity."

"Get out," Giovanni said.

"I can see that it worked even better than I'd hoped," he sang as he turned and left the room. "I'll be seeing you! Both of you. Soon." He sailed out of the reading room with a flourish, and in a second he was down the hallway. They heard the door to the stairwell click behind him.

Giovanni took a deep breath and finally turned to Beatrice. He had been able to smell the waves of adrenaline rolling off her during Lorenzo's visit and he could hear her heartbeat pounding, but he was not prepared for the tears that poured down her face.

"Beatrice?"

She choked and waved a hand in front of her face, trying to turn so he wouldn't see her crying, but he placed his hands on her shoulders to examine her, looking her up and down her to make sure she wasn't hurt. It didn't seem possible that she could be, but her reaction startled him.

She finally choked out. "He—he wants me. He wants my father. I can't...I've never been more—" She panted and tried to pull away from him. "I need a bathroom. I'm going to throw up."

"I'll take you."

"I don't need someone to take me to the bathroom," she shouted.

"And I'm not letting you out of my sight while he's around," he shouted back.

She lifted her hands and shoved him back. "This is your fault! I wish I'd never met you. He's going to kill me and it's your fault!"

He felt a twist in his heart and it gave a quick thump. He took a deep breath and tried to remain calm.

"One, he doesn't want to kill you. Two, the only one in the wrong is Lorenzo. Don't blame me—"

"Why didn't you just kill him?"

His eyebrows lifted in surprise. "So eager to collaborate in a murder? Ready to explain a rather large burn mark on the floor? It's a small room. Not that attached to your eyebrows, are you?"

She wiped the angry tears from her eyes and sniffed, her upset stomach apparently settled. "Well—"

"You have no idea what you speak of. I can't say I'm not impressed by your blood lust, *tesoro*, but you really must learn to pick your battleground." He rolled his eyes and walked to the table to pack the Pico letters away. Next he walked over to the scroll and closed the large document box it lay in.

"What are you doing?"

"These need to be put away, you need to lock up, and we need to go to my house. We'll stop on the way and get your grandmother."

"But it's not nine o'clock."

He turned to her, his irritation finally spilling over. "Are you serious? I'm going to assume you're still in some kind of shock, Beatrice, because I refuse to believe that after being threatened by a rather powerful, centuries-old, water vampire—who we just confirmed killed and turned your father, and now seems to have a sick fascination with *you*—you're not arguing with me about closing the reading room a couple of hours early!"

The color drained from her face before she turned and ran down the hall. He heard her throwing up in the bathroom and sighed, quickly packed up the documents and placed them on the counter before he walked down to stand outside the door.

Giving her a few moments to collect herself, he waited in the hallway and thought about his son's appearance at the library.

He had thought of the girl first.

It was…unexpected, even with his earlier reaction to Lorenzo's scent on her. He had been thinking defensively as his son entered the room, but his first instinct had been to protect the girl and not his letters.

He could still hear her sniffling alone in the bathroom. The urge to walk in and comfort her was also unexpected, though with his growing attraction it probably shouldn't have been. He had avoided long-term attachments to women for this reason. Once his protective instincts were triggered, he became much less rational.

He needed to call Carwyn and Tenzin. He would have to leave a message for the priest, as he would still be traveling. Hopefully, Tenzin was talking again, but he had no idea whether her airy visions would allow her to travel.

Then there was Livia in Rome. She had been brushing him off, and he needed to know what exactly had happened to Stephen De Novo. There was no longer time to put up with her dawdling attempts to draw him into a visit, which was no doubt her aim in putting him off in the first place.

He needed to talk to Gavin Wallace. For the right price, the Scot could tell him everyone who was new in town and who they belonged to. The man could probably tell him what their favorite drink was as well, but Giovanni didn't know if he really wanted to spend that much.

He needed to get Caspar out of Houston and up to the house in the hill country, along with Isadora. The last thing he needed to worry about was their well-being in this mess. Lorenzo had a passionate disgust for the elderly, so hopefully they hadn't even registered his attention.

Giovanni heard the sink running and knew Beatrice would be out in a minute. She had surprised him with her tears, but he sensed more anger than fear from her. He had dealt with this kind of danger for so many hundreds of years, he'd forgotten how shocking it was for someone so young.

She opened the door, and he saw her without the mask of her make-up for the first time. She must have washed it off, and a faint smudge of black mascara still marred the bottom of her right eyelid.

He had thought of her first. He crossed his arms and pushed down the urge to embrace her.

"Better?"

She nodded silently and walked back to the reading room. He sped by her, and quickly checked it to make sure no one had entered while his mind had been elsewhere.

"Let me shut down the computers and I'll lock up."

"Can I do anything to help?"

"Put the documents away. The combination to the stacks is the last four numbers of my social security number." She didn't ask if he knew it, and he would have laughed at her correct presumption if only she had not looked so shaken.

He quickly put everything back in its place, keeping an ear open to listen for anyone entering the reading room while he was out of sight. He noted the meticulous organization of the document shelves and the empty spaces where the boxes needed to be placed and the faint honeysuckle scent of her that lingered in the small room. For a brief moment, he considered simply taking the letters that were his, but he brushed the temptation aside and focused on the present danger. By the time he slipped out of the stacks, Beatrice had shut down the computers, grabbed her bag, and turned off the lights.

They walked down the hall together and silently made their way downstairs. She let him guide her toward his Mustang, and he unlocked the door for her, pausing before he opened it.

"Beatrice—"

"I know it's not really your fault," she murmured. "If anyone's, it's my dad's, though I'm sure he didn't plan on being attacked by a vampire when he went to Italy. You were just the closest one here, so it was easy to blame you."

He was surprised by her apology, but felt an unfamiliar tension ease when he heard it.

"Are you really sorry you met me?" he asked in a low voice.

She paused and glanced up at him in the dim lights of the parking lot before she reached out to grab the door handle, opening it for herself.

"I haven't decided yet."

He took surface streets to her grandmother's house, trying to give her time to collect herself before she saw Isadora.

"So he's really your son?"

"Unfortunately, yes."

"Why on earth did you turn him? Was he always so awful?"

Giovanni frowned. "He wasn't—no, he wasn't always like this. As a child, he was almost timid. He hadn't had an easy life. I thought I was doing the right thing when I did it. There was a time that I had a kind of affection for him. I had hoped with guidance, he would… Well, he had his own ideas about immortal life at a very young age. We only stayed together for around five years before we parted ways."

"Has he done this before? Has he tried to, I don't know, provoke you?"

"No. I know his reputation, of course, but we've spent hundreds of years avoiding each other. I'm starting to realize what a mistake that was."

"And he has your books? Your own son stole your books and letters from you?"

Giovanni nodded. "Before I turned him, he told me they had been lost. He told me that my properties were intact, but that my library had been ransacked and destroyed. It was during the time of Savonarola in Florence. It wasn't hard to believe. There was so much lost. I had to trust him. There was a time that I couldn't be around people like I can now."

"Why? The blood thing or the fire thing?"

He hesitated before he answered. "Either. Both. There were…many reasons. Can we talk about something other than my past, please?"

He saw her cross her arms from the corner of his eyes and angry tears came to her eyes. "Well, it seems like your past is affecting a lot of my future, Gio. So maybe I feel like it's kind of my business at this point."

Biting back a curse, he gripped the steering wheel a too hard and heard the plastic crack. *Damn.*

"I'll tell you what you need to know, just not right now. I'll take care of this, Beatrice, but you're staying with me for a while."

She snorted. "I am not. I have finals and classes and all sorts of shit to do. You're not locking me up in your house."

He frowned, irritated that she had predicted him so accurately. She was probably correct, and he didn't want to interfere with her completing her classes unless it was absolutely necessary. He had no doubt Lorenzo would linger in the city for some time, watching them and securing support before he made any sort of move.

In his mind, he recalled the small boy sitting in front of a basket, dangling a mouse by its tail. The rodent was intended to be a meal for the snake that was kept in the classroom, but the boy always asked to be the one to feed it. Not wanting to handle the task himself, Giovanni always let him, but soon became disturbed by how the angelic looking child taunted both the snake and the mouse before he finally offered the serpent its meal.

"Gio?"

"Hmm?" He broke out of his reverie to glance at Beatrice. "We'll figure something out. It would be best if you stayed at my house after dark. There's plenty of room. I'll increase your security during the daytime, as well."

"What about my grandmother?"

"There's a house that Caspar loves, up in the hill country around Kerrville. It's isolated and Caspar knows the area extremely well. He can take her there. I don't think it's in Lorenzo's interest to follow them. They aren't what he's after."

"He's after me?" she asked in a small voice. "I guess I knew that, but it hadn't really sunk in until today."

She seemed to shrink into the seat next to him as they made their way through the winding streets of Houston. He scented the air, pleased that the adrenaline had ceased pumping through her bloodstream and satisfied she wouldn't alarm Isadora.

"I really hate my dad right now," she whispered.

He wasn't shocked by her admission, but it saddened him. He felt the urge to hold her again, but he shoved it to the side.

"I understand why you feel that way, but you have to know I do not blame him for running from Lorenzo."

"You can't? Even though it's now messing with your life, too?"

Giovanni shrugged. "I'm the one who created the monster, Beatrice. And trust me, Lorenzo is a monster. Life as his child would be horrendous."

"Why? I don't get it. Carwyn told me he can't make his kids do anything they don't want to, so why would it be so horrible?"

He frowned at her. "It's not a mental compulsion, it's sheer physical strength most of the time. Strength for us is determined by age, mostly—though the age of your sire has some significance, as well. I'm old, but my sire was ancient. Combine that strength with my physical strength at the time of my change and my natural element—that makes me very strong.

"Lorenzo was never as strong as me when he was human, but my blood was very strong because of my sire and that was passed onto him. He has also trained himself particularly well in his elemental strength, though he'll never be quite as strong as I am.

"*Your* father—though very strong now by human standards—would be no match for either of us. He would never beat Lorenzo in a fight, and I'm sure my son probably tortured him in all sorts of inventive ways when your father didn't do exactly what he wanted."

He saw her eyes widen in horror, but he didn't want to soften the truth for her. "You have no idea how much power he would have over him, especially in those first few years when he was learning to control his bloodlust. Your father is almost five hundred years younger than his sire. And he could conceivably be under his control for eternity. You *must not* blame your father for running."

She seemed to shrink in her seat. "How about your sire?" she almost whispered. "Does he—I mean, was he good like Carwyn?"

Giovanni frowned. "My father...was a complicated vampire. And he's dead, so it doesn't have any effect on me now."

"Oh."

"Is there a proper anger, my son?"

"Aristotle said 'anyone can become angry, but to be angry with the right person and to the right degree, and at the right time. For the right purpose and in the right way—is not within every man's power.'"

"Are you the 'every man' that the philosopher spoke of?"

"No, Father, I am better than other mortals, and will be better still."

"Therefore, you must master your anger so you control it always."

"Yes, Father."

"Giovanni?"

"Hmm?" His eyes dropped their hollow stare as he glanced at Beatrice again.

"You missed the turn to my house."

He quickly turned the car around and made the right onto the street he had missed. As he pulled up in front of Isadora's small home, he noticed that all the lights lit up the first floor. He parked and walked around the car to help Beatrice out. Half way up the walk, the first scent of blood hit him, and he turned to Beatrice, pushing her back toward the Mustang.

"Go back to the car," he said firmly.

"What? No! What the hell—" Her eyes widened when she saw his face. She ran up the front walk, but Giovanni beat her to the door, blocking her path.

"Grandma!"

CHAPTER 16

"Let me in!" Beatrice beat on his chest. "Let me in, you bastard. Isadora!"

"Be quiet and wait. The smell of blood is not strong," he hissed. "Wait, so I can check the house, damn it!"

"Grandma?" She began to cry, continuing to try to shove past him, but his arms held her in a cold, iron grasp. She was beside herself, and could only imagine the worst.

"Beatrice, do you have your phone?"

She wanted to hit Giovanni, but she was too busy trying to get out of his arms so she could enter the house.

"Beatrice, calm down. You need to call this number." He rattled off a number, but she still wasn't listening.

"You stupid, asshole vampire!" She tried to jerk out of his arms. "Let me in my house. Make your own telephone—" She froze, suddenly realizing it was possible there were people or vampires still inside. She immediately fell silent and stopped struggling.

"What do you hear?" she whispered.

"Nothing suspicious, and I don't feel anyone. I do smell blood, but your grandmother's pulse sounds fine; her breathing is slow and regular. Are you going to be calm now?"

She took a deep breath and nodded, blinking the tears from her eyes.

He gave a quick nod and released her, turning the door knob to walk into the house. Beatrice couldn't see anything in the living room but the television playing a game show her grandmother hated.

"This way," he said, pointing down the hallway to the kitchen. Beatrice followed behind him.

"Grandma?"

She gave a strangled cry when she saw Isadora lying on the floor in a crumbled heap, but Giovanni pushed her back and went to examine the old woman.

There were vicious bite marks on her neck and others on her wrist. A small pool of blood appeared to have dripped from a wound on her forehead, but the bleeding had stopped.

"Please, please no," she cried and knelt down across from Giovanni, holding her grandmother's limp hand. "Not you too, no…"

Giovanni did a quick physical examination of the old woman, finally looking up to meet her eyes.

"She's going to be fine, it's not as serious as it looks."

Beatrice was still sniffing and holding Isadora's hand, rocking herself back and forth on the kitchen floor smeared with her grandmother's blood.

"Beatrice," his commanding voice broke through her growing panic, "you need to calm down now so you can help me."

Though her eyes welled with tears, she nodded and tried to get herself under control.

"What do I need to do? Should I call 911?"

He shook his head. "They drank from her, and made no effort to heal the bite marks. I could heal her outer wounds, but we'd still have to explain the blood loss to the paramedics. Do you have your phone?"

She nodded and pulled the mobile phone from her pocket.

"Good, dial this number." He slowly dictated the number and waited as it dialed. "Put it on speaker for me."

After a few rings, a male voice picked up.

"Hello?"

"Lucas, it's Giovanni Vecchio. I need you to come to my house now."

"There's nothing wrong with Caspar, is there?"

"No, I have a human suffering from blood loss." He looked at Beatrice. "Do you know her blood type?"

Beatrice shook her head. "No, she's always been really healthy."

"I'll bring universal," the voice on the phone replied brusquely. "Do you need transport?"

"No, I'll take her to my home. If you get there before me, do *not* tell Caspar anything, do you understand? He'll be angry, but just ignore him and tell him I sent you."

Beatrice could only imagine how Caspar was going to take the news that his boss's enemies made a meal out of his girlfriend.

"I'll see you in fifteen minutes. Goodbye." The phone went silent, and she looked down at her grandmother's pale face again.

"I'm going to lift her. I don't think anything is broken, so we'll put her in the back of my car. I'll hold her in the back so I can monitor her breathing and heart rate. Can you drive a manual transmission?"

She nodded. "Yeah, no problem. Just take care of her, okay?"

He grabbed her hand and squeezed it. "She's going to be fine, Beatrice. And as soon as she's able, we'll get her out of town."

"And I won't argue. I'll stay with you until you kill Lorenzo."

"Beatrice—"

"Because you are going to kill him, right?"

Giovanni bent to lift Isadora, cradling her tiny body as if she was a child. Nodding toward the door, he finally said, "Let's focus on taking care of your grandmother before we start plotting murder, shall we?"

When Beatrice pulled up to the house, she could see an unfamiliar blue sedan parked by the garage and Caspar pacing in the courtyard. As she stopped the car, he pulled the back door open.

"Oh no, please no—"

"She's going to be fine," Giovanni interrupted. "Calm down and help me."

Beatrice parked the car and got out, watching the two men fuss over her grandmother, who was still unconscious. She would have been insane with worry if Giovanni hadn't have been monitoring Isadora's heart rate aloud in the car the whole way over. She had seen him bite his finger and rub a bit of the oozing blood over her grandmother's neck and wrists in the backseat. The wounds, though red and angry, were already closed.

"Here," Caspar held out his arms, "let me take her. I thought—Lucas showed up and asked for a downstairs bedroom for a patient. I thought something had happened to Beatrice." Caspar glanced at her before he took Isadora's small body in his arms and walked toward the house. Giovanni raced over and opened the door for him before rushing back to her.

"You're doing very well," he whispered when he pulled her into his arms. "You drove her here safely and now Lucas will take care of her. He's Caspar's personal physician, and he's the best in the city. I trust him."

She nodded and relaxed, letting his arms hold her up. "I was afraid I was going to crash on the way over here."

"Nerves of steel, tesoro." He brushed a kiss across her temple as he walked her into the house with an arm around her shoulders. "You've handled yourself extremely well."

"Does this happen a lot?"

"No."

"You really need to kill Lorenzo."

She heard him give a small laugh. "You're quite bloodthirsty for a little girl."

"I'm serious," she said, pausing in the door between the kitchen and living room to look up at him. "I want him dead. If I could do it myself, I would."

He stared at her for a moment before nudging her toward the hallway. "Let's take care of Isadora first, then we'll talk."

When they entered the bedroom, the doctor had an IV set up and, within an hour, Isadora's coloring had improved. A half an hour later, her eyes fluttered open and she looked around in confusion.

"What am I...where am I?"

Beatrice rushed to her side. "You're going to be fine, Grandma. They just—I mean, you had an accident. But we're at Gio's house, and Caspar's here, and there's a doctor..."

Isadora's eyes searched the room, finally settling on Giovanni. She nodded, closed her eyes, and sighed.

"This has something to do with Stephen, doesn't it?"

BEATRICE HAD NEVER BEEN MORE FURIOUS IN HER LIFE.

"I cannot believe you didn't tell me!"

"He told me not to."

"You didn't think I had a right to know? Do you have any idea how messed up I was after all that shit he did to my brain?"

She paced the room, tugging at her hair as Isadora tried to calm her down.

"I didn't know about all that. Stephen told me he had tried to talk to you, and you couldn't handle it. He said you wouldn't remember. He told me not to tell you when you were older because we wouldn't see him again."

"But the depression—"

"Your grandfather and I never made the connection, Beatrice. Why would we? I was the only one who knew what was going on with your father, and you didn't tell me any of this about seeing him, or the dreams. You confided in your grandfather. This is the first I've heard of you having any memories of him after his change. I thought I was the only one who knew."

"Grandpa said it would just upset you if I told you I'd seen him."

Isadora shook her head and looked around the empty room. "You damn De Novos—so arrogant! You, your father, your grandfather...you all thought I was so fragile. Your father's the only one who figured it out, and he's dead."

"But he's *not* dead!"

"Yes, Beatrice, he is. He told me we would never see him again. He told me," her voice cracked, "he told me it was too dangerous. That he had to run away." Isadora paused. "I was so furious. I told him we could handle it as a family, but he just ran. He was determined to disappear."

She wiped angry tears from her eyes, and Beatrice stopped pacing and went to sit in a chair by the small fireplace.

"How did you not realize that Gio was a vampire when you met him?"

Her grandmother frowned. "He's much better at it than your father was. Other than the pale skin, Giovanni looks just like a normal human. You have no idea, B. Your father..." She paused and shook her head. "He was barely recognizable, even to me. He was gaunt and pale. His skin was cold to the touch. He looked *nothing* like a normal human. It's no wonder you found his appearance so frightening as a child."

Beatrice came to sit next to her grandmother. "How are you feeling now? Are you still feeling dizzy?"

Isadora smiled. "Fine. I'm going to be fine. I feel very lucky. When those men came to the door, I thought I was going to die. I saw their fangs and knew it had something to do with Stephen. What's going on?"

"The vampire that turned Dad, Lorenzo..." She paused, not wanting to tell her that Lorenzo was Giovanni's son. "He's after Gio, too. He's after—"

"He's after *you*, isn't he? Your father said he was looking for him ten years ago. If this Lorenzo still hasn't found Stephen, he'll want you. I'm only surprised he hasn't come after you before. If he knows your father at all, he knows the man would do anything for you. That's what this is about, isn't it?"

She nodded slowly, reminded again not to underestimate her delicate looking *abuela*.

"Well, what are we going to do about it? Can we run? Would it even make a difference? How about killing him? How hard would that be?"

"You De Novo women," Giovanni muttered as he entered the room with Caspar. "Terribly vicious, aren't you? Never underestimate the fury of an angry mother, Caspar. They're the most vicious creatures in the world."

Caspar went to take Isadora's hand. "How are you feeling, darling? You had me terribly frightened."

"I'll be fine. I *am* fine. I'm mostly concerned about Beatrice."

"We'll stay here for a few days to make sure you're recovered, then I'm taking you out of the city," he said.

"But B—"

"I'll be taking care of Beatrice," Giovanni said from the corner of the room.

Isadora's angry green eyes flared. "I'm supposed to trust you with my granddaughter, Giovanni Vecchio? How do I know you can keep her safe?"

"You don't, but I'm the best option you have."

"Isadora," Caspar murmured, "Giovanni is a good man."

"If it was your child, would you trust him?"

"My father did."

Isadora frowned and looked from Caspar to Giovanni, then finally at Beatrice.

"Mariposa, do you want to stay with this vampire? You're a grown woman, it's up to you."

Beatrice looked at Giovanni, then back to her grandmother as she sighed. "I think Gio's right, Grandma. I don't really like being bait, but I think he's probably my best bet at this point."

Isadora finally nodded, her eyes swinging back to Giovanni as he stood silently by the door. "Fine. Caspar, I'll go with you, but I want to be kept informed. I'm tired of people keeping me in the dark and thinking I can't handle things, do you understand?"

Giovanni nodded and withdrew from the room, leaving Isadora to the care of Beatrice and Caspar. Beatrice had no idea when Lucas had left, but she'd heard him say he would be back the next night to check on her grandmother's recovery.

"B?"

She looked up to see Caspar watching her.

"Hmm?"

"Why don't I show you to your room? I'll find some spare clothes for you to sleep in until we can go to your house tomorrow and get some things for you both. I've already adjusted your security, but it's better that we don't go during the dark."

"Okay." A sudden thought occurred to her. "Hey Caspar?"

"Yes?"

"What happened? I mean, where were the guys who've been watching the house when they attacked Grandma?"

His expression was grim. "They were the appetizers."

THREE DAYS LATER, GIOVANNI AND BEATRICE STOOD IN THE COURTYARD, waving to Caspar and Isadora as they drove away an hour before dawn. They were headed to a very private home in the hill country somewhere around Kerrville, Texas. A home, Giovanni had explained, that had never carried his name and would be almost impossible to find for anyone other than Caspar or himself.

She waved with a small smile, ignoring the twisted feeling in her stomach, and the little voice that warned this could be the last time she ever saw her grandmother. She walked back to the empty house, feeling Giovanni's eyes burn her back as she left.

As much as she was grateful that Caspar and Isadora would be safer out of Houston, Beatrice also dreaded the thought of living alone in a house with Giovanni, and no friendly buffer of Carwyn or Caspar to distract her. They had been avoiding each other since the night of her grandmother's attack, but she felt like he watched her almost constantly; she was more than aware of the building tension, and all that remained unspoken between them.

"Beatrice," she heard him call as she walked through the kitchen. "Your escort will be here at eight. You will have plenty of time to get to your first class."

She kept walking toward the living room. "Fine. I'm going to sleep for a few more hours."

"I'll see you tonight."

She walked up the stairs, never turning to look behind her as she went to her borrowed room on the second floor. "Yep, see you tonight."

"Beatrice."

She finally paused and turned around. In a flash, he was standing on the step below her, so they were almost eye to eye. His hand lifted to stroke her cheek and the familiar tremor ran through her as she stared into his green eyes. "Caspar will make sure she's safe. Nothing is going to happen to your grandmother. He's more dangerous than he looks."

She wanted to lean against him. She wanted to curl into his strong chest and feel his arms holding her as he chased away the chill of fear that had become her constant companion. She wanted to believe that nothing bad or scary was going to happen again. That her grandmother and Caspar were just going away for a vacation. That the world as she knew it had not ended the minute a beautiful blond vampire walked into the library. That it hadn't ended years ago when her father escaped a madman.

Most of all, she wanted to believe that Giovanni would keep her safe.

"Nothing bad is going to happen to her?" she whispered. "Promise?"

She saw the flicker of uncertainty in his eyes.

"Yeah, I didn't think so."

CHAPTER 17

"Only one more final left, right?" Charlotte grinned when Beatrice entered the reading room. "And then that's it for the graduate!"

Beatrice shrugged and set down her bag by the reference desk. "Until next semester. Then I can freak out about finals at the graduate level. Yay."

Charlotte chuckled and shook her head. "What is with you lately? Are you getting nervous about moving? I think I'm more excited than you are." The librarian continued sorting through the photographs on the counter.

"I guess I'm just missing my grandma." That much was true. Beatrice was starting to feel like graduate school in California, even if there was no fear of strange vampires, wasn't the best idea, after all. She had never imagined she could miss Isadora so much, though she was happy her grandmother seemed content and safe.

"How is she feeling? Have you talked to her lately?"

"Yeah, I just talked to her last night. She's feeling great."

"You know, I had no idea she had breathing problems like that."

Beatrice nodded. "It's...fairly recent. Her doctor suggested a few months in the desert. It's just lucky she has that cousin in New Mexico."

In reality, it was her grandfather who had cousins in New Mexico, but since Beatrice had to figure out some reason to explain her grandmother's disappearance, dry air seemed like a good one.

That excuse, along with a phone call from her grandmother, had been enough to assuage Isadora's friends from storming over to her currently empty house to investigate when she didn't show up for Tuesday dinner.

"It's such a shame she won't be here to see you graduate, you know? But, you always hear how bad the air quality is in Houston, especially in the summer, so I guess her doctor made the right call."

"It's not a big deal. The college graduations are a madhouse. She's not missing anything. I'll make sure she flies out for my master's, you know? The air in California has got to be better than here."

Charlotte giggled and winked at Beatrice. "And the scenery. You better date a surfer, at least once. I want pictures."

Soon the two women were laughing at all of Beatrice's imaginary romantic prospects in sunny Southern California. It felt good to joke around with Charlotte and listen to her tease about boys and suntans and rollerblading. It felt good to feel just a little bit normal after the overwhelming tension of the previous month.

Beatrice had done little beside school work, classes, and finals since moving to Giovanni's. The house was enormous and they both took care of their own cleaning and cooking, so other than the occasional meeting in the kitchen or the laundry room, she didn't even see him. She spent more time with Carl, her friendly neighborhood security guard, who always had a friendly smile and plenty of firepower.

Other than the research time they continued in the library, Beatrice didn't see her new roommate all that much, but she was definitely learning more about his habits by proximity.

Giovanni swam almost every night. She had woken once at three in the morning to hear a splash in the pool outside her window. She peeked outside and watched him swim laps for over an hour without taking a breath. She didn't stare the whole time, but his focus was impressive...as was his naked body. He really was the most perfect man she had ever seen. He looked like a Greek sculpture molded from a single block of pale marble.

He played several different instruments, but the piano and the cello seemed to be his favorites, and he often played through the night. It was always something quiet that soothed her and seemed to help her sleep through the nightmares that had begun to plague her sleep.

Other than whiskey, he did eat a little, rich foods like olives and avocados and cheese; ironically, she had never seen him eat any kind of meat. He liked sweet smells and spent a lot of time in the garden. He was fond of the gazebo where honeysuckle grew up and over, almost enclosing the small structure in vines. She had found him there a number of times, reading a book in the dark.

He also loved water, even the sound of it seemed to relax him, and if he was irritated or stressed, Giovanni would immediately go and jump in the pool. She remembered the way that the humid air Lorenzo manipulated had doused the flames that ran along his skin when he was angry, and she wondered if he was drawn to water for the same reason.

A HIDDEN FIRE

She was interrupted from her tangled thoughts by Dr. Christiansen's voice as he entered the reading room.

"Hello, ladies, I have another Pico letter."

"What? Really?" Beatrice was shocked. She had imagined, for some reason, that since Lorenzo was in town—even though he seemed to be laying low after their first meeting and her grandmother's attack—they wouldn't see any more of the fascinating letters. She had jotted down several other names in her notebook after filtering through what she remembered Lorenzo saying at the library.

Nic. *Niccolo.* He had called Giovanni "Niccolo's perfect boy" when he was taunting him. She needed to look at one of the early letters again. She was almost sure that one of them mentioned a Niccolo, but she couldn't remember which or what the context was.

"Yes, one more from the University of Ferrara. Apparently this one took a bit longer than the others for some reason. It's been delayed."

"Oh, so we were supposed to get it last month or something?"

Dr. Christiansen smiled. "No need to worry, B. We have it now, and there's plenty of time for you to look at it before you leave us next month. Would you like to make a few copies of the notes so we could put them out for the descending hordes?"

"Sure, I'd be happy to."

She walked over and grabbed the notes while the Dr. Christiansen and Charlotte chatted about the seventh letter. Beatrice walked down the hall to the copy and imaging room and quickly found a chair so she could sit down and read. Flipping through the notes to the translation, she immediately got out her notebook and started jotting down details.

Skimming over the mentions of Savonarola's return to Florence and other news of his friends, her eyes stopped when she read mention of the mysterious woman named G.

> *I received a letter from G. She seems greatly dismayed that you have cut off correspondence and mentioned your request to send the copies of your sonnets. I beg of you, Giovanni, whatever your intentions are toward the lady, do not take steps to destroy your work.*

He was going to destroy his poems? For some reason, even the thought of it made her want to cry. Just then, she caught a name that sparked her memory.

> *I spoke with Signore Andros when he returned from his visit with you in Fiesole.*

Signore Andros... she searched her memory and flipped through her notes until she spotted it. *Signore Niccolo Andros,* who had the fascinating library in Perugia where Giovanni had recovered with the young boy after his time in jail.

Could that be the connection to Giovanni's books? Were they really the property of this Niccolo Andros? Did Giovanni steal them? And what did all this have to do with her father? She flipped through her notes again to see what kind of books Signore Andros had and frowned. Why would her father be researching books about Eastern mysticism?

Beatrice took notes on the seventh letter, convinced that there was some piece of the puzzle that was just out of her grasp. She needed to study them together, but she could not waste any more time at work. She quickly made the copies, and walked back out to the reading room to see Dr. Scalia already poring over the newest letter with Dr. Christiansen.

"—and the progression of Savonarola's extreme ideas coinciding with Pico's apparent depression seems to be one of the most fascinating aspects. Along with the mention of his poetry. I believe the sonnets mentioned would be those Pico wrote to the wife of one of the Medici cousins. It was quite a scandal at the time, and caused his first imprisonment, but these letters certainly indicated they continued their relationship, at least through correspondence."

"What's so special about the sonnets?" she heard Charlotte ask.

"We knew Pico had written poetry, but we thought it was destroyed by Savonarola in the bonfires, or that Pico had destroyed it of his own volition as an act of penance. This seems to indicate that Poliziano—who was a poet himself—was trying to get them for safekeeping. It's all quite fascinating."

"What about the rest of Pico's library?"

All eyes swung to Beatrice as she entered the room and spoke.

Dr. Scalia frowned. "What library?"

"Well, the letters mention books and stuff, right? Didn't he have all sorts of mystical texts, too? Along with his own papers? All these nobles and philosophers had personal libraries, right? What happened to Pico's? Maybe the sonnets are there."

Dr. Scalia nodded. "Yes, from all reports, Giovanni Pico did have a very extensive library, though we don't know what happened to it. He had no heirs, you see. And when he died—"

"When did he die? How?"

The professor looked slightly shocked at her interruption, but only smiled a little and shook his head.

"We don't know exactly. We know Giovanni Pico died in Ferrara in 1494, but there is no record of him leaving an extensive library at his home, and he died under rather mysterious circumstances. As he had no heirs, it's probable that his library was taken by his family, the Mirandolas. It would have been theirs unless Pico had made other endowments."

Beatrice nodded, even more confused. "Thanks...sorry, Dr. Scalia. I don't mean to be rude, it's just..."

"Quite all right, my dear. I do love students who show curiosity such as yours. It makes teaching so rewarding."

A HIDDEN FIRE

She saw Charlotte watching her with narrowed eyes and was glad her shift would be over soon. As she walked back to check the dehumidifier, her mind whirled, more confused than ever by the pieces of a puzzle that seemed stubbornly jumbled in her mind.

SHE WAS HEATING A CAN OF SOUP ON THE STOVE WHEN GIOVANNI ENTERED the kitchen that night. He was wearing a black shirt and jacket with a pair of pressed black slacks. As always, he looked amazing and Beatrice looked away, trying to ignore the instant reaction she always had in his presence.

"Good evening, Beatrice."

She smiled as she examined him. "Going for the real inconspicuous 'no, I'm not a deadly creature of the night' look, are we?"

"Pardon?"

She raised an eyebrow and glanced back, looking him up and down. "It's Friday, right? Dinner time? Do chicks dig the whole man-in-black thing?"

He looked at her and cocked his head. "Do you really want to talk about this?"

She thought for a moment, and then shook her head. "No, probably not."

"I have to go out." A small smile teased the corner of his lips. "Unless you're offering, of course, then I could just skip the clubs. Much more convenient." He winked at her as he put his keys in his pocket.

She rolled her eyes and looked down at the stove, surprised and amused by his unusually flirtatious mood. "See this? It's soup. Soup is food." She looked back at him. "See me? I'm me, and I'm not food. Any questions?"

He looked her up and down. For a minute, she wanted to blush at his frank perusal. The appreciative look in his eye almost made her reconsider, but then she remembered the vicious bite marks on her grandmother's neck, and decided to stick with her first answer.

"Oh, Beatrice, I have many questions, but I'm not going to find an answer tonight, am I?"

It was far more suggestive than she had come to expect from him, and she figured it must have something to do with his hunger. She really didn't want to think about it all that much.

"You're in some kind of mood, aren't you?" she muttered, trying to ignore the flutters in her stomach as she stirred the pot on the stove.

She heard him take a deep breath, and she had a feeling he wasn't smelling the soup. Cursing, she glanced over her shoulder and caught him watching her. He definitely looked hungry, she just wasn't sure for what.

She cleared her throat and took a deep breath.

"Go, do your vampire thing. Don't kill anyone, okay?"

"I never do." He was still watching her, and she could see his fangs peeking out from behind his lips. She could feel her temperature rise when his eyes were on her.

"Gio!"

"Hmm?" He looked a bit startled, but stopped studying her ass like it contained the mysteries of the universe and met her eyes.

"Go, you need to...eat. I'll be here when you get back."

"Right." He cleared his throat and she caught him glancing at her neck. "Right. I'll just...be back later."

"Later."

"Right."

"Bye."

And he finally slipped out the door.

Taking a deep breath, she turned back to the stove.

"You do not want the insanely attractive vampire to kiss you, B. Nope, you don't. Just ignore that reaction and..." She trailed off as she remembered the sight of his long, muscular legs, defined waist, and broad shoulders as he cut through the pool the night before.

She let out a sigh and shook her head.

"Nope. You most definitely do not want him to bite you. And he's just hungry, anyway. He's not flirting with *you*, it's just your blood. It's a normal, natural—"

She gasped when she heard the door slam. Giovanni spun her around, pulling her into his arms before his mouth crashed down and his arm encircled her waist. He pushed her up against the cabinets and his other hand grasped the back of her neck. His hard body pushed against her own, and his arms lifted her against the counter. She gave in to her own desire and moaned into his mouth, tangling one hand in the dark curls at the nape of his neck as the soup spoon dangled uselessly from her other hand.

Giovanni kissed her for a few heated moments, stealing her breath and causing her head to swim. His fang nicked her lip and she felt his tongue swipe at the trickle of blood near the corner of her mouth before he gave a deep groan and pulled away.

He stared into her eyes, panting before he bent down to whisper in her ear.

"It's *not* just your blood."

She whimpered in the back of her throat, and his hands drifted down to her waist, squeezing once before he was out the door again.

This time, she stared at the kitchen door until she heard his Mustang roar down the drive. After a few moments, Carl and his partner began patrolling the grounds, and she saw the guard's familiar face pass by the window in the kitchen.

She was still breathing heavily when she heard the soup hiss on the stove.

"Damn it!"

. . .

HE RETURNED TO THE HOUSE THREE HOURS LATER, LOOKING flushed. His eyes had lost the hungry look from earlier in the night, but she still felt them as he walked into the living room. Beatrice had raided Caspar's cache of old horror movies; she was pondering whether their earlier kiss was something they needed to talk about.

Or possibly repeat.

She saw him sit down in his chair, which she often stole during the day because it was, by far, the most comfortable in the room. He took a deep breath and glanced at her.

"It's very odd."

"What is?"

He frowned a little and stared at the television. "Your scent is all over my house. Everywhere I go, I can smell you."

She cleared her throat, feeling suddenly self-conscious and wondering whether she needed to check her deodorant more often. "Sorry."

"No need to apologize." He shrugged. "You smell lovely. It's just different. Having you here. It's...nice."

They watched the rest of the movie in silence. Beatrice had turned the volume down so she could hear the comforting sounds of Carl and his partner as they patrolled the grounds.

"How was dinner?" she asked nonchalantly.

"Do you really want to know?"

She didn't. She didn't even know why she asked, and she shoved aside the irrational spurt of jealousy. "No, not really."

"Stale. Boring." He gave her a heated look. "Merely adequate."

"I said I didn't want to know, Gio."

"Well, maybe I want to tell you, Beatrice."

"Why?" She scowled. "Why do I need to know about that shit?"

"It's not always done in anger," he murmured, and she glanced back to the almost silent television screen. "Sometimes, it's done purely for sustenance, because a vampire needs blood to survive. Sometimes it is done in anger, but sometimes, it can be highly pleas—"

"I'm going up to my room." She shut off the movie and stood.

"You need to change your clothes. We're going out."

She spun around on her way to the stairs. "What? Why? Where are we going?"

He stood and walked toward her, his hands hanging casually in his pockets.

"We need to go to The Night Hawk."

She immediately flushed when she thought of the pub, and she started walking upstairs. "I don't want to go there again."

"You're going. We need to be seen there. I have information that Lorenzo is meeting with Gavin tonight, and we need to be there, too."

"Why?" Her discomfort with his flirtatious behavior fled, as her heart raced in fear at the thought of seeing the vampire again.

"We need to go there, and I'm going to act as if I'm feeding from you. I'm going to act like your lover, and you're going to play along if you know what's good for you."

Her pulse raced again, only it wasn't from fear. "Why? Why do I have to—"

"We don't have rules in my world. We don't even have conventions, really, but there is a kind of courtesy among those who are mostly civilized." He paused and watched her carefully. "Lorenzo is your father's sire, and in my world, that means he has...a certain claim over you. If he wanted to take you, no one would bat an eyelash as long as he didn't make it newsworthy. That's why no one cares that his people bit your grandmother in a very messy attack. She belonged to his child, so she belonged to him."

"So I'm just—"

"What you are, Beatrice, is *mine*, as far as anyone knows. My human, my 'food,' as you put it so eloquently earlier this evening. And I am Lorenzo's sire and far more feared, so my ownership trumps his. But we need to make sure he is forced to acknowledge that in order for you to have some measure of safety in this city. So he needs to see us together, and he needs to see us where there are witnesses, do you understand what I'm saying?"

"Yes," she whispered with a nod.

"I'm not doing this to torment either of us." His eyes dropped to her flushed lips. "I'm doing this because I think it's our best move at the moment."

"Are you going to bite me?"

She saw him swallow visibly and eye her neck. She could see his fangs run down behind his lips, but he turned and walked back toward the living room. "No. Get dressed."

"Fine."

"Wear the burgundy skirt."

"What? Why? Is there some dress code or something?"

He shrugged. "No, I just like how it looks on you."

She rolled her eyes and stomped up the stairs.

Twenty minutes later they were driving Giovanni's Mustang through the dark streets of Houston near Rice Village. He had been filling her in on the guidelines for acting like his regular meal. Beatrice thought they mostly consisted of her acting like a totally hypnotized doormat.

"And don't ever contradict me in front of another vampire. Carwyn or Tenzin are fine. Anyone else would put you at risk."

"So I basically have to act like I'm brainwashed and like it."

"If you were an average human, you would be, and I can guarantee that you would like it."

"I *am* an average human."

"Not to me," he murmured and she pretended to ignore him.

"Gio?"

"Hmm?"

"Is this going to end soon?"

He glanced at her from the corner of his eye. There was an odd, almost sad look on his face when he finally answered. "I will do everything in my power to make sure you can safely move to Los Angeles by the middle of August, Beatrice."

"That's not—"

"It's all I can promise. I don't want to start a war with Lorenzo if I can avoid it."

Her jaw dropped. "So you're not going to kill him?"

Giovanni just stared at the road. "Not if I can help it."

She sat, gaping at him, knowing she looked like a guppy the way her mouth moved in silent protest.

"S—so you're just going to let him get away with doing that to my grandmother? You're just going to let him treat us like *food*? Like property? I thought—"

She broke off when he jerked the car over onto a side street and slammed on the brakes. He grabbed her chin and forced her to look at him as his eyes blazed.

"Listen to me. Lorenzo has many powerful, *powerful* friends. As do I. And his friends owe him favors, as do mine. If I go to war with this vampire, people will be hurt, mortal and immortal. Do you understand that, little girl? People will *die*, Beatrice. So you tell me how many people need to die because of an insult to your grandmother. Because of an attack she survived. How many? Would you like my estimate? I don't think it would sit well with you."

She sat with her teeth clenched and tried to hold back the angry tears that wanted to fall from her eyes. "Fine."

"Do you understand what I'm saying?"

"Yes," she hissed, blinking. "I understand."

He released her and carefully pulled the car back into traffic. Minutes later, they were parking in the small lot behind The Night Hawk, and she was still fuming.

Giovanni leaned over and released her seatbelt before he grabbed her chin again. This time, his fingers were soft, and his lips ghosted over hers in a delicate kiss. The anger drained out of her at his unexpectedly tender gesture.

"Why—"

"Everything in there is for show." His accent was heavy and he wouldn't meet her eyes. "That was for me."

He stepped out of the car and went to open her door. As she stepped out, she said, "Giova—" but he stopped her mouth with a kiss.

He kissed her, pushing her body into the side of the car as she pressed her lips to his and clutched his shoulders. His tongue delved into her mouth and his hands gripped her waist. She was light headed by the time he let her up for air.

"Oh...damn," she breathed out.

His head bent and he whispered in her ear, "They're watching."

Giovanni placed his arm around her waist and walked her toward the back door of the pub. She had no problem leaning into him and acting like he needed to hold her up; her knees were still a little weak from the kiss.

Before they even reached the door, a dark-haired guard opened it from the inside and nodded toward them as he held it open.

He leaned down and whispered after they had passed by.

"I told you they were watching. Assume that there are cameras everywhere."

She nodded and tried to look casual. She slid her arm around his waist as they walked, and Beatrice thought she heard a low rumble of pleasure in his chest. He guided her toward the sofa near the fire, and Beatrice glanced up as he scanned the room.

"See anyone?" His hair, she noticed from that angle, had grown a little since they had met. His neck smelled like wood smoke and whiskey.

"Yes, he's here, in the corner with Gavin. And they've seen us, as have a number of other vampires in the pub."

Her breathing picked up at the thought of Lorenzo so close to them, but she forced herself to relax as his arm draped across her shoulders. She looked around the room, trying to seem brainless.

"Cool. They've seen us. Can we go now?"

He gave a grim laugh and sat back in the couch. "We'll have at least one drink, otherwise, Lorenzo might get suspicious, and...well, Gavin will just be insulted."

"Who is Gavin anyw—"

"Kiss me."

"What?"

"Kiss me, Beatrice, they're watching you right now," he murmured. "Kiss me like you belong to me."

She bit her lip before she turned her face toward his neck and began placing soft kisses there, slowly working her way up toward Giovanni's jaw. His skin was soft, with only a hint of roughness where stubble would normally grow on a man. He remained almost impassive, holding still as she slowly worked her lips along the line of his jaw and closer to his mouth, though she could feel his heart beat a few times under her hand.

At the last moment, his chin tilted down and his lips sought hers. She lost herself for a moment in the pure pleasure of it. Ever since their first kiss in

January, she had dreamt of the feel of his kiss, wondering what his lips could do to other parts of her body, but memory could not do Giovanni's mouth justice.

It was soft and drugging. He captured her bottom lip between his teeth and tugged gently as she felt the soft curls of his hair against her cheekbone. The vibrating energy she usually felt from his hands was far more potent on the sensitive skin of her lips and every touch only seemed to heighten the sensation. Just the feel of their skin brushing together was as arousing as any intimate touch, and she could tell he was as affected by the contact as she was because his skin was burning like he had a fever, and she felt the soft rumble in his chest.

She lost herself for a few more minutes before Giovanni jerked his head away. "That's enough, tesoro," he said clearly. "A glass of the eighteen year old Macallan for me, and a Laphroaig for the girl."

"Yes, Dr. Vecchio," she heard a waiter murmur behind her.

"You'll like the Laphroaig," he muttered quietly. "It has a smoky flavor I think you'll enjoy. Also, where the hell did you learn how to kiss?"

"What?" she asked. "Not playing the part well enough?"

She felt his lips ghost over her temple. "Playing it to the hilt, tesoro." His head bent down to murmur in her ear. "But back off a bit if you don't want me to really bite you." His mouth opened, and she shivered when she felt his fangs scrape along the edge of her jaw. "You're testing my instincts, Beatrice."

"Oh, okay." She took a deep breath. "Backing off, just a bit. Got it."

"Now relax."

"Kind of hard to do right now."

"Try, because they're coming over here."

His hand slipped down to curl around her waist, and he pulled her closer. She looked past the fireplace and saw Lorenzo and Gavin strolling across the pub.

"Giovanni," Gavin called. "How lovely to see you. You *really* should come in more often." She saw Gavin glance at Lorenzo behind the blond vampire's back. She had a feeling that Gavin Wallace wasn't terribly happy to see Giovanni's son either, and it made her like him, just a little. "What brings you out this evening?"

"Just out for a drink after dinner. How is Houston, Lorenzo?"

"Oh," Lorenzo replied, "it hasn't given up all its treasures just yet. I'll be around for a while. Don't worry."

"I don't. Worry, that is."

"Good to know."

She glanced between the two vampires as they stared at each other. She was trying to observe them while still looking vapid. She wasn't quite sure how well she did, but by the carefully controlled smile on Gavin's face, and the twinkle in his eyes when he caught her notice, she wasn't very convincing as Giovanni's brainless meal.

"Your drinks, Dr. Vecchio." The server placed the two glasses of amber whisky on the coffee table in front of them.

"Well," Gavin said, "we'll let you enjoy your drinks. Excellent choices for both of you. You must have very discerning palates." He winked at Beatrice behind Lorenzo's back and mouthed 'call me' to Giovanni with a slight frown.

"Goodbye for now," Lorenzo said. "I'll be seeing you around."

"Looking forward to catching up."

They walked away, and Giovanni and Beatrice both lifted their drinks.

"Cheers," she muttered and clinked the edge of her glass with his before she took a sip. "Here's to fooling no one."

CHAPTER 18

"**W**hat's that?"
He turned, embarrassed when she walked into the kitchen. Carl waved to him from the door then walked outside to make his rounds around the house.

"This is... a cake."

"You like cake?"

He frowned. "I was told you do."

Beatrice's mouth dropped open in shock. "You got me a cake?"

"You've just graduated, and your grandmother isn't here." He cleared his throat. "I called Caspar. He suggested a cake. I'm sorry if it's—"

"I love it."

The corner of his mouth lifted. He was pleased she was happy with the gesture, even if she hadn't tried the cake yet. "Your grandmother informed Caspar that your favorite flavor was lemon cake. I'll confess, I ordered it. I can't imagine you want me baking anything."

Beatrice grinned and set her school bag down before she walked over to join him at the counter.

"It'd be kind of cool to see you try to cook something with your hands, though."

He snorted and turned to take the small lemon cake out of the pink box.

"Have you ever done that? Cooked something with your fire?"

He shook his head. "Not anything you'd want to eat, Beatrice."

"What? Why—oh *ew*! You've killed things that way, haven't you?"

He shrugged. "What did you think when Carwyn said I liked my enemies 'extra crispy?'"

"I'll admit. I chose not to think about that too closely."

"Stick around for five hundred years or so, and you're bound to make a few enemies."

"I'll keep that in mind." She peeked over his shoulder and smiled.

Giovanni winked as he cut a piece of cake. He placed it on a small plate, and handed it to her. "Now, wait just a moment…"

He walked to the refrigerator and retrieved a bottle of champagne, which he twisted open before he grabbed two flutes from the butler's pantry.

"Come now. Dining room. You can't have your graduation cake standing in the kitchen."

She followed him to the dining room table, and Giovanni quickly flicked small flames toward the white tapers Caspar kept out. He poured the wine for them both and sat down next to her.

Lifting a glass, he toasted. "To you, Beatrice De Novo. Congratulations on your college graduation."

"Thanks!" She blushed with pleasure as she sipped the champagne and took a bite of cake. "It's delicious."

He nodded in satisfaction as he sipped the champagne. "Excellent."

"Do you want a bite?"

"Probably not. Most things with refined sugar are far too sweet for my taste."

"Really?" She cocked her head to the side in an adorable gesture.

"Yes, they didn't have anything that sweet when I was human. Not that I remember. Well…honey maybe. That's very sweet. Or fruit. I still eat that occasionally. I like some fruits."

She smiled and leaned forward, propping her chin in her hand. "Really? Like what?"

Giovanni frowned as he tried to think of the last person who had asked him personal questions. For some reason, he liked the feeling of sharing his likes and dislikes with her. "I like figs, fresh ones. And…apricots."

She smiled. "I like apricots, too."

"What are your favorite foods?"

She took another sip of champagne, and he watched the glass rise to her lips. He wondered if they were sweet from eating the cake.

"I like spicy things. Anything with chiles, especially my grandmother's food. And chocolate, but just dark chocolate."

He smiled. "I never tasted chocolate as a human. The new world had just been discovered, though I wasn't aware of it at the time."

Her mouth dropped open. "Wow, I guess not. So no tomatoes for you, either."

He shook his head. "No tomatoes or corn…or potatoes, for that matter."

"It's so funny because we think of tomatoes as an Italian food now."

"Oh," he smiled a little. "The food I ate as a child is very different from what is common in Italy now."

"Really?"

"Yes. Things were cooked more heavily. Lots of stews. I like modern food more. There are more ingredients and spices, and things to choose from."

"Yeah," she smiled sweetly. "I guess we're pretty lucky."

"Very lucky, Beatrice."

She sipped her champagne. "This is really good, by the way. What kind of champagne is it?"

He twisted the bottle so she could see the label. "This is Dom Pérignon."

She coughed a little, catching the wine that wanted to escape her mouth before she carefully swallowed. "Isn't that, like, super expensive?"

"This one was quite reasonable. I got it from the cellar. One of Caspar's, a 1985 vintage. I think he acquired it for around four hundred or so."

"A bottle?" she squeaked.

He shrugged. "Drink up. I have plenty of money. I might as well spend it on people and things I enjoy."

She was still eyeing the bubbling glass with trepidation. He rolled his eyes.

"Beatrice, just drink the champagne. I'll never be able to finish all of it myself, and it's your graduation."

Smiling a little, she took a tentative sip.

"Still good?"

She nodded and took another bite of her cake.

"Did you always have a lot?" she asked.

"Of money? Except for a brief period of my life, yes. I've had a very long time to acquire it, as you can imagine. I have extensive investments and property, as well as what money I make working for clients, which isn't insignificant."

"Investments? Cool. I know all about the stock market. My grandfather and I always used to play with it."

He laughed. "Really? That's a rather unusual past time. No fishing? Dollhouses?"

"No," she laughed along with him. "I think he did it instead of gambling, to be honest. If it wasn't the stock market, it would have been the race track. I got to be better at it than him, though."

"Were you?"

"Oh yeah, I'm pretty good. Ask my grandma. I invest all her money for her."

"And do you have money of your own invested?"

She nodded. "That's why I don't have any student loans. My grandpa and I invested all the money from my father's estate. There wasn't much, but it was years ago, and once online trading became more common, it was easy to play around with it. Online markets are great, and I pay a lot less in broker fees now."

He smiled in delight. "I should probably let you take a look at my financial portfolio."

"You should," she muttered as she took another bite of cake. "I could probably shift some of your stuff around and have you making double what you are now. Unless you've got a really good broker. Are you diversified into foreign markets or currencies?"

"I...don't know." He honestly had very little idea where most of his money was, other than the cache of gold he kept with him.

"You really need to be taking advantage of all the online trading there is now. I could show Caspar how to do it."

"I'll let him know."

"Cool." She smiled a little and took another drink of champagne. "It's pretty fun."

"And you do all of it on the computer now?"

"Yep."

He watched her, intrigued by the facets of her mind. "How did you learn so much about computers?"

Her smile fell, and she shrugged. "Antisocial teenager. I got one for my room, and my grandparents...well, they knew I liked being by myself, so they just left me to it." She cleared her throat and looked down at the table. "It was the place I felt most comfortable. On my computer. Or in my books."

"I'm sure your grandparents were happy you had it," he said, suddenly wishing he could ease the memory of the lonely child he saw behind her eyes.

"Good thing for you I did, right? You needed a computer whiz on staff."

"I most certainly did," he said with a smile and a nod.

They were quiet for a few minutes as Beatrice finished her cake. Giovanni poured another glass of champagne for them both.

"Gio?"

"Yes?"

"Why does Lorenzo want my father?"

He frowned, wishing she hadn't brought the topic up. "I'm sure he wants him back purely because he got away, to begin with. And I suspect he took something. Possibly something from the collection."

"Why would he do that?"

It was an excellent question; one Giovanni has asked himself many times.

"I don't know."

"And why would Lorenzo have killed him?"

The memory ambushed him; he could almost hear his father's voice.

"What do you hold in your hands?"

   "A book."

"No, you hold knowledge...and knowledge is power. Do you understand?"

"Yes, Father."

He shook his head.

"I... it could have been as simple as your father asking the wrong question to the wrong person, Beatrice. If Lorenzo considered him a threat, your father had no chance. It's more curious why he turned him, to be honest. For that, I think he must have had some use, though I don't know what it might be. Otherwise, he would have just killed him."

He saw a tear shining in her eye, but she brushed it away.

"It probably would have been better if he had, right? If Lorenzo had just killed him?"

"Don't say that," he murmured with a frown. "I'm not going to say that your father has had an easy start, but if this current problem can be solved, he can go on to live a wonderful, long life."

"If we can even find him."

He took a breath and put on a smile. "I'll find him. I'm waiting to hear from someone very knowledgeable right now. Someone in Rome."

"Would your friend Tenzin know anything about him?

"Tenzin?" he chuckled. "Why would Tenzin know? She lives in the middle of the Himalayas most of the time."

Beatrice blushed a little. "I don't know. You and Carwyn always talk about her like she's some all-knowing seer or something."

"And you thought—"

"I just thought she might have seen my dad." She looked embarrassed, so Giovanni was quick to reassure her.

"We do talk about Tenzin like that. She says she only sees people or vampires in our circle of friends. People she knows."

"But Carwyn said she'd probably had a dream or two about me?"

Damn sentimental Welshman. He paused, unsure of what to say and strangely uncomfortable with Beatrice's uncanny memory. "It's...possible, I suppose."

Her eyes darted around the room. "Oh, Carwyn was probably just teasing me. She's Chinese?"

"Who? Tenzin?"

"Yes."

"Tenzin is... old."

"What, so she's from way back when in China, huh?"

"Not exactly," he frowned. He wasn't sure where exactly Tenzin was from on today's maps. He wasn't sure his ancient friend knew herself.

Beatrice waved a hand in front of her face. "You know what, forget it. It's her story, right? I mean, I doubt I'll ever meet her, but if I do, it's her story to tell. I got it."

He smiled. "If you do ever meet Tenzin, that's the most important thing to remember. She's very, *very* old."

"Older than you? Than Carwyn?" She frowned.

Giovanni smiled. "Carwyn and I are children compared to Tenzin."

Beatrice paused, speechless as she stared at him, open mouthed. "How old do you have to be to make a thousand year old vampire look young?"

"Very old, Beatrice. Tenzin doesn't operate very comfortably in the modern world. That's part of the reason she's in Tibet."

"Wow."

"'Wow' is usually a good word to describe her, yes."

"I can't even imagine having that kind of life."

He shrugged. "It's not something you *can* imagine. When you are immortal, you see your life in years instead of days, and centuries instead of years."

She looked at him, searching his face for something he couldn't comprehend.

"Are you happy? Being a vampire?"

He blinked. "Am I happy?" He tried to remember if anyone had ever asked him that before.

She nodded.

Giovanni's mind raced as he thought of the challenge of keeping a constant, iron control over his instincts. He thought about how much he still missed the sun, and of all the human friends he had seen grow old and die over the years.

He also thought about the people he had met, and the places he had been. He thought about rescuing Caspar. And of an unmarked grave in the Tuscan countryside where his life would have ended had he never met his sire. He watched the curious girl who sat next to him, sharing a piece of cake and a glass of champagne. He nodded.

"Yes, I'm happy with my life."

"And I'm glad I met you."

They both smiled as they sipped the sweet wine. He reached across and touched the edge of his glass to hers.

"Congratulations, Beatrice. Happy graduation."

When Giovanni went to the library the following Wednesday, he had a smile on his face. It was Beatrice's final week of work, so she would no longer be dividing her time between the university library and his own.

Caspar and Isadora were doing well, and had so far garnered no attention in the mountains. And when he spoke to Caspar that evening, his butler had finally heard back from one of Livia's people in Rome.

According to her secretary, Giovanni could expect a letter from Livia sometime in the next three months. While it may have seemed slow for some, for the two thousand-year-old Roman noblewoman, three months was as good as overnight mail.

He was so cheerful, he almost skipped up to the fifth floor, only to halt in the stairwell as he caught the whisper of unfamiliar voices coming from above. He didn't sense any danger, but there were far more voices than normal. He tensed until he heard Beatrice; she sounded worried, but not panicked in any way.

Giovanni stepped into the hallway and listened, but the voices were too jumbled to sort through from a distance. He pushed open the door to see the director of Special Collections standing in the reading room with Beatrice and the librarian, Charlotte Martin. The president of the university was also present, along with the head of security, and two Houston Police detectives.

Charlotte spotted him immediately. "Oh, Dr. Vecchio, what a mess! Thank goodness your manuscript wasn't damaged."

"What is the problem?" He shot a look toward Beatrice, but she was giving a statement to one of the police detectives and only gave him a small shake of her head.

"The Pico letters, Dr. Vecchio. They're gone!"

CHAPTER 19

"And what time did you get here?"

Beatrice sighed. "I already told the other officer, I was running late, so I probably got here around five fifteen, or so. I didn't look at the clock because Dr. Christiansen and Charlotte were running around and there was security everywhere."

Detective Rose narrowed his gaze, and his tight smile failed to reach his eyes. "How long have you worked at the library?"

"A couple of years. I don't remember exactly what month I started working. It was my sophomore year."

"You're a senior now?"

"I just graduated. This is supposed to me my last week working."

"Isn't that nice? Congratulations."

Beatrice frowned. "Am I under suspicion or something? I would never steal anything from the library." She could see Giovanni lingering by the door, talking to Charlotte, but she could tell he was listening to her conversation with the detective.

"How many people have the combination to the document room, Miss De Novo? Or should I call you B?"

Her chin jutted out. "You can call me Miss De Novo." She saw Giovanni smile over the detective's shoulder. "I do, as well as Charlotte Martin, and Dr. Christiansen, obviously. Mrs. Ryan, on the first floor, would have it, as well as Karen Williams, who also works here sometimes. She's in Circulation, but she fills in when we're busy."

"That's a small staff."

"Well," she shrugged, "our hours are limited. It's not a very busy department."

"That makes a small suspect list."

"I suppose, unless you're counting anyone who knows anything about picking locks. This library doesn't exactly have cutting-edge technology."

"Do you know anything about picking locks?"

Her jaw dropped. "Are you joking?" He didn't look like he was joking. "I know *nothing* about picking locks. I know nothing about missing letters. I wouldn't even know what to do with them if I *did* steal them."

Immediately after saying this, Beatrice realized it wasn't exactly true. She was a fast learner, and had a feeling from talking with some of Giovanni's contacts over the past few months that more than one of them skirted the edges of legality. If she wanted to sell some stolen letters, she could probably figure out how.

"Where were you last night?"

"I was—um, I was..."

Having cake with a five hundred-year-old vampire that I think I might be falling in love with. Oh, and drinking really expensive champagne. And talking about my dead father...who isn't actually dead.

"She was having dinner with me," she heard from behind the police detective's back.

The officer turned and looked at the tall man approaching him, no doubt taking in Giovanni's professional appearance and friendly smile. He was wearing a white oxford shirt that night, a pair of studious looking glasses, and some of his seemingly endless supply of black slacks.

"And who are you?"

Giovanni smiled and held out his hand. "Dr. Giovanni Vecchio. I deal in rare books and I'm doing research here at the library. Beatrice and I are seeing each other."

Really? she thought. *Thanks for letting me know, Gio. Is that what we're doing?* Strictly speaking, she supposed it was true. They saw each other every day.

The police officer looked at Giovanni's extended hand for a moment before reaching his own out and shaking it. Beatrice watched to see if there was any physical evidence of the influence she knew he was using that very second—some sort of shimmer or spark—but there wasn't.

"I think you realize that Miss De Novo had nothing to do with this theft, don't you, Detective Rose?"

"Of course she didn't. What a ridiculous thought," the officer said in a warm voice, far more relaxed than he had been only a second before.

"And you were completely satisfied with her explanation."

"I was. She's a lovely girl."

Giovanni nodded and angled his head, looking into the officer's dazed eyes. "She is. No further investigation of her will be necessary."

The detective shook his head and turned to Beatrice. "Nope. I think we're done here." He folded up his notebook and saluted her with a small wave before he went to join his partner, who was talking to Dr. Christiansen.

She looked at Giovanni, whose face was grim as he watched the retreating officer.

"Not going to lie, that was more than a little creepy, Batman."

"Whatever keeps you out of this mess."

"Was it Lorenzo?"

He pursed his lips. "I imagine so. I have no idea how he got in, but you're right; this place has very little security. Anyone with a bit of skill could break in."

She hesitated, not wanting to voice the thought she'd had when she first learned of the theft, but feeling compelled, all the same time. "It wasn't you, was it?"

Giovanni frowned when he looked at her, but she forced herself to continue, "It's just...I know they *are* your letters. And I gave you my combination that time Lorenzo came here, and I would totally—"

"It wasn't me."

She felt horrible, as if she had betrayed him by even thinking it was a possibility. "Okay. I mean, I believe you. I don't know why...I just know how much you want them back. And I'd understand if you took them."

He looked at her with a suddenly blank expression.

"I need to go feed."

She glanced around, worried that someone had overheard, but Dr. Christiansen was still talking to the police officers, and Charlotte was talking with Dr. Scalia, who had come into the reading room while she and Giovanni had been speaking with the detective.

"Okay. Are you all right?" she whispered. "I mean, it's not Friday, and I know you—"

"It's best if I feed more." He glanced at the door. "If there is any sort of trouble, I'll be at my most effective if I've fed recently."

Beatrice swallowed, trying to ignore the tightness in her chest. She didn't know exactly what Giovanni did with the "donors" he fed from, but she had smelled perfume on him more than once when returned on Friday nights.

His eyes raked over her face. "Unless you're offering, of course," he said in a low voice. Giovanni stepped closer to her in the bright, florescent lights of the reading room, and she could feel herself react to him.

The small hairs on her body reached toward him as she fought their growing attraction. She felt the flush start in her face and her heart picked up, he had probably already sensed the hint of arousal his suggestion had produced.

She cleared her throat and shook her head. "That's all right. I need to...I'll see you later."

He paused, opening his mouth as if he wanted to say more, but then straight-

A HIDDEN FIRE

ened and stepped back a little. "I'll make sure Carl is waiting with the car when your shift is over."

She nodded and looked at her hands, twisting them together as he turned to go.

"See you," she called, but he was already halfway out the door.

Charlotte wandered over to her and gave her a small hug. "Can you believe this? What a mess! And poor Dr. Scalia, he's so upset."

Beatrice looked over Charlotte's shoulder and glanced at the small professor. He did look troubled, and Beatrice had the fleeting thought that sometimes academics put too high a price on old parchment. Then she shook her head and reminded herself she was supposed to be a librarian. Charlotte perched on the edge of the table next to her.

"I don't think there's any reason for you to stay."

"Why not?"

Charlotte shrugged. "We're just going to be talking to these guys most of the night. And Dr. Vecchio left. Dr. Scalia is hanging around, but he'll go in a few." She nodded toward the door. "Go on. Head home. I'll see you tomorrow."

Beatrice thought for a moment, but then decided she didn't really want to hang around the police detective who was questioning her earlier, even if Giovanni had worked his mind voodoo on him. "Okay. I might hang around downstairs for a while, but I'll clock out."

"Good, and don't hang out too long. Go do something fun. See if you can track down Dr. Handsome," she said with a wink.

"Right," she laughed. "Right."

Beatrice gathered her bag and book from behind the reference desk and checked her phone. As she waited by the elevator, she heard someone behind her. She glanced over, but realized it was only Dr. Scalia, who gave her a sad smile. She nodded at him before she dialed Carl's number. She was waiting for it to ring when the elevator doors opened. She frowned, knowing she would lose reception if she stepped inside, but not wanting to wait for the next unpredictable car. Beatrice hit the 'end' button on her phone and decided she could call Carl from the lobby and wait for him there.

They had just passed the fourth floor when Dr. Scalia reached forward and pushed the button for the third. She turned to him, startled by the interruption, and saw him standing in the corner, pointing a small handgun at her. His smile and his eyes were still sad.

"You are so perceptive, my dear. So very much like your father."

Her mouth gaped. "Dr. Scalia?"

The elevator door opened on the next floor and he scooted over to peer out.

"Come now, my dear. No need to linger in the elevator."

"W—what's going on?" She peered into the darkened hallway on the third floor. Beatrice knew that few students, if any, would be on the floor this time of

179

night. It contained an old section of the law library, and hardly anyone ever used it.

"You and I are going to meet some friends, Miss De Novo. Off the elevator now. I don't want to force you."

Her mind was reeling, and she kept looking between Dr. Scalia's sad smile and the gun, unable to comprehend why he was pointing it at her. "But Dr. Scalia—"

"No arguing," he said in a sharp voice, motioning toward the empty hallway with the dull, black weapon.

She stumbled out, her eyes glued to his hand. He propelled her forward, bypassing the main stairwell and heading into the stacks. Dr. Scalia walked close to her, making sure the barrel of his gun brushed against her if she slowed her pace.

"Did you know your father and I knew each other? We knew each other in school; we even worked together, for a time. It made everything so much harder. He never should have found those books in Ferrara."

She looked around, her heart beginning to beat in panic. The old law library was so seldom used, the staff didn't even keep the lights on through most of the floor, so the tall bookcases seemed to twist into a dark maze as they walked through them.

"Books? In Ferrara? Dr. Scalia, I don't know what you're talking about. What are you saying about my dad?"

"You look so much like him, too. Something about your eyes, I think." Halting for a moment, he looked at her with pity. "I hated to do it...but he had seen them, and he was asking so many questions. He knew they didn't belong there. I had to tell Lorenzo he had found the books. It was my responsibility to report him. You understand about responsibility, don't you?"

She nodded, trying to calm her racing heart as she clutched her phone. "Sure. Sure, I understand." She didn't understand. Beatrice didn't understand a word he was saying. She didn't know what was in Ferrara, except the—

"Wait, are you talking about the university where the letters were translated?" She spun around to look at him, halting in the middle of the stacks, totally forgetting about the gun. "So, you work for Lorenzo? Are you saying my father found Lorenzo's—I mean Gio's—books in Ferrara? He was in Florence, Dr. Scalia, he was killed—"

She broke off with a gasp when the small professor stepped forward and raised the gun to her chest. Her stomach dropped. "I don't understand what's going on," she choked out, suddenly looking around and realizing no one could help her. There wasn't a soul stirring on the third floor that night.

Dr. Scalia spoke in a soothing voice. "I know it's confusing, my dear. Hand me your phone, will you? I don't want to have to shoot you." He held out his hand, and Beatrice tried to think of a way to stall him so she could call Carl, but the gun seemed to grow larger in his hand the longer she stared at it. Eventually, she handed the small professor her mobile phone, and he stuck it in his pocket.

"It was such an honor to be asked to care for those books. You're a librarian, so you must understand. And no one seemed to mind me in the old building. I knew it like the back of my hand. The books never should have been found, I had taken such pains to hide them."

He continued to look at her with sympathy, but she noticed his hand never trembled on the gun. He pointed her toward the back staircase as they continued to weave their way through the bookshelves. The back stairs were rarely used, even by the maintenance staff.

"You stole the letters from the manuscript room, didn't you? You stole them for Lorenzo?"

"They were his to begin with, and it wasn't difficult. The combination lock is simple, and I'm such a trustworthy soul, aren't I? No one notices me darting around this place. Just like Ferrara," he said with a chuckle. "And he'll be so pleased to finally have *you*. He's been waiting for just the right time."

A picture of what her father had stumbled into was beginning to form in Beatrice's mind, but most of her brain was furiously searching for some way to escape the harmless looking old man with the scary black gun.

"Dr. Scalia," she stopped and turned, desperate to deflect his attention. "I don't know anything. I promise. You can tell Lorenzo." She tried to wear her most innocent expression. "This is all so confusing. Even the letters—the letters don't make sense to me. I don't know anything about the books. I don't know—"

"Of course you don't," he tried to soothe her, "but Stephen does, and he shouldn't have run. I know it's upsetting, but it's all so much bigger than our own small role. After all, I was the one that persuaded him to keep your father."

Dr. Scalia smiled then, and Beatrice could see the edge of madness in his eyes. "I told him how knowledgeable Stephen was, what a good scholar, and how many languages he spoke. I said he would be an asset." He looked at her and smiled. "I saved your father!"

She began to lose hope she would be able to elude him when she saw the stairwell approaching. She began to beg. "Dr. Scalia, if you could just put the gun away—"

He only walked more quickly. "Don't worry, he won't hurt you. He just needs you to persuade your father to come back. That's all. He promised he wouldn't hurt you."

"But—"

"Open the door, and no more talking," Scalia said in a cold voice. "We wouldn't want to echo in the stairwell."

Beatrice opened the door, praying fervently for some employee to find them as she slowly walked down three flights. They passed the door to the first floor, and she realized with dread that he was steering her toward the basement. She began to panic and tears came to her eyes.

"Please, Dr. Scalia, if you just let me go—"

"Quiet, we're almost there."

He shoved the gun between her shoulder blades as he forced her to the basement. The walls began to close in as he guided her down a long hallway with flickering lights. She'd never been in the basement of the library before; as they turned a corner, she almost ran into a grey metal door. No window revealed what was on the other side, but she could hear the sound of dripping water echo from somewhere beyond.

She felt tears begin to leak down her face.

"Please..." Beatrice turned and pleaded again. "Dr. Scalia, I don't want to go with—"

He put his fingers to his lips in a hushing gesture. "We all do things we don't want to sometimes."

She heard the door creak behind her, and a cold hand touched her shoulder. She felt the amnis creep along her collar, but unlike Giovanni's warm touch, it felt like a cold trickle of water crawling up her spine, until her eyes rolled back and darkness took her.

When she woke, Beatrice was disoriented and slumped in the back of a moving car. There was a pale vampire sitting next to her and a dark-haired one was driving. Neither one paid her more than a glance.

"Where are you taking me?"

She looked around, but both acted as if she'd said nothing. She sat up, just in time to see the car turn into the gates of Giovanni's home.

"Why—who are you?" she asked her captors. "Why are we here?" The sick thought of Giovanni being captured or hurt ate at her. She still felt dizzy, and her stomach was tied in knots. Nausea, either from the touch of amnis or from sheer panic, threatened to choke her. The only reason she wasn't sitting in a quivering heap was because she had hoped Giovanni was already planning her rescue.

The two vampires were silent as they parked behind the garage. They bared their fangs when she slapped at them, ignoring her protests as they pulled her out of the car and across the small courtyard to the kitchen door.

"Don't touch me! Don't—" She broke off with a gasp.

In the shadow of the bubbling fountain, tossed like yesterday's garbage, were the crumpled bodies of Carl and her other guard, still leaking blood where their necks had been torn open. Their guns lay scattered around their corpses like discarded toys.

"No—" Beatrice choked out a moment before she emptied her stomach near one of Caspar's potted plants. Tears she had smothered in the car leapt to her eyes at the sight of her steady, silent protectors laying broken on the ground. She spit out the gore that coated her mouth, and her captors pulled her inside.

She sniffed and wiped away the tears as they passed through the deserted kitchen and into the living room, where she saw Lorenzo sitting in Giovanni's chair. The water vampire had a roaring fire lit, and a glass of Giovanni's scotch in his hand.

Sitting across from him was Gavin Wallace, the owner of The Night Hawk, who glanced at her with bored eyes.

"How much longer are we going to be here?" Gavin asked, as they shoved Beatrice to the couch where she and Giovanni had watched horror movies the night before as they finished the bottle of champagne.

"I don't know." Lorenzo turned to her. "Beatrice dear, did your darling Giovanni tell you when he'd be back from feeding and fucking strange women? So lovely that you're not bothered by that, by the way, very progressive of you," he said with a wink. "Not like these silly girls in romance novels. I like that he's trained you so well."

Beatrice didn't know where Giovanni was, or how he was going to get them out of their current predicament, but she certainly wasn't going to give Lorenzo any clues, so she said nothing, curling her lip as tears fell down her face.

"Oh," Lorenzo said with a condescending smile. "Look how clever she is. No useless whining or begging for her. I like her; she reminds me so much of Stephen. He never cried or begged, no matter what I did to him."

He cocked his blond head, examining her before he smiled again. "So admirable. He was one still acquainted with honor. And that, my dear, is why you're such a wonderful prize!"

Gavin rolled his eyes. "Really, Lorenzo, it's not as if—"

"Oh! I hear Giovanni," Lorenzo broke in with an almost childish giggle. "He's almost to the gate. Listen, B—that's what your friends call you, correct? You and I get to solve a mystery tonight."

He scooted over next to Beatrice and put an arm around her, drawing her close to his side and stroking her long hair.

She noticed he made no effort to heat his skin as Giovanni and Carwyn did, and his clammy fingers made her skin crawl. She heard the soft growl of the car engine as it came up the drive, and she tried to dry the tears on her cheeks. She sniffed as Lorenzo watched her.

"Look at her. She's trying to be brave. Do you think she loves him, Gavin?" Lorenzo said. "It's so precious."

Gavin let his head fall back into the chair. "Shut up, you little prick. Why do I have to be here?"

"Witnesses, my dear man." Suddenly Lorenzo's tone took on a more serious bent. "I'm making a deal with my father, and I need an impartial observer. Everyone knows your reputation, Wallace. That's why you're here."

"Fine," the Scotsman huffed. "But I'm pouring myself another drink."

The room was quiet, except for the clink of Gavin's glass, and Beatrice could hear Giovanni's steps cross the courtyard. He paused before the door opened, and she wondered what he was planning as he looked at the bodies of the men he had hired to keep her safe.

Lorenzo gave her another giddy smile, and she was reminded of a Botticelli angel again. She looked away from him and glanced toward the dining room where she and Giovanni had eaten her cake the night before.

Instead of the usual candles that decorated the table, she saw stacks and stacks of books, bound in an assortment of dark leathers, spilling onto the chairs, even some that lay on the ground. They were assorted sizes and appeared to be different ages. There were scrolls and stacks of loose vellum, along with a series of large, identical books with a small stack of parchment on top of them.

"The books," she whispered.

Lorenzo followed her eyes. "Oh, you've spotted my surprise! I thought you'd appreciate them. I brought all of Papà's precious books. Now we will see why he was so excited at the library, won't we?"

Beatrice looked at the vampire, confusion evident in her face, but he only smiled at her, his eyes burning with delight.

She turned when she heard the door from the kitchen open. Giovanni walked in, and she could see the flush on his cheeks indicating he had fed. His eyes swept the two strange vampires in his living room, and he examined the stack of books on the dining room table with only a curious eyebrow before he turned to Gavin and Lorenzo lounging in front of the fire.

He curled his lip at his son then looked at Gavin, before finally, he let his eyes wander to her. He wore the same blank expression he'd often worn when they first started working together. She bit her lip, hoping to quell the tears that threatened to surface.

Giovanni walked to the sideboard and poured himself a glass of scotch before he sat down in his armchair. Gavin sat across from him, looking bored, but nodding politely toward his host. Lorenzo sat on the couch, almost bouncing in excitement, and Beatrice sat frozen next to him, willing Giovanni to give her some sign they would be okay.

"Why were you sitting in my chair, Lorenzo?" he finally spoke. "You know I hate that."

Lorenzo let out a shrill laugh. "I know, but I had to try it. Your scent and the girl's were all over it." He winked at Beatrice. "Naughty human."

"What do you want? I'm tired."

Lorenzo looked at the clock over the mantel. "It's barely nine-thirty!"

"Let me clarify. I'm tired of your company."

"Fine," Lorenzo said. "But you take all the fun out of everything."

"What do you—"

"I do wonder," Lorenzo interrupted, and took a moment to brush the hair away from Beatrice's neck, keeping his eyes on Giovanni as he leaned closer. "Where do you bite her? I've been looking and I can't see a mark on her."

"None of your business."

He paused to inhale at her throat and his soft blond curls brushed her chin, making her shudder and tense.

"Because you do bite her, don't you? I mean, why else would her scent be all over your house?" Lorenzo ducked his head back to her neck and took another predatory breath. "And I do mean all over," he said in a hoarse growl.

Gavin interrupted. "Lorenzo, I have things to do. Get on with it."

Beatrice was still blinking back tears, staring at the motionless Giovanni, who gave her no sign or acknowledgement. She bit her lip to hold in the cry that wanted to escape when she felt Lorenzo's hands. The cold that had started in her stomach when she saw the murdered guards had spread to her chest, and a chill crept across her skin everywhere he touched.

"I'm just wondering where you bite her. But maybe that's not your favorite place?" He smirked and stared into Giovanni's impassive gaze. "How about her wrists?"

Lorenzo made a show of checking both wrists. "Nope, nothing there…and nothing on her neck that I can see." A cold finger ran up her neck, starting at her collarbone and reaching her jaw. She jumped and a small whimper left her throat.

"And what a lovely neck she has," he whispered. Beatrice could no longer hold back, and tears began to trace down her cheeks.

"You curly haired git," Gavin groaned. "Hands off the blood until you make the deal. She's not yours, so stop acting like an ass and get on with it. Or I'm leaving and I'll let him burn you to a crisp if he wants."

But Lorenzo didn't stop, and nausea roiled in her stomach as his cold hand approached her thighs.

"No…" She gritted her teeth and tried to squirm away, but he held an arm around her shoulders. "Don't touch me!"

She kept looking between Lorenzo and Giovanni, expecting him to stop his son—to at least object—but he continued to stare at the vampire next to her with a completely impassive expression.

The tears fell faster when she realized Giovanni wasn't going to stop him.

"Maybe you like biting her down *here*," Lorenzo giggled, trailing a finger along her knee. "Shall we take off her skirt and find—"

"He doesn't!" Beatrice finally shrieked, pushing him away, unable to take the thought of the vampire's cold hands touching the skin of her thighs.

"He's never bitten me! There are no marks," she cried as she squirmed out of his grasp and scrambled to the other side of the couch. "Leave me alone! Don't touch me. Please, don't touch me again."

No one answered her. She began to cry angry tears; she felt like an object in the room. "Why aren't you making him stop?" She sniffed again and pulled her legs into her body, trying to make herself as small and casting her eyes around the room, looking for escape.

"For fuck's sake," she heard Gavin mutter.

Lorenzo scooted away from her, seemingly uninterested in her further discomfort. "So, not your property after all, is she, Giovanni?"

Giovanni sat, coldly sipping his scotch in the armchair. He glanced at Gavin.

"Why are *you* here, Wallace?"

"Shite, I'm here to witness a *supposed* business transaction that your little boy here doesn't seem to want to complete. Stop the gabbing, Lorenzo, and just do it."

"Fine!" Lorenzo sat back and crossed his legs. "You two are so boring. I'm going to allow that she's yours," she saw Gavin open his mouth to speak, but Lorenzo continued, "even though we all know I could press the point if I wanted to. Still, possession is nine-tenths of the law, or something like that." He shrugged. "Anyway, Papà, I do have a proposition for you."

He waved his hand toward the dining room table. "Over on the table, I have your books, the entire Pico collection. Manuscripts, letters, scrolls, blah, blah, blah. What I'm proposing—since possession is nine-tenths of the law—is that *you* give me the girl, who I have use for, in exchange for your books, which I don't."

Her stomach dropped. He wouldn't...

"The entire Pico collection is there?" Giovanni asked. Dread twisted in her stomach when she saw the interest light up his eyes. He glanced over toward the table and then let his eyes flicker to her.

"No," she whispered, but no one seemed to listen.

"Yes, yes." Lorenzo rolled his eyes. "All of it."

"And Andros's books?"

He snorted. "How valuable do you think she is?"

A sense of panic began to crawl over her skin the longer Giovanni looked at the books on the table.

"No," she said a bit louder. Still, no one even glanced at her.

"I've grown tired of lugging them around, so I thought I'd just throw them in this lovely fire if you don't want them. After all," Lorenzo leaned forward, "they are *mine*. Like the girl is yours. I can do with them what I want."

"What?" Beatrice looked around the room. "I don't *belong*—"

"Giovanni?" Gavin cut her off with a glare. "What do you think? He's offered a fair trade, property for property, do you want the books or the girl? It's up to you," Gavin said, as he played with a thread on his cuff.

"Gio," Beatrice started in horror. "No! You can't—"

"No trade," Giovanni murmured, finally looking at her.

Beatrice relaxed into the couch, leaning her forehead on her knees as she took a deep breath; her heart rate, which had been pounding erratically, started to calm.

"Unless you have Giuliana's sonnets."

Her head shot up.

She stared at him in horror. "What?"

He was looking at Lorenzo. She shook her head in disbelief.

"No," she said again, even louder.

Lorenzo reached over, drawing a thin book, bound in red leather, from the side table. It was small, no bigger than the size of a composition book, and the binding was intricately tooled; she could see the finely preserved gold script on the cover.

"As a matter of fact," Lorenzo said gleefully. "*I do*."

Giovanni cocked an eyebrow and held his pale hand out. "Let me see them."

She kept expecting him to offer her a look or a wink or...*anything* to tell her he was in control. That he was bluffing. That he wouldn't trade her for his old books. Anything to stop the cold feeling of dread and betrayal that began to climb her throat, choking her where she sat. She looked around the room in panic as Giovanni paged through the small book.

No, no, no, no, no, her mind chanted when she saw the interest in his eyes.

"They're all there. Angelo Poliziano had the originals bound after Giuliana sent them, heartbroken after her lover deserted her. Andros took them after he murdered Poliziano. These are her copies—written by her lover's hand. Now, would you like to trade? Or are these little poems destined for the fire?"

Giovanni looked at the small volume in his hands and a look of tenderness softened his features. Then, he wiped his expression clean and looked at Lorenzo.

"Fine. The girl is yours."

"No," she screamed. "No!" Beatrice looked around the room, but no one would meet her eyes. "I won't go with him!" She looked at the vampire she had trusted. "Gio? Don't let him take me! Giovanni?"

He wouldn't even look at her.

She crawled over the back of the couch, trying to flee toward the patio doors, but the dark-haired vampire grabbed her before her feet hit the ground.

"No," she screamed again, trying to twist away, but it was useless. She was bound in the iron grasp of cold, immortal arms. "You can't do this to me! No!"

But the sick feeling that crawled through her said that they could.

She observed the rest of the Lorenzo and Giovanni's "business transaction" as she twisted and bit the guard's arms, desperately trying to get away from him. "Let me go, you bastards! Let me go!"

They stood, and Giovanni shook Lorenzo's hand, then Gavin's.

She broke down sobbing when he refused to look at her. "Please, Gio!" she cried. "Please, don't let him take me. Please!"

"So," she heard Lorenzo say, "all that posturing at the library was about your books? I think I'm disappointed."

"I don't give a damn about your disappointment," Giovanni bit out. "And you're going to give me the rest eventually. Andros's books are mine and I will find them. Now get the hell out of my house and out of Houston. I don't want to see you for another hundred years, do you understand?"

Giovanni turned his back to her, and the tears fell swift down her face. Her screams had turned to painful whispers, and her head hurt from crying. She shook her head, trying to block out the betrayal that played out before her, and wishing for physical pain to block the deep cut of abandonment.

"I'm off!" Lorenzo chirped. "Lovely doing business with you."

There was no need for the guard to hold her tightly anymore. She sagged in his arms, and if she'd anything left in her stomach, it would have been emptied on Giovanni's luxurious Persian rug.

The whole time, she'd been a pawn. Only a pawn for the man in front of her to get what he wanted. His words months ago drifted to her memory.

"Don't be naive. For the right price, everything is for sale."

He'd told her.

She just didn't want to believe him.

Beatrice was propelled toward the kitchen door, but she refused to walk. Finally, her captor picked her up and carried her like a piece of luggage. As she left the room, she heard Giovanni speak.

"Gavin, care to stay for a drink? I've got a wonderful whiskey a friend sent for Christmas. I've been waiting to open it."

By the time they reached the car, she wished that someone would strike her or use their amnis so she could pass out and escape what must have been a nightmare.

Lorenzo got in the car next to her and shut the door. He smiled.

"Don't worry, my dear. I'm sure you and your father will be seeing each other very soon."

She glared at him, a bitter rage churning inside her.

"Go to hell."

A flicker of madness crept into his eyes.

"Already there."

Then cold hands touched her neck, and everything went black.

CHAPTER 20

Giovanni stood frozen, his fists clenched as he listened to Lorenzo's car wind down the driveway. When he finally heard it turn the corner toward Buffalo Bayou, he let out a roar and threw the glass of eighteen year old scotch into the fireplace.

"Dammit, man! The next time I give you a not-very-subtle message to get in touch with me, do it!" Gavin shouted.

"Not now," Giovanni snarled as he stalked past the table of books and crashed through the patio doors.

In the privacy of his garden's high walls, he let the rage envelope him. He'd kept himself reined since he scented the spilled blood coming up the driveway. He'd tamped down his anger when he caught the sharp tang of adrenaline in the courtyard, but he'd almost lost control when his son had placed his hands on her.

Blue flames erupted over his skin, burning off his clothes and turning them to charred rags as they drifted to the ground. He silently paced the length of the garden.

"Gio? Don't let them take me!"

The full weight of his anger unfurled, and the flames grew.

"You can't do this to me!"

He channeled the blaze toward a copse of cedars near the pool house, letting the intense fire burn them to ash in seconds as he heard Beatrice begging him to save her.

Please, Gio! Please, don't let him take me..."

He paced the yard, burning hands tugging his dark hair as the memory of her tears flooded his mind. His shoes turned to ash along with his clothes, and he seared the lush grass wherever his bare feet touched.

"*How valuable do you think she is?*"

Giovanni halted at the memory of his child's scoffing voice. He pushed the energy away from his body into the humid night air, loosing the fire within.

Priceless.

A thousand memories battered his mind. Her smile. The soft curve of her neck. The light in her dark eyes. The feel of her hands tangled in his hair. The soft, sweet smell of her skin.

In the shadow of her loss, he could finally admit the truth.

"*How valuable do you think she is?*"

She was priceless.

Remembering the sound of her defeated sobs when she realized his betrayal, he fell to his knees. His rage forgotten as the wave of loss washed over him. Giovanni stumbled to the edge of the pool, falling in and letting himself sink to the deepest part of the pool. He felt the water bubble along his skin as it cooled.

His rage ebbed as he floated in the cool water. The soft currents brushed through his hair, reminding him of her small fingers when she teased him the night before.

"*Your hair is so soft. I wish mine was soft like that.*"
"*I like your hair.*"
"*You do? It's so straight. I always wished I had curls like yours.*"
"*No. Your hair is beautiful as it is.*"

He lifted his hand and felt the singed curls float in front of his face. Pieces she had touched drifted away in the dark water.

After a few moments of self-indulgent grief, he gathered his wits and shot to the surface. He climbed out of the pool, wrapping a towel around his waist before he walked inside. Gavin was on the rotary phone in the corner, speaking in a low voice.

"He's just walked in...no, I don't yet, but I'll find out. Here, talk to him. Get him calmed down, and don't ask him that because the bastard had two of his lackeys with him, and at least two more on the grounds that I could smell. There was no way they were leaving without the De Novo girl."

Gavin handed the phone to Giovanni, who immediately took it and put it to his ear. He heard Carwyn's steady voice on the line.

"Hello, Sparky, you calmed down?"

He could only grunt, but the priest seemed to take it as an affirmative.

"It's a few hours before dawn here, but as soon as I'm able, I'll be on the next boat—"

"Don't."

"What?" Carwyn paused. "We're going after her, Gio."

"Of course we are, but we don't know where he's taking her yet. I'm sure Gavin can find out, but it will probably be in Europe, and you'll be closer if you stay where you are now."

"But—"

"I can't attack him here, Carwyn. There are too many unknowns and he's been planning this too far in advance. They're probably out of the city already, or close to it. And he'll have more people with him than just the four that were at my house." He saw Gavin nodding vehemently as he paced by the fireplace. "I'm better off...diffusing this right now and picking my own ground. I'll need to go to Rome and talk to Livia—probably Athens as well—and we'll need Tenzin."

"But Gio, Beatrice will be—"

"Terrified, I know." He clenched his jaw. "But he won't hurt her. Not yet. And I am no longer interested in resolving this peaceably. He ambushed me in my own home, and he took her from me. I was foolish to underestimate him."

There was a long pause on the line before Carwyn continued in a soft voice.

"Did you trade those damn books for her like Gav said?"

He cursed in a dozen languages before he answered. "He was experimenting like the sick little bastard that he is. He was going to take her, but I'd tipped my hand before. He was trying to determine if it was Beatrice or the books I was reacting to. It's better..." He cleared his throat before he continued. "It's better for her if he thinks I'm not attached to her."

He gripped the doorjamb, cracking the oak paneling and sending plaster dust crumbling to the floor.

"You're right," Carwyn said in a soothing voice, "he won't hurt her. He needs her to retrieve her father. We just need to get her back before Stephen De Novo hears about this and returns to Lorenzo. If that happens, all bets are off."

He couldn't find the words to speak to his old friend, so he took a deep, measured breath. The scent of her fear still permeated the living room, and he clenched his eyes in frustration.

"Giovanni," Carwyn was saying, "you realize, she might not understand. You know—"

"I know," he muttered. "I knew the minute I let him take her she might never forgive me for it. But it's better than her being injured or tortured to get back at me."

He turned and, leaning against the wall, slowly sank to his haunches. He paused, closing his eyes and breathing deeply, savoring her scent, even if it was tinged by the adrenaline he hated. He felt his heart give a sporadic thump as he stared at the sofa where Lorenzo had threatened her, and Giovanni had to fight back another wave of anger. He gripped the phone to his ear, anchoring himself to the sound of his friend's voice.

"Do you love her, Gio?"

He closed his eyes, but could only see her broken, empty stare as Lorenzo's guard carried her away.

"What do you think?" he asked in a hollow voice.

There was another long pause before Carwyn responded.

"We'll get her back."

"Yes, I will."

"And your son?"

Giovanni grit his teeth, letting his fangs pierce his lip as they descended, reveling in the taste of blood that filled his mouth and the sharp bite of pain.

"My son will burn."

"I'll wait for your call."

He hung up the phone and walked upstairs without a glance. In a little over a ten minutes, he had dressed, shaved off his singed hair, and walked back downstairs. He stopped on the second floor to sit in Beatrice's bedroom, soaking in her scent and the familiar traces of her that littered his home.

There was a stack of books on her bedside table. She left them everywhere, scattered around the house in little caches, always ready to be picked up and continued when a few moments could be stolen. Her boots stood by the closet. She hadn't worn them to work that afternoon, and he found himself wishing she had, as if the sturdy shoes could have protected her from the monsters who took her away.

A small picture of Beatrice and Isadora sat in a frame on her bedside table. He grabbed it, extracting the picture and putting it in his pocket before he walked down to the first floor.

Gavin waited in the living room, eying him as he walked down the stairs.

"I made some calls."

"And?"

"You know I'm only doing this because Carwyn is the closest thing I have to a friend, don't you? And because Lorenzo is such an ass. I'm not picking sides in any damn war. I refuse."

"I'm not asking you to."

Gavin rolled his eyes. "She'll be fine. It makes no sense for him to hurt her. Not now, and you know how little interest he has in human women."

"That is so very reassuring," Giovanni snarled. "What do you know?"

Gavin measured him as he stood on the staircase. Finally, he gave a small shrug. "She did seem amusing. And clever. Carwyn said you were less of an asshole when she was with you."

"Wallace, I would kill you without a moment's hesitation if it would make you give me this information faster. What did you find out?"

"You didn't hear it from me and all the usual speech, but that crazy plane he has took off from a private airfield north of Katy a half an hour ago, headed to

La Guardia airport in New York. They must have driven straight there. That's all my contact knew. They didn't file anything else."

"Could he be staying in New York?"

The Scotsman said, "Not likely. You know how the O'Brians feel about the little prick."

Giovanni frowned, remembering the surly clan of earth vampires that had taken over the New York area around the turn of the last century. They were notoriously hostile and suspicious, and Lorenzo had made them his enemies by throwing his money behind the old guard they had wiped out when they rose to power a hundred years before.

"No, it's most likely a stop-over on the way to Europe. Most of his allies are there," Giovanni continued to mutter, trying to wrap his mind around the fact that the peaceful life he'd cultivated for the last three hundred years was crumbling around him, returning him to the tumultuous early centuries of his life.

Just as he was about to kick Gavin out so he could go up to the library, he heard a crack at the French doors. He frowned, but stayed where he was, flicking off the lights in the living room and peering into the night. He thought he saw a magnolia branch sway, but no breeze stirred the other trees.

He heard another crack, but this time, he saw a pebble fall. He snuck out the kitchen door and around the side yard, reaching out with his senses to determine who or what was on the grounds. He scented the air, relaxing immediately when he recognized the familiar aroma of cardamom that always lingered around her. He walked to the back garden and scanned the trees.

He heard a chirp from the low hanging magnolia tree and glanced up to see the small vampire perched on a branch, her legs dangling and her feet bare. She appeared to be no more than sixteen or seventeen years old, and her glossy black hair fell in two sheets that framed her face. Her eyes were a clouded grey and beautifully tilted by an ancient hand, but when the girl smiled, vicious fangs curled behind her lips like the talons of some primeval bird of prey.

A strange calm settled over him.

"Hello, Tenzin."

"Hello, my boy," she said in Mandarin. "I thought you might need me."

"I've lost her."

The girl shook her head. "She was taken from you. But you'll get her back."

His eyes furrowed in grief, and she floated down from the tree to perch on his back, laying her head on his shoulder so she could watch his face.

"I've seen it. She is your balance in this life. In every life."

He whispered in English, "You know I don't believe in that."

"You put too much faith in your science, my boy. Science changes. Truth doesn't."

He paused before asking, "Do you know where she is?"

"Water. Lots of water. He'll go where he's strong."

He raised an eyebrow as he walked toward the house with her still clinging to his shoulders. "Is that a vision, or five thousand years of experience killing your enemies?"

She shrugged. "Whatever you decide to believe today."

Despite everything, he felt a small smile cross his face. "I'm glad you're here, bird girl."

She laughed, a tinkling sound that had always reminded him of a wind-chime. "I'm fate's messenger this time. That is all. I saw her long, long ago."

He halted near the doors, dropping her and spinning around.

"What do you mean?"

An impish grin crossed her face. "You are right to be patient. Where is the food? I'm hungry. It's very warm here."

Giovanni sighed, knowing he would get no further information from her. "We have to take care of Beatrice's guards first. Lorenzo killed them. Then we'll go hunting."

She switched to English. "You're sad about the humans?"

"Yes."

"Did they die protecting your woman?"

"Yes."

Tenzin shrugged. "They were warriors. That's a good death."

"It would have been better if they hadn't died at all."

They walked through the French doors and into the living room. Gavin was on the phone again, and his eyes widened at the sight of the small woman who skipped in front of him. He and Tenzin walked through the dark kitchen and into the courtyard with the burbling fountain.

Tenzin stopped, examining Giovanni's face as he observed the bodies of the two humans he had hired to guard Beatrice.

"This was their fate," she said gently.

"Tenz—"

He stopped when she held up a hand, her grey eyes pinched in sadness.

"Let's not argue while the crows can get them, my boy."

He sighed and bent to examine the two bodies, noting with dismay the deep gashes and bites that could never be explained to human authorities.

"We'll take them to the country where Carwyn hunts. I'll call his friend so he's expecting us."

Tenzin nodded. "This is good. Then we can hunt, too. We'll need it."

"He's probably going to Europe."

She paused for a moment and her stormy eyes seemed to swirl as he watched her. "Your son is in Greece, I think."

He frowned. "Why? Why Greece?"

Tenzin thought for a moment, but simply shrugged as she hoisted one large body to move it to the garage. "It sounds right."

He sighed, frustrated with her typically vague pronouncement. "But—"

"Think for yourself instead of doubting me," the small vampire said as she carried the guard into the garage. "Think about the water. You may wield fire, but you came from water, and so did your son. Does that water mean something to him?"

He thought of his sire and the ruins of the school where he'd held them. He remembered the stories they'd both listened to, the tales of gods and monsters. Tenzin walked back into the courtyard, and cocked her head.

He nodded. "Yes, it sounds right."

Just then, Gavin walked through the kitchen door. He nodded toward Giovanni and looked at Tenzin, who was hoisting the second body and carrying it to lie with the first.

"Is that—"

"Yes," Giovanni said. "It is."

"Amazing. I've heard stories."

Tenzin flitted back into the courtyard and over to Gavin, sniffing him a little. "Are you a wind walker, like me?"

"Well," Gavin said, "not like you."

"You get your flying yet?"

The Scotsman looked a little embarrassed. "Uh…no, not yet."

She shrugged and washed her hands in the fountain. "You will soon. And then, I think your life will change."

Gavin chuckled. "Well, I hope it doesn't change too…" He trailed off when he saw the serious look in Tenzin's eyes. He cleared his throat. "Right then, I'll be looking for that."

She nodded and started back into the house.

"Tenzin?" Gavin called. "Can I—"

She turned back to him with a quick grin. "You want to see my teeth?"

He smiled a little, before he gave a quick nod.

She floated up to stare him in the face and bared her curved fangs, which resembled nothing less than small scimitars. She grinned then darted inside the house. Giovanni shook his head at her theatrics and the normally unflappable Scotsman's shocked face.

"Now *that* is something."

"Yes, she is."

"And they're always out?"

"Her fangs?" he snorted. "Tenzin told me once that they used to retract, but she spent so much time killing her enemies her fangs forgot how to hide."

"Really?"

He shrugged. "Who knows? It's Tenzin. She likes telling stories."

Gavin stared off into the distance, while Giovanni stared at him.

"Well?"

"What?"

"Lorenzo?" he growled.

"Ah yes, back to the nasty business. Shipping. Water vamp. Gun running and seclusion. He's in Greece. Apparently, he has his own island. Sadly, it's probably going to take a while to narrow it down. There's quite a few of them."

He remembered her terror when they dragged her out of his house, and he felt the flames lick along his collar again. He closed his eyes and took a deep breath to calm himself. Tenzin had said he was right to be patient with Beatrice.

He could be patient.

Because when Giovanni found him, Lorenzo would burn.

CHAPTER 21

South Aegean Sea
June 2004

"Do you require another drink, Miss De Novo?"
She glanced at the small servant who stood next to her chair before staring back at the ocean that surrounded her.

"No, thanks."

"You must ring the kitchen if there is anything you need. Or let your guard know." Beatrice glanced at the sturdy Greek who stood near the entrance to her room. As far as she could tell, he didn't speak a word of English. She wasn't sure he spoke at all.

But he watched.

He watched every move she made during the day, unless she ducked into the small bathroom in the chamber where she had been kept for the past week.

"Sure. Thanks. I'll let him know." She looked back at the ocean, letting her thoughts drift in and out with the crashing surf.

The servant crept away, following the small trail that connected all the exterior rooms of Lorenzo's strange house. She watched him duck into what she thought was the kitchen area of the vampire's house, which had become her prison.

It was sprawling, built into the half-moon bay of what she had been told was Lorenzo's own island. Cliffs speared up from the surface of the water and the house was nestled in the crook above the rocky beach.

She knew there were other rooms, built back into the cliffs where the sun could not reach. All the exterior rooms faced the water and opened to the ocean with large doors not unlike a garage. She wasn't locked in, per se. But unless she wanted to jump fifty feet into the vast expanse of the Aegean, there wasn't anywhere she could go.

When she had woken after being dragged from Giovanni's house, she immediately heard the sound of large engines droning. She thought she was in the belly of a cargo plane of some sort, though it was outfitted luxuriously with plush seats, tables and beds.

She saw Lorenzo, lounging in a pair of white slacks and shirt that only emphasized his inhuman paleness.

"Where are we?"

He looked up with an indulgent smile.

"You're awake! On my plane, of course. Headed to what will be your home for some time. Do you want any refreshment?" She glanced at his own crystal glass, filled with a thick red liquid she assumed was human blood. Lorenzo noticed her looking.

"I'm not a heathen like Giovanni. I drink human, of course, but I don't like drinking from the tap." He shuddered. "So disgustingly intimate, in my opinion. I only like getting that close to someone when I'm fucking them or killing them."

He winked at her when she blanched. "No need to worry about that, my dear. I want you fresh and unharmed when your father comes begging for you."

"Where are we going?"

Lorenzo sighed with a smile. "Somewhere far more temperate than Houston. I don't know how you stand the weather in that horrid city." He shivered. "Absolutely horrendous. We're going to a little private island in the Aegean, my dear girl. A special place. Only a very few people know about it, so you should feel privileged."

"Be still my heart," she said dryly.

Lorenzo laughed, his sharp fangs falling down in his delight. "Oh, there you are, Miss De Novo, I knew I would like you once I got you away from my father. He's so stifling, isn't he? Terribly boring vampire. And I was sure you had that quick wit that so delighted me with Stephen.

"Even when I was torturing him," a wistful expression crossed Lorenzo's angelic face, "he would come up with the most inventive barbs. What a treat he was."

A sick feeling churned in Beatrice's stomach, and she thought she might throw up again, but she forced herself to take a deep breath and change the subject.

"How are you flying? I mean, doesn't your wonky energy mess up the plane and stuff?"

He chuckled. "What an excellent question. Yes, it would if the cargo compartment had not been especially designed for me. All sorts of wonderful, insulating materials they've come up with in the last few decades."

"Yeah? Well, God bless chemistry, I guess."

He chuckled, but continued paging through the magazine he'd been perusing. It appeared to be something about boats, but she couldn't read the language on the front cover; she thought it might be Greek.

"Just consider this trip a vacation, my dear. After all," an evil grin spread across his face, "you'll have an ocean view room."

Ocean view room, my ass. She stared at the endless sea that imprisoned her. The small interior door to her room was always locked. Any traffic in or out came by way of the large ocean-facing doors she was currently sitting in front of. They could be pulled up completely, so her room was always open. In the morning, her silent, watchful guard came and unlocked her, throwing open the room to the ocean breeze.

If she hadn't been a prisoner, it would have been beautiful.

She had no privacy except the small washroom that contained a toilet, a sink with no mirror, and a shower with no curtain. She could not lock the door, and lived in fear of someone walking into the bathroom if she lingered too long. The room had come stocked with clothing; when she arrived, two silent women undressed her and threw her clothes into a garbage bag, leaving her naked and crying on the floor of her room. She crawled to the bed, intending to cover herself with a sheet until one of them came back and wordlessly opened the small chest of drawers was filled with pure white clothes.

There were white pants and white shirts. Looking in the top drawer even netted her a wealth of white bras and panties, all in her size. There were bathing suits and sundresses, all in white, all without any other identifying feature on them. She hastily dressed herself and crawled into the corner of her room for the next two days, waiting for the other shoe to drop.

Beatrice had been captive a week and fallen into a monotonous rhythm. She woke. She took a quick shower and dressed herself in the white clothes, dumping the towel and dirty linens in a basket by the ocean door where another silent servant would carry them away at some point in the morning. No one ever talked to her. Her guard would open the door and she would sit in one of the chaises that faced the ocean, waiting for something to happen.

Nothing ever did.

When darkness fell, she could hear scurrying movements farther along the cliff to her left, but she never made any attempt to investigate the sick laughter or sounds of revelry that drifted to her room. Darkness meant vampires, and Beatrice may not have liked her human guard, but at least she didn't think tall, dark and silent was going to rip her throat out if he got hungry.

Her door wasn't shut until well after dark, so she often sat staring at the moon as it reflected off the dark water below her.

One night, about a week and a half after she'd been taken, she heard footsteps approaching. She tensed, but refused to run back to the corner, knowing that anything that came after her would just consider that an easier and more private meal.

To her surprise, it was Lorenzo who peeked his head around the corner.

"Hello, my dear. How are you enjoying your stay?"

Eying him warily, she took a moment to answer. Her own voice sounded strange to her ears.

"Well, I have no privacy, no human contact, and nothing to read or listen to other than the ocean. But at least your prison decorating skills are top notch, Lorenzo."

He walked over to her and stretched out on another chaise, dressed from head to toe in loose white linen that made his inhuman skin glow in the moonlight. "You like it? I'm so glad my home meets your approval."

"Oh, yeah, I mean, it's just so...white. And *white*. And with all those white accents."

Lorenzo smiled, his fangs dropping down. "Is this why Giovanni kept you around? To make him laugh? You smell as lovely as your father, so I'm sure he must have had to control himself if he didn't bite you. It does make me wonder."

She clenched her jaw for a moment. "I don't want to talk about him."

"Because he traded you?" Lorenzo shrugged. "Giovanni never cared for much besides his books and himself, to be honest. Don't take it personally."

Her mind flashed to a hundred different moments of kindness between them, but she didn't want to dwell on those memories when the reality had turned out to be so much different. "I just have better things to think about."

"I was expecting him to show up. I was so sure it was you he was smoking about in the library that day...but he hasn't by now, so he probably won't. If he cared for you at all, he'd be far more territorial."

She stared at the ocean, remembering Giovanni's fiercely protective behavior around Carwyn and Gavin. It had annoyed her at the time; but the moment she'd really wanted him to protect her, it had fallen away to nothing, so she didn't know what to think.

"Something tells me he still has something up his sleeve." Lorenzo flicked at a bug on his pants. "After all, one doesn't hire expensive security for dinner. So... yes, I'm expecting something."

"Yeah?" she muttered. "I'm not."

She suddenly remembered him laughing over a bite of lemon cake she'd forced him to try. He'd made the most hilarious face, and she had leaned over and kissed his cheek in delight, laughing at his disgust and tugging the ends of his hair.

"You need a haircut."

"I do not. Do you know how long it takes my hair to grow?"

"It falls in your eyes all the time and annoys you. Just a trim. I'll do it for you; I used to cut my grandfather's hair for him sometimes."

"You'd cut my hair for me?"

"Sure."

She felt tears come to her eyes, and she bit her lip until it bled, forgetting for a moment about the vampire sitting next to her in the dark. She glanced at him, worried he would try to bite, but he only handed her a white linen handkerchief and chuckled at her expression.

"I've had requests for you to join us in the evenings, but I doubt you'll do that. But there's a full library for you to enjoy, as well as plenty of music. I even have a music player you may borrow, if you like."

"What's the catch?"

His delighted laughter pealed out. "No catch, my dear. Xenos can come with you. He's your personal guard, you know, chosen by me. No one will touch you or harm you in any way. After all," he winked, "I need to have you in good condition when your father arrives."

Her heart dropped. "My father's coming? When?"

"I have no idea." He shrugged. "Crafty little boy to have eluded me for so long. I'd really find it quite endearing if I didn't want to kill him so much."

Beatrice shuddered at his matter-of-fact tone. "Why? Why do you want to kill him? You made him a vampire, now you want to kill him?" Her frustration boiled over. "I don't understand any of this! I feel like I got caught in some giant game all of you are playing, and I don't even know why."

Lorenzo's head cocked; he almost looked amused. "I suppose it would be confusing to a human—even a bright girl like you."

"So why don't you enlighten me, Lorenzo? Since I'm here and no one seems to be coming to my rescue."

He stared at her with the inhuman stillness she had come to associate with them. Finally, his lips cracked into a smile.

"You met my little mouse at the library, didn't you? Scalia has been my mouse for many years, long before you were born, and long before he met your father in Houston when they were in school. It was pure chance that they met again in Ferrara."

"My father wasn't in Ferrara, he was in—"

"Yes, he *was* in Ferrara, researching some correspondence about Dante, of all people, and his exile in Ravenna, blah, blah, blah. Very boring. He was in the old library and had the unfortunate luck to stumble upon some books of mine. Books I had hidden there." Lorenzo's expression darkened. "Books that my little mouse was supposed to be guarding for me."

"So you killed him? For finding some books?" She felt the tears slide down her cheeks. "He probably didn't even know what he was looking at. Why did he have to die? Why—"

"It didn't matter that he didn't know, Beatrice. Scalia found him and your father began asking questions of his old school chum—questions I didn't want *any* human asking. When Scalia told me about it, like the good little mouse he was, I decided to get rid of him. It seemed like the simplest thing." Lorenzo rolled his eyes. "It's my own fault I let myself be swayed to turn him. I thought he could be a replacement for Scalia, who had disappointed me, but sadly, your father was too bright."

"And he ran away."

"Yes, he did." Lorenzo grimaced. "Though not before taking some books he knew I valued."

"What books? Some of Giovanni's?"

His eyes narrowed. "Some of *mine*. Our father—yes, we had the same father, I only call Giovanni 'Papà' because it annoys him—and it is technically accurate. Our father left them to him, when he should have left them to me. It didn't matter what Giovanni thought. *I* was the one who had earned them."

Lorenzo broke off, making a disgusted noise and flipping his long hair over his shoulder. "The fool was so trusting."

"Who? Giovanni?" Beatrice was still confused. Was Lorenzo Giovanni's *brother*? His *son*? She wanted to ask, but wanted to know about the books more.

"I told him the mad friar had burned them all." A laugh bubbled up from Lorenzo's throat. "And he believed me! He thought they were all gone. All his books and letters, Guiliana's precious sonnets...all of it. Up in smoke in the 'bonfire of the vanities.'"

"In Florence," she whispered. "The bonfires of Savonarola."

"Of course, my dear." Lorenzo winked. "There were many things that didn't quite burn as Savonarola intended. It was a good time to be an opportunist. It all happened before Giovanni was turned. Even then, he couldn't run about like me. Andros didn't trust him. With good reason, as it turned out."

"Andros?" she muttered, but Lorenzo wasn't listening. She recognized the name from the letters. Niccolo Andros was the name of the strange associate of Lorenzo de Medici's who had shown such an interest in Giovanni Pico. Andros was Giovanni's sire? She wondered why Lorenzo called him his father, too.

"Father thought Giovanni was the clever one." Lorenzo chuckled, still reveling in his own deceit. "I was smarter than both of them. I fooled them both." His eyes narrowed as he looked over the water. "And soon, I will fool them all. All the silly, trusting fools with their delusions of grandeur. As soon as I find your father and torture him into telling me what he did with the books..."

Lorenzo smiled and turned to her. "But perhaps torture won't even be necessary. In fact," he chucked her under the chin as she cringed, "I'm absolutely counting on it."

Tucking all the vampire's cryptic revelations into the back of her mind, she swallowed and tried to remain calm. "How do you know he'll even come for me? How do you know he's even keeping track?"

"He might not be." Lorenzo shrugged. "But word will reach him eventually. Maybe tomorrow? Maybe in a few years? I'm sure it depends on where he is." Lorenzo smiled and scanned her with cold eyes. "I have no doubt he'll join you eventually."

A few years? She cringed at the thought.

"And then? What happens to me then?"

He looked at her, cold eyes raking over her throat and legs, lingering around her breasts until her skin flushed in embarrassment.

"Human women are too fragile for me. But maybe I'll have one of my children change you for me so we can play," he shrugged, carelessly nonchalant about the idea of her mortality.

"What if I don't want to be a vampire? Would you just kill me?"

His delighted laughter rung over the crashing waves. "Oh, my dear Beatrice, you're so amusing. Why do you think it matters what *you* want?"

He laughed again and stood, still snickering as he walked down the path.

When he was far enough away, she let the tears fall, soaking the linen handkerchief stained with her blood.

Despite Lorenzo's assurances, she didn't want to risk venturing out at night, so the next day she put a pair of pants and a shirt over a bathing suit and walked down the small cliff path to the area where she had seen the servants disappearing. She passed other rooms, all of them identical to hers, but none of them appeared to be occupied. There was a railing along parts of the path when it became too narrow, and even one place where a small bridge spanned a sharp drop into craggy rocks below.

She finally reached a series of rooms open to the ocean. They were living areas, and she saw a number of servants scuttling around, but nothing that resembled a library. She turned in confusion to her guard—who Lorenzo had referred to as Xenos—but he only shrugged.

Just then, an English accent rang from across the room.

"Oh, there you are!"

She turned and looked at a young man, also dressed head to toe in white, as he crossed the room. He was around her age, and wore a pair of wire-framed glasses on his tan face. His brown hair had gold highlights from the sun, and his smile was brilliantly white. He was handsome, in a catalogue model kind of way, and a friendly light shone from his eyes.

The stranger held out his hand. "I'm Tom. I'm one of Lorenzo's day people. I knew he had the daughter of a friend staying with him, but we hadn't seen you. Enjoying your stay?"

She choked out a stiff laugh. "The daughter of a friend? Is that what he told you?"

"Of course! Lorenzo's a good man, he wouldn't harm anyone."

She frowned at the startlingly false statement. "Um, no actually, he's a vicious vampire, who killed and turned my father and tortured him to get information. And then he flew to Houston, attacked my grandmother, killed some people who were protecting me, and then kidnapped me to get my father back."

Through her entire statement, Tom's smile never wavered. When she was finished, he only chuckled again. "Oh, don't worry. Lorenzo's a good man, he wouldn't harm anyone."

She looked at him, her eyebrows furrowed in confusion. "Did you not hear the part about him murdering and kidnapping and holding me hostage?"

Tom just shook his head again, still smiling. "Don't worry. Lorenzo's a good man, he wouldn't harm anyone."

She nodded, finally understanding that the man's cerebral cortex must have been altered by Lorenzo or one of his minions. "That's nice. What did you say your name was?"

"Tom. Tom Sanders. And what's your name?"

"It's B. Nice to meet you, Renfield."

The young man frowned, "Uh... no, my name is—"

"I heard you, Tom." Beatrice sighed. "Is there a library here?"

"Sure, just come with me; I'll be happy to show you the library."

"I'm sure you will."

"So, what do you like to read? There are computers here, too, if you want them."

"Computers?" her ears perked at the thought of contact with the outside world.

"Well, they're not online unless you have a special code. I do, but I can't give it to guests." The stiff set of his shoulders warned Beatrice they were treading on uncomfortable ground.

"No problem." She shrugged. "I'd rather read, anyway. What do you do for Lorenzo, Tom?"

He smiled, relaxing at her easy question. "I do some financial stuff. No biggie. Just things he can't do because of his disability."

Oh really?

"You mean the fact that he fries a computer just by touching it?"

"Yeah," he said. "Something like that."

Beatrice nodded, and decided to watch the young man more carefully. She was curious. As inept as Giovanni and Carwyn seemed to think Lorenzo was about technology, why did he have a financial guy who had online access in his super-secret bad guy lair?

They walked through a doorway to a dark paneled library.

Finally surrounded by something other than white, Beatrice took a deep breath, relaxing in the smell of leather bindings and old paper.

"If you'll excuse me," Tom said, "I have some work to do."

"Sure, do you mind if I read in here?"

"No problem," he said. "Don't let me bother you. And feel free to take books to your room, if you like."

She glanced around at the furniture which looked more like a typical English manor house then the cold, modern lines that characterized the rest of the mansion. The warm tones reminded her of Giovanni's library, but she frowned and turned toward the bookcases.

"No, I like it in here. It's warm." She smiled at him and went to explore the library, keeping an eye on the young man and the computer screen he studied.

She spent the next two weeks there. Or at least, that's what she guessed, since she had little sense of time in the strange, surreal world of Lorenzo's household. She would wake in the morning, dress in her white clothes, then go to the wood-paneled library to sit with Tom. She spent every moment she could in the library, and a grim satisfaction settled on her when she finally figured out what Tom was doing.

He was transferring money for Lorenzo. Cleaning it in clumsy ways and then moving it to offshore accounts that were far too obvious to be effective. She almost laughed at the young man's inept manipulations, but then, she hadn't had her cerebral cortex mangled on a nightly basis like Tom had.

When she had finally began creeping closer to the raucous parties Lorenzo hosted in the mansion on the sea's edge, Tom was the only human she recognized.

It happened every night, with Lorenzo lording over his men like some sort of modern day warlord. The music was loud, the lights were low, and the blood flowed freely. She had seen young Tom passed around from vampire to vampire on more than one night, though he always seemed to end up crumpled in a pile next to Lorenzo by the end of the evening.

The first time she snuck down to observe the parties, she looked at Xenos, who was following her, wondering if he would object to her furtive observation. He simply shrugged and continued to watch her. Apparently, as long as she wasn't trying to escape, she really did have free rein.

Lorenzo had a seemingly endless supply of humans who were brought out for his vampires to feed on. She guessed there were around twenty immortals on any given night, though she often saw different faces, so she suspected there were closer to thirty or forty around. Most nights, they would drain the humans to the point of unconsciousness and then toss them on a pile in the corner. Sometimes the oblivious people woke up and joined the party again, writhing on the vampires' laps and moaning as they were bitten. Other times, the pale men and women simply slunk out the door.

They were all young, beautiful things, tan and bleached from the sun, and she wondered where Lorenzo seemed to find such an endless feast for his men. On more than one occasion, tears slipped down her face when one of the humans was drained to death.

One night, a blond girl was killed, and the vampire who drained her laughed and pretended to dance with the limp body before tossing it over the side of the cliffs to be bashed against the rocks below.

Other than Tom, she never saw any of the house staff at the parties, so she imagined there was some kind of prohibition about feeding from the human servants. She hoped she fell into that category if any of the vicious looking vampires she saw at the parties ever found her.

Her life fell into a strange rhythm. Servants all seemed to look the same. Xenos hovered over her every move. Lorenzo would come visit her in the evenings, always with thinly veiled threats about her father hidden under his playful, angelic expression. She dreaded his visits most of all, but there was no way to avoid them.

The days and weeks dragged on.

She was sitting in her room one afternoon after her trip to the library, when an unexpected tap on the interior door startled her.

"Hello?" she called through the locked door.

"Miss De Novo?" a lightly accented female voice called out. It was daytime, so Beatrice knew it wasn't a vampire. She looked to Xenos, but he only shrugged and continued to watch the empty path by her room.

The door rattled open and she saw two small women, one of them smiling and the other looking somber and silent. The smiling one spoke some English.

"We are here for Miss De Novo."

"I'm Miss De Novo."

"The master wishes that we tend to you, miss."

Her eyebrows lifted. "What?"

The smiling woman, who was quite young, lifted a hand to her hair.

"Your beauty. Your hair and face."

"Oh," she said, feeling somewhat embarrassed. There were no mirrors in the mansion, and she'd forgotten that her hair must have had two inch roots showing at the base. She'd finally been given a wax kit for her legs—razors were not allowed—but her hair was probably a horrible mess. She put a hand up, feeling the limp lengths that hung around her face.

For some reason, this—more than the constant observation, more than the nightly horror of tossed bodies, more than the chill-inducing innuendo from Lorenzo—this small realization about her hair finally caused Beatrice to break down in loud sobs.

"Miss! We just make your hair pretty!" the woman said in a panic. Xenos frowned at her, but made no move toward the three women standing at the door.

"No," she sniffed, "it's fine. Come in. My hair's probably horrible."

"The master picked a color, so you sit down and we fix it."

"What?" Her head shot up. He may have dictated her every move in the mansion, but she was going to throw a fit if Lorenzo tried to make her blond.

Luckily, the woman held up a box of color that looked very close to her natural brown. Deciding it was better than walking around with roots—even if she couldn't see them—she sat down and let the two women get to work.

As they chattered in Greek, Beatrice couldn't help but think about the last time she'd had her hair cut and colored. Her grandmother had been with her and they'd gone to the salon where Marta's son worked. She had sipped a glass of wine and laughed at the jokes swirling around her and the comforting accents of home.

Tears began to pour down her face as she thought about the frightening new world she had been pulled into. She sniffed, biting back sobs, while the women silently colored and cut her hair. For the first time since she had arrived, Beatrice felt broken.

Eventually, the ever-present echo of the waves lulled her to sleep. When she woke, her hair felt soft and shiny at the tips, and the moon shone on a passive sea.

Unfortunately, she also had an unwelcome blond visitor.

He smirked. "You look lovely. That color suits you much better than the black."

She stared out at the ocean. "Why do you care if I'm ugly? I'm your prisoner here."

"I prefer to think of you as my guest."

"You can think that all you want, blondie, but I'm still your prisoner."

"'Blondie?'" he laughed. "I so enjoy you, Beatrice. Our chats are always amusing. But why are you so hostile, my dear? Did you not want your hair done? Would you rather walk around looking unattractive?"

She refused to look at him, staring as the glowing reflection of the silver moon was broken by the waves that rippled beneath her.

"I was supposed to start grad school in September," she murmured. "I was going to be a librarian."

She heard him laugh. "Why?"

She shrugged and wiped at the silent tears that slipped down her cheeks. "I liked it. I love books and helping people. It wasn't a big dream, but it was mine."

"That's your problem. Small dreams. Didn't anyone ever tell you to dream big? I figured that one out myself. I have dreams, too. But they're not small in the least. They're positively...world changing." She finally looked at him. He was looking at the water with a cold light sparking in his eyes. "And they will happen once I have your father back."

She found it difficult to gather any real anger toward him anymore; she had been exhausted by horror. "Maybe I would have gotten married. Gotten a cat. Maybe I would have written a book someday."

"Or you could have been hit by a bus on the way home from work. Humans are very fragile."

Beatrice didn't feel like there was any use fighting. No one was coming for her. If it wasn't for the faint hope her father might have some way of getting her out, she would have taken her chances climbing down the cliffs to be bashed on the rocks. In the end, she knew the chances of either of them escaping from Lorenzo were small; in all likelihood, she would remain under his thumb. Possibly for eternity.

"I heard a rumor that Giovanni was in Rome," Lorenzo said suddenly. "Talking with all his little allies." A demented giggle left Lorenzo's throat, and she tried to smother the faint hope that fluttered in her chest. "Do you think he'll try to come save you, Beatrice? Do you think he could? Do you even want him to anymore?"

Yes. Even if Giovanni only came for the books Lorenzo had stolen from him, maybe she could persuade him to take her, too. Surely not all of his humanity was a sham. Surely Caspar wouldn't—

"He tries to make himself so disgustingly good," Lorenzo mused. "So few people know the real vampire."

"Oh really?"

"Did he ever tell you why he made me? So unlike him to make a child. I'm his only son, you know. He doesn't care to 'form attachments.' That's what he told me when he sent me away," Lorenzo said. Though he tried to sound nonchalant, she still detected the faint edge of bitterness in his voice.

"Really?" Beatrice was having a hard time feeling sympathy for the bloodthirsty immortal next to her. "Poor you."

"Aren't you curious why?" he said with a glint in his eye.

"Not really."

"That's okay, I'll tell you anyway."

"Knock yourself out," she said, closing her eyes and trying to get lost in the sound of the surf.

"It was payment of a sort. Payment for killing someone."

"Yeah, right."

He grinned. "He comes across as so noble, doesn't he?"

Beatrice sat in silence, the rhythmic sounds of the waves enveloping her.

"But our Giovanni isn't nearly as virtuous as he'd like everyone to think. He wasn't always a mild-mannered book dealer. He's really quite vicious. And self-centered. Did he tell you he used to be a mercenary?"

She rolled her eyes in disbelief as Lorenzo continued. "Yes, he made a lot of money doing that. He was one of the best in the world. He killed many humans."

"Right."

"Ask him yourself, the next time you see him."

She finally sneered. "Because that's so likely, isn't it?"

He grinned, pleased to have finally sparked a reaction in her.

"We'll just have to see, won't we?"

She sank back in her chair, determined not to react to him again. He left shortly afterward, his interest in her dying along with her temper. He seemed disappointed by her defeated demeanor, but Beatrice had lost the will to spar with him.

The next day, she didn't leave her room.

She didn't leave it the day after or the day after that. And as the days stretched into weeks, she slowly shrank further and further into her protective shell.

CHAPTER 22

The three vampires rode the wind, the smallest propelling them forward as they swung lower toward the unnamed island in the South Aegean Sea. Tenzin hovered for a moment, her sharp eyes darting over the layout of the fortified mansion cut into the grey cliffs, scanning the patrolling guards and visible access points.

She looked to the red-haired man clutching her left hand. He nodded; then, concentrating his energy on a small, rocky outcropping that peeked from the water, slowly pulled the rocks up from the floor of the ocean, creating a small platform where they came to rest.

All three were barefoot, and when Carwyn's feet touched the rock, it seemed to pulse and swell under him, growing taller and elevating them just under edge of the cliff. Giovanni cocked his head, listening to the sounds of revelry above. As he listened, a thin human body was tossed over the edge of the cliff, landing directly at their feet.

Giovanni stared into the empty gaze of the discarded girl, narrowing his eyes and clenching his jaw, but letting the anger swirl around him until his bare torso and arms glowed with blue fire. His thick hair was cropped and his eyes were cold; he stood at attention, nothing less than the ideal warrior his sire had molded when he turned him five hundred years before.

The wind whipped around them, but Tenzin had wrapped them in a protective cocoon, blocking any trace of their scent from the guards above.

"Carwyn, do you remember?"

He nodded, his blue eyes gleaming in the moonlight. "I'll find her. And judging from the feel of these rocks, I should be able to tunnel under them until we reach the beach on the north side of the island."

"Get her away from here and out of the fire," Giovanni said in a low voice as his skin swirled with contained blue flames. "She's my first concern."

"I'll protect the girl. You two take care of the rest."

Giovanni nodded, and Tenzin grasped Carwyn's hand and took to the air, leaving the fire vampire glowing like a blue torch on the rocky outcropping.

He took deep breaths, crouching down and focusing his energy outward and away from his body. He meditated on the flames, feeling the powerful hum as they coursed over him. Every flare off his skin made him stronger, and he closed his eyes as he balanced on the heady edge of control.

"Father, will there always be war?"
"What did Plato say?"
"He said, 'It is only the dead who have seen the end of war.'"
"And if there is to be war, what is our role?"
"Victory."
"And nothing less."

He looked up when Tenzin landed next to him, her soft clothes fluttering in the wind. She held out her hand and he pulled back the flames to clasp her palm in his.

"Carwyn said he could smell her close to where we landed. Give him a few minutes and he'll send a signal."

Giovanni nodded and took a deep breath as he knelt to wait.

CARWYN SCUTTLED ALONG THE EDGE OF THE CLIFFS, THE ANCIENT ROCKS OF the Aegean coast reaching out to meet his bare hands and feet as he climbed along the face of the cliff. He could see the guards patrolling the trail that connected the rooms of Lorenzo's compound, but he was searching for the chamber where the girl's scent was strongest. He'd caught a hint of her as he landed, and he followed her trail farther to the end of the cliff where it was strongest around one room.

Reaching out with his senses, he could hear the faint sound of a human heartbeat and a murmur as if someone was talking in their sleep. He crawled nearer to one closed door.

"Dad...no. Don't want...no, Gio..."

She was inside the room, and she was having a nightmare. Waiting for the turn of the guard, Carwyn leapt onto the trail and rushed the door. He punched through the metal with ease, his two fists spreading and peeling back the steel door that held her.

Beatrice woke with a gasp, bolting up in bed. "No!"

Carwyn held out a calming hand. "There now, darling girl. Just me. Just old Carwyn."

Her pale face crumbled. "Am I dreaming?"

He shook his head, but held a finger to his lips when he heard the rush of guards coming back down the trail, drawn to the sound of wrenched metal from the door. With a wicked grin, Carwyn decided he would be more than happy to take care of a few of Lorenzo's minions before he got Beatrice to safety.

"Get your things." He winked. "I'll be right back. Don't leave the room."

She nodded and he saw her start to climb out of bed. She was reaching for the dresser when he left the room and ran directly into two guards.

"Hello, dead men." He smiled before he grabbed the first, ripping into his neck with thick fangs and whipping his head around to silence him. At the same time, he grabbed the other with lightening quick reflexes, crushing his throat so he couldn't make a sound. He spat out chunks of the first vampire's windpipe before he threw the second to the ground and stepped on his throat. With a quick turn of his powerful hands, he tore off the head of the first guard and tossed the remains over the cliff, into the ocean below.

Picking up the second guard, he wasted no time, twisting his head off like a screw-cap and tossing him into the ocean to join his partner. He paused for a moment to listen for any others approaching, but heard nothing but the howl of the wind. He was dripping blood from his mouth and chin, so he tore off his shirt and wiped his face, so he didn't alarm Beatrice.

"'*The wicked shall see me and grieve*,'" he murmured as he wiped the gore from his body. He glanced at the churning ocean. "'*They shall gnash with their teeth and melt away.*'"

When he returned to the room, Beatrice was dressed in strange white clothes, and her hair was pulled back from her face. She was thin, almost inhumanly pale, and her hair was different. She ran to throw her arms around him, and he felt her tears hot on his chest.

"I hoped," he heard her whisper. "I didn't know, but I hoped you'd find me."

He pulled back and looked into her face, framing her cheeks with his hands and kissing her forehead. "He moved heaven and earth to find you, darling girl."

He saw her eyes shutter at the mention of his friend, and he frowned.

"We have to go now. They're waiting for my signal."

"How—"

He turned and crouched in front of her. "Stories will have to wait. Climb on my back and hold on tight. I'll need my hands to get out of here, so I can't carry you. You have to make sure you hold on."

"Okay."

"No matter what happens." He looked over his shoulder. "Keep your head down and hold on to me until I let you down or Gio takes you off, do you understand?"

"Yes!" She glanced at the door. "Please, can we go now?"

He grinned when he felt her climb on his back and grip his neck. Her legs swung around his waist like a child.

Patting her leg, he said, "Ready to go?"

"I've been ready for weeks."

He strode from the room with Beatrice clutching his back. Walking over to a column of stones the size of an old Greek pillar, he gave a mighty shove and pushed the pillar into the ocean. There was a brief pause before he saw Giovanni's blue flames flare higher as he and Tenzin took to the sky.

"Remember." Carwyn grinned. "Hold on tight."

He felt her gasp when the ground beneath his feet opened up and swallowed them.

Giovanni watched as the grey rock tumbled into the surf. He could hear the shouts of the vampires above as they rushed to investigate the disturbance. He met Tenzin's steady eyes.

"My boy, is there anyone we need alive?"

Giovanni glanced at the dead girl who lay at their feet.

"No."

He grasped her hand and she leapt, pulling him with her as she took flight.

They landed on the edge of the cliff and Tenzin raised her arms, sending a great rush of wind into the open salons where Lorenzo held court. The vampires inside were stunned into momentary submission and Giovanni and Tenzin separated to begin their assault.

Lorenzo's guards spotted them, and no less than fifteen ran toward them, but as each approached, Tenzin reached out a small hand, capturing them in a swirling vortex of air as she lifted them into the sky. With a flick of her small hands, she grabbed half of them, flinging them toward Giovanni, who paused to toss roiling flames into each small whirlwind.

The captured vampires screamed and twisted as they burned in midair, lighting up the dark sky until their charred bodies turned to ash, and they drifted into the sea.

Giovanni took out the rest with a wall of fire he forced into a corner of the room. The guards tried to run, but were cornered by the flames. Their inhuman screams tore through the night air, as some of Lorenzo's guard ran toward them, and others fled into the rocks.

Tenzin and Giovanni worked together in brutal concert, capturing and annihilating each vampire that came at them until most ran in the other direction or fled to the churning water.

But as they leapt, Giovanni noticed the sea began to grow, pulled by an unseen force as the waves crashing at the base of the cliffs rose until they spilled over and flooded the luxurious rooms. The humans in attendance, who had been cowering away from the assault of fire and wind, started screaming and rushing toward the interior doors.

From the corner, Giovanni caught a flash of blond hair and Lorenzo's grin as the water vampire manipulated the ocean toward them.

"I see him," he yelled to Tenzin.

"Go!"

A stinging rain began to beat upon his back, dousing the fire before he could fling it at his son, and he saw a large wave surge over the edge of the cliff where it grabbed Tenzin before she could take to the air. She disappeared from view, and he stalked toward the corner where he had seen his child.

"Lorenzo!" he roared, striding toward him. Giovanni heard a demented giggle before his son pushed a panel in the back wall, and a door slid open. He ducked into a dark passage which must have led further into the cliffs. A surge of new guards attacked then, and Giovanni no longer had the ready flames at his fingertips.

He was twisting the head from one attacker when he felt a slashing pain across his chest. He looked down to see a bullet wound that had glanced off. He tossed the dead vampire to the side and grabbed the human holding the gun by the throat. With one quick toss, he flung him into the churning ocean before he turned back to the rest of the guards.

He hadn't seen Tenzin in a few minutes, and he cursed, knowing that if the five thousand year old wind vampire had any weakness, it was fighting in water.

He battled on, grabbing the rest of his attackers with long arms, pulling the guards to his fangs so he could rip and shred their throats. One by one, he twisted their heads from their bodies and tossed them on the ground, batting away the last of the humans who tried to defend their masters.

Most who came at him appeared to be water-born, but none of them had the strength of Lorenzo. The most they could do was keep him from building up any more flame as he crossed the room his son had soaked with a wave.

Giovanni paused when he got to the passageway, searching for Tenzin as he turned, and grunting in relief when he saw his old partner. She was perched on the edge of the cliff, darting over and around her attackers as she ripped at them with her talon-like fangs and tiny hands. She moved so quickly he could barely track her, but she paused in midair to meet his eyes.

"Go! Find him," she yelled before grasping two vampires by the necks and swinging them around until their bodies detached and sailed into the sea. Though her attackers were all larger, no vampire he had ever seen could overpower Tenzin in combat, and Giovanni had no fear she would fail to best the few determined guards that tried to defend their fortress.

"Go!" she yelled. "He's getting away!"

He nodded and ducked into the passageway, sniffing the damp air when he came to a turn. His path led him down twisting corridors until he smelled the ocean again. Listening at a heavy door where Lorenzo's scent had ended, he could hear the sound of a boat engine start up. He tried to push through, surprised when it would not budge.

The mystery was solved when he saw sea water leaking from under the edge. He realized Lorenzo must have walled off the door with ocean water, which meant there was a lagoon somewhere in the caves that led to the open sea.

He would never break through the wall before Lorenzo could escape, so he rushed back up to the cliffs, yelling at Tenzin as he ran.

"Boat! He has a boat, Tenzin."

She nodded and sank her teeth into one more neck before she tore her mouth away, dripping with blood and sinew from her opponent's throat.

She saw Giovanni running toward the edge of the cliff and started toward him.

"Catch me!" he yelled, as he flung himself over the edge.

She swooped down and caught him by the waist, grabbing his legs with her own as she flew them down to the base of the cliffs to search for a crevice where a boat could escape.

"It could be anywhere," she yelled. Giovanni could feel her struggle as she concentrated on keeping the air currents flowing around them so they stayed aloft.

"The cliffs only dominate the southern portion. It has to be here."

His eyes roamed over the dark cliff face, searching for the telltale flash of white from an emerging boat.

He heard it before he saw it; the black craft ripped out of the small cave, but its dark surface camouflaged it in the black sea. His ears followed the sound until his eyes caught the churning, white wake as it left the bay and sped toward the open ocean.

"Speed up!"

"I'm trying!" she yelled. "I would have fed on one of the humans if I knew I would be flying this low."

The lower she flew, the more energy Tenzin expended keeping them in the air.

"Just get me closer," he yelled. "I'll try to stop the boat."

He tried to build enough fire in his hands and arms, but the ocean air was thick and misty, dampening his energy when he tried to create a spark.

"Here!"

He snarled when Tenzin stopped abruptly, but calmed down when he saw her draw a cigarette lighter out of her pocket. Catching the flame, he coaxed it into a substantial fireball, and they sped off, cutting through the air toward the quickly disappearing boat.

"We're not going to catch him, Gio."

"Yes, we will!"

The trail of wake was getting farther away.

"Speed up, Tenzin."

"Gio—"

"Faster!"

"We can't catch him, my boy," she shouted over the wind.

He shouted every ancient curse he knew.

"Throw your fire. Try to catch the boat."

"I'm too far."

"Aim better!"

He narrowed his eyes, focusing on the small boat in the distance and aiming toward Lorenzo's white shirt he could barely see flapping in the wind. With a great roar, Giovanni flung the ball of fire toward his son and he felt Tenzin halt, throwing out her hands to speed the flames toward the distant vampire.

It grew and sped, finally finding its target, and Giovanni heard Lorenzo scream briefly before the flames engulfed him. He could see his son's clothes catch fire, and the flames burned his hair as Giovanni watched Lorenzo's skin slowly char to black.

The boat continued speeding through the water, but the water vampire stumbled to the side, flinging himself into the ocean where he sank out of sight.

He could feel Tenzin sag as she held him, and he bit into his own wrist, holding it up so she could drink and regain her strength. He flinched when he felt her curled fangs dig deep into his arm.

Soon after the first draw, he felt her strength returning, and they rose toward the shoreline. They landed in a heap on a grey outcropping to watch Lorenzo's black boat speed empty into the distance, its pale passenger still alive, and somewhere on the bottom of the ocean floor.

"We'll never find him in the water," Tenzin said.

"No." He cursed internally. "And he knows it."

"He's not dumb, your son."

"No, he's not." He curled his lip, narrowing his eyes as he searched the waves, though he knew Lorenzo could stay under the water for days, possibly longer, regaining his strength, safely cocooned in his element.

"Will he come after her again?"

"He'll be recovering for a while—years from the damage I saw. With his vanity and those burns, we may not see him for quite some time."

"But we will see him again," Tenzin said.

He shook his head and closed his eyes in frustration.

"I have no doubt."

"Another day, my boy. You'll get him another day."

He had to smile at her cheerful tone. For anyone as old as Tenzin, a few years was no time to wait.

"Is that a prophesy?" he smiled bitterly. "Or just experience, bird girl?"

She winked at him. "Maybe a bit of both. Now, let's go find your woman."

He tensed, simultaneously nervous and desperate to see Beatrice again.

"She's not my woman."

The small vampire laughed. "She will be."

Across the island, Carwyn and Beatrice pushed through the softer soil of the northern coast and emerged from the earth. Tunneling through the sheer rock of the southern cliffs, then the softer rock of the northern hills had been one of the strangest experiences of Beatrice's life. They had moved as if they were in a small bubble, the rock and soil parting in front of them, only to form again behind them as they maneuvered north. Every now and then, Carwyn would change direction, telling her they needed to avoid tree roots, or an underground stream. She clung to him throughout the journey, often burying her face in the back of his neck to avoid falling debris.

She looked like a cross between a monkey and a miner when she emerged, still clinging to Carwyn's back. Beatrice slipped to the ground and both of them brushed soil from their faces and cleared their throats.

"And that's how you travel earth-vamp style, Beatrice. Ready for that seaside cave in Hawaii yet?" Carwyn said as he coughed out dust. They walked toward the water, sitting down on the slope of a hill that led to the ocean.

Suddenly, she burst into laughter, which quickly turned to tears, the weeks of tension and fear overflowing as he put a comforting arm around her. Carwyn didn't tell her to stop or calm down, letting her release the horror of her captivity as he held her in his comforting embrace.

Eventually, he rubbed small circles on her back as she leaned into him, her tears creating small rivulets on his dust-covered skin.

"I thought I would die there. I thought you had forgotten about me."

"No." He cleared his throat. "Never, darling girl. We didn't forget about you."

She sat sniffing next to him, trying to compose herself. She wiped the tears from her eyes, smudging her face with streaks of salty mud.

"So, what's happening? Where do we go from here?"

"We're supposed to meet the destructive duo here, and we'll swim out to that boat and sail away." He pointed out into the water and she could barely make out the frame of a sailboat off in the distance. "How well do you swim?"

She snorted. "Not that well, but I guess I'll manage." She looked down at herself. "I might go wash some of this dust off. I'm filthy."

"Good idea." They walked down the hill, Beatrice enjoying the stretch of her legs and the beautiful sloping beach in front of her.

"So, B, what's with the all-white makeover?"

"News flash: Lorenzo is a sick, creepy asshole."

Carwyn halted and placed a hand on her shoulder. "He didn't—"

"No," she shook her head. "He didn't touch me. Just lots of mind games."

"Gio said he wouldn't," Carwyn muttered.

She clammed up at the mention of the vampire who had yet to arrive.

"I think," she paused and looked around, "I needed to stretch my eyes more than anything. I thought that room would be the last thing I'd see."

"Welcome back," he said with a smile.

They splashed into the water, Carwyn leaping like a dog before he stood and shook, droplets flying everywhere as he gave a joyful roar. Beatrice closed her eyes and sank down into the warm Mediterranean, caressing the tiny pebbles beneath her, letting her head slip underwater as she floated in the surf. She stretched and twisted, enjoying the natural buoyancy the ocean provided her sore muscles. Finally, she walked back up the beach and sat next to Carwyn to wait for her other two rescuers.

"Did it take you a long time to find me?"

She saw him nod out of the corner of her eye. "It took a while to narrow down the island. And then...it's kind of complicated. You should probably ask Gio."

She ignored his last statement. "How long has it been? I don't even know."

"Six weeks."

She took a deep breath and frowned, trying to remember what day that would make it.

"It's the last day of July."

"Right." She nodded. "Right. Is my grandma okay? Does she know what happened?"

"Isadora and Caspar are fine. Worried about you, but fine. Gio told them you had been taken, and—"

"But, I wasn't taken."

"What?"

She turned to him with hollow eyes. "I wasn't taken, Carwyn, I was traded."

His face fell. "Beatrice, you need to talk to Gio—"

"No, I don't." She shook her head. "I appreciate you coming to get me, but let's not pretend it didn't happen. Whatever his reasons, he traded me for what he thought was more important." Her voice was hoarse as she stared into the water, but the set of her shoulders was fixed.

"Hey," he said, leaning forward to try to catch her eyes. "I know you're resentful, and I understand why, but you need to listen to me."

She dragged her gaze to his, and she was reminded how ancient Carwyn ap

Bryn was behind his boyish charm. His blue eyes bored into hers, and his voice was low and even.

"Whatever you may be feeling right now, you need to remember this: No one goes to war for a pawn."

Tears spilled down her cheeks and she looked away. She saw him shake his head from the corner of her eye.

"You don't know…he's been *wrecked* with worry for you. The worst I've seen in three hundred years. Please believe that."

She choked out, "I'm not saying you would lie to me—"

"I'd never—" he cleared his throat, "never lie to you." He paused. "But he would. Gio would." He ducked his head down and forced her to meet his eyes. "If he thought it was necessary. If he thought it would keep you safe, I think he'd lie to Saint Peter himself."

It was too much. She shook her head, exhaustion beginning to creep up on her.

"I don't understand, Carwyn. And I don't want to talk about this…or about him."

His eyes were pinched with worry. "Don't you love him, B?"

The echo of the crashing waves tore at her. "Not anymore."

Carwyn said nothing, sitting next to her as she stared at the small boat in the distance. Soon, she heard the whisper of voices in the wind, and she braced herself.

Tenzin and Giovanni dropped to the beach and he stepped toward her, his eyes guarded when she lifted her gaze. She squinted, barely recognizing him. The forbidding soldier in front of her, wearing charred black cargo pants and slick healing burns across his chest, bore little resemblance to the polite academic who had charmed her in the university library. His hair was shaved close to his skull and his eyes were wary. Beatrice thought he looked like one of the busts of the Roman generals she had seen in museums. He looked as if he had just come back from a war.

"No one goes to war for a pawn."

He stood in front of her, waiting for a few moments before his composure cracked and he pulled her up and embraced her, clasping her to his chest as he buried his face in her neck and inhaled. His arms wrapped around her in an almost vice-like grip, and one hand cradled the back of her head.

Tears filled her eyes, but part of her wanted to grab onto him, and the other part wanted to strike him, so she stood confused and motionless in the circle of his arms.

He lingered for a few moments, but could not have missed the fact that she did not return his embrace. He took a step back, smoothing her limp hair from her face, brushing at the tears on her cheeks, and inspecting her from head to toe as Beatrice stared at the slowly healing burns on his chest.

"No problems getting here, Gio. Everything according to plan," she heard Carwyn murmur.

Giovanni nodded, his eyes never leaving her, and motioned to the small woman behind him. "Beatrice, this is Tenzin. She will fly you out to the boat; Carwyn and I will swim to meet you. Will that be acceptable?" he asked gently.

Beatrice glanced at the small woman, who really looked more like a girl. Tenzin had a friendly smile and curling fangs showing behind her lips. She glanced over her shoulder at Carwyn, who nodded reassuringly, so she held out her hand.

"Hi, I'm B."

"It's good to meet you. I've heard a lot about you." Tenzin grasped her hand, and Beatrice noted the delicate, cool flesh, just slightly warmer than Lorenzo's hands.

"You too. Thanks for helping get me out."

"My pleasure." Tenzin grinned, and Beatrice couldn't ignore the blood stains that caked the front of the small woman's shirt. Tenzin caught her looking, but only gave a shrug.

Beatrice blinked and looked across the ocean. "You can carry me to the boat?"

"Just hold my hand, the wind will carry us."

A small smile flickered across Beatrice's face. "Really?"

"Really." Tenzin nodded. "Let's get out of here. It's damp."

Beatrice nodded and looked for Carwyn, but her eyes were caught by Giovanni's penetrating gaze.

He was standing at attention, staring at her, his arms behind his back and his shoulders square. She had the sudden disarming impression that he was hers to command, and an unreadable expression filled his green eyes.

"Whenever you are ready, Beatrice."

Turning back to Tenzin, she held out her hand.

"Let's go."

CHAPTER 23

Giovanni watched as she slept, taking advantage of the last moments of calm before he knew she would wake, furious and argumentative.

He glanced around the plush compartment of the plane he had taken from Lorenzo. The weeks he had spent in Rome manipulating the ancient vampires of Livia's court, and the necessary maneuvers in Athens might have been maddening, but ultimately they had netted him exactly what he wanted, with a few unexpected extras thrown in.

He shifted closer to her, worried she would wake and relive her captivity with the madman he had sired. She had refused to speak to him for the most part, communicating mainly through Carwyn and Tenzin. To say it had not bothered him would have been inaccurate, though he knew it was to be expected after his perceived betrayal.

He lifted a hand, stroking her brown hair in a gesture he knew she wouldn't allow if she was awake. He hadn't had a chance to hunt before they left Greece, but he leaned closer anyway, drawing in her welcome scent despite the growing burn in his throat.

He dreaded her fury when she woke and discovered she was not back in Houston. She had screamed at him, refusing to board the plane when she discovered it wasn't going back to the United States.

"I want to go home. I don't want to talk to my grandmother on the phone, I want to see her. I want to go home."

"Beatrice, we need to get you somewhere safe until we can make sure—"

"You're still holding me captive, you bastard! You can go to hell, for all I care, but I want to go home. Take me home!"

Her words burned, and he'd almost given in and taken her back to Texas, but Tenzin had walked over, calmly placed a hand on Beatrice's arm and knocked her out, catching her as she slumped into unconsciousness.

Carwyn loaded her on the custom built airplane bound for one of his children's most remote territories in the south of Chile, where it would be winter and the days would be short. Giovanni had kept a safe house there for over one hundred and fifty years, and no one but the priest and his daughter's family knew exactly where it was.

He felt her begin to stir and stopped stroking her hair, backing away from her but staying within arm's reach in case she panicked. Tenzin had no clothes that would fit her, so Beatrice was dressed in a pair of sweatpants and one of Giovanni's black shirts.

She woke with a start, reviving from Tenzin's amnis and sitting up with a choking gasp. She searched the compartment with panicked eyes until they settled on him. He froze, not wanting to startle her, allowing her to take in her surroundings along with his presence. After a few seconds, her eyes narrowed and she flung herself at him, slapping his face and pushing his shoulders.

"I hate you! *I hate you!*"

He let her release her anger for a few minutes, finally grabbing her hands to halt her punches so she didn't hurt herself. Though Giovanni had not wept in five hundred years, he felt as if he might when he saw her useless rage and the tears that coursed down her cheeks.

"I know," he whispered.

"I want to go home," she cried. "Why won't you just take me home?"

She tried to hit him again but couldn't move as he held her, so she twisted away and threw herself on the opposite couch, glaring at him. He took a deep breath.

"It's not safe."

"You don't know that, asshole. And I can't believe you used your mind voodoo on me on top of everything else."

"That was Tenzin."

"Then I'm pissed off at her, too."

She fell silent, staring at a chair in the back of the compartment where he had noticed Lorenzo's smell was particularly strong.

"What did he do to you?"

"What do you care?"

He rushed over to kneel in front of her at vampire speed, ducking down and forcing her to meet his eyes.

"What do I care? I have spent the last six weeks doing nothing but trying to get you back, Beatrice. I spent weeks narrowing down where Lorenzo was keeping you. Then I spent weeks in Rome and Athens negotiating to make sure you weren't going to be caught in a war when I got you away from him. I called on centuries of alliances and personal debts so his allies would not try to take you back or retaliate against Carwyn, Tenzin, and all their families and allies for helping me."

He sat back on his heels, his eyes locked with hers as he began to see cracks in her angry shell.

"Be angry with me, Beatrice. Rail at me and slap me," he said more softly. "Feel betrayed if you want to, but don't ask me if I care. And *don't* ask me to take you someplace where I cannot assure your safety while you recover."

She looked away, unwilling to meet his eyes. They sat in silence for the rest of the flight over the Atlantic, and Giovanni began to feel drowsy as the pull of day dragged him toward sleep.

Tenzin had influenced the pilot, assuring them he would set the plane down in the private airfield outside of Santiago and safeguard it until the sun had set. From there, Carwyn's daughter, Isabel, had arranged a small customized plane to Puerto Montt, and after that, ground transport into the interior of Chilean Patagonia.

By dawn the next day, they would be in Giovanni's safe house in the Cochamó Valley.

Beatrice had slipped into fitful sleep by the time he stretched out on the ground next to her, finally succumbing to exhaustion.

When he woke, the plane was on the ground and she was staring at him.

"I've never seen you sleep before."

He frowned. "I don't think anyone has seen me sleep...maybe since Caspar was very young." He blinked to clear his eyes. "He would crawl all over me as a child, trying to wake me up to play. It's very hard to wake me, though it is possible."

"You don't breathe at all."

He shook his head slightly. "I only breathe out of habit when I'm awake. And to smell the air."

She continued to stare at him, and he lay motionless, letting her examine him from head to toe. He was still wearing the black cargo pants that had been burned in the assault on Lorenzo's compound, but he had changed into a clean black t-shirt that was not soaked in blood.

"Why did you cut your hair?"

"I burned it the night he took you."

"Because you got angry?"

He nodded, but remained silent when she frowned.

"But you traded me for your books."

He sat up and crouched in front of her as she perched on the bench. This time, she did not avoid his gaze.

"Do you really think he was going to leave without you that night? There were two of his own men in the house and two more you didn't see guarding the grounds. Don't think about what he *said*, think about what you know of him now. Would Lorenzo have left without you?"

She met his questioning gaze for a few minutes before she looked away. Giovanni waited to see if she would respond, but after a few minutes of silence, he rose to grab the large black duffel near the door. He stood at attention near the exit to the sealed compartment, until Beatrice stood and walked over to him.

"Where are we going?"

He held a hand out to her. "Someplace safe."

"For how long?"

He hesitated for a moment, but decided to take a chance. "As long as you want."

She looked down at the duffel bag and then at his outstretched hand. Finally, she grasped it, and he helped her off the plane.

Northern Patagonia, Chile

Six hours before dawn they were bumping through the rough terrain of the Lakes region on the way to the trailhead leading to the Cochamó Valley. It was pitch black on the forest road, but the skies were clear and Giovanni was grateful they would not have to battle any rain as they made their way to his most southern home.

She had fallen asleep again, nodding onto his shoulder where he had secured her with one arm so she would be more comfortable in the back of the Range Rover. She'd slept far more than seemed normal, and he suspected it had more to do with stress than physical exhaustion.

He tried to remember back to his first months of captivity after his sire had taken him, but the human memories were so clouded, Giovanni had trouble remembering exactly how he had felt.

As they approached the drop-off for the trail head, he began to feel the familiar excitement he always did when he approached the house he considered home more than any other.

Nestled in the Andes Mountains of Southern Chile, the Cochamó Valley was a U-shaped valley cut by glaciers and surrounded by towering granite peaks. Its remote location and lush forests had attracted one of Carwyn's more adventurous daughters over two hundred years before. Now Isabel and her husband,

Gustavo, made it their home, and their clan of vampires silently watched over the small local population. The incursion of tourism had proven to be a challenge, but not an insurmountable one, as the valley remained reachable only by foot, boat, or horseback.

The Range Rover neared the small turnoff, and Giovanni leaned forward, still holding on to Beatrice so she wouldn't fall over. He told the driver to halt and paid him, shaking his hand to make sure the human would have no memory of their trip.

He slung the duffel bag over one shoulder and reached across to lift Beatrice, who remained sleeping. He walked at human speed, so as not to startle her. As he crossed the bridge, he felt her begin to stir.

"Gio?" she mumbled. "Where are we?"

"The last part of the trip, tesoro."

"Why did we get out of the car?"

"There's no road into the valley. I don't suppose you know how to ride a horse?"

She was still half-asleep and rubbed her face into his chest when she responded.

"I rode a pony at the fair when I was little."

He pressed a kiss to the top of her head.

"No matter. I can carry you."

"At least you don't have to worry about breaking a horse like you do a car, huh?"

He smiled, grateful for the sleepy conversation that reminded him of their time together before her abduction.

"I told you once that I missed horses, remember?"

"Mmmhmm, I remember."

She fell silent, and he suspected she had fallen asleep again, but he felt a small shiver shake her frame.

"Are you cold?" He reached up to feel her cheek. It was chilled and her teeth began to chatter.

"Kind of," she said. Giovanni had bought a sweatshirt for her in Santiago, but in the damp, winter air of the valley, he knew it was too thin. He began to heat his arms and chest, taking care not to warm up too quickly and alarm her. She didn't seem startled, but burrowed into his chest and sighed.

"You're like a seat heater in a car."

He smiled again. "There should be more clothes at my house. Isabel said she would bring some warm things to fit you."

"It was so cold in his house," she murmured. "It looked like it should be warm, but I was cold all the time. Cold and damp."

His jaw clenched and he leaned down to brush his lips across her forehead. "I'll make sure you're not cold, Beatrice."

"I know," she said, and he could feel her press her cheek to his chest as he trudged over the muddy ground. "You're always warm."

He could hear the snorting of horses as he approached the trail head. Walking past the last stand of trees, he saw Gustavo standing between three mounts, who huffed and whinnied in the moonlight.

The dark-haired vampire walked toward them, holding his hand out and taking the duffel off Giovanni's shoulder, before he tied it on the back of one of the chestnut mares.

"*¿Está durmiendo?*" Gustavo asked.

"No, she's just sleepy," Giovanni responded in English. "I'll carry her in front of me. Can you lead the other?"

"Of course," Gustavo said with a nod.

"Can you stand for a minute, tesoro?"

She nodded, swaying a bit and blinking at Gustavo as Giovanni climbed on his mount.

"*Mucho gusto,*" she said to their burly host, who smiled in welcome.

"Welcome to the Cochamó Valley, Beatrice De Novo. You are welcome here."

"*Gracias,*" she said as Giovanni held out a hand. Gustavo helped her up and soon she had curled into his chest and fallen asleep to the rocking of their horses as they made their way into the secluded valley. He held her on his lap, making sure she was not chilled as he spoke quietly with Gustavo about local news.

A few hours later, they had reached a large wood-shingled house that butted up to one of the granite cliffs. A covered porch stretched around the low structure and jutted out over a green meadow surrounded by towering trees. The interior was lit, and Giovanni could see dark smoke coming from the chimney.

Beatrice woke when they stopped in front of the house and waited for Giovanni to dismount. He held out his arms and she slid to the ground, stretching muscles that would be sore from the four hour trek.

"I'll put these in the stable for you," Gustavo said as he grabbed the halter of Giovanni's horse. "You can use them while you're here, I'll send one of the Reverte boys over to tend them in the morning."

"Thank you, Gustavo."

Beatrice looked around. The house was clearly visible in the moonlight, and its small windows glowed gold. He could hear Isabel puttering inside and knew his friend would have already stocked the house with everything Beatrice might need for her stay.

"This is my home. Isabel and Gustavo let me build here many years ago."

She looked around. "It's beautiful."

He nodded and motioned her up the path. "It should be warmer inside. Isabel has already started a fire."

"She's Carwyn's daughter?"

"Yes, and Gustavo is her husband. Their clan watches the valley."

"Clan?" She frowned in confusion as they walked toward the house.

"They're earth vampires."

"What does that mean?"

He continued walking and she followed beside him. "Earth vampires are very domestic. Like Carwyn, they tend to settle and have big families. They usually prefer remote places like this."

They climbed onto the porch and she followed him when he stomped the mud off his boots and placed them under a bench. He opened the door and showed her in, immediately taking a deep breath to enjoy the familiar scent of home.

"Giovanni?" he heard Isabel call from the kitchen, walking toward them with open arms.

He glanced over at Beatrice, curious how she would perceive the friendly vampire. Like her father, Isabel was one of the most loyal and friendly immortals he had ever met, and her gracious demeanor spilled out in her greeting. Unlike Carwyn, she was Spanish, appeared to be in her late forties, and was around the same age Giovanni was in vampire years.

She kissed both his cheeks as they exchanged quiet greetings.

"Beatrice." She turned to the girl. "It's wonderful to meet you. I'm sure you're exhausted after your journey, so we must visit another time. There are clothes in the front bedroom, and the bathroom is stocked. There are no electric lamps, but there is running water and plenty of candles throughout the house."

Giovanni scowled, forgetting that Beatrice might be disturbed by the lack of electricity in the valley. She didn't say anything except a quiet 'thank you' as Isabel kissed both her cheeks and departed. He showed her down the hall and indicated two doors.

"This is your room for as long as you want it. The bathroom is across from it. My room is at the back of the house," he said. "Part of it is cut into the rocks, but your room has windows, so it won't be dark during the daytime."

"It's fine," she murmured.

He stood motionless, suddenly nervous to be alone with her and wishing he could secure her in his own room.

"Beatrice—"

"I think I'll wash up and go to my room. Are there books I could borrow?"

"There are always books." He nodded toward the front room. "Help yourself to any from the bookcases in the living room. I keep most of my personal collection here."

She smiled for a moment before her eyes clouded. "Fine, I'll figure it out tomorrow."

"Did you want me to—"

"Good night," she said abruptly. "I'll see you tomorrow."

He nodded silently, confused by the sudden shift in her demeanor. He checked the doors, windows, and any other access points, securing them before he went to his room in the back of the house. He was reluctant to leave her, even with the knowledge of Isabel and Gustavo's ever-present guards, but he sensed she wanted to be alone.

Giovanni could feel the pull of dawn dragging him under when he heard the first soft cries from her room, and when he dreamed, her accusing eyes haunted him.

He woke when the sun set and threw on a pair of pants before he went to Beatrice's room, noticing that her scent lingered in the hallway outside his door. He stood in the hallway, listening for her, but did not sense anyone in the house. Walking out to the kitchen, he noticed traces of her littering the main room, and a fire burned in the large stone hearth. No note indicated her whereabouts, and he immediately began to worry. He walked out to the porch, still barefoot, and searched the dim forest.

His ears picked up Isabel's voice calling through the trees. "Cálmate, Gio. You pace like an irritated cat. She's at our house; some of the boys were teaching her to ride. She's fine."

He halted on the porch, waiting for Isabel to emerge from the trees before he responded.

"She needs to leave me a note if she's going to leave the house. I was about—"

"Ay, yes, you'd burn down your lovely piece of forest with worry. You're such an old man. Calm down."

He sank into one of the large chairs that decorated the porch and scowled. "I am the same age as you."

Isabel rolled her eyes. "You know what I mean. And put some clothes on. You're not impressing me with your muscles and I'm cold just looking at you." She pretended to shiver as he opened his mouth to respond, but she only held up a hand. "I don't care if you're a walking space heater. Go get dressed."

Scowling, he went back to his room to change into a pair of the jeans he kept at the house and a long-sleeved thermal shirt. He walked back to Isabel, who sat on the porch, staring up at the stars and smiling a little.

"Father said she was bright, but I didn't really believe him." She winked at Giovanni as he leaned against a dark wooden post and stared into the forest. "A human? And after all, who in her right mind would get involved with you?"

"You're so amusing," he said as he scanned the tree line, searching for a hint of her.

"But she is. Very smart. And bold. She found her way to the lodge house today and tried to find someone to teach her how to ride a horse." Isabel let out a tinkling laugh. "She had this very elaborate story worked out for Esteban's family, because she didn't know what they knew about us. They let her know she didn't have anything to hide, and then one of the boys started giving her lessons."

"Which one?"

"Does it matter?" she asked with a curious brow. "Oh, I see that it does."

She smiled innocently and looked toward the trees again. "One of the big strapping ones that leads the rock-climbing trips, I think."

Giovanni growled and walked down the porch steps before she started laughing at him. "She's with Gustavo now, calm yourself. He'll bring her back shortly."

He curled a lip at her, but she just chuckled. He'd never had an older sister as a human, but had always imagined if he had, she would have been a lot like Isabel. He walked back onto the porch and sat next to her in a chair. He could feel the weight of unasked questions hanging over them as they waited for Beatrice to return.

"What happened to the girl, Giovanni? Her eyes are too sad for someone so young."

"I can't—" He cleared his throat. "You need to ask her that question. It's her story to tell when she wants."

"You infuriating man. I only put up with your secrets because I know you do it to everyone."

"It's not my place—"

"Blah, blah, blah. I've heard it a million times, you don't have to repeat yourself," she muttered. "At least I know if I tell you a secret, your lips are sealed."

He shrugged and watched the trail leading to the lodge. He could hear the faint sounds of Beatrice and Gustavo as they made their way through the forest, and his heart started a quick beat. Isabel must have heard it, and she looked at him.

"Are you in love with her?"

He stood up and walked to the railing, unwilling to share his feelings, even with someone he trusted as much as Isabel.

"I think you are." She paused before she continued quietly. "She's very young, my friend."

He nodded. "I know."

"And she's been hurt."

"Yes."

She stared at him until he met her dark, piercing gaze. He could hear Beatrice and Gustavo coming through the forest.

Isabel took a deep, calming breath. "I'll pray for you. For both of you."

His head turned when the two riders broke through the trees. He watched Beatrice ride the horse through the lush meadow. Her skin was pale and almost seemed to glow in the twilight. A healthy flush stained her cheeks, and a smile crossed her face as she listened to something Gustavo was joking about; but the light did not reach her eyes when they finally met his.

"Thank you, Isabel. For your help. For everything."

"You are welcome, my friend. You are both welcome."

Giovanni and Beatrice fell into a careful rhythm together in Cochamó, as they had from the beginning of their relationship. She explored the valley during the day, accompanied by one of the human family that worked for Gustavo and Isabel running the small tourist lodge. She would come back to the house to eat a quiet meal and read before going to sleep. There was no electricity in the house, but stone fireplaces warmed every room, and running water came from an old tower that stood next to the stable.

They spoke little, and her silence, which usually soothed him, began to tug at him the longer it continued. She would not speak about her time with Lorenzo, and only occasionally would their conversation venture farther than incidental information about the valley or its residents.

Worse than her silence were the weeping dreams she had every night when she finally fell asleep. He sat, silently crouched outside her bedroom door for hours, as she cried and murmured in her sleep and the memories tormented her. Her heart raced, and he could scent her panic throughout the house. As much as he tried to respect her privacy, eventually Giovanni tried to enter her room and wake her, only to find the door locked tight.

By the seventh night, he could no longer take the escalating nightmares.

"Dad...no," she sobbed. "Gio, don't...don't let them—" She broke off and he could hear her cries come through the thick wooden door.

He rose from his knees and pushed his way inside, breaking the lock in one swift shove before he walked to her bed and knelt beside her, anxiously stroking her hair.

"Beatrice," he said through gritted teeth, "please, wake up. *Please*—"

Her eyes flickered open and he cupped her face in his hands, brushing the tears away with his thumbs as she stared at him with swollen eyes.

"Tell me what to do," he whispered desperately. "I cannot...what would you have me do? I will do anything—"

"Don't let them take me," she said in a hollow voice.

Giovanni gave a hoarse groan and pulled her into his arms, clutching her to his chest as he rocked her. She tensed for a moment, but finally heaved a great sigh and let her head rest on his shoulder. He sat on the bed, stroking her hair and rocking her back and forth.

He cradled her as the waning moon streamed through her window. Finally, he reached over to the bedside table and lit a candle. He was wearing only a pair of loose pants, and he felt her tears hot on his chest.

"Do you want to forget?" he asked. "I can make you forget. Maybe everything. Is it better that way?" He ignored the ache in his chest, and waited for her to respond.

"Will *you* remember?"

He tilted her face toward his, memorizing the silver tracks on her cheeks and her swollen eyes. He locked away the sound of her nightmares in his mind, and took a deep breath, inhaling the scent of her panic as it stained the air.

"Yes. I will remember everything."

She nodded, and he finally saw a familiar hint of steel return to her eyes.

"If you can remember, I can remember."

He bent his head and kissed her softly on the forehead, then on each cheek, and finally laid a soft kiss on her mouth, as if sealing a promise. She made no move to leave his embrace, so he tucked her head under his chin and leaned against the headboard.

"Giovanni?"

"Yes?"

"Tell me your story."

He closed his eyes and hugged her, letting out a sigh before he began in a low voice.

"My name is Jacopo, and I was seven when my Uncle Giovanni found me..."

CHAPTER 24

She listened for hours, wrapped in his warm arms as he told her the tale of a small boy, plucked out of poverty by the friends of a beloved uncle. He had been an indulged child after his early years, fed a steady diet of art, philosophy, religion, and learning in a time of flowering human achievement.

Count Giovanni Pico della Mirandola, after adopting his older brother's illegitimate son, treated Jacopo more like a cherished younger brother than a bastard. His three friends; Angelo Poliziano, the scholar, Girolamo Benivieni, the poet, and Girolamo Savonarola, the monk; followed suit.

The four surrounded the boy with knowledge and love, each contributing a part to the young man he became, and each unaware of the hovering danger that lurked in the beautiful form of Signore Niccolo Andros, a water vampire of unspeakably ancient power.

"When did you first meet him? Your sire?" she asked as he carried her to his bedroom to escape the first stirrings of dawn. He settled her on top of his large bed, then walked back to her bedroom for blankets, since he slept with none.

"Andros?" he called. "My uncle first met him in Lorenzo's court in 1484. It was the same visit to Florence when he first met me."

Giovanni walked back in the bedroom, which was finished in plaster and wood on three walls. The far wall, at the head of the Giovanni's bed, was hewn granite and the candlelight in the room caused the black flecks in the stone to dance.

"I first met Andros when my uncle visited his villa in Perugia. He had collected an extraordinary library and gave my uncle many rare books and manuscripts to study, though I later learned he had always intended to take them back. Andros's books are the real treasure, tesoro. My uncle's books are valuable to me, but Andros's library was legendary."

He arranged the blankets over her before crawling in the bed, and settling a warm arm around her waist. "It had no equal I have ever seen. Greek, Roman, Egyptian, Hebrew, Persian. Even some Sumerian clay tablets. He'd amassed it over twenty-five hundred years, and inherited other manuscripts from his own sire, who I never met. It was an astonishing collection."

Since he'd woken her from the nightmare that had plagued her for weeks, Giovanni couldn't seem to stop touching her. As tumultuous as her feelings toward him were, she found his presence comforting, and his touch seemed to warm the persistent chill that had tormented her since the night she'd fallen into Lorenzo's hands.

"And Lorenzo still has it?"

He shrugged. "He must. It was all housed together after my uncle died. So if he has my uncle's books—"

"At least you got those back, right?"

She felt his arm tighten around her waist.

"I did."

There was a long silence as the memory of that night nudged at her. Finally, she heard him whisper, "I haven't even looked at them."

Her breath caught. "None?"

"Caspar had them shipped here for safekeeping, but..."

She nodded and put her hand over his arm, weaving her fingers with his.

"We should look at them."

"Not tonight."

"No, tell me more about when you met your uncle."

He paused before he continued. "It was all in 1484. It was a very eventful year."

"What else happened?"

She felt him sigh and she curled into his chest. "He met Lorenzo de Medici that trip, and then me, and then Andros, of course. Andros had been lingering in the Medici court."

"Why?"

"Why was my sire in Florence? He told me later he was ready to create a child—he never had before—and he wanted to pick from the brightest of the city." Giovanni propped his head up on his hand and looked at her. "He was looking for a 'Renaissance man,' I suppose. Initially, he set his sights on my uncle, but then my uncle disappointed him."

"How did he disappoint him? Not smart enough?"

"Oh no, my uncle was brilliant," he said wistfully. "No, Giovanni fell in love."

She swallowed the lump in her throat and remembered the slim book of sonnets he'd held in his hand the night she was taken. "With Giuliana?"

He nodded, and lay his head on the pillow next to hers, lifting a hand to play with a strand of her hair. "He met her in Arezzo, visiting an acquaintance. She was married...not her choice, of course, but it never was then. Her husband was cruel and dull. Even Lorenzo hated him, though he was a Medici cousin. But Giuliana and Giovanni...they were so beautiful."

"She was beautiful?"

He paused, and she rolled onto her back so she could see his expression. His eyes were narrowed in concentration while he thought. "It's difficult to say. My human memories are not always clear. I *remember* her as beautiful, but that could be a child's perspective. I remember the way my uncle smiled at her. She was very kind to me; she liked to play games. I don't think she could have any children of her own. She never did in all the time they wrote to each other."

"What happened?"

"She was married, and my uncle was thrown in prison when their affair was discovered. Though Lorenzo de Medici found my uncle entertaining, so he intervened."

"But they stayed in contact?"

He nodded and let his hand stroke along her arm. Everywhere he touched gave her goose bumps, but not from the chill. His energy, which he normally kept on a tight lease, seemed to hum along his skin as he reminisced. She could see him taking longer and longer blinks, and could only assume the sun was rising in the sky.

"They wrote beautiful letters to each other," he said quietly. "He locked them away; I never discovered where he put them."

"But why did that matter to Andros? They couldn't marry anyway, why—"

"My uncle fell into a depression toward the end of his life. After his imprisonment in Paris, he lost his spirit. He stopped writing Giuliana. He no longer had the same joy he'd always carried before. He destroyed his poetry. He burned many of his more progressive philosophical works and corresponded more with Savonarola, who had become so radical by then it taxed even Poliziano and Benevieni's friendship."

"When were the bonfires?"

"The 'bonfire of the vanities?'" he murmured, and she was reminded of the book she had been reading so many months ago when they had first met. His amusement at hearing the title finally made sense and she smiled.

"Yeah, those bonfires."

"It was after I had been taken, but before I was turned. My uncle left me everything; though he wasn't exorbitantly wealthy, his library was substantial and Andros wanted it, so he took it. When Lorenzo told me years later that everything had burned in the fires, it wasn't a stretch to imagine. Many of his books would have been considered heretical, and so many things were lost."

"What did your uncle write about?"

Giovanni smiled wistfully and placed a small kiss on her forehead. "He thought that all human religion and philosophy could be reconciled. That the quest for knowledge was the highest good; and that somewhere, between all the wars and debate, there was some universal truth he could discover which would bring humanity together."

Beatrice paused and watched his green eyes swirl with memories. "He sounds like a wonderful man."

"He was...an idealist."

She reached up to place a small kiss on his cheek, which had grown a dusting of stubble since she had kissed him so many weeks ago at the Night Hawk.

"The world needs idealists."

His hand trailed up from her arm and cupped her cheek. His eyes searched her own before he leaned down to place a gentle kiss on her mouth. It was soft and searching, and she felt his arm pull her closer. She also felt his eyelashes fluttering on her cheek, and knew he was struggling to remain awake.

"Sleep, Gio."

"Will you be here when I wake?" he mumbled, almost incoherent from the pull of day. "There's more..."

"Yes," she whispered. "I'll be here."

Though his arm lay heavy across her waist, and his head slumped to the side, Beatrice felt safe for the first time in weeks, so she closed her eyes and joined him in a dreamless slumber.

When she woke, he was still sleeping, so she pulled away from the tangle of his arms and went to the front of the house. She boiled some water and made black tea to drink on the front porch. When she went outside, there was fresh milk sitting on the porch, and a block of ice for the icebox.

She was surprised by how peaceful she found the simplicity of life in the valley. The house had no electricity, but she didn't miss it as much as she imagined. The fire in the main hearth was constantly burning, and it heated a small water heater by some mechanism she still didn't understand, but appreciated anyway.

Other than the dreams that had plagued her every night, Beatrice had never felt more peaceful, and she understood why Giovanni had wanted her to come to this quiet place. Her soul, as well as her mind, had been refreshed.

She could hear the rustle of someone approaching through the trees, and sat up straighter in instinctive alarm. She relaxed when she saw the oldest son of the Reverte family, who kept the lodge at the base of the valley. Arturo had escorted her over some of the gentler riding trails as she explored the valley. He was riding his favorite horse and leading another one for her.

"*Ciao, Beatriz!*" he called with a smile.

"*Buenos días, Arturo.*"

"*¿Quieres cabalgar?*"

"*No, grácias,*" she said, declining his offer to ride.

"*¿No? Estás segura?*" he asked with a wink.

She thought about getting some fresh air but was unsure of what time Giovanni would wake, so she nodded that, yes, she was sure, and waved him off with a smile. She realized she wanted to be there to hear the rest of Giovanni's story and didn't want to lose time when he woke.

To say she had been stunned to learn he was the orphan the count had adopted, instead of Giovanni Pico himself, was an understatement; though when she thought about her research into the life of the fifteenth century philosopher, the ages had never seemed exactly right. She still had many questions, but she was beginning to understand how valuable the correspondence of his uncle and friends would be to the boy who had loved them.

She ate a small meal and perused the bookcases in the living room. When Giovanni had mentioned his books the first night they'd come to the house, Beatrice had frozen, thrown back to the night he had callously traded her for the books he had sought for so long.

At least that's what she had thought at the time.

Her mind understood what he had been saying since he had rescued her, but a small part of her heart found it difficult to let down her guard around the magnetic man she knew she still loved, though she had trouble admitting it—even to herself.

Beatrice found a harmless paperback and crawled back in bed with the sleeping vampire, who had not moved from the position she left him in.

"Sheesh," she grunted as she shoved his arms over to clear a spot. "You're heavier than you look, Gio."

He just lay there, silent and unbreathing.

"It's probably really evil that I want to draw something on your face right now, isn't it?"

She examined his unmoving form. "I could draw a big, curly mustache, right on your upper lip, and you wouldn't be able to stop me, would you?" She lay down and traced her finger over his upper lip.

"Yep, that would piss you off for sure," she muttered. "You're so damn proud, Giovanni."

Ironically, his face looked childlike in repose, and she found herself wishing the soft curls still covered his forehead so she could brush them away.

"Or should I call you Jacopo?" she murmured.

She liked the feeling of his childhood name in her mouth, so she continued in a soft voice.

"Does anyone else know your name, Jacopo? Does Lorenzo even know?" she said. "I wonder…"

She began to feel tears prick the corner of her eyes, and she lay her head on his chest to stare at him. She heard one soft thud as his heart gave a beat before falling silent again.

"I thought I was in love with him, Jacopo. I think I still am." She blinked away tears. "But I don't trust him anymore, even though I want to."

Suddenly, his expression creased into a slight frown, and he no longer looked like a boy, but the hard man who had killed to get her back.

"Oh," she whispered, "there you are, Giovanni."

She sighed and decided she didn't really want to read, so she curled into his side and fell into another dreamless sleep.

BEATRICE WOKE TO THE FEEL OF A HARD BODY BESIDE HER, AND SOFT LIPS traveling over her neck. She sighed and arched toward it, purring in sleepy pleasure when a large hand cupped her breast. Though her eyes were closed, she could feel them roll back as a mouth traveled along her collarbone, a hot tongue licked up her neck, and she felt the gentle scrape of teeth behind her ear.

His mouth dipped lower, searching, and she could feel her heart begin to pound. The lips grew more urgent and a low rumble issued from the body next to hers. Beatrice's eyes suddenly blinked open when she felt the scrape of pointed teeth again the pulse in her neck.

Giovanni must have still been sleeping, but his body was hard and pressed into hers. His hand caressed her breast, and his other arm pulled her closer as they moved against each other. She was overwhelmed by the pleasure of his touch. Her skin hummed with the transfer of energy, and she could feel the brush of amnis wherever his bare hands or lips touched her flesh.

"Gio," she whispered softly. "Gio, I—" She broke off with a quiet moan of pleasure at the feel of his lips teasing behind her ear.

Giovanni's hand left her breast and moved up to cup her cheek. His thumb brushed against her lips before he wandered back down her body, touching places she had dreamed of for months.

"Tesoro," he breathed out, along with a string of sleepy Italian she didn't understand. They rocked against each other, and her eyes rolled back when she felt his teeth nip at her neck.

Bite me, she thought, unable to say the words aloud. Her heart pounded as his hands and mouth drove her into a frenzy of need, and she reached up to grasp his shoulder as he moved over her.

"Do it," she whimpered, unable to contain her desire as his lips teased her skin. "Please, Giovanni." She felt his mouth close over her neck, and his tongue teased her rapid pulse.

Beatrice thought, in the back of her mind, that it would hurt, at least a little. But though she could feel the quick burst as her skin gave way to his fangs, a wave of pleasure overwhelmed her, and she shuddered in his arms as his mouth latched on to her throat and sucked.

She cried out in release, and she sensed Giovanni rouse to full consciousness. He hesitated for only a second before instinct took hold, and he drew from her vein as his hands clasped her to his body.

Every pull of his mouth was answered as she arched into him, and she could hear soft growls of pleasure as he drank. Her hands dug into the hard muscle of his back, as his soft lips worked her neck and his hands stroked her skin. She was lightheaded, but had the feeling it had less to do with blood loss than the aftershocks of pleasure that coursed through her body.

It was probably only minutes until she felt his fangs retract and his tongue sweep over her skin, licking the last drops of blood as his body shivered, then fell still. He hid his face in her neck and lay next to her, silent and unmoving as a statue as her heart rate evened out.

"Gio?"

"I am...sorry, Beatrice," she heard him whisper. "That was—"

"It's okay."

"No, it's not."

"I wanted you to," she said, pulling his ear until he looked at her.

His green eyes were worried. "You did?"

She nodded and lifted a finger to the drop of blood at the corner of his mouth. She wiped it away, and he caught her finger in his mouth, licking off the last trace of her as his eyes closed in pleasure.

"That wasn't a good idea," he murmured.

"When was the last time you fed before tonight?"

"In Greece."

Her eyes widened in surprise. "You haven't had any blood since we've been here? Not even after you fought?"

"Pigs." He curled his lip. "There are mostly wild pigs in the valley. And I don't drink from the humans out of respect for Isabel and Gustavo. They don't allow it in their clan."

"So even after the battle at Lorenzo's—"

"No," he whispered and lifted a hand to her cheek. "I'm sorry I took advantage of you. It won't happen again."

She snorted. "I don't remember fighting you off. If I had wanted you to stop, I would have yelled at you."

"You didn't worry I would lose control?"

Beatrice took a moment to think. She hadn't worried about him losing control for a second. She had actually been more afraid he would wake up before he bit her, and stop the wave of pleasure that had begun with the feel of his mouth and hands on her body.

"No." She blushed. "I didn't worry about that."

He nodded, and leaned down to place a soft kiss on her mouth before he drew away and rose to leave the bedroom. He grabbed a change of clothes on his way out, and when he came back, he carried a glass of water and a plate of fruit.

"You should drink something, and have something to eat."

"Will you need to feed again?"

He looked at the floor when he answered. He had changed into a pair of loose pants and a t-shirt before he returned to the bedroom. "It depends on how long we stay."

"Oh."

"I don't need to drink as much here as I do in more modern places, and your blood is very rich, so it should satisfy me for a long time. I also drank quite deeply."

She paused and nodded a little. "I guess I taste okay, then. Good to know."

He coughed a little, and his eyes roamed over her body but did not meet her gaze.

"You taste...rather wonderful, actually."

She bit her lip and tried to contain a smile. "I wonder if I should put that on my resume."

He tried to contain himself for a second before bursting into laughter. He finally met her eyes and fell into bed next to her, covering his face with a pillow.

"Are you embarrassed?" she asked incredulously.

"Yes," came the muffled response from under the pillow. "I acted like a newly sired vampire, totally out of control."

"You didn't hear me complaining," she said with a blush. "And before I fell asleep this afternoon, I was thinking about finding a marker and drawing a big curly mustache on your face."

He lifted the pillow and frowned at her as she picked at the plate of dried apples and apricots.

"You wouldn't."

"I didn't, but I thought about it. Don't you feel a little less immature now?"

He cocked an eyebrow at her. "Quite."

Beatrice sat up in bed and began to nibble the fruit and sip the water as he watched her. "What were you really like? When you were new?"

He rolled over and lay on his stomach, crossing his arms under his chin. "Do you really want to know this? It's not pleasant."

"Have you ever told anyone?"

He shook his head, still watching her as she ate.

"Then tell me. Even the ugly parts."

He paused for a moment before he continued to tell his story. "My uncle was murdered in 1494, though I didn't realize it at the time. Andros had been watching us. He had decided that while my uncle would not suit his purposes, I would. He influenced one of the servants to put arsenic in my uncle's food, so he wasted away."

"How old were you?"

"Seventeen."

She tried to imagine him at seventeen, and her hand reached out to stroke the shorn hair that covered his scalp. She smiled when he moved into her touch. His eyes closed, and she could almost imagine him purring like a cat.

"He came to the door only hours after my uncle had died and took me. I was confused when I woke. He had taken me far away, and I was very disoriented."

"Where were you?"

"It was an old Greek settlement in the south of Italy. Crotone," he said the name with disgust. "He had made a kind of school there."

"He was Greek?"

Giovanni nodded, and she continued to stroke his hair. "He was around twenty-five hundred years old when he made me. A contemporary of Homer's, or so he claimed, I never knew whether he was lying or not. He was...crazy. Obsessed."

"With what?"

"*Areté. Aristos. Virtus*, to call it by its Roman name."

"Explain to the non-genius in the room, please."

He chuckled, rolling over and grabbing her hand which he placed over his heart and covered with his own. "Essentially, the perfect man. He wanted a child that personified the utmost in human potential."

"That must have been quite the ego stroke."

He shook his head and looked up at the ceiling, absently tracing the outline of her palm on his chest. "No, I wasn't perfect in the least. I was the raw material."

"You mean—"

"He had to create me, before he sired me."

She frowned. "I don't understand."

His head tilted back as he looked at her with sad eyes.

"Andros held me captive for ten years while he molded me into what he thought was the perfect man. He schooled me, trained me, drilled me to be the most perfect example of humanity he could create. It was...not pleasant."

Suddenly, Giovanni rolled up and knelt in front of her, pulling off his shirt and watching in silence as she stared at him.

"Do you think I'm handsome, Beatrice?"

She blushed, but looked into his eyes when she answered, "Yes, of course."

"Am I strong?" He crawled toward her on all fours, getting inches from her face. She took a deep breath, inhaling the faint smell of smoke that always seemed to linger on his skin.

"Yes."

He leaned into her neck, taking a deep breath before he whispered in her ear, "You smell like honeysuckle, did you know that?"

Her heart was pounding and her body reacted to him instinctively. She leaned toward him and felt his lips brush her temple before he sat back.

"Do I look like a statue? That's what he wanted. He wanted a perfect...specimen to turn, one who excelled physically, mentally, who had strong character."

"So, he made you into the ideal man, and then he killed you?" she choked out, still reeling from his scent and the energy that poured off him.

He gave her a sad smile. "No, then he turned me into a demigod."

"What?" she asked, suddenly wondering if she needed to call Carwyn for an immortal psych consult.

He snorted, "Well, that's what he thought, anyway. He thought vampires were the demigods of Greek mythology."

"Ah, so what you're saying is...he was completely nuts?"

"Absolutely *raving*, tesoro."

She shook her head and watched as he reached over to grab a bit of the dried apricot on her plate.

"And you lived with him for ten years?"

He nodded. "Ten years as a human, and then longer after I was turned. But Lorenzo..." He trailed off when he saw her shiver.

Placing the plate on the small table by the bed, he crawled over to her again, gathering her close and tucking her into his side when he stretched out under the blanket. "I don't know how long he had Lorenzo. And his name as a human was Paulo." Giovanni sighed. "He was a sad thing, always anxious for Andros's attention. Never quite good enough for my father."

"Why was he there?"

Giovanni shrugged. "As a servant mostly, though Father liked to insinuate he would turn Paulo, too, when it was time. Just to keep Paulo happy."

"But he didn't."

"My father..." Giovanni paused with a frown. "He was a complicated vampire. Cruel, horrible, and completely single-minded. But perceptive, as well. He was a genius in his own way, and he saw something in Paulo," he said. "Something I should have paid attention to before my pity overwhelmed my reason."

"What?"

"Cruelty. My father said that Paulo did not have the character necessary to be a good vampire, so he would not turn him."

"When did Lor—Paulo figure that out?" she asked as Giovanni's hand stroked along her hair. She curled into his side and he held her tightly.

He took a slow breath before he answered. "He found out five years after I was turned, the night I persuaded Paulo to kill my father."

Beatrice gasped, but Giovanni was staring at the ceiling, lost in his memories, and wearing a hollow look.

"You mean—"

"I knew I would never get away. He would always be stronger than me, and after he knew I could wield fire, Andros would never have released me. What he had planned, I wanted no part in. I couldn't get away on my own, but I knew I could get away with help. Andros was vulnerable during the day. He was vulnerable to humans if they knew where he rested. If it was someone he thought he had control of. And Paulo was so greedy...for gold, for power."

"What are you saying?"

"So I promised to turn him if he did it."

"Gio, what did you—"

"And I traded my father's life for my son's immortality."

CHAPTER 25

"I think it's time for us to go home."

Giovanni looked at her, nodding silently as their horses rode across the meadow near one of the rushing waterfalls that dotted the valley. They had been riding for two hours after waking in his bed that evening.

"I told you we would stay as long as you liked."

"It's been a month."

He smiled. "I'm impressed you put up with me for this long."

"Well," she said with a wink, "you're a bit of a bed hog, but at least your feet aren't cold."

He chuckled. "Good to know, considering I haven't slept next to anyone in well over a hundred years." In reality, it had been far longer since he'd trusted anyone to sleep next to him when he was defenseless—not counting Caspar as a child—but he didn't feel the need to elaborate.

"Really?"

He shrugged, and continued riding back toward the house.

Though it had tested his control, Giovanni refused to feed from her again, slipping out of the valley to find the nearest larger town to hunt the previous week. Her blood had sustained him for as long as he dared, but he did not want to risk losing control again.

While Beatrice showed no hesitance in furthering their physical relationship, he knew that once he had truly taken her to his bed, his territorial nature, combined with his deepening attachment to her, would make it practically impossible for him to allow her to leave.

"It's not that I'm unhappy here, it's just—"

"You have a life to get back to, Beatrice."

He could hear the hesitation in her voice when she finally answered.

"What will you do? Will you go back to Houston?"

He nodded. "I will. For now."

"Does that mean you'll have to move?"

"I don't know."

He stopped his horse near the small bridge over the stream near his house and waited for her to catch up with him.

"Do you know—"

"I know as much as you do. Carwyn and Tenzin are in Houston, waiting for us to return. I need to talk to them before I make any decisions."

They stared at each other and Giovanni could see the beginning of goodbye fill her eyes. He had not told her he loved her, though he knew he did. He still had doubts that her feelings were more than the product of a youthful infatuation and the stress of their tumultuous time together.

He grabbed her reins and reached across to pull her onto his lap. Giovanni settled his arms around her hips, which had filled out since they had been in Cochamó and rested his chin on her shoulder, drinking in the contact for as long as he could.

He led her mare beside them as they crossed the stream, and warmed her with his arms when a light mist began to fall.

"I love it here," she whispered.

"So do I," he said, thinking more of the girl in front of him than the valley they crossed.

They had spent their nights in peace, sleeping next to each other for most of the day and exploring the valley at night. He had shown her his favorite parts of Cochamó, and they spent hours in the company of Gustavo, Isabel, and their large family, who welcomed Beatrice like an old friend.

"Can I come back sometime?"

He brushed a kiss across her neck. "You can come back any time."

They fell into silence for the rest of the ride. When they returned to the house, he picked up a note someone had slipped under the door.

Father called the lodge.
  -Isabel

He closed his eyes, resigned to the intrusion of the outside world.

SHE LAY NEXT TO HIM LATER THAT NIGHT, CURLED PEACEFULLY INTO HIS SIDE as he read a book before dawn. She'd not had another disturbing dream since the night he had woken her and taken her to his bed; she had slept there every night since.

He thought about a quote from Aristotle he'd never paid much attention to until recent months. "'Love,'" he whispered in Italian, "'is a single soul inhabiting two bodies.'"

He stared at her, wondering if it was so simple, watching in fascination as her eyelids flickered with dreams, and a small smile played at the corner of her mouth.

She still said her father's name often, and he wished he had more answers for her. Stephen De Novo remained impressively elusive, despite Giovanni's most persistent inquiries. He had to admire the young vampire's skills in remaining hidden. He had evaded Lorenzo for years, and even now, remained stubbornly out of Giovanni's reach. He knew he would not stop looking for him, if only to let the vampire know that his daughter knew about him and wanted to find him.

"Gio?" she murmured and reached for him as she slept. Setting his book to the side, he slid down and took her into his arms, wondering again how he would ever let her go.

TWO DAYS LATER, THEY SAT NEXT TO EACH OTHER AS THE PLANE flew north to land at the small private airfield where Beatrice had left Houston over two months before.

"And my grandma and Caspar are at your house?" she asked, clasping his hand in her own.

"Yes, and Carwyn and Tenzin, as well."

"And none of his people are going to come after me?"

"We killed most of them. My negotiations in Rome and Athens should have secured your safety from the rest of his allies."

She nodded quickly, but tightened her grip.

"He's not dead though, is he?"

He felt his fangs fall. "No, I suspect he will be recovering for some time, but he still has resources."

"And he'll come after me again. To get to my father."

He tilted her chin up so she would meet his gaze. "I'll kill him before he gets to you."

She may have nodded, but Giovanni could see the infuriating doubt lingering in her eyes. She leaned her head on his shoulder, and held onto him for the rest of the flight.

His stomach dropped when the plane landed, but it wasn't from any turbulence. She stood as the plane came to a halt, but he grabbed her hand before she could exit.

Pushing her up against the door, he leaned down and kissed her. He felt the current of desperation run through him, but he held fast, clutching her back and gripping the nape of her neck. He forced himself to back away, suppressing his instinct to bite and claim her when he saw her red swollen lips and the desire that lit her eyes.

"Gio—"

"We should go," he breathed out. "Now, tesoro, before I tell the plane to take us back."

"I want—"

"Your grandmother, Beatrice," he growled. "She's waiting for us outside."

She bit her lip and her eyes narrowed in anger when she picked up the small leather case he had bought for her in Puerto Montt. She pushed past him and opened the thick door that shielded the plane's sealed compartment.

He closed his eyes, burying his frustration and breathing slowly until he regained his self-control. By the time he left the plane, Beatrice was wrapped in Isadora's fierce embrace as Caspar watched them with tears in the corners of his eyes.

"Gio," Caspar said as he strode toward him and embraced his old friend. "It's such a relief to see you both."

"Is everyone at the house?" he asked as he patted Caspar's back.

"Tenzin and Carwyn are both out hunting. They'll be back before dawn, but you need to rest. Have you fed—"

"I'm fine. We'll go back to the house. Tomorrow is soon enough to meet with them."

"Isadora has been staying at the house with me."

He nodded. "Of course, my friend. Of course."

They drove to the house and Beatrice sat next to him in the back of the car, keeping her hands carefully folded in her lap. When they arrived, Caspar and Isadora retired to his apartment, and Beatrice and Giovanni went upstairs. Beatrice went to her old room as he slowly climbed the stairs to his. He peeled off his rumpled shirt, petting Doyle as the cat curled around his legs in welcome.

"Hello, Doyle," he murmured as he bent down to pet the cat. He sat on the edge of the bed in his outer room and inhaled the familiar scents of Houston.

Caspar had left a window open to air out his room and he could smell the faint scent of honeysuckle drift in on the breeze.

Giovanni closed his eyes when he heard her footsteps on the stairs. He sat hunched over, his elbows leaning on his knees as she entered his room and came to stand in front of him. He sighed when he felt her small hands stroke his hair, run down his neck, and trace his shoulders as he lay his cheek against her and put his arms around her waist.

"Beatrice—"

"One night, Gio. One more night?" she asked softly as she placed her hand on his cheek, holding him against her. He closed his eyes for a moment and nodded. Finally looking up to meet her dark gaze, he pulled her into his lap and framed her face with his hands, searching her eyes before he kissed her. Their lips sparked when they met, and he could feel the heat rising on his skin, but he couldn't pull his mouth away, or stop his hands from pressing her closer as she moved against him.

Standing up, he carried her into the small room where he spent his days, and laid her on the narrow bed.

"One more night," he whispered before he shut the door.

The following evening, Giovanni, Beatrice, Carwyn and Tenzin gathered in the library. The priest and the small woman greeted her warmly, though Beatrice was annoyed Tenzin didn't even pretend to be sorry about using her amnis to knock her out in Athens.

"You needed to go. You're better now."

"And you knew this? Or you were just being domineering?"

The tiny woman shrugged. "I knew *and* I was being domineering. I'm much older than you, and far smarter."

Beatrice narrowed her eyes. "Are you always this arrogant?"

"No," Carwyn muttered. "Usually she's much worse."

"At least I don't have the arrogance to believe there is only one god, priest."

"But you do have the arrogance to believe that fate dictates—"

"Hush," Giovanni broke in. "I doubt Beatrice wants to listen to your old argument."

He had been sitting in one of the armchairs, sipping a glass of whiskey as he watched the three of them gather around the large library table in the center of the room.

She noticed that both Carwyn and Tenzin looked disappointed to be distracted from their debate. Beatrice pushed back her own smile and hopped on the edge of the table to sit cross-legged as Giovanni watched her from his chair.

"Catch us up," she said. "What did we miss?"

"Well, other than a sale at the Tommy Bahama store—don't worry, Gio, I helped myself to your safe when I ran out of cash—most of the big excitement is old news."

"Did you find Scalia?" Beatrice asked. She had briefed Carwyn on the professor's role in her abduction while they were on the boat to the Greek mainland, and he had promised he would look into the professor's background.

"The dear doctor met a rather unfortunate end." He raised his hands. "Don't look at me, he was found attacked and killed outside the library the day after you were taken. I didn't get a chance to question him. It looks like Lorenzo lost patience with the man, or he had just outlived his usefulness."

"He said he knew my father," Beatrice said.

"He did," Tenzin added. "We looked into it while you two were in South America. Robert Scalia had gone to school with your father years ago and must have met him again when he was working in Ferrara.

"As far as we can tell, Scalia had gone to the university as a guest lecturer and stayed, but no one seems able to remember what he did. He was doing some kind of research in the library, but all the humans we found appeared to have had their memories tampered with."

"So no one could give you any good information?" Giovanni asked.

Carwyn shrugged. "I wouldn't say that. From what he told B, and from what we could piece together, it seems obvious that Lorenzo was using the university library to hide your collection in plain sight, so to speak. Though nothing appears to be there now."

"No," Giovanni muttered. "I'm sure he moved it."

Beatrice asked, "Was it on the island? There was a *huge* library."

"No," Tenzin shook her head. "I flew back the night after you two left. There was nothing of any real value there. All the humans were gone or dead. The place was destroyed; he won't be going back there."

"Good," she said, shivering at the memory of the compound where she had been held. She glanced up to see Giovanni watching her, but she looked away. Instead, she looked over to Carwyn, who kept glancing between the two of them with a curious expression.

"So, what about Lorenzo? What should we do now? We know he's still alive, right? Are my grandma and I going to be safe?"

They all seemed to start talking at once.

Carwyn shook his head. "I really don't like the idea of you going to Los Angeles when he's still out there. We don't know—"

"It wouldn't be that hard to systematically assassinate his allies," Tenzin mused. "I'm sure between Gio and me, we could kill them all within a few years and then—"

"And *I* don't really feel like getting embroiled in more vendettas, Tenzin, no matter how easy it would be to kill them all," Giovanni said from across the room.

Carwyn snorted. "Besides the moral implications of killing immortals who may have no greater crime than being sired by someone who has allied themselves with Lorenzo a hundred years ago, Tenzin. I know you have your own notions about fate and—"

"It's not fate I'm talking about, I'm talking about protecting our own interests and—"

Beatrice rolled her eyes as she listened to the three old friends argue. Each had their own ideas about what she should do. Carwyn proposed going to some safe ground until the danger was eliminated, even offering his own isolated home in Wales. Giovanni believed that the political steps he had already taken would protect her until he could hunt down and kill Lorenzo himself; and Tenzin seemed to be suggesting eliminating anyone who'd ever had any sort of alliance with Giovanni's son—just to be on the safe side.

She watched the three arguing for a few moments and tried to remember what Giovanni had told her months ago about the loose organization of the immortal world.

"The strongest, smartest, and wealthiest have the most power. And power is the only law."

Vampires didn't have laws or governments. From what she could tell, their world ran on physical strength, wealth, and a tangled web of long term alliances. Beatrice began to think about how all this applied to Lorenzo.

Giovanni seemed to think he had neutralized Lorenzo's alliances. Tenzin and Giovanni had taken his strength by turning him into a crispy critter who would take years to recover. She couldn't attack his brains; that was impossible.

But, she *could* attack his money.

Beatrice walked silently over to her desk and turned to the one place she knew she had the upper hand on any vampire in the world. She may have been helpless to defend herself in the face of supernatural strength, and she sure didn't have much money...

At least not yet.

She closed her eyes, delving into her memories of captivity, and running through the list of accounts she memorized in the hours she sat in Lorenzo's library. The pitiful assistant had been sloppy, never noticing her careful study of the numerous account codes, passwords, and security questions she'd observed as she sat in the corner, pretending to read.

"Gio?" she called quietly as she turned on the equipment.

He glanced at her as he argued with Carwyn about the merits of meeting with the leader of a clan of water vampires that controlled London.

"Yes?"

"All these computers have security, don't they? Lots of firewalls?"

"Of course, tesoro," he said before he was distracted by Tenzin and something she was saying about a council of eight immortals that sounded like they controlled most of China.

"Good," she muttered as she dove online to access Lorenzo's accounts scattered over the globe.

The debate swirled around her for hours as she hunted, systematically eliminating Lorenzo's ability to access the money she had observed his lackey moving around. Beatrice searched, isolating each account that poor, addled Tom had set up for his master. She shifted and diverted, putting some of it in her own name and transferring other parts into overseas accounts she would have access to. For some banks, it was as simple as changing a password and electronically transferring funds into other, newly created accounts at the same institution. It was all completely illegal.

And she didn't care one bit.

As her fingers raced over the keys, she thought more about the clues Lorenzo had lain at her feet, no doubt thinking that she would never be out from under his thumb.

Her father had taken something from him.

"...not before taking some books he knew I valued."

And Lorenzo needed them for something.

"Soon, I will fool them all. All the silly, trusting fools with their delusions of grandeur."

Lorenzo had plans...big plans.

"I have dreams, too. But they're not small in the least. They're positively...world changing."

Beatrice had the feeling that those kind of plans wouldn't be derailed forever, but without the financial resources she was stealing from him, it would take Lorenzo a lot longer to get them back on track. She knew it wouldn't stop him, but she was buying herself time; and she hoped, giving her father the chance to find her. As for Giovanni...

"Beatrice?" Carwyn called over to her. "What are you doing over there? You're looking like the cat that just ate the canary."

She smiled and hit 'return,' typing the final, electronic nail in Lorenzo's coffin, and netting herself a hefty payday, though she had a feeling much of it would remain out of reach until she'd found a way to explain it to the IRS.

"Carwyn, the creepy blond canary is dead. Mangled by all of you, and finished by me."

Giovanni rose and walked toward her. "What did you do? If you've put yourself in more danger—"

"He's done, Gio, at least for a while." She sat back and kicked her feet up, resting her combat boots on the edge of the desk.

"What did you do?"

She stared into his worried eyes. "He's wiped out. Any easy money he had is mine now. He won't be able to access any electronic funds unless he had a whole lot his pitiful little accountant didn't know about, and I'm doubting that. They're mine. Safely tucked away where he can't get them."

Carwyn's face split into a giant grin. "Nicely done, darling girl. Very nicely done."

Tenzin walked over and peeked around Carwyn. "I like her."

Beatrice glanced at Tenzin and smiled, but quickly looked back to Giovanni, who had not taken his eyes off her. His face had shut down, and his expression was impossible for her to read.

From the corner of her eye, she noticed Carwyn tug on Tenzin's arm, and they both left the library. Giovanni walked to the table, leaning against it as he stared into the fire that crackled in the grate.

"I have to agree with Carwyn," he said, "that was very well done. Very smart. You'll have to talk to Caspar. He can help you clean the money...if you need any help, that is." The corner of his mouth lifted in a rueful smile.

Beatrice walked over to him, standing before him and lifting a hand to stroke his cheek. His smile fell, and he closed his eyes, leaning into her palm. She felt the ever-present crackling heat that ran along his skin as she held her hand to his face. Finally, he looked at her, and the stoic soldier met her gaze.

She took a deep breath. "I'm going to L.A."

"Yes," he murmured, "I know." He closed his eyes, and rubbed his face into the palm of her hand.

"Gio—"

"You have a wonderful life in front of you, Beatrice De Novo."

She felt the tears come to her eyes. *Ask me to stay,* she thought. *Ask to come with me! Tell me you love me as much as I love you.* She swallowed the lump in her throat. "Are you staying in Houston?"

He shrugged and took her hand from his face, threading their fingers together and holding them to his chest. "For now. Caspar seems to be very attached to this house," he said, "and this city."

"And you?"

He dropped her hand, and pulled her toward him. His fingers traced her cheek, his arms encircled her, and his warm lips met her own. They kissed slowly in the flickering light that filled the room. She could feel his energy hum along her skin, and she pressed closer, drawn to the hidden fire that burned between them.

After a few lingering minutes, his lips slowed and he trailed kisses across her cheek. She closed her eyes, and held him close as he whispered in her ear.

"Ubi amo, ibi patria."

EPILOGUE

Los Angeles, California
February 2005

The man walked under the shadow of the arch and into the flickering lights of the courtyard. He examined the bungalow-style apartments that surrounded him, and smiled at the calico cat perched near a bubbling fountain. It was an old complex, and brilliant red bougainvillea climbed the stucco walls. He could smell the scent of the ocean as the evening fog rolled up the Southern California hills.

The cheerful lamps near each door lit up the numbers of the apartments, and he scanned them until he found the one he was looking for. As he approached, he examined the windows, smiling when he noted the heavy bolts which secured her home.

"Excuse me? Can I help you?"

He smiled and turned to face the old woman who held the cat in her arms. Listening carefully to the surrounding apartments, he noted the lack of activity, and the faint sounds of sleep that issued from most. He held out his hand with a smile and the woman took it, opening her mind to him.

"Where is Beatrice tonight?"

"She went out with some friends from school," she said with a soft smile. "I heard them leaving earlier. Such a nice group of girls."

He smiled and led the woman over to the bench near the fountain, still holding her hand. "Do you know her well?"

"She comes over for coffee in the morning sometimes; I think she misses her grandmother. And she takes care of Miss Tabby for me when I go see my daughter. I'm glad she moved next door."

He smiled at the old woman. "Does she have many friends?"

"Not many. But the friends that do come by seem very nice. There are two other young ladies, and a young man I see."

He paused. "Are they dating? Beatrice and the young man?"

The woman tugged on her cardigan, but leaned toward him, as if telling a secret. "I asked her if she had a boyfriend, but she just looked sad. I think she left someone behind in Texas."

"I think she did, too," he murmured, before he cleared his throat. "Do you have a key to her apartment, Mrs. ...."

"I'm Mrs. Hanson, dear. You seem like a nice young man. Are you a friend of Beatrice's?"

He smiled softly. "Something like that, yes."

"That's lovely. You're very handsome."

He smiled, his green eyes lit in amusement. "Thank you."

"You should take Beatrice on a date. She's very pretty, you know."

"Yes, she is." He smiled. "She's beautiful."

"Are you going to wait for her? Would you like some hot chocolate?"

He reached over to pet the cat the old woman held. It purred under his hands and made Mrs. Hanson smile.

"I can't stay, but I was hoping to leave something for Beatrice. Do you have a key to her apartment?"

She smiled and nodded. "Oh, yes. Do you want to wait here?"

Planting the suggestion for her to bring him the key and then go to bed, forgetting his presence entirely, he let her go. She took the cat inside her small apartment, and returned a few minutes later bearing a small brass key.

"I'll leave this under your door before I go."

"That's fine."

Standing, he took her hand again. "Thank you, Mrs. Hanson. Time for you to go to sleep."

She waved absently and walked to her door. He watched her walk inside, before he turned to Beatrice's apartment, noticing the familiar fragrance that lingered near the entrance. He opened the door and slipped inside, making sure to leave the lights off.

He almost staggered when he entered the small room. Her scent infused the air, and he took a deep breath as his gaze traveled around the living area. There was a small armchair, a plush sofa, and stack of books piled on the coffee table. Following the honeysuckle trail, he lowered himself onto the opposite the end of the sofa where she must have sat.

He sank into the couch, imagining her across from him and lifting her small feet into his lap as she had so many months ago. He lingered only a few minutes before he peeked into the bedroom, smiling when he saw the tall, black boots that stood by the closet doors.

There was an old dressing table in the corner, and he walked to it, taking special note of the pictures tucked into the frame of the mirror.

A postcard from Dublin.

A picture of her grandmother from the previous Christmas.

A blurry shot of Beatrice with a group of girls at what looked like a night club.

A small picture of her sitting on a horse in a damp meadow, the sun glinting off her dark brown hair as she smiled.

In a corner of the mirror, he saw a small phrase written on a worn index card.

Ubi amo, ibi patria—Where I love, there is my homeland.

The man touched the card tucked into the mirror, noting its worn edges and smudged letters. He traced the edges for a moment before he stepped away.

He took the picture of her on the horse and tucked it into his pocket before he walked to her bed and sat on the side where he knew she rested. Hesitating for only a moment, he reached into his coat and withdrew two items. The man looked at the small, leather-bound volume of sonnets in his hand, and gently traced the gold lettering on the front.

I sonetti di Giuliana

Tucking the plane ticket to Santiago under the small book, he placed both on her pillow where she would find them. He looked longingly around the room for a moment, before he stood and walked out the front door, carefully locking it behind him.

He tucked the brass key under Mrs. Hanson's doormat and walked over to the fountain. Sitting on the bench, he looked around the old courtyard, trying to imagine her laughter echoing off the walls.

The man lingered for a few moments, letting her faint scent swirl around him along with his memories. Then he stood, walked back under the arch, and disappeared into the night.

END OF BOOK ONE

THIS SAME EARTH

All men are by nature equal, made of the same earth by one workman; and however we deceive ourselves, as dear unto God is the poor peasant as the mighty prince.

—Plato

PROLOGUE

Cochamó Valley
Chile

2005

August 3

I'm here.
　Where are you?
　And do you know it takes two days to get here from Los Angeles? I had to wait an extra day in Santiago so I could catch the plane to Puerto Montt. I thought you'd be the one meeting me at the trail, not Gustavo, but it was nice to catch up. Also, ouch. My legs are going to kill me tomorrow from all that riding.
　So, where are you?

August 4

　Isabel says you wrote her to say that I would be coming but didn't say when you would be coming. Should I be worried?

August 5

　And now everyone is doing the whole vampire clam-up-and-not-tell-me-anything thing. Screw you all. If Isabel and Gustavo aren't worried, then I'm not going to worry about you, either.

August 17

I've been here for two weeks now. Where the hell are you?

Ever since you came to my apartment (Do you know you always smell like smoke to me, by the way? I thought something was burning when I came home that night.) I've been looking forward to seeing you.

Is this you being pissed at me for leaving Houston?

You never once came to visit me in L.A. Not once. Except to break into my apartment and leave me the sonnets (which I brought by the way) and take one of my favorite pictures, of course. Would it have killed you to hang around for a while?

Haha. I just realized that was unintentionally funny.

August 20

Took a ride today.

You still aren't here.

Think I might go rock-climbing tomorrow—with the Reverte's oldest son. The really handsome one.

Why aren't you here?

I've been sleeping in your room, and I discovered that without any light to wake me up in the morning, I sleep a really long time. I'm very well rested.

Is that what this was? Just a getaway for Beatrice so she could relax? Not saying I don't appreciate it, but...

No, actually, I don't appreciate it. I love this place, but I came here to see you, not ride horses, and hike, and eat Señora Reverte's really excellent cooking.

So, where the hell are you?

I have a return ticket for the thirty-first. I'm not hanging out until you get here. If you even plan on getting here.

August 25

Why the hell am I even writing in this stupid journal? It was just lying open on the kitchen table when I got here. Did you know this whole place smells like you? It does. I kind of hate that at this point.

August 31

Go to hell. I never want to see you again.

THIS SAME EARTH

2006

Cochamó Valley
Chile

August 2

So, since I'm here again (and I'm just assuming you're going to be a no-show) I want to explain a few things.

1. I wasn't going to come this year until Dez (that's Desiree, my best friend, who you would know about if you communicated with me at all) convinced me that I should just take the free ticket because I love it here and I could use a vacation. So I'm here. That's why, and that's the only reason. Not because I wanted or expected to see you again.

2. I'm more than a little pissed that you seem to be able to communicate with everyone we know (Caspar, Carwyn, Tenzin—you even called my grandma on her birthday) but not me. Yay for you. You're traveling the world and won't tell anyone where you are. I don't even give a shit anymore, but it's just rude. I hope my grandma told you off. She probably didn't.

3. If you have any illusions about me "waiting for you" or some romantic crap like that, don't kid yourself. I'm dating. I'm dating a really nice guy, as a matter of fact. His name is Kevin, and I met him in my graduate program. He's handsome and smart and we have an amazing time together, and when I get back from this vacation, we're going to have sex. Lots of it. And that's going to be great, too.

August 15

I love this place. I really do. I mean, I love L.A. and I love school, but this place is just... magic. Do you come here when I'm not here? I bet you do. I'm betting you read this journal last year because it looked like it had been paged through, and I greatly doubt Isabel went to look under the pillows on our bed to set it out on the table for when I got here this year.

So I think you were here.

And I have no idea how to feel about that.

August 20

Does time stand still for you? Have you been living so long that a year or two is nothing? It seems so long to me, but it's probably like the blink of an eye to you. I remember you telling me once that a year was like a day when you are immortal.

So what does that mean? If I was just the blink of an eye in your life, why do you keep breaking into my apartment and giving me tickets to come here? Also, if you want pictures of me, you could call and ask for them instead of swiping the ones at my place. I really liked that picture of me at the beach. I actually had a tan.

August 23

I hate that everything in this house smells like you.

August 24

And I hate that I dream about you when I'm here.

August 29

I'm leaving tomorrow. I'm feeling very relaxed, so thanks for that.

I don't know what to think about you anymore. Were you really a part of my life? I'd say it was all a crazy dream except for the cryptic postcards that I'm assuming are from you, and the tickets, and the fact that I'm friends with all your friends now.

I'm going to finish my master's this winter. Only two and a half years. Not bad. I could have done better, but I was having a lot of fun. I learned how to rock-climb, kickbox, and I'm fairly good at a couple of martial arts, too. I'm even a pretty decent dancer now. Surprise, surprise. So I'm not going to regret the extra months.

Want to come to my graduation in December?

Yeah, didn't think so.

༺༻

2007

Cochamó Valley
Chile

August 1

I just got the best job! I'm in heaven. I think I might have finally found a library to top yours! I turned down a couple of positions because I was waiting for the right one and I got it! I'm starting at the Huntington Library next month! (I'm using a million exclamation points, but I don't care!)

I wasn't worried about money so much (thanks to my superior embezzling skills) but I wanted to find a place where I was really passionate about working. The Huntington is a private foundation, and its facilities are amazing.

Plus, they have this gorgeous botanical garden surrounding it, so it's a beautiful place to work, and it's an easy commute from my house in Silver Lake.

Oh, I bought a house. It's pretty damn cute. It's one of those Spanish bungalows built about eighty years ago and it has really nice architectural details. At least, that's what my realtor, Matt, told me. Now he's my neighbor, as a matter of fact. The house next door to his went on the market right after I met him, so I got a great deal because he found it right away and I could put in a quick offer. He's a nice neighbor. We're the only people on our block who are under eighty, I think. It's an old part of L.A. up in the hills, but I really like it.

We're not dating or anything. Actually, I'm pretty sure Dez has a crush on him, but she refuses to ask him out despite the fact that she's usually very outgoing. Oh, and I'm not dating that Kevin guy either. I mean, I did for a while, but... he was kind of boring, to be honest. And he snored a lot. Like... a lot.

August 17

You're missing it, but I'm a great rider now. Really. I even beat Gustavo in a race the other night. Still can't beat Isabel, though. Damn, she is good. And on sidesaddle, too. How does she even do that?

Oh, and I'm a pretty good rock-climber, if I do say so myself. I'm still studying tai chi and judo, but I'm taking jujitsu now, too. I'm going to be sitting a lot as a librarian (yes! I can officially call myself a librarian now!) so I want to keep active so I don't expand. You never have to worry about that, do you?

Jerk.

August 20

I have a boyfriend.

I don't know why that's weird to write. I just... I know we're not like that. I mean, I thought at one point that maybe we would be, but obviously, we're not. Don't get me wrong, I was really mad at you for a long time, but I guess I understand. I'm going to live, what? Another sixty or seventy years? And you'll still be here.

So, I get it now. I really do.

And my boyfriend is great. He's kind of your exact opposite (not that I was looking for that, it just happened) except he's tall like you. He's Hawaiian. And gorgeous. His name is Mano, which means 'shark' in Hawaiian. He surfs, and he's tan and has this amazing long, dark hair and black eyes.

He used to be a Navy diver, but now he has his own dive shop, and he and his friend run SCUBA classes and dive trips to Catalina. I met him in May when Dez forced me to take one of his classes. He has such a great smile. He's just... so open and honest and he's so... great. He's great, and he's really good to me, and everyone likes him. He wants to go to Houston and meet Grandma and Caspar this fall.

By the way, did Caspar tell you about Doyle and the Vietnamese vase in the entry way? I know you loved that vase, but please don't kill the cat when you get back from... wherever you are.

August 29

I'm trying to be really mature and well-adjusted here, but I'm crying right now, you jerk.

I miss you.

I miss you so much. Why the hell are you never here? Why? Where are you? I want to feel your arms around me and sleep next to you and talk to you and tease you and I hate you, Gio. I can't help it. I hate you.

But I don't really, even though I wish I did.

I still think about you every day. And I compare every man I meet to you. And every time I smell smoke or whiskey, I turn and expect to see you there. Do you know I studied Latin so I could impress you? How pathetic, huh? At least that one might come in handy professionally at some point.

When I bought my house, I checked how many windows were in the bedroom (just one) and imagined them with heavy drapes as if you might actually stay there at some point.

And it's pathetic. Because I will probably never see you again.

I'm leaving tomorrow. I don't know if I'm going to come back next year. I just don't know if I can keep doing this to myself no matter how much I love it here. Because when I'm in Cochamó, you're everywhere.

I should probably take this journal with me. I can't believe I just wrote that stuff.

2008

Cochamó Valley

Chile

August 5

Ah, ha ha. Very funny. So I threaten to take the last journal, so you take it (I'm assuming) and leave me with a new one. Clever.

Also, what are all these journals in the bedroom? There's got to be a couple hundred of them and they're all in Latin. Do you expect me to work while I'm here?

News flash: I don't work for you anymore.

I do love working at the Huntington, though. Such an amazing job. I only get three weeks of vacation, so only two weeks in the valley this year. Bummer. But if I skipped out on Christmas with Cas and Grandma, they'd kill me.

August 6

Holy shit. These are your journals. These are your whole life.

Why did you leave these here? Are they safe? Don't they need to be in a temperature-controlled room? And it gets really damp here in the winter. Though I suppose the bedroom is pretty good with the way it's cut into the rock.

I feel like I can't leave the house now, even though they were probably here for weeks before I came and I'm sure they're perfectly secure.

You knew Napoleon? Really?

Was he as insecure about his height as everyone says? You must have looked like a giant next to him.

August 10

These things are incredible. There's no way I'm going to get through all of them, though. My Latin is not that good.

So you've found an ingenious way of keeping me coming back here.

Bastard.

It's irritating how intelligent you are sometimes.

August 17

I have to leave tomorrow. I hate not having more time here, but I have to go.

Yes, I'll come back. You knew I would.

And just so you know, Mano and I are still together. Grandma and Caspar love him. Carwyn met him last winter when he came for a visit. I think he likes him, too. Carwyn made noises about Mano and I sleeping together, though. I forget he's a priest sometimes. Oops. Must be the Hawaiian shirts. You should have seen this green one he bought the last time he came to L.A. It was hideous. He loved it.

I got a letter from Tenzin last month. She's so... weird. In the best way, but... yeah, she's old. Did you know she calls me every three or four months? It's the most hilarious thing. I think whoever her human is puts it on speaker phone and Tenzin just yells. I have to hold the phone away from my ear so she doesn't break my eardrums. I think I'm the closest thing she has to a female friend. Not that we talk about braiding our hair or anything. She said she's going to come for a visit one of these days. Should be... interesting.

I'm not ready to leave. I want to read more about your life. You're very hard on yourself, Jacopo. Be kinder.

And wherever you are, be safe.

2009

Cochamó Valley
Chile

August 5

Four weeks of vacation now! Score. Well, I still only get three weeks paid, but they let me take an additional week off unpaid, so I'm using that to go see Grandma and Caspar for Christmas and I can take three weeks here.

By the way, could you surface at some point, please? I think Cas and Grandma would like to get married and they're waiting for you to be a part of our lives again in more ways than cryptic phone calls, letters, and postcards.

Just a suggestion. Going to read now.

August 11

I can't even... you have had such an amazing life, Gio. And now that I'm more used to your writing style in Latin, your journals are really hilarious at times.

And then sometimes they make me cry.

Don't worry, I'm taking good care of them.

August 14

I think Mano is starting to think about marriage and babies and all that stuff. I'm only twenty-eight, but he's older than me; he's already thirty-two. (And yes, I'm sure you're probably laughing when you read that, old man.)

I just don't know. He wanted to move in together last winter, but I like having my space. When he's there too much... well, we just get on each other's nerves, you know? I like having my alone time. We had a huge fight about it, but we worked through it. He's a good guy, and I love him a lot.

August 19

I'm so fucking mad right now, I can hardly write.

Was that you in the trees last night? It better not have been! I cannot believe you would come that close and not even—

Nevermind, I can believe it.

It was you. I could even smell the smoke. I can't believe you would do that to me.

Yes, I can.

Damn it, Gio. Damn it! Damn you. Damn this valley. Damn this house. Damn your journals. Damn everything.

I'm not doing it anymore. I refuse. What do you want from me? What? Just call me or write me or do anything! But I'm not doing this anymore. I'm done.

You know what? Don't write me. Don't contact me. I never want to see you again, or hear from you, or anything. I'm moving on with my life. I have a life! Do you realize that? And you're not in it, so leave me alone.

I'm not coming back here. I'm through.

You asshole! I've had enough of pale faces haunting me. I've done it before and I'm not going to let you get to me the way my father did. I'm leaving tomorrow and I'm not coming back.

Do you understand me?

And when Mano asks me to marry him, I'm saying yes.

CHAPTER 1

Los Angeles, California
October 2009

"B?"

"Hmph."

"Baby, the alarm already went off."

She looked over her shoulder at Mano, who appeared to be wearing nothing more than a lazy grin.

"It went off already?" she croaked, shutting her eyes against the morning sun.

He nodded. "Yep. I let you sleep in a little, but I knew you'd kick me if I let you miss work."

The morning sun streamed through the small window in the bedroom. Mano must have propped it open the night before, and she could smell the Meyer lemon tree blossoming on the patio.

"Why am I so tired?"

"Apparently, it was a scotch night last night," he snickered. "I came over and let myself in, but you were already asleep."

Beatrice rolled over and blinked at her gorgeous boyfriend. "You came over and crawled in my bed looking like that, and I missed it?"

"Your loss."

She groaned and burrowed into his warm chest. "Why did I drink the Laphroaig? It was not my friend last night. And I have to work late because Dr. Stevens asked me to help her close."

His low voice rumbled in her ear as she pressed her cheek to his chest. "How late? You want me to come over and cook dinner?"

She sighed and rubbed her eyes. "We've got that group visiting from USC right now and they've been staying as late as she'll let them, so...I don't know, probably not till eight-thirty or so."

"Leaving from work? So you won't be home till after nine."

She cuddled closer to him and reached up to brush the long, black hair out of his eyes. "Probably not. Can you come over anyway?"

"I can tonight, but not tomorrow night. We've got a group leaving early for an all-day dive, so I'll have to be at the boat by six."

She moved to lay kisses along his stubbled chin. "You know, we should be environmentally conscious this morning. There's a water shortage."

"Oh yeah?" he asked with a cocked eyebrow. He pulled her closer and hooked her leg over his hip. "Shower together, huh? You up for being environmentally responsible after last night?"

"Yes." She smiled. "Are you?"

Mano hugged her to his chest and rolled them out of bed before he stood and walked to the bathroom, his strong arms supporting her as she clung to him. "I'm always up for you, baby."

Beatrice giggled as he carried her to the bathroom, glancing at the bottle of scotch and the small book bound in red leather that lay on her desk in the corner. She hugged Mano closer and breathed in the scent of sun and ocean that clung to him.

SHE WAVED AS HE STOOD ON HER FRONT PORCH, STILL SHIRTLESS AND WEARING a lazy smile, while he held a cup of coffee as she sped away on her bike. She hopped onto Interstate 5 and gunned the engine, cutting lanes on her way to the 110 Freeway.

She'd bought the new Triumph Scrambler after Carwyn convinced her a motorcycle with a British pedigree was superior to an American bike. Since the Welshman had been the one to teach her to ride, and she liked the look of the matte-black bike, she'd relented and had it customized for her short frame.

Beatrice loved the freedom of being on the back of the bike, along with the ability to cut quickly through the Southern California traffic. While some moaned about their daily commute, for Beatrice, it was one of her favorite parts of the day.

By the time she arrived in San Marino—a small, wealthy enclave in the middle of South Pasadena—she'd made up for her late start that morning. She didn't know why she'd given in to the temptation to read Giuliana's sonnets the night before, but going down that road never led to a happy night.

She pulled off her helmet as she walked through the alley of jacaranda trees leading to the entrance of the library.

"Mornin', B!"

Beatrice waved at one of the guards as she climbed the white stone stairs leading to the grand entrance.

"Hey, Art. How are you today?"

The jovial man grinned and gave her a wink. "Oh, you know...just hangin'," he laughed. "Get it? Hangin'? 'Cause my name is 'Art?'"

She snorted and shook her head. "Yeah, good one."

"You closing with Dr. Stevens tonight?"

"Yup. You going to be here?"

He nodded and smiled, his brown eyes crinkling in the corners. "You betcha. I'll see you later then."

"See you."

"Hey, B?"

She turned before she reached the black glass of the library doors. "Yeah?"

"This is probably out of left field, but do you know a kid around twelve or thirteen named Ben?"

"Ben?" She frowned. "I don't think so, why?"

He shrugged. "Just a kid poking around the front of the gardens the other day. He was riding a bike and asked if I knew a librarian named Beatrice. That's your name, right?"

Beatrice's mouth dropped open. "Yeah, that's my name, but I don't know any kids that age. I don't really know any kids, period. I mean...maybe one of the school groups? That take the tours of the public exhibits? I've led a few of those."

Art nodded. "Yeah, that's probably it. Maybe he came last year with his class and remembered you or something."

"Huh." She frowned. "I guess. That's the only thing I can figure. Did he look...I don't know. What did he look like?"

"Just a kid. Hispanic, I think. Kinda skinny. He seemed smart, said his name was Ben, but didn't say anything else."

She paused, searching her memory for any hint of recognition. There wasn't one. "Well, if you see him again, let me know, okay?"

He nodded and gave her a small salute before he turned to help a guest that was signaling for attention. "You got it."

Walking into the cool of the library, Beatrice tucked her helmet under her arm, smoothed back her hair, and thought about what classes she might have led for that age last spring. She couldn't remember any that stood out.

"Weird."

The Huntington Library and Botanical Gardens was given to the city of San Marino by railroad magnate Henry Huntington when he passed away. While the gardens and house of the former estate were open to the public, the library, containing over six million rare books, manuscripts, and archived materials, was restricted and only open to special guests and Ph.D.s with recommendations. Beatrice had been more than fortunate her adviser at UCLA was willing to recommend her to Dr. Karen Stevens, a friend and colleague who happened to be the curator of the Western American archives.

The assistant's job didn't pay all that much, but it had decent benefits, and since Beatrice was independently—if quietly—wealthy, money wasn't her chief concern.

"Hey, B!"

"Morning."

"How's it going?"

She waved and smiled at the quiet morning greetings of her coworkers as she made her way to the small office where she spent her days. She was currently using her rather extensive knowledge of Spanish and Latin to translate early documents from the California missions. Many of the old papers were just storage records or letters between priests, but occasionally, she came upon something in the jumbled records that gave insight into the complicated political workings of California's early Spanish settlements.

"Good morning, Beatrice." Dr. Stevens poked her head into Beatrice's small office and smiled. An attractive blond woman in her mid-fifties, she wore a heather grey suit and a pair of stylish black glasses that framed her blue eyes. "Can you still help me close tonight?"

Beatrice nodded at her boss and grabbed her coffee cup, preparing to get a refill in the lunchroom. A headache from the night before started to gnaw at the space between her eyes.

"Morning. And yes, I can. I was wondering if I could take an extra hour at lunch today since I'm staying late. I'm supposed to meet a friend downtown, and if I had some extra time I'd appreciate it."

Dr. Stevens thought for a moment, then shrugged. "That shouldn't be a problem. I need you to finish those letters, but you'll be able to work late tonight. I really just need an extra body here to meet staff requirements. The group from USC doesn't need much help, and we've just got one other late appointment who's looking at some of the Lincoln archives."

She lifted an eyebrow as she turned on her computer. "Lincoln, huh?"

"Have you worked with those at all? The bodyguard's papers are particularly fascinating. Some of the letters—"

"Yeah, I did a whole project on some Lincoln documents as an undergrad. Not really relevant to what I'm doing now."

Dr. Stevens cocked her head. Beatrice immediately regretted her curt tone and looked up at her boss with an embarrassed smile. "Sorry. I'm feeling rotten this morning. Please excuse me. I appreciate the information."

The curator smirked. "Late night with the boyfriend?"

"I wish. No, just some...stupid stuff. And I think I might be getting sick." *...of thinking about a man I'm never going to see again and regretting words in a journal he'll probably never read.*

"I hope not. You just got back from vacation."

Two months ago. Beatrice offered her a tight smile and stood, brushing her hands along her slim-cut, black slacks. She picked up her empty mug and walked toward the doorway.

"I'm going to grab some coffee, can I get you anything?"

"No," Dr. Stevens said. "I'm fine. I'm supposed to be giving a talk with a visiting lecturer at ten, so I'm going to go prepare, and I'll let you get back to work. Take the extra hour at lunch, and I'll see you this evening."

Beatrice nodded and walked down to get more coffee, glancing at the framed art along the walls.

"Hangin' around, Art," she said. "Just hangin' around."

When she finally broke for lunch and sped down to Colorado Street to meet Dez at their favorite Spanish restaurant, she had moved past headache and into starving. She sat at one of the sidewalk tables and ordered a small plate of oil-roasted almonds to nibble on until her friend arrived.

Desiree Riley, or Dez as her friends called her, was the quintessential California girl. She'd grown up in Santa Monica and—if not for her parents insisting she leave for a few months to tour Europe after she graduated—would have happily stayed in Southern California her entire life. She'd gone to UCLA for both undergraduate and graduate work, completing her Masters in Information Science the same year as Beatrice.

They had become unexpected friends, the blond surfer girl and the quiet Texan in black boots and even blacker eyeliner; but as the years passed, they found their own friendly equilibrium. Beatrice stopped dying her hair pitch-black in favor of her natural, dark chocolate brown, and Dez had learned how to ride a motorcycle and even had a few piercings that mom and dad didn't know about.

"B!"

She heard her name shouted from a passing car and looked up to see Dez's silver Jetta slowing as cars honked behind her.

"Dez, stop blocking the road!"

"Oh," she waved a careless hand. "I will, but parking is *crazy* today. Order that sangria pitcher for two, okay?"

"I'm working today, you lush."

The honking behind the Jetta only got more persistent.

"Who says I'm sharing? I'll be there as soon as I find a spot." She lifted her hand to daintily flip off the driver behind her, who was shouting out his window.

"Red wine sangria for two, please," Beatrice said to the waiter, who had been staring at the commotion. He nodded with an amused smile and walked back inside. Dez huffed up the sidewalk a few minutes later and plopped down in the chair across from her friend, blowing a kiss to the waiter who dropped off the drinks.

"Okay, I'm drinking and so are you."

"Dez—"

"No 'buts.' You have been in a mood ever since you got back from Chile, and it's irritating. This is the first chance we've had to talk without Mano around, so spill. Everything."

Beatrice sighed in defeat and poured herself a glass.

An hour later, Dez was leaning on the table and staring raptly as Beatrice finished the story. Her best friend knew a very carefully edited version of the tale of Beatrice and Giovanni, as Dez liked to call it. But she knew that Beatrice went to Chile every summer only to return weeks later, alone and usually in a bad mood.

"So you think he was there? Watching the house?"

"Yeah, I'm pretty sure I saw him." *And smelled him.* She didn't really feel like explaining that part.

Dez sat back and frowned as she took another bite of her *tortilla española*. "Don't you think that's kind of creepy?"

Beatrice had never told Dez that Giovanni broke into her house at least once a year to leave plane tickets and occasionally grab a photograph. "Um ... no, it's not really. I mean, it is his house. It's not creepy to me. I was mostly just pissed off that he didn't come to the door."

"Yeah, I can see that." Dez took another sip of the sangria and silently munched on an olive.

"What?"

"*What* what?" Dez asked, the picture of innocence.

"You have something to say, I can tell."

She didn't deny it but folded her hands on her lap and sighed a little as she looked across the table.

"You need to stop going there."

"I am. I told you, I'm done."

"I know you have friends there, and I know how much you love it, but it just...you've got to move on from this guy."

Beatrice rolled her eyes. "Did you not hear me? I told you, I wrote him in the journal and told him—"

"Yeah, you told him you were done. Got it. You told *me* that, too. Remember?"

THIS SAME EARTH

Beatrice pursed her lips and looked away, biting her lip as Dez continued in a quiet voice.

"You told me you were done with him three years ago. And then you went back. And then two years ago, you said the same thing. And you still went back."

She bit her lip to keep the tears at bay as her friend recounted the last five years of an obsession she knew she needed to abandon.

"And then last year, even though Mano practically begged you not to go, you went again."

"I know—"

"I'm not sure you do, B. Because he and I are the ones who have to put up with your moody-ass, depressed behavior for a month afterward every time you go down there and get your heart broken again."

"My heart is not broken. You're being melodramatic," Beatrice muttered and took another sip of her water.

"Fine," she rolled her eyes. "Whatever you want to tell yourself. But stop, okay? For real. When you get the ticket in the mail next time, toss it. Donate it. Change it to a flight to the Bahamas and take your boyfriend, but do *not* go chasing that ghost again."

Beatrice swallowed the lump in her throat and clenched her jaw as she contained her tears. "I know," she whispered.

"Do you? Really?"

"Yes, I'm done. I'm...moving past it."

"You know I love you," Dez whispered. Beatrice could see the concerned tears in her eyes.

"I know."

"And I'm only saying this—"

"It's fine." She nodded. "I get it. Really, I do."

"You have an amazing man in your life, one who wants a future with you. That wants to move forward. Not everyone gets that, you know?"

Beatrice sniffed and brushed at her eyes. "And some people never know because they won't ask the person who's perfect for them out on a single date."

Dez straightened up and a flush rose in her cheeks. "I have no idea what you're talking about, Beatrice De Novo."

"Oh," she said with a smile, happy that the conversation had turned. "I can't imagine. Did I mention I saw my lovely neighbor, *Matt,* yesterday? Yeah, he was sitting on his front porch working on his mountain bike. It must have been hot, because Ken—I mean Matt—wasn't wearing a stitch more than a pair of little biking shorts. It was quite the view, I'll say that."

"He is not a Ken-doll," Dez muttered and threw an olive at Beatrice. She caught it and popped it into her mouth.

"You do some investigation about whether he's anatomically accurate, and I'll consider changing my opinion of him. Until then? Ken-doll."

Dez huffed, "Why do you even—"

"And you're a total Barbie. Librarian Barbie. Do you know how many naughty fantasies poor Ken—I mean Matt—has probably had about you already? You'd be putting him out of his misery. Besides, Ken and Barbie *belong* together," she said with a wicked grin.

"I hate you," Dez said in a prim voice, "and I hope someone scratches your ugly black motorcycle in the parking lot."

Beatrice reached down and threw an olive at Dez, but this time, her friend caught it and threw it back, hitting Beatrice right between the eyes. She snorted and then belly laughed at Beatrice's shocked expression.

"Forget Librarian Barbie," Beatrice muttered. "I'm going to go with Big League Barbie instead."

The two friends finished lunch and made plans to meet the following weekend for brunch at one of their favorite hangouts near the beach. Beatrice hopped on her bike and returned to the Huntington to finish the translation of the mission letter she'd been working on before lunch.

As the hours passed, she fell into a steady rhythm, speeding through not one, but two complete letters before Dr. Stevens called her to the reading room.

She packed up the document she'd been working on and moved it to one of the library tables in the quietest corner of the room. Dr. Stevens had asked her to be available if the group needed help, but she didn't really expect to be interrupted.

She was looking up a Latin noun she thought might have been misspelled when she heard the quiet footsteps. The smell of smoke reached her nose before she could look up into the green eyes that had haunted her for five years. An enigmatic smile flickered across his face before he spoke.

"I'm looking for Miss De Novo."

CHAPTER 2

"Hello, *tesoro*," he whispered.

Giovanni had expected her anger, but he hadn't expected the sheen of tears that touched her eyes when they finally met his own.

She stood, her fury palpable when she responded.

"You don't get to call me that anymore," she hissed before she looked around the room.

"I've introduced myself to everyone," he murmured, "shaken everyone's hand. You don't need to worry about anyone paying us any attention."

"So you used your mind voodoo on my boss and colleagues. Thanks."

He smiled a little. "I didn't want to be interrupted. Librarians can be such sticklers for rules."

"Why are you here?"

"For you."

Her mouth fell open before she finally sputtered back, "Well, you're about five years too late."

She bent over her desk and began to gather the letters she had been working on. He stood, watching her, taking in her appearance, and drinking in her welcome scent. He couldn't stop the smile. "You have no idea how much I've missed you."

She glared at him and glanced around the room.

"They won't remember us talking?"

He waved a careless hand. "No, they're barely registering my presence right now."

"Good." She walked around the table, drew back her hand, and slapped him across the face. "*You* missed *me?*" she spit out. "*You* don't get to say that."

She turned and picked up her materials to take back to her office, leaving Dr. Stevens in the reading room with the oblivious scholars from USC. Giovanni enjoyed the view of her walking away from him for a few moments before he followed.

"Beatrice?"

"Go to hell," she called over her shoulder as she made her way through the halls of the institution. She had changed in subtle ways he hadn't been able to detect in photographs. Her figure was fuller, and she carried herself with a grace and confidence she hadn't known five years before. Her walk was more assured, and the almost imperceptible lines that touched her face only added to the depth of her dramatic features.

She was absolutely stunning. And really, *really* pissed-off.

Her scent was the same, a sweet melange of honeysuckle and lemon that made his fangs descend when he thought of the single taste of her blood he'd enjoyed years before.

"Beatrice," he called again. "I've already told Dr. Stevens you'll be helping me on my project while I'm doing my research here."

She whirled around at her office door. "Well, you can just use that voodoo to change her mind then, can't you?"

He came to stand in front of her and took a deep breath, staring at her mouth, which was pursed in displeasure. "I could." He shrugged. "But I won't."

Beatrice looked like she wanted to slap him again, but her hands were full of documents and books, so he reached behind her and opened her door, scenting her as he leaned over her shoulder.

"You still smell like honeysuckle," he murmured before she shoved him aside so she could enter the office.

"Go away," she said. "I don't want to see you."

He closed the door and leaned against it. "Well, that's certainly understandable."

"Why?" she asked again as she put her work away. "Why are you here? Why now?"

Giovanni couldn't help but smile at her, despite her anger. He had to resist the urge to walk across the room and kiss her senseless; he had a feeling bodily injury would result. "I already told you. I'm here for you."

She paused in her work, and he could hear her heart begin to race, but her angry expression did not waver.

"Well, you can't have me. So what else are you here for?"

He let her entertain the notion she was unavailable for the time being. "I'm doing some work for a client who's looking for a journal that was carried to the new world in one of Father Junipero Serra's first missionary journeys in California." He smiled innocently when she looked up in shock. "I was told there was a very bright librarian here who could help me translate some of the Spanish and Latin correspondence from the era."

Her eyes narrowed. "Is that so?"

"She came very highly recommended by a mutual friend," he said with a wink.

"Remind me to call Carwyn and bitch at him later."

"Do I hear you're riding a motorcycle now?" He looked her up and down as she grabbed her backpack and helmet, staring at her legs in an obvious manner. "That, I really need to see, *tesoro*. Very sexy."

He smiled when he realized he had rendered her speechless again.

"I'm leaving now," she finally said.

He glanced at the clock above her desk. "Look at the time. I should finish up my meeting with Dr. Stevens before I go. After all, I'll see you tomorrow night."

Beatrice shook her head. "You bastard," she muttered through a clenched jaw.

He held open the door, but his arm shot out when she tried to walk past him. His hand curled around her waist, and he felt the familiar frisson of electricity run between them when they touched for the first time in five years. His temperature rose when he leaned over and murmured in her ear.

"I'm back, Beatrice. I'm back for *you*, and I'm not going anywhere. You're not a girl anymore, so run home for now but know that I'll see you again tomorrow. And I'm not leaving you again."

She turned her head to meet his green eyes and her mouth was only a breath away.

"What if I ask you to go?" she whispered. "Are you just going to hang around and be a nuisance forever?"

He paused, the words almost catching in his throat. "If you ever had any feelings for me, give me a chance. Please."

She didn't respond, pushing his arm away from her body before she rushed down the hall. He heard her pass through the reading room to say goodnight to her boss before she exited out the glass doors. When she left the building, the energy fled with her, and he slumped against her office wall.

"This is going to be harder than I thought."

HE FINALIZED PLANS WITH DR. STEVENS BEFORE HE LEFT THE HUNTINGTON that night, strolling the four blocks to the large Tudor-style home he'd purchased the month before. He was still getting used to the layout of the house but had been charmed by the dense trees that surrounded the property and the tiered gardens and ponds that filled the yard.

As he walked through the front doors, he looked around and listened for the activity that should have been going on in the library on the first floor. He heard nothing except the bouncing of a basketball behind the garage. Laughing under his breath, he turned and walked silently through the kitchen and out the back doors.

The boy was bouncing the ball in a pool of light that shone from the back of the garage. He was bent over, dribbling through his scrawny legs, his attention focused on the rhythmic bouncing of the orange ball in his hands. Just then, he crouched down and shot up, tossing a precise shot toward the basket mounted over the garage door.

"He shoots...he scores!" the boy shouted when the ball sailed through the hoop. "And the crowd goes wild for Ben Vecchio, lead scorer of the—" He turned then and spotted Giovanni, leaning against the wall.

"Scorer of the what?" Giovanni asked with a raised eyebrow.

"Um...of the top college in the country, which I will be getting into with no problem because I already finished my math and my Latin translation?"

"Reading?"

"Done before you woke up tonight."

"History?"

"Well, not quite..."

"Composition?"

"You know, you're back a lot sooner than I thought you'd be."

"How about piano?"

Ben's mouth gaped open and his shoulders slumped. "It hasn't even been delivered yet!"

Giovanni frowned. "I forgot that part. Did you call the movers today?"

Ben nodded. "Yep, they said that it'd be here next Thursday at the latest and to make sure that we had room for the truck."

"Excellent. Toss me the ball then."

"Pass, Gio. *Pass* the ball."

"Fine, whatever," he muttered as Ben passed the ball to him. He dribbled it, then tossed it toward the backboard, where it bounced off the rim before Ben ran over to catch it. He bounced it back to Giovanni.

"Okay, you need to square up your shoulders with the basket before you shoot. Try again."

Giovanni dribbled the ball a few more times before he tried again, squaring his shoulders like Ben had directed. "You know, if you put half the concentration into your composition that you do into this game—"

"Game, Gio. Remember? We're supposed to talk about non-school stuff when we play."

He rolled his eyes and shot again, this time getting slightly closer to the square behind the hoop.

"There," Ben encouraged. "That's better." The boy rebounded the shot and took some time dribbling it before he tossed it toward the hoop, where it sailed in. "So, did you talk to her?"

Giovanni watched as the boy ran around the small court, shooting baskets and chasing rebounds. His lanky limbs and awkward gait seemed to disappear on the basketball court, as he exhibited the natural confidence that had brought him to Giovanni's attention when he'd seen the boy in New York over a year ago.

"I did."

"Is she really mad at you?"

He nodded as Ben passed him the ball. "Yes, she's...fairly angry."

"Did you tell her about me yet?" he asked in a small voice.

"Not yet," he smiled. "I told you, Beatrice is far more apt to like you than me at the moment. Don't worry about that."

Ben gave a nonchalant shrug. "Girls always like me more, G. It's 'cause I'm so good-looking."

Giovanni laughed and passed the ball back to him. "I worry about your self-esteem, Benjamin. Really, I do. Have you eaten dinner yet?"

"Just a few more minutes?" His eyes pleaded. "Then I'll go in."

"Fine. But after that, you're finishing your homework."

"Sweet!" Ben shot a few rapid baskets. "So how long do you think it's going to be before she's not mad at you anymore?"

"How long was it before you started liking me after I took you off the streets and made you start bathing regularly?"

Ben snickered and passed the ball back to Giovanni. "Not as long as I acted. The food was a lot better at your house."

"Better than the randomly purloined hot dog? I should hope even *my* cooking beat that."

"Well, it was close, but—hey!" Ben dodged the ball that Giovanni threw at him. It hit the wall of the garage and bounced back toward Ben. Giovanni grinned at the boy's sharp reflexes, which had been part of the reason he'd been such a successful pickpocket until a little over a year before.

"I'll go start dinner. Come to the kitchen in a few minutes."

Giovanni walked back in the house and went to start a pot of water to boil. He had little interest in food that night, but because he was determined to civilize Benjamin as much as possible for a twelve-year-old boy, he had made nightly dinner at the table a priority.

When he'd found the boy in New York, Giovanni had spotted his wasted potential almost immediately. The urchin had stolen his wallet, and if Giovanni hadn't had preternatural senses, he would have easily gotten away with it. As it was, he'd let the boy have the wallet, followed him, and done some investigating.

Ben was the illegitimate son of a con woman and a cabbie. After looking into both parents and talking to the boy, Giovanni decided that neither one of them was deserving of his help—or their own child. One physically abusive and the other a manipulator, they had passed on to Ben little more than the ability to fend for himself and lie convincingly to authorities.

Giovanni, however, had seen the sharp intelligence and survival instinct the boy exhibited and decided he deserved more than to be chewed up on the streets of the city. On paper, Ben had become Giovanni's nephew, the son of his deceased brother and his wife, who had died in a tragic car accident the year before. They had spent the previous year resolving the details of the adoption and catching Ben up on the realities of his new world.

The boy barreled into the kitchen just as Giovanni finished putting the jar of sauce on the spaghetti. He set it on the table along with a salad he'd put together from a bag and a bowl of olives.

"Spaghetti again?"

He cocked an eyebrow at the boy. "Tomorrow night you can cook. Besides," he said as he flicked the back of the boy's ear as he sat at the table, "you're an Italian now, you need to eat lots of pasta."

Ben snorted and dug into the food. Giovanni watched him scarf down his food with gusto; it reminded him of how much Caspar had eaten at that age. It had been harder to find food for Caspar in postwar Britain, but with the proliferation of American all-night markets and Ben's natural independence, the two of them managed just fine.

"I'm not Italian, really," Ben said between bites. "I'm Leba-Rican."

Giovanni smiled at the boy's quick wit. Ben was half Lebanese and half Puerto Rican, but their coloring was close enough that no one questioned their relation. The only difference was Ben's dark brown eyes, which had always reminded Giovanni of Beatrice.

"You might have to be the one to convince her," he mused.

"Convince who? Beatrice?"

"Mmmhmm. You'll have to convince her I'm not a complete bastard."

"Well, technically," Ben said between bites, "we both are."

Giovanni flicked the boy's ear again. "You know what I mean."

Ben paused and set down his fork. "You know, if we were friends and then you went away and I didn't see you for five years, I'd be pretty mad, too."

"You don't have to worry about me leaving you, Ben."

"I know, but she—"

"It was important for her to have time on her own. Without all the vampire stuff, as you like to call it. That's part of why she came here." He paused. "It's complicated, Benjamin."

Ben smirked before he began eating again. "That's always what grown-ups say when they're not sure they're right. So did she decide all that? Or did you? 'Cause you're pretty bossy, you know."

He decided to change the subject. "It's a good thing I am, or you'd never finish school. Finish up your dinner, then go upstairs and do the rest of your work. Do you need help with anything?"

Ben shook his head. "I don't think so."

"If you do, I'll be on the patio talking to Carwyn."

"Okay."

"No video games until after your work is finished. None."

The boy rolled his eyes. "I got it, I got it."

Taking the bowl of olives and a glass of wine with him, he went outside to the large covered patio that spread across the back of the house. He'd set up a rotary phone connection there, which he used to dial his friend in Northern Wales.

"Uncle Gio!" Carwyn answered. "How's the boy doing?"

"Well," Giovanni sipped his wine. "Very well. His studies are coming along, and he hasn't run away since the last time I called you."

"That's progress. I knew he'd come around."

"He still runs off on his bike during the day, though. He had to talk himself out of a truancy ticket last week."

"I doubt that was a problem for him. He's got quite the smart mouth."

"He's conniving in the best way."

They both chuckled a little but quickly fell silent.

Giovanni took a deep breath. "I saw her today."

Carwyn made no response for a few moments. "How did it go?"

"About as well as I deserve, I suppose."

Carwyn was quiet as Giovanni sipped his wine.

"How did she look?"

"Beautiful," he murmured. "Stunning. Angry."

"I told you—"

"I know what you told me." He rubbed a hand across his face. "And you know I had my reasons for staying away."

Carwyn said, "You wanted her to have her own life? She does. She's got a damn good one, as a matter of fact."

"Tell me about the boyfriend."

"I realize you'd like Mano to be some kind of miscreant, but he's not. He's a very good man, and he absolutely adores her."

Giovanni sighed and pinched the bridge of his nose. "Tell me about the boyfriend."

Carwyn took a deep breath. "Ex-navy diver. Has his own business with one of his military mates. Does fairly well for himself. He's a hard worker and very well-respected. Not much family of his own, but talks about wanting one with our girl."

Giovanni had the sudden vision of Beatrice swollen with child, her face full and glowing as she smiled. His breath caught, knowing that if she chose him, it would never be his child she would carry, and for the first time in five hundred years, he regretted that. Then, thinking of the boy upstairs and a small boy hiding in an attic many years before, he reminded himself that family came in many forms.

"She's too smart to be with anyone for that long if he wasn't a good man," he muttered. "How does she feel about him? Really? Does she love him?"

"I can't answer that," the priest said. "I'm sure she does, but she's been half in love with your memory for more than five years now. I doubt she knows how to feel about either of you at this point."

He pulled the picture of her riding the horse in Cochamó out of his pocket and looked at it. The sun glinted off her hair and a huge smile spread across her face. "I'll just have to convince her then."

He heard Carwyn clear his throat and Giovanni could almost sense the lecture from his old friend approaching. "Gio, you have been my friend for over three hundred years, and I love you dearly, but that girl is precious to me."

"I know."

"Her father isn't here to ask you, so I will. What are your intentions toward her? She has a good life now. She has friends, and a career, and a good man that loves her, so—"

"He can't—" Giovanni cleared his throat and closed his eyes. "He can't love her like I do, Carwyn. He can't. Because I promise you, he doesn't know her like I do."

There was a long pause on the other end of the line. "That doesn't mean she'll agree with you, my friend. What you're asking of her…it's not a small thing. She may not want to give up her life, even if it means forever with you."

He shrugged, though no one could see in the dark yard. "She may not. It's her decision, but I wouldn't bet against me." His thumb brushed over her cheek as he stared at the photograph. "I've given her time. Time to grow however she needed, free from the complications of our world. You may not have agreed with me, but I did what I felt like I needed to. For her."

"And now?"

He lifted the picture to stare into her dark, smiling eyes, wishing she was next to him, as he had for the past five years. He took a deep breath.

"Now I plan to convince her she wants eternity with me."

CHAPTER 3

"I know, but Dr. Stevens didn't really give me a choice, Mano." She heard her boyfriend sigh over the phone. "Well, I suppose I'll just tell Dan that I can't handle the morning dives for a while. On my schedule right now, we're never going to see each other."

"I know."

"How long is this guy going to be doing research? And why does he have to do it in the evenings? Are you going to miss judo and kickboxing, too?"

She curled her lip; she'd forgotten about her martial arts classes that met twice a week. Damn vampire.

"I think he has to do nights because of his other job or something. It's probably only going to be a couple of weeks."

It better only be that long. Giovanni had two weeks to convince her of…she wasn't sure what, but two weeks was her limit. She clenched her eyes in frustration. She felt as if the careful wall she'd constructed between her past and her present, between the supernatural world and the normal one, was starting to crumble, and she didn't know where to draw the lines.

Mano was still talking. "I know it's not your choice. And it's great that this guy requested you specifically. I'm really proud of you, B."

Her heart twisted, and she couldn't help feeling like she was deceiving him by not telling her boyfriend that Giovanni was the scholar she was helping with translation. Mano knew an even more abbreviated version of the Giovanni and Beatrice story than she had told Dez, and she had never told him she'd been romantically involved with her former employer.

Or whatever they had been.

She felt the hum of energy when Giovanni entered the room and looked up to see the vampire approach the table where she was sitting. Beatrice cursed mentally when she felt her heart begin to race, knowing he could hear it. She met his intense stare as he crossed the room, but she didn't hang up her phone. Mano was still talking.

"—so I'll see you tomorrow afternoon. Hey, baby, I gotta go. Dan's waiting for me to close up the shop. Love you."

She stared back at Giovanni when she responded. "I love you, too. Have a great night! Miss you, and I'll see you tomorrow."

He sat down next to her and leaned his elbow on the table, propping his chin on his hand to watch her. He was wearing a charcoal grey button-down shirt, a pair of black slacks she knew would show off his incredible ass, and a small, satisfied smile.

"How's your friend, Beatrice?" he asked when she hung up the phone.

She gave him a tight smile. "My *boyfriend's* great. I'll have to apologize," she said as she yawned. "I'm so tired today; he kept me up pretty late last night."

"Is that so?" He leaned toward her, smiling when her heart picked up. "I'll remember that. I'm sure I can think of inventive ways to stimulate you."

She rolled her eyes and opened the document files he had requested through Dr. Stevens. "Fine. Whatever. Now, what do you actually want? Since I know you don't need my help with the translations."

"I really am looking for provenance on an old journal. I found it for my client, but he wants documentation on the origins," he said in a more professional voice.

Beatice felt her heart sink. "Oh, you mean, you really only came for—"

"Asking for your help with the translation was a pure ploy for your attention, of course." His eyes swept from her boots to her face, which she could feel heat up, much to her own annoyance. "I could have just requested the documents and not your help, but where's the fun in that?"

She fought the smile that wanted to surface. "Well, here they are. Do you want me to go through them with you? I'm familiar with this set."

"I'd appreciate your eyes. There are a lot to go through, and I know you're far more familiar with them than I am."

"Well, it's nice to be appreciated."

"Let me know what else you'd like me to appreciate," he whispered. "I'll be happy to oblige."

Beatrice bit her lip and ignored him as she began to sort through the letters on the table. She'd walked right into that one. She was having problems not reacting to the playful version of Giovanni she only had faint memories of from Houston. He could be very flirtatious when he let himself, but it was usually only when he hadn't fed for a while and let his guard down.

"Need to go grab a bite to eat?" she muttered. "You're in quite the mood."

He leaned closer and she could hear him inhale, even though she refused to look at him. "Are you offering? Because I could have feasted last night, and I still wouldn't turn that down."

The blood rushed to her face. "Stop."

"Stop what? Telling you how good you smell? How good you look? You look amazing, by the way. How about how good you taste?"

She could feel his breath on her neck.

You're not supposed to be here! Beatrice wanted to scream. *Where have you been?*

His voice only dropped. "Should I not tell you how many times I've replayed in my memory the one time I tasted you in my bed? How I've dreamt about your skin? Is *that* what I should stop, *tesoro mio?*"

She could feel the heat radiating off him, and Beatrice knew he was as affected as she was. The smell of smoke and whiskey was even stronger than the night before, and she clenched her eyes, trying to keep herself from breaking down and throwing herself into his arms. Nothing about their attraction to each other had dissipated in the five years they'd been apart. She forced her mind into the present.

"Don't. Just...*don't*. Let's get to work, all right?"

Please, she almost begged.

His green eyes raked over her face, and she saw the edge of his fangs peek out from behind his lips.

"Fine," he murmured. "I'll stop...for now."

She let out a ragged breath and started sorting through the letters again.

Since he'd shown up the night before, Beatrice hadn't been able to think of anything else. And she was furious with herself for not being able to give him the cold shoulder the way she'd imagined for so many years. She could lie to him, but he would know.

He'd *always* known.

She'd attacked Mano the night before, clinging to him as if he was a life raft. He'd been amused by her sudden rush of desire, but he was an enthusiastic participant, nonetheless. Afterward, Beatrice had lain awake for hours, shaking and confused. She felt herself slipping into the tangled maze of emotion that gripped her on rare occasions when she allowed herself to remember her last year in Houston, her abduction to Greece, and her time with Giovanni at his house in the Cochamó Valley. The persistent questions about her father's whereabouts and what Lorenzo wanted from him had surfaced along with Giovanni, and she was already having trouble sleeping.

In the years she had lived in Los Angeles, Beatrice had carefully constructed a "normal life," distancing herself from most of the more supernatural elements unless Carwyn or Tenzin happened to visit. She'd even been able to distance herself when she visited Cochamó, fooling herself that her visits could be part of her "normal" life since Giovanni was never there. Now sitting next to him, smelling him, sensing the familiar energy that always seemed to radiate from him like her own personal magnetic field, made her want to throw herself into his arms, wrap herself around him, and forget the past five years.

She took deep breaths, finally calming the beat of her heart and the rush of her blood. She focused her mind and tried to see him as just another visiting Ph.D.

"Well, Dr. Vecchio, let's get started."

They worked silently for another hour, quickly falling back into the unspoken communication they'd always shared. But then, Giovanni had always had an uncanny knack for understanding the way her brain worked, and she'd had the same understanding of him.

"Did you find that one letter from Governor Portolá to—"

"Yes, I did. Thank you, that mention of the young friar—"

"Yeah, I thought that might be what you were looking for there."

They skimmed through the first stack of documents from Mission San Diego and moved on to a stack of letters from Monterey. They continued to whisper back and forth throughout the evening.

"Have you seen any further correspondence from the priest in San Diego that—"

"You mean the young Catalán? I think there's something in this stack here..."

"Ah, exactly. That's what I'm looking for. Thank you, *tesoro*. Look at the year. That's promising."

As they worked, the years seemed to slip away. Strangely, Beatrice felt even more at ease than she had when she'd first worked with Giovanni. She supposed the years she'd spent at school and working with visiting scholars had given her much-needed confidence. She was no longer intimidated by his intellect or his experience, and she realized he no longer treated her as a bright student but more like a colleague.

When it was time to leave, she felt reluctant to go back to her empty house, even though she knew she should. He hadn't made any more suggestive overtures, but five years of questions tugged at her mind. Luckily—or unluckily, she couldn't decide—he was waiting on the steps outside the library when she exited holding her helmet and the black backpack she wore riding.

"So...a motorcycle?"

She sat down on the steps, keeping a careful distance from him. "It's easy on gas and good for traffic."

"And sexy. Beautiful woman on a fast bike? Very sexy, *tesoro*," he said with a wink.

Well, that hadn't taken long.

"Gio, you need to—"

"Don't shush me. I'm allowed to express an opinion."

"What—" Beatrice paused, waiting for Dr. Stevens to pass. "Where have you been? Since you have appeared out of nowhere, and apparently want back in my life, I think I have a right to know."

He leaned toward her and tucked a piece of hair behind her ear. "I definitely want back in your life. And I like the hair, by the way. It suits you, though I do miss the length. I had dreams about that long hair—"

"Damn it!" She slapped his hand away. "Stop saying shit like that, all right? I have a boyfriend, and I'm trying to have an actual conversation with you."

Giovanni leaned back, placing his elbows on the steps above and stretching his long legs in front of him. She rolled her eyes, wishing she didn't notice the way his shirt stretched across his defined chest.

"Fine. And of course you have a right to know where I've been. I've been traveling mostly—"

"Yeah, got the postcards, thanks a bunch."

He smiled. "Did you keep them? Those are all the places your father left me a clue, then disappeared before I could get there."

Her heart almost stopped. "You—you've been looking for my father?" she whispered, tears springing to her eyes. "All this time?"

He looked away, allowing her to wipe her eyes. "On and off, yes. I told you I'd find him. I have a great desire to meet your father. He is both impressively and irritatingly good at hiding himself."

When Beatrice had moved to L.A.—and the threat of Lorenzo seemed to disappear—she had hoped her father would find her. She'd waited, keeping a faint hope alive he could be part of her life again. But as the years passed, Stephen De Novo, and whatever mystery he carried with him, remained stubbornly out of reach. So, she tucked him away into a dark corner of her heart and tried to forget.

She was still trying to process the idea of Giovanni spending the previous five years looking for her missing father. "How did you know where to look?"

"Oh," Giovanni murmured, "I would get word through certain channels that he'd been asking questions of this associate or that acquaintance. Looking for records at a certain library or auction house. All little clues he must have known I would pick up on, if I was looking for him."

"Did he know you were looking for him?"

"Yes." His expression darkened. "I let it be known I wanted to meet with him. De Novo kept leaving traces, but by the time I would get to any location, he would be gone."

Beatrice frowned, twisting her hands together. "Does he think you want to hurt him? Is that why he's hiding?"

"I don't know, though it's fairly well-known that his daughter is..."

"What? His daughter is what?"

Giovanni cleared his throat. "To put it bluntly, 'my human,' and—

Her eyes popped wide. *"What?"*

"—I wanted to speak to him—"

"'Your human?'" she hissed.

"Beatrice."

"Was there some sort of memo I should have gotten about this?"

"Beatrice?"

"Because, it's been *five years*, and I sure don't remember—"

"Beatrice!"

She fell silent, glaring at him, but he only leaned closer.

"You stole an almost unspeakable amount of money from an immortal. One who still has many friends. You've been living here in peace for five years now. Do you think that was some sort of accident or luck?"

"I don't know! I thought you said I'd be safe!"

"You *are* safe, but did you think everyone in my world..." Giovanni glanced over at the trees and lowered his voice. "Did you think they had forgotten? You've been under my protection since I kissed you at The Night Hawk pub six years ago. That has never changed."

She felt like she'd been punched in the chest. "But—"

"It doesn't matter whether you have a boyfriend," he bit out, "or whether we see each other or not. You'll be under my aegis for as long as you live." He paused, but there was no amusement or victory in his eyes. "Or you're fair game, Beatrice. And that is not acceptable to me."

Beatrice whispered, "I wish you'd told me."

She'd been fooling herself. The graduate degree. The very respectable job. The little house in Silver Lake. Mano... All pieces of a life that was still under someone else's control.

Giovanni took a deep breath. When he continued his voice was hoarse, "Why would I tell you all that? So you could worry? So you could have nightmares again and spend your days looking over your shoulder? I didn't want that for you, *tesoro*."

She shook her head and glared at him. "What the hell *did* you want for me? Why didn't you ever come to Cochamó when you knew I'd be there? Did you want me to miss you? To wonder every night if you were alive or—" She broke off when he held up a hand.

"You should be quiet unless you want an audience," he muttered, looking at the trees again.

"What? What are you talking about?" She craned her neck, trying to see in the darkness.

Giovanni sighed. "Benjamin, stop hiding in the trees and come introduce yourself."

"Benjamin?" Her eyes narrowed. "*Ben?*"

"Are you going to be mad at me?" She heard a child's voice call from the shadows and looked back at Giovanni, who was sitting with an expression both sulking and amused.

"No." He stood and reached for her hand. "Just come out." He muttered something else in Italian she didn't understand.

"Will you please tell me what is going on?" Beatrice walked down the steps, clutching her helmet in front of her. At the edge of the trees, she saw a boy emerge holding onto a bicycle and looking at Giovanni with a crooked smile. He was thin and a bit clumsy as he emerged from the brush, but his sharp brown eyes looked her over, and a smile grew on his face.

"Are you Beatrice?"

"Are you the Ben who was asking for me last week?"

He grinned and nodded. "Yep. That guard actually told you? I didn't think he would."

Giovanni frowned. "What do you mean, you were asking after her?"

Ben looked at Giovanni innocently. "Well, you were so nervous about talking to her—"

"Tell me why you're out on your bike at nine-thirty, Benjamin." Giovanni interrupted.

Oh really? So Giovanni wasn't quite as confident as he seemed. She looked over to Ben, who grinned at her.

"I was wondering whether my uncle was going to provide a delicious and nutritious meal for me. Family time is so important and all."

Giovanni cocked an eyebrow in the boy's direction. "And I suppose you missed the note about the leftovers in the fridge?"

"Wait," Beatrice held up a hand. "Uncle? Am I missing something here?"

"Only me," Ben said with a mischievous smile, "but I'm here now, so no need to worry."

Giovanni reached over and pinched the boy's ear. "Don't be rude. Introduce yourself."

Ben propped his bike on the kickstand and held out his hand. "Benjamin Vecchio. Former pickpocket, con man, runaway, and fake nephew of the vampire to your right. You must be the beautiful Beatrice."

She held out her hand and Ben took it, bending down to kiss the back in a gallant gesture. She laughed and looked at Giovanni. "And you think *you're* charming?"

Giovanni rolled his eyes as Ben continued kissing up her arm. He reached over and tugged Ben's collar, pulling him away from Beatrice, who was still laughing.

"Stop it, she's too old for you."

"Well, technically," Ben said with a smile, "she's *way* too young for you, old man."

"Do you like that Xbox I bought you? How about the daily meals?"

"Shutting up now," Ben quipped. "But really, Beatrice, it's nice to finally meet you."

"Um..." She paused. "Likewise. And please call me B, only the professor here calls me Beatrice. So you're his fake nephew, huh?"

Giovanni put an arm around Ben's shoulders. "My poor, departed brother's child. Tragic accident."

"Very tragic," Ben nodded solemnly. "I still cry sometimes. Not really. My real parents were assholes."

She nodded along, trying to integrate this new, paternal side of the vampire. She knew it shouldn't surprise her—after all, he had raised Caspar—but it was still difficult to think about the man that made her blood boil with anger and desire in equal measure being, for all practical purposes, a father.

Despite the fact he was over five hundred years old.

"Okay then, well, on that very interesting note—"

"Do you ride a motorcycle?" Ben pointed at her helmet. "Cool! Can I see it?"

"Um, sure. I guess. I mean if it's okay with Gio..."

Giovanni nodded, probably glad he had managed to trap her into further conversation. They walked toward the parking lot and she looked over at Ben. "How did you get all the way here? Where do you guys live?"

"Well," Giovanni started, "I happened to find an appropriate house—"

"We just live a couple blocks from here! Gio thought it would be great 'cause he could walk to where you work instead of worrying about the driving thing. I keep telling him he should teach me to drive, and then he wouldn't have to worry about breaking cars, but he tells me I have to wait till I'm fourteen, or at least until my feet touch the pedals."

"So you could walk to where I work, huh?" she muttered under her breath, knowing he could hear her, even if Ben could not. He simply cocked an eyebrow at her and shrugged.

"I told you I was here for you. And the house next to yours was too small."

"You wouldn't—"

"Is that your bike? It's awesome! I've never seen one like that. Gio, can I have—"

"No," he said quickly and looked at her with a smile. Leaning down, he whispered in her ear. "Very sexy. I can just imagine your legs wrapping around—"

"So, Ben," Beatrice cleared her throat as she interrupted the thought she really didn't want him to finish. "Want to sit on it?"

"Cool!" Ben threw his bike on the ground and scrambled over to Beatrice's Triumph. As she helped the boy onto the back and explained some of the features of the bike, she could feel Giovanni's gaze as if it was a physical touch. She tried to concentrate on Ben's enthusiasm and ignore what the vampire's eyes were doing to her heart rate.

"So," Ben said, "are you going to take the job? He asked you already, right?"

"Wha—what job?" She looked over her shoulder at Giovanni, who was frowning and glaring at Ben in frustration. He closed his eyes and she thought she saw his lips move like he was counting.

"Oh." Ben grinned meekly. "I guess not. Oops."

She walked over and stood in front of Giovanni with her hands on her hips. "What job?"

CHAPTER 4

"Tell me more about my dad."

"Is this really the time, Beatrice?"

Giovanni looked up from the letter he was examining and around the reading room at the Huntington. They were finishing up the letters in the collection and, so far, he was relieved they hadn't found what he was expecting.

Beatrice whispered as she paged through a journal from a Franciscan friar in San Francisco. "Since you're not going to convince me to work for you, I think now would be an excellent time."

"I really wish you'd reconsider."

"I'm sure you would."

He slipped his hand over to trace along the skin of her forearm. She batted him away, but he could still feel her heart race.

"Stop it."

"I can almost promise my benefits package is better than the Huntington."

He saw her trying to suppress the smile. "Did you just say 'package?'" she snickered.

Giovanni cleared his throat and glanced at Dr. Stevens, who was looking at them. He smiled politely and nodded in the librarian's direction.

"You are never allowed to call me juvenile again, Gio."

"I never called you juvenile in the first place."

She cut her eyes toward him. "You thought it, though."

He let his eyes roam over her. "Not in a long time."

"Nice way to distract me, by the way. Tell me about my dad."

Giovanni rolled his eyes. "Your father is very good at hiding."

"He never contacted me. Do you think he even knows that I want to see him?"

She had cocked her shoulders in his direction and he wished he could reach over and smooth the frown that had gathered between her eyes. "Yes, I'm quite sure he does."

"So why wouldn't he—"

"He's avoiding me."

That only caused the frown to grow. "But why would he avoid you?"

"Oh..." He cleared his throat and glanced up to see Dr. Stevens watching them again. "You forget that he spent his formative vampire years with Lorenzo. I very much doubt my son has any nice things to say about me."

"But you said he would hate Lorenzo."

"And I'm sure he hates Lorenzo's sire, as well."

He saw her face fall a little. "But, you've protected me. You've...you said I was seen as 'yours' so wouldn't he know you were protecting me?"

Giovanni scanned one letter and began on another. "I'm sure he doesn't know what to think. And he's been quite elusive, so I'm sure he doesn't trust me."

Beatrice fell silent. They both worked quietly as the minutes passed. He was running out of time. He knew they would find the provenance on the journal eventually, or he would run out of research material, and then he would have no regular excuse to see her since she refused to quit her job and come work for him.

"I was in Shanghai a few years ago meeting with some old contacts. I was able to see some amazing martial arts demonstrations. You would have loved them." He knew Beatrice had developed an interest in self-defense and martial arts in the years they had been apart. Considering her kidnapping, it was not a surprise.

He saw her smile. "Are you trying to tempt me with exotic travel and intrigue if I come work for you?"

"Yes. Is it working?"

She looked around the reading room and over at Dr. Stevens, who was still watching her like a hawk, no doubt wondering why Giovanni had requested her specifically. He'd have to alter the woman's memories again before he left for the night.

"I like Southern California."

"Good, we'll make our base here and come back between research trips." He continued before she had time to interrupt. "Have I told you how nice it is to be working with you again? Or in a library at all, for that matter? I've been doing irritating political things in the past few years. Very annoying. I have to talk with all sorts of unpleasant people who like to hear themselves speak. Whining and simpering. They all remind me of my time with my father."

"What kind of political things?"

"Oh, visiting people that owe me favors. Trying to determine what my son is up to. A kind of intelligence gathering, I suppose. All those things I tried to avoid for the past three hundred years."

She said, "I'd apologize, but you're the one who made him."

"No apologies necessary. I put the matter of dealing with him off for too long."

"And your books? Andros's library?" She put down the journal she'd been working on and picked up another. "Any clues about that?"

"A bit. The majority of it remains a mystery, but he's sold off some of the more easily moveable pieces of the collection, so I've reacquired a few things. You really must have wiped him out when you took his accounts, *tesoro*."

"That's always nice to hear."

"And you appear to be doing quite well financially."

Giovanni saw her smile. "I don't have to worry about paying the bills, no."

He gave a quiet laugh. "So I've collected a few more of my father's books. I've tried to track your father. I've reestablished myself among some allies. Then I found Benjamin, and that's been quite the project."

"Sounds like you were busy," she said in a small voice.

"And I missed you every day."

She was silent for a few long minutes. He wondered if she would respond at all.

"You knew where to find me," she finally said.

Giovanni had no answer for her. He had known where to find her, but he had also known that she needed time to grow and mature. He only hoped he could convince her that it was worth giving him another chance.

"Beatrice—"

"So have you heard anything more about Lorenzo? He still staying under the radar?"

He sighed and picked up another letter. "He has been. I'll hear something every now and then about him or one of his children, but for the most part he's been quiet."

"Why do I find that disturbing?"

"Probably because it's easier to kill the snake on the path than the one in the rocks."

She looked at him. "That's an excellent description of him."

"A snake?" He cocked an eyebrow. "It's an accurate one."

She murmured under her breath, "He's like this ghost in the back of my mind. I try to forget him, but..."

He reached over and squeezed her hand quickly. "Don't forget about him until he's dead."

Beatrice shook her head. "Why did I ever fool myself?"

He frowned. "What? What are you talking about?"

She looked at him for a long moment before she turned back to the journal she'd been studying. "Nothing."

Giovanni knew it wasn't nothing, but he also knew she wouldn't tell him. They worked silently together for another half an hour. Finally, he saw her studying a page in the journal intently and her heart began to race.

"Here," she said quietly, but there was no victorious smile on her face. He took the journal from her and studied the page she had pointed to. "Found a mention in the Catalan's notes."

"Let me see," he said as he read the pages from the old book, reading about the young priest the father had met and how they compared journal notes on the journey up the California coast. It was consistent with the diary his client had acquired. It gave him a name and a year. It was as much as he could hope for from the Huntington collection.

"Guess I found your provenance," Beatrice said.

His eyes raked over her face. "I always knew you would."

BEATRICE THRUST HER HIP BACK, TOSSING HER SPARRING PARTNER OVER HER shoulder. The large man hit the floor with a loud *slap*, and she straightened with a grunt as her *sensei* smiled from across the mat. She held a hand out to her partner to help him up. They bowed to each other and shook hands as they finished the freestyle judo practice.

Pete called out, "B, you are on a roll today! What's gotten into you? Very nice *randori*, both of you. Very nice." The wiry, grey-haired man strode across the mat and shook both Beatrice and her partner's hands before all three walked to the lockers near the free weights. "B, you still have one of the strongest *harai goshi* I've seen. I know you were dissatisfied with your last teacher, but your forms are really strong."

She nodded and wiped the sweat from her eyes. "Thanks. He was great, I just felt like he'd taken me as far as I could go in my training. I felt like I was in a rut, you know?"

Pete nodded and slapped her shoulder. "No worries, I understand. Sometimes a relationship just runs its course. I hope you parted on good terms."

Beatrice nodded and untied her belt, taking off her heavy *judogi* and stripping down to a tank top to hit the punching bags on the side of the studio.

"How long have you been studying?"

"Judo?"

Pete nodded.

"Well, when I first moved out to L.A., I started studying martial arts. First, it was just some tai chi at the university. A friend suggested it. Then I decided to take a self-defense class—"

"Always a good idea for anyone."

"Yeah, I can agree with that. Anyway, the place I went to taught judo and jujitsu, too, so I got interested that way. I've been studying almost five years now."

She slipped on her gloves and Pete joined her at the bags. They both began hitting the teardrop shaped speed bags that hung from platforms in the low ceiling. Soon, Beatrice was zoning out to the sound and the rhythm of the quick punches as she tried to release the stress of the day and her last meeting with Giovanni.

Focus, focus, focus, she thought as she tried to wipe the image of his deep green eyes from her mind.

"Your focus is really impressive," Pete said as he worked the bag to her right. "You should be proud of yourself. You look like you've been studying twice as long."

"That's nice to hear." *Even though I'm completely distracted at the moment.*

Suddenly, he grinned. "What did you like about judo at first? I can almost guess."

Beatrice laughed. "I saw this little girl toss a guy about a foot taller and seventy pounds heavier than her."

Pete chuckled as he continued hitting the bag. "Yeah, that'll do it. It's pretty great when you realize you can take down someone way stronger than you if you know what you're doing and use their own strengths against them, right?"

She shook her head. "Pete, you have no idea."

"WHY AM I SO UPSET?" BEATRICE ASKED AS SHE DRANK ANOTHER GLASS OF wine at Dez's apartment.

Dez only raised an eyebrow. "Because you now have no handy excuse to see the man you've been in love with for five years?"

"I'm not in love with him."

"Yeah." Her best friend snorted. "Whatever."

"I'm not."

"Okay, then you're upset because...you're going to miss the challenge of the project? That is way cooler than most of the stuff we do." Dez couldn't contain the grin. "I mean, what a cool job! When you worked for him before, did you ever have a kind of treasure hunt like that? Or was it mostly research and catalogue work?"

Dez sat on the edge of her seat while Beatrice stared at her. "Uh...there may have been a mystery or two that we worked on, yeah."

"And did you solve it? I mean, how does that work? That's got to pay pretty well, right? It's like hiring a private detective to find something. Only it's someone who knows rare books! Do you think he's looking for an assistant? I would totally dig something like—"

"He's kind of a loner, to be honest." *Kinda.* "I doubt he'd hire...someone to do that stuff when he could just do it himself." She did wonder who he had doing his computer work for him. Did he just use amnis to get random people to search online? That wasn't very ethical. Maybe he did need—

"Yeah," Dez sighed. "I totally get why you're so hung up on him though. A good-looking Italian book collector who solves historical mysteries? That's just..."

"What?" *Implausible?*

"Hot. I can't believe Mano's not insanely jealous of all the time you're spending with him."

Beatrice felt her face heat up, and she caught Dez's wide-eyed look.

"He doesn't know, does he?"

She shrugged. There was no way on God's green earth Beatrice was telling Mano that she was working alongside a five-hundred-year-old vampire who was linked to her missing father and was the sire of the monster who had kidnapped her. There was no way she was telling anyone any of that. They'd think she was insane.

"Oh, he's going to be pissed, B!"

"Why? The research is done." And her heart still ached over it. "Why would I see him anymore?" She shook her head and continued quietly. "He'll probably leave town again now that he has it."

Dez frowned. "I thought you said he bought a house?"

So he had, and she'd been asked over for dinner more than once by the persistent Ben. It was both despicable and adorable that Giovanni seemed to have Ben on his team in his attempts to win her back. She had to admit, the boy was charming.

As was his fake uncle.

"So he's probably going to use Southern California as a base for work if he did that," Dez reasoned. "It would be a good one. Easy airport access and lots of international flights to both Europe and Asia. Big research libraries and plenty of resources."

"That's true."

"And a cute librarian he's obviously still got the hots for."

"Shut up, Dez."

"Not on your life."

BEATRICE WAS STILL THINKING ABOUT WHAT DEZ HAD SAID WHEN HER BEST friend dropped her off at her empty house. Would Giovanni leave? What if he really was serious about staying in her life? What did that mean for her? For him? For her relationship with her incredibly loving but clueless boyfriend? Mano had a dive in the morning, so she was alone when she picked up the shoebox she had brought from Houston five years before.

Beatrice opened the lid and pulled out a picture of her and her father. Stephen De Novo's dark brown eyes stared at her. She still missed him so much. It was worse knowing he was out there somewhere, and she just couldn't find him. What did it all mean? Why had he never come? Maybe her father didn't trust Giovanni, but couldn't he trust her? What was the secret he was still running from after fifteen years?

Was Giovanni her best chance at finding him?

Had Lorenzo already found him?

Would Giovanni's son find her again?

She shook her head and replaced the lid on the old box, shoving it back on the bottom of the bookshelf in the living room. She didn't have room in her life for another mystery. She had built a good life. A safe life. She didn't want to be pulled into the chaos of the past.

But when she closed her eyes that night, a dulcet laugh haunted her dreams, and her father's eyes pleaded with her to find him. Beatrice woke with a start to see the moon shining through the narrow window of her bedroom. In her drowsy state, she looked for Giovanni beside her.

Just as it had been for the past five years, he was nowhere to be found.

CHAPTER 5

Two weeks.
Giovanni's immortal life was measured in two-week intervals.
After her find at the library, Beatrice had given him two weeks to prove they could be friends again. While he knew he wouldn't be satisfied with only that, he realized she still had doubts about his intentions, so he tried to back off and give her some space. They had been friends first, and he could be a friend again.

For a while.

So they met for coffee and conversation. She came to dinner at the house with Ben acting as an enthusiastic chaperone. Giovanni waited outside the library when she worked late just to walk her to her motorcycle.

And at the end of two weeks, she told him he was allowed to be in her life... as a friend. So he gamely ignored her racing heart every time she saw him and the loaded looks she cast his direction when she thought he wasn't looking and pretended to be Beatrice's friend for a while.

Two weeks turned into four, and they met for coffee a few times each week after her judo class. She had recently begun practice with a new teacher.

"Pete's so good. I mean, he kind of beats me up—"

Giovanni couldn't contain the low growl, and she shot him a look.

"—but in a good way. Since I've changed to this studio, I've made a lot more progress. And I'm a lot stronger. They focus on conditioning more than my old place."

"You look stronger. And your balance has improved."

She smiled. "I love judo. It's so much fun. Have you ever studied martial arts?" She laughed. "Do you even need to?"

"My physical conditioning with my father was based on the Spartan *agoge*, so I learned about most military and fighting techniques that way, but Tenzin trained me more on hand-to-hand fighting styles. I picked up whatever she taught me, which was a strange mix of 'do whatever will kill your opponent the fastest,' and her sire's form of *wushu*, or kung fu, as humans refer to it."

"Cool. Tenzin's the one who recommended I take tai chi when I first moved to California. That's kind of what started me out. I still practice."

"Tai chi?"

"Yeah."

He nodded, letting a smile cross his lips when he thought about his old friend.

"And Mano studied martial arts in the military. He still does some kick boxing. Sometimes we practice together."

He made no response, choosing to ignore the existence of the boyfriend whenever she brought him up.

Beatrice had told Mano that Giovanni was an old friend from Houston who had recently moved to town and a mutual friend of Carwyn's whom she had worked for in the past. He had a feeling that the boyfriend was clueless about more than his and Beatrice's past relationship.

He leaned toward her in the crowded café. "So you really haven't told anyone? Not even Dez? About your father or Carwyn or... anything?" He blew on the fragrant coffee he held, heating his breath to heighten the scent since it had cooled.

"*No*, I didn't tell anyone. What would I say?" She lowered her voice. "Oh, hey, Dez, you know my friend, Carwyn? He's a thousand-year-old Welsh priest who hunts deer and drinks their blood. Oh, and my father is a vampire, too, but I haven't seen him for almost fifteen years so I don't know what he eats. And I was kidnapped by a vampire once, but don't worry, my boss—who I was kind of involved with, but not really—rescued me with his two best friends, one of whom can fly and the other who can tunnel underground like a giant gopher."

He shrugged. "Seems totally believable to me. And we were most definitely involved."

Beatrice rolled her eyes and took a sip of coffee. "Right, and were you going to swoop in and rescue me when they carted me off to the looney bin?"

"I will always swoop in and rescue you, whether from psychotic vampires or the men in white coats."

He caught the small smile she tried to hide and held up his cup of coffee, inhaling deeply.

"Why do you even order it, Gio?"

"I told you, I like the way it smells."

Beatrice shook her head and leaned back in the plush chair. She closed her eyes and he allowed his gaze to caress her face while she was unaware. He'd been dancing around his feelings for well over a month, and it was becoming increasingly harder to keep silent.

He forced himself to remain casual, more interested in regaining her trust than in satisfying himself. Tenzin's admonition to be patient seemed more and more apt every day.

"So," he cleared his throat. "I have a favor to ask, which you are in no way obligated to grant, but I thought I'd ask anyway."

She kept her eyes closed but mumbled, "Does it involve blood donation?"

"Are you offering?"

Beatrice cracked one eye open and grimaced. "No."

"Then how about taking Ben to the doctor?"

Her head shot up. "Why? Is he okay?"

"Nothing to worry about that I know of. He just needs a regular doctor. And you wouldn't even have to go in with him—I'm sure he'd be mortified if you did—just drive him. He needs a checkup and none of the pediatricians in the area have evening hours. I can write a note as his guardian, of course."

She thought for a moment before she nodded. "I can do that. Let me get my schedule for next week and I'll see what days would be best."

"Thank you. I appreciate it."

"Oh! Next week is Thanksgiving. That might not be the best week to go."

He nodded. "You are the one doing the favor, so you let me know what day will work for you. I'll make the appointment from there. And thank you again."

She shrugged. "I'm refusing to work for you, so it's the least I can do."

"I really wish you'd reconsider your—"

"I'm sure you would," she interrupted, "but I'm very happy at the Huntington."

He cocked an eyebrow. "Translating and researching for scholars with less intelligence than you? Taking orders from someone you could run circles around intellectually? It must be so stimulating, *tesoro*."

"Don't start, or I'll leave."

He exhaled and let his head fall back into the armchair. "Fine, I'll refrain from stating the obvious."

"Just..." she sighed. "It's only been a month. Give me time to have you back in my life like this. Give me some time to make room for you on my terms."

Why don't you get rid of the excess boyfriend? That should leave exactly the right amount of room. He thought it but bit his tongue and smiled. "Of course."

"So what are you and Ben doing for Thanksgiving? Going back to Houston?"

"No, no, we're going back to Texas for Christmas, but I thought we'd stay around here for a quiet meal."

Her mouth dropped open exactly how he had imagined the granddaughter of

Isadora De Novo's would. "What? You're going to feed the child spaghetti for Thanksgiving dinner?"

Giovanni shrugged. "Well, he's never celebrated it properly anyway. And I thought I'd try to make that macaroni and cheese he likes. I think I'd be able to manage that. We didn't do much last year, either." He frowned. "Of course, I think we were still fighting about stealing from my wallet last year."

"You're bringing him over to my place," she stated. "The boy's never even had a turkey dinner? What are you thinking, Gio?"

I'm thinking I wrangled exactly the invitation to your house I've been looking for. "Beatrice, you really don't—"

"Are you kidding me? Mac and cheese? You can barely manage spaghetti from a jar. And my grandmother would die if she heard I let you feed that kid junk food on Thanksgiving. Come over to my house. Sunset's before five now, I'll make dinner for six-thirty. Bring some wine."

He smothered his satisfied smile. "Thank you. I'm sure Benjamin will appreciate the decent meal. As will I."

She shook her head and muttered under her breath. "Macaroni and cheese..."

The following Thursday, he was trying to convince Ben that a collared shirt would not inflict bodily injury.

"She wears Docs! She'd like my CBGB's shirt way better. It's vintage. Vintage is better than a tux to a Doc Marten girl."

"It most certainly is not, Benjamin. And be grateful I'm not making you wear a tie."

"Oh man, I'm not wearing a tie. No way!"

Giovanni tucked in a dark green button down shirt and fastened the buttons at his wrists. "Trust me, women always appreciate a well-dressed man."

The boy looked at him suspiciously as he pulled on his hated dress shoes. "I don't know. She's not your girlfriend yet."

"Well, there's another lesson. Things and people of value are worth waiting for."

"If you say so."

"I know so."

"Hey, Gio?"

"Yes?"

Ben's face was free of its usual sarcasm when Giovanni looked at him. "I get why you love her so much. She's pretty great."

He smiled at the perceptive boy. "I have only the finest taste in people."

Ben looked embarrassed but quickly shot back, "Dude, I don't want to know about your blood-drinking habits."

Giovanni snorted and looked in the mirror before he walked over to the boy and mussed his hair. "Comb this mess. It's almost time to go."

They drove to Beatrice's small house, Ben carrying on a constant chatter in the old Mustang that had finally arrived from Houston, and Giovanni trying to prepare himself to curb his natural instincts so he could meet Beatrice's boyfriend without killing or maiming him.

They were met at the door by a blond woman Giovanni assumed was Beatrice's best friend, Desiree Riley.

"You must be Desiree." He held out his hand politely and nudged Ben to do the same. "It's a pleasure to meet you. I've heard a lot about you."

She smiled. "It's Dez. You must be Gio. I can almost promise I've heard more about you." She cocked her head and looked at Ben. "Or is this Gio? You're not that tall yet, but you've got the dark and handsome part down."

Ben grinned, winking at Dez and holding his arm out for her to take. She giggled and took it as they walked inside. "Well, Dez, my name's Ben, I'm the smarter and more charming of the Vecchio men..."

Giovanni shook his head as he followed them into the small 1920s era Spanish bungalow. He crossed the small living room and paused when he saw a large man bending over Beatrice's shoulder as she stood in front of the stove.

There were few times in his five hundred years that Giovanni had truly been grateful for the vicious training of his sire, Niccolo Andros. The fifteen years he'd spent under the vampire's thumb had been brutal and draining, both mentally and physically.

But as he watched former Navy diver, Mano Akana, put his hands on Beatrice's waist and pull her close, he knew he'd relive every one of those torturous training sessions if it allowed him to not kill the oblivious man holding onto his woman.

That level of violence would, no doubt, put most of the guests off their dinner.

He quieted the growl that wanted to escape his throat and cut his eyes toward Matt Kirby, his associate who had been living next to Beatrice on his orders for more than three years. Matt gave him a small nod and returned his attention to Dez and Ben. Ben was busy introducing himself.

"Gio!" Beatrice called, as she extricated herself from the grasp of the overmuscled behemoth who held her. She walked into the living room and gave Ben a quick hug before she walked to Giovanni.

She hesitated a moment but leaned forward and embraced him. He pushed his amnis toward her and felt the shiver travel down her back. Glancing past her, he noticed the boyfriend watching them intently and knew, without a doubt, that Beatrice was the only one fooling herself that they were nothing more than friends.

"Happy Thanksgiving, *tesoro*," he said quietly before he approached Mano in the kitchen. He held out his hand and tried not to imagine how many ways he could kill the man.

"Giovanni Vecchio. You must be Mano."

The man's hair may have fallen to his shoulders, but the eyes that examined him revealed his military background more than any uniform.

"Nice to meet you. You're a friend of Carwyn's, right? And B's old boss?"

"I'm both. And a friend as well. She's a remarkable woman. You're very lucky." *To not be dead right now.*

"Oh, I know I am," Mano murmured, a look of challenge in his eyes. "And this is your nephew?"

"Benjamin, yes. Ben, come introduce yourself to Beatrice's friend."

Mano cut his eyes toward Giovanni and smirked. Both men nodded toward the other, as if a challenge had been accepted, before Ben came over to introduce himself and the tension was cut.

The dinner was far better than anything he could have produced, and Giovanni ate more than he usually did. He'd been buying donated blood in Los Angeles and feeding on that unless the opportunity to feed from a criminal presented itself—which it did with fair regularity. In the past five years, he'd lost his appetite for random women and the blood they could offer him, so he'd been making do. He knew he was not at full strength, and it bothered him.

Giovanni wished that he hated the boyfriend but realized under other circumstances, he would probably like the man. No matter. After observing Beatrice and Mano throughout the evening, he had no qualms about doing everything in his power to separate them.

She was trying to convince herself she was in love with him. She most likely did love the human in some fashion, but she did not look at Mano the way she had once looked at him. Nor did she react to the man with the same physical intensity she did to Giovanni.

Mano, however, was very obviously in love with Beatrice. He could hardly blame the man, but his determination to make Beatrice his own suffered no setback at the thought of the human's impending disappointment.

"Giovanni? What are you working on right now? Are you settling in L.A. permanently?" Dez asked from across the table. He smiled at the blond woman, noticing the longing look Matt Kirby threw toward her every time she opened her mouth.

"I am for now," he answered. "It's a good place for research, and I like my house in Pasadena."

"It's totally awesome, and I have my own basketball court," Ben added.

"You should have a party!" Dez said.

Matt chuckled. "Gio's not really one for entertaining." His eyes widened and he added, "At least, you don't seem like the type to me."

Giovanni clenched his jaw and glanced at Matt's apologetic face before he looked toward Beatrice, who was glaring at him.

"Hey, Gio," she asked, "can you help me with something in the kitchen?"

He excused himself from the table, glancing at Mano's perturbed face as he left. He walked into the kitchen and leaned against the counter.

"Matt?" she whispered.

He shrugged. "I've worked with him on and off for a number of years. He's very trustworthy."

"But he's been watching me? This whole time?"

He rolled his eyes. "He's not a stalker, Beatrice. He's security, and he's very good. He likes you, as well, if you're curious. And I'm fairly certain he's romantically interested in your friend."

"This whole time?"

"I did what I needed to keep you safe. I'm not going to apologize for it."

She crossed her arms and glanced toward the dining room. "Well, did he 'save' me from anything? In all these years?"

He crossed his arms and mirrored her. "As a matter of fact, no."

"Then I think I deserve an apology."

"No. Absolutely not."

"Why not?" She was fuming. "Apparently he was unnecessary."

Giovanni stepped close to her, towering over her as she glared at him. "An apology would imply that I am regretful or sorry in some way, and I make no apologies for doing everything in my power to protect you."

He didn't expect the flash of tears in her eyes. "You wanted me protected? It was that important? Then why wasn't it you?" she hissed before she stormed toward the hall bathroom. Mano entered the kitchen a few minutes later wearing a smug look. Giovanni felt a small burst of flame rise near his hand, so he crossed his arms again and pulled his temper back.

"You managed to piss her off pretty well, Giovanni."

"Oh," he muttered. "That's nothing new. I've been doing that for years."

"Not for the past five, you haven't," Mano muttered. "That's how long it's been, right? That's how long she's been following your ghost to some old house in Chile?"

Giovanni smiled. "Did *she* tell you that?" He saw Mano deflate a bit. "No, I didn't think so. She's very good at keeping secrets, isn't she?"

"She's private."

"Call it what you will." Giovanni leaned back against the counter.

"Well, you don't know her anymore. Not like I do."

Giovanni laughed. "Oh really? And why do you say that?"

"Because you weren't here, asshole. Were you at her party when she bought this house? We'd only been dating a few weeks, but I made being there a priority. How about when she got her job at the Huntington? She was *so* proud of herself.

Or maybe when her grandmother had the scare with her heart a couple years ago? Miss out on that, too?"

He just stared in silence when Mano stepped closer in the small room.

"How about when her scum bag of a mother showed up last year and tried to get money from her? Did you know about that?" he asked. "Of course not, because you weren't here. Know who was? Me. I was here. And I'm not going anywhere."

He smiled at the tall man who knew so little. "You think you know her fairly well, don't you?"

"I do know her. And I love her."

"I'm sure you do. But you don't know her like I do." Giovanni shrugged. "It's not your fault. She hasn't allowed you to know her that well, has she?"

"You're so damn arrogant."

"I am, but am I wrong?" he asked and glanced toward the dining room, noting that Ben seemed to be entertaining Matt and Dez with some amusing story. "I know a lot about you, Mano. Can you say the same about me?"

"What does that even—"

"She's very protective of the ones she loves. So who is she protecting with her secrets? You?" Giovanni stepped closer and let his swirling green eyes bore into Mano's. "Or is she protecting me?"

Mano glared at him before he retreated, turning to walk down the hall in search of Beatrice. Giovanni could hear him knocking on the bathroom door when he walked back into the dining room.

"Benjamin, it's time for us to go."

TWO WEEKS.

She refused his calls for two weeks, until finally, Giovanni sat outside the library, waiting for her on the steps. When she walked through the glass doors and spotted him, she didn't stop, so he followed her.

"Beatrice."

She kept walking past the walkway to the parking lot and toward a small grove of isolated oak trees. She did not look back. For the first time since he'd come back into her life, Giovanni felt a hint of panic.

"I want to talk to you," he called as she paced through the trees.

She whirled around and he almost ran into her. "Yeah, I think that's a good idea, Gio. Let's talk."

"Fine. I think you need to tell Dez and Mano the truth about me. About everything."

She backed away from him and her mouth gaped open. "What?"

"You need to tell them." He cocked an eyebrow at her. "You say you love them and you want them to be a part of your life, so why don't you trust them?"

She might tell Dez... but he was betting she wouldn't tell Mano.

Beatrice only blinked at him. "I don't—you *want* me to tell them?"

"Do you love them?" She didn't answer, so he shrugged. "It's up to you, but you can't continue to live with these secrets. It's going to make you sick. It's already making you angry."

"No." She strode toward him, pointing a finger at his chest. "*You* made me angry. When you told Mano about us. It's none of his business."

"Why were you hiding it?"

"To protect you!"

"I didn't ask you to do that. I didn't ask you to protect me." He stepped closer and they circled each other under the oak trees.

"And I didn't ask you to protect me, but you did. Why the hell did you hire someone to live next to me all these years?" Her face was red and furious, but he could see the tears filling her eyes. "What was the point? Did he tell you when guys stayed over? Did he tell you when I flirted with him myself?"

His fists clenched, but he forced himself to remain calm. "It didn't matter, I don't care about that. I care about you." He approached cautiously, as if walking too quickly might scare her off. "You deserved a life. A normal life *without* me, so you knew—"

"I didn't *want* a life without you!" she exploded, tears finally falling down her face. "Don't you get that? Are you that dense? Don't you realize I was in love with you?"

His heart ached. "Beatrice—"

"Five hundred years and you couldn't tell?"

He walked toward her, desperate to take her in his arms, but she stepped back, dashing the tears from her eyes.

"*Tesoro*—"

"Why didn't you come?" She sobbed. "Why? I waited for *years*! I never loved a man the way I loved you. I've never loved anyone that way. I never wanted anyone that way."

For the first time in his immortal life, he felt as if his heart could bleed from another's pain. Giovanni could only whisper, "I know."

He stepped within arm's distance and put a single hand on her cheek, which was flushed and wet with tears. In that moment, Beatrice didn't look like a confident woman of twenty-eight; she looked like the girl he had forced himself to leave.

"So *why*, Gio? If you knew, why? Don't you realize I would have done *anything* for you? I would have run away with you."

"Beatrice—"

"Didn't you know?" She slapped his hand away, and her voice rose. "I would have left my family behind. I would have *begged* Carwyn to turn me so I could stay with you forever! Why?"

"That's why!" he yelled, grabbing onto her shoulders. "Don't you see, Beatrice? *That's* why I couldn't come to you!"

Giovanni dragged her to his chest, and their mouths crashed together. He wrapped his arms around her, his fingers gripping her back. He breathed her in, desperate to get closer, to take away the ache of her loss.

After a few moments, he backed away so she could draw breath, but his hands reached up to frame her face.

"Don't you see?" he pleaded. "I couldn't have denied you anything. I would have given you *anything* you wanted! You might have hated me in a hundred years, but if you had asked me, I would have done it." He leaned down and kissed along her eyelids, threading his hands through her hair as he pulled her into a more gentle kiss.

"Don't you realize how I adore you?" he whispered against her mouth. "But I couldn't steal the life of a girl when I wanted a woman's love. I wanted you to have a choice, not an infatuation."

"So damn arrogant," she whispered, clutching the collar of his shirt.

"I know," he said, as his mouth brushed over her skin, touching the face that had haunted his waking dreams.

"I loved you. It wasn't an infatuation."

He pressed his cheek to hers and whispered in her ear. "Then I will earn the woman's love, if I have lost the girl's."

Giovanni drew her into another kiss, and her arms reached around his waist as she kissed him back. He didn't know how long they embraced in the darkness, but he groaned when he felt Beatrice reach up to his chest and slowly push him back.

"I can't do this. It's not right."

"Yes, it is right. You know it is."

She shook her head. "What do you want from me?"

He blinked in surprise. "Isn't it obvious?"

"Five years ago, I would have said yes. Not now."

He closed his eyes and sighed. "Fine, let me make it clear." He reached up to hold her face between his hands and look into her eyes. "I love you, Beatrice De Novo. I fell in love with the girl I met six years ago, and I love the woman in front of me even more."

"Gio—"

"So you make the decision, *tesoro mio*." He murmured and his thumbs stroked the soft swell of her cheeks. "It's your choice. I want eternity with you, and I'm not leaving again." He gave her a sad smile. "You can't make me."

A storm raged in her eyes. Giovanni wanted to kiss her again, but he knew it wasn't welcome. Her tentative hand reached up and stroked his cheek; he leaned into it, a low hum of satisfaction rumbling from his chest, until they were interrupted by the ringing of her mobile phone.

"Who...?" She pulled away and reached into her backpack. Giovanni tensed when he heard the panicked voice on the other end, even before she put it to her ear.

"Danny? What—" she frowned. "Slow down, what's going on? A what?" The color drained from her face. "What kind of accident?"

CHAPTER 6

Beatrice didn't remember much about the ride to the hospital in Long Beach except for the familiar smell of leather and smoke that filled Giovanni's old Mustang. She remembered the first night she'd ridden in it, the night she had learned about vampires and blue fire and men who lived forever.

Men who wouldn't be in the hospital after a freak diving accident.

> "It was the weirdest thing," Danny said after he'd calmed down. "I've never seen anything like it. It looked like he was being attacked down there, but there was nothing around him. Then, it was like his mask was just sucked off of his face like the water was pulling on it."
>
> "I'm heading over there right now. What did the doctors say?"
>
> "I got him to the surface and got him resuscitated. Thank God we weren't that far from the marina. They're going to keep him overnight and release him in the morning if everything looks okay."

Giovanni wouldn't let her ride her bike to the hospital, much as he had refused to let her drive home the night six years before. She had never felt more confused in her life.

"Danny said it looked like the water was pulling on him."

"*Pulling* on him?"

She nodded. "Like he was being attacked, but there was nothing around."

She glanced over, and his face was grim. They drove in silence for a few more minutes.

"It's him, isn't it? It's Lorenzo. He's back."

He frowned. "The last time I had information on Lorenzo was a year ago; he was lurking around Northern Africa. None of my contacts have reported any movement from him." He shook his head. "He's very recognizable. It's more likely an associate of some sort, or someone he hired."

Someone Lorenzo hired to kill a man she loved. A combination of guilt and fury began to churn in her gut.

"Did I ever tell you Mano was a diver in the Navy?" she said. "He's really good. Danny says Mano's the best diver he's ever worked with, and Danny was a Master Diver before he retired."

"Beatrice—"

"Two and a half years we've been together," she whispered, "and he's never had an accident. I used to worry so much about him, especially at night, I worried...but nothing ever happened. Everything was fine. Mano was always so careful."

I did this, her mind kept repeating. *This is my fault.* She suddenly had more sympathy for her missing father and the complicated mess he'd inadvertently drawn her into years before.

Giovanni started to say something but paused and reached over to squeeze her limp hand. "I'll find out who it was."

"Who controls L.A.?" she asked in a whisper.

She could see his face harden in the passing streetlights.

"Are you sure you want to know? Sure you want back into this world? Into my world?"

"Do I have a choice?"

"Yes," he hissed. "You have a choice! That's what *all* of this was about, giving you a choice."

Beatrice shrugged, fighting back the tears in her eyes. She didn't feel like there was a choice. She felt like she'd been hiding her head in the sand and others would be the ones to pay the price. She didn't know what to do, and all she could think about was seeing Mano.

She forced Giovanni to go home to Ben after he dropped her off at the emergency room. Beatrice walked in and found Danny in the lobby, waiting to take her upstairs.

When she walked in, Mano was sleeping, and the quiet words of his doctor assured her that a week of rest and a break from diving were the only things needed for him to make a full recovery. Danny finally left them, and she curled up in the bed, squeezing herself into his side and laying her head on his chest as she listened to the steady beat of his heart.

Beatrice spent hours watching Mano sleep, seeing his steady chest rise and fall and listening to the faint murmurs as he dreamed. He had always looked so peaceful when he slept, his huge body relaxed and still in marked contrast to his waking vitality.

She called in to work and took some of her vacation time to be with him, though she knew he didn't really need her there the whole time.

"Hey, Mano, what do you want for lunch?"

"How about a break from hovering?"

She snickered and looked over at him. "I'm serious. There's some soup left, or I could make you a—"

"I'm serious, too." He gave her a slight frown. "Why are you being like this? You're not a hoverer."

"You... scared me." She frowned. "That's all. You've never had an accident and—"

"Accidents happen, baby. It was a weird one, but..."

"What?"

He tried to smile but could only shrug. "You don't seem like yourself lately."

"Don't be silly. I'm fine. You're the one who needs—"

"What's going on?"

Beatrice walked over and straddled his lap, pulling his arms around her. She put her ear to his chest, listening to his heartbeat as his strong arms held her. What could she say?

You know my friends Carwyn and Gio? They're vampires who drink blood and manipulate elements. Oh, and your accident was probably caused by a bad vampire who once kidnapped me because he's trying to get to my father...who's a vampire, too. But don't worry, the good vampires rescued me. Then I stole a whole bunch of money from the bad guy, which is why he's now trying to kill you.

And Gio says he's in love with me.

"Nothing's going on. I told you, you just gave me a scare. It's fine. We're fine. Nothing is going on."

She sat up and saw a bitter smile curling his lips. "You're a bad liar, you know that?"

Beatrice wanted to protest, to defend herself, but she couldn't think of anything that wouldn't be another lie, so she simply leaned forward, holding him closer and listening to the steady beat of his heart. Mano gently stroked her dark hair, and she felt his chest rise as he sighed.

"Lately, baby, I feel like being with you is like watching the tide go out."

"What?" She cleared her throat. "What are you talking about?"

"You don't notice the ebb at first, you're still listening to those waves go back and forth. They keep coming in, but...never quite as high as the last one."

"Mano—"

"And you know there's nothing you can do." He kept running his hands through her hair in long, soothing strokes. "You could try to hold on, to chase the waves, but the water's still going to slip away."

Beatrice bit her lip and felt tears come to her eyes as a portion of her heart began to crumble. "I don't...I don't—"

"I'd say it was this guy, but I think the tide started going out months ago. Otherwise, we'd be living together now, you know?" She heard him choke a little. "And I wouldn't be worried about your answer when I asked you to marry me."

She shook her head, still wishing she could deny the words coming out of his mouth as she turned her face and stained his shirt with her tears. Mano placed a warm hand on her cheek.

"I feel like you're on this wave, baby. And you're slipping away from me a little more every day. Slipping away somewhere you don't want me to go. Someplace I just—I can't quite see." He leaned down and whispered in her ear. "I want to catch you, but I don't think you want to be caught."

Beatrice cried, and her mind screamed, '*No*,' but she couldn't form the words.

"And I've been chasing the waves, thinking if I could just catch you, I could hold you back, and maybe you'd finally love me the way I love you."

She curled her fingers in his shirt. "I *do* love you, Mano," she whispered, wishing desperately that it was enough.

"But not—not the way you love him." He cleared his throat. "I wish it wasn't the truth, but it is."

He tilted her chin up and wiped her cheeks with the sleeve of his shirt, but Beatrice couldn't stop crying.

"Mano," she choked out, reaching up to touch his face with shaking hands. He stared at her with sad eyes.

"There's this huge thing you two hold between each other. I don't think you even realize how much I can see it. It's like all the dark places in you, the ones you never let me into, are open to him. And I'd chase away the dark for you— I've been trying for years—but I don't think you really want me to."

He cupped her cheeks with his warm, callused hands and pulled her tear stained face to his so he could lay a soft kiss on her mouth.

"I love you so much," Beatrice said as her tears rolled into his hands.

"But it's not enough, is it?"

She met his dark eyes and whispered in surrender, "No."

His face fell in pain, and his grip tightened on her jaw for only a second before his hands went lax and his arms fell to the side.

"You need to go now, B."

She choked on her tears but managed to nod as she climbed off his lap. Beatrice silently gathered the few things she kept at Mano's apartment and walked back to him. She leaned down to kiss his cheek but he turned away from her.

"Please, don't."

"Okay," she whispered. "Okay."

She was shaking by the time she made it to the door, and she heard his low voice for the last time. "Don't disappear completely. I want to know you're okay."

"Bye, Mano," Beatrice whispered before she opened the door, stumbling down the stairs as the tears ran down her face and the sun blinded her. She walked to the shade of the small carport and pulled out her phone to dial with trembling hands.

"Dez? Can you come get me?" She paused to wipe her eyes with her sleeve. "I think I need to stay with you for a while."

BEATRICE STAYED IN DEZ'S GUEST ROOM FOR THREE NIGHTS, IGNORING THE calls Giovanni made to her mobile phone and crying more than she had since her father died. Giovanni came to Dez's door every night, but she always sent him away.

She cried for days.

She cried for the guilt of not being able to love Mano the way he deserved. She cried for the lies she had told him and herself for so many years. And she cried because she already missed him.

She didn't allow herself to think about her argument with Giovanni the night of the "accident" or the stunning emotional revelations he had made. It was too much, and her heart, along with her head, felt like it would burst.

By the end of the week, she was utterly and completely spent by tears and the weight of decisions that hung over her. Dez couldn't comfort her, and she refused to call her grandmother while she was such a mess.

The one thing that kept echoing in her mind was the admonition Giovanni had given her the night they'd kissed.

You need to tell them. You say you love them and you want them to be a part of your life, so why don't you trust them?

She'd already killed her relationship with Mano with the weight of her secrets and the walls she had built, so she called Dez into the pale blue room where she was lying on the bed, determined not to lose another person she loved.

"Dez, I need to talk to you."

BEATRICE TOLD HER EVERYTHING.

She told her about murdered fathers and missing books. About mysterious men with blue fire and secrets. About blood and betrayal. Sacrifice and rescue. She told her best friend everything except Giovanni's secrets. Beatrice even called Matt to confirm the story, so Dez didn't feel like she had to call the men in white coats. Her friend was sitting on the bed with a dazed expression, looking like she'd just fallen down a very long rabbit hole.

"Was I wrong to tell you?"

Dez frowned. "I'm not quite sure at this point."

She nodded. "If you want, he can erase it all. Gio can, I mean. If you don't want to know. If it's too much."

"Did he offer that?" Dez looked worried. "Does he know you told me?"

"He told me I should tell the people I love."

Dez thought for a moment.

"Did you tell Mano? Is that why you broke up?"

"No." She shook her head. "I didn't tell Mano."

"Oh...okay," Dez stuttered. "Just give me a few minutes here."

"Okay."

They sat in silence for a few more minutes.

"B?"

"Yeah?"

"Why did Giovanni come back? Is it this Lorenzo guy? Is he back now?"

She took a deep breath. "He says he came back for me. He said..."

"What?"

"That he loves me. That he wants me to be with him."

"You mean like..."

"Yeah, I think so."

Dez paused again. "So, he wants you to..."

"It sounds like it."

"Because he loves you?"

Beatrice shrugged. "I guess so."

"But you don't believe him."

She shook her head. "I don't know what to believe anymore. I'm really..."

"What?"

"Confused," Beatrice sighed.

"Yeah...there's a lot of that going around."

"I'm so sorry."

Dez frowned at her. "Why?"

"I should have told you before. I shouldn't have lied about so much of my past."

"Oh, sweetie," Dez pulled her into a hug. "I totally understand why."

"And now that I told you, I feel like I'm putting you in danger."

Dez pulled away and a familiar, stubborn expression settled over her face. "That is not something that you should be worried about. If that's the cost of being your friend..."

"What?"

Dez reached over and enveloped her in another hug.

"Totally worth it, B."

She sniffed as the tears started again. "Thanks, Dezi. I love you. I don't know what I'd do if I lost you."

"I know. I'm pretty awesome."

Beatrice snorted, then they both laughed. Beatrice began to slump as the days of emotional exhaustion started to catch up with her. Dez, however, was looking surprisingly perky.

"So, Matt knows about all this stuff?"

BEATRICE CALLED HER NEXT-DOOR NEIGHBOR AND ASKED HIM TO DRIVE HER to the Huntington to get her motorcycle so she could go home for the first time in a week.

"Do you think she'll be okay?" she asked Matt as he drove her back to Pasadena.

"She'll be fine," he said with a smile. "Dez is tougher than she looks. And really smart. Don't you remember that crazy feeling you had when you first found out?" He shrugged. "She'll manage."

"How long have you known Gio?"

"About ten years. About vampires, longer. My father did some work for him back in the day, and Gio...well, he trusts our family, I guess."

"What do you actually do?" she asked with a frown. "You can't be a realtor."

He chuckled and reached a hand across the front seat. "Matt Kirby, private investigator. Nice to meet you, Beatrice De Novo."

She shook her head and slapped at his hand. He laughed and faced forward again, watching for the exit as they neared South Pasadena. Beatrice noticed that he was unusually chipper.

"You're going to ask Dez out, aren't you?"

"Yep," he said with a grin.

"Good. Why did you wait so long?"

He shrugged. "Too many secrets. You think I could keep all that from her and have a chance?"

She sighed and shook her head. "Probably not, Matt. Good luck."

"You too," he said with a smile.

BEATRICE SAW THE MUSTANG PARKED AT THE CURB AND GIOVANNI SITTING IN the dim light of the porch when she arrived. He looked at her, no doubt noticing the exhaustion that lined her face and her eyes, which felt like they had been swollen with tears for days on end.

She was irritated he was there, and she didn't know any of the answers he was probably looking for. She just wanted to be alone.

"Hi," he said.

"Hi."

"Kirby called me."

"Good for him." She attempted to walk past him as she dug out her keys. He shot up and tried to block her path to the front door.

"Beatrice—"

"Nothing you say," she bit out, "is going to make me feel better right now. *Nothing*." She took a deep breath. "I don't want to talk to you or see you for a while, so please leave me alone."

"I have information about who attacked Mano."

She closed her eyes and pressed the heel of her hand into her forehead to try to still the headache that began pounding.

"Just...give me a few days," she whispered. "I need a few days, Gio."

He tried to touch her shoulder, but she pushed him away.

"I understand," he murmured.

"No, you really, *really* don't."

He paused before speaking. "I'll put them off for a few days. Call me when you're ready to talk."

Beatrice still had her eyes closed when she heard him walk past her, down the porch, and toward his car. She didn't open them until she heard the Mustang pull away. Then she opened the door and retreated to her silent house.

CHAPTER 7

"Anything else?"

"I got a call from Ernesto's assistant today wondering whether you were going to bring B by this week."

Giovanni frowned and tugged on his hair. It still wasn't as long as when he first met Beatrice, but it had grown around four inches from the time he'd singed it off when Lorenzo had taken her.

"When does he need to know?"

"Kelli said he was going down to Mexico for some business next week so he was hoping to meet with you both tomorrow evening, if possible."

He nodded. "Let me ask her tonight. She and Benjamin are due back soon."

Matt smiled. "Spending time with the kid, huh?"

Giovanni grumbled, "He's been her preferred company for the last couple of weeks."

"Well..." The private detective shifted in his seat, looking slightly nervous. "Mano...he was a good guy. I mean, I know it's none of my business and all—"

"Do you consider yourself her friend, Kirby?"

Matt nodded. "I do."

"Then it's your business," Giovanni said, giving the tacit approval the man seemed to need. "And I'm not going to kill you for liking Beatrice's ex."

"Good to know," he said with a tight smile.

"How is the lovely Desiree? Beatrice said you two are seeing each other."

Matt chuckled. "Well, after the initial shock, she's fairly fascinated by all of it, to be honest. I think being part of the supernatural world gave me a leg up dating her."

Giovanni smiled before he burst into laughter. "Well, you've certainly taken enough risks over the years, I'm glad it finally paid off for you. Thank God for curious women."

Matt's head cocked when he heard the hum of the Mustang coming up the drive. "I should go."

"I'll call you about the meeting with Alvarez later tonight."

"Let me know. I'm sure he won't mind putting it off for the girl, with their connection, but it's getting close to Christmas and I know you're leaving for Texas..."

"No, I understand the urgency."

"And I'm not sure how long you want that guy to sit in the dry room, either."

"Oh," Giovanni murmured. "The longer the better as far as that goes. As long as he's conscious, he'll suit my purposes."

Matt nodded. "Just give me a call when you have a date. If it's not office hours for you, I'll take care of arranging the appointment."

"Thank you, Kirby. Your assistance, as always, has been excellent."

"No problem at all." He nodded toward the vampire, who showed him to the door.

"And give your father and mother my best."

"Of course. Have a nice night."

Giovanni closed the door and walked back to the kitchen, curious why he hadn't heard the stomping and shouting that normally followed Ben's return to the house. When the basketball began to bounce, he had his answer. He heated a glass of bagged blood and sat down at the counter to drink. Soon, Ben and Beatrice's quiet conversation drifted to his ears.

"—doesn't matter if you want to go. It's part of life. Just get it over with."

"But I hear really bad stuff about going to the dentist, and I've never been. My teeth are probably super bad, and he'll have to pull them all or something."

He could hear Beatrice laugh. "You're not going to get all your teeth pulled. I'll make the appointment with my dentist. She's really cool, and I'm sure she can fit you in next week."

"Hey, did you ask Gio if we could go to the blue alien movie?"

"Not yet." He could barely hear her mutter.

"Oh, come on, B! Will you guys stop fighting already? You could at least start talking to each other again."

He was tempted to go out and yank Ben's ear for talking to Beatrice that way, but he was too curious what she would say in response.

"Gee, Ben, I'm so sorry my disagreement with your uncle is cutting into your precious movie attendance. I'll see what I can do."

"It's not that, and you know it." Giovanni heard the basketball bounce a few more times and someone threw it toward the basket. "You guys are both just..."

"What?" she asked the question on the tip of his own tongue as he listened in.

"You're sad. Both of you. It sucks."

"Well," he heard her start, "sometimes shitty things just happen, Ben, and it takes time to work through them. It's not like I like being mad at him. Besides—" Her voice dropped. "—I'm mostly mad at myself."

His heart ached for her, and he had to fight the urge to rush out and embrace her. Giovanni knew his comfort was still unwelcome.

"Well, figure it out by Christmas, okay? This is my first huge Christmas with lots of grown-ups giving me stuff, and I don't want you two spoiling it."

Giovanni almost snorted blood through his nose, and he grabbed a napkin from the holder on the counter. Luckily, he heard the welcome sound of Beatrice's laughter, as well.

"I'll keep that in mind."

"You know he's listening to us in the kitchen right now, don't you? You should go say hi and stay for dinner. Actually, you should cook because you're way better at it than Gio is. Or we could order pizza! I know where he keeps his wallet."

Giovanni rolled his eyes and sent a small prayer toward heaven. Carwyn would be pleased, he thought, he hadn't prayed this much since Caspar started driving. Just as his eyes opened, he heard the kitchen door open and Beatrice walked into the house. He took a deep breath, enjoying the scent of her, fresh from the brisk air outside.

"Hi," she said.

"Hello."

"Apparently I'm a better cook than you are."

"I have a hard time imagining that's a surprise," he said with a smile.

He saw her glance at his glass. "Bagged blood?"

Giovanni shrugged. "Unless you're offering…"

Her eyes darted around the kitchen and she walked to the refrigerator to open it. "Uh, no. Not tonight. And there are tons of clubs in Los Angeles, why don't you just—"

"No thanks," he said. "Haven't gone that route in years."

Beatrice turned to look at him. "What? Years?"

He glanced meaningfully at her neck and sipped his glass. "Yes, years."

She turned back to the refrigerator and paused before she started pulling out what looked like the ingredients for a salad, or maybe tacos, which he knew Ben loved.

She worked quietly as Ben continued playing outside and Giovanni pretended to read a book. He heard her start to say something a number of times, but she stopped herself and continued working.

"Ben's doctor said he's healthy as a horse, by the way."

He nodded. "I assumed he was. I had him checked out in New York and his scent hasn't changed significantly."

"So, if a person is sick or something, they smell different?"

He nodded. "Yes, human scent changes quite significantly for all sorts of reasons. Health, hormones, even age ..."

She laughed. "I just had the realization that you have to smell adolescent boy on a daily basis."

Giovanni winced before he grinned. "You have no idea."

She shook her head, still laughing, and he suddenly realized they were smiling at each other for the first time in weeks. She must have realized it at the same time, and a sad smile replaced her laugh.

"So, your sense of smell is a little scary, to be honest. I always wonder if I'm wearing enough deodorant around you and Carwyn."

"I wouldn't worry. You usually smell lovely. Especially when you first wake up," he added quietly.

He smiled when he saw her pause, but she didn't get angry.

"You always smell the same to me," she said.

He cocked his head. "How? What do I smell like to you?"

She didn't look at him but turned on the burner to heat a pan on the stove. "Kind of like smoke. Wood smoke and whiskey."

"I remember you wrote that in the journal. About the smoke."

She looked up at him. "Did you read that? All of it?"

"Of course."

"Even the parts when I cussed at you? I wasn't very nice."

He shrugged. "Did you read my journals? Most of them are far harsher than yours."

"I haven't read all of them yet," she said as she put the ground beef on to cook. "You live in a rough world, you know?"

He folded his hands under his chin and put down the book he was pretending to read. "I don't want you to have any illusions, Beatrice. My world, and the world your father lives in, can be very brutal."

"I'm getting that impression."

"Good."

She glared at him. "Don't use the professor-voice with me, Gio. I'm not a kid anymore."

He allowed his eyes to run over her slim cut black jeans and the tight black t-shirt that hugged her breasts. It was her normal uniform on her days off and suited her to the ground. "No, you most certainly are not," he muttered. "I don't want to lie about anything to you, Beatrice. It doesn't do either of us any favors in the long run."

"The long run, huh?"

"That's what I'm talking about."

She paused to look at him, and he didn't flinch from her steady gaze.

"Yeah, we'll see."

Giovanni was annoyed by her dismissal, but he forced himself to remain calm. "Speaking of immortal matters, there is a certain vampire in town that you should meet."

The meat sizzled in the pan as she added the onions and chiles. "Who?"

"You asked who ran Los Angeles, but the answer is somewhat complicated. As a matter of fact, the reason I never worried much about you living here—"

"Hiring someone to move next door to me isn't worrying much?"

"—is because of who controls the city." He ignored her question and continued. "Tell me about your grandmother's family."

"What?" she frowned. "The Alvarezes? Why? They're from Mexico. Guadalajara. I've never even been there, but I hear it's pretty. I think Grandma has one cousin she keeps in contact with."

"Your grandmother is descended from a very old and very wealthy Spanish family that was once large land owners in Alta California."

"Okay," she said slowly as she alternated between stirring the meat for the tacos and chopping tomatoes.

"He won't eat those," he said, looking at the cutting board.

"He will if he wants me to feed him."

Giovanni grinned and continued talking. "Don Ernesto Alvarez was a very wealthy man, and he had a very large family. A tradition he continued even after he was turned into a vampire in the late 1700s."

She had looked up as soon as he said the name 'Alvarez.'

"Gio, are you telling me I'm related to another vampire?"

He smiled. "Well, if it makes you feel any better, probably ten percent of California and Northern Mexico is related to him in some way. It was a very large family."

She shook her head and continued preparing dinner. "So what? This Don Ernesto is my great-great-a whole bunch of times-great-grandfather?"

"Yes, he is. And you're a direct descendant, which is rare and brings out his sentimental side."

"And he runs the city of Los Angeles?"

"And most of the surrounding areas, yes. Most of the area between here and the Mexican border is under his and his clan's control."

"Is he an earth vampire? You told me once they tend to stay in clans."

"Ah, but they don't like politics much, and where there are cities and large populations, there are usually politics. No, most larger cities are controlled by water vampires. London, Athens, Rome, Beijing, Buenos Aires. Water vamps tend to be quite tricky. Very smart and they like manipulation."

"The perfect politician," she said.

"Exactly."

"What about Houston? Was there a lot of that there?"

He smiled. "Houston is a bit of an anomaly, to be honest. That's one of the reasons I like it. Because of the proximity of New Orleans, it has an extremely low vampire population. It's an easy place to lie low, if that's what you're looking for."

She gave him a rueful smile. "Kind of spoiled the lying low thing for you, didn't I?"

He winked. "You were worth every singed hair, *tesoro*."

"It's growing back," she said quietly, reaching over to run her fingers through his short locks. He leaned into her hand and she let it rest on his cheek briefly. Their eyes met again, and he saw hers soften.

"So," she said after a few quiet moments of contact, "this Don Ernesto knows about me? Does he know about my dad?"

He nodded and she continued fixing dinner. "He knows the basics, but not the specifics. I met with him the night I left the sonnets at your home. He was pleased to learn of the connection and more than happy to offer additional protection. An umbrella, of sorts."

She shrugged. "What's the big deal? You said he was related to a bunch of humans."

"But not any under my aegis, *tesoro*. He did me a favor by helping me protect you. And now I am in his debt."

She looked worried. "Is that a bad thing?"

"No," he shook his head. "He's a very decent sort, and if you're going to be related to a vampire, it's good that it's him. He's very protective of his people. Very old-fashioned. And he's pleased to have the connection to me, as well."

She smiled a little. "You really are kind of a bad-ass, aren't you? I read your journals. You and Tenzin made quite the reputation for yourselves for a couple hundred years."

Giovanni shrugged. "I did what I needed to survive and build a reputation that no one would question. The more you are feared, the more you are respected and left alone. It's the way of the world."

"The vampire world, anyway."

"It's the way of *any* world, Beatrice," he said grimly. "Don't let the politicians fool you."

Giovanni watched her grate the cheese for the tacos. He could hear Ben outside, still bouncing the basketball by the garage.

"So why did I need all the super-secret vampire info? Besides being well-informed."

"Don Ernesto has the vampire who attacked Mano in his custody. I will be interrogating him tomorrow evening, and he's asked that you accompany me so he can meet you. You will not go to the interrogation."

He could see the blood drain from her face. "What does he want from me?"

"I suspect Ernesto only wants to know you. As I said, he's very fond of his family and has been wanting to meet you for some time. It's only been out of courtesy to me that he has maintained his distance. He knew I wanted you left alone."

"And the guy who attacked Mano?" she asked quietly.

"He was apprehended after I spoke to Ernesto's enforcer, Baojia. The vampire is Greek, unknown, and not particularly valuable. He hadn't caused any trouble in the area but was spotted near the port the night Mano was attacked. They picked him up the next night."

Her mouth fell open. "So they've had him for two and a half weeks? What are they doing to him?"

"Do you care?"

She hesitated, frowning a little. "Not really, I'm just curious."

"They have him in a very ingenious little place called a dry room. Quite torturous for water vampires. Saps them of their power. It's a bit like a giant dehumidifying chamber."

"I don't want to picture that after two and a half weeks."

He shook his head. "It won't be pretty, but he should be miserable enough to give up any information about Lorenzo if he has it."

"Do you have any doubt about it being Lorenzo?"

He thought for a moment. "No."

Beatrice nodded. "So that must mean he still hasn't found my dad, right?"

"If you are still a target for him, then probably not. You did steal most of his money, though. That had to be irritating."

"And lucrative," she muttered. His only response was a snort. "And then what? After you interrogate this guy, what then?"

Giovanni watched her carefully. "I will kill him."

Her dark eyes seemed to lighten, her mouth a thin line. "Good."

"So, will you meet with Don Ernesto Alvarez tomorrow after work?"

"Sure. I'll come here and we can take your car. What about Ben?"

"The fewer people who know about Ben, the better. I'll see if Kirby and Dez can watch him. He seems to be fond of blondes."

Beatrice shook her head. "That kid is fond of females. Doesn't seem to matter what kind."

"He'll learn to be choosy in time. It only took me five hundred years to find the one I really want."

She blushed and tried to hide her smile. Giovanni was trying to keep the innuendo to a minimum, but he wasn't a saint. He knew she was grieving her relationship with Mano and blamed herself for the human's pain, but he also knew she would eventually see the wisdom of not dwelling in the past.

He'd had enough of the past; he wanted her future.

"Okay, I'll call Dez in the morning and then head over here after work. I'm sure she'll be happy to help. Then we can go over and talk to this Ernesto."

"He'll expect you to treat him like family, just so you know. He already knows all about you and considers you a granddaughter. He's quite proud of you."

Beatrice made a face and Giovanni started to laugh. "I'm not going to lie," she said, laughing along. "That's kind of weird."

"And he'll probably try to persuade you to let him sire you."

She fumbled the knife. "What?"

"He won't force the issue, far from it, he fears me too much, but he can be very persuasive. He loves having a large family and he particularly likes having human descendants in it. It's a peculiarity of his, but not an obsessive one."

Beatrice took a deep breath. "Okay, as long as he's not going to try to force me or anything."

"No, I'll be in his home with you. No one would dare."

"It's a date then."

He propped his elbows on the counter and watched her warm the tortillas, one by one, in the flame from the stove. "Maybe we should try the theater next time. Might be less stressful."

Beatrice looked over at him, glanced at his hands and held up another tortilla with a pair of tongs. "Little help here?"

He grinned, snapped his fingers, and let the warm flames fill his hands as he helped her finish preparing the meal.

"Ben wants to know if I can take him to that movie with the blue aliens."

"That movie looks horrible."

She shrugged and folded the tortillas in a clean dishtowel to keep them warm. "He's twelve."

"Remind me to make him read some Jules Verne."

She grinned and nodded toward the door. "You're such a snob. Can you call him in to set the table?"

Giovanni turned his head toward the door and yelled, "Benjamin! Come inside and set the table!"

She gave him a disgusted look.

"What? He heard me."

Beatrice rolled her eyes. "Boys. Five hundred or twelve. Mortal or immortal. Still kind of the same..."

He grinned, pleased beyond measure to have her in his kitchen, in his home, in his life. Giovanni couldn't help but imagine what it would be like to have her living with him, working with him, and helping him raise Ben.

Loving him.

His feelings must have spilled out of his eyes as he watched her take the food to the table, because she glanced over at him and quickly looked away. He stood, walked into the kitchen, and took the plate of food from her.

He leaned down and brushed a kiss over her cheek before he whispered in her ear, "*Grazie, tesoro*. For dinner. For being here."

She swallowed and opened her mouth as if she was about to speak, but just then, Ben barreled into the kitchen.

"Awesome, tacos—" And then. "— Ew, are those tomatoes?"

CHAPTER 8

The lights of the three-tiered yacht glowed in the harbor as Giovanni and Beatrice were ferried out in the small white boat. Don Ernesto Alvarez had spent his mortal and immortal life in the accumulation of wealth, power, and influence and had no qualms about enjoying and sharing that wealth with those he favored.

"So, the water vampire lives on a yacht, huh?" she leaned toward Giovanni and whispered.

"No need to be intimidated, *tesoro*, but do be careful."

"See, those two statements seem like they contradict each other to me, Gio."

He chuckled and slipped an arm around her, warming her when she shivered. She relaxed into his side and allowed herself to enjoy the simple comfort of his touch.

He'd been careful with her the past weeks, respecting the fact that she still grieved the loss of her relationship with Mano. No matter his own feelings, he had respected hers and was showing an extraordinary amount of patience.

And that, more than anything, softened the brittle wall she'd put up to protect herself.

It would have been as easy as breathing to fall into his arms. She knew he loved her and wanted her, but Beatrice also knew she was past the point in her life where she would jump head first into a situation she knew little about. She had been cautious six years ago; she was even more wary now.

Giovanni claimed he wanted her. Not just for this life, but for eternity. She was still trying to wrap her mind around the idea; what he was asking wasn't a decision she could make lightly.

"Señorita De Novo, Señor Vecchio, welcome aboard," the dark haired steward called down in greeting when they came alongside the anchored cruiser. They climbed up the large angled ladder that dipped toward the water, and she felt Giovanni's hand on the small of her back as she climbed. She was slightly unsteady on her feet, but she felt him behind her, steadying her legs as she climbed.

"I feel like I'm underdressed," she muttered, eyeing the formally dressed steward.

He chuckled and pinched her leg. "I told you to wear your boots."

"Haha. All the same, with this ladder I'm sure glad I didn't wear a skirt."

"I'm not," she heard him grumble.

"Oh really? Want me to share the view with all the boys in the boat below?"

She looked down to see one of the crewmen on the small boat wink at her. Beatrice snickered and Giovanni glanced over his shoulder to see the man quickly busy himself coiling rope.

"Fair point, *tesoro*. Skirts for my eyes only, if you please."

Beatrice rolled her eyes and continued climbing. Normally, she would consider his possessive behavior annoying, but in the unknown situation she was putting herself into, it was more comforting than anything else.

"*Tesoro mio*," Giovanni called from below, "can we hurry up a bit?"

"Why? You getting grey down there, professor?"

She squeaked when she felt him grab her by the waist and pull her into an embrace as he scooted up next to her. She clung to his neck and he shimmied up the ladder to the teak deck above. He held onto her a bit longer than necessary and bent down to murmur in her ear.

"It was getting hard to resist the temptation to sink my teeth in your thigh when I was staring at it for so long."

Her breath caught, her temperature shot up, and her heart raced at the rough sound of his voice. She made an effort to calm down so she didn't meet her great-great-however many great-grandfather completely turned on by her... whatever Giovanni was.

Beatrice saw two scantily clad women strolling along the deck; both of them shot Giovanni a look as they passed. He was dressed in surprisingly casual clothes that evening, though his dark jeans and black button-down shirt did nothing to detract from his good looks. The women swayed their hips as they walked past, but he didn't even glance at them. Instead, he held his hand out, searching for her own.

Whatever Giovanni was, she was beginning to realize he was most certainly *hers*.

She flushed when she realized she was more than a little possessive herself. The steward, who had been chatting with Giovanni in soft Italian, escorted them from the boat landing and up the stairs toward the decks above.

"Wow, how big is this thing?" she asked.

"The *Esmeralda* is over four hundred feet long, Señorita De Novo. It has forty cabins, twenty of which are interior and secured for our immortal guests."

"Does Don Ernesto live here full time?"

The man smiled enigmatically, and she sensed she wouldn't be getting a straight answer. "He stays here when it suits him."

"Okay then," she murmured as Giovanni slipped an arm around her waist. They left the stairwell and walked across a broad deck leading to what sounded like a party. In the distance, the lights of the Long Beach Pike glistened and she could see the giant Ferris wheel turn as families enjoyed Friday night at the pier.

There was a sudden gust of wind, and she pulled her leather riding jacket close to her body, tucking herself under Giovanni's shoulder. She felt the heat begin to radiate off him when he sensed her shiver.

"If you'll continue this way, Don Ernesto and his family will meet you on the veranda."

"Thank you for your help, Enzo," Giovanni said.

"Yeah, thanks." She followed Giovanni, taking tentative steps toward the sound of glasses clinking and quiet murmuring voices that drifted in the breeze. She was ambushed by a sudden memory of the wild parties Lorenzo had thrown on the island, and she tensed when she remembered the drained human guests who had been casually flung into the sea when the vampires were done with them. She froze and her heart began to race. Giovanni pulled her closer and whispered in her ear.

"It's not what you're thinking. If you feel uncomfortable, we'll go, but it's to your benefit if you meet him, Beatrice."

"No," she said, nodding, "no, it's fine."

He squeezed her waist and they continued walking. When they turned the corner, she saw what could only be described as a very elegant dinner party. Though she saw more than one glass filled with what she thought might be blood and more than one human sitting among the vampires, no one was being bitten, and everyone talked and laughed together.

"Ah, Giovanni!" A short, barrel-chested man rose from the far end of the table. He was small and stocky, but his pale skin was set off by dark hair, a thick mustache, and a pair of startling emerald eyes that made Beatrice catch her breath. She had only seen the unusual shade in one other person in her life, and she smiled automatically to see her grandmother's eyes wink at her from the face of her ancestor.

He reached over and took her hand in his. Unlike Giovanni's hands, which were always warm, Don Ernesto's were cool as they enveloped hers. They weren't clammy the way she remembered Lorenzo's when he had touched her, so she was able to relax.

"You have finally brought my granddaughter to me," he said with a delighted smile, shaking Giovanni's hand after he released her own. "And what a beautiful young woman she is, and so very accomplished. You are a credit to our family, *Beatriz*."

"Well..." She laughed a little nervously. "Thank you. I'm very...pleased to meet you."

"Giovanni has been hiding you in my own city, my dear." He nodded toward Giovanni, who maintained a position behind Beatrice's right shoulder. "His prerogative, of course, and I understand you've been very successful in your studies and in your career."

"I have, thank you."

"Please call me *abuelo*, or Ernesto, since you are family, *mi nieta*. Come, sit beside me so we may acquaint ourselves." He showed them to the long table where he had been holding court and Giovanni pulled out the chair to the left of Ernesto's for her while he took the seat on her other side.

As soon as she sat, a server brought her a glass of water with no ice, asking her in a quiet voice what else he might bring. She asked for a glass of red wine and waited for Giovanni to speak to the man before she turned back to her grandfather.

"O positive, if it's available," she heard him murmur to the waiter.

"And would you prefer a donor or a glass, Señor?"

"A glass, please."

She flushed, wondering what the correct reaction would have been if he'd ordered a donor. As she glanced around the table, she realized more than one donor sitting next to a guest was feeding them from their wrist. It had none of the darkly erotic feel of the biting she had seen at Lorenzo's, nor the passionate connection she had felt the one time she had fed Giovanni.

Thinking about that night in his bed made the flush rise on her cheeks, and she was thankful that no one seemed to be paying attention to her. Except for Giovanni, who had placed a hand on her thigh under the table, holding it palm up. She placed her hand in his and felt the slight hum of energy that always buzzed when their bodies touched.

"Giovanni," Ernesto finally called. "I know you are acquainted with my son, Baojia, but have you met my daughter, Paula, and her husband, Rory?" Ernesto nodded toward the beautiful female vampire sitting at the far end of the table. She was tall and regal, no doubt towering over Ernesto, but her dark eyes were friendly, as was her smile.

The man sitting next to her looked exactly how Beatrice expected a cowboy from the old west would look. He was tan, even with the natural paleness of his kind, and had the lean, wiry look of a man who had been used to working outside. His grey, handlebar mustache drooped on either side of his thin mouth, but his eyes twinkled with a silver light.

"I know Paula by reputation, of course," Giovanni nodded toward the end where the two vampires observed them. "And I had the fortune of meeting Rory many years ago."

From the smiled that touched the cowboy's face, Beatrice had the feeling that their meeting may have been of the violent kind. Nonetheless, they nodded toward each other like old comrades before Paula began to speak.

"Giovanni, your companion looks like a delightful young woman. It's so lovely to meet another member of the family. You are from Texas, are you not, Beatrice?"

"I am," she said. "From Houston. My grandmother, who is an Alvarez, was from Guadalajara, though."

That statement sent the vampires at the table into raptures about the beauty of Colonial era Guadalajara and the music and art it produced. The tone of the conversation had the same nostalgic bent as the dinners Beatrice remembered attending with her grandmother's friends, and she chuckled in amusement.

"And what has made you laugh, my dear?"

She turned to Ernesto with a smile. "Oh…I was just reminded of my grandmother. All the talk about Guadalajara." She felt Giovanni squeeze her hand under the table as he took a sip of his blood.

"Tell me about your grandmother. She is in good health?"

"Yes, very good. She has your eyes."

His green eyes lit up. "She has Esmeralda's eyes? How wonderful!"

"Esmeralda?"

"My mother had the same brilliant green eyes that I do, my dear. That is why she was called Esmeralda, for her emerald eyes. I named the boat after her. The green eyes are quite rare in the family now, but perhaps if you have children, you will pass them on."

Her mouth gaped in shock. "Uh…well—"

"But of course…so clumsy of me," he said with a sly smile. "You are with Giovanni, so children are, perhaps, not something you wish for."

"I…I mean—"

"We have much time to think about things like that, Ernesto," Giovanni said smoothly. "Beatrice is a young woman. Tell me more about the new casino I hear you are opening next month. Is one of your children running it for you?"

Their conversation drifted into business, and Beatrice took the opportunity to sit back in her chair, sip her wine, and observe the humans and vampires who filled the room.

What appeared at first glance to be a dinner party was, upon closer observation, a very well-orchestrated meeting. In each corner and each group, there were quiet words and bent heads as canny eyes darted around the room with measuring glances. The vampires obviously had the upper hand, sending humans to fetch and carry this or that across the decks.

It all seemed to be a quiet and persistent negotiation. She heard murmurs about business deals and quarrels. New children and old relationships. There was the odd mention of acquaintances who were passing through the area. With each quiet conversation, Beatrice played a mental game trying to determine who had the upper hand, and who was trying to attract attention. It was all a kind of dance, and she smiled to herself as she observed them.

"What a mysterious smile," she heard Ernesto say. She swung her eyes back in his direction to catch him watching her with a grin. "It's all quite fascinating, isn't it?"

She glanced at Giovanni, but he only cocked an amused eyebrow at her.

"It's interesting," she said to Ernesto. "Very...dynamic."

Ernest broke into a satisfied smile. "A politician already, *nieta*! What an interesting young woman you are. You have very perceptive eyes, Beatrice."

"She always has," she heard Giovanni say as he tucked a piece of her hair behind her ear and leaned over to kiss her cheek. "*Tesoro*, I believe the man I need to meet is here for me." She glanced around and saw an Asian vampire of medium build standing in the doorway, staring at Giovanni with a blank expression.

Ernesto turned to the man and nodded in respect. "My son, Baojia, is head of our security. He has helped to capture the stranger who assaulted your friend."

She looked at the mysterious vampire, who radiated a quiet menace. His eyes were dark when she met his gaze, and she found herself nodding at him out of respect, though she could not smile.

"*Tesoro*? Would you like to find a peaceful spot inside?" Giovanni asked. "Or would you like to stay with Ernesto? It is up to you if you would prefer the quiet."

She could tell from the slight narrowing of Ernesto's eyes that he wasn't pleased Giovanni had given her the option, but she could also tell from the way he looked at her companion, Ernesto would not cross him.

She lifted a hand and swept it across Giovanni's cheek, which was dusted with a hint of stubble. "I'm fine, Gio. I'd like to visit a bit more with Ernesto." *And observe the rather intriguing dance of influence that seemed to swirl around the room.*

"Very well, I'll be back when I can." He bent down and breathed into her ear. "Be careful what you agree to."

"No hurry," she said as she studied Ernesto, who was watching their every move.

The two men left the room, quietly chatting in what she assumed was Mandarin as they disappeared down the hall.

"Tell me, my dear." Ernesto leaned toward her with a glint in his eyes. "What are your plans for the future?"

. . .

BEATRICE SPENT THE NEXT HOUR IN A COMPLICATED CONVERSATIONAL GAME she found both stimulating and exhausting. Ernesto was completely open in his desire to turn her and make her one of his children.

"Just think of the benefits. You would have independence! If you wanted to continue in your relationship with the Italian, you certainly could or you could pursue others that might suit you more. But you would not be obligated to him or his protection any longer."

"No." She smiled. "I'd be obligated to you, right?"

He shrugged, smiling impishly. "But we are already family, *nieta*. I have only your best interests at heart. You could wait to turn and bear children with a human, if you like. Or if not, perhaps one of my own children might be more to your liking for a partner."

Skipping over the part about 'bearing children,' she frowned. "Wouldn't that be...I don't know, like dating your brother or something?"

Ernesto chortled at the question. "No! But of course you might think that. The attachment to your sire does not extend to all of his or her children, fortunately. There are bonds of friendship and loyalty between those of the same clan, but it is not like a human sibling relationship."

"Oh, that makes more sense, I guess."

"For instance, Paula and her husband are both my children, and I care for them both, but they are married. They have no greater bond than that."

"Ah," she nodded. "Got it. That's kind of a relief, to be honest."

She had been thinking more about the fact that her father had been turned by Lorenzo, who was technically Giovanni's son. If you were to extend the logic...well, it took Beatrice to an obviously uncomfortable place, so she was relieved that the connection only seemed to be between sire and child.

Anything more could get quite confusing.

"And if you were to remain in Los Angeles under my aegis," Ernesto continued, "what opportunities for study there would be. The academic institutions, the museums. Your skills would certainly face a challenge."

Beatrice looked around the table at the immortal beings surrounding her. Most were young, frozen in the prime of their life. Their eyes scanned the room with the kind of canny intelligence that could only come from years of experience. All carried themselves with a preternatural grace and confidence.

What would it be like to be frozen in time? Giovanni wanted her to join him in his life. She would never grow old or sick, never feel the sting of early death. She would be powerful, she thought, as she remembered the sick, helpless feeling of being held against her will in Lorenzo's mansion.

That kind of power was more than attractive.

"And perhaps, in time, even your father could come work with you."

A light shines in the darkness. She had been wondering at the dogged persistence of the water vampire, and suddenly his pursuit made sense. It seemed that Stephen De Novo held the interest of more than just Lorenzo and Giovanni.

"It seems like a lot of people want to find my father." She raised her eyebrow at her ancestor.

"Such a bright man. One does hear things..." Ernesto smiled. "I think he would be an asset to any family. As would his daughter."

Beatrice shook her head at his scheming. "Ernesto, you are an original."

"But of course," he said as he winked.

She felt no threat from the barrel-chested man with her grandmother's eyes. He seemed to enjoy their verbal dance as much as she did, though she had to admit his mental stamina outshone hers. Beatrice was beginning to droop by the time Giovanni found her an hour later.

The party was still going on, but she had retired to a bench near the edge of the deck, enjoying the quiet as she watched the human families on the pier.

Giovanni strode toward her on the open veranda and swept her into his arms, clutching her as he looked around the room. He glared at the party with heated eyes before he looked down at her.

His face held an inscrutable expression as he ran a hand down her arm, lifting her wrist before he opened his mouth and his fangs descended. Beatrice gasped as his tongue traced the blue vein that ran down the middle of her wrist, and she could feel the slight buzz under her skin where she anticipated his bite.

"Gio—" She could only utter his name before his fangs pierced her wrist. They didn't pierce deeply, it was more of a prick, but a few drops of blood leaked out and Giovanni caught them with his tongue, sucking them into his mouth as he looked around the room. She was lightheaded as his amnis flooded over her skin and she forced herself to hold back a moan.

Beatrice was more shocked than angry and confused by the uncharacteristic behavior. He bent down to kiss her, and she tasted the metallic hint of her blood as it lingered on his tongue. His mouth trailed to her ear and he whispered. "I'm sorry. Trust me, I'll explain in the car."

"Yes, you will," she murmured against his cheek.

He clutched her to his chest and raised his voice. "Beatrice is exhausted, Ernesto. We will visit more another time."

Ernesto frowned, glancing between Giovanni and Baojia, who stood in the corner of the veranda near the stairs. Beatrice watched him over her shoulder and saw the mysterious vampire give her a respectful nod. Ernesto caught it as well and cocked his head.

"Of course," Ernesto said with a cheerful smile. "You are both welcome anytime. Tend to my granddaughter, Giovanni."

In no time, he had lifted her and carried her down the stairs at vampire speed. Beatrice hardly registered anything until they were on the small boat racing back to the dock.

"Gio, what's—"

He pulled her into another breathtaking kiss as he smothered her question. She finally sighed into his mouth and relaxed, assuming he didn't want to tell her anything with an audience.

At least she could enjoy kissing an expert.

And kissing Giovanni was better than any memory she'd allowed herself. His tongue stroked hers, and he sucked her bottom lip into his mouth allowing his teeth to scrape it. She reached out with the tip of her tongue to stroke the fangs sharp in his mouth, and she could hear him quietly groan as he kissed her more deeply.

The boat sped toward shore, and within minutes they were back on the dock. Giovanni picked her up again and rushed toward the car, only to set her on the hood of the Mustang so he could stand between her legs and continue devouring her.

"*Tesoro,*" he murmured against her neck. Then his lips travelled along her collarbone. "Beatrice..." he breathed out. Giovanni pressed closer, but she was too conscious of their place and the questions swirling in her mind, so she held back.

"Gio," she whispered as she placed her hands firmly on his shoulders and pushed him back. She heard him growl quietly as he tried to pull her back, but she grabbed his chin and forced him to look into her face. "Giovanni, what was that on the boat?"

He blinked, shaking his head to clear it. His eyes continued to fall toward her neck so she pinched his chin.

"I'm serious. I'm exhausted, and I just had a verbal fencing match for the last two and a half hours. So calm your fangs, and tell me what the heck is going on."

"Sorry," he muttered as he stepped back and cleared his throat. "My apologies, Beatrice. Let's get in the car and I'll fill you in on the interrogation and the...biting."

Beatrice nodded, sliding down the side of the car, taking care not to scratch it. She paused before she got in when she noticed the side of his head.

"You singed some hair off again," she said. "What happened?"

He frowned and felt the bare spot behind his ear. "In the car. Let's get on the road and I'll tell you."

Giovanni drove back to the house since she was exhausted. If there hadn't have been news to hear, she probably would have fallen asleep.

"One of Ernesto's people is working for Lorenzo," he said. "Baojia discovered it last week, but he wanted to tell me in person because he's still not sure who it is."

"One of Ernesto's children is working for Lorenzo?"

He shook his head. "That's highly unlikely, since your connection to him is well known. It would be almost unheard of for a child to defy their sire like that."

She couldn't help but remember Giovanni had plotted his own sire's murder, but she didn't bring that up.

"But only a small portion of the vampires you saw tonight are his children," he continued. "Many are business associates, employees, or others who have connection to him and claim his protection."

"So Bao—whatever his name is—doesn't know who it is?"

"He'll be able to find out fairly quickly with the information I gleaned from the Greek. He was most talkative after a short time with me," Giovanni smiled grimly. "I wouldn't worry about it, *tesoro*."

"So what was up with the biting thing? Just feeling possessive?" she asked him with a curled lip. "You could have at least warned me."

"The bite on the veranda was a public display. I'm sorry I couldn't warn you, but for me to feed from Ernesto's granddaughter in front of him, and on his own ship, made a very strong statement, and since we don't know who it is yet—"

"I get it, I get it. You did the caveman dance, and we've covered our bases. Everyone knows who I 'belong' to." She rolled her eyes.

"Exactly," he said with a smile. "And, I'll confess, my blood was running after the interrogation. If I was human, you could say it was an adrenaline rush."

"Okay then," she cleared her throat. "Next time go punch something instead of biting me."

"I just had," he said in a hoarse voice.

"Oh."

"Yes, 'oh.'"

"So..." she hesitated. "Is the guy who attacked Mano dead?"

He paused before she heard his satisfied voice. "Ashes in the Pacific."

They exchanged a look Beatrice didn't want to think about too closely before he changed the subject. "So...how was your conversation with Ernesto?"

Her head fell back against the seat and her eyes drooped. "That was exhausting."

Giovanni smiled. "You did extremely well for your first small taste of vampire politics, Beatrice."

"That was a *small* taste?"

He smiled and reached for her hand, stroking the back of her palm with his thumb. "A small and rather friendly dip in the shark pool."

"Okay, well, it was interesting, but I could go on a vamp politics diet for a while, if you know what I mean."

"Fair enough. There's no reason I can think of for us to go back in the near future."

Beatrice must have dozed in the car, because when she woke Giovanni was lifting her from the passenger's seat and carrying her into the kitchen.

"What time is it?" she asked with a yawn.

"Around four in the morning."

"Good thing I don't have to work tomorrow."

He walked through the kitchen, still carrying her in his arms. Beatrice curled into his chest and thought of the first ride she'd made into Cochamó when he'd held her for hours in front of him on the rocking horse.

"Gio?"

"Yes?" He turned down a long hall she knew contained the guest bedrooms.

"If I stayed with you tonight…could we just sleep?"

His steps faltered, and she heard his heart give a quiet thump.

"If that's what you want."

"I miss you," she whispered as her eyes closed again. She burrowed toward the comforting smell of his skin. "I miss how warm your arms always are."

He paused in the hallway before he turned and walked up the stairs.

Beatrice didn't remember much except for his hands as they removed her shoes, the low buzz of his skin brushing against hers, and the comfort of being enveloped in his scent as he pulled the sheets around her. She heard him moving around the room before his long arms enfolded her and he nestled behind her in the bed. He whispered in her ear as she faded to dreams.

"I love you, Beatrice."

CHAPTER 9

En route to Houston

"If you're really from Texas—"

"Is that something people lie about? Being from Texas?"

"—then why don't you have an accent?"

Beatrice turned to Giovanni. "Is he serious?"

He shrugged. "I suppose so," he said, looking at Ben's curious face. "We've never been, he only met Caspar and your grandmother when they came to New York to stay with him."

They were sitting in the belly of Lorenzo's old plane, which now was stripped of its more ostentatious details. It sported a decent library, two twin beds, and the same couches, though Giovanni had made sure they'd been recovered. When he had inherited Lorenzo's converted cargo plane with the reinforced compartment that allowed him to fly, he had no idea it would be put to so much use.

Though he had spent much of the past year in New York and Los Angeles settling legal matters with Ben and preparing to reenter Beatrice's life, he had spent the four years previous flying across Europe, Asia, Africa, and South America, rebuilding old alliances and searching unsuccessfully for her father.

"I didn't know my grandmother and Caspar went to New York!"

He nodded. "They came in August when I..." When he had flown down to Cochamó, unable to resist seeing her. The farther he had pushed her to the back of his mind in their years apart, the more he had been able to successfully concentrate on preparing himself for the conflict he knew was coming.

But as the prospect of seeing her neared, he became almost desperate.

Though Isabel had verbally lashed him, he hadn't been able to resist lurking around the house to try to catch a glimpse of her or a hint of her scent.

As soon as he mentioned August, her eyes hardened, Giovanni knew she realized what he was talking about. Luckily, Ben was still chattering, so she wasn't allowed to shut herself off like she so often did.

"Will there be cowboy hats? Do I get one? No, that would probably look stupid. But maybe...Gio, have you ever worn a cowboy hat?"

"I never wore a cowboy hat when I lived in Texas," he said.

Ben and Beatrice looked between each other, their eyes glinting. "That wasn't a 'no,'" she said with a sly smile.

He shrugged, thinking back to the time he had spent in Argentina with Gustavo and Isabel in the late 1800s. "It wasn't, strictly speaking, a cowboy hat."

They both started laughing and Ben finally choked out. "You—a cowboy—Gio wore a cowboy hat!"

"I'm trying to imagine it, Ben, but I just can't," Beatrice snorted.

"It wasn't a western hat—it was a gaucho-style hat. Everyone wore them."

Her eyes lit up. "But *they* wore them to keep the sun out of their eyes, and unless I'm missing something, sun burns you to a crispy critter, so you wouldn't need one because you wouldn't be out during the day. Admit it, you liked the cowboy hat."

"It wasn't a cowboy hat."

"I bet it was a black one," Ben said.

Beatrice nodded. "Definitely black."

He rolled his eyes and opened a book, attempting to ignore them, but in reality, his heart lightened to see them laughing together. Though he never said it, Ben had been dreading the idea of Beatrice disrupting the tentative family ties the two of them had formed.

"And you know, the sun thing isn't totally true. He once chased me out of the house about twenty feet during the day when I was trying to run away in New York. He didn't burst into flames, he just got really sunburned and a little smoky around the ears."

She cocked an eyebrow at Giovanni. "Smoky ears, huh? I'll have to remember that."

"And then he fell asleep really hard after he had two bags of blood, and he kept saying your name over and—"

Like lightning, Giovanni reached across the small compartment and grabbed Ben's hand. The boy slumped over, instantly asleep, and Giovanni sat back in his chair as Beatrice gaped at him.

"Did you just use mind voodoo to shut him up?"

"Yes."

"That's..."

She just kept gaping, seemingly unable to comprehend Ben's slumbering form. He was now snoring, just a little.

"I gave him a very nice dream about flying," he said with a shrug.

"That cannot be ethical, Gio."

"Well, call me an unorthodox parent then, but do you really think we would both be here a year later, still un-maimed, if I couldn't do that on occasion? He's a twelve-year-old boy. Trust me, it's for the best. He'll wake up when we're in Houston."

She shook her head, then stood, crouched down over the sleeping boy and pulled him over her shoulder as she trundled him to one of the small beds.

He watched her in amusement; she was far stronger than he'd realized. When he pulled her in to kiss him on the boat the week before, he'd noticed the firmness of the muscles on her body. It felt foreign on her but not at all unpleasant.

"The judo has paid off. You're far stronger than you look," he said when she came back and sat on the couch across from him.

Beatrice nodded. "I told you, that new sensei has really been great. Between judo, jujitsu, and the tai chi I feel pretty well-rounded. I need to find a shooting class, though."

He smiled. "Gustavo mentioned that you were quite proficient with a rifle. He enjoyed shooting with you last summer. And the judo and jujitsu are good self-defense choices for you with your size."

"That was the idea. I didn't like feeling helpless."

His heart clenched at the thought of his own failure to protect her five years before. "I understand."

"I very much doubt that," she muttered.

"Do you?" he asked with a flash of irritation. "Do you forget that I was held against my will for over ten years as a human? That, even as a vampire, I was subject to a far more powerful sire. One who could easily overcome me, no matter how strong I was?"

Her mouth fell open as she stared at him in the low light of the plane. "I forgot. Sorry."

He looked back down at his book. "I have... a well of regret over what I have put you through that I doubt you'll ever understand, Beatrice." He swallowed the lump in his throat. "I am grateful you are now better able to protect yourself. It has given you confidence you lacked."

"Professor voice," she muttered under her breath.

He looked until she met his gaze. Then he allowed his eyes to travel suggestively down her body and back up until he met her eyes, which were heated with desire.

"You are no longer a girl," he murmured. "And I was never your professor."

"You just had the arrogance of one. Still do."

With lightning speed, he came to kneel between her knees. He could hear her sharp inhalation and the sudden rush of her pulse. Looking up, he met her dark eyes.

"You think I'm arrogant?"

"I know you are," she said breathlessly.

"Then what would you have me do, *tesoro*?"

She blinked and he saw her gaze drop to his mouth. "Wh—what?"

"Should I forget five hundred years of experience killing my enemies and protecting those who belong to me so that your modern sensibilities are not harmed?"

She was still looking at his mouth, and he forced himself not to smile.

"Would you have me confer with you before every move as if I was a mere boy looking for approval?"

"No, I mean—"

"You called all the shots in your relationship with that human, didn't you?"

He knew he had made a mistake bringing up Mano as soon as she twisted her mouth into a sneer.

"Yeah, I did. And he knew just how to make me happy."

He darted back to his side of the plane and draped his arm over the back of the couch. "Did he? Did he *really*?"

She paled and looked away from him, staring at the dark window over his shoulder and the stars that winked out.

"Fine," he conceded. "I shall do my utmost to consult with you on future matters of strategy and defense when it pertains to you."

"Good."

"But I reserve the right to overrule you based on my experience and superior knowledge of the immortal world."

"Bossy."

"Mortal."

They glared at each other in silent struggle for a few minutes before she walked to the other bed in the cabin and lay down, turning her back to him as she fell asleep. Giovanni watched for hours, memorizing the sound of her soft breath, steady heartbeat, and the small unintelligible murmurs that comforted him. He glanced at Ben and felt his dormant heart beat once as he remembered the interrogation of Lorenzo's man in Los Angeles.

"HE KNOWS ABOUT YOUR BOY, DI SPADA, AND YOUR HUMAN WOMAN. HE STILL HAS many friends," *the shriveled vampire had gloated as his limbs slowly charred under Giovanni's grip.* "You'll never find all of them before he kills your people."

"Is that so? Tell me more, Pirro. How did you escape the massacre on Lorenzo's island? Were you hiding in a corner? Did you run away from the fight?"

The small dark vampire grinned before another burst of flame from Giovanni's hands caused him to arch his back in agony.

"How—how does it—" He hissed, overcome with agony.

"The fire?" Giovanni leaned closer to the assassin, almost embracing the vampire as his lips murmured in his ear. "I've sent my fire through your dry veins, you fool. It's a slow burn. One that will eat you from the inside out." He gripped Pirro's arms more tightly, and he could see Baojia's approving nod from over the assassin's shoulder. "I'll stop it if you tell me who the traitor is on this boat."

"I don't know," he choked. "It burns. He didn't tell me how—"

"—badly I could hurt you? No, he likes to leave that part out because it makes him look weak, Pirro." Giovanni stepped away, keeping a hand on the vampire's shoulder and forcing the fire a little further into his veins. The gashes Giovanni had opened on the vampire's arms, face and abdomen continued to leak the sludge that was the last of his dehydrated blood. Still, he pushed his amnis onto the assassin and forced the silent fire deep into the dry body in front of him.

"Tell me," he said again. "Who is working for Lorenzo? Who gave you the information about the human diver?"

"Does it bother you that your woman keeps a lover, di Spada? Does it—" The vampire let loose a bloodcurdling scream as the fire reached his heart, which only tried to pump feverishly as the vampire curled in pain. Giovanni could hear the slow churning as it tried to move the bloody sludge through Pirro's body, which only pushed the burning further.

"Tell me," he murmured in the man's ear, "and I will kill you quickly."

"I don't know," Pirro finally croaked out of his dusty throat. Giovanni thought he could see a faint puff of smoke as the vampire spoke.

"I don't believe you." He hit him with another wave of fire, and the smoke poured out of the assassin's scream.

"I don't know!" he shrieked. "He was in Tripoli three months ago. We all knew he was meeting with the master, but none of us saw him."

Giovanni released the vampire's shoulder and allowed him to slump to the ground, where he curled into a small, smoking ball of pain.

"Tripoli?" he mused to Baojia.

The stoic vampire nodded. "I'll be able to find out who was traveling then. It's enough."

"Are you sure? I'm happy to take the time for further questioning."

Pirro whimpered on the floor, delirious from pain.

"We've been busy for quite some time. Do you know how much my father wants your human?" Baojia shook his head. "He knows you're going to take her soon. How hard do you think he's trying to persuade her to join us right now."

Giovanni's eyes darted up, as if he could see through the steel layers of the ship to the top deck where he had left Beatrice. He looked back to Ernesto's enforcer. "Why do you want her? Why is he so set on having her in his family?"

Baojia shrugged. "I have watched her these years—" The vampire was cut off by

Giovanni's snarl. "—and I understand her appeal. She has a certain type of perception that is rare. Her eyes see through the layers of things, don't they? That is a very valuable trait."

Giovanni's lips curled. "She is mine."

The enforcer's eyes locked with his. "Is she? Really? I think Beatrice De Novo belongs to no one but herself, di Spada, no matter who may taste her blood."

A feral sound crawled up from his throat and he reached down to pick up Lorenzo's assassin, pummeling him until he was a lump of smoking flesh.

"Do you have any more use for him?" he asked Baojia.

The vampire frowned and shook his head, so Giovanni threw the lump to the floor, where it was quickly engulfed in blue flames that turned the body to ash. Baojia opened the doors leading to the small balcony and turned on a fan that slowly sucked the remains of Lorenzo's assassin into the wet night air.

Houston, Texas
Christmas Eve 2009

"Da nobis quæsumus Dómine Deus noster: ut qui Navitátem Dómini nostri Jesu Christi mystériis nos frequentáre gaudémus; dignis conversatiónibus ad ejus mereámur perveníre consórtium. Qui tecum vivit et regnat in unitáte Spíritus Sancti, Deus, per ómnia sæcula sæculórum. Amen."

The familiar Latin of the priest poured over him like a balm as he sat next to Ben and Beatrice late on Christmas Eve. Isadora had insisted that the five of them celebrate midnight mass together, and Giovanni surprised himself by asking if there was one being celebrated anywhere in the old language.

He sat with his arm around Ben, who had slumped to the side in exhaustion, and his gaze rested on Beatrice's profile as she watched the priest deliver the last of the liturgy. Giovanni flashed back to the many human days he'd spent with his uncle listening to the same words spoken by ancient men who had taken the same vows as the young Irish priest standing in front of him.

It was good to remember that even some things in the human world did not change.

He may not have practiced regularly, but he had been Catholic in his human life, and in the deepest part of himself, Giovanni still considered it a part of his identity. There was little doubt in his mind that in two hundred years, he could sit in another church, thousands of miles away from this one, and listen to the same words spoken in a slightly different accent.

He heard the last of the ancient mass ring through in the stone church, and he gently shook Ben awake.

"Is it over?" he whispered.

"Yes, time to go home."

"It feels like home, even without a basketball hoop," he muttered. "That's kind of weird, huh?"

He smiled and mussed Ben's hair as the boy stood. "No. I don't think so. Home is about people." He saw Beatrice glance at him and knew she had heard him.

Caspar, Isadora, Beatrice, Ben, and Giovanni all drove back to the house in River Oaks where the humans quickly retired for the night. He went to the library and started a fire, content to sit on the couch and enjoy the quiet with Doyle, who was curled onto a chair. If he concentrated, he could still smell Beatrice's scent that seemed to linger everywhere.

The longer he concentrated, the stronger it grew until he realized he was ignoring the sound of quiet steps coming down the hall.

Beatrice entered the room, barefaced and beautiful, looking very young as she stood in the doorway. She was wearing an old Houston University t-shirt and what he thought might have been a pair of his boxers he'd left at the house years ago. He couldn't stop the smile that came to his face when he saw her.

"Couldn't sleep," she murmured before she walked over to the couch and lay down next to him, resting her head on his thigh as she stared into the fire with sleepy eyes. "I still miss you, even though I'm mad at you."

"I'll wear you down eventually."

"You do have forever, don't you?"

But you don't, he thought. "I can be patient. I told you to take as long as you need."

She continued to speak, unguarded in her exhaustion. "What if it takes a long time? What if I'm old and wrinkled before I love you again?"

A soft smile crossed his face. "I sincerely hope it doesn't take that long..." His hand lifted to stroke her hair and he could feel her begin to drift again. "But your beauty is not the reason I love you, Beatrice, even though it takes my breath away at times," he whispered as he watched the firelight dance across her skin.

"You don't breathe. Not that hard to take your breath away," she said, slowly blinking longer and longer as she stared at the fire.

"Harder than you might think. Sleep, *tesoro*."

And she did.

Early the next morning, he could hear Ben's shrieks as the boy woke for his first real Christmas. He smiled in satisfaction before the day pulled him under.

When he woke and left the small room he slept in, he could still hear Ben's incessant chatter. He dressed in a pair of grey slacks and a red shirt he remembered Beatrice complimenting before he made his way downstairs.

The changes to the Houston house were subtle but perfectly reflected Isadora's tastes. She and Caspar had lived at the house since Beatrice had moved to Los Angeles, and both of them seemed exceedingly happy. Though it was late in life, Caspar finally seemed to have found the right woman for him.

"Merry Christmas," he said to Beatrice's grandmother when he saw her on the second floor landing. She was arranging a vase of flowers, and she turned to smile at him.

"Merry Christmas, Gio! We've missed you today. Especially Ben; he's so excited." She stood on her tiptoes, and he leaned down to kiss her cheek.

"Where is everyone?" he asked politely, though he could already hear the television in the living room. Isadora had never quite accustomed herself to his preternatural senses the way Beatrice had.

"Oh, they're doing their awful Christmas horror movie marathon again. Only this time, Ben is an enthusiastic participant. It's quieter than normal without Carwyn this year."

He smiled at the reminder that their lives had moved forward without him. "He's dealing with some complications at home, I believe. He apologized for not making it for the holidays."

"I know he has a large family. Is everything all right?"

That was an excellent question, he thought. The priest had been uncharacteristically close-mouthed for the past couple of months, and Giovanni was beginning to worry.

"I'll ask him tonight. We've scheduled a call later."

He left Isadora humming as he walked downstairs and rushed into the living room at vampire speed, scooping Beatrice up and setting her on his lap before she could take a breath.

"Oh!" she gasped before she laughed. "I'll never get used to that."

Her mood was lighter; he could tell by the ease around her eyes and the quick tilt of her smile. "Merry Christmas, Beatrice."

"Gio," Ben bounced up and down next to him. "Cas and Isadora got me an iPod, and B got me an electric scooter, and there's a whole bunch more presents under the tree, too. And a lot of them are for you!"

Ben may have been a very streetwise twelve, but this morning, Giovanni thought he looked every bit the child he should have been for so many years. Then his words registered, and he turned to Beatrice, tugging her hair as she sat on his lap.

"An electric scooter?"

She grinned and leaned over to kiss his cheek. "He'll be fine, old man. I'll teach him to ride it. Just be glad it's not a dirt bike."

"A dirt bike?" Ben shouted in excitement. "I want a dirt bike!"

"If I could get headaches, I would have one right now. Thank you. I'll never hear the end of this."

"So stuffy," she muttered, but she leaned back into his chest and let him wrap his arms around her waist. They sat in silence for a few minutes, watching the old movie on the screen.

"Is this..."

"*Horror of Dracula*, 1958. I thought it was appropriate. Ben hadn't seen it."

"You have a sick sense of humor."

"But the vampires in this one have British accents. It's practically highbrow." She stared raptly at the screen and only wiggled in his lap when he pinched her waist. He bit back a groan before he leaned slightly closer to her neck, realizing he needed to feed if he was going to be this close to her. His fang pierced his lip, and he tried to shift in his seat.

"*Tesoro*," he said quietly. "I need to go."

"Why?" she asked absently.

He cleared his throat and waited for her to look at him. When she did, he let his fangs peek out from behind his lips and felt her pulse pick up.

"I need to feed." He leaned close. "Unless you're offering, in which case I'd be happy to go upstairs," he said with a soft growl.

She hesitated. "Do you have bagged blood here?"

He was tempted to lie but didn't. Instead, he nodded and tried to discern whether it was wishful thinking that he saw a hint of disappointment in her eyes. She moved off his lap, and he quickly retreated from her presence to feed himself from the bagged blood in the refrigerator.

An hour later, and despite his meal, he was still eyeing her neck as they opened presents around the Christmas tree.

"Sweet! Another video game!"

True to Ben's fantasies, the adults in the room had showered the boy with gifts. Beatrice gave him his first computer, and she assured Giovanni she would teach him to use it responsibly. Caspar supplied the boy with a wealth of comic books, video games, and movies; while Isadora gave him enough dress clothes to make Ben shudder.

None of it seemed to fascinate Ben like the computer, and Giovanni stared in pleasure as the boy and Beatrice huddled over it while she unlocked the mysteries Giovanni couldn't.

"I'd say you look like you want to eat her alive, my friend, but I think it's much more serious than that," Caspar said quietly, his eyes following Giovanni's as he sat next to him on the couch.

"Look at them. Look how beautiful they are," he murmured as he watched their dark heads lean toward each other.

He saw Caspar smile.

"She's so good for you. I can't remember the last time I've seen you this happy."

"I'd be happier if she returned my affections."

Caspar said, "Don't be blind. She's unsure, not indifferent."

He shrugged. "Aren't I being patient?"

"Mostly. What did you get her for Christmas? I didn't see a present from you."

"None of your business, you brat."

Caspar chuckled and nodded toward Ben. "It's so odd, to see you with another child. Was I anything like that?"

Giovanni frowned. "Yes and no. Some things are the same, but he's much more independent than you were."

"That makes sense."

"And much more canny, which is both good and bad."

"Yes, I can see that, as well. The two of you are much easier around each other than you were last summer. Has B helped?"

He looked at her, and her eyes lifted to his. She offered him a small wink and a smile before she turned back to Ben.

"Yes, Beatrice has helped." *Everything.*

After the rest of the house had gone to bed, they kept each other company in the library, waiting for Carwyn's expected phone call.

"I never gave you your present, *tesoro*. Do you want it now?"

She smiled. "I wondered. I have one for you, too."

Giovanni pulled out a large box wrapped in burgundy paper from under the side table and handed it to her. She opened it and pulled out a carefully packed book box with two small volumes inside. She looked at the spine in delight.

"*Persuasion?*"

"First American edition, 1832. I found it in Paris a few years ago and thought you might enjoy it. I remember you eyeing my Austen the first time you were here."

She carefully pulled the first volume from its original book box and opened it carefully. "It's wonderful, Gio. Thank you." She smiled again. "*Persuasion*, huh?"

He shrugged. "It seemed appropriate. There's another small item in there, as well."

She closed the book, carefully packing it away before she looked into the box again and pulled out a small leather bag. She opened it, and a familiar brass key fell into her hand.

She blinked. "Is this what I think it is?"

"Well, you like that house as much as I do, so there's your key."

"You're giving me the...the Cochamó house?"

He smiled. "You still have to share it with me. That's my favorite home, but your name is on the deed, so to speak. And Gustavo and Isabel know if anything ever happens to me—"

"*Nothing* better happen to you."

"—the house is yours, Beatrice. It's your house, too. You can go whenever you want to now."

He couldn't read the expression on her face until she looked up and there were tears in her eyes. "Thank you," she whispered. "I love both my presents, but this one especially."

"You're welcome."

She leaned over to him and kissed his cheek. He left his arms lying across the back of the couch so he didn't grab her and cart her off to his room.

"So," he asked, clearing his throat. "Where's my present?"

"You know, you're not really bouncing around like Ben was."

He grinned and bounced in his seat just a little, making her laugh uproariously before she stood.

"Hold on; it's in my room. I'll be right back."

"I'll be here."

Giovanni stared into the fire and tried to imagine her lying in their bed at Cochamó, her smooth skin lit by candlelight. He wondered when he'd be able to persuade her to go with him again. He wanted to go in the summer with her, so she could see the waterfalls running and the meadows filled with wildflowers. They were beautiful at night, though she would be able to enjoy them during the day, as well.

"Okay," she called from the hall. "I don't have it wrapped, so close your eyes."

He smiled and closed his eyes, hoping that when he opened them, she would be modeling lingerie...or just skin, but he had a feeling that was wishful thinking. Instead, he heard her fumbling with something that sounded rather large.

"Okay, open."

He opened his eyes to see a large framed color photograph. It was his favorite waterfall in Cochamó, the midday sun reflecting off the mist and scattering rainbows. He smiled when he recognized it and looked up to see her waiting expectantly.

"I thought you could put it in your room here to go with your picture of Florence." She set it down and propped it against the chair nearest to the door. "And I got you a case of your favorite scotch, too. I called Gavin last week—"

She was cut off when he pulled her into his lap and kissed her. Beatrice tensed for a moment before she relaxed and sank into his arms. She gave a small sigh as he caressed her mouth, and she finally seemed to melt in his arms. His hands grasped her waist as she straddled him and met each surge with corresponding need. Her arms twined around his neck to pull him closer, and his hands reached up her shoulders, pressing their bodies together.

"Thank you," he murmured against her mouth before his lips left hers to travel down her neck, nibbling in strategic places. "I love the picture."

"You sure it's not the scotch?" she asked breathlessly as she ran her hands through his hair and pulled his head into the crook of her neck.

"Positive. It's perfect. You're perfect," he said against her skin.

"I'm so far from perfect it's laughable."

"I love that you make me laugh."

"And I'm still kind of mad at you."

"I'm calling a Christmas truce. If soldiers in battle can do it, it shouldn't be that much of a stretch for us." His fingers lifted the back of her shirt and she shuddered as his hands caressed the skin at the small of her back.

He felt the normal buzz of electricity grow as his blood began to move through his veins and his fangs descended. He ignored his reaction and continued to explore the soft skin around her collarbone as her hands stroked his neck.

"Gio..."

"Let's not fight," he whispered. "Just for a little while."

"But, Gio—"

He cut her off with a deeper kiss. Giovanni felt her moan and move over him, and he became almost lightheaded with desire.

She finally grasped his shoulders and pushed back.

"Oh, *tesoro*," he groaned as his head fell to her shoulder. "Why are you—"

"The phone," she said breathlessly, "is ringing."

"Why?"

She smiled at him. "Carwyn, remember?"

"Damn that priest," he muttered. "I'm going to burn his Hawaiian shirts the next time I see him."

She grinned and stood. "Well, I'm going to answer the phone."

He slouched in the sofa, closing his eyes while she went to answer the phone.

"Carwyn." He heard her laugh. "You better lock up your Hawaiian—what? What are you—"

She gasped as he rushed to the phone and grabbed it out of her hand.

"—need to talk to Gio immediately. I can't—"

"I'm here," he said to his friend.

He'd heard the panic in his old friend's voice from across the room. His heartbeat sped in anticipation of danger. Carwyn hadn't panicked in two hundred years.

"I need you here, Giovanni di Spada. I need you in Ireland. It's Ioan...my son is missing."

CHAPTER 10

En route to Dublin, Ireland

Giovanni pulled Beatrice close as the plane took off, both of them glancing out the window to see Ben waving at the plane with a frightened look on his face. Her grandmother had one hand on the boy's shoulder and Caspar stood behind them. The three were leaving directly for the safe house in the Hill Country as soon as the plane was off the ground.

She huddled into Giovanni's side and buried her face in his collar. They had fought horribly about her going with him, but he finally relented when she threatened to fly to Dublin on her own if he left her behind.

Giovanni gripped her arm as the plane took off, and she was almost afraid he would leave bruises. She was beginning to realize he hated flying. He never said anything, but every time they flew together, he looked distinctly uncomfortable at takeoff.

"Tell me about Ioan," she said to distract him. She wondered whether he would break his usually reticent behavior to tell her anything specific.

"Ioan is...he's Carwyn's oldest son, and his biological great-grandson, I believe."

"Really?"

"Great or great-great grandson, yes. He's only about one hundred years younger than Carwyn. He's very powerful and very smart. His wife, Deirdre, is Irish and they've lived in the Wicklow Mountains for the last two hundred years or so, though they've been married for much longer."

"And they're both Carwyn's children?"

He nodded. "Yes, Ioan asked his father to change Deirdre. They met when she was human. I believe he was around five hundred years old at the time."

Beatrice fell into silence, contemplating a couple that seemed suddenly very familiar.

"So, if he's so powerful, how did he disappear?" she asked in a low voice. "Is it Lorenzo?"

Giovanni shook his head. "I don't know. I think it has to be, but this attack doesn't make sense. Ioan is not political. He's one of the most compassionate vampires I've ever met. He's also a superb scientist. Some of our conversations..." His face fell, and Beatrice realized that not only had Carwyn lost a son, but Giovanni had lost a friend if they couldn't find Ioan.

"He has studied medicine for around three hundred years," he finally continued. "And he will periodically go into Dublin for free clinics at night. He treats poor families, drug users, prostitutes...He has a very deep compassion for those on the fringes of society."

"But how does that—"

"Carwyn said he disappeared from Dublin during one of these clinics. He's weaker in the city. Earth vampires usually are. They draw their strength from the ground. And if he was put into a position where humans might have been hurt if he didn't comply, Ioan would let them take him." Giovanni sighed and closed his eyes. "He wouldn't even hesitate."

She swallowed and leaned her head on his shoulder. "Do you think he's already dead?"

He shook his head. "Deirdre would know. They've shared blood for over four hundred years. She would know if he was dead."

Beatrice fell silent, suddenly aware she knew nothing of the intimacies of vampire relationships. Though she had spent months with Isabel and Gustavo, it wasn't something they discussed, and she suddenly felt like an awkward school girl.

As if sensing her discomfort, Giovanni looked down and smiled a little. "I tried to explain once...about the biting. There are different kinds of bites, Beatrice. It's not always just to drink."

"Oh," she blushed, but he just pulled her closer, refusing to let her squirm away. "Well, I know that when you bit me...I mean, it didn't hurt. It felt...good," she said in a small voice. It had felt more than 'good,' but she didn't want to dwell on the details when she was stuck in a plane with him for the next eight hours. "I guess I always assumed that if vampires bit each other, it was just for, you know, siring someone."

When he spoke again, his voice was oddly formal, and it made her more comfortable to hear his "professor voice" when he was discussing something so intimate. "There are two different kinds of bonds that vampires will form with each other. Siring and, to use an old term, mating. When a vampire is sired, their blood is drained and replaced—"

"Does it hurt?"

He shrugged. "Not unless the sire wishes it. Andros had the odd theory, based only on his own madness, that a child sired in anger or pain would become unstable, but I've never seen any reason to believe that."

"So it didn't hurt when you were turned?"

Giovanni smiled and stroked her cheek. "No, *tesoro*. I knew what was going to happen. I can't say I was eager to drink blood, but I didn't want to die. Andros drained me...I don't remember much after that. I woke up the next night as an immortal. It was...an adjustment. I had to get used to my new senses and abilities, and I felt a very strong attachment to Andros."

He drifted off, lost in his own thoughts, and Beatrice took a chance on his talkative mood to ask something that had bothered her for years. "You seem like you have such complicated feelings for Andros; when you talk about him, it's almost like you love him."

"I did love him."

"But you bartered with Lorenzo to kill him."

"Yes," he said, and his eyes shuttered.

She rose onto her knees and straddled his lap on the couch, forcing him to look at her.

"I don't understand."

He began several times but paused before he could speak. Finally, he continued in a whisper, "He would have used me. He was already planning something. I don't know exactly what. You see, he never counted on me controlling fire. Once he knew...I think the temptation to use me for his own ends was too great."

She stroked his face and ran her fingers through his hair. He almost seemed like a large, fierce cat as he pushed into her palm and sought comfort in her touch.

"You had him killed so he wouldn't use you."

He nodded, but his eyes were still haunted. "I loved him, but whatever he was planning I wanted no part of. And I knew...I knew he would have been able to convince me."

"You can't feel guilty, Jacopo," she said gently, using his childhood name. "He was crazy. He murdered your uncle. He held you captive for ten years."

Giovanni nodded. "Yes, and without him doing all that, I wouldn't be sitting here with you. I would never have known Carwyn or Tenzin. No one would have been there to save Caspar. Benjamin would probably never have known a better life. So how can I hate him? His cruelty brought me to the people I love, Beatrice. What price can I put on that?"

She leaned forward and placed a gentle kiss on his forehead, smoothing the lines he created with his frown. Beatrice pulled his face into the crook of her neck and he wrapped his arms around her waist. He held her for hours until she drifted to sleep.

W*ICKLOW* M*OUNTAINS*, I*RELAND*
December 2009

T*HEY ARRIVED BY CAR AT THE SMALL LODGE TUCKED INTO THE* W*ICKLOW* Mountains a few hours after dusk the next night. There was a grouping of low, whitewashed houses around a central open courtyard, where small children ran and laughed. A large farmhouse spread out from the rear of the courtyard and a sheep dog sat by the doorway. She could see two human women walking across the garden, speaking and gesturing with their hands, as they corralled the children into the glowing houses.

"There are a lot of humans here," she said quietly to Giovanni, who had grabbed their bags and began walking toward the large farmhouse.

"Yes," he said with a nod. "Deirdre and Ioan are a poorly concealed secret in this area. The human population asks no questions, and the area is safe from almost all crime and poverty. The humans that live here are mostly connected to their children in some way."

"They have a lot of kids?"

He nodded again. "They are a large clan. Probably the largest in Ireland. And very influential. Even the water vampire that controls Dublin defers to them on most matters if they desire."

"So losing Ioan—"

"Is a very, *very* big deal, Beatrice."

He did not knock but pushed open the door of the large house, only to be greeted by a familiar furry face as they walked in.

"Bran!" she cried and immediately reached out to pet the wolfhound who was nudging her hip in a persistent manner. He was older and obviously near the end of his life, but the large dog still wore a friendly smile.

"*Och*, Bran," she heard a voice call. "Who is it now?" A stout, brown-haired woman with milky-white skin walked down the hallway. The roses in her cheeks marked her as human, and she wore a flour-dusted apron over her soft blue dress.

"Gio," she said with a smile. "It's been too long."

"Sinéad," he said softly, bending down to kiss her cheek. "This is—"

"You must be B." The woman held out her hand to shake. "Carwyn said to expect you both. Gio, your usual room is ready and, B, there's one upstairs for you. Give me a second to clean up and I'll show you. Such a dreadful, sad way to see old friends. Such a sorrow. The Father is on the warpath, though. If anyone can find Ioan, it'll be him."

"They contacted Dublin?"

Sinéad nodded. "Days ago. They've both been to the city, but the reports are unclear and they've not wanted to leave the valley unprotected."

Giovanni sighed and reached for her hand. She held it tightly and stood in silence, wishing there was something useful she could do. Sinéad was looking back and forth between them with a sad smile, but Giovanni didn't seem to notice.

"B, I'll take you up to your room. Gio, make yourself at home, of course."

He nodded and let go of her hand so she could follow Sinéad up to the second floor. Beatrice was led to a cheerful yellow room at the top of the stairs with a full bed, a small desk, and a set of drawers where she set her duffel bag. She sat on the edge of the bed and stared out the window. The stars had come out, and the clock read close to nine o'clock. She wasn't tired, but she felt lost in the unfamiliar room until she caught the whiff of smoke.

She turned and saw him standing in the doorway. He looked at her with grim eyes, and she held out her hand. He crossed the room, took it, and pulled her next to him, stretching out on the small bed as he enfolded her in his arms. They lay silently, watching the stars for a few minutes before he spoke.

"I'm glad you're here, but I wish you hadn't come."

"Not an option," she murmured as she stroked his forearm.

"Beatrice—"

"If you're so worried, train me."

"I've never studied judo."

"That's not what I'm talking about." He made an incredulous sound, and she looked over her shoulder. "What?"

"Train you? To fight vampires?"

She shrugged. "I know I'll never be as strong or as fast—"

"Or have keen senses, or control an element." She leaned down and bit his arm. "Ow!" He laughed. "Do it again."

She scowled. "Hush. I just mean, something is better than nothing. And it'll give you something to do until Carwyn comes back."

"What? You want to do it now?"

"What did you have in mind to pass the time?"

He raised a speculative eyebrow. "Well..."

"Yeah," she said. "Right. I have a feeling the house mom wouldn't be too keen on that idea." She nodded toward the door where she had no doubt Sinéad's ears were tuned toward them. "Otherwise, she'd probably have put us in the same room."

"True. I still—"

He sat up so quickly she almost fell off the bed.

"Carwyn's here," he said before he flew down the stairs.

Beatrice sat up and looked out the window, where she could just see the red hair of the priest as Giovanni embraced him at the edge of the road. She saw a blur streak by them both and the front door slammed shut. In the next heartbeat, a tall warrior of a woman stood in front of her, examining her with burning, blue eyes.

"Are you Giovanni's woman?"

Well, Beatrice almost said, *it's kind of complicated.* She thought better of it when she saw the fierce expression on the woman's face.

"I'm Beatrice."

"Your scent is unfamiliar."

"I didn't mean to surprise you."

"You didn't."

"Oh."

Deirdre seemed to take a step back. "I am Deirdre Mac Cuille. You are welcome in this house as long as you mean no harm to my own. You'll forgive me if I'm not a proper host to you."

Though she knew Ioan was Carwyn's blood relative, Deirdre looked like his daughter in every way. She shared the flaming auburn hair of the priest and stood at an impressive height. The planes of her pale face were regal as she stared down her nose.

Beatrice shook her head. "No, of course you wouldn't be. I'm so sorry about your husband."

Deirdre cocked her head. "He is not dead. Save your condolences, girl."

Just then, she heard a rushing on the stairs, and Giovanni appeared next to Deirdre in the doorway. They nodded toward each other, and Deirdre departed, leaving Beatrice staring in her wake.

"She's kind of scary."

He nodded. "Yes, she is. You would be too, if...well, if it was someone you cared about," he said quietly.

She looked at him standing in the door, and the wave of emotion almost overwhelmed her. She stood and walked to him. "If it were you," she whispered, knowing he could hear. "I'd be that way if it were you, Giovanni."

He said nothing as she slipped down the stairs.

CARWYN WAS FAR FROM THE CHEERFUL VAMPIRE SHE REMEMBERED FROM HIS last visit in May. She sat with him in the large farm kitchen as he ate the steak Sinéad had cooked for him. He tore into the bloody meat, not waiting for anyone to join him and barely speaking to her. Various members of the family, human and vampire, milled around him, but no one spoke.

"Carwyn," she heard Giovanni's voice as he walked into the kitchen. The crowd around the priest parted at his voice, and he came to sit beside his old friend. "Where's Deirdre?"

"She was in the garden for a bit, trying to scent him, but she couldn't pick anything up. They must know they're blood-bound and are keeping him away from open earth. I believe she's feeding right now."

Giovanni lowered his voice. "Human? I know she doesn't usually, but—"

"Yes, human. One of the farmhands. She knows she needs the strength."

"And you?"

Carwyn glared at Giovanni. "I'll not change who I am because of a madman. I cast no judgment, but—"

"For God's sake, Carwyn—"

"Do not take His name in vain among my people, di Spada!" the priest roared, standing up from the table and meeting Giovanni nose-to-nose as they squared off against each other.

"Fine," Giovanni spit out, "but I'm going to feed, as well. I've no interest in principle over survival."

Giovanni stormed out, leaving Beatrice gaping at them both as Carwyn sat down again, staring at the half-eaten meal in front of him. The humans and vampires in the kitchen dispersed and Beatrice sat silently, at a loss for what to say.

"I'm truly an ass sometimes, aren't I?" Carwyn finally muttered.

"He's worried about you. And I think he feels guilty."

"Why?" He began eating again. "I'm the one that agreed to help him get you back. Isn't it my fault? Oh, wait, you're the one we rescued, so maybe it's your fault." Beatrice felt tears spring to her eyes as she watched the surly vampire. "No...not your fault, after all, you were only targeted because of your father, so perhaps it's Stephen De Novo's fault after all."

"Carw—"

"Or," he finally looked up at her with a fierce expression in his blue eyes. "It's the fault of the man who kidnapped my son. Yes..." He nodded and took a gulp from the mug that Sinéad set by his elbow. "I'm sticking with this being Lorenzo's fault. Because that's the vampire I'm going to kill if I don't get my Ioan back." He wiped the blood from the corner of his mouth, smearing it across his jaw in an ominous red streak before he continued inhaling his food.

"What are you doing?"

She turned to see Deirdre walking toward her in the garden as she practiced her tai chi forms in the twilight. They had been in Wicklow for a week with little to no change in the situation. Giovanni and Carwyn had gone to Dublin the night before to meet with the leader of the city, and she had stayed in

Wicklow with Deirdre, who refused to venture far from her home, worried that more of her family might be targeted.

"It's tai chi. Martial arts. I study in L.A."

"It's quite beautiful. Why is it so slow?"

"Sometimes it's faster. But Tenzin told me when I practice forms, I should concentrate on the flow of energy and meditation so my movements are precise. It's relaxing that way, too."

"Tenzin?" Deirdre said. "How very...interesting."

She frowned as Deirdre sat next to her on the grass, taking a deep breath and sinking her hands into the soil of the garden that overlooked the green valley. Stands of trees lay in the creases where streams cut through, and a small herd of deer broke into a run as they scented danger at the edge of the forest. Beatrice could hear the sharp bark of the dogs and the lowing cows as the farmhands brought them in for the night.

She continued with her forms, moving slowly and trying to let the tense waves of energy from Deirdre wash over and around her. She heard the vampire take a deep breath.

"Why did Carwyn say you were trying to scent Ioan? Isn't he too far away?"

She saw Deirdre smile at her out of the corner of her eye.

"You don't know much about vampire relationships, do you?"

She blushed but continued practicing.

"Doesn't Gio tell you anything?"

"We're not—" Beatrice faltered. "It's not like that with us." *Yet.*

"He's in love with you. Don't you love him? You look at him like you do."

She frowned. "You know, forgive me if I don't feel like getting into the details with someone I hardly know."

Deirdre snorted. "Fine. Forget I asked."

Beatrice pushed down her irritation and focused on the slow and steady movement of her body. She could feel Deirdre still watching her.

"Sit down and talk to me, girl. It's not like I've never had this discussion with any of my daughters before. Ioan, despite being a doctor, has always been squeamish about these things. Typical male."

"I'm well aware of the birds and the bees, thanks very much."

"You asked how I could scent my husband, and I'll tell you how. It's either ask me or Giovanni eventually." Beatrice turned and Deirdre raised an eyebrow. "Well?"

She huffed and came to sit next to her on the grass, stretching out her sore muscles.

"Okay," Beatrice asked, "what's the big deal with smelling?"

Deirdre smiled. "You are amusing. I imagine you drive him mad in the best way. He has always taken himself too seriously."

Beatrice remained silent, at a loss for something to say to the vampire next to her, who looked younger but whose eyes held a kind of infinite wisdom she couldn't wrap her mind around.

"You know how our kind are sired, do you not?"

"Yes."

"When mates...when two vampires exchange blood in small amounts over long periods of time, a different bond is formed."

"A sexual bond?"

She shook her head. "Much more than sexual. You can have sex without exchanging blood, but when you do..."

"Yeah?"

Deirdre gazed out over the valley, still digging her hands into the earth. Her mood had shifted, and Beatrice could tell she was thinking of Ioan. "Blood exchanged in love and passion for hundreds of years. Over and over until it is so mingled..."

Beatrice's heart raced. "What?"

"We are two halves of a whole," Deirdre whispered. "Four hundred years we have been together. That's why I know he still lives. If he was dead, my own blood would cry out. There would be no question."

"So, when they said you could 'scent' him—"

"Our blood calls to each other if we are apart. I will be able to scent him because, if even a drop of his blood touches open earth, it will call to me."

Beatrice was silent, staring into the distance as the stars came out around them.

"I can't even imagine what you must be feeling right now."

Deirdre turned her head sharply. "Do you want to?"

"What?"

"You cannot look at him the way you do and not have thought about sharing this life with him."

She felt the tears spring to her eyes. "It's...too much. I can't—"

"You have to."

"Do you think so?" She remembered Giovanni had said Ioan asked Carwyn to change Deirdre when she was human. "You made the choice. Has it been worth it?"

Deirdre's blue eyes were wells of sorrow, as if she was staring into a grave.

"I have shared his blood for four hundred years. What do you think?"

CHAPTER 11

Dublin, Ireland

Giovanni rang in the New Year watching a young water vampire twist into a smoldering pile of ash.

"He's created all these children," Carwyn muttered. "Almost indiscriminately. But none of them know anything."

They were standing in a warehouse on the edge of the River Liffey that was thick with the scent of Ioan's blood and Giovanni's son, but other than faint brown smudges on the concrete floor, there was no sign of the missing doctor.

Giovanni pulled on his shirt after killing Lorenzo's useless minion. "Did you call Deirdre tonight?"

Carwyn nodded as he watched Patrick Murphy's people sweep the ashes out the open door of the warehouse.

"Gentlemen," said the solemn vampire in the three-piece suit. "We've come to the end of my leads. This warehouse was the last of the information my people had gleaned. We'll still keep our ears and eyes open, of course. The loss of Ioan—"

"Has not been confirmed in any way," Giovanni muttered, watching Carwyn pace at the other end of the warehouse.

Murphy tugged at the black curls on his head, obviously nervous. "If there is any further assistance I can offer to either of you while you are here..."

"It's fine, Murphy," he heard Carwyn spit out across the room. "I'll expect your cooperation in the future, but if we've ended our leads here, I want to go back to my daughter."

Giovanni tried not to sigh in relief. Though he knew Beatrice was perfectly safe in Wicklow, he still felt uncomfortable being without her.

"Boats," Murphy said. "My best guess would be boats. Lorenzo is a water vampire, and he would have the resources to transport him by boat. This warehouse has river access, and we are not far from the port."

Giovanni nodded. "We'll keep you informed."

"Please do. And safe travels to you both."

They drove Ioan's old car back to Wicklow, having located it near a church where he'd been running a clinic the night he disappeared. As they swerved through the hedgerows and over the bumpy roads on their way to the lodge, he could feel the weight of Carwyn's worry as if it was another passenger in the car.

"I think he is dead."

"You don't know that, Father. And Deirdre would have sensed it."

"She might not. Not if he was taken far away and never touched the ground."

"Carwyn—"

"What if he is in water? Or unable to touch the earth? Oh, my son," he whispered, gripping the wheel. "My Ioan. I don't want to contemplate this life without my boy."

Giovanni clenched his jaw, willing the road to smooth before them.

He saw Beatrice in the front garden, practicing her tai chi forms in the dark. He nodded toward the silent guard Deirdre must have assigned to her; the young vampire nodded back before disappearing into the night. Giovanni crept toward her, not wanting to disturb her silent meditation, and watched her for a few moments in the moonlight.

She was beautiful. And so much stronger than he ever could have anticipated. Though Beatrice was still weaker than him physically, it was the strength of her mind and her determination that impressed him. She was no longer afraid to stand up to him, their argument before leaving Texas a prime example. He loved her all the more for it.

A mischievous smile crossed his lips, and he snuck up behind her. Before he could anticipate it, she stepped back, shoved her hip into his groin, and threw him off balance. Beatrice reached around, grabbing his waist and sweeping her leg through one of his as she flipped him onto his back and landed on his chest.

He blinked, looking up at her with a shocked face before he roared in laughter.

"Oh," she said with a snicker. "It's you."

"Hello to you, too."

"Don't sneak up on me, vampire."

He was still laughing when he brushed away the lock of hair that had fallen into her eyes. "That was marvelous."

"I try."

"I'll be expecting it next time, so you better watch out."

A twinkle came to her eye. "Oh yeah? What are you going to do—"

She broke off when he reared up and jerked her neck to the side. His fangs were bared and he let them scrape lightly across the skin of her neck before he licked up to her ear.

"Just remember, never pin a vampire face-to-face." He rolled them over so she was lying under him, and she looked up with hungry eyes. "Unless you want this to happen."

"I'll keep that in mind," she choked out.

He bent his head down and brushed a kiss across her flushed lips.

"It's been on *my* mind for a while now."

He helped her up and they walked arm in arm back to the farmhouse. Giovanni was filling her in on what had transpired in Dublin when a blood-curdling scream rent the air.

Giovanni halted, a feeling of dread washing over him. He picked Beatrice up and rushed back to the house, setting her near the young guard as he sped toward the back garden. He felt the force of Deirdre's amnis slam into him as she wailed in Carwyn's arms. Giovanni almost fell to his knees, but he felt Beatrice come behind him and grab his hand. He pulled her into his arms and buried his face in her hair as he rocked her back and forth.

"He's dead," Beatrice whispered, holding him close. "He's dead, isn't he?"

Giovanni nodded. Nothing but the grief of losing half of yourself could tear a person in two the way that Deirdre Mac Cuille had been. Her screams were hardly that of a woman; they more closely resembled the death keen of the mythical banshee. She tore at her hair while Carwyn shouted, "Where, Deirdre? Where?" over and over again. She was unintelligible, gnashing her teeth and rocking back and forth as she dug her hands into the earth.

Finally, she shoved her father away, tore off her clothes, and stretched herself upon the ground. Giovanni felt the sudden jolt and sigh as the earth opened up and swallowed her whole.

BEFORE DAWN, LETTERS WERE SENT AND CALLS MADE. THOUGH DEIRDRE HAD not yet reappeared, some of their clan had already arrived, emerging from the valley confused and angry. Deirdre and Ioan's children converged on their parent's home as the scent of their father's blood travelled through the earth from which he had drawn his power.

Giovanni took refuge from his grief in the small stone room under the mountain. He pulled Beatrice with him, and the two retreated from the overwhelming sorrow of Ioan and Deirdre's family. Carwyn was surrounded by his children's children, both comforting and being comforted by his kin.

He held Beatrice for the rest of the night, and she lay with him, quietly stroking his hair the way she knew he loved, old wounds overtaken by the ache of new loss. He fell into his day rest next to her and when he woke she remained, staring at him with her deep brown eyes.

"There are so many vampires here."

He nodded. "Deirdre and Ioan sired or fostered many children over the years. They would take in anyone that needed a home unless they were dangerous. All their children had children, and so forth. Their clan numbers in the hundreds, probably."

Giovanni knew it had only begun. Soon, the trickle of friends and allies would become a flood as Ioan and Deirdre's people returned to the quiet mountain their parents had called home.

"Why did they all come? I mean, what do vampires do when..."

"When Deirdre returns and the family is gathered, Carwyn will say a funeral mass."

"I can't—" Beatrice choked and wiped at her eyes. "How will he be able to do that?"

Giovanni took a deep breath and hugged her closer. "It's the last thing he can do for his son."

He could feel her tears wet on her cheeks as she lay her head on his arm.

"Tell me about him."

He pulled her closer. She had been handling herself extremely well, considering how recently and dramatically her world had changed. For the past week and a half, she had been surrounded by humans and vampires she didn't know, and he had left her alone for much of the time, consumed by the need to search for his friend.

"Ioan was kind. Intelligent. Wise, *tesoro*. He had a kind of wisdom about life and family I could only hope to gain." He noticed the lines of stress that creased her brow. "Beatrice, there will be many vampires here and not all of them will be Carwyn's people. Some of the water vampires who run Dublin will be here, as well as others from around the country. They do not have the same attitude toward humans that we do, so make sure you stay close to me. It will be...somewhat overwhelming. It could be dangerous if tempers run high."

"Since I don't want to be a beverage during the vampire version of an Irish wake, I'll keep that in mind."

He tried to stifle a laugh, but couldn't.

"Sorry." She closed her eyes in embarrassment. "Too crass?"

He shook his head and leaned over, brushing a soft kiss across her temple. "I was just thinking how Ioan would have laughed at that. Having married an Irishwoman, jokes about his adopted homeland were some of his favorites. No one loves a joke like a Welshman."

"Will she survive?" she whispered. "Deirdre? How do you recover from something like that?"

He swallowed the lump in his throat. "You learn to deal with loss the longer you live. I have lost many people I cared for."

"But not like him. Not even *you* expected Ioan could die. I could tell. You all thought you'd be able to get him back somehow."

He frowned, thinking about her words, and realized she was right.

"Yes," he finally said. "It is difficult to think that someone so powerful could be cut down."

"This is Lorenzo, isn't it? He did this. Or someone he hired."

He pushed back the useless well of guilt. "It has to be. First he attacked someone important to you, then the child he knew would pain Carwyn the most."

"Is he—I don't know the right term—herding us? We were spread out before and now Carwyn, you, and I are together. If he wanted to attack us—"

"He won't be that direct, I don't think. He's not strong enough. He's going after the people we care about to distract us and throw me off balance."

"Should we warn Tenzin?"

He said, "Tenzin has four beings she cares for enough that Lorenzo might target them. Three are in this house, and the other is more protected than you could imagine. Don't worry about Tenzin. Lorenzo should be the one worried. Tenzin was…fond of Ioan."

He broke off, overwhelmed as grief ambushed him again. He gripped Beatrice against his chest, more afraid of loss than he had been in hundreds of years. If he could have allowed himself to weep, he would have at that moment. "I should call Caspar and check in, make sure everything is all right," he said hoarsely.

"I called my grandma a few hours ago," she said. "They're fine. In the mountains and hidden. Ben isn't causing any problems."

He relaxed a little. "Thank you."

"You don't have to do everything yourself, you know."

He smiled ruefully. "I'm not used to asking for help."

"Well…" She faltered a little before she continued in a quiet voice, "Get used to it."

He wanted to see her eyes in that moment, when her heart was racing and her face was flushed, but she was turned away, so he simply kissed the top of her head.

"Beatrice—"

Suddenly the air churned with the scent of power, and Giovanni turned toward the flurry of activity in the hall. He leapt up and opened the door. Beatrice peered out from underneath his cautious arm.

"Deirdre, wait!" Carwyn shouted in the corridor.

The scent of blood and dirt hit his nose as he saw Deirdre stride toward them, carrying what was left of Ioan's body wrapped in a dusty sheet. She walked down the narrow hall, still naked and covered with earth as she headed toward the chamber she had shared with her husband for over two hundred years.

She paused briefly and her eyes glanced over his shoulder where Beatrice stood behind him in the small stone room. The widow's eyes searched his out, and he shuddered at the utter desolation.

So quiet even he could barely hear her, Deirdre breathed out, "Are you sure?" Then she turned the corner, and he heard a door slam shut. Soon afterward, Carwyn walked down the hall and Giovanni could hear him enter the room. Then the low keening wail started again, and he pressed the door closed.

FOUR DAYS LATER, THE MAJORITY OF IOAN'S CLAN, HIS FRIENDS, AND THOSE who had known him had gathered on the small mountain. Carwyn and his daughter emerged the night after she brought Ioan's body home, the priest carrying the small wooden box of earth that contained all that was left of the nine-hundred-year-old vampire he had sired.

The mood on the mountain was cautious and confused. Ioan had been known not only as a powerful and ancient earth vampire, but as a scholar and a humanitarian. The idea of any immortal targeting him was seen by most of his friends and allies as supremely wasteful and far from shrewd, considering his alliances.

The moon was almost full, and the night was crisp and clear when Carwyn returned the remains of his last blood relative to the earth. Giovanni stood silently, grieving as his friend spoke the ancient rite over his child, and all those gathered felt the surge of energy as the clan reached down and touched the mountain together as the earth he had loved became Ioan's final resting place.

The following night, the clan of Ioan ap Carywn and Deirdre Mac Cuille gathered on the hilltop to grieve, as Carwyn and Giovanni met in the library of the main house with Deirdre and Beatrice to talk about what steps they needed to take. Deirdre had found Ioan's beheaded remains on the bank of the Liffey River, dumped by whoever had killed him.

"Murphy still has his people looking in the city and the port, and my people are scouring the coast of Wales to make sure they didn't escape in that direction," Carwyn said.

"The humans whose memories were tampered with were here," Giovanni pointed to a location on the map of Dublin spread out before them. "But the warehouse is here. Now that warehouse backs up to the port, so it's also likely that Murphy is right, and whoever did this is already out of our reach for right now. Beatrice?"

"Yes?"

"Is it possible for you to search online to see what ships were in the port the night Ioan died and where they went?"

"Absolutely." She nodded. "I just need an internet connection."

"Good, you do that and I'll give you the number of Murphy's day people so you can contact them if you run into any problems. He's offered the use of any of his resources—"

"Damn right he has," Carwyn muttered, obviously still unhappy with the water vampire who controlled the city where his son had been killed.

"—to catch whoever took Ioan."

"We know who took him," Deirdre said with a sigh. "We know who it is, Gio. Why are you wasting time?"

Giovanni's shoulders tensed when he heard her hollow voice; he braced himself for her recrimination, but her empty gaze was fixated on a canvas she had painted of Ioan, which hung on the wall near the small fireplace in the corner of the library. He looked at the painting, which had captured his friend's lively smile and the wicked humor he had inherited from his father.

"Deirdre—"

"I'll not be leaving the mountain, Gio. Not right now. There is too much to do and too many defenses to shore up. Our people need me here, so I'll depend on you and Father to kill him for me."

He nodded. "I understand."

"Though I'd rip his heart out of his body and feed it to the dogs," Deirdre said in a low voice, "just to rip it out again when it grew back."

The intense guilt from his son's actions almost threatened to overwhelm him, but Giovanni stood, stoically meeting Deirdre's vicious gaze.

"Kill him, Giovanni di Spada. I will not have you take his sin on your shoulders, but I do expect you to rid the world of this monster."

"I will," he whispered, as he fixed her burning blue eyes in his mind.

"I *demand* it of you."

"The right is yours, Deirdre, and I will honor it."

"For me, for Ioan, and for your woman as well."

He saw Beatrice's lip twitch minutely when Deirdre called her "his woman" and the grieving widow must have seen it as well, because she turned to Beatrice.

"Do I *offend* your modern sensibilities, Beatrice De Novo, to call you 'his woman?'"

An embarrassed flush rose in Beatrice's cheeks, and she opened her mouth to speak, but Deirdre continued, scorn dripping from her words.

"This *immortal*," she said, pointing to Giovanni, "who has never claimed a human woman in five hundred years, is not worthy of calling you 'his?' This vampire who wields the fiercest of elements with iron control is the one *you* dismiss?"

"Deirdre," Giovanni cautioned, but she brushed him aside with a careless wave.

"*You foolish girl!*" she bit out. "Why do you hesitate?"

"I know you're grieving," Beatrice said as she glared at Deirdre, "but our lives are none—"

"Do you think you have forever?" Deirdre finally choked and blood tinged tears rolled down her face. "Not even *we* had forever. And I only seek to live now that I may care for my people, otherwise I would join my husband in the grave."

"Daughter, that's enough," Carwyn murmured as he walked across to gather her up and hold her as she shook with silent sobs.

Giovanni watched Beatrice from across the room, noting her pale face as she watched Deirdre's grief. The fear in her eyes matched that which slashed at his own heart, and he fought back a wave of hot panic at the thought of being parted from her.

Deirdre finally wiped her eyes and pulled away from her father. She gave Beatrice a hard look, but before Giovanni could rebuke the widow, some unspoken communication seemed to pass between the women and the tension drained from the room. Deirdre turned to him with a veiled expression.

"Giovanni, forgive my outburst. I will leave you so that I may see to my family."

"Deirdre..."

"And you, Beatrice, thank you for helping to find those who killed my Ioan."

"Of course."

Carwyn and Deirdre walked out of the library to join the vampires who surrounded a bonfire lit in remembrance of their kinsman. Giovanni watched them through the window until he heard a quiet sniff behind him, and he turned. "Beatrice?"

"Is that what you want?" Tears were in her eyes, and her arms were folded across her chest.

"What—"

"Is that what you want for *us*? For me to give up my human life and be tied to you like that? So connected that either of us would want to *die* if something happened to the other?"

Yes.

No matter how painful Deirdre's loss was, Giovanni had also seen the incredible joy her bond with Ioan brought. "You know my feelings for you. And what I want."

"To become a vampire. Like you. To live in the dark and watch all my family and friends die around me." She dashed the tears from her eyes. "But I'd have you, right? And what if I lost you? Or what if you left me again?" Her eyes flashed out the window toward Deirdre. "What then?"

"I won't leave you again," he said gently, walking across the library. "And you see only the sadness, but what if we could have a thousand years together? More? Even if we had only one hundred years together, isn't that more than a mortal man could give you?" He stood in front of her, gripping her shoulders and willing her to see the devotion in his eyes. "What if we had ten? Or only one? Do you think Deirdre regrets any of her time with Ioan because of her grief now?"

"I don't know," Beatrice whispered. "It's *too much*, Gio. Everything's changing so fast. This is not my world. And it's so much bigger than anything I could have imagined."

He shook his head. "We live on the same earth, Beatrice. The world has not changed, only your perception of it."

"I don't know what I want," she whispered.

"And I *finally* do." He embraced her, feeling the race of her heart against his chest. "I've spent five hundred years waiting to feel toward anyone the way I feel toward you." He clenched his jaw when he spoke again. "I know you want to be cautious, but remember that, too."

Beatrice's pulse began to even out as she calmed herself, taking deep breaths until her shoulders relaxed. She took a step back and her hands unclenched.

"I feel like I'm falling sometimes. I feel like my life is out of control, and I don't know my way around." She shrugged helplessly. "I'm a stranger here."

He reached his hand out and she took it. "You're not a stranger to me."

CHAPTER 12

North Wales

A week later, Beatrice and Giovanni travelled by horseback through the rugged mountains of Snowdonia in northern Wales. They followed Carwyn, who was hospitable enough to travel above ground for the benefit of his guests. They were stopping in Carwyn's house in Wales for a few nights before continuing on to London to meet with his daughter and her fiancé, a water vampire who ran London and had extensive contacts throughout Britain and the continent.

The leads into Ioan's death had dead-ended in Dublin, but Beatrice had found two boats in the port that were owned by shadow corporations that looked promising. One was headed to London, and the other had been tracked to Le Havre. Either could have been Lorenzo, but they would have to go to London before they could find out more.

"I'm sorry you're visiting my home for the first time under these circumstances."

Beatrice looked over and smiled at Carwyn. "Don't apologize. I'm sorry I've been so moody lately."

He pulled his mount back and kept pace with her as they made their way along the trail. Giovanni had ridden ahead, familiar with the terrain and, she suspected, wanting to give her and Carwyn some time alone to talk.

He shrugged. "It's a crazy world you've found yourself in, darling girl. I can hardly blame you for not feeling entirely yourself."

"I'm glad to be visiting anyway."

"How's the bike?"

"Good," she smiled. "I'm happy you convinced me to buy the Triumph."

Carwyn nodded. "Anyone looking after things? While you're away?"

"Well, officially I'm still on my vacation time, though Dez and Matt know what's really going on and are watching the house. I'm going to have to figure out something to do about work, though."

"Ah, so Dez is finally in on the secret, is she?"

Beatrice nodded. "She is. And she and Matt are dating now."

"About bloody time," he muttered.

"Hey, watch the language, Father. Don't you have parishioners around here?"

Carwyn smiled and looked around the snowy valley. "That I do, though I hardly think any of them are out on a night like this."

Though she was bundled in the warm woolen clothes she had bought in Ireland, Beatrice still shivered as they made their way through the cold, desolate hills leading toward Carwyn's mountain home.

"So Matt and Dez are finally together," he continued.

"Yep."

"And you and Gio?"

She fell silent and looked sideways at him. "What about us?"

Carwyn shrugged and gave a wry smile. "Distract an old man with some juicy gossip. What's going on with you two? I know you and Mano broke up."

"Yeah," she said quietly, surprised by how much it still hurt, "we did."

"And you and Gio are obviously more than friends. You always were. Anything else is pure denial. So why aren't you two together now?" She may have been glaring at him, but the priest only offered a wink.

"He left me, Carwyn. For five years he stayed away, and he knew where I was the whole time. Am I supposed to just forget all that time because he comes back and tells me he loves me?"

Carwyn lifted an eyebrow. "He told you he loves you?"

She shrugged and looked at the mounded cairns that started to appear at regular intervals along the path.

"Do you love him?"

She wouldn't have answered for anyone but him, but Carwyn was one of the people she trusted most in the world.

"Honestly? I don't know. I think part of me never stopped, but the other part of me doesn't quite trust him to stick around."

They rode in silence for a while longer.

"I understand where you're coming from, B—and heaven knows I told him he was wrong to stay away for so long—but at the same time, I do understand why he did it."

Beatrice scowled at him. "You know, I'm pretty sick of everyone thinking they know what I want more than I do."

Carwyn chuckled and brushed at the red hair that fell in his eyes. "I'm sure you are, but let me tell you, the time you were in L.A., without him, you did a lot of growing. It was lovely to watch, you know, to see you come into yourself. Do you think you would have grown the same ways if he had been there? Or if you had stayed in Houston with him?"

She clenched her jaw. "It's not that I don't agree with what you're saying. I do, but—"

"Or what kind of life would you have had if you were traveling all over the world with him? The work he was doing, B—tracking your father, shoring up alliances—it was important. And then he found Ben—"

"I get it!" she blurted. "He had more important things to do than hang around and entertain my crush. Fine. I get it. Can we change the subject please?"

"Oh, so it was a crush, was it?"

She clenched her hands and spurred on her horse. "I am so damn tired of know-it-all vampires telling me how much more they know about life than I do! Maybe what I felt for Giovanni back then was a kind of hero worship. I don't think so, but *maybe*. Then he leaves, and I try my hardest to move on with my life, but I always feel kind of like I'm faking it.

"Then, when I *finally* feel like maybe I can have a life without him, he comes back!" She forced back the tears that gathered in her eyes. "And it's like everything I felt for him gets taken out of the closet, dusted off, and is stronger than ever. And he acts like it's no big deal."

"B—"

"Do you think that's fun? Do you have any idea how guilty I feel that I could never love Mano the way he deserved because I was so hung up on Gio?" She bit her lip and brushed at the angry tears that filled her eyes.

"B—"

"And I'm supposed to make this huge decision about being with him when it has so many implications. Because I won't be with him and grow old while he stays the same. I won't do it. It would be cruel to both of us. So, on top of deciding how I feel about him, I have to make the decision about whether I want to end my human life and drink blood for eternity."

"Beatrice—"

"You wanted to know? Well, that's how I feel, Carwyn!" She sniffed. "And I'm probably a giant shit for dumping all that on you right now, but you did ask."

"I'm sorry," he murmured.

She sniffed again. "If I become a vampire, will I stop crying every time I get pissed off? Because that would be a definite mark in the plus column."

Carwyn said, "I've no idea, but your tears would be kind of pink. Very... cute."

"Great," she swiped at her cheeks that were dusted with salty frost. "So I'd look stupid *and* I'd stain my clothes."

He snickered; then he laughed, and soon Beatrice was laughing along with him. After the tension of the past two weeks, laughing with Carwyn felt like coming up for air.

He reached over and squeezed her hand as they climbed the hill. "You'll figure it out between the two of you. I have to confess, other than the odd, unexpected emotional outburst—thanks for that—it's rather entertaining to watch. Don't give in too easily, I'm having fun needling him about it."

"Good to know we amuse you."

"Oh, yes. Better than wrestling," he snickered. "Well, maybe not quite."

"We could always make Gio wear one of those *lucha libre* masks while we bicker at each other."

"Excellent idea! I knew I liked you for a reason."

"You're ridiculous, you know that? Though he did confess to wearing a Zorro hat in a past life."

Carwyn shook his head. "Oh, he loved that thing. Looked absolutely ridiculous on him. Wore it for years in South America."

She snorted and looked across at him. "I missed you, Carwyn."

He winked at her. "Missed you, too. Despite all this, there's a light in your eyes I haven't seen for a long while."

She sniffed again and swallowed the lump in her throat. "If I do decide...I mean, if things work out with us and...I'm not even sure how to ask something like that."

He smiled gently. "Well, if you're *not* asking what I think you're not asking, then the answer would be...I'd consider it an honor to call you my daughter, Beatrice De Novo. I already consider you a part of my family." She looked across at him and realized his eyes looked a little red, too.

Beatrice reached over and squeezed his arm. "I'm sorry I never got to meet your son."

"I'll see him again, darling girl," he said in a rough voice. "Of that, I have no doubt."

The following night, she sat next to Giovanni on the bed, reading a manuscript she had found in Carwyn's huge library. The priest had mentioned she was welcome to borrow anything she liked while they were in his home.

Though Carwyn's house was built into the mountains like Isabel and Gustavo's, she could still hear the wind blow bare branches against the thick stone walls that protected them, and she shivered at the crack of ice as it hit the rocks.

She looked down and saw Giovanni begin to stir from his daytime rest. They'd slept next to each other every night since Ioan had died. Beatrice slept more soundly next to him, and he seemed reassured to keep her close and secure in his chamber. He never pushed, though his obvious desire for more was becoming harder and harder to resist.

Giovanni stretched beside her, looking for all the world like a very large, sexy cat waking from a nap. His eyes were closed and she took a moment to admire his body. She insisted he wear pants to sleep, though she knew he considered bedclothes of any kind irritating.

He refused to wear a shirt, so she had a clear view of his perfect physique, at least from the waist up. Knowing he had been kidnapped and molded by a madman to look like the ideal of male perfection still didn't lessen her appreciation for the end result.

She wondered if that was a moral failing of some sort.

"Mmm, *tesoro*..." he mumbled something in sleepy Italian as his eyes blinked open.

"Still don't speak Italian, Gio."

His hooded eyes raked over her breasts with sleepy languor as he whispered something else she couldn't understand. She could feel her face heating up, and decided from the tone of his voice, it was probably a good thing she didn't speak Italian.

Probably.

He began to reach for her, so she decided a drastic subject change was in order.

"How do you kill an immortal?"

Giovanni was obviously taken aback but looked surprised, not offended. He stretched again and sat up, crossing his arms on his chest as he leaned against the headboard of the sturdy bed in his room at Carwyn's house.

"Good evening to you, too. And how to kill an immortal?" he mused. "Well, that's obviously the wrong word, isn't it? Immortal."

Her heart faltered for a moment as she thought of Ioan. "You know what I mean."

"We like to call ourselves immortals." He reached over and played with a lock of her hair that had come out of her ponytail. "Makes the more civilized of us feel a bit better about feeding from human beings. Which we aren't anymore, but we once were. Makes us slightly less barbaric in our own eyes."

She leaned against his shoulder and let her cheek rest against his bare arm.

"You're not barbaric, Jacopo," she said. "You're one of the kindest men I know."

His skin automatically heated against her cheek. "Why do you call me by my human name?" he asked softly.

"Would you rather I didn't?"

"No, I...it is comforting to hear it again."

His hand came to rest on her left arm, and his fingertips traced gentle circles along the inside of her wrist.

"Am I the only one who calls you Jacopo?"

"You're the only one who knows my name."

Beatrice closed her eyes and gave in to the comfort of his warm hands. The low hum that always accompanied the touch of his skin on hers soothed her. As she sat in bed, enjoying the feel of him, she realized if she was robbed her sight, her hearing—of every sense she had—but could only feel his touch, she would recognize him by that alone.

She sighed and smiled, closing her eyes as she relaxed into him.

"*Tu sei tutta bella, amica mia, e non v'è difetto alcuno in te,*" he murmured.

"Hmm?" She roused herself from drifting. "What does that mean?"

He tucked her head under his chin. "It means you're beautiful."

She smiled and turned her face to press her cheek to his chest.

"Do you dream? I've always wondered that."

She heard him let out a soft chuckle. "I do sometimes. Not often though."

"What do you dream about?"

He hummed a little, still sounding sleepy as he played with the ends of her hair. "The past. The future. You."

She had no idea how to respond to that. *I dream about you a lot, too. Have for years. You're usually naked.*

"So." She cleared her throat a little. "I've been reading Ioan's book about vampire biology. I remember you said he was a doctor. It's fascinating." *Speaking of naked, did you pose for some of those diagrams? I'm pretty sure I recognize your abs.*

He reached his left arm around to the table where she had set the manuscript.

"Ah, I remember helping him with this one. Deirdre did some of the sketches. Excellent resource."

"I'm sure you get tired of answering all my questions, so I thought I'd just take advantage of the library since we have a few days here."

He smiled. "I don't get tired of answering because you ask good questions. So feel free to take advantage of me any time you like."

She swatted his arm playfully. "Haha."

He only pressed a kiss to the top of her head. "What a good little librarian you are, *tesoro*."

"Don't be patronizing."

"I'm not. Just teasing you a bit. So, what have you learned, Miss De Novo?"

"That you aren't immortal, but you are very hard to kill."

Giovanni nodded. "Yes we are. Fire and losing our head are the only ways I've ever heard of."

"Really? Definitely no wooden stakes, huh?"

He shook his head. "No, though that would take a long time to heal if anyone tried."

"Unless you're surrounded by your element, right? Like when you burned Lorenzo and he dove in the water, he knew he would heal faster that way."

"Yes, though burns still take years to heal completely, unless you're a fire vampire. But if Carwyn was injured, he could heal very quickly if he went to ground."

"So Tenzin—"

"Is practically impervious to serious injury unless she's buried or drowned."

"Wow."

"'Wow' is a common reaction, yes."

"And you?"

He shrugged. "Fire feeds me; fire destroys me. It's a very fine line."

"So, if you allow yourself to...what do you call it?"

Giovanni smiled. "Flame up? Manifest fire? Get sparky, as Carwyn likes to say?"

Beatrice quirked her mouth in a wry smile. "Yeah, that."

He stretched an arm against the headboard. "I'm not going to lie, *tesoro*, when I allow the fire to take over my body, it feels...heady. It's intoxicating, and it could be very addictive. It does feed something in me and it does help me heal, but at the same time, it's very, very dangerous."

"But you control it, Gio. It doesn't control you."

He shrugged. "And oddly, we have my sire to thank for that. Without the years of discipline Andros beat into me, I would probably have destroyed myself long ago."

She paused for a moment, frowning. "I don't like feeling grateful to him."

Giovanni gave her a sad smile. "He made me who I am."

"You made yourself who you are. I've read your journals."

"I wasn't a good man for a long time. It was Carwyn and then Ioan who helped to humanize me."

"And Tenzin. Kind of."

"Kind of, yes. But nothing like Ioan. He was the finest of us," he said quietly, slouching in the rumpled bed.

Beatrice wanted to erase the grief she saw fill his eyes, but she knew she couldn't, so she pulled him over to rest his head in her lap and began running her fingers through his hair like she knew he loved.

"How did you meet him?"

He lay with his head on her thigh, and she listened as he timed his breath to match hers. Finally, he spoke in a soft voice, "My father created me to be his idea of the perfect man: a scholar, an artist, a strategist, a soldier...after he was gone, when I had to make my way in the world, there was little need for strategists, artists or scholars. But there was always a need for soldiers. Especially with the talents and training I had.

"I was a known fire vampire. I knew I needed to make a reputation quickly, and I needed to make it frightening, so I used what Andros had given me, and I became the most efficient assassin and mercenary I could be."

"Who did you kill?"

"Whoever I was hired to," he said quietly.

She took a deep breath and tried to reconcile the gentle man she knew with what he was describing. Beatrice had read his journals, but it was so much more brutal to hear the truth from his own lips.

He continued when she did not speak. "After a while, I had built a decent reputation, though I was still targeted regularly. Then I met Tenzin and she wasn't what I was expecting. At all."

"Why not?"

"Well, I was hired to kill her—"

"What? Tenzin?" Beatrice laughed.

"Ridiculous, I know. She is one of the oldest and most powerful vampires I have ever heard of. But I did not know her reputation when I was hired. I was young—only fifty years old or so. I took the contract, but she is the one who hunted me."

"Why am I not surprised? Where did she find you?"

"It was in the mountains of southern Siberia, perched in the branches of an evergreen. She jumped on my back like she does, and I was too shocked by her appearance to do anything but try to run away."

"But she caught you?"

"Oh yes. She laughed and told me that she'd seen me long ago. That we were fated to be great friends, and that we would work together." He raised an eyebrow. "We would be more powerful than any other vampires walking the earth."

"Talk about appealing to your ego."

"I didn't believe her about fate, but she was persuasive, and I could see how powerful she was. She's always known how to get me to do what she wants me to. And then, well, she just knew things. It was Tenzin who took the contract in London that led us to Carwyn. She always seemed to know the exact moment to get out of one situation or into another. Tenzin always... Well, she always..."

He drifted off and she noticed an odd, almost childlike, look on his face.

"Gio? What were you saying about—"

"Why did I go to the library where you worked?"

"What? You went to transcribe that manuscript, remember?"

"Yes." His eyes lit up. "The manuscript for Tenzin. The one she just had to have copied."

"Gio?" she whispered, but he could only stare at her in wonder as his head lay on her lap. He reached up to smooth away the frown that had gathered on her forehead and slowly pulled her face down to feather a kiss across her mouth.

"You are my balance in this life. In every life," he murmured against her lips.

"Gio?"

"*Tu sei il mio amore,*" he said with a brilliant smile.

375

"I finally learn Latin and you switch to Italian on me, Jacopo? No fair." She frowned against his insistent lips.

"I don't want you to get bored."

"Because that's so likely, isn't it?"

He just grinned at her. "Were you bored without me?"

Beatrice didn't want to answer but knew she should considering how open he was being.

"Never mind," he said. "It's not my business. It's your—"

"Yes."

Giovanni cocked his head, as if surprised she had responded.

"I was bored without you," she continued. "I had a good life, but it wasn't anything..." *It was monochrome instead of color.*

"I hated being away from you, Beatrice. Even when I convinced myself it was necessary."

She blinked away the tears that tried to surface and pulled away from him. He still lay in her lap, looking up at her with an unguarded expression.

"What are we doing, Gio? I had so many questions for so many years. Why is everything suddenly not a secret?"

"Don't you know?" he murmured.

She looked into his eyes, which had once been veiled and enigmatic. Now, they were open, and Beatrice was beginning to realize that everything she thought she knew about the previous five years might have been wrong.

"I think... I'm starting to know," she finally said.

He shook his head; she could see the disappointment.

"Tell me more," she begged. "When did you meet Carwyn?"

A smile touched the corner of his mouth.

"I was a little over two hundred years old. Tenzin and I were still working together, but I had grown weary of it, no matter how efficient we were."

"You were tired of killing vampires."

"I was tired of killing *anything*. I mentioned a contract that Tenzin found. We'd taken a job from the old guard, the vampires that used to control London. There was a band of rogues that was terrorizing the human population in Cornwall, and we were hired to get rid of them and clean up the mess they'd left. By the time we got there, Carwyn and Ioan had already taken care of most of the problem. Carwyn had killed the young vampires and Ioan was altering all the memories of their human victims and healing those he could. It had been going on for quite some time, so there was still a lot we were able to do.

"Tenzin and I offered to share the bounty with them for the vampires they had killed, but they both refused. It intrigued us both, and we went to spend some time with them in Wales. Eventually, I decided to stay with them and leave mercenary work. I was exhausted."

"Was Tenzin mad?"

"Not really. She had begun to attract more attention than she normally liked, so she was ready to lie low for a few hundred years to let the rumors die down."

"Just a little while, huh?"

He smiled. "I told you, she's very old. I stayed with Carwyn's family for a time and slowly remembered what it was like not to spend every night looking for who would attack me next. I remembered how much I loved books, and music, and quiet. Eventually, I became convinced that I could choose to live another way. Carwyn and Ioan helped me see that."

"I'm sorry I'll never meet him," she whispered and rested her hand against his cheek.

"I'm sorry too."

"What happens when vampires die? The book was kind of vague."

He took her hand and knit their fingers together before he rested them on his chest. "If we're not burned, we return to our elements. What was left of Ioan's body lingered for a few days and then crumbled into earth. Water vampires almost melt away, but again, it's not instantaneous. And wind...well, they just disintegrate. Eventually, there is no trace of them."

"And fire?"

He shrugged. "I've never beheaded a fire vampire. I don't know. Usually, we burn."

She paused. "Why did you leave me your journals in Cochamó?"

"I wanted you to know everything. Like when I told you to tell Dez about your life. There can be no future with that many secrets, *tesoro*."

"But why didn't you tell me all that before?" she asked gently. "You always held back with me."

He sat up and moved to her side, looking into her eyes when he answered.

"When we first met, I didn't know if I could trust you. And when you left for Los Angeles, I wasn't sure you wanted to be part of my world. Which I understood. So I tried to shield you. There was no reason for you to be burdened with all of this if you were only going to touch the edges of it."

"Gio." She shook her head. "I think it's pretty obvious at this point..."

She didn't finish, and he leaned forward. "What? What's obvious?"

She stopped short of admitting she loved him. She still wondered, when the current mystery was solved, whether he would disappear from her life again. This time, she knew the hole she felt from his absence when she was younger would be dwarfed by the immense vacuum another departure would leave.

He reached over to nudge her chin toward him so she was forced to meet his eyes. "I take nothing for granted, but I will not have you make any decision blindly. I'll not have you resent me for hiding things from you."

"I don't want you to."

"Then why—"

"Are you going to leave me again?"

He drew back as if she had struck him. "What?"

"If we find Lorenzo—"

"*When* we find him."

Beatrice looked away. "Fine, when we find him. After he's been killed. After you find my father, will you leave again? What if you decide you don't want to feel grief like Deirdre's? What if I choose not to become a vampire? What if—"

"You'll have to be far better at evasion than even your father to lose me at this point, Beatrice De Novo."

She looked at him, and his eyes begged for her to believe him. She wanted to, she realized. More than anything, but five years still hung between them. "Are you *sure*? About me? About this?"

He cocked his head.

"What?" she looked down nervously, wondering at his expression.

"Deirdre asked me the same question," he said softly. "When she brought Ioan's body back. She asked me, 'Are you sure?' I didn't really understand what she meant at the time."

A memory of the fearsome woman carrying the body of her husband flashed to Beatrice's mind. "What did you answer her?"

"I never got the chance."

She swallowed the lump in her throat. "Will you answer me?"

Giovanni grasped the back of her neck and pulled her into a hard kiss; she felt the force of it down to her toes. Finally, his mouth traveled to her ear and there was no mistaking his answer.

"I am sure of the fire that runs through me. I am sure of the earth I stand on. And I am *sure* of you."

CHAPTER 13

"When are you coming home?"

"I'm not sure yet, Benjamin. I want to come home, but it's more important that I make everyone safe first."

"From Lorenzo?"

"Yes."

He heard the boy sigh over the telephone and knew that he was probably rolling his eyes as well.

"Tell me what you and Caspar and Isadora have been doing," Giovanni said to distract him.

"Lots of stuff. They're pretty cool for old people."

He chuckled. "They are. Has Caspar taught you how to shoot yet? He thought it would be good for you to learn. He's a very good shot, so make sure you pay attention when he teaches you."

"At first I thought it was going to be really cool, but then he made me clean all the rifles after we finished." Giovanni grinned. "And that wasn't cool at all. But we shot some cans for target practice, and he said I was pretty good."

"Excellent. And how is the rest of your schooling?"

Ben huffed on the other end of the line. "Dude, Caspar isn't very good at Latin anymore, Gio."

"Well," he said and laughed, "you can be his teacher then. And how is Beatrice's grandmother? Are you getting along?"

"Other than the cleaning stuff, yeah."

"Cleaning stuff?"

"She wants me to clean my room here, like, all the time."

He frowned. "Well, I'm fairly lax on that, so pay attention to her. Your room at home is something of a disaster area."

"She's a good cook, though. I'm gonna get fat hanging out with them, Gio. They both cook really good."

"They both cook very *well*, and see if Isadora will give you lessons while you're staying with them, will you?"

"If it means I'll have to help her clean up the kitchen, I think she'll be okay with it."

He smiled and sat back in the chair, feeling more relaxed than he had in days. Giovanni sat in the library at Carwyn's house, enjoying the fire and listening to the wind whipping outside. Beatrice had already fallen asleep, so he had taken advantage of the time difference to call Ben in Texas.

He was surprised by how much he missed the boy and his quick humor, though he was pleased Ben was getting along so well with Caspar and Isadora.

"Caspar said your friend died."

"Yes, he did."

"Did he have kids?"

Thinking of all the children Ioan and Deirdre had sired or fostered over the years, he nodded. "He did. He had a large family."

"I'm really sorry. Tell Carwyn I'm really sorry."

"Thank you, I will."

He could almost hear the wheels turning in Ben's small head, so he wasn't surprised by the next question.

"Are you going to get hurt? I thought you couldn't die."

"Benjamin, I will do everything in my power to prevent anything happening to Beatrice and myself."

"Can't you guys just come home and hide here with us?" he asked in a small voice.

He closed his eyes and thought how he wanted to answer.

"You know, Ben, in my own way, I hid for years. I minded my own business and tried to keep out of sight so I could live my life in peace. But sometimes, minding your own business isn't the right thing to do. Sometimes, you need to confront the evil in the world. I tried to ignore that for too long and people got hurt."

"Like B? When Lorenzo took her?"

"Yes."

"And your friend? Is that because of Lorenzo, too?"

The guilt and grief threatened to overwhelm him, but he cleared his throat and answered, "Yes, that was also because of Lorenzo."

"But you're going to get him, right?"

"Yes, I'm going to make sure he can't hurt anyone else."

"And find B's dad, too, right?"

He nodded, even though he was alone. "I'm going to find her father. Eventually."

"Good, 'cause he sounds like a good guy and she misses him."

He smiled, happy to hear the more relaxed tone of the boy's voice on the other line. He could hear Caspar and Isadora talking in the background, and Giovanni wished he and Beatrice could be relaxing with them in the Texas hill country instead of stuck at an old stone house in the cold Welsh mountains.

"So, is B your girlfriend yet?"

He frowned. "I'm working on it."

"Still?"

"I think I'm still on probation. She's making sure I'm really going to stick around."

Ben was quiet for a long time before he spoke again. "I guess that makes sense. You did go away for a long time."

Giovanni sipped at the scotch he'd poured before he sat down. "I did. I thought I was doing the right thing for her."

"Did you say you're sorry?"

He sighed. "I'm not sure what to say. I still think it was necessary to leave her, so I'm not sorry I did that."

"But you hurt her feelings!"

"I know," he said sadly.

"So you should say you're sorry for hurting her feelings then."

Giovanni frowned. He hadn't thought of doing that. Sometimes children really did see things more clearly.

"—and then ask her to marry you so she knows you're not going to leave again."

He inhaled his scotch. "Wh—what?"

"Well, you want to marry her and everything, right? I mean, you love her and all that stuff, and you don't want her to go anywhere, and you want her to know *you* aren't going anywhere again, so...you should just ask her, and then she'll know you aren't going to leave."

His mind whirled. Strangely, the thought of marrying Beatrice hadn't occurred to him, though he knew he wanted to spend the rest of his life with her. Suddenly, Ben seemed like a genius. After all, she couldn't ignore the inherent commitment in the request, could she?

"Ben, I'll consider that, my friend."

"Good. I think she's cool. She'd be an awesome fake aunt."

He smiled. "I should let you get back to your math work. Tell Caspar and Isadora I said hello."

"Okay," Ben sighed. "Tell B and Carwyn I said hi, too."

"I will see you as soon as I am able, fake nephew."

"I miss you and my basketball court, fake uncle."

He grinned and said goodbye. His ears perked up when he heard Beatrice stirring in their bed. Carwyn had muttered about them sharing a room while they were under his roof, and his housekeeper, Sister Maggie, had glared, but he and Beatrice ignored them. He suspected that Beatrice was afraid her nightmares might return, and he didn't like risking her peace of mind to appease the priest or the nun.

Besides, he thought, they were being frustratingly celibate.

Giovanni thought of how she looked curled into his side while she slept and the alluring scent of her blood when she woke, warm and sleepy as she stretched next to him.

He had gone longer without sex in his five hundred years—much longer at times if it was necessary—but he wasn't going to lie and say he enjoyed it. Especially when the object of his desire slept next to him every night and inflamed his preternatural senses with her every pulse.

Feeling his fangs descend, he decided that he should brave the cold and hunt. There was little wildlife to choose from this time of year, and Sister Maggie had stocked donated blood for him in the kitchen, but he needed the exertion of the chase.

So he gritted his teeth and braced himself for the sour taste of mountain goat.

He walked down the hall to check on Beatrice and put on a shirt, only to find her twisted in the covers, her eyes darting behind her lids in the beginning of a nightmare. He quickly slipped into the bed behind her and pulled her to his chest, murmuring soothing words and stroking the hair back from her face.

She started and turned in his arms.

"Gio?"

"You were having a bad dream," he murmured. "Do you remember?"

She took a deep breath and relaxed. "I...kind of. I remember hearing the ocean. It was echoing like it did when I was in Greece. The waves always echoed..."

She drifted off, sighing quietly as she relived the weeks she had spent as a captive under Lorenzo's control. The water vampire had kept her isolated and alone in his compound in the middle of the Aegean Sea. Beatrice told Giovanni later she had never felt more trapped than in the small room that faced the ocean. It was why she chose to live in the hills in Los Angeles instead of on the beach. The sound of waves, though soothing to most, gave her nightmares at times.

He held her tightly, humming a tune he remembered from his human childhood. It was a song about a cricket that Giuliana had sung to him in the garden of her home in Arezzo. He remembered her lilting voice and the sun as it reflected off the water of the fountain.

"Gio?"

"Hmm?"

"What is that song?"

"'Il Grillo.' It's a song about a cricket."

"I like it. I didn't know you could sing."

"Hmm," he breathed in her scent and pulled her closer. "My uncle liked it when I sang. Andros required it. I don't really sing anymore."

"It's nice."

"Thank you."

She was quiet, but he could tell she had woken from her slumber, at least for a while. She normally had trouble getting back to sleep if she woke in the middle of the night. Ironically, she often slept better during the day.

"Gio?"

"Hmm?"

"Did you call home?"

He nodded. "Ben said hello." *And that I should ask you to marry me. What do you think?*

"How's Grandma and Cas?"

"Doing well and pestering him about cleaning up his room."

She laughed quietly, and the shaking of her body against his reminded him why he had come to the room to begin with. The feel of her curves was starting to make his blood pulse.

"Beatrice, I need to go out."

"No," she murmured and pulled his arms more securely around her waist. "I'm too comfy here. Stay."

"*Tesoro,*" Giovanni groaned quietly and took a deep breath. It didn't help, he only managed to make his throat burn all the more and his desire spiked. "I need to go. I need to...hunt."

She stilled, and her fingers dug into his forearm.

"You're hungry?"

"Yes, I need to go out and hunt something. I need...I just need to hunt." He tried to pull away, but she clung to his arms and his jaw clenched in frustration. "Beatri—"

"Drink from me."

His blood roared when he heard her quiet voice and his fangs descended. "Are...are you sure?"

Beatrice rolled over and looked at him. "Yes. Will it be like before?"

"I won't drink too much," he whispered. "I promise." He could feel his skin heat and his heart begin to beat.

She blushed, and Giovanni stifled a low growl as the heat flooded her face. "Not that. I mean, I don't want to...you know. We probably shouldn't—"

"If you tell me 'no,' I'll stop." Giovanni clamped down his self-control. "No matter what."

"Okay," she whispered and tilted her head to the side, brushing the hair away from her neck. The scent of her skin washed over him, and he swallowed a groan. His hands reached under the camisole she wore, splaying across her back as his mouth dipped down to her neck.

He nosed against her pulse, rubbing his cheek across the delicate skin of her collar and reveling in the scent of her pounding blood. His tongue flicked out and began tracing the artery. He could feel the amnis that ran under his skin spread over her everywhere their flesh touched.

Her bare shoulders. The small of her back. Everywhere his hands went, her skin prickled in awareness. He could scent her arousal and he struggled to control his own. He fought the urge to plunge his fangs into her neck, determined to enjoy the rare pleasure of her blood and skin for as long as he could.

"Gio?" she panted, arching against him. "Are you going to—"

"Shh," he whispered. "Let me..." His tongue fluttered against the pulse point in her neck. "I don't want to rush."

"Oh," she breathed out and reached up to run her hands through the hair at the nape of his neck. Giovanni trailed his fangs along her skin. He closed his eyes and held her for a moment, feeling the beat of her heart against his chest.

"I love you," he whispered, as his hands stroked her back. He pulled her closer, but kept himself in check, determined to only take what she was offering.

He could, however, give her a taste of what she was missing.

Giovanni rolled over her, and his lips closed over her neck. He nipped at it, savoring the rush of blood to the surface. His fangs pierced around her artery, and she gasped in pleasure as the sensation of his bite combined with the electric current that ran from his lips and over her skin.

He was determined to drink slowly, but she cried out when he bit and her hands pressed his head to her neck. She arched under him as her rich blood filled his mouth. He moved against her, letting his hands roam as her blood ran down his throat, soothing and inflaming him at the same time.

It was nothing like the empty feeling Giovanni had experienced when he drank from random humans. Beatrice's touch, her smell, everything about her drew him in. When he moved, it was in time to her breath and pulse. It was need. Love. Nothing could compare to it.

He felt his amnis snap when she peaked, and her body shuddered underneath his. Her heartbeat hammered against his lips and he took one last draw from her neck before he pulled away. Their bodies slowed as he licked the last of the blood from her neck and sealed the small wounds. His hands stroked her hair, her shoulders, and down over the curve of her hips.

"Gio," she panted. "That was..."

Even as her blood coursed through his system, Giovanni hungered for more. Pushing down his own desire, he pressed her to his chest and breathed deeply, deliberately slowing the rush of his blood as he held her.

"Thank you, Beatrice."

"You're welcome. Did you get enough?" She was already falling asleep in his arms.

He smiled. "For now."

She rubbed her face into his chest and released a sigh. "Don't leave, okay? Stay with me. Just...stay."

He closed his eyes and sent up a silent prayer that she would do the same.

"Always."

"I CAN'T BELIEVE YOU TOLD HER THE STORY ABOUT ME AND THE BEAR," Giovanni muttered to Carwyn as the priest piloted the Range Rover through the twisting mountain roads.

Carwyn gaped at him. "I can't believe you didn't. I thought you were trying to impress this woman."

"I hardly think that story impressed her, you idiot."

"Well," Carwyn shrugged. "It made her laugh, anyway."

Giovanni glanced at Beatrice, who had fallen asleep in the back of the vehicle as they made their way to London. "I love hearing her laugh."

"She has a great laugh, doesn't she? Did she tell you the story about when she fell off the motorcycle when I was teaching her to ride? She was so terrible at first! She broke two fingers, and we had to wait six months for her hand to be strong enough to shift again. She had such a good sense of humor about the whole thing."

Giovanni glared at him. "You broke two of my woman's fingers?"

Carwyn cocked an eyebrow at him. "Careful now, you'd been gone for two years at that point. I doubt she'd appreciate you calling her 'yours.'"

Giovanni crossed his arms over his chest. "You knew better. You knew I was coming back."

"Oh, aye, but she didn't, did she?"

He was silent for a few minutes before he muttered, "Benjamin says I need to apologize to her."

Carwyn's eyes popped open. "You've not apologized to her? For leaving for five years? Why on God's earth is she even talking to you?"

He glared at the priest. "I've explained to her—"

"I want to punch you right now, di Spada. I really do," he whispered. "That's quite childish of you." Carwyn drove in silence for a few more minutes with a frown plastered to his face. "You don't deserve her."

"What?"

"You don't! For heaven's sake, is it that hard to say you're sorry? I've not been married for a thousand years, and I know that much."

"Can we talk about something else, please? This really isn't any of your business."

"Fine. But for the record, you're lucky she's even talking to you. And don't think I can't smell her all over you or see that flush in your cheeks."

"Drop it, Father. I'll not be leaving her again," he muttered, glancing over his shoulder to make sure she was still sleeping. "I don't even think I could at this point."

Carwyn glanced between them, muttering something in Welsh, a language Giovanni had never wrapped his brain around sufficiently, before he looked back to the dark road ahead. "Let's talk about London."

"Fine. What have Terrance's people found out?"

Carwyn shrugged. "It's been vague, but there seem to be enough reports of your boy lingering to make Terry think he's still around. It's a large port and with easy access to the French coast, it makes it harder to get a handle on him."

"Lorenzo had allies in Le Havre at one point. Has that been investigated?"

"It has, but not thoroughly. You know how tricky the French can be. Also, they're water clans in that area, so they're tight lipped to any that aren't their own."

Giovanni wracked his memory, trying to think of some connection he might use to get more information. "I could always ask Livia. One more favor to add to the growing list."

Carwyn said, "Do you have time for that? Besides, you know how she is. She'll not give you anything unless you come to Rome, and I doubt you want to take a side trip right now. Would you bring B? That would be interesting."

Giovanni sighed. "They'll have to meet eventually, and Beatrice handled the meeting with the Alvarezes in Los Angeles quite well."

"Ernesto Alvarez is a friendly guppy compared to the sharks that swim in Livia's sea. Don't dump her into that until you have to."

"I think you're underestimating Beatrice, Carwyn. She's a fast learner and I have a feeling that she'll have a knack for the political side of our life."

"Well, one of us should. I hate that stuff, and you piss people off too quickly. Don't get me started on Tenzin."

"Tenzin said something about Beatrice being my balance," he murmured.

Carwyn frowned. "You're not thinking—"

"I'm not thinking anything at this point. It's not an issue yet. She's handled herself extremely well so far. Ernesto was incredibly impressed with her. You could almost see him salivating at her potential." He looked over his shoulder at the young woman who still slept peacefully. "We'll see how she does in London. Meeting Terry and Gemma ought to be interesting."

"Does she know about you and Gemma?"

He paused, thinking about Carwyn's daughter, who was also a former lover. "I've told her we were involved, and that we are still friendly."

He heard Carwyn chuckle quietly before the Welshman laughed out loud.

"What?" Giovanni's voice dripped in irritation.

"You make it sound like the two of you were study partners at university!"

"Beatrice knows that I love her." He glanced at the sleeping woman in the backseat. "There was no need to go into detail."

"Well, don't let her imagine the worst. And she doesn't need to hear about your sporadic relationship with my daughter from someone else, either, so make sure it's from you."

"Gemma and I were never serious."

"I know that, but you two danced around each other for almost two hundred years, so don't just dismiss it."

"I can't believe she's marrying Terry. I would never have put them together."

"Well, sometimes we find our match in the most unexpected places, don't we?"

Giovanni turned to stare at Beatrice. Her head was slumped to the side of the car, and she was curled up with his coat covering her in the back seat. He had the urge to crawl next to her so she was lying against his side as she slept.

"I've never felt for any woman what I feel for her, Carwyn," he said quietly. "It's somewhat terrifying at times."

He heard his friend start to speak a few times, but he kept pausing. Finally, he heard him mutter under his breath.

"You're a lucky bastard, Giovanni Vecchio."

GIOVANNI WAS REMINDED WHY HE HATED LONDON AS SOON AS THEY ARRIVED, but he tried to enjoy it through Beatrice's eyes. Carwyn had woken her as soon as they crossed into the city and started pointing out the sights. She smiled and bounced, enjoying the historic town as he tried to smother his own displeasure.

He hated the city. The streets were too crowded. The traffic too rushed. Too many people pressed against him if he tried to walk around, and there was too much noise. The air quality may have improved, but he remembered when coal smoke hung over the dreary town and soured the air. More than anything, Giovanni hated the cold damp that reminded him of the school in Crotone where Andros had held him against his will for so many years.

"Don't be such an old man," she teased him. "How long are we staying, anyway?"

"As long as we need to, *tesoro*. I may not be very fond of London, but Gemma and Terrance are close allies and this is the best place to start looking for Lorenzo. If the information you found is correct, he's still in England or France. Between the three of us and all of their contacts, we have a very good chance of finding him. It may only take a few weeks if we're lucky."

She fell silent; finally, he heard her heave a great sigh.

"Beatrice?" He turned to look at her grim face.

"I'm going to have to quit my job."

Giovanni turned around so she didn't see his satisfied smile. "Oh no. Whatever will you do?"

She pinched his ear. "Shut up and don't gloat. I'm quite capable of surviving without a job, thanks to my superior embezzling skills. I haven't agreed to work for you yet."

Carwyn snorted, but Giovanni just grinned.

"Yet."

CHAPTER 14

London, England

"Another glass of wine...B?" Gemma arched an eyebrow at her in the formal sitting room of the house in Mayfair. They had arrived at the home of Terrance Ramsay only an hour before and been immediately welcomed by more household staff than Beatrice had ever seen outside a period film.

"No, thank you."

"Perhaps some tea?"

"No," she smiled stiffly at the extremely elegant vampire sitting across from her. "Thank you."

Gemma Melcombe may have been Carwyn's oldest daughter and second child, but her manners, accent, and wardrobe revealed none of what Beatrice suspected were probably humble origins. It wasn't just the staff that seemed to belong in a period film. Gemma's delicate features, gold-spun hair, and tinkling laugh made it hard not to imagine her in lace and petticoats, riding in a carriage to a ball.

Which she had most likely done on more than one occasion. Possibly in Giovanni's company.

Casually involved, my ass. Beatrice plastered a pleasant smile on her face.

"What do you mean, you were involved? She's an old girlfriend or something?"

"Nothing that serious, tesoro. *I just wanted to let you know. We're friendly now. She's apparently quite happy with her fiancé."*

"Oh."

"What?"

"Nothing."

"Are you jealous?"

"Why would I be jealous? You said it was years ago."

He had winked at her. "A vampire can hope, can't he?"

Beatrice hadn't asked more about their involvement, and she pushed away the cold lick of jealousy, knowing it was unreasonable. Giovanni, for all his keen intellect, could be startlingly obtuse about human nature at times. Because whatever he thought about their friendship, Gemma Melcombe was completely in love with him.

"Perhaps I should show you to your room," Gemma said with a polite smile. "I've prepared one of our guest suites for you. The windows are east-facing, so you'll be able to enjoy the morning—"

"Beatrice will share my room, Gemma," Giovanni murmured.

He had been sitting next to her on the small sofa, lost in his thoughts and absently playing with the ends of her hair. Upon their arrival, Carwyn and Gemma had taken a few moments together, presumably to talk about Ioan, before Terry and Carwyn had retreated to the study to speak to Terry's lieutenant about the current political situation, leaving Giovanni, Gemma, and Beatrice in the elegant sitting room to become acquainted.

Giovanni's skin, Beatrice observed with perverse satisfaction, was still flushed from feeding from her the night before, and she noticed he seemed quicker than he had been in weeks. His amnis was stronger, as well; she wondered how much his diet of donated blood had been affecting his health.

"You want her to share your room in the basement?" Gemma laughed, cutting her eyes toward Beatrice. "Surely she will want something brighter, Gio."

"We always share a room. We both rest better that way." Beatrice tried not to sound smug, but she remembered Giovanni telling her years ago that no one had seen him sleep in hundreds of years, so she knew Gemma was probably included in that. She placed a proprietary hand on his thigh and smiled.

"Well—" Gemma's blue eyes frosted. "—I'm sure that will be fine."

"*Tesoro*, if you want to rest, I will meet with Carwyn and Terry and fill you in at first dark. Gemma, will you be joining us in the study?"

"Of course," Gemma said. "Terry always asks for my opinion. It's what makes us such excellent partners."

"I forgot to offer my congratulations on your engagement. You and Terrance are a wonderful couple."

Beatrice could see the flash of hurt in Gemma's eyes and wondered again how Giovanni could be so dense.

"Thank you. We're very happy. I'm sure you can imagine how pleased Father is, as well."

"Congratulations," Beatrice added. "If you could show me to a phone, I have a few calls to make before I turn in." She turned to Giovanni, still resting a hand on his thigh. "I need to talk to Dez, and I'll call Dr. Stevens this afternoon."

He frowned and reached up to trace her cheek. "All joking aside, I am sorry about your job. I never intended—"

"Oh, yes you did," Beatrice laughed. "Don't lie. You wouldn't have forced the issue, but don't pretend like you're not pleased."

He winked at her and tugged at a lock of her hair. Beatrice saw Gemma watching them out of the corner of her eye.

"Sorry," she said. "I'm having job issues. If you could show me to a phone, it would be great."

"Of course." Gemma smiled politely. "Giovanni, I'll meet you in the study. Make yourself at home. You know where everything is."

"Of course."

They stood, and he leaned down to place a quick kiss on Beatrice's cheek before he stepped out of the room. Beatrice turned to her hostess, who had a hand held toward the door.

"I'll show you to Gio's room. We keep one for him since he visits so often. It's almost like a second home for him."

"I'm sure." Beatrice smiled and tried not to grit her teeth.

"There's a phone on the desk in his room."

They walked down the hall, and Gemma opened a door that led to a small landing and a set of stairs that curved down to the plush basement level of the house. Gemma walked at a leisurely pace, gliding down with preternatural grace while Beatrice felt like an awkward young girl trailing after her.

"Do tell me what dietary accommodation my cook will need for Gio. She's stocked some of the blood type he prefers, but let us know—"

"Oh, he won't be needing anything," Beatrice said. "He's taken care of."

Gemma halted on the stairs and raised a lofty eyebrow. "Is that so?"

"Very so," Beatrice said as she stepped past Gemma and continued down the stairwell. She halted at the foot of the stairs and turned with her hands in her pockets, tapping her boot on the floor as she waited for Gemma to reach her.

"So," she said, looking up and down the rich gold hallway. "Which room is ours?"

"CAT FIGHT! *HISS HISS HISS*," DEZ SAID. "WISH I WAS THERE TO SEE IT. DAMN, how do you get all these good looking men nuts about you, B? Tell me your secret."

"My secret?" Beatrice rolled her eyes. "I don't know. I smell good? At least Gio seems to think so. What about Matt? I thought Ken and Barbie were ready for their dream house."

"Shut up, you smelly man-magnet. We're not moving in together. And I'm just joking. Matt..." Dez gave a dreamy sigh. "He's so great. He's so fun and smart. I even met his parents at Christmas time and they're really cool, too. I can't believe he was into me for so long and I never knew about it."

"Yeah, imagine that. I've only been telling you to ask him out for three years now. I can't imagine what I was thinking. Who would have thought?"

"You know, some people say that sarcasm is not an attractive feature in a woman, Beatrice De Novo."

"Luckily, I don't give a shit about any of those people."

Dez laughed before suddenly turning serious. "So, I'm not going to be seeing you any time soon, am I?"

Beatrice settled back into the four-poster bed in Giovanni's chamber. It was decorated in dark burgundy and navy stripes, and rich mahogany furniture graced the room. There was an old-fashioned rotary phone on the bedside table, so she had kicked off her Docs and stretched out on the bed to call her best friend.

"I don't think so. It's not good. I don't know how much Matt's told you—"

"He told me that Lorenzo is back in business. And that he killed one of Carwyn's kids."

"Yeah," she sighed, relieved that Giovanni had kept Matt informed about the danger. "I want you to make sure you're not out by yourself at night, Dezi. I couldn't take losing a friend right now. I'm just..." She pinched the bridge of her nose as she began to feel the tension and exhaustion catch up with her. "I feel like my life is so crazy right now. I need to remind myself that the real world still exists."

"What are you talking about?"

"What?"

"What are you talking about 'the real world?' Have you been swept into another dimension? No one told me about that part if you have been."

"No," Beatrice frowned. "You know what I mean." She paused, looking around the dim, windowless room. "You know, you and Matt are part of my real life and—"

Dez laughed. "What are you talking about, your 'real life?'"

"Just all the non-vampire stuff. I know it's kind of crazy."

"Well, I don't know," Dez said. "I'm not an expert in any of this, but how is this not your real life?"

Beatrice said, "Maybe because there's vampires and villains and mysterious books and constant turmoil and danger?"

There was a long pause before Dez spoke again. "You could have stayed here, B. Matt told me Gio was having him watch you and all the security he had in place and even about the water vampires you're related to and everything—which, by the way, seems really cool, you should have told me about that—"

"What are you trying to say?"

She heard Dez take a deep breath. "You could have stayed here. None of this was *forced* on you. Gio didn't drag you away with him—you went. In fact, if I know you, you insisted on going."

Beatrice shifted on the richly appointed bed. "Yeah? So?"

"I just mean, I know you're human and that hasn't changed, but your world is bigger." Dez paused. "It has been for a while. You just weren't admitting it."

"So, you're saying—"

"Vampires and villains, danger and mystery...that *is* your real world. I mean, if you could forget all this and go back to the life you had before, would you even want to?"

"I don't know," Beatrice murmured.

"If it meant losing Gio? And Carwyn? Or missing the chance to find your dad someday?"

"No," she whispered. "I'd never choose that."

"Then I think you know what your 'real life' is, don't you? It's not the Huntington and the harmless boyfriend and a house in the suburbs."

She rolled her eyes. "Setting aside the suburbs comment, I know what you're saying, but I don't want to lose you, Dez."

"Please," she said. "Like you could. This shit is so damn cool, I'm dragging myself along with you."

Beatrice laughed, wiping tears from her eyes and swallowing the lump that had formed in her throat. "Oh, Dez, thanks for the perspective. I have to call and quit my job later today and I know that's not going to go well."

"Quitting over the phone from thousands of miles away? Nope, I don't think you're going to get a shining reference after that."

"No kidding. Well, I'm going to tell them it's an emergency, and it can't be helped. That's the best I can do. I have no idea when I'm going to be back in the States."

"Tell them it's a family emergency. Because it is."

"Yeah." Beatrice smiled, looking at Giovanni's coat, which lay on the back of a chair, tangled with her own. "I think it is."

They talked for another half an hour, chatting about mundane details like bills, houseplants, and cleaning out offices; but when Beatrice hung up the phone with her best friend, she felt like she had a new outlook on her life.

On her real, supernatural, hanging out with dangerous immortals, running from danger, plotting to kill, searching for elusive fathers and hidden books life.

And she finally felt like she could handle that.

"I want you to teach me how to fight better."

Giovanni arched his eyebrow at her as he stretched on the bed. "I'm not sure that's a good idea. You already have good self-defense skills; that's enough."

She sat up and crossed her arms over her chest. She had fallen asleep after an upsetting phone call with her former boss. Though she understood the woman's anger, Beatrice was longing for her kickboxing class; she really wanted to punch something.

"Why shouldn't I learn how to fight?"

He sat up next to her, raking his hands through his hair before he crossed his arms across his chest. "In what way are you equipped to fight a vampire, Beatrice? You are not as strong nor as fast. You don't have any elemental—"

"I know all that, all right?"

"So unless you're ready to talk about possibly turning—"

"*So* not ready for that discussion, Gio." She glared at him.

Giovanni examined her, looking every bit the five-hundred-year old, stubborn man that he was before he shrugged. "Then you learning how to fight vampires is a moot point."

"It wasn't a vampire who kidnapped me from the library. That was an old man with a gun that scared me to death and caught me by surprise."

"Beatrice—"

"It wasn't a vampire that guarded me on Lorenzo's island. It was a bunch of humans who were doing his work during the day."

He remained silent, staring into the fire with a stubborn set to his jaw.

"During the day," she reasoned, "I can be as strong, or stronger, than anything in this world, mortal or immortal. But I need to know more. I have self-defense training, but I don't know much about weapons or offensive fighting. You know about all that stuff, and I want you to teach me."

Giovanni didn't say anything, and she was beginning to think he was going to just ignore her request.

"I cannot help you learn to fight."

"Why not?"

He turned with a clenched jaw. "Because the mere thought of harming you, even while practicing, goes against every natural instinct I have! You *cannot* ask me to try to hurt you when everything in my being tells me to protect you. It is not an option for me, Beatrice."

She took a deep breath and lifted a hand to stroke his hair, calming him until she could no longer feel the flare of heat coming off his body.

"And don't ask Carwyn to help you. I would end up hurting him, and I don't want that."

She rolled her eyes but continued to stroke his hair, moving further down his bare back as she soothed him. A thought occurred to her. It wasn't pleasant, but she gritted her teeth and forced herself to ask.

"What about Gemma?"

"Have Gemma train you?" She could see him tilt his head as he considered it. "Well," he began, "that idea has some merit. I suppose if I told her to be very careful...If you're going to insist on it, she would be the person to ask. She's a fierce fighter, but I know she wouldn't be too harsh with you."

Beatrice forced herself to hold in the snort and focus on her goals. If anyone in the house would go easy on her, it most definitely would not be Gemma.

"Again!"

Beatrice blinked back the tears that dripped from her eyes and forced herself up to her knees. Even after years of martial arts training and a week with the vampire, she felt as if she was hitting a rock wall every time she came at her opponent. Gemma may have looked like a "lady of the manor," but her fighting style was far more "hooligan in the pub." It was nothing like she had imagined, and she was rethinking her determination to improve her fighting skills.

"Stand up and come at me, girl. Don't be so obvious in your attack next time. I saw that punch coming from a mile away. Go for the dirty punch. Always. And hit your opponent when they're down. There is no such thing as a fair fight."

"Fine," Beatrice muttered as she struggled to stand. Every muscle in her body ached and she tasted the blood in her mouth. She told Gemma not to bruise her in obvious places that Giovanni would see, but she was grateful it was wintertime. If he could see the series of bruises she was hiding under her clothes, Beatrice knew he would have lost it.

"You think you can take on a vampire? Currently, my lady's maid has better fighting skills." Gemma stood across from her, looking fresh and young in baby blue workout clothes that belied her ferocity. It was no wonder she had survived for over seven hundred years; the woman was lethal. Beatrice forced herself into position again.

"Remember, throw your attacker off-balance. It's the only way your small size can be used to your advantage."

"Got it."

They circled each other, both eyeing the other for weaknesses.

"I imagine Gio has to be quite careful with you, doesn't he?"

"What—" She ducked to the left as Gemma's arm shot out. "Are you talking about?"

Beatrice winced as Gemma landed a punishing fist to the shoulder. "Oh, you must know. He was always quite...vigorous if I remember correctly." The vampire gave her a wicked, knowing grin.

Bitch, Beatrice thought, dodging the blow Gemma aimed at her chest, only to miss the one that struck her abdomen. She doubled over for a second before she stood, trying to keep a clear eye on the vampire.

"Well, he certainly doesn't seem to have any complaints," Beatrice panted. "At least, he didn't last night." *When we did nothing but sleep because I was sore and could barely handle an arm around me.*

Gemma grinned as if she could read her mind. "You're such a sweet little thing. I'm sure you'll miss him when he's gone to France."

"Yeah," she grunted as she managed to block a swift kick to her knee. "Because God knows I was waiting in my bedroom, crying, for the five years we were apart."

Gemma cocked an eyebrow at her before she flipped backward over Beatrice's head.

"Hey!" Beatrice said as she spun around and avoided Gemma trying to sweep her leg. "I thought you were keeping it to human speed." She darted to the side and grabbed the edge of Gemma's shorts, pulling the vampire closer as she tried to throw her off-balance.

"And I thought," Gemma laughed. "That you wanted to learn how to fight vampires, little girl."

"Fine." Beatrice grunted when Gemma punched her side. Even though she was only using half her strength, the blow caused tears to spring to her eyes.

Gemma stepped back and wiped at a spot of blood Beatrice had spilled on her arm, allowing the human to catch her breath.

"I forget sometimes that you two are only recently reunited. Terry hasn't left my side in twenty years, at least." She darted in and landed a kick to Beatrice's hamstring. "He's so devoted."

Okay, that one hurt a little. Beatrice was determined not to show any mental weakness before the woman, even if physical fortitude wasn't an option.

"You need to toughen up," Gemma continued. "And you need to get faster. Watch me." Gemma attacked one of the training dummies in the large studio on the second floor of Terry's house. Beatrice watched in awe as Gemma laid a flurry of punches, elbows, and even a few head-butts to the dummy in the corner. Though she had slowed to human speed, Beatrice still recognized the utter ruthlessness of the attack.

"Now, try that on the dummy, and then you can try it on me. After that, you need to run some more; your stamina is still not up to snuff. And be quicker. Make yourself so fast they can't grab you. If they do, you're dead."

"Fine," she grunted, approaching the dummy in the corner. Beatrice had been training for over two hours that night. She was exhausted but tried to rouse herself so she didn't meet Gemma's mocking eyes when she finished.

She imagined the face of her old boss for a moment, but that didn't raise as much ire as it had the week before. Then she imagined Gemma's face, but not even the sneering blonde could raise her out of her exhaustion.

Finally, she imagined the look on Deirdre's face when she felt Ioan's death. She remembered the howl of her cries before the ground swallowed her; then she imagined pale hands restraining Giovanni.

A cold calm settled as she cleared her mind and focused the way Tenzin had practiced with her. She sprang, first into the combination Gemma had shown her, but she couldn't stop. She rained down blows over and over until she felt her knuckles slip wet against the plastic skin. Beatrice paused to catch her breath, leaning down and bracing her hands on her knees. As she wiped the sweat from her eyes, she realized her knuckles were bloody and the skin of her knees was torn.

Beatrice glanced over her shoulder to look for Gemma and found the blond woman watching her with narrowed blue eyes. Her stance was relaxed and a small smile played on her porcelain face.

"You'll do fine," she said. "Now run."

"Ow, ow, ow," Beatrice whined as she sank into the bathtub. She was exhausted, sore, bloody at the joints, but relieved as well. She was finally getting a little less battered every night. Beatrice and Gemma had been training together for over two weeks, and as much as Beatrice resented her, she had to admit the vampire was giving her a lot of precious time.

Beatrice had realized soon after she learned Giovanni was a vampire that, as much as their strength and speed gave them physical advantages, the fact that vampires were housebound for half of the day put severe limitations on their immortal lives. Even older immortals like Carwyn who could be awake for much of the day were groggy and weak, exhibiting barely human strength and even less speed.

For Gemma to devote as much of her limited night hours to training Beatrice as she had—no matter how much satisfaction she got from beating her up on a regular basis—was not something Beatrice could forget, and she was reluctantly grateful.

She relaxed into the heat of the bath, wishing that she could share how sore she was with Giovanni, but knowing instinctively that he would not react well. He and Carwyn had been in France for a week, trying to determine what connections Lorenzo still had and meeting with possible allies. It was a delicate balancing act, since most of the French immortals seemed to hate Terry, Gemma, and all their people simply because they were English.

"Vampire drama," she muttered. It still reminded her a little bit of high school.

She heard the door to the bedroom open and Giovanni's voice when he walked in. Her eyes popped open. He was back early.

"Shit," she whispered and stuck her bloodied hands under the water.

"Beatrice? I'm back."

"Hey, just taking a bath. I was training tonight," she called through the door. *Shit, shit, shit.*

"How are you feeling? Gemma was quite complimentary of your determination when I talked to her. She says your speed is improving as well."

He sounded impressed, and she hoped he wasn't breathing too deeply.

"That's good to hear," she said and ran the soap over her knees, trying to clean the blood from her skin even though it made her wince.

Owwwwww.

"Beatrice?"

No!

She panicked and ducked under the water, remembering all the blood that had stained her hair from her broken knuckles. She heard him snarl from the other room.

"Why do I smell so much blood?"

Too late.

She surfaced to see an irate vampire standing over her.

"I'm naked, Gio! *Naked!* Get out of here."

He ignored her, his eyes raking over her bruised form and bloody joints.

"What the hell is going on?" he roared. "You look like you've been attacked."

"I was. On purpose. That's kind of the point, isn't it?"

She sat up in the bathtub and crossed her arms over her bare breasts.

"What has Gemma been doing to you? She was supposed to take care of you. She was supposed to make sure—"

"We've been training. And I don't want her to go easy on me, that's not helpful. Now will you—"

"I told her not to hurt you!" he yelled. "I told her to temper herself and make sure—"

"The last person in this house that's going to temper herself around me is Gemma! That's the only reason—"

"What is that supposed to mean?"

She finally realized he wasn't going to leave the bathroom while they were arguing, so she swallowed her embarrassment and continued washing up.

"Do you really not know she's in love with you, Gio?" she whispered, conscious of the sensitive ears that filled the house. She rinsed out her hair as Giovanni stood over her, glowering. "Gemma is *in love* with you. And you love me and she's not going to cut me any slack in the training room. That's the only reason I suggested training with her."

He wore a furious expression when he finally spoke. "You're being ridiculous and jealous, Beatrice. And this is beneath you."

She stood up, water sloshing out of the tub as she grabbed a towel from the stand.

"I am not. Stop being a pretentious ass and get out of the bathroom right now." She shoved his chest when she caught him glancing at her breasts. "We will argue about this when I'm dressed."

He turned and stormed out of the room. She heard the bedroom door open.

"And do not go looking for Gemma right now!"

She heard a pause before the door slammed shut. His heavy footsteps paced the bedroom. Beatrice toweled off, grimacing at the broken skin on her knees, elbows, and fists. She ached badly but forced herself into her soft sleep pants and t-shirt without a sound. Finally, she grabbed her hairbrush and went to sit on the bed to work the tangles out of her knotted hair.

Giovanni had stopped pacing and was standing with his back against the door, the scent of smoke pouring off him.

"You better calm down. You'll burn that shirt if you don't."

His jaw unclenched enough for him to speak slowly. "I am not interested in the state of my wardrobe, Beatrice."

"Well, calm down anyway." She started working the brush through her hair, but he darted behind her and sat with his legs on either side, running one hand down her arm to grab the brush.

"Let me," he said in a gentle voice. "You're hurting. Just try to relax."

He started to pull the brush through her tangled hair, stopping to work out the knots as she tried not to wince. She was sore and beginning to get stiff in the cold room.

As if sensing her discomfort, Giovanni tossed small blue flames toward the grate, where they lit the wood that was waiting to be kindled. She sighed and tried to relax her shoulders.

He spoke softly as he worked. "Why do you say she's in love with me? We were involved, but it was never serious."

"Well, obviously it wasn't for you, but from the way she looks at you, it was for her."

"But I never felt for her what I feel for you. I have an affection for her; I consider her a friend."

"And I'm not trying to interfere with that, Gio. I understand, I'm just—"

"Did she beat you like this because I love you?" he asked in a whisper.

Beatrice stopped his hands and turned so she could look him in the eye. She placed one hand on his cheek. "No. We were sparring, and she's a good teacher. My sensei in L.A. would have treated me just the same. Well, if he was a vampire." She shook her head. "It wouldn't do me any favors for her to go easy on me. I need to know how to fight." She turned back around to face the fire, and he continued to brush her hair out.

He finally spoke again. "Is this because you don't trust me to stay? The fighting? Is it because you think I'll leave you again?"

Was it? It was a fair question, but the more she thought about it, the more she realized that even if Giovanni didn't leave, she would still feel like she needed to be able to defend herself.

"You can't be with me all the time. You have to sleep during the day, and I don't want you following me around all night, either. We'd both go nuts."

He put the brush down and laid his hands lightly on her waist.

"Maybe I'll lock you in with me during the day," he said in a teasing voice, pinching her waist and putting his chin on her shoulder. "I think I could keep you occupied."

She rolled her eyes. "You wouldn't dare. I would draw all over your face while you slept. I'd write, 'I'm a pretentious ass' on your forehead."

Beatrice felt him chuckle and his skin was cool, so she knew he was no longer angry.

"Where does it hurt, *tesoro*? Let me help."

"Can your blood do anything? What if I drink a little?"

"Unfortunately, it only works on open wounds for humans." He turned her and rolled her pants up to her torn knees. He bit his finger and started rubbing the blood into the cuts. She felt a tingle as it spread over her skin; then she saw the wounds start to knit together before her eyes.

"That is wicked cool."

"If you were a vampire, some of my blood would help heal your bruises, too. But your human metabolism would break it down before it could take effect. It will help on any open wounds, though. Give me your hands." He held out his hands and she placed her palms into them as he bit his thumbs and spread the healing blood over the cuts there, as well.

"Thanks."

He shrugged and finished looking over her arms, healing, then cleaning any wounds he found. Finally, he tilted her face up and she saw him pierce his tongue. He licked from her chin, mending the cut there before he traced along her bottom lip. She could feel the tingling before he caught her lips in a gentle kiss.

Giovanni sighed into her mouth and wrapped his arms around her. Even though his embrace was gentle, Beatrice winced when he touched her shoulder, and he backed away.

"Sorry, sorry," she muttered. "I'm still pretty sore."

He picked her up and laid her down on the bed, stretching out beside her and rolling up her shirt.

"Don't apologize. Just tell me where it hurts."

"What are you—"

"Heating pads for hands, remember? Tell me where it hurts."

She slowly relaxed as he kneaded her sore body, making his hands almost painfully hot at times to treat the battered muscles. By the time he was finished, she was limp as a rag and half-asleep.

"Tell me what happened in France," she murmured.

"Shhh. Tomorrow, Beatrice. I'll be here when you wake up."

"Okay...night."

He wrapped his warm arms around her, and she drifted away.

CHAPTER 15

The Swan with Two Necks was not a pub where tourists would venture. In fact, as Giovanni looked around, he thought even the fiercest of immortals would balk at entering the dark bar in London's Docklands, if for no other reason than to avoid tasting a human with Hepatitis, which was never a pleasant experience.

But the dark pub was the known meeting place for the canny water vampire he and Gemma were finally meeting that night. Tywyll only had one name, as far as anyone knew. And his name was the only thing most humans or vampires knew about the dark vampire whose skiff moved up and down the River Thames, trading and controlling the valuable flow of information Giovanni needed to access.

He had brought Gemma along because Terry had jokingly informed him the night before that Tywyll had a rather unexpected, and very unrequited, infatuation with his old friend. He had been avoiding spending time alone with Gemma since Beatrice's revelation of Gemma's feelings for him.

"So, ye' want to know whether yer boy ha' been on the river, do ye'?"

Tywyll took a gulp of the porter in front of him. He was a small, dark man with an enigmatic middle-aged face that indicated he could have been turned anywhere between ages twenty and fifty, depending on when he had lived his mortal life.

Giovanni had long suspected Tywyll could give Tenzin competition in the age department. He glanced at Gemma, nodding toward the old vampire.

"If you had any information about Lorenzo, Tywyll, we'd be most grateful for it." She smiled. Gemma was perched precariously on the bench in the small booth where they had found the man, and her legs were pressed to his as she scowled at Giovanni across the table.

"Eh, lass, I'm sure you and yer man would be most grateful, but what of the Italian next to ye'? Is he wantin' the goods as well?"

Tywyll stared at Giovanni with hooded eyes. He knew that Giovanni wanted the information, but what he needed to know was if the fire vampire recognized the favor that would be owed for his cooperation.

Giovanni nodded. "I would be grateful for any information you could obtain about my son's whereabouts or activities, Tywyll."

Understanding offered, Tywyll sat back in the booth and took another sip of his pint. He eyed Giovanni with dark delight, happy to be doing a favor for the feared immortal.

"I'll not lie to ye', he's not been upriver that I've heard. And I'd know. I might be makin' my way down to the mouth of the river in the next week or so. If I hear anything of value, I'll let ye' know."

It was as close to a promise of investigation as they would get from the old vampire. Tywyll had a reputation as a loner, which was unusual for a water vampire, but Giovanni had long suspected that, like Tenzin, the vampire was simply too old to comfortably socialize with others more steeped in the modern world.

Instead, he maintained an extensive list of contacts up and down the river who owed him favors of one sort or another. If Lorenzo was in London, he was probably in a boat. If he was in a boat, then Tywyll would be able to locate him.

"Thank you ever so much, Tywyll," Gemma started. "As always, it's a pleasure to see you. Of course—"

"We'll be staying to finish our drinks," Giovanni added quickly. "I'm living near the water now and I'm considering buying a boat of some kind. I'd greatly appreciate any insight you could give me."

The old vampire grinned and glanced at Gemma from the corner of his eye, keen to play along with Gemma's discomfort if it meant he could spend more time with her.

"Well, now...it all depends on what yer wantin' the vessel for, doesn't it?"

"You know, Giovanni, I used to consider you a friend. That time has passed."

He laughed and twisted the woolen scarf around his neck as he and Gemma walked the damp streets. They had left the car and driver in one of the more recently gentrified areas of the Docklands where the old Bentley wouldn't be as conspicuous.

"Whatever could you mean, my dear? He was a delightful companion for drinks. If I lived in the area, I'd surely make a habit of meeting him for a beer now and then."

"You're a miserable, spiteful man, Giovanni Vecchio. And if it was your knee he was not-so-subtly brushing against, you'd be humming a different tune."

"I'm sure I wouldn't be humming at all." He grinned as they approached the car. "Nonetheless, I'm grateful you came. I doubt he would have trusted to meet with me otherwise. I know I don't have the best reputation here."

"If you hadn't have been so damn lethal during the sixteenth century, people might have forgotten by now."

"Fair enough. I appreciate the favor."

He opened the car door for her and she immediately raised the privacy screen Terry installed in all his vehicles. Not only did it provide complete sound insulation, it also protected the mechanics of the car more effectively from the energy that coursed through the vehicle if more than one vampire was present.

"So," he asked. "How is Beatrice's training going? She's very close-mouthed about the whole business with me."

"Probably because she knows how overprotective you are."

"Protective, not overprotective."

She fluttered a dismissive hand. "Beatrice is doing quite well for a human. I'm glad she's meeting with Terry tonight for firearms training. She's ready for it. I have a feeling she'll be an excellent markswoman."

He nodded with a smile on his face. Sometime after they had arrived in London and she had quit her job, Beatrice seemed to gain a new sense of resolve. As much as he disliked it initially, she had thrown herself into her training with Gemma; she had also taken an active part in the search for Lorenzo, which he did appreciate. Though Giovanni hated that she was constantly bruised, he sensed her physical confidence growing.

She was also becoming more affectionate with him, and Giovanni often rose in the evening to find her curled into his side sleeping or reading a book. He couldn't forget the picture she had made under the water, naked and floating in the large tub with her hair drifting around her. Though he had seen her in damp clothes more than once and had a good imagination, it was the first time he had seen her completely bare and, if not for the bruises covering her body, he would have had a hard time controlling himself at the sight.

Thinking of their argument that night, he looked at the woman next to him and frowned; Gemma caught his eye and squirmed.

"Gio?"

"Hmm?"

"I've been wondering...are you angry with me for training her?" Giovanni looked at Gemma's hands, which were twisted in her lap. "I know you're not pleased about her fighting, but it really is her choice. I don't want you to be angry."

She's always been so supremely confident with everyone but me. Gemma's age, her strength, and her intelligence made her a force to be reckoned with, but she had always seemed to lose her nerve around Giovanni at odd times.

And he suddenly realized why.

"Are you in love with me?"

She stared at him with wide blue eyes.

"What are you talking about? I'm marrying—"

"Are you in love with me, Gemma?"

Her eyes narrowed and grew colder.

"You really are a right bastard," she said harshly, her cultured accent slipping in anger. "You have no idea, do you?"

"You *are*," he muttered with a frown. "You are, and I had no idea. She's right, I'm really quite obtuse at times, aren't I?"

Gemma curled her lip. "Well, that's something your perceptive little human and I agree on, Giovanni." Then she shrugged and faced forward, crossing her arms across her dove-grey suit and lifting her chin.

"Why are you marrying Terry?"

"Because he's a good man, an excellent partner, and he knows me and cares for me as I am."

He frowned. "Do you love him?"

Gemma rolled her eyes. "For a five-hundred-year old vampire, you're remarkably sentimental at times, do you know that? Perhaps it's because you were raised during the Renaissance." She shook her head. "For most of human history, marriages were arranged and almost none of them were based on love. I have a huge amount of respect for my fiancé, a real affection for him, and the sex is surprisingly good. Nothing explosive like we were, but for long-term prospects, I doubt I'll see better. I foresee Terry and I working well together for hundreds of years. Past that?" She shrugged. "Who knows? Nothing is permanent in this life. If we choose to part ways after that, then I'm sure we can reach an amicable arrangement. We're both very pragmatic people."

"But Deirdre and Ioan—"

"Had something very few people ever find." She cut her eyes toward him. "Don't tell me about my brother and sister. What they had..." She turned away, but not before he could see the sheen of tears in her eyes. "What they had was unique. I've never...even what I may feel for you is nothing like what they had. Ioan and Deirdre were special, Gio."

A single tear slipped down her cheek, and he reached across the car to take her hand in his.

"I know, Gemma." He squeezed her fingers. "I know. I miss him, too."

They sat in silence the rest of the drive to the house, and Giovanni knew they would never speak of her feelings for him again.

Beatrice straightened his tie for him before they went upstairs for dinner.

"As long as you've lived," she muttered, "and you still make it crooked."

He smiled down at her. "How did you learn to tie a necktie, *tesoro*? Was it a rebellious fashion statement in grad school that I never caught wind of?"

"My grandfather, you goof," she said as she continued to tie the perfect Windsor knot. If he was purposefully making them subpar so she would fix them…well, he decided she didn't need to know. He enjoyed her fussing over him too much.

"My Grandpa Hector was a plumber, but he loved dressing up. He would take Grandma for dinner and dancing every month." She smiled wistfully. "It was their thing. And he always dressed in a suit for church on Sunday. He was…"

"What?" She hardly ever talked about her grandfather, and he knew they had been very close.

"He was my ideal man," she said with a soft smile.

"You loved him very much."

She sniffed and wiped at the tear in the corner of her eye. "I adored him."

Beatrice finished up with his tie and then went to the bathroom to change into the deep burgundy dress she had bought the day before. It was high necked and long-sleeved, which would cover the bruises that still dotted her pale skin.

Giovanni was happy to see her injuries gradually decreasing as she gained strength and speed. She had also acquired the faint smell of cordite and gun oil since learning to shoot with Terry. According to their host, she had a natural and "typically American" affinity for firearms and was becoming a very good shot.

"Speaking of grandfathers, *tesoro*, did you call Ernesto today?"

"I did," she said through the bathroom door. "Why did you want me to talk to him again?"

"He requested that I keep him updated on our progress, and I thought he would enjoy talking to you, as well. Keep in mind, he's a powerful vampire who has a real affection for you. That's not something to take for granted."

She peeked her head out the door and he caught a tantalizing glimpse of bare shoulder. "I just met him that one time. I don't want him to think I'm looking for anything from him." She shut the door and continued her preparations.

"You should. He would expect you to." He came to sit on the edge of the bed closest to the bathroom and picked up a long, dark hair that lay on her pillow, twining it around his finger as they talked.

"What do you mean, he expects it?"

"He considers you family, remember? He will enjoy providing connections for you. He'll consider it a privilege."

"That seems kind of opportunistic."

Giovanni chuckled. "Trust me, he'll use his connection to me now if he needs it, and I'm happy to give it to him. He won't get anything I'm not willing to give."

"So why—"

"He's a powerful and wealthy man. Part of his wealth is his connections. He offers you connections and...pedigree, if you want to call it that. You offer him connection to me, to Carwyn, to Gemma and Terry now...even to the legendary Tenzin. It's all part of how the game is played."

The door cracked open and she stood with a hand on her hip, which was cocked ever so slightly in his direction. He pushed down the satisfied rumble that wanted to leave his chest as he stared at the luscious curve he knew would be pressed against him when he rested later.

"Gio."

"Hmm?"

"Up here."

His eyes moved up her body to meet her amused gaze.

"Yes," he said with an innocent smile.

She only rolled her eyes. "So, what you're saying is, don't be afraid to drop names at dinner."

"Name dropping is an art in immortal society, particularly among water vampires. So no, drop away."

"Good to know."

"Happy to tell you."

She left the door open, and his eyes traced the lines of her body through the form-fitting dress. He darted over to rest his chin on her shoulder as she applied make-up in the mirror. He disliked when she put anything over her skin, but he enjoyed the brush of gold that accented her dark eyes.

Giovanni placed his hands on her waist and bent down to nose along the nape of her neck where she had pulled her hair up in a simple ponytail.

"You look beautiful."

"Thanks." She winked in the mirror and reached back to tug his tie. "You look pretty good yourself."

JEAN DESMARAIS HAD CONTROLLED THE PORTS OF LE HAVRE AND MARSEILLES for over two hundred years. His ruthless ascension on the French coast bore witness to both his canny political skills and his ferocity as a fighter. He was renowned for his business acumen and his negotiating skills; his wealth and connections were some of the best in France.

What Giovanni hadn't counted on was his charm.

"Surely, *mademoiselle*, they cannot pretend to make wine in Texas. California, I grant you, may have some passable vines, but Texas? How could a cowboy produce something so fine?"

Beatrice laughed along with him.

"I don't know, Jean, some of the Chardonnays I've had from the Hill Country have been pretty fantastic."

"Far be it from me to disagree with such a charming recommendation." He winked and sipped his glass of red from the bottle he had brought for dinner.

Jean was decidedly rakish in his appeal and appeared to have been turned in his mid-thirties. His brown hair and dark eyes spoke to as much Spanish blood as French, and the ladies at the table seemed to melt when he flashed them his roguish grin.

When Giovanni and Carwyn had wrangled a meeting with the busy water vampire over a month before, he had agreed to come and meet with Terry and Gemma in their home, which was a testament to both Jean's confidence and his curiosity. The French and the English, like their human counterparts, did not often agree. But since the swarthy vampire had arrived, he had charmed the party with his wit and humor.

Giovanni stared at Beatrice from across the table. She had been nervous at first, glancing at him as if checking for proper protocol, but he only nodded and shrugged, curious how the evening might progress.

In very short order, she had the shipping mogul eating out of the palm of her hand.

"I haven't seen him eye her neck once." Carwyn leaned over and murmured into his ear. "He's playing this very well."

"As is she," Giovanni said. "I told you, she has a knack for this. She doesn't even realize she's doing it."

"—so I was riding through the hills and I had my helmet on. Now, granted, it was winter and I was wearing a bulky jacket."

"Winter? In Hollywood? I thought you only had sunshine and palm trees?"

They both laughed and Giovanni smiled, pleased to see others appreciating her quick wit and humor.

"We get a little bit cold. Nothing like here, of course—"

"My own home is quite damp. Perhaps I need to come to California to see the surfers."

She smiled. "Perhaps you should."

"Please, continue my dear."

"So I was riding my bike and my helmet was down. I pull up to the stoplight and no less than three girls in a convertible—don't ask me why they had a convertible in December, they were probably tourists—start cat-calling me!"

"Cat-calling?"

"Oh, you know, 'Hey, handsome, I'll give you a ride,' stuff like that."

"They thought you were a man?" he asked, finally catching on before he started chuckling.

"I didn't know whether to be insulted or flattered, Jean."

The whole table seemed to find the story amusing, and the small side-conversations continued as the roast beef was served. Giovanni bypassed it, never caring much for roast meat, which reminded him too much of his days as a mercenary. He focused quietly on Beatrice and the Frenchman across from him.

"Di Spada," Jean called. "How were you so lucky to find this lovely woman, and why does she pay you any attention?"

"I must have been born under an auspicious star." Giovanni winked at Beatrice, smiling when he saw the slight blush on her cheeks.

"Truly, you must have been. Now, Mademoiselle De Novo, if I were to visit Los Angeles, what must I see?"

"Well, it all depends on your interests…"

She continued to explain the various sights in Southern California as the table hummed around him. Giovanni exchanged cautious nods with Jean's silent enforcer, who sat near the door to the dining room and glanced occasionally at Terry who, he noticed, was also observing Beatrice and Jean. Gemma caught his eye, and he saw a small smile cross her face. Despite their initial dislike, he had seen a grudging respect grow between the two women in the weeks they had spent in London.

"My daughter would love to meet you," he heard the Frenchman say.

"Oh?"

"She was born during the twenties, my Louise. She absolutely adores the cinema. And anything American, for that matter. She even talks about acting on the screen, but that, of course, is impossible."

"Is she interested in other aspects of working in film? I'm sure there are a lot of things she could do that wouldn't be in front of the camera."

Jean gave a typically Gallic shrug. "She has expressed an interest in costumes; but of course, there is nothing like that in Marseilles. And the vampires in Paris and Lyon…they are not particular friends of mine. No, French cinema is not for my Louise, I'm afraid."

Giovanni saw the minute Beatrice recognized the opportunity, and he suppressed a smile.

"Has she considered moving?"

"Out of France? My dear Beatrice, where could she go where I would be assured of her welcome and safety? I am very fond of my daughter. She is my youngest child."

"I wonder…are you familiar with my grandfather, Don Ernesto Alvarez?"

A slow smile spread across the Frenchman's face. "What are you proposing?"

"YOU WERE BRILLIANT." HE SHOVED THE DOOR CLOSED AND REACHED FOR her, pulling her to his chest and kissing her passionately before he drew her to the chair in the corner of their bedroom.

"That *was* kind of fun," she said when he finally let her up for air. She was perched in his lap, and he was running his hands over her waist and kissing her neck, tasting behind her ear as he pulled the tie from her hair.

"I knew you'd be a natural at this."

"I kind of am, aren't I? It's like a big game board. Or a puzzle. You just have to figure out how everyone is connected."

"Mmmhmm," he murmured as his lips wandered over her collarbone.

"And you're sure Ernesto won't mind?"

"He'll consider it an honor to introduce the girl to Hollywood if it means Jean's cooperation on the French coast, I'm sure of it."

"And you think Jean will help us look for Lorenzo?"

He nodded and ran his fingers through the hair that fell down her back. She hadn't cut it since they had been reunited, and he wondered if she knew how much he liked the length. "He's in shipping, smuggling, all the same circles. They were allies of a sort, for a while. If Lorenzo goes to France, he'll call Jean."

"Okay then. Yay me."

He pulled her closer, and his mouth moved along her neck as his fangs ran out. "Yay you, indeed," he said as his tongue fluttered against her racing pulse.

"Go ahead," she whispered and pulled him toward her neck, tilting her head as his fangs pierced the skin.

He moaned and pulled as the sweet blood entered his mouth. Giovanni pulled her hip against him, knowing she could feel his arousal.

"Gio," she whispered. "Wait—"

"Can you feel how much I want you?"

He licked at her neck, sealing the wounds after a few quick drinks that slaked one hunger while feeding another.

She gasped, "Gio—"

"Let me make love to you, Beatrice. I've wanted to for so long. I love you. Let me show you." One hand pressed at the small of her back, while the other stroked over her breasts. Her arms lifted and she clutched at his shoulders.

"I don't..." She whimpered in pleasure. "Not here."

"What?" He blinked and pulled away.

"Not in Gemma and Terry's house. I just..." He saw the blush flood her face and he only imagined it spreading further down her body. "And...it's too soon."

He sat back and let his arms drop to the side.

"Too soon? For what? For this? For *us*?"

"We've only been...together for a few weeks now," she stammered. "I mean, we've never even talked about—"

He pushed her off his lap and stood up to pace the room. "What? What do you want to talk about?"

"Well—" she was still blushing. "—us, I guess."

"I love you." He crossed his arms as he leaned against the desk. "I've made it quite clear what I want, Beatrice. If anyone should have doubts about our relationship, it's me."

She stood as her jaw dropped. "Excuse me?"

"You are the one holding back. You've held back for months when I know how attracted you are to me. I know how aroused you are right now. Why do you push me away?"

"I told you—"

"You tell me..." He broke off and lowered his voice, which had risen as they argued. "You tell me nothing. I know *nothing* of your feelings for me because you refuse to tell me anything."

She stood gaping at him, furious as she struggled for words.

"You—you haven't even apologized."

"For what?"

Her face flushed with anger. "If you don't know, then I'm not going to tell you, you stubborn ass."

Giovanni walked over and sidled next to her. "You know, you talk a lot about me being an ass: a pretentious ass, a stubborn ass. Seems like you think about my ass a lot, Beatrice." He yanked her hips to his and pressed their bodies together, pulling her arms around to place them on the ass he'd just mentioned. She trembled, and her breath came in quick pants. He could sense her arousal through her fury.

"What are you—"

"Are you missing something?" He leaned down and purred in her ear. "Something you know I could give you? Don't be coy, *tesoro*."

Giovanni was frustrated and angry, but he still wanted her.

"Stop it," she hissed. "Not like this. Not—"

"Not good enough for you? I think you might be surprised. I've had a few hundred years to practice—"

"Stop it!" She pushed away from him and walked across the room, standing by her side of the bed. "Why are you being like this?"

He forced down the snarl that wanted to erupt. *Because I've been the equivalent of a monk for almost six years, and you're driving me crazy. Especially when you've been flirting with another vampire for the better part of the night.*

He didn't say it. Giovanni only frowned and shook his head. Beatrice's face was pale, and she looked angry and on the verge of crying. He took a deep breath and shook his head. "This...this is a mistake. I'll find another room."

Giovanni spun on his heel and walked toward the door but stopped when he heard her heart go wild. He turned to see a hollow look on her face, and she started to shake. He suddenly realized the rash words he had uttered.

"No!" He rushed to her side. "I'm not leaving you. Not like that. I would never...I just meant that I am frustrated tonight, and you're angry—"

"Don't leave me," she whispered as the tears sprang to her eyes. "Don't. I don't think I could handle it again. You left me and..."

He grabbed her, wrapping her tightly in his arms. "I won't. I promise."

"Everyone leaves."

"What?" He frowned and pulled away so he could see her face. "What do you mean?"

"Everyone. Dad left. Grandpa. My own mom never even wanted me."

Her small voice tore at his heart, and Giovanni finally realized the enormity of his actions five years before.

"And then I left you." His chest ached when he pulled her against it, pressing her against his heart as if it could heal the wound.

"I don't want to be left again."

"I won't! I'm sorry I even said it. I'm so sorry..." Beatrice looked up at him with tear-filled eyes, and he brushed at the shining tracks that ran down her cheeks. "I am sorry, Beatrice. I am sorry I was so... *arrogant*. I'm sorry for hurting you when I left."

She gripped his waist as he held her, sighing before she pressed her cheek to his chest. Finally, she nodded. "Okay," she whispered. "Okay."

He stood, rocking them back and forth before they lay down in bed, still in their dress clothes. He didn't want to release her, even to take off his shoes. Giovanni finally felt her retreat into sleep an hour before dawn took him.

He woke the next night to the clamor of the old phone in their room. He was still wearing his dress shirt and slacks, though his shoes, coat and tie had been removed sometime during the day. He saw Beatrice's burgundy dress hanging on the back of the chair, but he did not sense her nearby.

He reached over and picked up the phone.

"Is this the Italian?" Tywyll's creaky voice greeted him on the other end of the line.

"It is. Do you have information for me?"

"I have a question for ye', fire-starter."

"What is it?" He rubbed his bleary eyes.

"Do ye' know where yer woman is?"

CHAPTER 16

Somewhere on the English Chanel

"Stupid, stupid, stupid," Beatrice chanted, punctuating each utterance with a quick kick to the side of the small room where she had been stashed. The four walls seemed to close in on her with each passing hour. She glanced at the fading light through the porthole.

She guessed that she was on a freighter of some kind, after being snatched from the streets of Mayfair while shopping on Thursday morning. Now it was nearing Thursday evening, from the look of the sun, and she braced herself for her inevitable appointment.

It just figured that the one time she left Gemma and Terry's house without her guard was the day she would be kidnapped.

"Stupid, stupid, stupid."

She just couldn't stand the idea of the rough-looking thug they'd hired to tail her during the day following her to the lingerie shop on Conduit Street.

Beatrice had been shaken by her argument with Giovanni the night before. She'd thought they'd been doing well, and her trust in him had been growing each night they spent together. When his frustration boiled over, she had been unprepared.

Not that she wasn't frustrated, too.

He was right—she was attracted to him; that had never changed. And it was maddening to sleep next to him every night and morning knowing how he felt about her. Knowing that he wanted her. Knowing that making love to him would be amazing. She'd certainly had a taste of his passion during the infrequent feedings they shared. He never seemed to take much, but just the touch of his lips at her neck sent her shuddering toward release.

But Beatrice had held back, not wanting their physical attraction to overwhelm what she knew was the most important part of their relationship. She still needed to trust him.

"Stupid, stupid, stupid," she chanted as angry tears gathered in her eyes.

In the dim light of morning, when she'd finally removed her rumpled dress, she forced herself to confront her feelings for the vampire she shared a bed with every night.

She sat next to him in her robe, stroking his face before she rolled him over and removed his jacket. Her hands pressed against the iron weight of his chest, and she lifted his muscular arms to pull it off.

This immortal being that slept next to her every night was almost unimaginably powerful. His hands could snap her like a twig if he wanted. Even more, one simple touch from him could render her malleable to any whim he could imagine. Yet, Giovanni knew how she feared mental manipulation and had always restrained himself.

"Don't you realize how I adore you? I wanted you to have a choice."

He was waiting for her. He had been waiting for months. He had never wavered in his promise not to leave her again, and he had done everything in his power to make himself a permanent fixture in her life.

"I will earn the woman's love, if I have lost the girl's."

She pulled his shoes off and set them at the foot of the bed before she leaned over to remove his tie. He purposely made it crooked so she would fix it. Such a small, human thing. He did it purely for her attention.

"Why do you call me by my human name?"

"Because I love you, Jacopo," she whispered.

Beatrice felt tears on her face as the walls she had carefully constructed for the past five years fell, and she finally let herself imagine a future with Giovanni. Could she give up the life she knew to join him? Even more, could she imagine a future without him?

She curled next to him in bed, wishing for the sun to fall faster so he could be with her again. She lay next to him and considered trying to wake him but decided it would just be frustrating. She had tried more than once to rouse him during the afternoon to give him some important message, only to be disappointed when he had no memory of it when he woke.

And now, she sat in the bowels of the creaking ship, banging her head against the wall.

"Stupid, stupid, stupid." *Just letting him wake up next to you naked probably would have been a better idea than new lingerie, Beatrice.*

They must have used chloroform or something similar, because she hardly remembered anything besides thick arms and something soft covering her nose and mouth. Then she'd woken in the swaying boat, alone and unharmed, which probably meant she was due for a visitor as soon as the sun set.

She stood up, pacing the room and trying to imagine any form of escape. There had to be something. There had to be someone. Someone she could plead with. Someone she could bribe. Someone who...

Her attention was drawn to the porthole. The sky was deep blue, and the setting sun turned the clouds gold.

In the distance, she could see land, closer than she would have expected for such a large ship, but then, she really didn't know much about boats. She stopped pacing and started jogging in place, trying to loosen her stiff muscles and think.

Beatrice muttered to herself, "No way in hell am I spending another month of my life under this sick bastard's control."

She knew he wouldn't hurt her, which dispelled some of the fear she'd felt five years before and gave her renewed confidence. No doubt the humans he had guarding her were under orders not to harm her either. She walked to the small bathroom in the corner of the room, relieved herself, and prepared to do everything possible to make keeping her a major annoyance.

She jumped up and down, doing as many of her warm-up exercises as she could in the limited amount of space. She mentally ran through the throws she had learned in her judo class, the hits and kicks she had learned from Gemma, and tried to quiet her mind the way Tenzin had always advised her. She hoped one of the humans had guns; she might be able to steal one.

As the sky darkened, she realized that the possibility of avoiding a vampire was probably non-existent. She sat on the bed, closed her eyes, and listened for the approaching footsteps. In the back of her mind, she realized that Giovanni would be waking soon. He would realize she was gone, but would he have any idea where she had been taken?

Beatrice heard footsteps coming toward her room. She could tell it was more than one person, but she couldn't tell how many. The door swung open, but she remained on the bed, trying her best to look calm. A young, dark-haired vampire of medium build walked in and looked around, only glancing at her as his eyes swept the room. He was completely unremarkable except for the twin fangs she could see in his mouth. He murmured something over his shoulder in a low voice. She had noticed Giovanni and Carwyn using the same tone when they didn't want her to hear something.

With some ceremony that was probably meant to frighten her, Lorenzo swept into the room. His blond curls were shorter than she remembered, and his Botticelli face bore the smudges of healing scars around his mouth and left eye. He was still wearing the ridiculous white wardrobe he had favored in Greece, though he was dressed for the colder winter weather of Northern Europe.

"Beatrice, my dear, it has been too long," he said as he looked down his nose.

"You look like a ski bunny. Nice sweater."

"Ah!" his face brightened. "You have regained your delightful sense of humor. Excellent. You were so dreadfully dull when we parted in Greece."

"You mean when your dad came and spanked your ass with his two friends? Yeah, that was awesome. Nice scars. You getting a *Phantom of the Opera* mask to go with those? They're white too, if I remember correctly."

He smiled, his cold blue eyes examining her as he leaned against the open doorway.

"That lovely De Novo sarcasm. I do so miss that about your father. And now that I know how much Giovanni loves you," he sneered, "I'll enjoy torturing you as well. As soon as we've secured Stephen, of course. You see—" He darted over and leaned down so she could feel his cold breath against her neck when he spoke. "—I'm going to find him first."

"Good luck with that," she choked out, disgusted by the chill that seemed to course over her skin at his proximity. "Even Gio—"

"Does not have the resources I do when it comes to finding people," he said with a condescending smile. "He's too virtuous. And once you tell me exactly what he knows about your father from his search, the combined information should be enough to put me well ahead in the race."

"Don't count on it. What makes you think I'm going to tell you—"

She choked on the words when his cold fingers grasped her neck, and she began to shake when she realized he was right. She would tell him anything.

Anything he wanted.

He knelt before her and let the cruel smile twist his lips as he forced his influence on her.

"No wasting time with friendly banter, Beatrice. I've been waiting too long to get what is mine, and I have little faith that our location is a well-kept secret. I need that book your father has. I've made promises that some are starting to doubt. And I will *not*—" She winced when his grip around her neck tightened. "—be denied any longer."

His touch was not the soft caress of Giovanni or even the sick, teasing touch she remembered from the last time he'd held her. It was the cold burn of ice that gripped her throat; the sensation quickly spread over her skin and nausea turned her stomach.

The ache spread from his fingers, around her neck, and up to the base of her skull as she stared into his frigid, blue eyes. She couldn't speak, but her teeth began to chatter and the goose bumps spread down her body. It was as if his touch had frozen her and, as the creeping cold slipped into her mind, Beatrice knew she was powerless to stop the invasion.

"Where is your father?"

Her teeth chattered when she answered. "I—I don't know."

"Has Giovanni been in contact with him?"

Her mind screamed at her to tell him nothing, but she couldn't stop the words as they tumbled out of her mouth.

"Postcards."

"Explain."

"Dad left clues for Gio, and he sent me…postcards."

"Who sent you postcards, Beatrice?"

"G—G—io sent me postcards," she rattled. "From the places he f—found clues."

Beatrice could feel the tears trickling down her cheeks, and she was surprised that they didn't freeze against her cold skin. But as she saw the spotted condensation on the porthole, she realized that no one in the room was cold except her. In fact, if someone touched her skin, she imagined it would still be its normal temperature. But Lorenzo told her nerve endings she was freezing, and her body reacted accordingly.

"What kind of clues?"

"He—he wouldn't tell me." Beatrice wondered if the knowledge of her vulnerability was what had caused Giovanni to hold back the information, and she was suddenly grateful for his stubborn, determined, forward-thinking ass.

"He sent you the postcards?"

"Yes."

"From where? I want every location he sent a postcard from. List them all."

And with trembling lips and tears in her eyes, Beatrice gave Lorenzo the location of every place Giovanni had found a clue left by Stephen De Novo in the previous five years.

Warsaw.

Johannesburg.

Lima.

San Francisco.

Tripoli. Santiago. Shanghai. Stockholm. Budapest. Novosibirsk.

She told him everything she knew.

And as she told him, Lorenzo came to sit next to her on the small bed, putting an arm around her as he played with her hair. He twisted it in his right hand while his left hand played with her fingers.

"Your skin is so lovely, Beatrice. Have I ever told you that?"

"N—no."

"It is. It's no wonder he likes you. I can see his bite marks on your neck now." He bent down to run his lips against her skin, inhaling deeply. "Do you like it? When he bites you?"

She wanted to pull away. To strike him. But she was utterly frozen and had no choice but to answer as the cold fingers of Lorenzo's amnis stroked her mind.

"Yes."

"Does his bite make you come?" he purred into her ear.

Beatrice tried to resist. She pictured walls going up in her mind, blocking the creep of his influence, but the twisted fingers flowed over and around the walls, forcing her to answer.

"Y—yes," she whispered.

"How delicious you smell. Sweet, but not overpowering. Very much like I remember your father tasting. Maybe I should have kept him like my father keeps you. Quite convenient having a regular meal."

The angry tears still fell down her face as she realized how powerless she was.

"Of course," he whispered her hidden fear as his fingers slid up her arm. "I could just keep *you*. Maybe my father is on to something with his human women. Who cares if you bruise a little when I'm done with you? If you're interesting enough to keep him occupied, perhaps you are worth my time."

"N—no!" Just the thought churned her gut. "I don't want—" And yet it didn't seem to matter what she wanted. She could feel the suggestion take root in her mind, and her arm lifted until her fingers were nestled in the soft golden curls on his head. She stroked them, and he hissed in pleasure.

"Such lovely, delicate hands, Beatrice. Why are your knuckles so bruised, precious girl? Surely you haven't been practicing your ridiculous martial arts like you did in California. Surely you know..." His lips brushed against her cheek, and he whispered into her ear, *"You cannot fight me."*

He snickered a little and pierced her earlobe with one fang, quickly lapping at the blood with his cold tongue before he rose and straightened his clothes. She immediately felt the chill leave her, and Beatrice resisted the urge to shake.

"Delicious. You are a treat, my dear. I've already fed this evening, but hopefully we'll have time tomorrow night."

"Where are you taking me?" she asked, shrugging the tension from her body and drying her eyes with the back of her sleeve. He thought she was going to wait around to let him feed on her? In his dreams.

"Don't be silly. It's very possible that Giovanni will have found you by tomorrow night, and I don't want to give him any new information."

She glared at the monster in front of her.

"Why did you kill Ioan?"

He giggled and looked around the room. Beatrice finally noticed that there were four other vampires present beside Lorenzo and no other humans beside herself. All of Lorenzo's men were dressed in black, and none of them seemed remarkable in the least.

Lorenzo finally stopped his ridiculous giggling. "One, I did not kill the kindly doctor, these lovely gentlemen did. Two, the reason I killed Ioan is between Ioan and myself. So you'll have to ask one of us, and since I'm not telling, and he's little bits of dust at this point, I suppose you'll just have to live with disappointment."

In that moment, Beatrice De Novo decided that she would become a vampire. If for no other reason than to kill the evil creature in front of her, who shattered lives on a whim. A cool calm settled over her, and a smile flickered across her face.

"I am going to kill you, Lorenzo."

He only laughed. "You're precious. Now, will my father kill me?" He shrugged. "Perhaps. He's definitely powerful enough. The problem for him is, he lacks a certain...we'll call it 'devious intent,' that allows me to be far more ruthless. Oh, he's quite violent when provoked, as my lovely house on the island can attest, but he doesn't really *enjoy* it like I do. Now you..." He lifted a curious eyebrow. "You might be a force to be reckoned with, Beatrice De Novo."

The smile fell from his face, and he cocked his head to the side. "I can see the calculation in your eyes, and it's very intriguing. What could you accomplish with power? It's almost worth changing you to find out."

The thought of his blood running through her veins sickened her, and she curled her lip. He quickly plastered on a sick smile.

"Oh! You're so darling. I missed you."

"I can't say I feel the same, Paulo."

She didn't even see the slap coming. His quick backhand would have knocked her unconscious if she hadn't become accustomed to Gemma's even more ruthless blows during their training. Lorenzo was eyeing her with a new light in his eyes.

"So, my darling Papá confided my human name to you, did he? What else did he confide?"

Beatrice kept her expression neutral, suddenly aware that she'd made a horrible mistake. No one had known how much she knew about Giovanni, and she realized that his secrets were completely open to any vampire that wanted them if they could get their hands on her.

The same thought seemed to occur to Lorenzo, but he didn't put his hands on her. Instead, smirked and blew her a kiss before he swept out of the room with his entourage. Beatrice released a breath when she was alone again and settled into the bed to rest and wait for dawn.

CHAPTER 17

The sun was pouring through the porthole when she woke, and small droplets of condensation cast tiny rainbows around the small room. Beatrice remembered Giovanni's favorite waterfall in Cochamó and how it looked during the day with the sun reflecting off the spraying mist. It would be late summer right now, and she decided that if she could pick one place to be, it would be at their house in the valley with him.

They would wake in the early evening and make love in front of the fireplace in their bedroom, the flecks of mica sparkling in the hewn granite wall. She would sleep next to him all day and spend the night riding through the meadows in the moonlight. Maybe there would be wildflowers. She would have to remember to see as much of the valley as she could in the sunlight and take pictures for after she had turned. Since it was summer, maybe they would implement a no clothing rule in the house. She knew Giovanni wouldn't mind.

Beatrice rubbed her eyes and stretched. She was going to get out of the room today. She wasn't sure how, but it was daytime. Granted, it was morning, which meant that some of the vampires could still be awake if they stayed out of sunlight, but by afternoon, she knew they would be sleeping. That meant anyone up and walking around would be human. And she was pretty sure if she could land the odd blow on Gemma, she could kick some human ass.

Hours later, when the sun was hanging lower in the sky, she beat on the thick metal door.

"Hey!" she shouted. "Anyone?"

She paused to hear if there was any movement.

"Anyone out there? I've been in here all day, you gonna feed me?" She pounded some more. "Hey, I'm starving!"

She wasn't starving, she was sickeningly nervous, but she needed someone to open the door.

"Open up! I need some food."

She finally heard steps approaching, and Beatrice stepped back, grasping the sheet she had twisted into a thick rope.

"Hello?" an accented voice called. "You are hungry?"

"Yeah, I'm starving, all right? Will you feed me already?" She braced herself on the corner of the bed. When the door opened, whoever came through would see her immediately, there was no avoiding it, so she stepped up on the small bed, knowing that she would get one chance for surprise.

"Okay. I get food," the voice called. She felt a brief pang at the thought of harming the voice, which sounded fairly friendly, but there was no way in hell she was going to show mercy to her captors when Lorenzo was waiting at sundown.

The footsteps walked away, and she put down her sheet to take off the jacket she had been wearing. It was cold on the ship, and she knew it was cold outside, but the jacket was too bulky for her to move freely, and she knew that the less an attacker had to grab, the better.

Beatrice took deep breaths, preparing her mind for the rush at the door. She focused on her hand-to-hand training with Gemma and all the advice the woman had given her over the past month.

"Go for the dirty punch. Always. And hit them when they're down."

"Throw your attacker off balance. It's the only way your small size can be used to your advantage."

"Be quick! Quicker. Make yourself so fast they can't grab you. If they do, you're dead."

She took a deep breath.

The footsteps approached.

She heard a key in the lock.

The door cracked open.

She saw a tray.

Spotting her opportunity, Beatrice braced her arms on the narrow walls and kicked up, knocking the tray into her captor's face as she swung the twisted bed sheet around his neck and, holding it securely, jumped off the bed.

The force of her momentum knocked the large man off balance and he stumbled into the wall. She aimed her boot at his groin and kicked him as hard as she could. Then she kicked him again.

He was on the ground, grunting in pain, so she stomped.

Beatrice was surprised how little noise he made. She must have knocked the wind out of him. After the first low grunt, the crewman curled into himself while she continued battering his kidney area with her boot the way Gemma had taught her. She shoved the door mostly closed and paused to survey the writhing man at her feet.

There was a gun in his belt. *Score.*

She reached down to his doughy waist and grabbed it. It was a Heckler and Koch nine millimeter, exactly like the one she had practiced with the previous week.

"God bless you, Terry," she muttered as she popped the magazine out and checked the ammunition. The crewman hadn't fired his weapon since he'd loaded it, so she slammed it back, racked a bullet into the chamber, and took the safety off.

She aimed it at the belly of the large man who was looking at her with wide eyes.

"Funny thing, guns. Six foot tall man with a nine millimeter, five foot tall woman with a nine millimeter...pretty much the same, aren't they?"

He didn't speak, but he was panting and she saw his mouth start to open. She kicked him in the kidneys again.

"You stay quiet. You yell? Everyone's going to know I'm busting out, and I'll have no reason not to just shoot you. Noise is noise, right? I don't particularly want to shoot you, but I really hate the creepy asshole that put me in here, so if I have to, I will. Is this making sense?"

The silent crewman nodded and closed his mouth.

"Good, what language do you speak?"

"*Español*," he whispered.

"Fine." She switched to Spanish. "I want off this boat. Like I said, I don't particularly want to shoot you, but I will if it'll get me off the boat. Is that a cell phone?" She nodded toward his pocket, where she could see a slight bulge.

"Yes."

"Give it to me. One hand, in your pocket. No sudden moves, or I'll shoot you."

"Yes," he said as he reached down. "Please, I just work here. I don't want to hurt you. I don't even know—"

"Shut up."

"My name is—"

"Shut. Up." If she had to shoot him later, she sure as hell didn't want to know his name. She didn't know if she could kill him, but the thought of shooting his legs didn't bother her at all.

The more Beatrice examined the nameless crewman, the more she realized that he looked like a normal guy. He didn't react or assess the room like someone trained in security, and she smiled a little when she realized she had lucked out.

It also made her feel slightly bad about scaring the shit out of him—she could smell that he had peed his pants—but she wasn't going to back down.

Let him think she was a big badass; Beatrice was feeling like it at the moment.

He handed her his phone and she stuck it in her pocket. "Thanks. Now, where are we, and how far are we from land?"

"We're still in the Channel. We had to stop in Le Havre before dawn. We are...maybe fifteen miles off the coast of France? Near Cherbourg. I'm not sure." His voice shook just a little.

"Shit." The land didn't look that far away. She was going need a boat. "Where are the lifeboats?"

Would a lifeboat be enough on the English Channel in the middle of February? She had a sudden thought. "This is a freighter, right?"

He nodded, looking confused when she smiled. "So it's got those big, orange life rafts with navigation and engines and all that stuff? The contained ones?"

"Yes."

Thank you, Discovery Channel. She shoved the gun closer. "You ever launch one?"

"I—I've seen the drills, but there's never been an emergency—"

"Good enough for me. We're headed for the lifeboat, mister. If you try to get away, I'll shoot you. If you try to yell for help, I'll shoot you. I don't really have a lot to lose at this point, and I'm sure the creepy, blond asshole that hired you told me you can't hurt me, so don't even try."

She nodded toward the door and the crewman scrambled up, still clutching his groin from where she had kicked him.

Beatrice hadn't heard anyone pass in the hall, which fit with the deserted feeling she'd gotten from the ship through most of the morning. She nudged the large man in front of her with the barrel of the H&K, taking comfort in the sturdy grip in her hand. She snagged her thick jacket on the way out the door.

Nameless Crewman walked in front of her.

"Where are you taking me?"

"The lifeboats, remember?"

"Honestly, I've seen the drills, but there's never been an emergency, so I don't know—"

"Feel this?" She nudged his back with the barrel of the gun. "This is an emergency. You're launching it, and you're taking me to the nearest stretch of land. And I suggest we get there before nightfall, 'cause that's when the monsters come out."

"Monsters?" She could hear his voice quiver a little, and she shoved down the flicker of sympathy.

"Yeah, monsters. And my boyfriend? He's the scariest one, so as long as you help me get out of here, you'll be fine."

They wound through the corridors of the creaking ship, heading upward at a steady pace. Nameless Crewman didn't halt and seemed to be cooperating, so they reached the deck in short order. She could smell the fresh sea air when he stopped by the last door.

"Wait, Miss. Let me check outside to see if anyone—"

"I will have this gun at your back the whole time, do you understand? If I think you're messing with me, I'll shoot you." Beatrice was impressed by how firm her voice sounded. She was probably going to fall apart later, but at the moment, the adrenaline and the firearm were making her feel like Superwoman.

He nodded and cracked open the door, only to close it almost immediately.

"There are men out there I do not recognize! With guns. Lots of guns," he said in a panic. "What is going on? The captain has been acting so strange; he never used to—"

"Shut up! Men? What did they look like?" Giovanni couldn't have found her already; she had seen the crack of sunlight at the door. Would Lorenzo have hired security that Nameless Crewman didn't recognize?

She crowded him, shoving the gun into his belly. "Do you know everyone on this boat? What about passengers? Are there any?"

He frowned. "There are the strange people renting the interior cabins. They are odd and they come and go at night while I am off duty—"

"Okay, but the guys out there aren't them?"

"No. And they're speaking French. This is a Spanish vessel. We all speak Spanish."

"French?" Her eyes lit up.

Jean.

She remembered him bragging about his extensive human staff when he gave her his card.

"Day or night, B. If you are in France, call these numbers and someone will help you. I have people everywhere," he'd said proudly.

She wracked her brain for the numbers he had given her and pulled out Nameless Crewman's phone. The signal was faint, but it might just be enough. She punched one in and practically cried in relief when she heard the phone ringing on the other end.

"*Allo?*" a polite woman answered.

"Do you speak English? This is Beatrice De Novo, and Jean Demarais—"

"Ah! Madmoiselle De Novo," she tumbled off a ridiculously fast stream of French before Beatrice heard another voice on the line.

"Miss De Novo?" a deep voice asked. "Am I speaking with Beatrice De Novo?"

"Yes, you are. I met your boss a few nights ago, and I had a quick question."

"We have been looking for you since this morning, where—"

"Do you happen to have a whole bunch of guys looking for me on the deck of a freighter in the English Channel right now?"

There was a deep chuckle. "As a matter of fact..."

She sighed in relief but gasped when she felt the cold barrel of a gun at her neck. She dropped the phone when she heard a low voice hiss in Spanish, "You're not supposed to be out of your cabin, are you?"

Beatrice turned to Nameless Crewman, who was staring in horror at the group of men gathered behind them. He looked at her in panic right before one of the crewmen raised a gun and shot him in the chest. She cried out when the man slumped forward and the pool of blood spread under him.

"No!" *I'm sorry...I'm so sorry.*

It was Beatrice's last thought before she felt something strike her temple, and she blacked out.

CHAPTER 18

The freighter's hatch started to glow, and the heat radiated from the center of the panel until the metal was cherry red. The steel turned the consistency of wet cardboard as it slumped in his hands. Giovanni pushed aside the soft metal, blocking the three vampires behind him as Terry sent a blast of cold water to cool it.

Jean's human assault team had remained, standing alert on deck to grab any humans they found. The team had already secured the bridge but had been told not to go belowdecks until Giovanni, Carwyn, Gemma, and Terry arrived at first dark. When they had, the team leader gladly let the silent immortals dressed in black take the lead.

Giovanni reached down the dark passageway with his senses, stretching his hearing and sense of smell to detect any danger. He could smell the faint scent of honeysuckle near the top of the stairs, along with the scent of adrenaline that made the blue flames jump on his bare torso.

He felt Terry's cool hand on his shoulder, dousing the flames as the salt air was drawn to him.

"Watch yourself. Narrow corridors. Flammable cargo. We don't know what's down there."

"Beatrice is down there," he said.

"So she is, and we're getting her back tonight."

Giovanni touched the melted edges of the door, nodding as he ducked his tall frame through the opening. He could hear Terry, Carwyn, and Gemma crawl through behind him. He walked down the corridor and halted at the top of a stairwell.

He could hear a scuffle somewhere in the bowels of the ship, as if humans were scrambling, and he heard the soft *shush* of immortals as they swept through the ship at inhuman speed.

"Father and I will go forward," Gemma murmured. "You and Terry go to the rear of the ship; with this damp air, he'll have no trouble extinguishing you if things get dangerous."

"Just stay behind me, Terry."

"Right."

She nodded. "We've all seen the layout of this ship from Jean's man, but I think it's important to note that many of the small interior cabins could be good hiding spots, as well."

Carwyn said, "We're sending humans above if they cooperate—"

"And it doesn't waste too much time," Giovanni added.

"Fine, and let's remember that there are twenty men listed in this crew, and only four of them are being held above," Carwyn said.

"And we don't know how many vampires Lorenzo has with him," Terry added.

"Is he here?" Gemma looked to Giovanni. "Do you get any sense of him, Gio?"

"Not of Lorenzo, but there are four other energy signatures. Young, not very strong."

Though all vampires could sense electricity, much as sharks could in the water, Giovanni's senses had always been more keen than most. Since his particular element made him highly reactive to electronics, he could also sense vampire signatures at far greater distances than even most ancient vampires. It was one of the reasons he and Tenzin had been such effective mercenaries.

"Lorenzo's scent is here, but I don't feel him. He might have left."

"Rats do tend to flee when they smell fire," Carwyn muttered.

"Let's go," Terry said. "No need to be quiet if we find them." He leaned over and pulled Gemma toward him, planting a rough kiss on her mouth before chucking her chin. "Make sure you leave some for the rest of us, luv."

The four nodded toward each other before breaking apart to search. Giovanni clamped down the instinctive rage and forced himself to think rationally. Beatrice was smart and brave, and he knew Lorenzo needed her unharmed as bait for her father. If she was still on the ship, she would be fine. She had to be.

He traced the scent of honeysuckle and adrenaline down to the starboard side of the ship, halting before a small cabin where the smell was strongest. Terry caught up with him just before he cracked open the door.

"Here." Giovanni stepped through the door, almost falling to his knees at the scent of her panic and a faint trace of blood. A cocktail of Lorenzo's scent and cloying energy combined with the smell of blood, adrenaline, and Beatrice. Blue flames burst out over his body. Giovanni heard his growl echo through the small room, and his fangs punched through his lower lip.

He felt Terry slap at his burning shoulder and steam rose. "Gio, focus. I smell blood, too, but it's not much. Calm down and track her." The water vampire sent a cooling blanket of air over his torso, extinguishing the flames as Giovanni wiped the blood dripping from his chin.

He walked back to the corridor, focusing his senses on the scent of Beatrice and a male human. It drew him down the hall and through twisting corridors, slowly working its way toward the top deck.

"She had a man with her," Terry noted. "A pissing scared one, at that."

"Caught that, did you?"

"She's no wilting flower, your girl."

"Neither's yours."

Beatrice's scent stopped right before a steel door that he knew led to the top deck, and he caught the thick musk of four male humans along with the stronger scent of human blood. It was not hers. He looked down to the pool of blood on the floor, following the trail to a small supply closet where a large body had been stowed.

Terry peered in. "This is the one she took up from her cabin by the smell of him. Look at his holster, empty. I bet she took his gun. That's why he pissed himself. Good girl, B."

"But they were intercepted. Beatrice wouldn't have shot him in the chest if he was cooperating. Other humans must have found them."

"Rough smelling ones at that."

"Let's go." Giovanni turned. "Their scent leads down this way."

They moved down to the lower decks, and Terry let a sharp whistle echo down one corridor. In a few seconds, Carwyn and Gemma had joined them, and all four snuck through the freighter, following behind Giovanni.

There was a scuffle in the cabin to their right. Carwyn turned and ripped the door off its hinges, throwing it to the side.

Terry caught the first crewman who tried to scurry out, tossing him to Giovanni while Gemma found the other trying to hide in a closet. The man was trembling in fear, so she used her amnis to calm him and send him to the top deck with his hands on his head.

"Where is the girl?" Giovanni growled, as he held the small man up by the throat. Flames flared on his shoulders, and the crewman's horrified gaze flicked farther down the hallway to a pair of large, steel doors.

"Forward cargo hold," Terry murmured before Giovanni squeezed the man's neck and sent the human into unconsciousness before dropping him on the floor.

The four approached the door cautiously, Giovanni reaching out with his senses, searching for Beatrice's distinctive scent in the confused mass of immortal energy, human scent, and growing commotion behind the steel doors. The flames flared on his arms as his frustration grew.

"Carwyn..."

"Focus on her, Gio. Is she in there?"

"Yes," he hissed and reached for the door. His hands were already flaming as he placed them on the metal, but Carwyn put a firm hand on his shoulder, halting him.

"We don't know what's on the other side of that. Hold back the fire, my friend. Now, what's behind there?"

He closed his eyes and focused. "Beatrice is there. Four vampires...too many humans. More than ten, that's all I can tell."

"Is she frightened?"

"Everyone is frightened. I can't tell where she is." His patience snapped. "Just get the damn door open before I melt it!"

Terry pulled him back from the doorway and let Carwyn forward.

"Hold back, mate. We'll take care of the rest. You just find your girl."

Carwyn placed his ear on the door and closed his eyes before nodding with satisfaction. He reared back and punched both hands through the layers of steel, ripping them apart and pulling the door off its hinges as it broke apart.

All four rushed into the room, darting around the confused humans, who were running to one corner of the cavernous hold where boxes were stacked in a kind of barricade. The four vampires rushed toward them, and Gemma and Terry confronted them as Carwyn began knocking out humans who darted by and tossing them in a pile.

Giovanni only looked for one thing.

"Gio!"

He heard her call his name, but he could not see her in the confusion. One of the vampires escaped Gemma and rushed him, sending a blanket of wet air and extinguishing his flames before he could send them out. The young water vampire drew a sword and slashed at him but only succeeded in cutting Giovanni's arm before he was grabbed by the throat.

Giovanni eyed him, trying to determine whether he was worth interrogating. The vampire sneered, and Giovanni almost snapped his neck, but Carwyn reached over and snatched him away.

"No. This one feels the oldest. I want to question him."

Giovanni grunted as he continued stalking toward the corner with the boxes. He saw Beatrice peek out before she was pulled back by a large human holding a gun on her.

"Gio!" she shrieked again before the human tugged her behind a stack of crates. He heard her yell, "Let me go, you bastard!"

Giovanni was tracking her so intently that he barely registered when one of the human crew members to his right pulled a handgun and shot him in the chest.

The blast punched through him, but missed his heart, which would have knocked him over. Giovanni grunted and reached over to grab the man, annoyed as he twisted his neck and let him fall to the ground. He strode to the crates where the human had taken Beatrice only to find her twisting away from her captor. He watched as she drove her elbow into the large man's gut and her knee into his groin. She had already disarmed him, and the gun lay on the ground as they struggled.

Giovanni rushed over, grabbed the human by the neck, and squeezed. The man's face turned red as he struggled helplessly in his iron grip. Beatrice reached down to grab the nine millimeter and aim it at the dangling human. He examined her quickly.

She was pale and had bruises on her arms, several cuts to her face, and a swollen knee. She also had the beginning of a black eye and an ugly bruise spread over her temple, but her hands were steady.

"*Tesoro*, are you all right?"

"Fine. I'll be fine. I'm really glad to see you guys, though." He saw her glance over his shoulder. "There's four vampires here. They came down as soon as the sun set, but they didn't say anything to me. They just herded us down here and told this guy to keep me quiet."

"Gemma, Terry, and Carwyn are taking care of them."

"You're bleeding a lot," she said in a shaky voice as she glanced at his chest.

"I was shot. It missed the heart, so it shouldn't take long to heal." In fact, he could already feel the wound beginning to close, so he reached in his chest with his fingers, grunting until he had pulled the bullet from the torn flesh.

"Oh, Gio!" she cried as she watched him toss the bullet to the ground and wipe at the bleeding cavity. "Are you going to be okay?"

"I'll be fine. Did this human hurt you?" The man was barely conscious, but his eyes widened when he heard Giovanni.

He saw her clench her jaw from the corner of his eye. "He's the one that hit me. He was trying for something else, but my boot met his balls."

The man desperately tried to pry Giovanni's fingers from his throat. His terror-stricken eyes met the vampire's gaze when he cocked his head and spoke in a low voice.

"Did you lay your hands on my woman? That was very foolish. You're going to wish she had killed you now. She would have been quicker than me."

His heart began a slow thud of anticipation, but Giovanni wanted to be fair.

"Beatrice, do you wish to kill him yourself?"

His green eyes remained locked on the struggling human's, and he refused to allow any amnis to spread over him to soften the terror.

"No," he heard her murmur. "You need the blood."

Giovanni bared his fangs in the man's face, cutting off the human's scream as he twisted his neck to the side and sank his fangs into the soft, warm throat. He closed his eyes and took long, dragging gulps as his bloodlust collided with the pain that finally slammed into his chest.

He opened his eyes to see Beatrice looking around the cargo hold, watching for any threats. He could hear Gemma and Terry rounding up the last of the humans behind them. Beatrice came to stand in front of him as he drank, and he bit harder, piercing the carotid as the blood flooded into his mouth. His green eyes locked with hers and blood ran down his chin, but Beatrice did not flinch as she watched him drain the human who had threatened her life.

He felt the blood pumping through his system as his stomach filled, and a feral growl rumbled in his chest. The flames began to lick at his arms as his body grew stronger.

Beatrice never took her eyes off Giovanni, watching as he slowly sucked the life out of the man. Her hand reached toward him, and an instinctive snarl ripped from his throat, but she only paused for a moment before she placed a hand on his forehead, sweeping her fingers back through his hair as his eyes remained on hers. Gradually, the rage lessened, and the fire along his arms began to die down.

The human's heartbeat slowed, then stopped, and Giovanni dropped the dead man on the ground, wiping his mouth on his forearm before he stepped toward Beatrice, gripped the back of her neck, and let his bloody mouth crash down on hers.

He almost expected her to push him away, disgusted by his animalistic display, but she did not. She wrapped her arms around his waist and pressed close, careful to avoid his chest wound. He pierced his tongue and licked at the cut on her chin and at the corner of her mouth until they were sealed and healing.

"Gio," she finally murmured as he buried his face in her hair, inhaling her scent and holding her as his heartbeat slowed. "You came for me."

"I will always come for you. I love you," he murmured as he nuzzled his face into her neck, covering her in his scent before the smell of blood and Lorenzo hit him.

"What did he do?" he hissed and brushed back her hair searching for the source of the blood. He saw a small wound that looked like a piercing on her earlobe, and he looked at her. "Did he hurt you, Beatrice?"

She took a deep breath and lifted a hand to his hair, soothing him with her touch. "Just that. He bit my ear, but that's all. Other than that, it was just mind games again."

"If there was only a way to kill him more than once," he muttered as he pierced his tongue again and sucked her earlobe into his mouth to clean and heal the small wound.

He held her for a few more minutes until he heard Terry walk over.

"Nicely done, B. Gio, you hurt?"

"Nothing serious. The vampires?"

"Gemma killed two. Carwyn and I grabbed the others so we could question them."

"And the humans?" Beatrice asked.

"Most of them are dead. A few surrendered willingly, and Carwyn sent them up to Jean's men."

"I need to heal myself," Giovanni said as he pushed away from Beatrice. "Terry, you and Gemma take the vampires up to the deck and wait for me there. Beatrice, go to Carwyn." He could sense the earth vampire hovering nearby.

Terry nodded and crossed the hold, grabbing the other vampire that Gemma held before they walked out. Carwyn walked over to the corner.

Beatrice just stared at his bleeding chest. "How do you heal yourself?"

"Stand back," he said as he turned and nodded toward Carwyn, who reached out his hand to Beatrice and drew her away toward the far side of the hold.

"How do you heal yourself?" she asked again.

"I need to let it take me, Father. Keep her away."

"You're going to set yourself on fire?" Beatrice was starting to sound panicked.

"Darling girl," Carwyn soothed her. "Come stand with me. Did you get shot, Gio? You're getting slow in your old age."

He closed his eyes, trying to focus on something other than the pain in his chest. "Keep her away. Maybe you should both go up on deck."

"No," they said together.

"I won't leave you," she said.

Giovanni thought about the resolute look in her eyes as she watched him drain the human and nodded before he stepped to the far corner of the empty compartment. He stood motionless and lowered his head, taking deep breaths before he allowed the static electricity to start snapping along his skin. After a moment, he began pacing, keeping one eye near the door where Carwyn and Beatrice stood. They were at least ten meters away, but he was still cautious, which was, no doubt, part of Carwyn's plan in keeping them close by.

He flexed his arms and curled his shoulders in, focusing his energy to run along his skin and push outward as he felt the flames begin to lick along his chest and arms. He could feel himself start to walk the thin edge between control and chaos. The last of his clothes burned away, and he stood naked as the blue fire covered his body.

As Giovanni's energy grew and the flames rose, he could feel his chest ache and start to knit together. He glanced up to see Carwyn holding onto Beatrice with an iron grip. He turned and faced her, focusing on her dark eyes as he stood motionless and let the fire wash his injuries away.

He heard the hiss as his hair singed, and the acrid scent drifted to his nose. He kept himself focused on the sour smell of burning hair to counteract the heady sensation of power that threatened to overwhelm him. The blood rushed through his body and his heart raced, but the higher the flames grew, the stronger he became.

His power peaked, and Giovanni could feel his chest muscles stretch and smooth out. He flexed them, feeling only an edge of pain. He continued to stare at Beatrice as he let the fire fall back and finally dissipate into the cold salt air.

He gave a quiet grunt and fell to his knees as they rushed over. Beatrice put her arms around him, flinching from the heat that still radiated off his skin, but she only pulled him closer and rocked him as her hands tangled in his singed hair.

"That was..." She sniffed. "It was—"

"Cracking as always, Gio," Carwyn said with a laugh. "By God, you'll manage to kill me someday, but that's absolutely brilliant."

Giovanni sighed and slumped against Beatrice, burying his face in the cool skin at her throat and wrapping his arms around her waist.

"I hate getting shot."

CHAPTER 19

"Just the two left?"

"We were lucky to save those before Gemma got her hands on them."

"And no trace of my son?"

"No, but he left his lackeys here. And he must have known we would take them."

"Interesting and deliberate."

Giovanni and Carwyn were walking up the stairs, Giovanni growing stronger with every step. He wanted to feed again, but didn't want to weaken Beatrice more by asking. She was still limping, and her bruises were more vivid. It irritated him that he could do nothing more to heal her. She had been handling herself extraordinarily well, but he could tell she was starting to crash.

"*Tesoro*," he said as he slipped a hand around her shoulders while clutching the blanket wrapped around his waist. "Will you stay with Jean's men on the top deck while we question them? I'm sure you could handle it, but—"

"I'm okay with skipping the torture part, thanks."

He nodded, relieved she had not insisted on being present for what would be, no doubt, a brutal interrogation.

As they walked through the melted door and onto the open deck, he saw Jean's men securing what was left of the crew, and Gemma held two battered, young vampires by the throat. Terry tossed him a pair of black pants he found somewhere, and Giovanni turned to Beatrice as he saw the three vampires walk away with the captives.

He leaned down and kissed her. "I'll be back soon."

She threw her arms around his neck and whispered in his ear, "Don't be too long. There are things to say."

He nodded and gave her one more lingering kiss before he walked away.

THE INJURED VAMPIRES WERE OBVIOUSLY DISPOSABLE; GIOVANNI WONDERED why Lorenzo had even left them on the ship. They dragged them to the rear deck among the maze of containers the freighter carried.

"No one else?" he asked as he slipped on the borrowed pants.

Terry and Carwyn shook their heads.

"Jean's men searched all the containers," Gemma said, pounding on one that echoed in the dark. "Nothing. Not even a drained human or a bit of clothing."

"*Cazzo*," he muttered and turned his attention back to the vampires at Gemma's feet. "Why did he leave you?"

"Are you the master's father?" One croaked and took a deep breath of the salt air. Giovanni suspected they were both water vampires, turned by Lorenzo to replace the personal army he and Tenzin had destroyed in Greece. Both looked to be in their early twenties. One had an American accent, and the other sounded Irish.

Giovanni knelt down and braced one arm on his knee. "I am Lorenzo's sire."

"We have a message for you," the American said.

"Thought you might." He let the blue flames flare on his torso as the young vampires watched. The American, a young blond man with brown eyes and an innocent face, looked at Giovanni as if he had never seen anything more terrifying. The other wore a placid expression, and his hard, blue eyes did not flinch. "Well?"

It was the Irishman who spoke up. "Lorenzo says he will burn your books, take your woman, turn your child, and one day, you will call him master...and you will love him."

Giovanni cocked his head. "He sacrifices your lives to boast?"

The young American vampire could not seem to look away as the fire grew. Again, it was the other that spoke for them. "We are his humble servants."

Giovanni stared into the young one's frigid blue eyes. He whispered, "Did you kill Ioan ap Carwyn?" He could feel Gemma and Carwyn looking over his shoulders. "Did you kill my friend?"

The young vampire's calm mask finally faltered, and he stuttered when he answered.

"W—we are his humble servants."

Giovanni grabbed him by the neck and took the knife that Terry held out. "You are nothing. But you will tell me everything you know."

He slashed the vampire across the neck and the side, placing his burning hands on the wounds as the young one began to scream.

. . .

Giovanni interrogated them for hours, Terry reviving both with seawater when they fainted.

The two vampires confessed to luring Ioan away from the clinic he had been running in the slums of Dublin. The young Irish vampire, named Sean, had been a patient of Ioan's as a child and used the connection to put the doctor at ease. Then the other vampires, two of whom Gemma had killed in the cargo hold, kidnapped three children who had come to the clinic, threatening to kill them unless Ioan cooperated.

As Giovanni had suspected, his compassionate friend had not hesitated to sacrifice his freedom for the innocent girls. It was the American boy with the guilty brown eyes named Josh who finally broke down and confessed how Ioan had been killed.

Lorenzo met them at the old warehouse, where he tortured the doctor for days about some kind of research he had been conducting on vampire blood types. None of it made sense to the young ones, and Josh broke down sobbing when he confessed that he and his friends had drained the little girls instead of letting them go.

By the time Giovanni finished, he could hear Gemma sniffing quietly in Carwyn's arms as Josh explained how Lorenzo forced Sean to behead Ioan before he tossed his body onto the riverbank on their way out of Dublin. It was the only time the young Irishman showed any sign of guilt.

Giovanni continued questioning them about Lorenzo's plans, but the young water vampires knew nothing of value. Terry checked the time on the reinforced pocket watch he carried and glanced at him.

"We're wasting time. They don't know anything else."

Giovanni left the crumpled vampires twisting on the deck and walked over to Carwyn and Gemma.

"They are yours. Finish them for Deirdre."

He watched stoically as Gemma and Carwyn walked over to the two boys, forcing them down on bloody knees as Josh sobbed. Sean lifted his head defiantly. Carwyn twisted Sean's head off first, tossing it into the ocean before he kicked the body over the railing. The priest stood over the sobbing American boy for a few minutes before his shoulders slumped. Finally, Carwyn knelt down and quietly offered the boy last rites.

Giovanni turned his head away as the boy finished confessing his sins and asking for forgiveness. Carwyn walked away, and Gemma twisted Josh's head off and tossed his remains into the ocean before rushing into Terry's waiting arms.

The four vampires walked back to the front of the boat, using one of the deck showers to wash off the worst of the blood so they didn't startle Beatrice.

"Gio?" Terry called. He was walking behind Giovanni with an arm around Gemma.

"Yes?"

"Your boy knew we were coming."

"Yes."

"Why didn't he take her?"

Giovanni shook his head at the question that had plagued him since they failed to find any trace of his son on the ship. "There is something he wants more than Beatrice at the moment. That is my only guess."

"He's traveling light," Carwyn said. "Only four other vampires with him."

"And now none."

Giovanni muttered, "Who knows where he is? I can't do anything about it right now. I need to see Beatrice."

Carwyn nodded. "Go. We'll question the crew."

He sped across the deck, only slowing when he had her in sight. He walked to a small metal table where she sat huddled, blinking back tears from the wind, which whipped her dark hair into her face. He waved Jean's men away, picked her up, and settled her on his lap as he tried to block the wind.

She sighed and laid her head on his chest before she pulled away. "Oh! Is it okay?"

"It's fine." He drew her back and tucked her under his chin.

"Lorenzo?"

"They knew nothing."

"Did they kill Ioan?"

"They helped."

"Are they dead?"

"Yes."

She paused for a moment before she squeezed his waist and whispered, "Good."

They sat silent for a few moments. He drank in her scent and rocked her when she hugged his waist.

"I told him things, Gio. About my father. About you. I couldn't help it."

It was nothing he hadn't been expecting.

"It's all right. What you knew is not...it's fine. Your father's location is still a mystery to me, so I doubt it will make much sense to Lorenzo, either."

"I thought maybe you hadn't told me everything because you worried about him taking me again."

"There were a few things I held back, but not much."

Giovanni could feel her start to shake, and he held her securely as he examined her, stroking his hands along her limbs and torso, noting every minute flinch or hint of tension. Soon, the shivers overcame her, and he knew the adrenaline that had fueled her for hours was wearing off. The aftershock collided with the stress of the day and caused her to shake.

"Shhh," he soothed her, sending a mild current through his hands to relax her muscles. He rocked her in his warm arms until her breathing had returned to normal and her heart no longer raced.

"I...shit, Gio. I thought..." She sniffed, stuttering for a moment until she took a deep breath. "I thought he was going to bite me. Maybe turn me. He threatened—"

"I'll kill him." He kissed her forehead and tilted her chin up. "As many times as I can."

She snorted before he heard her mutter, "Not if I kill him first."

Giovanni smiled as she placed her cheek over his heart. "That's the spirit of competition, my bloodthirsty girl."

They sat in silence for a few more minutes, rocking in the cool night air.

"Man, I am glad you're here," she said in a shaky voice. "I'm exhausted."

"You are extraordinary. I saw you disarm that man. You didn't even need me there."

He felt her smile. "The librarian finally kicked some ass, didn't she?"

"She most certainly did. And I'm sure you've made Terry and Gemma quite proud." He winked when she looked up.

"And you?"

He shrugged. "I've always been proud of you. I always knew you were extraordinary."

She smiled and relaxed back into his chest. "I slipped and called Lorenzo by his human name. He knows you've told me about your life."

"Don't worry about it."

"Why did you tell me? Why?" She almost looked a little angry. "You knew I would be vulnerable to any vampire who got his hands on me. Why did you tell me?"

He simply smiled. "Because you asked."

"What?" She looked up at him, blinking as the wind made her eyes tear up again.

He leaned down and brushed at the tears. "I told you. I can't deny you anything. You asked. I answered. I like that you know. It's good to be known."

She pressed her hands to his cheeks and looked into his eyes. "You should take the memories away so you'll be safer. I never want to—"

He stopped her with a hard kiss. "Not in a thousand years."

Beatrice stroked his cheeks and let her fingers trail to the back of his neck where she played with the singed ends of his hair.

"I love you, Jacopo."

He blinked, wondering whether he had imagined it.

"What?"

She placed her hands back on his cheeks. "I *love* you, Jacopo...Giovanni... whatever name you choose in a hundred years...or two hundred. I'll love you then, too. *Ubi amo, ibi patria.* Where I love, there is my home. You..." She blinked back tears and gave him a smile. "You are my home."

Giovanni was speechless, so he crushed her to his chest. He held Beatrice for a few moments before pulling away so he could kiss her. He kissed her over and over again, nipping at soft, swollen lips as his heart pounded. "I love you," he whispered. "*Per sempre.* Forever."

"I love you, too. I never really stopped. I can just admit it now."

He broke into a low chuckle that turned into a full laugh. He was happy. More. Joyful. She loved him. He kissed her again.

"I really wish we didn't have an audience right now," she finally said when they came up for air.

Giovanni tucked her head under his chin. "Someday, woman, I will have you to myself."

"We need to get away, just us. Soon. But right now..." She hugged him close. "We have a crew to interrogate and strategy to plan. We still need to murder Lorenzo and find my dad, remember?"

"Somehow, you are not any less sexy as you say this, Beatrice," he said with a smile. "I love you."

"I love you, too. Now, let's go interrogate some Spanish sailors."

"Darling girl," Carwyn walked over and embraced her. "Gemma says you disarmed a six foot man. If I promise not to make you watch wrestling anymore, will you promise not to hurt me?"

She punched Carwyn's side and smiled. "Very funny, old man."

"That'll teach you to run from your bodyguard next time you visit," Terry muttered. "I had to keep your man there from turning the poor sod into a pile of ash last night."

"I'll remember. Thanks to you both, by the way," she said, nodding at Gemma and Terry. "Thanks for beating me up, Gemma. Humans have nothing on you."

"What do you Americans say? 'It was a tough job, but someone had to do it?'"

"Right." Beatrice said and rolled her eyes.

"You should keep that gun, by the way. It's a nice piece," Terry said, nodding to the nine millimeter handgun tucked into her waistband. "Your first spoils of war, B."

"That *is* a good weapon," Giovanni's eyes narrowed. "Why does a Spanish sailor have an H&K?"

"Well, while some of us..." Carwyn waggled his eyebrows at the two of them.

"Were snogging on the deck, others were questioning what was left of the crew. None knew anything about your son, of course."

"It seems like they took Lorenzo and his people on in Rotterdam, but they didn't really know what they were getting into," Gemma added. "Lorenzo was directing the captain off his usual route. London was not a scheduled stop, so thank God for Tywyll's informants, whoever they are."

"Where *does* that little bastard get his information?" Terry muttered.

Carwyn shrugged. "From looking at the ship's records, it looks like they were headed to North Africa. The details are a bit fuzzy, but Lorenzo outfitted the crew with weapons, probably thinking he could use them as fodder if he was threatened."

Giovanni looked between Carwyn and Terry. "Then why is he not here? What tipped him off?"

"Well." Terry glanced at the French humans. "It's more likely 'Who?' is the better question."

Carwyn shook his head. "Apparently, they stopped in Le Havre early this morning, just before dawn. Someone on our side or Jean's must have warned him we were sending a daylight team. There were three containers dropped off and put on trucks. Gemma called Jean. He has people at the port checking where they went, but Lorenzo could have been in any of them."

"And that explains why the bastard didn't take Beatrice," Terry said. "He would never have left himself alone with a human during the day."

"Damn, now I wish he had taken me," Beatrice muttered at his side. Giovanni put an arm around her and stroked her arm, more relieved to have her back than angry at the missed opportunity.

He bent down and kissed the top of her head. "We'll get another chance at him. The most important thing is that you are safe."

"We'll have some questions for Jean's people. And my own, for that matter. Unfortunately, it's probably the human staff," Terry said, shrugging. "They're always the most vulnerable."

"It could be a vampire," Giovanni added. "Lorenzo still has resources we don't know about."

Gemma piped up, "Anything's possible. We'll just have to keep our ears open."

Carwyn looked over at the group of humans surrounded by Jean's men. "What should we do with the crew?"

Giovanni looked at Beatrice, who only shrugged. "Let Jean look into them," he said. "If they were only being used by Lorenzo, I have no quarrel with them, as long as they did not harm Beatrice."

"All the ones who hurt me are taken care of."

The five of them looked around the deck, and Giovanni noticed that the sky was already beginning to lighten with a hint of dawn. They needed to return to Terry's secured boat in the port of Cherbourg.

"Can we go now?" Beatrice asked. "This human is cold and really, really tired."

Terry motioned toward the zodiac floating nearby, piloted by one of his sons. "Your chariot awaits, ass-kicking librarian."

"Haha," she said with a slight blush as she tugged Giovanni in the direction Terry and Gemma were walking. Carwyn walked beside them, looking out toward the sea, and Giovanni wondered whether he was thinking of the two boys who lay at the bottom of the ocean, finally dead after stealing the life of his oldest child.

His friend looked over at him, glancing between him and Beatrice with a bittersweet smile. Carwyn reached a hand over to stroke her hair. "You're safe, darling girl, you're safe."

CHAPTER 20

Cherbourg, France

They took refuge an hour before dawn on the secure yacht one of Terry's lieutenants had brought to Cherbourg harbor for them. When they arrived on deck, they were greeted by a steward that informed them Jean Desmarais was waiting in the saloon, along with two of Terry's people.

"Beatrice," Jean said as she stepped through the door of the luxurious room. He rose from the leather couch, setting down a glass of something red. Whether it was blood or wine, she couldn't tell. "I'm so very relieved you are unharmed. I hope my men were helpful."

"Yes," Giovanni said as they walked across the wood paneled saloon. "It appears I am in your debt, Desmarais."

The keen water vampire cocked an eyebrow. "It was a pleasure to do a favor for a friend."

"I'm sure it was," Terry muttered from behind them. "Now, if you could inform us how exactly *your* old friend managed to hear we were on our way, that'd be greatly appreciated."

Jean stiffened and his narrowed eyes swept the room. "I do not care for your implication, Monsieur Ramsay."

"Like it or not," Carwyn added as he walked in with Gemma. "Lorenzo was taken off that freighter in Le Havre. Someone told him we were coming, and he bolted. Who has the closer tie to the little bastard, hmm?"

Jean's eyes flared, and Giovanni pulled Beatrice closer to his side as the three vampires circled the Frenchman.

"I know nothing of this. I am insulted—"

"Fine," Carwyn said. "Be insulted. You'll answer our questions or we'll know why."

"Hey, guys," Beatrice held up her hands. "Let's calm down. I think we need to—"

"Yes, Jean," Gemma piped up. "Why exactly were the only vampires on that ship sacrificial lambs that died too quickly for my brother's death?"

"I offer you my help and you ambush me?" Jean glared at them. "Do you think if I am harmed you will leave this harbor alive?"

"I reckon we've got a fair shot," Terry said, crossing his arms as his men shut the door.

"As do I," Carwyn added. "Besides, what do you care? You'll be dead if you betrayed us."

Beatrice braced herself against Giovanni, clutching his hand and scanning the layout of the room. It was open, but there was no way Jean could escape. He was completely outnumbered.

"I did not betray you." Jean's chin jutted out arrogantly. "I do not dishonor myself by turning on an ally. Unlike *some* here, I—"

"You were allied with Lorenzo for two hundred years," Terry growled.

"Do you know *why* I broke ties with him?" Jean spit out. "Do you know why I am supporting you? As charming as the De Novo girl is, she's certainly not my *only* motivation."

Beatrice leaned forward. Jean was tense, Terry and Carwyn stood across from him with their arms crossed on their chests, and Gemma stood at the door, guarding it like some lethal angel with eyes trained on the rakish Frenchman. But when Beatrice glanced up, she noticed that Giovanni was completely relaxed. His arm slid around her waist, and he wore an almost bemused expression.

"Tell us why we should believe you," he said. "For some reason, I think I do."

Carwyn glared. "Gio—"

"He's not the only one who could have told Lorenzo," Giovanni said with a shrug. "I want to hear what he has to say."

Jean stepped toward him. "No, I did not give Lorenzo any information. Nor would I have. My daughter will forgive me for speaking of this." He glanced at Beatrice before looking away. "Louise had one child while she was still human. The boy was raised in my home, and his family was under my aegis. Louise remained very close to her son's children and grandchildren. One of her granddaughters was on holiday in Greece ten years ago."

A sick feeling began to churn in Beatrice's stomach. She saw Jean's eyes swing to hers and they locked. The truth was written on his face.

"Oh no," she whispered as the tears came to her eyes.

"Julie had met Lorenzo before, so she accepted his invitation. She thought she was safe. She was not."

Beatrice's face fell as she flashed back to the young bodies Lorenzo's men had tossed over the cliffs in Greece to be swallowed by the Aegean Sea.

"There were so many," she whispered, blinking back tears. "I believe you."

Giovanni squeezed her waist. "As do I."

At Giovanni's quiet declaration, Beatrice felt the tension drain out of the room, though all parties kept their guarded positions as the questions flew.

"Lorenzo killed a girl? One under your protection?" Gemma asked from the doorway. "Why would he be so stupid?"

"Or so arrogant?" Terry added.

Jean was staring at Giovanni. "You have been fooling yourself, di Spada, hiding away in your books. Your son has many powerful friends. In the last ten years, his influence has grown. I do not know why. It is a testament to your connections that you were given the girl five years ago." He nodded toward Beatrice. "You think you damaged him? He is still more powerful and connected than you know."

"What do you mean? What do you know?" Giovanni asked.

Jean only shook his head. "You think you have allies? Everyone has an agenda. Everyone."

"What's yours?" Beatrice asked.

The Frenchman turned. "My family. Nothing remains except family. Power. Wealth. All these change, but my family remains. My daughter was distraught. Her family lost faith in us. My own reputation was damaged to have lost one under my protection. Trust me." He looked around the room. "None in my company bear Lorenzo any goodwill."

"And I vouch for my people," Terry said.

"So where does that leave us?" Carwyn asked, looking around the room in frustration. "Someone told him. One of our humans? Someone manipulated? Bribed?"

Jean shrugged. "I will have the port checked immediately. If there is any indication where the containers went or who arranged the shipment, I will find it. I have many people in Le Havre."

"Don't most shipping containers have GPS now?" Beatrice asked.

"These wouldn't," Giovanni muttered. "I think you taught him a lesson about technology, *tesoro*. It would be easy enough to make them untraceable, and since there were three containers—"

"He could be on any one of three trucks going to any one of three locations," Gemma sighed.

Beatrice looked around the room. "But there has to be a way of finding out more."

Everyone was silent, standing around the room with the strange blank expressions she hated, each vampire lost in their own thoughts.

"Gio?"

"Beatrice—"

"Who told you?"

He frowned. "What?"

"*Who?* Who told you that Lorenzo had taken me? You knew what ship I was on; Jean's team found the boat too fast for you to be looking very long. Someone told you which one I was on. I was barely there for a day. Whoever told you knew where I was and had to know you were coming for me, so *who told you?*"

"That little bastard," Gemma murmured.

She felt Giovanni's skin heat.

"Tywyll."

Gravesend, England

BEATRICE LOOKED AROUND WITH A POORLY VEILED LOOK OF DISDAIN.

"This is the dirtiest pub I've ever seen."

"It definitely ranks quite high, *tesoro*."

"Is it…floating?"

Beatrice looked at the floor, which seemed to rock and sway under their feet. She saw a beer bottle roll in the corner as the pub near the mouth of the River Thames rose with the swell of the water. Then she looked into Giovanni's taciturn face.

"Are you going to kill him? Can you?"

He thought for a long moment before he shrugged. "Doubtful, and definitely not until you get your information. I have a feeling that Tywyll has a bit to tell us."

"He's really old, isn't he?"

"I believe so. No one knows. I've never met anyone that claimed to know him before he became what he is now."

She frowned and pulled his arm to sit next to her in the dark booth with its cracked leather seats. Giovanni sat with his back to the wall and his eyes on the door as the dark pub rose and fell.

When they had returned to London just before dawn the night before, they were met at the door of the Mayfair house with a handwritten note.

Mariposa—

Come to The Cockleshell in Gravesend with the Italian tonight at nine o'clock. I have information for you.

—Tywyll

"What is he?"

"A trader. A conduit. And apparently, someone who knew your father."

She whispered, "My dad and my grandma are the only ones that have ever called me 'Mariposa.' And it's not something he would have shared with just anyone."

"Which is why we are meeting him alone at the dirtiest pub in Gravesend, instead of being accompanied by twenty of Terry's most vicious minions."

She smiled and tried to lighten his mood as she slipped an arm around his waist. "You should totally get some minions."

He smiled despite himself. "Isn't that what Benjamin is for? He's a minion-in-training."

She snickered and pulled him down for a kiss. Between rushing back to London, seeing a doctor for her injuries, and questioning Terry's human staff, Beatrice had little to no time alone with Giovanni, and she could tell the stress of the previous three nights was wearing on them both.

"I'm exhausted," she whispered as she laid her head on his shoulder. He pressed a kiss to her forehead.

"I know."

His restless eyes continued to scan the dark, almost empty, pub. She sat next to him and left a hand on his knee, needing the connection. Giovanni had been eager to escape the city, wanting to whisk her away somewhere safe and away from prying eyes and ears as soon as they had returned. But after they received the note, Beatrice and Carwyn had insisted it was important to meet the mysterious water vampire—even if he was the source of the betrayal—and Giovanni had reluctantly agreed.

She heard the door open and an electric current radiated up her arm. She could feel Giovanni's skin heat against hers.

"Tywyll," he said in a low voice.

"This is Stephen's girl then." She looked up. "Ay, ye' are. Look at the eyes. Just like yer father."

She stared at the unassuming man wearing dirty work clothes. To anyone else, he would have fit right in, a hardworking middle-aged man out for a pint at the pub after work. Beatrice, however, took note of his inhuman paleness, the energy that seemed to vibrate off him, and the fangs that peeked from the corners of his mouth.

"How do you know my father?"

"Can I sit without fear for meself, fire-starter? Do I have yer word?"

She could tell it was a struggle for him, but she saw Giovanni give a slight nod out of the corner of her eye.

"For now, yes."

"Fer now'll do fine." He sat across from them and raised three fingers toward the bar. "I reckon we'll stay out of each other's way after that, eh?"

"It depends very much on what you say, waterman."

"How do you know my father?" Beatrice asked again.

The old vampire turned his eyes toward her.

"Yer father is a fine one, miss. I don't like many, but I liked him. Met him at this very pub."

A shiver crossed her neck and she felt Giovanni's hand squeeze hers under the table. "My father was here?"

Tywyll paused as an old man came to set three dark pints on the table in front of them. Tywyll took his and drank before he answered.

"He was. Ten years ago. He'd just come from the North and he was makin' his way out of the country. Needed a bit of help. Someone gave him my name. Had gold and he didn't talk too much. I like that in a vampire."

Giovanni leaned forward and passed one of the pints to Beatrice as he set the other in front of himself. The glasses were surprisingly clean.

"I heard rumors about him ten years ago," Giovanni said. "About the books he had. He was referred to me for a job, but no one seemed to be able to find him."

Tywyll's eyes almost twinkled. "Well now, that might ha' been my doin'. He was awful young then, and he didn't know much. I may ha' kept him out of the way for a bit from those lookin' for him."

"Why?" Beatrice asked. "You protected him? Why? And if you protected my father, why would you sell us out to Lorenzo?"

"Did I sell you out?" Tywyll's head tilted to the side and she could feel the heat start to radiate from Giovanni. She squeezed his knee and felt the energy in the air dissipate slightly. "You were taken, but it looks like yer here and safe to me, girl."

Giovanni's voice was taut. "Do you deny informing my son we were coming after Beatrice?"

Tywyll squinted as he took another drink. "I may have...repaid a favor, fire-starter. I *always* repay my favors. But I wouldn't be bringing harm to Stephen's dear girl." Tywyll's eyes darkened and Beatrice saw the cold-blooded killer beneath the unassuming demeanor of the small man. "Now, my debt is repaid, so I'll ask you: were you hurt, Mariposa?"

Giovanni spit something out in a language she didn't recognize, and Tywyll glared at him before responding in kind. She didn't recognize the language, and she was beginning to get frustrated with their quick, heated exchange. She saw tension lift from Tywyll's shoulders before his eyes shuttered closed. He fell silent and took a long drink of his beer.

"Interesting," Tywyll muttered.

"What?" She turned to Giovanni, irritated and confused. "What was that?"

"I'll tell you later. Tywyll knew your father. He hid him from Lorenzo for a time. He has an...interest in you. Nothing to be concerned about."

"Do you know where my dad is?" She turned to Tywyll, reaching across the table to grab his cold hand. She saw Giovanni start, but Tywyll only squeezed her slight fingers. "Please, do you know—"

"No, girl, I don't. I taught him well. You'll not find Stephen unless he wants to be found. That was my gift to him. In my many years, I've not considered many friends, but yer father was one."

Giovanni put a hand on her shoulder and drew her back. "Why did you tell Lorenzo we were coming for Beatrice?"

"Did the *mariposa* figure it out?" Tywyll asked with a small smile. "I'll bet she did. She's got the look of her father; I'll bet she has his mind, too. Ye' are the butterfly, aren't ye?" Tywyll said. "I'll be keen to see what happens with ye."

"I don't know what you're talking about," she whispered. She was lying, she knew exactly what he was talking about, and from the look in his eyes, Tywyll did too.

"Don't ye'?" Tywyll took another drink and turned to Giovanni. "Why did I tell yer son? I owed a very old favor to him, Giovanni Vecchio. One he was keen to collect. I do have a reputation to maintain, and I'll not be backing out of a favor owed. However, I don't owe him anymore. The ship he was on before I got word to him was bound for two ports—Port Said in Egypt and Shanghai, China."

Tywyll directed his words to Beatrice. "Now, I've no idea where he was goin' after that, and I don't know his location now. Not my job. But he's still after my friend, so I've got no objection to answering what ye' want to ask, if it suits my mood, and ye' ask the right questions."

Beatrice could sense the buzzing anticipation from Giovanni. She still didn't know what she wanted to ask, her mind was whirling from the night's revelations, so she looked up and nodded at him. A small smile quirked Giovanni's mouth as he began questioning Tywyll.

"What did Stephen De Novo take from my son?"

"Good question. Gold, for one. And a lot of it. Unusual stuff. Old. Some of it melted down. All unmarked, not that I minded."

She caught the minute flicker in Giovanni's eyes and she knew he recognized what the other vampire was talking about. "What about the books?"

"*Books?*" Tywyll cocked his head. "Not a good question."

Beatrice whispered, "Book. What about the *book*?"

Tywyll nodded. "Better question."

Giovanni looked confused. "Only one?"

"Only one he kept with him. Only one yer boy really wanted."

They all seemed to lean toward each other, and her heart pounded.

"What book does my son want?"

Tywyll smirked. "If I could read ancient Persian, I'd have a much better idea. Unfortunately, Stephen didn't teach me. Don't know that he could read it himself—though, I've no doubt he can by now. When he escaped yer son, he only knew that this book was the one Lorenzo guarded most carefully."

"He didn't know what it was?"

"Oh—" The old vampire's eyes twinkled. "He had an idea."

Tywyll paused to finish off his beer as Beatrice fought the urge to reach across the table and shake him. "Well?" she finally asked.

"What do you know of alchemy, Mariposa?"

Giovanni shook his head and slumped in his seat. "Spells and magic," he muttered. "Ridiculous. What does that tell us? Nothing."

"Arrogance, fire-starter. It's an old science."

Beatrice looked between them, confused by their demeanor. "Wait, isn't alchemy just an early form of chemistry?"

"Yes," Tywyll said, as Giovanni muttered, "No."

She could almost hear the "professor voice" before Giovanni opened his mouth. "Alchemy is magic, not chemistry. And most certainly not a real science. Philosopher's stones. Gold from lead. Elixir of life. Not science. Magic."

Tywyll cut his eyes toward her. "Oh...immortality, manipulation of the elements, the creation of life itself. I can't imagine why a curious vampire would find those things worthy of further study."

They all fell silent around the table while Giovanni and Tywyll exchanged looks she couldn't quite decipher. "So—" She looked back and forth between them. "—what is it? Is it science, like amnis? Something natural we just don't understand yet? Or is it magic?"

Tywyll chuckled while Giovanni looked chastened.

"Ye've nabbed yerself a smart one. You two won't bore each other anytime soon."

Giovanni shook his head. "We will have to consider what Lorenzo may have found."

"Or what my father did," she added. "If he was willing to risk himself for this book..." Beatrice felt her throat tighten up. "I have to think it's all been worth it."

Giovanni pulled her into his side and she felt him press a kiss to the top of her head. She glanced at Tywyll across the table, but the old vampire only wore a mysterious smile.

"Well," he said as he shrugged. "I'm tired of answering questions. This is the most I've talked in years. I've a mind to get home now."

Beatrice leaned into Giovanni's shoulder. "Where is home, Tywyll?"

He winked. "Here and there, girl. The river, that's my home."

Giovanni tossed a few pounds on the table and they rose to leave. They walked out of the dark pub to see their car and driver waiting a block away and a long, wooden skiff tied up to the side of the floating pub.

She looked at the cagey vampire, who had given her more clues to her father's whereabouts than she'd had in the five years she'd searched for him.

"Thank you, Tywyll."

"Yer welcome, Mariposa. He gave me that name, you know. I have a feeling he thought you might come looking for me."

"Smart man." She heard Giovanni murmur.

"Smarter vampire," Tywyll said.

The river surged beside them and Beatrice heard a glass fall to the floor and shatter inside.

"Why on Earth did you want to meet here?" Beatrice asked as she looked from the ramshackle bar to the old water vampire. "This bar is just…" She curled her lip as the strange man chuckled.

Tywyll stood on the dock, his hands tucked in his pockets, and she could feel the sudden energy that charged the air.

"Oh," he said, "it has its features."

Looking over his shoulder, Beatrice noticed the boats moored nearby begin to drift to the bank. There was a soft ripple, and a squawking rose as a flock of ducks took off from the center channel. In the distance, she saw a fishing boat begin to change course. Then Beatrice gasped as the The Cockleshell pub itself began to rise as the river pushed it up and toward them.

Beatrice could only gape as the whole of the River Thames waited at attention for the old water vampire. He rocked back and forth, and the river, and everything floating, mirrored his small movement.

"Wow," she whispered.

Finally, Tywyll shrugged and the river seemed to heave a sigh before the boats drifted back downriver, and the current flowed out toward the sea. The pub settled back into its slip and the ducks landed over the rippling reflection of the moon.

He winked at her. "I like the beer, too." Tywyll walked toward his skiff and stepped aboard. He untied the ropes and stood watching them as the boat began to drift away.

"Find yer father, Mariposa. He needs ye.' And Giovanni Vecchio, don't let your arrogance blind ye to the schemes of others."

Giovanni frowned. "What aren't you telling me, waterman?"

"Oh…" He smiled. "A lot."

Tywyll tipped his hat toward Beatrice as she clutched Giovanni's hand. "Ye' know more than ye' realize, girl. Yer father wants ye' to find him."

Tywyll drifted away, and the moon rippled in the quiet wake. Beatrice and Giovanni stood on the dock and she wrapped her arms around him, burying her face in his chest and inhaling his dark, smoky scent. She could feel his arms embrace her, and she tilted her face up for a kiss.

"Do we believe him?" she whispered.

His eyes narrowed as he searched the inky night. "I think we do."

"We've got a lot to think about."

"Yes, we do. But not here."

She paused and held him tighter as the exhaustion ate at her. She could feel his arm holding her up as they began the walk back to the car.

"Gio?"

"Yes, *tesoro*?"

"I want to go home. Take me to Cochamó."

Giovanni looked down and met her tired eyes. She saw a flare of excitement in his gaze and a smile teased the corner of his mouth. He nodded. "We'll leave tonight."

CHAPTER 21

Santiago, Chile

He stared at her profile in the dim light of the theater, admiring how the lights from the stage caught bits of red in her hair and made her skin glow. Giovanni had seen the play before, but Beatrice had not, and she stared at the actors with a small smile flirting around her mouth.

She must have caught his gaze from the corner of her eye.

What? she mouthed.

"I finally took you on a date," he whispered.

She laughed silently, and he reached across to cup her cheek before he bent and pressed a kiss to her mouth. He felt the curl of her lips against his own as she smiled and placed her cool hand on his jaw. He pulled away so she could continue to watch the performance of the Lorca play, and she felt for his hand, laying it on her lap and knitting their fingers together.

Beatrice was stunning in a black silk dress, her neck and shoulders bare. He could see the flutter of the pulse in her neck, and a flush rose in her cheeks. He made no show of hiding his hungry stare. Her dark eyes kept glancing between his rapt face and the stage; he could hear her heartbeat quicken as his amnis reached out to her. The air was lush with her scent in their corner of the dark theater. After another twenty minutes, she silently rose from her seat and took his hand, pulling him up and out the door. As soon as they reached the dark hallway, she pressed him against the wall and lifted her mouth to his as he met her in a passionate kiss.

The blood had already begun to pulse in his veins when she whispered, "Take me back to the hotel."

Giovanni said nothing as he wrapped an arm around her waist and escorted her down the stairs of the theater and into the starlit night.

They rushed through the lively streets of the Providencia district, ignoring the flow of pedestrians and the call of music from the clubs, stopping only at lights where they kissed without thought of the people around them. It was eleven o'clock, and the warm streets of Santiago were filled with late summer crowds, but they ignored all distractions as they hurried back to the private entrance of their hotel.

Giovanni paused when they were finally alone, pulling off his jacket and taking a calming breath to cool his skin. She stood near the open terrace doors, looking out on the lights of the city. The night air was soft as he placed his hands on the bare skin of her shoulders.

"Tesoro mio," he murmured. "My Beatrice."

He bent down to kiss behind her ear and closed his eyes as he felt the heat rise between them. He brushed at her dark hair, smoothing it away as it fell loose down her back. He could feel the rush of his blood as his heart picked up pace. Giovanni struggled to control the fire that wanted to burst from his skin.

"Do you know how I love you?" she whispered.

He wrapped both his arms around her waist and held her to his chest for a few moments, breathing in her scent and listening to the rush of her pulse. His lips kissed above the single button that held the halter of her dress in place. "How do you love me?" he murmured against her skin.

Beatrice turned in his arms and placed a hand on his cheek. "I love you forever."

He paused, staring into her eyes. They no longer held even a trace of doubt. She had said that she loved him, but for the first time, as Beatrice looked at him, Giovanni felt as if he held her heart in his gaze. There was no caution. No reservation. His breath caught in his throat and his heart raced.

"Don't you know," she said with dancing eyes, "how I adore you?"

Giovanni smiled to hear his own words from so many months ago repeated on her lips.

"Do you love me?" he asked.

"You know I do."

"And do you trust me?"

A slow smile bloomed on her face. "Yes."

"Finally." Giovanni's lips swept down to meet her own, and his left hand came around her waist and pulled her away from the window. He returned to her bare shoulder, trailing his hand up to slip the button of her halter loose, then down to catch the edge of her dress.

He felt her quick intake of breath, and she gave a small cry when both his palms cupped her breasts and his mouth bent to her collarbone.

"Too long," he groaned against her skin. The current raced over his skin. "Beatrice, I—"

"I love you, Gio," he heard her whisper. "One life is not enough."

His hands slipped the rest of her dress down her body. Most of her bruises had healed, and Beatrice stood before him with nothing hiding her from his eyes.

"I have seen masterpieces," he said. "But nothing that compares to you." It was the truth, because no work of an artists' hand could compare to her when she looked at him with trust in her eyes.

Beatrice smiled and reached for his shirt, undressing him as his hands trailed along her arms and his ancient heart beat for her. Her skin was flushed, and he felt his fangs grow long in his mouth, but he was not hungry for blood.

Careful. Careful. Careful.

She was mortal, exquisitely, delectably mortal. If he let loose the full breadth of his desire, the fire would consume them both.

"I've waited so long," she murmured, running her hands over his chest. "And you are everything I ever dreamed."

Giovanni shuddered under her hands, reveling in the sight of her fingers tracing his chest. His stomach. Down to his waist...

"Enough." He lifted her in his arms and walked to the bed, setting her down, naked and spread before him.

A roar of hunger.

Careful.

He took a measured breath.

Giovanni lay down facing Beatrice and let his fingertips explore the dips and curves of her body before his mouth followed, tasting and licking along her skin, letting his amnis spread where they touched until their senses were so heightened he thought the flames would burst from his fingertips. He sated himself on the taste of her, careful not to let his fangs cut her skin.

'Love is a single soul dwelling in two bodies.'

He could feel the blood in her veins; even the tiny hairs on her arms reached for him as they embraced.

"Kiss me." She sounded as desperate as he felt.

Giovanni rose to meet her lips again; he deepened his kiss, exploring her mouth as her hands traced along his jawline and the back of his neck. She pulled him closer, her heart pounding against his heated chest.

"The heat," he panted as he pulled away to let her breath. "Is it too much?"

"I'm fine." She pulled him back down. "We're fine."

He focused on her eyes, her mouth, her breasts, and the pulsing life he held in his arms. He braced himself over her, threading his hands with hers and ducking down to taste her again before he whispered the question he had waited so many years to ask.

"Forever?"

A brilliant smile spread over her face. "Yes."

He pressed his cheek to hers when he entered her, and she cried out. The needy sound tripped some long-buried instinct and he drove in to the hilt, bucking between her hips with a barely concealed growl. He wanted to sink his fangs into her neck; he wanted to make her scream.

He held back.

Mortal, a softer voice whispered. *Mortal.*

But for how long?

Holding tight to the control that had become the law of his eternity, Giovanni focused on Beatrice. Her heat. Her heart. The catch in her breath as she approached her climax. Giovanni focused every sense on her.

"Giovanni!" she gasped as she came. "I love you. I love you so much."

Giovanni could smell the scent of smoke surrounding them when he reached his own climax, but he did not let the fire take him. If the flames took him, they would take Beatrice. And that could never, ever happen. So he clamped down on his control and let the sounds of the city mask their cries as they made love through the night.

Cochamó Valley, Chile

"You really are a better rider."

"Told you."

He smiled at her flushed cheeks and tousled hair. Only the thought of hiding away in the Cochamó house could have pulled him away from the quiet hotel room where they spent the past week. They had scarcely come up for air. She teased him that it was a good thing he didn't have to breathe. Giovanni had to agree.

"You should see her with a rifle, Gio," Gustavo remarked as he led them into the valley. "She's an excellent shot."

"I got to be pretty good with a nine millimeter, too!"

Giovanni smiled as she and Gustavo caught up on news. In many ways, Beatrice was more familiar with his friends than he was. He had spent so much time flying around the world the previous five years that he was out of touch with those he cared for most. As he looked at the woman who had captivated him, he let out a contented sigh.

"Gio," he heard Gustavo say, and he looked over to the burly earth vampire. "Tell me what the current news is. Should Isabel and I be on our guard? Should we alert our families?"

He frowned at the reminder that all was not right in his world. "The last time I talked to the Frenchman, he had tracked the three cargo containers that left the ship, but he had no idea which one Lorenzo was in. The best indications we have say he has gone east. We've already sent word to Tenzin, but until we know more—"

"And B's father? Is there any news of him?"

Giovanni glanced at her. "No." The flushed, happy look Beatrice had worn fled with the mention of her father and Lorenzo.

He sidled his horse next to hers and reached an arm around her waist. She leaned into him and allowed him to pull her across his lap. He nodded toward Gustavo, tossed him the reins, and watched as the other vampire spurred his horse, leaving them behind. They rode in silence for a few minutes as she leaned her head against his shoulder.

"I'm starting to think he's really dead."

"We have no reason to think that, *tesoro*."

He helped her swing a leg over and scooted back so she sat comfortably in front of him in the gaucho saddle. He handed her the reins and placed his arms around her waist. They rode in silence over the summer meadows lit by moonlight, past the rushing waterfalls, and through the dense forests on the trail to their house.

She finally spoke again. "What was your happiest time?"

"Ever?"

"Yeah? Did you like it better before electricity and all the modern stuff that trips you up?"

He only chuckled, and she looked over her shoulder.

"What?"

"My happiest time is now, woman. Isn't that obvious?"

He could see the flush creep onto her cheeks and down her neck. He smiled wider and let his chin rest on her shoulder as his hands trailed up her torso, teasing under her breasts.

"Hey now." She nudged him. "I'm not sure I'm *that* good at riding."

"We could find out. It's good to challenge yourself."

"No." She laughed. "Besides, you can control yourself for another couple hours until we get home."

"But can you? Remember..." He reached down to tickle the inside of her knee and she squirmed. The horse gave a disapproving whinny.

"Behave!"

"You never should have let me find out where you are ticklish. That was a strategic error, Beatrice."

"I'll figure out your weakness one of these days."

You, he thought, though he remained silent. She was, perhaps, his greatest weakness. They rode quietly for a few more minutes before she spoke again.

"Really, though? Now? With the mortal danger and running everywhere?"

"Well." He frowned. "I won't miss that. But you're with me now. And you are safe."

She looked over her shoulder and lifted her mouth for a kiss. "I'm happy, too."

"How long do you want to stay?"

"How long *can* we?"

He shrugged. "We probably shouldn't leave Benjamin with Caspar and your grandmother for much longer, or they'll never agree to babysit again."

She burst into laughter, and he joined her. He knew she missed the boy, too. They had spoken to Ben that afternoon and he was doing well with the closest thing he had to grandparents, but he did mention that he missed his basketball hoop.

"When all this is over, *if* it's ever over—"

"It will be over someday, I promise you."

"When it's over, what do you want?"

"To do?"

"Yes."

He thought for a few moments. "Just to have my life back. With you. Like it was when we first met."

He felt her sigh in front of him as they crossed the last bridge before they reached the house. "I want that, too. Just working with you and being normal."

"Oh yes." He snapped his fingers and tossed a blue flame into the night. It hovered in front of them, lighting the way so she could see as they passed through the overhanging trees. "Very normal."

She smiled. "You know what I mean."

Kissing her cheek, he hugged her around the waist as they broke through the last of the trees and into the meadow that surrounded their home.

"I know what you mean."

MOONLIGHT POURED OVER HER BARE SKIN AS SHE MOVED OVER HIM AT THE edge of the secluded pool. The mist from the waterfall surrounded them, cooling his skin as they made love. She was a vision as she rode him, her head thrown back in the cool night air as the water dripped down her neck. He reared up, letting his fangs scrape the valley between her breasts before he teased her neck, flicking his tongue behind her ear until she moaned.

"Yes," she panted. "More."

Giovanni felt her hands run through his damp hair and down his neck as she drew his head toward the pounding pulse in her throat. His tongue traced over her skin as they moved together, and he wrapped one arm around her back to steady her as he tugged her neck to the side, exposing the lush vein.

"Gio," she whispered. "*Now.*"

He emitted a low growl before he sunk his fangs into her, drawing on the rich blood she offered as he felt her tense and shudder around him. She cried into the night as she came, and he grasped the ends of her dark hair as she arched back.

She didn't stop moving and he hissed when he felt the edge approaching. Her fingers bit into the thick muscle of his shoulders, and he pulled away from her neck to taste her mouth. He moaned into their kiss, then bent to lick the small wounds at her throat before he buried his face in her hair and groaned in release. He didn't pull away, but stayed linked with her, enjoying the shivers that coursed over their skin as they rocked together under the stars.

"*Tesoro.*" He listened with satisfaction to her racing heart. "Remind me to suggest swimming more often."

"It is your favorite waterfall."

"Even more so now," he said with a grin.

They were soaked, and he framed her face with his hands as the water collected on their skin, running down in rivulets as they smiled and laughed together and the moon reflected in the ripples of dark water beside them.

Later, they stretched naked on the wool blanket she had tucked into their saddlebag, and he wrapped his body around her, chasing away the night chill. His hands explored each curve, leisurely studying her unique topography. In five hundred years, he'd had lovers he'd cared for, but none like her. Never before had one woman captured his heart, his body, and his mind as Beatrice had.

"What are you thinking right now?" she asked as his fingers traced over the soft rise of her belly.

"I am thinking, for the first time in five hundred years, I wish I could give you children. I regret that I cannot. It is not possible."

She lay back, silent as she looked up at the stars. Finally, he heard her soft voice.

"Have I ever told you about my mom?"

"Not really."

"She didn't want me. She and my dad were never married, though I think he did ask at some point. But she didn't want to be pregnant or married. She kind of... had me for my dad. Then she took off."

"She was a foolish woman."

Beatrice shrugged, and he clamped down on his instinctive anger.

"She didn't want to be a mom. She could have gotten rid of me. She could have abandoned me to some stranger, but she didn't. She gave me to my dad and my grandparents. And they loved me. So I can't be too angry with her. I was probably better off."

"My mother died of a fever. I think I was around five years old. I'm not sure. I know I was very young."

"And then your uncle found you."

"And then my uncle's friends found me—purely by chance—and apparently I was a replica of my father, so they knew I was his bastard."

"But your uncle was kind."

"Yes." He nodded. "Very kind."

"So, Jacopo…" She rolled him over on his back and laid a slender arm across his chest as she met his gaze. "We know better than anyone that family is what you make it."

"You would make a wonderful mother," he whispered.

"Maybe I will be one day…somehow," she said with a soft smile. "I think I have time."

He tucked a strand of hair behind her ear and brought his mouth to hers for a soft kiss. "Yes, you will have time."

A WEEK LATER THEY WERE LYING IN THEIR BED IN THE EARLY EVENING AS A fire burned in the grate and reflected off the mica in the hewn granite wall. Beatrice was watching the lights dance and laughing at a story Ben had related when she'd called him that afternoon.

"So he was reading the recipe and somehow read one quarter *teaspoon* as one quarter *cup*," she said as she held back the laughter.

"And?"

The incredulity covered her face as she looked up at him.

"Really?"

"What?"

"Haven't you ever baked?"

He cocked an eyebrow at her. "Only the bad guys."

She rolled over to fold her arms on his chest.

"Well, there was a little bit of cleaning to do when the brownies ran all over the oven."

"As long as he was the one doing the cleaning."

"I have no doubt of that. My grandma has been forcing reluctant men to clean for years. My grandpa. My dad…"

She choked, and he caught her chin between his fingers, forcing her to meet his eyes.

"Do you want to know?"

"What are you talking about?" she muttered.

"You have very carefully not asked me any more about your father. You know I was looking for him. I know you received the postcards, but you seem reluctant to ask any other questions."

She pursed her lips and wiped at a tear that had come to one eye. "I'm not sure what I thought. I guess part of me always hoped *he* would find *me*. That he would come to L.A."

"He was in San Francisco once, but that was the closest he ever came that I know of."

She thought for a few more minutes as he played with the ends of her hair.

"Okay, tell me what you found."

"Whatever tricks Tywyll taught your father, he learned them well. Combine that with a brain like yours, enhanced by better vampire processing and memory...he's stayed one step ahead of me for years."

"But you found—"

"What is the saying? Breadcrumbs, *tesoro*. I found breadcrumbs."

He pulled her closer as he continued. "As I told you before, in each location I found some clue. I would get a call, or a note, or some indication that he had been inquiring after one of my books or my services, something like that."

"But when you got there—"

"He would be gone. I would always find a hotel room, recently occupied, with some trace—a note, a receipt, something that would tell me it had been his."

"And that's where you sent the postcards from?"

"Yes."

"So he didn't try to hide that he'd been there."

Giovanni shook his head. "Quite the opposite. It was almost as if he was waving a flag, then ducking out of sight."

He could almost hear the wheels turning in her head.

"So what if the locations were the clue? There has to be a—a method. A pattern, some—"

"I thought the same," he said, shaking his head. "I thought the locations must be some kind of code or pattern, but there was nothing. I even played with the latitude and longitude for each city, looking for some kind of method to the seemingly random appearances."

"So why did you send the postcards?"

"In the back of my mind, I thought that perhaps the cities would mean something to you. I thought that perhaps you would see something I wasn't."

He could feel her sigh as he stroked her back to try to ease the tension building in her muscles.

"No," she finally whispered. "Those weren't even places he talked about going. I mean, some of them were, but they were all fairly major cities, so there wasn't anything that stood out."

"Yes, after that first sighting in Iraklion, all the cities were major urban—"

"Where?"

"Iraklion or Heraklion. Crete. It was the first place I got any news of him. The director of the Archaeological Museum—"

"You didn't send me a postcard from Iraklion."

He blinked. "I'm sorry. I didn't think to start sending them to you until I'd left Crete, and by then—"

She bolted up, staring into the fire, and he heard her heart begin to race. "Crete?"

He sat up next and placed a hand on her shoulder.

"I'm sorry I didn't send one from Iraklion, but it's hardly a major city. He didn't even stay very long—"

"But it's *Crete*!"

He frowned. "Beatrice, I don't understand—"

"Knossos. Minos." She turned to Giovanni with burning eyes. She clasped his face between her hands. "It's Minos, Gio. The minotaur!"

"Beatrice, what are you trying to tell me?"

She began shaking her head and a desperate look came to her eye.

"Not breadcrumbs. Not breadcrumbs... it's a *labyrinth*."

CHAPTER 22

Beatrice's heart raced.
"Daddy! Daddy, the string game, Daddy!"

She tore out of the bedroom, searching for the unassuming reference book she'd spotted on the bottom shelf in one of the living room bookcases years ago.

"Beatrice, slow down. You're going to trip if you don't—"
"I'm going to find the treasure!"
"You think you're clever enough to solve the puzzle, Mariposa?"

She searched for the blue binding as Giovanni rushed out of the bedroom to join her. "Beatrice—"

"The string game. I called it the string game when I was little," she muttered. The book wasn't where she remembered. Her eyes raked over the shelves in the living room, searching for the familiar book as the memories poured over her.

"What?" Giovanni's voice called from the edge of the room. "The string game?"

"Stephen, are you two playing that silly game again? I'm going to trip and break my neck one of these days!"
"Relax, Mom. But don't go in the living room, okay?"
"Grandma, I'm in the maze right now!"

She finally spotted it on the bottom shelf in the bookcase closest to the front door; she rushed over. "It used to drive my grandmother nuts. She was always tripping over the strings that we put up."

"*Tesoro*, what are you—"

"Theseus and the Minotaur. My dad read me the story...I don't know how many times. It was my favorite." Her hands pulled the book out and raced over to the large kitchen table, slamming it down.

"Beatrice, if you need an atlas, I have much better editions—"

"No, no, this is the one we had." She waved her hand as she opened it. "We had this one in our house. It would be this one."

"Look for the clues, Mariposa. I left you clues all over the house; find them and follow the string to the treasure."

"Like Theseus. Follow the string out of the labyrinth."

"When I was a child, my father would read me the Greek myths. I loved them. He read them to me over and over again, but my favorite was the story of Theseus and the Minotaur."

"The minotaur in the labyrinth?"

"Yeah." She nodded. "Theseus goes to Crete, right? His father sends him to King Minos of Crete."

"In Knossus, the ancient excavation site right outside of Iraklion."

"Exactly. Theseus kills the Minotaur in the middle of the labyrinth, but then he has to find his way out of the maze again. Luckily, he was smart. He tied a string near the entrance and held onto it so he could find his way out again."

She opened the atlas and flipped to the large map of Greece, pointing toward the island of Crete. "There's no way my father picked that location at random. It was our game; he was telling me to play the string game."

"What's the first clue?"

"'What goes up when the rain comes down?'"

"Solve the riddle, Beatrice."

Giovanni was standing in a corner of the living room, his arms crossed as he stared at her like she was a crazy person. "Can you please explain from the beginning? What is the 'string game?'"

She looked up at his beautiful, confused face and smiled. "I love mazes, always have, partly because of that story. Solving mazes, building mazes. I told my dad one time that I wanted to build a labyrinth at our house, but how do you make a maze in a little, tiny house, right?"

"...'comes up when the rain'...an umbrella!"

"Where do we keep the umbrellas?"
"By the door!"
"Go find my umbrella and tie your string."

Giovanni was shaking his head. "I still don't—"

"So he made up this game, the string game. He would leave me clues to random places in the house. I would have to tie a string when I found the first clue and that would start the game. Then I'd find the next clue and tie the string there."

She began to see Giovanni's eyes light in understanding. "And you would find the clues and keep tying."

Beatrice nodded. Her heart pounded in her chest. "They could be any location in the house. There was never a pattern. Totally random locations. There would be riddles, or drawings, or...anything, really. The goal of the string game was to find the locations and tie the string—"

"And then follow it." He rushed to look over her shoulder as she found the world map in the center of the book. Her eyes raked over the pages crowded with cities, borders, latitude, and longitude.

"The cities where you found my dad *were* random. They were meant to be."

"But where does it lead?" He shook his head. "I stopped getting clues from him after he showed up in Santiago two years ago. I thought he had found our house here and that's why he was so close. I stayed here for months in the middle of summer that year thinking that he would show himself before I gave up and went to New York."

"Did you find it, Beatrice? Did you find the treasure?"

She grabbed his arm. "No, no, you're missing the point of the game. Once you mapped out the points and tied off the string, you had to—"

"Follow it back!" he said with a smile. "Clever man. You follow the string back like Theseus out of the labyrinth, but..." His face fell.

"At one point in the web—" She held out her two index fingers and crossed them. "—the strings would touch. *That's* where the prize was."

"Found it, Daddy!"

"And that's where your father is," he murmured.

She shook her head and fought the tears that she felt pricking the corner of her eyes. "It was our game. I'm the only one who would be able to figure it out."

"And you would only solve it if you were cooperating with me."

"Exactly."

They both looked down at the map on the table. She grabbed a pencil from the counter, put the tip on the small island in the middle of the Mediterranean Sea, and looked at Giovanni.

"Do you remember where he went next?"

He nodded. "Budapest. The next sighting was in Budapest."

She began to drag the pencil north.

"Wait." He held up a hand. "You need something—"

"Oh, a straight edge, just give me a magazine or—"

"Got it!" He tossed her a thin book from the end of the table.

"Okay...Budapest, Hungary."

Her pencil stopped on the map, and she looked up.

"Then Warsaw."

She moved the book and her pencil tip traced a light line over the soft, pastel colors of the map, each thread drawing them closer to the mystery of her father's whereabouts.

"Stockholm."

"Novosibirsk."

She could feel his crackling energy fill the room as he listed the cities. "It will be a major city," he mused. "It's much easier to stay hidden in a major city."

Beatrice looked up at him. "Okay, next?"

"Shanghai."

"Madras."

The line dipped and traced over the world, zagging north and south as each city was reached, slowly working east, then south.

"Johannesburg."

"Lima."

"San Francisco, right?"

"Yes, then El Paso."

"Boston."

"Tripoli."

"Santiago," she whispered, and her breath hitched when she saw the faint lines finally cross in front of her. Tears spilled down her face and she felt his hand on her shoulder as he took the shaking pencil from her grasp.

"Very well done, Beatrice! There's my clever girl."

"Found it, Daddy! Can we go for ice cream now?"

He held her as she cried, her tears soaking the front of his shirt.

"So close," Giovanni murmured as he stroked her hair.

"Brasilia. He's in Brasilia."

Brasilia, Brazil

"Why would he come here?" she asked over the steady hum of the engine.

"In a way, it's very much like Houston," Giovanni said as he steered the old car through the wide streets of the Brazilian capitol. Though it was built in the 1960s as the modern ideal of contemporary city planning, Beatrice thought the capitol and fourth largest city in Brazil seemed empty.

"What do you mean, it's like Houston?"

He turned right at the small road leading to the resort where Isabel and Gustavo's contacts had informed them a quiet vampire going by the name "Emil Gonzales" owned a cottage on the shore of Lake Paranoá.

"If you are trying to remain anonymous, you go to a city like Brasilia. With the popularity and proximity of Rio de Janeiro and Sao Paulo, the immortal population here is very low and tends to mind its own business."

"So not very much politics?"

"Practically none. It's like a ghost town," he said quietly, his eyes scanning the low, red painted cottages with dark roofs. "There," he said, "the one on the end."

She gripped her seat as he parked along the curb, almost unwilling to step out of the car, afraid of what she might find. Giovanni hadn't had any sign of her father for the last two years. He'd dropped off the radar when he finished giving the clues to his location. If they had been together two years before, she thought, she might have seen it sooner.

As if reading her thoughts, she heard him say, "If we've lost him because of my own stubbornness—"

"Can we save that for another time, please?" she murmured as she eyed the small house surrounded by low palms. The cottage was part of a larger resort, though some of the apartments and cottages were privately owned. The gardens surrounding it were well tended, but because it was part of the hotel property, there was no way of knowing who took care of them.

She took a deep breath and reached across the car to squeeze Giovanni's hand. "I'm fine; let's go see if anyone's home."

He pulled her toward him and laid a gentle kiss on her lips before giving her a small smile. His eyes were shuttered, and his shoulders were fixed. She knew he thought they would find nothing.

They walked toward the low cottage tucked into a quiet corner at the edge of the lake. Streams ran through the grounds, under small footbridges, and trickled over rocks through the lush gardens.

"Definitely a water vampire," he muttered, taking her hand as they crossed a small bridge. "And a smart one."

"Why do you say that?"

"He's surrounded himself with his element. The lake, the streams. For him, this is an excellent defensive position."

"Oh."

They drew closer to the small house and she heard him drawing deep, testing breaths.

"Sense anything?"

His nose twitched. "I smell guava. Coffee. No vampires."

She could feel the clench in her chest, but she continued to walk toward the house. They stopped in front of the green door, and Giovanni shot her a sad look as he took a fist and punched, splintering the frame near the lock and pushing it open.

Beatrice stepped into the dim cottage, immediately hit by the musty scent that clung to the room. She reached to flip on the lights but Giovanni's hand stopped her.

"Not a good idea. Better not to draw attention to ourselves, even if it is a quiet location."

"Okay." She pulled out her mobile phone and turned on the small flashlight.

"I'm afraid no vampire has been here for many months, Beatrice."

She sighed. "I was getting that feeling."

They both walked around the small living area, and she noticed the lack of dust on the surfaces, and the quiet hum of the refrigerator and air conditioner.

"Appliances running."

Giovanni sniffed again. "I do smell a human. Older. He smells sick. Cancer maybe."

"A caretaker?"

"Possibly. If he planned on leaving, it's something he might have arranged." He lingered in front of the wall of bookcases that lined one side of the room. "And these books are not molded. In this climate, they would be unless the air conditioner was usually on."

"So why the musty smell?"

"Just the perils of a closed house by the lake, I imagine." He was already lost studying the texts in front of him.

Beatrice roamed through the small house. There was nothing in the modern kitchen, not even any canned food. A drip coffeemaker sat on the otherwise empty counter, and nothing was in the refrigerator. There were no indications of life anywhere.

She pushed open the door to the bedroom and was surprised to find traces of the man she remembered. A pair of shoes sat at the end of the bed where he would kick them off. A pile of books lay on the bedside table, and there was a note propped on top of it. Heavy curtains were pinned around the large French doors, and one window was covered with carefully cut plywood.

Picking up the note on the bedside table, she noticed it was written in Portuguese; the signature read, 'Maria.' She tucked it in the pocket of her jeans and went to the small desk on the other side of the room.

Under a sheet of glass were several pictures of her and her grandparents, along with blank spaces where some had been removed. There was a finger painting she remembered had been tucked into a childhood scrapbook, along with a poem she had written when she was ten, signed by a juvenile hand.

Beatrice sniffed and rubbed at the tears on her cheeks. She pulled open the single drawer and began to look through it. There were receipts and scraps of paper; most of the notes had been written in Portuguese. Spare change rattled around the bottom of the drawer. Occasionally, she would find something that looked more personal. A single cufflink. A disposable lighter. A rosary twisted into knots.

She heard Giovanni approach and relaxed a little as his arms encircled her waist. She turned and buried her face in his chest, breathing in the comforting smell of wood smoke and whiskey.

"He's not here, *tesoro*."

"I know," she whispered.

He tilted her face up and she was struck by the anguish in his expression.

"I was wrong to stay away from you for so long. I didn't know. And I hurt you. This is my fault."

"We don't know if we would have found him even if we had been together." She ran her hand up his chest and into the hair at the nape of his neck. "We don't know. He may have left before we could get here years ago. There's no way of knowing."

"I think you need to see a few things on the bookcase."

She sighed and hugged him closer. "Just give me a minute."

They stood holding each other for a few more minutes in the empty bedroom. She heard the trickle of a stream running outside the terrace doors. Eventually, she took Giovanni's hand and walked back out to the living room and the wall of books.

"Here." He pointed toward a corner of the room. "These are textbooks for the study of old Arabic and old Persian. It appears he taught himself how to read both."

"Why?"

"Alchemy. Remember what Tywyll said? The manuscript was about alchemy. Much early medieval alchemic work was done in the Middle East, so if he wanted to learn more, he might have started there."

She paged through the books, looking at her father's familiar scrawl in the margins of each volume. Most of it, she couldn't understand.

"Aristotle," Giovanni murmured, dragging his finger along the spines. "Zosimos, Mary...did your father read classical Greek?"

"A little," she muttered, paging through a dense history of the burned library of Alexandria in Egypt.

"He appeared to be well-versed in Greco-Roman roots of alchemy and was studying the work done in the Middle East. Khalid ibn Yazid. A lot of Geber."

"Who?"

"Ah...he was known during my time as Geber, but he was a Persian, possibly Arab, medieval alchemist. Jabir ibn Hayyan was his Arabic name. It also appears he was looking into Bön, Spagyric—"

"What?" she asked with a frown. "I haven't even heard of those."

"Bön is an ancient Asian belief system. I'm only familiar with it through Tenzin. Spagyric refers to a subset of alchemy, plant alchemy. Again, Tenzin studied it at one point." Giovanni stepped back and shook his head as he surveyed the wall of books. "What were you up to, Stephen?"

She looked through the section in front of her. "I'm also seeing stuff on Newton and Boyle. I know Newton, who's Boyle?"

"Early modern chemistry." He walked slowly, his head cocked to the side as he moved down the wall.

"So, chemistry, languages, philosophy, religion...what *wasn't* he studying?"

He said, "Alchemy is a *very* twisted subject. It blurs lines between science and superstition. Chemistry and magic." He heaved a sigh, and she could see the air stir in the light of her small flashlight.

"Gio?"

"*Sì, tesoro?*" he asked, absently bending down to the far corner where something appeared to have caught his eye.

"Why don't we—"

"Beatrice, look at this."

She walked over and knelt down next to him.

"What?"

Giovanni pulled out a small book. It was a black and white composition book, like the ones she remembered using in high school. It had no label, only the number "1" written on the front cover in black marker. She pulled it from his hands with trembling fingers, knowing somehow that this book was different from the others.

Beatrice sat on the floor, cross-legged in the corner as Giovanni knelt next to her. She opened it to the first page.

"'August 20, 1996,'" she read in a shaky voice. "'Dear Mariposa, I had to say goodbye to you tonight—'" She choked on the sob that tore from her throat and before she could blink, Giovanni had picked her up and was rocking her in his arms on the floor of the lonely cottage.

Beatrice wept, deep, gut-wrenching sobs that tore at her heart and shook her small frame. Giovanni held her as she emptied her sorrow, fear, and frustration into his chest. He didn't try to calm her, only stroked her back as she let six years of anger and grief pour out into the still night air.

"Why isn't he here?" she finally choked out. "Why?"

"I don't know."

"Is he dead? Is he hiding again?" She shook her head and clutched at his neck. "I want my father! I want all this to be worth it, somehow. Carl and the other bodyguards, and—and the blond girl in Greece. And all the people he killed. And Ioan and Jean's granddaughter and who knows how many other people who had nothing to do with this," she practically yelled. "Why is this happening to me? To *us*?"

"I don't know."

"Why?" She raised her tear-stricken face to him, but he could do nothing but cup her cheek and wipe at the tears that fell fast and hot. "I'm past sad. I'm just pissed-off now! I want this to end so I can get on with my life—with *our* life. Is this ever going to end?"

"Yes," he pressed his cheek to hers. "This is going to end. I told you six years ago that I would find your father, and I will, Beatrice. *We* will find him."

She sniffed, and he reached down to hand her a handkerchief from his pocket.

"Why do you always carry handkerchiefs? You never need them."

He didn't say anything, but she could feel him press the cloth to her cheeks as she lay her head on his shoulder and allowed him to hold her up.

"Beatrice, don't read the notebooks here," he murmured. "There are too many of them. Take them back to Houston. I know your grandmother would want to see them, too."

She clutched the notebook to her chest and nodded. "Okay."

"We should go. I don't think there's anything more."

"Will you remember all the books? Should we make a list?"

"I'll remember."

"Okay," she said before she paused. "Let's go then. There's nothing here."

She sat with her back against a chair as Giovanni pulled out the stacks of composition books. She didn't stop to count them as she dried the last of her tears and piled them by the door along with the few personal items she'd found in the bedroom and small bath.

"*Tesoro*, look at this."

She glanced over to see Giovanni standing over the same blue atlas that they'd used to play the string game sitting out on the small cafe table near the kitchen.

"Where was that?"

"Behind the notebooks. Tucked against the wall."

She looked at his raised eyebrow and then back to the book.

"There's something in there."

"I believe you're right."

Beatrice walked over to the table and started paging through the atlas in front of her. She grew progressively more frustrated with each map she turned, only to find it devoid of any clue to Stephen's whereabouts. Finally, she felt Giovanni's hand still her own.

"Let me. I have an idea."

"Fine," she muttered, ready to leave the small, empty cottage and go home. He opened to the large map at the center and pointed to Greece.

"He has already studied the roots of alchemy." His finger slid east. "And he told Tywyll the manuscript he took from Lorenzo was Persian."

He looked at her, locking eyes for a moment before she heard his finger move across the page again. This time, it slid farther east, through the heart of the Middle East, past northern India, and over to the far edge of China.

"He had books about Asian alchemic traditions and study, and another that related to Bön. I know of one vampire who is revered for his knowledge of both."

"One vampire? You think my father would have looked for him? Who? Where?"

He frowned and flipped to the page showing a larger map of the Northern Chinese coast and pointed to a small gulf east of Beijing. She leaned down to look closer and her mouth fell open when she saw a lone pinprick in the center of the Bohai Sea.

"What is that?" she whispered.

He stared at her for a moment before he looked back to the atlas Stephen had left for them to find.

"That, *tesoro*, is Mount Penglai. That is the residence of the Eight Immortals."

"Who?"

He sighed and closed the atlas.

"Tenzin is going to kill me."

CHAPTER 23

Houston, Texas
May 2010

"Caspar, do you take Isadora to be your lawfully wedded wife? Do you promise to love, honor, cherish and protect her, forsaking all others as long as you both shall live?"

"I do."

Giovanni felt his heart give a quiet thump as Caspar and Isadora exchanged the vows they had chosen for their ceremony. As it turned out, it was Stephen's presence the two had been waiting for, but when Beatrice and he had returned from Brasilia and given them the news that Stephen remained out of reach, Isadora had nodded in understanding and called her friend Marta's husband to perform the simple ceremony.

Judge Voorhies stood in the beautifully lit gardens of the house in River Oaks, standing under the gazebo with the bride and groom as a few of their closest friends watched the early evening ceremony.

Caspar wore his best charcoal grey suit, and Isadora looked stunning in a deep green dress that set off her beautiful eyes and silver-white hair. He glanced to his side to see Beatrice watching them both with a smile. She squeezed his hand, and he smiled before drawing her closer and kissing her temple. His eyes returned to the bride and groom in the garden. To say he was pleased for his old friend would be an understatement.

After a few more heartfelt words, Isadora and Caspar turned to the group with a smile.

"Caspar and Isadora chose a short reading from the Song of Songs, chapter four. 'You have stolen my heart, my darling, my bride; you have stolen my heart with one glance of your eyes, with one jewel of your necklace ...'"

Giovanni leaned down, whispering the same sweet words into Beatrice's ear in soft Italian.

"I still don't speak Italian," she whispered.

He only smiled. "You will."

"'How delightful is your love, my darling, my bride, how much more pleasing is your love than wine,'" the judge continued. "And I think we all know, as much as Caspar loves wine, what a truly bold statement that is."

Giovanni smiled as their friends laughed around them and Isadora and Caspar met each other with a sweet kiss. The judge pronounced them husband and wife. Giovanni and Beatrice smiled, Ben gave a little whoop, and the group clapped before going inside to share a meal.

Ben raced in circles, almost knocking Beatrice over in his enthusiasm. The boy had been ecstatic to see them both when they returned from South America, though he'd tried to play it off nonchalantly. He was bouncing with excitement and chattering nonstop about getting back home. Giovanni realized it was going to be a rather complicated discussion.

He was almost sure that Stephen had gone to China. The more he and Beatrice studied the journals the vampire had left behind, the more he became convinced that Stephen had sought the help of one far more ancient. The knowledge was both a comfort and a concern.

He was also growing more certain that Lorenzo had somehow discovered Stephen's plan. All indications from Jean Desmarais and his contacts seemed to indicate that the vampire was heading to the Far East. He was brought back to the present by Beatrice's arm around his waist.

"Hold on to those deep thoughts, love. Not for tonight, okay?"

He looked down at the woman beside him. Beatrice had pulled herself up from the disappointment that ambushed her in Brazil and dove into research, trying to recreate her father's library in the hopes that the books Stephen had chosen to study would give her insight into the manuscript Lorenzo was so keen to recover.

"What?" she asked with a frown.

"I love you very much, Beatrice. I'm very fortunate to have you."

She blushed and bumped his arm with her shoulder.

"Yeah, you are. I love you, too." She paused for a moment, then pulled him down for a quick kiss. "You're getting sentimental in your old age, Gio."

He smiled and bent down to kiss the top of her head.

"Must be the weddings."

"So—" She grinned as they walked toward the house. "—how are you feeling? Your oldest is finally married off. Soon Ben will be dating..."

He clutched his chest dramatically. "I shudder to think."

"You're going to be an empty-nester soon."

He said, "They grow up so fast."

"They do," she said with solemn nod.

He could feel her laughing at him for a moment before they both started chuckling.

"Is Carwyn going to be pissed off they didn't wait for him?"

He shrugged. "I don't think so. He's fairly busy at the moment."

"Back in Ireland?"

He nodded. "Deirdre is...coping. But he needs to be there right now."

They walked in silence, strolling hand in hand through the gardens lit with tiny lights. Giovanni could see the gathering of friends through the French doors, spilling out across the patio. The scent of honeysuckle and roses hung in the air.

His eyes found Ben as the boy gave Isadora a hug and a sweet smile. Caspar leaned over them both to place a kiss on his new wife's cheek. More than ever, Giovanni felt the weight of responsibility to keep them all safe. He wouldn't be able to remain in Houston for long. He felt Beatrice squeeze his waist, and his heart thumped again. At least, he would no longer travel alone.

"'You have stolen my heart, my darling, my bride,'" he whispered again as he pulled her closer.

Beatrice was also watching the group inside. Ben darted through the adults, who were all laughing and enjoying the plentiful wine that Caspar poured for the well-wishers.

"How are we going to keep them all safe?" she asked in a small voice.

"We'll figure something out."

She looked up at him, steely determination in her eyes. "We have to."

HE FOUND HER READING LATER THAT NIGHT, HALF ASLEEP IN THE LIBRARY AS she studied one of Stephen's journals in front of the cold fireplace. Their company had left hours before, but the house still hummed with quiet activity. Caspar and Isadora were in the kitchen, finishing the wine and enjoying their time together after a busy day. Ben had finally collapsed on the couch in the den, and Giovanni had carried him to his room before making a call to Carwyn on the phone in the study.

"Beatrice," he whispered, picking her up and setting her on his lap. "Why don't you go to bed?"

She looked at the clock over the mantle. "But it's only one a.m."

He smiled, amused by her convenient habit of keeping vampire hours. "It's been a long day. You should get some rest."

"Is Ben in bed?"

"Mmmhmm." He ran his lips along her temple.

She paused, and he could feel her head nodding against his chest. "Maybe I will."

"Or just stay here. I could probably find a way to distract you."

He felt her shoulders shake with quiet laughter. "I'm sure you could. How is Carwyn?"

"Doing well. He says hello, and he won't hold it against Isadora and Caspar for too long that they got married without him."

"I'm sure they're relieved."

"He also said that we had better not pull something like that."

She raised an eyebrow. Giovanni just shrugged, and she snuggled back into his chest.

"Have we heard from Tenzin yet?"

"Not yet."

"How about...what's his name?"

"That could take some time. Zhang Guo and his court operate on their own timetable."

"He's older than Tenzin?"

He chuckled. "Oh yes."

"Wow."

"I don't want to go to China until we know more. It's not in our best interests to arrive without some sort of introduction."

"But we will go."

"Yes, I think we must."

"What are we going to do about Ben?"

He sighed and shifted on the couch. "I don't know. I don't like leaving him, but the safest place for him to be is away from us. Lorenzo has already discovered him; I don't like the idea of leaving Caspar and Isadora here alone with him when we know he's a target. Then there's Dez and Kirby in L.A. I think we should speak to your Grandfather Alvarez and—"

She pulled him down and stopped the rambling list with a kiss. Slowly shifting on his lap, she continued kissing him until he forgot about the worries swirling in his mind and all he could think of was her soft skin, sweet mouth, and the feel of her hips under his hands. She ran her fingers through his hair and along the back of his neck, searching for his heated skin as her hands slipped under his collar.

"Tomorrow," she said. "We'll worry about it tomorrow."

"Beatrice," he groaned. "Careful, *tesoro*. I'm getting...hot. The fire—"

He broke off with a groan and his eyes rolled back as Beatrice's teeth found his ear and bit the lobe between her teeth.

"Gio," she whispered. "I need..."

"What do you need?"

He pulled her closer as she murmured in his ear and rocked against him.

"You guys are so gross."

They both froze when they heard Ben at the door.

"Benjamin, why aren't you in bed?"

"Are you guys going to be doing that stuff all the time now? 'Cause I really don't need to see that."

"Benjamin," they said in unison. Beatrice moved to crawl off Giovanni's lap, but he held her in place, shifting and clearing his throat with a meaningful glance.

"I couldn't sleep," Ben whined before stretching into one of the armchairs. "I think I drank too much Coke at the party."

"Remind me to forbid that beverage when we get home," he muttered.

Beatrice curled up against his chest again, and he tried to distract himself as he played with the ends of her hair.

"Are we going home soon? I miss L.A."

"You miss your basketball hoop," Giovanni said.

"And the neighborhood girls," Beatrice added.

"Well," Ben thought for a moment. "Yeah. I miss those. But I missed you guys, too."

Giovanni smiled at the sleepy boy stretched out in the chair next to them. Ben had a happy, contented look on his face, and he immediately began nodding off again.

"I think he missed his Uncle Gio," Beatrice whispered.

He smiled and kissed her forehead. "I missed him, too."

They sat for a few more minutes, enjoying the quiet.

"Benjamin?" he asked. "Are you asleep?"

"No, what's up?" The boy sat up in his chair.

"We should talk."

Ben's face fell a little before being replaced by a determined expression. "Because you're going to leave again?"

Giovanni frowned and felt Beatrice squeeze his arm.

"It's okay," Ben said. "I get it. I know Lorenzo's still out there. And you haven't found B's dad yet."

Beatrice said, "We don't want to leave you again, Ben."

"But you have to."

The boy met his eyes and Giovanni was both relieved and saddened by the understanding he saw there. If he could, Giovanni would wipe away the sad memories that colored the young man's childhood, but he knew it wouldn't be fair. Just as his own childhood had shaped him, so would Ben's. He only hoped he and Beatrice could make life a little easier in the end.

"So," Ben sighed and seemed to rally himself. "What are we gonna do? Am I gonna stay with Caspar and Isadora here? If we do that, can I get a basketball hoop before you go?"

He smiled at the boy and nodded. "Yes, Benjamin. I will make sure you have a basketball hoop."

"Who's getting a basketball hoop?" Caspar asked as he entered the library.

"Ben is. That way, when he stays here while we are traveling, he will not be deprived of his greatest love. The girls, however, he'll have to see to himself," he said as Ben did a small victory wiggle in the chair.

"Ben's staying here?" Isadora came in behind Caspar. "But when will you leave for Asia, Beatrice?"

"We don't know, Grandma. We'll stay as long as we can, but we want to make sure you and Caspar and Ben are safe in case we need to leave quickly."

"We're still waiting for word from Tenzin. She should be able to smooth channels for us," Giovanni said quietly. "As for security—"

"Caspar," Isadora said. She gave him a look before linking her hand with her new husband's. Caspar smiled down at her and nodded before he turned to Giovanni and Beatrice.

"Isadora and I have been talking about this. As much as we love this house, we feel like we need to move to Los Angeles with the rest of the family."

Giovanni blinked when Caspar said, "family." He looked from Ben's sleepy face to Isadora's warm smile. His eyes paused on Caspar for a long moment before he looked back to Beatrice, who was watching him with loving eyes. His arm tightened around her, and he felt his heart thump twice. Giovanni suddenly realized it was exactly what they were. For the first time in over five hundred years, he had a family.

A fierce wave of protectiveness swept over him, and Beatrice ran her hand over his jaw, soothing him as the heat rose to the surface.

"Yes," he said hoarsely, "the family should stay together."

"And if everyone's in L.A., Matt can keep an eye on things if we have to leave," Beatrice said quietly.

"Don't forget Ernesto," Giovanni added. "I'm sure he would be as pleased to meet your grandmother as he was to meet you, *tesoro*."

"Are you kidding?" she snorted. "Grandma's way more charming than me. Ernesto will love her."

Caspar only nodded. "So, that's settled then. Who wants a drink?"

Isadora smiled and began a rapid-fire conversation with Beatrice in Spanish about the Alvarez clan while Caspar moved to the sideboard to pour drinks.

"So everyone's moving to L.A. after all?" Ben piped up. "Sweet!"

A strange peace settled over him as he began to plan, strategizing to ensure the well-being of the four people who had become, quite unexpectedly, more important than anything else in the world.

He and Beatrice would go to China in search of her father and the manuscript, but Lorenzo was still a threat. Luckily, with the help of his contacts in Los Angeles, he would be able to ensure the best protection for Caspar, Isadora and Benjamin.

Beatrice would go with him, adding her keen intellect to his own as they worked toward solving the puzzle of Stephen De Novo, the missing manuscript, and what his son was trying to accomplish by taking them both.

Giovanni heard the phone in the back of the library start to ring. He frowned at Caspar, who went to answer it.

"Hello? Tenzin, my dear!" Caspar paused as Beatrice's eyes swung toward his. They both rose from the couch and walked to the phone.

"They're right here...yes, here you are."

Giovanni picked up the phone, holding it away from his ear so Tenzin's voice did not deafen him.

"Gio!" he heard her clearly. "Is B there?"

"Yes, did you get our e-mail?"

"E-mail? I never check that stuff."

Giovanni frowned at Beatrice, who only shrugged.

"Gio?"

"Still here, bird girl." Everyone was looking toward the back of the room as he spoke.

"Can you tell me why I'm getting a summons from my sire to meet him at Mount Penglai?"

Giovanni's heart sank. It was happening much faster than he'd anticipated. He looked at Caspar and Isadora, then at Ben's wide eyes from across the room. Finally, he looked to Beatrice, who reached out to grasp his hand. He took a deep breath.

"We'll meet you there."

EPILOGUE

From the journals of Stephen De Novo

HOUSTON, TEXAS

August 20, 1996

Dear Mariposa,

    I had to say goodbye to you tonight. It was the hardest thing I've ever had to do. Harder than controlling the bloodlust that still ambushes me from time to time. Harder than escaping the madman who killed me. Harder than ignoring my mother's pleas to stay.

    I doubt you'll ever read this, but I feel stupid writing "Dear Diary" when I'm an immortal bloodsucking predator, so I'll address it to you. On the off chance you do read this, then you know what I've become.

    I thought I could be part of your life, at least for a little while, but the first time you saw me, I was reminded of what a monster I am now. I tried to erase the memory from you and try again, but it was no use. Hopefully, you remember me the way I was.

    I want you to remember the good things.

    I am going away now. Whatever happens to me, I just hope I haven't made you a target. That's the other reason I'm leaving. I couldn't stand if you got pulled into this. I want you to have a good life. I want you to grow up strong and smart. I know Grandma and Grandpa will do their best. They're amazing. I want you to find someone to love, who loves you back. I want you to live a full life and have a big family, with lots of people who love you and challenge you and bring you as much joy as you brought me just by being your dad.

I may live a thousand years. Hopefully, I'll do something good with that time. Whatever purpose God has in all this, I hope I find it. But no matter what else I do in the endless time that's been given to me, you will always be my greatest accomplishment.

I love you so much,
Dad

DUBLIN, IRELAND

March 1998

Dear Beatrice,

I finally met a vampire tonight who wasn't out to get me. Funny, right? I'm sure I've met others, but this was the first one I found that gave me hope I might not have to be a lowly, manipulative bastard who only uses humans for the rest of my existence. I was doing some research at Trinity last night, and on the way back to my hotel, I sensed another vampire around me. I tensed up. You never know who you can trust.

But when I finally saw him from a distance, he just smiled. He was a doctor, and he was running a free medical clinic in the lobby of an old office building. It was just him with a bunch of poor humans, so I felt like I could relax. I don't know why, but he saw me through the glass and motioned me over to ask if I could help.

See, when I touch people now, I can get a sense of their general health. That, and their smell makes me able to tell if they're sick. I guess he just wanted some company... and some help. The line of people was out the door and it was almost eleven o'clock.

He didn't ask much about me. Just if I was American and if I was visiting anyone in town. I think he could tell from talking to me that I was trying to lay low, so he didn't pry. He asked if I needed any help. He was so nice, I was tempted to spill the whole crazy story, but something held me back. I didn't want to get him involved. Knowing that there was someone good out there, that maybe I could eventually do something useful with this life was enough. It made me grateful to have met him.

After the clinic, he asked if he could pay me for my time. It was nice to say no and just feel good about myself for the first time in years. All the humans that I've fed from since I was turned, I finally felt like I gave something back without taking.

He gave me his card and told me to call him if I ever needed any help. I hope I won't have to use it, but I took it, just in case.

Love,
Dad

GRAVESEND, ENGLAND

January 20, 2000

Dear Beatrice,

I found a friend today.

Sounds silly, right? Like I'm the new kid at school. But in the last seven years, I've discovered how rare it is to find a friend you can trust. Do you have those kind of people around you? Do you have good friends? I hope so. You're nineteen now. Maybe you have a boyfriend. You better be going to college. I wonder what you'll study. Probably not Dante.

Do you still love Greek myths? Maybe you'll study literature. Or archeology. I'm sure you'd be good at anything, you were always so smart. I bet you're beautiful, too. The last time I saw you, you had that gawky, uncomfortable look that kids have when they're teenagers, but you were only fifteen. I bet you're beautiful now. You always looked like Mom, and she's so lovely.

This new friend of mine is teaching me how to hide better. He's old. Older than you can even imagine. I'm not sure they even measured time when he was human. He's also incredibly powerful. He can control water like me, but much better. He's a good friend, and I feel like I might finally have time to study this book and not spend all my time running around trying to hide.

Love,
Dad

BRASILIA, BRAZIL

October 2001

Dear Beatrice,

I'm writing to you from my home. After eight years of running, I finally feel like I've found a new home. It's quiet here. No one pays attention to me. With all the tourists around, I can feed without bothering anyone, and no one even remembers me.

I feel strange talking to you about feeding, even though I know you'll probably never read this. I tried feeding from animals, but after a while, it got to be too much work. I have to feed a lot more often and drink a lot more blood than if I just take a quick sip from a human.

Forgive any unfortunate juice box comparisons.

I don't look down on people like most vampires do, but it's the easiest way for me to survive. If it makes you feel better, I always pay them. They don't remember where the money came from, but hopefully they just think they forgot about it in their pocket.

It's not all bad. I'm learning so much faster now. I wish I knew a neurobiologist who could study it. It's like my brain can absorb information and my memory—which was always good—is amazing now. I've become fluent in Portuguese, French, Ancient Greek, Old Arabic, Old Persian, Mandarin, and my Latin and Italian are much better, too. My recall and processing are faster; it's easier to make connections. I'm simply smarter than I was as a human. Honestly, I can see why some vampires, after hundreds of years, do feel superior to them.

I'm much stronger. I've been told that if I was in better physical condition when I was turned it would be even better, but my sire was old, so that helped. But he also made a lot of 'children,' which depletes their strength. So unless I find a much stronger vampire who is willing to exchange blood with me, which is unlikely, I'll always be weaker than him.

I think I'm starting to understand this book. I still can't figure out why he wants it, though.

Love,
Dad

August 2004

Dear Beatrice,

I received a letter from a contact in Rome today.
How can you ever forgive me?

This is my fault.

Please forgive me.

If I didn't need to keep this book safe, I would walk into the sun on his sick little island right now, just to make him leave you alone.

Maybe he's dead. I hope like hell he's dead.

This vampire that petitioned for you in Rome... he's frightening, Beatrice. I don't know why he wants you, but he's Lorenzo's sire, and the stories I've heard make my blood curdle.

A fire vampire?

What does he want from you?

They all want something.

Forgive me!

I can only hope what I've heard is wrong. My contact said di Spada was 'uncharacteristically impassioned' in his claim, that he offered a lot in exchange for you. At least this makes me hopeful his intentions toward you are good. It is hard to imagine, from what I have heard, but I can hope.

Forgive me,
Dad

ATHENS, GREECE

December, 2004

You're in L.A.

You're in grad school.

You're safe.

From what I hear, you're really safe.

I'm not sure what Giovanni Vecchio is to you, but whatever he is, he's protecting you more than any human I've ever heard of.

Maybe he can be trusted. He's powerful enough.

I don't know if I can trust him.

But I think I can trust you.

IRAKLION, CRETE

February 2005

Dear Beatrice,
    Please understand. Please get the message.
    Please remember the game.
    I want you to find me.
    Please remember.
    I can't do this alone.
    Dad

SHANGHAI, CHINA

June 2006

Dear Beatrice,
    I haven't written in a while. I think I may understand why Lorenzo wants this. But it doesn't make sense. Not really. There's something I'm not seeing. For the first time since I was turned thirteen years ago, I don't feel smart enough to handle this.
    I need more information, but I don't know who to trust. Everyone has an agenda.
    Remember that.
    Everyone has an agenda.
    Love,
    Dad

EL PASO, TEXAS

September 2007

Why does anyone live in El Paso? It's so hot. I don't even sweat anymore, and it still feels hot.
    I'm so tempted to go see your grandma. She's so close.
    Is she okay? I heard about Grandpa a couple of years ago. I hope she's not lonely. She and Dad... They had that kind of love you always read about, you know?
    Is that what you've found with this immortal?
    Is it even possible?
    You're twenty-five now. I've missed so much of your life. Even the hints I get

now, the reports and the notes, they're not enough. I just need to be sure he can be trusted.

I have to be sure.

Love,

Dad

BRASILIA, BRAZIL

March 2008

Dear Beatrice,

Okay, game played. Did you follow the clues? Can you find me?

Please find me.

I'll wait for you.

I've found some new avenues for research. I finally understand the basics of this manuscript, but the alchemy is still beyond me. There's just not enough research done on vampire biology. I may contact that doctor in Dublin if I can. Maybe he would be able to make better sense of this.

I just know that there's a piece I'm missing. Something doesn't quite fit. It seems like it should work, but if it does, then why does he want it? The more I learn, the less sense it makes.

Back to my books.

Love,

Dad

August 2008

Dear Beatrice,

This is the last time I'll write in these journals. I was stupid to depend on a game we played when you were a child. It wasn't fair of me.

I'm leaving Brazil, but in case you ever find this place, I'll leave my journals here. Where I am going, it's best not to bring them anyway.

There is an elder I need to see. I don't trust him personally, but I think I can trust him with the manuscript. I think, from what I've learned, he may be my best chance to keep the book safe from Lorenzo, and to help me make sense of all this.

 I'm leaving tomorrow. August 8, 2008.

 I'm going West to the East. You know me; I like to be in my element.

 Find me, Mariposa.

 Love,

 Dad

END OF BOOK TWO

THE FORCE OF WIND

*The little reed, bending to the force of the wind,
soon stood upright when the storm had passed.*
—Aesop

PROLOGUE

Wuyi Mountains
Fujian Province, China
September 2008

Fu-han watched the passing boats in the late afternoon sun, carrying their people and wares to the small town just a few miles away. The sun glinted off the surface of the Nine-Bend River and a breeze stirred, swirling the air and tickling the red and gold leaves from the trees. They whirled and twisted in the wind, fluttering down to lie along the edge of the water and drift downstream, carried away by the burbling river.

"Master, do we need more of the moss?"

The old man brushed a few leaves from his faded grey robes and glanced down to the young brother who was gathering moss from a rock along the bank. The young man had good eyes, stronger now than the eyes of the old man who taught him. Fu-han held his gnarled hand out and motioned to the young man, asking him to bring the basket closer to his eyes.

"No more."

"Is that all we need from this part of the forest? Are the mushrooms here the correct ones or do we need to go upstream?"

The old man gave a crooked smile. Elder Lu was wise to choose this young one to be his apprentice, despite his impatience. Impatience, Fu-han knew, could be mastered, but perception such as the boy's could not be taught. The young man already perceived even a slight difference in the hours of shade could impart a different character to an ingredient.

"We have enough for this remedy. These mushrooms are fine for healing. Do we have all the other ingredients?"

The young man glanced at the slip of paper in his hand. "Yes, Master."

"Then, let us begin our walk back," he said with a smile.

The young man held out his arm for his teacher, who grabbed it along with his walking stick. They started up the small dirt path to the monastery, which was tucked into one of the creeping river valleys of the Wuyi Mountains in Southern China. The humid air was soft in the early evening, and the old man was glad that one of the young brothers had already come down to light the lamps along the path.

"Is it true we will have visitors coming tonight?"

"Yes," the old man nodded, "Elders Zhang and Lu. They are bringing another immortal with them, a scholar. The scholar carries a book we will have the opportunity to study."

"What is the book?"

"It is an old manuscript. From the West. The Elders think we may be able to help the young immortal to interpret it."

"They honor us."

The old man chuckled. "They do. But then, I am only an apprentice to Elder Zhang."

"Why does he not study the book himself?"

"The Elders have many important things to do." *Like indulge in the new wine*, the old man thought with a private smile. "And I am Elder Zhang's oldest student. I accept the honor with happiness."

They walked for a few more minutes, slowly climbing the old stairs as twilight fell and the mist crept up the mountain.

"Master Fu-han?"

"Yes?"

"Why did you not join the Elders when they asked?"

The old man glanced at the setting sun and then up at the tall young man who helped him along the path. It was an important question, so he took his time in answering.

"You will choose your own path, but I am happy to know I have only a short time more in this body. It has been a good life, and I have learned much. I will be ready to move on when death comes for me."

"But the gift of immortality... is it not an opportunity for even more study? Think of the years you could teach others. Someday, you could be as wise as Elder Zhang."

He only offered the young man a knowing smile. "Ah, but the gift of mortality offers its own lessons, as well. And though I will never have the wisdom of Elder Zhang, he will never have the wisdom of Master Fu-han."

The young man's cheeks reddened at the old man's apparent arrogance. Fu-han was quick to continue.

"Do not mistake me, I do not compare myself to the Elders. Their wisdom is beyond our comprehension, but they have chosen to step off the path of enlightenment that mortality offers. Just as there is wisdom to be gained from a long life, there is wisdom to be gained from a short one, as well."

"I do not understand."

The old man gripped the young monk's arm as he avoided a thick tree root that had worked its way through the old stone staircase. "The immortals carry the wisdom of our ancestors, but their own enlightenment is slowed by their long life." As they climbed the stairs leading to the monastery, a small bird came and landed on one of the stone lanterns. Fu-han nodded toward it with a smile.

"Look at the thrush."

The young man glanced at the small speckled bird as it cocked its head to the side, observing the two men as they moved up the stairs.

"What of the thrush?"

"What lessons might be learned from living in such a small, weak body?" The old monk smiled at the bird, which flicked its tail before flying to perch on the branch of a low-hanging conifer.

"The thrush has a most beautiful song, Master. One could learn to appreciate that."

"You are correct. And is it a powerful bird?"

The young man smiled. "Of course not. It darts along the branches and eats only seeds and insects."

"And yet, it does not worry about its life. It is a humble bird, as many small creatures are humble, but it has a beautiful song." He paused to catch his breath on the stairs and looked up at the young man beside him. "We gain more enlightenment from weakness and loss than we do from strength and victory. That is the wisdom of mortality that our immortal elders cannot grasp. It is only the youngest of them that remember such humility."

"But that wisdom is lost when you die," the boy said with a frown.

"As it should be—to be discovered again by the young." He reached a gnarled hand up to pat the young man's cheek. "You will learn this. And when the time comes, and Elder Lu asks you if you would choose an immortal life, you will make your own choice, as all of those in your order do."

They continued to climb, and Fu-han felt every creak of his joints. Soon, he would not be able to join the young monks as they gathered the plants and roots in the forest. Soon, he would take refuge in the collected wisdom of all those who had come before him and stay in the library and workrooms of the monastery.

"Master?"

"Yes?"

"Which of the elements is most powerful?"

Fu-han smiled. It was a young question.

"There is no one element more powerful than the others."

"But surely—"

"It is *balance* that is most powerful. The elders know this; that is why there have always been eight, two from each earthly element."

But it was the fifth element, the space between, that Fu-han thought of as he climbed the stone stairs. It was the elusive energy he felt quicken his own senses as he looked to the top of the stairs to see his old teacher jump from the branch of a tree to land on his toes.

Fu-han smiled as his companion took a sharp breath.

"Elder Zhang Guo," the young monk said with a respectful bow.

The ancient wind vampire floated down the stairs, his white robes fluttering in the dark along with his long, black hair. Though he was called 'elder,' Zhang had been frozen in the prime of his human life. His broad face was open and jovial as he greeted Fu-han and reached out an arm to help him.

"How is my old student this evening?"

The old monk smiled and gave a deep nod. "I am well, my teacher. We were not expecting you until much later."

Zhang shrugged. "We took refuge in one of the caves today so we could be here early. Our guest was most eager to bring his book to the safety of the library."

The old man frowned. "Does this guest bring trouble?" He glanced at the young man beside him and thought of all the boys who trained at the monastery school.

The ancient wind immortal only smiled. "And who would dare harm the monks of Lu Dongbin? Your patron is far too powerful for anyone to challenge."

Fu-han bowed. "We are grateful for the protection of *all* the council, Elder Zhang."

Zhang laughed. "Some more than others, my old friend."

The three walked slowly up the stairs after Fu-han waved away the offer of a quick flight from his old teacher. The two friends spoke of the young monks and the school, about the visitor who would be staying with them and the curious book he was bringing.

"I am eager to hear your thoughts on it," Zhang mused. "You are familiar with its author, though I can promise you have not seen anything like this before."

"Oh?"

"I need your eyes, my friend."

"Have you asked your daughter to look at it?"

Zhang smiled a little. "My daughter has taken a vow of silence for many years. She has no time for me."

THE FORCE OF WIND

Fu-han chuckled. "I will always have time for you, Master."

"No," the vampire said as he looked at the bent, old man. "I'm afraid you won't."

"I suppose that is true enough," Fu-han said.

They reached the gates of the monastery to find a group of young monks scurrying about, preparing for their visitors. They were rushing in expectation of their patron and only a few stopped and stared at the three men as they made their way through the stone courtyard and the meeting room, winding their way back into the mountain and toward the library.

The dim hall was lined with books, scrolls, and manuscripts, a mix of modern and new writings, and small alcoves branched off into study rooms strewn with cushions. It was lit by some of the few electric lamps in the ancient building, the risk of fire outweighing the preferences of their immortal patrons.

The young man escorted Fu-han to his favorite corner of the room and left him to go put the herbs and other ingredients they had gathered in the workroom. He promised to return with tea.

Fu-han could feel the eyes of his old teacher on him as he arranged his aching body on the low cushions. Zhang stretched his legs out and relaxed against the cool, stone wall of the library.

"It's not too late to change your mind."

The old man laughed. "And spend eternity with an old and creaking body? I was tempted when I was thirty, considered it at forty, but at ninety-eight years?" The old monk shook his head. "I will welcome death when it seeks me out."

Zhang scowled. "You waste yourself."

"I move on to whatever is next." Fu-han shrugged. "That is all. Tell me about the young immortal."

"He has been hiding for many years, afraid of the knowledge he has."

"Why be afraid of knowledge?"

"This knowledge is power, and others seek it. His mortal life was taken because he found it."

"Ah," Fu-han nodded. That changed things. To be thrust into an immortal life without a choice was a harsh fate. "He is welcome here."

"I hear him approaching with Lu now."

"And his element?"

"He controls water, but is not very powerful. His sire was unwise and too prolific."

"And his mind?"

"Impressive," Zhang said with a slow nod. "Very impressive."

"I look forward to meeting him."

They paused when Fu-han felt the stirring of energy that signaled the presence of a powerful immortal. Zhang rose as Lu Dongbin, patron of the monastery and ancient water vampire, swept through the doors of the library, followed by a thin man in Western clothes. The proper greetings were offered along with quiet words of welcome as the three vampires situated themselves on low cushions in front of the old man, who examined the newcomer.

The young immortal was of moderate height, and his dark hair and dramatic features indicated Spanish or Mediterranean blood. He did not carry himself with the confidence typical of his kind, but his keen eyes darted around the room, taking in the massive library that Fu-han's order had tended for over a thousand years. He carried a wrapped bundle clutched to his chest that looked like a small book or box.

He was younger than Fu-han, in mortal years as well as immortal, and the old scholar could feel the vampire's nervous energy fill the small alcove, causing the lights to flicker.

This one, he thought, had not forgotten his own humility. This one was open to a greater wisdom.

When Fu-han's kind eyes finally met the brown gaze of his guest, the old man smiled.

"Stephen De Novo, you are welcome here. And you are safe."

CHAPTER 1

En route to Beijing, China
August 2010

Giovanni Vecchio eyed the impassive water vampire from across the compartment, casually draping an arm around Beatrice's shoulders as she sat next to him on the plush couch.

"Remind me why he is here."

She rolled her eyes and refused to answer, so Baojia spoke for himself.

"I am here because Beatrice has a very concerned grandfather who offers her the finest protection of his clan."

"Are you sure you're not just homesick?"

The Asian vampire's face betrayed no emotion when he replied, "Unless we have changed course to San Francisco, I do not understand the question."

Beatrice snorted and laid her head on Giovanni's shoulder. "Leave him alone, Gio."

"I dislike having someone else on the plane." Particularly someone who looked at Beatrice the way her grandfather's enforcer did. Beatrice may not have noticed, but the quiet water vampire watched her every move with keen interest.

"You're overreacting," she murmured. "Besides, Ernesto wouldn't send anyone with us who wasn't on our side."

He saw an almost imperceptible smile flicker across Baojia's face, and there was a wry amusement in his eyes when he looked back at Giovanni.

"And it is always beneficial to have another interpreter," Baojia said in perfect Mandarin.

When Don Ernesto Alvarez, Beatrice's powerful ancestor whose clan controlled Southern California, had offered to send his child with them to visit the legendary Eight Immortals of Penglai Island, Giovanni could hardly refuse.

Baojia's prowess as a fighter was almost as well known as Giovanni's, despite his youth, and the offer was evidence of both how highly Ernesto viewed his granddaughter and how valuable he saw her connections in his world. Giovanni couldn't deny the offer without alienating a powerful ally and causing a rift in Beatrice's family.

Though she had initially been intimidated by the silent water vampire, Baojia made every effort to set Beatrice at ease in his presence. From casual observation, the vampire, who was only known by his given name, did not seem particularly intimidating, and his medium build and even features were unremarkable.

But the minute a canny opponent looked into his black eyes, Giovanni knew they would reevaluate. Baojia was one of the most lethal water vampires Giovanni had ever known, including his own sire. His mastery of his element, combined with a natural grace and training in various martial arts, had quickly become legendary. He was known for his ruthless and efficient combat and was also an exceptional swordsman.

The enforcer had monitored Beatrice for her grandfather in the years before Giovanni's return, and he could tell Baojia's interest in the young woman had been piqued.

"Gio?"

He looked down at Beatrice, whose eyes had begun to droop. "Yes, Tesoro?"

"I'm going to go lay down. When will we be in Beijing? Do I need to be awake?"

He shook his head. "We'll arrive mid-afternoon, but we'll remain in a secured hangar until nightfall. Sleep as long as you like."

She leaned over to place a kiss on his cheek, but he turned his head and captured her lips. Giovanni heard the small hum of satisfaction she made and the contented sigh when she pulled away. He let his eyes rake over her face, delighting in the slight blush that colored her cheeks.

"I'll join you soon," he said with a wink before she turned, gave Baojia a slight wave, and walked back to the secured bedchamber he'd installed in the belly of the cargo plane.

Giovanni watched her go, letting his eyes wander over her supple body and ignoring the instinct to follow her. Then he turned back to Baojia; he still had a few questions for the enigmatic man.

"Why are you really here?" he asked in Mandarin.

The water vampire offered a placid smile before responding in the same language. "As I said, I am here on orders from my father to guard Beatrice. As you have the same goal, I'm sure there will be no conflict. We will... cooperate, di Spada."

He flinched at the name he had used as a mercenary and assassin. Giovanni had chosen a different name for a reason.

"Please," he offered a stiff smile, "call me Giovanni."

Baojia nodded with respect before his eyes flicked to the room where Beatrice had gone to rest.

"So, you are here to guard my woman?"

He smiled again. "Does she like it when you call her that?"

Beatrice didn't like it in conversation, but he knew without a doubt she liked it in other, more intimate, moments. "She prefers it."

"That surprises me."

"Do you think you know her?"

"She's an interesting human," Baojia said, avoiding the question.

"She is." Giovanni paused. "And to what lengths will you go to protect my woman, Baojia? What did Ernesto ask of you?"

"That is between my father and me."

Giovanni cocked his head. "Is that so?" He looked between Baojia and the door Beatrice had walked through. "He told you to turn her if she is in danger, didn't he? Ernesto told you to sire her if her human life is at risk."

A shadow flickered in his black eyes, and Giovanni leaned forward. It was the truth, but Baojia was not pleased by the command from his sire.

"I was instructed to protect her by whatever means necessary."

Giovanni gave a rueful smile. "Not particularly pleased by that, are you?" He wasn't either, which was one of the reasons he was so eager to join Tenzin. The reassurance of Beatrice having the protection of another immortal—one he trusted implicitly—was vital to him.

"I have no desire for children," Baojia said.

Particularly not a human you are interested in.

Giovanni decided he was tired of parrying with the vampire, so he stood up and stretched his tall frame. "I'm going to retire for the day. I hope you're comfortable on the couch."

"I am perfectly comfortable, thank you."

Giovanni grunted and walked to the bedroom door, opening it, then locking it behind him with the multiple deadbolts, safety latches, and bars he used to secure the room. He turned to see Beatrice watching him with a sleepy smile.

"You're in a mood tonight."

He shrugged. "I don't trust him."

"I think he's fine." She yawned, reaching across the bed toward him. He stripped off his clothes and climbed in next to her. Tugging her arm, he pulled her on top of him and began kissing along her neck. Beatrice continued, "As interested in me as Ernesto is, I hardly think he'd send anyone to guard me that wasn't trustworthy."

He tugged at the small shorts and tank top she had put on to sleep. Her habit of dressing for bed annoyed him. Sleep clothing was an unnecessary layer, in his opinion, and highly uncomfortable against his skin.

"I'm going to donate all your night clothes to charity," he murmured against her neck as his hands slipped under her shorts, sliding them down her hips.

"And you know how much Ernesto is scared of you and Tenzin, so I hardly think—"

"Beatrice?"

"Hmm?"

He rolled them over and pressed his hips into hers, smiling when the sigh left her throat.

"I don't want to talk about your grandfather."

His gaze traveled from her dark eyes, across her pale skin, and down the slim column of her neck before his mouth followed.

"Okay," she breathed out.

"I don't want to talk." His mouth moved down her body, and he enjoyed the rush of energy that followed his lips and hands as he explored her skin. "At all."

"Okay." Her voice was higher pitched, and he smiled in satisfaction as he nipped at the inside of her thigh.

She may not have kept quiet, but he decided he didn't mind after all.

Giovanni woke the next evening to see her smiling at him.

"You think you're so sneaky."

"Hmm?" He rubbed at his eyes.

"I don't think you wanted me to be quiet at all, Mr. Possessive."

He grunted and blinked as she propped her head on his chest.

"I don't know what you're talking about."

She gave an adorable snort. "I should be pissed off, but—"

"We're going to a place with far thinner walls and far more vampires, so I suggest you get over any unnecessary modesty," he said as he ran a hand along her back.

She rolled her eyes at him, and he grinned at the gesture. The previous months had been the happiest in his memory. The move to Los Angeles had gone smoothly for the whole family, and he was satisfied with the security he had arranged for Ben, Caspar and Isadora while they were gone. Matt Kirby and Desiree Riley were aware of the situation, and Ernesto Alvarez had arranged his own security for Beatrice's grandmother, who had charmed him, to no one's surprise.

His family was as protected as it could be, and Beatrice was with him. Despite the danger and uncertainty he knew they were facing, Giovanni was content.

THE FORCE OF WIND

"I love you," he said quietly as he ran his fingers over her skin, causing her to shiver.

She sighed and laid her cheek on his chest. "I love you, too."

He knew the plane had landed, but he delayed leaving the safe cocoon of their cabin, knowing that an uncertain reality would face them as soon as they unlocked the door. They weren't meeting the boat to the island until midnight. Her fingers played along his chest, waking him and arousing his hunger. As if she could sense his fangs descending, she moved up his body, tilting her head to the side.

"You're hungry."

He growled low in his throat as her scent washed over him. Giovanni loved the fragrance of her skin when she first woke. His fangs descended, but he shook his head.

"I took too much yesterday. I'll drink a bag later."

Beatrice frowned. "I don't like it. You're not as strong from the bagged blood. I can tell."

She was right, but he shrugged anyway. "I'll be fine."

"I don't want you 'fine,' I want you as strong as you can be."

"Beatrice—"

"I know you don't like feeding from other humans, but we're going to have to figure something out eventually."

He rolled away from her, annoyed she had brought up the argument that had plagued them for months. "Can we not talk about this here?"

"You're not going to be able to feed from me forever. Not if you want me to—"

"I don't want to talk about this when we are about to go into a very unknown situation!"

She glared at him and sat up in bed. "And I don't want you going into an unknown situation at anything less than your strongest. It's not smart."

He snarled, pacing the small cabin, but she didn't back down. Instead, she rose to her knees, brushed her dark hair to the side, and took a fingernail to her neck, scoring it so deeply she bled.

Giovanni hesitated only a second before he rushed her, licking at the thin line of blood that marred her skin for a second before he latched on. He could feel the quick bite of her nails on his shoulders when he pierced her neck, but the flash of pain was quickly overwhelmed by pleasure as his amnis spread across their skin, and the rich, warm blood flowed down his throat.

She held his head to her neck and arched her body against him, but he took only a few deep swallows before he stopped and sealed the wounds by piercing his tongue. He closed his eyes and looked away from her, angered by her actions.

"Gio?"

He shook his head and walked to the small washroom attached to the cabin.

"Don't do that again," he said before he shut the door.

The boat from the mainland left at midnight, ferried by a young water vampire who greeted them with a nod and a polite smile. They climbed aboard the small junk and walked toward the seats the pilot indicated near the bow of the vessel. Giovanni's senses were on alert, but he could only feel faint traces of old energy signatures and the expected hum of their escort.

"Just us," Baojia murmured in English, his eyes scanning the water around them. "Nothing in the sea, either."

He nodded and placed a hand on Beatrice's back to lead her forward. They had come to an uneasy truce since their argument earlier in the evening, and he caught her eye, giving her a slight smile as they took their seats. As soon as they were seated, the young water vampire held out his hands at the stern, propelling them forward in the dark water and toward the hidden island in the Bohai Sea.

"How does he know how to get there?" Beatrice whispered, looking around the boat, which was devoid of any modern navigation equipment.

She had dressed in her typical uniform of slim black jeans and a black T-shirt before they left, but had failed to bring a coat in the warm summer air of the city. The wind on the water was brisk, so he put an arm around her and drew her closer as he answered.

"Penglai Island has a particularly strong energy signature because of the high immortal population. Even I can feel it, and it is not my home."

"And you're sure they're expecting us?"

"We wouldn't be going if they weren't."

"Tell me what to expect again," she said. "I feel like I'm going to forget."

"There will most likely be some sort of reception when we arrive, since we are expected and friends of Tenzin's."

"Why is Tenzin so important?"

Baojia chuckled quietly. Even Giovanni had to smile.

"Tenzin's sire is one of the Eight Immortals, Beatrice. The one I think your father sought out, Elder Zhang Guo."

He heard Baojia mutter something under his breath, clearly displeased by their destination.

"So, what? Tenzin's really important, then?"

"Tenzin could be one of the Elders if she wanted," Baojia said. "Unfortunately for them, she's too smart and has too low a tolerance for bullshit."

"She's older than most of them, Beatrice. And far more powerful."

"And her father's one of the main guys? Is he a good guy?"

Giovanni glanced back to their pilot. Though he was smiling and looking straight ahead into the night sea, he knew the vampire was memorizing their every word.

"Elder Zhang Guo is a great and powerful immortal. We are fortunate that he chooses to see us. He is deserving of great respect." He nudged her shoulder when she frowned at his rote answer, and she looked up at him. Giovanni made sure she caught the long look he gave the unknown vampire out of the corner of his eye, and he saw her mouth part as she nodded in understanding.

"I'm looking forward to meeting him, then," she said in a cheerful voice. "And to seeing Tenzin. It's been weeks since I've talked to her."

Giovanni smiled. Beatrice had proven to be a natural at the more political side of his life, and there was no way their pilot had missed the implied intimacy between the legendary wind vampire and the young human woman.

The sky had become strangely overcast, and a swirling fog covered the surface of the sea the farther they sailed away from the mainland. He glanced to the side to see Baojia curl his lip. The water vampire lifted a hand to reach out in front of him and, with a broad sweep of his arm, brushed the fog away. The dark blanket parted to reveal a great, glowing mountain, rising out of the water. Its stone walls were lit with golden lamps, and a wide avenue curled around, leading to a large palace that spread across the summit. The whole island shone like a jewel in the moonless night, and Giovanni could feel the energy rolling out from it in waves.

"The Elders do like their fancy castles," Baojia said as he stared at Penglai.

Giovanni turned to him. "You really didn't want to come here, did you?"

Baojia shook his head.

"I thought you were Chinese," Beatrice said.

"I've been an American far longer than you have, Beatrice De Novo." He curled his lip again as he stared ahead. "There's a reason I was willing to enslave myself to the railroads in order to leave this place."

Giovanni glanced back at the silent water vampire who piloted them. Baojia caught his look, but only shrugged, seemingly unconcerned to make his opinions public.

They entered a small bay and approached the dock that reached into the ocean. A crew of humans met the junk and tied it up before helping them off with quick movements and near-constant smiles.

The sounds of Mandarin filled the air, though the humans looked to be a mix of ethnicities from all over China. Giovanni pushed the humans back to help Beatrice off the boat and up the walkway, only to be met at the road by two hand-drawn carriages that were pulled by even more human servants. He tossed their small bags into one, which Baojia boarded with a quick nod, then Giovanni helped Beatrice into the second, and they started up the cobbled road toward the castle at the top of the hill.

Taking advantage of the weak human ears, Giovanni whispered to Beatrice in English.

"Remember what we talked about. Be very cautious what you say or what you commit to when talking with anyone. You are taken at your word here and must always follow through or you will lose face."

"Got it. I'll be careful."

"And remember, everyone will smile. Even if they want to kill you, they'll do it with a smile to your face and a knife to your back."

He felt her begin to tremble and he pulled her closer.

"I won't ever leave you unless I absolutely must. Trust me and Tenzin. No one else."

"And now I'm scared."

Giovanni was too, and he hated bringing her into such an unknown situation, but he knew that the possibility of open conflict on the sacred mountain in the middle of the sea was also very low.

"Don't be scared. Be smart. You'll do fine. Just remember, everyone has an agenda."

He tucked her head under his chin and stroked her hair. A part of him wanted to force the carriage around and take her back to the safety of the plane, but he knew that running was no longer an option. Lorenzo had forced their hands with Ioan's death and Beatrice's abduction. Giovanni was convinced they had to find her father and the book he carried if they were ever going to end this.

Their carriage approached the grand gate to the Temple of the Eight Immortals. Two giant stone lions guarded the steps leading to the entrance and Baojia waited nearby. He held a hand out for Beatrice and helped her down when the carriage came to a stop. Two human servants in dull brown robes rushed off with their bags, and the carriages sped away, leaving the two vampires and the human woman standing at the gate of the palace.

Giovanni heard Baojia sigh. "Let's get the circus over with. I'm hungry."

The two vampires flanked Beatrice, Giovanni walking slightly forward and to her right, while Baojia stepped behind her and took up her left side. Their eyes scanned the long staircase and the surrounding forest as they began climbing.

When they reached the top, two human servants met them and swung open massive doors painted gold and decorated with semiprecious stones set in elaborate patterns. The entrance to the palace was designed to impress, and by the look on Beatrice's awestruck face, it was working.

A hum seemed to come from beyond the antechamber when they walked in and two smaller, but more richly decorated, doors swung open. They walked into a massive stone courtyard lit with more golden lamps and decorated with ancient stone statues. Fountains and pools cut through the space and a huge open lawn ran down the center.

The flaming lanterns and flowing water, the open earth and empty sky all combined to provide a perfect balance of the four elements mastered by the immortal Elders that dwelled in the palace. Giovanni, Beatrice, and Baojia crossed the lawn dotted with tall, twisting rocks and walked up another set of steps leading to the main hall of the complex.

Through it all, Giovanni kept an eye on Beatrice, watching her as she took in the grandeur of the palace and the wealth on display. She was subdued and looked around with curiosity, but no great outward reaction. She was handling herself perfectly, he thought as he reached back and gave her hand a quick squeeze.

They climbed the steps and waited for an even more elaborate set of carved doors, overlaid in pure gold, to be pulled open by saffron-robed monks. Finally, they entered the Hall of the Elders and Giovanni paused, taking a deep breath to sense the air.

The few times he had come to this place in his five hundred years, the sheer spectacle of it was enough to start his heart. The hall was lined by enormous malachite pillars, and the walls were coated in silver. The oil lamps were gold, and the floor was a pure, white marble. Deep red rosewood benches lined the walls, but his eye was drawn to the end of the hall, where eight ancient thrones were placed, each from the era and province of the immortal who sat upon it.

His eyes moved from left to right as he faced them.

Elder Zhang Guo, the oldest of the eight, was Tenzin's sire and a warlord of some kind from the ancient steppes of the North.

Royal Uncle Cao, the youngest of the eight, was still over twelve hundred years old. An earth vampire of unknown origin, he usually wore a pleasant smile.

The Immortal Woman, He Xiangu, sat next to Cao. Giovanni met the eyes of his fellow fire vampire, who nodded at him with respect.

Lu Dongbin, the ancient water-master, scholar, and reluctant leader of the eight, sat near the center next to Zhongli Quan, a wind vampire who met him in an uneasy truce. The two had been embroiled in a somewhat-polite tug-of-war for power for almost two millennia.

The earth-master and legendary healer, Iron Crutch Li sat next to Zhongli, and next to him was possibly the most enigmatic immortal Giovanni had ever met.

Lan Caihe was a fire vampire who had been turned at a very young age, but that was all anyone knew about him... or her. No one even knew that much, and Lan wasn't sharing.

The last of the eight was the philosopher and water vampire, Han Xiang, a watchful immortal with a smile that never reached his eyes.

Giovanni estimated that at least sixty other vampires and numerous humans milled around the room, positioned in relation to their allies and associates. All of them paused and turned when Giovanni, Beatrice, and Baojia entered the room.

As one, the Eight Immortals, wearing identical white robes, rose to greet them, and the rush of energy that rolled through the room was enough to make Beatrice stumble back.

"Welcome, Giovanni Vecchio," Zhang greeted him in Mandarin. "And welcome, Baojia. Your presence is unexpected, but not unwelcome."

Baojia nodded, but refrained from bowing toward Zhang.

He Xiangu, the Immortal Woman, smiled as she surveyed the group. "It is pleasant to have such respected vampires in our midst, particularly a famed one of my own element." She nodded toward Giovanni. "But who is this young human you have with you? Who is this girl who warrants protection from both the lion and the dragon?"

Giovanni stepped forward. "Elder He, may I introduce the granddaughter of Don Ernesto Alvarez of Los Angeles, a friend of Tenzin, and my companion, Beatrice De Novo." He motioned Beatrice forward, and she nodded respectfully toward the Eight, as Giovanni had instructed her. When she spoke, it was in English, which Giovanni knew all the Elders spoke.

"I am honored to be introduced to the hall. Thank you for your invitation, Elder Zhang Guo."

"You are welcome here, Miss De Novo," Zhang answered with a smile. "It is my pleasure to meet my daughter's dear friend." He looked to Giovanni as if searching for a reaction when he continued. "I believe there is another present in the hall who is even more pleased to see you than the Elders."

Zhang looked at Lu, who lifted an open hand and motioned to the side of the enormous room. The crowd parted to reveal a slim vampire dressed in the blue-grey robes common among scholars of the court. Giovanni recognized him immediately and turned to Beatrice to hold her hand as she gasped in recognition.

"Dad?"

CHAPTER 2

He looked exactly the same. Beatrice's mind flashed to the last time she had seen her father the summer she was twelve. She'd been angry with him because he was leaving for Italy and worried because he wouldn't be there for her first day of junior high school.

> "You're always leaving. You love books more than me."
> "Don't be ridiculous. I'll be back on Friday afternoon. You and Grandma can pick me up at the airport and we'll meet Grandpa for dinner to celebrate your first week of school."
> "I can't believe you're leaving again! You just got back from Boston."
> "And I was only there for the weekend. I can't turn down this invitation, Beatrice. Try to understand."

She hadn't understood. Beatrice hadn't understood anything except the last words she had ever spoken to her father had been in anger. Five weeks later, her grandparents sat down with tears in their eyes and told her she would never see him again.

And fifteen years later, Stephen De Novo looked exactly as he had when he'd stepped out the door that summer morning.

"Daddy?"

Beatrice could feel Giovanni's hand on her arm, and she knew he wanted her to stay still. He worried so much. He shouldn't have. Her feet were as frozen as her gaze while she stood, staring at the man she thought she would never see again.

His thick, black hair was shorter, and he was paler, but no wrinkles touched the corners of his eyes. No grey sprinkled his hair. His dark brown eyes, the exact color of her own, stared at her as he stood in utter, immortal stillness. Her father was thirty-five years old for eternity.

Her hand slid down to Giovanni's, gripping it in her own as she heard him start to speak.

"Elder Zhang, you can imagine that you have... surprised us, though I am pleased to see Mister De Novo in good health. I'm sure his daughter is eager to meet with him, and—"

He broke off when the doors to the hall swung open and an irritated stream of Mandarin rung out. Beatrice tore her eyes from her father and turned to see the disturbance. For some reason, the sight of Tenzin's tiny figure stalking into the hall brought tears to her eyes and an overwhelming wave of relief.

Giovanni pulled her closer, slipping an arm around her waist and sighing. "*Grazie a Dio*," he whispered.

Beatrice leaned into him, her eyes darting between Tenzin and Stephen, who had stepped forward with a smile.

"Why are they doing the bowing thing again?" Tenzin barked in English. "Did you get new humans? Don't you tell them I hate the bowing thing?"

Elder Zhang stepped forward. Beatrice could have sworn he rolled his eyes when he saw his daughter. He issued a very polite-sounding stream of Mandarin that Beatrice didn't understand a word of until Tenzin interrupted him.

"Don't be rude in front of B. You know she doesn't speak Chinese, and your English is perfect. And why is Stephen in the hall? I told you I wanted to be here when he was introduced."

She could feel Giovanni start next to her, and she looked up at him in confusion. Tenzin had known her father was here? How long? She could tell the same questions were running through Giovanni's mind at lightning speed. The minute she saw his face, she realized he was furious, and she could feel his skin heating as she held his hand.

"I knew you were coming tonight," Zhang said with a shrug. "Why would I delay their reunion for your whims, my daughter?"

"Because I asked you to." Tenzin let loose a string of incomprehensible words that Beatrice couldn't even begin to translate. It didn't sound like Mandarin. It didn't sound like any language she'd ever heard before. She looked around, but no one looked as if they understood a word.

Zhang was arguing with his daughter in the same guttural tongue. Beatrice looked up at Giovanni, whose eyes were darting between Tenzin, Zhang, and Stephen with steadily mounting anger.

She slipped her hand along the small of his back, trying to soothe him. Beatrice was starting to feel overwhelmed. The last thing she needed was to worry about Giovanni bursting into flames while she was in a completely foreign environment, her father had suddenly appeared, and her friend seemed way more familiar with him that she ever would have expected.

"What, um... what language is that?" she whispered, trying to distract Giovanni, as Tenzin and Zhang continued their argument, seemingly oblivious to the audience in the hall.

"What?"

"What language are they speaking? No one looks like they understand what they're saying."

"They don't." Beatrice saw him take a deep breath and a calm mask fell over his face. "It's their own language. I suspect anyone who speaks it died long ago... or Tenzin and her father killed them so they could converse without eavesdroppers."

Somehow, that didn't seem implausible.

Most of the vampires were riveted by the loud argument. The humans skittered to the edges of the room, but the vampires were still and utterly silent. The Elders in the front of the room looked bored, except for Elder Lan. The childlike immortal's mouth was covered by his or her hands as the vampire looked on with laughing eyes.

"Enough. I'm taking them to my rooms," Tenzin cut her father off. "You can meet with them there if you want. Tomorrow night."

"Of course, dearest daughter," Zhang said with an indulgent smile. "There has been enough excitement for tonight. We have disrupted the business of the court long enough." He looked over to Beatrice and Giovanni with a smile. "Giovanni Vecchio, Beatrice De Novo, Baojia, you are welcome here. My daughter will see to your needs."

She felt her arm being pulled toward the back door, but she was still frozen in confusion. "What? Where are we going now?" She looked back toward where her father had just been standing, but he was gone. Beatrice started to panic. "Gio, where's—"

"Shh, Tesoro, he'll meet us there. Follow Tenzin. Follow her now."

"But—"

"Beatrice, do not linger. We have been dismissed."

His arm was like iron around her waist, but she craned her neck, trying to see where her father had gone. Over her shoulder, she spotted Baojia, who shook his head slightly before catching her eye and giving her a nod toward the door and a quick wink.

Beatrice swallowed the feeling of panic and leaned into Giovanni as he led her from the room, following behind Tenzin, who swept the doors open with a flick of her wrist and a gust of wind. She strode into the dark night, growling at the humans who bowed before her.

. . .

He still looked exactly the same.

They were sitting in one of the windowless rooms in Tenzin's wing of the palace. Beatrice and Stephen sat on low couches across from each other in awkward silence as Giovanni and Tenzin carried on a vicious argument in yet another unknown language. Baojia lounged on another couch across the room, glancing up from his book occasionally with a smile.

Beatrice stared at her father for a few more minutes until the silence became overwhelming. "What language are they speaking?"

Stephen blinked, apparently shocked that she'd spoken to him.

"I—I think it's Mongolian. Or some variation of it. There are several dialects that Tenzin speaks."

His voice sounded different. Deeper, somehow, but then she wondered if she had only forgotten what he sounded like in the fifteen years they'd been apart. He stared at her and a pink sheen came to his eyes. He smiled.

"You're so beautiful."

Blinking back her own tears, she crossed her arms and took a deep breath, wishing that Giovanni would finish his argument and take her away so she could collapse. "Thanks."

"You look like Mom… but different, too."

She stared at him, completely confused by the churning emotions in her gut.

"You look exactly the same."

He gave her a wry smile. "Part of the package, you know?"

"Yeah, I know."

He had no response, only nodding as he continued to stare at her.

"Grandma's doing okay?"

"Yeah. You know about Grandpa, right?"

"Yes. I… uh." Stephen cleared his throat the same way he always had when he was nervous. "I heard a few months after he passed away. But Tenzin said Mom got remarried earlier this year?"

"Yeah." She gestured toward Giovanni. "Gio's friend… well, kind of his son. But not a vampire son. But he raised Caspar, so he's like his son. But he's not a vampire. I mean, that would be weird, because he's old. Like Grandma. Well, a little younger. They're good. Great, really. Really in love and… happy. They're really happy." Beatrice couldn't seem to stop rambling, and her father was looking at her the same way he had when she would tell him a story as a child.

"I'm happy for her." Stephen nodded. "Tenzin has nice things to say about Caspar. And Giovanni, too."

She wanted to hug him. She wanted to hit him. Beatrice wanted to break down in tears and beg his forgiveness for her childish anger when he left. Then, she wanted to scream at him for putting her life in danger so many times.

"I don't know what to say to you," she choked out.

THE FORCE OF WIND

His eyebrows furrowed, and she saw a pink tear slip out of the corner of his eye as he shrugged his shoulders.

"That's okay. You don't have to say anything. I'm kind of enjoying just sitting across from you right now."

She fought back tears and twisted her hands together. "There's just... so much. There's so much that's happened. I'm really different than I was when I was little. And you're..."

"What?"

"You're just the same! But you're not. I just—I don't know who you are anymore."

Stephen nodded and took a deep breath before he spoke in a hoarse voice. "I know it's confusing, Beatrice. And I know we have a lot—a *lot* to talk about, but... I'm still me, Mariposa. I'm still me. And I love you so much. That has *never* changed."

Tears rolled down her face, and her father held out a tentative hand.

"Dad—" she cried before she stood up and met his arms as he embraced her.

His hands were cool when they brushed the hair out of her eyes and tucked her head under his chin as he had when she'd had nightmares as a child. She felt the rush of energy as Giovanni sped toward her side. He didn't pull her away, but Beatrice felt his quiet presence at her back as her father rocked her silently.

"I missed you so much," she whispered.

"I missed you, too. More than I could ever say."

Beatrice let him hold her as she soaked the front of his grey robes with her tears. After a few minutes, she heard him softly singing a lullaby she remembered from childhood.

"*A los niños que duermen, Dios los bendice...*" His low voice took her back to the small bedroom where she'd grown up. *The children who sleep, God bless them...*

"*A los padres que velan, Dios los asiste,*" she whispered along, remembering the old words as if he'd sung them to her the night before. *The fathers who watch them, God helps them...*

"I missed you every day, Beatrice. Forgive me for putting you in danger. Forgive me—"

"Don't," she said, pulling back and wiping her eyes. "Don't start apologizing for that. This has all been..." She shook her head. "I know it's not your fault, Dad."

She saw her father glancing over her shoulder and knew he was looking at Giovanni. She could feel his heat radiating on her back and knew her lover was showing enormous self-control to be standing still instead of whisking her away. Giovanni hated to see her cry. It seemed to disturb him on a very deep level, and he often reacted in anger toward the perceived cause. Feeling for his hand, she grasped it and pulled him closer.

"I think Beatrice needs some answers, Tenzin." She heard Giovanni speak in a low voice as he pulled her away from her father and into his arms. She kept hold of Stephen's hand for a moment, squeezing it before she retreated into Giovanni's embrace.

"What were you two arguing about?" She sniffed. "It better not have been about me."

"Of course it was." Tenzin snorted. "You know how he is."

Tenzin walked over and motioned toward a grouping of plush cushions on the far side of the room. A small fountain trickled in the corner, and Giovanni sat next to it, pulling Beatrice into his lap as Tenzin and Stephen sat across from them.

"Tell her how long."

Beatrice's eyes narrowed at her friend. Tenzin sat, perfectly relaxed and looking like the queen of her own personal castle. Which, in a way, she was. The palace complex was two-tiered, and Tenzin's rooms took up a full half of her father's buildings. Giovanni had explained it as they walked out of the Great Hall, trying to distract her from her whirling emotions.

The two earth Elders and their clans stayed below ground in a complex series of caverns that had been dug thousands of years before. The four wind and water Elders each took a wing of the outer palace walls with their retinues; and Mistress He and Elder Lan, the two fire vampires, lived in smaller homes within the palace walls, since they preferred to keep less company.

"Tell her how long you've known where her father was."

"Don't be rude. I don't have to explain myself to you. You're in my home."

"Tenzin," Giovanni growled.

"And, I'm here in this crazy house as a favor to you. You know how much I dislike being around my father and all the bowing people."

A bevy of servants scurried about, most of them overseen by a quiet, sweet-faced woman named Nima, who was a personal assistant of some sort. She was older than Caspar, easily in her eighties or nineties, and issued quiet orders as each human servant hung on her words.

"Tenzin," Beatrice finally said after a silent woman brought a tray of tea. It was hot and sweet-smelling, suffusing the air with the scents of honey and cardamom. "Please tell me how long you've known my father was here. You know we've been looking for him."

"You even asked me to call you when we got back from Brasilia, Tenzin. You knew then how upset she was, and you still said nothing," Giovanni bit out, obviously still angry with his old friend.

"You found my house in Brasilia?" Stephen asked, looking at her with delight. "You did remember the game!"

"Yes, it might have been a bit easier to just leave a note, De Novo," Giovanni replied. "Or show up to expected appointments. Either one would have worked so your daughter didn't have to worry that you were dead."

Stephen's eyes flashed. "And how was I supposed to know *you* were trustworthy, di Spada? How was I supposed to know you wouldn't take advantage of her?"

"Dad..." Beatrice squirmed.

"Maybe because I protected her. Which is more than what you did. Maybe because—"

"Stop it, both of you," Tenzin broke in. "This is ridiculous. Save your posturing for another time, or leave B and I alone so we can talk."

"Don't get mad," Beatrice said as she grabbed Giovanni's hand. "Just... let's talk for a bit, then I want to go to bed. I'm exhausted." In the back of her mind, she felt as if she should be slightly embarrassed to talk about going to bed with Giovanni when her father was right across from her, but she was too tired to be mortified. "Tenzin, tell me what's been going on."

Tenzin looked at Stephen and something passed between them that caused Beatrice to sit up slightly straighter. It wasn't exactly—

"If you found the house in Brasilia, then I'm assuming you found my journals," Stephen said. "So you know I came here in August of 2008."

"And what have you been doing since?" Giovanni asked. "You've been here for two years."

"Working, mostly. I was in a monastery in the Wuyi Mountains for over a year, studying with one of the Bön scholars trained by Elder Zhang. Then I came back here when I was called."

"And Tenzin? When did you meet her?"

Tenzin curled her lip and reached her foot across to kick Giovanni's shin.

"Shut up. It's none of your business, and you don't ask him. Ask me."

"Fine." Beatrice saw the collar of Giovanni's shirt start to smoke and she put a hand on his shoulder, willing him to calm down. "Tenzin," he said through gritted teeth, "when did you meet Stephen and why didn't you tell me you'd found him?"

"I met him about a year and a half ago, and I didn't tell you because it wasn't time to tell you yet." She gave a slight shrug and reached for her tea again.

"Okay!" Beatrice jumped in, knowing Giovanni was about to lose his temper with his oldest friend. "I'm exhausted, and I want to go to bed before I collapse. Gio, where are we sleeping?"

Giovanni pulled back from the argument he was about to jump into and rested his chin on her shoulder. He and Tenzin appeared to be in some kind of staring contest for a few moments until she heard him take a steadying breath. He brushed a kiss across her temple and helped her up before standing himself. She put an arm around his waist and almost pushed him away from her father and Tenzin.

On their way out the door, she paused by Baojia. Giovanni waited next to her with a blank expression, his mind obviously elsewhere.

"Are you calling Ernesto tonight?" she asked.

Baojia cocked an eyebrow at her. "Perceptive as always. Did you have a message for him?"

"Yeah, tell him he has a new family member around."

"Already on the agenda," he said before giving her a wink.

"Goodnight, then."

"Gio," Tenzin called across the room, still drinking tea with Stephen. "Nima put your bags in the same room as last time."

"Please, tell me it has more than chamber pots now."

"Yes," she sounded bored. "I made Father put a full bathroom in all my rooms here."

"How very modern of you, Tenzin," he muttered as they walked out the door.

"CAN WE PRETEND ALL THAT STUFF OUT THERE DIDN'T JUST HAPPEN?" Beatrice asked when they were finally alone. "I just need to be normal with you tonight. That was... too much. There's a million things to talk about, but I don't want to talk about any of them right now."

Giovanni nodded and gave her hand a quick squeeze before he started looking around the room. Even though they were in his friend's home, he did his typical precautionary search, zipping around the room, pulling back any draperies and generally searching every corner for any unknown threat.

While he did that, Beatrice fastened the series of locks on the heavy wooden door and slipped off her shoes. She sighed when she turned around to survey the room where they would be living for... she had no idea anymore. "Wow, this is so beautiful."

"It's different. It's all red."

Giovanni was looking around their room with some confusion, but she could do nothing but admire the space. The ceilings were vaulted, and she could see what she guessed were the original dark wood beams crossing the center. The rest of the room was a stunning mix of modern simplicity and Chinese elegance. There were no windows, but carved wooden screens lined the walls and an intricately worked arch lined with silk curtains separated the bedroom from the sitting area.

Giovanni was still frowning. "She definitely redecorated since the last time I was here."

"When was that?"

"About... a hundred years ago? I don't remember exactly."

She took a deep breath. "I forget how old you are most of the time."

"*I* forget how old I am most of the time."

Beatrice walked over to a low chaise, covered in red shantung. The whole room was decorated in rich crimson and black fabrics. "Somehow, I never pictured Tenzin having a flair for interior design."

He smiled. "I can almost promise you this is Nima. As rough as Tenzin can be, Nima is as cultured. They've been companions for many years."

Thinking of the odd mood she'd picked up between her father and Tenzin, she asked, "Is Tenzin... well, were she and Nima *together*? Or... I don't know anything about that part of her life, to be honest."

He shrugged. "Neither do I."

"Really?"

He cocked an eyebrow at her and walked over, placing his hands at her waist. "It's not something she talks about. You have to remember, Tenzin has been alive for over five *thousand* years. I expect she sees those kind of relationships in a very different way than you or I do."

She sighed and embraced him, wrapping her arms around his waist and putting her ear to his chest. His heart gave a single, quiet thump.

"Are you very angry with her?" She cursed herself for asking, but she had to know.

"You were crying."

"That's not her fault."

"No, it's your father's fault."

"No..." She looked up at him and traced around his lips with her finger. "It's not anyone's fault. You can't blame anyone this time."

He frowned as if her explanation was unsatisfactory, so she asked another question.

"Who are the lion and the dragon?"

He pulled back. "What?"

"Elder He, the other fire vampire?"

"Yes?"

"She said, 'Who is this human who's protected by the lion and the dragon?' Was she talking about you and Baojia?"

Giovanni chuckled. "Yes, she's quite dramatic, isn't she? She always has been."

"So, are you the dragon?" Beatrice teased, pulling at the back of his shirt as she walked backward toward the silk-covered bed beyond the arched doorway. "The dragon that breathes fire?"

He bent down and hitched up her legs around his waist, carrying her toward the bed and laying her on the red pillows. "We're in China; the dragon is a water symbol here."

"Oh?" she asked as his warm hands stroked along her waist. "So you're the lion? Why are you the lion?"

"I'm from the West, and the lion is a symbol of the sun," he said as he laid gentle kisses along her collar. "The sun is the mother of fire."

"But..." She sighed as she felt the quick lick of amnis wherever his lips touched. Her heart began to race. "That seems kind of cruel. You can't go out in the sun."

He only smiled, and she could see the length of his fangs gleaming in the low light of the candles that lit the room.

"*Tesoro mio,* the lion may be a symbol of the sun..." He bent down, lifted her body toward his, and gave one long, slow lick from her collarbone to her ear. "But he hunts at night."

CHAPTER 3

Giovanni left Beatrice sleeping a few hours before dawn, after exhausting her body and quieting her mind. She wouldn't talk about her feelings toward her father yet. He knew it was too soon. As she did with all new developments, she would take her time observing and thinking before she came to a decision.

But Giovanni could still be angry.

He was angry with Tenzin, who had kept the secret of Stephen's location for her own cryptic reasons. He was angry with Stephen for running and questioning his motives with Beatrice. He was angry that he had to be in this place that tried his patience and set every instinct on edge. He knew exactly why Tenzin avoided her father's court. It reminded him of the strictly choreographed social scenes of his human childhood, where even the color of a hat could have some hidden meaning.

Giovanni walked out of Tenzin's rooms and into the central courtyard, spending a few quiet moments breathing the night air and wandering among the large limestone rocks placed around the garden. The scholar's stones had been shaped by wind and water and were a popular symbol among the Eight Immortals, as they combined three of the four natural elements in harmony.

He stepped over a small footbridge and spied Beatrice's father reading a book near the edge of a stream. The vampire must have sensed the changing energy because he immediately looked up and narrowed his eyes. Giovanni walked over, sitting on a stone bench opposite Stephen. He looked around the garden, but picked up no indications they were being observed.

"How's my daughter?" Stephen asked.

Giovanni debated for a moment, but decided he would answer him. "She'll be fine."

Stephen nodded and closed his book. He set it on the bench next to him and folded his hands, the picture of practiced serenity.

"Have you had any word of Lorenzo?"

"I suspect he knows you are here. Or at least has some suspicion. The last time we had information about him, it indicated he was heading to Eastern Asia."

Stephen took a deep breath. "I've been in this place long enough that I knew it would trickle back to him."

"Then why did you stay?"

"I was tired of running." He sighed. "And I hoped that Beatrice would find me somehow."

Giovanni felt a spurt of anger. "You knew that I was looking for you. You must know my reputation. Why did you not seek me out? I was protecting your daughter; I could have protected you, too. And then you wouldn't have worried her."

"And how did I know you were trustworthy?" Stephen asked. "Do you know the stories your son tells about you? The picture Lorenzo painted of you would make a thousand-year-old vampire run screaming, much less someone as young as me."

"Good."

"Do you know what it did to me to think that Beatrice was under your aegis? I had the most horrifying thoughts and conflicting reports. I had no way of knowing what the truth was."

Giovanni snorted. "Your daughter is more than safe with me, De Novo."

"I realized that when I met Tenzin."

"Tenzin..." Giovanni curled his lip. "I'm quite angry with both of you."

"She said you would be, but that we were doing the right thing and that things had to happen in a certain order."

He shook his head. "Damned mystic. Who does she think she is?"

"Your friend," Stephen said as he leaned forward, "and a friend to my daughter."

Giovanni remained silent, sitting with a stoic expression as he examined Beatrice's father. Stephen had the thin countenance common among those who spent their lives immersed in books, but he also looked as if he had been feeding regularly, and he no longer wore the gaunt look Beatrice had described from her childhood. There was something about his energy signature that bothered Giovanni. If he had no idea who the vampire was, he would have guessed he was much, much older.

Perhaps even older than him.

THE FORCE OF WIND

"Is Beatrice very angry with me?"

Giovanni shrugged. "You'll have to ask her."

Stephen sighed. "You explained to her what he's like, didn't you? Lorenzo?"

"She didn't need me to describe Lorenzo's madness for her. Unfortunately, she's quite well-acquainted with it on her own."

Stephen's face fell, crumbling with guilt as he remembered why Beatrice was familiar with Lorenzo's cruelty. "I know she may not forgive me. I understand that." He looked up. "Do you understand?"

"Why you ran? Of course I do. I could even feel some guilt for it, since I created him, but ultimately, Lorenzo is a creature of his own making. And frankly, Stephen De Novo, you are only as important to me as you are to your daughter. If she did not want to find you, you would be nothing to me. A mere annoyance in my otherwise very long life."

Stephen looked at him silently, taking a deep breath and closing his eyes for a moment. "You really do love her, don't you?"

"That is between Beatrice and me. I do not know you well enough to confide in you; however, Tenzin may decide to trust you. And if I think that your presence is a danger to Beatrice, I will not hesitate to be rid of you, manuscript or no manuscript."

"You killed to get her back. You've spent vast sums to protect her. Does she even know?"

Giovanni shifted slightly. "It is irrelevant."

Stephen only nodded. "I'm glad you found her. She could have come to a far worse end."

"Yes," he murmured, "she could have." The rage Giovanni had suppressed for over five years bubbled to the surface, and he felt his skin begin to heat. "Do you have any idea what you did? How you endangered her? What it did when you abandoned her?"

"What? Abandoned—"

"How could you be so careless? With your own daughter? Do you realize what could have happened to her?"

Stephen scowled. "I didn't plan on being murdered by your son, di Spada. If he hadn't killed me, my daughter never would have been in danger."

Giovanni rose to his feet. "And if you hadn't left her unprotected, she wouldn't have been, either."

Stephen shook his head. "What do you even know about—"

"You are not a man without skills, Stephen De Novo. You could have sought protection for yourself and your family through someone more powerful of your choosing. Then she and your mother—"

"I thought I was doing the right thing!" Stephen rose to his feet. "I thought—"

"You thought like a petulant child!" Giovanni glared at him, clenching his hands and trying to restrain himself. "You gave no thought to your daughter. Do you realize that every man in her life has abandoned her at some point?"

Stephen blinked, cocking his head at Giovanni before he sank back to his seat. "But I thought you—"

"I left her, too. Like a fool. After I came back, it took me months to realize what I had done, how I had hurt her." He took a deep breath and calmed the rush of his heart, taking a seat on the bench once again. "I was arrogant, probably even more than you. I thought I knew what was best for her, what she could 'handle.'"

Stephen sat with his arms resting by his side and his shoulders slumped. He took a hand and waved it in a scooping motion toward the stream. A ball of water floated toward him, and he tossed it in the air between his upturned palms like a baseball.

"I never thought about it that way. I really didn't think she'd remember me."

"Don't get me started on your clumsy mental manipulations. You're lucky that I'm feeling generous and she has such a strong mind."

Stephen winced and let the ball of water splatter on the neatly trimmed grass. "My father, Hector—"

"Your father was a good man, De Novo, but he died. He didn't want to leave her, but he did anyway. You left her. Your father left her. I left her. Don't even get me started on the woman who calls herself her mother. Frankly, some days I think it's a miracle she'll talk to either of us."

Stephen looked at the ground, nodding. "I understand what you're saying."

"She's far stronger than either of us gave her credit for. Just remember that."

"Will she..." Stephen looked at him with pleading eyes. "I mean, does she want this life? Have you talked about it?"

Giovanni looked away. "You'll have to ask her. It is not my business to speak for her."

"I understand," Stephen said, nodding again.

"Do you?" Giovanni leaned forward, capturing Stephen in his vivid green gaze. "Make sure that you do."

Stephen did not flinch under his stare. "She's lucky she found you."

Giovanni shook his head and muttered, "I am the lucky one." Just then, his eyes darted to the right as he registered an ancient immortal coming toward them. Giovanni held up a hand to silence Stephen and took a deep breath, waiting for their host in a pose of meditation.

"Giovanni Vecchio. Stephen." Elder Zhang spoke as he approached them. "You are enjoying the hours before dawn in my favorite place."

Giovanni smiled. "I thought your favorite place was the banquet hall."

Zhang chuckled. "You know me too well. I have to thank you both for giving my daughter a reason to come visit me. It has been too long since I have seen her."

THE FORCE OF WIND

"You know Tenzin only does what she wishes, Zhang." Giovanni had always liked Tenzin's sire, enjoying his jovial personality that often reminded him of Carwyn. But he knew Zhang and Tenzin's history was complicated, so he didn't often express his feelings to his old friend.

"My daughter has always done what she wishes," the ancient wind vampire said. "I suppose I should be grateful she visits at all."

Giovanni fell silent, wary of saying the wrong thing. Zhang looked Stephen up and down. "Stephen, have you fed tonight?"

"I have, Elder Zhang. Thank you for asking."

"And how are you finding the palace after the austerity of the monastery?"

"I am grateful for my time in both, Elder Zhang. I am grateful for your hospitality, as well as the hospitality of Elder Lu Dongbin's monks."

So, Beatrice came by her political side naturally.

Stephen answered graciously, with none of the hesitation that would typically mark a vampire speaking to one so much older than himself. In fact, Stephen had carried himself with a surprising amount of confidence in the main hall earlier in the evening, as well.

Interesting.

"And your book has remained safely at the monastery, has it not?" Zhang said, looking at Giovanni out of the corner of his eye. Giovanni cut his eyes toward Stephen, curious what the young immortal would reveal with his expression, but Stephen had mastered the art of the impassive face. His expression revealed nothing but contentment.

Giovanni spoke up. "It is quite safe, from what Tenzin tells me. No one knows the location of the monastery except the Elders, is that not true, Zhang? Even Stephen was prevented from knowing where he was going on his journey."

"Very true." Zhang quirked a smile and shrugged his shoulders in an unusually dramatic fashion. Tenzin's sire was from the ancient steppes of Northern Asia and had always been more expressive than his younger Chinese peers. His mannerisms reflected it. "I feel the pull of the dawn coming. I believe I will retire."

Zhang nodded at them both before taking his leave, lifting off the ground in front of them and skipping across the top of the stones as he flew toward his rooms.

Giovanni looked at Stephen. "A good suggestion for all of us, I think."

Stephen and Giovanni rose and walked across the lawn.

"We'll talk about the book tomorrow, Stephen. At first dark, when Beatrice and I are awake."

Beatrice's father nodded quickly. "Fine, I'll be expecting it." Then he smiled as he watched Zhang's retreating figure. "You realize he doesn't really sleep, right? Neither he nor Tenzin have to sleep more than an hour or two a day."

"I know." *But I find it curious that you do, Stephen.*

519

He couldn't help but notice, as they walked toward the windowless rooms of Tenzin's palace and the morning sky began to lighten, that Stephen hadn't slowed at all, as a younger vampire normally would as he felt the pull of day.

Very interesting.

"Tesoro," Giovanni whispered into Beatrice's ear the following evening, trailing a hand from her knee, over the curve of her hip, and slipping it around her waist as he pulled her back to his chest. He had woken before her, which was unusual. She must have been overwhelmed from the night before.

"Beatrice," he whispered again.

"Hmm?"

"Time to wake up."

"Okay." He felt her shift into his chest as she stretched. "Can you rub my legs?"

"Of course." He sat up and pulled back the sheet. "Were you practi—what the hell?" His mouth dropped open as he saw the bruises on her legs. There was one particularly large one near her hip. He let loose with a string of old curses she probably didn't understand.

"I was sparring with Tenzin today," she said in a sleepy voice. "You know, Gemma has nothing on Tenzin. Tenzin's mean." Beatrice smiled a little. "And did you know she doesn't have to sleep hardly at all? She never mentioned that when she visited me in L.A."

He was still speechless as he examined her. There were fat bruises along her torso and arms, though none so severe that they could cause internal injuries. He continued muttering in Italian and he felt his skin heat up.

She must have sensed his anger, because she turned and narrowed her eyes. "Don't do the thing again. And calm down, you're getting hot."

"Beatrice, if you—"

"If I what?" She sat up, glaring at him. "I'm the one that asked her to practice with me. And it's not the first time we've sparred, Gio. Remember? You were gone for a few years. We always practice when we're together, and I usually get pretty bruised. It's nothing to worry about."

"Does she always treat you as her own personal punching bag?" He was angry. All he could see were the startling bruises that marred his lover's fair skin.

"You know what? Forget it. I'll take a bath and find some aspirin." Beatrice sat up and swung her legs over the edge of the bed. "I'm sure one of the bowing people—"

"Don't," he said as he pulled her back. He wrapped his arms around her, gently heating his body to soothe her aching muscles when she winced. She began to relax, but he kept her on his lap, pulling her legs around to straddle his waist as he heated his hands and placed them on the worst of her abdominal bruises. He buried his face in the crook of her neck.

"Warn me next time," he said. "I was surprised. You know my reaction to seeing you hurt."

"Okay, consider yourself warned." She played with the hair at his neck, twisting the curls in her fingers as she slowly relaxed her muscles. "When Tenzin and I hang out, I end up bruised from practice. But she's a great teacher, and she never does more than I can handle."

He made no reply, but moved his hands down her legs and began to massage them.

"Gio?"

"Mmmhmm?"

"Maybe... maybe we need to think about doing it sooner."

His breath caught and his hands halted. "I thought we were going to wait until Benjamin was older, so at least one of us—"

"I think we could work around it." Her fingers twisted in his dark hair. He took a deep breath and continued her massage.

"And I think it's not something I want you to do because you're fearful for your life. That's not a good reason to—"

"It's not the reason. You know that."

"Then why—"

"Because it's still a factor, love." She tilted his head back so they were eye to eye. "Gio, my safety is still a huge liability."

He took a deep breath and stared into the eyes of the woman he loved. "I think..."

"What?"

Giovanni frowned as he met her worried brown eyes. "I feel like we're rushing this. You're still young. You should have time—"

"Ugh." She rolled her eyes and looked away. "Not this again."

"It's not a small thing, Beatrice."

"I'm not saying it is. But it's not a big thing—not for me."

"I just think we should wait. Don't you trust Tenzin and me to guard you?"

She took a deep breath. "Of course I do. That's not the issue."

"Then—"

"We should get out of bed." She climbed off his lap. "I want to ask my dad a few questions tonight. I think I deserve some answers from him."

He sighed when she made the obvious subject change, but smiled at the determined expression she wore as he rose to join her.

"Are you feeling better?"

"I am, thanks." She squeaked as he scooped her into his arms and walked to the bathroom.

"Good. I think a nice, warm bath is in order, Miss De Novo. Just to be safe, I'll join you."

"Well," she laughed. "If it's for my own safety…"

"Oh yes," he said with a pinch to her knee, which was thankfully not bruised. "Safety first."

GIOVANNI WAS FAR MORE RELAXED AN HOUR LATER WHEN THEY MET WITH Tenzin and Stephen in the main room. Baojia was out hunting, no doubt informed that they had planned a private meeting. Stephen and Tenzin were already sitting at a table, sipping tea, when they walked in.

"Good, Nima had dinner prepared for you," Tenzin said, nodding to one of the servants standing near the door. "Did I bruise you too much?"

"I'm fine," Beatrice said with a wave.

Tenzin cocked an eyebrow at Giovanni, as if challenging his cool demeanor, but he didn't rise to the bait. "She's very good, you know. When she changes, she'll be formidable. We should have Baojia give her weapons training while she is here. I have a full practice room with many options."

"Oh?" Beatrice perked up. "What kind of weapons?"

He sat down and waited for Tenzin to stop teasing him. Though, really, it wasn't a bad idea. Because he had such a ready weapon in his fire and rarely needed to behead an enemy, Giovanni wasn't as well trained in swordsmanship as most vampires were. He was proficient in fencing and the older Greek and Roman forms of hand-to-hand combat, but he suspected that Beatrice would take to the Asian styles better, considering her background in martial arts. Baojia, despite Giovanni's personal reservations, would be an excellent teacher.

"We'll talk later; I'm sure she'll consider it," he said. "In the meantime, try not to bruise any internal organs on my woman, Tenzin."

"Hey!" Beatrice scowled and smacked his arm. "Enough with the 'my woman' stuff already."

"Really?" He lifted an eyebrow in her direction. She blushed and looked at the bowl of noodle soup the servant had just placed in front of her.

"Well," Stephen said when the servant finally closed the door. "Speaking of awkward silences, let's talk about what's been keeping me running around the globe for the past thirteen years, shall we?"

Giovanni leaned forward. "First, do you know where Andros's library is?"

Stephen shrugged. "When I escaped, it was in Lorenzo's villa in Perugia, but who knows where it is now! I'm sure he moved it; it could be any number of places."

Giovanni sat back, stunned into silence by the simple confirmation of the mystery he'd followed for so long. He felt Beatrice's hand grasp his own, and he

THE FORCE OF WIND

looked over at her. She had tears in her eyes as she stared at him, but he gave her a small smile and squeezed her hand.

He heard Stephen still speaking. "You knew about the library, right?"

Giovanni looked up, his voice a little hoarse when he finally spoke.

"No, Stephen. I have suspected for some time, but when Lorenzo and I parted many years ago, I thought my father's and uncle's collections had been lost or burned in Savonarola's bonfires."

Stephen's mouth dropped in horror. "No wonder you were looking for me. Andros's library was... magnificent! It would take a thousand years to detail it. The tablets. The scrolls." Stephen turned to his daughter. "Beatrice, Andros had scrolls from Alexandria. Things from Baghdad that he'd rescued from the Mongols. Books humanity thought had been lost for—"

"Dad," Beatrice interrupted. "Trust me when I say, we could talk about that library for years—and probably someday, we will. But right now, I think there's one book we really need to know about."

"Of course." Stephen nodded, taking a deep breath and leaning back in his seat, though Giovanni could still see the energy snapping off him. "Of course. I just... I had no idea you had no confirmation of its existence, Giovanni. I'd be happy—"

"Another time, Stephen." Tenzin rolled her eyes. "Tell them about the manuscript. Tell them about Geber's work."

"Geber?" Giovanni's ears perked up. "I wondered. So it was alchemy, or early chemistry? A lost manuscript? An experiment?"

"An incomplete work, but his greatest achievement. Of that, I have no doubt."

"Okay," Beatrice broke in. "Geber. I know I've heard the name, but remind me."

Giovanni turned to her. "Jabir ibn Hayyan. He was called Geber during my time, Tesoro, but he was an eighth century Persian alchemist."

"One of the first to apply modern scientific methods to his work," Stephen said. "He was hugely influential in the Middle East and later in Europe."

Tenzin piped up. "His work mostly related to the artificial creation of life. Not achievable, that we know of, but his formulas held promise and were better tested than others of the time. He wrote in deliberately cryptic ways, so many of his original formulas are still a mystery."

"But what is so special about this book? The book you stole, Dad? Why is it worth killing for?"

"'Knowledge is power,'" Giovanni murmured, still haunted by the words of his father. He shook his head and squeezed Beatrice's hand. "Humanity steals it. Trades it. Covets it. Many have killed for it. What is the knowledge that Lorenzo seeks from this, De Novo?"

Stephen sighed and spread his hands on the table.

"Life. The secret mankind has sought for centuries. Geber found the elixir of life. He discovered its source."

Beatrice shook her head. "That's not possible, that's—"

"And it's not just for humans."

CHAPTER 4

"The elixir of... life?"

Beatrice could hear the skepticism dripping in Giovanni's voice.

Stephen only nodded. "Yes, the elixir of life."

"Let's pretend I believe that this is possible," he said. Tenzin barked something in Mandarin, but he just waved a hand in her direction and continued looking at Stephen. "I'll pretend this is possible, and you tell me why on earth an immortal vampire like Lorenzo wants this elixir enough to start a war with me."

"I told you, it's not just for humans."

Beatrice's eyes were darting around the table. She was as skeptical as Giovanni, but she knew her father had never been easily fooled, and he looked dead serious.

"I'd like to know why you think this is plausible, Dad." She spoke quietly, but every head at the table swung toward her. She had forgotten about her food almost as soon as it was set in front of her, but she played with her chopsticks nervously. "I mean, from all accounts, alchemists have tried for thousands of years to create a magic formula to prolong life, but none of them ever accomplished it."

Tenzin finally spoke. "But, none of them—as far as we know—had the advantage that Geber had."

"And what was that?" Giovanni leaned back in his chair as he spoke.

Stephen said, "Four vampires willing to work with him."

All attention was on her father again.

"What?" Giovanni narrowed his eyes, glaring at Stephen.

"Geber had four vampires, one of each element, that he was working with. I finally figured it out by reading one of his journals in Andros's library. It's one of the other books I took. I took the manuscript with the formula, along with three of Geber's journals and a few books I knew I would be able to sell for quick cash."

"Some of *my* collection."

He offered Giovanni an embarrassed frown. "I'm sorry. I'm sure some of them were yours, but I had nothing."

"I'll get them back. Continue."

"The key to the elixir is the blood. No one knows why we have an affinity toward the elements, but all vampires do. And it's our blood that seems to hold the key. Geber was smart and probably knew that his contemporaries would doubt his use of blood that wasn't even supposed to exist—except in myth—so he never names the ingredients in the formula, but from reading his journals, I was finally able to figure it out."

"But why would that even—"

Stephen turned to Beatrice. "You have bruises all over, why can't Giovanni heal them?"

She frowned. Surely her father knew that much. "Because I'm human. Gio says my digestive system would break down his blood before it could have any positive effect. That's why it only works on open cuts or scrapes."

"Exactly, your human system doesn't know what to do with it. Whatever magic animates our blood—"

"It's not magic," Giovanni spit out. "We just haven't figured out what it is yet."

"Damn it!" Tenzin said. "You're so damn arrogant, Gio. Do you think your science can explain everything? There are things in this world—"

"That haven't been explained yet. And once upon a time, humans didn't know what the stars were, either. But that time has passed. The mysteries of the natural world—"

"Are not going to be revealed at this table," Beatrice interrupted. "But the super-secret mystery of the elixir of life might be if you all quit arguing and let my dad talk."

Stephen chuckled, but Giovanni and Tenzin looked annoyed to have been interrupted. Still, they fell silent and Giovanni gestured to Stephen. "Continue."

Her father turned to Tenzin. "If you were injured, would you go to another wind vampire for blood?"

"You know I wouldn't." She seemed content to play along with the rhetorical question. "I would go to a vampire of another element that I trusted if I needed strength. The blood of your own element—"

"Does very little to heal, unless it is your own sire," Giovanni said, a sudden light of interest coming to his eyes. "It is the combination of elements that seems to heal. Tell me about the four types of blood."

Stephen took a deep breath. "Geber must have researched extensively, and his subjects must have been very open with him. What he discovered was that, combined, the four elemental bloods would create an elixir that would heal and prolong human life. Possibly indefinitely."

"Oh, wow," Beatrice whispered. "So—"

"How?" Giovanni asked. "How would a human even be able to ingest it?"

Tenzin spoke softly. "That's where his alchemy came in, my boy. It seems that somehow, Geber was able to stabilize it. That's what the formula is for. It's the formula to stabilize the four combined immortal bloods in a way that will allow the human body to reap the benefits in the same way that a vampire body does."

"But..."

She could tell from looking at him that Giovanni had been rocked. She was feeling a little overwhelmed herself. He looked at her and traced a hand along her cheek, letting his thumb rest at the pulse in her neck.

"Beatrice," he whispered. "This could be..."

"Gio, we don't know enough about this."

Tenzin spoke up again. "No, we most definitely do *not*. And I'm highly suspicious of the next part of the findings."

"What findings?" Beatrice asked.

"Geber tested it for almost a year," Stephen said, "and the results seemed very promising. He gave it to a human that was diseased—he only described it as a 'wasting disease'—but the recovery was almost instant. The human was observed for another few months before Geber sent him home, apparently totally healed. Another subject was very elderly. While the elixir didn't reverse the aging process, it seemed to halt when he took the blood, and his quality of life improved. He was healthier and exhibited a 'younger' level of health."

"But you said this was not just for humans," Giovanni said, leaning forward over the table. "What did you mean?"

"I mean that one of the vampires that drank from a human who had taken the elixir only had to drink once."

Beatrice frowned. "Drink once for what?"

Stephen looked at her, spreading his hands across the table. "I mean, he only had to drink once, Mariposa. He drank once in the year of testing."

She still didn't understand what he was trying to say. "And then what?"

"And then he didn't have to drink again," Tenzin said. "At all."

She turned to Giovanni in shock. His face was completely frozen.

Beatrice said, "What? At all? As in, he drank once from a human that had taken this elixir, and he didn't have to drink any more blood in the entire year of testing?"

"That's exactly what I mean," Stephen said. "He drank once, ate the amount of food he normally would have, and never had to take another drop of blood."

"There's something we're not seeing," Tenzin said. "Gio, I can see the look on your face, and I know what you're thinking, but this is not a cure for bloodlust. It's not. There's something—"

"But what if it is, bird girl?"

Beatrice didn't think she had ever heard him sound more vulnerable.

Despite his pragmatic views on vampire life, she knew it still bothered Giovanni every time he had to feed from a human, even a criminal. It made him feel barbaric, like a parasite. When they were together and she received pleasure from him, it was one thing; but he couldn't drink from her all the time, it simply wasn't healthy. That was why he bought donated blood, even though it affected his health.

"It is not the answer. There's something we're not seeing here."

"But what if it's true? What if—"

"Then why would your son want it?" Tenzin shouted. "Why would he kill for this? He has no need of eternal life, and he has no compunction about drinking, or even draining, humans. He's no kind of humanitarian, so why does he want it so badly? I'm telling you, there's something here we are not seeing!"

They broke into a heated argument in Mandarin that Beatrice couldn't follow, while Stephen watched, occasionally glancing at her as if she might know what to do. Tenzin and Giovanni had both risen to their feet and showed no signs of stopping.

"Enough!" Beatrice finally said, standing to join them. "This isn't something we can solve tonight. Even I can tell this book needs more investigating before we all run out and drink the Kool-Aid, so to speak."

"That's why it's still at the monastery," Stephen added. "Zhang wanted his oldest student and Lu's monks to take a look at it. Their knowledge of alchemy, particularly plant alchemy, which is what the formula required, is far better than my own."

"Or even mine, to be honest." Tenzin stepped away from the table. "Now, I'm going to find Baojia. I want to talk to him about training Beatrice. B, take him away and calm him down, will you?"

She could hear Giovanni growl next to her, but he didn't feel hot, so she wasn't overly concerned. She glanced at her father.

"Um... Dad—"

"I'm going to the library; then I'll be in the Great Hall," Stephen said. "I'll talk to you both later."

He slipped out of the room, and she and Giovanni were alone. He stared at her with the most tender expression she had ever seen.

"Tesoro, if this means—"

"We don't know what it means yet, Gio. And we don't know if we can trust this information. There are too many unknowns."

He put a warm hand over her heart. "But, if you didn't have to give up the sun, if you didn't have to be a slave to your own hunger to be with me forever..."

She drew him down for a gentle kiss. "There's still a lot to think about, love."

He nodded, but pulled her into his arms, wrapping her up in his warm embrace as she tried to think past the feeling of dread that still churned in her gut when she remembered Tenzin's warning.

Beatrice had to agree. There was something they weren't seeing.

"I DON'T TRUST THAT DAMN FORMULA," TENZIN MUTTERED AS THEY practiced late that afternoon. Beatrice was still astonished by how comfortable she was in the middle of the day. Though she couldn't go out in the sun, the ancient vampire showed not a hint of reduced strength, although Tenzin claimed that flying wasn't a very good idea.

They were taking some time off from heavier sparring to concentrate on tai chi forms.

"I don't really want to talk about the formula any more right now, if that's okay. I think there are too many questions."

"Thank you for being skeptical. It's a relief. I was worried that you were going to go crazy at the possibilities, and I'd have to restrain you both. I don't trust it."

Beatrice moved deliberately, focusing on the slow movement of her limbs and the steady rhythm of her breathing. "I'm skeptical of anything that seems too good to be true, and this formula falls into that category. Why are we doing basic forms again? And why are we doing them even slower than normal?"

"Because, when you turn, my friend..." Tenzin moved in front of her and started to mirror her in the "push hands" technique she employed when she wanted Beatrice to slow her movements. The technique always made Beatrice feel as if she was moving through heavy water.

Languorous. Flowing. Forceful, but still fluid in her body and mind.

"You must remember how your body feels right now. How you control every muscle, every bone, every joint and tendon. Deliberate. Everything must be deliberate. That is what will enable you to control yourself when your senses have been heightened, so you will not become overwhelmed. If I had known this discipline when I had first turned, my younger years would have been much more pleasant."

They moved as mirrors of each other, an achingly slow ballet of combat forms, pared to their most essential movements. This was not about speed or strength; it was about the total focus of the mind and body. The meditation of the mind was as central as the physical control.

"What were you like when you were younger?"

Tenzin paused, and Beatrice wondered if the secretive vampire would answer her.

"I was very angry and very violent. Why doesn't Giovanni want you to turn?"

She sighed and closed her eyes, moving through the familiar movements.

Bend. Sweep. Push. Yield.

"He's sentimental, for one. He uses the idea of one of us being available during the day for Ben as an excuse, but it's not really what's bothering him."

"What is it, then? Your human life is a liability at this point."

"I agree, but he's pretty stubborn."

"Why?"

"I think he's worried about the motherhood thing, to be honest. He thinks I'm going to turn and then regret not having children."

Tenzin snorted. "So you'll adopt."

"That's what I told him. We already have Ben, for heaven's sake. If we want more children someday, we can adopt, but he thinks I'll regret not giving birth or something. It's not something I take *lightly*, but being pregnant, especially when it wouldn't be his, isn't something that I consider vital to happiness."

"It's not. And pregnancy doesn't make you a mother. I gave birth to three children, but I was only mother to one."

Beatrice stumbled back, stunned by Tenzin's admission. The vampire just looked at her, clearly annoyed she had fumbled their practice. She stepped closer, pushing Beatrice to mirror her graceful movements.

Bend. Stretch. Push. Yield.

"How old were you?"

"When I birthed my children?" Tenzin shrugged, moving into a more complex routine. "*Focus.* I have no idea. We didn't celebrate birthdays back then. I'd been bleeding for one winter when I became pregnant with my first child."

"What—"

"She was small. She didn't survive the winter. Neither did her father."

Bend. Sweep. Push. Yield.

"Your husband died, too?"

She frowned, folding at the waist as they swept down into a new form. "I suppose you could call him my husband. His older brother took me after that. He already had a wife, but she hadn't given him any children, so he took me. I was luckier with him. My babies were born in the spring the following year, and both survived."

"What happened to them?" Beatrice concentrated on keeping her tone easy as they moved. She was shocked Tenzin was sharing as much as she was.

"The oldest one, the stronger one, was given to my husband's first wife. I was allowed to keep the second child. He was small, but strong."

Her mind was still reeling at the casual tone in which Tenzin was relating her story. She almost sounded like she was talking about an acquaintance. They continued to move with each other, as Beatrice focused on her breath and the stretch of her muscles.

Bend. Stretch. Push. Yield.

THE FORCE OF WIND

"Where did you live?"

"It was on the Northern steppes. I have no idea where exactly. I lived in a village that was raided a lot. That's how I was turned."

"What happened?" She held her breath, half expecting Tenzin to clam up. She didn't.

"We were raided one day, and the first wife sent me out to check the goats. They never took everything—how else would we have more goats for them the next time they came? But she wanted to know how many we had left and if any kids had dropped, so she sent me out after dark. I was happy to go. My son had been crying and he always liked it better when I walked, so I tied him to my back and went out to check the pens. There were three men there."

"The raiders?"

Tenzin cocked an eyebrow and moved into a new routine. "No, definitely not. These 'men' didn't need horses to get around."

"They were vampires," Beatrice whispered.

"Yes, they were vampires."

She fell silent for a few moments, and Beatrice saw her close her eyes as she moved through the forms.

Bend. Push. Sweep. Yield.

Even though her heart ached, and part of her didn't want to hear the rest of the story, Beatrice still asked.

"What happened?"

"They were feeding on the goats, but stopped when they heard me. My son started crying, and I tried to hush him so I could run away, but they were already coming toward me. I thought they were demons of some kind; they moved so fast. They swept me up and took me away."

"And your son?" she whispered.

Tenzin paused for only a second in her silent exercise.

"He fell to the ground. He was crying when they took to the air. It's possible someone from the village found him. Probably not."

Tears fell down Beatrice's cheeks, but Tenzin's eyes were still closed, silently practicing the meditative forms of the tai chi routine. Her face was serene, and her hair flowed around her, brushing her shoulders as they moved together.

Bend. Stretch. Push. Yield.

"And Zhang?"

"The men who took me were Zhang's sons. His own band of raiders. There were four of them then. He turned more as the years passed. His sons sired sons. Eventually, my father had over fifty wind vampires to do his bidding."

"Why did he turn you?"

"For his men. They usually killed the human women they took, so Zhang turned me. He thought I would be more… resilient."

Beatrice's stomach twisted in horror, but she took care not to halt her steady

531

movements. She could not comprehend the cruelty of Elder Zhang turning a young girl, just so she could be a plaything for his other children. No wonder the vampire disliked her sire.

Tenzin was still moving with her eyes closed, her face a picture of placid meditation as she practiced.

Bend. Sweep. Push. Yield.

"How long were you with him?"

"Two or three hundred years. Just long enough to kill off all of his children."

Beatrice was speechless, but Tenzin never stopped moving through the complex combat forms. Eventually, she continued without prompting.

"They would take turns with me. At first, I was frightened. After all, I was a child. And I had no idea how to use my new body. But I slowly gathered more skill. I was probably twenty years immortal when I killed the first of his sons."

Bend. Stretch. Push. Yield.

"Eventually, they avoided me. But I didn't stop until I had killed them all."

"What did Zhang do when they were all dead?"

"He laughed. Then he told me I was his finest creation, his fiercest warrior, and sent me out into the world with half of his wealth. He came to Penglai soon after that, and I was on my own. I never had another companion until I met Giovanni."

Finally, she slowed her movements, finishing the routine before she bowed to Beatrice, who mirrored the movement. Tenzin opened her storm-grey eyes.

"Do not pity me, Beatrice De Novo. My life has been as fate dictated, and now I am master of it. Do not waste your regret on the past."

Beatrice nodded as they moved to the benches that lined the room and drank from the pitcher of water that had been set out. "Why didn't you kill Gio when you met him? He told me that he'd been sent to kill you. Why did you have mercy on him?"

She smiled. "I saw him. I saw his eyes in a dream. They were the same color as my son's. I knew our fates were intertwined."

Beatrice gulped down the water as Tenzin looked over her shoulder. She smiled just a few seconds before Beatrice heard the door open.

"Nightfall," Tenzin said. "You boys will have to wait to play with her," she shouted at the door. "She's still mine for another hour."

Beatrice turned to see Giovanni and Baojia leaning against the wall of the practice room. Her heart skipped a beat when she saw the two handsome men outlined against the pale walls. Baojia wore a look of amusement. Giovanni's eyes were narrowed at her; he looked hungry.

"Give me back my woman, Tenzin. You've borrowed her for too long."

Tenzin rolled her eyes and turned back to Beatrice. "How do you put up with him? That's so annoying."

She laughed. "He just hates it when I'm not there when he wakes up."

The small vampire lifted up and flew toward the two men, swiping at them and smacking both on the back of the head before she flitted back to Beatrice's side.

"Well, they'll have to learn how to be patient. You have more important things to be doing than entertaining his libido." She looked up at Beatrice and gestured toward the mat. "We're running out of time."

CHAPTER 5

The longer he watched her, the faster his heart beat.

She was astonishing.

A vision of her transformed assaulted him. Lithe grace turned into preternatural strength and speed. Fangs gleaming in her mouth as she pierced his skin. Her smooth, pale skin crackling with energy when she touched him.

Imagining Beatrice as an immortal was undeniably alluring. Yet, it still filled him with guilt.

"She'll be stunning when she turns," Baojia said as he sat next to him.

Giovanni glared at him, irritated that his thoughts had been so closely mirrored by the other vampire.

"She's stunning now."

Baojia just cocked an amused eyebrow at him.

"She plans on it. Why else would she practice as she does?" He folded his legs and hands in a meditative pose. "I think it was in the back of her mind even before you came back."

"Oh?"

"I remember the first martial arts class she took. Introductory tai chi. Ernesto was very pleased. Beatrice says Tenzin suggested it. Very forward thinking of your old partner; it will help immeasurably with physical control."

Giovanni wanted the water vampire to shut up. He disliked being reminded of the years where Baojia had watched over Beatrice, and he had not. He decided to change the subject.

"What weapons do you plan on introducing?"

"I'll start her with the *jian* and *dao*. She doesn't have any experience with weapons yet, and those will be a good start for her."

Giovanni nodded. The double-edged straight sword, or *jian*, and the curved single-edge saber, or *dao*, would be light enough for a human and versatile enough for Beatrice to carry regularly. Moreover, both were weapons he had some experience with and would be able to practice with her.

"Eventually, she will wield the *shuang gou*."

"What?" Giovanni looked up, frowning. "The hook sword?"

"Two," he said, watching Beatrice move in the faster *wushu* that Giovanni remembered practicing so many years before with Tenzin. Baojia leaned forward, tracking Beatrice with his eyes. "She'll carry two. Watch her move, di Spada. She's quick as a human; imagine her after. And she doesn't favor either side. She's adaptable and smart enough to wield them effectively." Baojia smiled. "Yes, we will start with the *dao*, but the *shuang gou* will be her weapon."

Giovanni frowned. The wicked curves of the traditional hook swords used in the northern part of China may have been brutally effective, even Zhang favored them, but they were also dangerous.

"Any sword is dangerous," Baojia murmured, as if reading Giovanni's thoughts, "but the *shuang gou* has many advantages to the one who can wield it effectively."

In the end, Giovanni had to admit that the water vampire's knowledge of weapons was far more extensive than his own. "I will accede to your expertise, Baojia, as long as it is what Beatrice wishes."

"I will make sure to demonstrate a variety of weapons with Tenzin. That way she will be able to observe them all."

"But keeping the *jian* and *dao* for her weapons at first?"

Baojia chuckled. "I never would have taken you for such a cautious immortal."

Just then, Beatrice's laugh rang through the practice room. Tenzin had picked her up, flown her to the corner of the room, and was hanging her by her feet.

"You crazy vampire," she called out, laughing. "Put me down, Tenzin! No fair."

Giovanni smiled as his old friend flipped her upright and floated them both toward the ground. Beatrice looked toward him with laughing eyes and a brilliant smile, her face flushed and happy. She winked and blew him a kiss before walking over to the bench to drink a glass of water.

He glanced at Baojia. "And what fool would risk that?"

Baojia opened his mouth, as if to speak, but suddenly, Tenzin barked at him in Mandarin.

"Get over here. Do you want my help demonstrating or not?"

Baojia tossed a few insults back at her before he stood and walked to the thin mat that spread across the center of the room. Tenzin's practice room was exactly as Giovanni remembered it. He doubted it had changed in five hundred years. The ceiling was retractable, the walls were bare except for the impressive collection of weapons that covered two of them, and a small channel of water cut through the room, diverted from the gardens outside.

Giovanni caught the look of obvious interest that Baojia directed toward Beatrice as she crossed the room and headed toward him. She was covered in sweat, and her skin was flushed. She was still breathing heavily when she plopped down next to him.

"Hey," she said, kissing his cheek. "Sorry I smell."

He shrugged and pulled her into his lap. "You forget that I lived long before people bathed regularly, Tesoro. A little sweat won't scare me off." In fact, as he kissed her neck, he realized that her natural scent was only heightened. She smelled of salt, soap, and the unique honeysuckle and lemon scent that had drawn him from the beginning.

"I love practicing with Tenzin."

"No bruises today?"

She shook her head. "We were mostly doing tai chi earlier." A shadow fell across her face, but her gaze was quickly drawn toward the center of the room as Tenzin and Baojia parted and went to opposite walls to choose weapons.

Tenzin selected the long Chinese *jian* and skipped the ancient curved scimitar she usually fought with. She was ruthless when she carried it, but it would not be a good choice for Beatrice since she could not fly.

Baojia chose the *dao* he had spoken of, a single-edged weapon with good reach and a subtle curve. It had greater slashing power and, since beheading was the intention, Giovanni thought the choice was a good one.

"I'm really excited to start learning this," she whispered, wiggling on his lap.

"Of course you are."

"Relax. I doubt I'm in any danger from my grandfather's favorite son."

"I'm not worried about him hurting you."

"Then why the surly vampire act, old man?"

He bared his fangs playfully, pulling her head to the side as if going for a bite. She only laughed and reached up, pulling his head closer until his lips met her skin in a kiss. He was suddenly distracted by the steady beat of the pulse in her neck and the warm fingers entwined in his hair.

If she didn't have to give up the sun...

"Hey, why so quiet?"

"I'm thinking about the elixir."

"Gio—"

"I know there is more to investigate, but I am allowed to have some hope that you might not have to become a vampire to be with me."

She paused a moment, a slight frown creasing her forehead.

"What?" he asked.

"I've chosen *you*, Gio. I've chosen this life. I knew what it meant. I haven't changed my mind about turning."

"But, Beatrice, if you didn't have to—"

"If I could drink this elixir and remain human forever, then I would always be your physical inferior."

"That's not important to me; you know that."

"Who said it was up to you?" she asked. "This is something *I* decided." She turned in his arms, placing her cheek against his and whispering so they couldn't be overheard.

"I know you have to hold back with... so much. I don't want that forever. I want to be your partner. Your equal. I don't want to live a life separate from you, even in the hard things."

She pulled away and stroked his cheek as he looked at her.

In five hundred years of life, he had rarely met a human more stubborn or independent than Beatrice. It wasn't a foolish kind of disregard; she simply took her time to make up her mind, and when she did, she was determined. And he loved her for it.

"We'll talk about it more later."

That didn't mean he wasn't just as stubborn.

He felt her small elbow in his ribs, but she turned back to the mat, watching Tenzin and Baojia as they practiced with their chosen weapons. Eventually, they bowed toward each other in the way common among older immortals, bending from the waist while never breaking eye contact, arms outstretched so that all weapons were visible.

They began circling from their bow, both eyeing the other as Baojia murmured instructions to Tenzin about the techniques he wanted to demonstrate. Tenzin held the *jian* high in a pointed stance while Baojia's arm came out and his elbow pulled the *dao* back as if preparing to strike. They began moving in concert, demonstrating the most common strikes for each weapon as Baojia narrated to Beatrice what they were doing with each thrust or parry.

Giovanni glanced at her as she sat on his lap. She was completely enthralled. Her eyes lit up and she leaned forward, her complete focus on the two masters in front of her.

"This is so cool."

He saw them relax into the combat, and they began moving in more natural fight patterns for immortals. Baojia would use the water as a second weapon, sweeping his arm out to spear it in Tenzin's direction as she leapt into the air, dodging out of reach. At one point, Baojia sent a thin stream of water toward her as she flew above his head. The silver ribbon curled around her ankle, almost too thin to see, until Baojia reached a hand out and touched the stream, sending a shock of amnis through it, which brought Tenzin to the ground.

"Oh!" Giovanni cried, leaning forward and forgetting Beatrice on his lap. He had never seen a water vampire with that kind of control. "That was brilliant! Clever dragon."

Tenzin didn't seem to agree; as she rose up, she snarled at Baojia before launching herself into the air again. Baojia smiled, but Giovanni knew the vampire would only be able to use that trick once.

Not long after, they began to vary their routine, tossing weapons back and forth, calling out to Beatrice as they did, explaining each one as they demonstrated the proper way to use it.

Swords, pikes, axes, chains, daggers, spears, poles. Beatrice was transfixed.

"Oh," she drew out a breath as her eyes followed Baojia, who was drawing two ancient swords from the wall. "What are *those*?"

Giovanni growled when he saw the two wickedly curved swords that Baojia wielded. They were the length of the *jian*, but each had a long hook on the end. The hilts were sharpened into daggers, and the hand guard on each was a sharp crescent moon, suitable for either blocking or slashing an opponent.

Damn, prescient vampire.

"Those are *shuang gou,* Beatrice. Hook swords."

As Giovanni spoke, Baojia leapt toward Tenzin, whirling in dizzying circles toward her, as she parried with the *jian* and a chain, which she threw toward his neck. Baojia hooked the chain with the end of one sword, pulling it away as he slashed at the blade in her other hand. Giovanni could barely follow their movements, and Beatrice held her breath as they continued to fight for several minutes. They were a blur of movement as they spun around the room.

In one final flurry, Tenzin came to a halt, *jian* held out as Boajia pressed the *shuang gou* to her neck, the hooks curved toward her bared throat, and the blades crossed in a scissor formation.

"No way," Beatrice whispered.

Giovanni narrowed his eyes. "It's debatable whether she let him win, but that was still very impressive."

"I want to learn how to use those."

He shook his head as Baojia looked toward him and laughed. His eyes only said one thing.

Told you.

"You let him win, didn't you?"

Tenzin shrugged as they walked through the garden. They had left Beatrice with Baojia in the training studio. His woman scarcely gave him a second glance before she rushed toward the weaponry, peppering Baojia with question after question. Tenzin pulled him out of the palace and forced him to walk through the grounds so he didn't hover.

"Maybe. He's very good, and he'll be a much better instructor than I would."

"Why is that?"

"I revert too quickly to flying, and she won't be a flyer."

Giovanni halted, leaning against a wall of carved stonework.

"Oh, she won't?"

Tenzin turned and smiled, her face a picture of innocence.

In the back of his mind, Tenzin had always been Giovanni's first choice to sire Beatrice, though he knew Beatrice and Carwyn had discussed it, and the choice was Beatrice's in the end. Still, there was no one he trusted more than the small woman in front of him. Tenzin was his oldest friend, and she had one other advantage that Giovanni greatly desired.

Tenzin was immeasurably powerful.

She had lived for over five thousand years, and as far as he knew, she had never sired a child. Her blood would be unspeakably potent, and any vampire child she sired would be a force to be reckoned with. If Giovanni guessed correctly, Beatrice turning from Tenzin would put her almost immediately on par with his own physical strength. She would quickly outstrip him, but she would be able to defend herself from almost any other immortal, and that was all he cared about.

He narrowed his eyes. "Are you so averse to siring your own friend, bird-girl?"

"Did I say that?" She shrugged in her irritatingly vague way. "Even if she is sired from wind, the flying always takes time to develop."

"Not for your child, it wouldn't."

They continued walking. He knew Tenzin wouldn't tell him anything more, even if he pestered her, so he switched to a topic he knew would irritate her.

"I'm very curious to learn more about the elixir."

Her string of Mongolian curses was impressive. Most of them had something to do with horses and obscene acts. Giovanni smiled. "You have such a foul mouth for a little girl."

Tenzin punched his side. Then she threw him several meters away purely out of irritation.

"I knew you were going to be excited about that. If I could have destroyed that book when I learned about it, I would have been far happier, but Stephen was too attached to it."

"Not to mention that it rightfully belongs to me. Why destroy it? Maybe it really would allow us to stop feeding off humanity like parasites."

She shook her head. "It's so ridiculous, this guilt you feel. And don't pretend that it has anything to do with being a humanitarian, Giovanni."

"What?"

"You don't have a problem feeding from Beatrice, do you? You don't have a problem buying blood from banks when you need to. No, you just don't like being dependent on anyone, even a human, for your own survival. That's why you would prefer to conquer the bloodlust."

He frowned, unwilling to admit that part of her judgment was correct.

"It would be better for Beatrice if—"

"You didn't try to dictate her actions again?" She cocked an eyebrow at him. "If you allowed her to make her own decisions? I agree. The choice has always been hers."

"Damn you, woman."

"Stubborn old man."

"That's highly amusing, coming from you."

She laughed the tinkling, wind-chime laugh as the breeze picked up. "Why do you fight your own fate, my boy? She is your balance in this life."

"In every life. I know."

"Do you?" She stopped and placed a hand on his cheek, looking up at him with the loving, almost maternal, gaze she allowed herself at times. Giovanni didn't know much about her human life, but he knew that at one point Tenzin had mortal children of her own. He had a feeling their fate had not been pleasant.

"I know you sent me to her, Tenzin," he whispered, sensing the approach of a servant. "I know you saw her."

A slow smile grew on her face. "I thought you didn't believe in that stuff?" She winked and flew up, perching on one of the scholar's stones as she looked across the garden at the servant hurrying toward them in brown robes. She closed her eyes and turned her face into the breeze.

"Trouble is coming," she murmured into the wind. "No..." She shook her head and looked down at him with stormy eyes. "Trouble is here."

"Mistress Tenzin," the servant said as he bowed low, "your father requests your presence in the great hall with Dr. Vecchio." The man did not look up, and Giovanni had the impression he was purposely avoiding Tenzin's gaze. She floated down from the top of the tall limestone pillar.

"Stop bowing. Has Stephen been called to the Elders?" Her eyes darted across the dark garden toward the glowing lanterns in the center of the complex.

"He is already there, Mistress."

"I said stop bowing. Go to my chambers and inform Nima."

"Yes, Mistress." He started to scurry off. "Wait!" she called before she turned to Giovanni. "Have you fed tonight?"

He frowned. "No, I fed last night. I don't need—"

"Feed." She pulled the servant in front of him. The man immediately held up a wrist, bowing his head so as not to meet Giovanni's eyes.

"Tenzin, I told you, I don't need it."

"Giovanni..." She glanced toward the glowing lanterns again. "*Feed.*"

Narrowing his eyes, he took the servant's wrist and bit, numbing the man's skin so it wouldn't be painful. Despite his initial irritation, he couldn't help but enjoy the rich flow of blood from the servant, who obviously kept to an older diet free from processed foods. The surge of strength was immediate, and he felt his amnis pulse within him as he opened his senses and sent them across the palace grounds. A faint energy signature caught him off guard, and he pulled away from the man's wrist, quickly sealing the wounds he had made.

"What is this?" he hissed before taking off at a run. He felt Tenzin's amnis at his back and forced himself to hold back and wait for her. He paused before entering the hall, pulling back his fury and calming the rush of fire beneath his skin. Tenzin put a hand on his arm, pulling him back so she could enter the Great Hall ahead of him.

"My boy, I cannot emphasize how important it is for you to let me speak. Whatever you hear, remain silent."

She strode forward, the jeweled doors swinging open with a flick of her hands that made the human servants scurry. The silk curtains blew back as Giovanni followed her into the glowing hall. It was filled to capacity with curious humans and wary immortals, and he could feel the tension roiling when Tenzin spoke.

"Lorenzo!" she called out as the press of immortals parted in front of her. "Get your hands off my mate."

CHAPTER 6

Step, thrust, sweep, turn.

"Again."

Baojia mirrored her movements, guiding her in the steps of the drill as she worked the *jian*. It already felt natural; the light balance of the old sword allowed her to move through the complicated routine with ease. It was as if some long ago muscle memory had been awakened.

Step, thrust, sweep, turn.

"Again."

She realized about halfway through the lesson that Baojia had switched to giving commands in Chinese, but by then, his instructions were so predictable that she hadn't even noticed. They moved in concert, both wearing the loose black pants and shirts that Tenzin had provided for them. Beatrice may not have liked most of the bland food that the palace provided, but she really liked the feeling of going through the day in what felt a lot like pajamas.

"Stop after this series and watch."

She finished the last turn and moved to the benches to watch him. Baojia was not an ordinarily eye-catching figure. His even features were handsome, but not striking. He spoke even less than Giovanni did, but she had discovered that when he did, he had a dry humor that put her at ease.

It wasn't until he moved that her eyes were drawn to him. If she hadn't been studying martial arts for years, he might have made it look easy. But Beatrice could detect the iron control and carefully restrained ferocity of the vampire. No matter what move he made, he looked smooth, effortless, as if the complicated sequences he performed came as naturally to him as breathing did to her.

He had picked up the shorter curved saber Tenzin used earlier and was going through the basic movements when his eyes darted to the door. A few moments later, she heard Nima quietly enter the room, and the two had a quick exchange before Baojia returned the sword to its place on the wall and walked to her, his face unreadable and his gaze distant.

"What's going on?"

"Come with me."

"What's going on?" she asked again, standing when he held out a hand. He pulled her up and stepped close. Beatrice suddenly realized that he was not much taller than she was, and she only had to glance up to meet his dark stare. She could see the barely concealed tension in his face, and for a second, she felt as if she could not breathe.

"Baojia... what's going on?"

"There is"—he hesitated—"a new guest in the Great Hall. Tenzin has requested our presence."

"Who—"

"No more questions." He hooked her arm with his own and shuffled her toward the doors, grabbing a red robe hanging by the door.

"Maybe you don't know this about me, but I really don't like being kept in the dark," she said as she pulled on the silk robe.

He snorted. "Maybe you don't know this about me, but I don't really care."

"Would Ernesto care?"

Baojia laughed bitterly. "I am very clear on what my father wants from me, Beatrice De Novo. Why don't you spend a little time worrying about your own father?"

"My own..." She fell silent as a sick feeling began to churn in her gut. "Where's Gio?"

"With Tenzin in the hall."

They left Tenzin's wing of the palace and strode across the grounds, Baojia almost dragging her behind him. As they climbed the steps, she could already hear Tenzin's stream of angry words pouring out of the hall, though she had no idea what her friend was yelling.

Beatrice knew not to open her mouth. She simply followed along, her fists clenched at her sides as Baojia ushered her into the opulent room with a hand at her back, his quick eyes sweeping the room.

Beatrice spotted Giovanni's tall figure immediately. He stood at attention at the foot of Zhang's throne, his gaze flickering over the crowd that had gathered toward the center of the room. She saw him glance at her, nod, then he locked his gaze with Baojia and tilted his head toward the left side of the hall, where Beatrice noticed some of the humans and vampires in Zhang's retinue had gathered. She couldn't see Tenzin, but she could hear the woman arguing in Mandarin from the center of the mass of vampires.

They picked their way through the crowd, and Beatrice was glad that her dark hair and short stature allowed her to blend in far better than Giovanni's striking figure. They stopped about ten feet away, their backs to a large green column, and Baojia seemed to relax slightly at her side.

"Where's my dad?" she whispered.

Baojia leaned over to murmur in her ear. "He's in the crowd with Tenzin. I can hear him."

"Can you translate for me? What's going on?"

He sighed, and she could tell he didn't want to do it, but he continued leaning over, translating as the argument progressed.

"Tenzin says, 'You've always been needlessly worried about me. I have no interest in your throne…' and she calls him a foul name."

"Who?"

"Zhongli Quan."

"The other head guy? The one below Lu?"

"Some may say so. He is a wind vampire, like Tenzin. Do you understand?"

"No."

"There are only two of each element on the council."

'No interest in your throne…' "Oh, he thinks Tenzin wants to take his place or something?"

He only cocked an eyebrow at her and tilted his head back toward the crowd.

"Zhongli responds that Zhang may invite his guests without fear of them coming to harm, and he may do so, as well."

"What? Guests? Who—"

She broke off when an eerily familiar voice rang out. Beatrice may not have recognized the language, but she would never forget the dulcet tones of her former captor.

"Lorenzo," she gasped as her heart began to race. Her eyes searched for Giovanni's; he was looking at her, his lips pursed in a hushing motion, and she began to move toward him. He gave a tiny shake of his head at the same time that Baojia gripped her forearm.

"Let go!"

"No. You need to calm down and look at me." She couldn't look away from the front of the room; her eyes darted between Giovanni, who stood in a position by Zhang, and the clutch of people who surrounded the arguing voices. She could feel the vampires pressing around her begin to react to her agitation, and it only made her more nervous.

"Beatrice," Baojia said, "you need to look at me. Now. Take a deep breath and look at me."

She finally tore her eyes away from the crowd and looked at Baojia. She let herself rest in his calm, dark gaze as he continued to speak in a soothing voice.

"Giovanni needs to stay by Zhang. He is publicly allying himself with the

Elder right now, so he must stay there. You are here under his aegis, and under the protection of Tenzin, Zhang, and all their allies, who are more numerous than you can imagine. He will not touch you here."

"But—"

"Beatrice," Baojia continued, "he will not touch you. I will not allow it."

Something in his eyes pulled her in. Some flare of emotion touched his normally placid face, and she pulled away in surprise, only to have him move with her. She leaned back against the pillar and made a conscious effort to calm her breathing. Baojia stared at her, his hand still holding her forearm, and she could feel his finger brush against her wrist. A calm began to steal over her, and her breathing smoothed out, so she was able to look back at the group at the front of the hall.

The crowd had thinned, but all eyes were on the ongoing argument between Tenzin and Elder Zhongli. She could see her father through the crowd and relaxed more when she saw his calm expression. She looked at Giovanni, whose eyes continued to scan the room, glancing from her and Baojia, to the back doors, across the crowd, over the arguing immortals, and back again.

For a moment, his eyes met hers and he gave her a quick wink. She tried to smile, but she was worried it came out more pained than optimistic.

"What did you study at university?"

Beatrice turned at the sound of the unexpected voice to her left. The odd Elder Lan Caihe had sidled up to her in the crowd and was staring at her with a curious expression. He... or she glanced at Baojia, and the two exchanged a friendly nod. Lan was no longer wearing the brilliant white robes of the Elders, but a dull grey set that blended with the crowd.

She frowned. "What? What did I study?"

"Yes, what was your course of study at the university? Your father says you are very bright for a human. What did you study? Medicine? Theology?"

"Um... library science."

Lan laughed. "You did experiments with books?"

"No." Beatrice had to smile. "Information Technology. I studied... well, how to be a good librarian. The best ways to preserve books and manuscripts and how to get that information to the people who need it. It's called 'library science,' but—"

"Oh!" Lan smiled, his or her round face creasing into a delighted smile. "You are a scribe."

She smiled, happy to be distracted by the strange vampire, even if she was confused why exactly Lan was talking to her. Lan's dark hair was pulled into a topknot, and while she had heard the immortal was mysterious, his or her face seemed open and friendly. Beatrice, like everyone else, was at a loss to guess whether 'he' or 'she' was the correct pronoun.

"Um... I guess that's accurate. I don't write the books, though. I just take care of them."

"But that is a heavy responsibility, as well. A scribe was a very honorable position when I was a human. Only the wisest could write and were given care of the scrolls."

Beatrice smiled, a little embarrassed by Lan's eager face.

"I don't think people take librarians quite that seriously anymore."

"That's because humanity is foolish," Lan said with a shrug. "And what do you do with my brother fire-vampire?"

She smiled when she heard the casual acceptance in Lan's voice. Most vampires, even those who knew and seemed to like Giovanni, spoke about him with a kind of reservation, almost as if they expected him to erupt at any minute. Lan's gentle voice held no judgment, and even though she didn't know the vampire, she was immediately set at ease by Lan's manner.

"I had to quit my job a while back. So I'm traveling with him and currently hoping I can stay away from Lorenzo. We don't get along very well."

Lan squinted at the mess of arguing vampires. "I do not think you should be concerned for your safety. You have many protectors."

"But my dad doesn't."

Lan's eyes twinkled. "I do not think your father looks worried, Mistress Scribe. And you should not, either."

She cocked her head at Lan before glancing at her father, who she was surprised to realize really didn't look concerned. He seemed completely relaxed and... taller, if that was even possible. She frowned and glanced back to her left, expecting to see Lan there, but the elder had disappeared into the crowd and the only one to her left was one of Zhang's guards, who began a quiet conversation with Baojia that she couldn't understand.

She really needed to learn Chinese.

By that time, the arguments had died down, and more vampires had dispersed, allowing her to see Tenzin and Zhongli speaking more quietly. Tenzin held an open hand toward Stephen, who reached out to grasp it in his own.

"Well," she heard Baojia murmur, "that is... interesting."

"What? What's interesting?"

Zhongli looked irritated, but resigned. Elder Lu Dongbin, who she remembered Giovanni telling her was a close ally of Tenzin's father, looked quietly pleased, and the Immortal Woman looked as if she wanted to laugh.

Elder Zhongli turned to Lorenzo, who was still arguing quietly. Suddenly, Zhang Guo stood from his throne and walked toward the center of the room with a scowl on his face. The crowd parted as he approached. When he reached his daughter, he grabbed her hand and bit. Tenzin curled her lip and pulled her hand away, but lifted Stephen's hand toward her sire, as well. Zhang bit Stephen's hand, licked at the blood, then dropped it before he spoke to the hall.

"My daughter is telling the truth. I want no more of this arguing," he said in English, glancing at Beatrice before he looked back at Lorenzo with a pointed glare. "You cannot have him. He is my daughter's mate, under her aegis and my own."

Everyone in the hall seemed to disperse after Zhang issued his proclamation, but Beatrice was frozen stiff.

"What just happened?" she asked.

"Well, it seems—"

"Shhh." She held up a hand to Baojia's mouth, cutting him off before he could finish his sentence. She felt him smile beneath her fingertips. "Just... hush. I need to think. I need everyone to be quiet so I can think for a minute."

Beatrice heard Baojia chuckle, but she couldn't tear her eyes from her father, who stood next to Tenzin, tall and confident in the face of his sire, the vampire he had run from for fifteen years. She felt warm fingers grasp her own, and she looked over her shoulder to see Giovanni standing behind her. He looked down at her with an expression that told her he was carefully concealing his feelings from the rest of the room.

"Tesoro," he murmured, bringing her hand to his lips and brushing her knuckles with a kiss.

She dropped her hand from Baojia's mouth and the vampire took a careful step back.

"What just happened there?"

"Tenzin has claimed your father as her mate," he said quietly, "and Zhang just confirmed that they have exchanged blood. Therefore, Lorenzo's claim on your father, and his request to take him, has been overruled."

"That's a lot of stuff happening."

"Yes, it was an eventful meeting."

"That's kind of an understatement."

"Beatrice—"

"Can we kill Lorenzo now?"

"Unfortunately, he is here as a guest of Elder Zhongli Quan. Unless we want to risk the wrath of—"

He was cut off by Lorenzo's voice ringing through the hall in clear English.

"I have another request for the great court of the Eight Immortals."

All eyes swung back to the center of the room, and Beatrice could finally see Lorenzo clearly as he stood on the steps in front of Zhongli's throne. He looked the same as he had when he had taken her five months before. His curling blond hair came to his shoulders, and he still had faint smudges of scarring along the edges of his Botticelli face. He stared right at her with a smile before he spoke again.

"There is a book that my son stole from me. A very valuable manuscript that I petition the court to return to me. I understand that it has been taken for study by the scholars of Elder Lu Dongbin, and I would like it returned. My child did not have permission to take it."

She glanced at Giovanni, whose eyes had narrowed. He dropped her hand and stepped forward toward the center of the room.

"The book in question is mine, wise Elders of Penglai." Giovanni was the picture of calm respect as he stood before the hall. "My son took it from me without permission, and his son took it from him. I have no objections to Elder Lu's wise scholars keeping it for study."

No one spoke after that. It was almost as if the whole room waited for... something. There was so much tension in the air, Beatrice almost felt as if she would choke on it.

Finally, it was the Immortal Woman, Elder He Xiangu, who spoke. It was in Mandarin, and Baojia leaned over to translate.

"Honored Elder Zhongli, it appears that there is some disagreement regarding the owner of this valued book."

Royal Uncle Cao, the earth vampire who sat between the Immortal Woman and Tenzin's sire, leaned forward, finally showing some interest in the proceedings. "Perhaps this is a disagreement we could help to resolve, for your guest, Elder Lu. And yours, Elder Zhang."

There seemed to be a murmur of agreement around the hall. Baojia laughed quietly.

"Clever imp," Beatrice heard him whisper.

"What?" she asked, leaning toward him. "Is there going to be some kind of trial or something? What are they going to do?"

"Oh," Baojia nodded, "there will be a trial, but not now."

"Why not? Why—"

"Alas," Zhang stood, once again speaking in English and glancing at Beatrice. "It appears that Honored Elder Lan has departed the hall. If only I had known, I would have asked our fellow Elder to stay. Lan was departing on a journey of some kind. Of course, I did not question the Elder's plans."

"What?" Lorenzo hissed before glancing at Zhongli and falling silent again. There was a murmur of dissatisfaction from the right side of the hall where Zhongli's allies had congregated, and many vampires seemed to be searching the hall for Lan's small, white form.

But Beatrice knew the elder would not be found; Lan's earlier appearance in the inconspicuous grey robes suddenly made more sense. For whatever reason, Lan had delayed Zhongli and Lorenzo. To what end, she had no idea, but as she looked around the room, she realized that Tenzin, Giovanni and her father looked pleased, and Lorenzo and all the vampires on the other side of the room looked annoyed.

That was probably a good thing.

"We cannot decide this matter without Elder Lan," Zhongli conceded in

THE FORCE OF WIND

English. "Lorenzo, you may remain at the palace as my guest until his return. All here"—he glared at the six elders surrounding him—"will guarantee your safety upon this sacred island. And to Elder Zhang's guests." He turned to Tenzin. "And to yours, Mistress Tenzin, we will guarantee safety as well."

Giovanni stood casually in the center of the room. He nodded toward Elder Lu and Elder Zhongli in the center thrones. "No one under my aegis would doubt the honor of the Eight Immortals. We stay here at your leisure."

After that, the hall turned back to the business of the night and hummed with energy again. Lorenzo was whisked away by Zhongli's entourage, and Tenzin walked over to speak to her father, leaving Stephen and Giovanni in the center of the room, both wearing completely blank expressions. Finally, her father nodded to Giovanni and brushed past him, walking toward Tenzin, who reached her hand back to grasp his.

Beatrice wondered whether she was just noticing, or whether they were now being more open, but the intimacy between the two was apparent. They almost seemed to circle each other, reacting instinctively to the other's movements as they passed through the room and out one of the side doors, leaving her alone with Baojia.

Giovanni was speaking with one of Zhang's people in a low voice, and the room began to swirl around her. She turned to Baojia, who was watching her. His steady, silent presence remained at her elbow as she felt her exhaustion begin to creep up. She gave one last look at Giovanni, who was still deep in conversation, before she raised her eyes to her silent guard.

"Can we go now?" she asked.

Nodding, he took her arm and led her toward the back doors, where other vampires and human servants were exiting the hall and dispersing through the palace grounds.

"I will wait outside your room until Giovanni can join you. You should get some sleep."

"Will Lorenzo—"

"Do not worry about Lorenzo."

"You know," she said, shaking her head, "I'm pretty tired of people telling me that when he's kidnapped me twice."

Baojia pulled her to a halt near the base of a large white limestone rock dotted with tiny shells. He stared at her for a few minutes, and she was beginning to squirm under his steady gaze.

"Giovanni is embroiled in this," he finally said. "He has many roles to play in this game. I respect that."

Beatrice frowned. "What are you trying to say?"

"I have one role to play here, Beatrice De Novo. I have one objective and one purpose. I was entrusted with your safety by your grandfather, my sire. I have one job, and it is you. So I tell you, do not worry about Lorenzo."

He stepped closer, and the same flare of emotion she had seen earlier in his eyes leapt out again. Her heart began to beat more quickly, and a faint heat rose to her cheeks. Baojia's eyes never wavered from hers, and she forced herself to tear her gaze away before she continued walking toward her room, his ever-present footsteps trailing behind her.

CHAPTER 7

Giovanni gritted his teeth as she left. The fact that Baojia had been the one to comfort her in her distress had not escaped his notice, even as he stood watch over the hall. His need to claim her had been overruled by caution, but he wasn't pleased.

"Doctor Vecchio? Did you have any other questions?"

He turned back to Zhang's administrator. "None. As long as Zhang can spare the extra security to make sure Miss De Novo is fully protected through the daylight hours, I am comfortable remaining on the island."

The old wind vampire gave a respectful nod. "You honor us with your presence. And your support of Zhang's interests will be remembered."

"Thank you, Quan. Your master's offer of protection will be remembered, as well."

"Is there anything else?"

"I will return to Tenzin's quarters at this time. I have some phone calls to make. I understand there is a phone connection on the island now?"

"Yes, a custom satellite system was installed last year. There are insulated phones that connect in each wing of the palace. I believe Tenzin does have one." He leaned in a little closer. "The connections, of course, are shared. One must always keep that in mind."

In short, don't say anything on the phone that you don't want spread around the palace. Giovanni received the veiled message with a quick nod before he took his leave from Elder Zhang's efficient administrator.

He walked across the grounds, glancing toward the opposite side of the compound where Lorenzo was carefully sheltered within Zhongli's entourage. He gritted his teeth and kept walking.

What was the wind immortal's purpose? Why would he invite the water vampire to Penglai? Had his jealousy and paranoia of Tenzin finally reached its limit?

Elder Zhongli Quan may have been the second-ranking political leader of the Eight Immortals, but the old wind vampire had long been insecure of his position and suspicious of Tenzin. Zhang's daughter dwarfed him in age and power, and it was only her disinterest in politics and her desire to avoid her sire, which kept her from attaining a position of leadership in the hall of the Elders. She could have had Zhongli's throne with a flick of her small wrist, but had always been quite vocal that she had no desire for it.

Had her recent activities on Giovanni's behalf caused suspicion that Tenzin had taken an interest in political life? If it had, he regretted it. He'd had no quarrel with Zhongli in the past, but now, the wind vampire was an enemy.

He was mentally running through the web of alliances within the council as he entered Tenzin's quarters. He immediately turned down the hall to check on Beatrice. As he passed their room, he saw Baojia sitting on a bench, reading, nearby.

He looked up briefly. "She's sleeping. She was exhausted."

Giovanni came to a halt. He had nothing to criticize, even though an instinctive protest at the vampire's presence wanted to leap to his mouth. The water vampire was doing the job his sire had assigned him, and as much as Giovanni may not have liked the interest Baojia showed his woman, he knew that Beatrice was safe under his care.

He finally nodded. "I have some calls to make to Southern California. Do you know where the phone is located?"

"It's in the front library. You have to put it on speaker phone to use it, even with the insulation for the wiring, so be careful what you say."

"Has Ernesto been informed?"

"I told her I wouldn't leave the door until you returned, so no."

"I'll make my calls and be back shortly."

Baojia shrugged. "It's morning there anyway, so I can only talk to his secretary. Take your time."

Giovanni frowned. "I'll be back shortly." He turned and walked toward the small library just off the main sitting room. The walls in Tenzin's rooms were all decorated simply, with pale paint, sparse wall hangings, and a few wood screens. It suited her while still being formal enough for her father's tastes.

He passed Nima in the hall, and the old woman nodded in his direction. Her face, as always, was set in a pleasant expression that concealed the calculating mind he knew she possessed. Nima had been in Tenzin's company for so long,

THE FORCE OF WIND

she was almost like another half of his friend, though Tenzin took care to not place the old woman in any position she feared could be dangerous.

No, Nima had always been carefully protected. As the old woman continued down the hall, he turned to watch her slow gait. Giovanni had always assumed that Tenzin and Nima had been more than merely companions at one point, and he wondered what Nima thought of her mistress's involvement with Stephen. Giovanni had to wonder himself.

He walked into the library; there was a small man working; a servant of Zhang's was dusting the books.

Giovanni spoke quietly. "You may leave now. Shut the door." The man bowed silently and left.

He spotted the phone and walked over. It was a speaker unit, as Baojia had said, in some sort of bulky, protective case with a stylus sitting next to it for dialing.

The fact that there was any phone on the island was a huge advance. For thousands of years, Mount Penglai had been cut off from the modern world, with electricity only coming in select locations fifteen years before, and most correspondence was still sent by courier. The human population of the island was just as isolated, though all stayed by their own desire, as far as he knew.

He quickly dialed Matt Kirby's number in Pasadena.

"Hello?" The connection was slightly delayed.

"Kirby, it's me."

"Gio?" His tone was cautious. "How's everything?"

"Going well." *In a manner of speaking.* "How are Caspar and Isadora?"

"Enjoying the gardens here, which look amazing. They're both enjoying the house and the weather. Dez and Isadora are thick as thieves and are spending a frightening amount of time shopping lately. They miss your girl, though. Give her our love."

"I will. And how is the puppy?"

Though Lorenzo knew of Ben's existence, the knowledge that Giovanni had adopted a human child was not widespread, so he and Matt had agreed that, if lines were not secure, Ben would only be referred to as Giovanni's "puppy."

"Active as always. His obedience classes are going well, but he still has discipline problems occasionally." They had enrolled Ben at an exclusive school used by many of the human families under Ernesto's aegis and others involved in the immortal world. Some of the students boarded there, though Ben lived at home. Most importantly, it was private, and the security met Matt's stringent requirements.

"Any accidents in the house?" *Any fights with Caspar or Isadora?*

"Nothing serious."

"Well, give him a scratch behind the ears from me."

"Will do," Matt said. "Anything new there? Was everyone there that you expected?" *Was Stephen there?*

"All the expected players. Beatrice was pleased. And then we had some unexpected company tonight."

"Oh?"

"Yes."

"The one I thought?" Matt had been convinced that Lorenzo would make an appearance while they were in the East; Giovanni hadn't been as sure. Luckily, "I told you so" wasn't Matt Kirby's style.

"You may have mentioned him."

"Do we need to make adjustments?" *Did Giovanni need Matt to fly out?*

"It's not anything I'm not equipped to handle. Things seem secure on our end. I just wanted to let you know."

"Thanks. I'll take appropriate precautions." Realistically, if Lorenzo was in China, it was unlikely that he or his associates would target Giovanni's family in Southern California. Still, it never hurt to be cautious.

"Thank you, Kirby. Please give my regards to everyone."

Giovanni wanted to talk to both Ben and Caspar, but it wasn't smart to advertise his human attachments. They were simply too vulnerable. Sending greetings through Matt was the best he could do.

"I will," Matt said. "Take care, and say hi to B for me."

"I will."

He hung up and immediately called Carwyn in Ireland. The priest was staying with Deirdre and helping the widow cope with losing her mate. He was also looking through Ioan's library in the hopes that it would reveal some sort of clue why he was targeted.

Lorenzo's child had confessed that his master had tortured Ioan while questioning him about vampire blood types, and Giovanni wondered whether Ioan had somehow stumbled into the mystery of the elixir, or whether there was some other reason Lorenzo had wanted the information from the doctor.

"Carwyn?"

The tricky delay caused him to talk over the priest when he answered, "Hello?"

"Carwyn, it's me."

"Gio, are you there?"

He frowned. "Yes, it's me."

"Are you calling from Penglai?"

"Yes."

There was a crackling pause. "When did they get a phone? Also, the connection is horrid."

Giovanni chuckled. "I'll let them know. It's fairly recent."

"Have they finally put bathrooms in that crazy palace?"

"Yes, even showers."

"Will wonders never cease?" He heard Carwyn laugh. "And how's the ancient and drafty one? Has she killed anyone yet?"

"Not yet, but we haven't been here that long."

"She's got time, then. Excellent. Is the food still awful?"

"Even you would have trouble eating it."

Carwyn laughed again. "And has her dad been there?"

"Stephen *is* here, Father."

There was a long silence on the line. Carwyn was one of the few people that knew how much finding her father had meant to Beatrice. His voice was slightly hoarse when he spoke again. Or, it might have just been the connection.

"How is she?"

"Well. She was shocked, of course, but they're catching up. It's... good."

"And he's safe?"

If Stephen had been exchanging blood with Tenzin for some time, it would explain the strange level of energy from the young vampire. Simply ingesting a little of Tenzin's ancient blood would strengthen Stephen immeasurably. If the point of the blood exchange had been to make him stronger than Lorenzo, it was most likely already accomplished. The young vampire was no longer holding back, and the strength of his amnis had been evident from across the room that night.

Giovanni had to laugh. "Oh, yes. I think Stephen is very safe."

"What do you mean 'very?'"

"He and Tenzin are mated."

There was nothing but silence on the other line.

"Um..." Carwyn finally sputtered. "Well, that's... what? Tenzin and..."

"Stephen, yes. They're mated." It was probably common knowledge on the island within minutes of the revelation, so Giovanni had no qualms revealing it over the phone.

"Has she... I mean, has Tenzin ever taken a mate?"

"Not that I know of."

"That is very... interesting."

"I thought so, too." Giovanni heard shouting in the background. What was his old friend up to?

"Well, on that very interesting note, I should probably go. It's nightfall here, and I have much to do tonight. Lots of news, but it can wait."

"Anything vital?"

"No, it can wait. If you need to contact me, I might be in Scotland visiting the boys for a bit. So try there if I'm not here."

"Are you sure everything's fine?" Giovanni heard a crash.

"Oh, nothing I can't handle. Give my best to B."

"I will. And hello to Deirdre and the boys, too."

"Goodbye, my friend."

Giovanni ended the call and hung his head. He took a deep breath. Something odd was going on with Carwyn. Stephen and Tenzin were essentially married by ancient tradition. His son had arrived with an unexpected and very powerful ally. It was too much. He thought he had escaped this life three hundred years before. He did not relish returning to the wily manipulations of politics or the constant danger and tension he found himself embroiled in.

He just wanted Beatrice.

So, he left the library and sped down the hall, waving at Baojia as he unlocked their room and entered. He heard the vampire slip away, and Giovanni locked the reinforced door behind him, leaning against it for a moment as he listened to her soft breathing while she slept.

He smiled and crept silently into the room, gazing at her as her chest rose and fell. The tension had left her face, except for her eyebrows, which were slightly furrowed. He undressed and slid behind her, grateful that she hadn't worn nightclothes so he could feel the warmth of her skin against his own. He wrapped his arms around her waist, cradling her against his body and taking comfort in her scent and the soft beat of her heart.

"Beatrice," he whispered against her shoulder. Giovanni knew he should let her sleep, but he needed her. He needed the comfort of her touch, and he needed to see himself in her eyes.

"Tesoro," he murmured, as his lips trailed down her back. His hands brushed along her sides, tracing over her hip under the red silk sheets. She shifted onto her back, and he was able to see her small form. Her pale skin was luminous in the soft lamplight. Her breasts peeked above the sheet, and her hand was thrown over her head in a plaintive gesture. He drew the sheet down and kissed along the ripples of her ribs as her brown eyes flickered open.

"Gio?"

"Hmm," he hummed when she tangled her hands in his hair. He had cut it again, so she wasn't able to grab the length of it as she liked, but her fingers played along his neck as he tasted the skin on her belly.

"I missed you," she said, her heart already racing. "Come here."

She tried to pull him up, but he slipped under the sheet, determined to continue his leisurely exploration. Her soft cries filled the silent room as he slowly brought her to climax, piercing her thigh with his fangs as she arched her back and whispered his name. He drank her sweet blood before he slid up her body and into her, finally meeting her mouth as they moved together. Beatrice's hands gripped his shoulders, and she met his gaze, staring at him as he moved over her.

She was worth it. Worth every worry, every pain. Her safety and security was everything to him. After five hundred years of existence, she had become the singular desire that animated his immortal life.

He drove her harder when he felt her peaking again, and he chased her pleasure, burying his face in the crook of her neck as she stroked his back and he shuddered. They lay together in silent communion, his body and mind refreshed from her love.

Giovanni finally rolled onto his side and pulled her under his arm, cradling her head on his chest as he played with the ends of her hair and ran gentle fingers up and down her back. He smiled to see the way the small hairs on her body reached for him.

"I'd say I was sorry to wake you up, but I'm not."

He felt her shoulders shake. "You can wake me up that way anytime."

Giovanni laughed quietly and hummed a tune he knew she liked.

"I love it when you hum."

"I know."

They lay in peace for a few more minutes.

"Have you called Matt? Did you let him know? How's Ben?"

"Yes, I called Matt. Benjamin is fine. It sounds like school is going well. Caspar and your grandmother still love the house."

"Carwyn?"

"Still in Ireland."

"How's Deirdre?"

Giovanni shrugged. "He didn't say much." He paused. "I'm sorry I couldn't be with you in the hall."

"Shh," she whispered, reaching a hand up to stroke along his cheek. "It's fine. I was fine. After the initial surprise, I was fine."

"I should have expected it. Matt said he would make an appearance."

"But we had no way of knowing. Just like we had no way of knowing..."

She trailed off, and he knew she was thinking of her father and Tenzin.

"Beatrice? Do you want to talk about it?"

"Did you have any idea?"

"No. I sensed there was something we weren't seeing, but with Tenzin, you never know."

"Why? Why would she—"

"Your guess is as good as mine. It's possible they simply have a connection. I'm not going to lie and say it's not odd to me, but she certainly doesn't have to ask my permission to have a relationship."

"With my dad."

"Is it that strange?"

She screwed her face into an adorable frown. "You have to understand, he never dated when I was young. Not that I ever knew of. So to see him again, after so many years. And he looks exactly the same as when I was thirteen. We look like we're almost the same age. And then Tenzin, who I know is way older than you or even Carwyn, but she looks like she's a teenager..."

"It's strange to you."

"Yes!" She shook her head. "And I know it's my own problem. But she's my friend, and he's my dad. And it just feels…"

"What?"

"Weird." He began shaking in quiet laughter, and she hit his shoulder. "Shut up. I know I'm being ridiculous, but it's weird. There's no other word for it."

"What if they have found love together? As we have? Would you begrudge them that?"

"No." She propped herself up and lay a gentle kiss on his mouth. "No, everyone should be as lucky as we are."

"Lucky? We've been kidnapped. Blackmailed. Chased around the globe. Targeted because of who we are and what we know. We're lucky?"

She smiled and laid her head on his chest, looking at him and trailing a finger along his lips. He opened his mouth and let a fang peek out. She flicked it with her fingertip, and he growled in pleasure.

"Born five hundred years apart? Finding our way to each other through pain and loss. All that so we can have hundreds, maybe thousands, of years together? Lucky."

This time, it was Beatrice that moved, stroking his face and kissing his lips as they lost themselves in each other again. After another hour, he had exhausted her, and she was sleeping again. He dressed and slipped from the room to walk through the gardens, calling one of Tenzin's guards to watch Beatrice's room. Baojia showed up anyway.

Giovanni strolled through the palace grounds, working his way across the gardens until he was wandering through the stones in front of Elder Zhongli's wing.

"Well, *you* smell like you've had a good night."

He turned to his son, who was sprawled on a bench, pleased to have found him so quickly.

"I've had an excellent night, thank you."

"Your human is very alluring, but I'm surprised you haven't killed her yet. I tend to break human women. That's why I gave up on them years ago. Too fragile."

"Not all of us are barbarians."

"Oh"—Lorenzo threw out a laugh—"yes we are. Just because we fool ourselves with the trappings of courtly life does not mean we're not monsters."

"Becoming a philosopher in your old age, Lorenzo?"

"Oh no." His blue eyes gleamed in the darkness. "I quite enjoy being the thing that goes bump in the night. In fact, I revel in it."

Giovanni stepped closer to his only child. At one point, he and Lorenzo had been almost like brothers, lashed together, trying to survive the whims of a madman. That they had gone such drastically different directions still bothered him.

"Why do you want this elixir?"

Lorenzo's eyebrows lifted. "Ah! So Stephen did figure it out, did he? I thought he would, especially when I discovered he was here. I wonder how he put the pieces together to come here. It's very curious."

Giovanni had wondered that himself, but he did not voice his suspicions to Lorenzo. "How did you know he was here?"

"Oh, what's the saying?" Lorenzo glanced over his shoulder toward Zhongli's guards that shadowed him on the palace grounds. He smiled. "'A little bird told me.'"

"Of course." So Zhongli Quan did have some ulterior motive inviting Lorenzo to the island. Otherwise, why would he have tempted him with Stephen's whereabouts?

"You never answered my question. Why do you want this elixir?"

Lorenzo grinned. "I'm a humanitarian."

"You're a monster."

He shrugged. "I'm a monstrous humanitarian?"

"Why?"

Lorenzo only rolled his eyes. "As if I would tell you, *Papà*! What do you think? I'm going to reveal all in some strange, enlightening monologue? What makes you think I even have a reason? Maybe I just want it so others can't have it?"

"You're too calculating for that."

Lorenzo stood in the blink of an eye. "Yes, I am."

His son stepped closer, and Giovanni could feel the heat running along his skin. It would be so easy... But he saw Lorenzo's guards step closer, so he smiled and turned to go.

"I'll see you around, Lorenzo. We'll have to have some father-son bonding time when your guards aren't around."

"So sentimental, Giovanni. I do love a good family reunion. If only Niccolo was here."

Giovanni turned, cutting his eyes toward the guards before he looked at Lorenzo. "If Andros was here," he whispered, "you wouldn't be."

"Oh, I know." Lorenzo's mouth curved into a wicked smile. "I remember. Everything."

CHAPTER 8

"Stupid, irritating, obscure, dead, Persian guy." Beatrice muttered as she scanned a copy of a sixteenth century manuscript, searching for the exact ingredients of a curative concoction that her father thought might be similar to one of Geber's ingredients. "Why couldn't he just write in clear language instead of putting everything in code?"

Stephen glanced up. "Trust me, I understand. Having his journals was the only thing that let me decipher the manuscript at all. Otherwise, it would have been complete gibberish."

They were buried in Zhang's personal library, which Stephen said rivaled the monastery library where the manuscript was being kept. Zhang Guo's selection of manuscripts and scrolls was... intimidating.

Beatrice stretched her neck and looked around. "Is this library bigger than Lorenzo's collection? Well, it's rightfully Gio's, I suppose."

"It's comparable." Stephen nodded and looked around. "The subject matter is just wildly different. I really could go on for ages about Andros's collection from the ancient world. He seemed to have a particular fascination with the near East and Minoan culture." Stephen laughed. "If *you* got your hands on it, you could spend an eternity cataloguing its contents. It wasn't exactly organized in any fashion. And, of course, Lorenzo moved it periodically, so I'm sure some things have been lost or damaged."

She shook her head. "So, in addition to kidnapping and murder, the bastard's guilty of putting ancient documents at risk. I really have to kill him now."

Stephen shook with laughter. "Oh, Mariposa..." He reached across the table and brushed her cheek. "I'm so lucky to see you again." Stephen sighed a little, and she could see his eyes line slightly with pink tears. "I never really thought I would, you know? I hoped, but I never thought it would be safe for us to be in contact. If you hadn't come under Giovanni's aegis—"

"My life would be..." She laughed. "I can't even imagine."

"You'd probably be safer."

"Yeah, but I'd be bored silly. I'd get myself into trouble."

"I doubt that. Though you do seem very suited to all this. It's rather amazing, if you think about it."

She shrugged and continued scanning the pages. There were numerous mentions of mercury, but she had yet to find the original formula for "mercury of life" that Tenzin had recommended she look for.

"Dad, why didn't you just memorize the damn formula with your super-duper vampire brain? I'm trying not to be judgmental here, but—"

Stephen barked out a laugh. "It wasn't exactly a cookie recipe. There were so many steps, and I didn't know half of what the terms were, much less how to concoct them or process them. I mean, I was an assistant professor of medieval literature, for heaven's sake. It probably would have made more sense to a chemist or a holistic doctor, though so many of the ingredients were obscure, even a trained alchemist might have had problems."

"But Lu's monks seemed to understand them?"

"I spent most of my time at the monastery learning Mandarin first, then translating the book from Arabic into Mandarin so Fu-han could read it. Then, I had to explain what a lot of Geber's codes were, and all of his journals were written in Persian." Stephen shook his head. "I had a feeling things were becoming clearer to him, but then I was called here. I'm still sending letters back and forth to him, explaining this or that word or phrase. And he and Zhang are the Spagyric experts, not me."

"And that's the plant alchemy, right?"

"Yes, which is a specialty even within normal alchemy. If Geber hadn't written his findings in his journals, I'd have had no idea what the book was or what the formula was supposed to do."

"But Lorenzo knows?"

"He doesn't know what the formula is, clearly, but I believe he knows what it's supposed to do. I saw him examining the journals and smiling that creepy, satisfied grin he has."

Beatrice shivered involuntarily when her father mentioned his name. "Did he really torture you?"

Stephen's eyes clouded in pain. "Beatrice, I don't want to talk to you about that. It's not... it's just not something..."

She shook her head and looked back to the book. "It's okay. Never mind. I know. Gio said it was probably pretty bad."

He paused, staring down at the table where they sat. "It's in the past. He can't hurt me anymore. I'm too strong now."

"Okay."

"I don't want you to worry about me."

The corner of her mouth lifted. "You're my dad."

"Exactly. It's my job to worry about you, not the other way round. You were always an old soul, even as a child."

She snorted. "I must have been so obnoxious. Grandma always said she turned grey early because of me."

"You were a joy. Just... headstrong." He grinned. "And frighteningly perceptive for a cute little girl."

Beatrice looked up at her father. She was still struck by how young he looked, frozen in time the same age he had been when she was young. "Was I?"

"What?"

"A joy? Was I? Was it worth it being a single dad when Holly left me with you? I must have been a surprise. And you couldn't hit the clubs with your friends when you were twenty-two, could you? Not with a baby and no one to help you."

"Oh." Stephen shrugged. "I had Grandma and Grandpa. Who needed to go out dancing when I had toothless baby smiles at home? You made things plenty exciting."

She thought of all the Friday nights when she was young when her father had taken her to the skating rink or the movies, instead of spending time with other adults. Though she hadn't recognized it at the time, his whole life had revolved around her. "Thanks, Dad. For not... you know. When I met Holly a couple years ago, she said she knew I'd be better off with you. That you'd take care of me. So... thanks."

His voice was hoarse when he finally replied. "You are completely welcome, Beatrice. Your mom is the one that missed out."

A booming voice came from the hallway. "Agreed."

Beatrice turned when she heard Giovanni. He walked over and sat down next to her, kissing her cheek.

"Hello, Tesoro," he whispered in her ear. "I missed you."

"Sorry, I got caught up here."

"No problem at all. Let me help your father. Baojia is waiting for you in the practice room. More weapons training tonight."

She leapt up. "Oh! He said I could try out the *dao* and maybe some other stuff tonight. Cool." She was halfway out of the room before she turned back. She skipped over to Stephen and leaned down, brushing a kiss across his cool cheek. "See you later, Dad."

"Bye, Mariposa. Have fun with the swords. Don't stab anyone." Stephen paused and frowned. "Well, unless you're supposed to."

"See? You're still such a dad," she said as she winked and darted out the door. She could hear the two men chuckle as she raced down the hall.

"THE SABER, OR *DAO*, HAS A DIFFERENT BALANCE THAN THE *JIAN*," BAOJIA SAID softly as he circled her. "You must learn to carry it in a different way. Your stance will be different. Your thrusts will be different. Remember, the sword is not a weapon; it is an extension of your arm, and you must balance yourself with that in mind."

She took a deep breath, moving slowly through the tai chi forms as he instructed. Painfully slowly. Her muscles were tense and quivering. Beatrice tried to focus on her balance and the weight of the blade in her hand.

"Would it be better if I just stayed practicing with the *jian*?"

"And be limited to one weapon? What do you think?"

"I think it's always better to have options."

Beatrice took a deep breath as her instructor stepped into her line of sight, eyeing her up and down as she moved. "Yes, it is," he said in a rough voice.

Beatrice blushed, not sure if they were still talking about swords.

"So"—she cleared her throat—"after this, do I get to try out the pike? I've been curious about that one spear with the thick base."

"So *many* jokes." She heard him say under his breath. She burst into laughter and stumbled, shaking her head when she saw his eyes dance.

"Okay, I walked into that one."

He laughed. "You, my dear, walk into them all the time." He grabbed the saber from her and hung it back on the wall. "I'm just forcing myself to be on my best behavior."

"Oh really?" She blinked at herself when she heard the flirtatious tone of her voice. What was she doing? She shook her head and turned back to her teacher.

Yes, Baojia was her teacher.

Her instructor.

Baojia was... distracting.

He narrowed his eyes as he looked over the weapons Tenzin had decorating the walls. She saw a devious smile cross his face as he walked to a rack of spears and chose two. He held them up for her.

"So, spears..." He lifted one eyebrow. "European or Asian? What's your preference?"

She rolled her eyes and reached for the one in his right hand. "This is your best behavior? And European, if you're asking."

He shrugged. "Pity. You really should try both."

"I'm sure the European will suit me fine, thanks." She examined the weapon, enjoying the razor-sharp point and smooth wooden grip. Baojia brushed past her.

"Strange that you chose the Asian one, then." He walked to the other side of the practice mat and bowed. "Now, watch, and I'll show you how to handle this."

HARMLESS FLIRTATION WAS THE FURTHEST THING FROM HER MIND AN HOUR later when she finally handed the spear back to Baojia. He had demonstrated the hook swords, or *shuang gou* for her, knocking the long wooden spear from her hands at a distance when he hooked the two lethal weapons together to demonstrate their reach. The spear had splintered in her hands as she held it, and she was more determined than ever to learn to wield the complex weapons, no matter what Giovanni thought.

Baojia was encouraging and smiled a little as they put the weapons away. "You'll be ready within a year after you turn, I think. Given what you are learning now and your natural aptitude for weapons, you will be ready to wield these as soon as your reflexes catch up with your mind and your amnis."

"What do you mean, 'catch up with my amnis?'"

Baojia shook his head. "It's impossible to explain to a mortal. Even a bright one like you would not understand it."

She grimaced. "Oh, well, I guess I should be flattered you're willing to teach a mere mortal like me anyway."

"Yes." He smiled and walked behind her to stretch her arms. "You should be. I usually don't bother with humans."

"So why me? Ernesto's orders, huh?"

She couldn't see him as he lifted her arms, stretching them before they moved into hand-to-hand combat practice.

"Why you?" he murmured. "What an interesting question..."

That I notice you're not answering.

"Yeah, well, I'm Miss Popular for some reason. Even the bad guy wants to hang out with me."

He lifted her arms, running a hand down her tricep to knead it. His fingers were cool and strong against her sore muscles. "I told you not to worry about Lorenzo. Take a bath later. Soak your arms, or they will be stiff."

She cleared her throat. "Well then, I'll just put all those icky thoughts about murdering him out of my pretty little head, won't I?" She pulled her arms away and walked across from him. They bowed and began practicing. Baojia never *really* hit her. Not like Tenzin. He seemed more interested in teaching her how to attack. If he did manage to land the odd blow, he usually apologized very formally.

"You should leave killing him to Giovanni or Tenzin. Or me, if he threatens you."

"Oh? Why is that?"

He frowned as if she was speaking Farsi, which was on her list of languages to learn after she turned. Come to think of it, she thought, it was entirely possible that Baojia already spoke Farsi.

"Why should you leave killing Lorenzo up to Giovanni, Tenzin, or myself? Because he's a vampire and you're not, foolish girl. Don't kill yourself by being an idiot."

"Now there's the kind of sweet talk I expect," she grunted as she struck his shoulder. She went to land a kick, but he grabbed her leg and held onto it.

"I'm serious, B." He waited until she met his dark eyes. "Don't think you can challenge him. Compared to Giovanni or myself, he's not that strong, but he is *very* smart. He's a survivor, and in our world, strategy counts as much as strength."

She scowled at him. "It's not like I'm going to go hunt him down right now. Let's just say it's... on my list."

He raised an eyebrow. "Does Gio know you have a list?"

Did he? Probably. She often thought Giovanni could read her mind, he knew her so well. Baojia and Beatrice went back and forth for a few more minutes until she heard the practice room door open. His scent reached her nose even before she turned.

"Hey," she said, and a smile spread across her face. *Now there was a distraction.*

Giovanni leaned against the wall of the practice room. He had changed into a pair of loose, black pants and a shirt that hung open at the neck. The sleeves were rolled up, and Beatrice could see the muscles of his forearms as he crossed them over his chest and watched her.

He smiled at her, a languorous, easy grin that made her insides melt. His eyes raked over her flushed body, and she felt her heartbeat pick up. *The things that vampire could do with a single smile...*

He curled a finger, beckoning her. Beatrice walked toward him, making another list in her mind, when Tenzin darted into the room.

"Stop right there." Tenzin held up a hand and nodded toward Beatrice. "You, practice. You"—she glared at Giovanni—"I told you not to distract her. You'll get her back later. She needs to work."

Giovanni narrowed his eyes, while Beatrice scowled. "Tenzin," she said, "I don't like you very much right now."

"Nor do I," Giovanni muttered. "Ignore her. You've practiced enough for one night."

Tenzin pulled his collar. "She has not."

"I really think..." Beatrice pouted when Tenzin shoved Giovanni into the hallway. She turned to see Baojia watching her with a smile. "What?"

"Options," he almost sang as he picked up a long, wooden pole and tossed it toward her. "Always good to have options. Now, let's talk about the staff."

CHAPTER 9

"The water vampire is interested in Beatrice."

Tenzin snorted. "Which one?"

Giovanni glared at her as they walked through the palace grounds. "You know which one I'm speaking of."

"Well, Baojia is interested in her. Lorenzo is interested in her. I think half the palace is fascinated by the strange American girl, so you might want to specify."

He stopped and watched her as she hopped along the top of a carved stone wall. "You know, I forget how irritating you can be when I don't spend time with you for a while."

She flew over him, stepping on his head once before she lit on top of one of the giant, limestone pillars. "I hate it here."

"I know you do."

"You know how you feel about Rome?"

"Yes, Tenzin."

"That's how I feel here. Everyone looking at me with expectations."

"I know."

"And my father is the worst one."

"He cares about you."

"That is... debatable."

He continued walking as she flitted from one stone to the next. Finally, she set herself down on the grass to walk beside him. "You're not jealous, are you?"

"Of Baojia? Not really, it's just irritating."

"She loves you very much. She wants to be your mate for eternity."

He eyed her tiny form as she walked next to him. "And what of you and Stephen? I confess, that—"

"Stephen and I are none of your business. Just because you confide in me does not mean I confide in you, my boy."

He paused. "Who *do* you confide in, bird-girl?"

It was often hard to imagine how long she had lived, but when Tenzin turned her deep grey eyes on him, Giovanni saw millennia in her stare. "No one. I confide in myself alone."

He had the strange urge to embrace her, which he had never once done in all their years as friends. "Are you lonely sometimes?"

She tilted her head and smiled. "I don't remember."

Giovanni shook his head and continued walking. "I am glad that Beatrice and Stephen have this time together."

"He missed her very much. Family is very important to him."

"It has become important to me, as well."

"Family was always important to you. Why else would you look for your uncle's books for so many years?"

"I suppose that is true."

"You were always looking for a family. Now you have one. It is good for you."

A familiar drift of amnis wafted on the breeze, and he turned his head. Lorenzo was walking with Zhongli Quan and a group of six guards. The Elder nodded toward them with an unreadable expression in his eyes before he turned. Two of the guards followed him while four stayed with Lorenzo as he approached Giovanni and Tenzin.

"If it isn't my father and his miniature companion."

The black-clad guards halted abruptly. They looked toward Tenzin with wide eyes, but she only waved at them and shrugged.

"Lorenzo," Giovanni said, "you're becoming even more foolish as the years go by."

"Why? Is she going to attack me here? I have been promised protection, just like you. Penglai is neutral ground; we both know it."

Tenzin's eyes were impassive as she stared at Giovanni's son. "You are irritating, and it will be good when he kills you."

Lorenzo's fangs flashed in the lantern light. "Do you think so? I think we are a long way from my father killing me. After all, we both know I have information he wants."

How much Giovanni was willing to put up with to get his sire's library back was debatable, but he wasn't in the mood to confide in the blond bastard in front of him.

"Go away and do something useful, Lorenzo," he said. "Never mind, that's probably not possible."

"So sullen, *Papà*. Where is your toy human? Has she taken another lover again?"

With one sweep of her arm, Tenzin blew the four guards halfway across the grounds before she rounded on Lorenzo. She lifted the vampire by the collar and shot into the air.

"Be careful what you say about my friend, little boy. You may think you are safe here because it is customary to respect the Elders, but do not forget that my sire is the oldest of all. And while I may bow to his wishes at times..." She dropped Lorenzo a few feet before grabbing him again. "...in general, I am a *very* disrespectful daughter."

She spoke just loud enough for Giovanni to hear. He noticed that Zhongli's guards were taking their time walking back across the grounds, and Lorenzo's dangling form was beginning to attract attention.

Giovanni smiled and sat on a bench to wait.

"Let me down." Lorenzo was trying to sound nonchalant, but Giovanni could hear the quiver in his voice.

"Fine," Tenzin said and she dropped him. His son landed in a heap at his feet before he shot up and walked back toward Zhongli's guards, never sparing Giovanni a glance. Tenzin flew down and sat next to him.

"You really need to get rid of him."

"I know."

"What were you thinking?"

"It's a long story."

GIOVANNI WATCHED BEATRICE PACE THEIR BEDROOM, RECOUNTING IN DETAIL the different weapons she had tried in practice that night. It was a few hours before dawn, and he could tell she was exhausted. But still, her heartbeat was jumping.

"—and then I tried the other spear, and it kind of had this hook on the end, too. Like on the side? And it was a lot lighter than it looked, something about the way the shaft is balanced or something, and then there was the *shuang gou*. Oh, Gio, I can't wait to learn those. Baojia said that once I turn—"

"Which may be unnecessary. We don't know yet."

She only rolled her eyes and continued. "Yeah, so once I've turned, I'll pick up the hook swords no problem."

He cocked an eyebrow at her. "Really? He said, 'no problem?'"

"Well, he said something about my body catching up with my amnis... or my amnis catching up with my mind. Something like that, but after that, he said I'd pick it up easily."

Giovanni thought she was probably being optimistic, but he had to admire her enthusiasm. He smiled. "Well, even if it takes some time, it sounds like you're getting a good idea of what options you'll... what?"

She had turned red in the face when he said the word "options."

"Beatrice?"

"What?"

He didn't know what. It was strange, but she almost looked...

"Why are you blushing?"

"I'm probably just... tired. You know, I should take a bath and go to bed, I've—"

"You're not just tired." He frowned. For a brief flicker, she had looked... "Why do you look guilty?" He felt his temperature begin to rise.

Her mouth dropped open, but there it was again. Just a hint in her eye.

"I do not look guilty."

"You do." He sat up. "And your heart is racing. Why? Did Baojia do something inappropriate?" While he knew the vampire was interested in Beatrice, Giovanni could not imagine him acting inappropriately toward Ernesto's favored granddaughter. Nor did he think that Beatrice would be unfaithful, but...

"No! No, Baojia was just... kind of flirting. That's all."

"Flirting?"

"Yeah." She waved a hand. "He was joking about 'knowing your options' about weapons and, you know, there's some kind of obvious jokes and... yeah, just being silly."

"Silly?"

"Why do you keep repeating the last word of everything I say? That's annoying."

He couldn't keep the smile from his mouth. "Annoying?"

She picked up a pillow and threw it, hitting him dead in the face as he started to laugh. "We were just joking around!"

"I believe you, so why are you throwing things at me?" He couldn't stop chuckling at her consternation. "You're very cute when you're embarrassed."

"I'm not embarrassed. I'm irritated."

"At Baojia?"

"At you!"

He kept laughing and pulled her onto the bed as she tried to walk past. "Did he ask if you wanted to play with his sword?"

"Stop," Beatrice said as she began laughing, too. Soon, they were wrestling on the bed and he had her arms pinned above her head so she had to stop slapping at him. "I'll have you know," she said, gasping, "I told him that I only liked European spears."

Giovanni burst into laughter again and leaned down to kiss her. His head fell forward as he buried it in the crook of her neck. "Beatrice, I'm not jealous."

"Why not?"

He lifted his head and met her mouth, stealing her breath when he kissed her. "Because no one, *tesoro mio*, will ever love you the way that I do. Of this, I have no doubt."

A sweet smile spread across her face. "No?"

"No."

The next evening, Giovanni passed Baojia in the hallway. The water vampire nodded at him politely. He paused. "Baojia?"

"Yes?"

He turned toward the water vampire. "I just wanted to thank you for all the time you have spent training Beatrice."

"I am at her disposal."

"I have never been able to quell my protective instincts enough to train with her as she deserves, but I know she is progressing, and it pleases me. I also know you usually do not train humans."

Baojia curled his lip. "I'm not doing it as a favor to you, di Spada."

"I know. I appreciate it nonetheless."

Giovanni saw Baojia smile a little. "And she has good things to say about her weapons practice?"

"*Weapons* practice?" Giovanni nodded. "Oh yes. She quite enjoys weapons practice."

Baojia's eyes narrowed. "Yes... she's very skilled."

Giovanni chuckled and continued walking. "You really have no idea."

CHAPTER 10

Despite the slow pace of life on the island, time seemed to slip away with a whisper. It had been three weeks since Lorenzo made his appearance, but Beatrice had scarcely noticed. Her nights were occupied training with Baojia, and her days were occupied with Tenzin or her father, who had absorbed Tenzin's ability to stay awake almost effortlessly through most of the day. Stephen scarcely needed sleep, so the long separated father and daughter spent hours hidden away in the library of Tenzin's quarters, getting to know each other again.

Other than her training, Beatrice's nights were spent with Giovanni. He was doing his utmost to keep her occupied during any hours Lorenzo might be active, keeping her away from the practice room, as well.

"Come back to bed."

She rose from the silk pillow, intending to take a quick shower at nightfall before she met Baojia for practice with the sword. She'd taken an afternoon nap and woken to Giovanni's lips again.

"I need to go practice."

He stretched with a lazy smile and hooded eyes, knowing what the slip of the silk sheet did to her as it crept down his sculpted chest.

"*Tesoro mio*," he purred, "come back to bed. You're not dressed yet; we have time."

His hand crept out, fingers slipping around her thigh as he drew her back to the luxurious bed.

Beatrice allowed herself to be pulled. "I know what you're trying to do, possessive vampire."

"Yes?" he asked as he laid a kiss along her bare hip. "What is that?"

"You're trying"—she sighed and gave in, falling into the curve of his arms—"to distract me."

"How am I doing?"

"Very, very well." She gasped when he ran his fangs along the curve of her shoulder and his hands teased her body, sparking as they pulsed with amnis. Beatrice leaned her head to the side and moaned when his tongue teased her pulse.

"Well, I wouldn't want to disappoint."

They decided to make use of the luxurious marble tub much, much later.

TENZIN WATCHED BEATRICE AS THEY PRACTICED.

"You're getting much more limber."

"Thanks." She panted as she executed a complex series of kicks and punches from the wushu technique Tenzin's father had developed hundreds, maybe thousands, of years before. Her legs were aching, but she reveled in the stretch in her hamstrings as her leg lifted in almost a full split.

"Maybe Gio's libido *is* good for something."

"Tenzin, please!" Stephen called from the side of the practice room where he was studying.

"Your ears are just as good as mine!"

Beatrice may have unconsciously held the pose longer than she intended. Tenzin ignored the crimson flush on her face and batted her leg down to the floor.

"Let's work on flips."

"Tenzin." She shook her head. "There's no way I'm going to be able to do most of those until I turn."

"You can still practice. Don't be lazy."

Beatrice heard Stephen snort. "Why don't you give her a break so she can help me with this Latin passage?"

"Lazy De Novos!" Tenzin stormed toward the door. "Fine, take fifteen minutes while I go find someone to eat. And, Stephen, don't pretend you need her help."

Stephen only looked up and winked at Tenzin before she left the room. Beatrice grabbed a towel and a glass of water before she sat down next to her father.

"Do you really need help?"

"No." He grinned. "I'm not even reading Latin. This is a Greek manual on alchemy from Alexandria. Have you learned any classical Greek yet?"

She shook her head. "No, it's so dense."

"You'll learn fast enough when you put your mind to it. Especially after you turn." He glanced up, and a serious expression blanketed his eyes. "You're sure about it?"

"What?" She patted her face with the towel. "About turning? Yeah. I mean, Gio and I... well, you know we're serious, and I wouldn't commit myself to him without being sure about the vampire thing."

"But do *you* want it? Or is it just because of him?"

She leaned back against the cool wall. "Dad, I know you're being the good dad here and looking out for my interests, but you realize that there's no way I can answer that, don't you?"

"Why?"

She frowned, trying to think how she could explain. "I have no idea what my life would be without him. Without all this. I can't even imagine. This is reality now. My dad became a vampire through no fault of his own. I was drawn into it by virtue of being your child. And no." She held up a hand. "I won't allow you to apologize. It's not your fault either."

"I still feel guilty."

She rolled her eyes. "Well, get over it. Life happens. You were taken. I was targeted. I met Gio. We fell in love. We have a family. I wouldn't have said this even a year ago, but... all this happened for a reason. God, fate, destiny. Somehow, it was meant. Our lives are so intertwined, I can't even imagine it any other way at this point. And I want it."

She leaned forward and grasped her father's cool hand in her own. "Do you understand? I know there are sacrifices. I know there are limitations. I still want it. I'm tired of always being the one that needs protecting."

Stephen looked at her for a long moment. "Okay."

"Okay?"

"Tenzin told me exactly what you'd say. She says you'll be an extraordinary vampire. Greater than me, no doubt."

Beatrice smiled and shook her head, still patting sweat from her face. "I have no illusions. I know I'm still going to be the slow one."

"Oh, I don't know about that." He chuckled and flicked his wrist, and she felt a cool spray of water at her back. "There, that better?"

She closed her eyes and grinned. "Much. Thanks."

"Controlling water does come in handy occasionally."

"You're really powerful now, aren't you? From exchanging blood with Tenzin?" She saw him glance away and squirm in discomfort. "I'm not asking about... anything, really. It's none of my business, I know. I just... I'm happy that you're stronger now."

"I am," he said quietly. "I'm very strong. Tenzin has been... well, she's—"

"Back." Beatrice turned when the door opened and Tenzin strode in. "And you need to practice your flips, lazy De Novo."

She wrinkled her forehead and turned back to her father.

"Don't look at me," Stephen said with a smile. "You said you didn't want to be protected."

Beatrice stuck her tongue out at him, but Stephen only laughed.

"You really... I have to..." Giovanni cut her off by sinking into their kiss. They were tangled in bed, and he was distracting her again. He moved over her, his iron arms boxing her in as he kissed down her body.

"Beatrice," he whispered before muttering something unintelligible in rough Italian.

"I really need to learn that language." She sighed as her eyes rolled back.

"Hmm." He lifted his mouth and gave her a wicked smile. "I'll just switch to another language you don't know then."

"I'll catch up with you eventually."

"You don't need to catch up." He moved up her body so he could whisper in her ear. "Just stay. Stay with me. Stay here."

"I can't... oh"—she arched her back in pleasure—"stay here forever."

"Yes, you can."

Giovanni set about proving why staying in bed with him really *was* the best plan, but he was interrupted by a loud knock at the door.

He looked up with a snarl and sped naked to the door in the sitting room. She heard it open.

"Go away," she heard him say before he slammed it shut.

Beatrice sat up in the bed, covering herself with the sheet. He walked back in the room and dove into the bed.

"Who was that?"

"No one," he said before he pulled the sheet away.

"Giovanni!"

He rolled his eyes and lay back on the bed, pulling her on top of him and running his hands through her hair. "That was your fencing teacher."

"Baojia?"

"Yes."

"You slammed the door in Baojia's face?"

"Yes." He obviously didn't consider this rude or unusual as he began investigating the freckles that dotted her cleavage. "He's probably standing out in the hall now if you want to tell him something," he said before his mouth returned to her skin.

She rolled off of him. He only sat up and tried to pull her into his lap.

"Sorry, Baojia," she called loudly, knowing he would be able to hear. "Sorry my... Giovanni is a rude vampire."

"Fine." Beatrice heard his muffled reply from the hall as she hid her face in her hands. "I'll be in the practice room when you escape his clutches."

Giovanni gave a satisfied laugh, but she slapped at his shoulder and pulled away, standing to walk to the bathroom so she could take a shower.

"What?" he called out, still laughing.

"You can't keep me occupied every single hour that Lorenzo is awake. I have things I need to be doing."

"Yes," he said as he lay back on the bed, stretching his legs. "I can think of several right now, in fact."

She shook her head and shut the door, only to hear it open as she stepped in the shower.

"I really need to go practice, love." She felt him run the ginger-scented soap over her back.

"Consider this a warm-up," he said as he ducked under the water.

HER FACE WAS STILL FLUSHED WHEN SHE FINALLY MADE IT TO THE PRACTICE room.

"Sorry," she said when she spotted Baojia in the corner of the room.

"No need to apologize. We practice on your schedule." He stood and handed her the practice *dao*, which had become her favored weapon for practice. She hadn't switched to the full-weight weapon yet. Soon. The thin steel blade curved wickedly in the lamplight, and she began her regular warm up routine, spinning and thrusting in the style Baojia had taught her.

He made quiet corrections to her form before he grabbed his own weapon and began demonstrating a new series of maneuvers. He rarely spoke, and the vampire's near silent instruction became a kind of meditation, focusing her mind as her muscles memorized the intricate steps.

They practiced almost silently for another hour before she spoke again.

"He'd prefer it if I never left our quarters after dark."

Baojia gave a quiet laugh. "I can't blame him for that."

"No, really, he doesn't like me being out when Lorenzo might be around."

"Are you sure that's his only motivation?" he teased quietly.

"Haha. Men."

Baojia laughed again. "Like I said, I can't blame him for that."

He came to a halt and she followed his lead, standing at relaxed attention and mirroring his stance. "Were you my woman, Beatrice"—his eyes darted down to her mouth—"I would hardly let you leave the room." He grabbed her *dao*, brushing a finger against her wrist as he took it from her suddenly limp hands. "For safety's sake, of course."

He walked calmly over to the wall of weapons, placing both sabers back in their cradles before he looked over his shoulder with a smile.

"Safety's sake." She gulped. "Right."

He caught her eye and tossed a *jian* in her direction. Her arm reached out instinctively and caught it.

"Switch weapons."

BEATRICE STRADDLED GIOVANNI'S LAP IN THE LARGE TUB, WORKING A LATHER up as she shampooed his hair. He just watched her, smiling as his blinks became longer.

"You better not fall asleep in here, old man." She laughed. "There's no way I could carry you to the bed."

"Well, at least you know I couldn't drown."

She smiled and pinched his shoulder to rouse him. He sat up and put his hands on her back, warming them to soothe her sore muscles as he laid his head against her shoulder.

"Thanks, Gio."

"Your back feels tense. Good practice? And did you have dinner with your father this afternoon? I forgot to ask."

"Yep. He hates the food here, too."

Giovanni chuckled. "Just because there's no hot sauce."

"You can take the girl out of Texas…"

He laughed against her neck as she poured the water over his hair, rinsing the soap out and soaking them both.

"I'm still amazed that he can stay awake so well."

Beatrice shrugged. "It must be Tenzin's blood."

"It must be. It's no wonder his amnis seemed so strange when I first met him."

She pulled back. "You never told me that."

"I didn't know what to make of it," he murmured. "It seemed different, but I couldn't pinpoint how. It makes sense now."

"Why?" She stood and reached for one of the towels, handing the other to him when he followed her.

"I would have guessed that he was much older. Easily my own age, but perhaps even more."

"Wow."

"It was definitely odd. And the fact that he can stay awake for most of the day now, it's extraordinary. My sire could stay awake except for a few hours in the middle of the day, but he was over two thousand years old."

She frowned as she patted her hair dry. "So my dad is the equivalent of a two thousand year old vampire?"

"Well." Giovanni shrugged. "His energy feels that way. He doesn't have the life experience, memory, or skills, of course."

"Still… wow."

"Yes." He rubbed the towel across his shoulders before he grabbed Beatrice's, hanging both on a hook by the door. "It's quite a strength."

"I'll say." She grabbed a brush to comb out her hair, but Giovanni picked her up and took her to the bed, tossing her in the middle with a playful grin. He grabbed the brush and settled behind her, kissing her shoulder as he let the heat build on his skin to warm them both in the cold bedroom.

"Gio?"

"*Sì, Tesoro?*"

She leaned back and pulled his warm arms around her. "I feel like this is the calm before the storm."

He took a deep breath and rested his chin on her shoulder.

"I do, too."

"Stupid, stubborn vampire jerk," she muttered under her breath, stabbing the air in the dark garden.

"Focus. You're not going to hurt him, but by all means, visualize that if it improves your focus. Plus, it's just sort of amusing."

Baojia's droll voice drifted across the lawn as she whirled and stabbed the air, focusing on a spot in front of her that had a stubborn, five hundred year old man floating in it.

"Stupid, overprotective..." She thrust into a tall camellia bush that was beginning to bud with white blossoms.

"Please don't kill the shrubbery, my dear. The Elders might get annoyed and not let us practice out here again."

Normally, any kind of sparring was disallowed on the palace grounds, but Elder Zhang had overheard Beatrice whining about feeling cooped up one night and generously offered the gardens for her to practice, promising he would smooth any ruffled feathers in the court as long as she and Baojia were careful.

Beatrice had been overjoyed she would be able to escape the confines of Tenzin's quarters.

Giovanni had not.

"Stupid, overbearing—"

"Beatrice, if you hack that scholar's stone, I will disarm you! Focus."

She shook her head and brought her mind back. The fight with Giovanni could wait. He had certainly stormed off in a huff, smoke pouring from his collar as he stalked back to the library, ostensibly to help Stephen translate more of some Greek manual for Elder Lu's monks to examine.

The two scholars were sending letters back and forth to the mysterious monastery that no one knew the location of except for the Eight Immortals. Stephen had visited, but had been blindfolded for the journey. Not even the highest-ranking administrators knew the secret site of the protected library where the book was being kept.

Nor did anyone know where Elder Lan had gone. No word had reached Mount Penglai about the strange immortal's whereabouts, so the whole palace was in a kind of holding pattern. Tension blanketed the grounds, affecting everyone.

Especially Beatrice.

Her martial arts were improving exponentially, mostly because practicing was all she could do. She had progressed in her weapons training to the point that Baojia had moved her from dull weapons to sharp and was practicing more aggressively with her. The strange chemistry Beatrice sensed from her teacher had not dissipated in the tense atmosphere, which only added to the overall stress she was feeling. Even the weight of his stare was starting to bother her.

"Again." Baojia's blade slapped hers and she backed away. "Try that combination again, only this time, try not thinking about your boyfriend."

"Shut up!"

He snarled at her, getting in her face when she glared at him. "Do not order me around, little girl. Do you think I care about your hurt feelings? You wanted to learn from me, so pay attention."

She didn't back down, stepping closer as she tossed her blade to the ground. "I'm done. Go bite something, Baojia."

He grabbed her arm and spun her around when she tried to walk away. "You want me to bite something? I'll tell you—"

"Well, isn't this interesting." Beatrice stiffened when she heard the mocking voice. "Whatever would my *Papà* say if he saw this little scene?"

She turned slowly to see Lorenzo sitting on a bench nearby, surrounded by guards.

"Beatrice," Baojia warned quietly. "He's baiting you. Ignore him."

"Gio wouldn't say anything to you, you slimy little bastard." She spit at the blond vampire. "Leave me alone. Or were you going to try to grab me again? Not so brave when you don't have others doing your dirty work, are you?"

Lorenzo's blue eyes narrowed, and a smile flicked at the corner of his lips. In the blink of an eye, he stood before her, leaning down and hissing before Baojia could pull her behind him. Her bodyguard pressed her into his back, standing his ground as the palace guards intervened and stepped between the two water vampires. They pushed Lorenzo back and Beatrice heard a low snarl come from Baojia's chest.

"Back away, Lorenzo." She heard him say. "I have orders to protect this one, and I don't care who your patron is. I will happily end you if you interfere with my assignment."

"Everyone is in love with the little human." Lorenzo laughed. "It's all so amusing. Such a precious little girl. I do hope she wanders in my direction soon."

"I very much doubt that will happen," Baojia said as Beatrice slumped against his back, suddenly exhausted and wishing she could run away. Despite her fear, she didn't want to show any weakness in front of her old antagonist, so she straightened up and stepped out from her protector's shadow.

"Run along, Lorenzo," she called. "No one wants to play with you today."

"I'll just have to see if I can change your mind," he said with a wink and a smile before he jumped across the stream and strolled back to the opposite side of the palace gardens.

They both watched him until he was out of sight. Baojia finally turned to her.

"Don't be brave. Bravado will get you killed."

Beatrice only shrugged and turned to walk back to Tenzin's. "So will fear."

He caught up with her. "I request that you do not make my job more difficult for me, Beatrice De Novo."

"Afraid of my grandfather's wrath if I get hurt?"

"Of course I am. I'm not an idiot. Also..."

"What?" She stopped and turned to him, suddenly desperate to know why he watched her the way he did. It had become more than just the obvious male appreciation she was used to. His dark eyes searched her face.

"I find you... worthwhile. For a human."

She snorted. "Worthwhile?"

He frowned. "I would find it very unpleasant if anything were to happen to you, B."

Beatrice had no idea what to say to him, and her heart was racing in her chest. Baojia looked as if he was on the edge of saying something else, so she turned abruptly and retreated to her room.

CHAPTER 11

Stephen and Giovanni paged through the books in Tenzin's library, looking for any further connections between Geber's research in the elixir manuscript and existing alchemic practices in the far East. They had been looking for any precedent for the attempt to stabilize vampire blood for human consumption, but had found none.

"Did you see this?"

Stephen handed Giovanni a book. "It was written in the eighteenth century, comparing Aristotle's theory of aether and the traditional fifth element in Indian alchemy. A contact mentioned it years ago and told me it might be worth looking into. This is the first copy I've found. Might be relevant."

"I hadn't seen it, thank you." Something caught Giovanni's attention. "What contact?"

Stephen shrugged. "Someone in Rome."

Giovanni frowned, but continued working.

The two vampires had come to an uneasy truce in the time they had spent together in the library, and Giovanni was forced to acknowledge that Beatrice's father cared for her deeply, even though he had left her for so many years. Stephen De Novo was as open and honest as Giovanni could expect, and he found himself looking forward to seeing the man more with each passing day.

In addition to his deep love for Beatrice, Giovanni could also see how much Stephen cared for Tenzin, though he still could not classify their relationship. Since it was Tenzin, he accepted that he probably never would. Whatever had drawn his old friend to Stephen, they seemed to care for each other, and Stephen had grown immeasurably more powerful as a result. His already keen mind had been sharpened, and the vampire seemed to have a photographic memory for detail. Giovanni wondered if he was seeing a preview of how Beatrice's fascinating mind would develop after she had turned.

If she had to turn. He still held out some hope that the elixir might negate her need to give up her mortal life, though they still disagreed on the subject. He knew, far better than she did, the sacrifices that vampire life called for, and he would spare her if he could.

"Giovanni, have you given any more thought to why Lorenzo might want this?"

He looked up from his book. "What? The elixir?"

"Yes."

He took a slow breath. "Money is the most obvious answer. If this was made viable and could be marketed in the health industry, he could become tremendously wealthy. And since your daughter stole the majority of his fortune, I'm sure that is attractive."

"I still can't believe she did that."

Giovanni smiled. "I can."

"And she still has it?"

He shrugged. "We don't talk about it all that much. She's a very canny investor, and I know she and Caspar cleaned it through mostly legitimate channels, so she's extremely rich now. I believe they invented a wealthy uncle of some sort." He looked up with a wry smile. "Congratulations, you have a dead brother."

Stephen laughed. "She gets that from my father, I think—that deviousness. My father would have been an excellent con man if he hadn't been such a good Catholic."

"She talks about him occasionally. I know they were very close."

A wistful smile crossed Stephen's face. "I deeply regret not being there at the end of his life. I hate that Mom and B had to deal with that alone."

Giovanni paused, thinking about all the friends he had lost through the centuries. "That is the way of the world, De Novo. People die. Their loved ones continue on."

"But my daughter won't die, will she?"

He looked up, meeting Stephen's brown eyes. They hadn't changed when he was sired. They looked exactly like Beatrice's.

"No, she won't."

"Would you stay with her? If she had wanted to remain human?"

His heart gave a quick beat. "I would have stayed with her as long as she would have allowed me."

Giovanni saw Stephen nod. "Yeah, I know what you mean."

They continued working together and Giovanni could hear Beatrice arguing with Baojia down the hall in the practice room. She stormed outside, but he also heard Baojia follow her. He forced himself to remain in his seat, knowing she was well-protected on the palace grounds, even if Lorenzo was lurking. They had argued more than once about what she perceived as his "hovering."

"There could be another reason that we're not seeing."

He turned at Stephen's soft voice. "What? For why Lorenzo wants the elixir?"

"Yes."

"There's much we don't know, so his motivations could be endless."

"I still think there is something we're not seeing about the effects. I agree with Tenzin."

Giovanni leaned back in his chair. "I'm also curious how he thinks he might produce it. He would need reliable immortal blood donors, and he can only create water vampires, so he must have some plan for that."

"And he would need a lab to create the elixir once the formula was decoded. It wouldn't be easy. My contact in Rome—"

"Who is this contact you mention?" Giovanni had noted it before, but now, he went on alert.

Stephen only shook his head. "I don't know, to be completely honest. It's someone that found me years ago when I was still running from Lorenzo. There was a note in my hotel room in Warsaw when I came back from the National Archives. It just said, 'I'm here to help.' I was terrified at first, thinking that someone had found me and would reveal me to Lorenzo, but he always seemed to step in at exactly the right time to help. Since then, he has left me information at hotels, or sent it to my address in Brasilia. Tips about research. Clues leading me to Geber's other work. It was all… rather friendly, to be honest. I came to think of him as a friend, even though I really didn't have any way to contact him. I haven't received anything since I've been here. The last communication was the mention of Elder Zhang's name."

"But how do you know he's from Rome?"

"He mentioned it once. He either lives there or visits a lot, I'm sure of it. I'm assuming it's a man only because the handwriting looks masculine. He's the one that told me when you went to Livia's to negotiate for Beatrice after Lorenzo took her. He's kept me apprised of Lorenzo's movements so I could keep one step ahead of him. He told me you were tracking me. One of his last letters to me said that Lorenzo had been researching private pharmaceutical labs in Eastern Europe."

Giovanni's mind raced. He tried to think who in Rome could be so well-connected that he would have access to all that information. Not only did this immortal know Stephen's whereabouts, but he also seemed to have intimate knowledge of the manuscript.

Stephen's voice broke through his internal reverie. "Has Beatrice been to Rome?"

THE FORCE OF WIND

Giovanni shook his head. "No. I'll not take her until... well, it's not time for that yet."

"Does Livia know about her?"

"I've kept her apprised of the situation."

Stephen smiled. "I'm sure it's a comfort to her to know you have found someone after so long."

Giovanni gave a tight smile. "Yes."

"I'm sure she will love Beatrice. And your father would, as well."

And I'm sure he wouldn't have.

Andros's blanket disdain for women was something that his sire had hidden fairly well, but Giovanni only said, "There are few that meet your daughter that don't love her."

"When was the last time you were in Rome?"

Giovanni chose another book, wishing that Stephen would choose another subject. "When I went to petition for her release. It was a complicated visit."

"I'm sure it was. The two of you should go back after all this is over. I know it has been a joy to me to see the two of you together. We always want our children to find someone that loves them with such devotion."

He flashed back to a memory of his father and Livia, the blanket of manipulation lying heavy over their last visit to Rome in 1506. There had been no joy between them. Any affection Livia had ever had for Giovanni was layered in self-interest.

"I'm sure we will go eventually."

"There have been many times over the years when I wished I could have met your father. His library was an inspiration to me."

Giovanni smothered his instinctual reaction, as he had for over five hundred years. "I'm very pleased Andros's collection has been preserved. Even if it is not in my hands. You have no idea where it is now?"

Stephen shook his head. "When I first discovered it, it was in Ferrara. But after Lorenzo took me, he moved everything to an old villa in Perugia. That was where I was held for the first three years after I was turned. And where I escaped from."

Giovanni's eyes darted up. "Perugia?"

Stephen smiled. "Yes, a beautiful old place. I heard it was the site of a medieval fortress of some kind that had burned down. The villa was built in the seventeenth century."

"Brigands, Livia. Everything was destroyed. The servants fled. If Father *had not sent Lorenzo and I to Crotone on that errand, we would have been destroyed, too.*"

She had sobbed in the middle of the court. "It cannot be! My Andros, my Niccolo! How will I survive without him?"

"I am so sorry."

She had embraced him in front of the throngs, his newly turned son standing behind him. "You are such a comfort to me, Giovanni. Such a comfort. To have Niccolo's beloved son in my court is... such a comfort." Her eyes lit with calculation. "You must stay for a time."

"I—of course I will stay. For a time."

"Yes." She had stroked his arm. "Of course you will, my darling Giovanni."

HAD LORENZO REBUILT ANDROS'S OLD VILLA? GIOVANNI HAD GIVEN HIM property nearby, but had his son recreated the villa where they had murdered his sire? Giovanni shook his head and focused back on Beatrice's father, who had been staring at him.

"I'm sorry to bring up your father. I forget that some losses can still be painful, even after so many years."

Giovanni cleared his throat. "Yes, I don't think about him much anymore."

"You were fortunate to have had the time with him that you did." Stephen smiled. "Not all of us had such excellent examples of immortal life."

Giovanni forced a smile. "Fortunate. Yes, Stephen. I was very... fortunate."

Hours passed, and it was just before dawn when he heard a commotion in the courtyard. An unwelcome scent hit him, and he rose swiftly to rush out the door. His ears tuned to Baojia's voice.

"Get back! I have her. Just stay back and someone get the Italian, dammit!"

He raced down the hall, flames erupting along his collar when he saw Baojia carrying Beatrice in his arms like a child. She was unconscious. Her face had a grey pallor, and she was bleeding from a cut on her forehead.

"What the hell happened?" he shouted.

"She got away from her guards. I found her in a creek outside the palace grounds. She was face down, but I drew the water out of her lungs. She's stable now."

Baojia handed Beatrice's limp body to him, and he forced back the flames when he heard her rasping breath and steady pulse. She was still unconscious, but the color was returning to her face. He placed his palm on her temple, but her mind felt only as if it was sleeping, and he sensed no damage, so he heated his arms to warm her cold body.

Tenzin came down the hall with Stephen on her heels. "I will kill those guards. How a human could escape them is beyond me."

"Where were you?" Giovanni growled at Baojia. The water vampire glared at him.

"I thought it best to let someone else protect her for a few minutes so we didn't kill each other, di Spada. Trust me, she was in a foul mood. Someone would have been injured."

"Someone was injured, you fool!"

Giovanni strode to their room, laying her on the bed and covering her with the thick blankets before he turned on Baojia, Tenzin, and Stephen, who had followed them.

"All of you, go away." He spotted Nima in the corner. "Nima, can you bring her some broth, please?"

Tenzin only cocked her head, examining Beatrice's limp form. "You're lucky it was Baojia that found her. If there hadn't been a water vampire around—"

"I'm well aware of the consequences, Tenzin."

"I'm just saying you shouldn't be so mad. She was lucky this time."

"Tenzin, get out."

His old friend didn't leave. "You need to get over this attachment to her pulse, my boy. Her mortal life—"

"Out!"

Stephen grabbed Tenzin's arm and pulled her to the door, but not before sending his daughter one longing glance over Giovanni's shoulder. Fortunately, he didn't try to approach the irate, territorial vampire who hovered over her. Baojia followed them, and Giovanni knelt down beside Beatrice and stroked her forehead. The cut was oozing blood, so he pierced his tongue and healed it, cleaning the wound and the blood that was smeared on her forehead. His hands framed her face, and he could feel her start to wake.

"Gio?" Her voice was rasping.

"You're in bed, Beatrice. You fell. Or were pushed. You almost drowned. Do you have any memory of it?"

He suspected she wouldn't. The water had washed away any scent on her, but her mind bore the telltale smudge of amnis. A vampire had attacked her. His son, probably, but there would be no proof. Lorenzo had been waiting for his opportunity, and Beatrice's stubborn and independent nature had provided it.

"I was... taking a walk in the forest."

"By yourself?" He tried to tamp down his anger.

"Yes, by myself." She must have seen his expression and she scowled. "Do you know what it's like to go weeks with people hovering around you? I was going crazy."

"So you left the palace grounds and left yourself open to attack?"

She winced and brought a hand up to her forehead. "Can we not argue about this right now? Can we just... I have a headache."

He glared at her. "We are talking about it now, because you might have been killed. How could you be so foolish?"

She curled her lip. "How could I be so... you know what? You try having people hovering over you twenty-four hours a day and see how you do." She sat up in bed, color rushing to her face as her temper built up steam. "You try being the one constantly protected! Having your mind open to anyone that can get their hands on you. Being constantly under the threat of manipulation from any vampire who even brushes your skin. Have you thought about that?"

"Beatrice—"

"Have you ever thought about the fact that one touch from anyone untrustworthy would make me their puppet? Let them discover any of the secrets I know? And I'd have no way of protecting myself or the people I love! I might not even remember telling them."

His stomach churned at the thought, but his mind fought against the words she threw at him.

"I'm sick of it! I'm sick of all of this." Giovanni knew what she was going to say before her mouth even opened. "Gio, I'm ready."

He sat back on his heels, as his heart began to thump. "No."

"What is your problem? What?" She leaned toward him. "You wanted me to have a choice? Well, this is my choice. I want to be a vampire. And I don't want to wait. This vulnerability—"

"Beatrice, you have no idea—"

"I have a very good idea what I'm giving up. I'm ready."

He shook his head and began pacing the room. "No."

"Why?"

"Because you're not ready."

"I am."

He tugged at his hair as he paced. "No!"

"It is not your choice."

Giovanni knelt by the bed, placing both hands on her cheeks. He could feel her pulse pounding in her neck, and his desperate heart raced along with it. "Don't I have a say in this? Haven't I earned that? Why does it have to be right now?"

She shook her head, her eyes pleading with him. "You know why," she whispered.

"I don't! If you would just stay with me—"

"I can't do that, love." She shook her head, tears building in her eyes. "I can't live my life under constant protection. I want to be able to protect myself. I don't want to be vulnerable anymore. I don't want my mind to be someone else's open book!"

For a brief moment, he panicked at the thought of Beatrice being forced to give up the secrets she held. His conversation with Stephen had reminded him that if his and Lorenzo's secret were ever discovered, their lives would both be forfeit to a very powerful immortal. Only one human knew the truth about his father's death.

Only Beatrice.

And her mind *was* an open book.

Her eyes pleaded with him. "Jacopo, you know I'm right. You know—"

"There has to be another way." She still had no idea what she would be giving up, and the tears fell down her face.

"There isn't!"

They were interrupted by a quiet knock at the door. Nima came in, bearing a bowl of broth with a soft smile and a gentle pat on Beatrice's cheek. She looked between the two of them before she slipped out the door.

Giovanni walked over and secured the room, twisting the locks closed as he heard Beatrice go to the washroom. He heard the shower start to flow, but he stayed in the bedroom, listening to her as she washed the attack from her body.

She thought she knew so much, but as mature as she was, he knew she didn't truly understand how much her life would change. It was impossible.

He was still sitting in the armchair when she came out, wrapped in a soft white towel. There wasn't much time before dawn. Beatrice walked over and sat on his lap, curling into his chest.

Giovanni stroked her hair. "How do you feel?"

"Other than a sore throat, I feel fine."

"Baojia had to pull the water from your lungs."

"But he did. And I'm fine."

"You might not have been. This is Lorenzo, please don't underestimate him."

"I know who my enemy is." She didn't. Not really. She only thought she did. "Don't be angry with me," she whispered as she kissed his neck.

His brow furrowed in frustration. "I love you. More than you can imagine. Don't put yourself at risk. Do you have any idea what it would do to me?"

"I need to do this."

"You need to wait."

"I know you think that."

He gritted his teeth and remained silent. The full force of her attack suddenly hit him, and he clasped her to his chest.

"I need you," he whispered, peeling off the towel she wore. He needed the pulse of her heart against his chest. He needed the smell of her blood as it rushed through her body. He wanted to see her skin glow in the lamplight as he moved in her.

She met his kiss with equal fervor, gripping his shoulders as she straddled his lap. They made love frantically, face-to-face in the low light of the oil lamps, and she pulled him to her neck, asking without words for Giovanni to bite her and send her over the edge.

"You're injured."

"Please," she whispered. "Please." With a low growl, he gave in and bit, her warm blood coursing over his tongue as they both climaxed. He held her wrapped in his arms, rocking back and forth as he sealed the tiny wounds and pressed his ear to her pounding heart. He held her and walked to the bed, tucking her into his side as he began to feel the pull of day in his limbs.

Beatrice stroked a hand over his heart, feeling the slow thump as his body warmed with the rush of her blood. His hunger sated, Giovanni's eyes began to droop, and she sat up, watching him as he fell into his daytime rest.

"I love you, Jacopo."

He struggled to stay awake. "*Ti amo*. Stay. Stay with me today. Don't leave."

"I will stay." Beatrice stroked his hair, and their eyes met. He recognized the familiar look of resolve. "I'll never leave. I'm going to be with you forever."

Giovanni's lips tried to form the words of protest, but they lay silent in his mind before he blacked out, her flushed face the last thing he saw before he closed his eyes.

CHAPTER 12

Beatrice watched Giovanni for a few minutes before he ceased breathing, and she knew he would not rise until just before dusk. She left his scent on her skin as she dressed in a pair of loose pants and a T-shirt. Then she left the room, locking it behind her. She ignored the chill in the air when she walked out to the garden and sat in the sun, closing her eyes as the warm rays touched her skin for the last time.

She let her mind drift to the night before. She had been practicing with Baojia, frustrated with her own fumbling attempts to best him.

"Deflect, girl!" He slapped at the blade of her dao *with an open palm. "Where is your mind tonight?"*

Her mind was on Lorenzo, who she had seen walking across the garden as they left earlier to practice outside. As soon as her heart began to race, Giovanni had rushed to her side, arguing with Baojia until the vampire had relented and taken their practice back to Tenzin's rooms.

"I'm just... my arm is really sore; can we take a break? This full-weight sword is kind of killing me."

He frowned. "You didn't take this long switching from the practice jian. *What's your problem?"*

She lost her temper. "Maybe I'm not an immortal, badass vampire, Baojia! Maybe I just need a fucking break for once. Is that too much to ask?"

He curled his lip in disgust. "You're acting like a child. I should send you to your room until you have improved your attitude."

She threw the sword on the ground. "Go to hell! I am not a child, and maybe I have a bit more on my mind than just your dumb sword practice. The last thing I need—"

"You will not treat your weapon in that manner," he hissed.

Beatrice gasped when Baojia rushed to her. He stood, glaring into her eyes as he flipped the dao up with his foot, grabbed her hand, and slapped the handle into her palm. As the sword flipped in the air, it caught a finger, and she winced as she felt the blade slice her skin.

Baojia grabbed the sword from her hand immediately and brought her palm up to his face, his eyebrows furrowed in alarm.

"Beatrice, I..." Immediately, he brought her finger to his mouth and licked at the blood as it trickled down her hand. She saw his tongue flick out, piercing a long fang, and he sealed the wound in a matter of seconds.

As soon as he had, he froze. His eyes lifted to hers, and she saw his fangs grow longer in his mouth. Her breath rushed out of her body as she felt the soft caress of his amnis spread over her palm and tease the skin of her wrist.

"Stop," she whispered. "Let go of my hand."

But he didn't, nor did he move. Baojia stood inhumanly still, and his eyes never left hers. For a brief moment, she could imagine falling into them, and she pulled away, stunned by the rush of her own pulse.

"Stop." She wasn't sure whether she was talking to him or herself.

"I'm sorry, B."

"Forget about it."

"I most certainly will not."

She flushed in embarrassment, furious at the idea of Giovanni or Tenzin walking in and seeing them in such proximity. "Really, forget about it. All of it."

"Beatrice—"

"I'm done practicing for the night."

"We're not finished here."

She huffed out a breath. "Yes, we are." She reached down and grabbed her dao, then tried to walk past him, but his arm shot out and grabbed her wrist. She felt the creep of his energy again when their skin met, and she wrenched it away.

"Don't! Don't touch me."

"B, just listen—"

"I'm done. Got it? You..." She was still blushing, and she couldn't forget the intimate feel of his tongue and the teasing caress of his amnis. "Just forget about it."

"You cannot deny that there is something—"

"Shut up!" she shouted. "What? You getting tired of the donated blood? Need a little refreshment? I'm not a fucking appetizer."

He blinked in surprise, but anger quickly overtook his features. "You arrogant little—"

"Leave me the hell alone! I'm going for a walk." She continued toward the door. "Don't worry. I'll take my precious sword."

"Get back here, girl!"

Beatrice turned, gave him a bitter smile, then flipped him off, noting absently that the *finger he had healed was the one now raised in ire. She continued walking backward, straight out the door. She turned down the hallway and out to the gardens, ignoring Baojia as he called her name. She heard him call for Tenzin's guards, so she ducked down a corridor she had seen the servants using.*

She followed it toward fresh air. With the lack of windows in the palace, it was hard to tell which way led outside, but she felt a gust of cool air waft across her heated face, so she followed it, eventually opening a door that led to the outer perimeter of the palace grounds.

She saw a path leading through the forest that surrounded the compound, and a few monks were walking in the grey hours before dawn. She followed them, but soon got lost in the dark maze of the shifting bamboo. Following the sound of water, she came upon the creek that fed the streams that cut through the gardens. Heaving a sigh of relief, Beatrice began to follow it back to the palace gardens.

"A beautiful woman carrying such a weapon. What is the world coming to?"

She whirled, gasping when she heard his voice. She immediately raised her sword. Lorenzo only smiled and stepped into it. Lifting a hand to prop the heavy dao *on his shoulder, he laughed.*

"There, now you're quite safe. You can chop off my head if I threaten to harm a hair on yours. Feel better?"

"What are you doing here?" *She debated whether to try chopping off his head, or at least trimming the hair he seemed so fond of.*

"Do you think you could? Chop off my head?" *His full mouth pouted in concentration.* "I'm not sure you could. You might not realize how much strength that actually takes. There are all these pesky bones and tendons. It's harder than it looks. I should know."

"Would you like to be my test subject? What do you say, you bastard?"

"I just want to talk. Since you seem to be the most rational of your little group, I thought I'd give you a try. You see, my attempts to reason with my father have failed."

"Gee, I can't imagine why."

Lorenzo shrugged. "I can't either. I tried to explain that I no longer wished Stephen any harm, or you for that matter, and he just ignored me. I think he's still blinded by his desire for our father's books. That vampire is quite single-minded when his attention gets focused on something." *Lorenzo gave a lascivious smirk.* "Of course, you probably know that by now."

She swallowed, struck by something Lorenzo had said. "What do you mean? You've said over and over that you wanted to torture and murder my father. And me. Why would I believe that you no longer want to hurt us?"

He cocked his head. "You're a very perceptive woman, Beatrice De Novo. Look into my eyes, and see if you believe me. I do not wish any harm to come to you. Nor do I have any interest in your father. All I want is—"

"The book."

He smiled. "I knew you would understand. All my interest in you and your family will cease if I get my books back. That's all I want. Well—" *He smiled.* "I'd be lying if I said that was all I wanted." *He let his gaze rake over her body.*

She snorted. "Right, like *that's going to happen.*"

"I deeply regret not tasting you... really *tasting you the night I had you on my boat.* That was foolish of me. Tell me, do you plan on turning, Beatrice?"

She couldn't help the smile that flickered across her face at the thought of being as powerful as the monster across from her.

"Ah, I see you smile. Excellent idea, if you ask me. And refreshing. So nice to see a human that's not attached to breathing or breeding. Very forward thinking of you."

"I don't really give a shit about your opinion. I really doubt that comes as a surprise."

He chuckled. "Enough chatting. It's quite addicting talking to you, you know. I do love good banter. But I'll return to my original point, I promise to leave your father and all your relations in peace as long as I get that manuscript and the journals."

"And what about Ioan? What about him?"

Lorenzo merely shrugged. "Was he your lover? Your father? Your child? Leave Ioan's vengeance to his family; it is no concern of yours."

"But Gio would never—"

"*Giovanni*"—he stepped closer and let the blade run along his skin, drawing a line of blood—"*will do what* you *want.* You know you could persuade him to give it to me if it meant he could go back to his quiet, uneventful life. He can bury himself in his books and research again, just like you know he wants to."

Beatrice would have been lying to say the idea was not tempting. On one level, she knew she could probably convince Giovanni if she really tried. But...

"I don't make deals with the devil, Lorenzo. Even when the devil looks me in the eye." She stepped forward and let the blade cut deeper into his skin. His lip curled in disdain.

"Fool." And she gasped when his cold hand reached up and grabbed the back of her neck.

The next thing she remembered was looking into Giovanni's tormented green eyes.

It was the idea of mental manipulation, even more than physical harm, that Beatrice feared the most. The period of her teenage years when she was afraid she was losing her sanity had been the most frightening of her life.

Until she was immortal, Beatrice knew she was vulnerable.

The morning sun poured over the garden, lighting the gleaming limestone pillars and flashing across the streams that cut through the grass. The air was lush with the sound of morning birds, and brilliant fall leaves lay scattered along the lawn as servants spread across the silent grounds, raking the paths in their orange robes.

Beatrice sat on the damp ground under a weeping maple and watched the sun rise in the East. She sat for hours, watching it track across the garden and memorizing the way the shadows shifted and the light danced on the rippling water. She let her mind roam to the waterfalls of Cochamó and the rainbows in the mist. She let herself remember the sunset over the Pacific and the searing heat of hiking in the desert with Dez as the light painted the rocks red.

She spent hours staring into the bright garden and never closed her eyes.

When she felt the soft touch on her shoulder, she turned to see Nima standing with a cup of cardamom tea. Though she had hardly spoken to the woman in the weeks they had been at the palace, her quiet human company was welcome. She sat next to Beatrice on the ground, surprisingly flexible for one with such a wrinkled face. Her dark eyes looked over the sun-lit grounds.

"I have painted many gardens for Tenzin over the years," she said in quietly accented English, "but it's never exactly the same."

"There are photographs."

Nima nodded her silver-grey head. "Yes."

"Still not the same, though."

"No."

Beatrice sniffed, swallowing the lump in her throat, before she gave up and let the tears fall down her cheeks.

"Sorry," she sniffed again.

Nima just smiled. "I understand the grief."

"But I know I'm ready."

"Tenzin said you would be. That was one of the reasons she asked me to be here. I don't usually like to leave the mountains."

Beatrice frowned, curious why Nima's presence was important, until she looked into the old woman's eyes and understood the quiet sadness that lived there.

"You said no, didn't you?"

"Yes."

"Oh," she breathed out.

"And I regret it every day."

"But why—"

"By the time I really understood the regret, my body was old. I would not choose it now. It is not vanity, simply... not what I wish for eternity."

"Was she angry?"

"Yes."

"But you are still together."

Nima smiled and nodded. "Yes."

"Someday, she'll watch you die."

"And that is the sadness I live with."

Beatrice swallowed the lump in her throat. "So I'm making the right decision?"

Nima smiled. "I can't tell you that, but I think you already know."

Beatrice looked over the sun-washed garden again and closed her eyes. "Yes, I know."

"It is still understandable to grieve."

"Thank you for being here."

"You're welcome."

Nima tucked her feet under and sat next to Beatrice as the sun rose to the apex of the sky. The two women sat silently in the sunlight, listening to the chirp of the birds and the buzzing bees. They watched the wind tease the orange, red, and purple leaves from the trees, and the clouds drifted across the sky, their slow-moving shadows falling across the earth.

It was close to three o'clock when Beatrice rose, helped Nima to her feet, then walked inside, shutting the door to the sun for the last time. She walked down the hall to the practice room to find Tenzin sitting there with her father. She looked into the storm-grey eyes of her friend.

"Are you ready?"

"Yes."

"I CAN'T." STEPHEN SHOOK HIS HEAD. "I CAN'T DRAIN HER, TENZIN."

"It has to be you. That's what needs to happen. Her fate lies with water, not air."

"I can give her my blood. I just can't *drain* her."

Tenzin scowled. "You'll be very weak if you don't."

Stephen still shook his head. "I can't do it."

Beatrice put a hand on her father's arm. "Tenzin, is it that important who drains me? As long as I have Dad's blood to turn, right?"

"Yes, but his amnis will be drained from giving you his blood. I don't like the idea of him being so weak."

"Then you can give me some of yours later. And I'll feed after," Stephen said, "but you cannot ask me to drain my daughter to the point of death."

"Fine," Tenzin rolled her eyes. "I'll probably need the strength when he wakes, anyway."

Beatrice shuddered at the thought. "He's going to be furious. Tenzin, I'm sorry for anything Giovanni—"

"Please," she said. "It's not like he can hurt me. This is one of those situations where it is better to ask forgiveness than permission. Besides, he knows it's coming."

"That's not going to make him any less angry." She felt a churning in her gut as she remembered his plea before he fell asleep. She felt like she was betraying his trust, but she also felt as if she had no other choice.

Tenzin grabbed her arm. "Are you ready? Really?"

She nodded. "Okay, dirty details time."

"Fine. I'll drain your blood, you'll probably pass out, but your father will feed you his. It won't be instinctive for you to drink from him at first, but don't worry, we'll make sure you get enough. He'll be able to use amnis to make you swallow the blood until you latch on."

She bit her lip. "And I won't remember any of it?"

"Probably not much. I'll use my amnis to keep you from struggling. Your body will fight the blood loss instinctively, so it's better if I use it to keep you calm."

Beatrice hated the thought of that, but agreed it was probably for the best. "Okay. What happens after that?"

Tenzin and her father exchanged a look. "Your body will go through quite a few changes at first. The first couple of hours it will expel anything from your digestive system. But you won't be awake for that."

"Oh, *ew*." She took Tenzin's hand. "I want you to promise me that you will not let Giovanni be here when all that stuff is going on. One, gross. Two, he'll freak out."

She shrugged. "I'll be able to keep him away. Once it's done, he'll understand."

Beatrice thought Tenzin might have been a bit overconfident on that one, but she didn't have much choice but to trust her. "Okay. Then what?"

"Your body will shut down for about twenty-four hours, or until first dark. Then you'll wake up and be a vampire."

"Am I going to be hungry right away?"

"Not immediately, but definitely the first night." Tenzin just shrugged like it was no big deal.

She sighed a little and saw her father's mouth quirk into a small grin.

"And?"

"What? We'll find someone to feed you. It's not a big deal. There are lots of bowing people around."

"Um... that's not exactly... can I have donated blood at first? I don't want to drain anyone."

Stephen was quick to reassure her. "We won't let you kill anyone. We'll make sure you have some fresh blood, but you will need a lot."

"How much?"

Tenzin said, "About a person's worth."

Her mouth fell open. "That much?"

"Just at first. The first year or so, you'll have to drink a few cups every night and then you'll need much less."

She began to feel her heart rate pick up. "Don't let me kill anyone. I... I can't—"

"You won't." Tenzin reassured her. "We'll have you fully stocked with fresh blood that hasn't been preserved. No preserved blood for a while. You need the fresh stuff to be strong. Animal will do if you must, but human is always the best."

"Okay." She nodded. "Okay."

"Any other questions?"

"What will it be like? At first?"

Tenzin frowned. "I don't really remember. It's been a long time. Stephen?"

Stephen took a deep breath. "You'll feel very overwhelmed. All your senses will be heightened. Your hearing will be better. Your sense of smell. You'll feel the electrical currents almost like a web around you. This place is ideal because there is so little electricity, it won't be as overwhelming as—"

"Oh!" Beatrice gasped.

"What?" Stephen looked at her in panic. "B, you can change your mind at any time, you don't have to—"

"Yes, she does!"

He glared at Tenzin. "No, she doesn't."

"She really does."

"Stop." Beatrice held out a hand. "Don't fight. I'm just... It's silly. I just realized I won't be able to use my computer anymore."

Tenzin rolled her eyes. "Is that all?"

"Yeah," she frowned and felt her father reach over to squeeze her arm. "That's all."

For a moment, the unexpected grief welled up again. She felt childish to feel grief about something that seemed so inconsequential, but it wasn't. Then she remembered the feeling of helplessness she'd had again when she woke the night before, weak and shivering from another attack. She thought about her conversation with Nima in the garden and about the flicker of grief she saw in Giovanni's eyes every time he looked at Casper.

She didn't want to be vulnerable. She didn't want to leave Giovanni.

She was ready.

"I'm ready."

Beatrice looked up and realized they were waiting for her. Her father stood and pulled her into a fierce embrace.

"I love you, kiddo. It's going to be fine."

"I'm glad you're here, Dad. This is the best thing. Right? I mean, you're my dad."

"Yeah," he smiled, and his eyes crinkled just like she remembered as a child, "I'm your dad."

She whispered, "And you always will be."

"Yep."

"Sentimental De Novos," she heard Tenzin call. "The very angry, territorial fire-vampire will be waking up very soon. If we want this to happen, we need to do it now."

Beatrice nodded and went to sit on the grouping of low cushions in the corner of the room. Stephen sat across from her, and Tenzin sat to her left and pulled her hair to the side. She gave her a full, fangy grin. Beatrice cocked her head at an angle.

"Okay, drink up."

"I have to say, you do smell delicious. I kind of get why he wants to keep you."

Beatrice frowned. "Tenzin, please don't make me feel any more like dinner than I already do."

Her friend laughed long and hard. Finally, Beatrice did too. Then Tenzin reached over and stroked Beatrice's hair back from her face, and the soft look she occasionally allowed herself peeked through.

"It will be all right. Relax." Beatrice could feel the amnis start to creep across her skin as she stared at Tenzin. Her father held her hand and she allowed the soft brush of her friend's influence in her mind. She closed her eyes and listened to the hypnotic voice.

"Meditate. Just like we practiced. Calm. Let yourself relax."

She drifted, focusing on a picture of Giovanni she held in her mind. It was the single-minded look he gave her sometimes. When he was angry. When he made love to her. When he killed for her. It was the look that told her she was the center of his world.

"I am your balance in this life," she whispered to him, even though he was not there. "In every life."

Her eyes flew open when she felt Tenzin's fangs strike.

Beatrice could feel her body jerk once at the attack before Tenzin's influence drifted over her limbs and caused her to fall still. She could still feel her father holding her hand, and her senses were on alert, but she couldn't speak, nor could she move.

She was paralyzed. Cut off from reaction to the fierce attack her mind fought against, but her body was powerless to stop. Tenzin's bite wasn't painful, but her vicious, curled fangs buried themselves in her artery and Beatrice felt her heart race at the unwelcome intrusion. It was as if her body had been forced into a whirlwind, and she knew there was no escape. The blood rushed to her head as she felt the hard draw of Tenzin's mouth at her neck.

Drums beat in her mind. It was nothing like the soft, drugging bites that Giovanni took. It was hard. Violent, no matter how Tenzin tried to reassure her. Her mind began to scream '*No*' as she felt the life drain out of her.

It wasn't quick.

'*There are an average of ten pints of blood in the human body,*' she heard the echo of her high school biology teacher in her mind as her thoughts scattered.

Ten pints.

Twenty cups.

How long would it take to drink that much water?

But blood was thicker than water.

Or whiskey.
How long had he known he would sire her?
Did he know?
Who knew?
Was that why?
Her heart pounded. A ringing grew in her ears.
Her mind began to flash, and the lights danced across the room.
A sunrise.
Her grandparents slow dancing in the living room.
Her father reading her a bedtime story in a purple-painted room.
Hiding in a tree to read *A Little Princess.*
Sunset on Galveston Bay.
The pictures flashed like an old film reel.
Her father. Webs in the living room. Grandma's swollen eyes. Hands twisted in rage. A knife at her leg. His pale face in the streetlamp. Grasping hands.
Books lined the walls of her mind, all falling open to different pages.
"There's a position open at the library."
A pair of vivid green eyes.
"What's your real name?"
The taste of whiskey filled her mouth.
"That was for me."
A thundering silence washed over her.
She heard nothing but his voice.
Her heart.
His voice.
"My name is Jacopo."
Thump.
"I'm here for you."
Thump.
"I will always come for you."
Thump.
"Don't you know how I adore you?"
Thump.
"You are my balance in this life."
Thump.
"In every life."
There came a force of wind in her ears.
"Forever."
Thump.
Forever. Forever. Forever.
The wind grew louder, filling the room as she felt the first falter of her heart.
She dimly heard her father say something as Tenzin's mouth pulled away. Her

body was passed from one set of arms to another, more familiar, pair. The wind still roared through the room.

Forever.

Forever.

Forever.

The shriek grew. There was a banging and clamoring as the whirlwind took over, and she heard a door burst open. The roaring filled her ears as she felt the drip of blood at her lips.

Her eyelids fluttered closed.

Her heart fell silent.

His inhuman roar was the last thing she heard before the black void took her.

CHAPTER 13

Giovanni was engulfed in flames. His roar shook the room.
"*Beatrice!*"
Tenzin held his shoulders against the wall as the fire unfurled around him.
"No!" he raged as the smell of her blood filled the air.
He couldn't hear her heart.
He couldn't see her eyes.
Giovanni was trapped in Tenzin's iron grasp as his lover's blood flooded his friend's body and turned her cheeks red. The blue fire burned his clothes and spread up the wall behind him as he continued to struggle.
"Let me go!"
He couldn't hear her heart.
"No."
The snarl ripped from his throat. "Release me, or I will kill you."
"Her father is feeding her."
Giovanni's roar was inhuman. Stephen looked up in horror as he pressed his wrist to Beatrice's mouth. Her lips weren't moving.
He couldn't see her eyes.
"You need to calm yourself."
"I will kill you both!"
He heard another vampire enter the room, but his eyes never left Beatrice's crumpled form. She lay lifeless on the cushions as her father forced his blood in her mouth.
He couldn't hear her heart.
"Well, this was stupid."

"Shut up, and help me hold him."

He felt the pinch of a metal pike pierce his shoulder and the wall behind him, holding him as Tenzin's wind forced the flames up the side of the practice room. The air was filled with smoke and fire.

"A little help with the flames, please."

He saw Beatrice's throat move once before Baojia blanketed him with a sheet of water drawn from the stream that cut through the room. He relaxed slightly when he saw her lips begin to move and latch onto Stephen's wrist. Her father cradled her in his arms as Beatrice began to drink.

Giovanni slumped against the wall, Tenzin holding his shoulders while Baojia tugged the spear out of his flesh. He could not tear his eyes from her.

"Tenzin, let me go."

"No."

"I won't kill Stephen."

"I don't really trust you right now."

The flames flared again on his torso.

"Let me go!"

Baojia doused him again, but he still struggled against Tenzin's hold.

"Calm down, my boy."

"Let me go to her."

"Her father is feeding her. Let him take care of her."

"Tenzin!" He took a deep breath and closed his eyes. "Please, bird-girl. Let me go." When he opened his eyes, he stared into her grey ones, trying to ignore the flush of her cheeks, rich with Beatrice's blood.

"Are you calm?"

He finally heard her heart give a faint thump, and a new trace of amnis began to drift across the room as Stephen's blood entered her system. A familiar honeysuckle smell reached his nose.

"Please," he begged. "Let me go, Tenzin. Let me go to my wife."

She drew back in surprise. "What?"

"My wife," he pleaded. "Let me go to Beatrice. I need to go to her."

Her hands released him. "I did not see that."

Giovanni rushed over, taking her limp hand and pressing it to his cheek as she continued to drink from her father's wrist.

It was cold. The human warmth gone from her forever.

He pushed down the instinctive rage and grief to focus on Beatrice.

The new whisper of her energy comforted him, and he put his hands to her temples, searching for the familiar signature of her mind. Her scent was the same; fainter, as he knew it would be. Giovanni brushed her cheek with soft fingers as her father took his wrist away, biting it open again before he put it back to her mouth. Beatrice's lips were stained with blood and rivulets dripped down her neck, mingling with Tenzin's angry bite marks. He resisted the urge to heal her, knowing that any of his blood mingling with her own before she was fully turned could be tragic.

Stephen looked at him cautiously. "Did you say 'my wife?'"

"Yes." He brushed the hair away from her face. She was deathly pale.

"When?"

"We were married in Santiago months ago."

Silence blanketed the room. The only sounds came from the new vampire suckling at her father's wrist. Giovanni watched her with a single-minded focus, memorizing the rhythm of her lips and throat as she drank.

"Why didn't you tell anyone?" Tenzin asked.

He shook his head, continuing to stare at Beatrice. "Her idea. She wanted a more formal ceremony after all this was over. I thought it was silly, but she insisted. Why are we talking about this?"

"Because they are waiting for you to erupt again." He heard Baojia's stiff voice from the edge of the room. He could feel the vampire leave, but Tenzin remained, moving closer to him and placing a hand on his shoulder.

"I'm very, very angry with you both, but now is not the time for that." He continued to stroke Beatrice's hair, tucking it behind her ear so it wouldn't fall in her face.

"It was her idea."

He whispered, "I'm angry with her, as well."

No one said anything. All three were focused on Beatrice as she drank. He could feel her amnis begin to pulse, and he knew she was almost finished feeding. She would not wake until nightfall the next day. He finally tore his eyes from her and looked at Tenzin.

"Have you informed your father?"

"Stephen and I told him months ago."

He just shook his head, stunned by her audacity. He shoved her hand from his shoulder.

"Get away from me."

"You need to leave her with us and go to your room."

"I'm not leaving her," he scoffed.

"Giovanni." She sat next to him, but he refused to look at her. "You know what changes her body will be going through as she turns. She didn't want you to see that. You know this. There is a reason a sire takes care of his child."

He swallowed once. "Don't ask me to leave her."

"I didn't ask it. She did."

A new ache pierced his heart, and Giovanni looked at Stephen, who only nodded before he returned to watching his daughter, cradling her as if she was an infant. As much as he wanted to stay with Beatrice, he knew her father was probably telling the truth. He would honor Beatrice's wishes, even if she hadn't honored his.

THE FORCE OF WIND

Watching Stephen hold her, he realized he felt more at ease leaving Beatrice in the care of her father than with his oldest friend. Tenzin tried to touch his bare shoulder again, but he brushed her off.

"My boy—"

"I'll go," he whispered. "Bring her to me before dawn. I don't want her waking with anyone but me."

Stephen nodded. "Fine."

Beatrice stopped drinking and curled instinctively into her father's arms. Giovanni gave one last brush to her cheek, leaned over to kiss her temple, then stood to go with clenched fists. He turned at the door to watch Tenzin crouch beside Stephen and Beatrice, guarding the room with watchful eyes. Then, he forced himself to walk back to their room and wait.

Tenzin knocked on the door hours later, and, without a word, Giovanni took Beatrice's sleeping form from Stephen's arms. They had bathed her, but a faint human smell still clung to her body. She seemed lighter than normal, and he was reminded how small she was beneath her bravado. He kicked the door closed before he walked to the bed and nestled her in the silk sheets. He secured the room, double-checking every safety measure, before he lay down with her. He took the sheet from her body and wrapped her in his arms, pressing her cold skin to warm her.

When Giovanni touched her, her energy twined with his, reaching out even in the black void of the deepest sleep. The touch of her amnis flooded him, and it was as if he could feel the brush of her small hands over his body. He lay utterly still, closed his eyes, and waited for her to rise.

When he opened his eyes an hour before dusk, Beatrice was pulsing with amnis, her senses already heightened though she wasn't yet conscious. The hairs on her body stood on end and her skin was damp, the water in the air drawn to her as she rested. There was no question, she was most definitely her father's daughter. And with Stephen drinking as much of Tenzin's blood as he had been, she was going to be very, very powerful. He could read her energy signature already.

He rose, threw on a robe, and went to open the door. Nima was sitting on a bench outside.

"Nima?"

She looked up. "Yes, Gio?"

He paused, unsure of what to say.

"Has Tenzin informed you—"

"I know. I talked to Beatrice yesterday morning."

He blinked. "You did?"

"Yes." She smiled. "She was very peaceful about her decision. Only a little worried how you would react."

"Of course." He didn't know how to respond to her. He was angry. Relieved. Furious. Unavoidably excited. He shook his head. "Is there blood available?"

"Tenzin has already arranged fresh donors. Beatrice was quite concerned about not draining anyone."

"She would be."

"It's taken care of. We will keep it warm for her." She motioned to one of Zhang's younger vampires who he saw standing at the end of the hall. "Send for someone when it is needed."

"Thank you, Nima."

For the first time, he was grateful he was in Penglai, that she had made her change there. No other place in the world was more of an island for immortals. Everything in the palace revolved around their particular needs and foibles.

"And please let Beatrice know that all the human staff has been moved to another part of the quarters, so she doesn't need to worry about them. I'm leaving now. I just wanted to speak to you before I left."

"Thank you again."

"We are at your disposal. It is our honor to help." She gave a nod and walked down the hall, giving quiet instructions to the young vampire at the end of the hall.

Giovanni shut the door and checked the clock on the wall, before he walked back to the bedroom. He paced for a few minutes, determined to push back his anger and frustration. It was not something she could deal with her first night. Taking a deep breath, he peeled the sheets back to really look at her for the first time since her change.

He had been right. She was stunning.

Her skin was smooth and pale, a luminescent pearl that glowed in the lamplight. Her hair was the same, a thick, shining wave of brown that would hopefully still match her eyes. It wasn't uncommon for eyes to change, but her father's had not, so he hoped Beatrice's wouldn't, either.

He pulled her lip up to see the delicate fangs peeking at him. For the first time in days, he smiled. They weren't fully extended yet, but he could imagine them gleaming in her mouth, and he shuddered in anticipation.

Her body was the same, preserved for all eternity as it had been on her last day of human life. The marks in her neck from Tenzin's bite had healed, but he could still see the tiny scars left on the rise of her right breast where he had bitten her while they made love on their wedding night. She had asked him not to heal that bite, wanting the tiny reminder that only they would see.

The small scar on her knee remained, a token of childhood that he kissed, along with the small, sad scars that marked her thigh. She could have had them removed, but she had chosen not to. He traced over each mark on her body that remained unchanged.

"*Tesoro mio*," he murmured as he stroked her face. "So stubborn. How I love you."

If there was one thing he remembered from waking, it was the pain along his sensitive skin. Every nerve ending was heightened in a vampire, particularly a new one who hadn't fully mastered their amnis and the shield it could provide. It was that sharp, overwhelming pain that had first caused the fire to bloom on Giovanni's skin as a newborn vampire. He would never forget the look of fascination and glee in Andros's eyes when he saw it.

He knew she would be most comfortable surrounded by her element, so he left her in bed and drew a warm bath in the large, marble tub. Then he walked back to the bedroom and gathered her up to wait.

He could feel it in her skin first, the twitching, shuddering sensation that rippled wherever his fingers touched. It started on her arms, then traveled down to her fingers, which twitched under the warm water. His arms encircled her as she lay against his chest. He felt her rouse, and she took a deep, gasping breath.

"Ah!" she cried, scooting away from his arms and turning as the water sloshed out of the bath. She put her hands over her ears to shield them from the sound of her own voice, but winced at the movement. "What's wrong with me?"

He held his hands up, soothing her as her eyes darted around the room. He almost sighed in relief that they were the same deep brown.

"Shh," he whispered, conscious of her newly keen hearing, "what is the last thing you remember?"

Her eyes finally settled on him, and she stared rapt at his face.

"Your eyes are different. Why are your eyes different?"

He smiled. "You're just seeing more light, Beatrice. I'm the same."

She shivered, and blood-tinged tears fell down her face. "It hurts. Why does it hurt everywhere? I'm sorry, are you mad at me? Please, don't be mad at me."

His heart ached at her confused plea, and he swallowed the last of his anger in the face of her need. "Take a deep breath. It will calm you, even though you no longer need the oxygen. It's habit."

She took one, a look of confusion coloring her face when she realized she didn't need to breathe it out. "Now let it out." She did, then took another. "Your skin hurts because the nerve endings are much more sensitive. Your whole body is like an exposed nerve."

"Yeah," she moaned. "No kidding."

He continued to make soothing noises, humming quietly as she took a few moments to compose herself.

"Why are we in the bathtub?"

"It should help with the sensitivity. Does it feel good?"

"Yeah." She breathed out. "Really good."

"Do you feel the water around you?"

"Yes," she said, looking down in fascination. "It loves me."

He smiled. "Yes, it does. Water will always be your element now. You will have more control over yourself when you are surrounded by it. Do you feel your amnis?"

Beatrice wasn't paying attention. She had lifted a hand out of the water, drawing rivulets of it up to meet her fingertips where she made them dance like puppet strings. Giovanni was amazed by her control. The mere fact that she could be sitting in the water and not have it rushing uncontrollably over her body was remarkable.

"Water loves me."

"Yes, it does."

"I love water."

Giovanni chuckled. Her mind was probably so flooded with new sensory information, she was focusing on the one thing that seemed to make sense. He remembered the same feeling looking into a candle on his first night of immortal life.

"I love you," she said. She was staring at him again.

"I love you, too." As if it was even a question.

"You're mad at me."

As if it was even a question.

"We'll talk about it another time. Now is not the time."

"I can agree with that."

He saw her staring at the lamps, probably fascinated by the new light spectrum she could see. "Can I kiss you?" he whispered.

She cocked her head. "Will it hurt?"

He leaned forward, tentatively reaching for her. "I'll try to be very gentle."

She nodded, still staring at him. He braced himself on the sides of the tub and bent down to give her a whisper of a kiss.

"Oh." She breathed out with a small smile. "Wow."

"Didn't hurt?"

"No." She blinked back more tears. "Kiss me again."

"I love you," he said before his mouth met hers in another soft kiss.

"I can feel your amnis," she whispered. "It's like another layer of skin. All over. Moving."

"Do you feel yours?"

He could see her eyes narrow as she filtered through the flood of senses. Then, she smiled and looked up. "Yes."

"Soon, you'll learn how to make it cover your skin like me. That's what will let you heat your skin, keep your senses manageable, all of that. Your amnis is both a weapon and a shield. A second skin is an excellent way of thinking about it."

Even as he spoke, he could see her close her eyes and furrow her eyebrows in concentration. When he reached out to touch her hand, she didn't flinch. A layer of amnis already covered it and she knit their fingers together, palm to palm.

"Do I look different?" Her eyebrows shot up, and she lifted fingers to her mouth. "I have teeth!"

As soon as she touched them, her fangs descended even more, and it took every bit of control he owned not to lean over and lick them. He wanted to pierce his tongue on her teeth and let his blood flood her mouth. He wanted her to sink her teeth into his neck. Into his chest. He wanted her to feed from him as he had fed from her. Giovanni pushed back the growl in his chest and focused on her eyes.

"Ith kin' of hard to talk with theeth," she mumbled, speaking around her descended canines.

Her strange lisp broke him out of his trance, and he laughed. "You look the same, Beatrice. Just... paler skin and longer teeth. You'll get used to the teeth."

He kept chuckling, and she flicked her fingers at him. A splash of water rose from the tub and hit his face.

"Okay," she grinned. "Thath's going to be awthume."

He couldn't stop laughing. "And you'll be able to save my shirts if I lose my temper now."

She swallowed and her fangs seemed to retract. "Just... all sorts of benefits to controlling water, aren't there?"

Giovanni smiled as she leaned back against her side of the tub. He reached for her foot underwater and touched it. She flinched for a moment before her toes relaxed and he set both her feet on his lap.

"Are you really mad at me?"

He stared. He didn't want to argue with her on her first night as an immortal. She would be far too volatile. "There's no use in anger toward you. It's done." He paused. "And I know it was your decision."

"Are you mad at Tenzin and my dad?"

"Yes," he growled.

"Why?"

"Because they were planning this and they didn't tell me. They went behind my back."

"So did I."

He sighed and let his head fall back. "Maybe I just don't want to be angry with you. It's easier to be angry with them. I don't like it when we fight."

She smiled and reached a hand over to pat his as it lay on the side of the tub. "Just as long as you realize it's not logical. I'm more to blame than they are."

"Tesoro, I realized long ago that logic departs me when it comes to you."

She grinned again, which exposed her fangs. He couldn't help himself. He leaned over and cupped her face gently before he kissed her. His tongue delved into her mouth and searched for them. When he found the slick lengths, he flicked the tip of his tongue against them and purred when he heard her moan. She moved into the kiss, and her fangs fell more. They were long, sharp, and slick with the taste of his blood as he cut himself.

He recognized the moment the blood touched her tongue. She tried to pull him closer, but he pushed her away gently. "Hungry?"

She nodded, still eyeing his mouth.

Giovanni wanted to take her right then, but he knew she needed to feed. Plus, the minute she left the tub, her senses were going to overwhelm her again. It would be days before she was even partially in control of her body. He certainly hoped there were no emergencies they would have to deal with. He rose from the tub, feeling her hungry eyes on him as he wrapped himself in a towel.

"Stay here. I'm going to find you some blood."

"No people!"

He smiled. "I've already made arrangements with Nima. She has fresh donors waiting. Nothing to worry about."

Her mouth fell open as she stared at him. "Oh, blood sounds so damn good."

Giovanni cocked an eyebrow at her. "Well, Beatrice, that's hardly a surprise. You're a vampire."

She grinned with two gleaming white fangs. "Yes, I am."

CHAPTER 14

"When are you two going to start talking again?"

"Well," Tenzin blocked a kick that Beatrice aimed at her left knee by taking to the air. "There was a time about two hundred years ago that he stopped talking to me for five years because I killed one of his servants."

"You what?" Beatrice's mouth dropped open. Tenzin landed a few yards away and rushed her, sliding to her side along the mat as she pulled Beatrice's legs out from under her. The two women fell into a heap before Tenzin shot up again.

She shrugged. "He was a very dishonest human. He'd been stealing from Gio. And he was taking advantage of a servant girl."

"So you killed him?" Beatrice shook her head as she jumped to her feet, continually amazed by Tenzin's rather interesting take on morality.

"He was diseased anyway. And the servant girl was pregnant. He was trying to beat the baby from her by striking her stomach. An entirely worthless human. I'm not sure why your husband was so upset." Tenzin landed a blow to her shoulder and Beatrice stumbled back and grimaced.

Tenzin had been slipping the "your husband" phrase into conversation as often as possible. Always with a slight smile or a snort. "I'm not sure why he was angry, either."

Tenzin dodged a quick blow she aimed at her head. They had been practicing Zhang's style of kung fu that evening and Beatrice was still amazed that the movements came so naturally.

"He started talking to me again when I explained why I killed the human. He wasn't completely unreasonable."

Beatrice rolled her eyes. "So you took five years to tell him why you killed his servant?"

"Yes."

"Well, that kind of explains it, Tenzin."

The small woman shrugged one shoulder before her hand reached out and landed a jaw-shattering blow to Beatrice's face. Beatrice winced, but shook her head and continued to fight, feeling the water in the air automatically draw to her skin as her bones knit together.

"I hate talking to your husband when he gets self-righteous and flame-y. I gave him a few years to cool off, then I had a rational conversation with him. It's not my fault he always assumes the worst."

"Stop it."

"Stop talking to your husband?" Tenzin grinned. "Not really a problem at the moment."

"Stop with the 'your husband' thing, all right?"

Tenzin burst into laughter. "I think it's hilarious."

"What?" Beatrice asked as she ducked down to avoid another blow. "That we didn't feel like sharing personal news that was really no one's business but ours?"

"No," Tenzin said, "that you two participated in an arcane human ritual that was completely unnecessary. It's not like you need a piece of paper. You're mates."

Beatrice frowned. "Do you have to make it sound quite so scientific?"

Tenzin laughed so hard that Beatrice managed to land a blow to her torso that knocked the vampire to the ground. She skidded and came to a stop near the stream in the practice room, still laughing. Beatrice went to sit next to her and lay on her back, staring out the open ceiling, the roof drawn back to show the sparkling night sky.

"Was it his idea or yours?"

Beatrice sighed, knowing she wouldn't get out of answering. Tenzin was fascinated by the whole situation, for some odd reason.

"Getting married was his idea. Keeping it to ourselves was mine."

"That doesn't surprise me. He's remarkably sentimental for a vampire."

"He's a five hundred year old Italian Catholic, Tenzin. Of course he wanted to get married. He's just annoyed that we only had a civil ceremony. Among other things."

Tenzin was silent, and Beatrice finally looked over to see her staring at her with a sympathetic look. She reached over and tucked a strand of hair behind Beatrice's ear.

"He adores you. You must know that."

Beatrice bit her lip and tried to keep the bloody tears from her eyes.

"It'd be nice if he started acting like it again, you know?"

The first nights after Beatrice had turned, Giovanni had been perfect.

Strong, tender, supportive, he was everything she had needed him to be as she made the awkward, often painful, transition from human life to immortal.

He had helped her to master her amnis so she could walk around the room without cringing from a gust of air. He stayed by her side as she saw her father and Tenzin again, supporting her through the roller coaster of intense emotions that seemed to be her constant companion. He had been quick to make sure she never had to wait when hunger struck her and made sure that all humans were kept at a safe distance. He had been the steady, quiet presence Beatrice had needed him to be.

But as the days passed and she grew more confident in her body, as she regained her composure and her control, Giovanni had drawn away, sinking into a shell of polite resentment. They slept in the same bed every night, but he had not touched her in weeks, and he refused to speak to Tenzin. He conversed only in the most polite way with Stephen and Baojia. And only when it was strictly necessary. He was most often in the library, still searching for the key to the elixir formula, or in the Great Hall, strategizing with Tenzin's father and his allies.

"Do you think it will be five years before he forgives me?"

"Please, you're his wife. He'll get horny. You'll fight. The two of you will make up. We won't see you for a few days. You'll be fine."

She glared at Tenzin. "Thanks, that's reassuring."

Tenzin shrugged. "It should be. I've been alive for over five thousand years. If there's one thing predictable about the male of the species, it's their sex drive and their fascination with fire."

Beatrice smiled. "That's it, huh?"

"Most advances in technology occur because they're either trying to impress women or blow things up. It's as predictable as the sunrise."

The two women stared at each other for a few seconds before they burst into laughter. Even Tenzin was wiping blood stained tears from her eyes.

"I'm being mostly serious, my girl. He really does adore you. He's angry right now. He feels like you went behind his back. That we both did—"

"We *did* go behind his back."

"But it was for the best."

Beatrice fell silent, wiping new tears from her eyes. "You sure?"

"I'm positive." Tenzin sighed. "Some things just have to happen a certain way. He will understand that in time. And he hates being angry with you, I can tell."

"I'm not a big fan of it, either."

Tenzin waved her concerns away. "You'll both be fine. You love each other too much to be angry for long. Plus"—she held a finger up—"you didn't kill anyone. That's a definite point in your favor."

Beatrice sighed and looked back up at the stars, gleaming and multi-colored in the night sky. How had she ever thought the night was black? It was a million shades, none of them as dense or unyielding as she'd thought.

Eternal night was a million swirling shades of grey.

SHE WAS DRINKING A LARGE MUG OF WARMED BLOOD THE NEXT TIME SHE SAW him. Giovanni passed in the hall, stopping when he saw Beatrice and Stephen at the large dining table.

"Good evening, Beatrice, Stephen. How are you tonight?"

The mouthful of blood stuck in her throat.

"We're doing well," Stephen said. "Thank you. Tenzin said Beatrice's kung fu is becoming quite exceptional."

"That's excellent."

She forced the blood down, almost choking on the thick liquid as it slid down her throat. He was wearing a pair of grey slacks and a white oxford shirt, open at the collar so she could see the rise of his chest. She tried to read his eyes, hoping that their brilliant green depths might have softened to her since she had risen that evening.

They had not.

"I... I'm practicing later with Baojia," she said, looking down at the small plate of food in front of her. It looked even more unappetizing than it had a few minutes before. "You should come by. We're doing weapons and water practice."

"I'll try."

"Gio, are you hungry?" Stephen offered. "The cooks prepared a very mild—"

"I'm fine, thank you." Giovanni glanced at her briefly. "I've already fed this evening."

A thick spike of jealousy cut through her. Beatrice wondered who he had fed from. It was just as likely Giovanni was making use of the donated blood in the palace as she and her father were, but a small part of her wondered whether he would be spiteful enough to drink from a human without telling her.

Stephen was speechless, looking between the two of them awkwardly.

"I have a meeting with Zhang in a few minutes. I'll see you both later."

Her father said, "Have a good evening."

"Bye," she said, never looking up and holding in the tears that wanted to escape. She heard his steps retreat down the hall, and she gripped the mug so tightly that it cracked, leaking blood over the ebony table before it dripped to the floor.

Beatrice rose and rushed to her room, never having finished her meal.

SHE REGRETTED SKIPPING HER RATION OF BLOOD LATER THAT NIGHT WHEN she sparred with Baojia.

THE FORCE OF WIND

"Shit!" she yelled as he sliced through her arm with the razor-sharp *dao*. She had been distracted by the burning in her throat.

"Pay attention before I put another slice in you," he yelled. "Where is your head tonight?"

"I've got a lot on my mind," she spit at him as she walked to the wall to replace her *dao* in its scabbard. "Can we do water practice for a while?"

"Fine. But only because I'll probably take your head off at some point for pissing me off. Then I'd have to deal with Giovanni trying to take mine."

"Doubt he'd even care at this point," she muttered as she took off her outer shirt to reveal the black tank underneath. It was skin tight, but since water practice usually involved both of them getting soaked from head to toe, the last thing she needed was to have wet practice robes flapping around while she tried to move.

"Let me count the ways I'm completely uninterested in your lover's spat with your husband, Mrs. Vecchio," Baojia sneered. "Don't waste my time."

She swung an arm at him, reaching out with her amnis to fling the water from the stream to his face. "Don't call me 'Mrs. Vecchio.'"

"Fine." He spat out the water from behind bared fangs. "Let's play."

With a quick flick of his hand, she was soaked by a thin wall of water that materialized behind her. She rolled closer to the flowing stream, avoiding the charged air he aimed at her face. Since her change, Beatrice could sense the amnis in the air almost like floating currents that filled the room. And on each floating current, she could send her element. While she was only beginning to understand the force of it, Baojia was an expert.

The water vampire, though relatively young among his kind, was an expert fighter, and his mental control, along with his control over his amnis, was masterful. He could send a thin stream of energy anywhere in the large room, almost beyond her detection, and the water in the air was drawn to it. If the stream was solid enough, he could send a bolt of electricity through it, rendering her useless until she could manage to throw up a shield of her own to counter the attack. He had shocked her in this way countless times, though she was beginning to get a better handle on detecting the trace of his amnis brushing against hers.

"Now," he lectured as they moved through the room, circling each other and trying to use the water in the room to their own advantage, "water tricks are a waste of time. That is Lorenzo's problem; he's too showy. Don't bother with showing off. Over seventy percent of the Earth's surface is covered in water. It suffuses the air around you. It makes up a portion of every living being on the earth. And you are that element's master. You can control it. You can manipulate it, Beatrice."

"Does that mean I can manipulate bodies?" She had never even considered it.

"That's more difficult, because there is muscle and will involved, but eventually, yes, you will."

"Even vampires?"

"Only if they let you." A whip of water wrapped around her legs, throwing her to the ground as he answered her. "Remember, we all have amnis. If a vampire is protecting himself, your amnis will not break through unless you are far, far more powerful. It's almost unheard of. Humans, on the other hand, are your toys to play with." She rolled away and climbed to her feet.

"That's kind of creepy." Beatrice attempted to trip him with a thin strand she drew from the tip of her bare foot. He caught it in the corner of his eye and jumped over it with ease.

"Clever one."

"Thanks."

They spent another half an hour trying to best each other with water, combining it with kicks or punches as it benefited the fight. Baojia dominated her, and she spent most of her time on the defensive, but slowly, Beatrice began to predict his movements.

"You're a fast learner," he said with a playful smile. She was embarrassed by how that smile affected her. It had been weeks since anyone looked at her with that kind of approval or admiration.

"That's good to hear, considering how completely inept I feel most of the time."

"You're not inept," he said with a sudden scowl, as he almost knocked her over from the right. The water splashed her eyes, and she struggled to blink it out. "You're just young. And you're far more powerful than I was at less than a month old."

"Did you really leave China to work on the railroads?" She had been curious about the vampire's history from the beginning, but he was even more secretive than Giovanni.

"What? You think because you are a vampire now, I will confide in you?"

If she could have blushed, she would have. He knocked her back with a punch to her shoulder. "No! I'm just... sorry, I was just curious."

"Curiosity killed the little water vampire, you know." He smiled and she wondered what, exactly, he was referring to.

"I may be immortal now, but I don't think I changed *that* much."

"I don't think you did, either." She was distracted by their conversation and blinked in surprise when she twisted instinctively to dodge a kick to her midsection. "Sadly, Mrs. Vecchio, you have lost none of your... unusual appeal."

"What's that supposed to mean?"

His lips curled into a smile, but it wasn't a lighthearted one. "You'll give me a run for my money one of these days... Mrs. Vecchio." His arms lifted, calling the

THE FORCE OF WIND

water from the stream into a thick coil that wrapped around her torso and spun her before knocking her over.

"Stop." She spat out the water that slapped her face as she fell. "Stop calling me that."

"Stop calling you 'Mrs. Vecchio?' But that's your name, isn't it?" He circled her, and his dark eyes held a trace of bitterness.

"My name is Beatrice."

"Not 'B' anymore, huh?" he said softly. She stood and they eyed each other, continuing to circle, each looking for any sign of weakness. The hairs on the back of her neck stood on end. "You are what he calls you?"

She narrowed her eyes, confused by his shifting moods. "What the hell is your problem?"

She felt the thin brush of amnis stroke the small of her back a second before he sent the shock. She winced and instinctively blocked it with a surge of her shield.

"Didn't fall over that time, did you?"

"No!"

"Stop thinking so damn much, B. You're stronger when you're angry."

Suddenly, Baojia came at her, a fury of fists and kicks that she tried to block, but even with her new speed, his blows knocked the air from her lungs. She couldn't keep up. He was aggressive; and, despite his iron control, she sensed an edge of anger in his blows.

"Hey—"

She was cut off by a fist.

"Defend yourself."

"What—"

A slap hit her cheek.

"Don't think about it. Hit me."

She stepped back, shaking her head to clear it. It didn't hurt the way it had as a human, but it still hurt. She could feel the cut on her lip closing even as he landed another blow.

"Hit me!"

"What are you—" A flurry of water pounded her. Beatrice tried to block each surge, but they soon knocked her to the ground. In a flash, Baojia had grabbed a sword and had the edge pressed against her neck.

"And you're dead."

She shoved the blade away, ignoring the bite of the blade against her skin, crawling to her knees and glaring at him as the blood rushed through her veins. Anger reared up and her fangs descended. "What do you want from me?" She felt her amnis swirl along her skin, out of control as her fists clenched. The water in the air quivered around her.

"You're more powerful than they realize, but you're not using it."

"What?"

"Instinct," he spat out. "You're still a human in vampire skin. Your muscles know these patterns, but your mind hasn't caught up. If Lorenzo attacked you tomorrow, he would kill you. Let your instincts take over and fight!"

"You want me to fight?"

"Yes!"

"Fine!" She hopped up and took a deep breath. She stood in her normal ready stance, but Baojia only sneered.

"Such a cute little girl, Mrs. Vecchio."

A thin red veil fell over her eyes, the fangs grew long in her mouth, and she felt her amnis pulse. Her heart beat its own unique rhythm, no longer bound by the trappings of biology. She felt the water in the air around her. Beatrice stopped concentrating on moving her limbs deliberately, as she had in *tai chi,* and just felt.

Baojia was crouched across from her.

"Hit me."

She let the amnis flow down her arm. Her fist landed in a blur, and Beatrice grinned.

He wiped the trickle of blood from the corner of his lip and smiled.

They started circling faster. She bent over, weaving back and forth, ready to strike. The amnis took over her limbs, and she began to move even faster, dipping and bending. In the back of her mind, she realized she was moving in ways she never would have attempted as a human, but there was no pain.

"Faster," he whispered.

She spun faster. Punching. Kicking. Flips and rolls did not challenge her immortal body.

It was effortless, she realized, as she took a deep, unnecessary breath. Her body was made for this. Her limbs moved without thought, the long practiced muscle memory colliding with her amnis as she moved in her own lethal ballet. Her amnis crackled as the water in the air was drawn to her, creating a thin sheen over her skin.

She flipped toward him, and her foot struck his face before she rolled away and shot up again. He sent another stream of water toward her, but she lifted a hand and blocked it with ease. Beatrice crouched down and swept his legs from under him before she rolled away. Then Baojia leapt on her shoulders. She bent back, nearly folding in half until he lost his grip and rolled away.

He reached out and grabbed her wrist, pulling her back to his chest. She could feel his cool breath at her neck.

"More," he whispered.

A swift hunger rose in her, and she thought of the blood dripping to the ground from her cracked mug. She wanted more.

More blood.

More fight.

More...

She bared her fangs, hissing as he shoved her away.

Beatrice stumbled for only a second before she was on her feet, spinning into a kick that landed near Baojia's ear. She smiled as her heart raced. She heard the door to the practice room swing open and was distracted for a second when she saw Giovanni enter. Baojia's kick landed on her jaw, knocking her back as she heard a snarl rip from her mate's throat.

A heartbeat later, she had been shoved back, and Giovanni pounced on Baojia, rolling across the floor in a tangle of limbs as the fire flared on his back and arms. She sent a wave of water over the two vampires, who were twisted in a growling heap.

Baojia pulled away and the two immortals began to circle each other. The water vampire's shirt was half torn from his body, and Beatrice could see burns healing at his neck. Giovanni eyed him, snarling as he placed himself between Beatrice and the perceived threat.

Beatrice knew instinctively that Baojia had triggered Giovanni's most territorial instincts, and she shook her head, trying to clear her mind so the practice session didn't end in death or serious injury. With her blood roiling, she was having difficulty focusing on anything other than the rippling muscle that spread over her mate's back, bared through the burned shirt and dripping water from the shower she had thrown at him. She could already see steam rising from his skin as his ire spiked.

Giovanni was magnificent. Pulsing energy and raw power. Beatrice could sense the amnis surge over his body. She could see the low flames licking along his chest. She could hear his blood roaring in her ears and smell the smoke pouring off his skin.

"Gio," she breathed out.

His head lifted and his eyes darted toward her voice and scent. Baojia leapt on him, but Giovanni only batted him across the room before he moved toward her, nostrils flared and fight forgotten as the blue flames swirled along his arms.

Not a word passed his lips when she pounced on him. Beatrice heard the hiss as her damp skin met his burning arms. He grabbed her, his fingers digging into the soft flesh of her hips and burning through the cloth that covered her before he strode toward the doors. As they sped down the hall, she saw Baojia, watching them with bared fangs from the door of the practice room. He narrowed his eyes and glared before he ran in the opposite direction.

They reached their chamber door, and Giovanni kicked it open.

"Fight later," he growled before he slammed it shut.

CHAPTER 15

"Fight now," she panted as her fingers clutched his neck. Their mouths crashed together as they stumbled through the room. She felt his fangs run along her neck.

"Later."

"Now!"

He reared back, glaring at her before he threw her on the bed. Giovanni paced, silent and furious around the room. Finally, he spoke in a tightly controlled voice.

"How could you do it?"

"You know how!"

"No, I don't." He bent down and grabbed her chin, forcing her face to his. "Why don't you explain it, Beatrice? Explain why my *wife* would conspire with my best friend to turn herself without even telling me or letting me be involved!"

She rose onto her knees. "You know why. And I told you over and over again, you just didn't listen. You weren't the vulnerable one. You weren't the weak one. I was done with it. I was *ready*."

"You were not! You have no idea what you're giving up."

"I do, too. Don't be so arrogant. Do you think I don't know my own mind?"

He paced, still glancing over his shoulder toward her. She could see him struggling to extinguish the swirling flames that covered his torso.

"I can be your equal now," she continued, peeling the wet clothes from her body. "I'm not weak anymore. Look at me. My mind is my own. My body is my own. He can't make me do anything anymore."

Giovanni pounced on her, rolling in the sheets as he trapped her under his

THE FORCE OF WIND

body. She reached out with her amnis, throwing a layer of cool air over his back as they were enveloped in a cloud of steam.

"Your body is mine," he growled through clenched teeth, "as mine is yours. You are my wife. My mate. We are *one*. And you shut me out." His angry eyes suddenly furrowed in pain. "Did it hurt? Were you frightened? Who held your hand as the life drained out of you? Whose eyes did you see before your heart stopped?"

She had no answer.

"That should have been me, Beatrice. Even if I could not turn you, it was my right to be there to care for you."

Bloody tears filled her eyes, and she lifted a hand, the cool water meeting the burning skin of his cheek. Tendrils of steam rose from the contact.

"I'm sorry," she whispered. "I'm sorry I shut you out." She reared up and captured his lips with her own, rolling them over with inhuman strength so she was straddling his hips. "But I'm not sorry I did it. I'm not sorry that I'm a vampire. And your anger is worth being with you forever."

He shook his head, fury still swirling in his eyes.

"And even if it takes years for you to forgive me, I'm not going anywhere. I have eternity now." She swallowed the lump in her throat. "But, please don't make me wait that long."

Giovanni lay motionless as she splayed her hands across the thick muscle of his chest. Both watched in fascination as the vapor rose where they touched. Their room was like a sauna, and thick clouds hung around them, making the lamps glow in the dark room. She could feel his heart pound beneath her hands, and she closed her eyes, arching her back in pleasure when his burning fingertips traced the bite scars that marked her breast, slowly swirling over her preternaturally sensitive skin.

Her fangs grew longer in her mouth, cutting her lip as they descended. She felt him rear up, tasting the trickle of blood that fell from her lips and down her throat. Giovanni licked up from her collarbone, locking his mouth with hers before his tongue invaded. She gasped when he stroked along the length of her fangs.

"Yes," Beatrice hissed as the hint of his rich blood filled her mouth. She pulled him back, fusing their lips as she traced along his own sharp teeth. The taste of their mingled blood seeped down her throat.

Smokey.

Sweet.

Hot.

Cool.

His blood reminded her of the rich taste of the whiskey they had shared before their first kiss, years before when he was hiding and she was human. The memory gave her pause, and she drew back, licking the last of their blood from his lips before she looked at him.

Giovanni's eyes were closed, and he seemed to sway in her arms. She peeled the scraps of his shirt away and pressed their skin together. His chest burned against hers. Their hearts pounded together, the usually slow movement of their veins excited by blood and anger. His eyes were still closed as she began to rock against him, trailing her fangs across his chest until he shuddered.

"*Beatrice...*" His voice was rough, his hands smoothed down her shoulders, kneading the small of her back as she pressed their hips together and he loosed a low moan. Her fingers threaded through his hair and she brought her mouth to his in a whisper of a kiss, flooding her lips with amnis. Their energy twined, and Giovanni took a deep breath, arching his back and opening his eyes, which finally met hers with tenderness.

"I missed you," she whispered.

"You are my balance in this life," he said before he pierced his tongue and kissed her again. She pulled back and drew blood in her own mouth.

"In every life," she finished.

Their lips met, and they drank the other in, their amnis twisting and melding so that Beatrice couldn't feel where she ended and he began. Giovanni picked her up and pulled at the thin leggings she wore to practice. She pulled at the buckle on his belt, struggling as he held her.

"*Beatrice...*" He finally stood up to rid himself of the last of his clothing as he eyed her in the center of the bed. The urgency returned, along with her hunger, and she eyed the thick vein in his throat.

"Gio?"

"Yes?" She heard the low growl in his throat as he stalked toward her.

"I need..." She swallowed the burning in her throat.

Giovanni braced himself over her as she backed against the headboard. "Tell me what you need."

"I need..." She eyed his neck.

"*Sì, Tesoro,*" he purred, and his tongue stroked the fangs that peeked from her mouth. "Feed from me; I have only one request." He caught her lower lip between his teeth, biting down as her heart raced.

"What?"

When he whispered, his fangs nicked her ear. "*Do not be gentle.*"

Beatrice hissed before she reached up, pulled his hair to bare his neck, and struck.

GIOVANNI ROARED, PULLING HER CLOSE, AND FUSING THEIR BODIES AS SHE drank. He rolled them over and she lay on top of him, drawing the thick blood from his neck as he writhed beneath her.

He grasped her hips, sheathing himself deep in her body. She pulled away and arched back with a gasp of pleasure. He reared up and Beatrice clutched his arms before leaning down to sink her fangs into him on the other side, piercing the curve where his neck met his shoulder.

"Yes." He hummed in pleasure before he bared his own fangs and lifted her arm, biting his teeth into the soft flesh above her elbow as she gripped his hair. He felt her shudder for a moment before her mouth returned to the thick muscle at his shoulder. They drank from each other, their blood fueling the heated release they both sought. The room began to fill with steam as her skin touched his, each pushing the other closer to ecstasy.

Beatrice pulled away and searched for his mouth. He met her kiss, both of their lips wet with the other's blood. Fire and water, they met each other as equals as they reached their release together.

They lay together for what could have been days. Nothing else existed for them. Lost in each other, they drifted, their energy spinning them in a thousand silken threads. He lost count of how many times she drank from him, but his hunger for her bite was never sated. Again and again, he pressed her closer, his amnis seeking hers as his blood traveled through her body.

The room filled with clouds as they moved together, only to gather on Beatrice's body as she rested, an endless cycle of heat and release coalescing around them. Giovanni drank from her, her energy swirling and pulsing in waves. She fell into daytime rest, but he woke her, a cup of fresh blood near the bed and his mouth traveling over her body. He had no idea how much time had passed.

It didn't matter, he thought, as they moved together.

They were eternal.

"I FEEL... DRUNK."

Giovanni chuckled as she lay boneless across his chest, her arm draped across his waist in their bed. The steam had finally dissipated in the room. "I'll take that as a compliment."

Beatrice blinked, but didn't make a characteristic smart remark. He smiled. She did sound drunk.

She asked, "Is it the blood?"

"I have no idea. I've never shared blood with anyone before. It's probably a combination of that and our amnis combining."

She stretched out next to him, and her energy flowed over his body, touching each corner of his skin like a feather.

"You feel so good," he breathed out, shivering at her touch. "Is that what my amnis always felt like to you? Soft? Like feathers or silk?"

"Hmm," she mused. "Kind of, but hot. Your energy is always hot, even when your skin isn't."

He frowned. "Not painful?"

"No." She shook her head. "Just warm. I've always loved to feel you. From the beginning, I've loved that."

"I love it, too," he whispered, brushing the hair from her face, in awe of the startling creature next to him. It was Beatrice, but stronger. Delicate, but not breakable as she had been.

"Beatrice?"

"Hmm?"

"I understand." She looked up at him, her eyes wide at his quiet declaration.

"You—you do?"

He gave her a small nod. "It still hurts that you chose to go through that without me. And I still think there are reasons you should have waited, but I understand why you did it. And I understand why you wanted to do it here."

She shook her head. "I never wanted to hurt you, Gio, but you're so stubborn. And I was so worried—"

"Shhh," he whispered, leaning over to kiss her. "I know I can be stubborn." He lifted an eyebrow. "But so can you."

She smiled. "You're stuck with me now."

"And I am *eternally* grateful," he whispered.

Her hand began brushing over him again, combining with the current to arouse him. Giovanni had little hair on his body, most of it burning off when the fire took over, but what little there was lifted and followed her fingers, as if pleading for attention.

"I had no idea you liked biting so much," she murmured as her lips trailed down his chest.

He took a deep breath, releasing it as he enjoyed the feel of her mouth and the scrape of her teeth. "I had no idea I did, either. Maybe I didn't until it was you doing the biting."

She gave a throaty laugh and looked up, her fangs gleaming in the candlelight. "I like it."

"Good," Giovanni said with a hoarse voice as she bent her head, sinking her fangs into the V of muscle that ran from his waist. He arched his back and gave a low hum of pleasure. "What do I taste like, Beatrice?"

"Your blood?"

"Yes."

Her tongue lapped at the punctures in his skin, licking the blood before the wounds closed.

"Like smoke. Spicy. Rich."

He smiled. "Like your favorite foods."

She cocked her head, smiling at him. "Yeah, I guess so. That's convenient." She grinned, then leaned down to taste again. "You're like... my own hot sauce."

He burst into laughter. "That's what I get for marrying a Texan."

Giovanni pulled her up to kiss her lips and taste his blood on her tongue. It was startlingly arousing.

"And I think I discovered why the food here is so bland."

"Yes," he brushed a hand through her hair. "When they cook for vampires, it's very mild. Your taste buds will be heightened for quite some time. I think it was ten years before I tasted any food that didn't seem too strong. Like everything else, you will adapt."

"Gio?"

"Hmm?" His lips moved along her neck, nipping and testing the soft skin.

"What do I taste like? Is it different now?"

"The same," he breathed out, "except perhaps a little stronger, sweeter."

Giovanni had always loved the flavor of her blood and had worried about taking too much for that reason alone when she was human. Now, it wasn't an issue. What they took from each other couldn't harm them when they were exchanging blood. He could already feel his energy swirling inside his mate, heightening their connection and their pleasure.

Beatrice slid down and nibbled across his waist before she sank her teeth in the other side of his waist, her fang marks mirror images in his perfect, sculpted body.

He pulled her up to meet his mouth again, as his fingers fluttered along the crease of her thigh.

"I'm keeping you locked in our room for the next several nights. Just in case you had any plans, cancel them. No working. No training. You're *mine*."

"Oh?" she gasped as he rolled her onto her back. "Are you sure that's a good idea?"

"Yes. I'll have them deliver some blood to us. That's all we need."

Her fingers traced the arch of his brow. "I just need you."

Giovanni pressed his hips into hers, and she wrapped her legs around his waist. They kissed leisurely for what could have been minutes or hours. Time had lost all meaning to him.

"I want to stay with you forever," he whispered, looking into her eyes. "I want the world to go away."

Beatrice lifted a hand to his cheek, stroking it and igniting another surge of desire. "I do, too." She closed her eyes and arched up. "Love me now."

"I will love you always."

It was a quiet knock on the door some days later that finally roused them out of their safe cocoon. Tenzin stood in the hall with a solemn look on her face. Giovanni wrapped himself in a sheet and stood silent in the doorway, listening, but still refusing to speak to her.

"I have a message from the Elders."

He cocked an eyebrow.

"Lan is on the way home."

His heart dropped in his chest, and he finally spoke.

"How long?"

"Two weeks."

Giovanni nodded and shut the door. He walked back to the bedroom, wrapping Beatrice in his arms as she drifted in her daytime rest.

CHAPTER 16

"I need to talk to you about something."

Beatrice looked up from the bowl of noodles. She was eating a light meal after rising for the evening. "What's up?"

She had discovered she was better able to eat some mild foods and was more comfortable with a little in her stomach. Between that and all the blood she had been drinking, both his own and human, Giovanni was satisfied Beatrice was as strong as she could be. Her control was impressive, her amnis was surprisingly powerful, but she was still young. He only hoped she could avoid any sort of serious physical confrontation for some time, though her intense training with Tenzin and Baojia seemed to be paying off.

"Tenzin came to the door as you were falling asleep this morning. Elder Lan will be back in two weeks."

She didn't look frightened, only resigned. "I guess we have two more weeks of what I'm considering our honeymoon, then."

Giovanni laughed. "*This* is our honeymoon?"

She shrugged. "Well, we did spend time in Cochamó, but that just feels like home. And with the move and everything, we didn't really get to take one after we came back. Then we came here and I started training so much... so, yeah."

"I would like to point out that if you had let me tell anyone we were married, they might have been more understanding and allowed us some time away."

"You *did* tell a few 'someones' we were married." She rolled her eyes. "Apparently when I was unconscious. I haven't heard the end of it."

Giovanni only laughed and came to sit next to her on the chaise. He pulled her feet into his lap. "I want to take you to Italy when all this is over. I'd like to take you there for a long trip. Maybe that can be our real honeymoon."

"Can't be too long. Ben's going to forget about us one of these days. We are the worst fake aunt and uncle in history."

"I very much doubt that he'll forget us. He'll be fine. Maybe..." He cocked his head. "Maybe if we go, we could take him with us."

"Huh?" She curled her lip.

He laughed. "Not as much of a honeymoon, but we could make it a group trip. Maybe Kirby and Dez would want to come with us and help with Ben. I don't know that Caspar and your grandmother would want to leave home for that long, but if Kirby and Dez come, we could go for the summer. They could look after the boy during the day. We'd still get plenty of time to ourselves, but we'd be able to spend time with them, too."

Her face suddenly fell, and tears sprang to her eyes. "I'm not gonna be able to see any of them for a while, am I?"

Giovanni shook his head when one of the harsher realities of her new life struck her. She set her food down and crawled into his lap. He wrapped his arms around her and kissed her temple. "My grandma," she whispered. "Caspar."

"They are both in very good health. And you're very strong for a new vampire. Very strong, Beatrice. After a year or so..."

She nodded her head, still tucking herself into his chest.

"I need to talk to you about something else. Something I should have spoken to you about years ago." Giovanni took a deep breath. "Speaking of Italy... of Rome, that is, I need to tell you about Livia."

"Livia? Your friend in Rome?"

He shook his head. "I wouldn't call her a friend. Livia is... well, it's complicated. You remember"—his voice dropped to a whisper and he murmured in her ear—"you remember about my father. Don't say anything, remember there are many sensitive ears in the palace."

Beatrice nodded again, pressing closer.

"You must know, you and my son are the only beings on earth that know the truth about Andros. And it *must* stay that way."

She drew back and looked at him, the question evident in her frown.

"What we did... what *I* did... it is a very grave crime. To kill your own sire is a very grave crime."

"So, everyone thinks—"

"Lorenzo and I told Livia that the villa was burned by marauders. That Andros was killed in the fire."

They were still speaking in whispers, but his ears were alert to the sound of any passerby in the hallway. They had been left alone, for the most part, but he could take no chances.

"But really, Lorenzo killed him, right?"

"He sent all the servants away and dragged Andros into the sunlight when he was in the depths of daytime rest. I saw the ashes in the courtyard when I woke. Paulo was sitting in the corner, weeping and shaking. I took him to Crotone the next night and turned him. We burned the villa before we left."

"And the library?"

"That is more complicated. And I don't know what happened to all of it, only Lorenzo does. It's one of the reasons I'd like to take him alive, if possible."

"But your uncle's books were safe, so your father's—"

"Paulo told me that after my uncle's collection was burned in Florence, Andros became paranoid. He kept some of his books in Crotone. Some of them at the villa my uncle left me near Ferrara. Some at the property in Perugia. It was scattered, and since Lorenzo was the one who oversaw the property and the human servants, I did not keep track of it as I should have. When he told me later that most things had been lost, destroyed or stolen, I believed him. He must have been planning for some time."

"Wouldn't Andros have noticed?"

"I don't know what he told Andros. After he died, I was focused on survival, and I foolishly trusted that my father would have kept track of Paulo. He had been with Andros since he was a child and my father trusted him, possibly even more than me."

"Why?"

"Andros thought he could control Paulo. He thought... my father had little respect for humans, Beatrice. He didn't really understand them anymore. He thought Paulo adored him. He couldn't see the resentment because he didn't really look. And Paulo was very good at presenting a front, just like Andros."

"So, everyone in the vampire world thinks your father was... a good guy?"

Giovanni shrugged. "Define 'good.' Andros was highly respected. Feared. Admired. Most never saw his madness or his cruelty. He was the consummate politician, a master manipulator. Even adored in some circles as the highest example of learning and culture. If it was ever known that we killed him..."

"What would happen? And why hasn't Lorenzo told anyone in all these years?"

Giovanni said, "Paulo would be killed first. He was human when he killed Andros."

"But you—"

"My life would also be forfeit."

She spoke in an angry whisper. "To who? You're the one he tortured. You're the one he kidnapped and held captive for ten years. Who has the right—"

"Livia," he whispered, leaning so his lips brushed her ear, "is not just one of the most powerful vampires in the Old World. Not just the vampire who helped me to get you back. Who spoke for me with the council in Athens. They never would have allowed me to attack Lorenzo the night I took you unless she had intervened on my behalf. But Livia has always had a strange sort of affection for me, because Livia..." His breath caught for a moment, and he pressed Beatrice closer. "Livia was my father's wife."

A FEW NIGHTS LATER, TENZIN, STEPHEN, AND BAOJIA JOINED THEM IN THE living area to talk about Lan's return and what it would mean when the council met.

"It's a sort of trial, but not one you would recognize, Beatrice." Tenzin was sipping tea and looked bored. "They do it mostly for their own amusement. Everyone knows how they will decide before they go in; it's all worked out ahead of time in private negotiations."

"Well," Stephen added, "except for Lan. In this matter..." He only gave a shrug.

Beatrice looked around, confused. "What? What does that mean?"

Giovanni leaned forward. "No one knows how Lan will vote, and he's the most unpredictable."

"Or she," Beatrice whispered. The whole table laughed. "Really?" she asked. "No one knows?"

Tenzin smirked at Giovanni. "Have you ever seen Lan get angry?"

"Only once," he grimaced. "Not pleasant."

"It doesn't happen often." Tenzin's eyes danced toward Beatrice. "Try to imagine an extremely old and powerful fire vampire having a temper tantrum. It takes a lot to get Lan truly angry, but when she does, numerous vampires usually end up dead. Lots of humans, too."

Giovanni saw Beatrice's eyes grow wide. "But that doesn't happen often, right?"

"No, Tesoro, it takes much to provoke Lan. Despite his playful appearance, he's one of the canniest vampires on the council."

"I'm not going to lie, the whole he or she thing is kind of annoying."

"Agreed," Stephen added quietly.

"He," Baojia smiled, "or she doesn't feel the need to inform anyone. Are you going to be the one to ask?"

"No," Stephen and Beatrice said together.

"Getting back to the trial," Tenzin said, "the council is fairly evenly split. My father and Elder Lu are firmly our allies. The Immortal Woman will side with Giovanni, because he's a fire vampire, and she's like that. Royal Uncle Cao will go along with Lu because he doesn't want to disagree."

"What about Elder Li?" Stephen asked.

Giovanni shook his head. "You know how the earth vampires tend to be. It seems that he will most likely follow Zhongli Quan since they are typically allies and he won't want to disrupt that. Since Zhongli is the one who invited Lorenzo to Penglai, we can assume he'll vote with him."

"Han Xiang?" Baojia asked after the second water vampire on the council.

"He'll vote with Zhongli," Tenzin said. "He always does, just to spite Lu."

"But," Stephen directed himself to Beatrice, "Earth vampires also tend to be the ones most amenable to compromise, so if a reasonable one is offered, Iron Crutch Li and Royal Uncle Cao would probably go in that direction."

"What kind of compromise could there be?" Beatrice asked. "Lu's monks have the books. Lorenzo wants it. Giovanni wants it. Someone has to win." No one spoke, and Beatrice looked around the table. "So, by my calculation, that leaves four elders on our voting side and three on theirs. And no one knows what Lan will do."

Giovanni said, "He could vote for us."

"She could vote for Lorenzo, too." Tenzin shrugged. "I've known Lan for years and I don't even know how she'll vote."

"Again with the he and she thing..." Beatrice muttered under her breath. "So, if Lan votes against us, that leaves it at a tie. What happens then?"

Giovanni's eyes darted to Tenzin's and both of them smiled.

"What was that look?" Beatrice asked. "That was a look."

"A tie means that your husband could challenge Lorenzo," Baojia said.

"I don't like that option!"

"Neither would Lorenzo," Tenzin snorted. "Giovanni would put an end to him quite easily. It's really the best thing that could happen."

Beatrice leaned forward. "But then we'll never know what happened to the books. Or why he wants the elixir. I think we need to know that stuff, don't you guys?"

"You aren't worried, are you?" Tenzin looked scornful. "Have you ever really seen your mate fight? He's ruthless. Lorenzo wouldn't have a chance. I trained him myself."

"And he has that irritating habit of bursting into flames," Baojia said.

Stephen raised a hand. "I have to agree with Beatrice on this. As much as I'd like to see my sire dead, I think he has information we need. Lorenzo wants this elixir for a reason, and I think it's obvious at this point that there are others involved in his scheme. We need to know who they are, or we're back in the same boat of not knowing who may be after us."

"Lorenzo said he had made promises to people. When he had me on the freighter, he said he had 'made promises to people who were starting to doubt he could deliver.' There's obviously someone else involved. At least one other person, maybe more."

"And," Stephen added, "if my contact is correct that Lorenzo was researching pharmaceutical labs in Eastern Europe—possibly to produce it—then he must have someone who can fund him. That wouldn't be cheap, and B stole most of his money."

"You did?" Baojia turned to Beatrice with a look of amusement. "I always wondered why a college girl had that much cash. Ernesto never said. How clever of you."

"Thanks!" She smiled.

Giovanni swallowed a growl, but he caught Baojia's eye and threw an arm around the back of Beatrice's chair.

Tenzin crossed her arms over her chest. "So, killing the annoying one is not the ideal outcome. But, if it happens, it happens. If there's a tie, Gio has to challenge Lorenzo; that is what's done. And if he challenges him, he *will* kill him."

"He can't just like... take him captive or something?"

Tenzin shook her head. "Nope. All or nothing. Only one of them would be allowed to leave the island."

"Great." Beatrice sighed.

Giovanni was torn. He wanted to find his father's books so badly he could taste it, but the prospect of killing Lorenzo was also rather alluring. Since it was out of his control, he chose not to torment himself. He would do what he needed to do. Soon after, the group split for the evening; Beatrice kissed him goodbye before leaving with Tenzin and Baojia for more training. He and Stephen went to the library and dove back into research again.

A WEEK AND A HALF FLEW BY, AND THE FIVE OF THEM STAYED BARRICADED IN Tenzin's quarters except for one brief trip to the open ocean for Giovanni and Beatrice. She was ecstatic, ebullient in her joy and surrounded by her element. She dove under the surface, playing for hours. She wasn't as strong as she might have been, and Giovanni suspected that, like her father, she would draw more elemental strength from fresh water, though she could easily manipulate both.

Late on Friday night, Tenzin, Beatrice, Stephen and Baojia were playing a game of poker by the fire while Giovanni read a book. He saw Beatrice's nostrils flare a second before a knock came at the door. She burst up from the table, rushing toward the door, but Stephen quickly caught her, holding her back from the human servant someone had foolishly sent.

Giovanni walked over and took Beatrice's arms, braceleting her wrists with one hand before he grabbed her around the waist and took her from her father, carrying her to the corner. She snarled at him, baring her teeth and whipping around in an attempt to get away and hunt the human. He waited patiently for Tenzin to send the servant away.

"Order some blood, at least a liter," he called over his shoulder to Stephen as Beatrice cursed at him in Spanish. Baojia stood behind him, ready for her to break away. Giovanni was reluctantly grateful. A newly turned vampire in the midst of bloodlust could be surprisingly strong. When he could hear the human's steps receding, he shoved her into the corner, braced his legs around hers, and brought his wrist to her mouth. She tore at it, biting hard into the flesh as she glared at him with narrowed eyes.

"Shhh," he murmured. Soon, she was calmer, and he let go of her wrists, bringing his hand up to stroke her hair. "Drink what you need, my love. Your father is getting you more blood."

He could tell when reason grabbed hold of her again because her eyes cleared and bloody tears leaked from the corners. She let go of his wrist and wrapped her arms around his waist, leaning into him.

"I'm sorry," she whispered. "I'm so sorry. That was the first time I've smelled a live one. Their blood—"

"I know. Don't apologize; it's perfectly natural, and we were unprepared. It's fine, Beatrice." He still stroked her face as he heard Stephen enter the room and Baojia faded back. Giovanni could smell the warm blood from the corner. "Go, drink. You hadn't fed tonight. We've been too casual about it, being isolated like this. You'll need to be more prepared in the future."

"What about the trial?" She sniffed and wiped her eyes as she sat at the table. "There are usually humans in the hall. I don't want to hurt anyone."

Tenzin came to sit next to her, holding a folded piece of paper. "There won't be any during the trial. It's vampire only. If you were still human, you wouldn't be allowed in." Giovanni caught the quick gleam in Tenzin's eye.

"What is it?" he asked.

"Lan's back. They're meeting tomorrow night."

Giovanni nodded. He had no sense of nervousness, only a grim kind of resolve. Whatever happened, he would be getting his way. Either the council could vote with him, or he could kill Lorenzo.

GIOVANNI TRIED TO IGNORE THE PERVASIVE SENSE OF FOREBODING WHEN HE rose next to Beatrice the following afternoon. By nightfall, they were both fed and dressed in the formal clothing that Zhang provided them. They wore the soft blue-grey robes and pants that the scholars of the court wore. Their collars were adorned with a single jewel indicating their element, deep blue lapis lazuli for Beatrice and a blood-red jasper for Giovanni. Beatrice tied her hair back into a subdued knot at the nape of her neck.

They met Tenzin, Stephen, and Baojia in the front room. Stephen also wore the grey scholar's robes, but Tenzin wore a silver robe similar in style to her father's formal white, which was decorated with an ornately jeweled Mandarin collar with dotted moonstones and pearls. Her hair, which she usually tied back, flowed around her shoulders in a long, black sweep. Baojia looked severe in the plain black robes worn by the palace guards. They were met and escorted by one of the green-clad administrators who worked for Zhang.

"Gio?" He heard Beatrice speak softly as they crossed the gardens.

"Yes?"

"My dad was explaining all the color meanings to me. If yellow is supposed to be the most beautiful color, why do the servants wear it around here? Wouldn't that be reserved for the Elders or something?"

He smiled. Trust Beatrice to be curious instead of nervous on the way to meet an enemy. "Many of the servants here are monks, Beatrice, so they wear their yellow or saffron robes. Most of the other humans dress in brown. But the ones you have seen tending the gardens are almost all monks. It is considered a great honor to serve in the palace of the Eight Immortals."

"Oh, I guess that makes sense."

"The elders wear white because it is the symbol of death."

"That... doesn't make much sense."

He smiled again. "But they are the masters of death, aren't they?"

They climbed the stone steps leading to the great hall, even Tenzin was oddly subdued as they made their way to the front of the room and took their place in front of Zhang's leather throne.

The elder was already seated, looking calm and fearsome, his hair loose and long as his daughter's. At times, it was easy to forget that Tenzin and her father belonged to a far less civilized past than the one represented by most of the sophisticated vampires of the Chinese court. With his hair flowing around him, seated on his saddle-like throne, Elder Zhang Guo looked like the ancient warlord he was. Tenzin stood behind her father, playing the loyal daughter for appearance's sake. Even the most powerful of immortals would tremble to challenge the pair.

Giovanni glanced at Beatrice, who was taking in everything with her perceptive eyes, measuring each Elder and the people who scurried around them. Baojia stood behind her, watching, always watching, anyone that came too close. Once again, Giovanni found himself reluctantly grateful.

"Baojia, will you be able to translate for Beatrice?" he asked quietly. "I'm sure this will all be in Mandarin, and I will have to speak at some point."

"Not if you want me to be able to concentrate on protecting her."

"I can translate," Stephen whispered.

"Anything you don't want overheard, say in Spanish," Giovanni said. "It's not widely spoken here and will be the most secure."

Stephen nodded as Zhongli's guards entered the hall. The Elder was already at the front of the room, but the guards ushered Lorenzo between them. Giovanni scoffed when he saw his son wearing scholar's robes like their own. Though the pursuit of knowledge was far from a priority with him, Lorenzo was nothing if not a master of appearances. In that way, Giovanni supposed Lorenzo truly *had* become Andros's heir.

Giovanni was curious about the company he was keeping. There were eight guards around Lorenzo, all wind vampires from the look of their robes, which bore the milky moonstone associated with the wind element. Eight. A lucky number, particularly when associated with business. He had a feeling that the selection was not without calculation. All the Elders were superstitious, but none more so than Lorenzo's host, Zhongli Quan.

Little by little, the hall filled, until eventually, every elder was on his or her throne and their entourages filled the room in front of them. Energy buzzed, the collision of electrical currents charging the air. The torches and lamps that lit the room flickered, and a soft wind brushed through the crowd. Everyone was there and waiting.

Except for Elder Lan.

Giovanni exchanged a look with Baojia, who only shrugged. "No one's surprised, are they?"

Suddenly, every head turned when a laugh rang from the back of the room, and a high-pitched voice called out, "Are you all waiting for me? How amusing!"

The childlike elder tripped into the room with a huge smile adorning his or her face. Just as Lan passed them, Giovanni saw the elder pause for only a fraction of a second. Lan caught Beatrice's eye as she stood next to Giovanni and gave her a playful wink.

Giovanni looked down at Beatrice, then back to Lan, who had already moved up to the throne at the front of the room. Beatrice looked up at Giovanni with an expression of equal confusion.

"What the hell did that mean?" she murmured in Spanish between clenched lips.

"Tesoro... I have no idea."

CHAPTER 17

"There's still something I'm not getting about this," Beatrice whispered to her father in Spanish as the formal greetings of the court began. Each elder was standing to greet the assembled vampires and most of them seemed highly impressed with their own voices.

"There's a lot about this that I don't understand," Stephen whispered back.

"Why did he agree to this?"

"Who?"

"Lorenzo," she said. "Why did he agree to this? Everyone seems to be sure that the Elders will either vote for Gio or tie, both of which leave Lorenzo at a disadvantage, so why did he ask for this trial?"

Stephen shrugged. "Perhaps he didn't plan for it. When he made the request, it was right after Lorenzo discovered he had no claim over me. Maybe it was not well thought out."

"I'm not buying it," Beatrice whispered as the Immortal Woman began to speak. Like Lan Caihe, He Xiangu was not as long-winded as the rest of the council. Thinking about her own terse mate, Beatrice wondered if it was a characteristic of all fire vampires. "Lorenzo plans everything. He may be totally different from Gio in a lot of ways, but not that. They both plan for every contingency."

"Beatrice, I don't know what to tell you."

"Shhh," Giovanni turned to them and made a shushing motion as Tenzin's father stood to speak.

"Immortal brothers and sisters of the council, I would take this opportunity to introduce an immortal sired in my household these past weeks. Most of you know the dear friend of my only child, Tenzin, was turned by my daughter's mate in my home. We welcome you to our honored company, Beatrice De Novo. Daughter of water, mated to fire. Kinswoman of Don Ernesto Alvarez of California. Honored friend of my house and learned scribe."

Though Beatrice had been briefed on the importance of her formal introduction, she still felt like blushing, even though she couldn't. Her heart began to beat as she stepped forward, nodding deeply to Zhang, then turned to the rest of the room and gave a slight nod. She stepped back next to Giovanni, with her father standing behind her. Her eyes scanned the room, searching out Lorenzo to gauge his reaction.

She finally spotted his blond curls in the middle of a group of Zhongli's guards. Far from the anger she had expected, Lorenzo looked positively gleeful, and his eyes looked her over with clear interest and approval. She knew Giovanni had spotted him when she felt his hand brush hers. His amnis reached out and wrapped around her waist.

Stephen leaned over once Zhang had stopped speaking. "Why do they call us scribes, B? It makes me feel old."

She snorted a little under her breath. "Because it sounds cooler than assistant professor and librarian?"

"Laugh if you want," she heard Baojia say as his eyes scanned the room, "but Zhang gave you that title deliberately. It is now part of who you are here, and it's not something this court takes lightly."

"Come to think of it, B, I've never been named a scribe in any formal way," Stephen said. "That is significant."

"And I was not informed of it," Giovanni muttered. All four were speaking in Spanish, and Beatrice could see the curious looks from the few vampires around who could hear them.

"I think we need to shut up now," Beatrice said.

"Quite right, Tesoro."

Zhongli was speaking. "It is my guest, Lorenzo, who has brought this petition to us. He claims the right of ownership on a certain book that is in the possession of Elder Lu Dongbin's monks." Zhongli nodded toward Lorenzo, who stepped forward.

"The book in question belonged to the sire of my own father, Giovanni di Spada of Florence, Giovanni Vecchio to the company here. Though it was intended for my father, the great library of Nikolaos Andreas was scattered five hundred years ago. It is only with great care and much time and expense that I have managed to find a few valued pieces from my grand-sire's collection."

"Liar," Beatrice whispered.

Giovanni shot her a look. "Shh."

"Imagine my dismay when those same books were stolen by my own son when he ran from my home. He took this manuscript, along with several others that were worth a considerable amount of money. I'm sure he has sold many of them." Lorenzo shook his head sadly. "But this one in particular was very dear to Andreas and it is my hope that it may be returned to my rightful ownership."

Royal Uncle Cao, the earth vampire, leaned forward. "But if it was intended for your sire, then why do you have a claim on it?"

It was Zhongli that responded. "Surely the Elder must recognize that my guest is the one who found the book. If Giovanni Vecchio wanted it, surely he would have been the one to find it."

"Perhaps he would have," the Immortal Woman spoke, "if he had known it had survived the destruction of Andreas's library."

"Indeed," Elder Lu added. "It seems to me that the original intentions of the owner, the scholar, Nikolaos Andreas, should be honored in this matter. He intended it for his only son; it should belong to his son. I'm sure Giovanni Vecchio would reimburse his child for any expense he incurred while searching for the book."

"Indeed," Giovanni spoke up, "I would be happy to reimburse Lorenzo for any expenses, though I sent him into the world with wealth, as is the custom."

"I was wondering," Elder Zhang spoke, "why your son took these books, Lorenzo. You imply that it was for money. Did he not have an allowance from his sire?"

"Why would you?" Beatrice whispered.

All eyes turned to Stephen as he spoke to the hall. "Sadly, my father did not send me into the world with anything, Elder Zhang. I had to fend for myself."

A low murmur of disapproval filled the room. Beatrice looked at Giovanni. "What? What's the big deal? I mean, not every vampire is turned by their choice, right? It's not always friendly. Why would Lorenzo give my father anything?"

"Even in cases where the vampire is unwilling, Beatrice, it is still customary after a certain number of years to send a child into the world with some degree of independence if they want to leave. Since I was Andros's only child, he would have given at least a quarter of his wealth to me if he had sent me away."

"What? Really?"

"Yes, I wouldn't have gone—he had far too much influence over me—but when I sent Lorenzo out on his own, I sent a third of my wealth with him."

"It is the custom among our kind," Baojia whispered. "If you send a child away from your care, out of your aegis, it is considered very shameful to send them away with nothing."

"But Dad escaped."

The room was still milling, and Beatrice could see a sour expression on Lorenzo's face.

"My son," Lorenzo spoke over the crowd, "Stephen, ran away from my aegis.

If he had told me his desire to leave, I would surely have given him gold, as is proper."

A few vampires on Zhongli's side nodded, as if that explanation was satisfactory, but Beatrice could tell by the subtle frowns and veiled expressions of the vampires in the hall that the mood of the room had shifted against Lorenzo.

"Perhaps he took these books out of spite," Elder Han, the water vampire, said. "Why should we honor the actions of a spiteful child?"

"Why should we deliberate at all?" Elder Lan finally spoke, and the attention of the room swung toward the previously silent vampire. "Why shouldn't it remain with Lu's monks? I'm sure they are taking good care of it."

More nods were seen among the Elders, and Lorenzo pursed his lips.

Beatrice didn't like the idea. They needed to find out more about the book, and currently, it was being held at a monastery of unknown location, and they couldn't even examine it. If they were ever going to find out what the secret of Geber's elixir was, they needed the manuscript.

"What is this book that we deliberate over? What makes it so valuable that it warrants the time of the council?" Iron Crutch Li asked.

Lorenzo stepped forward, confident again. "It is an unfinished manuscript of the alchemist, Jabir ibn Hayyan, or Geber, as he is known in the West. It is not among his published works, but Geber was an acquaintance of Andreas, and it was given to him for safekeeping. It had... sentimental value to my grand-sire."

Beatrice asked. "Is that true?"

Giovanni shook his head. "I have no idea. It's possible, but my father had little regard for alchemy when I knew him. He considered it more superstition than science."

"This claim seems very straightforward to me," Lorenzo's ally, Zhongli, said. "The book is clearly Lorenzo's."

"Of course it is," Beatrice muttered.

Elder Han spoke. "This book may have been intended for Andreas's son, but he forfeited his rights by not pursuing the manuscript when it was lost. I see no claim here by Giovanni Vecchio."

"I see no claim here by Lorenzo," the Immortal Woman spoke up. "Can we not honor the intentions of the great Andreas and give his property to his only child? Let this conflict be between sire and child. The book belongs to Vecchio."

At that point, whispers began to circulate the room, and Beatrice looked around. The hall seemed to be split exactly as Tenzin had predicted, and Beatrice's eyes sought out the one elder that no one seemed to be able to predict. When she found Lan, the enigmatic vampire was looking straight at her. Lan scanned the crowd, propped herself up on her knees, and addressed the gathering of immortals.

"Brothers and sisters," Lan said with a smile. "I feel at a disadvantage after my travels. It seems that so much has passed in my absence. May I be permitted to ask a few questions?"

Lu Dongbin leaned forward and nodded to Lan. "Of course, Elder Lan. The hall is yours."

"Oh good!" Lan clapped and grinned. "Dr. Vecchio, did you send your son into the world with wealth?"

"Yes," Giovanni answered respectfully. "I sent him with half of my gold, and I gave him property in our homeland, as well. It is what my own sire would have wanted."

"You honor your father, Dr. Vecchio. And did you send him with any of your father's library?"

"It was my own son that had the care of my father's books when he was human," Giovanni said.

Careful, careful, careful. Beatrice's heart raced.

"After my father's home had been raided, and Andros died in the fires, Lorenzo gave me the grave news that my father's property near Ferrara had also been ransacked by brigands and the majority of the library lost. Rumors abounded for many years that this piece or that had survived, but there was little fact. My own business now centers on finding lost books and antiquities, in part to find what I can of my father's collection. But I had no knowledge of this manuscript until a few years ago. I have been searching for it since I learned of it."

"So you *were* searching for it?"

"Yes, Elder Lan."

"And found it here?"

"In the stewardship of Elder Lu's monks." Giovanni nodded at Lu. "I have full confidence they have handled it with care and respect."

"And do you ask for it to be returned now?"

Giovanni paused, as if considering. "Though I would prefer that the book return to my own library, I ask only to be able to examine it. I am willing to leave the book in the care of Lu's monks if that is what the council desires."

It wasn't the ideal outcome, but if they were allowed to examine the manuscript more carefully, Beatrice realized that Giovanni would probably be able to memorize it enough for their purposes.

"Lorenzo?" Lan turned to Giovanni's son.

"Yes, Elder Lan?" Lorenzo stepped forward with an ingratiating smile.

"How many children have you sired?"

Beatrice blinked at the unexpected question.

"What does that have to do with anything?" she whispered to Stephen.

"Canny vampire," Baojia murmured.

"Why?"

"The Eight Immortals have been outspoken against those who sire many

THE FORCE OF WIND

children, Beatrice." Giovanni looked at her with a subtle smile. "They consider it irresponsible and unwise."

"Oh."

Lorenzo didn't look pleased. He looked nervous. "I... I have had the joy of siring many children in my life, Elder Lan. I cannot give you an exact number at this time."

"Or he doesn't want to," Baojia said.

"You have sired so many children that you can't remember the number?" Lan said with a raised eyebrow. "That is... unusual."

"Is it?" Beatrice whispered.

"How many children does Carwyn have, Beatrice?"

"Um... eleven, right?"

Giovanni nodded. "Eleven in over a thousand years. And that is considered a very large family."

"Oh... so Lorenzo—"

"Is not making himself look very responsible if he can't even remember the number of humans he has turned."

Lan still questioned Lorenzo. "Have you ever taken a mate to help care for all your children?"

"What? Are we questioning his family values here?" Beatrice asked between clenched teeth. "Is Lan going to ask if he uses corporal punishment next?"

"Well, the answer to that is yes, but I have no idea where Lan's going with this," Stephen said.

Lorenzo looked confused, as well. "I have never taken a mate, no."

Lan broke into a huge smile. "But your father has!"

Lorenzo returned a tight smile of his own. "Yes, he has a mate now."

"I have met her. She is a scribe. She spent many years training to care for books in her university. I like her very much. Do you?" Lan leaned forward with a dancing smile. "You must like her, too! I heard she was a guest of yours for some time. Is that true?"

Lorenzo spoke carefully. "Yes, Miss De Novo was a guest at my home in Greece for some time."

Beatrice's ire spiked, and she whispered, "Why do people keep forgetting the whole kidnapping and murdering thing?"

"Calm down, B," Stephen said behind her. She could feel the water in the air drawn to her, and her skin became damp.

"She's very intelligent, is she not?" Lan continued. "And your own child, Stephen, sired her. You must be pleased since you like having a large family."

"Of course, I'm very pleased." Lorenzo didn't look pleased; if anything, he looked a little green.

"And so Mistress Scribe is part of your family and mated to your own father, as well. It's all so wonderful, is it not?" Lan clapped again, seemingly delighted by the happy circumstances. The rest of the council looked either confused or disinterested, most of them accustomed to Lan's odd outbursts.

"Yes, it's... very wonderful," Lorenzo forced out.

Just then, Beatrice caught a strange light in Lan's eyes. "It is, isn't it?"

She was bewildered, and Giovanni looked as lost as she did. Her father placed a protective hand on her shoulder, and Baojia seemed to stand at attention. Beatrice glanced at Tenzin and Zhang, but both wore completely impassive expressions that were impossible to decipher.

Beatrice looked back to Lan, who had sat back on her throne and seemed to be thinking. Finally, the elder piped up, "I have no idea which vampire should have the book! It's all quite confusing."

A collective breath seemed to leave the crowd. Everyone had been waiting for Lan's judgment, but if none came...

She looked around. "Does that mean Gio and Lorenzo will fight?"

Stephen leaned forward. "If the council cannot come to some agreement, that is the only option."

Even as he said it, Beatrice sensed a buzzing from the crowd. What had been anticipation and interest was slowly building into a more heated energy. The vampires that surrounded them seemed to be preparing for a confrontation. She could see some silently moving to the edges of the hall, slowly shifting position as a new current swept the room.

Giovanni was tense, and she could feel the heat building on his arms. Beatrice reached a hand out for him, only to hear the hiss of steam when their fingers touched. Her own body seemed to be preparing for a fight without her mind thinking about it; she felt damp air at her collar.

"What's happening?" Stephen asked.

Through it all, Beatrice kept watching Lan. She sensed, somehow, that the small vampire had not finished, though the crowd's attention had left the elder. Lan lounged in her throne, examining her fingernails and playing with the ends of the hair that had slipped out of her topknot. Suddenly, the innocent-looking vampire took a breath and Beatrice tensed.

Lan murmured, almost under her breath. "Unless..."

Every eye focused on Lan as the small vampire spoke. Lan's eyes lifted and sought Beatrice again.

"Perhaps there is some sort of compromise we can reach, after all."

CHAPTER 18

Giovanni blinked. Though he tried to remain impassive, the unexpected statement from Lan startled him. His mind raced, trying to predict and plan around the unknown.

"What kind of compromise could there be?" Zhongli asked. The wind vampire was looking around the room with suspicion. "Either the book belongs to Vecchio or Lorenzo. What compromise—"

"Perhaps the book belongs to the world." Lan sat up on his knees again. "It sounds very important. A book of universal knowledge? Wisdom to be preserved and shared? I don't know..." Lan flicked his wrist carelessly. "Perhaps it needs only a caretaker. Someone"—Lan's eyes swept the hall, landing briefly on Beatrice before he looked at Lorenzo—"who both parties can agree is a learned and able steward. A scribe who could care for the book. One that has a connection to both Lorenzo and Dr. Vecchio."

Giovanni's eyes flicked to his wife. *They wouldn't...*

In a flash, Lan's peculiar questioning made sense. He had constructed the trap perfectly, and Lorenzo would be forced to walk in. Giovanni's heart began to race, though his face remained blank.

"A scribe?" Elder Zhongli asked with a slight smile. "Who could..." His eyes fell on Beatrice and grew wide. It was only a fraction of expression, but the whole hall began to stir. Furtive glances were directed at Giovanni's wife, who still stood next to him, apparently clueless to the web she was being drawn into.

"Now that's an interesting development," Baojia muttered.

"What?" Beatrice whispered. "Who are they talking about?"

Lan smiled and clapped. "There is a scribe present who has a connection to both the parties! She has even been acknowledged by the Elders. The daughter of Lorenzo's son. The mate of Giovanni Vecchio. She has even studied book science at a modern university. Beatrice De Novo is clearly able to care for the book. It is the perfect compromise."

"What?" Beatrice whispered. "Not... not me. It's not my—" Giovanni reached over and clutched her hand, willing her to be silent as the Elders deliberated.

Lorenzo looked livid. "And where exactly would she keep this precious book? Has she a monastery like Elder Lu? A library of her own?"

"As a matter of fact," Giovanni stepped forward before Beatrice could speak, "Miss De Novo has an extensive library in Southern California, in the territory of her grandfather, Don Ernesto Alvarez, a noted scholarly and artistic patron. While the facilities do not have the history of Elder Lu Dongbin's monastery"—Giovanni nodded toward Lu and the Elder nodded in return—"they are extensive and modern, the very finest in the New World." He could feel Beatrice squeeze his hand. If he was a mortal man, his fingers would have been crushed by the pressure.

"See?" Lan clapped again. "It's perfect! She can take care of the book and then both of them can see it."

Zhongli leaned forward, his tight smile the only evidence of his discomfort. "It is a most excellent compromise, Elder Lan, but can Miss De Novo truly guarantee that Lorenzo would remain safe when he is examining this book? Surely you are aware that Lorenzo and his sire have a... complicated relationship."

"I am sure that Miss De Novo would guarantee Lorenzo's safety in her library. After all"—Lan's eyes darted between Lorenzo and Giovanni—"are not places of knowledge sacred to those immortal? As are places of worship? They are the outer reflections of our inner wisdom." Lan rose to his feet and turned toward Beatrice. Suddenly, the childlike elder did not look like a playful boy or girl; and the wisdom, power, and amnis of the ancient vampire swept over the room.

"Beatrice De Novo," Lan said in a deeper voice, "if it is the will of this council, would you keep this book? Would you guarantee safety to these two parties who wish to claim it? Would you guard the knowledge therein with honor? What is your answer, Mistress Scribe?"

Giovanni could hear Beatrice's heart pounding, and her fingers still clutched his. He turned toward her as all eyes in the room searched her out. The air was still, but alive with energy. When their eyes met, Giovanni's heart soared in pride and respect. Far from the panic he had expected, Beatrice looked calm, peaceful even. She met Lan's eyes with confidence.

"I will, Elder Lan. It would be my honor to do this for the Elders of Penglai. I would guard this book and guarantee the safety of all those who examined it while in my library."

THE FORCE OF WIND

Giovanni could almost hear Carwyn in his mind. *Clever, clever girl...*

Though part of Giovanni rebelled at the thought of Beatrice guaranteeing Lorenzo's safety in any way, his more practical side realized that he would likely kill Lorenzo long before his son ever had the chance to examine Geber's manuscript. As long as Lorenzo wasn't killed while trying to examine the book under Beatrice's care, no one could challenge her honor.

"What a truly excellent compromise, Lan," Tenzin's father stated with a wide smile. "How fortunate that you were here to present such an amiable resolution to this issue. I wholeheartedly support giving the book into Beatrice De Novo's care. I can vouch for her excellent character and wisdom, and the honor and wisdom of her kinsman, Don Ernesto Alvarez, whose own son accompanies her. Though she is young, Miss De Novo spent her mortal life preparing for this role, to be a caretaker of knowledge. It is only fitting that she take the role of scribe and steward in her immortal life, as well."

Elder He, the Immortal Woman, leaned forward. "I, too, like this compromise. It respects both parties, as Miss De Novo has connections to both Lorenzo and Vecchio. Indeed, we have just heard from Lorenzo's own testimony how much he admires his father's mate."

"Yes," Iron Crutch Li smiled from the opposite side of the room as he sat between Zhongli and Han, both of whom wore sour expressions. "It is always best to compromise so both parties feel that they are treated fairly. I will support this as well."

Brilliant Lan. Giovanni would never underestimate the savvy of the odd immortal again. By presenting a compromise to the council, Lan had practically guaranteed the outcome they wanted without bloodshed. Both earth vampires on the council were known to support almost any compromise that avoided taking a clear stand. This decision would not only be acceptable to all those who had taken their side before, but would also sway Zhongli's former ally to their seemingly moderate solution. It would leave the council voting six to two in favor of giving the book to Beatrice. A clear victory for Giovanni with the appearance of moderation.

Clever Lan. His eyes darted back to his wife, whose eyes were glowing with victory. She wore only a hint of a smile, and Stephen watched her proudly. *Clever Beatrice.*

Finally, Giovanni sought out his son, and he blinked in surprise. Far from the anger or bitterness he had expected, Lorenzo seemed placid. He wore a pleasant expression that revealed nothing of his thoughts. He whispered with the wind vampire closest to him, one of Zhongli's guards. Giovanni narrowed his eyes in suspicion.

Elder Lu stood. "Lorenzo, Giovanni Vecchio, are you amenable to this compromise? Will you abide by the terms set out by Elder Lan and agreed to by the scribe, Beatrice De Novo?"

643

Giovanni stepped forward. "I will, Elder Lu. I respect the will of the council."

He looked at his son. Lorenzo looked at him and smiled for a second. A calculating glint came to his eye. "I will abide by the decision of this honored council, as well. I am most pleased by this resolution." He bowed deeply, then stepped back, melting into the crowd of grey and black-clad vampires on the far side of the hall.

"Very well," Lu continued, outlining the agreed-upon plan. Lu would send for the book by one of his guards, who would bring it to Mount Penglai to be given to Beatrice, who would then take the book back to her library in Los Angeles, where it would supposedly be accessible to Lorenzo and safely preserved.

Giovanni stepped back and motioned to Baojia. The vampire stepped toward him.

"See what you can find out. I don't trust Lorenzo."

"Agreed. This was too easy. He already has a plan to take it from her, I can almost guarantee it. I'll call Ernesto and let him know what has happened." Baojia's eyes danced for a moment. "I'll tell you right now, my father will be crowing about this honor to his granddaughter for a hundred years, at least."

The corner of his mouth lifted. "As will I."

Baojia's smile fell a fraction, and he leaned closer, speaking in Mandarin. "I hope you realize what a fortunate bastard you are, di Spada."

"I do."

"Feel free to piss her off, though." Baojia smirked. "A lot can happen in eternity."

Giovanni couldn't stop the reluctant smile. "Go check in with Ernesto, then find out what the gossip is among the guards. I'll take care of my wife."

Baojia smiled and stepped back, vanishing into the crowd in a heartbeat. Giovanni turned to Beatrice, who was surrounded by Stephen and Tenzin. For a second, he saw Tenzin's eyes examine Beatrice with a pride and care he had rarely seen. He wondered if Beatrice even realized how deep her connection to the wind vampire was. With the blood Tenzin and Stephen had shared, almost as much of Tenzin's blood ran through Beatrice's immortal veins as Stephen's. If Beatrice had been sired to wind, it would have been unexpected, but not unheard of.

"Tesoro," he murmured, and she immediately turned to him, reaching out a hand to grasp his own. "I am..." He smiled, at a loss for words, overwhelmed by love and pride.

"I guess I'm still a librarian, huh?" She gave a crooked smile. "Thanks for giving me the library, by the way."

Giovanni shook his head. "It's yours. Of course it's yours."

She pulled him closer, but only squeezed his hand, mindful of the attention of the milling vampires around them. "It's ours."

They both spoke to Lu Dongbin for a few minutes. The elder was sending a group of guards the next night to retrieve the book, which would then be given into Beatrice's care. Giovanni urged him to send more guards than he thought necessary, but Lu seemed confident that, though Zhongli was disappointed, he would control Lorenzo while he remained on the island.

Beatrice was pulled away by one of Zhang's administrators, as Giovanni tried to persuade Lu. "I have confidence in the excellence of your guard, Elder Lu, but I do not trust my son. I do not doubt the honor of the Elders, but it is not like Lorenzo to give up like this."

Elder Lu only smiled. "I do not wish you to worry. I will send double the guards. The book will be quite safe."

Giovanni was not satisfied, but knew he could not press the issue without offending the elder. He nodded and retreated to Beatrice's side. She was still speaking with Zhang's administrator.

"—a most excellent resolution, Miss De Novo. Elder Zhang considers it an honor that one so close to his aegis, and a close friend of his daughter, has been given this distinction."

"Please tell Elder Zhang thank you for all the help. I'm really glad I could be part of the resolution in this situation. And I'm very pleased to assist the council."

Ever the politician, Giovanni thought. Though it all seemed very casual, Beatrice continued to amaze him with her instincts. She seemed to have a gift for knowing exactly what people were looking for and how to offer them what they wanted while still getting her own way in the process. He congratulated himself again on persuading her to become his wife. He felt a tug on his arm and turned to speak to another administrator, this one belonging to the Immortal Woman, Elder He.

When Stephen, Tenzin, Beatrice and Giovanni finally returned to their quarters an hour later, all pretenses dropped.

"Shit! I am *not* happy about this." Beatrice pulled at her collar. "I know he has a back-up plan. What the hell is Lorenzo up to?"

"Agreed," Tenzin said. "That was far too easy; he is planning something."

Giovanni said, "We all agree Lorenzo is going to try to steal the book, correct?"

Every one of them nodded.

"The question is," Stephen asked, "is he going to try to intercept Lu's guards? Or try to take us on directly?"

Tenzin said, "He'd be a fool to take us on directly unless he has a private army we don't know about."

Beatrice asked, "Is there any way he could find the monastery?"

Tenzin shook her head. "I don't think so. All the Elders know where it is, but if anyone revealed the location, their life would be forfeit. I can't imagine Zhongli taking that chance."

"But *you* know where it is, don't you?" Stephen asked.

Tenzin snorted. "Of course."

Giovanni rolled his eyes and sat at the table, pulling Beatrice onto his lap and tugging at her collar while Stephen and Tenzin argued about something under their breath.

He felt his wife relax a little bit. "You're very covered up in all this, Tesoro."

"Watch it now," Beatrice said as she snuggled into his chest. He could feel the tension begin to drain out of her shoulders. "Don't start getting handsy with the honored scribe."

He chuckled and nipped her ear with his fangs. "Do I have to call you Mistress Scribe now?"

"Only if you're really good," she whispered.

He smiled before he captured her mouth in a kiss. "I sent Baojia out to see what he could learn from the guards. They gossip like old women."

"They do, huh? Do—" She broke off, and they both turned toward a commotion in the hall. Baojia stormed into the room carrying four swords and scabbards. He tossed Tenzin her curved scimitar, a *jian* toward Stephen, and a *dao* to Beatrice. She stood and caught it instinctively. Giovanni could already feel the fire teasing along his collar.

"What's happened?"

"Lorenzo left the island over an hour ago with a large group of Zhongli's guards. They were flying and left fully armed. We need to go. Now. It's already getting close to dawn. They will have a head start because they are only carrying one and the rest are flying, but we may be able to catch up if we take the plane. We can have the pilot fly us to..." Baojia looked at Tenzin, who actually looked speechless.

"Nanping," she whispered. "How could he... The monks. All the monks are there." She reached back and grasped Stephen's hand.

"The word from the guards is that Zhongli has a human mistress who has refused to turn," Baojia said. "He will do anything to keep her, including fund Lorenzo in his search for the elixir. Including revealing the location of Lu's monastery."

Giovanni's fangs burst forth along with the fire that he smothered along his neck. He rose to his feet and began to pace.

Beatrice sent a cooling mist toward him. "So Lorenzo is going to take the book from the monks?"

"He is on his way to the monastery right now. Hurry up." Baojia tossed the odd straps toward Giovanni, who caught them. "I've adjusted these so we should be able to swim with them fairly easily." Baojia walked over and began to buckle the scabbard around Stephen as Giovanni helped Beatrice with hers. "We have to—Tenzin!"

The small immortal had rushed out of the room.

"She's gone to tell Zhang," Stephen said. "He must be told of Zhongli's treachery. And Lu will need to be told, as well. Zhang can send some immortals to help."

Baojia shook his head. "They're going to be too late. *We're* going to be too late unless we can get on that plane before dawn."

Giovanni walked down to the library to call the pilot of the plane in Beijing. He and Tenzin would fly while Baojia, Beatrice, and Stephen swam to the mainland. They would just be able to make it to Beijing before dawn; then they could fly during the day and land in Nanping by nightfall. With any luck, they would make it to the monastery within a few hours. When he returned to the meeting room, Tenzin was speaking.

"—and they have already taken Zhongli before the council. They found the mistress, as well. My father has sent out his guards in pursuit of Zhongli's, but even he admits they are not as fast, and they will have to rest during the day. We are even farther behind."

"We won't be by evening," Giovanni said, striding into the room. "I've already contacted the pilot. He can have us in Nanping in six hours. Where do we go from there?"

Tenzin paled at the mention of the plane, but straightened stoically. "Up the Nine-Bend River. I will fly you, but the rest will have to go by river."

"Shouldn't be a problem," Baojia said. "I haven't spent much time with Beatrice in the water, but—"

"I'll be fine," Beatrice said. "I'll keep up."

Giovanni nodded. "So we'll fly to Nanping today while we rest. By nightfall, we'll be headed upriver. If we're lucky, we'll beat them there."

Baojia said, "I don't think we'll be *that* lucky, but we may just get there in time."

At that grim statement, the room fell silent. Giovanni could only imagine what Lorenzo would do when he arrived at the monastery. He had little respect for vampire life, and none when it came to humans. If he would defy the council of the Eight Immortals to retrieve Geber's manuscript, he was capable of anything. Giovanni felt for Beatrice's hand, and she looked up at him with frightened eyes.

"We have to go *now*," she said. "We're running out of time."

CHAPTER 19

Fujian Province
November 2010

Beatrice woke with a burning in her throat. She rose from the bed in the plane, baring her fangs as her eyes darted toward the door. In a heartbeat, she had the handle half turned and Giovanni at her back. He locked an arm around her throat and threw her on the bed.

"You're up early." He fell on top of her, pinning her to the mattress and pulling her mouth to his neck. She struck hard and fast, the thick taste of his blood slaking her instinctual hunger, though it didn't kill it completely.

"Shhh," he soothed her, stroking Beatrice's hair until she was calm again. As soon as she was thinking rationally, she took a deep breath, only to be hit with the unremitting scent of sweet human blood. She could even hear the pump of the pilot's heartbeat, though she realized, for the first time, that the bloodlust was not overpowering.

"Where are we?" she grunted out after she took one last draw from Giovanni's vein.

"A small airfield outside Nanping. Tenzin says it's the closest to the monastery, but we will have to go upriver. It's an hour and a half until sunset, so we can't leave the compartment."

She felt like weeping. "So I have to smell the pilot for another hour and a half?"

"Shh," he whispered again. She buried her face in his neck, sealing the bite marks she had made and trying to block the smell of human with her mate's own, smoky scent. "If it helps, Tenzin is more miserable than you. This is her first time in a plane, and I'm surprised she hasn't peeled the walls off yet, despite the threat of sunlight."

She tried to laugh, but it only exacerbated the burning.

Giovanni continued, "You're beginning to wake earlier and earlier. Just like your father and Tenzin. You're awake ten minutes earlier than last night, and that was ten minutes earlier than the night before."

"What does that mean?"

"It means that unless something changes, soon you will need as little sleep as Tenzin and your father. Maybe only a few hours."

"But that's less than you!"

"I know." He did not sound displeased. "That's means your amnis is already very strong, and growing stronger by the day. This is good. Eventually, you won't need sleep at all."

It also meant that for a good portion of the day, she would be without the support she had come to depend on from her husband. If Giovanni was not awake to distract her or stop her, Beatrice feared what she was capable of.

As if reading her mind, he spoke in a soothing voice. "Don't worry. We'll figure something out. Perhaps your father can stay with us for a time, or Tenzin. One night at a time, Beatrice. Don't borrow trouble."

"Okay," she whispered, burying her face in his skin again.

"Let me up, and I'll get you some blood. That will help your thirst. We have some in the main cabin, I was just about to get it when you woke."

"Have someone block the door."

"Of course." He rose and paused over her, examining her eyes, which were still hazy with hunger.

She gripped the sheets and nodded. "I'm fine. Go."

Giovanni rose, pulled on a pair of pants, then darted out the door in the blink of an eye. In a few seconds, he was back with three pints of blood, cool, but still smelling fresh. He tossed one to her and she caught it with one hand, piercing it with her fangs before she sucked it dry. By the time she was finished with the third bag, she realized that, though the pilot's blood still called to her, with some effort, she could think around it.

"How long?"

"Will the bloodlust last?" He took the bags from her, placing them on the small bedside table before he slid next to her. He wrapped a steadying arm around her waist. "If you progress the way I expect you to, within a year, you'll be able to be around people with ease as long as you feed when you wake."

She took a deep swallow, still distracted by the burning sensation at the back of her throat, though the ache in her gut had been satisfied. "That's not too bad."

"It will pass more quickly than you can imagine."

Beatrice closed her eyes and bit her lip. "Unfortunately, the next hour and a half is going to be torture."

"Well, we can't leave the secured compartment until the sun falls, which means we have no way of making the pilot leave until then. I'm afraid there's no escaping the scent, but..."

She looked up to see a smile teasing the corner of his lips.

"What?"

He leaned down to nip at her ear.

"Let's see if I can't distract you, hmm?"

THOUGH SHE HAD TO ADMIT GIOVANNI DID AN EXCELLENT JOB DISTRACTING her, there was also a hint of desperation to their coupling. She knew they would be plunged into the most dangerous race she could imagine as soon as the sun crept below the horizon, and she had no idea what to expect. Her *dao* sat propped by the door in the sling that Baojia had fashioned that would allow her to carry it while swimming.

She lay across his chest in the last minutes before sunset. "Am I going to be distracted by humans while I'm in the river?"

He frowned as he ran his fingers up and down her back. The water had been drawn to her skin as they made love, so his hot fingers left trails of steam where they touched.

"You'll be fine. The water will help your control. And I doubt there will be many humans in the river after dark. I'll tell your father and Baojia to watch out for you. Any animals should be fine, they won't smell as appealing."

"I don't want to slow anyone down."

"The key is to let your amnis connect with the water the way it wants to, then allow it to move you upriver. It will be instinctual, so don't try to control it too much. Just let it happen. The way you move already and the way you fight, I think you'll be very fast as long as you allow yourself."

"Okay."

"But I'm going to tell Baojia to swim as fast as he can. If you fall behind, Stephen will stay back with you. I'm sorry, Beatrice, but the priority—"

"Is the monks." She nodded. "I understand, Gio. They're defenseless against Lorenzo. Of course they're the priority."

They both fell silent then, and Beatrice's eyes darted to the clock that hung on the wall. They had ten minutes till sundown.

"We should get dressed," she whispered.

He held her tight to his chest for a moment before he pulled her up and kissed her. They stared at each other for a few more minutes before she rose from the bed. Beatrice focused on the task at hand, pushing the still-present scent of the human to the back of her mind. Giovanni watched her dress in a slim pair of jeans and a tight T-shirt that would not drag in the water.

"Beatrice."

She looked up. "Hmm?"

"I love you."

Her breath caught, and her heart gave a quick thump. "Don't say that like you're saying goodbye."

He frowned and shook his head quickly, but she could see him blink away a red gleam in his own eyes. He rose and dressed in the black combat pants he wore when fighting and nothing else. Though the pants were fire treated and would usually stand up to his element, any other clothing would be nothing but ash, so he did not waste time with it. Giovanni strapped a curved dagger to his thigh and he was ready. He helped her buckle her sword onto her back, making sure she could easily draw it to fight.

Five minutes.

She began to feel a pressure in her chest. "I love you, too," she whispered.

He moved to stand in front of her. "This is no longer sparring. These vampires will kill you, and you must not allow that to happen," he murmured. "There will always be war. It is your job to survive it. No matter what. That is your victory, do you understand?"

Beatrice nodded, staring at his chest and wishing she could bury her face in it to avoid the coming bloodshed. Giovanni grasped her face in his hands and forced her to look at him. He did not look at her with the soft eyes of her lover; he wore the fierce expression of a soldier.

"You must survive, Beatrice. Do you understand? Do *not* sacrifice yourself for any other. Do *not* be meek in battle. Do *not* hesitate to kill anyone that threatens you. Eliminate them swiftly and without remorse. Do you understand?"

"Yes."

A desperate light came to his eyes and his hands tightened on her jaw. "Do you understand?" he asked again.

She reached up and put her hands over his as she stared into his eyes. "Nothing will keep me from you."

They stared at each other for a minute more before Giovanni pressed his lips to hers in a single, fierce kiss before he drew back and reached for the door. He pulled it open and everything seemed to happen at once.

They rushed into the main compartment. Tenzin had the door open and waiting for them. Baojia streaked out, followed by Stephen and Giovanni carrying Beatrice in a headlock as they passed the human in the cockpit. As soon as they reached the deserted runway, Tenzin sealed the door, eliminating the alluring scent of blood; then she grabbed Giovanni and took to the sky in one sweep. Giovanni and Beatrice's fingers touched for only a second before he disappeared into the night.

Beatrice turned to Baojia, but the vampire had already bolted toward a thick stand of forest calling, "This way!" as he ran.

Stephen grabbed her hand, and Beatrice ran at full speed for the first time in her immortal life. Her heart pounded in excitement. The wind rushed around her and, if she had been human, it would have stolen her breath. She squinted her eyes, closed her mouth and ignored the swarm of insects she swam through as she and her father rushed to keep up with Baojia. She could only assume he had been briefed during the plane trip and knew where they were going.

They darted through the thick stand of trees, dodging around tree trunks and skipping over rocks with a swift grace she tried not to think about. The less she allowed her mind to analyze how fast she was going, the easier it was. Her heart pumped, but not with effort. It was pure excitement.

Later, Beatrice would realize she had never truly understood instinct until the moment the scent of the river hit her nose. The rushing water called to her, and when she saw Baojia leap into its depths, she followed without hesitation, her father close on her heels. She had no need to hold her breath; she simply closed her mouth and let the water envelop her, keeping Baojia's murky form in front of her as they sped up the rushing stream.

Beatrice struggled for a moment to keep up with him, trying to force herself forward under her own preternatural power until she remembered what Giovanni had told her.

"...let your amnis connect with the water the way it wants to... allow it to move you... it will be instinctual..."

She forced the thought of kicking from her mind and focused on the rush of amnis over her skin. The moment she did, it was almost as if her energy unfurled into a thousand long tendrils, spreading out in the water as it reached to push her upstream. She had no conscious thought of maneuvering around rocks or the odd raft she came across, she had only to think of where she wanted to go and her amnis reached out to bring her there.

After a few moments, she was fully enveloped in the ecstasy of the river, moving with a single thought just under its dark surface as she tracked Baojia. She barely registered her father trailing behind her or the bends and creases of the river as it wound up and through the deep river valleys of the Wuyi Mountains. She could feel the energy signatures of the fish and small animals that darted away from her, but their blood did not distract her as human blood did. She felt the water shallow out before it grew deeper again.

They sped upriver for miles, and Beatrice had little sense of time. She knew only the water, her amnis, and Baojia's faint shadow in front of her as she followed him. After what could have been hours or minutes, she felt him slow, and she moved silently behind him along the edge of the river. Her eyes broke the surface as they approached the bank where a long bamboo raft was pulled up.

Baojia held a hand out for silence as they walked to the edge of the riverbank. Beatrice could feel the mud between her toes and fought the instinct to remain in the safety of the water. She felt Stephen pick up her hand and tug her along when she hesitated.

None of them said a word as they walked along the muddy bank, finally stepping onto the soft grass that lined the clearing on the edge of the forest.

Baojia smelled it first, and his gaze lifted toward the rise of ancient stone stairs and the scent of blood and smoke. Both hit Beatrice's nose at the same moment, and her eyes darted around, looking for danger. The smell of blood and fire surrounded her.

"The monastery is in flames," Stephen whispered. He looked over her shoulder to a set of stairs buried in the hill. They led up into the dark forest and Stephen started for them before he was pulled back by Baojia.

"We need to find the source of the blood. Di Spada and Tenzin are already up there, I'm sure of it."

Stephen shook his head. "Of course."

Beatrice's nostrils flared. "It's not human."

"No."

They walked cautiously toward where the scent was strongest. As they breached the laurel trees on the edge of the riverbank, she saw them. A mass of twisted bodies and rolling heads, Zhongli's guards were piled into a low depression just beyond a clearing. Their blood sprayed across the dead leaves and detritus that layered the forest floor, and Beatrice gagged at the tangled bodies of the dead vampires.

"Lorenzo must have had men following them," Baojia said.

"But how?" Stephen looked up in confusion. "They flew."

"I don't have any idea, but we'll talk about it later. Take Beatrice back to the river, and I'll go up to the monastery."

"I don't want to wait by the river!"

His eyes cut toward hers. "Too bad. You're not going up there unless there's no avoiding it. It's already a bloodbath from the smell of it, and I'll not have you distracting di Spada with your presence and endangering lives. You're not ready yet. Stay here and keep your head down, little girl."

Baojia turned to Stephen. "And you stay here, too. Keep her away and out of trouble."

"The monks—"

"Are probably already dead. By the smell of them, these bodies have been dead at least an hour. Stay here and keep her out of it. That's the most you can do."

"Baojia," Beatrice still protested. "I'm not going to stay down here when—"

He tackled her and bared his fangs as he gripped her around the neck. "Stay here! I do not have time to argue with you. I shouldn't have come here. I shouldn't have let *you* come here. So don't make me regret it. Stay here and keep your head down, or you'll get someone killed. Probably yourself."

She opened her mouth to protest, but he bared his fangs again and she shut up. No matter how much she wanted to help, she knew much of what he was saying was true. She had little experience in actual battle and would probably only hurt herself.

"There will always be war. It is your job to survive it. That is your victory..."

She nodded tightly and Baojia leapt off, racing up the stone stairway and toward the growing cloud of smoke. Stephen gripped her hand and pulled her up. He drew Beatrice away from the bodies of Zhongli's guards and toward the riverbank where they crouched in the shadows to wait.

"Do you worry about Tenzin?" she asked.

Stephen paused before he answered. "Yes. I know I probably shouldn't. She's lived for five thousand years, right?"

"Yep."

"Right."

"I still worry about Gio," she confessed in a whisper. "Even though he's survived more than I could even imagine."

"You're very lucky, Beatrice." Stephen looked at her in the dim light of the crescent moon. "You're lucky to have found each other. You know that love that I was talking about in my journals? The kind Grandma and Grandpa had? That's the way he looks at you. Like you're the most important thing in the world to him."

She blinked back tears. "He's everything to me."

Stephen gave her a soft smile. "You're very lucky."

They waited in silence as the smell of smoke only grew stronger. Every now and then, Beatrice thought she could hear a shout from the top of the stairs, but nothing was clear. Stephen explained that the majority of the old stone temple was hewn into the side of the mountain, and the hallways were like a puzzle.

"Even if Lorenzo gets there, there are many false corridors and passageways. It was designed as a defensive fortress, so there are escape routes and dead ends; the monks know all of them. It would take him hours to find his way to the library alone." She wasn't sure whether he was convincing her or himself.

But she nodded anyway, even though Beatrice had a hard time feeling very reassured as the smoke grew thicker, blotting out the stars in the night sky. She had little concept of the passage of time, and she sat up straight when she heard a whistling tune.

It was the children's song about a cricket that Giovanni would often sing to her, but as the sound of the whistle grew louder, she shrank back, dreading its approach. It was not Giovanni.

Lorenzo's blond hair shone silver in the moonlight as he bounced down the stairs carrying a wrapped package clutched to this chest. Three guards followed him as he descended. He still sported the grey scholar's robes he had worn in the Hall of the Eight Immortals as he stepped toward the bamboo raft.

Beatrice turned to her father in panic.

"The book," Stephen breathed out as he watched his sire with wide eyes.

Lorenzo's steps halted immediately, and he turned and eyed the bushes where they were hiding. Beatrice heard a taunting laugh come from his throat.

"A book in the hand," he called as he stepped toward them, "and it sounds like *two* De Novos in the bush."

Her father rolled to the right and into the clearing, drawing his sword in one swift movement. Beatrice drew her own and darted around the trees behind Lorenzo's guards as Stephen rose to face his sire.

"Well," Lorenzo chirped, "this night just keeps getting better!"

CHAPTER 20

Giovanni threw fire into another whirlwind that Tenzin tossed his direction, the scent of blood and ash thick in his nostrils. The bodies of Lu's monks lay scattered in the courtyard as he and Tenzin eliminated the last of Lorenzo's water vampires who guarded the outer gates of the monastery.

"One more!" Tenzin swung her arm around, tossing the vampire toward him.

The dark-haired guard fell in a crumbled heap, only to rise and run toward Giovanni. These were not the ineffectual spawn that Lorenzo had been creating; these vampires were far more formidable and bore European features that were further confirmation that Lorenzo had allies that remained a mystery. Allies with deep resources to hire or inspire the loyalty of such fierce opponents.

It was taking longer than he'd planned for Tenzin and him to work through them.

Giovanni sidestepped the guard, who tried to spray him with water to extinguish the fire that coursed over his body, but Tenzin drew the wind from the attacking vampire, sucking the water toward herself and allowing Giovanni to light his opponent on fire. He screamed and ran toward the stairs to escape, but Tenzin caught him up in a gust, pinning him to a stone wall as he turned black and flaked away.

"This is taking too long!"

"That's the last one."

"I smell blood in the monastery." He tried to suppress the flames on his body. "Let me just..." He took deep breaths, forcing the fire back so he could enter the stone rooms without harming Tenzin or any remaining monks.

They had seen the crumpled bodies of Lu's monks from a distance as they

THE FORCE OF WIND

approached. The journey through the mountains had gone swiftly, but not swiftly enough to beat Lorenzo's men. At least twenty human bodies littered the courtyard and five vampires had patrolled the gates.

"Are you ready to go inside?" Tenzin asked with cold eyes.

He nodded, taking a deep, calming breath. "Yes."

They stole silently through the doors, searching, but quickly bypassing the meeting hall where the monks had met to pray. He forced himself to ignore the lifeless bodies that lay in the shadows. Giovanni followed Tenzin, who quickly wound her way back into the mountain, following tangled corridors and dark passageways that always seemed to end with more bloodied corpses. The sheltered monks of Lu Dongbin's order had been decimated.

Finally, at the end of one corridor, Tenzin's eyes darted to the right. She took a deep breath before she ducked under a thick tapestry that hung on one wall. There was a small stone door, no bigger than a gravestone, that she pulled back before she ducked inside.

Giovanni followed. He heard a scuffling in the chamber and quickly lit a flame that shot to the top of the small room. A young monk, no more than sixteen or seventeen, stood, spreading his arms to guard the clutch of small boys behind him. The young monks wore saffron robes and tears in their eyes.

"We are not here to hurt you," Tenzin said softly. "Where have they gone?"

The young monk examined them before he seemed to decide they were trustworthy. "I do not know. Master Fu-han woke me and told me to gather the young ones here to hide them while he went to the library. I only did what he told me."

"And you have not seen the strangers?"

"I saw no one. But many have come through the halls before you. What has happened in the monastery?"

"There has been an attack. You cannot stay here—" Tenzin's eyes darted toward the door in panic before she relaxed. "It is Baojia." She turned to Giovanni. "I will find a safe place for these boys, and then we search for Lorenzo."

Giovanni nodded and stepped into the corridor where he found Baojia waiting for them. "Where is Beatrice?"

"At the riverbank with Stephen. It was deserted. All of Zhongli's guards were there, dead."

The boys filed into the passageway and began following Tenzin down the corridor.

"I wondered what had happened to them. There were others in the courtyard," Giovanni murmured. "We killed them."

"I saw the ashes."

"They were not Asian. European."

Baojia cocked an eyebrow. "Interesting."

"I thought so."

They ducked under another tapestry that led to a narrow earthen passageway lined with unlit torches. Giovanni quickly lit one and handed it to the young monk before he turned back to Tenzin.

"I don't feel anything here," she said. "You?"

"I feel nothing in this direction," he said, looking down the dark corridor. "No vampire has been here tonight."

She nodded. "Excellent. This one is very old, I was hoping they would not know of it." She turned to the young man. "This tunnel leads to a river landing. There is a cave at the base. Continue down the corridor and then wait at the riverbank. Take shelter in the cave if you feel danger. Elder Zhang is sending his guards, they will find you and keep you safe."

The young monk nodded.

"Go. We must return to the monastery and continue searching."

"If you find Master Fu-han—"

"Do not worry about your master, worry about these boys. Keep them safe."

She nodded to the young man and then ducked back under the tapestry and ran in the opposite direction from where they had come. Baojia and Giovanni followed her.

"Where are we going?" Giovanni asked.

"There is an older part of the monastery," she yelled. "That is where the library is. Your senses are better than mine in the mountains. Open up and look for them, my boy."

Giovanni tried to focus his amnis to detect any latent energy traces, but the stone walls, along with the mass of blood, adrenaline, and old tangled signatures were confusing.

"They've been all over, it's almost impossi—"

He broke off and swerved to the right, drawn to a clutch of energy in a large empty space.

"Here!"

Giovanni burst through an old wooden door to see three vampires huddled over a group of bodies, feasting on the blood of Lu Dongbin's monks. They looked up in surprise, snarling at the three vampires who entered the stone courtyard that looked like an outdoor kitchen.

Baojia, Tenzin, and Giovanni spread out, surrounding the vampires before they attacked. Baojia drew his sword, immediately cutting off the head of one while Tenzin took to the air and swooped down over the group, hacking at another with her scimitar. Giovanni grabbed the third by the neck, twisting it until the head came off and the three vampires lay in a bloody heap over the bodies of the monks.

"Where the hell is he?" Giovanni said as he scanned the courtyard.

Baojia began to shake his head. "There are more. More than I had imagined.

It was a bad idea to leave Stephen and Beatrice by the river. If Lorenzo's not here, he may be anywhere."

"Go," Tenzin said. "He's probably still in the library somewhere. It's a maze. We'll search the rest of the monastery. We weren't in time to stop their murder, but let's hope the monks might have saved the book."

Baojia nodded and ran back out the way he had come, while Tenzin and Giovanni ran deeper into the mountain fortress, searching for Geber's manuscript.

Stephen stood with sword drawn, tense and ready. "Give me the book, Lorenzo."

Lorenzo rolled his eyes. "And why would I do that? I finally got it back, and I had to get rather messy doing so."

Beatrice could see the blood spatter on Lorenzo's robes, even in the darkness. The smell of human blood covered her father's sire and the three guards that surrounded him. She was having trouble concentrating. She gritted her teeth, gripped her sword, and tried to focus on the two vampires that stood across from her in the small, grassy clearing.

"What are you doing, my Stephen?" Lorenzo laughed. She heard him draw his own sword. "Do you actually think you and your little girl are going to stop me? My friends and I just killed all of Zhongli's guards—they were a bit squeamish about killing all the monks, you see—and ransacked a very valuable library to get this book back. I'm certainly not intimidated by you and the girl." He glanced over his shoulder at Beatrice. "Though I do find her very attractive when she's bloodthirsty like this. Nicely done, Stephen. She turned out beautifully."

"Dad?" She didn't know what she was asking. She shifted back and forth on her feet as her eyes darted between the two guards who licked their lips and grinned at her. She had never faced two opponents before.

"Tenzin and Giovanni will be here shortly, Lorenzo."

Lorenzo only laughed. "I very much doubt that. We left... well, a bit of a mess, really. I was worried about her Chinese dragon, but he seems to have run off and abandoned his post."

Beatrice glanced at Stephen again. They were separated on opposite sides of the clearing with four vampires between them.

Her father still spoke calmly. "Baojia will be coming back soon, as well."

"I'm sure you hope so."

Beatrice was starting to panic, and the scent of the human blood covering the guards was flooding her senses, causing her head to swim. There was too much going on. She could see everything, hear everything, smell everything. Far from making her more aware, the flood of sensory input was only confusing. Her fangs were long in her mouth, and she could taste the blood where they had pierced her lip.

Beatrice saw one guard curl his lip and move to attack, and she reacted automatically, cartwheeling to the side. As she hit the ground with one hand and popped up, she brought her *dao* down on the back of the attacker's neck.

Her sword sliced through the thick muscle and bone with a sickening, wet sound, and the head fell to the grass with a soft thunk. Beatrice stared for only a second before she fell to her knees and regurgitated what was left of the blood in her stomach over the headless corpse. She saw the other guard come toward her and rolled to the side, standing in a ready pose.

Lorenzo must have been watching.

"Well, that was fun." She heard him say. "And somewhat disgusting. Must have been her first. She's better than I would have thought for a young one. Looks like those lessons paid off, Beatrice."

"I try." She hoped she sounded braver than she felt.

"I won't make the mistake of underestimating you."

Stephen was still speaking calmly. "Give me the book and no one has to get hurt, Lorenzo. Zhang's vampires are already on their way." Stephen began circling his sire. "Zhongli's treachery has been revealed. The council knows what you are doing."

"As if I care about the council!" Lorenzo scoffed, and she heard the clang of swords. She glanced over and saw Lorenzo and her father parrying. A breeze wafted the scent of blood toward her, and her throat burned. Her opponent only grinned.

"Hungry, little one?"

"You're not really my flavor, thanks."

He chuckled and his fangs ran lower. "But I think you might be mine."

"Yeah?" She feinted to the right before she swept her arm back to slice his thigh. "I really don't agree."

She took a second to find her father. Stephen was facing Lorenzo and one other vampire. He had his sword drawn on Lorenzo's guard and Lorenzo was looking on in amusement. She blinked and missed the quick thrust and parry of her father and his opponent before she turned her attention back to her own fight. The blond vampire she faced had used her distraction to sweep her leg with his own, and Beatrice was thrown off balance as she stumbled back. She quickly regained her footing and returned thrusts as he grinned with bared fangs in the moonlight.

It was all so quick. And yet everything seemed to happen in slow motion. She saw a head with short, dark hair roll near her feet and realized that her father must have killed the vampire he was fighting. She was distracted by the gaping mouth and empty eyes that stared at her, and her opponent took the opportunity to leave a deep gash in her right arm.

THE FORCE OF WIND

"Argh!" Beatrice cried out when she felt the sharp clank of his blade against her bone. She lost her grip on the *dao* and rolled away from the vampire, scurrying toward the bushes as her opponent turned and joined the fight between Lorenzo and her father. Stephen was once again facing two attackers.

"No!" She stood again, clutching her arm as she tried to dive toward her weapon, but Lorenzo saw her. He stepped back and ran toward her sword, snatching it up and tossing it into the river.

"Look who lost her sword!" he gloated. "Didn't Giovanni teach you better? Never lose your weapon, girl. That was beaten into my brain more times than I could count. He must be getting soft not to have trained you as well."

Beatrice's eyes darted around, looking for help from any direction. She had no sword. She was ravenously hungry, and her panic was beginning to overwhelm her. She saw the victorious light in Lorenzo's eyes, and it only made her more frantic.

"Dad?" she called, but Stephen was still dueling with the other guard. Lorenzo was walking toward her. She looked at the river with longing, wishing she could run toward its dark depths and swim away, but she knew she couldn't leave her father. In a last ditch effort, she ran toward Lorenzo, diving down and curling into a ball at the last minute to knock his legs out from under him. The ground felt like nothing. The only pain she registered was the sharp slice in her arm, which had been healing, but broke open again.

"Oh," Lorenzo said, laughing in a heap on the ground. "Are we supposed to fight hand-to-hand now because you've lost your weapon? Precious thing, don't you know I don't fight fair?"

He popped up, grabbing his own saber where it had fallen. Beatrice was crouched on the other side of the clearing, clutching her arm and waiting for his approach. She could still see her father battling the last guard, but now, both were drawing from the water in the river, throwing waves toward each other as they tried to throw the other off balance.

"Giovanni and Baojia are coming," she panted.

"But they're not here *now*, are they?" Lorenzo kept walking toward her. He curled his lip and ripped at the front of his robe, tearing it from the collar and tossing the blood-soaked rag in her direction. Beatrice caught the sweet smell and turned toward it instinctively, snapping at the cloth as it covered her face. She was blind when he kicked her to the ground.

"Did you think to challenge me?" he yelled. She tried to gather her energy. The world swam around her. She was hurt. Hungry. Her head swam from smoke and blood.

It was too much.

Her father grunted at the edge of the clearing opposite her.

Her arm throbbed, itching and aching as it tried to knit together.

The edge of a blade hooked the blood-soaked rag and pulled it from her face. Lorenzo stood over her with a grin, laughing at the tears in her eyes.

Too much.

Beatrice felt the tip of his sword slowly pierce her stomach, thrusting into her gut as he ran it through her body and deep into the ground below. Blood spilled out beneath her. She coughed once, and it flooded her mouth.

"It's all quite overwhelming, isn't it?" he whispered, bending down to stroke a finger along her jaw. She felt his finger gather up the blood as it dripped from her mouth. He lifted it to his lips and tasted. Then he grinned and bent down, licking the drips that ran down her neck.

"Mmm," he growled as his cold tongue drank her in.

"Go—" She tried to turn away, but the blade dug in deeper and she choked on her own blood.

"So sweet, my precious girl. Just wait... just wait." She could feel his cold hands run over her struggling body, and she cried in agony as the blade tore at her stomach.

Lorenzo laid a single kiss at the corner of her mouth before he rose, snapped off the handle of the sword, and ran toward Stephen, grabbing a weapon from one of the dead guards.

No! her mind screamed. She tried to grab at the blade and realized why he had snapped off the handle. Her hands quickly became slick with blood, and she could not grip the metal with enough force to pull it from the rough ground beneath her. She was pinned and weak from blood loss. It seeped out around her, and every time she struggled, it only tore her wound more.

"Dad?" she choked out, looking for her father. "Dad!"

Stephen had been holding his own against the guard, but once Lorenzo joined in, he was battling on two fronts with only one weapon. Their eyes met for one panicked moment.

Too much.

Beatrice sobbed and struggled against the sword pinning her to the ground, only to hear the quick snap when it finally cut her spine. Her legs fell still. She could no longer feel them. She closed her eyes.

Stephen yelled, "Beatrice!"

Too much.

Lorenzo was going to win.

GIOVANNI AND TENZIN PICKED UP LORENZO'S SCENT JUST PAST THE courtyard where Baojia had left them, tracking him deeper into the mountain. They struggled through the scent of human blood, meeting only a few survivors. A few monks had hidden in corners, but most had rushed out to the courtyards, only to be cut down as Lorenzo's men found them.

THE FORCE OF WIND

The two friends entered the dim library. Old energy filled the room, but Giovanni could sense that no vampire remained. Scrolls, books, and tablets lay tossed on the floor. Two monks lay near the door, their necks snapped. Giovanni immediately picked up a faint human heartbeat on the far side of the room.

"Fu-han," Tenzin whispered as she rushed across the room. She picked up the old man, cradling him as his eyes flickered open.

"Tenzin?" he croaked. "My dear, why... what has happened? Who were those immortals? Why..."

"Shhh," she soothed the old man, rocking him as she held his head in her lap. "Fu-han, the book? Did they get the book?"

"They wanted Stephen's book," the old monk whispered. "I don't know why. They won't understand it. I finally..." He stopped and coughed up a little blood. "I finally found..." The monk's eyes flickered closed.

"What?" Giovanni asked. "What did you find, old man?"

He ignored Tenzin's sharp eyes, realizing that this must be Zhang's old pupil, who had been interpreting Geber's manuscript for them.

"He won't be able to... it's simply not what it seems. And he does not have the humility to see." Fu-han was looking into the distance, his eyes open, but empty, as the life drained out of him. "He is too arrogant. Too arrogant..."

"Who is too arrogant?" Giovanni knelt next to him. He heard the old man's heart falter, and he put his hands on his chest, sending an electric jolt through his body, which started the heart again. "What are you talking about? What did you discover?" he practically yelled.

"Giovanni!" Tenzin pushed him away, but he only crawled back, bending toward the monk in supplication.

Fu-han's eyes opened and locked with Giovanni's, momentarily lucid in the flickering light of the library.

"Learn humility, immortal. Look for the space between. The secret of the elixir lies in what is not there."

"What—"

"Do not forget the fifth element," he whispered as his eye flickered closed and his heart stopped.

The fifth element?

His mind raced and his heart pounded. There was something... something that Lorenzo did not see. Even if his son had the book, the old monk said he could not understand it. If Lorenzo could not understand it, there was still hope they could keep the elixir from him.

He felt the blow as Tenzin threw him across the room.

"Who do you think you are?" she yelled. "Have you no respect for my father's pupil?"

She raged, and he knew it was as much in grief for the destruction of the monastery as it was in anger for his actions. Tenzin tossed him around the library, and he did not try to resist, letting her vent her ire as she battered him against the cold, stone walls. Papers whipped around the room, churned by the wind she summoned.

"Tenzin—"

"This is your fault, you arrogant boy! Did you think your suffering so much worse than others? Did you think you were unique? This is the monster that *you* created!"

The whirlwind swirled around her, an outward manifestation of her anger and frustration. It was rare for Tenzin to lose her temper like this; he had only seen it once.

"I'm sorry, Tenzin."

"You are sorry? You're *sorry*? Your sorrow does not make this right!"

He narrowed his eyes. She was emotional. Too emotional. He suddenly realized his own blood was churning, and a twisting fear filled his stomach. He felt a phantom pain in his back, and his blood ached as it rushed through his body.

His blood... Beatrice's blood. His eyes darted to Tenzin, baffled by her uncharacteristic show of emotion. Her blood. *Stephen*.

"Tenzin!" He rose to his feet and rushed toward her. She batted him back with an angry wall of wind, and he fell into the alcoves that held the books as more paper whipped around him. "We must go to Beatrice and Stephen," he roared. "We must make sure they are safe. Something is wrong!"

The wind stopped and she cocked her head toward him. "Stephen?"

"Stephen." Giovanni nodded, rising to his feet. "There is something—"

"Stephen," she said again, blinking her eyes as if waking from a daze. She frowned at Giovanni and started toward the door. He followed her, only to halt when she suddenly stopped right before the open door of the library. Giovanni almost ran into her when he heard her gasp and buckle forward, as if something had punched her in the gut.

"Tenzin?" He placed a hand on her shoulder and she slumped to the ground. "Tenzin!"

He caught her and turned her in his arms. Her eyes were glazed over, hollow as the grave. The flames burst over his back when he heard her plaintive whisper.

"*Stephen...*"

CHAPTER 21

"How shall I kill you, my Stephen?" Lorenzo slapped at his child's face with the flat of his sword. Stephen was hanging, trapped in a wall of water from which he couldn't break free. Lorenzo paced nearby, as his guard watched the stairs.

"You're so stupid. You have all this power, but no idea what to do with it. You should have spent less time with your books and more time practicing, like your daughter."

"Let me out of here," Stephen grunted, "and fight me like a man."

"Oh," Lorenzo laughed, "but I am not a man, you silly child. You're such an American. Can you do a John Wayne impression, cowboy?" Lorenzo chuckled at his own joke, and the silent guard smirked.

Beatrice was still trapped on the ground. Her hands continued to struggle with the blade that Lorenzo had run through her, but her palms slipped on the bloody sword, cutting her fingers as she struggled.

Stephen looked resigned. "Lorenzo, you already have the book. What else do you want?"

"To kill you, of course. I just can't decide… quickly or slowly? I would normally take my time since you've been such a bother the last few years, but I have a feeling"—he looked toward the stone stairs leading up to the monastery—"that we'll be having company soon, which makes me sad."

Beatrice saw Stephen's arm break free from the water and her father flicked his hand toward the river, summoning a stream of water that knocked Lorenzo over as he stood near the riverbank. The distraction was enough to break Lorenzo's hold on the water that had trapped him.

"Oh, you are a clever boy!" Lorenzo laughed. "I suppose you're right, a fight is much more fun."

Stephen fell to the earth, reaching out and grabbing his sword before he sprang to his feet and met the silent guard who rushed him.

"Dad!" She had to get free. She had to help him. Beatrice tried to grab at the sword again, but she did not have the strength to pull it from the ground beneath her. She continued to spit out the blood that poured into her mouth as she struggled.

"Beatrice, hold on!"

"Enough," Lorenzo growled, looking toward the stone steps. Just then, there was a flurry of movement on the edge of the river as Beatrice saw her father leap up, sweeping down and beheading the guard he battled. He landed on the ground and started in her direction, only to have Lorenzo dart behind and slash the back of his thighs, cutting his hamstrings and bringing him to his knees.

"No!" Stephen cried out as he fell to his knees. Beatrice fought back the urge to scream when Lorenzo kicked her father's sword away from him.

No, no, no! Beatrice struggled harder, bloody tears coursing down her cheeks as she tried to break free. She choked on the blood that continued to fill her mouth. If she could just break free... Even if her legs wouldn't work, she could drag herself—

"Enough of this." She heard Lorenzo say as he bent over her father. "Enough playing, Stephen."

Beatrice spat out the blood. "Dad?" she choked. She could feel her wounds close around the blade in her stomach, but even that pain no longer registered as she watched Lorenzo circle her father with one hand gripping his neck.

"Dad!"

"Look at her, Stephen, isn't she beautiful?" Lorenzo ran a sword through Stephen's stomach and forced his neck around so Beatrice met her father's eyes as he began coughing up blood. She saw his lips form her name.

Mariposa...

"No, no... Lorenzo! Get away from him!"

"She's so lovely," Lorenzo murmured. "I have plans for her, you know? Such wonderful plans." He pulled the blade from her father's stomach and the blood poured out.

Stephen muttered through bloody lips. "Leave... leave her, Lorenzo."

"Take me! Leave him alone and take me if you want me!" Beatrice cried into the night. "I'll go. I promise."

"You have the book. Leave my daughter."

Lorenzo was watching her as his blade slid around Stephen's neck, drawing a thin collar of blood. "So touching. And I won't kill her. I have plans for her. If I could only keep you around, you could see them."

"No! Daddy!" Beatrice screamed as Lorenzo drew back the sword. Her eyes locked with Stephen's, and she saw a strange euphoria fill her father's face. Her eyes raced to Lorenzo, who only cocked his head as he stared at her with a small smile.

"Sadly," Lorenzo said. "I have to travel light."

The blade descended, cutting off Stephen's head in one swift stroke. It rolled toward her, coming to rest a few feet away as his lifeless brown eyes stared into the dark heaven above.

Beatrice screamed as her father's lips moved in one last silent prayer.

She heard Lorenzo walking toward her, and she stopped struggling when the pain caused her head to swim. She thought she was strong, but what use was her strength in the face of this monster? Lorenzo's black dress shoes came to stop in front of her face.

She heard Giovanni's voice in the back of her mind. *"Survive... that is your victory..."*

Lorenzo knelt beside her. He held the manuscript in his hands; Beatrice stared at it. It wasn't as big as she thought it would be, no larger than a typical hardback, and not even as thick. The dull, leather cover was stained with her father's blood. A single drop trickled down the side. It smeared when Lorenzo placed the manuscript in a large plastic bag and stuffed it in his shirt, securing it to his body as he ran a bloody hand through his blond curls.

"Oh"—he curled his lip as he saw the smeared blood on his fingers—"that's disgusting. Good thing I'm going for a swim. Tell *Papà* I said hello, and I'll see him later. I wish I could take you with me right now, but like I said, I am traveling light, so we'll have to catch up later."

"I hate you," she spit out through bloody lips. "I hate you, I hate you. I'm going to kill you if it's the last thing I do."

"Do you think so?"

She couldn't stop the sob that escaped her lips when she saw her father's lifeless eyes. "You will die, Lorenzo, and I will make it painful. You will scream in agony."

"So much anger," he murmured. "It's beautiful."

"It is my only purpose in this life, do you understand me?"

He leaned down and left a lingering kiss on her cheek before he whispered in her ear. "I know you think that you'll kill me, but I'm quite sure there will come a day when you will be putty in my hands. I'm quite looking forward to it."

"Never."

"Oh." He stood and wagged a finger at her. "Never is a long time in our world, precious girl." He winked before he ran and jumped into the river, sinking out of sight beneath its black currents.

"No!" she screamed in frustration before she caught sight of her father's head again. "No, no!" She sobbed bloody tears as she continued to struggle against the blade that pinned her to the ground. The night was silent, marked only by the soft sounds of night birds and her own cries. A few moments later, she heard a rushing sound and Baojia leaned over her.

"No," he groaned. "No, Beatrice. Not this." His voice as pained as she had ever heard it.

"He killed my dad." Beatrice couldn't tear her eyes from Stephen's head.

"Hold still, B. You're going to be all right, but hold still."

"My dad's dead, Baojia."

She heard him choke, but her eyes were still locked on her father's staring face.

"Damn it to hell!" he yelled as he stood. "Hold still, this is going to hurt you again. You're healing too fast."

"It won't hurt. I don't feel anything anymore." It wasn't strictly true; she was beginning to feel twitching in her toes as her nerves knit together around the blade in her spine.

"I'm going to pull the sword out and it's going to break your spine again, so just hold still."

She finally looked up at him. His eyes were red and there was a deep cut around his neck, as if someone had cut his throat from ear to ear.

"What happened to you?"

He shook his head. *Anguish*. He was anguished. "It's not important," he whispered. "Hold still." He gripped at the sword in her stomach, grasped it with both hands while his blood ran down, and pulled.

Beatrice screamed as her shoulders bucked up. She fell back to the earth with a thud, feeling the blood spill out beneath her again. Baojia tossed the sword away and came to cradle her head as she lay on the ground.

"Hold still, B. Please, hold still." There was a gaping wound in her stomach where the sword had torn her abdomen, and she couldn't feel her legs again. He stroked her hair back. "Shhh. Don't move. Give your body time to heal."

"Gio," she whispered, aching for her mate. "I need..."

"Giovanni Vecchio!" Baojia screamed into the night. "Where are you?"

No sooner had he called out than she heard quick footsteps on the stairs and felt his familiar energy rush toward her. She looked up and saw him, pale face and furious eyes, cradling Tenzin in front of him.

"Take her," Giovanni called to Baojia before he rushed over. Baojia gathered Tenzin in his arms, but she lifted a pale hand, reaching toward Stephen's body by the riverbank.

Beatrice began crying again as Giovanni knelt beside her.

"My dad, Gio. He killed my dad." She clutched at his shoulders as Giovanni cradled her in his arms and lifted her from the cold ground.

"Please, Tesoro, you need to go in the water."

"My dad."

THE FORCE OF WIND

"I know," he choked out. "Tenzin collapsed in the library. I came as quickly as I could. I had to carry her."

"He took the book and jumped in the river."

Beatrice heard the splash as Giovanni waded in. He dipped her down, submerging her in the river as the water swirled around her body, embracing her in its cool, healing depths. She looked up at Giovanni through the rippling surface of the water. For the first time, she saw his own tears fall as he watched her pain. They dropped into the water over her face, meeting her drifting tears before the river washed them away.

"Take the water in, Beatrice. As much as you can. Let it heal you." He shook his head and blood scattered over the water.

"My dad," she mouthed, as the water filled and covered her.

"I know."

He lifted her head out and pressed their cheeks together, leaving her body in the water to heal. She felt tears on her cheeks, but she didn't know who was crying.

"Lorenzo killed him."

"I know."

"Where was everyone? I tried. I tried so hard, but there was so much blood and there were too many of them."

"Shh, don't talk." He held his wrist in front of her mouth and she bit into it, taking in his blood as her body floated in the stream. She could feel her bones knitting together. Her flesh stretched over her wounds. The prickling in her legs grew as her spine healed. Soon, her body was itching all over as her amnis joined the water to make her strong again. She continued sucking at Giovanni's wrist, and he watched every wound, examining them as they healed.

A few minutes later, she released his wrist and reached out, leaving the safety of the water as she threw herself into her mate's embrace. He lifted her up, and she wrapped her legs around his waist as they trudged to the edge of the riverbank. She dropped to the ground and looked for her father.

Stephen's body was laying on the edge of the river, and Tenzin was crouched beside him, stroking his lifeless cheek. She had laid Stephen's head next to his body and Baojia stood over them both, watching the night sky.

"Where are Zhang's people? They should be here by now."

"They had to travel fifteen hundred kilometers by air in one night," she heard Giovanni say as she sat by Tenzin and took her father's hand. Tenzin's eyes darted to her, and Beatrice saw her tense before her shoulders relaxed.

They all sat silent over Stephen's remains before a low keening began from Tenzin's small form. She rocked back and forth, one hand on Stephen's cheek and the other braced on his chest. Beatrice heard her murmur a low chant in the old language she shared with Zhang, and she felt her tears fall again.

Giovanni knelt down behind her and tried to pull her away from her father, but she shrugged him off and reached over to embrace Tenzin. The small vampire curled her shoulders, but Beatrice kept her hands out until finally, the small woman turned to her and Beatrice could see the desolate look in Tenzin's grey eyes.

"Tenzin?" Beatrice whispered. Tenzin reached over, pulling her into a fierce embrace. The two women rocked together until they heard a sound like a flock of birds flapping in the wind. Tenzin quickly dried her eyes.

Zhang's men landed in a crouch, eyeing the bloody clearing and the bodies of Stephen and the three guards that lay around them. The leader approached cautiously as Tenzin rose to her feet, stoic again in the face of her father's men.

"Mistress Tenzin." He nodded deeply to her. "Your mate... Elder Lu's monks?"

"The monks are dead. There is a small group of boys who escaped out the southern passageway. Follow the river down, and you should find them. Help them to find shelter in the nearest village until we hear from Lu. They should not go back to the monastery."

"Yes, Mistress." The leader motioned toward two of his men, who took to the air.

"Zhongli's guards are in the forest. His 'honored guest' slaughtered his men before he went up to the monastery." Beatrice watched as a flicker of confusion passed over the vampire's face at Tenzin's words. She could see Tenzin sag almost imperceptibly, and Giovanni's hand reached out for her arm.

"The monastery was ransacked," he said. "Most of the monks were killed. Master Fu-han among them."

"And Miss De Novo's property?" the guard asked.

"Stolen by Lorenzo," Beatrice said as she looked down at her father's body again. As if she cared about the book. Part of her knew it was important, but she was frozen in her grief.

"Mistress Tenzin." Zhang's guard bowed again and spoke softly, "may we help you with Stephen's body?"

"No!" Tenzin bent down, then looked at the body and shook her head. "I mean... yes. Take him up to the monastery." She turned and glanced at Beatrice before she took to the air.

Zhang's guard split up. Some of them followed Baojia to the edge of the forest where Zhongli's men lay; others gently lifted her father's remains before they followed Tenzin up the mountain.

She felt Giovanni grasp her shoulders. "Beatrice, we need to find you some blood. Most of the monks were killed and you need fresh—"

"I don't—" She broke off, overwhelmed again. "I'm not hungry. I don't want blood. I just want my dad. I want to be with Tenzin. Can we follow—"

"Beatrice," he broke in with a hoarse voice. "You need blood. You drank from me, but you had a terrible injury. I'll find an animal in the forest if you want, but you need to feed."

For some reason, the idea of killing a helpless animal seemed to break her. She slumped into Giovanni's chest as his arms wrapped around her, and she shook with tears.

He held her close. "You survived, Beatrice. You survived. That is a victory. You and your father faced four opponents, and you *survived*. Even Baojia was gravely wounded by those men."

"But my father didn't survive."

She heard him clear his throat and sniff. He pressed a kiss to her forehead and whispered, "I would take this pain from you if I could."

"I need to go to my father."

"Beatri—" Giovanni broke off and turned toward the forest. There was a rustling sound as a monk walked through the trees. Giovanni grasped Beatrice's shoulders, holding her still as the scent hit her nose. Though the smell wafted over her, and her fangs descended, she had no desire to pursue the human.

"You should be with Zhang's men," Giovanni said.

The boy answered in Mandarin, and the two had a quick, heated exchange she couldn't understand. She stared at the guard she had killed and the blood she vomited over his corpse. She imagined that it was Lorenzo's head that lay next to the body. The thought brought her some comfort and a hint of satisfaction.

Beatrice felt Giovanni's hands tighten on her shoulders.

"Tesoro, this monk has offered to feed you. He will hold out his wrist—"

"No!" Beatrice had no confidence that she could eat without harming the young man. He had come closer, and the churning in her stomach increased. Her fangs were sharp in her mouth.

"You will drink from his wrist, and I will make sure you do not take too much, but it is the best thing for you."

"I'll hurt him."

"No, you won't. I'm here. I won't let you hurt him."

"And I am, as well." She heard Baojia approach. The two grasped her shoulders as she turned and faced the young man. He was no more than sixteen or seventeen, and his head was shaved like the monks she remembered from Mount Penglai. He wore saffron robes and a resolute expression. She hissed instinctively, but shrank back when she saw the look of fear enter the young man's eyes. Still, he held up his wrist to her face, and Giovanni held her hair in his iron grasp as Beatrice leaned forward and latched on to the young man's wrist.

It was heaven. Thick, sweet blood flooded her mouth, slid down her throat, and filled her angry stomach. She could feel the boy's pulse, and she sucked in rhythm to it, watching him with hungry eyes as she struggled against Baojia and Giovanni's grasp. She eyed the pulsing vein in the neck, watching it like a predator as she drank. Soon, she could feel the aching in her throat lessen, but she did not release. She could see the boy pale in front of her, and a surge of satisfaction ran through her as the hint of fear permeated the air. If she could just get free of their hands...

"Enough!" Giovanni's fingers pinched her nose and pulled her away from the vein.

"No!" she snarled, lunging at him before Baojia pulled her back. Giovanni quickly healed the boy's wrist and spoke quietly to him in Mandarin before the young monk disappeared into the forest. Then he turned to Beatrice, and Baojia released her into his embrace.

"We must go up to the monastery. Dawn is coming and Tenzin needs you."

She blinked as her reason returned. She walked toward the stairs, holding his hand as they climbed the old staircase together. Baojia trailed behind them.

Beatrice turned and gave one last look at the clearing where her father had died. Though his body lingered, she knew Stephen's soul had fled. She clung to the vision of his peaceful face the moment before he was killed. Whatever her father's last vision had been, it had brought him joy, and she sent a silent prayer that his soul had found the home he had sought for so long in life.

She turned back to Giovanni. Her husband met her gaze, then bent down and picked her up, cradling her in his warm arms as they made their way to shelter.

CHAPTER 22

They were ensconced in the library when dawn came. Giovanni carried Beatrice past the reek of blood by the door, guiding her to an alcove where low cushions lay scattered.

"Where are Tenzin and my father?"

"Here," he said as he laid her among the cushions. "At the back of the library. Tenzin is with him."

The monastery library was a long hall, dug deep into the mountain and carefully lined with shelves for the books and scrolls. Small alcoves branched off from the main hallway, most lined with low cushions and some with tables, the ideal location for quiet study and contemplation.

"I want to go to her." Beatrice couldn't explain it. It wasn't just that she wanted to see Tenzin; it was as if she needed to. She felt a pull of longing past understanding, even as she fought against exhaustion.

"You need to rest."

"Please, Gio."

He knelt down next to her, studying her face before he nodded silently. He stood and walked down the hall. A low murmur reached her ears before a rush of air and then Tenzin was beside her. She placed her arm around Beatrice and lay next to her; the comfort was instantaneous. Giovanni silently paced the hall while Beatrice blinked back tears.

Tenzin spoke in a low voice. "It is his blood, do you understand?"

"Yes."

"I will guard him today. You will help me prepare the body tomorrow night when you rise, as a daughter should."

"Yes."

"My father's guards are here. They are numerous, and I have sent for more."

Beatrice could only nod.

"Rest, my girl. Let your mate care for you."

"You'll be nearby?"

"Yes."

After a few more minutes, Beatrice could feel her eyes start to droop as the sun rose in the sky. Tenzin slipped away, and she felt Giovanni come to her, lying down and gathering her in his arms as the dawn took them both.

HE WAS THERE WHEN SHE WOKE, HIS ARMS WRAPPED TIGHTLY AROUND HER. Beatrice blinked for a moment in confusion.

"Where are we?"

He paused. "The library at the monastery."

In a harsh second, it all flooded back. Lorenzo and the four vicious guards. The current that radiated up her arms when she cut the head off one vampire. The sickening realization that Lorenzo had felt the same when he cut off her father's head.

Her father.

She began to shake, burying her face into Giovanni's chest; he stroked her hair until she was spent. Though her body was refreshed from sleep, her mind was still weary with grief.

"Wait here," Giovanni said. "Zhang's men brought blood."

"I'm not hungry."

His grip tightened on her shoulders.

"You must not stop eating."

Just then, Tenzin appeared in the hallway bearing two mugs of blood. Beatrice's fangs descended as she caught the sweet smell.

"Eat." She handed both to Beatrice.

Beatrice nodded and drank as Tenzin turned to Giovanni.

"Go get Baojia. I want to speak to him about yesterday."

Giovanni rose and walked down the hallway. Beatrice finished the first mug and started on the second as Tenzin sat across from her.

"You must not refuse to eat. He is worried because it is a common reaction of our kind to grief, but a dangerous one, especially for a new vampire."

"Okay."

They both fell silent as Beatrice drank. Though the burn in her throat lessened, she felt no satisfaction from her meal. After a few minutes, Giovanni returned with Baojia. She saw her mate inspect the cups she drank from. "I finished them both," she murmured. He sat next to her and took her hand as

THE FORCE OF WIND

Baojia sat across from them. The deep cut across his neck had healed and the only evidence was an angry red line and his grim expression.

All four were silent until Tenzin spoke.

"Explain."

He nodded. "I was on my way back to the river when I caught the scent of vampires and human blood from another corridor. Thinking there were more humans being drained, I followed the passageway. It was similar to the one you had sent the boys down, but on the opposite side of the mountain."

"The northern route." Tenzin said. "Continue."

"The further I followed, the more scent I picked up. I smelled Lorenzo and the river, so I knew where he was going. I didn't want to turn back and waste time." His eyes narrowed. "I met six vampires at the exit."

"That must be the route Lorenzo took back to the river," Giovanni said. "That's why we did not detect him." Tenzin only nodded as Baojia continued.

"I killed them... eventually. It took longer than I had hoped. These were not raw warriors. They had training and most of them, I would guess, were my age or older."

Beatrice whispered, "You killed six on your own?"

Baojia's eyes softened when he looked at her. "I have had many years fighting, Beatrice. You and your father did well against your opponents. Four against two. One of whom was your father's sire? Do not blame yourself for his death. Others bear that responsibility."

But Beatrice did. It was unavoidable. Her mind kept replaying little things she could have done differently. If she hadn't panicked. If she had been faster. If she had better control of the bloodlust that had ambushed and distracted her.

"When I got to the river, Lorenzo was already gone. Stephen was dead. B was pinned—"

"Pinned?" Giovanni squeezed her hand.

"He pinned me to the ground with his sword. I tried to pull it out, but it was so deep. He broke off the handle so I couldn't... And then, I'm pretty sure it cut my spine and—"

She broke off when Giovanni grabbed her and pulled her into a fierce embrace. She heard Tenzin and Baojia quickly leave them as Giovanni rocked her back and forth.

"Tesoro," he whispered as he rocked her back and forth. "Beatrice, I should never have left you."

"You can't say that. You were trying to find Lorenzo. You were trying to protect the monks. I'm not the only person in the world, you know."

He said something low in Italian before he cleared his throat.

"Do you want to rest? Do you want to help Tenzin with your father? What would you do?"

"I'll help Tenzin. What... what will happen to his body?"

He paused. "It will linger for two more nights. On the third night, we return to our element. We will take him to the river."

She nodded. Beatrice was glad they were near a river. Some instinctual part of her recoiled at the idea of her father's remains dissolving into the earth. She peeled herself away from Giovanni, rose, and went to find Tenzin.

GIOVANNI AND BAOJIA WERE SILENTLY SORTING AND REPLACING THE SCROLLS on the shelves while Beatrice and Tenzin sat next to Stephen's lifeless body. Giovanni kept an eye on his wife even as he worked. He also watched in fascination as Tenzin performed the ancient mourning ritual over her mate.

She chanted a low, droning song, first washing, then covering his body in oils she had gathered from the monks' workrooms. She had closed his eyes and bound his mouth closed with a piece of saffron cloth, before covering his face with a white fragment torn from her own tunic. Tenzin rose to her feet, leaving the library on some errand, while Beatrice remained watching over her father.

Giovanni came to sit with her.

"I wish we had a priest."

"Rituals are for the living, not the dead." He knew Stephen had been Catholic, and he wished that Carwyn was there to comfort Beatrice.

As if reading his mind, she spoke. "Have you called Carwyn?"

"I sent a letter out to him and one to Kirby last night. Zhang's men will see that they are delivered."

"And Matt will tell my grandma."

"Yes."

"Because I can't."

He hesitated. "You can't see her right now, Beatrice. You're too volatile."

He heard her begin to cry again, and he put an arm around her, drawing her into his chest. He was grateful for the black robes that Zhang's guards had brought for them, as his shirt and her own were stained with bloody tears. Tenzin came back with a large white cloth and Beatrice pulled away from him, sniffing and wiping her eyes.

"What do we do now?" she asked.

Giovanni rose and let them continue. Beatrice tore the linen cloth into long strips, which Tenzin used to bind the body and head together. He watched in fascination as his friend took a dagger and cut her long hair at the shoulder, twisting it into a braid that she placed over Stephen's chest before she crossed his arms and began wrapping him in his shroud, tucking fragrant herbs among the linen. He had no idea where Tenzin had found the white cloth with which she wrapped her mate, but he watched carefully as Beatrice helped, following Tenzin's murmured instructions as they cared for Stephen's earthly remains.

Giovanni wondered what ancient rite they were following. He had never seen

Tenzin grieve. Giovanni doubted anyone ever had, and he wondered if any human or vampire in the last five thousand years had sung the low song she chanted in her mother tongue.

No one entered the library or disturbed their quiet sorrow. Giovanni left briefly to check with Zhang's men, who were clearing the human remains and waiting for the company of humans and vampires that Lu Dongbin would send.

"The young monks?" he asked Zhang's lieutenant as he stood near the gates and watched them work.

"Have been taken to Penglai. They will go to another monastery. One only Lu has knowledge of."

"Please tell Elder Lu that we are sorting the library as best we can. It was left in shambles."

The wind vampire said, "The elder will be most grateful. After Mistress Tenzin has mourned her mate, his people will take care of the rest."

Giovanni nodded and slipped back into the dim hall.

Beatrice and Tenzin sat silently next to the wrapped body the rest of the night, while he and Baojia continued to put the library in as much order as was possible. Much had been destroyed in Lorenzo's frantic search for Geber's manuscript, but much still remained.

"I DIDN'T LOVE HIM, YOU KNOW."

"What?" Giovanni looked up from sorting the next night.

Tenzin was still sitting by Stephen's body while Beatrice and Baojia swam. Like most of her kind, Beatrice was drawn to the water, taking comfort from its presence. She and Baojia had slipped away when the sun had set and they had fed. The water vampire had refused to leave Beatrice's presence since her attack, even sitting within eye distance while she rested for the day. Giovanni had allowed it, understanding the other vampire's burden.

"Stephen. When we started exchanging blood. I did not love him. We did not have what you and Beatrice... It was not the same."

Looking into her grief-stricken eyes, Giovanni knew that his friend had loved Stephen, no matter what she said. He only shook his head. "You do not have to explain yourself to me."

"I exchanged blood with him to protect him. And for Beatrice. I knew it was his fate to sire her, and he needed to be strong."

"He was as strong as you could make him, Tenzin."

"I was overconfident."

"We all were."

She fell silent before she left Stephen's body and came to sit next to him. He handed her a stack of loose paper, which she began paging through.

"What will you do now?" she asked.

"Try to get it back."

"I think you need to find out who his partner is. Someone provided him with those guards. Someone other than Elder Zhongli."

"Yes, I know."

They worked steadily for another hour.

"You will take Beatrice to Cochamó?"

"Yes."

"I know you think it was a mistake to turn her. That it left her vulnerable to the bloodlust, but—"

"I don't want to talk about it."

She looked up. "Surely you must see that she would not have survived if she had not turned."

Giovanni clenched his jaw in frustration. "Did you see the council giving her the book? Did you see them forcing Lorenzo's hand? Causing this confrontation? Did your mystic eye see that, Tenzin?"

"Lan would have voted with you if there was no other option," Tenzin said in a firm voice. "They would not have allowed you to kill him on the island, you know how they are."

"And then Lorenzo would have done this anyway."

She made no response, only continued to quietly leaf through the old papers.

"Stephen told me he would not live long."

He frowned. "What?"

"He told me months ago that he felt he was 'living on borrowed time,' as he put it. That he would not escape this fate. He was peaceful about it. Stephen claimed that he should have died years ago when Lorenzo turned him. That all this time was only a gift."

"Because he saw Beatrice again."

She nodded.

"But you did not see this fate for him?"

"No, I did not see this."

"Or you did not choose to."

Tenzin looked at him with guarded eyes. "Perhaps, I did not choose to."

Giovanni cleared his throat. "Will she... will she join him?"

It had weighed on his mind more than he wanted. As much as Beatrice loved him, new immortals were impulsive and irrational, and he clearly remembered his own sense of despair hundreds of years before when he had murdered his own sire. Despite Giovanni's loathing for him, there was a gaping hollow where he felt Andros's loss.

"Gio, you know her better than that."

"Do I?"

Tenzin frowned. "How can you ask that?"

"She is the same to me, but more. Surely you can see it."

His friend placed her hand on his arm, squeezing slightly. "She is... exactly who she will need to be, my boy."

He took a deep breath. "Beatrice is as much your daughter as she was Stephen's, Tenzin. Please, don't disappear."

Giovanni saw her grey eyes shutter. She slipped away and went to sit by Stephen's body again, and in his heart, he knew she was already gone.

TWO NIGHTS LATER, A SOLEMN PROCESSION SLIPPED DOWN THE STEPS FROM the monastery. Giovanni walked ahead and lit the stone lanterns on the path before four of Zhang's men, who carried Stephen's body. Tenzin and Beatrice followed them. Lu's water vampires had arrived the night before and stood near the edge of the river, watching the procession in silent respect.

The four wind vampires carried the body to the edge of the river where Tenzin and Beatrice, both dressed in white robes, held out their hands and cradled Stephen between them, waiting until the water claimed its own.

He felt a flutter of wind and looked to his right to see Zhang light on the stone steps and walk to him. They nodded toward each other.

"Giovanni."

"Zhang."

"How is your wife?"

"Beatrice will be fine. She is very strong."

He heard a slight hoarseness in Zhang's voice. "And how is my daughter?"

Giovanni paused. "She will be fine."

"The elder has been executed. Lu carried it out himself. The whole council was displeased by his actions."

"He broke their trust."

"And sacrificed a sacred place of learning for a human."

Giovanni couldn't help but think that he would have done the same if the human had been Beatrice, but he remained silent.

"Does your son have Beatrice's book?"

"Yes. She saw him take it."

"You will retrieve it. The book was given to Beatrice as a scribe of Penglai; it is rightfully hers. If the council of the Eight Immortals can help you, we will. We do not care to have our will averted."

"It is the Seven Immortals now, isn't it?"

Zhang was silent for a moment. "Surely you must know that the council is immortal. There will always be eight."

"But—"

"Elder Zhongli is more than the vampire who wore his name."

Giovanni nodded in understanding. So, another Elder Zhongli Quan would be chosen. Giovanni wondered how that would come about, but chose not to ask, knowing he would receive no answer. He wondered if Zhongli had been the original vampire of legend, or whether he had been a replacement himself.

"Of course, Elder Zhang. Continuity is important."

"As is balance."

"Yes." Giovanni looked to his mate. She stood proud and solemn across from his oldest friend. He thought of Beatrice and Tenzin. Of Carwyn and himself. Water, wind, earth and fire.

Balance.

Four elements.

Always four.

His eyes narrowed and he glanced at Zhang, who only looked at him with a slight smile.

"Balance," Zhang said again, "is the key, Giovanni Vecchio. The wisest of immortals have always understood this."

A thought began to bloom at the back of his mind. A path in the darkness began to grow lighter.

Balance.

He nodded at Zhang a little more deeply. "Of course. Thank you, Elder Zhang."

Giovanni turned back to the river; he could feel the change in the air. Beatrice's heart began to beat more rapidly, and he and Zhang stepped closer as the air became charged.

It was only a ripple at first. The solid shroud of Stephen's earthly form seemed to shudder in the current. Then, little by little, it grew thinner. The strips of cloth that had bound his feet came loose, curling in the water as the river teased them. Then, as if by silent command, the white cloth slipped away from the women's grasp, unfurling like a silken cocoon as the pure white linen was washed away in the stream. He watched it spread, a silver web scattering in the curls and eddies of the Nine-Bend River, washing down the mountain and into the sea.

He watched Stephen's shroud until the turn of the river took it out of sight, then his eyes sought his mate. She was standing in the shallow water, watching with dark eyes. He could see the longing in them, and he knew that she felt the call to follow him, to lose herself within the soft embrace of her element. He sent a silent plea to her, willing her eyes to turn toward his.

She was poised on the riverbank. One foot on the muddy ground and the other sunk in the water. Finally, her head turned, she looked at him, and he felt her return. Beatrice climbed from the edge, and he caught her in a tight embrace.

"I want to go home," she whispered. "There is nothing here. Take me home."

"We will leave tonight."

Beatrice pressed her face into his chest as Giovanni watched Tenzin walk toward them. His friend stopped and spoke a few words to her father in the old language, then walked to them. Beatrice turned, and Tenzin put one hand on her cheek, wiping the tears that stained it as she pulled Beatrice toward her, laying a soft kiss on her forehead and whispering in her ear before she stepped back.

Tenzin met Giovanni's eye, nodded once, and took to the air, silently disappearing into the black shroud of night.

CHAPTER 23

Los Angeles, California

"Where is she?"

"A small airport outside of Chino. It smells more like cows than people there."

"And she's alone?"

Giovanni paused, looking at Beatrice's grandfather. Ernesto's measuring gaze bored into him. "She prefers the solitude. She asked that I lock her in while we had our visit."

Ernesto waved a dismissive hand at him. "I will be by to visit later tonight. She will see me."

Giovanni cocked his head. "You are welcome to try. Kirby is guarding the hangar. Call him for directions."

"And the boy?"

"I've already sent him south. He's being looked after."

Ernesto nodded, quietly tapping the arm of the leather chair in his study where he met with Giovanni. They were sipping red wine in Ernesto's mansion in Newport Harbor. Quiet servants scuttled about in the background, but no one disturbed their quiet conversation.

Beatrice and Giovanni had arrived in Southern California the night before to return Baojia to his sire. Giovanni was meeting with family and associates for the next two nights; then he and Beatrice would leave for Chile.

"You'll be in South America for a year?"

"Yes."

"And where can I reach my granddaughter if I want to contact her? I need an address of some kind."

Giovanni smiled and avoided the question. "You may reach us through Kirby, of course. And we'll also be making sure that Isadora is kept informed of Beatrice's progress."

Ernesto narrowed his eyes, but Giovanni suspected the old vampire knew he would not get more, no matter who he was related to.

"You may be sure that I'll be keeping a close eye on Isadora while you are away."

Threat or promise? Giovanni suspected that for Ernesto Alvarez, it was a promise. "I'm sure Beatrice will appreciate it. As do I."

"I'm not doing it for you, di Spada." It had not escaped Giovanni's notice that Beatrice's grandfather was using his more notorious name. "Beatrice may be under your aegis—"

"She is under no one's aegis but her own."

"—but she is still my granddaughter. It is my responsibility that Stephen was lost, and I will not risk her. I only let her go with you now because you are her mate, and I know your reputation."

Giovanni forced down the instinctive surge of fire that flowed under his skin and narrowed his eyes at the old man. "Let me be clear, Alvarez, no one will be allowed to interfere with my family. Particularly with my wife. She is no one's pawn, no matter how they may care for her. Be very careful in your presumptions."

The old man's eyes gleamed for a moment before a smile curved his mouth. "Excellent. She has chosen a good mate in you." Ernesto sighed and leaned back into his chair, showing his age more in the slump of his shoulders than the lines that marked his face. It was the least guarded Giovanni had ever seen him.

"How is she, really?"

Giovanni took a deep breath and tried to release the tension. "She is grieving. Her father and her sire."

"It would have been better if I had sired her." Ernesto waved a hand as Giovanni opened his mouth to protest. "I know you think I have my own designs on her future, and I will not deny it. She was an extraordinary human, and she will be an even more extraordinary immortal, even the Elders of Penglai recognized it."

"She already is."

"But now she grieves doubly for Stephen De Novo. It would have been better if I had been her father in this life."

Tenzin's words echoed in his mind. *"She is exactly who she will need to be."*

"I think," Giovanni began, "things had to happen exactly as they did,

Alvarez. Some things happen for a reason. Even if we cannot see the purpose of it."

Ernesto looked amused. "You have been spending time with the holy men, di Spada. That is not the rational man that I have come to know."

Perhaps not. But Giovanni only shrugged.

"Or." Ernesto smirked. "Has marriage softened you?"

"If it has, I'd better toughen up. Your granddaughter is not a woman, or a vampire, to be underestimated."

The old man burst into laughter. Giovanni only smiled as the immortal took another sip of wine.

"My son"—Ernesto curled his lip briefly—"says that her fighting skills are quite advanced."

"They are. And she says Baojia is an excellent instructor."

Ernesto's shoulders straightened. "Baojia failed in his mission. He will be dealt with."

Giovanni frowned. "He was a fierce ally in our battle. I would gladly fight at his side again."

"My son had one job. To protect my granddaughter from harm. It was not to rescue some humans or retrieve a book. One task was required of him, and he failed. He will be dealt with."

Giovanni's instinctive reaction was to defend the water vampire, but he closed his mouth. Beatrice may have been under her own aegis, but Baojia was not. He still answered to his sire, and Giovanni knew he must respect that.

So he nodded and rose to his feet. "I hope you understand, but I must leave you. I have much to do to prepare for our journey."

Ernesto rose and shook his hand. "Of course. I'll call Kirby and go by the hanger to see my granddaughter tonight."

"Of course." Giovanni turned to go, but halted when he heard Ernesto's voice.

"You will take care of her, di Spada. You may be her husband, but I am her kinsman. If any harm should come to her—"

Ernesto halted when Giovanni turned. The waft of smoke that drifted across the room matched the low growl of his voice when he finally spoke. "It would be wise of you not to finish that sentence, Don Ernesto Alvarez."

The two vampires stood, measuring each other from a distance. Finally, it was Ernesto that let a smile touch his lips. "Welcome to the family."

Giovanni turned and left the room, shutting the door firmly behind him. He had only taken a few steps when Baojia appeared out of a dark hallway.

"Di Spada."

"Baojia."

They stood in silence. When Baojia finally met his eyes, Giovanni saw the flash of quick grief the water vampire carefully smothered. Then, as before, his dark gaze revealed nothing.

"You will give my regards to your wife."

"I'm sure she would return the sentiment."

The shorter man offered a rueful smile and looked over Giovanni's shoulder, down the dark hallway were he had emerged. "I'll be going to San Diego for some time. I may not see you when you return."

"San Diego?"

"As you may imagine, my father is displeased with me at the moment. I go where he chooses to send me."

Another silence filled the hall until Giovanni finally spoke. "She does not blame you."

Baojia only hummed a little and nodded. "She should." He walked past Giovanni, toward the study where Ernesto waited. "She *should* blame me."

Cochamó Valley, Chile
December 2010

"When will I be able to see her?"

"Probably not for some time. Around a year. But I put a radio at our house, so you'll be able to call from the lodge."

Ben sat silently for a few minutes, playing with a torn seam on Isabel and Gustavo's couch.

Giovanni cleared his throat and knit his hands together. "How is your room here?"

The boy shrugged. "Good, I guess."

"You realize that I'm only a few minutes away if you need me."

Ben rolled his eyes. "Gio, I'm not a little kid. Isabel and Gus are cool. And the Revertes are cool, too. I'll be fine."

"We'll continue to study as we used to, and we'll take a trip into Santiago after the New Year. I'll show you some of the city."

"Yeah," Ben nodded. "Sounds fun."

"And you can teach the Reverte boys how to play basketball."

Ben snorted. "Really, I'm fine."

Giovanni still felt guilty pulling the boy away from the friends he had made in his semester at school. Ben was a social child, and Dez said he had thrived at the private school he had been attending.

"It's only for a year; it will be a good experience. Your Spanish will get much better. You can learn how to ride a horse, go mountain climbing. I'll teach you to shoot, and we'll start training soon, as well."

"Gio," Ben squirmed. "I really don't think I have to learn all the sword stuff, you know? I mean, we're not living in the dark ages, I—"

"It's not an option, Benjamin." He crossed his arms. "I will not have you unable to protect yourself."

"It's just, swords are kind of old, you know? I mean, the martial arts stuff is cool, and I'm excited about jujitsu with Gus. But swords…"

"Are very practical in our world. You need to learn how to use one, and you are fourteen now. By the time I was fourteen, I could already handle a blade. You're more than capable. You're strong now, and you'll get stronger. It is important to train your muscles young."

"I just mean, I'm already pretty good with a rifle, and if you teach me how to shoot better—"

"Do you think that any gun will kill a vampire?"

Ben reddened at Giovanni's harsh tone. "No, I just—"

"It is not an option. We are taking this year to regroup, but that is all. You are old enough to know now. You are old enough to defend yourself and others." Giovanni tried to soften his voice. "Do you know what it would do to her… to both of us if anything were to happen to you, Benjamin?"

The boy blushed a deep red from either anger or embarrassment. "Okay."

"We will start after Christmas."

"I said okay."

Giovanni let the hint of defiance pass unmentioned.

"What does she do up there all by herself? Is she bored? She can't use her computer anymore, can she?"

He looked up at Ben, noting the look of concern on the boy's face. "She reads. And runs at night. Or swims. She likes both."

Benjamin smiled. "I bet she's super fast now, huh?"

"Very super fast," he said.

"Is Carwyn really coming for a visit?"

"Yes."

"That's good. She'll be happy to see him."

Giovanni nodded. His wife had been quiet, speaking more with Isabel than with anyone else. He hoped that Carwyn's visit would help to heal her wounds. He knew from his own experience that most healing only came with time.

"Hey, G?"

He looked up at Benjamin's plaintive tone. "Yes, Benjamin?"

"She's going to be all right, though. Right?"

He stared at the boy for a long moment, wishing he could will the months away.

"She'll be fine."

. . .

THE FORCE OF WIND

He entered the house quietly, careful not to disturb her as she sat near the fire, reading.

"How is he?"

Giovanni slid behind Beatrice on the couch, picking her up so she sat on his lap. "He's fine. He likes Isabel and Gustavo. He'll get to know the Revertes soon enough."

"Does he know they have a very cute daughter his age?"

"I have a feeling that information will brighten his outlook considerably."

She nestled back into his chest, and his skin hummed happily wherever she touched.

"You're going to start training him soon, right? You and Gus?"

It had been Beatrice, even more than Giovanni, who had been adamant about Ben receiving self-defense, shooting, and weapons training. He had been reluctant to force the discipline on the boy, but she had insisted to the point of tears. Giovanni knew it was a good precaution, so he had pushed the memories of his own forced training from his mind and focused on what was best for Ben.

"We will start after the holidays, Tesoro. Don't be anxious. Give him some time to get adjusted."

"Okay." She fell silent again, and he looked down to what she was reading. It was a collection of C.S. Lewis essays he had seen her paging through more than once. He pulled the book from her fingers, making sure to mark the page she had been reading.

"Carwyn is coming in a few weeks."

"That's good. It'll be nice to see him."

"I thought so."

She was silent for a few minutes more, staring into the fire as he stroked her hair.

"You should see whether Gus and Isabel can get a wrestling match on their satellite dish."

He chuckled, pleased to hear the spark of humor that lit her voice. "I should."

There was another silence, and the only sound was the pop of the logs crackling in the fireplace. Even in the middle of summer, Beatrice asked for a fire if he was leaving the house. She seemed to be almost constantly chilled.

"I'm fine, you know. I'm going to be fine."

He nodded and tucked her head into his shoulder. "I know."

"So don't hover."

Giovanni grinned and picked her up, carrying her to the bedroom. "Wanting my wife's attention is hovering?"

"Oh... I just realized." Her head fell against his shoulder. "We're going to hear it from Carwyn about the wedding thing, aren't we?"

"I'm sure needling us about that is on the agenda right after wrestling."

She kissed his jaw and leaned up to whisper, "Can we un-invite him at this point?"

"No." He kicked the bedroom door closed. "But you can feign irrationally losing your temper as much as you like. He'll be expecting that from a young vampire."

She put her hand on his cheek, turning it so she could look into his eyes. For the first time in weeks, Giovanni saw a glimpse of the warm joy that usually marked her gaze.

She smiled. "Excellent. It's good to have a plan."

He tossed her in the middle of the bed with a mischievous smile. "Yes, it is."

London, England
March 2011

THE SWAN WITH TWO NECKS HAD LOST NONE OF ITS GRIMY DOCKLANDS charm in the year since Giovanni's last visit. As he sat in the booth, waiting for Tywyll, he looked at the printout of the e-mail Carwyn had sent through Benjamin.

> *Giovanni,*
>
> *We're having far more fun without you here. No lessons are being completed. Ben and I are drinking, smoking, and chasing women in Santiago next weekend. Please stay in the cold weather as long as you like, it's nice and warm here. Also, I've bought my nephew an off-road motorbike. I am now his favorite uncle.*
>
> *Your wife is fine. I'm only calling her your wife now because I was able to properly marry you two. Thank the heavens you're no longer living in sin. Sadly for you, she has finally decided that I am more fun to be with, so we will promptly be tempting God's wrath to run away together to Hawaii. Also, we went hunting last week. She likes pigs as much as you do.*
>
> *Carwyn*
>
> *P.S. She's well. But take care of things and come home. You are missed.*

He felt Tywyll enter the pub and looked up. The old water vampire motioned to the man behind the bar before he sat across from Giovanni, taking out a brown-wrapped parcel from under his arm and setting it on the table.

"This is for yer wife. Some journals that Stephen left with me."

"What kind of journals?"

"Did ye ever buy that boat you were talkin' about?"

"Why did I need to come all the way to London for these?"

"Did ye go with a powered vessel, or a sailing one? I always recommend sails, less mechanics to go wrong fer our sort. Of course, with the *Mariposa* being as she is, any further form of propulsion is somewhat redundant, isn't it?"

He placed his hand on the package, sliding it across the scarred table and looking into Tywyll's eyes.

"Why," he asked again, "did I need to come here for these? You could have sent them with Gemma's father. Why did I need to leave my wife to come fetch these like an errand boy?"

Tywyll paused, a look of sadness flickering over his rough face. "How is she?"

He paused for a moment. "She's coping. She's adapting very well to this life. She is extremely strong."

"Did I hear correctly that your old partner had a hand in that?"

He paused before deciding to confide in Tywyll. In reality, the old vampire seemed genuine. And if Stephen had trusted him...

Giovanni had received a letter from him the previous month, volunteering the information that Beatrice's father had left things with Tywyll in the event of his death that Stephen intended for Beatrice. Tywyll, much to Giovanni's annoyance, had insisted he collect the items in person.

"She did. Tenzin and Stephen were mated, so yes, Beatrice is partly of her blood, which is... very strong."

"Oh," Tywyll grinned. "Clever Stephen. Well done, lad. And well done, Tenzin."

As always, Giovanni wondered how extensive the immortal's connections were. He seemed to know a little bit about everyone and everything, though Giovanni had never heard of the old man traveling farther than up and down the river.

"She'll be a day-walker, as well. As Stephen became."

A smile lifted the corner of Tywyll's mouth. "Excellent. You'll give her my regards and my condolences."

Giovanni nodded. "My condolences to you, as well. I know you considered him a friend."

Tywyll paused as the barman set down two pints on the old table. "I did. I *do*. I don't happen to believe that significant things like souls just disappear. That's energy, isn't it? That's our element. And if there's one thing we know, the elements always remain."

"Nothing remains, save us and the elements."

The old memory from his father startled him. Giovanni blinked and took a sip of his beer, enjoying the sharp bite of the hops on his tongue.

"Tywyll?"

"Aye, lad?"

He paused before he took a chance. "Do you consider me a friend?"

The old man cocked an eyebrow at him. "Not yet."

"Do you consider my wife a friend?"

"I consider her a responsibility. But a pleasant one."

"I know you told Stephen you would care for her if he died."

"Ye've known that for over a year." He took another drink. "What do ye want, fire-starter?"

Giovanni paused, weighing the odds before he spoke. Someone had found Stephen. In the years he had hidden from the immortal world, one vampire had always found him. Whatever Tywyll may have said, if the old vampire had taught Stephen how to hide, then he could teach someone else how to find him.

"Who was Stephen's contact in Rome?"

A minute flicker in Tywyll's eye let Giovanni know that he'd hit his mark.

"Who says I know what yer talking about?"

"I do. There was a contact. An information source. One who knew exactly what Stephen had and whom he was hiding from. One who knew how to find him and get in contact with him when he wanted to."

Tywyll didn't look at him; he quietly sipped his pint as his eyes scanned the pub.

"And what if he did? What business is that of yers? You don't have Stephen's book now, do you?"

"No." He leaned forward. "I don't, but my son does. And I don't know exactly what was in it. I don't know the formula that Geber wrote, but I know what Stephen claimed it contained. And I know that Zhang Guo's most brilliant student told me that there was something that my son wouldn't understand, even if he got his hands on the formula."

Tywyll narrowed his eyes. "I'm not interested in formulas or elixirs, fire-starter. I have no use for them. What is it that you want? Speak plain or leave me to my beer."

"I want the name of Stephen's contact. And I think you know who it is, because I think you told him how to find Stephen."

Giovanni sat back in his seat, watching Tywyll deliberate in silence. Stephen's contact had pointed him in the right direction too many times for his involvement to be coincidental.

"And if I do know of this contact's name, why would I give it to you? You've no need to stay one step ahead of Lorenzo."

"On the contrary, I have even more reason to stay one step ahead of him. My son has this book. If it does what Stephen thought it did, he has a purpose for it, and it won't be a good one. Anyone who has truly studied it is dead or missing. Anyone who had any sort of understanding of it is gone... except for four vampires that I can think of."

A strange gleam came to Tywyll's eyes. "Four, eh?"

Giovanni nodded slowly. "Four immortals, who are hopefully still living.

Balanced. One water, one wind, one earth, and one fire. Whomever Geber used in his research knew about the formula, possibly better than Geber himself. If Geber's manuscript is out of reach, then I will make it my mission to find the immortals who helped author it, and I think Stephen's contact was one of them."

Tywyll took another drink. Then he smiled. The old vampire chuckled and slid the brown-wrapped parcel across the table.

"Well then, Giovanni Vecchio, I suppose ye have some reading to do."

EPILOGUE

Plovdiv, Bulgaria
March 2011

Dr. Paskal Todorov shut off the light in the empty lab and shrugged on his brown overcoat to face the brisk wind outside. He sighed as he looked around the empty laboratory that had once employed so many men and women making high-end cosmetics for the European market.

Though their corporate office in Rome had given them enough funding to keep the building in good repair and to employ a few of the highest-grade chemists, they had not worked on a new project in months, and the majority of the employees had sought work elsewhere in the city's growing economy.

He was walking out of the lab and to his warm office late on Friday night to shut down the computers when the lights in the hallway flickered. He frowned and made a mental note to ask the janitor about the wiring. It had been replaced only the year before, right before they had ceased regular operations.

Todorov turned into his office and started when he saw the corporate representative who had visited them right before the shutdown sitting in the chairs and playing with one of the perfume samples that sat in a small beaker on his desk.

"Signor Andros! What a surprise. I was just closing the lab and getting ready to return home for the weekend. I hope you have not been waiting for me long. Did you call the office to tell them you would be arriving tonight? If you did, I am sorry. I was not informed."

The blond head covered in curls turned. A smirk twisted his mouth. "This is rose oil?"

Todorov frowned. "Yes, it is. The finest Bulgarian rose oil. My country is known for it."

Andros nodded and set the beaker back in its wooden cradle. The young man had always set him on edge, though Todorov could never say exactly why. Andros smiled, then held a hand toward the doctor's chair, but no warmth reached his vivid blue eyes.

"I came quite at the last minute, Dr. Todorov. I hope you don't mind. I am only glad I was able to catch you before the weekend."

"Well." The chemist took off his overcoat and sat behind his desk, picking up the silver letter opener his wife had given him for his birthday and fidgeting with the handle. "How can I help you, Signore? I hope that our reports have been favorable. I confess, we are eager for a new project to keep our employees busy. I hope that there has been no irregularity that has caused—"

"No irregularity, Doctor. None. Your records indicate a very well-run lab with seven chemists on staff. Your specialty was in botanical cosmetics, was it not?"

Todorov nodded. "Indeed it was. We had excellent results using the traditional botanicals produced locally and incorporating them into high-end cosmetics. Our products were very well received."

"And were all the botanical ingredients produced organically?"

Todorov nodded again. "Yes, it is what the corporate office requested. It costs more, of course, but the results and marketing made it—"

"Cost is not an issue on this proposed project."

The scientist brightened. "So there is a project from Rome? How excellent. The chemists will be—"

"There will be a project." Andros reached into his coat. "Providing you have ready access to these ingredients produced organically. And you have the quantities indicated."

Todorov took the paper from Andros's pale hand and looked it over. Some of the ingredients were unusual. A few, almost medieval. He frowned. "I'm afraid, Signore, that some of these are not produced commercially in Bulgaria." He glanced up to see the pale Italian's eyes frost over. "However," he continued quickly, "most of them are, and the others can be quite easily obtained. In fact, I know of a farmer we have used for specialty products who works primarily for the perfume industry. He can grow almost anything if it is ordered. Indeed, that would be ideal because we could ensure all the ingredients meet your particular requirements for quality. He even has extensive greenhouses."

Andros's smile immediately warmed. "Excellent. And when can we expect those ingredients to be ready?"

"It is March now." Todorov shrugged. "If money is no object, we could, perhaps, have some within a few months. I will have to talk to the grower."

693

"Of course, Todorov. I'm so happy I chose you; I was told you had a... flexible mind."

"Oh?"

"Indeed." Andros rose and turned to leave the office. "We will start production on the formula next winter, if all goes according to projections."

"May I ask, Signore?" He examined the odd formula at the bottom of the page. "What is it that we are producing? I confess, I have never seen anything like this. It is most…"

Andros cocked his blond head innocently. "Yes?"

"Unusual, Signor Andros. It is quite unlike any other formula I have worked on."

"Oh," Andros chuckled. "I'm quite sure of that."

A niggling fear began to work its way into Todorov's mind. "Signore, while none of this appears dangerous, I feel I have a responsibility to my employees and your customers to make sure that nothing we produce could ever be considered—"

Andros's laugh cut him off. "Oh, it's quite harmless, Todorov. It's an old beauty formula. A 'lost secret' so to speak. It was recently discovered and our marketing team thought it worthy of investigation. The sales pitch alone was enough to tempt them. 'An ancient formula for health and rejuvenation.' Buy the wisdom of the ancients for a reasonable price!"

"Oh." Todorov almost laughed at his own paranoia. "So it is a beauty product?"

"Oh yes." Signor Andros smiled again and an inadvertent shiver ran down Paskal Todorov's spine, despite the warmth of his cozy office.

"One could almost call it… the elixir of life."

END OF BOOK THREE

A FALL OF WATER

The fall of dropping water wears away the stone.
—Lucretius

PROLOGUE

Cochamó Valley, Chile
2011

JANUARY

"What's that?"

Giovanni winked over his shoulder as he backed into the living room. "Another bookcase."

Beatrice rolled her eyes as Gustavo stumbled into the room. "Ha ha. Funny, it sure looks like a piano."

"And not one that was easy to get here," Gustavo said.

"Gio, why did you bring a piano to the house?"

"Because we're going to be here for at least a year, and I like the piano."

She shrugged and turned back to the fire and her book.

"And I thought maybe you would like to learn, too."

She glanced over at the two vampires. "I'm not very musical."

"I know," Gustavo said. "I've heard you hum."

"Hey!" She tossed a pillow at him, but he only laughed as he and Giovanni maneuvered the piano into a corner of the living room near the bookcases. It was a small upright, shiny black, and blended nicely with the dark wood and wrought iron, which decorated their mountain home. Much smaller than Giovanni's grand piano at their house in Los Angeles, she knew he would enjoy playing it just as much.

Beatrice heard footsteps crossing the meadow and rose to meet the visitor at the door. It was Isabel, carrying the bench for the piano.

"They forgot this!" she called as she climbed the steps. "I'm amazed it all made it into the valley in one piece."

Gustavo walked over and took the bench from her. "We didn't forget it, woman. We may have inhuman strength, but we still only have two hands apiece."

Isabel sat next to Beatrice and put her arm around the younger woman. "How are you? I haven't seen you since Christmas."

"Fine." She nodded. "Good. I've been doing a lot of reading."

"Ben's doing well. He and Father are thick as thieves."

Beatrice smiled. "Well, that's not a surprise. They're about the same age, mentally."

Isabel's laugh pealed out and Beatrice saw Gustavo look up, watching his wife with a small smile as he helped Giovanni.

"You're right, you know; you missed the wrestling match. I've never... I don't think there are words to describe that scene."

"I was sorry to miss it, but I didn't want to spoil Ben's fun by, you know, draining him or something."

Isabel nodded. "Good point. Nice of you to be so thoughtful."

"I try."

Isabel raised a knowing eyebrow. "Really?"

Beatrice took a deep breath and swallowed the lump that had risen in her throat. "I'm... trying."

Isabel leaned over and squeezed her shoulders in a quick hug before she rose from the couch. "I'll see you later. If you want a break from this one"—she pointed at Giovanni—"just use the radio."

"Thanks."

Giovanni scowled at Isabel. "Why would she want a break from me?"

Beatrice snickered as Isabel gave him a dry look, then pulled Gustavo out the door, muttering under her breath about "stubborn, donkey men."

Giovanni sat next to her on the couch, tossing more flames toward the dwindling fire, even though it was summer. He frowned and looked into the bright flames, which lit the dim cabin. "So, you really don't have any interest in learning the piano?"

Beatrice leaned into his shoulder and shrugged. "Like I said, I'm not musical."

FEBRUARY

"I'm sick of you!" Beatrice threw a copy of *Moby Dick* at Giovanni.

He caught it and slammed it on the coffee table, wincing at the crack of wood underneath the book. "It's a good thing that was a mass market edition, woman! And I'm not particularly thrilled with you right now, either."

She stalked toward him, shoving a finger in his chest. He could see her fangs descended in anger and feel her heart racing. "You know, at least you're not stuck up in this cabin, miles away from any other person. I can't even visit most of them because I'd probably end up drinking them for dinner! Add to that, I'm awake in here all day with nothing to do but read. You, at least, get to sleep for longer than a few hours!"

Giovanni stepped closer, ignoring Carwyn, who stared at them from the couch with wide eyes. "At least I don't blame you for things that are entirely out of my control, Beatrice. It's not my fault that you're awake most of the day."

"You don't even *try* to stay awake."

His mouth gaped. "You're being completely irrational right now. I refuse to continue this discussion—"

"Don't you use the professor voice on me!"

Giovanni saw Carwyn sneaking toward the door. "I'm just—" the priest stammered, "I'll be..." He slipped out and they paused, waiting for the sound of their friend escaping through the forest.

Giovanni waited for only a moment before he grabbed Beatrice, lifting her up as she wrapped her legs around his waist. "Nicely done, Tesoro," he murmured as his lips devoured the skin along her neck.

Her hands were already ripping his shirt. "I thought he was never going to leave."

"Mmm." He growled as she nipped at his collarbone. "Why is it so sexy when you yell at me?" They stumbled toward the bedroom and Giovanni nudged the door closed with his hip.

"Probably"—she panted as Giovanni tore her shirt down the front—"the same reason I find the professor voice strangely hot."

"Let's not question it, shall we?"

MARCH

She sat alone on the porch, staring into the clear night sky. Carwyn had gone back to Isabel and Gustavo's house to watch a movie with Ben, so Beatrice sat, holding the printout of the e-mail from Giovanni in London.

Six more days.

It was the longest they had ever been apart since he had returned to her. Three weeks. Considering they could be together for hundreds, if not thousands of years, Beatrice knew she should probably be grateful for the solitude.

Six more days.

She sensed Isabel coming through the trees. Even though they could move swiftly, it was considered rude to just appear at someone's doorstep in the quiet valley commune. So even vampires usually approached at human speed unless there was an emergency, or they were expected.

Isabel said not a word as she sat next to Beatrice on the carved wooden bench that Gustavo had made for them as a wedding present.

"Deirdre and Ioan used to separate for months at a time when they were first together... well, after the first fifty years or so. They were both so independent. They once went a year and a half apart, totally by choice, just sending letters to each other. Ioan was at our brother's castle in Scotland and Deirdre was on some island in the North Sea."

"Really?" If Isabel intended her words to be some strange comfort, she wasn't successful. Beatrice felt even more feeble thinking about Deirdre and Ioan's resilient marriage.

"My Gustavo and I though..." Isabel smiled to herself. "We can't be without each other that long. It just doesn't suit us. He is my other half. I went a month without him once and almost went insane. I snapped at everyone. I was so cross."

Beatrice gripped Isabel's hand. "Thanks."

"It doesn't make us weak to need them."

"No?"

Isabel looked over with a smile. "If your right hand was lame, wouldn't your left miss its mate? You might get along without it, but you'd always be aware that something was missing. That's natural, not weak."

"I'm not used..." Beatrice struggled to articulate what had been bothering her for months. "I just feel so tied to him. And to my..."

"Your father. You miss the tie to your father."

"Yes," she whispered, blinking back tears. "I mean, even more than when I thought he had died when I was a girl. There's just this big, empty void in my chest. When Giovanni's here, it helps. Especially when we—" She broke off, suddenly reluctant to continue.

Isabel chuckled. "No need to be embarrassed. When you exchange blood, it's very intimate. It's a tie of another sort, and one that will eventually surpass the tie you felt with your father. It's natural. And it's natural that you feel this void from your father's loss." She put an arm around Beatrice's shoulders and pulled her into an embrace. "If I even think about losing Father... It's too horrible to contemplate. And I was sired over five hundred years ago. For you? You were a newborn when he was lost, his blood still fresh in your veins. I cannot imagine it, Beatrice. You should never feel weak. I believe you are one of the strongest young women I have had the privilege of knowing."

Beatrice sniffed. "So I'm not a big baby for missing my dad like this? Some days, I feel like I barely want to leave my room. And then when Giovanni left... Honestly, if Carwyn would leave me alone more, I would curl up under the covers and never come out."

"And that is why he pesters you so much."

She snorted. "Yeah, I kind of figured."

"You are loved, Beatrice De Novo. By so many. On your darkest days, don't forget that."

APRIL

He woke in their bed, alone; her sheets were not even rumpled.

"Beatrice?"

There was no answer. He raced out to the living room, where all the windows had been blacked out and covered by curtains so she could have the freedom of the house during the daylight hours.

"Beatrice?"

She was sitting by the fire, staring into it with blank eyes. There was an open textbook on her lap.

"Tesoro?"

She finally blinked and turned to him.

He walked toward her slowly. "Did you sleep at all today? Have you been reading this whole time?"

Beatrice looked down to the book on her lap, then over at Giovanni, who sat down beside her.

"I can read Greek now." His heart sank when he saw the lost look she wore. "Do you think he knows?"

Giovanni reached over and closed the book, taking both her hands in his before he pulled her onto his lap. "Yes."

MAY

He teased her as she stood in the kitchen, warming the blood before she drank.

"Come outside. Swim with me. We'll go to the waterfall." He stood behind her, wrapping his arms around her waist and nipping at the hollow behind her earlobe.

She shrugged as she stirred the blood. "It's getting cold now."

"So I'll heat up the pool. You're married to a fire vampire; take advantage of me however you like. I'll make it a hot tub if that's what you want. Just come swimming. Go running. Leave the house."

"Gio, you're acting like I'm a hermit or something. I've just got a lot to read right now and I'm working on my Persian so I can read the journals, and—"

"And you haven't left the house in a week."

She frowned. "It hasn't... it's only been a couple of days." *Hadn't it?*

He turned her around so she was facing him. "The last night you left the house was the night Carwyn had to leave, and that was over a week ago."

Beatrice took a drink of the blood. It wasn't as fresh as she liked it, but they had to order blood from Puerto Montt or drink pig's blood, so she was willing to put up with the stale taste if it meant no pigs. "Fine. I'll go swimming."

Giovanni cocked an eyebrow. "Don't sound so excited."

She mustered up a giant, fake grin and plastered it on her face. "There," she said through gritted teeth, "see how excited I am?"

He narrowed his eyes, then pinched her waist and stuck his tongue out in her direction. Her jaw dropped. "Did you just stick your tongue out at me?"

"Yes," he said. "I've been wanting to do that for years."

She only looked at him, confused, before she burst into laughter. Beatrice laughed and laughed, bending over as bloody tears came to her eyes. She heard Giovanni chuckle a little, but knew he was only laughing at her own amusement.

It was the loudest she had laughed in months.

JUNE

"Have you bitten anyone yet?"

She cleared her throat. *Well, Ben, just your uncle, but you really don't need to know about that, do you?* Beatrice took a pencil, pressing on the button on the front of the radio phone to reply. "Nope. I'm clean so far."

"Good." She heard Ben reply. "Just remember, if you do need to drain someone, make sure it's someone really evil or really annoying. Or my geometry teacher, though that would be a pretty long way to travel for a meal."

"Got it. And, of course, there's the whole 'killing an innocent human being' thing, too."

"Oh, he's not innocent; he gives pop quizzes."

Beatrice laughed. "Ben, I'm not going to kill your math teacher."

"I'm just saying, when we get home, keep it in mind. I'm pretty sure no one would miss him."

"Right." She played with the edge of her book, trying not to notice Giovanni hovering in the corner. He wore a small, satisfied smirk that she was interacting with the outside world again. "So, how's school? How's everything going?"

"Can Gio hear us?"

She muffled a laugh and pressed the respond button again. "Yes."

"Oh, well then, it's going magnificently. I'm so fortunate to have a knowledgeable and patient teacher like my uncle, who is imparting his centuries of wisdom into my eager young mind."

Beatrice was rolling on the couch, laughing, when Giovanni walked over and pressed the respond button. "Tell me more, oh eager young nephew, who will be translating an extra passage of Virgil tomorrow afternoon."

"Dude!" Ben protested. "Gio, that's not cool. Hear her laughing? When was the last time you made her laugh like that?"

Giovanni cocked his head at Beatrice and let an evil grin cross his face.

Beatrice stopped laughing and leaped on him. "You better not!" she hissed as they tumbled to the floor, breaking one of the dining room chairs as they rolled.

"Whatever could you be talking about?" He laughed as he trapped her legs between his own and rolled on top of her. "I was simply going to tell him how much you like it when I—"

Beatrice cut him off with a kiss, rolling them over so that she was lying on his chest. She pinned him at the shoulders as the speakerphone squawked in the background.

"Guys? Gio? Did you short out the phone again?" Giovanni and Beatrice continued to roll across the dining room and into the living room, taking out another chair as each tried to best the other in their playful wrestling match.

"B? Can you hear me?"

Giovanni gripped her hips and rocked against her, ignoring the voice in the background.

"You guys are fooling around, aren't you?" Ben sighed over the line. "That's so gross."

They didn't notice when the phone clicked.

JULY

"What were you thinking?" He patted her face with cool cloths, more for his own peace of mind than anything else. She was already healing.

"I just wanted to see a glimpse of it," she said sullenly. "Just a... sliver. I didn't think I would burn that fast."

He fought back the scream he wanted to level at her. "You're too young, Tesoro. You just—" He broke off and clutched her to his chest, frightened beyond words. "Do you realize what would have happened if I hadn't been quick enough?"

"Crispy critter," she said as she pulled away from him. "I'm fine."

"Do not make light of this."

"Don't order me around."

He clutched her shoulders again and spoke in a hard voice, holding fast when she tried to squirm away. "Do you realize what it would do to me? To Benjamin?"

"Not fair."

"To Isadora? To Caspar? How about Carwyn?"

"Shut up!" She shoved him away and tried to stand, but her eyes were still blinded from the seconds of sun she had felt on her face.

"How about Dez? Matt? Isabel? Gustavo? Tenzin?"

"Tenzin does not give two shits about me, Gio!" She rose to her feet and grabbed the back of the couch.

He grabbed her hand. "You know that's not true."

"Then where the hell is she?"

AUGUST

He was playing again. He often did right before dawn. Relaxing things. Slow melodies by Bach or Satie or Chopin. Things he knew she loved. She wondered if it was an attempt to quiet her and let her rest, even though she rarely took comfort in sleep anymore. There were only a few hours a day that she was able to sleep. She didn't tire, but she did envy the peaceful oblivion that slumber had once provided.

And dreaming. She missed dreaming.

Beatrice approached the piano, sliding next to Giovanni on the narrow bench he had pushed back to fit his long legs. He didn't cease playing the Nocturne when he leaned over and kissed her.

"Hello."

"Hey."

"Want me to show you a few things?"

"Nope."

"A little Mozart melody?" His fingers tripped up the keys. "You'll be amazed by how fast you pick it up."

"Still nope."

SEPTEMBER

"How could you?" She threw him into the face of the cliff, tossing him as if he weighed nothing when he finally caught up with her on the road back to the valley.

"He was old. He was going to die within a few weeks, Beatrice."

She paced back and forth in the small clearing. "But *I* didn't need to be the one to kill him." Streaks of crimson tears marred her perfect white skin. The rain beat down on them and the wind whipped through the small pass.

He tried to speak in a low, calming voice. "You broke out of the bloodlust much quicker than I had imagined. You're doing very well."

"But I still killed him, Gio! I did. And you stood there and let me. You stood by and let me kill that old man doing nothing more than sitting in his garden."

Giovanni slowly stood, still keeping his distance. "If he had been in good health, you would not have killed him. But he was sick, Tesoro. Surely, you must have tasted it in his blood. He was in pain. Your amnis calmed him as you drank. He didn't feel anything."

She screamed and pulled at her hair. "How could you let me kill him?"

"It was a mercy."

"No!" she yelled and rushed him, knocking him over and pummeling his face.

She loosed her rage on her mate until he grabbed her hands. He could barely contain her; Beatrice had become almost immeasurably strong. "Why? Why did you let me murder him?"

With a surge, he rolled over until she was lying under him, sobbing in the rain as the bloody tears ran down her face and into the mud.

"This is why! Do you understand? Look at me, Beatrice." He finally caught her narrowed eye and she bared her teeth at him. "Look at me and listen right now. Did I let you kill that old man? Yes, and I'll tell you why."

He took a softer hand and brushed at the tears that stained her cheeks. "Because one day, very soon, it's not going to be a sick stranger in a garden that tempts you." He sat back and pulled her to sit in front of him, the rain still beating on their backs.

"Someday very soon, it's going to be Benjamin. Or your grandmother. Or Caspar or Dez or Matt. It's going to be someone you love. An innocent stranger on a train or walking down the street at night. And the temptation is going to knock you over and every instinct in you is going to be screaming to take and drink and not to stop because there is *nothing* in the human world more powerful than you. Do you understand what I'm saying?" He grabbed the collar of her soaked overcoat and pulled her closer. She still stared at him with sullen, tear-filled eyes as he continued.

"And when that moment comes, I want you to remember how you feel right now. I want you to remember this moment for the rest of your existence because that is what will keep the humans around you safe from the monster that lives inside you. That lives inside all of us."

Her eyes were dull as she stared at him. Her hands limp and lying at her sides.

"I hate you."

"I love you."

OCTOBER

"Beatrice?"

She glanced at him, but didn't speak.

"Have you fed tonight?"

He looked so calm as he wrapped his needless scarf around his neck and prepared to go down to the lodge for Ben's lessons.

She nodded.

"Call if you need anything."

She shrugged and turned back to the fire. They hadn't exchanged blood since she had killed the old man. Her logical brain understood why Giovanni had allowed her to do it, but the gaping void in her chest, the hollow that never seemed to be filled, was only growing deeper the longer she let her anger fester.

And she couldn't see a way to bridge the gap that had opened between them.

An hour later, there was a knock at the door. So focused on the fire, she failed to register the approaching energy. A storm system had moved into the valley, bringing thunder, lightning, and causing her senses to go haywire in the charged air.

Beatrice rose and went to the door, gasping when she recognized the smell of cardamom on the other side. She flung it open and Tenzin was there, silent and soaked from the rain. Her shorn hair hung in thick chunks around her face as she waited on the porch.

Simultaneous rage and love reared up in Beatrice. She raised her hand to strike, but Tenzin only reached out and caught her fist before it made contact. Beatrice shook, then she crumbled to the ground, sobbing out her grief, anger, and heartbreak as her father's mate knelt down and gathered her in an embrace. Tenzin kicked the door closed and tucked Beatrice's head under her chin, rocking her back and forth as Beatrice clutched at her dirty white robes.

"I'm here, my girl. I'm back."

NOVEMBER

"It's normal to feel that, you know."

Tenzin and Beatrice were sparring on the edge of a clearing as one of Gustavo's men looked on. A human, one of the guides that worked in the valley during the summer months, sat at his feet. While Beatrice had very good control around humans most of the time, Tenzin had emphasized the importance of learning how to fight while the distraction was nearby. Considering Lorenzo had used the scent of human blood to pin her and kill her father, Beatrice was quick to agree to the practice, no matter how much her throat burned.

"Feel what?"

"That void from Stephen's loss. It will fade with time, but there will always be a trace. You were sired from his blood; it would be unnatural to not feel the lack of him."

They moved in a dancing fight, Beatrice's style having developed into something uniquely her own in the year since she had turned. It was a melding of the martial arts that she had practiced as a human, Gemma's vicious street-fighting, and Tenzin's flowing, but lethal, ballet. Though Tenzin was still faster, Beatrice was more than able to keep up.

"Do you still feel it?" Tenzin cut her eyes toward Beatrice before she punched out in a swift uppercut.

"Sorry," Beatrice muttered through her fractured jaw. "Stupid question."

"Have you talked to Giovanni about it?"

"Why?"

Tenzin smacked the back of her head. "Are you stupid, girl? Do you forget that he lost his father, too?"

"Oh, well..." Beatrice had no idea how much Tenzin knew about Andros's death, but she wasn't going to say. Giovanni had told her that no one could ever know that he had a hand in the death of his sire. She would not reveal his secrets, not even to Tenzin.

"And however that came about—" Tenzin looked down at the ground. "And I have always had my suspicions—your husband understands the loss you feel. He has felt it himself. If you need to talk to someone, he's the one vampire here that would understand. If you haven't talked to him about it, you're stupid."

Beatrice held a hand up and paused. "Are you coming back with us to L.A.?"

Tenzin frowned. "I suppose I am. Why?"

"Because apparently, I need you to tell me when I'm being stupid."

DECEMBER

She was glowing. Her face may not have blushed anymore, but his wife had been glowing as she sat next to Ben and opened presents earlier that evening. They had gathered at Isabel and Gustavo's house, Beatrice and Giovanni, Tenzin, Carwyn, and Ben. All together, and she had not struggled to control her bloodlust once.

Giovanni imagined that he was glowing, too.

She lay on the couch, stretched out and listening to him play bits and pieces from the Nutcracker Suite as dawn approached. She hummed along, horribly out of tune, as always, but he didn't care. He heard her stand and walk toward him. She placed her hand on his shoulder and he leaned into her arm, rubbing his cheek against her flesh and enjoying the crackling, excited energy that filled the house.

They would go back to Los Angeles soon.

"Gio?"

"Hmm?"

She sat next to him for a moment before she ducked under his arms and straddled his lap. He pulled his hands away to grab her waist, but she winked and placed them back on the keyboard. "Keep playing."

Giovanni chuckled. "What game are you playing, woman?"

She put her arms around his neck, nipping at his ear and nuzzling into his neck. "I think..."

"Yes?" Despite his preternatural concentration, he was having trouble focusing on the Tchaikovsky.

"I think that maybe I do want to learn to play."

His eyes rolled back as she let her fangs scrape along his neck. "Oh, I think you're quite adept at playing already, Tesoro."

"No." She giggled. "An instrument."

"I'm allowing that joke to pass. Too obvious."

She laughed and cuddled into him, wiggling on his lap as he struggled to concentrate on the keyboard. "Not piano though."

"No?"

"No, maybe... guitar. I could be a rock and roll chick. Not electric, obviously... well, maybe I could figure something out. I mean, if I really tried, I could probably figure out a way to make it work. Maybe an insulated case of some kind, but I'd have to make sure it didn't damage the guitar... What?"

He grinned and ceased playing, wrapping his arms around her and pressing his mouth to hers in a long kiss. His hands reached up, running through her hair and teasing the pins out that she had used to put it up earlier.

"I love you madly, Beatrice De Novo."

She smiled and nipped at his chin. "I love you, too."

"Welcome back."

CHAPTER 1

Los Angeles, California
March 2012

Giovanni woke with a start, and Beatrice looked up from across the room. He sat up and swung his legs over the side of their large bed to stare at the photograph of the Ponte Vecchio, which hung on the wall of their bedroom.

"Hey."

He blinked before he looked over at her. Beatrice smiled. Her husband looked as if he was still halfway dreaming.

"Good evening. Did you rest at all today?" He rose and walked to her, bending down to kiss her bare shoulder. He still refused to wear any sort of clothing to bed. Since their room was blocked by a sturdy, reinforced door, multiple locks, and an electronic monitoring system that she'd had custom made for them, Beatrice just decided to enjoy the view. No one would be breaking in.

"I rested a few hours. You looked like you were dreaming. What was it about?"

He shrugged and walked to the small kitchen area, heating a bag of blood and leaning over to sniff the coffee pot she'd added in the corner of their room.

"Was it about your father again?"

He was silent for a few minutes, but she didn't try to fill the space. Giovanni finally turned with a frown on his face. "I don't know why I'm having so many dreams about him."

She cocked her head. "Because of me? Because I lost my dad? Because we've been talking about that?"

"Perhaps."

She had finally taken Tenzin's advice and confided in Giovanni about the gaping wound that Stephen's loss had left. As predicted, he understood completely. Just sharing the hurt had done more to lessen the grief than any of her own efforts.

"Gio... there's no chance that Andros could be alive, is there? I mean, you didn't actually see him die. He was just ash when you woke up. Lorenzo was the one who saw—"

"Beatrice, how did you feel when your father was killed?"

Tears sprang immediately to her eyes. "Like... something was ripped from my chest. Empty. Physical pain would have been a relief."

He only looked at her and nodded. "I felt the same. Despite how much I hated Andros, I loved him, too. And the pain of my father's death woke me from my day rest, even though it was practically impossible to wake me when I was that young. I know he is dead."

"Okay," she whispered. "I'm sorry. I just—"

"It's a valid question. Don't apologize."

He turned and picked up the bag of blood he had heated in warm water, drinking it quickly before he walked across the room. He picked her up and brought her back to the bed. Though she didn't need to sleep, his presence—the silent meditation of his touch—allowed Beatrice to rest her mind.

The sun still peeked through the edges of the windows, so they lay silently, curled together as her amnis wrapped around its mate. Though he didn't move, she could feel Giovanni's invisible energy stroking along her back and neck, fluttering over her skin and soothing her.

"What are you doing tonight?" she asked in a drowsy whisper.

"I'm introducing one of Gustavo's sons to Ernesto. Diego has some business in Los Angeles and he asked for an introduction."

"Oh, you get to play politics. Lucky you."

He pinched her side when she snickered. "Your grandfather asked for you to come, as well, but I made an excuse for you. I'm not going to next time."

She leaned over and kissed him. "Thank you. You're the best husband in the whole room." Beatrice squealed when he dug his fingers into her sides. Immortality had not lessened how ticklish she was. If anything, it had made it worse.

"Why? Why did I sign up for this abuse for eternity? What have I done to deserve this woman?" He chuckled as he continued to tickle her. Soon, she was gasping under him.

"Stop!" she panted. "Stop. I'll..."

An evil grin spread across his face. "You'll what?"

She brought an arm around and trailed her fingers down his back, teasing his spine as he shivered. Giovanni may not have been ticklish, but she knew exactly how to torment him.

"I'll... save some hot water for you!"

Beatrice darted out from under him and into the luxurious bathroom, locking the door behind her. She laughed and started the shower, only to hear the door splinter behind her. Giovanni tossed the broken wood to the side and strode into the room.

"We didn't need that door."

She drove the grey Mustang through the busy streets, pulling up to the old warehouse where Tenzin had set up a practice studio. The ancient wind vampire was already there, and Beatrice could hear her pounding on one of the training dummies.

"You're coming later, right?" Ben grabbed his gym bag and opened the door.

"Yeah, I'm just meeting Dez for dinner, and then I'll come back and practice with you guys for a while."

"No rush. I think she's meaner to me when you're there."

Beatrice laughed and reached across to ruffle his hair as he tried to squirm away.

At fifteen, Ben Vecchio had all the marks of a boy on the verge of manhood. He had shot up the year they had been in Chile and was far taller than she was. Beatrice guessed he would rival Giovanni's height when he was full-grown. His chest was starting to fill out and lose its scrawny appearance, helped along by the intense physical training that Beatrice and Giovanni insisted on for his safety. His curling hair, deep brown eyes, and quick smile already attracted enough female attention to keep a grown man happy, much less a teenage boy.

Ben was well on the way to breaking a few hearts, and Beatrice absolutely adored him.

"Tell Dez I said 'Hi' and let her know I'm here when she gets tired of the old fart."

"She told the old fart she'd marry him, so I have a feeling you're out of luck."

He leaned down and winked. "Engaged is not married, B. There's hope until there's a ring on her finger."

She shook her head. "You're shameless."

"Yep. But I'm cute, too. See ya!" He slapped the top of the car and walked into the warehouse, whistling.

"Shameless," she said as she pulled away.

She turned at El Molina Avenue and parked on the street, glad to have found a parking spot so near the cafe where she and Dez met on Thursday nights. She could already hear a new band warming up inside, and no one was sitting on the patio, so she grabbed a table, glad for the clear night sky. Dez arrived a few minutes later, and Beatrice shoved down the instinctive hunger that tickled the back of her throat.

Though she was used to the scents of her family, close contact with other humans still awakened her instincts. She could easily control it, but that did require some concentration. Her best friend, for whatever reason, smelled particularly appealing that night.

"How are you, hon?" Dez chattered as they both settled into their seats. A waiter came out and they both ordered a coffee and dessert. "How was your week? Matt and Gio are both at that thing at your grandfather's tonight, right? What's Ben up to?"

"Other than still plotting how to steal you from Matt?"

She giggled. "Of course."

"He and Tenzin are practicing tonight."

"How's school going?"

Beatrice nodded. "Good, he seems to have swung right back into his classes since we've been back. Of course, Gio's way more demanding than his high school teachers, so that's not really a surprise."

"Of course."

"The boy could probably pass most college level classes at this point."

"Has he thought about early admission anywhere?"

Beatrice shrugged. "It's not a priority for him. He likes his friends the most now. He still does most of his learning at home with Gio. He only goes to school for girls, basketball, and to have something to do during the day."

They paused to let a group enter the cafe. The lively music spilled out as the door opened, quiet to Dez, but almost distractingly loud to Beatrice's immortal ears.

They chatted as they sipped their coffee, Dez happily filling Beatrice in on her wedding plans. She and Matt had been engaged the previous summer, but had waited until Giovanni and Beatrice had returned from Chile to get married. The wedding was only a few weeks away.

"—so the guests will have the option to eat either chicken or beef. I liked the idea. Of course, the cake looks amazing, but then, it's chocolate, so how it looks isn't all that important. B?"

"Huh?"

"You've been staring at my neck for the past couple minutes, hon."

She blinked. "Oh, sorry."

"No problem. Did you forget to eat before you came? You haven't touched your coffee."

Beatrice wrinkled her nose. "It's really strong. Are you wearing a new perfume or something?"

"No, nothing different."

"Are you…" Beatrice struggled, trying to determine what it was that was triggering her awareness. Scent had taken on an entirely new dimension for her since becoming a vampire. Everything smelled. She had quickly learned to block out as much as possible, so as not to become overwhelmed, but there was something about Dez that night...

"You're pregnant."

Her best friend's mouth gaped, just a little. "Uh... what?"

"I think that's it. You smell... more. I don't know what else it could be. You don't smell sick, and I know you went off birth control a while back, so—"

"How did you know that?" Dez almost looked offended.

Beatrice just shrugged. "Your scent changed. Matt liked it; I could tell."

Dez rolled her eyes. "And I thought being your friend was weird before... and I'm not pregnant. It's only been a couple months, and I haven't even missed my period."

"Well, you will. I'm pretty sure that's it."

Dez just shook her head. "How... I mean, what—"

"I told you, you smell different." Beatrice shrugged again and sipped at her coffee. It really did smell better than it tasted now. Unless she was at home and she could make it watered down, it was overwhelming. "You don't smell *bad*. You smell more... female, if that makes sense. I'm sure it's the hormones. Matt's probably been going nuts around you lately, huh? Humans react to that stuff even if they don't know what it is."

Dez cocked an eyebrow. "Humans, huh?"

"Yup." Beatrice smiled. "So you believe me?"

She shrugged. "Well, since you're a big, bad vampire with a super-strong nose, I guess I have to, though I think I'll still wait for the pathetic human doctor to confirm before I tell my fiancé."

She grinned. "Congratulations! So were you trying?"

Dez flushed. "We weren't *not* trying, if you know what I mean. Matt's older than me; he didn't want to wait. I was game for whatever. I knew I wanted kids and I'll be thirty next month. We're getting married in a couple weeks. No one will care we started a tiny bit backwards."

"I bet Matt's going to be really excited."

"I bet he'll be surprised. I don't think he thought it would happen this fast." She paused. "Heck, I didn't think it would happen this fast, but I suppose this is the logical result of all that sex."

Beatrice snorted. "You're so smart for a human."

Dez narrowed her eyes. "'For a human,' huh? I'm smart for a human?" She tossed her hair, picking up a menu and waving her scent toward Beatrice. "Oh, look at the poor, pathetic human tempting the big, bad vampire. Poor vampire. Hungry are we?"

Beatrice growled low in her throat, feeling her fangs descend, even though she knew she wasn't hungry. "Thtop it."

"Oh!" Dez gasped in mock surprise. "Are those your fangs? How embarrassing. Is there anything you can do about that little situation?"

"You fink you're tho funny."

"I *am* funny." Dez grinned. "Know what else is funny? Your lisp when you talk around your fangs."

Beatrice swallowed the burn in her throat and willed her teeth to ascend. "One of these days, I'm going to bite you. Then you won't think it's so funny."

"You better not. According to your accounts, I might like it a little *too* much."

"Haha."

Dez cackled. "It's hilarious, you look like you *should* be blushing, but you can't."

"Why am I still friends with you?"

"Because I'm awesome. And you're going to be an auntie."

Beatrice couldn't stop the smile that spread across her face and the tug at her heart. Though she had no desire for children, she was thrilled for her friend. "You're going to be an amazing mom, Dez."

"Oh..." Her face fell. "I'm going to get totally fat now. And you'll never get fat. I kind of hate you for that. I wonder if Matt's going to get totally grossed out."

Beatrice shook her head. "Please. Matt adores you. He's going to be thrilled—"

"B?"

She halted at the familiar voice of her ex-boyfriend.

"Beatrice?" She heard him again, but she didn't turn around. Beatrice looked across at Dez, who just looked panicked. "Dez, is that you?"

She could hear Mano approaching the table. Before he could get a good look at her, Beatrice reached out and grabbed his hand, clasping his bare skin in her cool palm and letting her amnis crawl up his arm. She stood and faced him, never easing her grip.

"Hi, Mano," she whispered. She looked over his shoulder, but he appeared to be alone. She looked back into the eyes of the man who had loved her. Who had seen her through one of the loneliest parts of her life with caring and self-sacrifice.

He blinked at her, his eyes already swimming with her influence. "You look different, baby."

"I know."

"You need some sun. Let's go out on the boat tomorrow."

She shook her head. "No, Mano. I'm fine."

"Where have you been? I've missed you."

She swallowed the lump in her throat, searching his face, pained at the loneliness she found. The longing. "I'm fine. And so are you."

"I am?"

"Yes. You saw me and you realized that you had moved on."

"But I love you."

Beatrice gripped his hand, stroking her thumb along the calluses on his palm "No, you've moved on. And you're ready to meet someone new. Someone who will love you as much as you love her."

"I am?" He blinked at her.

"Yep. You saw me, and we caught up. And you heard that Gio and I are married and really happy now, and you were happy, too. Because you realized that you don't love me anymore."

He shook his head, and she forced her influence further into his mind, pushing back the tears at his familiar scent. Mano still smelled like sunshine and the sea.

"Right," he finally said with a small smile. "You look great. I don't love you anymore."

"Nope," she choked out. "And you're going to meet someone great. And you're going to fall in love."

"I am?"

"Yes, you are."

"I've missed you, baby." He smiled at her again, the soft smile he wore when he was sleepy.

"I missed you, too." It wasn't a lie. She had missed Mano, even though she loved Giovanni with all her heart. She forced out a smile. "Bye, Mano. You're going to go home now."

He nodded and leaned down as if to kiss her, but she backed away. He still smiled.

"Bye, B."

She finally let go of his warm hand, and he turned and walked away down the dark street. Beatrice turned back to Dez, pulled her wallet out of her pocket, and threw down some cash. Dez reached over and squeezed her hand. "You okay?"

"Yeah. I need to go."

"That the first time?"

She nodded, forcing back the tears that threatened her eyes. "Yeah, it was just a surprise, you know? I was surprised."

"Well, you did great. And you were really kind to do that. He, um, he called Matt for months. He was worried about you. Will he remember anything?"

Beatrice waved her hand as Dez stood. "Just... vague stuff. He should remember he saw me, but the exact memories will be kind of cloudy. Hopefully, I did it right."

"Are you going to tell Gio you saw him?"

"Yeah, I wouldn't try to hide it. And he'll smell him anyway."

Dez just stared at her before she walked down the street, Beatrice following after. "Vampires are weird."

"I'll remind you of that when you have a giant human parasite sucking the life out of you and making you ill."

"Shut up, bloodsucker."

Beatrice walked into the kitchen behind Ben, who immediately ran upstairs to shower and call one of the girls who had been texting him during his practice.

"Ben," she called, "it's eleven o'clock, and you practiced hard. You better get some sleep."

"Sure thing, B!"

"Goodnight."

"'Night! Night, Isadora!"

She glanced at her grandmother, who was sitting at the kitchen table, reading a book. "Good night, Benjamin."

Beatrice leaned down and placed a soft kiss on her grandmother's delicate cheek. At age seventy-eight, Isadora Alvarez De Novo Davidson had lost none of the liveliness from her vivid green eyes; though her step was slower, her mind was not.

"And how is Dez?"

"Pregnant, but don't tell anyone. It's early."

"Oh!" Isadora smiled. "How wonderful. And the Kirbys will be thrilled."

"It's really early, so Matt doesn't even know. That's why you can't tell anyone."

Isadora frowned. "How early? Matt doesn't know?"

"Nope. I just told her tonight." Beatrice munched on an almond from the bowl her grandmother had out. "She smelled different. I got all fang-y."

Isadora was quiet for a minute. "You know, sometimes it's easy to forget you are a vampire, and sometimes, it's not."

Beatrice grinned and let her fangs run down. Isadora slapped at her shoulder. "Stop it, Mariposa!"

She giggled and took two almonds, sticking them on her fangs and muttering around them. "Yep, thcary, thcary vampire here."

They both broke into giggles, until Beatrice finally calmed down. "Where's Caspar?"

"He drove Matt and Gio to the meeting at Ernesto's."

"Ah."

"I'm going to go to sleep soon. I just thought I'd stay up to say hello. I missed you this afternoon."

"I was in the library."

"Looking at Geber's journals?"

"Yup." The journals, which her father had left in Tywyll's care, were all written in the alchemist's own strange code. In addition to learning Old Persian,

Beatrice was also trying to decipher the peculiar phrases and code words the medieval scientist had used to disguise his research. If she could decode them, they might learn the identity of Geber's original test subjects and be that much closer to solving the mystery of the elixir. Though they hadn't heard a peep from Lorenzo, his presence lurked in her mind, teasing her that the book Stephen had taken was in his possession again.

"Mariposa?"

"Hmm?" She looked up at her grandmother.

"I said I'm going to bed now."

"Oh." She rose and kissed Isadora's cheek. "Night, Grandma."

"I'll see you in the morning."

"I'll probably be in the library around ten or so."

"Have a good night."

Isadora shuffled through the door and down the hall toward the ground floor rooms that Giovanni had converted into a suite for Caspar and Isadora. She could hear Ben walking around upstairs and felt the quiet hum of the electrical currents and waves of Wi-Fi that Matt had installed for Ben. The house may have been quiet, but it was never really still the way their house in Cochamó was, and Beatrice realized why Giovanni would get frustrated if he was surrounded by technology for too long. The modern world, to the senses of an immortal, was relentlessly noisy.

She was happily lost in a novel and curled up in the living room when the sound of the Mercedes broke through. She smiled at Caspar when he walked through the door. The clock on the wall pointed toward one and the old man bent down to kiss her cheek.

"Good night, my dear. I'll see you in the morning. This old man is exhausted."

"Night, Cas."

"What time did she turn in?"

"A few hours ago."

"I'll be joining her. Have fun with him."

"Oh?" She said, "What's that supposed to mean?"

Caspar shrugged. "Don't ask me. He's being terribly silent tonight."

"Huh, weird. He was fine earlier. Did everything go all right with Ernesto?"

"I believe so. He didn't seem upset. Just... quiet."

"Okay. I'll see you in the morning. Night."

He gave her a small salute and walked down the hall just as Giovanni walked through the door. He wore a strange expression and sat beside her. She stared at him as he looked off into the distance. Finally, he reached into his jacket and pulled out a thick, cream envelope with a broken wax seal. The interior was filigreed in gold leaf, and she could see a swirl of calligraphy peeking out from the letter inside.

"Hi. What's this? Caspar said you were doing the moody, silent thing. What's up?"

Giovanni tossed the envelope on her lap and leaned back, throwing an arm around her on the couch.

"Beatrice, how do you feel about Rome in the springtime?"

CHAPTER 2

Crotone, Italy
1494

"Where am I?"

"Your new home."

Jacopo looked around the room, blinking. It looked nothing like the warm chambers of his uncle's villa in Ferrara or the bustling of Benevieni's house in Florence. The dim room where he woke was dark and damp. Though there were clean rushes that littered the floor, the chill of the air seemed to seep in through his bare feet and the smell of the ocean was everywhere. He sat on the edge of a small bed that smelled of sweet straw and herbs.

"This is not my home."

Signor Andros only smiled at him indulgently. The strange man had always bothered Jacopo, though never the same way as the teasing courtiers of Florence or Rome. He had learned at a young age to escape their stealthy hands and avoid their attention, but from the beginning, Niccolo Andros had seemed to be a different sort. Jacopo had never understood his uncle's fascination with the Greek, despite his wealth, knowledge, and connections.

"This *is* your home. And will be until I decide you are ready to move on."

"And when will that be?"

Andros only shrugged. "There is no rush. We must complete your education first. You are very young, even for a human. You have not yet reached your prime. That is why I have chosen you to be my student."

Jacopo may have been young, but he watched Andros with canny eyes. The boy had managed his uncle's servants for many years and had been an observer of human nature for far longer. Jacopo had never mingled with the other young men at court or even the servants his own age. He had always felt most comfortable among his uncle's books or in the company of Giovanni's friends.

He sat up a little straighter. "I am already well-educated. My uncle saw to my education. You know this, Signore."

"I do. That is why I chose you. You are extremely bright for a human." Andros stepped back, examining Jacopo as if he was an animal for sale. "Of fine form. Healthy. Yes, I'm very satisfied with my choice."

Jacopo cocked his head, and his mind began to spin. Andros had called him a "human," as if there was some other option, and there remained a faint, dull ache at the base of his skull. He felt as if he had woken from a strange fever, but his body did not ache, only his mind. His memory flashed to the strange preachers on the streets of Paris, raving about demons and spirits. His uncle had dismissed them as lunatics.

"You are young," Andros continued with a nod. "You will adapt nicely."

"What do you want from me?"

The odd man smiled. "It is not what I want *from* you. It is what I want to give to you.

Instinct caused Jacopo's stomach to churn, and his eyes darted around the room, searching for escape.

"Don't panic." Andros laughed. "I mean you no harm. Your uncle is dead. Florence continues its descent into madness." He came and sat next to Jacopo on the small bed, but kept a comfortable distance. "You will be safe with me. Cared for."

"Cared for?" The reality of his isolation hit him at last. Jacopo wondered what the servants thought had happened to him. His uncle had only been dead a few hours when the footman had announced that Signor Niccolo Andros had come to the villa. He remembered meeting the man in the study, but nothing else. "What has happened to my uncle?" Jacopo asked in a soft voice.

"Your uncle is dead," Andros said. "His family will bury him. The servants have sent for them already."

A slow ache twisted in his chest. "I am his family."

"No, you aren't."

Jacopo's eyes closed in pain. He was weary. He wanted nothing more than to curl up and go to sleep. If he woke, perhaps this would be revealed to be a strange nightmare. If he woke, his uncle might be alive. His warm feather bed would be beneath him. He would hear the maid singing a lilting song in the courtyard.

Andros's voice brought him back to reality. "As much as your uncle may have loved you, he was never *really* your family. Did he ever name you as his heir? Of course not. You were his brother's bastard. He would have married eventually and, if you were very fortunate, he would have made you steward of some house or property. You, my dear boy, were never his family."

Jacopo's eyes furrowed in pain. He knew in his heart that his uncle had cared for him, but the twisted words of his captor needled his insecurities. "I *was* his family. I was."

Andros rose, and Jacopo's eyes followed him. At first glance, Niccolo Andros did not look exceptionally strong or powerful. He was black-haired and bore the even, Mediterranean features shared by most men of Jacopo's acquaintance. He had a medium build, though his arms were thickly muscled, more like those of a laborer than a successful merchant. The only startling things about the man were his pale complexion and vivid blue gaze, which sparked with intelligence and calculation. When Jacopo looked into Andros's eyes, they radiated a quiet menace.

"No, my boy, you *weren't* his family, but you will be mine." Andros stepped closer in the small room, towering over the tall, young man as he sat on the edge of the bed.

"Do what I say, and I promise you I shall call you my son. In front of a far more powerful court than the piddling salons of the Medici, I will stand up and call you my child."

Jacopo frowned. "What do you speak of? What court is more powerful than the Medici? Are you a priest? Do you claim the Holy Father's favor?"

The older man chuckled. "Oh, my dear boy, how your eyes will be opened! Your world has been so small, even with all your uncle's travels. That which I speak of is beyond your comprehension. But you will understand. I promise, very soon, you will understand." Andros's voice grew gentle. "You have never truly had a home, a family. I will be your family. I will call you my son, and someday, all that I have will be yours, do you understand?"

Despite his fear, a strange kind of desire began to fill Jacopo. He had watched many men lie, and was more than proficient at the art himself, but Andros's eyes held none of the telltale signs of a deceiver. In fact, despite the ridiculous promise of the words he spoke, Jacopo almost believed him.

"You would call me your son?"

Andros smiled and stepped forward, placing a cool hand on Jacopo's cheek. "Trust me, my child. I am your family now."

Los Angeles, California

HE WOKE SUDDENLY, TWITCHING HIS NOSE AT THE MEMORY OF THE SALT AIR. Giovanni blinked the sleep from his eyes and immediately searched the bedroom. As was her habit, Beatrice sat in the large chair by the fireplace, reading a journal and taking notes in a small book. Her forehead crinkled in thought as she puzzled over some mystery. He took a silent moment to examine her.

She was stronger than he was now, though she lacked his experience, discipline, and control. For whatever reason, the cocktail of blood that had flooded her mortal body during her change had effected a truly spectacular transformation. In the year and a half since she had turned, Beatrice had grown in power and confidence. She rarely acted impulsively, and her grace was that of someone ten times her age.

Happily, she was still the same woman he had fallen in love with.

"Tesoro."

She looked up and a slow smile spread across her face.

"Hey, handsome."

He cocked a finger at her, squinting his eyes as he caught the teasing light in her own. She rose and sauntered toward him as he continued to beckon her. Once she was within arm's reach, he pounced. Beatrice laughed and rolled across the floor with him as they played.

"You're in a mood for just waking up." She laughed as they came to a stop halfway to the fireplace. Giovanni braced himself over her and looked down. "Do I dare ask what you were dreaming about?"

Sadly, not what you're thinking of. He kissed along her collar and nuzzled into her neck. "Have I told you tonight that I love you?"

"No."

"I do. I love you." His lips explored the nape of her neck, where her soft, honeysuckle scent was strongest.

"I love you, too."

He rolled to the side and let his hand trail along her shoulder. "And I love our home."

She laughed. "Okay."

"And our family."

She caught his chin and forced his eyes to hers. Giovanni met her gaze, bathing in the comfort of her energy as it wrapped them both. "Where are you tonight?"

He still marveled that she could read him so well. "Just... thinking about the past."

Beatrice's eyes held nothing but the soft light of understanding. "Anything you want to share?"

He shook his head. She paused for a minute, examining him before she leaned in for a gentle kiss. Giovanni kissed her back, letting his amnis spread over her skin to tease her senses. He could feel her desire twine with his, and he sat up, pulling her with him and pressing her mouth to his neck.

"Bite," he growled. "Feed from me."

"Thought you'd never ask."

"Since when have you ever waited for permission?"

Giovanni heard a low purr before her fangs pierced his skin.

"What is on your agenda tonight?" he asked as he dressed in his uniform of black slacks and a dress shirt. Beatrice lounged in the bath, enjoying the calm of the water before she left their room.

"I've got some translation to do on the journals. I already helped Ben with his homework today, but I'll drive him to Tenzin's later tonight and practice for a while."

"I wanted to talk to you about that. I asked Ernesto to call Baojia back from San Diego."

Beatrice raised her eyebrow. "Oh, really? Did Grandpa decide to let him out of time-out?"

Giovanni grimaced. "I asked Ernesto to bring him back so he could continue your training. I spoke to Baojia last week and he wanted to know how your weapons were progressing. He says Tenzin is not a good enough teacher."

She smiled. "It's going fine. I'm always grateful for help though. I was talking about it with Tenzin the other night. She says I'm more than proficient with the *dao*, and I'm fine with the *jian*. I never really liked using a *jian* much, to be honest, so I'm not too concerned—"

"Baojia says you're ready for the *shuang gou*."

Her eyes lit up. "The hook-swords?"

"Yes."

"Wicked."

He smirked and walked over for a quick kiss. "Glad you agree. I'll probably be in the library most of the night. I want to go over some of my uncle's correspondence before we leave for Rome."

"This trip is going to be safe, right? I know you want to bring Ben, but it's not worth it if you think there's any danger of—"

"Nothing we can't handle, Tesoro." He leaned against the edge of the counter. "We'll see Livia, and I'll introduce you to her people. We'll play nice for a week or so, and then she'll lose interest. That's what she always does. She's always after the shiny new toy. Right now, she's curious, that's all. Honestly, I should have taken you to see her right after we got married, but we had a bit on the schedule."

"So no reason to worry?"

"No." He frowned. "Are you worried?"

Beatrice shrugged. "Well, she's the closest thing I have to a mother-in-law. From all reports, she's also an incredibly beautiful, two-thousand-year-old, Roman noblewoman. And she is, according to you, one of the most powerful vampires in Europe. Nope, nothing intimidating about her at all."

Giovanni bent down, ignoring the water soaking his knees. "Nothing to worry about. She'll love you."

"Yeah?" She couldn't hide the skepticism in her voice.

He grabbed her chin and laid a hard kiss on her mouth. "Since when is my woman afraid?"

Her eyes narrowed. "I'm not afraid."

"Good." He stood and straightened his collar. "You'll love Rome. And since Kirby and Desiree can come along with Benjamin, we'll all have a grand time. Tenzin will... she'll put up with it for your sake. Try to persuade her not to kill anyone."

"Hmm."

"What now?"

"Just thinking. We'll need to figure out something about accommodations. We're going to be there for three months and there's six of us, so—"

"We have a house in Rome. It has plenty of room."

Beatrice blinked. "We do?"

"I have a large house in Rome, an estate outside Florence, and a smaller flat in Milan. Didn't I tell you that?"

"Anything else?"

"That's all that I have in Italy. I have a few other places scattered around Europe."

Beatrice paused. "Was that on your husband profile right under your ability to burn pasta? Because, I'll be honest, anything after the description of your sexual skills I just skipped over."

He burst out laughing and tossed a hand towel at her. It hit her in the face.

"Hey!" She flicked her fingers and a spray of water crossed the room, soaking him.

"Thanks for that." He stripped off the wet shirt.

"Aha! My devious plan worked; you're naked again." She grabbed his hand as he walked past and pulled him into the tub.

"Tesoro?"

"Yes?"

"Are we going to accomplish anything tonight?"

"Probably not."

Hours later, he managed to pull himself away when Ben resorted to calling their room, threatening to steal the car to drive himself to practice. Though Giovanni was agreeable to that scenario, Beatrice was not. She muttered something about "stupid teenage drivers" as she pulled on her practice clothes and left the room, blowing him a kiss over her shoulder.

He wandered down to the library on the first floor, where he had shipped most of his uncle's collection of books, letters, and artwork. He had expanded the original library during the year they had been in Chile and added a pool house, as well. All the windows had lightproof shutters, which allowed Beatrice to have use of most of the house during the day. He had spared no expense making sure their home suited his wife's somewhat unusual needs.

Just as he was sitting down with a collection of letters between Girolamo Benivieni and his uncle, Giovanni Pico, the phone rang. Looking at the clock, he realized it was probably Carwyn calling before dawn.

Giovanni picked up the phone. "Hello, Father."

"That would have been awkward if it was Livia."

"You know she never uses the phone. She can barely stand using the postal service instead of uniformed messenger."

"And yet she does love her fancy lights and indoor plumbing."

"No one can ever claim she was anything but an aristocrat."

"So, speaking of your mummy—"

"Please, don't call her that," he said with a wince. Carwyn only chuckled. "Ever. I'm serious."

"Fine. Speaking of the Roman she-devil, when will you be there?"

He rolled his eyes. Carwyn had always had a clear disdain for anything having to do with Rome. The Welshman barely put up with his own friends at the Vatican, who had known about the priest's existence for centuries, and he delighted in making snide remarks about the arrogance of ecclesiastical and military empires.

"We'll be there at the beginning of May. Will you be joining us?"

"Will Tenzin be there? And the boy?"

"Of course."

"Well, I wouldn't want to miss out on the party. I'll see you there. I could use a visit with a few people in red bathrobes anyway."

That was unexpected. Carwyn usually avoided Vatican City if possible. "Oh? Anything I need to know about?"

"Just some... personal details. Collar-type things you'd have no interest in."

The priest was being uncharacteristically cagey, but Giovanni let it rest. He knew if his old friend wanted to share, he would. Carwyn had few secrets, but those he did have, he kept very close. Giovanni decided to change the subject.

"How's Deirdre?"

Carwyn paused. "She's doing well. As well as can be expected. She's keeping busy. Has quite a few projects she's juggling at the moment."

"Good."

"And how is your wife?"

"Doing extremely well. She's practicing with Ben and Tenzin tonight, though I believe she'll be training with Baojia again in the near future."

"Oh, you must be thrilled."

"I can... appreciate his usefulness."

Carwyn only laughed. "And the bloodlust? How's she doing with that? Any slips?"

He shrugged. "Doesn't seem to be a problem. She still feels it, from what she says, but her control is so good you wouldn't know it was ever a problem. She's extraordinary."

"Well, that's no surprise."

"I suppose not; she's always performed beyond expectations."

"Speaking of things I don't need to know about..."

Giovanni snorted. "Aren't you amusing?"

"Sometimes."

He frowned. Something was bothering his friend. "Are you sure you don't have things at home you need to take care of? We'd all love to see you in Rome, but it's not necessary if you're busy."

Carwyn paused. "I'm sure. I've been here too long as it is."

"Where are you? I thought you were calling from home."

"No, I'm in Ireland."

"Still looking through Ioan's library? If he's the doctor that Stephen mentioned in the journals, it's possible that they were in contact. Have you looked through his letters?"

"Deirdre has. I've been through his library, and so far, there's nothing. Nothing about the research that Lorenzo tortured him over, either. In fact, anything related to vampire blood seems to be gone, though I know he had at least one book that he wrote, detailing its uses in treating humans. Deirdre is quite certain that no one has been in their library except their immediate family and nothing seems disturbed. I've been writing letters to the rest of the family and his other colleagues to see if he lent his work to anyone, but as you can imagine, the list is fairly long."

"I hate to pull you away if you're needed there. Are you sure—"

"Yes, I need to get away from here for a bit." Carwyn sighed. "I'll see you in Rome the beginning of May, Gio. Keep out of trouble and say hello to B for me. I need to go."

"You're acting strange."

The priest laughed. "When do I not act strange?"

Giovanni scowled. "Fine. Keep your secrets."

"Just following your excellent example. I'll see you in a month or so."

"Good night, Carwyn."

"Good night."

He hung up, but couldn't shake the feeling that something was very wrong. Carwyn had lost much of his normally affable demeanor since Ioan's death, and Giovanni knew that witnessing his family's grief was even more wrenching than his own. Reminding himself that Lorenzo still walked the earth, free to hurt others, he dove back into research. He pulled out the letters and turned to one dated 1488, written from Benivieni to his uncle when they were in Paris.

"My dear Giovanni, I saw the odd Signor Andros in Rome last month. He was speaking with the Moor who is visiting with the governor on some trade issue. He really is a most strange gentleman. I cannot ascertain your preoccupation with him..."

CHAPTER 3

In the four years since Ben Vecchio had lived with his adopted uncle, it wasn't unusual for him to pinch himself to make sure he was awake. It wasn't when he saw his uncle dart by so fast that his eyes blurred or noticed his aunt's new fangs peek out of her mouth. The fact that he had been adopted by vampires no longer fazed the young man. No, it was the mornings he woke in a warm bed, surrounded by the sounds of family and signs of comfort that he pinched himself.

But pinching was the last thing he needed to do to remind himself he wasn't dreaming when it came time for practice with Tenzin.

"I'm going to keep beating you up until you get this," Tenzin said as she punched his shoulder. "You're horrible today. Very distracted."

"Hey." He scowled and threw up an arm, instinctively blocking the strike she aimed at his face. "Can we take a break and watch them already? It's kinda hard to concentrate."

"What? Them?" Tenzin glanced over her shoulder at Baojia and Beatrice as they practiced with the new swords that Baojia had brought. Ben snuck in a quick jab to her knee while she was turned.

Tenzin's leg buckled and she looked back with a smile. "Good. Opportunistic is good. Fine, we can watch them for a while. I'd better make sure that vampire doesn't slice her up before Gio gets here anyway."

Tenzin walked over to the wall opposite the weapons training area in the industrial building. When she'd moved to Los Angeles, she had bought the nondescript complex off Allen Avenue and gutted it, turning the majority of the large area into her own personal training studio. She had shipped many of her own weapons over from somewhere in China, and now Giovanni, Beatrice, Tenzin, Ben, and currently, Baojia, used the large space to work out and train.

Beatrice and Baojia were sparring in the corner, Beatrice using the curved *dao* she usually trained with, while Baojia used the twin blades of the *shuang gou* he had brought to introduce into her training regimen.

"Why isn't she using them?" Ben asked. "I thought she was supposed to be learning."

"Watch and learn. He's showing her how to defend herself against them before he teaches her how to attack. Watching Baojia use them will be the most effective way for her to learn."

The longer Ben watched, the more he could see the wisdom of it. Initially, Beatrice was cautious, weaving and ducking away from the other vampire, darting in occasionally with a quick thrust of her saber, but mostly, dancing around him. He saw Baojia hook the swords together in one swift movement, sweeping the blades over his head and then down toward Beatrice's legs as she jumped to escape the broad reach of the wicked edge. He swung them around like a chain or rope, and the double-sided blades cut through the air, lethal from all angles as they sought their target.

Ben frowned. "He wouldn't actually hurt her, would he?"

Tenzin only shrugged. "He won't cut her head off. He's more careful than that. If he slices her up a bit, well... that's just part of training."

Ben had a feeling that his uncle might have a distinctly different attitude about the whole matter, but that was probably why Giovanni rarely joined them when Beatrice was fighting. As cultured and calm as his uncle usually was, Ben had witnessed his rare fury once when he thought Tenzin had attacked his wife too fiercely. The flames from his outburst had singed the hair off Ben's forearms from ten feet away. Beatrice was furious, but Giovanni only snarled and told Ben to run faster next time.

Secretly, Ben thought it was the coolest thing he'd ever seen.

"How long will it be before she's really good with them?"

"Watch her now," Tenzin murmured. "Watch, boy."

It irritated Ben that Tenzin always called him "boy," but he supposed he couldn't really say anything about it. Even if she only looked a few years older than him, he knew she was the oldest vampire he would probably ever meet. The funny thing about Tenzin was she still acted like a little kid at times. Beatrice said it was because she was so old and didn't get out in the modern world all that much, but Tenzin was still amazed by weird stuff like TV and cars. She hated cars, but she liked the television. She really loved going to the movies, and she and Ben had fallen into the habit of going to see one at least once a week. She liked 3D pictures the best.

Tenzin reached over and whacked his arm. "Boy, are you watching?"

"My name is *Ben*," he grumbled, but turned his attention back to Beatrice and Baojia. He could see what Tenzin meant. Beatrice was no longer simply reacting to Baojia's attacks, she was now actively attacking him, spotting tiny opportunities to throw the other vampire off balance, or make his grip on the *shuang gou* waver.

"Oh, wow," he whispered as they picked up speed. Soon, both vampires were whirling in an almost sickening blur, whipping around each other, jumping and leaping, while the blades caught the glint from the overhead lights. Finally, Ben had to look away. He was starting to get motion sick from the speed of their movements.

"Ah... ah..." From the corner of his eye, he saw Tenzin lean forward and laugh. Ben chanced a look up, only to see Beatrice standing in front of Baojia. She had taken one of the *shuang gou* from him and held it, along with her saber, at the other vampire's neck as he was pressed against the wall.

"And she's got him," Tenzin said. She turned to Ben with a grin. "Did you see? She's very good. No one will stab her again."

As soon as she said it, he saw the flicker of sadness in her grey eyes. Tenzin quickly looked away as Ben watched the expression drain from her face.

"Nope," he said, teasing. "That's my fake aunt, toughest vampire around."

Tenzin turned back to him with a smirk. "Now, you're just asking me to beat you up again."

"What?" he scoffed. "You're a little girl. What kind of—okay, ow!" Tenzin pounced on Ben and twisted his arm behind his back. "Ow, *ow*... Tenzin, I was joking."

"'Little girl?' You are an infant."

"I'm not going to be able to practice if you take my arm off. Ow!" His eyes rolled back until he heard a swift, whooshing sound. Suddenly, her grip loosened.

"Please don't damage the boy, bird-girl. He whines when he's in too much pain."

Ben rolled on his side to see his uncle's leather dress shoes by his face.

"Hey, Gio." He looked up at Giovanni's amused face.

"What did you say to piss her off?"

"I called her a little girl."

His eyebrow cocked, and Giovanni glanced at Tenzin, who had flown over to speak to Baojia and Beatrice as they were putting the weapons away.

"You're a brave fool, Benjamin."

Ben snickered and took the hand his uncle held out. "You should have seen B. She was awesome. She totally beat Baojia with the hook swords."

"Excellent." Giovanni smiled. "I am almost sorry I missed it."

"Yeah? Well, I'm glad I still have all my hair, so thanks for keeping away."

"What are you doing tonight?"

Ben's eyes darted away. "Oh... you know, just gonna head home and maybe hang out for a while. I got a history test on Monday. Stupid French Revolution stuff. Nothing major, but..."

"Ben, I can hear your heartbeat; I know you're lying."

He huffed. "I'm just... sheesh, man. I don't ask you what you're doing every hour of the day."

"Are you meeting a girl?"

"What?" Ben's face reddened. "No, I'm not." *This time.*

Luckily, Giovanni must have decided that Ben was lying about his true intentions because he just grunted and leaned toward the boy. "Be careful. Be respectful. That's all I require. And be in your bed by morning."

"I'm not—never mind." Let him think he was going out to meet Heather or Brianna. Ben walked over and picked up a towel, wiping the sweat from his forehead before he walked to the small locker room to wash up. "Whatever. I'll see you guys later."

Ben showered, grabbed his helmet, and walked out to his scooter. At fifteen, he was still breaking the law by riding it, but Giovanni and Beatrice both turned a blind eye since their schedules and his were so screwy, and Caspar was getting older. Besides, Ben just felt weird making Caspar drive him around when he was perfectly capable of doing it himself. With his height and his deep voice, Ben had never attracted attention riding the stripped-down Honda Ruckus, and he always kept it on surface streets. He couldn't wait till he was sixteen, and he could finally get Beatrice's old motorcycle.

Ben made a show of riding off, only to double back and wait in an alley, watching for his aunt and uncle to exit the building. He saw Baojia and Tenzin leave. Baojia walked toward a parked car with a driver in front, and Tenzin ducked toward the back of the building before he saw her small form take to the sky in a blur.

Still, he waited.

Ben didn't know why, but recently, the idea of how Beatrice and Giovanni were feeding was starting to bug him. Did they feed on random strangers? Criminals? He was starting to entertain crazy notions of them stalking gang members in dark alleys like modern day superheroes, and he knew he was being ridiculous. He felt awkward asking, so he decided that the easiest way to find out would be to trail them when they went out. It was Friday night, and he knew they would feed, because both of them always looked flushed on Saturday, and Beatrice usually slept a little during the day, which she rarely needed to do.

Ben waited in the shadows until he saw them walk out, hand in hand. They were on foot, so he left his scooter in the alley and prayed that no one would bother it. He followed behind them as they turned the corner and headed toward a clutch of storefronts. They must have walked a mile, both of them strolling at a human pace, chatting and laughing together like any other couple out for a date. Beatrice had her hand tucked around Giovanni's waist, and his hand occasionally reached up to play with the ends of her hair. Ben envied the easy love he saw between them and wondered if he would ever find someone that loved him like that.

No matter, he thought with a grin. There was plenty of time for that and plenty of interested girls in the meantime.

Ben saw them turn a corner and walk toward a bar where a loud group of what looked like college kids gathered on the patio outside, drinking and smoking. They paused across the street, then looked at each other. Giovanni gave Beatrice a small nod, and they crossed the road.

"What are you doing?"

Ben almost fell over when he heard the voice at his ear.

"Dammit, Tenzin!" he gasped and spun around. "You scared me to death!"

"Why are you following your aunt and uncle?"

"I'm... not. I'm not following them. I'm just..." He cleared his throat and stared into her skeptical grey eyes.

She looked across the street, then back at him. "Yes, you are. And you are a bad liar."

"You know, I'm actually a really good liar unless I'm talking to a vampire who can hear my heartbeat."

She shrugged. "Well, it's too bad that half of your family are vampires then. Why are you following Gio and B?"

"I'm just... I was just... worried."

"About?"

"Them. You know, with all the danger and... stuff." He was flailing. Ben could charm his way out of practically any situation imaginable. He could charm the harshest teacher at school with a flash of his smile. He could get any of the girls to do his boring homework for him by batting his long, dark lashes, but Tenzin...

He sighed. Tenzin was uncharmable.

She waited, standing with preternatural stillness that seemed to wrench the truth from his gut.

"I'm just curious, all right?"

"About?"

"How they... you know..."

She furrowed her brows. "Are you one of those strange boys who likes to watch people do personal things? A 'Peeping Tim?'"

"Tom! It's 'Peeping Tom,' Tenzin."

"Oh, and you are one of them?" She didn't look disgusted, just curious as she cocked her head to the side.

"No!"

"Then why are you following them?"

"I'm just curious about... the eating thing."

"About what?"

A FALL OF WATER

Ben flushed to the roots of his hair. "The eating—feeding thing, you know? Who do they eat from? What do they... I mean, do they kill people? Do they... I don't know!"

She scowled. "They don't kill people. Why do you think they kill people?"

"I don't think they kill people."

"But you just said—"

"I'm just curious, okay?"

"So why don't you ask them?"

He shrugged. "I don't know. It just seems rude."

Tenzin curled her lip. "It's rude to ask them, but following them is not? You are a very odd boy."

"I'm not—"

"Come on." She waved at him and started walking back down the street. "I'll walk back to your bicycle with you."

He frowned and started to follow her. "It's not a bicycle, Tenzin."

"It has two wheels, doesn't it? Bi. Cycle."

"You're so weird."

"I'm not the one following my aunt and uncle and being a Peeping Tim."

"Tom."

"Who?"

Ben reached over to tug at a chunk of her dark hair. "Never mind."

"IS HE GONE?" BEATRICE SIPPED A GLASS OF WINE AND PEEKED AT GIOVANNI from the corner of her eye as he sat across from her at the small table.

"Yes, she grabbed him. They're walking back to the warehouse now."

"Why do you think he was following us?"

Giovanni shrugged and picked up the glass of Jameson she had ordered for him. "I heard him asking Caspar—in what he probably thought was a subtle way—about what we're eating. He's probably curious. He knows we're not feeding from bagged blood anymore. Do you think he's worried we're draining the innocent and wreaking havoc on Southern California?"

Beatrice snorted. "Well, will you have a talk with him tomorrow, so we don't have a repeat of this?"

Giovanni curled his lip, but nodded. "I avoided the sex talk, so I suppose it's only fair."

She looked at her mate, amused by the uncomfortable expression on his face. It was the oddest things that seemed to be an issue for him. Teaching Ben how to kill someone silently and with minimal blood spray? No problem. Telling him about sex or feeding? Immediate squirm.

Beatrice laid a comforting hand on his shoulder, but her ears perked up when she heard the booming voice of the college boy at the table next to her. The young man was regaling his friends with some highly unlikely sexual exploit. He was also, apparently, familiar with a surprising number of professional athletes, Hollywood starlets, and at least one dangerous African warlord.

Her eyes lit up, and she looked at Giovanni. "Go ahead," he said with a smile. "He's your favorite flavor."

She grinned. "I do love the sweet taste of bragging liar."

Her husband chuckled, shaking his head and leaning back to watch her work. As soon as the bragging boy went back to the bar, she followed him. He was taking a long draw from his imported beer when Beatrice sidled up to him. His eyes raked over her breasts before he finally looked up to her eyes. She smiled, careful to conceal her fangs.

"Hi, how are you?"

SHE HELD HIM BY THE NECK IN THE BACK ALLEY. "AND WHAT ARE YOU DOING in your classes?"

The boy's dazed eyes swam. "Well... not much."

"So you're wasting all the hard-earned money that your parents are putting into your education?"

"Yeah, I guess so."

"Do you think your mother's proud of you?"

The drunk boy shook his head sadly. "Probably not."

"But you're going to turn over a new leaf, right, Dave?"

"Oh, yeah." He nodded with a smile. "Totally."

"Good. Make your parents proud of you."

"Okay."

"And the next girlfriend you have, you're going to be respectful and faithful, right?"

"Right."

She heard the back door open and felt Giovanni's energy as he walked toward them.

"Are you being a guidance counselor again? Stop playing with your food."

She glanced over her shoulder. "I get blood; he gets some good advice."

"Can't you just drink him so we can do other, more *interesting*, things?" She heard the low growl in his voice and decided the college boy had been given enough advice for one night. She looked back at Dave, letting her amnis wash up his neck.

"Give me your wrist."

He lifted his wrist and she grabbed it, turning to stare at her mate as she bared her fangs and struck. She heard the boy give a low sigh of pleasure as she drank from him, but she kept a firm grip on his throat, monitoring his pulse as she locked her eyes with Giovanni's.

Her mate watched her with hungry eyes, pacing a short distance away, and she saw his fangs grow long in his mouth. His tongue darted out and licked his lips as he watched her drink, and Beatrice knew that she would not be the only one feeding that night. She took a few more deep swallows of the boy's blood before she sealed the wounds and whispered instructions in his ear, keeping her eyes on Giovanni the whole time.

The mindless boy wandered back into the bar, and Giovanni waited for the alley door to click before he sprung on her. He shoved Beatrice up against the wall, pushing her arms over her head as he attacked her mouth. One hand held her wrists against the sharp brick while the other slid down her side, dragging her hips to his as he pushed their bodies together.

Beatrice hissed and bared her fangs, reacting instinctively to his attack. Her hands fought against his iron grip, and she finally worked one free only to reach around and drag Giovanni even closer, pulling at his shirt and digging her fingers into the hot flesh at the small of his back. He whipped her around so that he was leaning against the wall and she climbed his body, locking her thighs around his hips as they moved together.

"Home," he snarled.

"Here. We'll hear anyone coming."

"Fine." Giovanni grabbed her hair, angling her neck to the side as she gasped. "You listen, I have other things to do."

Her eyes rolled back when his fangs struck. If anyone interrupted them after that, Beatrice just didn't notice.

"They're babies! It doesn't count!"

"Yes, it does."

Beatrice frowned when she heard Ben and Tenzin arguing from the living room as she and Giovanni walked through the kitchen door hours later.

"Babies can't help drooling, so it doesn't count."

She raised an eyebrow and looked at Giovanni, who only shrugged his shoulders.

"I think you're wrong." They heard Tenzin speak again. "And I am older, so I am right."

"Do you think that B and Gio will ever adopt a baby?"

"I certainly hope not. They're very messy, and they smell horrible."

Beatrice shook her head and walked toward the living room. Giovanni locked the door behind him before he followed her.

"If we do," she said as she entered the room, "you two will be last on the babysitting list, that's for sure."

"Hey!" Ben raised his hands. "I was defending the human babies. Tenzin is the barbarian here."

Tenzin rolled her eyes. "I was simply saying that once a human has reached the drooling stage, it is a valid question whether they should be considered a real human or not."

Ben just stared at her, shaking his head. "So not cool, Tenzin."

Giovanni sat in his favorite chair and pulled Beatrice to sit in his lap. "You two bicker more than old married people."

"Hey! You're the only old married people I see," Ben said.

Tenzin curled her lip at Giovanni. "We do not."

Beatrice shrugged. "Just be nice to Dez and Matt's baby when it gets here, that's all I'm asking."

Dez and Matt had been married the previous week, and the couple was vacationing on one of Ernesto's yachts before they returned to Los Angeles and accompanied Beatrice, Giovanni, and Ben to Rome. Beatrice had some concern about her friend traveling so early in her pregnancy, but Dez seemed nonchalant about the matter, so she was trying not to worry.

"Is Tenzin coming on the plane with us?"

"No," Tenzin said firmly. "I will meet you all within the week, but you will not get me on that flying contraption again. It's unnatural."

"Who's coming on the plane, then?"

Giovanni leaned back and closed his eyes. "Desiree, Kirby, and the three of us. Carwyn will meet us there."

"Cool," Ben said as he stood. "I'm going to bed."

"Good, it's late."

Tenzin piped up from the couch, "We are watching movies tomorrow night."

Beatrice asked, "What are we watching?"

"We're going to Rome." Ben shrugged. "*Gladiator. Spartacus.*"

"*Ben Hur. Cleopatra,*" Tenzin said.

Beatrice grinned. "*Roman Holiday?*"

"*The Life of Brian?*" Giovanni suggested.

"No," Tenzin and Ben said together.

Beatrice said, "You two are so predictable." She leaned back and laid her head on Giovanni's shoulder. She felt his hand comb through her hair, and she closed her eyes, content and sated in her lover's arms. Soon, Ben walked up to bed, and Tenzin retreated to the den with the television.

"Everything's going to be okay in Rome, right?"

"Yes. Whatever happens, we will handle it."

Beatrice still had the sneaking suspicion that their trip to the Eternal City was going to be far more interesting than Giovanni predicted, but she kept silent. They had to go, and they might find out more about her father's informant when they were there. Stephen De Novo had received too much valuable and accurate information on his hunt for Geber's elixir of life for it to be merely coincidence. The ancient city held secrets, and hopefully, a few answers as well.

For almost a year, she had been studying Geber's journals and jotting down characteristics the alchemist had noted from his immortal "donors" when she found them. With enough time, and with Giovanni's knowledge of the intricate immortal court in Rome, Beatrice might have a chance of identifying the original four vampires who had contributed to the elixir. If they could find those four, then they were one step closer to understanding the mystery, and just maybe, they would be a step ahead of Lorenzo.

She felt Giovanni's skin heat up, and he began to nose against her neck.

"More?" she murmured.

"More."

CHAPTER 4

Crotone, Italy
1494

Jacopo was starving.

He pulled himself up from the thin pallet on the floor and crawled to the door where a jar of water stood. He had eaten the four thin wafers that had been slipped under the door, but his stomach still growled. The flavorless bread was the only food he had been given in the previous week, though his water had been replenished on a daily basis.

Jacopo reached for the door, pulling on it again before he paced the room. Just then, a timid knock sounded. A few moments later, he heard the key turn, and the door cracked open. He saw the edge of a vivid-blue eye in the darkness of the corridor, and then a mop of shining blond hair poked though.

"Hello?" The boy was small, perhaps ten years of age, and he held a large loaf of bread in his hands. He was dressed in clean clothes, costly: the clothing of a servant in a fine house.

"Who are you?" Jacopo crouched in the corner, watching the small boy come closer. His stomach rumbled as the smell of the warm bread wafted toward him.

"It's morning, so the master is in his chamber," the boy said. "He won't come out until nightfall. I brought this for you."

Still, Jacopo eyed him warily. "Who are you?" he asked again.

"I'm Paulo." He smiled and held out the bread. "Master told the servants not to feed you, that you had to steal food for yourself, but no one had seen you, so I thought you might be sick."

A FALL OF WATER

Bits of information clicked into place. The week before, Andros had come to him and told Jacopo that he was strong enough to start his training. *You need to be taught self-reliance,* Andros had said with a strange glint in his eye. The next morning, there was water when he woke, but no food.

Jacopo frowned at the boy and ignored the gnawing in his stomach. "He wants me to steal food from him?"

Paulo nodded. "I heard him telling the cook. He told her if she found food missing, not to be alarmed, that he wanted you to learn how to escape your room and steal it."

"Crazy old man," Jacopo muttered. "Fine, he wants me to steal; I'll steal from him. And I will learn how to escape this wretched chamber, as well." Though he hadn't been forced to steal since his uncle had adopted him, he had once been adept at picking locks. If Andros wanted Jacopo to escape his room, it wouldn't be a problem.

"So"—Paulo held out the bread—"do you want it? I brought it for you."

Jacopo looked at the seemingly innocent boy with the wide, blue gaze. Why would he bring him bread and risk the anger of the master of the house? Was this boy a spy of some sort? Would Jacopo receive a beating for taking the bread from him? Perhaps it was a test.

"I want nothing from you," Jacopo said. "Why do you bring me bread when Andros wants me to steal it? Do you run to him and tell him of my weakness later?"

As soon as he said it, Jacopo knew it had not been the boy's intention. Paulo's face fell, and a hard mask slipped over his previously open features. Jacopo regretted that he had rebuffed the boy's kindness, but he had no desire to attract the wrath of Niccolo Andros by defying him.

The boy straightened his shoulders. "I brought it to tempt you," Paulo said with false bravado. "It's only a shame you can't taste it for yourself." The blond boy took a large bite from the fragrant loaf, and Jacopo could smell the herbs the cook had used in the bread. His mouth watered.

He leapt up, pouncing on the boy and knocking him to the ground. Jacopo slapped his face and grabbed the loaf from his hands. Paulo's eyes watered, but he twisted his mouth into a sneer as Jacopo tossed the bread to the corner.

"Go. Tell the cook I stole your bread and beat you. She will not blame you for the loss." He stood and held out a hand to the boy, but Paulo rolled away and stood on his own.

"You're a filthy animal." Paulo curled his lip. "I can smell you from here. Signor Andros will surely get rid of you when he smells you through the house."

"Oh?" Jacopo cocked his head. "Has he brought boys to his home before?" What was this madness Niccolo Andros had planned? Were there other boys like him hidden in this cold, stone castle?

"No," Paulo said. "Signor Andros is a most cultured and honorable man. When he sees you, I'm sure he will be displeased and send you away."

Jacopo smirked. "So, I am the only one he ordered the cook not to feed?"

"Yes," Paulo said with a shrug.

He wandered to the corner and grabbed the bread, tearing off a chunk and stuffing it in his mouth. It was the finest thing he had ever tasted. "So I am the only one he keeps like this? The only... prisoner."

"He calls you his student."

"Is that so?"

"Yes." Paulo was backing toward the door as Jacopo tore off another chunk of bread.

"And I am the only student?"

"Yes, but he will send you away when he smells you, *animal*."

A grim smile curled Jacopo's lips. "Paulo, how many servants does Signor Andros have?"

"Many." He sneered again. "He has many servants."

"And how many 'students' does he have?"

Paulo's eyes narrowed. "Just you."

Jacopo walked toward the haughty boy, towering over him. At seventeen years of age, he was taller than most grown men, as tall as the father he had never met. He stared down at the blond boy in his clean clothes and scrubbed face.

"Well, if I am your master's *only* student, and you are one of many servants, then I think we know the one who is expendable, no?"

En route to Rome
May 2012

Giovanni woke, brushing the dream from his mind and looking around the compartment for Beatrice. He could hear the low hum of the engines as they flew. He spotted her sitting in a chair in the corner, notebooks spread over her side of the bed.

"Where are we?"

She looked up with a smile. "Hey! You know, you're sleeping a lot less now, too."

"I don't find that surprising, considering how much blood we exchange." His wife's blood was powerful, more powerful than even he had predicted, and his waking hours were growing longer as a result. Though the phenomenon had its advantages, he did not envy her lack of rest.

"I've found something interesting in the journals."

"Oh?"

She nodded with a grin. "I think I've finally identified the four original donors."

He sat up and leaned over the spread notebooks. "How? You've been looking for months."

Beatrice opened her notebook and handed it to him. "I don't have them exactly, but I've been making notes every time he mentions them in his journals, and I finally found a reference to the one I'd been missing, the earth donor."

"What did you find?" He began paging through her notes, deciphering the strange shorthand she had developed since she had turned. Most vampires developed some sort of unique language for their thoughts over time. Since their minds moved more rapidly than mortals, it was the best way to record thoughts and had the added benefit of concealing their meaning from the casual reader. To anyone else, Beatrice's writing would have been gibberish; Giovanni alone could read it.

"What is this?" He pointed toward an unknown symbol. "This is new."

"It stands for '*Aethiop*.'"

"'Aethiop?' You mean the earth donor was Ethiopian?"

She nodded with a grin. "Yep, and she—"

"She?"

"Uh-huh, another surprise. The others were clearly male, but this one was definitely female because Geber notes that preliminary testing on her blood showed no discernible difference because of sex."

"Which would only be notable if her sex was different." Giovanni smiled. "Nicely done, Tesoro."

"So, we have his names for the four, which all indicate their origin... except for his friend."

Giovanni paged through the notebook. "The Greek, the Numidian, the Aethiop, and 'my dear friend.'"

Beatrice sighed. "I don't want to make assumptions, because medieval Kufa was so diverse."

He nodded. "It was in decline, in a political sense, during Geber's lifetime, but it was an active center of learning and scholarship, so it could have been a friend from any number of backgrounds. Arab and Persian are the most likely, but many vampires were drawn to the Middle East during that period because there was so much going on."

"He does use the medieval Persian word for 'friend' so that could be significant."

Giovanni shook his head. "It could just as easily *not* be significant. All his personal journals were written in Persian. And if we are looking for your father's contact in Rome, it could be less than helpful. Livia has always kept a very diverse court... well, diverse for a Roman."

"What do you mean?"

"She takes pride in having tokens from all areas of the Roman Empire, thinks it adds to the 'imperial' quality. Shows how magnanimous she is. So, all of these, Greek, Numidian, Ethiopian, any of these would be common in the Roman court. Nothing particularly notable there. We'll have to wait and see who's been keeping her company the last few years. It changes all the time with a few notable exceptions. Rome is probably the most 'international' of the European immortal courts."

"But old. We're looking for older vampires, for sure."

He shrugged. "The experiments were conducted around 800 A.D.? We're looking for four vampires over a thousand years old. In Rome, it's not uncommon. Though the majority of the population is fairly young, there are so many older vampires who come and go that one of a thousand years would not stand out."

She scowled. "Well, thanks for raining on my parade, Captain Sunshine."

He chuckled and put the notebook down. "However, this is exceptional work, as always. I don't tell you enough how brilliant you are."

"No, you really don't."

Beatrice was still pretending to pout, so he pushed the notebooks aside to grab her hand and pull her toward him. "You're brilliant... beautiful."

"Yes, keep it coming," she said, waving her other hand.

"Smart, sexy." He pulled her to straddle his lap and began running his fingers along her spine, enjoying the shiver of excitement that rose between them. "Very sexy."

"More," she whispered, and Giovanni grinned, not sure whether she was talking about the compliments or the caresses.

"Thorough. Thoroughly lovely, that is..." His lips nibbled along her jawline as her hands tangled in his hair. "You're just so..." He breathed out along her skin, causing her to shiver. "*So...*"

"What?" She panted as his fingers teased her.

He pulled back and traced his tongue along her lower lip. "You're so... *meticulous.*" He drew the word out sensuously.

Finally, she giggled and tackled him to the bed.

"Giovanni Vecchio, you sure know how to seduce a woman."

"No." He rolled over and tucked her into his chest as his hands continued to tease. "I just know how to seduce you."

It was after ten o'clock when they landed in Rome. The plane had touched down without incident, but Matt and Giovanni were both wary in the foreign territory. Luckily, neither was unfamiliar with the city; Matt had spent plenty of time in Rome, and for Giovanni, Rome was like a second home. His knowledge of it was trumped only by his knowledge of Florence, which had a very low vampire population. Rome, on the other hand, was teeming with the creatures.

They exited the plane, only to be met by a dark car that Matt had ordered. As planned, Beatrice stood guard over Dez and Ben, her watchful gaze sweeping around as Giovanni and Matt thoroughly checked the vehicle for any listening devices or explosives. He knew their arrival was expected, and Giovanni would take no chances with his family's safety. Rome was a city with a long memory.

"Clear for bugs," Matt said quietly.

"And I don't sense any energy signatures or smell any explosives. Beatrice?" Beatrice, like most water vampires, had developed an extremely keen sense of smell.

"I don't smell anything suspicious."

"Excellent." Giovanni walked over to the driver, shaking his hand and quickly asking him a few questions that reassured him the man had been sent by the usual car service he used in Rome. The five passengers squeezed into the small car as Matt sat in the front, directing the driver to Giovanni's home near the Pantheon.

"How old is your house?" Ben asked as they sped through the streets. The driver swerved to avoid a horde of passing Vespas, and Giovanni could hear the man cursing under his breath. It was Friday night in Rome, and the streets were alive with activity.

"Wow," Beatrice said. "And I thought New York was busy at night."

"My home was built in the sixteenth century, Ben."

"Wow, that's old. It has bathrooms and stuff, right?"

He grinned. "Yes."

"And I have my own room?"

"Yes, Angela said she had prepared a room just for you."

"Sweet." Ben grinned and settled back into his seat as he watched the lights speed by. "Dude, I need a Vespa."

"I do, too!" Dez said.

"No, you don't," Giovanni and Matt said together, while Beatrice laughed.

"There's really no need for a scooter." Giovanni tried to reason with them. You will be within easy walking distance of most of the sites. My home is very centrally located."

"And, Honey," Matt protested, "the baby—"

"Likes going fast. He told me." Dez patted her still-flat belly and grinned at her husband. "Just like he told me that he hopes there's food at Gio's house 'cause he's starving."

Giovanni chuckled and turned back to watch the streets. They zipped through Rome, drawing closer to the neighborhood where he had kept a home for almost as long as he had been immortal. The area around the Pantheon was in the oldest part of Rome, and his unassuming home there took up half a small block. He kept it deliberately plain from the outside, but it was an excellent defensive position with many passageways and access points he had built over hundreds of years. He kept two staff members in residence, his housekeeper, Angela, and a butler, Bruno, who he saw waiting as they turned up the small, twisting street that bordered the house.

"Here we are."

Matt, who had visited before while on business for Giovanni, nodded at Bruno as he hopped out of the car and opened the back door for Dez and Ben to climb out. Bruno and the driver grabbed their bags and carried them through the green door that led to a small open courtyard paved by marble mosaics. A fountain almost identical to the one at the Houston house bubbled there, and he saw Beatrice walk in front of him, strangely nervous for her to see his oldest home.

"Gio, this is so beautiful," she murmured as she took in the arches that lined the lush courtyard and the climbing plants that Angela lovingly tended.

"Welcome home." He leaned over and brushed a kiss along her cheek before he spotted his housekeeper waiting in a corner by the front door. A smaller door leading to the kitchen and the servants' quarters was on the other side of the courtyard. Angela was wearing a simple blue dress and a warm smile, her dark eyes and silver hair shining.

"Giovanni!" She walked over, pulling him down with wrinkled hands to kiss him in greeting.

"*Ciao,* Angela," he said with a smile. Angela had grown up in his home. Her parents had been his housekeeper and butler, though Angela had never married. He had hired Bruno fifteen years before.

"And this is your beautiful bride," she said as she walked over to fuss over Beatrice. His wife squirmed in discomfort, but returned the friendly kisses Angela gave her in greeting. "I never thought I would see you married! My prayers finally are answered."

"Angela..." He didn't want to make Beatrice uncomfortable, but he knew that Angela had been thrilled when he'd sent her the letter that they were coming for a visit.

"And this is your boy," Angela said as she greeted Ben and introduced herself to his other guests. Soon, Dez and Angela were chattering away, his housekeeper thrilled to have so many people to look after. Giovanni spotted Bruno paying the driver and sorting their luggage. He was a stocky man, happily sliding into middle age, but he was efficient and an excellent handyman, which was vital when you owned a five-hundred-year-old building.

"Bruno," he called, and the man walked over. Giovanni shook his hand and patted his shoulder in greeting. "How is the house?"

They spent a few minutes going over details, Bruno describing the leaking in the first floor bathroom that had been repaired the week before while Giovanni held onto his hand.

"Bruno, I want you to take the rest of the month off. I will call you if necessary."

He could see the man's eyes swim under his influence. "But, the guests—"

"I will call you if you are needed, but my wife is American and not accustomed to so much domestic help. You understand, I am sure."

Bruno blinked rapidly. "Of course."

"And there will be no interruption in your salary."

"Yes, Signor Vecchio."

"Gather your things and take a holiday. Use the house outside of Florence. I'll let them know you are coming."

"Thank you, Signore."

"Think nothing of it," he said. By the time Giovanni turned around, Matt was the only one left in the courtyard.

"Did you get rid of him?"

Giovanni nodded. "As soon as he has left, we'll check the house."

Matt chuckled and the two men walked inside, both keeping quiet until they heard the courtyard door close as Bruno left. He caught Angela's eye and the old woman nodded before she herded Beatrice, Dez, and Ben into the large kitchen.

"I'll take the top two floors," Giovanni said. "And the south passageway."

Matt frowned. "Does Bruno know about the passageways?"

"I don't know." He shrugged. "It is better to be cautious. He always seems to plant a few in places I haven't thought of before. He's surprisingly resourceful."

The human and the vampire scoured the house for electronic bugs, cameras, and any other surveillance equipment. They found a few, but it was a half-hearted effort. Bruno had worked for Livia the entire time he had been in Giovanni's employ, but he knew that the butler had gathered little intelligence for his mistress. It was an expected game; one Giovanni and Livia would both pretend to be shocked over if they ever spoke about it. Which they wouldn't.

After another half an hour, Matt was satisfied that the house was clean, but Giovanni still felt uneasy. He had a sudden thought.

"Benjamin!" he called down the hallway.

He heard a quick scuffling before the boy appeared. "Hey, you guys done? Angela made some awesome food. It's like the best spaghetti I've ever had. I can't believe how much Dez is eating. I bet she's—"

"Be quiet. If you wanted to hide a bug somewhere, where would you put it?"

Giovanni had learned from experience never to underestimate the instincts of his nephew. He also wanted to accustom the boy to thinking defensively. He saw Ben cock his head to the side.

"You said Bruno's in charge of fixing stuff, right?"

He smiled. "He is."

"Well, has he fixed anything lately? That he mentioned? He'd mention it, right? So you wouldn't get suspicious if you noticed something."

"Good thinking. Yes, the first floor bathroom was just repaired." Giovanni and Ben climbed the stairs, and Giovanni led the boy to the recently repaired bathroom. Ben turned and looked at his uncle.

"Well?"

Giovanni opened his senses, searching for the faint buzz, almost like a vibrating thread, that he would usually pick up from a small electronic device. It was small, but appeared to come from just behind a patch of new plaster.

"Well, damn." He'd have to have it repaired again. He punched through and plucked the small bug that was hidden behind the wall, holding it up so that Ben could see it before he crushed it between his fingers.

"Cool! Got one."

"Excellent thinking, Benjamin. And I don't feel anything else in here. Go tell Matt it appears the house is clear."

Ben rushed downstairs while Giovanni brushed at the plaster dust on his hands. He felt Beatrice come to stand in the doorway behind him.

"How is Angela's cooking, Tesoro?"

"Fantastic. And tell me again why you don't just fire him?"

"Oh"—Giovanni chuckled as he walked past and squeezed her waist—"she'd be expecting that, and I'd just have to look for a new butler."

"Yep, Gio." He heard her call down the hall as he followed the scent of herb focaccia that Angela knew he loved. "I can't imagine why I'm nervous about meeting Livia!"

CHAPTER 5

There were certain things about having gobs of money that Beatrice had become used to. She never worried about paying her bills. She liked being able to buy her own house when she was single. And she never went crazy with her money; in fact, she ended up giving a lot to charity just because she felt guilty for robbing Lorenzo. She had pretty simple tastes, but liked being able to buy what she wanted, when she wanted.

Which, that morning, happened to be another computer keyboard.

"Damn it!" she yelled, tossing the keyboard on the floor where it shattered.

Ben rushed into the small library, which had been light-proofed like most of the rest of the house. "What's up?" He looked down. "Oh."

She sighed. "Bring me another one. This time with the rubber keyboard cover and see if Angela has any of those big freezer bags that the keyboard might fit in. I think moisture in the air is becoming a problem."

"If you need help looking for something—"

"No!" She shut her eyes. "Sorry, Ben. I appreciate it, I just..."

"It's okay." He nodded and backed out of the room. "I get it."

"Thanks." Beatrice bent and picked up the pieces of the keyboard, tossing them in the waste bin before she sat down at the desk again. She took a pencil and manipulated the roller ball attached to the computer at the desk. They had learned their lesson in Chile about Beatrice and laptops, but she still had hope that she would find some way to use a desktop computer, since she had less contact while operating it. So far, she was only on her second monitor, though the keyboard was proving a challenge.

Yes, she decided, money did have its privileges.

She smiled at Angela as the housekeeper passed in the hall, still giving her a slightly wary look. Beatrice knew the fact that she could be awake and alert during the day freaked the woman out. Despite that, Angela was so sweet that Beatrice could hardly blame her for it. She knew she was an oddity. She had the strength of an ancient vampire wrapped in the coordination and attitude of a baby. She had never fit in during her human life, why start now?

"B, got it!"

Ben barreled into the library and dropped off a new computer keyboard, a neoprene case she had cut out to fit it, and a large plastic bag that looked like a large version of the bags they received when they bought donated blood.

Speaking of blood...

Her fangs popped out when Dez entered the room. Beatrice had no idea why it was still happening. She had absolutely no desire to drink from Dez, but the longer her friend was pregnant, the more Beatrice reacted when she was near. Tenzin had speculated that, far from bloodlust, it was a latent protective instinct for Dez and her unborn child.

"Hey, I think we're going to take Ben to the Colosseum this afternoon. He keeps asking to see where the lions ate the Christians. Think we should worry?"

"I doubt it. And you know that there's no specific historical accounts of—"

"Yes, yes." Dez rolled her eyes. "I know. Next you're going to tell me Russell Crowe never really fought there, either."

Beatrice snorted. "Well, you guys have fun. Want to meet somewhere for dinner later?"

"Don't you and Gio have the meeting with the mother-in-law of doom later?"

She shrugged. "There's some sort of cocktail party at her place later tonight, but not until one or two in the morning, so we could meet you guys for dinner."

"Okay, cool! We'll call the house after the sun sets. Also, I'm very curious what a Roman aristocrat serves at a cocktail party."

"Um, I'm going to guess... cocktails."

Dez narrowed her eyes. "And the blood of her enemies."

"Oh, well that too, of course."

"Of course!" Dez skipped out of the room and Beatrice wondered when the fabled exhaustion of pregnant women would hit her friend. So far, Dez seemed to have *more* energy, not less. Though apparently, from the agonized whining she heard from their room every day, the morning sickness was in full swing. Angela just clucked her tongue at Dez and fed her grapefruit for some reason.

Beatrice was reading through the journals again when she heard Giovanni start to wake. She set them down and slipped upstairs. She was trying to be better about being next to him when he woke because she knew he liked it. She was also worried about him. He seemed to be dreaming more, though when he woke, she suspected the dreams were more like nightmares. His eyes held a lean, haunted look that was only growing worse.

A FALL OF WATER

She slid under the covers next to him just as he began to move, tucking herself under his arm as he pulled her tight, even as he slumbered.

"Mmm." He began to murmur something in Italian. His accent, she noticed with pleasure, was heavier since they'd arrived. He slipped into his native language more, and she was grateful that understanding him was no longer a problem. Beatrice had already been able to speak English, Spanish, and Latin before she turned. But now she could speak Italian and a lot of Mandarin, too. She could also read classical Greek, Persian, and Arabic. She was still working on her Hebrew.

Giovanni stopped speaking and nuzzled into her neck as he began to tease her clothes off even before he was fully awake. Now that, she decided, was talent.

"You move differently here."

"I what?" Giovanni blinked and looked around as they walked up the Via dei Condotti, past the luxury shops, headed toward the *ristorante* where Matt had chosen to meet them after their walking tour with Ben.

"You move differently." She slid an arm around his waist, keeping pace with easy strides. "I don't know, you're more... Italian, I guess."

"Beatrice, I am a Florentine. I will always be a Florentine."

"But see"—she poked his side—"Like that. In L.A. you would just say you're Italian. But here, you're *Florentine*."

"So?" He frowned. "I'm in Rome. There is a difference. Is there something wrong with this?"

"No, it's cute."

"Cute?"

"And you walk different, too. You're not in as much of a hurry here."

He just grunted at her, no doubt thinking she was imagining it, but she wasn't. He looked... lighter, somehow. Comfortable. In California, she often thought Giovanni seemed more British than Italian, but here, he gestured more. His accent was stronger. His shoulders were more expressive, and his eyes more languorous.

"Whatever it is, it's hot. So go with it."

"Oh?" He grinned. "Is that so?"

"Yes."

He leaned down and whispered something very dirty in her ear. If she could have blushed, she would have. Then he nipped at her ear and murmured, "Does it sound better in Italian?"

"Yes."

He pinched her waist and kept walking. "I'll keep that in mind."

They spotted Matt waiting outside the restaurant. He waved at them and jogged over.

"Hey, guys. Dez and Ben are inside. I just wanted to catch you before you went in. Gio, Emil Conti's inside."

Giovanni only raised an eyebrow. "Interesting."

Matt shrugged. "He does live around here, so it's not that unexpected."

Beatrice looked between them. "Emil Conti? Who's that again?" The name sounded vaguely familiar.

"Old Roman," Giovanni said. "Water vampire, very old family from the Republic. He's older than Livia, but has never enjoyed her popularity. He's not the attention-seeking kind."

"Brilliant guy, though," Matt added. "He could easily take Rome if he really tried."

Giovanni hummed. "That's debatable. I'm not certain what his support would be like. He and Livia have entertained a low-key rivalry for a few centuries, so I know she considers him a threat, but I'm not sure he has the ambition. Is Donatella with him?"

Matt shook his head. "No, a female companion. No one I recognize."

"Probably just out for a meal." Giovanni tugged on her waist and walked forward. "Tesoro, nothing to worry about. Let's say hello, then we'll join you, Matt. Thank you for the notice."

"No problem. He nodded at me. Recognized me, so I'm sure he's expecting you."

"Oh my, Kirby," Giovanni said. "Don't tell me we've become predictable. I might have to fire you."

"Eh." Matt shrugged. "I'm not worried. Who else would keep the secret of your embarrassing pro-wrestling addiction?"

Beatrice laughed and squeezed her husband's waist. "He's got a point."

Giovanni scowled, but she could see the smile flirting at the corner of his mouth. "Blackmail is an ugly business."

"But so lucrative." Matt held the door open and a mustached host, who nodded toward Matt and Giovanni, greeted them. She saw her mate scan the restaurant, but her own senses had already located the energy signature in the corner. They walked toward the vampire, who rose to greet them when they were a few feet away.

Like everything else in immortal society, Beatrice had discovered that greetings usually mirrored the culture and time where the vampire originated. She briefly wondered what the form of greeting had been in the Roman Republic, but was surprised when Emil Conti simply held out a hand to Giovanni. The two men shook before Beatrice was introduced.

"Emil, I would introduce my wife, Beatrice De Novo."

"A pleasure." Emil bowed slightly over her hand as he took it. Emil Conti looked nothing like an ancient Roman. He looked like a very formal, very successful, Italian businessman. He was handsome and wore clothes straight out of a fashion magazine. His dark hair was trimmed neatly, and his broad smile was gleaming white. Beatrice wondered whether dental care was really that good in ancient Rome, or whether he'd had work done.

"Beatrice, this is Emil Conti, a very old acquaintance of mine."

"May I call you Beatrice?" the vampire asked politely. "A beautiful name."

"Sure." She couldn't help but smile back. "It's nice to meet you, Signor Conti."

"But you must call me Emil, of course." He turned to Giovanni. "May I congratulate you on your marriage? I cannot deny I was surprised by the news, but very happy for your fortune. It is a blessing to find one's true mate."

Giovanni glanced at the blond woman still sitting at the table silently. "And where is Donatella this evening?"

Emil gave a careless shrug. "Shopping, probably. I think she's in town, but she's getting ready to leave for the lakes for the summer. You know how the city can be."

"Of course."

"I don't want to keep you; I saw your friends waiting for you, but thank you for introducing me to your lovely wife."

"Will you be at Livia's later?"

"Of course," he said. "Who would miss it?"

"You, Emil." Giovanni chuckled. "If you could avoid it graciously."

Emil gave another shrug and waved them off. "Go, enjoy your meal. I'll see you at the circus later. The squid-ink capellini with lemon and caviar is excellent tonight."

"Thank you."

Beatrice smiled. "Very nice to meet you."

He gave her a little bow and a wink. "And you as well, Beatrice De Novo. *Benvenuto a Roma*. May you have a pleasant visit in our beautiful city."

They walked back to the table and she could feel Giovanni's fingers in the small of her back.

"Benvenuto a Roma," he muttered. "Welcome to the shark pool, Tesoro."

Castello Furio, Lazio

"So, this is a *castle*?"

"Yes." He looked out the window as they twisted through the country roads northeast of the city. "Livia keeps a rather lavish apartment in the city during the winter, but she leaves the city in the summer when it starts getting warm and there are more tourists."

"Well, that makes sense."

"And she likes to make people come to her."

"That kind of makes sense, too."

He laughed and draped an arm around her in the dark car he had ordered. They were seated in the back with the privacy shield raised so they were not disturbed. Livia had offered to send a car for them, but Giovanni had demurred, stating that he didn't know how long they would be able to stay. He had done the polite dance over the phone the evening before with Livia's social secretary, the secretary pressing Giovanni to spend a few days at the castle, while Giovanni insisted that they could not neglect their own guests in the city. In the end, her husband's polite stubbornness had prevailed.

"So, we will go. We will introduce you to everyone. She will try to persuade you to persuade *me* to stay for a few days at the country house—"

"You mean, the castle."

"Why are you stuck on the 'castle' bit? This is Europe. There are castles everywhere."

"But not all of them are owned by my mother-in-law."

He frowned. "Livia is not my mother."

"But you said she kind of acts like it."

Giovanni shrugged. "She tries to."

Beatrice sighed and leaned into his shoulder. "This is so damn complicated. I thought my family was dysfunctional."

"Tesoro, you don't know the meaning of dysfunctional until you have spent time in an ancient Greek or Roman family."

"I'm starting to get that idea."

They turned into a small lane leading to an elaborate gate that didn't open by electronics, but by two uniformed servants who swung the gates out when Giovanni rolled the window down to identify himself. She saw the quick look of deference on the servants' faces before she caught the sheepish expression on Giovanni's face.

She narrowed her eyes. "You're kind of a big deal here, aren't you? Even more than your usual bad-assedness."

He cleared his throat and squirmed a little. "That is not a word, and I am somewhat well-known."

"Kind of how Tenzin is well-known at Penglai Island?"

He actually tugged at his collar. "Perhaps. Have I told you how beautiful you look tonight? That dress suits you. The color is... appropriate."

"Nice try, handsome. And what do you mean, 'appropriate?'"

"Really, there is nothing to worry about. They will all be dazzled by you."

"Right."

They pulled into a long, circular driveway in front of the biggest house Beatrice had ever contemplated entering. It was, as advertised, a castle. Round, stone towers marked the corners and huge walls rose between them. A massive iron gate was swung open as women in glittering dresses and formally-dressed men walked or darted across the lush green lawn in front. She gripped Giovanni's hand harder and wished, for some reason, that she had her *shuang gou* strapped to the back of her plum-colored cocktail dress.

"Missing your swords?"

"What?" She looked at him, amazed by his perception, until she realized that she was reaching over her shoulder as if to draw a weapon. Her husband only wore a sexy smirk. Well, that and a very nicely cut jacket and shirt over a pair of slim-cut black slacks. He looked...

"Like a prince."

He cocked his head at her as if she was crazy. "What?"

Beatrice took a deep, unnecessary breath. "Nothing. Let's go."

They left the car and walked along the pebbled pathway leading to the iron gate. They crossed under the arch and found themselves at the beginning of a long path that led over a lush green park dotted with olive trees and classical statuary. The paths were lined by immaculately cut boxwoods and the gravel paths were raked. The house itself lay spread across the back of the park, pure white, with red, terra cotta tile roofs. The arches and pillars of the facade welcomed them, but the dark hills that rose behind the castle cast an ominous shadow over the grand home.

The party was already in full swing, and tables and chairs were gathered in small groups in front of the house. The trees were lit by tiny lights that provided more than enough illumination for the vampire guests, though she doubted the humans could see very well. Small torches also lined the paths. She saw Giovanni glance at them with interest.

"Nothing to be afraid of," he murmured as he put an arm around her, nodding to the odd passerby. All the humans or vampires they passed seemed to glance at her husband with wide eyes. She saw their lips moving, heard the soft whispers, and knew that they were the subject of speculation.

"I think you may have downplayed how big a deal this was," she whispered.

"I think that Livia has gone to more trouble than I would have liked to 'welcome' us. I do apologize, but we seem to be the main attraction for the evening."

"Yeah, no kidding."

Just then, the glittering crowds seemed to part, and an immortal appeared at the end of a long pathway. She was stunning. Her dark curls were piled high on her head, and Beatrice saw diamonds glittering in the waves. She wore a vivid amethyst-colored goddess dress, one shoulder was bare, and her pale, luminous skin glowed in the moonlight and the flaming torches. Her almond shaped eyes were lined with kohl, and her lips were full and smiling.

"Oh... wow," Beatrice murmured.

"Livia," Giovanni called, tugging on her waist. She was rooted in place for only a second before she forced her feet to move toward the regal woman who lifted a hand in greeting.

"*Mio caro Giovanni*," Livia said with a smile, approaching Giovanni. She reached up and kissed him in greeting, murmuring endearments and pinching his chin. Beatrice raised an eyebrow. Either Livia was a *very* affectionate maternal-type person, or there were some Greek myth dynamics going on in her mind. Giovanni, for his part, seemed to be barely putting up with her affections, and he never let go of Beatrice's hand.

"Livia, let me introduce you to my wife."

She threw up her hands in apparent delight. "Of course, the beautiful Beatrice!" Livia turned to her, the picture of welcome. "Let me greet you, my daughter." She kissed her cheeks, embraced her, and Beatrice felt the cool stroke of amnis gently run down her arms. Livia stepped back and looked into her eyes. "So, you are the woman who has finally captured my Giovanni's heart. I thought it would never happen, but I see the love between you. The devotion. And it fills my own heart with joy. Welcome to *Castello Furio*, Beatrice De Novo. Let my home be yours. You are most welcome here."

If Beatrice's breath could have been stolen, it would have been. Livia was vibrant. Magnetic. Beatrice had the almost uncontrollable urge to hug her, just to get closer to the warm hum that seemed to emanate from the beautiful woman.

"Thank you." She breathed out. "I'm so happy to finally meet you."

Somehow, Livia appeared to blush. "You flatter me, my dear. It is my honor to meet you. And I simply adore your dress. Come, let me introduce you to my people." She pulled her away from Giovanni and linked their arms as she guided Beatrice through the clutches of eager vampires and humans at the party. Beatrice panicked for a moment until she felt Giovanni's fingers reach out and his amnis caressed her arm, holding her even as they were separated.

Beatrice felt like a celebrity. Everyone wanted to meet her. Everyone complimented her dress. Everyone hung on her every word. It was strange. It was terrifying. Giovanni fared no better. Though he hung behind them, he had his fingers twined with hers while they greeted more people than Beatrice could ever remember, even with her improved memory.

"And you are sired from water, too. As all in our family are. What more could I ask from a daughter?" The group around them seemed to titter at Livia's quip. Beatrice glanced over her shoulder to see Giovanni roll his eyes slightly. She hadn't thought about it before, but unlike the hum of energy at Penglai, Livia's party had a very low energy signature except for a few bright spots. As they moved through the party, Beatrice began to take note of the strongest signatures, noting whom they belonged to and who was gathered around them.

There was a tall woman with strong Germanic features that held court with a

A FALL OF WATER

group of tall vampires around her. She was stronger than most, but not as vibrant as Livia.

A regal man with ebony skin and a booming laugh caught her attention from one corner. His signature was very strong, but he didn't feel very old. He also had an entourage gathered around him.

Another, quieter immortal drifted around the edges of the party. He stopped to talk to others every now and then before quickly moving on. He looked North African, his features a fascinating blend of Arab and African. His face was scarred, and he didn't seem to attract much attention, but his energy swirled and drifted in a fascinating way. The vampire felt old. Very old. She noticed Giovanni hadn't acknowledged him before her attention was drawn to a familiar voice.

"Signora De Novo, how did you like the restaurant?"

"Signor Conti," Beatrice smiled. "It was lovely. How nice to see you again." Beatrice could tell her familiarity with Livia's rival came as a surprise to her hostess, but Livia's eyes flickered for only a second before the happy mask descended again.

"You are acquainted, then? How lovely. Signor Conti is from one of the oldest families in Rome. Our people have known each other for centuries."

"It is a pleasure to see you again, Beatrice." Emil bowed again, this time kissing the back of her hand, a gesture common among the immortal men she had met. Every time it happened, she stifled a snicker as Giovanni's amnis tightened around her waist as if he was a second away from pulling her back into his arms.

They continued to circulate for hours, and it was growing late when Giovanni finally pulled Beatrice from Livia's company. He promptly gathered her under his arm and found a quiet corner.

"Are you ready to go? Please say yes."

"I think we better if we're going to make it back to the house before dawn."

He nodded. "Stay here. She'll draw you into another round of socializing until we're forced to stay here at the castle. She keeps rooms for me here, but I don't want to stay unless you do."

"No." She shook her head. "I want to go home."

"Excellent. I'll be right back."

Beatrice watched him cross the party to speak to Livia, and the conversation of gestures began. She watched for only a moment before her eyes scanned the crowd again. She was hiding in the shadows, trying to avoid notice, but one set of eyes caught hers. It was the North African vampire with the pockmarked face. He gave her a deep, respectful nod before he seemed to disappear into the shadows on the other side. She searched for him, but did not see him again.

"All right. We're free." Giovanni pulled her under his arm, shuffling them along the edges of the party-goers and out the grand iron gate toward the car.

"So, when do we have to come back?"

He grimaced. "Wednesday. She's hosting a concert here, and I somehow agreed that we would come."

Beatrice chuckled. Something about Livia definitely bothered her, but at the same time, it was kind of funny to see Giovanni put at a disadvantage. Usually, he was unbending.

"I see you laughing at me, Tesoro. Watch out"— he pinched her thigh—"or I'll be forced to assert my 'bad-assedness.'"

She winked as he opened the door for her. "Promise?"

Beatrice heard him tap on the driver's window. The window rolled down and Giovanni threw two hundred Euro notes at the man. "Drive fast."

CHAPTER 6

Giovanni almost missed telling the driver the last turn to the house, he was so distracted by his wife's attentions. They had both discovered the benefits of having a lover with shared blood. As long as they maintained skin contact, they could send their energy over each other to tease their mate's senses. It had become a kind of game for Beatrice, and she enjoyed trying to break his concentration in public. The car was almost as fun.

He was ready to tear her beautiful new dress by the time they got back to the house, and he almost snarled when they exited the car and heard the telltale skid of the football in the courtyard along with the low laugh of his old friend.

Beatrice blinked, as lust-hazed as he was. "Wha—who's that?"

"Carwyn's here." He glanced at her red, swollen lips, knowing they'd have to pretend to be polite for at least a few minutes.

Damn priest.

Beatrice sighed and pushed the courtyard door open, only to immediately dodge the football that came in her direction.

"B, kick it back!"

She glared at Ben. "In these shoes? I don't think so."

"So fancy, you two." Carwyn stepped from the shadows with a grin. "You didn't really need to get so dressed up for me." He walked over and embraced Beatrice. "You look lovely, though. I appreciate the effort. Oh, and you smell nice, too." He only grinned when Giovanni growled at him. "You ready to run away with me yet?"

Giovanni picked up the football and tossed it at his friend's head. "No, she's not."

Carwyn only batted it away, not letting Beatrice out of his embrace. "And *you* definitely didn't need to get fancied up, Gio. I've told you a thousand times, I'm not interested."

"Haha. Why are you playing football with my nephew at four in the morning?"

He saw Ben begin to speak, but Giovanni only raised a finger to silence him. The boy was smarter than the priest.

"Well..." Carwyn placed a kiss on Beatrice's forehead before he ran after the ball and kicked it toward Ben again. "I'm playing football with *my* nephew because I just got here, and I am the cool uncle. You are the boring one."

He heard Beatrice and Ben both snicker, but Beatrice said, "Honestly, Ben, how long have you been up?"

"Just an hour or so." He kicked the ball back to Carwyn. "We were talking."

"Well, it's time for you to sleep."

"No." The boy whined. "You're going to talk about interesting things, and I'll miss it all."

Beatrice grabbed him around the collar and shoved him toward the door. "Say goodnight. I promise we won't plot murder and mayhem without you."

"Promise?"

"Promise. And you..." she turned back to Giovanni. "Don't be too long. I'm going to bed."

Ben made gagging noises as Carwyn let out a wolf-whistle. Giovanni grinned and gave her a wink. "Goodnight, Benjamin," he said, then whispered something suggestive in Italian that made Beatrice bite her lip and Carwyn roar with laughter.

"What?" He heard Ben say as they walked up the stairs. "Oh, I don't want to know, do I?"

"Nope."

Giovanni's ears tracked for a few more minutes until he heard the door to Ben's room shut. He turned to Carwyn, who kicked him the football. "Well?"

"Well, what?"

"What's going on with you?"

Carwyn shrugged. "It's nothing for you to be concerned about. And my trip here was nicely boring, thanks. I caught one of Jean's boats to Genoa and came from there. That Frenchman's not half bad, after all. Fantastic food—"

"Why were you so eager to come here?"

"Aren't you happy to see me?"

The two old friends kicked the ball back and forth in the low light of the courtyard, the skidding and bouncing the only sound in the still morning air. Giovanni could smell the scent of bread baking at the *paneterria* on the corner.

"Of course I am. And you know how happy Beatrice is to see you. I just wonder—"

"She looks amazing, by the way."

"I know. That dress does suit her."

Carwyn shook his head. "I'm not talking about her damn dress. You probably don't notice because you see her every day, but she looks extraordinary. She's very comfortable in her skin. Doesn't have that awkward, hungry look the new ones usually do."

"Ah. Yes, she's doing extremely well."

"If I didn't know her, I'd think she was twenty years immortal, at least."

"That old?"

Carwyn nodded, still kicking the ball back and forth, dribbling around the courtyard to amuse himself. He was dressed in black. Black pants, black T-shirt, black leather jacket, but no collar, which he often wore when in Rome.

"So, the meeting with the empress went well?"

"Yes." Giovanni said. "Livia's fine. We're going back on Wednesday for a concert. It's supposed to be good. Care to come along? I know Beatrice would like some company she didn't have to perform for."

Only a careful observer would have noticed the slight hitch in Carwyn's step. "Wednesday? Can't."

"Oh?"

"Meeting with the men in bathrobes on Wednesday night."

"Oh?" Giovanni chuckled at his friend's pet name for some of the Vatican staff he usually met with if he came to Rome, which wasn't often.

"Yes, one red bathrobe in particular."

"A cardinal?"

"A friend."

Carwyn passed him the ball, but Giovanni stopped it and held it under his foot, waiting for his friend to meet his eye. "What's going on, Father?"

Carwyn took a deep breath and frowned. "I'm not sure yet. Something... maybe long overdue. I'll let you know. It's nothing to be concerned about." He walked over and placed a hand on Giovanni's shoulder before he grinned and kicked the ball out from under his foot. "If there's something to worry about, I'll tell you. Now, go shag your wife like you were planning before I interrupted you with my arrival."

"Fine." He turned toward the door. "You'll let me know?"

"Of course I will. Go away."

He walked through the door, calling back, "Your room is ready for you when you get tired. Don't damage any of Angela's plants."

"Go away!"

When Giovanni walked through his bedroom door, he was greeted by the sight of his wife, naked, sitting in a chair and draped over the cello he kept in the closet of the Rome house.

"You've never played this one for me."

He fastened the series of locks on the door and walked toward her slowly. "No?"

"Nope." She looked up with hooded eyes. "You should. It would be..." He took a finger, running it down her spine as she curled over the body of the instrument.

"What would it be?"

He heard her heart begin to pulse. "Relaxing."

"Do you need to be relaxed?" He knelt beside her, placing soft kisses along her side. Her shoulder, the crook of her arm. Her hip. Her knee. His fingers trailed up from her ankle.

"Maybe," she gasped. "But not just yet."

His hand gripped her knee as he pulled the instrument from her, propping it against the wall before he lifted her and sat in the chair, letting her naked body straddle him as he sat fully clothed.

"I love you," she said as his mouth began exploring her skin. He rubbed his lips along the rise of her breasts and let his fangs scrape her delicate collarbones. His fingers trailed down her spine, over her hips and down her thighs.

She gripped his hair hard, but Giovanni remained silent, watching her in the low light as his fingers slowly brought her to release. She gasped his name into the silence of their bedroom before he bent his head and let his fangs pierce her skin, just above the delicate scars on her breast.

"More." She panted as her back arched and he drew harder on the small wound.

More? It would never be enough.

He did play for her, hours later as the sun rose in the sky and Beatrice drifted in a haze, awake, but sated and quiet. He could feel her energy level out to a hum that told him she was meditating in the way that allowed her mind to rest, even if her body could not.

Giovanni did not envy her waking days. Even though his recent dreams had plagued him, he still took comfort in the sweet oblivion that rest brought. Though he needed less now that they shared blood, he fervently hoped that sleep would never abandon him completely.

THE NEXT EVENING, BEATRICE AND GIOVANNI, MATT AND DEZ, CARWYN, Ben, and even Angela gathered in the large kitchen of the house. Ben had slept until past noon before wandering out of the house with Dez as they explored the neighborhood and ate copious amounts of gelato. Angela was feeding them another full dinner. Giovanni smiled as he watched her enjoy the humans in the house with normal appetites.

"I can't believe how much I'm eating," Dez said, as she shoveled more pasta in her mouth.

"Neither can I." Beatrice stared at her in amazement.

"Hey." Dez glared. "I'm growing a human here. What's your superpower?"

"Speed. Strength. Night vision. Lightning fast reflexes. Water manipulation—"

"Okay, stupid question."

Ben piped up, "Don't forget allergy to electronics and sunlight."

Carwyn looked amused. "How have you managed to remain unbitten, boy?"

"It's been close a couple times with Tenzin."

Giovanni examined Dez, knowing that Beatrice worried about her friend. He knew she had been experiencing some morning sickness. "Dez, how are you? Did Angela point you toward a pharmacy? I know you're not very familiar with the city."

Dez smiled. "I'm great! And Ben gets around in Italy a lot better than me. We found a drug store the other day that has the stuff I forgot at home. But thanks for that basket in my room, too. That make-up is so nice."

He waved a hand. "Thank Livia. She has some sort of cosmetics company that makes all those things. She always sends over baskets when she knows I'm bringing guests.

"Well, please tell her I said thank you. B, did you get one, too?"

Beatrice looked up. "Get what?"

"The basket of make-up, perfume, lotions..." Dez rolled her eyes when Beatrice looked back in confusion. "Am I the only girl here? I swear, you and Tenzin are hopeless."

The priest looked around the house. "Where is she, by the way?"

Beatrice shrugged. "Not here yet. You know Tenzin."

"Okay," Giovanni said. "We met with Livia last night and met many vampires. Beatrice, who do you want to know about? Matt, this might be beneficial to you, too."

She leaned forward. "First off, why isn't that place humming the way Penglai does?"

Carwyn burst into laughter, but Beatrice shook her head. "Really, it's so weird! There were at least as many vampires at Livia's little party last night, but it didn't have half the energy of a 'low hum' day at Penglai."

Giovanni nodded. "I'm glad you noticed. Did you notice what else is missing from Castello Furio?"

She thought for a minute before her eyes lit up. "Water."

Dez looked around. "What? She doesn't have plumbing there? Even the Romans had aqueducts, right?"

Giovanni shook his head. "No, what Beatrice noticed, and I'm glad she did, is that for a water vampire, Livia does not surround herself with her element. It's an odd quirk for an immortal, because most of us draw strength from our elements. In Penglai, there's a careful balance of the elements. Many fountains and streams, gardens and rocks, most of the palace complex is open air, they even have torches lit at all times for those of the fire element. The idea being a kind of balanced threat."

"Ah." Dez nodded. "Got it. So if everyone has easy access to their element, no one's going to go crazy and try to take over."

"Like mutually assured destruction," Ben said with a full mouth. "I learned about that in school."

Matt said, "You learned something in school that you didn't already know?"

"Haha."

"The point is," Beatrice continued, "Livia's place should have all sorts of water around her house, but she doesn't. And all the vampires in her court seem really weak."

Carwyn said, "Tenzin would say it's because most of them drink donated blood and live in such a modern environment. The longer I live, the more I think she may be on to something."

"If anything," Beatrice said, "her house would favor earth and wind vampires, with all the open ground and the stone castle."

"She has a castle?" Ben asked. "Cool."

"Maybe that's why Matilda has always seemed so haughty," Giovanni mused.

"Who's Matilda?" three voices asked at once.

Carwyn spoke. "Tall. Blond. She's German. About my age. Very powerful wind vampire. She and Livia hate each other."

"Too many queen bees." Dez nodded. "There can be only one."

Matt snorted. "You watch too much T.V."

"Okay, so that's the blonde I noticed," Beatrice said. "Yeah, she felt strong. Who's the huge guy? Really tall. Big laugh. He looked African? His energy was strong, too."

Giovanni nodded. "He is. That's Bomeni. He's Ethiopian, but he's not as old, maybe my age."

"Who's his sire?" Beatrice leaned forward with interest. He suspected she was thinking about Geber's four blood donors. The Ethiopian he had written about was an earth vampire and a female.

"I don't know. It's a possibility we should investigate. He *is* an earth vampire from the right part of the world."

"Okay, so the most powerful vampires I noticed were Matilde, Bomeni, and Emil Conti, who is... water?"

"Yes."

"And then the weird guy."

He frowned. "What weird guy?"

"You didn't notice him?"

Giovanni shook his head. "Notice who?"

"There was this old vampire. He didn't just feel old—he *looked* it. Scarred face. Maybe North African? He was wearing these long robes. He looked out of place, to be honest. His amnis was weird. Kind of swirling around him, almost visible in some strange way. If I had to guess, I'd say he was a wind vampire, but I'm just guessing. Something about him reminded me of Tenzin."

Carwyn looked at Giovanni. "That sounds like Ziri."

"If Ziri was there, how could I have missed him?"

Beatrice looked between them. "Who's Ziri?"

Carwyn shrugged. "You hear strange stories about Ziri. With his age and power, it's hard to say what's true. I know one vampire, who is not an imaginative sort, say that Ziri melted into the air in front of him."

Giovanni scowled. "Impossible."

Matt piped up. "Hey, they say that at some point transporter technology may be feasible. We *are* creatures made up of mostly empty space at an atomic level. Maybe Ziri has just taken a leap."

Giovanni said, "Be that as it may, it sounds like Beatrice saw him last night. He's the only one that fits her description, and he does visit Rome on occasion."

"He doesn't live here?" Ben asked. "In Rome?"

"He doesn't really live anywhere that I know of," Giovanni said. "He was probably a nomad in his human life—he's very old—and couple that with a wind element... He roams."

"And right now, he's roaming in Rome." Ben snorted, looking around when no one laughed. He slumped in his seat. "Tenzin would have laughed."

They quickly finished their meal and cleaned up the kitchen before they went to the living room for drinks.

"So," Beatrice asked, "no fire vampires in Livia's court?"

"No." He shook his head. "Just me. She doesn't like them."

"Just you."

He shrugged. "Just me."

Carwyn said, "Oh, she loves Gio, all right."

Beatrice raised her eyebrows. "Okay, so it's not just me that was getting the incest vibe. Good to know."

"She's not my mother!"

"Still, Sparky." Carwyn leaned against the fireplace. "You have to admit she's always been very... affectionate with you."

"Ew," Ben said as he sat on the couch and began to nibble at the dish of dry, sugared fruit that Angela set out. "That's so gross."

Matt grinned. "You probably wouldn't say that if you saw her."

Dez elbowed him. "What's that supposed to mean?"

"It means she's incredibly beautiful," Beatrice said. "Really, stunningly beautiful. She looks like she should be a model, or something."

Giovanni cleared his throat. "Let's get back to business. Now that Carwyn's here, we have enough people to start getting some information. Matt, your main job is still going to be security, but Ben is old enough that he can do some, as well."

"Really?" Ben sat up straighter.

"Yes, Matt will get a firearm for you. Carry it with you when you go out, especially if Dez goes with you. And your knives. Carry those, as well."

The boy suddenly looked nervous. "Am I going to get in all sorts of trouble if I get caught with them, though?"

"On the slight chance you have to use them, we'll worry about getting you out of police custody after you've defended yourself. Priorities, Benjamin."

Matt elbowed the boy. "Hey, I've got some friends in the police here. Don't worry about it. Just keep yourself safe and remember: money and amnis erase criminal records."

Giovanni continued, "Matt will be our day man if we need information or investigation during the day. Our main objective on this trip is identifying Geber's four vampires, which will mainly be up to Beatrice and me. Chances are that Stephen's contact is a member of Livia's court, or a frequent visitor, and since we believe he is one of Geber's four, finding him is our starting point."

Carwyn said, "I'll be looking into finding more about what Ioan was researching. I have some avenues here since he had colleagues in the city that I know he corresponded with, and I'll be looking into private pharmaceutical labs in Eastern Europe, as well."

Dez frowned. "Why pharmaceutical labs?"

Beatrice said, "Lorenzo has the formula. He's going to want to produce it. It may be in production already."

"Speaking of Lorenzo," Matt said. "What are we doing there? Have we had any word?"

Giovanni spoke quietly. "Tenzin has requested we leave locating Lorenzo to her."

"By herself?" Ben asked.

"It is her mate that was killed, Benjamin."

"But no one's going to help her?"

Beatrice leaned toward the boy. "If she finds him, she won't need help."

Dez was sitting silently with narrowed eyes. "But would modern labs even have what you needed for a medieval alchemic formula? We're talking about plant ingredients, mainly. Produced in Persia in the early ninth century..."

Beatrice smiled. "I always forget your thesis was on medieval science, Dez."

"I'm just doubting that your modern chemistry labs are going to have the kind of ingredients you would need. And for the formula to work as intended, they would have to be organic..."

Giovanni began pacing the room. It was an angle he hadn't considered. The woman was right. Modern chemistry labs wouldn't have access to traditional plant ingredients like Geber had used in the formula. Though he didn't know the exact preparation, Stephen remembered the majority of the ingredients were plant-based and Zhang Guo confirmed it before they left China.

"So," Carwyn said, "who would have access to those kind of ingredients, if not a chemistry lab? What should I be looking for? Are we still talking about Eastern Europe? Stephen's contact in Rome—"

"Botanicals!" Dez stood and looked at him with a look of triumph in her eyes. "The baskets, Gio!"

Beatrice looked up. "What?"

"Of course." Giovanni breathed out before he strode over to Dez, placed two hands on her shoulders, and kissed her full on the mouth. "Dez, you brilliant, beautiful genius. I think you're right."

She grinned. "They're organic. Plant based! The packages even say, 'Using Traditional Botanical Ingredients,' also..." She took a deep breath and brought a hand to her lips. "Wow, I mean, B said, but... wow."

Giovanni smirked at her and both of them turned back to the rest of the room, all of whom were looking at the two of them in frank confusion.

Ben spoke first. "That was... weird."

Beatrice had her head tilted to the side. "I'm missing something. What about botanicals?"

Dez was still blinking a little. Matt narrowed his eyes. "Are you swooning?"

She shot him a look. "Hey! There's this tingly kind of... thing with the amnis that just kind of... you know, when the lips touch, just... shut up."

Beatrice smiled as Dez moved back to sit next to Matt on the couch. "B, if you were more of a girly-girl, you would have figured it out ages ago." Dez pulled a tube of lip balm from her pocket and tossed it to Beatrice. "Finally, my make-up addiction has been put to good use. This is the lip gloss from the basket Livia sent over. Botanical ingredients. Read the label. It's the trendy thing right now; no one would question it. Organic plant extracts in beauty products. It's super popular. A chemistry lab isn't going to have a ready supply of botanical ingredients or suppliers, but—"

"A cosmetics company might." Carwyn grinned. "I want to kiss you myself. Good thinking, Dez."

Matt put an arm around his wife. "No, really, I got this." He leaned over to place a long kiss on her mouth. "Way to go, honey. You're brilliant."

Dez was glowing. "It's perfect. Nothing out of the ordinary. They would have labs, suppliers, packaging, even a distribution network..."

"Wait," Beatrice raised a hand. "What are we talking about here? Or rather, *who* are we talking about? Dez, are you saying what I think you're saying?" Her eyes sought out Giovanni's.

He shook his head. "Beatrice, I don't know."

Was it possible? As conflicted as his feelings toward Livia were, as complicated as their relationship had always been... would she betray him that way? Would his father's wife even consider it a betrayal?

Beatrice turned the tube of lip gloss in her fingers, shaking her head. "There are many cosmetics manufacturers in the world. Lots of companies produce this kind of thing. There are many—"

Matt broke in. "How many of those companies are owned by vampires?"

Carwyn walked toward him. "We knew that Lorenzo was supported by someone with far more money and power than just Zhongli Quan. We guessed that it was someone in Europe because of the vampires Lorenzo brought to the monastery. You have to consider it, my friend."

"It's... possible." Giovanni nodded. "It's possible that Livia might be behind it all."

CHAPTER 7

"Ah... ahahaha!" Beatrice stood and danced around the library. "I did it. I did it," she chanted, wishing Ben or Dez were there to witness her triumph.

Through a combination of plastic bags, keyboard covers, and rubber kitchen gloves, Beatrice had finally managed to type on the computer without starting a fire or shorting it out. She was dancing around the library and singing "We Are the Champions" at the top of her lungs when she heard a commotion in the hall.

"You know, you forget that I don't sleep as soundly as your husband, and my room is right down the hall," Carwyn muttered as he stumbled in the library and collapsed on the sofa. "Why am I awake?"

"Because I..." She continued to strut, a smile plastered on her face, as she sat down and hugged him. "Figured out how to work the computer by myself."

"Well, aren't you the big girl?"

"Cranky, cranky."

Carwyn glanced at the clock on the mantle, draped his arm across the back of the sofa, and gave Beatrice a squeeze. "It's twelve o'clock in the afternoon. Of course I'm cranky. But congratulations anyway."

Beatrice couldn't stop grinning, and she leaned into her friend's shoulder as he sat at her side, blinking. As silly as it may have seemed to Carwyn, being able to use a computer again felt like a huge victory.

"I should wake your husband up, just for spite. I'll pound on the door. Threaten to harm his piano. Flush his first-edition Gatsby. Something horrible like that."

She snickered. "Don't. And don't even think about the Gatsby. He hasn't been resting well lately."

"Hmph," he said and pinched her neck. "Been drinking too much daywalker."

He took a deep breath and relaxed, drifting in a hazy state as she leaned against him. Beatrice knew that, at over a thousand years old, Carwyn would often wake during the day, but unlike Tenzin or her father, he was groggy and slow. Still, it was nice to not be alone like she usually was.

"Carwyn?"

"Hmm?"

"How did your meeting go last night?"

"With the cardinal?"

"Mmmhmm."

"It was fine. About how I expected."

"Were you in trouble or anything?"

He said, "Not exactly. I'm the second oldest priest in the church. They don't really reprimand me anymore. They leave me to myself."

"*Second* oldest?"

Carwyn simply cocked an eyebrow before he closed his eyes again.

"Are there a lot of immortal priests?"

"There are a few. It's not unheard of. The church has known about vampires for hundreds of years. Perhaps longer."

Beatrice really didn't know what to think of that, except that it wasn't as surprising as it should have been. "But everything's okay?"

He squeezed her shoulders again and leaned over to kiss the top of her head. "Everything's fine, darling girl. Or it will be soon. Why is your man not resting well?"

"Dreams. He's been dreaming."

"Ah."

"He won't talk about it, though."

"Gio's always been a quiet one about things like that."

"I think he loves it and hates it here."

Carwyn chuckled. "I think you know him very well."

"I think I feel the same way."

"Well, you're both ahead of me. I just hate it."

"So why were you so eager to come here?"

He gave her a side-eye and clammed up again.

Interesting.

"Come with us to this crazy party she's throwing next week."

Carwyn groaned. "Oh, don't use the pitiful voice on me, B."

"Please." She hugged his waist. "Please. Everyone is so..."

"What?"

"Fake."

Carwyn let out a snort.

"And weird."

"You always have been a perceptive girl."

"And they all look at me like I'm some sort of cross between a celebrity and a sideshow freak. I don't care. I really don't, but it'd be nice to have someone to talk to while Gio has to play the dutiful... whatever."

"Son? Ward? Strange and inappropriate escort for his stepmother?"

"Yes, exactly."

Carwyn groaned again, but Beatrice knew she was wearing him down. "Please. Come with us. You can help me make sense of all the players in this crazy game."

"I'll tell you now. Who do you want to know about?"

"Nice subject change."

"I thought so." He sniffed and sat up, rubbing his eyes a little.

Beatrice searched her mind. "Emil Conti."

"Not a bad sort for a Roman. Far better than Livia. He's a Republican, of the ancient Roman variety, and a fairly solid businessman. He's got diverse interests. Lots of shipping, since he's a water vamp. Most of his business is run out of Genoa, and he has ties with Jean Demarais, but like most aristocrats, he farms out most of the day-to-day and stays here to dabble in politics."

"Matt said he could rule Rome if he wanted."

Carwyn frowned. "I think it would be more accurate to say that he could rule Rome if he wanted to, and Livia didn't. He's not as ambitious as she is and, as much as he dislikes her, he's not willing to go to war with her over the city, though some would like him to. The Vatican likes him. Would back him in a conflict, for what it's worth."

"How much influence do they have?"

He shrugged. "Now? Not much. In the past? Enormous. Livia courted whoever the Holy Father happened to be when it suited her in the past, but the Vatican isn't the political power that it once was. Thank heavens."

"That sounds kind of funny coming from a priest."

"Why? When I became a priest, the church wasn't a global power. It was a church. Its purpose was to shepherd the faithful, not influence worldly governments."

"This sounds like a much longer discussion than we want to have at twelve thirty in the afternoon."

"Very true." He patted her head. "What other gossip do you want? I know most of it."

She laughed. "Okay, Livia. Honestly, is she that bad? Do you actually think she could be the one behind Lorenzo?"

"Yes," he said immediately. "If it suited her purposes and enriched her holdings, yes. Gio is sentimental, but she is completely self-serving, and she's very, very greedy."

"You think—"

"I think I don't trust her to fetch my boots. She'd most likely put a scorpion in them."

She smiled. "So... good friend of yours, then?"

"Oh yes," he said. "We correspond regularly. Plus, she hates me because she blames Ioan and me for Gio retreating from public life, as she sees it."

"Oh?"

"She rather liked being the stepmother to one of the most feared vampires in Europe and Asia. Gave her a certain cache. She's been trying to convince him to move back and be her personal enforcer for centuries."

"'Personal enforcer.' Is that what they're calling it now?"

Carwyn's laughed cracked the still air. "Oh, B, I can tell you've bonded with her already."

"I'm pretty sure the feeling's mutual. She has that bitchy 'I'm pretending to like you, but I'd actually like to stab you in the eye' look I remember from high school."

Carwyn shook his head. "Heaven help me." He was silent for a few moments, drifting in the warm afternoon air. "Women are... gloriously tangled creatures, aren't they, Beatrice?"

She looked up with a smile. "You having woman problems, Father?"

Carwyn didn't answer, and Beatrice leaned back, studying his still face. She didn't know whether he had drifted off, or was just avoiding her question. "Carwyn?"

He sighed and let out a string of soft Welsh, his eyes still closed.

"Carwyn, you awake?"

"Shh." He put a heavy arm around her shoulders and pulled her a little closer. "Shh, love. Rest now, Brigid."

Beatrice's eyes flew open, and her mouth dropped. "Who's Brigid?"

At the sound of the name, Carwyn's eyes popped open. "Hmm?"

"Who's Brigid?"

He only frowned and cleared his throat. "Sixth century Irish bishop. Patron saint of Ireland. Who else do you want to know about? Matilda? Bomeni?"

"You're *so* not getting out of that question!"

He shifted and scooted forward, as if to go. "I should go back to sleep. Keep your celebrating down, B."

She pulled on his arm. "No fair."

He stood and turned back to her. "If I recall, once upon a time, you weren't quite so forthcoming about a certain vampire and *your* feelings, so leave it be."

"Carwyn, what—"

"Leave it be." His voice was rough, and a light flared in his eyes.

She sat, looking up at him. He didn't look angry, or even irritated. He looked... peaceful. And maybe a little resigned. "You'll tell me someday?"

A smile crept across his face. "I'll tell you when there's something to tell."

Beatrice couldn't help meeting his smile with one of her own. "Yeah?"

"Yes."

"Okay." She rose from the couch and gave him a quick hug. "Do you really need to sleep?"

He shook his head. "I can stay awake for you, if you've a need for company."

"'Night of the Living Dead?'"

"Romero?" He slowly walked toward the doorway.

"Of course."

"Well"—Carwyn raised his arms and stumbled down the hall—"Zombies do seem strangely appropriate at the moment."

"You try to eat my brain, and I'll get the swords out."

"Oooh, scary."

"I can't believe how much gelato I'm eating."

Ben eyed Dez as she scooped up another spoonful. "It is pretty amazing. But then, I think we just need to accept that we are no longer eating lunch while we're in Rome."

"Yep, gelato is its own food group here."

Dez leaned back against the cool pillar as they sat in the shade in front of the Pantheon. They had woken that morning as they did most mornings since they had come to Rome. Late. Angela fed them breakfast before Dez and Ben struck out to explore the Temple of Hadrian, which was fairly close to the house. Every day, they would take in some site that the guidebooks recommended before they found a suitable *gelateria* and a shady place to people-watch.

Even though Ben made a game of flirting with Dez, she and Matt were two of his favorite people, and the three were having a great time exploring the city. If he was free, Matt came along, but most times, he was running an errand for Beatrice or Giovanni. That morning, he happened to be meeting with some of his "friends" to procure a suitable weapon for Ben to carry when he was in Rome. Ben slipped a hand into his pocket and felt the cool grip of the knife his uncle had given him the night before.

"Carry it whenever you go out. Particularly if you're with Dez. Get to know the neighborhood. Learn the streets. We're relying on you. Be smart, Benjamin."

His eyes darted around the square, watching the bustling crowd. Tourist season had already started, but Ben knew enough about cities to be able to spot the locals. He may have spent the previous few years taking it easy in Houston and L.A., but he had been born in New York and raised himself on the streets. And big cities, he knew, were remarkably similar in a lot of ways.

He could still spot the tourists with the fattest wallets. He could spot the savvy local girls. And he could definitely spot the guy with the shiny forehead wearing the unseasonably warm jacket who was trying a little too hard to be inconspicuous.

"Okay, I'm stuffed." Dez stood and stretched, shoving her sunglasses up her nose and looking around. Ben could hear the trickle of the fountain in the background, and the murmur of the crowd, but he kept an eye on the suspicious man out of the corner of his eye. The guy was definitely eyeing Dez, and Ben didn't think it was because of her California-girl looks.

"Ben?"

"Huh?"

"Let's head back to the house. I'm getting sleepy. Do you mind?"

Ben stood and casually slung his backpack over his shoulder. "Nah, that's cool." He slipped his hand into his pocket and started toward the street that would lead them to Giovanni's house. Very subtly, he noticed the man shift in their direction before he looked down at the newspaper he was reading. As Dez and Ben left the shade of the temple, they turned right and Ben caught the man following them at a distance.

"Hey, Dez?"

"Yeah?"

Ben grabbed her hand and hustled down a side street he had mapped out the week before. It looked like an alleyway, but led to a triangular-shaped piazza surrounded by office buildings. Also headed in that direction was a blond girl who was similar to Dez in height.

Perfect. "Let's go this way, okay?"

"What?" She followed Ben, her pace matching his as they turned left into the cobblestone piazza. Ben hurried to catch up with the blonde, glancing over his shoulder. The man was definitely following them.

The triangle-shaped piazza opened up before narrowing down into a driveway leading out to a larger thoroughfare. Though that was the direction most of the pedestrian traffic was flowing; there was also a twisting walkway past a parking lot leading through the houses and to the primary school behind the Pantheon. Ben had found it when he was scoping out the neighborhood. It was roundabout, but the best way he could think of to lose whomever it was that seemed to be tailing them. The blond girl went straight; Ben tugged Dez's hand and turned left.

"Ben? Where are we going?"

"I think I saw a bookshop that had English books in the window."

Dez perked up immediately. Though Giovanni had a full library at the house, his selection of books in English was somewhat limited, so Ben and Dez had been on a hunt to expand it. He glanced over his shoulder as they turned the corner. He could see the man following the blond girl to the main road. Ben pulled Dez into a small shop that sold postcards and cigarettes. The man behind the counter, with the universal wisdom of all convenience store owners, eyed Ben with suspicion, only relaxing when he saw Dez walk in behind him.

"Signore, uno... uno cappelo, per favore?" Ben motioned to Dez. "Per la signora?"

The older man shrugged and pointed to the back of the shop where a few rows of tacky caps with pictures of the Colosseum were lined up. Ben grabbed a navy blue cap and tugged it on Dez's head.

"Ben, I don't see any books here. I think you—hey!" She was looking around and jerked back when Ben pushed the hat on her head. "Ew! I'm not wearing this."

"You should." He kept hold of her hand and pulled a few euros from his pocket, handing them to the shopkeeper on the way out of the store. "It's getting warm and you don't want to overheat." He peeked his head out, but couldn't see the man anywhere. "I think I was remembering a shop on the other side of the Pantheon. Where we were this morning."

"Oh." Dez looked around. "Yeah, that was a big triangle like this one. Ben, I'm not wearing this hat. It's ugly. Why did you waste the money?"

He pulled her out into the parking lot and to the left toward the alley that led to the school.

"Oh, just humor me until we get home, will you?" His eyes never stopped glancing around, looking for the shiny forehead of the man who had been watching them before. He was nowhere in Ben's sight, and he allowed himself to relax a little.

"Ben?" He finally turned and looked at Dez. She was no longer smiling. "Who was following us?"

Ben was moments away from denying it, not wanting to seem paranoid or worry her, but he stopped himself. Dez was too smart to buy the quick lie.

"I'm not sure. I remember his face. I'll try to draw it when I get home."

She just nodded and squeezed his hand. "Okay. Which way should we go back?"

Ben let out the breath he was holding. He knew he wasn't overreacting, but he'd been afraid that Dez would think so. He let her hand go, reaching back into his pocket to grasp the knife. "Down here. I checked it out last week."

She smirked and tugged the cap lower on her head. "Lead the way."

"AND HE HADN'T SEEN HIM BEFORE?" BEATRICE QUESTIONED DEZ AS THEY stood in the enormous walk-in closet in the guest room where Beatrice kept her wardrobe. She had acquired more clothes in the past month than she had in the previous three years, thanks to Dez's shopping habits, her suddenly active social calendar, and Giovanni's habit of losing his patience with buttons and zippers when the mood struck.

"No, he drew a pretty good sketch, though. He gave it to Matt as soon as he got home. Matt, Gio, and Ben are talking in the library right now."

Beatrice sighed and glanced longingly toward the door.

"Nope, not on your life. You have to figure something out to wear to this party next week, and if you're serious about not wearing that... grand occasion of a dress that Livia sent, then you better stay here." Dez pointed toward the magnificent Renaissance era gown that Livia had sent by uniformed courier the day before. It was a sixteenth century style, rich with priceless fabric and stunning detail. The wine-colored brocade would set off Beatrice's pale, luminous complexion. The gold cording around the collar would make her brown eyes and hair glow. It was stunning.

"It has a hoop skirt. Are you kidding me?"

"Technically, it's called a..." Dez looked over to the laptop on the desk. "Farthingale."

"Well, farthingale or hoop skirt, I'm not wearing this thing. It's ridiculous."

Dez grinned. "The corset's kind of hot, though."

Beatrice gave her most ladylike snort. "Okay, I'll wear the corset with a nice pair of black jeans and some kick-ass boots."

"Have you seen what Gio's wearing? Is it tights? Please tell me it's tights."

"Should it weird me out that you want to ogle my husband's ass in a pair of tights?"

Dez just shook her head. "Not appreciating that ass would be like walking through the Sistine Chapel and not looking up. No, really, what's he wearing?"

Beatrice laughed. "It's pretty simple. She probably knew she couldn't get away with anything too elaborate. And no tights. There are these kind of fitted leggings, but they go just above his knee. The jacket looks similar to mine, but plainer. Mostly, he was grumbling because she's doing this whole party in his honor. She has this party every year, but usually people just dress up in whatever costumes they want. Livia made it a Renaissance theme for Gio."

Dez stood, blinking at her. "There are some serious issues going on there, B."

"You're not joking. And his outfit is right here. Take a look."

Dez unzipped the garment bag that contained the sleeveless leather jerkin and black leggings that Giovanni would wear to the party.

"Okay, not gonna lie, that's kind of hot."

"It's going to be *really* hot. This party is outdoors in June. Thank goodness it's at night."

"Haha. Seriously, that leather..."

"I'm definitely not complaining about the leather. So, what am I going to wear to this? You think I can I get away with wearing my Docs?"

Dez laughed for a few minutes before she looked back at Giovanni's clothes. Then she looked at Beatrice's dress, then back to Giovanni's. She narrowed her eyes and smiled.

"No Docs, Beatrice De Novo di Spada Vecchio whatever the heck your name is now. But I may have an idea."

CHAPTER 8

Crotone, Italy
1497

The lash struck again, and Jacopo could feel it cut into his flesh. Still, he did not cry out, steeling himself against the pain that had become part of his daily life. His flesh, though dripping and bloody, would be healed shortly. Andros always made sure to preserve the perfect body he had created by healing him with his demon blood.

"Good. You are no longer even flinching."

Jacopo made the mistake of letting his shoulders relax slightly, only to be struck on the back of the thighs with Andros's staff. He grunted and his knees buckled, but he did not cry out.

"Cato may have been a Roman, but he was correct in one thing: The first virtue is to restrain the tongue. Do you know why, my son? You may speak now."

Jacopo took a deep breath and flexed his arms and shoulders. He could feel Paulo wiping at the blood on his back so Andros could heal the open wounds. The muscles, unfortunately, could not be as easily mended and would ache for days.

"Why is silence the first virtue, Father?"

"Because words can be twisted. And they should be. I will teach you how. Words are to manipulate and fool, but when you hand them to your enemies, they will be used against you. Your Bible may not be worth much, but Solomon did speak some wisdom. 'Even a fool is counted wise when he holds his tongue.'"

"Yes, Father."

He felt the cool lick of Andros's blood as he pierced his finger and began to seal the lashes. Giovanni could feel the strange tingling sensation of the wounds closing.

"Nothing will inflame your enemies more than your silence. Give them nothing. Nothing to accuse you with. Nothing to condemn you. Let your actions speak for themselves. Never talk to an enemy, but listen always."

"Yes, Father."

"And let your actions be your words. Is it better to reason with an enemy or kill him?"

"If I could reason with him, he would not be an enemy."

Andros stepped in front of him and looked up. He smiled and patted Jacopo's cheek. "Excellent. You have done well. You had your music class today. Do you like your new instructor?"

"Yes, Father."

Andros scowled. "I said you could speak, my son."

Jacopo's face, as always, was impassive. It was the only defense against the mercurial moods of the ancient Greek. The monster would be as loving as his uncle some nights, then turn in an instant and beat him. Always, Andros said, for his own good. For his education. His training. Jacopo examined the man's eyes. They were relaxed. Amused even, and his mouth may have been turned down, but his fangs were not descended. It appeared that Andros wanted a debate instead of rote answers.

"The music teacher is a heathen, Father. He teaches me profane songs. I do not care for them."

Andros smirked. "There is no profane music. Only music. Some is good. Some is bad. Sometimes the coarsest peasant tune is the one most pleasing to the ear."

Jacopo blinked. He had been exposed to the finest composers of the Basilica di San Lorenzo; and while he had heard beautiful madrigals sung in Paris, nothing could compare to the breathtaking experience of the holy mass.

"I would prefer learning music that edifies the spirit, Father."

"That is your pathetic uncle talking, boy."

His temper flared, as it always did when Andros criticized Giovanni Pico.

"You are a heathen demon," Jacopo spit out. "And God will condemn you for your madness."

Andros curled his lip and picked up his staff again. "I wonder about you sometimes." Walking behind Jacopo, he struck the back of his thighs again. "Don't you know? There is no god. The Greeks stole their gods from the Minoans. The Romans stole their gods from the Greeks. It's all nonsense, and your Hebrew god is no different."

Jacopo remembered the gentle instruction of his uncle, reflecting on the common strands of faith that wove through the ancient world. "You're wrong."

"I'm not, and you know it. You know more now, more than your pitiful uncle and his friends. More than the deluded mortals who plot and plan." Andros came to stand in front of him and looked up into Jacopo's defiant eyes. "They build cathedrals for their immortality. But you will have no need for buildings made of stone."

Jacopo bit his tongue and decided to take Andros's earlier advice. In the three years he had been with the strange man, he had learned the lesson of silence. The vampire reached up and grabbed Giovanni by the ear, pulling him down to his face.

"You know the truth, my son," Andros whispered. Jacopo could feel the creature's vicious fangs scrape his skin. "You know who the ancients saw that made them believe that the gods were among them, don't you?"

Jacopo forced his jaws to part. "Yes, Father."

"They saw *us*, my boy. They saw the water vampire move the ocean, and Poseidon was born. They saw the wind immortal fly on the night storm and draw the lightning to his hands, and Zeus came to be."

"Yes, Father."

"Never forget." Andros patted Jacopo's cheek and gently stroked the dark curls on his head. He looked up into the young man's vivid green eyes and smiled. "I *am* god."

Castello Furio, Italy

GIOVANNI LEANED BACK IN THE PLUSH SEAT OF THE SEDAN AND EYED Beatrice in the slim leggings and fitted bodice. The black boots she wore rose over her knees and hugged her calves, flaring just below the tight muscles of her thighs as she sat across from him.

"Tesoro," he murmured, "if the women of the court dressed anything like that, I would have had a much harder time keeping my reputation unsullied."

She only grinned and glanced at his lap. "You're not having a hard time right now?"

"Oh, I knew I should have taken my own transport." Carwyn groaned and closed his eyes. "Or better yet, avoided this fiasco all together. Why? Why did I let her sway me with the pitiful voice?"

Beatrice bumped Carwyn's shoulder. "You love me, and you know it."

Giovanni smiled at his old friend and his wife. They bantered back and forth as they made their way to Livia's party, and he reflected on how different this trip was than the last time he had been in Rome. Then, he had been desperate and pleading. He'd had no time for parties or pleasure when his every waking moment had been focused on manipulating different parties at court—Livia most of all—to negotiate for Beatrice's release from Lorenzo.

After all that, could Livia have taken up supporting Giovanni's own estranged son? It was something they would have to determine. He frowned and shook his head, contemplating the idea of staying in Rome longer than their original plan of three months. If the answers were there, they would need to stay as long as necessary.

"Hey, Professor." Beatrice nudged his knee with the toe of her boot, which he grabbed and pulled into his lap. "Stop brooding. We're going to a party."

"And one in your honor, Sparky. You should be grateful."

"Why do I like either of you? Please, remind me."

"Aww." She teased him, slipping across the seats to cuddle into his side. "Poor Gio. Forced to play nice with the empress for the night."

He rolled his eyes. "Not you, too. It's bad enough that the priest calls her that." He sighed and waved a hand. "Fine, get it out of your systems now, so you can both behave."

For the next twenty minutes, Carwyn and Beatrice thought of every needling joke about royalty, Romans, and incest that they could. By the time they pulled into the park, all three of them were laughing.

"B, I swear, if you call her a cougar to her face, I will buy you a car." Carwyn snickered. "A house. Maybe an island. Something ridiculously extravagant, just so long as I can see the look on her face."

"Hush!" She giggled and turned to Giovanni. She cleared her throat. "Okay, we're done."

"Are you sure?" He cocked an eyebrow at them, which threw both of them into fits of laughter again.

"Okay, okay, we're really done." She gasped and grabbed his hand, pulling him toward the iron gates, lit by a thousand tiny lights.

"Yes." Carwyn coughed. "And I promise not to mention any Greek plays."

"*How* many times must I state that she is not my mother?"

Beatrice and Carwyn barely controlled themselves by the time they entered the main hall. While more casual gatherings were held in the gardens, Livia had decorated the main hall of the castle for the party that evening. Candles and torches were everywhere. The room was draped in rich tapestries, and demure human servants darted about, offering wine or blood from their wrists.

Part of the way that Livia controlled the huge Roman population of immortals was her decree that feeding from live donors was only allowed at her parties or festivals. While most of the more prominent vampires ignored her, she had enough influence over the younger and weaker of the court that she was rarely defied. It kept the majority of the population under her thumb and relatively weak compared to the older minority. It also ensured her parties were very well attended, which fed her already gargantuan ego.

He heard Carwyn mutter under his breath. "Heaven help us, she actually has a throne now."

Giovanni looked down the length of the room. Livia's table had been set up to look very much like the head table at a fifteenth century feast. She was dressed in a burgundy dress that would have far outshone his wife's—that is, if Beatrice had not paid a seamstress top dollar to butcher Livia's gown and make her a costume that was more fitting for her personality.

"She does put on a good show—I'll give her that." Beatrice looked around the room, seemingly oblivious to the stares her costume drew. Giovanni knew better. His wife, in her own way, was making a statement to Livia and the entire Roman court.

She bowed to no one.

Grinning, he tucked her hand under his arm and walked toward the front of the room. The crowd parted automatically. Livia rose, all smiles as they approached. Only Giovanni caught the acid glint to her eye as she examined the remains of the priceless gown she had sent.

"Beatrice!" Livia smiled, her fangs peeking from the edge of her mouth. "What an... interesting ensemble. I'm so glad you both could make it."

"Thanks, Livia. I just love my new corset." Beatrice glanced down at her black leggings and leather boots. "I hope you don't mind. I don't really do hoop skirts."

Livia forced a smile. "How American of you."

Beatrice feigned naiveté. "Thanks!"

"And, Giovanni, your priest friend came as well, how amusing."

"Always a pleasure, Livia." Carwyn stepped forward, snagging a passing glass of champagne. "I do love spending time in your incredibly ancient and imperial presence."

She only lifted an eyebrow at the dig.

"Not that you really have an empire, anymore. Thank heaven and the Gauls."

Giovanni cleared his throat, but Carwyn only continued.

"And the Goths. The Vandals, too, I suppose. You *have* been sacked a lot, haven't you?"

Giovanni broke in. "Beautiful party, Livia. Do excuse us while we say hello." He dragged Carwyn away with Beatrice following. They both wore smiles.

"You just can't help yourself, can you?"

Carwyn only laughed, drained the champagne and looked around. "Where's the bar?"

An hour or so later, they had greeted all the appropriate people and left Carwyn chatting with Emil Conti, who he did get along with, surprisingly enough. The priest had also been instructed to keep an eye out for the presence of Ziri, the ancient wind vampire, in case he decided to make an appearance. Giovanni approached Beatrice from behind as she chatted with a younger group of immortals who had congregated near the fountain in the massive entry hall.

He snuck behind her and grabbed her around the waist.

A FALL OF WATER

"Tesoro mio," he bent down and murmured in her ear. "What have you been doing without me for so long?"

She turned and winked at him. "Everyone likes my boots."

He slipped his hand along the stays of the bodice she wore and over her smooth backside, teasing the back of her thigh. "I'm rather fond of them myself."

He felt the frisson of energy rise between them and drew her away from the gaping vampires she'd been talking to, throwing them a wink before he tucked Beatrice under his arm. "Come with me; I want to show you something."

"Come on, you can think of a better line than that."

He chuckled, shuffling them past the guards, who nodded at him respectfully as they made their way through the labyrinth of a castle. Finally, he reached the tower rooms he called his own on the rare occasions he stayed with Livia. He opened the door, slipping the latch closed behind them. A tall, circular staircase ran around up the sides and he pulled her upstairs.

"Where are we?"

He grinned. "This, Beatrice, is the vampire equivalent of my childhood room."

"What?" She laughed. "You stayed here?"

"Yes, after my sire's death, I stayed here with Livia for around ten years or so, getting my bearings, meeting the right people. She wanted me to stay longer, but..."

"I'm surprised she kept it for you."

They reached the top of the stairs, which opened onto a richly appointed library with curved bookcases that lined the walls. Narrow windows looked out over the park and the full moon shone through.

He left her in the center of the room and walked around, tracing a hand along the bookcases, which had not a hint of dust.

"She wants me to move back, you know?"

"I know."

He laughed low in his throat. "As if anything here could tempt me." He looked over his shoulder to see her looking around in wonder. The room looked like the fairytale version of a tower library, complete with dark oak cabinetry, velvet armchairs, and a fireplace he took a moment to light.

"It's sure beautiful. This whole place is."

He turned to her, watching as she took it all in. The gold leaf picture frames and jeweled clocks. There was a Faberge egg on a side table and a Lalique decanter with the finest whiskey. He had seen it all before, and he only had eyes for his wife.

"Beautiful."

He circled her, slowly drawing closer as her busy eyes memorized the room. "Yeah, everything's gor—"

He darted in and stopped her mouth with a kiss. "Beautiful."

She smiled, strangely shy in the opulent surroundings. "Gio, this is still so—"

"Fake." He looked around, then placed his hands around her waist and looked into her eyes. "Real."

She nodded in understanding, and Giovanni leaned down, drawing her mouth into a leisurely kiss. They stood in the center of the tower as the moonlight streamed in the windows and the faint sounds of the party drifted to their ears. He nipped at her lips, tasting them and enjoying the sweet wine that lingered.

His hands roamed down to cup her bottom, and he lifted her against his body. Their kisses grew heated, and Giovanni felt her heart begin to beat against his chest. Her hands tugged at his neck and he could scent her arousal as it filled the room. It was heady, intoxicating. He wanted nothing more than to feel her skin on his and her flesh against his tongue.

"You were right," he murmured in between soft bites of her swollen mouth.

"About?"

He backed her up against the nearest bookcase, propping her on the edge of one deep shelf as his hands stroked down her legs, fingers teasing under the edge of her boots to tickle the sensitive skin behind her knee.

"Hoop skirts would make this problematic."

"I think ahead that way," she panted.

"Beatrice..." He hissed as his hands clutched at her thighs. Beatrice's fingers tugged at the laces of his pants, as her other hand stroked him through the thick fabric. He bit back a groan when her hand closed around him. Desire? He had never known desire until he had known her.

"Now," she whispered. "Gio, I need you."

One hand reached up to the nape of her neck, angling Beatrice's mouth to his as the other pulled at the drawstring that held her leggings tight. His hand slipped under the fabric and searched for her heat as she bit down on his lower lip.

Feeling how ready she was, he freed himself and drove into her with one swift stroke. Her satisfied cry echoed off the cold stone of the tower library, but Giovanni didn't care who heard them. He pulled back and gave her a wicked smile. He'd dreamt about taking her in this room for years.

A few books fell to the floor as they moved faster, and his hand reached back to cradle her head so it wasn't bashed against the hard oak shelves. He dove back toward her mouth, swallowing the cries of pleasure as he drove her toward the edge.

"I love you," he whispered as she clenched around him. "*I love you so much.*"

Beatrice's fingers dug into his shoulders. He could feel the painful dig of her nails, but he stared into her eyes as the pleasure blinded her. His hand gripped her bare thigh. If she hadn't have been a vampire, they would have left bruises.

He felt his own climax approaching and slowed, pressing his mouth to hers and pouring his pleasure into their kiss as his amnis flooded her body. He felt her hands reach up to frame his face, and her own energy flowed over his skin in a soft wave. He closed his eyes and came with a groan.

Giovanni laid his head on her shoulder and put his arms around her waist, pulling Beatrice closer as their hearts beat in unison. He could feel her stroke his hair, running her fingers along his neck where she drew the moisture against his skin, cooling him as he relaxed into her touch.

"I love you, Jacopo," she whispered.

He matched her breaths and laid soft kisses along her neck.

"I wish I could write as my uncle did." He pulled away and looked into her eyes, sparkling with love and satisfaction. "I don't have the words, Tesoro mio."

She smiled at him anyway and pulled him down for one more quick kiss before he set her down on the floor. They righted their clothing, smiling and sneaking glances toward the stairs and the sounds of the party.

"Do we have to go back?" she asked.

Giovanni grinned. "Unfortunately, yes." He pulled up his pants and quickly tied the strings that held them in place, shaking his head the whole time. "I hated wearing these clothes when they were in fashion."

She giggled and snuck a hand around to pinch his backside. "I kind of like them. And don't you like my boots?"

He eyed the curve of her calf, the smooth line of her waist, and her breasts riding high in the stiff bodice. "I like your costume far better than mine, that is no question."

She only laughed, and he watched her struggle to get the drawstring tight enough. He finally reached over and grabbed her waist, drawing them tight with a smirk.

"I'm going to have to dance."

"What?" She laughed.

"Dance. Move in a regular pattern to the rhythm of music. Surely you're familiar with the concept." He pulled her hand and led her down the stairs, in no rush to rejoin the party.

"We have to dance?"

He chuckled. "You certainly may, if you like, but listen to the music."

Giovanni paused and cocked his head. He heard the strains of the violin and the guitar. "Unless you are well-acquainted with the *galliard*, feel free to sit this one out."

"The gall-what?"

He pulled her down the hall. "The galliard. It's a dance Livia was particularly fond of, and she'll want me to dance one with her."

"I'm biting my tongue here..."

He snorted. "It's not exactly the tango, Beatrice. It's all very formal."

"I'm just trying to imagine you dancing."

"Me?" He raised his eyebrows in shock. "My wife, I am an excellent dancer."

"Oh, really?"

"Really. I had a dance instructor from the time I was a boy."

She snickered. "This, I can't wait to see."

"So happy to amuse you."

"Also, you better teach me the tango."

He reached down and pinched her as they passed two of the solemn guards. "That, my love, will be my pleasure."

GIOVANNI BOWED TOWARD LIVIA, PLEASED THAT THEY HAD BEEN JOINED BY A group of twenty or so other immortals as they danced. He looked at the edge of the crowd, where Beatrice leaned against a pillar, watching him with an amused smile. He winked at her before he turned his attention to his partner. He saw Livia's gaze flick toward his wife, then she lifted a hand, and the musicians paused.

"We should dance *la volta!*" The other dancers smiled with delight, pleased to take part in the vigorous, but more intimate, dance. He smiled stiffly and bowed toward her again as the music resumed.

They began the intricate steps. At the first turn, Livia sprang, and he lifted her, waiting the few beats of the music before he turned and set her down again. They repeated the steps, weaving among the other dancers as they moved in formation.

"Are you enjoying the party?" she asked during one lift.

"Quite. I can't remember the last time I danced."

They separated for one turn, then were back next to each other.

"And how is your wife liking Rome?"

"Very well. Thank you."

"And your guests? You should bring them to the house one evening. We'll have a quiet dinner in their honor."

Giovanni suspected that a "quiet dinner" could easily involve forty or more people.

"I'll keep that in mind." He spotted his opportunity. "Speaking of guests, Beatrice's friend wanted me to thank you for the cosmetics you sent over. She was quite taken with them. How is your business?"

She smiled and her eyebrow lifted slightly. "Business has been very rewarding lately. Thank you for asking. And how is your search?"

He was about to answer when he saw a flash of gold hair at the edge of the crowd. Giovanni was swept into another turn, and when he spun back, the gold was nowhere to be found. His eyes searched for Beatrice. He could not find her.

"Giovanni?"

He frowned down at Livia. He had lost step in the dance. She laughed.

"It *has* been some time since you've danced."

Giovanni picked her up into another turn. When he set her down, he spotted Carwyn leaning against the bar, flirting with a redhead in a brilliant blue dress. His friend was grinning, not paying attention to anything but his conversation.

"You seem distracted. Am I boring you?"

"I... no, Livia, of course not." There it was again! A flash of golden curls under a brocade hood.

"You never answered my question."

"What question?"

He finally heard the music drawing to an end.

"How goes your search for your son?"

Had he told Livia he was searching for Lorenzo? She knew he was searching for Andros's books. The music stopped. The crowd clapped. And he looked down into her scheming brown eyes. Giovanni's heart began to pound.

"I don't know, Livia. Perhaps *you* might be able to tell me."

Just then, he heard Beatrice gasp. He recognized her sharp inhale from across the room, and his hand reached down to grasp the dagger tucked into his boot. The fire flared along his collar. He looked up to see Lorenzo smiling at Beatrice with bared fangs while two of Livia's guards held his wife back.

Giovanni hissed and flung the dagger across the room, aiming straight for Lorenzo's neck, only to have it intercepted by the chest of another guard. The vampire grunted and turned to look for the source of the blade.

Within seconds, Giovanni's fire burst out, lighting his arms, though the thick leather jerkin Livia had sent for him prevented the fire from spreading over his torso. His arms reached out and grabbed the two guards who approached him, immediately engulfing them in flames while the crowd ran screaming and the guards turned to ash. He heard Carwyn shout, and the marble beneath his feet shifted. Another swarm of guards ran for him as he looked for Beatrice.

"Stop now, *Papà*!"

Lorenzo held a sword to her throat as Beatrice snarled and Livia's guards restrained her. Giovanni stilled immediately. The ground beneath him grew still. Everyone froze exactly where they were.

"I'll cut her head off given the word."

"Hold, Lorenzo," Livia said as she stepped between them. "I have no reason to harm the girl."

His eyes darted to Beatrice, who was held by four guards, arms twisted behind her back. The water of the fountain had risen behind her, but it did nothing but spill over the sides, drenching the floor and trickling down the stairs. Giovanni growled, but forced the fire back. He looked for Carwyn, who was surrounded by more guards, though they did not touch him. His old friend was watching the scene with a calculating blue stare.

"Livia!" Emil Conti pushed forward. "What is the meaning of this? What kind of violence have you allowed in your own home? And toward your guests?"

Giovanni could tell the crowd was as confused as Conti was. A low murmur began to rumble and a frantic energy filled the air, causing his heart to beat faster.

"Emil, thank you for asking." Livia raised her voice, the small woman speaking with authority as she continued to stare at him. "I am taking Giovanni di Spada as my prisoner. It is my right."

Conti sputtered. "What? What ri—"

"I accuse him here as the murderer of my husband, Niccolo Andros, his own sire."

The murmur grew. Emil Conti drew back, a horrified look on his usually placid face. Livia stepped closer, standing in front of Giovanni and looking up as the fire coursed along his collar and the guards held onto his leather-clad torso and legs.

"You foolish boy!" Livia spat out and slapped him. "Don't you know? No secret stays hidden forever."

A red haze fell over his eyes, and Giovanni opened his mouth to speak, but a breath of air whispered in his ear.

"Silence, Jacopo."

His eyes darted around the room, stunned by the sound of the name only one other knew. The glittering immortals of Rome were tittering like panicked birds as Livia and Emil argued. The whisper came again.

"Say nothing to her."

Giovanni blinked and looked again. Carwyn was staring at him in shock. Beatrice was standing by the fountain, but the sword had been lowered from her neck. Everyone around them was frozen, as if waiting for a command. He was sure that no one else had heard the ghostly whisper.

He looked to Beatrice and her eyes met his, pleading with him. She was furious. Frightened. He mouthed, *'Ti amo'* at her, frowning when she began to struggle again. Just then, an apparition took shape behind her; a man appeared from the shadows of the room.

He was dressed in long, flowing robes, and he held a finger up to his lips. He glanced at Beatrice, and his mouth moved in a silent murmur. A moment later, the whisper came to Giovanni's ear.

"Do not worry for your woman, Jacopo. Be still. Be silent. Give your enemy nothing."

Giovanni stopped struggling, and a strange calm stole over him.

Because when an immortal as ancient as Ziri spoke, he listened.

CHAPTER 9

She wanted to scream. She wanted to cry. Everything seemed to move in slow motion around her, as if the castle had been plunged to the bottom of the sea. Silent. Why was it so silent?

Beatrice stood frozen as Livia's guards pulled Giovanni away into the twisted maze of the castle. Finally, what felt like dozens of hands released her, and she lifted her arms with an unspoken scream. A roaring filled her mind, like a river rushing over a cliff, and she felt the pulse of energy behind her.

The water in the fountain rose, trembling and quivering at her command. Beatrice narrowed her gaze on Lorenzo and Livia, who stood next to each other. The vampires of the hall seemed to drift like lost sheep in the confusion.

Her rage driving her, she stepped toward her enemies, only to be tackled from the side. When she realized it was Carwyn, the scream died in her throat, but she still struggled.

"Stop," he whispered fiercely. "Contain yourself for now."

"Can't."

"You must."

In the safety of his arms, the roaring began to clear and sound filtered back to her. The confused murmur of the crowd. Emil Conti's voice arguing with Livia. Lorenzo's arrogant laugh.

The laugh caused her rage to bubble up again, and Carwyn's grip on her grew even tighter as he pushed her to a small alcove.

"Lord in Heaven, you are strong, B."

"Let me go." Her voice sounded foreign to her ears. Quiet. Feral.

"That's really not the best move right now. If you were in your right mind, you'd know that."

"Let me go."

"We have to find out more. She won't harm him. Look around the room. Everyone's in shock. She's going to feel out the crowd before she makes a move. I have a feeling she's not pleased. I somehow doubt Lorenzo was supposed to show up tonight. She's not happy with him."

His arms embraced her, but they were not Giovanni's arms. She began to shake again.

"My dad... Ioan. They took Gio. They took him."

"Christ, we've got to get you out of here. Now. You're going to collapse or explode. Possibly both."

She felt wind at her feet, and a sharp longing for Tenzin rose in her. Tenzin. She needed Tenzin now. Where was Tenzin?

"Come with me, priest. Bring the woman."

Who did that voice belong to? It was cold and comforting at the same time. And... familiar. Her eyes flicked to the silhouette at the entrance of the alcove. Amnis swirled around the voice, filling the small niche.

"Ziri." Carwyn's voice was cautious, but she recognized the hint of optimism.

"This is a surprise. I did not see her making a move for weeks. Lorenzo has not pleased her by appearing like this."

"What are you—"

"We must get her out of here. Her rage will not be contained for long. Come, Mariposa."

Her eyes darted to his when he spoke her childhood name. Ziri stepped toward her, and she could finally make out his eyes. The whites shone in his dark face. Despite her shock and anger, she blinked. The vampire's irises were a pure, deep black.

"Who are you?"

He held out a hand, and she felt the whisper of air stroke across her cheek.

"I am Ziri, and if you allow it, I will call you my friend."

Carwyn had darted out of the alcove to go look for Emil Conti. Ziri swept Beatrice down a dark hall that led outside. Once out of the suffocating walls of the castle, the wind vampire picked her up and flew her to the car. He tucked her into the backseat and waited outside for the priest.

Beatrice blinked, as if coming out of a dream. What was she doing? They had taken her husband! She was just about to shove her way out of the car when the door opened and Carwyn slipped in, grasping her wrists the minute they raised to shove him back.

"Ah-ah. Calm yourself, Beatrice De Novo. Now is the time to listen."

She had found her voice. "They took him. Let me go!"

"No." He let go of one arm to pound on the divider, and the car jerked forward. Beatrice reached over and punched him in the jaw.

"Let go of me, damn you!"

He grabbed her wrists again. "Beatrice, look at me."

She was shaking with anger.

"Beatrice, you need to understand that Gio is in no mortal danger right now."

Her fangs descended and she tasted blood in her mouth. "You say that when he was taken by that *bitch*? By that backstabbing bitch? With Lorenzo there? With—"

"With hundreds of witnesses watching her take him. He is, right now, a political prisoner. And no one knows anything. There are factions within factions that will all try to manipulate this situation to their own advantage. She has accused him, but everyone knows that she'll lie if it suits her purposes."

Her face fell. "But—"

"Whatever you're about to tell me, don't. Right now, your husband is a bargaining piece to Livia. He is safe." Carwyn locked his eyes with hers. "Do you understand? He is safe. No harm will come to him as her prisoner. At least not right now. She won't make any rash moves; she's too smart for that."

The reality of the situation began to take hold, and Beatrice felt the rage slipping away. In its place was a bone-deep pain. Carwyn must have caught the shift, because he let go of her wrists and pulled her into his arms. She shook with suppressed grief as the dark car made the twisted journey back to Rome.

When they pulled up to the house by the Pantheon, Ziri was already waiting by the gate. Carwyn paid the driver and the black car sped away. They stepped through the green door and the smell of cardamom hit Beatrice's nose.

"Tenzin!" she cried into the courtyard and felt the rush of wind as Tenzin sped to her.

"What has happened?" Small arms encircled her, embracing and lifting her when she stumbled. "What has happened tonight? Where is Gio?"

Ziri stepped into the courtyard. "Livia arrested him. It was unexpected."

Beatrice felt Carwyn on one side, holding her, when Tenzin dropped her arms. Her hiss was vicious. "What? That arrogant dog took my boy? I will kill her!"

"Lorenzo," Beatrice muttered as they made their way into the silent house. "She's the one helping Lorenzo."

Tenzin said, "I know."

"How?"

"What do you think I've been doing for the past few weeks? It doesn't actually take me that long to get across the ocean."

Beatrice heard Ziri's low chuckle as they made their way up the stairs, careful to keep silent as they walked to the library so they wouldn't wake Ben.

"What am I going to tell Ben?" she whispered. As tough as Ben pretended to be, she knew he adored Giovanni. Depended on him. Giovanni was the constant. Nothing could harm him. She felt frozen by grief and confusion.

"Shh, my girl," Tenzin whispered. "I will get him back. Do you hear me?"

"They took him. How could they take him?"

"With trickery and surprise. That is how." Tenzin's arm slipped around her waist. "But they have lost the surprise, and no one will hold him for long."

Dawn was close when the four of them settled into the library. Beatrice collapsed on the couch. Carwyn sat next to her. Ziri and Tenzin both stood by the cold fireplace. Beatrice was reminded of the fireplace in the tower that Giovanni had lit. Other memories assaulted her. The warm grasp of his hands. His burning kiss. Would that be her last memory of him? The last time he touched her?

"Whatever dark, depressing thoughts you are entertaining, B, snap out of them." Carwyn's voice was brusque and, surprisingly, exactly what she needed to hear. "Taking political prisoners is commonplace in our world. She won't hurt him. She might torture him, but it won't be anything he hasn't endured before."

A glass of water she'd been watching on the coffee table shattered. Water scattered over the table, but the pieces of glass were swept up in a gust and immediately tossed into the fire. She looked up to see Ziri smirking at her with his terrifying black gaze.

"Who are you?" she asked.

His dark head bowed, and he swept back the striped robes he wore. "I am Ziri."

"I know that. Who are you?"

Ziri said, "You are very much like your father, do you know?"

She felt Tenzin's tension from across the room. Beatrice's eyes darted to her father's mate, who was watching her fellow wind vampire with suspicion. Tenzin remained silent and let Beatrice question him.

"I am. How did you know my father?"

The ancient vampire looked thoughtful for a moment, tilting his head while Beatrice examined him. He was definitely the ancient immortal she'd seen at Livia's garden party. His skin was pockmarked and looked dusky from the sun. His features were a curious blend of Middle Eastern and African. Beatrice was reminded of a library exhibit she had helped curate about the Berber people of Morocco. But Ziri looked old, far older than the Berber people. He was ancient and curiously regal. Not a Berber, but then, North Africa had not always had the same names. She remembered Geber's journals.

"Are you the Numidian?"

A FALL OF WATER

Ziri smiled again. The swirling amnis that surrounded him reached out to her hand, but she did not flinch when she felt the press of his ghostly greeting.

"I am Ziri. I am the Numidian of Jabir's journals, and I was your father's guardian... for as long as I was able."

A FEW HOURS LATER, MATT STUMBLED INTO THE LIBRARY AND LOOKED around in confusion.

"Who's the vampire sleeping in the second floor guest room? Hi, Tenzin. Who are you?" He looked at Ziri, then around the room with sharper eyes. "And where the hell is Gio?"

Beatrice sighed. "Sit down, Matt. I'll explain."

Tenzin spoke, "The vampire isn't awake, is he?"

"No."

"Good, he needs to rest."

Carwyn and Beatrice both looked at her in confusion.

"What's that?" the priest said.

Beatrice asked, "What are you talking about?"

Even though most vampires rested during the day, they didn't 'need' to. Beatrice had never grown tired in a bodily sense, even though she rarely slept. She would weary, exhausted by her own thoughts, but that was why she meditated. Tenzin, she knew, was the same way.

"I'll let him explain, but Lucien... He is..." Tenzin stammered, looking disturbed. "It's difficult to say exactly. He is not... well."

"Lucien Thrax?" Carwyn asked. He looked confused. Tenzin looked strangely nervous. Beatrice looked to Ziri. The old wind vampire looked like... nothing. She had never seen a face so carefully blank.

"Who's Lucien?" Beatrice asked.

"Lucien Thrax—an old friend of mine. A very old friend. And he was a friend of—"

"Ioan's." Carwyn interrupted. "Lucien and Ioan were close correspondents. Lucien is a doctor, B. The son of the greatest healer the immortal world has ever known."

"She's also the oldest," Tenzin said.

Carwyn nodded. "Lucien and Ioan were friends for many years. He's one of the contacts that I was going to look for while I was here. He's often in Eastern Europe."

"He was in Bulgaria when I found him. I'd heard rumors." Tenzin frowned. "He hadn't heard about Ioan."

Matt spoke up. "Bulgaria?"

Tenzin nodded.

Beatrice said, "Why do you ask, Matt?"

"Dez was doing research into Livia's businesses. One of her companies owns a very small plant in Bulgaria. From what she could find out, it was pretty busy until about three years ago; then it was shut down. But not exactly. It was kept in operation, but with a skeleton staff and no product being shipped out, then a little over a year ago, they put out a hiring notice again. Nothing's been shipped out yet, but the plant is in operation."

Tenzin nodded. "That fits the timeline I've been thinking of. If Livia is using this plant to produce the elixir, that means they started just a few months after Stephen was killed and Lorenzo took the manuscript."

Beatrice asked Matt, "What was the cosmetics company making? Before it was shut down, what did they produce?"

Matt scowled. "High-end cosmetics for the European market. Using traditional, botanical ingredients."

"That's it." Beatrice sighed. "It has to be."

"B, I need to talk to Gio, there was something else—"

"Gio's not here, Matt," Beatrice said quietly.

She had never seen the man look more shocked. "What? It's past dawn. He stayed at Livia's? What the—"

"He stayed at Livia's, but it wasn't his choice," Carwyn said. "She accused him of murdering Andros in front of the Roman vampires. She's taken him prisoner."

Matt's mouth gaped. He looked at Beatrice. "B, is it—"

"Shut up!" Tenzin walked over and stood in front of Matt. The small woman looked up into the human's shocked face. "Whatever you were about to ask, don't."

"But—"

"Does it matter to you? If Giovanni killed his sire? If he didn't? Does it matter to you? Does it change your opinion of him or your loyalty to him?"

Matt just blinked. "No, of course not. I know what a good man he is."

"Then don't even ask. If you ask B, you're forcing her to reveal information she holds in confidence or lie to you. Do you understand?"

Matt paused before he spoke. "Yes, Tenzin."

"Good. Now, go get your wife. I want to know more about this company."

Matt looked abashed when he was dismissed, and Beatrice tried to catch his eye, but she could tell the man was already focused on the task at hand. The thought of Matt and Dez working with them almost brought tears to her eyes. Part of her wanted to force them to return to Los Angeles with Ben, but the other part knew that she needed them more than ever.

"Hey." She heard Ben's voice at the door and turned. "What's going on?" Ben yawned and rubbed his eyes. "And who's the weird guy?"

Ziri smiled. "My name is Ziri, boy. And I am a friend of your aunt's."

"What's going on? Matt looked really upset. Is everything alright?"

Beatrice waved him over, and Ben came to sit next to her. She blurted it out, knowing that nothing she said would soften the loss of his uncle. "Gio's been taken prisoner, but he's going to be fine."

All the bravado fell from Ben's face, and he looked like the insecure child she'd first laid eyes on in the bushes outside the Huntington Library years ago.

"What? He... he's—"

Carwyn stepped in and put a hand on Ben's shoulder. "He'll be fine. We're going to get him out. It'll just be—"

Ben shot out of his seat; anger spread across his face. He stalked over to Tenzin. "Where the hell have you been, Tenzin? If you were here, this wouldn't have happened!"

Beatrice rose. "Ben, she was working on—"

"What does it matter if you find Lorenzo if Gio gets killed? Don't you care about him?"

Tenzin said nothing, staring at the boy through her dark curtain of hair.

Ziri spoke quietly from the other side of the library. "Lorenzo is here, Benjamin. He's working with Livia. He's the reason your uncle was taken."

Ben's eyes darted between Ziri and Beatrice. He looked back at Tenzin. Beatrice could see his anger flee. "Is it true?"

Tenzin only nodded; she stiffened when Ben threw his arms around her. Tenzin waited for a moment, but finally lifted her small arms and hugged the young man back. Beatrice could hear Ben whisper, "Get him back, Tenzin. Please, get him back." Then he spun on his heel and rushed out of the library. Beatrice could hear him climb the stairs to his room.

THEY SPOKE ABOUT DETAILS FOR A FEW MORE HOURS. ZIRI ASKED FOR THE USE of a bedroom with a desk and some paper to write a few letters. Beatrice was still confused about what, exactly, his part in all this was. She got the impression that there was a lot that Ziri wasn't telling them. She also got the impression he was waiting for the mysterious Lucien Thrax, who Tenzin thought would wake a few hours after dark. Beatrice was still confused why such an old vampire needed so much sleep.

Matt had already been on the phone with Emil Conti's people, arranging a meeting with Carwyn and their boss for the following night. Dez and Tenzin were talking about the details of the Bulgarian cosmetics company.

And Beatrice felt lost.

Finally, she realized she would be useless for anything until she could spend some time alone. She climbed the stairs to their room, only to find Ben sitting outside on the floor by the door. He looked up with red eyes.

"I know you usually don't let anyone in your room, but—"

"Come in."

Beatrice unlocked the door and she and Ben entered. She fought back the tears when she saw the rumpled bed Giovanni hadn't made because they were rushing to get ready for the party the night before. A damp towel was tossed on the floor by the couch. She picked it up and inhaled the distinctive smoky smell of her mate's skin a moment before she crumpled to the floor.

She felt Ben's hands lifting her and pulling her to the couch. He grabbed a linen handkerchief from his pocket. He had taken to always carrying them, just like his uncle. He joked that it impressed the girls.

"I need to calm down," she whispered, patting the bloody tears from her eyes. "He needs me to be thinking straight. To be calm and smart and—"

"It's okay, B. It's just us, okay?" She could hear the hitch in his voice. "For right now, it's okay. It's just me."

She sniffed and tried to remember when Ben had grown up. It had happened without her even realizing it. The young man threw an arm around her shoulders, and Beatrice allowed herself to lean into him. Ben rocked back and forth, comforting his aunt and sniffing back his own tears.

Beatrice looked over to their bed and knew that she would not lie in it again until her husband returned to her. Ben was murmuring comforting words in her ear, his arms tight around her shoulders. Beatrice finally let herself close her eyes and let go of the sorrow that she'd held back for hours.

Ben was right. It was just them.

CHAPTER 10

Crotone
1504

He heard Andros's heavy step in the hall. Jacopo looked up for a moment, but quickly returned to the translation of the Arabic manuscript he was working on. It was one that his father had rescued from the destruction of the Mongols in Baghdad.

The door swept open and Andros walked over and patted his shoulder. Jacopo heard Paulo follow, carrying a heavy trunk.

"Son, it is good to be home."

"How was Rome?"

"As expected," Andros said. "She grows more pompous every century. I can't imagine why Livia thinks so much of herself when this detestable country is run by thieves, mad priests, and inbreeds."

Jacopo glanced at Paulo, but the young man only rolled his eyes. Jacopo had been with Andros for almost ten years, Paulo even longer, and both the men were used to the unpredictable moods of the vampire.

A visit to Rome, however, only ever raised Andros's ire.

"But the trip to Florence was a pleasure. The ugly sculptor finished his statue of David, and it was installed in front of the civic house while we were there. A true masterwork. A pity the human is so detestable in his form. Otherwise, he might be worth turning for his talent."

Jacopo's ears perked up. "You went to Florence?"

Andros only glanced at him. "We did."

Jacopo waited. He had known for years that his uncle's friend, Poliziano, had died only a few months after Giovanni Pico. Savaranola had met a gruesome end, along with most of his uncle's collection of books and papers, during Florence's descent into madness six years before. The only survivor of the four men who had raised him was the poet, Benivieni. But Andros was always careful to dole out only the information he wanted Jacopo to have.

"Benivieni is in good health, from what I heard."

Jacopo kept his face carefully blank. "Thank you."

"Of course."

Andros began to unpack books and papers from the trunk Paulo had carried in.

"I have more translations for you to do if your current work is up to standard."

"It is."

He heard Andros chuckle. "Your confidence pleases me. And your Arabic is quite good. After you have turned, you will start your study of Sanskrit."

Jacopo's head jerked up. "After I have turned?"

Though Jacopo had known of his father's intentions for years, he rarely mentioned it and never referred to it directly. It was implied—an eternal sentence that hung over Jacopo's shoulders.

"Yes, you have been with me for ten years now. I have started to note some mild deterioration of your physical form. It is time."

Jacopo's heart raced, and he cursed internally, knowing that Andros could hear it. The old vampire looked up.

"Have you changed your mind? Would you prefer that I kill you, instead?"

Jacopo looked over Andros's shoulder and saw the pathetic hope flare on Paulo's face. He knew the young man wanted immortality in a desperate and hungry way. He also knew that Andros would never turn the young man, whom he considered "defective." Jacopo forced himself to smile.

"And waste the fine education you have given me, Father? That would be a mistake, would it not?"

Andros watched him with careful eyes. "It would. But, I suppose, I could always find another student."

Jacopo rose to his feet. In his late twenties, he was taller than his uncle had been, taller than Andros, and far taller than was common for most men of fifteenth century Italy. His shoulders had filled out, and the strict exercise regimen that Andros had forced on him had molded his body into perfect form. Jacopo looked at the ancient statues of demigods that Andros used to decorate the stone fortress where he resided, and he saw a mirror image of himself.

He gave his father an arrogant smile. "You could find another student, Father?" A cold smirk flicked across Andros's lips as Jacopo continued, "You would never find another like me."

A FALL OF WATER

Castello Furio

GIOVANNI'S EYES OPENED. FOR A MOMENT, HE WAS IN HIS FATHER'S FORTRESS in Crotone, the cold, stone walls echoing the damp room he had woken in his last days as a human. He sat up into a crouch and eyed his surroundings.

The room where Livia's guards had thrown him was surrounded by a thin fall of water, an effective counter to any of his elemental power, which also filled the underground chamber with a pervasive chill. He could heat his skin, but could do nothing to create a spark. The door had no handle, and the walls mimicked the diameter and shape of the tower where he had slept in apparent safety so many years before. In the back of his mind, he wondered if his current prison was built under the very tower that had sheltered him in Livia's castle. He did not find it hard to imagine.

Though he could not use fire to escape the chamber, he had immediately tested the walls when he had been thrown in the night before. He sensed no weakness and no nearby energy signatures. Giovanni was completely isolated in the cold room. He could hear the rushing of an underground river somewhere close. No doubt, it fed the waterfall that trickled down the walls.

He wished he had fed the night before. He and Beatrice had planned to feed once they returned to Rome after the party, not trusting any of the blood that Livia would provide. Thinking about his wife made his blood rush, and he was more grateful than ever that Carwyn had accompanied them the night before. His friend would protect Beatrice. His mate would be safe.

He detected a familiar signature approaching, so he stood and braced himself against a stone pillar.

The door opened, and Livia strode in, tailed by two guards dressed in the same clothing that he remembered the vampires at the monastery wearing on the night they had slaughtered the monks and ransacked the library with Lorenzo. At least Giovanni finally knew who was backing his son.

She stood in front of him. Gone was any pleasant facade; her disgust lay plain on her face.

"I suppose you think you are quite safe because I was forced to take you in front of witnesses."

He said nothing, but a small smile touched his lips.

"Your son changed my plans, but did not ruin them, you know. I will still kill you."

Giovanni still said nothing. Livia smiled back at him and approached.

"You see, Giovanni, I will be very, very fair." She reached up and ran a finger along his jaw. "I have spent two thousand years manipulating this city into thinking of me as its queen. I know exactly the words to use." Her hand ran back and tangled in the hair at the nape of his neck.

"There may be some objections, at first. You have plenty of your own allies and a very honorable reputation. But by the time I cut your head off and throw it in the river that flows under this castle, all will think of you as a murderer and a liar. A thief of one of the greatest collections of knowledge our world has ever seen. A greedy vampire who would keep the best interest of our kind for his own profit."

He opened his mouth to speak and saw her pause, waiting for the words of protest to leave his lips. She was waiting for him to object or defend himself.

Giovanni asked, "How is my wife?"

The flash of fury confirmed that Beatrice was, as he suspected, quite safe from the she-demon in front of him. Giovanni's smile grew.

"I have no interest in your common wife. She may be seen by some as extraordinary, but it is not evident to me. A human of questionable breeding with little to no grace? I'm still wondering what you see in her."

The impassive expression blanketed his face again.

"Lorenzo has expressed an interest in using her as a plaything once our plans are complete. I'll most likely give her to him. She won't be any use to me."

Still, he let no expression flicker over his face.

Livia forced his head down and whispered in his ear.

"Let this all be a misunderstanding, my darling boy. Show me your contrition and I will let you live." He felt her fangs flick along his earlobe. Giovanni reached back to his earliest memories and emptied himself of all emotion, as he had under his father's sword.

"I would bear you no ill will. I, of all people, understood his temperament. His particular foibles were my friends for a thousand years. Let me free you of him once and for all. Confess to me, my Giovanni."

He closed his eyes and pulled away, opening them to meet her gaze. Finally, he spoke in a soft voice. "Livia?"

"Yes?"

"Do you know what my father called you?"

Her eyes frosted over. Livia stepped back and pulled the sword from the belt of one of her guards. She ran it into Giovanni's gut, but he only smiled. Even as the blood spilled out, he smiled.

"He called you the Roman whore, Livia."

She reached back and pulled the other guard's sword from his waist. He felt it pierce higher, closer to his heart as she ran the thin blade between his ribs. As his father taught him, he did not even flinch.

"The Roman whore," he said again, feeling the pull of the blades against his skin and muscle. "That is what your dear husband called you in the privacy of our home."

"I will kill you, Giovanni di Spada."

He smiled. "My name is Giovanni Vecchio, son of Niccolo Andros. Mate of Beatrice De Novo. And you will not kill me."

"Dead man."

"Whore."

She raised her hand and slapped him before grabbing a blade from his body and ramming it in again. Giovanni smiled, but said nothing more. She turned on her heel and strode from the room. The silent guards walked over, drew their weapons from his body, and left behind her.

He heard the heavy clanks of metal as the unseen locks fell into place. Livia knew almost as well as his father how easily he could escape most places. As he looked around the room, Giovanni realized that she had constructed this dungeon with him in mind. He also noted it did not look new.

He reassessed his options. He would not underestimate Livia's intelligence; he would not be able to escape on his own. Luckily, he was not alone. Carwyn was in Rome. Beatrice was stronger by the day. Tenzin would arrive soon, if she hadn't already.

Giovanni tore off strips of cloth to stuff into the stab wounds. With no blood and no ability to manifest his fire, he knew he would heal slowly. He took a deep breath of the damp air, pictured his wife's laughing face in his mind, and closed his eyes to wait.

CHAPTER 11

Beatrice was meditating to the strains of a Bach concerto when Tenzin came in her room. The wind vampire looked at Ben, stretched out at Beatrice's feet, sleeping in the late afternoon. The boy had refused to leave his aunt, even when he needed to rest.

"Get up. Get dressed. We're going to Livia's castle."

Hope flared in Beatrice's eyes. "We're going to get him?"

"No. Not yet, anyway. But she doesn't know I'm here, and she needs to."

"Why?"

The small vampire smiled. "Because I scare the shit out of Livia. I always have. She hates me." Then the smile fell. "Plus, she has Lorenzo with her. I have a few things to say."

Beatrice stood and looked over her wrinkled clothes. She was still wearing the loose shirt and leggings from the party. "What should I wear?"

"Whatever you want. Whatever you think she'll hate. And bring your *shuang gou*. If we're lucky, we'll get to kill something."

She hopped to her feet. "Hell, yes."

Beatrice ran to the bathroom to take a shower. As she reached down to untie the drawstring on her leggings, her fingers twisted in the knot. For a moment, she clutched it, remembering Giovanni's hands tugging at the drawstring in the tower room. She lifted the front of her shirt and inhaled the sweet and heady fragrance of their combined scents. Then she stripped off her clothes, stepping into the shower as she locked her sorrow away.

A few minutes later, she poked her head out the door. Ben was gone, and

Tenzin sat at the desk in the corner of the room, poking through Geber's journals.

"We should give these to Lucien to look through. He'll be able to read them."

Beatrice went to the closet and began to dress in a pair of black jeans and a skin-tight black T-shirt. She slipped on the leather boots she'd worn to the party. "I doubt it. It took me months to wrap my head around Geber's writing."

"Trust me, he'll be able to read them."

"Is he awake yet?"

Tenzin shook her head. "He probably won't wake until well after sundown, and we'll already be in the air."

"Oh, right, you can fly us. Much better," Beatrice muttered as she tied her hair back and strapped on the scabbard Baojia had made for her to carry the twin hook-swords that had become her weapon of choice. She slid the two blades into the black leather sheaths and stretched back over her shoulders to make sure she could draw them easily. She thanked her vampire strength and flexibility that she was able to wield them at all.

"Ready?"

Beatrice nodded. "We have a few minutes before sundown. What are we expecting to happen?"

"We'll fly up there. Scare her. If we're lucky, some of her guards will attack us and we'll get to kill some of them."

Beatrice hesitated as she remembered Carwyn's admonition to be patient. "As much as I'm looking forward to killing something, are you sure this is a good idea?"

"If they attack us, we can defend ourselves. No one will question it, particularly since you have been put on the defensive, and I am a known ally of Giovanni's."

"And you're sure going there is the right move?"

"It's the only move. Currently, Livia has all the bargaining power. We need to shift the balance and throw her off her plan. Making her appear weak is our main objective."

They left the bedroom and walked down the stairs.

Beatrice asked, "So how are we going to do that?"

"When we get there, let me do the talking. I may hate politics, but I know how to play the game when I must."

"What do I do?"

"You'll stand behind me and look pissed off and menacing. Like I said, if anyone threatens you, kill them."

"Even Lorenzo?"

Tenzin cut her eyes to the side. "He's not that stupid. He might not even be there. It depends on how much attention he's looking for."

Beatrice paused at the base of the stairs. "Tenzin, why are we *really* going?"

The small woman looked up at Beatrice with furious eyes. "For almost a thousand years, the Eastern immortals have left her to her pretense of an empire. She kept to herself. We had no interest in her. Lorenzo changed that. Livia needs to realize that as long as she harbors a vampire who killed my mate and defied my father's court, she has lost any pretense of disinterest."

"She's powerful."

Tenzin gave a wicked smile, baring her curved fangs. "Never forget, Livia has tasted defeat in the past. She's vicious, but she's become soft on her cushioned throne."

Beatrice nodded, feeling nervous and elated at the same time. She watched as Tenzin strapped her ancient scimitar to her waist and opened the door to the garden. Twilight had fallen.

Tenzin held out her hand for Beatrice to grasp as they took to the air with a quick jerk. "My girl," she called out. "I believe we should remind her what it is to fear."

A FEW MINUTES LATER, THEY LANDED WITH A SOFT THUD AT THE GATES OF Castello Furio. Beatrice could hear the sounds of a party going on in the house.

Tenzin's eyes swept the grounds. "She's thinking more defensively."

As soon as the words left her mouth, two guards rushed them. They came to a halt a few meters away, but Tenzin kept walking at a steady and determined pace.

A guard spoke. "Stop, both of you! You may not enter the castle with weapons."

Tenzin drew her sword in the space of a heartbeat, sliced off the head of the guard who spoke, and kept walking as the body crumbled to the ground. "Oh, really?"

The other guard immediately snarled and drew his weapon, but Beatrice reached back for the *shuang gou*, drew them, and cut off the head of the vampire in one smooth movement. She hooked the swords in front of her and kept walking.

Four guards came at them next. Tenzin took to the air and swiftly killed two as Beatrice reached out to either side and hooked her blades around the necks of her attackers. She pulled both of them toward her, feeling the cold blood spatter on her face as their spines were severed and their heads fell at her feet.

By the time they were halfway across the garden, more guards had gathered but had stopped attacking them. They walked up the stairs, and Tenzin sent a great gust of wind to slam against the doors, pushing them open.

The two vampires entered the grand entryway and halted as every eye in the room turned toward them. Beatrice walked to the fountain and tore off a sleeve, flicking her fingers to spray a sheen of water over her blood-splattered face. She patted it dry, staring at the gaping immortals in formal wear that watched them. The music had died, and a path opened through the crowd, guiding them forward.

Beatrice bared her gleaming white fangs and let her amnis churn the water in the fountain until it splashed over the edges of the stone basin.

"Sorry about that." She sniffed and flicked the water back in. "We left a bit of a mess on the front lawn, too."

Tenzin hushed her as they walked to the right and into the great banquet hall of Castello Furio. It looked like the party the night before had not stopped with Giovanni's arrest. Beatrice could see Livia sitting on a plush chaise with a group of admirers in one corner. The noblewoman was dressed in another rich amethyst gown, her hair piled in a tower of curls. She looked up, and the smile fell from her face. She stood as Tenzin came to a halt and sniffed the air.

Out of the corner of her eye, Beatrice saw Lorenzo emerge from a doorway to the right with a company of guards. The guards spread along the edges of the room and Lorenzo stood behind Livia. His smiling eyes never left Beatrice. She glanced at him, then turned back to Tenzin, who stood quietly in front of the Roman. No one spoke until Tenzin opened her mouth.

"Livia."

"Tenzin."

"Give me Giovanni Vecchio."

Livia curled a red-painted lip. "Don't be ridiculous."

"In thousands of years, I've been called many things, but 'ridiculous' is not one of them, Roman dog."

Livia narrowed her eyes and scanned the two vampires, noting their bloody clothes. "Why do you come to my house to insult me, barbarian? To kill my guards? What kind of civilized person comes to a party with bloody weapons?"

"You will give me my friend."

"Why? Giovanni di Spada killed my husband and mate, Niccolo Andros, his own sire. I have every right to keep him as my prisoner. He is a murderer, a liar, and a thief. His own son confirms it."

Even though the accusation had been made before, Beatrice could still feel the shock roll through the room, and her own rage mount. She glanced around at the crowd, all of whom were keeping a safe distance. No one seemed to be able to take their eyes off of Tenzin and Livia.

"I do not know the truth of this accusation, nor do I care." Tenzin lifted her bloody saber and pointed it toward Lorenzo. "I know that *you* harbor a vampire who has defied a judgment of the immortal elders of Penglai Island. What have you to say to that?"

Livia shrugged. "I have received no official correspondence from that court. Who are you to speak for them?"

Beatrice could hear a few gasps around the room. Apparently, Livia was surprising even the jaded Roman population with her arrogance. From the corner of her eye, she saw Emil Conti approach with watchful eyes.

"Who am *I*?" Tenzin bared her fangs. Beatrice could hear the rustle of alarm spread through the room, but Livia remained still. "I am Tenzin. That is all the explanation you require."

Livia lifted an eyebrow. "Oh? And who makes these ridiculous accusations of my associate?"

Beatrice forced back the angry words that wanted to burst from her mouth. Her fangs grew long, and she tasted blood. She glanced over at Tenzin, but the small vampire looked eerily calm as she turned her back on Livia and addressed the Roman crowd.

"This vampire who Livia favors, Lorenzo, defied an official judgment of the Eight Immortals when he stole a manuscript from their scribe, Beatrice De Novo. Further, he and his vampires slaughtered the learned monks of Elder Lu Dongbin in the Wuyi Mountains. They killed humans under immortal aegis, none of whom had provoked such an attack."

A growing wind built in the room, lifting Tenzin as she surveyed the crowd. Beatrice looked on, unable to tear her eyes from the frightening specter of her friend wielding her power. Tenzin turned to Livia, but her voice echoed off the stone walls.

"The vampire *you* shelter defied the Elders, slaughtered the monks, and then..." Tenzin swooped down and grabbed Lorenzo by the throat, lifting him in the air and beyond the reach of his patroness. "Then, this bastard killed *my* mate."

The reaction was instantaneous. The Roman vampires, still even in the face of Tenzin's frightening power, began to whisper and scuttle to the edges of the room. The black-clad guards stepped forward, surrounding Beatrice, but keeping their distance from her drawn weapons.

Livia calmly walked down the steps and came to stand in front of Beatrice. She looked up with haughty eyes. "And what immortal accuses Lorenzo of this murder?"

Beatrice made sure she spoke loud enough to be heard over the rushing wind.

"I do. He killed my father and my sire, Stephen De Novo."

Livia was silent for a moment before she burst into laughter. "Lorenzo killed your father? How predictable. And why should we believe the accusations of an angry child?"

Beatrice let a satisfied smile curve her lips when she realized the trap that Tenzin had so carefully laid. Lorenzo dropped from Tenzin's grasp a moment before the wind vampire landed next to Beatrice. Tenzin kicked the blond vampire to the corner and stepped between Beatrice and Livia.

"Quite right, Livia." The Roman inched back as Tenzin crowded her. "You are *quite* right. Who would believe the angry accusations of a grieving child?

Even more"—Tenzin aimed a glare at Lorenzo—"who would believe the accusations of a *spiteful* child? One who has always coveted his father's wealth? Why, to believe something like that without question, would be... madness."

The air was suddenly still and not a whisper could be heard. Livia took a step back. Anger churned in her eyes, but her face was otherwise placid. Finally, she turned and sat on the brocade sofa where she had been holding court. Lorenzo brushed his clothes off and came to sit next to her. She placed her hand in his.

"So, Tenzin, what do you want? We all know your power, but you are in *my* court now, not an island in the sea. You know I will not release your friend, and you cannot have Lorenzo. There is obviously some investigation to be done in this matter, which I trust you will allow me to pursue. I'm a very fair person. Are you?"

"Not particularly."

Beatrice heard a few laughs in the crowd. One of them, she was almost certain, belonged to Emil Conti. Tenzin continued watching Livia with cold, calculating eyes.

"You know what I want, Livia. I want Giovanni Vecchio returned to his wife, the daughter of my mate. I want the head of the vampire on your left. I've considered killing you, as well, but I'm willing to let you live as long as you meet my demands."

"I could kill Giovanni with a snap of my fingers." Livia raised a hand and Beatrice could not stop the snarl that left her lips. Livia smirked. "But I won't, of course. Some of us aren't barbarians."

"And some of us are." Tenzin stepped closer and pointed at Lorenzo. "He exists at my pleasure. I could kill him quite easily; I'm sure you know this. If any harm comes to my friend, I will."

"As I said, I'm not—"

"And if that is not enough incentive to keep Giovanni Vecchio safe..." Tenzin again raised a swirling wind that lifted her in the air as she faced the Roman immortals. She lifted her arms, raising her bloody sword. "Vampires of Rome, I am the only child of Zhuang Guo, warrior king of the ancient steppes. I am the daughter of the Northern Wind. It has been many years since the hordes from the East have descended on your land, but make no mistake, we can and will raise them again."

Faster than the eye could follow, Tenzin darted down to twist the neck from the guard who stood next to Livia, splattering blood across her purple gown. A group of guards rushed toward them, but Beatrice raised her swords, twisting them in a razor-sharp whirl until they fell back.

Tenzin snatched the head of the guard and flew to the top of the room, then dropped to the ground in a crouch and tossed the guard's head at Livia's feet. Then she stood up, smearing the blood across her cheek as she tucked her hair behind her ear.

"Make no mistake, Roman. I am not civilized. Giovanni Vecchio remains safe, or I will call the Golden Horde. And remember, no ancient power remains to guard your Eastern gate."

Then Tenzin grasped Beatrice's arm, and the two vampires flew from the room in a rush of wind.

A few miles outside of Rome, they suddenly dropped to the ground. Beatrice looked around at the small, deserted piazza with a fountain in the middle. Judging by the position of the moon, it was probably around ten o'clock.

Tenzin pointed toward the fountain. "Wash up. You don't want to scare Dez or Ben. And you did well back there."

"You know, I always thought you were scary, but if I were Livia, I'd be metaphorically shitting my pants right now." Beatrice walked over and began washing. She was grateful for the deserted fountain and the moment to gather her thoughts. She took a calming breath and lay as much of her body in the water as she could, wrapping herself in the soft comfort of her element. Tenzin sat on the stone ledge.

After a few silent minutes, Beatrice spoke. "How did you leave him alive?"

She saw Tenzin look up at the moon. "I can be patient."

"You'll kill him soon enough."

"Or you will."

Beatrice shook her head. "He killed your mate. If it was Gio—"

"My girl, he killed your father. Your sire." Tenzin blinked a few times. "If you have your opportunity, take it. I will not be angry."

"Are you sure?"

Tenzin stood and held a hand out to Beatrice, lifting her out of the water. "There are more important things than my vengeance. That is why I could leave him alive. That is why you will kill him one day."

Beatrice frowned. "But, Tenzin—"

"Come, we need to get back to Rome. Lucien will be awake now. You need to talk to him."

GIOVANNI HEARD HER APPROACH. LIVIA SWEPT INTO THE ROOM AND SHOVED the guard back that tried to follow her. She paced, and he could see the water in the air drawn to her as her amnis swirled.

For a moment, Giovanni felt fear. He had not fed and was still weak from the injuries she had inflicted on him earlier in the night. But he braced himself against the stone pillar and remained silent, watching her stomp around the room.

Suddenly, Livia turned to him and screamed at the top of her lungs. Then she flew at him, stabbing him in the gut with a dagger she pulled from her bodice. She kicked his knees and slapped his face. She loosed her rage on Giovanni as he stood utterly still, not understanding what had caused the usually composed vampire to lose her temper.

Livia stabbed him over and over, until his leather jerkin hung in bloody strips, and he began to blink, lightheaded from the blood loss. Still, he said not a word and barely flinched, determined not to give her the reaction he knew she was looking for.

"Say something!" she screamed in his face, her fangs cutting her lips. He felt a spatter of her blood touch his face and she eyed his neck.

She paused, then a sick smile twisted her lips. She sprung on him and tried to latch onto his neck to drink, but Giovanni raised his arms and batted her away, throwing her as far across the room as his weakened body would allow.

He said only one word. "No."

Livia stood again and screamed, stamping her foot. Giovanni began to think she would finally kill him, but as soon as he thought it, she took a deep breath, pushed the mangled hair from her face, and looked at him with her typical look of contempt. Then she turned her nose up and walked from the room.

Only when he heard her steps retreating down the hall did he allow his shoulders to slump. If he did not get blood soon, he would fall into sleep, his body shutting down to protect his mind.

A few moments later, Giovanni scrambled to his feet when he heard footsteps in the hall. The locks twisted and a human servant entered the room. The young man raised an arm, clearly indicating that Giovanni was allowed to drink. His fangs slid down and he grasped the man's throat. Then he took a deep breath and backed away, clamping down his control so he did not drain the donor. He could see the fear evident in the young man's frightened gaze.

Keeping one hand on the man's throat and letting his amnis flow to calm him, Giovanni pressed his lips to the offered wrist. He took deep, slow draughts of the fresh blood until he felt his wounds begin to heal. Finally, he sealed up the man's wrist and released him.

"Thank you."

The young donor blinked, then said, "The mistress says to tell you another will be sent tomorrow."

Giovanni narrowed his eyes. "What?"

"Another will come to feed you, Master."

He nodded slowly, then waved the man away. The guard opened the stone door and let the donor out before the locks clicked in place again. Giovanni took a deep breath as the strength began to flow through his limbs and his wounds began to knit together.

He thought about Livia's strange fury as he healed. Her violence. Her attempts to drink from him. She had looked...

"What was that, Livia?" He paced his stone cell. "What was that in your eyes? What was—" He halted when the answer occurred to him. She hadn't been angry. Livia had been... frustrated. Like a child whose mischief had been thwarted.

Giovanni began to smile. Then laugh. Soon, his deep laughter echoed off the stone walls that held him. Someone had spoiled Livia's plans.

It appeared Tenzin was back in Rome.

CHAPTER 12

When Tenzin and Beatrice reached the house in Rome, they dropped into the courtyard to see an unfamiliar vampire sitting near the fountain talking to Carwyn and drinking a glass of golden wine. The immortal may have appeared to be young, but his long, angular face and deep-set eyes gave him an ancient stare.

Carwyn smiled and waved them over.

"Beatrice, meet Lucien Thrax."

"Finally." She smiled and held out a hand.

The vampire rose. He was lean and weathered. His shaggy brown hair fell over his forehead when he bent over Beatrice's hand and clasped it with both his own. "Many thanks for your hospitality, Beatrice De Novo. I am sorry I retired before we could be introduced last night. Your household has been gracious to me."

She found herself clasping his fingers, which were unusually warm for a vampire. His energy felt different from any she had ever sensed, but his eyes were open and honest.

"You're very welcome. I understand you're a friend of the family, in a manner of speaking."

Lucien closed his eyes and smiled slightly. "I was honored to call Ioan ap Carwyn one of my dearest friends. Carwyn and I were taking a moment to catch up on news. I met your lovely friends Desiree and Ben earlier this evening while you were..." His smile broadened. "Otherwise engaged."

Carwyn snorted as he rose, motioning Beatrice to his seat while he and

Tenzin gathered more chairs from the other side of the courtyard. "Speaking of that," Carwyn said, "I don't suppose you saw Gio?"

Tenzin shook her head. "No, but we did get to kill some guards."

Carwyn patted her small shoulder. "That's my small, ferocious girl."

Beatrice smiled. "You missed it, Father. She scared the proverbial shit out of Livia."

"I miss *all* the fun."

Tenzin only looked him up and down. "If you weren't such a behemoth, I'd fly you, too."

Carwyn just shuddered while Beatrice and Lucien laughed.

"We earth vampires," Lucien said, "aren't terribly fond of air travel, if you haven't noticed yet, Ms. De Novo."

"Please, call me Beatrice. And yes, I've noticed."

"Horrid, unnatural way to travel," Carwyn muttered.

"Yes, it's far more pleasant to tunnel underground like a giant rat."

Beatrice shook her head. "You two really do bicker like siblings."

Lucien burst out laughing. "Beatrice, you haven't seen half of it!"

"Both of you, stop." Carwyn waved a hand at them and looked back to Tenzin, suddenly serious. "Really though, what is the mood in the court?"

"Livia knows she's backed into a corner, which means anything is possible. We need to get him out of there. She's become more unstable than the last time I saw her. She's still frightened by me, but she's keeping Lorenzo at her side like a favorite pet, which means that he's valuable to her right now. We have to assume it's because of the elixir."

"Or something to do with Geber's book," Carwyn said.

"No doubt, but that's not the point. We need to get Gio out, and we need to do it in a way that she'll not be able to point to us. My introduction should be arriving any night now."

Beatrice said, "Your introduction?"

"Yes. Despite the way I charged in today, I will be very properly received the next time we're there. It should drive her crazy." Tenzin grinned. "One of Elder Lu's children is coming in the next week to discuss mutual textile interests in Southern China, and Livia will be forced to acknowledge him as they have business. He's naming me as a member of his retinue as a favor."

"What?" Beatrice looked around. "Really? And she'll just have to welcome you back? Even after the stunt we pulled tonight?"

"You mean the stunt *I* pulled? Remember, B, you did nothing but defend yourself. She'll have no excuse to keep you out of court. With their natural sympathy for Gio and the Roman fascination with the new girl, you might be our most valuable asset."

She just shook her head. "This makes no sense."

Carwyn said, "You have to remember, as powerful as Livia is, she's not the only member of the Roman court. There are many others with their own interests, and she has to placate them, too. She can't piss everyone off and remain in power. Tenzin, what did you think of Conti?"

Tenzin paused for a moment to think and Beatrice thought about the quietly confident water vampire. Like Carwyn, she was curious what Tenzin would think of him.

"Conti may be poised. With the right push, he could take power. He'd be far better than Livia and his connections are more consistent."

Beatrice asked, "More consistent? What does that mean?"

Carwyn leaned forward. "Emil Conti is a bit older than Livia. He was born during the Republic, not the Empire, so he has more... democratic ideals. He's an elitist, but he tends to keep the same friends over the years, unlike our favorite empress. He's also a much better businessman, which means he likes stability and avoids drama. If Livia was pushed out of power, it would be best for everyone if someone was poised to take her place so there wasn't a vacuum."

Beatrice said, "And, Tenzin, you think he's ready?"

She nodded. "He's positioning himself in all this. He senses an opportunity. He could be an ally, so you should get to know him."

Beatrice said, "But does that help us get Gio out?"

"Oh," Tenzin said, "none of *us* can get Gio out. We'll need to be in her presence when he escapes. That way, Livia can't point to any of us."

"But then how—"

Carwyn broke in. "Leave that to me." He gave her a quick wink. "Just a few days and I'll have something worked out."

Beatrice looked over to Tenzin, who was exchanging some kind of wordless communication with the priest. All of a sudden, her friend nodded. "Ah, yes. Send him to me when he gets here, and I'll fill him in on what I know about the castle."

"Good."

Beatrice felt her anger spike. "Will someone clue me in, please? It *is* my husband we're talking about."

Carwyn reached over and patted her hand. "Not just now. I'll fill you in, but I have a feeling our friend here is tiring."

Beatrice looked at the sky, which was still pitch black. Then she looked at Lucien, who had been listening silently to their conversation while leaning his head back and letting his fingers brush through the tangled ferns that lined the edge of the fountain.

"Oh," he murmured, "don't mind me. I'm quite comfortable and quite happy to stay out of all of it."

"Lucien," Tenzin said, "you're neck-deep in all this, and you know it."

He opened his eyes, looking around the courtyard for a moment before he locked his eyes on Beatrice. Eyes that could never belong to a mortal man. They were stone-grey and ringed by a deep brown. Like bits of rock emerging from the earth. Despite the lack of lines on his face, she knew Lucien Thrax had seen many centuries.

As if guessing her thoughts, he said, "I'm almost as old as this one." He winked at Tenzin.

"Where—"

"I come from the mountains, like my mother. But farther north. Not all that far from here, as the crow flies."

Beatrice took a deep breath. "Not that you're unwelcome, but *why* are you here? I know you're not one of Geber's four if you're an earth vampire. You're old enough, but Geber's earth immortal was a woman."

"What a wonderful mind you have, Beatrice." He smiled and drifted in the cool night air. "And you ask an excellent question. Ever since Tenzin found me near my home, I've been hoping I might be able to help you. You see, in addition to being a good friend, Ioan and I were colleagues, as you would say now."

"Colleagues?"

"Yes, though we trained centuries apart, the healing of vampires and humans was our shared interest, and we often corresponded. I've brought some letters and papers that might be of use to you."

"Letters? From Ioan?"

"Yes, there were a number of books and papers he sent some time ago that he asked me to look over. They concerned his research into vampiric blood and his theories on what might alter it. His ideas were interesting, even going back to our origins, as mysterious as those are."

Beatrice sat forward, enthralled by Lucien's quiet voice. "What do you mean?"

"Why do we live as we do? Why do we have an affinity for the elements? Why must we drink from the blood of living humans or beasts to remain as we are? Why do we heal from injury?"

"And why," Carwyn asked in a quiet voice, "is our blood unable to heal humans as it heals others of our kind?"

Lucien nodded. "Ioan and I both researched this question over the years. We both had our own theories. He was convinced that there must be some way that we could harness the power of our blood to make humanity stronger. A trade, if you will. That we might drink from them, but that we could offer something good in return."

"Just like Geber."

Lucien offered her a sad smile. "You speak of the elixir."

Beatrice blinked. "Yes! How do you—"

"Oh, my dear Beatrice." Lucien nodded and slumped in his chair, staring into the burbling fountain. "I'm very well acquainted with Geber's elixir. You see..." He looked back to meet her eyes. "I've taken it."

A FALL OF WATER

. . .

By the time Beatrice noticed Ziri had joined them, she was immersed in Lucien's story. The old wind vampire drifted around the edge of the courtyard, watching Lucien as he spoke.

"I looked over her charts, spoke to her doctors, but there was nothing more that I could do. Pancreatic cancer is one of the most vicious, you see. And very fast moving. By the time Rada was able to reach me, she was almost gone. Her family was devastated. And I knew that she would never accept immortality. We had discussed it many years before, but she..."

Beatrice spoke softly. "She was a friend?"

Lucien smiled wistfully. "A research assistant. For many years. And a... a dear friend, as well. She left me to go to medical school, marry, have children. It was good. It was what she wanted. But we kept in contact over the years, though her family never understood, as she did, what I truly was."

"And she died?"

For a moment, a gleam of joy lit Lucien's face. "No, she didn't."

Beatrice frowned, "But—"

"I was sitting in a cafe in Plovdiv, sipping a glass of wine and mourning her. You see, I thought that I had seen her for the last time that evening. I felt sure she would not last the next day. Her body was ravaged. Then, Lorenzo walked through the door."

"Lorenzo?" Beatrice whispered, her fangs dropping in instinctive alarm. She could feel a brush of air soothing her shoulder, but didn't know if it came from Ziri or Tenzin.

Lucien shook his head. "I remember thinking later that it was as if an angel appeared. Oh, I knew his reputation, of course, but you never know exactly how much of anything is true in this world. We started to chat. He was sympathetic when he heard of Rada's illness. Who among us has not lost a multitude of human friends?"

Beatrice was willing to bet that there were no humans Lorenzo mourned, but she didn't interrupt.

Lucien continued, "He seemed to sense that Rada was special to me. And then, he made his offer."

A creeping suspicion took root in Beatrice's mind. "When was this?"

"Eight months ago. October of last year."

She whispered. "Almost a year after he took it."

Lucien smiled bitterly. "As Tenzin informed me a few weeks ago."

"He had the elixir."

He nodded. "A form of it, anyway. He said that he was developing it for the pharmaceutical industry. That it was experimental, but would have miraculous effects." Lucien shrugged. "What could it hurt? I thought. She is dying already.

Practically a ghost in my arms. I took the elixir for Rada without hesitation. I gave it to her within hours of talking to Lorenzo."

"And?"

"It was just before dawn on a Monday morning. I went to my home to rest and meditate, trying not to retain too much hope. I didn't *really* think it would work, despite the gold I'd paid for it." Lucien paused and brought a hand up to rest on his chin before he spoke again. "But that night, when the sun set, I still ran to the hospital. To her room, and there she was."

Beatrice could see his red-rimmed eyes, and her heart ached.

"She had cheated death! She was still thin, but the color had returned to her face. The doctors called it a miracle. The cancer was completely gone. Her blood tests showed normal results." He sighed and looked up at Beatrice. "I was convinced. How could I not be? It *was* a miracle. Lorenzo had developed the elixir of life."

"Tell them," Tenzin said gently. "Tell them the rest, Lucien."

"I stayed at my home nearby for a few months. Rada seemed to be thriving, and I met with Lorenzo again to learn more about this medicine he had developed. He told me about Geber and the four vampires, though he did not tell me who they were. My instincts are always to be skeptical, but how could I be? I had seen the results with my own eyes. And it fit with much of what Ioan and I had theorized over the years. That blood had always been the key. The combination of elemental blood which linked to the four elements present in human blood—"

Beatrice broke in. "What do you mean? What do you mean the four elements in *human* blood?"

"Ioan and I had always speculated that there was something about human blood that fed the elemental energy in all vampires, which was why we must have it. Human blood, in a way, *contains* all four elements. The cells are made up of matter, as earth is. There is water, of course."

"And then the oxygen it carries is the air," she nodded. "I get those. But what about—"

"Fire?" Lucien grinned, and she saw the spark of the scientist in his eyes. "More elusive. But blood carries heat, does it not? It carries the energy of the entire human body, an energy grid of far more ancient design than the ones humans have developed."

"So, what Lorenzo told you fit with what you and Ioan already speculated, so you bought into the elixir?"

He shrugged again. "As I said, how could I not? I had seen Rada's results. And it wasn't until later that he told me of its other benefits." Lucien took a deep breath and let it out, slumping into his seat. "I cannot tell you what it felt like to hear, after *thousands* of years, that I might be free from the demands of bloodlust, Beatrice De Novo."

"I don't understand. Did you feel guilty? Truly? After *thousands* of years being who you are?"

Lucien smirked. "You live in a very luxurious time, my dear. A time where there is donated blood for the newborn. A time when you can carry a reserve, if you will. You never had to conquer bloodlust while feeding from an innocent. An innocent who looked you in the eye. Talk to me after a few thousand years and let me know if feeding from humanity still holds no shame for you."

She bowed her head, humbled by Lucien's words. Beatrice knew she was young, though she often forgot it when she was in her friends' company. "So, you drank from Rada?" she said. "After you'd heard?"

He took a deep breath and nodded. "I discussed it with her. She was a scientist herself, after all. She offered." Lucien's eyes drifted away. "I kissed her, as I had so many years ago, and then I bit. It was only a few drops. She was still recovering, and... we were not as we once were."

The vampire fell silent. His eyes seemed to glaze over, and he stared at the flowing water in complete stillness until Tenzin leaned over and touched his shoulder. "Lucien?"

He blinked and came back. His eyes narrowed on Tenzin. "How long?"

"Just a few moments this time."

He nodded. "I finally left the city and went to my home in the mountains earlier this year. Just after Christmas. It was then that I began noticing odd things happening."

Carwyn leaned forward. "What things?" Beatrice noticed that Ziri had come closer, as well.

"I needed to sleep. Much more than just a few hours in the afternoon as had been my custom. I thought, perhaps, it was the consequence of the lack of bloodlust. Truly, I felt none. I *still* feel none, though I try to drink. I never feel the burn in my throat, nor the ache in my belly from the lack of it. I have no hunger."

"None?" Beatrice asked.

"None. So I decided, for lack of bloodlust, more rest is surely not so great a sacrifice. If I need no food but a bit of bread, now and again, I am willing to pay that price."

Beatrice had a suspicion that more rest was not the only problem. "What else? It was more than just the bloodlust, wasn't it?"

Lucien nodded. "I began losing time. I would wake in a room that I had no memory of entering. I woke once, thinking it was the next evening, to find that I had no memory of three days past."

Carwyn gaped. "Three days?"

He nodded. "Three days had passed. I don't know if I sleepwalked. If I simply slept? I have no memory of it at all."

Beatrice asked, "And you live alone?"

"I had. I can no longer. I have a fear that I would simply wander out of the house and lose time, meeting the dawn without any knowledge of it. I have lived the past five months in fear, my friends." Lucien ran a hand through his shaggy hair, pushing it off his forehead in a frustrated gesture. "I have no idea what has happened to me. I must assume that it is the result of drinking Rada's blood, but I have no idea why. I force myself to drink now, but it is difficult. I have no taste for it, and I'm not sure my body is drawing any strength from the blood I ingest, no matter how fresh it is."

"And it's getting worse?" Beatrice whispered.

Lucien paused, looking around the courtyard. "Yes. And I have no idea how much worse my condition will grow. I tried to find Lorenzo when I started noticing symptoms, but I heard he was in Rome. He did not answer my letters. In truth, I did not expect him to."

"What about Saba?" Carwyn asked. "Have you written to her?"

"I have sent a messenger to my mother, but, as you know, she is difficult to find. I do have hope that some of my sire's own blood might heal me. But even if the messenger finds her in the mountains, it would be some time. I have no idea how fast this illness might take me. And the distance from Ethiopia to Rome—"

"Ethiopia?" Beatrice sat up straight. "Did you say—"

"It might not matter." Ziri's quiet voice came from the edge of the courtyard. He drifted over and stood next to Lucien, running a hand along the man's cheek in a tender gesture. "Even if you found my old friend, dear Lucien, I don't know if your mother's blood would heal you."

"Uncle..." Lucien took a deep breath. "You have knowledge of this, I think. But not knowledge that will comfort me."

Ziri nodded. "I have knowledge about the elixir, yes. We were foolish to keep it a secret. We truly thought it had been lost, that our children were safe from our folly. We should have known better."

Beatrice murmured, "No secret stays hidden forever."

Ziri nodded. "You speak truth, Beatrice De Novo."

Lucien gripped Ziri's fingers. "Uncle, am I dying?"

"I don't know." Ziri's eyes furrowed in pain. "But I know that something is wrong. Something that can even hurt the most ancient among us. Something that I and my closest friends are responsible for creating."

CHAPTER 13

Crotone
1507

Jacopo was crouched in the corner, his throat aching and his eyes glued to the small, lit candle. He reached a finger out, and the flickering flame reached toward him. For a moment, he held it, then it began to spread as if by its own will, up his finger, quickly engulfing his hand. The sharp bite of pain caused him to wince, and he quickly reached for the basin of water Andros had left for him.

For the first time in ten years, he was grateful for the damp air of the craggy castle his father called home. The wet soothed his aching skin and helped him to tame the blue fire that wanted to rush over his body.

Andros had told stories of those fabled immortals who could control fire. His education in both mortal and immortal history had been exemplary. But he had never expected to carry the burden of it. He closed his eyes again and tried to forget the terror of the flames bursting out on his aching body and the quick flash of water his father had used to douse him. Every hair on his body had been burned away within seconds after he first woke, and he rubbed a hand along the bare skin on his scalp.

He heard a commotion in the hall, and a sweet scent reached his nose, causing his new fangs to drop in his mouth. They pierced his lip and the pain caused his skin to heat. Steam rose from his arms as the door opened. Andros entered, dragging one of the servant girls.

She smelled like food.

It was the smell of an orchard when the fruit was ready to drop. The tantalizing aroma of new bread and freshly pressed olives. It was everything. He heard the rush of her blood, rich and sweeter than new wine, as a low growl built in his throat.

He spoke around his long fangs. "Why is she here?"

Andros held the girl up like a prize. "For you. My blood is gone from your system and you need sustenance."

Her name was Serafina, and she was Paulo's lover. Jacopo struggled to look into her eyes, forcing himself to look at her and remember her voice, her laugh, and her smile before she became nothing more than blood to him. He had known he would need to feed from one of the servants, but he had not known which it would be.

He closed his eyes and tried to block her scent.

"I don't want—"

"You will not drain her. That only exhibits a lack of control. Though you are young, you must never be without self-control, do you understand me?"

"Yes, Father."

Jacopo rose to his feet and approached, a small fire burst out on his shoulder, causing the once-friendly girl to look at him in horror. Though Andros quickly doused the flame, another pain twisted his heart. Serafina had once sung and laughed while she cleaned his room.

He held a hand out toward her, trying to calm the terrified girl who had reminded him of his uncle's lover, Giuliana. She had the same dark brown hair and fair skin. The same sweet disposition. Tears streamed down her face, though she bit her lip and smothered her cries.

Andros tossed her toward him and he caught her in his arms. She slumped against him and he heard her whispering under her breath. *"Per piacere, Signore. Abbi pietà. Per favore, per favore."*

Andros's voice slipped over her cries. "Now feed."

Jacopo tried to soothe the burn in his throat. He embraced Serafina, running a hand through her long hair. He could do this. The iron control that enabled him to stand the harshest beating from his sire would let him drink from the girl without killing her.

It had to.

"Shhh," he whispered. He nosed against her neck, forcing himself to become accustomed to her scent before he bit. "Be still. I will try not to hurt you."

As if by its own volition, he felt the energy flow from his fingertips, soothing the girl who ceased her struggles. Serafina lay limp in his arms as he put his mouth to her neck, felt for her pulse, and bit.

Heaven.

He moaned against her neck, pulling her closer as her blood poured down his throat. He pressed her body to his, feeling his flesh rouse as he drank the girl's

A FALL OF WATER

blood. For a few moments, he was lost in lust. Blood. Body. Desire for both wound him in iron coils until the girl's cries broke through.

She was praying.

So Jacopo pulled his fangs from her neck, forcing back the monster inside that wanted to take her. He willed down his arousal and let his fangs pierce his own lips, pushing her away while he dug burning fingers into his arms.

The girl stumbled before she fell to the floor. He backed away from her and into the corner of the room. The scent of her open wound called to him. Her dress was torn at the neck. He swallowed the lingering burn in his throat and closed his eyes, licking the last of her sweet blood from his mouth. He stopped breathing. Anything to keep from killing the helpless girl.

"Nicely done. Your control is impressive. Exactly what I would expect of my son."

Jacopo's voice was a hoarse growl. "Thank you, Father."

"Do you need another?"

Another? He needed thousands. A vision of the Arno River came to him. If the Arno was a never-ending stream of blood, he would swallow it whole. But that was not what Andros wanted to hear.

"I am fine."

The old water vampire smirked as if he knew the truth, but appreciated Jacopo's lie anyway. Then he walked over and picked up the girl by her arm.

"Grazie, Signor Andros," she gasped. "Grazie per—"

Her words stopped when Andros twisted her neck. Jacopo heard the tiny snap before she fell to the ground, lifeless.

"No!" He started toward her, his heart breaking as he looked into the girl's lifeless eyes, but Andros intercepted him. "Stop." He put a hand on Jacopo's chest and shoved him into the wall. "This will not do. She was human. You are a god. We do not control ourselves to have mercy, but to conquer our own lusts. To be master of them."

"But she was an innocent."

"She was a whore. She had no honor. The girl lay with anyone who paid her attention."

A vision of Serafina and Paulo came to his mind as he stared at her body. They were whispering in the kitchen at night while Paulo snuck some bread and a few kisses from the pretty servant. It was the only time Jacopo ever saw the young man truly smile.

"She wouldn't have been useful much longer, anyway. She was carrying Paulo's bastard in her womb." Andros curled his lip and shook his head, patting Jacopo's cheek in a friendly gesture. "Remember, never keep the same woman for too long. They begin to have expectations."

He couldn't take his eyes from her. Andros walked to the door and opened it.

"Paulo!"

Jacopo heard the steps approaching. Had Paulo known that the girl carried his child? The young man stepped into the room and his fangs dropped again. Jacopo bared them viciously when the scent of the human's blood reached his nose. He heard the faint intake of breath when Paulo spotted his lover's body, but he made no protest.

"Clean this up. Take it out to the sea and dispose of it."

The young man was frozen, his eyes fixed on Serafina's body. For a moment, Jacopo saw his fists clench, then the young man deliberately relaxed them and bent down, kneeling beside his lover. His eyes darted to Jacopo's in the corner of the room, and his lip curled in disgust.

Andros brought a basin and a rag over and began to wash the blood from Jacopo's chin, neck, and chest where it had dripped down. "There, my son. Let me help you. You did well. I am proud of you, so very proud."

Jacopo watched as Paulo closed Serafina's eyes and smoothed her crumpled dress behind Andros's back. For a moment, the young man's hand halted over the girl's belly where his unborn child had grown, then he lifted her slight frame in his arms and walked from the room.

Jacopo felt his fangs retract, and the taste of her blood was bitter in his mouth.

Castello Furio

GIOVANNI STARED INTO THE HATEFUL EYES OF HIS SON AS LORENZO accompanied Emil Conti and Ziri into his dungeon. He knew, from all outward appearances, that he was being treated well. Though he refused to speak, the two men would have seen the simple, comfortable furnishings that Livia had brought to his cell the previous evening.

He was being fed every evening. He needed it; otherwise the nightly rage that Livia loosed upon him would have been far more evident. Luckily for her, his freshly washed clothes hid the red slashes across his chest, back, and thighs from where she tortured him.

"As you can see, *signores*, Signor Vecchio is being treated well, despite his refusal to speak or confess his crimes. Livia provides him with plentiful meals and all the necessary comforts, and she will continue to do so until a determination of his guilt can be provided to the court's satisfaction."

Emil nodded. "I do see, Lorenzo. And while I am satisfied that Giovanni is well—"

The canny water vampire drew Lorenzo into a detailed discussion of Giovanni's "case" leaving Ziri to mouth his ghostly whispers from across the room.

'Is she feeding you? Blink once for 'yes.'

Giovanni blinked.

'Is she torturing you?'

Giovanni did not blink.

'You are lying. I can see a mark on your chest. But I will not tell your wife.'

Giovanni mouthed, *Thank you.*

'She is well, and your friends are working toward your release. Do you understand?'

He blinked once.

'Keep strong. You will be in your mate's arms soon. And remain silent, as much as you can.'

He blinked again.

'Your grandsire would be very proud of you, if he could see your strength.'

When Giovanni blinked, it was not in response to anything the old wind vampire had asked. A frown spread across his face.

'Keep silent. I knew your grandsire well. We will speak—truly speak—soon, Jacopo.'

"—and so I am satisfied for now, but this matter must be resolved quickly. I do not care for this drawn-out process. It disrupts business and becomes an unnecessary distraction for the younger members of the court."

Lorenzo nodded at Emil with respect. "I will make mention of your concerns to Livia, Signor Conti. And Ziri?"

The old vampire glanced toward Lorenzo, seemingly disinterested in his surroundings. "Yes?"

"Are you satisfied that the prisoner is being taken care of in a proper way? Do we have your testimony to this? Your opinion would go very far in assuaging some of the more squeamish members of the court."

Ziri waved a hand. "Oh, yes. He's fine. I was simply curious. The design of this chamber..." He looked around in an academic way. "It is most unusual. Will it hold him, do you think?"

"I cannot go into the specifics, of course. But be assured, it is very secure." Lorenzo's lip curled as he eyed Giovanni in the corner. "Even against a vampire as ruthless and cunning as my father."

When Giovanni woke the next night, Livia was in his chamber, staring at him.

"I told him to kill you," she said.

Giovanni only shrugged.

"When Andros wrote to say he had sired you to fire, I told him then that he should spare himself the trouble and kill you."

He blinked and felt along his bare chest to see if the new wounds she had opened the previous night had already closed. They had.

"He didn't listen to me, of course. He rarely did."

She walked over to the side of his bed and sat on it. He lay still and silent, stretching his arms up and knitting his fingers together behind his head. Livia's eyes roamed his chest, and she reached down to trace along the red marks she had made the night before.

"I understood, of course. You were always so beautiful. He was so proud of you. Bright. Strong." She dug her small hands into the defined muscles along his abdomen. "So strong. Stronger than him, as it turned out."

He still said nothing, letting her voice whatever tormented thoughts crowded her mind.

"And I once thought he was the strongest being I would ever meet. I adored him, you know. The first time Andros snuck into my bedchamber, my husband was snoring in my bed, the fat pig. But Andros..."

A wistful smile touched her lips as she gazed into the past. "I had seen him at the banquet that night. He was so handsome. *Strong*. His dark hair was thick and his belly was flat. And no matter how much wine touched his lips, he did not grow drunk. I saw him looking at me, so I encouraged him. Why not?"

Her fingers stroked his skin, drawing damp circles as she reminisced.

"He snuck into our villa that night and fucked me against a wall as my husband snored beside us. It was magnificent."

Though his stomach churned, Giovanni remained motionless and silent. At least she wasn't stabbing him.

"When he finally brought a vampire to turn me, Andros tied my husband up and made him watch. That was even better. Andros fucked me and drained my blood, then my sire gave me his before Andros killed him so he would not interfere. He was nothing. A pawn. I was Andros's *mate*. From the first night of my immortality, I belonged to him."

Livia smiled and ran a finger across his throat.

"My first meal was my stupid, fat husband. I can still taste his blood. It tasted like revenge. While it wasn't cold, thank the gods..." She bent down and whispered into his ear. "It was very, *very* sweet."

Livia took both hands and traced along Giovanni's arms.

"But you, Giovanni... Andros loved you. He adored you. Almost as much as me, I think."

Far more, you stupid cow. Giovanni rolled his eyes.

She curled her lip and slapped him. "If only he had listened to me and killed you."

Livia rose and stepped away from him. "Do you know who built this chamber? Your father did. I told him if he was determined to keep you, then he must build a chamber here that could contain you. I never trusted you, do you understand that? In five hundred years. Never."

Giovanni sat up and looked around. So, this chamber was of his father's design?

"He could be such a genius. Turning me. Using my human connections and my dead husband's gold. Finding the book. We were made to rule, he and I. We *would* have ruled, if you hadn't killed him, you stupid boy."

He swung his legs over the side of the bed and sat silently, examining her. Finally, he opened his mouth to speak.

"The. Roman. Whore."

She pulled a dagger from between her breasts, walked over, and stabbed him in the neck. Bending down, she whispered, "I will enjoy killing you. Then I will drink your blood and the blood of your little wife, you bastard."

Livia spun and left the room as Giovanni sat stunned and blinking.

So, his father had built this chamber.

Giovanni pulled the dagger from his neck and pressed a sheet to the wound.

And Livia had left him a blade.

How generous.

CHAPTER 14

It was late afternoon, and the house was buzzing with activity.

Ben and Dez were doing research into Bulgarian cosmetics companies and their not-exactly-public financial information. They were trying to determine who else might be funding Livia's enterprise, or if she was in it on her own. So far, Elder Zhongli was the only other immortal they'd found any evidence of and, according to Tenzin, he was most decidedly dead.

Matt seemed to be making phone call after phone call in the downstairs study. She couldn't tell whom exactly he was talking to, but Beatrice thought he was speaking French.

She could hear Carwyn and Ziri making plans downstairs in the library. Carwyn had an appointment to speak to someone at the Vatican about unrelated church business, and Ziri was speaking with Emil Conti about a visit to see Giovanni wherever Livia was holding him. Apparently, no one knew of Ziri's connection to Beatrice or Stephen, so he could be presented as an impartial observer and gain access to the dungeons. Emil Conti was willing to play along.

Angela had been cooking all day. The whole house was suffused with the smell of herb bread, lemon, and fresh basil from the pesto she made.

If she listened closely, Beatrice could hear the soft rise and fall of Lucien's breaths in the second floor guest room. He had been at the house for over a week and Beatrice was still surprised by how weary the simplest tasks seemed to make him.

Tenzin left just before dawn, saying she had some business to take care of and would take shelter with the Chinese delegation she would be joining with Elder Lu's son.

A FALL OF WATER

So Beatrice sat in her empty bedroom, wearing one of Giovanni's shirts she'd stolen from the laundry, and going quietly mad as another day passed without her husband resting in their bed.

Finally, she picked up the phone and called Los Angeles.

"Hello?"

"Caspar?"

"Beatrice, darling—Isadora, B's on the phone." She heard the quick shuffle of feet and her grandmother picked up the other line.

"Mariposa?"

Beatrice smiled just hearing her voice. "Hey, Grandma."

"How are you, dear? Matt called us a few days ago, and Dez called us yesterday, but they didn't seem to know much."

"No change, really."

"But it's been over a week now! Has anyone been to see him? Does he get a—a lawyer? A doctor? Is there anyone that you can call or petition?"

"It's not really that kind of arrest, Grandma."

She heard Caspar soothing her grandmother in the background.

"Beatrice." His calm voice soothed her, as well. "I know Tenzin and Carwyn are there. Are there any other vampires who have publicly voiced support for Giovanni?"

"Not publicly. At least not right now. She's really powerful, Cas. These Roman vampires are like sheep or something. There are a few who seem to stand up to her, but for the most part, they all just follow along."

"She's still being careful. Gio has enough of a reputation for her to be very cautious about all of this. I expect she's quite angry about having to arrest him as she did. It doesn't sound as if that was her plan. Please be patient, my dear."

Beatrice knew all of it. She had heard the arguments for patience and prudence. She had listened and followed the instructions of those far older and more experienced than she, vampires she knew loved Giovanni, too. Still, she could feel the tears well up in her eyes, and she cleared her throat. Caspar trailed off.

"How are you holding up, dear girl?"

Her voice caught. "Um... can I... can I just talk to my grandma for a little bit, Caspar?"

"Of course." She heard him put the phone down, followed by a few murmurs in the background and a closing door before Isadora came back on the line.

"Beatrice?"

At the sound of her name, silent tears began to stream down her face. Soon, she was choking on her cries as Isadora made soothing noises in the background.

"Oh, my girl. If I could only be there for you now."

"I can't do this, Grandma. I can't be who I'm supposed to be without him here."

"Yes, you can."

"No! Everything's wrong. I can't think straight. I don't feel like myself. I have to force myself to eat, and I know it's not good for me. I can usually sleep a little bit when he's here, but now, it's just... *nothing*. And everything is wrong, and I can't do this."

"Beatrice, you can. And according to what everyone says, this is upsetting, but—"

"It's not upsetting! It's infuriating!" She stood and tried pacing the room, but the rotary phone wouldn't let her get far. She gripped the back of the chair so hard that the wood splintered. "I'm so angry, I want to kill something, Grandma. I want to kill *her*. I want to tear her heart out. I want to rip Lorenzo's head off his body and toss it to a pack of dogs. I want to round up all the spineless weaklings that follow her orders and tear every last one of them apart. I want to burn this damn city to the ground and spit in its ashes. And there is nothing—*nothing*—I can do except sit here and wait for ridiculous protocol and negotiations!"

By the time she had vented her anger, her grandmother was speechless.

"Well..."

"Grandma?"

"Beatrice, this is one of those times when I am reminded that you are a vampire now."

A harsh laugh broke from her throat, but it quickly turned to tears again. She brushed at her tears. "I'm pretty sure I'd feel this way if I was still human, too."

"Possibly, but the potential to carry out the bloodshed would not be as likely."

She grabbed another of Giovanni's handkerchiefs and cleaned her blood-streaked face.

"Beatrice, you must be strong. For him. For yourself. For Ben. Control your anger. Nothing good can come from losing control. I'm sure they're probably expecting you to be foolish and out of your mind with your Gio in prison, so prove them wrong."

"I know you're right."

"Of course I am. I'm your grandmother."

She couldn't help the smile. "Thanks, Grandma." There was silence over the phone as both women seemed to catch their breath.

"Hey, Grandma?"

"Yes, dear?"

"Distract me, okay? Tell me what trouble you and Caspar have been up to lately."

Isadora's tinkling laugh did more to soothe her weary heart than all the kind words from her friends.

"Well, I went to a wonderful painting workshop at the Huntington the other day. Did you know that Caspar has started volunteering in the gardens there? All those little old women just adore him. I'd be jealous, but it's too adorable how he preens for them. It's rose season now, and you know how he loves his roses. Oh! And I should tell you about the art opening that Ernesto took us to the other night. It was wonderful, the girl who was featured..."

As Isadora chattered about roses and art galleries, Beatrice closed her eyes. The familiar voice of her grandmother and the everyday news she spoke of was its own kind of meditation. A reminder that, past the blood and the intrigue, beyond the danger and the heartache, another kind of life waited for her and Giovanni. A life filled with family and love. With their own pursuits and challenges.

If only they could get there.

Finally, she broke into her grandmother's news, anxious to rest her mind on one more subject.

"Grandma, I know Matt usually keeps an eye on things if we're not there—"

"Don't worry about us, Beatrice. We have quite a bit of company, if you know what I mean. Baojia is usually here in the evenings and then there's a lovely woman and a gentleman that Ernesto introduced us to that help with the driving and taking care of this and that around the house during the day. They're quite understanding of us old people!" Isadora laughed, but the keen edge to her voice let Beatrice know she was well aware of the security that Ernesto had arranged.

"Well good. I hope you don't give them too many problems. The two of you are troublemakers, I know."

"But only the best kind of trouble!" Isadora laughed.

By the time she hung up the phone an hour later, Beatrice thought she could just about make it through a few more nights without killing anything.

Unless a good opportunity presented itself, of course.

SHE WAS STUDYING SOME OF GEBER'S JOURNALS LATER THAT EVENING AND watching Ziri and Lucien from the corner of the library. The old vampire patted Lucien's gaunt cheek as he rose. He walked over to Beatrice.

"I will be visiting your mate later this evening with Emil Conti. It has all been arranged. I will be able to send my voice to him without anyone else hearing. Did you have a message?"

I love you. I miss you. Don't die. You cannot leave me alone in this world. I will kill anything that harms you. I will raze a thousand castles to get you back.

"Tell him," she said, "I will see him soon."

Ziri smiled as if he could read her thoughts, but only nodded and walked out of the library.

"He admires you."

She turned toward Lucien's voice. "Oh?"

"He admires your resolve and control. It is unusual in one so young."

Beatrice closed the journal. She hadn't really read anything anyway. "What is he to you? Ziri? You call him 'Uncle.'"

"He's not an uncle, not in the human sense. But he is one of my mother's dearest friends."

"Your mother is the earth vampire who worked with Geber, isn't she?"

Lucien smiled and rose. He walked toward Beatrice and settled into the chair across from her. They were sitting in the corner of the library closest to the fire. As always, Beatrice found the sound, scent, and presence of the flames soothing.

"She is. There is more to the story, but Ziri says he will fill us all in when Giovanni is back. He doesn't like telling stories twice."

"Okay. I suppose. Since I don't seem to have any choice in the matter, I'll be patient. How are you feeling?"

"As well as I have been." He raised an eyebrow. "Ziri keeps telling me that he will explain more soon, but he is being irritatingly close-mouthed about it. He has always been like that. Maybe that is why he and my mother get along so well. They can sit in a cave and not speak for fifty years and be totally content." He closed his eyes and sighed. "I am not sure... well, I am not sure." He looked up and shrugged. "I suppose that sums up my life, lately. I am not sure of much."

Her own curiosity burned, but Beatrice forced herself to remain calm and strove for the patience she knew her husband would expect. "Who's your mother? Will you tell me about her?"

He smiled fondly. "Her name is Saba. And I may complain about her, but she is wonderful. She is a phenomenal healer and is very wise. She lives in the highlands of Ethiopia."

"You're pretty old. She must be ancient."

He smiled. "She is the oldest of our kind I have known."

"Truly?"

"Truly. I have never met her equal in power."

"How old is she?"

He shrugged. "I doubt even she knows. She says that she simply was. She no longer remembers being human."

It was impossible to fathom. "Does she have a big family?"

"She did at one time, but she stopped siring children many years ago. I am one of the youngest of her direct clan, and one of the last still living. But most vampires, if they looked back far enough, would hold some relation to her."

"Interesting." Beatrice contemplated the idea. Some of the oldest traces of human life had been found in Africa. Why would vampire life be any different? Then another thought struck, and she smiled. "She's kind of like Eve."

Lucien nodded and smiled. "The comparison is probably quite apt. In a way, I suppose she is our own Eve. A common mother from the times when elemental affinities were far more fluid."

"What do you mean? I thought we always inherited the element of our sire, unless you become a fire vampire."

"Now this is true. It is very uncommon for a vampire to sire out of their own element. It occasionally happens, but it's quite rare. But many years ago, it wasn't as uncommon, especially if the sire was mated to one of a different element and they shared blood. Saba's mate, when she made me, was a wind vampire. His blood is probably the reason I am not nearly as established as most earth immortals. I like to travel and do so frequently."

"Until recently."

"Yes," Lucien said. "Until recently."

"I'm not going to lie, Lucien, I'm having a hard time being patient with all this. I need to know what all of this means. If this elixir is so dangerous, why did they keep it a secret? Why didn't they destroy the book to begin with?"

"Well..." He leaned back and closed his eyes. "We have many strengths, our kind, but the longer we live, the more weaknesses become evident, too. We're not very good at sharing. Part of this is a survival mechanism, of course, but part of it is simply habit. We get so accustomed to hiding from the human world, we tend to hide things from each other, as well. And we're quite greedy for information. Art, ideas, philosophy... these are the things that make immortal life interesting for those that live for centuries, because they are the only things that change. Humanity"—he grinned—"really does not change that much, you will learn. But stories, the ebb and flow of ideas, creativity, all of these things are always changing. It's why we tend to congregate in certain places when there is an explosion of art or science. Anything new, really."

"Like Italy? During the Renaissance when Gio was born."

Lucien leaned forward, his eyes lit. "Exactly. Giovanni probably had no idea at the time, but Renaissance Florence was teeming with vampires. Ziri was there. Even I was there for a time, though I'm not very fond of cities."

"That's interesting. Any other times?"

He folded his hands and relaxed, a wistful smile crossing his face. "Hmm, Greece, for a time. Baghdad, before the libraries burned, of course. Egypt, on and off for centuries. India in the fifth century. I am quite fond of Russia, but not many are."

"Rome?"

"Yes and no. Some, like Andros, were attracted to Rome during the Republic and later, of course, but it was not my favorite time. It was wonderful during the Renaissance. Japan in the sixteenth century. The American colonies during the Revolution."

"What about the times of conflict? Wars? Do vampires like wars?"

He shook his head. "Not usually. We're very self-interested, and wars are not interesting. Plus, we've all seen so many of them that they become repetitive, I suppose."

She shook her head. "Lucien, you're one interesting guy."

He shrugged. "I am, and I am not. I like talking about the past more than most immortals. I don't mind reminiscing. Most older vampires won't."

"I've noticed that. Both Carwyn and Tenzin don't talk about the past. They hardly even mention it."

"It's survival. You'll probably become the same way, after a time. Dwelling in the past can be very depressing. You should always be looking ahead." He smiled. "Look forward. Where is the next great idea or invention? That is what makes immortal life interesting."

"And family. Friends."

He nodded. "Yes, those are the most important. It has always been so. And it will remain. Another constant."

"Constant... right." She bit her lip and tried not to let the overwhelming loneliness envelop her.

"You are thinking about your mate."

"Of course."

"He is your constant. As, I'm sure, you are for him."

"I hope so."

Lucien grinned. "He was always so formal and distant, your Giovanni. I never knew him very well, but he was always so..."

"What?"

He grimaced. "Polite."

Beatrice burst out laughing. "Yes, he is."

Lucien laughed along and shook his head. "But irritatingly so. It was like he was saying, 'Nice to meet you' and 'You're beneath my notice' all at the same time."

"You can't accuse him of being a humble man, no."

"That's good." Lucien nodded. "Good. That means that he'll be fine. Even if she tortures him, he'll be fine. He is above her."

Beatrice fell silent. "Yes, I suppose so."

"I have no doubt he's dealt with worse."

Thinking of some of the more horrible stories she'd managed to pry out of him, and some of the other things that Beatrice had inferred, she had to agree. "Yes, he has."

Lucien only nodded. "He'll be fine."

Beatrice smiled when she heard Carwyn barrel into the house. He walked into the kitchen to bark at Ben about doing his homework, charm a plate of food from Angela, and then she heard him stomp up the stairs.

"Ah! There's my favorite girl. Oh, and, Beatrice, you're here, too."

Lucien chuckled and flipped up a surprisingly modern hand gesture at the noisy vampire. Carwyn put a plate of food on the library table and started eating. "So, what did I miss while I was meeting with the bathrobes?"

"How did the meeting go?"

"Fine. *Great*, actually." He grinned and took a drink from the bottle of beer he'd brought.

"Yeah?"

"Yes. I'm feeling like a new vampire. Fangs are sharper. Growl is scarier. And still, just as good-looking. Watch out, Livia."

Beatrice and Lucien exchanged amused looks.

"What's gotten into you, Father?"

For some reason, that question made Carwyn burst into laughter. Finally, he calmed down and said, "Enough about me. What kind of mischief can we make? I feel like causing some trouble."

"Well, Ziri and Emil went to the castle to make sure that Giovanni is healthy and being kept safe. Beatrice and I were reminiscing about history and talking about how polite her husband is. And then you interrupted us."

Carwyn darted over to them both and smacked the backs of their heads.

"Hey!"

"What kind of evening fun is that? You two are boring."

She stuck out a foot and tripped him before he could make it back to the table. "Well, some of us are trying to be patient and not kill anything."

"Oh ho!" Carwyn grinned from the ground. "I know what you need, B."

"What?"

He just kept grinning.

She rolled her eyes. "Other than that."

Lucien and Carwyn both laughed. Beatrice started for the door, only to feel Carwyn tackle her from behind. He picked her up and ran down the stairs.

"What are you doing? Put me down!"

"Nope. Your husband isn't around for you to shag. You're being a good girl and not killing things. So…" He opened a door she hadn't been through before and tossed her down the stairs. She bounced and tumbled until she came to a small landing.

Beatrice scowled and looked around before gasping in pleasure. "Oh!"

It was a stone basement. Damp and gloomy. Stacked with odds and ends, it looked like the catch-all room for a very large, very old house. But along with old furniture, boxes, and chairs were a rather startling number of weapons mounted on one wall and a large mat that looked like it was used for training.

"You"—Carwyn marched down the stairs and went over to the mat—"need to beat something up. So let's go. We haven't fought in months and your husband isn't around to kill me if I punch you, so have at it, my dear."

Beatrice could have cried; she was so happy. "You're the most awesome friend in the world, Carwyn!"

"I know. Stop gushing like a little girl and hit me already."

She pounced.

Despite his larger size, Beatrice was much faster, so they were evenly matched as they fought. They kept it to hands, fists, and elbows, for the most part, and they laughed and joked as they both tried to beat each other within an inch of their immortal lives. It was exactly what she needed.

Three hours later, she was still not tired, but the soul-crushing tension had been partly relieved. They finally stopped, neither one really winning, and Carwyn leaned against the wall while Beatrice slumped against his shoulder.

"Thanks."

"No problem. Happy to help."

"I miss him so damn much."

"You're just like him, you know."

"How do you mean?"

He patted her head. "Remember when Lorenzo took you the first time? Gio had to dance this dance for almost a month while you were gone. Remember that?"

"Oh, yeah. I'd almost forgotten. That seems like so long ago."

"I think we came down here every day while we were in Rome, and he did the exact same thing. We'd beat each other up just so he didn't go mad. It was the only thing I could do for him."

She blinked back tears. "You're a damn good friend, you know that?"

"I do." He put an arm around her and pulled her close. She wrapped her arm around his waist and let him hold her up for a little while. "He never gave me a cuddle afterward, though, so you've definitely got him beat in the 'thank you' department."

She pinched his waist. "You need to find yourself a woman, Carwyn. If you don't, I'll be too tempted to run away with you."

"I've been telling you for years what a catch I am."

They laughed quietly, and Beatrice found that, for a few minutes, she could rest. They sat silent until she was distracted by a faint noise. A low rumble seemed to be coming from behind another door in the basement, and she sat up straight.

"What was that?"

"Hmm?" Carwyn sat up and looked around. "Oh, the noise. What day is it again?"

"It's—what? What day is it? It's Friday. Why?"

"Ah! They're a bit early. Excellent."

She scowled at him. "Who?"

Just then, she heard familiar voices behind the door. They were raised in irritation and she heard a scuffling sound before the door cracked open. Beatrice couldn't contain her grin.

Gavin Wallace stumbled through the door. "I don't care how you try to pretty it up, woman. It's a strange and unnatural way to travel. The fact that we had to go underground is bad enough, but then water? Do you have any idea how—"

"Shut up, you whining Scot. Do you think I enjoyed having you carry me across the Channel? It's not like you're very practiced at the whole flying bit anyway. I'm surprised you didn't drop me in the sea."

Gavin and Deirdre continued to bicker at each other as Jean Desmarais swept into the room. Beatrice rose and rushed toward them. "What are you doing here? Why—"

"My Beatrice," Jean grabbed her hand and kissed her cheek. "The reports do not do you justice. You are stunning, *ma cherie*."

Deirdre grabbed her shoulders and embraced her. "We're here to help, B. You're looking well. How are you holding up?"

"I'm..." *Stunned. Happy. Relieved.* A smile broke across her face, and she turned to a very sour-looking Gavin.

"I can't believe the red-headed demon pulled me into this. I'm *not* glad to be here. I'm positive this is going to end badly for me, and I've never liked Gio all that much to begin with. He's an arrogant bastard, who has horrible taste in whiskey." A reluctant smile quirked his lips. "He does, however, have rather fantastic taste in women. You're looking well, Beatrice."

"It's good to see you, too, Gav."

Gavin sighed and crossed his arms. "Fine. Now that we're here, what kind of trouble are we in for?"

Carwyn stepped forward and slapped his hands together. "The best kind, of course. And the kind that needs your area of expertise."

Gavin cocked an eyebrow. "Breaking and entering, then. Excellent."

CHAPTER 15

When he woke, Beatrice was sitting on the edge of the bed, playing with the ends of his hair, as she knew he loved. Giovanni blinked once.

"I'm dreaming."

"Yes."

He reached a hand up and let it ghost down her arm. "This is much better than most of the dreams I've been having lately."

She smiled. "I'm sure it is."

He lay quiet, reveling in the vision of her beside him. He was afraid to move. Afraid that the dream would shatter, and he'd be back in the cold cell alone. She had no such worries and angled herself toward him, leaning over his chest to look into his face.

"Why do you let him haunt you?"

"Andros does not haunt me."

"Not Andros."

"Lorenzo does not haunt me."

"Not Lorenzo."

He frowned and chanced a single finger to trail along her cheek. "Who then?"

"You. You let the memory of who you were haunt you."

He paused. "I did many things wrong."

"You look back at the actions of a child and expect the wisdom of five hundred years."

"It is far easier to forgive others than to forgive yourself."

She sighed and laid her head on his chest. "I forgive you."

A FALL OF WATER

"I am dreaming?"

"Yes."

He fell silent, the protest dying on his lips as he enjoyed the weight of her body pressing against his unbeating heart.

"I love you, Beatrice."

"I know."

"Loving you has been the finest thing I have done in five hundred years."

"You have done many good things."

"I do not tell you enough."

She looked up and smiled. "You tell me every night."

"It is not enough." He rose and twisted her in his arms, flipping her so that she lay under him. Desperation colored his words. "It is *never* enough."

"It is enough."

"No." His lips touched the swell of her cheek. They whispered down to her jaw and explored the delicate line that led to the tip of her chin. "Never enough. It should be the unceasing prayer on my lips. The echo in every breath I take."

"It is enough."

He drew back and looked into her dark eyes. "I would level empires to be with you again. It is never enough."

"Mine is not the only love you have."

"It is the only one that matters."

"You know that is untrue."

He ignored her quiet voice and kissed her again. His mouth met hers in growing hunger, his lips and teeth and tongue fighting to hold on to the vision of her. He could feel himself waking.

"I love you, Beatrice. *I love you.* I thank God for bringing you into my life."

She grinned then, the mischievous smile Giovanni had fallen in love with when she was a lonely girl in a library, and he was frozen in time. "You don't believe in God. Not really."

He narrowed his eyes. "I do."

"You don't."

He scanned her face. Her luminous skin. Her dark eyes and hair. The slight bump on the bridge of her nose. The tiny scars and imperfections that marked her as the only woman in the world. The only woman. For him.

"I believed in God when He brought you to me."

"You don't believe in coincidence."

He could see her fading. The fall of water in the room grew louder, and she began to melt away. Her eyes drifted around the room, but she was the only thing he saw. "Don't leave," he whispered. "Don't leave me."

Her eyes were filled with tears and her hand lifted to his face, holding his cheek in her soothing hand.

"*Ubi amo; ibi patria.* Come home to me, Jacopo."

"Don't leave me." He blinked to suppress the tears that came to his own eyes. "Please."

When he opened them, she was gone, and Giovanni lay silent in his cold cell, the sound of rushing water surrounding him.

He might have lain still for hours; he did not know. He waited to hear the unseen lock turn in the stone door, signaling Livia's entrance. No sound came, only the falling water that dripped down the walls. His fingers played along the edge of the dagger she had left. It had been over a week and yet his keen senses had detected no weakness in the room. It was round, and the water was fed through some channel that coated the walls with a constant stream and filled the air with a swirling dampness. There was a slight opening where the water flowed, but it was far past his reach. Though he could jump, he could not suspend himself long enough to take advantage of the weakness and because it was round, it contained no corner that he might brace himself.

Giovanni could hear the rushing of some underground stream that flowed beneath the room. The chamber was probably set on a pile foundation of some kind, as had been used to build Venice. Between the river below him, and the water flowing around, it was as if he was floating in a stone bubble. If he was an earth or water vampire, an enviable prison. For a fire vampire... a very effective one. His father always had done quality work.

He stared at the ceiling, trying to determine what lay beyond it. It was impossible to sense past the stone. He was concentrating so intently, he almost missed the scratching sound coming from the floor. Suddenly, he felt the floor buckle beneath him and a shock of red hair pushed through. He sat up, and his heart raced when he saw his visitor.

Muddy. Disheveled. The cloud of red hair fell into her face, but she pushed it back, and Giovanni grinned when he saw the wicked gleam in Deirdre's eyes. She put a finger to her lips and reached down, pulling a very annoyed looking Gavin up behind her. The wind vampire looked about as happy as a drenched cat.

"This is the most humiliating, most—"

Deirdre slapped a hand over his mouth and pulled Gavin away from the hole that was starting to crumble along the edges. Giovanni saw another hand reach up and Jean Desmarais lifted himself gracefully out of the river. Unfortunately, as soon as Jean entered the room, the force he had been using to push the water back faltered and the room began filling with water. Rapidly.

"Oh, for fuck's sake! Can this get any worse? I thought I was going to be able to dry off for a bit."

Deirdre curled her lip. "Thank you so much for alerting the entire castle to our presence, Gavin."

Giovanni could already hear shouts coming from past the door. "Whatever stealth you had was lost when the water started leaking under the door, so whine away as long as you have some plan to get us out."

"Well, in that case—"

"Yes, feel free to continue," Jean said as he looked around the room. "Especially if you're keen for Livia to know exactly who is breaking out her favorite prisoner."

That thought seemed to shut Gavin up, and he also began to look around.

Deirdre said, "It's exactly as he described. Gavin, I know you're wet, but you're going to have to fly me up there. Can you do it?"

Gavin scoffed and lifted Deirdre in his arms. The two vampires flew to the top of the chamber as Giovanni turned to Jean. "Why can't we go out the way you came?"

Jean shook his head. "Very strong current and a nasty drop off somewhere just past this chamber. I have no idea where it leads. I could drag one person, but not three and none of you are strong enough to swim back upstream without my help. No, our contact said there is a large, empty chamber above this. He felt it."

"Who—ah, I see." Giovanni nodded. Ziri must have been able to get a feel for the surrounding space when he visited the chamber to see him. "And so Deirdre will break through the ceiling..." His eyes looked up to see Deirdre pushing against the stone, tossing pieces away and digging her hands into the solid chamber walls.

"If she and Gavin don't kill each other. They've been bickering ever since they showed up in Le Havre."

Deirdre had dug about a foot and a half into the rock when she motioned for Gavin to fly her down. The water was almost up to their knees.

"It's very thick. I think I have another foot and a half to go. It's dry set and mostly solid. Very few joints and very tight. There's no soil here, so it makes it more difficult." She was paler than normal, and Giovanni could tell tunneling into the river, then through the floor of the prison had tired her. She needed blood, but no humans were available.

Giovanni nodded and tried to push back the impatience that wanted to grab hold of him. "Deirdre, do you need—"

"Here." Gavin stuck out his wrist, baring it to her face. Giovanni could see her fangs descend, and Deirdre almost skittered back. He knew without asking that she had not drunk from another immortal since her husband had died. Giovanni frowned at Gavin. For him to even offer...

"Here, woman." The gruff Scot huffed and pushed his wrist closer to her face. "Don't be stubborn, unless you want to die. I don't, and neither do I plan on failing a job this simple."

Deirdre hesitated another moment before she grabbed his wrist and dug in. Giovanni glanced at Jean, who was watching with interest, one eyebrow cocked at the pair. Gavin's face was carefully impassive, but Giovanni saw him swallow once. After a few deep draws, Deirdre pulled back and Giovanni could feel her amnis flex in the air around them. She grabbed onto Gavin's shoulders and the two wordlessly flew up to the top of the room again.

After a few more moments and a few more pieces of stone, the marble came crashing down, and Giovanni could scent the stale air as it rushed into the room. He and Jean were floating in the water. Someone was trying to push the door open, but they had tossed the loose stones against it. Between that and the press of water against the door, they were secure.

Finally, Gavin pushed Deirdre up through the passage she had made. Then, he flew down and pulled on Giovanni's arm first and flew him to the top of the cell. He crawled through and lifted himself into an empty chamber that was even higher than the first.

"How deep was that room?" He looked at Deirdre as she walked around the second stone-lined room.

Deirdre said, "I'd estimate twelve meters? It was about three stories down. And it looks like I'm going to have to break through another—"

"No." Giovanni's eyes had spotted something up in the corner of the vaulted ceiling. He heard Jean and Gavin climb through the floor, but his eyes were glued to a tiny ledge and small door he had spotted. "My sire built this room, and Andros didn't believe in one way out. There would always be an escape hatch. Always another way out. Look." He pointed up and turned to Gavin. "Nice flying, by the way. When did that happen?"

Gavin only gave a roguish grin and a wink. "Handy, no?"

"Very. Can you fly up to that corner? I believe there is a door up there."

Gavin nodded and flew up quickly before he dropped back down. "Well, yes, there's a door, but it's rather thick—maybe a foot or more of solid oak. Can you burn through?"

He frowned. "It's locked?"

"Yes. Odd kind of thing. Not one I've seen before. Almost looks like a sundial with a—"

"Starburst along the outer edges and a kind of rippling channel that runs around it?"

"Not unfamiliar, then?"

Giovanni shook his head. Trust his father to use his most difficult lock to secure the door. He pulled the dagger from the small of his back. "Andros loved designing locks I would have difficulty breaking. He tried for years to find some design I could not master."

Deirdre asked, "And did he?"

Giovanni walked over to stand by Gavin and flicked the end of his blade. "No."

Jean's low chuckle echoed in the empty room. Giovanni held a hand out. "Gavin, if you please?"

"Well, you're not as pretty as the last one that asked for a ride, but I suppose you'll do." Giovanni heard Deirdre snort. The wind vampire flew up to the corner of the room and held him, hovering while Giovanni carefully picked the lock. It occurred to him that while Livia had never trusted Giovanni, Andros had never trusted her. Why else would he create a way for him—only him—to escape? No other being he knew of could pick the lock in front of him. He couldn't have escaped without help, but perhaps Andros had more faith in him than he'd thought.

After a few tense moments, he pulled the starburst from the thin channel and pushed the door open, revealing a dark, earthen passageway. Gavin, who must have been tiring, tossed him through. Then he flew back. Giovanni waited only a few moments before Jean entered the tunnel behind him. They both waited longer—much longer—before Gavin and Deirdre entered. Gavin, Giovanni noted with some amusement, looked decidedly more energetic.

"I can smell fresh air," Gavin said. "Deirdre, can you tell where it leads?"

She held her hands out and ran both along the walls as she walked forward. "Southwest. It's long and sloping. If it keeps at this angle it would exit... past the castle wall, I imagine."

Jean said, "Let's keep to the plan. The party must still be going on, which means that Carwyn, Tenzin, and Beatrice are still upstairs."

His heart leapt. "Beatrice?"

Gavin held a hand out. "You'll see your woman soon, but not here. Livia has to find you missing and discover that none of them—"

"Fuck Livia," he almost shouted. "I want to see my wife."

Deirdre stepped in front of him and put a hand on his chest. "Calm down, Gio. She's the one that came up with this plan."

"Hey!" Gavin looked rather offended, but Deirdre only rolled her eyes.

"With input from our resident thief, of course."

"Retired," Gavin said. "Mostly."

Giovanni could still feel his skin heating in anticipation. The smell of smoke was sweet in his nose, and he imagined Livia's skin turning black as she screamed. The steam began to rise from his wet arms.

"Gio, listen." Deirdre spoke more urgently, sensing his growing tension. "Jean and I will tunnel back down to the river and escape that way. Gavin is going to fly you to his house... somewhere. No one knows but he and Beatrice. Your wife has spent days planning this with my father and Tenzin to orchestrate some particular outcome, so don't spoil this plan by losing your head."

Giovanni took a deep breath and tried to shove back the fire that wanted to burst out. He smothered the desire for Livia's blood for the moment. She would still burn, he vowed, but he would respect his wife's wisdom in this and wait to hear her plan. "Fine. Gavin, take me out of this damned place."

"Don't order me around. You already owe me one. More than that if we're—"

"Be quiet. This is not the time to argue," Deirdre cut in. She gave Giovanni a quick hug before she turned to Gavin and halted. The two stood in awkward silence until she said, "Don't drop him." Then she turned to the wall of the tunnel, lifted her hands, and the earth moved in front of her. Jean gave Gavin and Giovanni a smile and a small salute before following.

"Well..." Gavin cleared his throat. "Let's get going. I'm starting to hear voices below."

Giovanni could hear both voices and water as the large, empty room they had flown through began to fill from the chamber and the river below. The two men rushed up the passageway; the walls and floors were smooth, even if the air was stale and ancient. When the smell of fresh air became more evident, they slowed and listened. Gavin shook his head and whispered, "I hear nothing."

"Agreed." Giovanni pushed through a loose pile of rocks that blocked the passage and peeked out. They were on the side of a hill, and he could see the lights of the castle in the distance. They had wound south and then west to a slope that overlooked Livia's stronghold. He swallowed, imagining his wife sitting in the glittering salons of Livia's court. So close, yet still past his reach. He swallowed the growl and turned back to Gavin. "Get me out of here. If I can't see her, take me to where I can."

"Orders, orders. Why must he always issue orders?" Gavin shook his head. "I'm not one of your minions, you know. And I'll be more than happy to be done with my part in all this."

"Fine. Then get me out of here."

Gavin picked him up under the shoulders and lifted into the air. "You try to do a favor for someone—"

"How much are you getting paid, Gav?"

He could feel, rather than hear, Gavin laugh as they cut through the air, heading north. "A rather princely sum, of course."

"Carwyn or my wife?"

"Your wife drives a hard bargain, Dr. Vecchio. And she's cute. It's deceiving really, hardly fair."

Giovanni felt the smile curve his lips. His wife. He would see her soon. Within hours, hopefully. As if anticipating the question, Gavin said, "I'll drop you off and then go back for her. I should be able to get her to you by dawn."

"Good."

"And yes, you will be somewhere very secluded."

"Good."

"Do me a favor, though, and try not to break any *retaining* walls, please."

He smirked. "I'll try my best, but I can't make any promises."

A FALL OF WATER

"You know what? You're just going to buy this house from me. It's sure to sustain damage, and I'll never get the mental pictures out of my mind."

"Done."

"It's not her, mind you. Picturing *her*—"

"It's very important that you shut up now, Gavin."

They were whipping over the Italian countryside, flying well out of range of human eyes. The air was cold, but the anticipation of seeing Beatrice warmed him to his soul. They flew over the rolling hills of Tuscany, past the lights that illuminated Milan, finally climbing the foothills, then the mountains of Northern Italy and into the Alps. They passed high above the water, and the lights from the homes along the lake's edge glowed in the darkness. The long, uninterrupted line slowly scattered as they approached a large inlet where a single home was nestled between the hills and the water.

"Home, sweet home." He heard Gavin sigh.

"You don't actually have to sell me the house, if you don't want to."

"No, it's for the best. I've been here too long, as it is."

Giovanni thought for a moment, then smiled. "You mean you've slept with all the attractive women nearby?"

"Exactly. I've ruined them for all others, so it's perfect for an old married man like you."

"Thank you so much."

Gavin dropped him off on the sloping dock that stretched into the water and flew into the house. He emerged a few minutes later with a bag of blood for himself and tossed another to Giovanni. He bit, ignoring the stale taste of the refrigerated blood and enjoying the peace of mind that came with not worrying about whether his meal was poisoned or not.

His reluctant host tossed him the empty bag and then took to the air without further ado as Giovanni paced the dock and tried to imagine how he would pass the hours until he saw Beatrice again. Deciding that he needed to cool down and wash the stink of Livia's prison from him, he stripped off his tattered clothes and dove into the lake.

Giovanni swam for what might have been hours, up and down the lake. He went in the house and drank another bag of blood. He swam to the bottom of the lake and watched the moon track across the sky. The minutes dragged into hours while he waited for her.

He was floating on the surface of the water and staring up at the stars when he heard the splash. Startled, he sat up, only to be tackled from behind by two familiar arms.

"You're here!" she cried, wrapping herself around him. "You're really here."

"Tesoro." He groaned a moment before their mouths met in a furious kiss.

Her legs tangled with his. The force of her embrace took his breath away. He held her close, aching to feel her amnis spread over his skin. Giovanni tore his mouth from her kiss and stripped the clothes from her body until they were pressed together and their energy combined again. His hands raced over her and held her in an iron grasp.

Beatrice's hand tugged at his arms, his back, pulling him close. Closer. Not close enough. In the blink of an eye, he grasped her hips and slid into her. She bit into his shoulder as they sank beneath the surface of the water.

And suddenly, he was home.

CHAPTER 16

Lake Maggiore, Switzerland

Water. Blood. Warm blood running down her throat. The grasp of hands. His hands. Her mate's hands. Her mate's blood.

He was back.

Beatrice felt his feet hit the lakebed a moment before Giovanni's long legs began striding toward the shore. She remained wrapped around his body, clutching him tightly. He held her as they rose from the water only to kneel in the long grass at the lake's edge. Steam rose from his body as he began moving in her again. Her hands dug into the earth around them and she arched her back, desperate for his touch.

Her first climax hit like a sudden wave, and she cried into the night. Her mate said nothing, only growling as his arm reached behind her, lifting her body as her head fell back. His fangs struck hard and deep in her throat, and he drank from her. The sharp bite threw her over another crest, but he did not halt feasting from her neck as she sobbed in relief and pulled him even closer. Her nails dug into his shoulders until he reared back, blood dripping from his lips and fangs gleaming white in the moonlight.

Blue fire swirled across his body, illuminating his arms and chest. His hands gripped Beatrice's hips and she lifted her body to move with him. Fast. Faster. Every layer of civilization burned away in their desperate need. She could feel the water drawn to her skin, protecting it from the scorch of Giovanni's hands, but nothing could protect her from the passionate assault of her mate's body.

She didn't want it to. His eyes held hers as he moved, pinning her to the ground as effectively as his touch.

He finally pulled her up and pressed her against his chest. His hands tangled in her dripping hair and she felt him pull at the nape of her neck, angling her face up to his. Her skin hissed and a cloud of steam enveloped them. His hands and hips set a punishing rhythm, but his mouth was tender as it explored her face. He kissed her forehead, the swell of her cheeks, the arch of her brows. She felt his lips burn across the line of her jaw before his mouth dipped down and his fangs pierced the other side of her neck. She came again, and he clutched her closer as he drank. A low growl grew in his chest until he threw his head back and roared his release into the night.

Beatrice collapsed in his arms as the fire covering his skin waned, and the cloud of steam drifted away on the night breeze. His movement slowed. The iron cage of his arms softened, and his hands began to stroke down her back as Giovanni murmured in a hoarse voice. She sobbed in pleasure and relief, but he only pressed her closer.

"*Ubi amo; ibi patria. Calma, Tesoro. Ti amo, Beatrice. Calma.*"

She blinked away the tears and buried her face in his neck, inhaling the rich smoke of his skin. She could feel her blood leaping within him, and his amnis pulsed and swirled around her. Beatrice felt Giovanni tilt his neck to the side and press her mouth closer.

"Drink from me, Beatrice. Please, drink."

Beatrice gave a small cry before she bit into the thick vein at his neck. His blood burned down her throat, inflaming her desire again. She reached down and felt him grow hard in her hand as the muscles of his chest tensed.

She pulled away from his vein with a contented sigh, licking his rich blood from her lips and letting her fangs scrape over his chest.

"More," she whispered.

He laid her down in the long grass and stretched out next to her. This time, they were slow. Languorous and lazy with soft hands and long strokes. She pressed her mouth to his and inhaled his breath when he entered her. Tears ran down her cheeks, but he kissed them away. They moved together as the night birds sang to warn of the dawn.

Hours later, Beatrice still felt like she could not stop touching him. They had finally taken shelter in the house when the morning chased away the stars. The bedroom lay at the very center of the home, surrounded by winding hallways that shielded it from the sun. They had laughed and joked as they wandered through the labyrinth of a house, turning first into the kitchen, then an office, a sitting room, and a library before they finally discovered a room with a bed.

"I hope you like this house, Beatrice, because I believe we're buying it from Gavin. He said something about mental pictures."

"Well, seeing as we... *enjoyed* his kitchen—"

"And his library."

"I think you punched a hole in one of the walls in the hall."

"You tore up some of the carpet in the study."

"Then I can't blame him." She laughed. "And I like it. It's like a maze. Only, instead of a minotaur at the middle, you finally get to the bedroom."

"And a comfortable bed is far better than being gored to death."

She snorted. "Is that supposed to be a joke about your sexual performance?"

He barked out a laugh, but then grew very quiet. He pulled down the sheets to inspect her. "I wasn't too rough was I? Did I hurt you?"

"Don't be silly." She stroked along his shoulders, running her fingers through his hair. "I needed that as much as you did. I was a mess without you."

He buried his face in her neck and took a deep breath. His skin was still warm, but comfortingly so. And his amnis wrapped around her tightly, curling and twisting as it met hers, binding them together as surely as their bodies were linked.

"I dreamt about you."

"In prison?"

"Yes." He paused and his fingers encircled her wrist. "I think it was the only thing that kept me sane."

"Did she hurt you?"

He was silent, and the fury ran hot within her. Beatrice gritted her teeth and hissed. "She will die."

"When we get back to Rome—" He broke off when he felt her tense up. "What is it?"

"I don't want to talk about Livia. You should get some sleep. There will be plenty of time to talk about this stuff later. Right now, I just want to lie with you and try to rest."

He pulled her chin around and forced her to look into his eyes. He was frowning, and Beatrice knew that he was not satisfied with her answer.

"Fine, but you're explaining that later."

"Okay."

He tucked her under his arm and pulled the sheets up to cover her.

"Do you want me to sing to you?" he asked softly.

"Just sleep. Having you here is enough."

"Try to rest, Tesoro."

She smiled and buried her face in his chest. She felt him drift away into a bone-deep, contented sleep. Beatrice watched him for hours, wiping at the tears that fell down her face and drinking in the sight of him, determined to make it last.

. . .

"Why does chamois blood taste so much better than other goats? It's not sour at all."

Giovanni shrugged and continued field-dressing the dark-skinned animal they had hunted the following night.

"The meat is very good. I know the right way to cook it. You will like it."

Though Gavin had the house stocked with blood and there were many towns nearby, Giovanni had wanted the exertion of the hunt, so they had slipped away from the balmy edge of the lake to run miles north into the mountains. Giovanni enjoyed the fresh, dry air of the Southern Alps and Beatrice enjoyed Giovanni. All she had to do was catch a glimpse of him from the corner of her eye, and she smiled.

He wore some of the clothes Gavin had at the house, small on him, but still better than the rags he'd worn away from the castle. One look at the shredded tunic he'd thrown on the dock, and her rage against Livia had bloomed again.

"Come." He held out his hand after washing his hands in a small stream. He made a small satchel from the shirt he had worn and carried the best cuts of meat down the mountain for them to share. She grinned at her shirtless husband carrying the game they had just killed. There was still a drop of blood at the corner of his mouth.

"You know, I feel very frontier woman right now."

He laughed. "This is how people got food for most of history. It is good to know these things."

Beatrice wrinkled her nose. "Well, when the coming zombie apocalypse hits and there aren't any more grocery stores, I'll just let you take care of the hunting and the gathering, all right?"

Giovanni laughed again and sped down the game trail they had followed. It was a clear night and the moon was full. She could see the distant lights of the town as they came down out of the hills, enjoying the stretch of her legs as she ran. As they approached the small road that led back to the house, Giovanni slowed to a human pace, so as not to attract attention. "Beatrice?"

"Mmhmm?"

"Why did you tense up when I talked about going back to Rome? Do you think she will be able to capture me again? Are you afraid?"

"No! No, I don't—"

"She surprised me last time." He halted on the path and narrowed his gaze. "I was not on my guard. You should not fear that I will be taken again. I do not make the same mistake twice."

Her eyes widened. "I'm not afraid that she'll take you again."

"No?" He frowned and started walking, muttering under his breath. "You have lost confidence in me. You fear—"

"Gio, you can't go back to Rome." She halted in the middle of the trail. "I mean... at least, not yet."

A FALL OF WATER

His nostrils flared in anger. "I am going back to Rome."

"No, you don't understand—"

"I understand that you no longer think I am strong enough to protect those under my aegis."

Her jaw dropped. "What? That's not—"

"But I will. Do you know what I have planned for that Roman bitch? Would you like to hear it?"

"Stop, Gio. That's not what I'm talking about! I know you're strong enough."

"Obviously you don't, if you think I'm going to hide from her."

She clutched at her hair, frustrated and angry that the argument had devolved into her husband thinking she lacked confidence in him. "Giovanni, it's not that we can't go back."

He picked up the bundle of meat he'd dropped and stalked down the trail ahead of her. "Damn right, it's not. I may live quietly now, but there's a reason—"

"*You* can't go back."

He halted again, slowly turning until he faced her. "What did you say?"

Her heart thundered, and she felt tears run down her cheeks. "I said, *you* can't go back. I have to, but you can't. Not yet."

His eyes flared, and he stepped toward her. "This is... what? Some plan you've come up with?"

She swallowed and nodded tentatively. "Yes. Me and Ziri."

"Ziri?"

"And Carwyn. And Tenzin, too."

"And this plan involves you going back to Rome and me... what? Staying here safely tucked away?"

"No." She walked toward him. "We need you to find someone. Two people, actually."

He stepped back, and a blank mask fell over his face. "So, you will return to Rome and I—"

"Carwyn, too. He's going to go with you."

"But you won't."

Beatrice shook her head, and her heart fell in her chest when he took another careful step back.

"So, we would separate again?"

Her throat felt frozen, but she nodded with effort.

Giovanni's eyes were glacial. "Unacceptable." He turned and sped back to the house.

"Gio!" She called after him, but he did not turn back. She walked at a human pace, knowing that he needed time to think.

When Beatrice got back to the house, he had put some of the meat away and was cooking two thick fillets over the built-in grill in Gavin's kitchen. He must have heard her walk in, but he did not turn around. Her nose twitched at the scent of the savory meat.

"Do you know why I don't often care to eat roasted meat, my wife?"

She had always suspected, but it wasn't something they talked about. "Why?"

"Roasted meat has a distinctive aroma, doesn't it? Something about that combination of flesh and fire."

"Gio—"

"Strangely enough, the smell of human and vampire flesh is not that different. Well, not that most would notice. The essentials are the same. Flesh. Fire."

She cleared her throat and bit her lip. "I'll take your word on that."

He nodded. "Good. You *should* take my word on that. Do you know why?"

Beatrice whispered. "Because you've killed many—"

"Hundreds, Beatrice." He threw a bloody knife across the room where it lodged in a wall. "I have killed *hundreds*. Yet, apparently, my wife and my closest friends only think that I am capable of fetching someone for their little plan."

"You're the only one who can do it."

He sneered and shut off the grill, tossing the meat onto a plate. "That's bullshit, and you know it. Carwyn or Tenzin could easily deal with finding—"

"Arosh."

His eyes widened. "Wh—what did you say?"

"Arosh," she whispered. "We need you to find Arosh."

He shook his head, anger forsaken for confusion. "He is dead, Beatrice. The fire king has been dead for centuries."

"He's not."

He crossed his arms and leaned back against the counter. "I think you had better explain."

"Arosh was one of Geber's four. It was Ziri, the Numidian. Saba, the Aethiop, Arosh, the Persian, and... Kato, the Greek."

Giovanni shrank back when he heard the last name. "Kato?"

"Yes, Kato."

He rushed over and clutched her shoulders. "Kato, the ruler of Minos. King of the ancient sea. *Kato* is the Greek? You are telling me that the water vampire that Geber used... is my own father's sire?"

"Yes."

"He is not dead as I was told?"

"No. Ziri will explain it to you. There's still a lot I don't understand."

He let out a harsh breath. "And you want *me* to go find two of the most ancient and deadly vampires to ever walk the earth? Two unopposed rulers of the ancient world, thought to be dead for centuries?"

"They're not dead," she whispered. "And we're pretty sure we know where you and Carwyn need to look. Ziri will be here in two days to explain it all."

The harsh expression fell from his face. "Two days?"

A FALL OF WATER

She nodded, and he pulled her to his chest.

"Two *days*, Tesoro?"

"It's all we can afford."

"I just got you back. You cannot ask me to—"

"Tenzin and I need to be back in court in that time. Livia won't be able to prove anything, and Ziri will vouch that I spent the last few days at his estate examining some books, but any longer than that…" He wrapped his arms around her and she buried her face in his chest. "I don't want to leave you," she whispered. "I don't ever want—"

"Shh." He stroked her face and rocked her as the tears slipped down her face. "We cannot do this." He framed her face and brushed back the hair that had fallen in her face. "You must come with me. If we are going to find these immortals, then at least we should be together."

"Someone has to stay back in Rome, Gio. We think she may already have the elixir. Rumors are starting to circulate, and I—"

"But *two days?*"

His lips began a frantic race as he held her tighter. Her eyes. Her cheeks. His hands tilted her face toward him before he attacked her mouth. He inhaled her gasp and lifted her in his arms, walking them to the counter where he set her on the edge. He paused and wove his fingers into her hair as he looked at her with a haunted stare. "How can I leave you again?"

"Gio—"

"How can I leave my heart?" He ducked down and pressed a kiss to her neck. "My love?" His hands drifted over her shoulders. "My life? Beatrice, how?" He buried his face in her neck and pulled her closer so she wrapped her legs around his waist.

"I don't want this either."

Their desire was a desperate, frantic call. He lifted her and walked to the bedroom where he slowly slipped off her clothes, letting his fingers memorize the texture of her skin. His mouth followed every dip and curve, and she held back tears when he lay down next to her and let his head rest on her abdomen, wrapping his arms around her hips as he whispered her name over and over.

She pulled him up and rolled them over, so she rested on his chest. "Some day," she whispered. "We will come here when things are peaceful. And we will swim in the lake every night."

"Yes?"

She sat up and spread her hands along his chest, tracing the line of his arms until her hands met his. She nodded and knit their fingers together.

"Yes. And we will buy a boat and you will teach me how to sail it." Her fingers were enveloped by his warm hands, and she felt his thumb stroke the back of her palm.

He whispered, "How do you know I can sail a boat?"

"You can do everything."

A sad smile crossed his lips for a second. "And you will show me the strange contraption you have created to use the computer."

"And you'll finally be able to check your own e-mail."

He twisted their arms around, so that Beatrice was curled on her side facing away from him and his arms encircled her. "And I will make love to you every night in our boat." He kissed along her shoulders, and his hand drifted over her hip.

"And you will read me Giuliana's sonnets and sing me beautiful songs," she whispered. The tears slipped down her face as he lifted her thigh and slid into her. He pressed her back to his chest and kissed the side of her neck. She leaned back into his embrace and turned her face to his, kissing his lips as he made love to her.

"And you will make me laugh." He smiled against her mouth and his hands stroked her breasts, her belly, the soft skin at the juncture of her thighs. "And tease me and remind me not to be so serious. And not to burn the food."

She laughed, but it turned into a sob as pleasure collided with the heartbreak of losing him, even for a little while. "And in a hundred years, when we get sick of each other—"

"I will never tire of you," he said frantically as he approached his own release. "Never."

"We'll take separate vacations." She knit their hands together again, wrapping his arms across her breast. "And then—"

"I will find you!" He gasped as the climax rolled through him and his arms banded around her. "I will find you, Beatrice. Wherever we go—"

"We will find each other," she cried out, and he turned her so that she was sheltered in his warm embrace. Beatrice felt him press a kiss to her hair.

"We will find each other."

CHAPTER 17

Giovanni spread his arms across the back of the couch in the lake house study. Beatrice sat next to him, nestled into his side, still reluctant to stray too far from the comfort of his presence. They had spent two days wrapped in each other, both avoiding what he was now beginning to suspect was their inevitable separation. The ancient wind immortal, Ziri, took a chair opposite him and his wife, and Carwyn sat near the fire, looking grim.

"Ziri, thank you for coming. Please, explain. Particularly about my grand-sire."

Ziri folded his hands in his lap. "Your grand-sire, Kato, is alive, as far as I know. My friends and I deliberately misled the immortal community regarding his death. I don't know his condition, and we don't know how the book came into *your* sire's possession, but that is why you must find Arosh. Only someone who rivals him in power will stand a chance of getting close enough. And Arosh will have Kato with him."

"I understood that Arosh is the one who killed my father's sire. He and Kato were legendary enemies."

"Yes, of course they were. For many years they battled each other for land, resources, power... that is why they became such close friends."

Beatrice leaned forward. "You're going to have to explain this part a little more clearly to me, Ziri."

The old vampire smiled. "You must understand that this was the age of empires. The pale shadows of empires that came later, the Greeks, the Romans, the Roman church, none of them *truly* understood empire as we did. Zhang, before he changed his name to be civilized, ruled the East with his Golden

Horde of vicious immortals and their people. Arosh held Zhang back at the gates of the Western world. Saba, the most ancient of us, kept her peace in the flourishing African highlands. I ruled the deserts, and Kato... Kato ruled the waters. We were rivals. Enemies. Our power kept each other in check. There was death and conquest, but there was balance, as well."

Beatrice asked, "What changed?"

"We grew tired of empire. All of us had ruled for thousands of years, sometimes as gods, but humanity was growing stronger, more sophisticated. They were becoming more interesting to us, and the age of the immortal empire began to wane. Zhang was first. His horde dispersed and he parted company with his child—your friend, Tenzin—and retreated to form the council of the Eight Immortals in Penglai Island. Saba... well, Saba hadn't ruled in any real sense for ages. She just retreated farther into the mountains. I gladly let my people fracture as they had wanted for years. Wind immortals never really take to any kind of central government."

"And what of Kato and Arosh?" Giovanni asked.

"They held out the longest, but finally, your grand-sire traveled to his great rival and they met. I don't know what they spoke of, but I think they both must have realized what we had was passing. Human thought and development had reached the point where they had become more than ragged bands of hunters and gatherers. Civilizations were beginning to flourish. Observing them had become more interesting than ruling them."

Giovanni cocked his head. "And you expect me to believe they just gave up this great power you speak of?"

"In a way, it was a relief. To give up the burden of rule and to sink into a more leisurely life. We all had our pursuits and, as centuries passed, the four of us came to a kind of understanding. A camaraderie of those who understood what it had once been to be a god." Ziri's black eyes twinkled. "Not many understand what that once meant. Arosh and Kato became very good friends, over the years. Their legends passed into our own peculiar history, but few remembered the particulars. None of us wanted to."

"But they were supposed to be dead. My father said that Arosh was the one who had killed Kato, and in doing so, killed himself. So how is it that you say they are living?"

Carwyn broke in. "Start at the beginning of the tale, Ziri. You must go back to Kufa."

Ziri nodded. "Of course. As I was saying, humanity had become interesting. There were periods of great enlightenment, often followed by periods of ignorance and destruction, but thoughts were changing. Kufa, in the eighth century, was in the heart of the Islamic Golden Age. There was a wonderful confluence of thought and technology. Theology and philosophy. Arosh had been living there for many years. He was Persian, but had been intrigued by the new ideas.

Kato joined him. Eventually, we were all drawn there, and we spent a century watching the region flourish."

"When did you meet Geber? Was Arosh the "dear friend" he wrote of in his journals?"

Ziri smiled. "We knew him as Jabir, but yes, Arosh and the alchemist had become very good friends. They enjoyed debating science and faith. And Jabir was so bright for a human, eventually Kato joined them in their discussions and the three of them became very close. The idea of the elixir was born from their friendship."

"Who thought of it first?" Beatrice asked in a quiet voice.

"It was Jabir's idea, though we all latched onto it very quickly. He was fascinated by how we could heal, particularly if we shared blood, which the four of us did freely."

Carwyn smirked. "You must have been... very close."

Ziri shrugged. "As I said, there are few who understand each other as we did. It was, and still is, a kind of intimacy that extends beyond the understanding of most humans or even younger immortals. We gave no thought to sharing blood in order to nurture that."

"But Geber—*Jabir* noticed it?" Giovanni asked.

"He was fascinated by the science of us. By the properties of our blood and what it could mean. He was the one who wanted to stabilize it for human use."

Beatrice shook her head. "And you all agreed? Didn't you have any reservations?"

Ziri shrugged. "Not many. We all had our own reasons for wanting it. Saba thought it could be used to heal humans. She has always been a healer. Arosh thought that somehow it could be used to conquer bloodlust and grant him independence from needing humanity, even as food. Kato had taken a lover who refused to turn, though he was very attached to the young man. He hoped to make him immortal with it."

"And what of you?" Giovanni asked him. "What was your agenda, Ziri?"

"I was curious," he said.

Beatrice said, "Curious?"

The old wind vampire chuckled. "I believe that it is not a condition you are unfamiliar with, Beatrice De Novo."

Giovanni pinched her waist and smiled. "No, indeed not." He pulled her under his arm and turned his attention back to the story. "So, you all agreed to help Geber in his research. And you were successful?"

"That, I'm sure we can all agree, is debatable. Jabir *did* stabilize the blood. It took years, but the formula appeared to work. He had tried it on several servants who were diseased and it had proven to be useful for healing. As for the bloodlust, we weren't as certain. And we were all very cautious. It was your grand-sire" —Ziri nodded toward Giovanni—"who eventually tried it. His lover, a very kind and loving young man, was ill. A wasting disease, probably some kind of cancer. But it was spreading and Kato became... strangely emotional. He forced his lover to take the elixir, then drank from him. He said if the young man did not live, that he did not care to, either. It was shocking to us, to risk himself for a mortal, but it was his choice, after all."

All three vampires were riveted on the old immortal as he spoke. "And then what happened?" Beatrice said.

"We thought it was a success. The young man, Fadhil, grew strong again. Kato drank his blood and claimed to need no more. He claimed he was no longer thirsty. That he no longer felt the pull of hunger or the burn in his throat."

Carwyn asked, "So why didn't you all try it? If it appeared to be a success, why not?"

Ziri raised an eyebrow. "Kato was in love with this human. In raptures over the possibility that his lover could live forever, and he would no longer have to feed from humans. The best of all worlds. No sacrifice. No trade-off. The rest of us... we were more cautious. I wanted to give it time. Perhaps, I thought, in one hundred years, if the human was still living, perhaps then I would try it. I left shortly after the initial tests. I was bored in Kufa and needed to travel."

Giovanni said, "But how did it end? Why did you deceive the world about Kato? What happened to him?"

"I received a message from Saba a few years later. She did not say much, only that Arosh and Kato had gone away. That she was taking Geber's research for further study and that I should not try to replicate it or drink from any human that had taken the elixir. She said—and this is how I know it is very dangerous— that she had *killed* all those who had been test subjects. There were dangers. She said that Arosh had asked her to spread the word that he and Kato had killed each other, and she wanted my help in spreading the rumors."

"And you agreed?" Giovanni was angry. "Without asking for more information? Without confirming—"

"What would I confirm?" Ziri broke in. "Who would I ask? Saba only tells you what she wants you to know. Arosh? I had no idea where he was at the time. And, most importantly, I trusted my friend. If Saba said this was necessary, then it was. We had been friends, the four of us, for thousands of years. If she asked me to spread this rumor, it was for Arosh and Kato's protection."

Giovanni stood and paced. He was angry with the vague picture that Ziri had painted. Angry that he knew so much... *but still not enough*. Why did Lorenzo and Livia want this elixir? No one even truly knew what it did.

Beatrice said, "Well, if it did to Kato what it's doing to Lucien—"

"Lucien?" He spun toward her. "Lucien who?"

"The Thracian, Gio," Carwyn said gently. "Tenzin found him in Bulgaria. He's drunk from an elixired human and there's something very wrong. Whatever is happening to him seems to be weakening him dangerously."

A FALL OF WATER

Giovanni looked at Beatrice. "What has happened while I was gone?"

She looked embarrassed. "Well, I was going to fill you in, but... two days, you know?"

He couldn't argue with her. Catching up on news hadn't even crossed his mind. He heard Carwyn snort as Giovanni sat next to her and pulled her onto his lap.

Carwyn muttered, "Haven't you two done anything besides shag this entire time?"

Giovanni shot him a look. "Two days."

"Fine, but yes, since you didn't know, Lucien Thrax is staying at the Rome house, and he's not well. Tenzin is with one of the Chinese delegations. You and I are going to go off looking for two supposedly dead vampires so we have some sort of proof that Livia is trying to... whatever she's trying to do. And your wife and Ziri are going back to Rome to keep an eye on the court and find out if Livia actually has any of the elixir like the rumors are claiming."

Giovanni could think of a dozen objections to that plan immediately, but there was one question his brain couldn't file away. He turned back to Ziri. "How did my father get this book? I thought Saba had taken it, so how did it come to be in Andros's possession?"

"Your guess is as good as mine. I had met your father a few times while I was spending time with Kato. They weren't close, you know. Kato regretted turning Andros, though he never said so directly. He thought Andros was too greedy for power and knowledge. Your father was a voracious book collector, but not out of any altruistic reasons. He was greedy for knowledge, but he stored it away like he was stealing secrets. And he had become obsessed with creating the perfect vampire. A foolish quest—what interest is there in perfection? The next time I saw him was during the Renaissance." He smiled at Giovanni. "You probably don't remember, Jacopo. You were quite young, but I met him in Rome during the Giovanni Pico debates. I was there to meet with your uncle, but I remember you, as well."

Carwyn bolted up. "What? That was your uncle? I always thought that was you!"

Beatrice said, "I figured that out when I was human, Carwyn. What makes you so slow?"

He sat back with a sulky look on his face. "I just don't choose to be nosey, unlike some people."

"Both of you, stop," Giovanni said. "So you were watching the debates in Rome and you met Andros there? I remember him being there. He was trailing after my uncle at the time, though I didn't understand why until later."

Ziri nodded. "Yes, I met him there. He had acquired the majority of your father's books after his 'death' and had some questions. He knew Kato and I were friends, so he was cautious. But I could tell from his questions that he had somehow laid his hands on Geber's research. He was too curious. He would not let the subject go. It was at that point that I knew I would have to kill him and get the books back. I left Rome and went to seek Saba. I needed to know what she did."

The air had left Giovanni's lungs. "So... you would have killed Andros? And taken the book?"

Ziri's eyes drifted to the fire. "By the time I returned from Africa, years had passed. I had met with Saba and we were both in agreement. Though she claimed to have no idea where Andros acquired the book, she did not tell me what she had done with it. She did tell me where I could find Arosh and Kato if I felt like I needed their permission to kill Andros. I did not go. From talking with her, I knew Andros could not live. This knowledge *had* to remain a secret." He looked up and met Giovanni's gaze. "Imagine my surprise when I returned to Italy to find that a young immortal had done the job for me."

Carwyn sighed. "So it's true?"

Giovanni turned to his friend. "My father was not who people thought he was. He was—"

"Hold, Gio." Carwyn held up his hands. "You don't have to explain yourself to me. I know it's not something you would have done lightly."

Giovanni turned back to Ziri. "How did you know? How did you know that it wasn't an accident? A robbery, as we claimed?"

Ziri smiled. "Because I recognized *you*, my friend. I recognized the boy who had grown into a man and then been transformed into one of us. I remembered the bright child and I heard about your uncle's death. I could guess what had happened. Andros had finally made himself the perfect child. And that child was so perfect, he knew that his sire needed to be burned from the earth. So I say, *well done,* Giovanni Vecchio."

Guilt still burned in Giovanni's chest and anger toward the placid immortal who seemed so detached, but Beatrice rubbed his thigh comfortingly. "And the book?" she asked. "Geber's research?"

"The fires," Giovanni murmured in understanding. "You thought as I did."

"Everyone knew that the library of Niccolo Andros had been scattered. Some books burned in Savonarola's fires. Others lost or destroyed... I had no reason to think that Andros had shared the information with anyone. Whom did he trust besides himself?"

Giovanni's mouth was a grim line. "No one."

"No one." Ziri nodded. "And until Stephen found the books, I doubt Lorenzo knew what he had, either. They were artifacts to him. But when Stephen found them, Lorenzo took a closer look. And, as your father learned, he found something quite unique."

Now, it was Beatrice who spoke. "You never told me how you found my father."

"Tywyll the water vampire is an old, old friend. I have used him for information many times in my travels. He is as old as Arosh or Kato or any of us, though he's always preferred the solitude of his British rivers and his dirty pubs. When Stephen came to him to exchange gold for safe passage, he recognized what your father had. He did not know the whole of it, but he must have remembered our work in Kufa. I had told him about the time I'd spent there, though I never told him why. He put the pieces together and contacted me. I told him... enough. He wasn't very curious, but he wanted me to help Stephen."

Ziri turned to Beatrice. "I will not lie to you. My initial intention was to find your father, kill him, and destroy the book. But I became interested in his mind. In his research. I thought... why not another? Perhaps another could succeed where we had failed? Perhaps this search had not been in vain. So, instead of killing him, I watched him. I protected him." Ziri leaned back in his chair and crossed his arms over his chest. His face was carefully blank. "I suppose, in the end, I was still curious."

Giovanni sat, staring at Ziri for a moment as he tried to process the revelations the ancient had given them. Finally, he spoke. "Ziri, if you would leave us, please."

Ziri gave a regal bow. "Of course."

Beatrice sat next to him. Carwyn stood across the room. He could tell that some of the information had been new to his wife and friend, but not all.

He said, "I can see that much has been discovered and planned in my absence."

Beatrice tried to interrupt. "Gio, we—"

He cut her off. "You have all made your plans, but now I am back. And I will tell you what I will do."

CHAPTER 18

Beatrice opened her mouth again, but Carwyn caught her eye with a warning glare. He shook his head slightly, so she shut her mouth.

"I am going back to Rome. I am going to find Livia and kill her. Then, I am going to find my son and kill him. I will take the book back, destroy it, and see to it that any of the elixir that has been made is destroyed. I will maintain my reputation so that others who threaten my family will fear me. If that means that I have to kill half of Rome, so be it. If that means I have to travel to Greece and kill the council there, I will." His voice rose. "If that means that I have to spend the next hundred years killing, maiming, and burning the European immortal community to the ground, I will. I will not run and hide. I will not stand for others shielding me, and I will *not* stand for Livia to live while I walk the earth. Is that understood?"

Beatrice was speechless. She could handle Giovanni's fiery anger, but the cold rage that poured off her husband was something she rarely encountered. Again, she opened her mouth to speak, but Carwyn spoke first.

"Fine, Gio." Her eyes widened, but Carwyn glared her into silence before he continued. "You know you have my backing, as well as the support of Jean in France and Terry in London. The Germans may have a problem with it, but I have a feeling that you could make your case to Matilda. It's too bad you're married already. A political marriage could have solved that problem, but I'm sure you can work something out. Greece will be tricky, but they're not strong enough to really oppose you once you control Rome."

Beatrice's head began to swim, and she felt Giovanni stiffen beside her. Carwyn just continued on in a deadly quiet voice. "I can secure the support of the Vatican. Emil Conti would be your most likely rival for power. We had planned on cultivating him as an ally, but that is easily cured. You'll probably need to eliminate him and most of those under his aegis to avoid any future problems. A takeover in Rome is long overdue. Most of the other centers of power have switched to a new guard in the last hundred years or so. Rome was the only holdout. Once you're established, you'll need to start thinking about whom you want as a lieutenant. I have some ideas, but you might want to bring in entirely new people. After all, you are an outsider, so it wouldn't be nearly as simple as an internal coup. Still, it's manageable."

She wanted to protest. Her heart was racing, and the words were on the tip of her tongue, but Carwyn just kept talking in a steady voice. "You'll need to send Beatrice and Ben back to the States, of course. She's strong, but as she'd be targeted constantly, her presence would be a distraction for you. She'll be far safer in Los Angeles under Ernesto's protection until things are stable. If everything goes well, in fifty years she'll be by your side again, my friend."

Carwyn finally leaned back and crossed his arms over his chest. "Really, not all that long in the vast span of things. Excellent plan, Gio. Let me know when you want to leave."

Giovanni shot out of his seat and across the room, plowing his fist into the wall and shouting, "Damn it!"

Carwyn said, "You want to blaze into Rome and take out Livia. That's what you're looking at. You know I'm right."

She saw him glare. "I'll hand it over to Conti."

Carwyn snorted. "Brilliant plan. Conti will take it and then try to kill you. He'd have to, or no one would respect him, and he'd be battling rivals for the next hundred years."

"I'll..."

"What?" Carwyn rose and walked over to stand next to him. Beatrice was tempted to speak, but knew that Giovanni needed to reach the same conclusions they had weeks before.

Carwyn leaned closer and spoke softly. "What are you going to do, Gio? You want to kill Livia? You get Rome. That's the way it works. You'll be embroiled in politics for the next three hundred years, at least."

"I have no desire to rule Rome."

He took a deep breath. "Then you need to listen to Beatrice's plan."

Giovanni pulled his fist out of the wall and turned around. He leaned against it and crossed his arms. "Livia still needs to die."

Beatrice finally spoke. "She will. And hopefully, you'll be able to kill her, but this needs to come from someone in Rome, unless we want the city to descend into chaos that you'll be expected to clean up. In the long run, it's the easiest way. Emil Conti has been making moves to return the city to a more republican form of leadership for years. He's sensible. Stable. Given the right circumstances, he could take over and we wouldn't be stuck with it. We just need to create the right opportunity for him."

Giovanni smirked. "You sound so very American right now, my dear."

"Hey." She shrugged. "We do love our revolutions. But this time, we'll try to make it slightly less bloody."

He took a deep breath and let it out slowly. "What's your plan?"

"Dez and Ben have discovered where she's been producing it. It's a cosmetics factory in Bulgaria. We need you and Carwyn to go shut it down. Find the humans she's been working with. Find out how much they know. From what Ziri remembers and looking at Lucien Thrax's condition, we know that this elixir is harmful to immortals, but she's been circulating rumors that she has some great revelation. A secret that will make Rome the center of the world again and make her even wealthier. We need to get people doubting her. Questioning her intentions. If we can make people distrust her—"

"We can try, but who will believe us?" Giovanni shrugged. "She's charismatic. Powerful. Even if we find out the elixir is poison, she could play it as if she was a victim. She's very good at manipulation."

Carwyn spoke up. "If we can find Arosh, Ziri's certain we'll find Kato. If we can find Kato, we'll know the truth about the effects."

"The truth doesn't matter," Giovanni shouted. "It only matters what people believe."

"Then we'll *make* them believe. Listen Gio, she either knows what the effects are, or we'll make it sound like she does and didn't care. Saba, the greatest healer in our history, killed everyone who had taken it. *Killed* them, Gio. Ziri thinks the truth will be damaging enough for her allies to abandon her. Once that has happened, Conti can step in with minimal conflict, because he is the obvious successor. There will be some bloodshed, of course, but we'll be able to let him take the lead so that he's the one stuck with the city. We'll be backing him up, instead of acting as usurpers. Jean and Terry will throw their support behind him. The Vatican likes him already, which will lend him further legitimacy with the younger Roman vampires, most of whom identify as Catholic. It's the easiest way."

"You're forgetting that we have nothing as proof. *Nothing*. We have guesses and the memories of one of the vampires involved. We have one sick vampire. Memories and suppositions. Even Lucien doesn't know what's really going on with his own health." Giovanni paced the room.

"And then you have Livia! She has a lost secret. The elixir of life. And no doubt she'll have mocked up some kind of lab results to make this elixir look legitimate. She'll make it sound like we're trying to stir things up against her, and no one is going to trust us."

Beatrice murmured, "Well... that's why you're going to have to bring Kato back."

A FALL OF WATER

She could have heard a pin drop.

"Oh, of course!" He threw up his hands. "So, not only are Carwyn and I supposed to *find* these two vampires—who aren't supposed to exist—but we need to bring them back to Rome, as well!"

Beatrice forced a smile. "Ziri's pretty sure Kato will like you."

Giovanni turned to Carwyn. "Tell me she's joking."

"She's not joking. Ziri says Kato would love you." Carwyn slapped him on the shoulder and moved across the room.

Giovanni's eyes darted between him. "Are we forgetting about the deadliest fire immortal in history? Are we forgetting about Arosh? If Arosh took Kato away for his own protection, then I'm fairly sure he's not going to be pleased about being found."

"Well, that's true." Beatrice nodded. "And that's why *you* need to go."

"Tesoro..." He rushed to her side and took her hands. "I'm very strong. I'm very powerful, Yes, I could probably hold my own against him in battle for longer than any other, but *no one* is as powerful as Arosh. He is the oldest fire vampire in immortal legend. He ruled Persia and Eastern Europe for thousands of years. I stand very little chance of actually making him listen to me!"

"But Ziri says he hated Andros."

His face was frozen. "That just means he'll kill me faster."

"But what if you tell him you killed him? We're pretty sure he'll listen then. Also, Ziri has a letter for you guys to take."

"Oh, of course. A letter!" Giovanni brushed a hand over his exasperated face. "Do we even have an idea where he might be after all this time?"

Carwyn said, "Ziri has the location that Saba gave him when he first decided to kill Andros. It's somewhere in the Caucasus."

Giovanni blinked. "So, we have the location that a notoriously vague immortal gave a friend over five hundred years ago to track down two vampires who have managed to remain hidden from the immortal community for a thousand years?"

Beatrice cleared her throat. "Well, if you're only going to look at the down side—"

"Forgive me if I am less than optimistic about our chances of finding them."

Carwyn said, "Do you really think that, once they'd found a good hiding place, they'd move? You know how the old ones are. Five hundred years is little to them. They're probably tucked into the Northern Caucasus, happily feeding on the local population and playing chess."

Giovanni stared at his friend.

"See that," Beatrice said. "That's his skeptical face, Carwyn."

"I'm familiar with it."

Her husband said, "I agree that I would probably have the best chance to find him. And you'd need a fire immortal to approach Arosh if you're going to get close enough to deliver any sort of message. A female would be better, but... it might work. We will need a letter from Ziri. And we trust him?" His eyes turned back to Beatrice.

She nodded. "We do. Tenzin vouches for him and so does Lucien."

Giovanni sat for a moment, thinking. Then he sat next to her on the couch. "The Thracian has always been trustworthy."

She could see him begin to really consider their plan, and she felt herself relax. "So?"

"So Carwyn and I will go shut down this factory in Bulgaria and then find Arosh and Kato, who are in..." He looked toward Carwyn.

"It sounds like the mountains in the Republic of Georgia."

"Lovely. And after we avoid being killed, we're going to convince Arosh and Kato to come out of hiding in order to go to Rome and testify that Livia knew about this elixir and whatever harm it can cause. Which we're still not sure of."

Carwyn said, "It would have to be damn serious for Saba to kill any human they had tested it on and for Arosh and Kato to fake their deaths."

"Agreed." Giovanni paused, and she could see his mind churning. "So while we're doing this, Beatrice and Tenzin will be stirring up revolution in Rome?"

She nodded. "I'll be getting closer to Emil Conti. He's already displeased with the actions Livia took against you. The population seems to be split, but given some encouragement, he could probably turn the tide against her. He's already becoming more popular. He senses an opportunity, and I'm surprisingly... well, I'm kind of popular in Rome."

Carwyn said, "Everyone is enamored of the new girl Livia doesn't like."

Beatrice grinned. "I'm driving her crazy. Tenzin and I killed a bunch of her guards and she couldn't really do anything about it."

Giovanni sighed and rubbed his temples. "So, I'm going to let you and Tenzin create havoc in Rome and destabilize a dangerous and powerful vampire even further while I go off on a dubious errand to find two legends who I'm still not entirely convinced even exist anymore."

Carwyn walked over and slapped him on the back. "Yes, you are. Tenzin and B are brilliant and between the two of them, along with some help from Lucien and Ziri, they're going to be fine."

Giovanni reached up and touched her cheek. "And we will have to say goodbye."

Beatrice blinked back tears. "For now."

"We have to say good-bye *tonight*."

Carwyn cleared his throat. "And I think that's my cue to go. Gio, I'm going to procure a car for us. Hopefully, something older that you won't break. I'll be back later. B, I'll see you later, darling girl." He leaned down, brushed a kiss across her cheek, and left the room.

As soon as they were alone, Giovanni pulled her into his lap.

"I still don't like this."

"It's either this, or we face you killing Livia in a bloody coup as an outsider and becoming even more tangled in politics for the next few hundred years. Do you want that?"

"No."

"Then..." She tucked her head into his neck. "This is the best way."

"Do you feel safe? Around Livia? Around Lorenzo? He's still there, isn't he?"

"Yes, and I don't like it, but I'll be fine. Tenzin is teaching me patience."

"Yes, she's good at that. I remember once we hid for over six months in a cave in Russia waiting for a target. She played this dice game against the wall of the cave constantly. Almost drove me mad."

She smiled and took a deep breath, drinking in the smell of his skin, trying to soak up enough of his presence to last her through the weeks, and maybe months, ahead. He held her, playing with her hair and letting his lips trail over her skin.

"Is Ben all right?"

"He's fine." She smiled a little. "He's been taking care of his aunt."

"He's a good boy."

"He's becoming a man through all of this. Keeping me company when I'm sad. Helping Dez with research. Helping Matt with security."

"Tell him I'm very proud of him."

She blinked back tears. "I will."

"And I'm proud of you, too. This is... as much as I do not like aspects of it, this is a good plan."

"It is?"

She felt him nod and press a kiss to her temple. "It is. If everything goes well, we'll be home by Christmas."

Beatrice smiled a little. "Yeah, maybe."

"Let's plan on it, shall we?"

"Okay."

They held each other for another hour. The fire in the grate crackled in the still night air. They could hear Ziri pacing out on the dock, though he did not interrupt them. Beatrice knew that they would need to leave soon if they were going to make it back to Rome before dawn.

"I love you so much it hurts sometimes," she whispered.

His arms tightened around her. "Love should never hurt."

A wave of panic flooded up, and she was suddenly overcome with doubts. Her heart began to pound. "This—this is stupid. You're right. We need to stay together. We'll go back to Rome. We'll just take everyone away and say to hell with them all. You and Tenzin can come back and kill Livia and Lorenzo later. I don't—"

"Beatrice—"

"I don't give a shit about the rest of the vampires! Let them kill themselves with this drug. We'll go back to the States. We'll—"

"Beatrice." He soothed her, pressing her face into the crook of his neck. He rocked her back and forth for a few moments as her heart evened out. "You know that we must put an end to this. If this elixir is as dangerous as everyone seems to think, it could spread through Europe. Asia. Africa. On the surface, it looks like a miracle. Imagine how many would be taken in. Eventually, it would reach our own home. It could endanger the people we care about. This secret has been in the shadows for too long. We need to uncover the truth—the whole of it—and it needs to come to light. Whatever the consequences. You know this."

She clutched his neck. "Why did it have to be us?"

"Who else could it be? This is the secret that brought us together, Tesoro mio. Some things have to happen—"

"Exactly as they do."

"Yes."

She only held him tighter, feeling his hands stroke her back. He hummed a song in her ear and she closed her eyes and took a calming breath. "You better come back to me, Giovanni Vecchio."

"I told you already. *Ubi amo; ibi patria.* Wherever you go, I will find you."

GIOVANNI WATCHED HER FROM THE DOCK AS ZIRI GRASPED HER HAND AND took off into the clear, dark night. They would have enough time to get back to the safety of the house in Rome before dawn. He felt Carwyn stand behind him.

"She'll be fine."

"That's not your wife flying off to go play politics in the viper's nest."

"No, you managed to fool her into thinking that you were the better choice. How did that happen?"

Giovanni smiled. "Natural charm, I guess."

"Keep telling yourself that if it makes you feel better, Sparky. I'm still betting you used amnis on her."

He couldn't stop the low chuckle that came to his throat. "Did you bring me any clothes that fit, by the way? I've been wearing Gavin's miniature wardrobe for the past few days."

"Don't lie. You haven't been wearing clothes at all."

They started toward the house. "I have a feeling you might not like that wardrobe option as much as Beatrice did."

"Good thing I brought you some clothes then."

"Hawaiian shirts?"

"Of course. We're being men of mystery."

"How are we going to find two vampires who are supposed to have been dead for centuries, Father?" Carwyn burst into laughter, and Giovanni turned to him, confused. "Did I miss the joke?"

"Oh..." Carwyn tried to calm his features, but couldn't seem to help himself. He was bent over, laughing and wiping tears from his eyes. "I suppose you *have* been gone for a while, haven't you?"

Giovanni shook his head, still confused. "What the hell are you laughing about?"

"It's a good thing we're taking a road trip. We need to catch up."

"I've been a bit busy."

"As have I, my friend, as have I. The joke, as you say, is on... well, everyone." Carwyn slapped him on the back and pulled open the door. "You see, strictly speaking, I'm not exactly a Father anymore."

Giovanni stopped in his tracks and his eyes widened. Carwyn was still chuckling.

"Come on. We'll talk in the car. Might as well get going; it's a long drive to Bulgaria."

CHAPTER 19

"You need to let him stab you."

"I'm not letting him stab me."

"He needs to learn."

"Forget it, you mad vampire. It's not going to be me."

"He has been raised to have too many manners. He won't stab a woman. Even me."

Ben's eyes darted between Tenzin and an angry Gavin. "For the record, I really don't want to stab anyone."

Tenzin's eyes swung toward him. "Too bad. We're practicing hand-to-hand combat with knives. That's what you need to do." Gavin just huffed and leaned against a wall in the basement.

"I'm not stabbing any of you guys. Forget it. We'll practice with…"

Tenzin crossed her arms. "What?"

"I don't know, but I'm not stabbing anyone!"

She rolled her eyes. "It's not like you can kill us."

"I agree with the boy," Gavin said. "Just pretend."

Tenzin said, "You have obviously never trained anyone to fight before."

Gavin looked indignant. "Yes, I have."

"Are they still alive?"

The two started bickering again and Ben sighed. For the past few weeks, ever since Gavin, Deirdre, and Jean had showed up in Rome, everyone had been stuck in Giovanni's house, trying to be inconspicuous. Deirdre spent most of the time on her phone or visiting with Dez and Angela. Jean was either talking on the phone or meeting with an assistant who ran errands for him. Gavin, Ben had decided, was the most fun to hang out with. And he let Ben drink. Well, he did until Beatrice caught them in the library and went ballistic.

The rest of the time, Gavin helped Tenzin with Ben's training. Matt had given him a handgun to carry, but Tenzin still insisted that knives were often more reliable and better because of their silence.

'Remember, boy. A knife never runs out of bullets. You can use it anywhere. And it doesn't announce its presence.'

Ben touched the grip of the hunting knife he carried. He had a simple sheath tucked into the inside of his waistband that made it invisible, even under summer clothes. It definitely beat the rusty old steak knife he'd carried with him on the streets when he was a kid. That one he'd found behind a restaurant in the Bowery when he was eight, but it had come in handy more than once.

Gavin and Tenzin were still arguing, so Ben spoke up. "Listen, both of you, I really don't think I need to stab either of you. I know you may find this hard to believe—"

Ben felt the cold slip of a hand at his neck a moment before the barrel of a gun hit the small of his back. In a heartbeat, Ben leaned back into his attacker, ducking down and to the left as he twisted his body under the arm that was reaching around his neck. In one smooth movement, he drew the hunting knife from his waist and turned so that he came behind his assailant. His arm reached around, slicing up the front of the man's shirt until it was poised at the neck.

The whole maneuver had taken just a few seconds.

Cocky vampires, Ben thought as his other arm braced itself against the rock hard back of Jean Desmarais.

Jean chuckled and patted the hand that held the knife at his throat. "Nicely done. See? Neither of you needs to bleed. The young man is well-trained already. Boy, if we were on the streets, would I be breathing?"

"You don't breathe." Ben's heart was racing, but he kept his voice in check. He let his hand fall and stepped from behind the Frenchman.

Jean merely shrugged. "You see? Tenzin, you have taught him well. The boy is very good with a knife already."

Tenzin eyed him with the guarded expression Ben had come to expect from her. "I can't teach reflexes like that."

Ben ignored her and tucked his knife back in his waistband. "Jean, sorry about the shirt."

"Think nothing of it. Perhaps you could procure one of your uncle's for me. My wardrobe is rather limited."

He slapped the Frenchman on the shoulder. "No problem, man. I'll go grab one. You sure you don't want one of Carwyn's?" Ben heard Jean laugh as he jogged up the stairs.

He walked through the kitchen where Lucien, Angela, and Dez were involved in a conversation about baking or something. He wandered up the stairs and past the library. Deirdre, Matt, and Ziri were there, speaking some language he thought might have been German. Or Russian. He couldn't really tell. All three sounded like they needed to gargle.

By the time he got to the third floor, Ben could hear the cello recording coming from Beatrice and Giovanni's room. He knocked lightly on the door and waited for her voice.

"Come on in, Ben."

He was the only one who ever disturbed her when she was up here. Not even Dez was really allowed. Tenzin came up sometimes, but she never knocked. He poked his head into the bedroom. Beatrice was sitting at the table in the living area of the suite and tapping her pencil against a notebook.

"What's up?"

"Can I borrow one of Gio's shirts for Jean? I kind of sliced his up in the basement."

She frowned. "Do I want to know?"

"Probably not."

A smile flickered across her face. She was better since his uncle had escaped from Livia's castle, but still not herself. She wouldn't be until Giovanni was back. He missed his uncle, too, but the thing they had? Ben thought he would probably never feel that way about anyone. His aunt and uncle were the center of each other's universe. Even he could see that.

"Yeah, there's a bunch that came from the cleaner's a few weeks ago. Pick any of those. Except the green one."

"I'll just grab a black one. That's what he was wearing."

Ben went to the closet and ignored the few crumbled Oxford shirts that lay on top of the dresser. Giovanni's clothes hadn't really been touched. Everything was still as it had been that first horrible night his uncle had been arrested. Ben shook his head and grabbed a random black shirt, hoping it would fit. Jean was a little smaller than his uncle, but not by much. He wandered back out to the bedroom.

"What are you working on?"

"Huh?" She looked up. "Oh, I'm just taking some notes. I'm going to that reception thing that Livia's hosting at this club in town later."

"Like a dance club?"

"Kinda. It's more like a social club. I'm not sure, but Emil Conti's going to be there along with most of the most influential vampires in the city. Ziri said that she's trying to be more visible since word got out that Gio escaped."

"That probably made her look pretty bad, huh?"

"Yes. But Emil requested another visit, so she had to admit he'd escaped. And she knows we were at the reception the night it happened." A satisfied grin spread over her face. "It's driving her crazy. And yes, it makes her look really bad."

He sat down. "Well, that's good, right? That's what you want."

"Yep, that's what we want. And that's why she's hanging out in the city more and having this reception. She's trying to show off and make sure people remember she's still the queen. But Emil's going to be there, along with his wife, who I haven't met yet."

"So you're gonna go make nice?"

"I'm going to go hang out and try to boost his ego and his reputation. The more people think of him, the more likely he's going to be able to make the moves we want to get Livia out of power. Hopefully, flattery will get us everywhere."

Ben asked, "Anyone going with you?"

"Not this time." She glanced up into his worried eyes. "It's fine, Ben. Nothing's going to happen to me. It's a very public event. I'm not even going to be very far away from here."

"You sure? Maybe Matt—"

"This is a vampire thing, Ben."

"Tenzin?"

She dropped her pencil and reached a hand across the table. "Ben, honey, I'll be fine."

He shrugged and tried to act nonchalant. "Okay, whatever."

She smiled and patted his hand. "Now, go take that shirt to Jean. He's a little too proud of that hairy French chest. We don't want him scaring Angela."

Ben burst into laughter and stood. He walked out and looked back at his aunt. Beatrice was sitting at the table, looking pensive, and staring at the moon through the open window. He gently closed the door.

"My dear, if looks could kill, then you would be a splatter on the wall."

Beatrice glanced up to see Emil Conti standing over her with a martini and a cool smile. "Emil, I doubt you're complimenting my outfit, so I'm going to assume she was glaring at me again."

He chuckled as he sat next to her in the plush velvet chairs that lined the VIP section of the club.

She had been mistaken, Livia *was* entertaining them at a nightclub. It was one she owned, and Beatrice could feel the vibrations of the music from the dance floor below. The favored vampires who had received an invitation stood at the edge of the darkened glass, surveying the humans who crowded the club like their own, personal buffet.

Which, Beatrice thought, they kind of were. The few humans allowed upstairs were swimming in amnis and quickly taken to the private rooms. The grunts and moans of pleasure were dampened by the thick walls, but not completely drowned out.

"A vampire-owned nightclub," she said. "Kind of a cliché, isn't it?"

Emil smiled. "It's a cliché for a reason. It's a good business to be in and provides an excellent cover. She's had this one since the seventies. Thankfully, the decor has been updated."

"You own any?" They were somewhat isolated in their corner of the balcony. Beatrice had staked out a spot earlier where she could keep an eye on the whole party, but still be heard if she lifted her voice. It also had a great view of the table where Livia and Lorenzo had set up court.

"I don't. I have very boring businesses like shipping companies. Fishing. Though I do own several small cruise lines."

"That could be fun."

"If I had a taste for retiree blood, I'm sure I'd get my fill."

They laughed together, but both of them looked over to the head table.

Both Livia and Lorenzo had humans draped over them and made no disguise about taking a sip openly. The vampires surrounding them looked on like a hungry pack. Even Emil narrowed his eyes, but Beatrice had a feeling it wasn't in envy.

"Doesn't that piss people off?" she asked, her voice raised to allow the sensitive ears around them to hear. "I mean—I don't like to compare—but at my grandfather's parties in Los Angeles, everyone is allowed to bring their own company, if you know what I mean." Beatrice noticed the subtle attention that had shifted in their direction. So had Emil. A smile flickered across his mouth.

"In truth, Beatrice, most cities do not have the strict discipline about feeding that Rome has." His voice was very carefully neutral. "It is one thing that sets us apart."

You're definitely not saying that's a good thing, are you? His dark eyes were narrowed in calculation as she continued. "It's definitely unusual. I know I'm young, but I've traveled quite a bit. Other than the feeding thing, you're lucky to live here. I love Rome. The energy. The sights. It's an amazing city."

"I'm glad you're enjoying your stay. Despite the unpleasantness earlier this summer."

"I'm sure things will all be sorted out. I'm relieved that Gio is no longer confined, but then, no one contains my husband for long."

"And you have no idea where he is?"

She smiled. *Are you asking for me or the silent audience we've attracted?* "None at all."

Laughing eyes met hers. "Of course not. After all." Emil looked around the room. "I can scarcely keep track of my own wife, and she's never been arrested."

"Are you talking about me?" A graceful vampire slinked over and draped herself across the arm of Emil's red velvet chair. Donatella Conti was, according

A FALL OF WATER

to Ziri, a very keen water vampire with very good instincts. She had been turned during the Renaissance, the same as Giovanni, but was a distant relative of the Borgia family. Her union with Emil Conti was a political manipulation of her sire, who had died shortly after the match. Beatrice couldn't quite figure Donatella out.

She was a gorgeous chestnut brunette who wore designer fashions like they were loungewear. She made no disguise of her disdain for Livia, but still seemed to live in a charmed bubble of popularity. She and Emil had both come with other dates, but gravitated toward each other throughout the evening.

Emil ran a possessive hand over her thigh. "Of course we are talking about you, my love. Who else?"

Beatrice said, "I love your dress. That color is amazing on you." It was a blood-red cocktail dress that Beatrice remembered some skinny actress in Hollywood wearing to an awards show the year before. The actress looked anemic in it. Donatella looked stunning.

"Thank you," Donatella said, as her gaze raked over Beatrice's uniform of black jeans and a skin-tight black shirt. She'd dressed it up for the night with a satin top that Dez had picked out and her tall, black boots. "I like your boots, Beatrice De Novo."

Beatrice let her fangs run out and smiled. "Thanks. These are Gio's favorites. I'm pretty sure I don't match Livia's dress code, though." It was true. She was the only woman wearing jeans in the club, but no one dared turn her away at the door.

"And, I suppose, that is why Rome loves you." Donatella smirked. "And you are American. You can get away with it."

"Oh?" Beatrice said. "I think Roman women can get away with a lot more."

Emil smiled and ran a hand up the curve of his wife's calf. "You are quite right."

"Maybe it's time for a change," Beatrice said. She could hear the chatter around them drop off and she was fairly certain Livia, Lorenzo, or both were listening as well.

The smile fell from Emil's face and he glanced around. "Change can be dangerous. Disruptive."

"Change can also be healthy."

"If done for the right reasons, I suppose so."

Beatrice looked up at Donatella, who was watching her with narrowed eyes. "For instance, Donatella, I saw a similar dress on an actress last year. She looked like a little girl playing dress-up. You, however..." She trailed off, hoping that the vampire had picked up her cue.

As if she had orchestrated it, Donatella slid into Emil's lap. A smile flirted at the corner of her mouth. "It's all about finding the right person, isn't it, Beatrice? The right person can wear the boldest colors."

871

"They can. It's good to shake things up every now and then."

Emil stroked his wife's hair while Donatella and Beatrice exchanged a private smile. "You ladies," Emil murmured. "Always talking about the newest trends."

Beatrice cast her eyes around the club at their silent audience. "Emil, I am *all* about new trends."

SHE WAS ON THE STREET, WAITING FOR HER CAR TO PICK HER UP, WHEN EMIL caught up with her.

"Beatrice, please, allow me to offer you a ride home."

She looked around. Livia's guards watched them from the front of the club. Her driver pulled up, but she waved him away and turned back to Emil. "That would be nice, thanks. Where's Donatella?"

He shrugged. "I believe that she is seeing her companion home. Mine brought her own driver."

They slid into the dark blue luxury sedan, and Emil immediately raised the privacy screen, encasing them in silence. He swung his eyes toward her and bared his teeth.

"You play a dangerous game, Beatrice De Novo. No one is sure how you got him out, but we know that Giovanni did not escape on his own. There was no way it could have happened. I saw his cell myself. I don't know what he has planned, but—"

"Neither my husband nor I have any interest in ruling Rome." Her fangs had slid down in reaction to his aggressive stance, but Beatrice curbed her natural instincts and tried to relax. This was their potential ally, she reminded herself, and he had every reason to be suspicious.

"Then what are you insinuating? Surely you must have noticed that others were listening to you tonight."

"I think you know exactly what I'm insinuating."

"Assistance only?"

"Let's just say, we like to help our friends."

Emil sat back and relaxed his stance. "What you're talking about has many risks."

"Like I said, change always does."

"We're not talking about fashion crimes anymore, Beatrice."

"I never was, *Emil*." She tapped her finger on her knee and watched him. "She can't remain in power. It will not be allowed. If there is no other option, Giovanni will remove her. But we're hoping there are other options."

Emil watched her with a measuring stare. "Other options would prove to be far less trouble for you. But I don't know that you're aware of how much power she really has."

"You're talking about these rumors circulating. About her cure for bloodlust?"

He shifted in his seat. "It's never been stated quite that succinctly, but everyone knows she has ties to the pharmaceutical industry. If that is something she has attained, the cure could bring her immense wealth and influence. Every vampire in the world would pay to be free of the one thing that controls us. Only a shield against the sun would be more valuable." He cleared his throat. "Some of us may have tried to discover the truth of these claims, but so far it's been rather—"

"It's a cosmetics factory in Bulgaria." Beatrice took a chance. If Emil was going to risk his neck, she had to give him something. "They started production earlier this year."

He narrowed his eyes. "How do you know this?"

"Put it this way, I'm very good at research."

She saw him deflate in his seat, but still, his eyes flared. "So, it is true? She has discovered a cure?"

"Not exactly."

He frowned. "Please, continue."

"This formula was given to me by the Elders of Penglai Island. They wanted it protected. Not even their most skilled alchemists really understood it. And then Lorenzo stole it. And make no mistake, Emil. He *did* steal it. He *did* kill my father. He almost killed me."

Emil snorted. "I doubt he'd kill you. Have you seen the way he looks at you?"

"Please, he'd want anyone that Giovanni had. That has nothing to do with me."

"I wouldn't be too sure about that, but tell me more about this. As much as I dislike Livia, this does sound like something that could be good for our kind, Beatrice. Whatever our personal rivalries, we should think of the greater good of all—"

"See that!" she interrupted. "That right there? That's why *you're* the best person to lead Rome. You really do care about the city. You care about the vampires who live here. You feel a responsibility to them."

He drew himself up, almost as if she had insulted him. "It is my belief that those who have power have a responsibility to—"

"It's good! I'm not saying it isn't. It's nice to meet someone who's not completely self-interested. But the thing is, this formula is not safe. And she knows it." Actually, Beatrice had no idea whether Livia knew the effects of the elixir on amnis, but that didn't matter. Getting Livia out of power was more important. "We think it's a poison, Emil."

He looked skeptical. "Why would she want to poison her own people? I know she's not benevolent, but it's hardly in her best interests to kill all of them."

"We're not sure, but we're trying to find out what, *exactly*, it does."

He sighed. "Beatrice, I like you. I think Livia is a bad leader. And I believe your claims against Lorenzo. In fact, after Tenzin's speech, I'm fairly sure all of Rome knows that he murdered your father, but the fact remains that Livia has many allies. Allies here and abroad. She has done many favors for many people in her two thousand years. Unless those people decide to cut her off..."

"Well," Beatrice said quietly. "I guess we'll just have to make them realize that it's time for a change."

Emil crossed his legs and leaned back in the seat. He tapped his fingers restlessly on one knee as he glanced between Beatrice and the lights of the Eternal City that flashed past the car. He was silent until they pulled up to the Pantheon. Beatrice heard the driver get out and walk around to open her door. It opened, but Emil grabbed her hand as she was climbing out.

"You're right," he said. "You're right. Change is good. Change is... necessary."

She smiled and nodded. "I'll be in touch."

Beatrice whistled as she walked up the street and watched Emil's car turn the corner. She had just made her most important ally.

CHAPTER 20

Plovdiv, Bulgaria

Giovanni stepped out of the telegraph office tucked into a corner of the Kapana district and strolled up the cobbled streets. Summer nights were warm in Plovdiv, and pedestrians crowded the walkways of the neighborhood on their way to the clubs and restaurants of the graceful old town. Bulgaria's second largest city, and one of the oldest in Europe, had enjoyed a surge of prosperity since the last time Giovanni had visited. Like much of Eastern Europe, the city had always maintained a fairly high immortal population, with Lucien Thrax being one of its oldest inhabitants.

He and Carwyn had received a polite, if muted, reception from the vampire who ran the city after a letter of introduction from the old Thracian had paved the way. Their business in town was not questioned, which was all Giovanni wanted. If everything went as planned, they wouldn't be in Bulgaria long.

He caught the red of Carwyn's hair against the dark green wall of an outdoor cafe. The former priest was drinking a glass of plum *rakia* and writing a letter at a small table. A smile flirted at the corner of his mouth. Giovanni sat down next to him and Carwyn tucked the letter under the edge of his book.

"Who were you writing, Father?"

Carwyn smiled. "I told you—"

"I've been calling you that for three hundred years, Carwyn. I'm not going to just stop, you know."

"Fine, but I may stop answering."

Giovanni chuckled. "So?"

"What?"

"Who were you writing?"

"None of your business."

"You are quite the mystery lately."

The vampire shrugged and sipped the fruit wine. "What's so mysterious? I decided that a thousand years of service to the church was enough. After all, when I took my vows, I was only expecting to live forty or fifty."

"I'm not questioning your decision, my friend." Giovanni cocked an eyebrow. "Are *you*?"

Carwyn smiled and looked over at the fountain that trickled in the small square and the flow of young people that passed by. "No. I'm not going to deny it feels a bit odd, but I'm at peace about it. I'm... excited. It's a new chapter in life. There are going to be some changes for me."

Giovanni nodded. "So, is this the immortal version of a mid-life crisis?"

Carwyn snorted and waved over a young man to order two more glasses, then he turned back to Giovanni. "I blame the girls, you know."

"Why?"

"I'm warning you, never make daughters. You raise them. Give them hundreds of years of guidance and love, and then they think they know everything. Try to tell you what to do. Very irritating."

"What? All of them?"

"Not Carla, thank God, but then, she never speaks to anyone but me and Gus. No, it's the rest of them, Gio. They plot against me."

Giovanni smiled, thinking of the most likely culprits. Deirdre, Isabel, and Gemma may have been scattered around the globe, but he had no doubt the three sisters could gang up on their father if they put their minds to it.

"I'll keep that in mind. No daughters. Have you told anyone else yet?"

"Other than the cardinals? No."

"How did they take it?"

"How do you think? Officially, they weren't pleased. But they can't say anything when, *officially*, I've never existed in the first place. Besides, I've always been an oddity. Most immortal priests were turned from the Roman church and have far more respect for the Vatican."

Giovanni slapped his friend's shoulder and thanked the waiter, who set down the wine. "You'll be fine. This is good. You're right; it's a new life. I'm excited for you. So, who were you writing a letter to that you needed to hide it?"

Carwyn just grinned and took another drink. "Our friend is still inside with his wife. They look like a lovely couple, if I do say so. In no way does he resemble a minion of Satan."

"The best minions never do." Giovanni turned his eyes toward the large windows of the restaurant where Doctor Paskal Todorov was dining. It hadn't been difficult to track down the chemist or the cosmetics factory, but they had

A FALL OF WATER

decided they needed to question the director to find out precisely what he knew before they destroyed the factory.

"He seems like a nice enough fellow. It's possible he has no idea who he's in business with."

"Considering that it's Livia, it's likely that he's completely unaware. She's never been very forthcoming."

"Particularly with humans."

"True."

Carwyn grimaced. "I'm beginning to feel bad about destroying the factory."

"Start another one and hire him to run it. It's not like you don't have the money."

"I'm not—"

"Don't lie." Giovanni shook his head. "You were always sketchy about that 'vow of poverty' thing. Don't even pretend you don't have the funds tucked away."

Carwyn's only response was a wicked grin. "Now, what kind of vampire would I be if I didn't tuck a bit away?"

"None. So, don't feel bad about the good doctor; you can always give him another job. Most likely, he'll find another on his own anyway."

"Fine."

The two vampires waited. Watched. The chemist ate a leisurely meal with his wife before they saw him finally stand and start toward the door. Carwyn threw a few euros on the table to pay for the wine before he and Giovanni stood and started following.

They allowed the humans to turn down the street leading to their home before they approached. It was late enough that most of the street was quiet, and Giovanni couldn't detect any observers.

"Doctor Todorov?" he called out. The doctor turned, frowning at the two casually dressed men who approached him. "Aren't you Paskal Todorov?"

"Yes? Can I help you?" the doctor replied in English.

Giovanni smiled warmly. "Forgive the intrusion, but I believe we have a mutual acquaintance in Rome."

"From Rome?" The human was clearly confused, but must have sensed no danger from their approach. He stood patiently as Carwyn and Giovanni walked toward them.

Carwyn immediately approached the doctor's wife and held out a hand in greeting. Giovanni held out his hand, as well. "Yes, I believe you know my associate, Lorenzo."

As soon as Giovanni's hand met Todorov's, the amnis flooded over him. He glanced to the left, and Carwyn was quietly engaging the wife in some pleasant chitchat she was completely oblivious to.

"Paskal Todorov, do you know a man named Lorenzo?"

877

"I know a Lorenzo Andros. He works for my company in Rome. He has inspected the factory."

Right on the first question, he thought. Giovanni curled his lip, annoyed that Lorenzo had used his father's name in his business dealings.

"And what are you producing at your factory, Dr. Todorov?"

"It is a cosmetics formula. A serum of some sort. I believe it is intended to combat aging."

"I see—"

"But it is dangerous." A frightened look came to the chemist's eyes, and Giovanni knew that he was tapping into the doctor's unconscious thoughts about the project. Possibly, thoughts he wouldn't even recognize.

"Why do you say it is dangerous?"

"I... I don't know."

"Did Lorenzo say it was dangerous?"

"He is not a trustworthy man."

So, not a minion after all. Giovanni wondered if, confronted with the truth, the doctor would voluntarily shut the factory down. Was it worth taking a chance to keep Livia in the dark about their actions? The minute the factory was destroyed, she would probably be aware that Giovanni was behind it. Could they shut it down without alerting her?

He looked over at Carwyn. "Keep the wife occupied, but don't make it obvious. I'm going to talk to him."

Carwyn nodded and began to ask the doctor's wife about local sightseeing while Giovanni lessened his influence over the chemist. Todorov blinked at him when Giovanni released his hand.

"Yes, Doctor, as I was saying, the health commission has some concerns about this cosmetic serum. And I'm sure you can understand our reluctance to make our concerns public. It's not an immediate health threat, but we do need your cooperation."

"Oh... of course." Todorov still looked confused, but amenable, and Giovanni knew that the doctor's human instincts, even as dull as they were, had picked up some danger from Lorenzo. "But... who did you say you were with?"

"It's a joint inquiry between our two countries. No one wants to make the concerns public as we do our investigation, but it is vital that we control the output."

"Oh... of course. I did understand that the trials had positive results. Were there problems I was unaware of?"

Giovanni thought back to Lucien's story that Carwyn had related on their drive to Bulgaria. "The immediate testing did have positive results, but there are some concerns about long-term use of the product."

"I see, I see." Todorov reeked of worry. "I do hope the commission knows that all proper procedures were followed by our labs. Our chemists are some of the finest, and I would hate if—"

"Your facility is not under scrutiny, Doctor Todorov. We know you manufactured the product in good faith."

The doctor looked sheepish. "In all honesty, the formula... well, it was unusual. But since all the components were botanical in nature—and Rome was very strict about quality—well, it was unusual, but not enough to worry me. Not really. Though..."

"Yes?"

"I did think it odd, Mr...."

"Rossi. Doctor Guiseppe Rossi." He took out his wallet and flipped it open, brushing Todorov's hand to create the illusion of impeccable credentials in the human's mind.

"Of course, Dr. Rossi. I did think it odd that the office in Rome was so insistent on security for the factory. Any time you have employees, there can be theft, but they were most persistent in their measures. I even had to hand count the first shipment to ensure that the product was completely accounted for."

A chill spread over his skin and he heard Carwyn's friendly voice falter.

"What shipment?"

"The first shipment of Elixir. It went out on the trucks last week, Doctor Rossi. It's on its way to Rome right now." Todorov frowned. "I... I thought you knew."

THEY STARED OVER THE BOXES CONTAINING THE BLOOD-RED LIQUID. IT WAS packaged in frosted glass and deluxe, gold-trimmed boxes with ELIXIR stamped on the outside. The small vials held no more than half an ounce. According to Lucien, a few drops was all it took. A few drops to cure a human being of ravaging cancer. A few drops to weaken a three thousand-year-old immortal in a matter of months.

"We destroy it." Giovanni picked up a box, almost cringing just to touch the plain brown cardboard.

"We'll drive out to the country and you can burn it. Can you destroy it fast enough to eliminate flames and ash?"

"There will be ash, but we'll try to contain it."

Carwyn nodded. "And make sure we don't breathe any of the smoke."

"Agreed."

"Thank God they haven't made more than this."

"They made enough for one shipment, Carwyn. A shipment that's headed toward my wife and our friends."

"Do you suppose there's any way it's detectable?"

"I don't know." Suddenly the idea of destroying all the computers seemed less than ideal and he wished he had Dez or Benjamin available to hack into the mysterious technology and find out more about it. He felt sick and desperate. "This is a disaster."

Carwyn bent to help him and they began carting the small stack of brown boxes to the back of the Range Rover. "It's not a disaster. We just need to find the truck."

"And the boxes of Elixir. And make sure none of them went missing. Because that never happens at border crossings, does it?"

"Livia isn't going to produce something she can't detect, Gio. There has to be some way to detect it. Just calm down."

He exploded. "She doesn't know what the hell this does! None of us do! There is some sort of—of poison headed toward my wife and family, and I have no idea what it does or what danger it really poses, Carwyn. Do not tell me to calm down!"

The vampire's blue eyes flared. "Don't pretend you have any more at stake than the rest of us, Gio. We need to get in contact with Rome and let them handle it so we can keep going."

"We need to go after the—"

"Jean and Gavin are still in Rome and those two smugglers know more about tracking down shipments of dodgy goods than we ever will. You're right; we don't know what this does. The most important thing for us to do is find the answers."

Giovanni took a deep breath and nodded. Carwyn was right. "We need to find Arosh and Kato."

"If we find them, then we know what to worry about. If we find them, we find the truth."

They burned the boxes on an empty stretch of road outside the city a few hours before dawn. They stood upwind of the fire, blocking their mouths and watching as the smoke rose from the pit that Carwyn dug. When the flames were finally out, the earth vampire sunk the remnants and covered the ashes with dirt and rocks.

"There. It's gone."

"That bit is, anyway." Giovanni sighed and turned his face west.

The lights of the city glittered in the distance and he could still see smoke rising from the fire at the factory. Hopefully the small fire he'd set would conceal the destruction of the computers and the theft of the boxes and the computer that Dez told them she would try to access. There weren't many computers. Only seven. And they fed into an unassuming tower in Todorov's office. The metal box was swathed in blankets in the back of their vehicle. They would ship it to Rome as soon as they reached Istanbul.

Hopefully, the computer would give Beatrice and Tenzin a better idea of how the formula had been manufactured and what its effects were. They had tracked down the registration of the truck that had taken the small shipment to Rome and sent it to Matt. Giovanni only prayed that his friends could find the truck before it reached Livia.

"Come on, Sparky. We've got to get down the road a bit before dawn."

"What if they can't find the truck, Carwyn?"

"You can't think that way. You just can't. Besides, Jean and Gavin will track it down. When has Gavin ever failed to steal something he really wants?"

"I suppose that's true."

Carwyn slapped him on the shoulder. "Come, my friend. Let them do what they do best, and we'll get on with finding the legendary missing vampires in their mythological fortress in the Caucasus Mountains using only vague directions and landmarks that haven't held the same names for four hundred years. If we're very lucky, Arosh will burn us before Kato pulls the water from our bodies and leaves us shriveled husks of the vampires we once were."

Giovanni nodded. "But we have a letter."

Carwyn turned and walked to the car. "We do. And it better be a damn good one."

Giovanni followed him. "Speaking of letters…"

"I'm not going to tell you who I was writing, so stop asking."

CHAPTER 21

"Yes," Ziri said, "that is the formula that I remember."

Lucien and Dez were sitting at the desk, going over the printouts from the hard drive that Giovanni and Carwyn had sent from Istanbul. Dez had spent the previous week going over the contents with a fine-tooth comb. Since Beatrice still had trouble accessing electronics, the printer had gotten a workout.

Dez had quickly pinpointed the shipping information of the single truck that had taken the first shipment from Bulgaria to Rome. There were only five boxes on the manifest. Apparently, someone hadn't wanted to wait. Jean and Gavin had immediately called contacts in the area, and the truck had been delayed in Serbia. They left the following night, hoping to intercept it before their favors were preempted by whomever Livia had in her pocket.

Ziri was still speaking. "It is amazing to me that they manufactured it so quickly. It took us months to put it together, even after Jabir perfected the formula."

Beatrice perked up from her chair by the fire. "Ziri?"

"Yes?"

"How *did* Jabir perfect it? Did he test it on humans before Fahdil and Kato tried it? What did he do?"

Ziri walked over and sat across from her. Beatrice could feel Lucien and Dez's eyes on them.

"He did test it on humans first. There was no shortage of ailing people in that part of the world, but he only tested it on the sickest of them. The first attempts did little. The human's metabolism destroyed any benefits our blood might have offered. But slowly, there were small improvements. An extra hour

A FALL OF WATER

before the blood was rejected. Then a day. It took over a year, but he finally found the exact formula to keep the human body from rejecting the blood. From there, the results were quite startling. One elderly woman in particular showed an amazing recovery."

"Yeah, I remember reading about her in the journals."

Ziri smiled. "He was always so careful with his language in those. Careful to conceal what we were and what we were doing. I'm very impressed you and your father figured them out."

"I doubt we would have had we not known about vampires already."

"True." Ziri sat back in his chair and stroked his chin in a thoughtful manner. "I do wonder how Livia and Lorenzo were able to interpret them so quickly."

"Gio thinks that there were notes that the monks made that Lorenzo stole when he ransacked the monastery. He said that Fu-Han had made progress."

"That was Zhang's old apprentice?"

"Yes. Giovanni said he had figured it out. Lorenzo must have taken his notes."

"Interesting."

"But Gio also said that Fu-han told him right before he died that there was something Lorenzo would not understand about the elixir."

Ziri cocked his head. "What? What wouldn't he understand?"

Beatrice shook her head. "He didn't say. He just said something about the fifth element. Not even Gio knew what the hell he was talking about. There are only four elements."

Dez piped up. "No, there's not. There's five."

Beatrice's head swung around. Dez was still sitting at the desk, and her eyes were glued to the monitor. Lucien was sitting to her left, studying the screen intently. He turned in his chair to address her.

"Dez is right," Lucien said. "The four elements are more philosophical than scientific. There are consistencies and variations across history. While four elements were named in ancient Western tradition, Aristotle added a fifth, *aether*."

"Aether?"

"The essence. The... *aether*. It's hard to explain. Aristotle described it as that which the heavens were made of. The eternal elements. All earthly elements are, in reality, unstable. They can be changed in many ways. Aether, the essence of the eternal, could not." Lucien smiled. "Call it what you will. The soul. The spark of God. Eternity. Aether is that which does not change."

"That's not science."

Lucien chuckled. "My child, God has existed long before science. He created it, after all."

"The fifth element was more prevalent in the East, Beatrice." Ziri broke in.

"The ancient Babylonians had five elements, the sky being one, which you could relate to the Greek concept of aether."

Lucien continued, "Hindu philosophy and Bön have five elements as well. Bön has always held a fascination for Eastern vampires. Its study is what Tenzin's father is so well known for—well, that and bloodshed. Bön names five elements: fire, earth, wind, water, and space. The philosophy says that everything is related to these five elements. The four earthly elements influence everything about an individual, with the fifth, the space or aether, tying all things together."

"So, there *are* five elements." Beatrice nodded. "Okay, but how does that relate to the elixir of life? What could Fu-han have found?"

Ziri shrugged. "Who knows? The four earthly elements are all that truly pertain to our biology. There are no *aether* vampires. None possess a fifth power."

"What element is the most common?" Dez asked, looking up from the computer. "Just curious. Are there roughly the same number of all the different vampires around?"

Beatrice shook her head. "Not fire. Fire vampires are pretty rare, right Ziri?"

"Yes, I would say that there are roughly the same number of wind and water immortals. Earth vampires are more numerous."

Lucien said, "We do like our big families."

Dez patted Lucien's hand. "That must be why you guys are so easy to hang out with." She laid a hand on her swelling abdomen. "Family oriented."

Lucien watched Dez with a warm gaze. The human and the vampire had bonded over Dez's pregnancy, which was progressing with no complications. Matt had arranged an Italian midwife and hospital for his wife, but Dez also had the benefit of an immortal doctor on call. Lucien had been a healer for thousands of years and had grown very fond of Dez.

"How are you feeling, my dear?" He held a hand out. "May I?"

"Of course!"

Lucien placed a hand on Dez's stomach. Beatrice felt her fangs descend involuntarily and tried not to growl.

"Relax, Beatrice." Lucien glanced over his shoulder. "I'm not going to hurt her."

She took a deep breath. "I don't know why that keeps happening. You're her doctor, for goodness sake. I'm so sorry."

Ziri spoke. "It's instinct. It's natural for you because you consider Dez under your aegis. It's nothing to be concerned about. It just means that you will protect her and the baby."

"Aw." Dez winked at her. "I knew you were gonna be the best auntie."

Lucien smiled. "Have you felt the quickening?"

"Huh?"

"The baby. Have you felt the baby move?"

"Oh, yeah! Just a little. It kinda feels like bubbles."

"You'll feel more and more. He's very active."

Dez sat up straight. "It's a boy?"

"I'm not sure," Lucien said with a smile. "Extra strong senses, remember? No vampire ultrasound. And I can't smell the little one. He or she is very well protected in there." Lucien gave one last pat to Dez's little rounded belly. "Aren't you, *bebe*? Stay nice and snug until it's your time."

Dez melted. "Lucien, you are a big vampire sweetheart."

"Please don't let that get out. Well, you can tell my mother. She would laugh." He winked. "And this vampire sweetheart is exhausted, I better—"

Deirdre blew through the door in her typical, abrupt way. "I need to leave," she stated.

Beatrice sat up straight. "Everything all right?"

The redheaded vampire nodded. "Everything is fine. But there is nothing more I can do here. I need to return to my family."

"Oh." Dez stood and walked toward her. "I'm going to miss you!"

Lucien said, "You need to leave tonight?"

She nodded as she embraced Dez. "Matt has been looking for a ship that could carry me back. There is one leaving out of Genoa in the morning, but I'll need to leave tonight. Soon."

Beatrice glanced around the room. Ziri was unmoved. Dez was disappointed, but Lucien looked... lost.

"Deirdre," he said.

Deirdre's eyes swung toward him and she held out a hand. "Lucien."

And Beatrice suddenly recognized the anguish in his voice. The two friends had known each other for hundreds of years. Lucien and Deirdre's husband had been the closest of friends and colleagues. And Lucien didn't think he would see her again.

Deirdre walked over and embraced him. "You must not think this way, my friend. You must not."

"I do not know if I will see you again in this life."

Blood tears touched Deirdre's stoic face as Lucien enfolded her in his long arms. "Do not make me say good-bye to another loved one, Lucien. Whatever this is—"

"It is not goodbye. Not really, Deirdre. You and I both know this."

Beatrice just tried to hold herself together. At times, it was easy to see the mystery of Geber's manuscript as academic. It was a research project. A problem to be solved.

But it wasn't.

She watched the friends say good-bye, and her mind flashed back to her father's anguished face as he faced off against Lorenzo on the banks of the Nine-bend River. The scattered bodies of the monks in the Wuyi Mountains. The memory of the woman before her, wailing on the ground as she mourned the loss of her mate.

It would never be just academic.

The memories of loss were still fresh as Beatrice made the journey to Castello Furio later that night. Deirdre had left for Genoa. Dez and Matt had finally collapsed in exhaustion. They were both working day and night, trying to help solve the mystery and keep track of Ben while Giovanni was gone. Lucien had also taken to his bedroom. He'd had a bad spell after Deirdre left and drifted in a kind of fugue state he couldn't seem to wake from. It was happening more and more. Ziri and Beatrice had helped him to bed before Ziri flew ahead of her.

The last place in the world she wanted to be was Livia's castle, but there was a party that night in honor of the Chinese delegation that Tenzin told her she needed to be present for. After all, she had been named a scribe of Penglai, so she gritted her teeth, took a quick drink from the clueless driver, and headed out of Rome.

As they pulled up to the castle, she could see the glittering lights in the olive trees and the bevy of guards that only seemed to grow with each passing week. Whatever Livia was planning, she was gathering more and more guards. Beatrice debated, but left her shuang gou in the back of the car, tucking a few daggers into her boots, and another in her waistband before she walked through the gates.

The grounds were glittering with immortals and humans dressed in festive red outfits in honor of the Eastern guests. Beatrice was wearing her uniform of black jeans and a T-shirt. She still enjoyed flouting Livia's snobbish fashion sense. Plus, it was easier to hide knives in jeans and a T-shirt than a cocktail dress.

"Beatrice!" Donatella Conti called her name from across the lawn. Beatrice nodded and walked over. In the weeks since she and Emil had made their tentative alliance, Donatella had proven invaluable. Beatrice knew now that the seemingly frivolous manner of the immortal hid a very keen mind and a vicious loyalty to her husband and his interests. Donatella had cultivated Beatrice as her new pet in the Roman court, and most of Beatrice's communications to Emil were channeled through her.

"What are you wearing, my friend? What are you doing to me? Jeans?"

"I'm just not into dresses, Donatella." The Roman vampire leaned over and kissed her cheeks in greeting while Beatrice whispered, "The better to hide weapons, my dear."

"Oh, Beatrice." Donatella winked. "You just have to use your imagination." Scanning the woman's skin-tight designer gown, Beatrice had to really use her imagination to figure out where Donatella could be hiding anything.

"So, what's the gossip tonight?"

"Oh, she's saying she has some big announcement she wants to make."

"The Chinese delegation still playing nice with her?"

"As far as she knows, yes." Beatrice had learned through Tenzin that the small trade group, which was headed by Elder Lu's son, may have been there for business reasons, but quietly, they were supporting Beatrice and Giovanni's plan to destabilize Livia's power base. The Roman aristocrat had finally pissed off enough of the wrong people.

"Cool. We need to keep her happy until we hear more from Gio and Carwyn."

They strolled through the crowds arm in arm, whispering to each other. "Any news?"

Beatrice and Tenzin had told no one outside of their small circle where Giovanni and Carwyn were headed. And no one other than their closest allies really knew who they were looking for.

"We received some information from the factory in Bulgaria."

"Oh?"

"Which is shut down, by the way."

"Good to know."

"There was one shipment, which our sources do say contained a successful sample of the product."

"Coming to Rome?"

"Headed here, but hopefully it will be detained."

"Excellent."

"I'll keep you informed, but in the meantime—"

"Ladies."

Donatella and Beatrice both turned to look at the interruption.

The gall.

Lorenzo leaned casually against a stone pillar, watching them and holding two flutes of champagne. He held them both out. Donatella took one, but Beatrice only glared.

"Donatella, you are looking delicious this evening."

"Oh, Lorenzo." She let out a tinkling laugh. "You are too kind. And stupid. You are very, very stupid."

The vampire only lifted a blond eyebrow. "Oh?"

Donatella quickly covered the venom in her voice with a layer of honey. "To not have noticed my friend, of course! My beauty is nothing to her bold style. I am learning from our young American friend. She is so fearless."

When Lorenzo opened his mouth, Beatrice could see his fangs descended behind his full lips. "I'm well aware of Miss De Novo's fearlessness. She is a rare treasure, indeed."

"Your sire is a lucky man, Lorenzo."

That was bold. The disappearance of Giovanni Vecchio was the giant, blood-red elephant at all of Livia's parties. It seemed by mutual unspoken agreement that no one spoke of it. His name was not even mentioned except behind closed doors.

Or by his wife, of course.

She narrowed her eyes at the blond murderer who taunted her with his presence. "Oh, Lorenzo has always been jealous of Giovanni, haven't you, blondie? Giovanni's always had more class. More power. More... well, just more." She let a smile cross her lips.

"Are you sure of that? After all, you've never really explored your options, have you?"

"My grandma told me I don't need to taste piss to know I'm drinking wine."

Lorenzo only offered her a sympathetic look. "How is your family, Beatrice? I was so sorry to hear about Stephen's disappearance. Tragic."

The rage burst forth. "You fucking bastard! You know—" She cut herself off when she felt Donatella's arm restraining her.

"Come, my friend, let us find more pleasant company. I have a companion with me who would be to your liking, I think. His blood is very rich."

Beatrice relented at Donatella's touch. Lorenzo lifted his glass of champagne in a silent toast. As he brought it to his lips, Beatrice reached out and forced the liquid in the glass to expand, shattering the champagne flute at Lorenzo's lips and opening a small cut at the corner of his mouth. He smiled and reached up with an elegant finger, swiping at the cut and holding the finger out to her.

"Care for a taste?"

She turned her back on him and walked away.

The night wore on, and she managed to find Tenzin, who was crouched on a corner of one of the towers, pouting.

"Tenzin, come down."

The small wind vampire glared at her and floated to the ground.

"If I don't kill something soon, I'm going to go crazy."

"I thought you were supposed to be the patient one."

"I hate all this shit."

"You think I don't?"

The two friends leaned against the stone tower and watched the crowd, conscious of the numerous eyes that followed them constantly.

Tenzin said, "How much longer are we going to have to drag this out? I'm bored."

"Well, you're not the one trying to avoid..." She looked around and lowered her voice. "Further complications, so to speak."

Tenzin switched to Mandarin, which Beatrice could speak passably well.

A FALL OF WATER

"Would killing everyone really be that bad? I'm not saying it wouldn't be a pain in the ass to deal with the fallout, but at least you'd have some fun in the meantime."

"We're not really in the mood to rule a city, Tenzin."

"It would just be for a few hundred years."

"Do you know how crazy that sounds to my ears?"

"You'll get used to it, my girl."

Beatrice sighed. "Tenzin…"

"I know. I know."

They watched the party for a few more minutes, and Beatrice detected a strange energy building among the crowd.

"Tenzin, something—"

"I know. I feel it, too."

They both walked closer. There were murmurs of excitement. Whispers flew around and a strange buzz of energy enervated the immortals gathered. She felt the approach of a particularly strong energy signature and turned to see Emil Conti approaching her with Donatella hanging on his arm.

"Beatrice."

"What's happening, Emil?"

"You young people with your slang."

"No, really. What is *happening*?"

He blinked. "Oh. I believe our fair patroness has an announcement of some kind. I'm bubbling with excitement, can't you tell?"

Beatrice's eyes widened. "Not…"

Emil only cocked a lazy eyebrow, and Donatella smirked.

Livia mounted the stairs of a small stage where a string orchestra had been playing and tapped on her champagne flute to gather everyone's attention. It was completely unnecessary; the whole party was riveted to her before she even reached the top of the stairs. She was glowing with excitement when she started to speak.

"My friends, we are joined tonight by esteemed guests. We welcome them to the Eternal City. The Immortal City. Rome has long been a center of culture and learning. Of sophistication and enlightenment. I am happy to announce tonight that another achievement has been added to her crown."

"Pompous bitch," Tenzin muttered.

"As most of you know, I have been a patroness of the human sciences for hundreds of years. For in the prosperity of the human world, we find our own continued success. I am happy to announce that an ancient secret, a *stunning* discovery has, this past year, been recovered from the lost library of the great immortal, Niccolo Andros. It is in his honor that I announce a mystery of the ages has been solved. Long have humans and immortals sought the elixir of life. The unique formula that would offer our human friends the longevity and health that we immortals enjoy. Now, we have accomplished this." A buzz began to build among the crowd. "And in doing so, an even greater achievement has been made."

"She's going to do it." Beatrice shook her head. "She's going to announce—"

"My scientists have discovered not only the elixir of life, but the cure to bloodlust, as well." The buzzing stopped, and an eerie silence fell over the castle grounds as Livia continued. "And it will be available to all of you. This secret is a secret no longer. It belongs to us." Beatrice saw Livia's eyes light up. "It belongs to the world!"

The silence lasted only as long as it took for the first burst of applause to erupt from the excited crowd. It had to have been the humans in attendance who started it, Beatrice thought. Vampires weren't usually an enthusiastic crowd. But soon, everyone around them, including the immortals, was applauding and moving toward the stage. Livia was enveloped by vampires and humans vying for her attention.

Beatrice and Tenzin exchanged a grim look, and Emil said quietly, "Look how they gather around her now."

"Why?" she asked. "All of these vampires are blood drinkers from what I've seen. Why is it so important to find a cure for bloodlust? Are they all humanitarians? They can't all care about the good of mankind *that* much."

Donatella was the one who answered. "They're not being altruistic, Beatrice. And most of them enjoy blood as much as we do. But they *need* it. They don't just choose to drink, they *have* to. It controls us. Even the oldest vampire is a slave to hunger in the end. They all clamor for Livia's favor, but it's not a cure they are seeking. They crave control, and she offers it. So more will come." Donatella looked at Beatrice with a hard stare. "*Many* more will come."

CHAPTER 22

Svaneti, Georgia
Caucasus Mountains

Giovanni nodded at the old woman who refilled his wine glass and smiled at the young woman who set down the bread. The women left the room, retreating into the kitchen to whisper quietly about the foreign visitors and leaving the two vampires alone with the three humans gathered in the dark room. Giovanni's attention was drawn to the head of the family and leader of the small village in a remote mountain valley in Northern Georgia.

The man was seated in a richly decorated chair. Giovanni guessed that it was hundreds of years old, but had been lovingly oiled and tended, a mark of pride for the small village and the man who sat upon it that night. The head of the village, a Svan in his early fifties, was dressed in the curious blend of ancient and modern typical in the mountains. His jacket sported an American logo, but his head was topped by the grey felt hat typical of all men of the region high in the Caucasus Mountains. A long dagger hung at his belt and an icon of Saint George graced the wall. The cold wind whistled around the old house, and Giovanni was grateful not to be out in the wind, at least for a little while.

Carwyn was still exchanging stories with the man, laughing over ribald jokes in Russian, since neither of them spoke Georgian or the strange, old language of the Svans. Giovanni's Russian was passable, but not nearly as good as the priest's, so he sat back and listened.

"This region you speak of," the human said. "No one goes there." He waved a dismissive hand. "You want hiking or climbing, I will have my son, Otar, show you to some of the lower trails. It is too cold in that part of the mountains anyway."

Carwyn steered the conversation back toward the mountain pass they were now almost certain led to the forgotten fortress of Arosh that Saba had mentioned in her letters to Ziri. It had been first dark when Giovanni and Carwyn entered the village. They had taken shelter in a cave the earth vampire had carved out at dawn the day before. The tiny town was nestled at the base of several passes. They knew that Arosh's fortress lay in the mountains, but they weren't certain through which of the three gorges they needed to pass to get there.

Carwyn spoke. "This mountain we speak of is unique. And we will not need a guide for the hike. We ask only your permission to climb there and direction to the proper trail."

"Your horses will not make the journey this late in the year," the man continued to protest, as Giovanni's eyes scanned the room. The house was not a wealthy one, but the art and icons on the walls gave testament to the man's position of authority in the community. His son stood at the doorway, watching the two foreigners with cautious eyes.

"I appreciate your concern." Carwyn nodded respectfully. "But we must go there. It was recommended to us by a very dear friend. A climbing partner who insisted we must see the vistas from the peak."

The man's eyes narrowed. "I do not know who you might speak of. That mountain is not a good place; I am telling you, no one travels there."

Giovanni broke in. "Why? Why doesn't anyone go there?"

The Svan hesitated, glancing between Giovanni and Carwyn. "Bandits. There are bandits in that part of the mountains."

The man's son broke into the conversation, murmuring in their own tongue, as he and his father seemed to have a low-voiced debate. Finally, the father raised his hand and his son fell quiet. "If you want to go there, I will not stop you. But I must know that no one will come looking for you and causing us trouble."

Giovanni said, "No one will come after us. We do not wish to bring trouble to your home."

The older man nodded and sat back in his chair. "Otar will take you as far as the base of the trail, but that is all. He will not accompany you up the mountain."

Carwyn's eyes darted toward Giovanni's, and he nodded. Carwyn said, "That is more than we ask; we appreciate your hospitality."

"Tell me again," Giovanni said. "Why do you not want us to go there?"

Otar spoke from behind them, surprising Giovanni when he spoke in English. "That mountain is cursed. No one goes there. Or at least, no one comes back."

"Cursed by what?"

The younger man shrugged. "The old people tell legends. And sometimes, the girls disappear if they go too close."

"Only the girls?" Carwyn asked.

The young man was about to speak, but his father interrupted. "There are still robbers in the hills. It is better now than it was, but... we keep our children close to the village. Especially at night."

Giovanni turned to the father. "Tell me about the legends."

"They are nonsense."

He smiled. "I am curious. I am a literature professor in Italy. I love stories and myths."

The father shrugged. "The old people say that an angel appeared to Queen Tamar hundreds of years ago when she visited the mountains. He shone like fire and fell in love with our queen, so she gave him this mountain and let him build a stone tower. He stayed in the tower when she returned to the lowlands and her castle, but she returned here every summer to visit him. Many years passed in peace, but when the messengers came to the mountains, telling the people that the queen had died in her castle, the mountain she had given the angel was engulfed in flames. All the trees burned and none grew again. The angel continued to live there, but he grew angry with the Svan people. Hundreds of years passed, and the village that once thrived in the gorge beneath was deserted. Now, no one goes there. It is cursed."

An angel of fire.

Giovanni wondered what Arosh would think of the legend. He wondered if he would even get to ask or whether these dark hours in the small village would be his last before he was killed by the legendary immortal.

"You will stay in my son's house tonight, my friends. You may leave in the morning for your trek."

Carwyn smiled and demurred. "No, no. We must travel at night. My friend's skin condition makes it necessary to travel at night. And we only need your son to point us toward the trailhead. We will be happy to find our own way."

Giovanni was glad he was so pale. The men had been suspicious of his 'sunlight allergy,' but had been more than happy to take the money for their hospitality without too many questions. As they made their way out of the small home and toward the horses they had ridden into the remote village, Carwyn and Giovanni were careful to shake hands with the men, ensuring their cooperation through subtle amnis and removing any suspicion from their minds.

"You are sure you want to go there?" Otar asked Giovanni as he saddled his packhorse.

"Yes, very sure."

"I'm not sure what you're looking for, but if it's treasure, I don't think you will find any in those mountains."

"Do people come looking for treasure?"

The young man's eyes held a playful kind of mischief. "Many things have been hidden in these mountains over the years. Often, they are found. More often, they are not."

Giovanni's mouth lifted at the corner, wondering what treasure hunters had been disappointed. In the old man's house alone, he spotted several icons that any museum in Western Europe would love to have in their collection. Here, they hung on the walls, watching over humble families and simple meals.

"Truly, my friend"—Giovanni slapped the young man on the shoulder—"you must not worry about us. We are not here to look for anything that might bring harm to your family."

"I'm not worried about my family, but I'll be surprised if I see *you* again."

Carwyn left the small house with a bottle of wine and a wrapped package that smelled like the flat bread they had eaten earlier. An old woman patted the vampire's rough cheek and waved at them from the glowing door of the kitchen as they mounted their horses and followed the young man up to the trailhead.

"Leave it to you to think of your stomach, Carwyn." Giovanni spoke in Latin, hoping the young man didn't have any other surprises.

The vampire grinned. "If it's my last night on earth, and I'm not in the company of a beautiful woman, then wine is the next best choice. Well, beer would be better, but wine will do."

Giovanni chuckled and followed the soft padding of the horse in front of them. Otar led them up the western trail and into the hills. After a few miles, the young man stopped.

"This is as far as I will go with you. Keep to this trail and when you get to the dead tree line, you'll know you're at the right mountain. It will rise on the west side of the trail. Trust me; you won't miss it. I have been there only once. It was during the daytime, when it is safe."

Giovanni said, "I thought you said that no one went there."

The young man smiled. "Only brave little boys and unhappy girls go to this mountain. The boys go during the day. The girls, at night. The boys we see again."

Giovanni's eyes sought Carwyn's. What treachery was Arosh involved in? Was he feasting from the women of this small, mountain town?

Carwyn said, "Thank you, Otar."

The young man nodded and turned his horse around. "Good luck finding whatever you're after!"

"Thank you."

Giovanni and Carwyn continued up the trail. It became narrower, and thick stands of forest rose on either side. Despite the peaceful surroundings, Giovanni could feel the steady thrum of energy that grew stronger the farther they traveled up the mountain.

"Do you feel it?"

A FALL OF WATER

Carwyn nodded. "Oh yes. These hills are... different."

Eventually, the two vampires dismounted their horses, who were quickly becoming agitated by the crackling energy that permeated the air. Giovanni and Carwyn took their packs and strapped them on their backs before they turned the horses and shooed them away. The animals sped down the trail, and the two friends continued in silence until Carwyn started singing.

Giovanni smirked. "Really, Father? I'm trying not to think about the fact that I may never see my wife or family again, and you start a drinking song?"

"Well, it's no use meeting somewhat certain death in a bad mood, is it?"

"I suppose you may have a point."

"And why are you so certain that he's going to kill us, Gio? You've become so cynical in your old age."

"I've always been cynical. And tell me, my friend, have you ever seen two male fire vampires in the same room? The same building? The same city, for that matter?"

"Does Lan Caihe count?"

Giovanni snorted, thinking of the young, androgynous fire vampire of Penglai. "No, Lan doesn't count."

"Well then... no." His mouth twisted. "That's odd. I've never thought about it before. I haven't. Not that I know many fire vampires at all."

"There's a reason for that."

"Don't get along?"

"We tend to kill each other on sight. It's a very hard instinct to quell. Females do far better than males."

"Good to know." Carwyn paused, then took a long drink of the wine the old woman had given him before passing it to Giovanni. "Drink up."

Giovanni grabbed the bottle and took a drink. It didn't taste a fraction as sweet as his wife's mouth, but he tried not to think about that. He tried not to think about Beatrice at all. Otherwise, he'd be too tempted to turn himself around and abandon the whole crazy plan. The farther they traveled, the heavier the air seemed to grow. If he was human, he doubted he could have stood under the pressure. The air was thick with amnis when they spotted the first charred trees.

Otar had been right; there was no mistaking this mountain. Unlike the surrounding hills, the slope that rose up from the gorge was a vast, wasted ruin. Rocks tumbled down and sharp spires of blackened conifer trunks dotted the landscape that glowed grey under the full moon.

"Think this is it?"

Giovanni took his foot off the trail and stepped up. As soon as he touched the base of the mountain he caught a whiff of almond smoke. The unmistakable scent of another male fire vampire filled his nostrils, and a certain dread fell over him. "This is it."

They went slowly, not wanting to surprise whatever presence dwelled at the top of the mountain. Even Carwyn, who was usually at home in remote hills, seemed grim. Giovanni heard him praying under his breath as they climbed.

"Father?"

"Didn't I tell you to stop calling me that?"

Giovanni turned to him and held out a hand. "Thank you. For everything."

He saw Carwyn's eyes glow bright in the moonlight, and his voice was hoarse when he grasped Giovanni's hand. "Don't be so morbid, Sparky."

Just then, a rushing sound filled the air. The wind whipped by as if churned by some great flying beast. They turned, but nothing showed itself in the night. Giovanni took a deep breath and continued their silent climb.

They had just climbed over a scarred knoll when they heard the rushing wind again. This time, it was closer. Then, he felt a great rush of wind, as if the air around him was being sucked up toward the summit of the mountain. His heart faltered for a moment.

"Carwyn, duck."

They both dropped to the rocks before the wave of scarlet fire swept down the mountain. Carwyn's amnis pushed up, and a wall of rock rose before them. They pressed against it as the flames rolled down the slope. Giovanni could even feel the rock they sheltered behind begin to heat, and he struggled to rein in his own instinctive reaction. The fire bloomed on his skin and burned away his shirt and coat. His fangs ran out, but he bit his lip and tried to control himself.

"Carwyn?"

"Yes?"

"I know you're not, strictly speaking, a priest anymore—"

"Trust me when I say I'm rethinking that decision just now!"

"Pray anyway."

The flames halted for a minute and Giovanni stepped out from behind their earthen shield, the blue flames swirling along his skin, but contained for the moment.

"Arosh!" he called.

He felt the slow suck of air again, and he darted back behind the rock as the flames swept down the mountain again. They were slower this time, creeping and testing, and Carwyn rolled the rocks and earth up around them to smother the flames before they reached their feet.

A whispering Persian voice came on the wind. "Who seeks Arosh?"

Giovanni took a deep breath and answered. "I am Giovanni, son of Nikolaos Andreas, sired by Kato of Minos."

The flames were no longer testing. They came in furious waves. Carwyn roared as one curled up his leg. He sank his foot in the rock to kill the burning tendril.

"I don't think that helped much, Sparky!"

"Apparently, I'm not the only one who hated my father."

The flames halted again, so Giovanni tried another name. "We have been sent by Ziri, the Numidian. We come as friends!"

The deep voice came again, closer this time. "I have no quarrel with the holy man. Tell Saba's son to depart from this place. I have no wish to anger her or the immortal's god. But the son of Andreas is mine."

Carwyn looked confused. "Saba's son?"

"He must mean because you're an earth vampire. If you want to go, go."

Carwyn reached into his coat and pulled out the wine bottle, uncorking it and taking a long drink. "Tempting, but no."

Giovanni's heart was racing and he could no longer contain his own flames. He could feel them rushing over his body, and his heavy canvas pants were burning at the cuffs. "He's going to kill us."

Carwyn nodded. "That seems to be more likely by the moment, yes. I wonder if it would help if he knew you killed your sire."

Giovanni swallowed the growl that wanted to leap from his throat when he felt the heavy amnis press around them. He quelled the flames as much as he could before he stepped out from behind their rocky shelter, but the blue fire swirled as he held his arms out. He threw out a burst of flame when he saw the spear of fire heading toward him.

The battling flames met and burst high into the night sky, flooding the rocky slope with red light. Then they stopped, and a great roar erupted from the top of the mountain, as Giovanni's fire leapt forward. He fought the instinct telling him to strike back and called on every ounce of self-control as he forced himself to pull back. Then he stood bare and smoking on the rugged cliffs as he cried out:

"I am Giovanni Vecchio, murderer of my sire, Nikolaos Andreas! I am sent from Ziri, seeking his friends Arosh and Kato. I ask for an audience with the great kings. I mean *no harm* upon this mountain or the immortals here!"

A gaping silence followed his pronouncement. He could hear Carwyn's soft prayers coming from behind him and suddenly, Giovanni heard footsteps.

Emerging from the smoke, the ancient fire vampire approached, his black eyes raking Giovanni's blue fire and his amnis sparking in the air around him. Red flames licked along his ruddy brown skin, and long, black hair flew out behind him. His regal forehead needed no crown to speak its authority, and mysterious symbols were tattooed on the rise of his cheekbones. He wore brown leather leggings, but nothing else except an angry glare. He came to a halt a few meters above Giovanni, hands fisted on his hips as he examined the younger immortal in front of him.

"Did you really kill Andreas?"

Giovanni took a deep, calming breath and pulled his fire back further. "Yes."

The vampire arched a black eyebrow. "And Ziri sent you?"

He took a deep breath and nodded. "Are you Arosh?"

Giovanni felt a fluttering wind behind him, and a vampire came to light behind the ancient one. The silent immortal crouched down and eyed him with a feral gaze. The fire vampire reached down and petted the wind vampire's head as he would a beloved pet, and he calmed. Then the vampire looked at Giovanni, and his mouth turned up at the corner.

"Some have called me Arosh, but I am known by many names."

"I seek Arosh, ancient king of the East, friend of Ziri of Numidia, and friend of Geber, the alchemist."

There was a flicker in the old one's eyes. "Geber, you say?"

"Are you the Arosh I seek?"

"I am." Arosh craned his neck to look over Giovanni's shoulder. "You may come out, holy man."

Giovanni heard Carwyn call out, "Is the posturing done?"

Arosh looked amused. "Yes, for now."

"Good." Giovanni heard Carwyn stride toward them, packs clutched in his hands and wine tucked under his arm. "And, strictly speaking, I'm not a holy man anymore. But I do have wine."

A smile broke over Arosh's fearsome face. "Wine, my friend, is always welcome. I think I will like you. What is your name?"

"Carwyn ap Bryn. Son of Maelona of Gwynedd, daughter of Brennus the Celt."

"You are well met, Carwyn ap Bryn. And you, Giovanni Vecchio, if you are who you both say. Come with me, my son will follow us." He motioned to the wind vampire, who took to the air and circled above them. "I hope you brought no men with you," Arosh said, "or Samson will kill them."

Carwyn and Giovanni exchanged a cautious look. "We are alone."

"Good. He doesn't harm the girls, but he's been trained to kill the men."

"Understood. It's just us."

They walked up the mountain, their host skipping over rocks and rubble as he climbed. Arosh made no pretense of human speed, so they didn't either. As they crested the summit, Giovanni could see a house in the distance. As they approached, they were met with a square tower surrounded by a lavish estate. Lush trees surrounded the home, and Giovanni could hear laughter and music coming from inside. The grounds were lit with torches and gravel paths ran through neat gardens. He could hear a fountain burbling somewhere and a murmur of female voices.

Their host yelled out, "Nothing to fear, my jewels."

Suddenly, a bevy of women poured out of the fortress, tumbling and laughing over each other in their rush to greet Arosh. They gathered around him, nubile teenagers and lush women of all ages, all stroking his arms and hair as he walked into the house. He pulled them along, kissing their eager mouths and running his fingers through their hair as they made their way into the glowing home.

Giovanni and Carwyn both stood, gaping at the vicious fire vampire surrounded by the crowd of women. Samson, the silent wind vampire, landed behind them, cocking his head when they stared. He held out a hand and motioned them toward the house. They followed cautiously, and Giovanni's eyes roamed the lavish house and the girls who came out to greet them, grabbing their hands to lead them into the house with cheerful smiles.

"Gio?"

"I'm as confused as you are, Father."

"Why do I feel like we just found the vampire version of the Playboy Mansion?"

"Because I'm fairly sure we did."

CHAPTER 23

"Wow, look. It's another priceless and culturally significant work of art."

"Stop with your gushing enthusiasm. It's embarrassing to walk next to you."

"You're the one letting yourself go."

Dez turned and slapped Ben's shoulder as they strolled through the Galleria Borghese.

"Shut up, you brat. I'm pregnant."

"You may blame the baby, Dez, but I'm pretty sure the gelato has something to do with it, too."

He laughed and ducked away as she swung her purse at him. The gallery was mostly deserted that Thursday afternoon, the summer crowds had dissipated to nothing, and the damp weather was making their usual stroll through the villa gardens less than attractive, so they had decided to take in the collection of paintings.

"I'm kidding! Sheesh, I'm kidding. You know you're gorgeous. I'd still steal you from Matt if I thought I could get away with it." Ben winked and threw an arm around her slender shoulders as she pretended to pout.

"You're mean, Benjamin Vecchio."

"Yeah, but I'm cute, too." He kissed the top of her head as they continued to walk. "And you really are beautiful."

The smile spread across her face as she beamed.

"Are you missing school?"

He snorted. "What do you think?"

She laughed a little. "Are you missing your girlfriends?"

A FALL OF WATER

"Well, probably not as much as I should be. You know what I really miss?"

"Basketball?"

"Besides basketball, that's a given."

"What?"

"Getting my license." He groaned. "I can't believe I'm finally sixteen and in a foreign country where I can't even drive."

"Aw, Benny." She hugged his waist a little. "Maybe Gio will get you a Ferrari for all your hard work."

"Oh, that's *so* likely! Why don't you suggest that to him when he gets back?"

They both fell silent after that. It was a subject they tried not to bring up. After the last communication from Istanbul, no one had heard from his uncle or Carwyn in over three weeks. Ben's world felt like it was balanced on a very thin edge. He could only imagine how Beatrice felt.

"I will," Dez said quietly. "As soon as he's back, I'll tell him how helpful you've been. You're a first-rate hacker."

"Shhh. Don't tell B that I'm better than her now. It'll hurt her feelings."

"Your secret is safe with me."

Dez and Ben had spent weeks sifting through all the information on the hard drive from the Bulgarian plant. Then they'd systematically been going through all the public records of Livia's companies. It was a good thing that Italian seemed to come so easily to Ben. Between his knowledge of Spanish, which he'd taught himself to read as a child, and his Latin education with Giovanni, he had picked up a working knowledge of Italian within weeks of arriving in Rome. In the six months they'd been there, his fluency had only grown. He and Dez had been a vital part of discovering Livia's holdings and assets. They were still tracing the money that had funded the cosmetics factory, but so far, the Roman noblewoman seemed to be the only immortal with a concrete tie to the place, which was both frustrating and reassuring.

"You know," he said. "I was thinking about that German corporation we found that she funneled money through last April, if we could—"

"Hey, this is supposed to be our non-work time, mister."

"I know, I'm just..."

"What?"

He stopped in front of what looked like a Renaissance era oil painting on wood. "Bored," he said. "I'm really, *really* bored."

"I know the computer work isn't exactly the most thrilling, but—"

"Maybe if Matt would let me, you know, help with some other stuff."

Dez cocked a skeptical eyebrow in his direction. "Ben, not even *I* know most of what Matt does. He gets information in... slightly less orthodox ways, you know? I don't think you want to get mixed up in any of that."

But he did. He stared at the painting of the men carrying the body of Jesus to his tomb. He glanced at the small plaque. Rafael. Then he looked more closely at the painting.

"Hey, Dez?" He tilted his head to the side and leaned forward. "Is that..."

Her eyes were narrowed at the painting, too. "Looks kind of like..."

"Emil Conti?"

"That's what I was thinking, too."

They exchanged a glance and stepped back.

"Dez, our lives are really weird."

"And you're bored anyway."

"What can I say? I have a high tolerance for weirdness."

They had detoured down a street near the train station to check out a bookstore that catered to English speaking tourists later that afternoon. Both were sorting through their finds when the scooter almost knocked Dez over.

"Hey!" Ben shouted at the driver in Italian. "Watch where you're going!" The driver didn't turn around or even notice them. Ben turned back to Dez. "You okay?"

She was staring at the retreating man on the scooter with a frown on her face. "Yeah... yeah, I'm fine."

"What's the look?"

"That driver."

"What about him? He was an asshole." Ben took the bag from her hand and helped her back onto the narrow sidewalk.

"No, not the driver, exactly. The uniform. I recognize—that's the service she uses!"

"What?" Ben shook his head and wondered how fast they could leave the somewhat rough streets of the Termini neighborhood. "Who?"

"Livia. I've been wondering—you know how Gio and Carwyn joke about how she'll only send stuff by uniformed messenger? Well, it's kind of true. Back when they were getting invitations and stuff from her—when we first got here—I noticed that they never came in the mail. They always came by delivery. Even that crazy dress she sent for B, it was the same uniform that guy had. That must be the company she uses."

Ben looked around, scanning the shops along the Via Marsala and wondering how fast they could walk back to the house. Even though the area was improving, Dez was still dressed far too nicely to go unnoticed by the dark, familiar eyes of the pickpockets and thieves that trolled the neighborhood. He looked around and wondered if he should just call for a cab.

"Let's go check out the shop!"

His head jerked around. "What?"

"The shop! Look." She pointed down the street. "I can see those same scooters, a whole bunch of them, down there in front of that shop. Let's just go hang out for a while. If we watch, maybe we'll recognize someone. Maybe she uses the same couriers and stuff. It sounds like something she'd do."

He felt a nervous twinge in the bottom of his stomach. "Dez, I don't really think—"

"Come on." She tugged his arm. "We're just going to go watch it for a while. Didn't you say you were bored?"

He was, but watching a messenger service that was used by Livia, all while Dez was with him, wasn't exactly what he had in mind. She was already walking toward the shop.

"Dez!"

She didn't turn around, and Ben had to hustle to catch up with the petite blonde, all the while cutting his eyes at the men who watched her as she passed. He strode quickly to catch up with her, but refused to run. Dez was already attracting too much attention. Finally, his long legs reached her and he pulled her arm, tucking her a little behind him while he slipped his hand in his pocket and hooked a finger in his waistband, flicking the handle of the knife he carried. He saw a scrawny thief's eyes dart to his, then down to his hand before he turned away, looking for an easier mark.

"Let's just walk a little slower, okay? Try not to shout, 'I'm a rich tourist' at the top of your lungs."

She just looked confused. "I wasn't saying anything."

"Yes, you were."

He took her arm and they walked closer to the shop. A group of men sat in chairs outside as young couriers darted in and out of the storefront. Judging from their posture, Ben thought they wore weapons. He sighed and looked farther up the street, spotting a small café that looked like it catered to backpackers. It had an outdoor seating area and a few tourists were sitting around, drinking coffee.

"Dez, if you're determined to watch the place, let's go up here."

"Where?"

"That café."

She squinted. "We won't be able to see much from—"

"We'll see enough."

The tension in his stomach was growing as they walked opposite the shop. Ben tried to distract her, but he could tell the men in front of the shop had noticed Dez's eyes on them. Still, he didn't want to draw more attention to either of them by telling her to not be so obviously curious. They took a seat at one of the small tables and Ben asked Dez to go grab two drinks.

"Big ones. American coffees so we'll be here a while."

"Okay!" She was so damn cheerful it almost killed him. He sat down in the chair that had the best angle to observe the shop. It seemed to do a brisk business, and he could hear the phone ringing from inside all the way up the narrow street. The men in front glanced over at them a few times before they returned to their coffees and papers. A few of them talked on cell phones and their eyes darted around the street. Dez finally came out carrying a plain, black coffee for him and some sweet concoction for herself. He wondered if she'd had to instruct the barista how to make the drink. No doubt she had, by the friendly wave she gave someone through the window.

"They have decaf here!"

He couldn't help but smile. "Cool."

"I know, right?"

"Good for the baby and less likely to get you completely wound up." Dez on a caffeine high was truly something to behold.

"Now, what can we—" She began to turn around to look at the shop, and Ben grabbed her arm.

"Don't."

"But I can't see."

"Well, I can, so you'll just have to put up with my eyes."

"But I'm the one that's seen the messengers! And if there's one I recognize, we could follow him or something."

"That sounds like a spectacularly bad idea that Matt would kill me for letting you do."

She grimaced. "He's not the boss of me, Ben. Come on. It's daylight! It's not like any of the really bad guys are even up."

"I'm not worried about the *really* bad guys. Just the normal, everyday ones are enough to handle, thanks."

He sipped his coffee and watched the shop. Ben had skirted the edge of violence for most of his childhood. When he was younger, he'd picked the pocket of the wrong type of mark more than once. He was good at running away; he was better at avoiding a fight in the first place. As he'd gotten older, he'd learned how to spot the bullies he could handle and the ones he wanted to avoid. Dez, apparently, had not. He cursed under his breath as she tried to sneak a surreptitious glance at the shop. Her eyes followed every scooter that went up the street.

"Okay, that's it." He stood and finished his coffee in one gulp. He grabbed the bag of books and held his hand out for Dez. "We're going."

"What?" She looked over her shoulder again, drawing the attention of the men in front of the shop. "But we—"

He pulled her up and tugged her close. "You're attracting too much attention," he muttered. "We need to *go*."

"Oh." She looked embarrassed, and Ben felt bad for the harsh whisper. "Sorry, I... sorry."

"It's fine." He scanned the street. *Damn.* He wasn't as familiar with this neighborhood, but the street they were on looked fairly busy. He didn't want to walk back past the shop and draw more attention, so he took Dez's hand and walked farther up, hoping to catch a cross street that would lead them back to something more familiar.

"Ben, I'm sorry."

He didn't stop. "It's fine."

"No, really, I—"

"We just need to get back to the..." He heard the heavy steps echo along the narrow road, but he kept walking.

"Should we go back to the train station?"

In retrospect, they probably should have. The street, which seemed busy near the café, was slowly growing more deserted. The few shops they passed seemed to be closed for the afternoon. The rain started picking up again and small puddles formed in between the cobblestones.

"Ben, should we..." Dez trailed off, and her eyes widened. Ben knew she was also hearing the steady footsteps behind them. He risked a glance over his shoulder to see who was following. It was two men from the front of the shop. Both were wearing loose jackets that blocked the rain and probably concealed guns, too.

Shit, shit, shit. They were following them for sure, and Ben wasn't familiar enough with the neighborhood to plan a good escape, especially considering that the street they were walking up was becoming narrower and more deserted with every block.

"Ben?" Her voice was frightened.

Not good, Dez. Don't sound scared when they can hear us.

He took a chance and turned right by a closed shop, only to find a dead end.

Shit.

"Hey!" He heard one of the men call from behind them in Italian. "Boy!"

Ben turned and plastered on his most innocent smile when he replied in English. "Hey, do you guys know how to get back to the train station? My friend and I got kind of lost."

Dez picked up the theme. "Yeah, we just stopped for coffee, and I told him this would be a short-cut." She forced out a laugh. "Oops! We're still getting to know the streets here, and..."

The men were still approaching, but one of them was speaking quietly on a mobile phone. His eyes narrowed at Ben and he pulled his partner closer.

"*Il ragazzo Vecchio,*" one said in the other's ear.

"*E la donna?*"

"*La amica della Americana.*"

'*A friend of the American woman.*' Well, Ben thought, at least they knew it was definitely one of Livia's shops. Someone must have taken pictures, or there were cameras he hadn't seen. More troubling, they knew who he and Dez were. His eyes immediately scanned the narrow alley they found themselves in. There was a fence behind them, but there was no way Dez would be able to jump over it. The men were blocking the exit, and they were still speaking and gesturing. Unfortunately, the one on the phone was also slipping his hand in his pocket.

His senses triggered, Ben quickly skimmed through his options. They didn't look like they wanted to kill them, but those fingers dancing in the man's pocket were making him nervous. Very nervous.

"Just scare them," he heard one say in quiet Italian. "He says to rough them up a little. Send a message to the American woman."

"*Sì?*"

Ben whispered to Dez under his breath. "When you see an opening, run back to the train station as fast as you can. Do not argue with me. Just run straight to the police." The man had slipped his hand in his pocket again and was looking at Dez with a smirk.

She whispered frantically, "But Ben—"

Ben sprang on the unsuspecting man, looking at Dez before she could finish her protest.

"Dez, run!"

His fingers slipped in the man's pocket and pulled out the gun, tossing it as far as he could down the street before the man twisted around and slugged him in the gut. Ben stumbled back and the man kicked his knee, sending him to the ground.

"Ben!" Dez hesitated for only a second before she ran toward the mouth of the alley.

He saw the other man moving toward her; luckily, he didn't look like he was pulling out any weapons. Just as Dez was about to slip past him, her heel caught in one of the cracked cobblestones that lined the street and the other man caught her arm and dragged her closer as Ben watched helplessly from the ground. The thug drew his hand back, punched the small woman in the face, and Dez crumbled to the ground.

Ben barely registered the pain in his stomach when his attacker kicked him. His eyes were trained on Dez, the swell of her belly where the baby grew, and the man whose foot was drawing back to strike her. His uncle's voice whispered in the back of his mind.

'Protect Dez.'

He blinked once and rolled to the side as Dez curled her body to protect herself and her unborn child. Ben grunted when his attacker's foot met his knee; then he deflected the blow and reached into his waistband, pulling out his hunting knife. In one swift stroke, he reached up and sliced the back of the man's knee, severing the tendons and causing the man to fall over him in pain.

'Neutralize the immediate danger.'

Ben blinked and shoved the knife into the man's stomach as he pushed the heavy body to the side. He didn't hear the curses of the man he had stabbed. The wet suck of the blade was the only sound he heard as he came up to a crouch and rushed toward the other man who was kicking Dez as she lay helpless on the ground.

'Do not *hesitate.*'

He blinked again and reached around the man's heavy body with the knife. Just as Dez's attacker began to turn, he struck. Once. *Suck.* Twice. The blade entered the man's soft abdomen, angling up under his ribs between the muscles exactly where Giovanni had showed him. Ben gave a quick twist of the knife when his hand met flesh, and he could feel the spurt of warm blood as he severed the artery he'd aimed for.

'Never leave your weapon.'

Ben pulled the knife out and kicked the man to the side. The first man he had stabbed lay cursing on the ground. The man who had been kicking Dez and the baby said nothing. A growing pool of blood leaked out of him and into the cobblestones that paved the street. The rain fell harder, and a rivulet of blood joined the small stream that flowed down the middle of the alley. Ben blinked again and tucked the knife into his waistband before he knelt and picked up the wounded woman.

Dez was moaning and her face was bleeding.

"The baby," she mumbled. "He kicked the baby."

"Hang on. I'm going to get us out of here."

Ben had no idea how he carried her. He didn't remember leaving the dead-end street or which direction he turned. He paid no attention to the pain in his knee or the strain in his arms. But he felt the warm blood soak his arm when Dez began bleeding between her legs, and he felt the warm tears that fell from her bruised face to stain his shirt.

The moment he came within sight of the train station, he started yelling at the dark blue coats of the police who stood at attention near the doors.

"*Help her!* She needs a hospital! She's pregnant and she's bleeding!" He wasn't sure whether he was speaking English or Italian, but he could hear the sharp cries of the men who rushed toward them. They grabbed Dez from his arms and laid her gently on the ground. A radio began to squawk in the background as he knelt beside her.

"Hold on, Dez. It's gonna be okay."

She looked up at Ben, holding her stomach as tears fell from eyes that were quickly turning black from the bruising. "The baby…"

"They're calling for an ambulance right now, okay?" His hand stroked her cheek, and he cringed when he saw the smear of blood his fingers left.

"Call Matt. You need to call Matt right now."

He nodded and tried to reach for her fingers, but rough hands pulled him away.

"Ben?" Dez looked around in alarm, but Ben could see the paramedics running toward her as the police began shouting and searching his pockets.

"It's okay, Dez. It's gonna be okay. Just give the doctors Matt's number, okay?"

"What's going on?" She looked around and tried to grab the coat of one of the police who hovered over her. "Stop them! He's the one who saved me. He kept the men—"

"Dez!" She looked to Ben and he gave a sharp shake of his head. "Don't worry about me. Just call Matt!"

Tears continued to streak down her face, but she nodded. Ben could see the gentle hands of the paramedics lifting her up as they secured his wrists behind his back and shoved him into the small police car.

CHAPTER 24

"And your friend, she is stable?" Beatrice could tell that Emil was trying to be soothing over the phone. She could also tell he was angry.

Not as angry as Beatrice.

She spoke around fully elongated fangs. "She appears to be. She is in the hospital right now. Her husband called just a few minutes ago. The bleeding has stopped and they have her under observation."

"That is welcome news."

She paced the library, barking at the speakerphone and willing the sun to set faster. "She's pregnant, Emil. She's *pregnant,* and they attacked her. Her husband said that they aimed kicks at her stomach. There was—" She choked on her own rage. "'Extensive bruising.'"

There was a grim silence. "But the baby is fine?"

"They're monitoring both of them."

She could hear him take a breath. "Beatrice, I am glad that your friend is being cared for. If you have any concerns about human doctors or the hospital, you need only call my people. It pains me that she was not able to walk the streets of my city in safety. I hope you know... this *will* be dealt with, I assure you."

She picked up a vase and threw it into the fireplace, reveling in the crash. "You bet your ass it's going to be dealt with, Emil!"

There was a long pause over the line before he spoke in a cool voice. "I'm going to ask something of you, and you're not going to like it."

Her fangs cut her lower lip. "What?"

"I want you to stay away from the castle tonight."

Her jaw dropped. "*What?*"

"I know what you are feeling now. I know someone has attacked a valued member of your household, but I am asking you to stay away." Beatrice tried to quell the roaring in her ears so she could listen to Emil's crisp voice. "I can turn this against her, Beatrice. Donatella is furious. I am in shock that she would go to this extreme. This was very foolish of Livia, and I can use this to paint her in a very bad light, but *not* if the court is focused on your reaction."

"I want that bitch to die!" Beatrice screamed across the room. "I will kill her for this!"

Emil's voice was suddenly hard and sharp. "And that would be very foolish. You know this."

She closed her eyes and tried to calm herself and focus on more than her own rage.

Matt had been frantic, but Angela had called from the hospital to let her know that Dez was awake and talking. She had told the police the details of the attack, which brought Beatrice back to the reason she had called Emil in the first place. He was still speaking.

"Stay in the city tonight. Take care of your friend. Let me bring this in front of the court without the distraction of your rivalry with Livia. The vampires of Rome know better than to attack tourists. It is bad for everyone and risks exposing us all."

"Do you think she even cares about that anymore?"

"I do not know. That, in itself, is disturbing." Emil paused again. "This will look very bad for her, but you must stay in the city and let the focus shift to her and her actions. Or Lorenzo's. I think this sounds more like him than her. He has proven himself to be quite rash. Let me take care of this. Do you agree?"

She took a deep breath and tried to think about taking care of her family. "Fine."

"Is there anything else I can do? Any help my human staff can give you right now?"

"Yes. My nephew was arrested. He speaks some Italian, but we've told him never to talk to the police. Matt would usually take care of it, but—"

"Your head of security must take care of his wife. Let me handle this. The police will be no problem. What is the boy's name?"

Her heart ached when she thought about Ben. Dez said she thought he might have killed one of the men. She said he had stabbed both to protect her. "His name is Ben. Benjamin Vecchio. He's only sixteen, Emil. He was protecting her, and he was... he was covered in blood, so the police thought—"

"Do not concern yourself. He will be out of police custody in a matter of hours at the most. I'll have my men take him to the hospital."

She closed her eyes in relief. "Thank you. I will—*we* will owe you a favor."

"And I'll be sure to collect when the time is appropriate, which is not now.

This attack has the potential to expose all of us to scrutiny. Let my people take care of this. I will call you when I know more."

"Thank you."

"Good-bye, Beatrice. Be well."

She hung up the phone and sat on the couch. It was late afternoon and the house that was usually filled with life was utterly and completely silent. No Dez. No Ben. Matt was at the hospital with Angela. Tenzin was wherever the Chinese delegation was staying. Ziri was... somewhere. Lucien was sleeping, completely unaware of what had transpired only hours before. It would be hours before the sun set.

She took advantage of the empty house and screamed at the top of her lungs. Beatrice wanted her husband. She wanted her friends. And she was completely cut off from the outside world as she waited for a call back from Emil with news about Ben.

She was tempted to walk down to the basement so she could punch the stone walls, but there were no phone connections there.

So she sat. She paced. She glared at the thin line of light she could see around the heavy shutters that covered the windows. She ached with rage and frustration. She suddenly remembered something Lucien had talked about just the day before.

"I think I offended God."

Beatrice had frowned. "What? How?"

"By drinking from Rada. Trying to conquer the bloodlust."

"How would that offend God?"

"Perhaps we are meant to struggle against it. Perhaps..."

"What?"

"There is a price, isn't there? There has to be. Strength. Immortality. Wisdom... it must have a price."

"What kind of god would demand a price of blood?"

"It is not blood He demands. It is humility. The knowledge that even as powerful as we are, we will never be gods."

As powerful as they were...

Beatrice didn't feel powerful. She felt helpless.

The phone rang.

"Yes?"

"Your nephew will be on his way to the hospital shortly. They were trying to interrogate him, but he refused to speak. That is a very clever boy you have. And very skilled. It appears he took out two of Livia's human staff. They found one of the men dead at the scene. The other my people are attempting to track down.

There was an impressive amount of blood in the alley. The police were trying to contact the U.S. Embassy when my contact intervened."

So, Ben *had* killed one of their attackers. Possibly both. The thought both satisfied and pained her at the same time. "Who do we need to pay, Emil? I want this to disappear."

She heard him give a quiet laugh. "Don't be absurd. It is my responsibility that the boy had to use force to defend himself on our streets. Do not think of repaying me with money."

"You're not responsible for everything that happens on the streets of Rome."

There was silence over the line. "Not yet, anyway."

"Thank you."

"Stay away from the castle tonight. Take care of your people. I will have my head of security coordinate with Mr. Kirby regarding his wife's protection."

"I won't forget this."

"Neither will I."

He hung up the phone and Beatrice immediately dialed the number Tenzin had given her weeks before. She hadn't wanted to call until she had more information. A polite voice answered in Mandarin, and she asked for her friend. She heard a rustling as the phone was switched to the echoing quality of the speakerphone.

"Who is calling me?"

"It's me, Tenzin."

There was a long pause. "What is wrong? What has happened?"

Beatrice blinked back tears. "Um... Dez and Ben were attacked today. Ben killed one, maybe both, of the men that attacked them, but Dez is in the hospital. The doctors say she's stable."

"What does that mean? Dez is all right? What about the baby?"

"Stable means she's not bleeding anymore. It looks like the baby's going to be okay. I don't know that much, but—"

"Where is Benjamin?"

She cleared her throat. "I contacted Emil Conti's people. He's out of police custody now and on the way to the hospital."

There was a long silence on the phone.

"He killed one of the men who attacked them?"

"Yes. Maybe... maybe both. There was a lot of blood at the scene and—"

"Where was it?"

She frowned. "Where?"

"Yes! Where did this happen?"

"Near the train station. Why—"

"I will take care of this. I'll find you at the hospital later."

And Tenzin hung up the phone.

. . .

A FALL OF WATER

Beatrice arrived at the hospital a half an hour after the sun set. She struggled to control her fangs amidst the smell of blood that permeated the building. The sour antiseptic smell helped. Dez had been put in a private room at Matt's insistence, and she could see two armed guards standing outside. They were probably Emil's men. They nodded at her respectfully as she entered the room.

There were lines and IVs and monitors beeping, but her friend was smiling and flowers filled the room. Matt was sitting next to her, looking quietly furious and Dez was patting his hand and speaking in a low voice. She turned when Beatrice entered.

"B, I'm fine. Look." She pointed to the monitors. "The baby's fine. Told you growing a human was my superpower. I must have a uterus of steel. And the doctors have been awesome. And both my heroes are with me now. No one is allowed to freak out."

Beatrice had barely noticed a pale Ben sitting in a corner of the room. He lifted his hand in a small wave, but didn't attempt a smile. He was staring at Dez like there was no one else in the room.

She halted and pushed back the bloody tears of relief she couldn't let herself cry. "You're awesome, Dez. I've told you a thousand times."

"Good." The small woman in the hospital bed looked around the room with a glare. "Now tell everyone to take a chill pill and let me sleep. And this is no one's fault but my own. Ben warned me it was a bad idea, and I went ahead anyway."

Matt growled at her. "Dez—"

"Don't even start again. I know you're pissed at me and everyone is freaked out, but I'm fine." She looked around the room at all of them. "I am fine. The baby's fine. And if I'm going to have to sit my ass in a hospital bed for the next month or so, at least I'm in Italy. I'm betting the hospital food is way better here."

"Dez, I just..." Beatrice gave up and walked over to her best friend, being careful not to jostle the network of wires and tubes that were attached to her. "I was so scared for you," she whispered.

Matt spoke in a low voice. "Beatrice, I want to talk to you."

She sniffed and wiped her eyes with the handkerchief in her pocket. "Right."

"In the hall. Ben?" Matt stood and pointed to the chair he was vacating. Ben jumped up and went to sit beside Dez. Matt patted Ben on the shoulder before he walked out of the room.

Dez looked at her with worried eyes. "Don't be mad at each other. He was really worried, B. He was pretty frantic."

"I deserve anything he throws at me." She patted Dez's hand and stood.

Matt was pacing in a small waiting room down the hall. He didn't even glance up when she entered.

"If she didn't have to be in the hospital for the next month, I'd have her ass on a plane and out of here so fast your head would spin, Beatrice De Novo."

"I know. I would, too."

"*Don't!*" He spun on her. "I know she's your friend, but that is my *wife*! Do you understand me? My wife and my child and no amount of money or friendship or loyalty is worth the kind of hell that she has been put through, no matter how much she's trying to play the cheerful fucking patient right now!"

"Matt, I know. I would never, *ever* put her or the baby in danger. You know this."

He kept pacing, glaring at the ground. "Conti's people are on her until the baby is born. After the baby is here and the doctor gives the okay to travel, we are out of here. I don't care what you need or where Giovanni is. Do you get that, B? We're out of here. She is my priority, and I will *not* have her in danger again. Thank God Ben was there. And just so you know, when we go, I'm taking him, too. He doesn't need to get mixed up in this any more than he is. He already... he had to—"

"*I know.*" She walked toward him. "You're not getting any arguments from me, Matt. I wish we'd sent all of you back weeks ago."

He was still pacing, but she could see his reason returning. "Conti knows what happened? I'm assuming, since his men brought Ben back and his people have been stationed out there for the last few hours. His human security guy left me a message, but I haven't called him back yet."

"He knows. And Tenzin knows. I called them both. They all know how much Dez means to me. How important she is."

Matt paused in his pacing and looked up at her. His arms were still crossed, but she saw the anguish in his eyes.

"She's my life, B. She's *everything*. I can't... Nothing can happen to her, do you get that?"

Beatrice nodded and walked over to him. Finally, he reached his arms out and embraced her.

"I get it, Matt. Trust me, I get it."

Ben watched over Dez as she drifted to sleep. The nurse had just come in to give her some medicine that was supposed to kill the pain. The goons at the door had checked over the nurse's badge like they were the Secret Service or something. He thought that was good.

The doctors all said she was going to be fine, but Ben still watched all the monitors and took note of any unusual jump or extra beep. He had liked hearing the tiny thrum of the baby's heartbeat when they brought in the machine to check. It sounded kind of fast to him, but it made Dez smile, so he thought that fast was probably okay. Her face was swollen and both of her eyes were black.

A FALL OF WATER

She was all covered up, but he knew she had bruises on her legs, abdomen, and even her chest. It made him sick to even think about it.

He heard a rustling sound in the hall, then the goons started to block the door.

"Get away from me. I'm with them, you idiots."

It was Tenzin. He walked to the door and put a hand up on one of the guard's broad shoulders.

"It's okay, guys. She's with us."

They parted to let her pass, and Tenzin stomped in the room.

"Idiots."

"Calm down. They're just guarding Dez. That's what they're supposed to do."

She looked around with narrowed eyes. "I've never been in a hospital before."

"What, never?"

"No."

Tenzin walked over to the sleeping Dez and put her hand on her forehead. Then she pushed back the blanket that covered her and laid her ear against Dez's belly, dislodging some of the monitors. Ben rushed over.

"Hey! Tenzin, that's—"

"Shhh." She put both hands on Dez's belly and held them there for a minute, listening to whatever mysterious sounds the baby was making. Then she straightened and pulled the blanket up.

"I'll let the healers put the electrical equipment back. She's going to be fine. The baby sounds active and her heart is good. Does she have any cuts that need healing?"

"No. Matt said... well, she has to be here for a while, so it's probably not a good idea to heal anything they would really notice. None of her cuts were major. Just scrapes from the street and stuff." He fell silent and went back to his chair beside Dez. Tenzin pulled a chair over and sat next to him.

She said, "I went to the alley."

Ben couldn't say anything. The police had told him. They'd told him he'd killed a man. In his heart, he'd known it the second the knife plunged in the man's belly. He'd meant to kill him, and he knew exactly what he was aiming for.

"I tracked the other man who attacked you both. It's been taken care of."

He nodded. Was he a bad person for being relieved that Tenzin had finished off the other man instead of him? He felt frozen. He didn't know how to feel. He shouldn't have taken them into that alley. He shouldn't have done a lot of things. Dez might not have known better, but he should have. He stared at the monitors above Dez's head.

Tenzin's voice was uncharacteristically soft when she finally spoke. "Was this the first?"

The first person he'd ever killed? Ben nodded.

He was familiar with violence. It had been a constant, lurking shadow his whole life. Ben had seen a lot. He'd watched a man kick another to death and leave him broken in an alley. He'd seen a gloating man stabbed, his blood spilling out in the mud as the money was stolen from his body by greedy hands. But Ben had never killed anyone.

"Ben?"

He whispered, "Yeah?"

"Was the man attacking Dez?"

He nodded.

"Was he hurting the baby?"

"He..." He swallowed the lump in his throat. "He was kicking her. He had to see she was pregnant. Her shirt was up, and her belly... He couldn't have—"

"You were defending Dez. You were protecting the baby."

He blinked back the tears, but they fell down his face anyway.

Tenzin slipped her hand in his, and Ben gripped her small fingers.

"You did well, Benjamin. You did right."

Ben held on to Tenzin's hand, and the two sat in silence as Dez slept under their watch.

CHAPTER 25

Giovanni decided that the home of Arosh—which could only be described as a palace—was an odd, but not uncomfortable combination of museum and harem. Silks and tapestries hung from the windowless walls. The rooms were lit by golden oil lamps and heated by glowing braziers. The rooms they had been shown to when they arrived were equipped with luxurious baths and opulent furnishings. The only electricity in the palace seemed to be in the bedrooms, a nod to the humans who occupied most of the rooms.

And by humans, Giovanni meant women. Dozens of them. Hundreds, possibly. Women of every age, shape, and color ran laughing through the house. They cooked Giovanni and Carwyn rich meals and offered their willing wrists for the vampires to drink. They tended the house and the gardens. They read books in the vast library. Many were beautiful, but not all. Some bore the scars of past abuse or injury, but all seemed content. Most appeared to be between seventeen and forty, but a few older women passed them in the halls, as well.

And one woman, a regal beauty named Zarine, ruled the house.

Her accent was Armenian. Her long, black hair curled down her back and her brown eyes were warm and wise. She appeared to be in her fifties or sixties, and she was fiercely protective of her master.

"Doctor Vecchio, are you sure that you will not take sustenance from one of the girls? You have been here for several weeks now. Arosh would be most disappointed that you have not fed properly."

He leaned forward on the silk-wrapped chaise. "And where is our host this evening, if I may ask?"

Zarine's eyes lit with amusement. "He is... occupied this evening."

"He is occupied *every* evening."

"He does not deprive himself. It is not his nature."

Giovanni bit his tongue and glanced at Carwyn, who was sipping wine and frowning at a group of passing women.

As soon as they had arrived at the house, Carwyn had given Arosh the letter from Ziri. The ancient fire vampire had taken it, glanced at the unbroken seal, then promptly disappeared into the palace with a dozen girls.

They hadn't seen him since.

Giovanni and Carwyn had been fed and watered. They had been given luxurious rooms and a tour of the house, which was filled to the brim with ancient treasures from all over the world. Arosh was a collector of all sorts of beautiful things. Art and women just seemed to top the list. There were also many treasures that looked Greek or Minoan in origin, but there was no sign of Kato, the fabled water vampire.

"Zarine, I do not wish to seem ungrateful—"

"Then don't. You are being given the finest hospitality of my master's home. It would be most unfortunate if you were not satisfied with that."

Though her voice and pleasant expression never wavered, he could see the glint of steel in her eyes. Zarine, as much as the silent wind vampire, Samson, was Arosh's most fervent and devoted security.

Carwyn spoke up. "Zarine?"

She turned toward the friendly vampire. "Yes, Carwyn?"

"All the women here... they *do* come willingly, do they not?"

She smiled. "And leave when they wish to. Samson simply alters their memories depending on where they want to go. He's very gifted in that trait. Most are placed with one of my associates in the city if they want to work. Some desire husbands and families. They all receive what they wish. If they wish to leave."

"But many don't."

She shrugged. "These girls... most of them did not have good lives before they came here. Here, they are my master's treasures. His 'jewels.'" She turned as Samson swept silently through the room and toward the front door.

The wind vampire was an enigma. He never spoke, and the Eastern European man had wild, grey eyes. He had been sired young, but his head was covered by an alarming shock of pure silver hair. Arosh called him his child, Zarine looked at him with affection, but the vampire moved through the house like a ghost.

Samson stopped for a moment when a younger girl caught the edge of his cloak. She pulled him down and whispered in his ear. The bruises on her face were still healing and one arm was set in a brace. She had appeared in the house the week before and been enfolded by the women of Arosh's palace. The wounded girl placed a soft kiss on the vampire's pale cheek. Samson gave the girl a slight nod before he disappeared into the black night without a word.

Zarine turned back to her guests with a smile. "As you can see, the girls are not mistreated here. Though, I appreciate your concern."

The earth vampire only shrugged. "I have daughters of my own."

Giovanni broke in. "Why doesn't he speak?"

"Samson?"

He nodded.

"I do not know. He never has in all the time I've been here. He has a tongue." Her eyes danced in amusement. "Of that, I'm quite positive. But I've never heard him speak."

"And what about your master?" asked Carwyn. "Should we expect to see him soon? My friend here is trying to be polite, but that's never been an affliction of mine. I cannot complain about your hospitality, but we really do need to speak with him."

Zarine's eyes softened. "I understand your impatience. Truly. And I know that you have traveled a long way, but Arosh is a king." She shrugged. "He comes and goes as he pleases and currently, he is enjoying the pleasures of his women. He may not appear for days. Or weeks."

Giovanni's eyes widened. "Weeks?"

He tried not to think of his own woman waiting back in Rome. He missed his wife. He missed her teasing voice and her soft touch. He missed waking with her and falling asleep wrapped in her arms. He even missed their arguments. And, he was worried. He couldn't deny it.

A particularly sweet-smelling girl walked past and his fangs lengthened in his mouth. A low growl built at the back of his throat. Arosh carried no stored blood. Why would he? He had a walking, giggling supply running around his palace. Carwyn's voice broke through his hungry reverie.

"Gio, I'm going to hunt tonight. I already let Samson know. There are wolves and bears in the mountains around here. Would you join me?"

Unlike Carwyn, Giovanni's system was not accustomed to subsisting on animal blood alone. He could hunt, but he knew he wouldn't be as strong from animal blood as he would be from just a few drinks of one of the many willing women who surrounded him.

"I..." He looked toward his friend.

Carwyn looked back with understanding before he rose and patted Giovanni on the shoulder. He leaned down and whispered in Latin, "Drink. Make yourself strong. We both need to be strong. She will understand."

Giovanni blinked and pushed back his longing for Beatrice. He nodded to a girl who had offered herself to him the day before.

"Fine. Send her to my room."

Zarine's lips curled into a smile. "Excellent. I hope you enjoy your time with her."

"Just feeding, Zarine."

She shrugged. "The girl will be disappointed, but it is your choice, of course."

He returned to his room, pushing back the flames that danced at his collar. Giovanni wanted to leave this place. He had been battling aggression from the moment he stepped through the door. Arosh's distinctive smell was everywhere, and the scent of burning almond wood filled the rooms. He had never been under the roof of another fire vampire. The only males he had ever met, he had killed or avoided as much as possible. Being around another male triggered the worst of his natural aggression and territorial instincts. He had to constantly fight back the fire that wanted to erupt. Perhaps, as much as he disliked it, feeding would help.

The girl tapped at the door and he clenched his fists to control his hunger. "Enter."

It was two days later when Arosh finally appeared. He stretched out on a low couch and drew Zarine to his chest, stroking her hair and feeding her an orange he had peeled.

"How has your stay been, my friends?"

Carwyn said, "Clearly not as pleasant as yours."

Arosh threw his head back and laughed. "You amuse me, holy man! I understand your own odd beliefs, but why has the son of Andreas not taken his pleasure with the beauties of my home? I'm sure Zarine has pointed out those who are acceptable."

Giovanni forced back the instinctive curl of his lip and banished the memory of the disappointed girl he had fed from. "I am mated, Arosh."

"And you are faithful?" Arosh's eyes lit in amusement. "How odd."

"Not odd. No woman is appealing when compared to my wife."

Arosh's eyes narrowed for a moment before he smiled. It was the most sincere smile he had seen from the ancient. "Kato would approve of you. He took a number of mates over the centuries and was always very faithful to them when he did."

"Where is my grand-sire?"

Arosh ignored the question. "Your sire, however, did not hold others in such esteem. He had little regard for family. He had little regard for anyone but himself."

"I am aware of this."

"You would be. Tell me, why did you kill him?"

"Wouldn't you have? He had plans for me. I'm sure you can imagine."

"And you wouldn't have defied him."

Giovanni said, "I'd like to think I would have, but probably not. Could you have ignored your sire?"

Arosh shrugged. "I do not know. My earliest memory is of a fire-scarred cave. There was no one."

Carwyn frowned. "What? No one at all?"

"If there was, the fire burned them." Arosh slipped another piece of orange between Zarine's lips and ran a finger along her cheek. "That is too long ago to matter. All of my children have been sired to wind, so that must have been my own origin. Perhaps he left me. Perhaps he had no interest in my future. Unlike your sire, Giovanni Vecchio. Am I correct?"

"Yes." Giovanni did not let his eyes wander from Arosh's keen gaze. "My father was very... involved."

"I can imagine he was." He sat up and pulled Zarine with him, whispering in her ear that she should leave them. She nodded silently and backed out of the room, closing the doors behind her. Arosh watched her leave, then turned back to them.

"I knew your sire, Giovanni. I did not like him. His own sire didn't like him. Ironically, you seem like the type of child that Kato *would* have wanted. He valued loyalty above all, but had the wisdom to appreciate others and respect them. Kato felt a deep responsibility toward those under his aegis. He was not only feared, but loved. A true ruler must have both."

"I do not want to rule anything. I want only to live my life in peace and protect those who are mine."

"Ah!" Arosh grinned. "You are a wise child. You have learned early what it took Kato and me thousands of years to learn. Peace is a treasure beyond earthly price."

Giovanni took a deep breath. "Where is my grand-sire, Arosh?"

Arosh pulled the letter from his cloak, fingering the broken seal and staring into the fire. "Do you know, Giovanni, I asked your sire for a favor once?"

He and Carwyn exchanged glances, and he threw a careful mask over his face to hide the shock. To most, Arosh's admission would be nothing remarkable, but for a king of legend to admit that he had once asked another immortal for a favor was shocking.

"No, I did not know this. You honored him by ask—"

"He refused."

Giovanni almost choked. To be asked for a favor from a legend like Arosh was awe-inspiring enough. To refuse? *Unthinkable.* Arosh would have owed Andros a favor of his own. A favor from the ancient king was not something to be dismissed. Or refused. Ever.

"I offer my apologies, Arosh. My sire's audacity—"

"Is not your fault!" Arosh only looked amused. "And you have killed him for me, so that is very pleasing." He held up the letter that Ziri had written. "But it appears that you did not kill him on your own. You sired a child. And now you have a problem, Giovanni Vecchio."

He nodded carefully. Now was the time for bargaining. "Yes, we have a problem."

"And Ziri asks me to expose myself and my dearest friend to this annoying vampire in Rome."

"Not for her. To keep the world safe from the—"

"Yes, the elixir." Arosh curled his lip. "I had hoped to never hear about that dreaded concoction again. What a mess."

Carwyn, ever fearless, piped up. "What were you thinking?"

Giovanni was tempted to muzzle the priest, but Arosh only laughed. "It seemed like a good idea at the time, holy man."

"Ah well." Carwyn sat up straighter and looked at the ancient fire vampire with suddenly keen eyes. "I'd very much like to kill the bastard that murdered my son. Or watch someone kill him, I'm not picky. So, if we could get on with it, please?"

"Yes, holy man, let us 'get on with it' as you say." Arosh cocked his head and looked at Giovanni. "I have read Ziri's letter. I know what my friend asks of me, but what about you, Giovanni, son of Andreas?"

The ancient fire vampire wanted something. And though Ziri had already asked for the favor, he wanted Giovanni to ask it as well. That way, a favor would be owed. He had no choice.

"Arosh, I would ask a favor of you."

The dark eyes of the old king lit up. "And I may grant it. We shall see."

Arosh led them down into the mountain and through a twisted maze of passageways that Giovanni couldn't help but think Beatrice would enjoy.

"Kato always liked mazes," Arosh called as he led them forward. "And this one keeps the more curious girls away. I only let a few attend to him, though he's not dangerous to human women."

To human women? Giovanni couldn't help but notice that he and Carwyn didn't fall under that particular category.

They finally exited the maze and were led toward a chamber that reminded Giovanni of an old tomb. The large, stone doors were intricately carved and painted, and a channel of water fell from a hidden stream.

"The cisterns feed the waterfall and the fountains. He can't reside near the sea, but I can keep enough water here to keep him content."

What the hell were they walking into? Arosh pushed the doors open and the three vampires stepped into a large open chamber. The tiled ceiling was held up by richly painted columns and fountains flowed through the room. The walls were bare stone. Cold, but painted with rich murals depicting beautiful scenes of the ocean and sea life. They walked along a bridge that led them toward the sound of soft voices. As they crossed over a long pool, Giovanni spied his father's sire and gasped.

Andros had been right. Ancient peoples had seen this immortal and the legends of Poseidon were born. Kato sat submerged to his chest in a large, Roman-style bath. He stared straight ahead and quiet women circled around him, pouring water over his thickly muscled chest, curling hair, and long beard. His eyes were a deep, sea blue. His hair was the color of bronze. The immortal didn't appear sickly or ill. Kato, the ancient water vampire, looked like a god.

Giovanni heard Arosh shift behind him a moment before Kato moved. It was infinitesimal, a twitch. But suddenly, he was looking into the eyes of his grand-sire and he realized that something was very, very wrong.

The brilliant blue eyes held nothing; they were vacant and wild.

Kato's mouth opened. Long, thick fangs speared behind his lips and in a blink, he had flown out of the water and toward the intruders. Arosh stepped back again, taking Carwyn's arm and pulling him behind his body. A snarl ripped from Kato's throat, and Giovanni could scarcely draw a breath before he was overtaken. Kato grabbed him by the throat and lifted him into the air.

"Gio!"

"Stay back, holy man."

At Kato's touch, the water was drawn from Giovanni's body. He could feel it wicking away as the water vampire drew it out of him. No shield or energy could stop it as Giovanni's skin dried. His lips cracked. It was as if he was a sponge being wrung out by the hands of the old king.

And he was choking. Kato held him up and Giovanni knew that with one squeeze, the hands of this vampire could end him. He had no fire in this watery tomb. The air was too thick with moisture. His dry hands reached up to the iron grip of his grand-sire, but did nothing. It was like pawing at solid rock.

However, just as quickly as Kato had lifted him, the water vampire froze, took a deep breath, and lowered Giovanni to the ground. A soft look stole over the immortal's face, and he pulled Giovanni closer. The iron hand tilted his chin up, and Kato leaned over, placed his face at Giovanni's throat, and inhaled. Then he smiled and lowered his chin. He placed soft hands on his grandchild's shoulders and kissed his forehead.

Giovanni remained motionless. He had no idea what had just happened. Arosh, as if reading his mind, strode over and placed a hand on his ancient rival's shoulder. Kato flinched under his touch, but turned a beatific smile on Arosh, as well.

"You have enough. Excellent. Otherwise you would be dead. Kato smells his blood. He reacts to most strangers like this, which is why your friend should not approach." Arosh was almost whispering, as he placed a hand on Kato's forehead and stroked his friend's hair back with the gentlest of touches. "But you are of his direct line, and he smells his blood in you. This is why you are not in danger. I carry his blood as well, though it is not as strong."

"What has happened to him? What is this?"

"This, son of Andreas, is the result of curing bloodlust. Your grand-sire's amnis is shattered. Barely functioning. His body is as vital as it ever was, but the brilliant mind that was nurtured by the fifth element is broken. He is a creature of instinct now."

Giovanni was reeling. "How is this possible?"

"Come with me, and I will tell you."

CHAPTER 26

"Pride, my friends, is the deadliest of fires. While other flames burn the surface, pride burns from within. It works its way from the heart until it consumes you. And like any fire, it will eat its prey until it is smothered or quenched."

They were sitting in Arosh's private rooms. A low fire burned in an earthen fireplace, and silk-covered couches encircled it. The panels of the ceiling had been drawn back, and the night sky was cold and clear. Smoke drifted up to be carried away by a breeze as Giovanni, Arosh, and Carwyn sat around the fire, drinking the sweet red wine the ancient fire vampire poured.

"My three friends and I were more proud than any other immortals who walked the Earth. We had reason to be. We were kings and queens. Civilizations existed at our pleasure. And in our arrogance, perhaps we forgot…" A smile lifted the corner of Arosh's mouth. "We were not gods."

Giovanni stared at him. "How did it happen?"

"I will go back to the beginning. I do not know all that Ziri has told you. He only wrote that I should answer any questions you had about the elixir."

"How did it come to be? What has it done to my grand-sire?"

Arosh took a sip of wine. "I was the first to reach Kufa at the beginning of the eighth century as the Romans counted, but Kato followed soon after. The city was becoming rich with ideas. Innovation. An interesting atmosphere in a region that hadn't seen such enlightenment for too long. Years later, I was introduced to the alchemist. Jabir was from Khorasan, a province in Persia where I had kept a home for hundreds of years. I was familiar with his people."

Arosh's dark eyes were amused. "Jabir was so bright for a human. Our discussions quickly progressed to the point where I confided in him my true nature. I suspected he was trustworthy. And if he proved not to be?" Arosh shrugged. "He was easily disposed of. Kato joined us in our discussions soon after I revealed myself. Jabir was enthralled with us both."

Giovanni asked, "What of Ziri and Saba?"

"They arrived years after we did. Ziri already had a home in the area with some distant members of his clan. Saba lived as my wife while we were there. She chafed at the ridiculous restrictions of that culture regarding their women, but tolerated it for us."

"So..." Carwyn cleared his throat. "You and Saba were..."

Arosh smiled. "Saba takes whatever lover she chooses. The four of us have always been close, but she only tolerates me for brief periods." His smile widened. "We are too much alike and value our independence too fiercely."

Giovanni said, "But you were all in Kufa with Geber—Jabir at the end of the eighth century?"

"Yes. The alchemist was doing fascinating experiments regarding the artificial creation of life. Ridiculous premise now, but at the time, it was a serious study. Jabir was the first who saw the possibilities that combining our blood could have."

Carwyn reached for the bottle of wine. "How did he get the idea to begin with?"

"He saw how we healed each other. Kato and Saba had been fighting with daggers one night—she has always had a fondness for them—and Ziri and I were sharing wine with the alchemist. Kato managed to put a slice in Saba's face." Arosh laughed. "She was so irritated with him! Of course, he simply bit his tongue and cleaned the wound for her without a thought. Jabir noticed it and became fascinated."

"With the healing properties?" Carwyn asked.

"Yes. He began interviewing us. Making many notes about us. Our blood. How we healed. How we fed. He asked so many questions. Jabir noted four unique properties of vampire blood. Our blood healed, sustained life, and sated hunger. But it could not be consumed by humans. He tried, and it made him quite ill."

Giovanni held his glass out for more wine, and Arosh filled it. "And he combined the blood?"

"Yes, we already knew that blood of the same element did little to heal a serious injury. The four of us had discovered that through the centuries, but we had never made the connection between that fact and our elemental affinity."

Carwyn's eyes narrowed on Arosh. "What do you mean?"

"Jabir concluded that the dominant element in immortal blood—fire for me, earth for you—is what gives us our strength. To feed our own strength does little to repair our bodies, but to strengthen the other elements within us? *That* is what gave further strength and healing."

Carwyn said, "I'm still not understanding this."

Arosh leaned toward the fire. "Think, holy man! Blood contains all four elements. My blood has the strongest heat, the fire. Yours has the strongest *substance*, that is what enables you to control the earth as you do. Samson's blood connects him to the air. Kato's to the water. I have no need to feed the fire within my blood—"

"Because you are strongest in fire," Giovanni said. "As I am. So to strengthen ourselves, the blood of a different element helps more."

"It is all about *balance*. As much as it may wound our pride, immortals are stronger together, sharing our strength, than we are in isolation."

"Four elements together," Giovanni murmured. "Fire, earth, air, and water. Arosh, Saba, Ziri, and Kato."

Arosh nodded toward him. "Giovanni, Carwyn, Tenzin, and Beatrice."

He was reminded of Zhang's cryptic statement months before. *'Balance, Giovanni Vecchio. Balance is the key.'*

Giovanni looked up. "So, you theorized it would work for healing and, according to Ziri, it did. He found a formula to stabilize the blood for human consumption. How did you make the connection to curing bloodlust?"

"It was my idea. I guessed that if a human was strengthened by this elixir, it was possible that their blood—treated blood—might cure our insatiable hunger."

Carwyn asked, "Did you really care at that point? None of you must have had to feed very often. As ancient as you all are, why did it matter?"

A grim smile crossed Arosh's lips. "Pride."

Giovanni nodded. "As strong as we are, we still need humans. Whatever disdain some may hold for humanity after hundreds or even thousands of years, we all still need them to survive."

"Yes." Arosh's shoulders seemed to droop. "Only a cure for the sun is more greatly desired, but there is no hope of that. Trust me, many have tried. And will continue to try. It will not happen. Whatever god created us designed us to be mortal. The very source of this world's energy will kill us within minutes. Even the oldest immortal cannot avoid this sentence."

Carwyn said, "But you thought you could cure bloodlust?"

Arosh smiled at him, but turned to Giovanni. "You waited long to feed from one of my women. Tell me, my friend, do you and your mate exchange blood?"

Giovanni frowned and answered, "We do."

"And you both feed from humans, as well."

"Yes, but..."

Arosh cocked an eyebrow. "Not as much as before, is it? While you may have needed to feed every week before you took your wife's immortal blood, now you can go several weeks, a month even. How does human blood taste to you now?"

He shrugged. "Pleasant, but weak."

"Not like your mate's blood."

"No, her blood..." Giovanni cleared his throat and tried to rid the longing from his voice. "It is the sweetest wine. Nothing compares to it."

Arosh's eyes danced. "Some of what you say is sentiment, but some is not. Your wife drinks the blood of humans. You drink blood from her. In her blood, both bloods sustain you. But what if that human blood was even more strengthened by this immortal elixir? What then? Could it sustain us even longer? Could it cure us, even?"

Giovanni's eyes narrowed and his energy snapped in the air. "Can it? Ziri said that Kato drank the blood of his human and look what it has done to him. How did this happen, Arosh? What did Geber miss? What did *you* miss?"

Arosh's nostrils flared, but just then, a gust of winter wind blew from outside and cooled the room. "We *all* missed it. The elixir worked. It cured the humans —unfortunately, its effects were short-lived."

Carwyn shook his head. "So, even the successful cases that Geber documented—"

"Died. Yes. The effects of the elixir lasted anywhere between two to five years by our best estimates. Then, whatever illness had afflicted the human came back. Stronger than ever."

"Kato's lover?"

Arosh sighed. "Kato had taken blood from Fahdil two years after the elixir was tested and appeared successful. As proud as we all were with ourselves, we were still hesitant to drink from one of the test subjects. But Kato was too attached to this human. When the young man grew ill, it affected him. He gave the elixir to Fahdil and then drank from him. But, though we had reservations, none of us thought it could *really* be harmful. After all, it was only a potion! And made from our own blood. Where could the real danger be?"

Giovanni tensed. "You said something in the room with Kato. You said something about the fifth element. What were you talking about?"

Arosh's dark eyes glistened in the fire. "Something our pride did not see. We were never meant to conquer the bloodlust, son of Andreas. We only looked at what was seen, not that which is unseen. By focusing on the earthly elements, we forget that which *truly* animates us. The energy that sustains our immortality."

It was a whisper on Giovanni's lips. "*Amnis.*"

Arosh's mouth lifted in the corner. "Energy. Current. It has been called many things. Magic. Aether. Your holy man would call it the soul. Others in the East would call it the void, that which is not there, but permeates all things." Arosh stared into the crackling fire. "Whatever you call it, in immortals, it manifests as the energy that animates our bodies." He reached out a hand and tossed the flames higher. "It lets us control our element. It lets us manipulate the thoughts and memories of humankind. It is our weapon. Our shield. And, as I have learned, it preserves our mind. This 'amnis,' as you call it, is the fifth element that we all share. And no elixir can replace it."

"So blood sustains not just our bodies, but our minds and our souls, as well," Carwyn murmured. "And we must draw it from humanity."

Arosh nodded. "Or animals. As many, including you, have learned, the wild things of this world do carry a spark, but it is not as strong. You must drink more often."

"And preservation kills it," Giovanni added. "That is why we grow weak if we drink too much preserved or stored blood."

Arosh nodded again. "We must feed on the *living* to sustain our bodies, but even more importantly, our minds and energy."

"So by killing the bloodlust—"

"We found a way to preserve the body, but the elixir of life cannot preserve or sustain the mind. Though Kato does not grow physically weak, his amnis is almost gone. And that is why he operates on instinct."

Carwyn sat up and leaned forward. "So, when Kato drank from his lover it... what? It *broke* him? It damaged his amnis past the point of repair? Why couldn't he just start drinking human blood again? Wouldn't that have fixed it?"

Arosh shrugged. "He has no desire for it. Any blood he drinks I must force on him. And I do not know why it no longer feeds his amnis when he drinks human blood. Perhaps we may never know, but yes, it has broken his amnis somehow."

Giovanni said, "But his mind isn't completely gone. He did recognize me. He does still have some consciousness."

"He does *now*." Arosh took a deep breath and refilled his glass. "When I first found him, it was not so." He took another sip of wine. "Kato stayed in Kufa with Fahdil long after the rest of us had left. Ziri was the first to leave the city. Saba left. Eventually, I did, as well. I went north to my home in Persia. I did not know about Kato's decline for several years. His energy—his amnis, as you call it—was very strong. It sustained him, but it could not maintain his mind forever. When Fahdil finally contacted me, it was because his own health was failing. The human had protected Kato as well as he could, but he knew he was dying. When I arrived back in Kufa, Fahdil was dead, and Kato had been locked in a windowless room." Arosh frowned at the memory. "I was confused. Why was my friend confined? What chamber could even hold him? When I opened the door, I understood."

Carwyn asked, "What had happened to him?"

Arosh's eyes furrowed in pain. "Kato was crouched in a corner of the room. He *growled* at me, his oldest friend, but then cringed from the sound of his voice. He flew at me like an animal, but fell back in pain when I touched him. It was when I touched him that I realized... His amnis was almost gone. He had no shield from his senses. The slightest gust of air frayed his skin. A whisper hurt his ears. He was as a newborn vampire without any shield. Water was the only thing that soothed him."

"So his blood still connected him to his element..."

"But he had no control of it. Not as he had before."

Carwyn said, "So that is why he stays in the bath."

"Yes. The water still protects him from some of his senses, so he is most comfortable there. Back in Kufa, I immediately sent for Saba. She and I had argued before she left and she was angry with me, but that was typical for us. I wrote her and told her to gather Jabir's notes and come to my home in Persia. She is the oldest of us and the most skilled in healing. I hoped that she would know how to cure him."

"But she didn't?"

He shook his head. "She had some ideas. From the beginning, Saba was most reluctant to drink from the elixired humans, though she never said why. Perhaps some ancient instinct warned her where our reason and intellect did not. We finally realized that Kato's body remained vital, but the human blood we forced on him did nothing for his mind. It was then that we tried our own blood. Since human blood did nothing, we hoped that immortal blood would help heal his mind. After all, Saba and I were both very powerful, very rich in amnis."

"Did it?" Carwyn asked. "If human blood no longer fed his amnis, did vampire blood?"

"It did help some." Arosh nodded. "He was less aggressive and seemed to have some recognition of us. You saw him with Giovanni earlier. It was like that. So, we tried blood of other elements. I tried giving him Samson's blood, but it showed no improvement. I found other vampires. Older ones. I killed them if they refused. Drained them of life in the hopes that it would do something for my friend. It didn't matter. Their blood did nothing. Finally, it was Saba who suggested that it was Kato's own blood in *us* that had helped him the first time."

Giovanni lifted his eyes from the fire. "His own blood?" His eyes darted toward Carwyn's and he could see the expression in his friend's eyes sharpen. "You mean that his own blood *did* revive his amnis? Restart him, in some way? Is his sire—"

"Kato's sire is no more. We suspected, as you do, that the untainted blood that had sired him could heal him. Remake him in some way. It only existed faintly in those he had exchanged with, like Saba and me, but we had one other hope. If his own blood in us could heal him, then the blood of his direct line could, as well."

Carwyn broke in again. "So, since Lucien's amnis is damaged—dying, as it seems it is—if we could find Saba, his mother, he could be healed?"

"I believe he could, yes. Has he tried to contact her?"

A FALL OF WATER

"He has, but..." Carwyn shrugged helplessly.

Arosh nodded. "She appears when she wants. I know this better than any other."

"But *Kato* had a son," Giovanni said. "My father. Did he have any other children?"

"None living. Your father was the only living child of his line, and at the time, he had sired no children. His blood would be undiluted and strong. He was our best hope to heal our friend. Kato had cut Andreas off years before, so I was the one who sent for him."

Giovanni let out a measured breath. "So, that is the favor you asked of Andros. His blood."

Arosh leaned forward. "I invited him to my home in Persia. I asked him for this favor. I never dreamed he would refuse. I considered killing him and taking his blood, but who knew if one ingestion would be effective? Saba and I had given Kato our blood many times over a period of months. But your father was unwilling." The ancient leaned back and shook his head. "I should have kept him captive. I thought Kato would regain his strength as time passed, and I didn't want the irritation of Andreas as my captive. He was annoying and rather surprisingly powerful."

"So you took Kato away and asked Ziri and Saba to tell the world you had killed each other."

"The last thing I wanted was Andreas to come back and try to assassinate his father. I wanted to give Kato time. I believed, in my arrogance, that no affliction could weaken my friend for long. After all, he had been as strong as I was! Surely, he would heal."

Carwyn said, "But he didn't."

Arosh cocked his head and stared at the fire. "No, he didn't. I brought him here. I made sure he was safe and left him in Samson's care along with a few trusted humans. When I went back to my home in Persia—this was after the word had spread that we had killed each other—" His eyes lifted to Giovanni's. "My home, particularly my library, had been ransacked."

Giovanni closed his eyes and clenched his hands in anger. "And that is how the book came to my father."

Arosh nodded. "Saba left Jabir's manuscript and notes in my library. I doubt your father had any idea what he took. Maybe he discovered it. Maybe he didn't. He was always a bright child, however detestable his character was."

Giovanni slumped back, exhausted by the revelations. Had his father known? Did it even matter? The damage had been done. The poison had already spread, and Arosh was staring at him.

"So now, Giovanni, son of Andreas, you will ask me for your favor again, and I will tell you what you must give me in exchange."

Giovanni leaned forward and stared through the fire to meet the ancient immortal's gaze. "Arosh, will you expose this truth, and my grand-sire, to stop this evil from spreading? Will you take Kato to Rome and show the immortal world the true price of this 'cure?'"

Arosh's gaze was guarded. "You ask me to expose my closest friend, Giovanni Vecchio. You ask me to show the world what he has become. To show them his weakness?"

"To stop this? Yes. I ask you to expose the dangerous secret that you, Kato, Saba, and Ziri hid."

He could feel the heat from the other vampire roll from across the room. "Why do *you* not kill this vampire and take the city? Destroy the book. Destroy those who know of it. Why should I expose my friend to scrutiny? To spare you the inconvenience of battle? I fought many battles I didn't choose because I had to. What makes you above me?"

The flames threatened to burst from his collar, and it was Carwyn who answered while Giovanni fought to maintain his control. "This elixir, Arosh, this *secret*, has been released into the world! Who knows whom Livia has told? Who knows if there have been copies of the book or the formula made? We don't need to just stop the elixir, we need to tell the world the *truth*. Enough secrets! Expose the danger. That is the *only* way it will be stopped."

Giovanni managed to push back his own anger as he rose to his feet. "You have warned us of the dangerous fire of pride. This secret that you and your friends created has remained hidden for too long. Others have been hurt. Killed. Saba's own child has fallen ill from it. Do not let your pride blind you to what must be done to stop this."

Arosh gave him a long, measuring look before he rose. "You are asking this of me?"

His heart gave a quick beat. "I am."

"Then you know what I will want in return."

"Yes."

"Your blood, Giovanni, son of Andreas. Your blood to heal your grand-sire. For as long as he needs it. Your blood and the blood of your children. The blood of any and all of Kato's line." His eyes flared, and he stepped through the fire toward Giovanni. "Promise me your blood, and I will grant you your request."

CHAPTER 27

Beatrice had spent most of the day in the bath. The house was quiet. Lucien was sleeping. Gavin and Jean were due back any night with the truck that held the ELIXIR shipment, but it was anyone's guess when they would actually show. Dez remained in the hospital on bed rest per her doctor's orders, so Ben and Matt spent their days there and Beatrice wandered the halls of Giovanni's house with little to do.

She had kept away from Livia, letting Emil take the lead as more and more vampires flooded into Rome. News of the Roman noblewoman's startling announcement had quickly spread through Europe, and the Roman court was suddenly the most active in the Old World. Most European leaders had either sent delegations to Rome to investigate Livia's claims, or had issued statements praising her. Emil Conti could no longer pretend to be impartial. The lone voice of dissent, he had come out weeks before with a strong public statement, warning those who would listen about the unknown dangers of any formula that claimed to cure bloodlust.

Distinct lines were being drawn and, unfortunately for Beatrice, the personal grievance of a young American vampire received little notice to the major players of the European immortal community, no matter what her connections were.

She dabbed at her face with a towel as she walked back into the bedroom and saw Giovanni stretched out on the bed. He reached an arm out as she walked toward him.

"Come. Lie down and try to rest, Tesoro."

She blinked back tears and dropped the towel before she went to lie next to him. "That's it. I've finally lost it, haven't I? I'm hallucinating."

He tucked her into his side and wrapped a warm arm around her.

"Hush. You're dreaming."

"Thanks for trying to make me feel better, but I don't really sleep anymore." She closed her eyes, resigned to the illusion if it let her imagine he was next to her again. "I haven't slept at all since you've been gone. It's okay. I'm okay with being crazy."

"You're not crazy."

"I am," she said. "I am, but that's okay because you're here."

Warm fingers trailed up and down her arm as she reveled in his touch.

"Dreaming, I tell you. Not hallucinating."

She opened her eyes and looked up at him. "You're not really here, are you?"

He gave a sad shake. "As much as I may wish it, no."

"I guess I'm okay with crazy then."

He tapped a finger against her forehead. "Not crazy."

"I am, a little. Why do you love me like you do? I've never been able to figure it out. I'm really not that special."

Giovanni smiled mischievously and tapped her forehead again. "Maybe I like crazy."

"Told you."

"No." He breathed out. "I recognized you. Here." He leaned down and kissed her forehead, then let his finger trail down her nose, over the slight bump and down around her lips. His fingertips danced across her bare skin until they rested lightly over her heart. "And here. I recognized you. Your mind. Your heart. We recognized each other."

"Like Aristotle said."

"One soul. Two bodies. My soul recognized its own. That is why I love you as I do. All the mysteries. All the secrets. That is the one truth we can hold to."

She sighed and buried her face in the crook of his warm neck, inhaling the ghost of scent that covered him. "You are my balance in this life. In every life."

He tangled his hand in her hair and held her closer. "In every life. Remember that, Tesoro mio."

She took a deep breath and dug her fingers into his arms, desperate to hold him there. "I can't do this without you. I'm so lost. Nothing is right without you."

"You are exactly who you need to be."

"Not without you. Never without you. Come back to me." She closed her eyes and tried to stop the tears that welled up. "What if you don't come back to me?"

"Then you will go on."

"I won't want to."

"But you will."

She felt his lips on her forehead, softly pressing kisses along her hairline, down across her cheek until his face was buried in her neck and he could breathe in her scent. She twisted his hair around her fingers as their hearts beat together and they breathed in unison. In. Out. She inhaled the scent of sweet smoke and held it as long as she could.

"You can't leave me."

"I didn't want to."

"Please, Jacopo."

"Why did you send me away?"

She choked on her cry. "Please... please come back."

"Whatever happens, you will go on, Beatrice."

"No."

"Yes."

She closed her eyes and held him close, but when she opened them a pillow was crushed to her chest, and the ghost of his scent barely clung to it.

Night had fallen when Ben tapped on her door. "B?"

She was still holding the pillow and wrapped in the sheets that held the last of his scent. "Yeah?"

"Jean's here. He's in the library."

"Gavin?"

"I guess he's guarding the truck wherever they left it."

She grabbed the dark handkerchief she kept by the bed and swiped at her eyes. "I'll be down in a minute, okay?"

"Okay." She heard him hesitate. "You all right?"

Beatrice sat up and swung her legs over the side of the bed. "I'm fine."

She heard Ben walk back down the stairs, and she rose to walk into the closet. On impulse, she grabbed one of Giovanni's black Oxford shirts and threw it over a black tank and a pair of jeans. She slipped her old boots on and pulled her hair back into a quick knot. Then she took a deep breath and walked out of the bedroom and down the stairs.

She heard Jean's deep voice as she approached the library. He was chatting with Angela and complimenting her on the wine. When Beatrice entered, he rose and offered a guarded smile. "Beatrice."

"Hey, Jean. So, what's the news?"

Angela slipped out of the room, probably to join Ben, who she could hear in the kitchen on the ground floor.

"Well, as they say, do you want the good news? Or the bad news?"

She sank into the couch and Jean took the seat across from her. Leaning forward, she tugged at her hair. "Can't we get one, single break, Jean? Hit me with both. Whatever."

"We have the truck. We have the boxes of ELIXIR. But we only have four of them."

"And there were five in the shipment."

"*Oui*. Whoever was holding the truck for us in Zagreb must have taken one off. Or Livia managed to get one of her people in."

"So, there's one box of this stuff floating around?"

He shrugged. "Chances are, she also had people watching, though she does not have as many *interesting* associates as Gavin and I do. Prior to this, the majority of her business has been legitimate."

Beatrice bit her lip. "What's your best guess? I'm bowing to the experts on this one. Do you and Gavin think she has it, or is this the kind of thing that was randomly stolen?"

Jean squinted and took another sip of his wine. "Honestly? If it was ordinary thieves stealing from a truck carrying what appeared to be high-end cosmetics... I suspect they would have taken all five boxes. Things like that are easily sold. Thieves would know this. I suspect that this was a single individual, one probably sent to fetch a box for Livia when she realized we had located and stopped the truck. A human who could only carry one before being detected. There was no scent of another immortal lingering in the area."

"So, chances are good that she has a box of ELIXIR now."

He nodded. "I would work from that assumption."

A voice spoke from the hallway. "I'm going to Castello Furio." Beatrice and Jean turned to see Lucien enter the library. He was paler than normal and appeared exhausted, but his voice was strong.

"Lucien, you can't."

"Yes, Beatrice, I can. I am no longer waiting for my mother. I don't know when, or even if, she will show up. And I am through hiding the truth of my illness."

Jean stood and held an arm out. Though Lucien was still strong, he often seemed to have strange sensitivities to light or sound. His balance was no longer reliable because the strange fugues that took him could hit at any time. Jean helped him to a chair and gave him his own glass of wine.

"My friend, may I send for some blood?"

The earth vampire only shrugged. "I am not hungry."

He was never hungry.

Beatrice reached out a hand. "Lucien, please—"

"It's been a year. I took the elixir a year ago and this is what it has done to me. I have lived thousands of years, and it is defeating me." He shook his head. "I will probably die anyway; what use is my pride? My reputation? If any of my enemies wanted to take advantage of this to harm me, they will anyway."

"Lucien, you know that we will take care of you, no matter what." As much as she tried, Beatrice couldn't help but feel like part of this was her father's fault. If Stephen hadn't shown interest in the manuscript, would it have drifted into obscurity? Would Lorenzo have damaged or destroyed it, ridding the world of its evil? It was useless speculation that still haunted her.

Lucien shook his head. "No. Enough. I spoke to Emil to let him know I am in town, and he told me the clamor of praise grows around her every day. The enthusiasm is boundless. I need to tell people the truth of what has happened to me."

"Did Emil put you up to this?"

Lucien scoffed. "I'm not that far out of my own mind, Beatrice. I can make decisions for myself."

Jean said, "Hold, my friend. We are only concerned that you may be endangering your—"

"I'm dying, Jean!" He clenched his jaw. "I am *dying*, and she would offer up this poison as a cure. Our kind must know the truth. Beatrice, take me to her. Take me to court. I will speak before I die. While I still have a voice, I will tell the truth."

Beatrice couldn't ignore him. "Okay, Lucien. If that's what you want, I'll take you." She could see Jean begin to protest, so she held up her hand. "It's his choice. Can you and Gavin guard the boxes of elixir until we get back and decide what to do with them?"

Jean nodded. "Of course. Should one of us stay here at the house with your humans?"

She nodded. "If you could. I don't trust anyone in this city right now. Matt and Dez are at the hospital, and I'm pretty sure of the security there, but the house is too big to be left without at least one of us here."

"I'll let Gavin know. We won't leave the residence unguarded."

"Thanks, Jean. Now." She rose and walked toward the door. "I better call a car if we're going to make it there with enough time for some ass-kicking. Lucien, you need anything before we go?"

He took a deep breath, and she noticed that he looked peaceful for the first time in weeks. "Nope. Just point me in the direction of the asses. I may pass out, but I'll try to get a few kicks in before I do."

Beatrice wanted to laugh, but it stuck in her throat.

This wasn't going to end well.

It took over an hour to reach the castle. When they pulled through the lavish gates, she noticed the number of uniformed drivers and luxury cars that crowded the lawn. Beatrice got out of the car and debated wearing her *shuang gou*. Unfortunately, there was no way she could carry the weapons inconspicuously. She tucked a few daggers into her boot and put the rest of her weapons away.

"Look at them all," Lucien murmured as he looked around. "This is insane."

"Well, Gio did say she loved it when people came to her."

"He's right."

"He usually is. It's very annoying."

Lucien chuckled. "Let's make sure we have an introduction. Do you think the party's inside?"

"In this weather?" She looked around at the damp mist that was falling. "Yeah, they're inside."

"Does she still have that grand hall where she likes to sit like a queen?"

"Yup."

"Lovely."

They stopped inside the gates of the castle grounds and flagged down a servant. They asked for someone to give their names to Emil Conti while they waited under the watchful and plentiful eyes of Livia's guards.

"When did she get so much security?" Lucien asked.

Beatrice looked around. Her back itched where her swords would usually hang, and she twisted her leg to the side, taking comfort in the solid press of metal against her ankle. "She really started piling them on after Lorenzo showed up and she arrested Gio."

He frowned. "Where is she getting them? These do not look like young vampires." He trailed off, muttering as she watched for a sign of Emil. Within a few minutes, she spotted a blur crossing the grounds and Emil stood before them. He nodded toward Lucien and bent to greet Beatrice with a kiss. He did not look pleased.

"My dear, this is unexpected. And probably quite foolish. Livia has taken advantage of this reception to announce what she is calling a 'partnership' with a few other vampires. I'm really not sure this is the proper place to—"

"Hey, don't look at me." She raised her hands, palms-out. "Lucien insisted."

"Lucien, your call this afternoon was very unexpected. What do you have to do with all this mess?"

Lucien took a deep breath. "It's the elixir, Emil. They found the truck, and there was a box of elixir missing. She has it. I know it—it…" He drifted off and Emil looked between Lucien and Beatrice in confusion.

"Lucien? What are you talking about?"

"He's taken it, Emil." Beatrice took Lucien's hand and held it as he drifted.

Emil's eyes grew wide. "The elixir? Lucien has taken the elixir?"

"He drank from a human who had taken it. Now, he is… ill. We're not sure how or why, but that is where Gio and Carwyn have been. They've been trying to find more information from the vampires who helped develop it. And hopefully, they'll find some kind of cure for Lucien, too."

She was still reluctant to detail Giovanni and Carwyn's attempts to find Arosh and Kato. For one thing, she had no idea whether they were having any success. They hadn't heard any news from them in weeks. For another, the vampires they were looking for were supposed to be dead.

Emil was staring at Lucien in confusion. "So, Lucien drank from a human who had taken this drug and now he is... what?"

Lucien blinked and came back. "I'm still here. For now. But my mind is not right. I must tell the court what this elixir does. I must warn them."

Emil shook his head. "My friend, I know how trustworthy you are, but I can only vouch for you as my friend. Many of the younger Romans do not know you. They don't know your sire or your reputation. There is no guarantee they will listen to you when Livia and her three associates have been telling them they hold the keys to a miracle."

Beatrice's eyes darted away from Lucien's disappointed face. "Associates?" she asked. "What associates?"

"She has just announced that she partnered with Matilda from Germany—"

"She's wind."

"Bomeni from Ethiopia."

"Earth," Lucien said.

"And Livia holds water." Beatrice's eyes darted back to Emil's. "Who else?"

"Oleg, the Russian."

Lucien said, "Fire."

Beatrice nodded. "And she's got her four now. We knew she'd have to find willing donors."

Emil asked, "Do you think they know the effects?"

Beatrice nodded, even though they were far from sure. "She knows. Lucien has tried to contact them with no success. They're obviously avoiding him." Though Lucien raised an eyebrow, he did not correct her.

He said, "Whether she knows or suspects, I must have an audience to speak to the vampires of the court. I must at least try, Emil."

The Roman nodded. "I understand. And I will introduce you tonight so you may speak. Beatrice..." He looked toward her with an apologetic expression. "I think it would be better if—"

"Not on your life," she said. "Lucien's not going anywhere near that bitch without me. I don't make the same mistake twice."

Emil sighed. "I will introduce you. Please understand though, the matter of your friend—"

"Is a minor human problem according to these guys," she said. "I get it."

"I am truly sorry. It would not happen if I—"

"Not your fault, Emil. Let's let Lucien have his say so I can get him home. The last thing we need is to be stuck here for the day."

The three started toward the castle, and Beatrice couldn't help but notice how many more guards were dotted around the grounds. "Are Ziri and Tenzin inside?"

"I believe so. Tenzin is with the remnants of the Chinese delegation, though I believe most of them are leaving or have left already. Ziri is... around."

"Somewhere?"

"Yes, but I've only seen him once tonight."

They sped over the grounds and, in no time, they were climbing the stairs toward another of Livia's glittering parties. And once again, Beatrice was distinctly underdressed. She caught the stares of the vampires inspecting her jeans and tank top covered by her husband's shirt, which draped her body almost to the knees. The stares didn't bother her. However, the idea that a good number of these vampires could be going out of their mind if Livia had her way did bother her.

She glanced sideways and caught Emil's frown. "What?" she whispered.

He spoke in a whisper. "Why does she want this?"

"Money? Power over her enemies? Who knows?" Beatrice kept walking through the whispering crowd. "Currently, she's the one that has the knowledge, and knowledge is power. People have fought for this. Died for it, even." She tilted her head toward Lucien. "What would you sacrifice to hold a power that could turn your keenest enemy into a shadow of himself?"

Lucien whispered, "I'd be offended if I didn't agree with you so much. Emil, imagine a bottle of this in the hands of your enemy. They wouldn't even need to attack you. They could influence any human you drank from and send that poison back to you with a healthy flush on their face. You would have no idea."

She didn't miss the hairs that lifted on Emil's neck as they made their way through the crowd. Still, his face was impassive and his stride was purposeful. Many of the vampires they passed seemed to want his attention, but didn't feel confident enough to approach him. He acknowledged the crowd with a polite nod, though he did not stop his steady pace. Beatrice smiled. She had chosen a good leader for Rome.

As long as putting him in power didn't get them all killed.

They arrived in the main hall, which was teeming with vampires. Glittering lights dripped from the ceiling and the rich colors of fall decorated the room. Red and orange dresses were everywhere along with purple, green, and gold decorations. The human servers carried flutes of champagne and tiny hors d'oeuvres as they moved through the crowd. Other humans held up wrists that Beatrice saw more than one vampire take advantage of as they mingled. A thought suddenly struck her.

"You know, all she'd have to do is dose up her donors, and she'd have

A FALL OF WATER

everyone here under her thumb. Think about it, Emil. None of the younger immortals drink from anyone live unless it's here."

She could tell he'd never considered the possibility. "My god, you're right."

Beatrice heard Lucien say, "This is ridiculous. All this ridiculous protocol. Have we become humans after all?"

Lucien pushed them both back and strode toward the front of the room.

"Lucien!"

He didn't stop. The crowd parted and she could see Livia seated in another richly draped chaise at the front of the room. Lorenzo was beside her, along with Matilda, Bomeni, and a scowling vampire Beatrice did not recognize.

Livia rose as Lucien approached.

"Lucien," she said, clearly shocked, but trying to cover it. "What a wonderful surprise to—"

"Shut up, Livia."

Livia didn't just shut up; the whole room did. If there had been a record playing somewhere, Beatrice imagined it would have made a screeching noise. Lucien raised a hand and pointed toward Lorenzo as he sat at her side.

"Did your errand boy tell you he's given out samples of your great discovery?"

Livia's face was blank, and Beatrice suspected she hadn't known, after all. No matter, Lucien was still speaking, but he had turned to address the crowd.

"Oh yes, my friends, I have tried this elixir she calls a miracle! Lorenzo gave it to cure a human under my aegis. Then he told me of its other benefits." His eyes swept the room and Beatrice could tell the ancient vampire had the attention of all in the room. "I drank from her. I drank from her over a year ago. Do you know what it has done to me? Shall I tell you, or perhaps I should just wait here with Livia until I fall into a coma and do not wake?"

The muttering began to circulate around the room. Livia stood, doing her best to keep the peace.

"Lucien, my old friend. Whatever are you talking about?" Her laugh was brittle. "If you have received something purported to be my elixir, I apologize, and I will make sure the finest healers see to you, but this cure has been tested, my friends!" Her gaze swung away from Lucien to the crowd that surrounded her, trying to reassure them. "This is not some magic potion; this is science. A breakthrough of historic significance..."

Beatrice's eyes drifted as Livia started her sales pitch again. She searched through the crowd to examine those who surrounded the water vampire. There was security, definitely. A lot of that. And her three partners stood next to her. None of them looked shocked in the least. All their faces were very carefully blank.

She continued to scan the room. In addition to the tiered fountains that dotted it, a discreet channel of water had been built since the last time she had visited. To most, it would have looked like a very beautiful water feature, but

Beatrice knew what it really was: a weapon. Luckily, it was a weapon for more than just Livia. She stepped closer to Lucien and the wary vampires of Livia's court kept their distance.

"Livia!" Lucien was shouting over her. "Stop your speeches and listen! I'm willing to believe that you may not have realized how harmful this all was, but for the good of your people, you must stop this madness now. Admit that this elixir is harmful. Stop the production until more research can be done. What kind of leader are you if you cannot look past your own self-interest to the good of Rome? To the common good of our kind?"

Beatrice noticed a flicker on the edge of the crowd. *Tenzin.* Her ancient friend nodded toward her and Beatrice slowly relaxed. She glanced at Emil and noticed that he was subtly making eye contact with a number of other vampires in the room who she guessed were his allies. There were more than she had expected.

Livia's eyes narrowed. "Lucien, perhaps you are ill. Or at least ill-informed. Apparently, your association with..." Livia looked toward Beatrice with a blatant sneer. "Less than trustworthy immortals has influenced your usually clear head."

"It's not Beatrice or Giovanni who have clouded my mind, Livia. That was done by this poison you are trying to convince—"

"Stop your lies!" she exploded. "Your reputation for questionable connections has long haunted you. You are no longer welcome in my home."

"I am not leaving until I am heard!"

"Guards, escort the vampire, Lucien Thrax, out of my home, along with his detestable companion. Emil, I cannot believe you even offered them an introduction here."

Silent vampires stepped forward and laid their hands on Lucien's shoulders, pushing him toward the doors. Beatrice saw him blink and stumble once.

"Lucien!" She rushed forward, only to be grabbed by several guards before she could reach him. She quickly grabbed the daggers from her boots and slashed out, cutting two of them at the throat. She could feel the blades meet their spines, but the bone did not snap. Blood sprayed out as guards rushed them and Livia shrieked.

"Murderer! She brings weapons to my home to assassinate me. Seize her! Arrest Beatrice De Novo. Take her away!"

Beatrice heard Emil shout out over the gathering furor. "Hold, immortals of Rome! Listen to me and hold!"

Rough hands grabbed for her. She whirled, slashing at any that came close. Two went down at her feet, their blood spilling over the marble mosaics on the floor as she severed their spines. Another. Two more. Beatrice cut and kicked at anyone who approached her as she fought her way toward Lucien. He was crumpled on the floor, and she feared he could be trampled as the crowd began to panic and churn.

A FALL OF WATER

She felt water dash her face and glanced over her shoulder to see Livia raise her arms to command it. Beatrice raised an arm, swiping the wave that Livia aimed at her back toward its source. As she did, she felt multiple hands grab her legs. She growled and kicked them away. She needed to get to Lucien, but kept tripping over vampires in her path. She looked around in confusion. The hall had turned into a near riot as humans fled toward the doors, but where was Tenzin?

Beatrice reached Lucien, only to kneel down and have four of Livia's guards dive on top of her, kicking her face and hitting the sick vampire in the process. She screamed and lashed out, but more still came.

"Seize her!" Livia continued to scream. "Seize her and bring her to me!"

It seemed as if dozens of hands grabbed her and tore her from Lucien's side. She was dragged in front of Livia, but the crowd still churned in confusion and she couldn't see Tenzin anywhere. Suddenly, Lucien disappeared from in front of her. Beatrice looked around in panic, only to see Tenzin hovering in a corner of the room, cradling the tall man in her arms. She relaxed for a second before they dragged her in front of the screaming Roman matriarch.

Emil was shouting over the crowd. "Livia, you must not do this! She is protected. Do not lay a hand—"

The crowd drowned him out and the guards pushed him back. Beatrice stood in front of Livia, secured by Livia's guards. The Roman was spitting mad, but Beatrice ignored her as she noticed the new addition to the room. Lorenzo. He was standing behind Livia, surrounded by guards, and his canny eyes watched the chaos breaking out across the room.

Beatrice finally caught his eye and grinned. She mouthed, *'You're next,'* and kicked at one of the bodies near her feet. Her boots were sticky, and she could feel the spray of blood cooling on her face. Giovanni's shirt hung in tatters and trailed thick drops on the intricate mosaics at her feet.

Beatrice no longer cared.

The hall finally seemed to quiet down, and she could hear Emil's shouts again. "Do not allow Livia's rash actions, immortals of Rome. Beatrice De Novo is the favored scribe of Penglai Island. She is the granddaughter of Don Ernesto Alvarez. A favorite of those in power across Europe and the East. Do not let Livia's vindictive actions go unchallenged!"

Just then, Beatrice heard it. The water in the fountain near her quivered and shook in excitement. A hush fell over the room as a gusting wind approached. She heard a commotion in the outer chamber and the smell of smoke reached her nose. Her eyes followed Livia's, glued to the giant doors at the back of the hall. They suddenly burst open with a rush of wind and fire. Humans around the room screamed as three immortals passed over their heads and the room filled with heat.

Carwyn dropped to her side with a crash. The marble floor burst open beneath his feet.

Tenzin circled overhead, hissing and spitting at any guard that drew near.

And coming through the crowd, blue fire swirling over his body, Giovanni walked. He looked for her, and Beatrice reached out a hand to her mate. Their fingers twined with a hiss as water and fire met, then both of them turned to Livia.

CHAPTER 28

As his fingers tangled with hers, Giovanni thought that there was no other time in five hundred years of life when he'd had so much to say and so little ability to say it. He linked his fingers with hers as their friends flanked him. Their amnis tangled together, twisting in relief that mirrored the sense of relief he'd felt as soon as he entered the hall and sensed her.

The room was frozen in shock for a few precious moments until Livia screamed out, "Arrest him!"

Giovanni glanced up at Tenzin. She nodded. He let go of Beatrice's hand and shoved her behind him. Then he snapped both fingers, immediately bringing the fire to his hands. He threw out two streams of flame that Tenzin whipped into a circle, surrounding them, holding off Livia's guards and causing the vampires in the hall to skitter back in fear. He could hear the few humans left in the hall weeping as Livia bared her fangs and hissed.

She raised her arms, calling the water in the room. It rose up, a glistening shower over their heads, the tiny droplets poised to spear down on them, but then Giovanni felt Beatrice's amnis rise behind him and the water halted, suspended like a quivering chandelier, frozen as it scattered the light of his flames.

Matilda took to the air to face Tenzin. Bomeni crouched down in front of Livia. Giovanni recognized the Russian standing behind her, surprised to see Oleg in Livia's company. He met his fellow fire vampire's gaze and saw the other man's eyes narrow to a calculating stare. Giovanni's collar began to smoke as he caught the smell of the other immortal's fire.

He looked back at Livia as the hall reached a standstill. The once beautiful woman had never appeared more animalistic. Her fangs had pierced her lips and blood dripped from her mouth and down her chin, staining her intricate gown. He stepped forward, the fire moving with him as Tenzin tracked his pace.

Livia pulled back her rage and spoke to him in a low voice. "Why are you here?"

To kill you. Giovanni whispered to Beatrice. "Conti?"

"He's ready," she whispered. She held the water almost effortlessly above them.

Giovanni looked at Emil Conti, who stood at the edge of the crowd, eyeing Giovanni with suspicion. No doubt, the vampire was wondering if the fire vampire was there to take his place.

"Signor Conti," he asked in a respectful voice. "I would like to address the immortals of Rome."

Emil straightened his shoulders and nodded with a smile. "Please, Dottor Vecchio, the Roman court will listen."

Giovanni looked back at Livia, who was curling her lips in anger. "Step aside, Livia."

She bared her fangs. Giovanni could see black-clad guards pouring into the room from the two doors behind her. "Never," she said. "This city is mine."

"Admit that this 'elixir of life' is a poison."

"You are as ridiculous and delusional as the Thracian. I seek only the good of my people; you seek to deceive. No one will believe your lies, murderer." She raised her voice. "*Murderer!*"

Giovanni turned back to Emil. "Signor Conti, if you would send the humans out of the room?"

Emil nodded. "Immortals of Rome, this is a conflict among our own kind. Send your humans away. They are not welcome here."

Giovanni could see eyes darting around the room. Many of the older vampires looked to Livia for confirmation, but she ignored them. Then the few humans left in the room were herded toward the doors near the back.

"Oleg!" Giovanni addressed the Russian. "I have had no quarrel with you."

The Russian responded with caution. "Nor I with you, di Spada."

"This water vampire has deceived you."

Giovanni saw Oleg eyeing Livia with suspicion. The Russian had been sired from earth. He usually minded his own business and had never been the trusting kind. He had also been an associate of Lucien Thrax, who Tenzin had flown out of the hall earlier. The vampire was obviously reconsidering his alliance with the Roman aristocrat after seeing his ailing friend. Oleg looked up at Tenzin, then at Carwyn, and then over Giovanni's shoulder where Beatrice stood holding back Livia's water. Oleg looked to Emil Conti and nodded. "I seek no quarrel with Rome or those who dwell here."

Oleg stepped away from Livia, and Emil called out, "Depart in peace, and consider yourself a friend of Rome."

"Traitor!" Livia screamed. "I will have your head for this, Russian."

Oleg only looked amused as he and his retinue headed toward the doors. "We shall see, Livia." The doors opened one last time as the fire vampire headed out the doors, then they slammed shut and a low murmur began to fill the room. Livia's guards surrounded them. Bomeni and Matilda guarded their leader. Swirling amnis charged the air, and Giovanni lowered the flames that surrounded him as he looked over the nearby vampires.

There were immortals from all over the Old World. Romans, but also those from the Middle East, North Africa, and Europe and Asia. Familiar, friendly faces and unfamiliar, suspicious expressions combined. Some of them had obviously cast their lot with Livia, and he could almost feel their anger floating in the air around him.

"Immortal brothers and sisters," he said. "I am not your enemy! I come here as one of you. Not to lead. Not to conquer. I come seeking the truth. I am the only son of the great scholar, Niccolo Andros, and I am here to warn you of a great danger." He reached over and grasped Beatrice's hand and her amnis met his again. "One that could affect all of us and all those under our aegis."

Emil Conti spoke. "Dottor Vecchio, your skills as a scholar are as renowned as your skills as a fighter. Please, tell us what you know of the elixir of life."

Giovanni nodded. "I learned of this elixir years ago. I know that Livia has told you it is a cure for the bloodlust that stalks us. That it is an answer to humanity's ills, as well. It is not."

His eyes swung back to Livia. "Step down now, Livia."

"Don't be ridiculous," she scoffed.

Beatrice squeezed his hand as he continued to address the crowd. "The vampire who leads Rome tells you that with this elixir, you will no longer be a slave to your hunger. She tells you that any humans you may care for will live forever, without pain or illness. We have all suffered from bloodlust. We have all lost human companions or friends that were useful or even loved. But I tell you now, this is no cure."

Livia began to laugh as more guards entered the room. They lined the walls, and he could see the vampires around him start to tense. Some with anticipation. Some with fear. The guards blocked the door. All of them were armed with swords, though none of the crowd appeared to carry any weapons.

"Last chance, Livia." Giovanni still wouldn't let her live, but he might kill her in a more private location if she complied. The problem was, she knew it, too.

Livia said, "You are a murderer, a liar, and a thief. No one believes you, Giovanni di Spada."

"You are right," he said. "I *am* a murderer." He heard the gasp that swept the room, but he continued. "I will hold back no truth! I admit that I killed my sire, Niccolo Andros, with the help of my son, Lorenzo, who stands behind you."

"You forced him to help you with amnis, Giovanni! He was only a human."

Giovanni laughed. "I did no such thing. Lorenzo knew of my father's cruelty. As did you. Andros's own sire had cut him off. It was only the rest of the world my father fooled."

"Andros was not cruel." She addressed the crowd. "He was a great immortal and my beloved mate. Let me kill this rebellious child who has admitted to taking him from us."

"Niccolo Andros had no more use for you than he did for his money purse, Livia. You were a tool. Nothing more. We both know it."

She screamed. "Liar!"

He narrowed his eyes and a smile curled the corner of his lip. "Perhaps you were deceived by him. Perhaps he fooled you, as well. Did Andros keep his secrets from you, as he did from us all?"

"Foolish child, Andros was my mate. We had no secrets from each other."

She had stepped into the trap with such ease that Giovanni had to force himself not to grin. His face was a picture of sympathetic understanding. "There is no shame in being the victim of deception, Livia."

"I knew him better than you ever did."

Perhaps not even Livia knew the truth. She had created her own history, and Giovanni would not fight it. In the end, it did not matter; she would burn with the rest of his enemies. "Then, my dear, you will not be surprised by our guests! Emil?" He turned back to the old Roman, who was watching the exchange with a guarded expression. "I would like to invite to the court three of our most ancient brethren." Giovanni angled his shoulders toward the door a second before they flew open. A few of the younger vampires rushed toward the open doors, only to be thrown back by a strong wind as Ziri flew into the hall.

The ancient wind vampire carried Giovanni's grand-sire, who looked around the room with a slow blink. Giovanni had fed Kato his blood before they left Arosh's mountain fortress, and the effects were immediately evident. The old water vampire was less aggressive and seemed to already have more awareness of his surroundings. Though he still did not speak, he seemed to exhibit a growing recognition of Giovanni and Arosh. He had even allowed Carwyn to remain in his presence.

The fire vampire strode into the room with a lazy gait and looked around in amusement. He ignored the whispers that began as he entered, and the crowd parted for him. He calmly walked through the circle of fire and came to stand beside Giovanni as Ziri landed behind him and set Kato on his feet.

Arosh looked around the room; then he nodded at Emil Conti and narrowed his eyes at Livia. His deep voice filled the silent hall when he finally spoke. "So, this is Andreas's woman who calls herself the leader of Rome?" He curled his lip. "We shall see."

CHAPTER 29

At the mention of Andros's name, the massive vampire next to Beatrice bared his fangs and hissed. She looked up with wide eyes. This had to be Kato. He looked like the statue of Neptune that ruled over the Trevi fountain in the center of Rome. His hair flowed over his shoulders. His beard was long and curling, and he wore only a loose pair of pants. She clutched Giovanni's hand, but he calmly pressed her fingers between his own.

Despite everything, the blood in her veins sang. *He is back.* He was near! Her mate was next to her again, and her heart sped in delight and anticipation even as she looked at the frighteningly powerful immortal that towered over her.

The water in the air clung to Kato's skin. She could even feel it wick away from her as she stood next to him. The delicate skin of her lips cracked, causing blood to spring up. She shivered, and a small breath escaped her, but as soon as Kato heard her small gasp, he turned his eyes to Beatrice, and they softened. His fangs disappeared, and he lifted a large hand to touch her cheek. Her skin immediately plumped with moisture again.

"Gio?" she whispered.

"It's fine, Tesoro. He won't hurt you. He smells his blood in you. Remember, you are of his line."

"Isn't Livia, too?"

At the mention of Livia's name, Kato's eyes swung back toward the front of the room and he bared his fangs again. Ziri placed a hand on the giant's shoulder, and Kato calmed. Beatrice clutched Giovanni's hand in hers, determined not to be separated from him. She heard the long-haired vampire with the crackling energy address the crowd.

"I am Arosh. The vampires of Rome know who I am. I need no permission to speak to this hall."

Livia, as if sensing the situation slipping out of her control cried out, "This is *my* hall! And I do not—"

She was cut off as a sharp spear of fire shot out of Arosh's fingers. Livia pulled a guard in front of her, who immediately turned to ash.

"Shut up, woman. I am speaking."

Beatrice might have imagined the slight shake in Emil's voice, but she didn't think so. Still, Emil stepped forward with an outstretched arm that didn't tremble once. Beatrice was impressed.

He said, "Though you need no permission, my lord, I would welcome you to my city. We had heard of your demise, but I am very pleased to hear that the rumors were false."

Arosh waved a careless hand. "My thanks, Roman. I have come to your city in return for a favor granted by Giovanni Vecchio, the son of Andreas, sired of Kato."

The low chatter began as Kato's name moved around the room. This was the ancient king of the Mediterranean, she realized. As soon as he had stepped into the room, many of the vampires had probably recognized him. All of them had thought their legendary king was dead. And though he definitely wasn't dead, there *was* something wrong with him. As powerful as he was, his amnis, when he had touched her, had felt very wrong.

Arosh continued, "I come here with my friend, Kato, your ancient king, and our friend Ziri, who is often among you, to tell you what I know of this elixir that the alchemist made for us."

Beatrice held on to Giovanni's hand and felt his warm energy run up her arm. He stepped back and put his arm around her shoulders as she breathed in the rich scent of his skin. Then, she caught the bobbing blond head of Lorenzo from behind Livia's guards. He was watching them with narrowed eyes. She tensed for a moment, but then heard the soft, steady thump of Giovanni's normally silent heart. He was poised, but calm, so she tried to relax.

Arosh continued his speech. "I will not stay long. This is not my fight, but I do know this elixir and it is no cure. It is quite harmful and has made my friend, this ancient immortal before you, sick. Though it nurtures the body, it destroys the very energy that animates us. Do not believe this deceiver who claims to lead you."

The low chatter in the room grew louder, and Giovanni stepped forward to speak.

"Vampires of Rome, I was trained by my sire to be the most rational of our kind. He desired that I exhibit knowledge and reason alone. I did not subscribe to superstition or magic. I believed only in what could be tested and tried." Giovanni looked around the room, then down to meet her eyes. "But some things, I have learned, have no rational explanation. Some things are far greater than what can be seen."

He looked around the hall. "We are not only creatures of the elements. Though these elements preserve our bodies, they are *not* the eternal energy of our souls. We are *more*. All of us. We are more than creatures of the physical world." Giovanni turned to his grand-sire, placing a hand upon the giant's shoulder. "We are creatures of the heart and the spirit. Of energy and things unseen. If we seek to preserve our bodies without accepting our need for humanity and what they offer us, *we will be lost*."

He turned to Arosh, who gave him a respectful nod. Giovanni said, "We are *not* all-powerful, my friends. Even the greatest among us have been forced to acknowledge this."

Arosh spoke again. "Be rid of this poison and be rid of your foolish pride. Though the great Kato grows strong again..." He glared at the vampires who surrounded them. "And will soon be as strong as ever—not even he could heal himself. Giovanni Vecchio has helped to heal him."

A brave voice called from the back of the room. "But Giovanni Vecchio killed his own sire!"

Arosh frowned. "If he hadn't, I would have. Andreas refused to grant me a favor."

The room fell silent again. Beatrice wanted to ask why refusing a favor was such a big deal, but decided that it wasn't the best time. She finally heard Livia speak. The favor thing must have been serious, because for the first time, the scheming water immortal's voice held a note of calculation.

"My lord Arosh, forgive my ignorance. And forgive my earlier outburst. I was enraged by the thought of my mate's murderer standing before me. But if you say Giovanni Vecchio has your good will—"

"I did not say he had my good will," Arosh scowled. "That is not easily bestowed. I said he had granted me a favor, one that his sire would not."

Livia nodded respectfully, her face a picture of accommodation.

Unbelievable, Beatrice thought, she was actually trying to get out of it. Livia continued in an ingratiating voice, "But if you would only forgive my earlier surprise. I had no idea that my husband had displeased you, or that his sire was in need of—"

"But Livia"—Giovanni stepped forward, still holding Beatrice's hand—"you just finished telling this court that Andros had no secrets from you. Arosh, did you not tell me that Andros knew of the elixir and its effects?"

The ancient king shrugged. "Of course. I told him when I asked him to help his sire. He knew exactly what the elixir did. And, I'm assuming he would have told his wife when he stole the book containing this formula from my library and brought it back to Rome."

Giovanni looked around the room. "Then surely Livia knew as well! For she and Andros had no secrets. Surely her 'dear friend' Lorenzo knew when he gave Lucien Thrax the fatal dose. They have deceived you, Rome. They hope to profit from this formula. To become rich as their enemies grow weak. They would use this elixir, not to cure bloodlust, but to kill us. To kill the humans we value. It is not the elixir of life. It's the elixir of death."

The water in the air that Beatrice had been holding began to shake again, as Livia quaked with rage. Beatrice pulled away from Giovanni and held her hands out, forcing the water away from the ring of flame that protected them from the multitude of black-clad guards. She eyed the one nearest her, measuring how quickly she could take his weapon from him.

Giovanni's skin began to heat, and she saw the smoke rise above his collar. Arosh was looking around the room in amusement. "I see great fear on many of your faces. I believe some of you have taken this elixir already. Foolish vampires! Is your sire alive to heal you? I hope so, for your sakes. Come, my friends, you have wise immortals among you." Arosh gestured toward Emil. "You are the people of the great sea! Kato's heirs. Rid yourselves of this poison she has spread and appoint a leader worthy of you."

Beatrice's eyes flew to Livia. She was livid. The appeasing expression on her face had vanished and her arms were raised over the crowd.

Beatrice felt Giovanni's hand tighten around hers and knew he had seen the insane glint in Livia's eyes, too.

Not good.

The water in the air crept along her skin. The flames around her surged. And Beatrice's heart sped for a moment, then fell completely still as Livia whispered, "Kill them all."

CHAPTER 30

As if they had choreographed it, Ziri grabbed Kato and Arosh, then took to the air in front of Giovanni as soon as the words left Livia's mouth. He looked up and caught the other fire vampire's eye, and Arosh grinned as the room erupted in violence.

"Do not get yourself killed, Giovanni Vecchio! Remember, we have a deal."

So they would fight Livia and her guards without the help of the ancients. Giovanni wasn't surprised. Arosh and Ziri had their own agenda, and risking their lives in a fight that was not their own was not part of it. Giovanni could see Emil calling to those vampires loyal to him as they rushed Livia's allies.

His eyes swung toward Beatrice, but she had already leapt through the circle of flame, bashing in the head of one guard with a swift kick before she grabbed his weapon and the weapon of another guard she quickly beheaded. He felt a spray from overhead and looked up to see Tenzin with her scimitar out, locked in struggle with a ferocious Matilda. A moment later a long, pale leg dropped to the ground between Giovanni and Carwyn, and the earth vampire bared his fangs and grinned.

"Can't let the girls have all the fun, can we?"

"Never!" He dropped the circle of flames that protected them a moment before the water Beatrice had been holding showered around him, soaking him to the skin and dousing his flames. Carwyn rushed Bomeni, and the two crashed together like twin boulders before they rolled across the floor and the ground buckled beneath them.

Giovanni scanned the room. Where was Livia? The front of the room was a mass of swirling black as Livia's guards protected their queen. He cut through the crowd, slashing with the dagger he had brought, the same one she had plunged into his body in rage. He felt a sword slash at the small of his back before a spray of blood hit him. He turned to see his wife grinning with bared fangs as she took down another guard.

He took two strides to her and grabbed his mate in a fierce kiss.

Beatrice bit his lip and said, "Hey, handsome. Nice to see you."

He elbowed a guard that tried to attack them, grabbing the vampire's sword as the guard fell to the ground and Beatrice cut off his legs. Giovanni licked the blood from his lip and smiled. "I missed you, Tesoro."

"Same here. Now let's kill this bitch so we can go home."

She pulled him down for one more swift kiss before she spun away, slashing with the twin sabers she had stolen.

Giovanni headed toward the front of the room. He had a sword but no fire. His hair was wet and moisture clung to his body. Giovanni looked up for Tenzin and yelled, "Bird girl? A little wind, please?"

Tenzin curled her lip, but grabbed Matilda by her long blond hair and swung her across the room where the vampire was bashed against the wall and slid to the ground. Tenzin directed a strong gust that dried him as he walked toward Livia's position. The flames sparked on his skin, and Tenzin's wind fanned them higher as he looked for his prey.

A streak of red darted by and he saw Donatella Conti rush toward the back doors where she battled the guards who were cutting down those running to safety. Many of the younger, weaker vampires were desperately trying to escape the battle, so he abandoned his search to help Donatella. She saw him approaching and shouted, "The doors! They're oak!"

He nodded and summoned two streams of flame. With one, he blasted back Livia's guards. The other, he aimed at the giant arched doors that sealed them in. The smoke began to fill the room as the lacquered oak caught fire. Within a few moments, the doors were crumbling, and the drapes in the room had been set aflame. Donatella flung water from the fountains to douse the flames and quell the growing panic.

"Go!" she yelled, and the younger vampires ran from the room. Donatella plunged back into battle, her brilliant red cocktail dress slashed and ragged. She grinned at him as she ran past, grabbing a sword from the ashes near the door.

"I like your wife, Giovanni. *Fantastic* boots."

He gave a hoarse laugh. "I'm fond of them, myself." Donatella disappeared into the melee of vampires still battling, cutting toward her husband who was in the center of the battle. They were greatly outnumbered once the younger vampires had fled, but were still holding their own.

Tenzin was battling in the air. He didn't see Matilda, but some of her entourage were keeping his old partner occupied. Sprays of blood rained around him as Tenzin cut them down, one by one. Carwyn and Bomeni were evenly matched, and the floor buckled as each tried to best the other. Though Carwyn was as occupied keeping up the support pillars in the room as he was trying to best the other vampire.

Beatrice was cutting down the guards that swarmed near the front, slowly but surely making her way forward. Most of the guards were water vampires, but were no match for his mate's power. She slapped at them with the water from the fountains and spun gracefully. Giovanni saw her take out two guards with one slash of her sword.

But he still didn't see Livia.

As he walked through the room, he sent out his fire, trying to avoid allies while killing enemies. Battling in enclosed spaces had always posed a problem for him, unless he wanted to kill everyone in the room. He cut back a few guards with his sword as he searched. He caught a flash of blond hair and saw Lorenzo dueling with Emil Conti.

Just then, he felt water splash against his feet. Giovanni looked down to see a few inches of water had covered the floor.

A lot of water.

He felt the ground shake and looked for Carwyn.

Bomeni, playing to the strengths of his allies, had opened a crack in the floor, splitting the foundation and the earth below it. Giovanni finally spotted Livia. She was standing in the corner of the room, pulling groundwater from the river that flowed under the castle.

Too much water.

It splashed up around his feet. At the speed and power with which she was drawing it, the room would be filled in no time. The fire along his torso sizzled out. There was no way Tenzin would be able to dry him when she was battling six of Matilda's guards in the air. Carwyn was holding off Bomeni with one arm and keeping the ceiling from crashing down with the other. Emil was dueling Lorenzo, as his allies battled Livia's.

As Giovanni dispatched four of Livia's guards, he saw a red-clad arm float by. He spun just in time to see Donatella Conti take a deep breath. Her eyes were wide and hollow when the sword slashed her neck and her head sailed across the room, landing with a splash as Emil roared out at the death of his mate.

Giovanni's eyes sought Beatrice. She was holding her own, trying to make her way toward Livia, but he saw her arms were bloody and torn. The room continued to flood with water. They had lost one of their fiercest fighters. And the black clad guards poured into the room like a never-ending stream of death.

He needed to end this.

"Beatrice!"

CHAPTER 31

She heard Giovanni call her name from the back of the room. Beatrice cut off the heads of the two guards in front of her before she sped back to where he stood. Livia's guards did not follow. They were completely focused on protecting their mistress, who seemed to be pulling water from the ground itself as the battle raged around her. Giovanni grabbed her and slashed at the vampires that fell on them.

"Beatrice, I need to end this. Now!"

"How?" she cried. "There's too much water!"

Beatrice glanced toward Carwyn. The earth vampire seemed to have finally stabilized the pillars that held up the room, so he turned his attention fully on Bomeni. The fierce immortal bared his gleaming white fangs and sprang on her friend, but Carwyn caught him and locked his long arms around the man's chest, crushing his ribs with an audible crack before Bomeni howled in pain and fell to the ground. Carwyn stood over him, took the vampire's head between his hands, and twisted it off in a spray of blood and gore. Then he roared and started into the mass of twisted bodies where Emil still fought.

The room was filling with water. Massive blocks of marble had fallen in front of the doors, so they were blocked, and Livia's guards still outnumbered them.

Giovanni yelled, "Carwyn!"

The earth vampire turned and looked to them. Then he sped back, tossing away the vampires that followed.

"We need to do something!" he panted. "This water, Gio—"

"It's filling up the room." He shook his head. "I can't build any flame, and even if I could, our allies are scattered. It's not safe. I would kill our own people."

"Carwyn," Beatrice said. "Get to Emil. I'll try to push the water back, but I'll need his help."

Carwyn nodded, but before he could leave them, a drenched and tattered Tenzin appeared with Emil gripped in her arms. He was wounded and bleeding from a deep cut to the neck.

"Your son almost killed him, my boy. I managed to grab him, but I think Lorenzo has fled."

Giovanni said, "Forget him right now. We need to kill Livia. Can you get to her?"

She shook her head. "They're watching for me. She has guards that are covering her from the air while she pulls this damn water up."

"Go. Get as many of our allies as you can and bring them here to the back of the room. Then I need you to bring the wind."

Tenzin cocked her head. "Truly?"

Giovanni's voice was hoarse. "I need a hurricane, bird girl."

Tenzin narrowed her eyes, but nodded before she took to the air.

A kind of barricade built up as they killed and tossed the bodies of Livia's guards around them in the back corner of the room. Carwyn continued to protect them as Emil gathered his strength in the corner. Beatrice saw the ancient Roman grow stronger with each breath as the water grew higher. He grabbed a passing guard and bit his neck as the vampire screamed in agony. Then he broke his victim's spine and tossed him on the growing pile.

She felt Giovanni tug on her arm. "Tesoro, we need to end this. We have to kill her."

Beatrice wiped a spray of blood from her face. "How—"

"As soon as Tenzin gathers as many of our allies as she can, she'll bring a whirlwind to this side of the room. That will block her guards; they won't be able to get through."

"But the water. She's pulling from the river; there's no end to it. I've tried! I can't hold it back."

He turned to face her and shook her shoulders. "*Don't* hold it back! You and Emil must pull the water away from her."

"I can't!" Tears came to her eyes. She was exhausted, and Livia had not lifted a sword.

"You have to. Tenzin's wind will help. As soon as the room is dry enough, I can finish this."

A sick feeling rooted in her stomach. "How?"

"You will take shelter in the water. The wind and the water will protect you from the fire. You will be in the eye of the whirlwind with the water around you. The flames will *not* get through."

She hacked the head off two guards and spun on her mate. "What are you going to do?" she screamed.

Taking advantage of a brief moment of calm, Giovanni cupped her bloody cheek in his hand. In the background, she heard the fall of their allies as Tenzin tossed them to safety. Then the air grew eerily still as the ancient wind vampire began to stir the wind around them.

Beatrice looked up to meet her husband's eyes. "Gio, please..."

He leaned down and pressed his lips to hers as the wind grew stronger. Soon, Beatrice, Giovanni, and all their friends were surrounded by a screaming vortex that Tenzin whipped into a frenzy. Giovanni wrapped her in his arms, and Beatrice held him tightly, refusing to let go. He finally pulled away, and she could see his look of resolve.

"Pull the water into the whirlwind, Beatrice."

She choked back the tears. "You can't."

"I must." He stroked her cheek tenderly. "Pull the water in, Tesoro. Emil cannot do it alone."

She looked over her shoulder as the tears fell down her cheeks. Emil was pulling the water in, and the air around them grew damp and humid as he forced the water away from Livia and into Tenzin's storm. Carwyn's arms held up the ceiling as the floor trembled. In the distance, Beatrice heard Livia scream when she realized what Emil was doing.

"Pull the water in, Beatrice. You have the strength. *I love you*," he whispered. "So much. And you are exactly who you need to be. All of this has happened for a reason. Now let me do my part."

She sobbed as she reached up and clutched his neck, pulling his mouth to hers in one final kiss before she let go with a hoarse cry and lifted her arms. Beatrice felt the rage and the power well up from the very center of her being. She grabbed Emil's hand and held onto it as the amnis rushed between them and they pulled the water into the storm. The room around them grew dark as the lights went out, but they stood protected in the eye of the small hurricane. The wind around them grew thick with mud and ash, until all she could see was the swirling black of wind and water, and the grim resolve on Giovanni's face.

He caught her eye one last time before Tenzin plucked him from the center of the storm and lifted him up and over the wall of wind and water. Beatrice let go of Emil's hand and screamed in rage as she pulled at the river. She could feel the water around her, flexing and answering her call. It danced and sang, waiting for her command.

Immortals around her gaped in silent awe as strings of water reached down to touch each finger, and Beatrice lifted her face to see Tenzin floating in the air above. Her friend hovered for a moment with tears in her eyes, before she came and landed in front of Beatrice, who continued to hold the water in the wind.

"Pull it in, my girl. All the way. The room is dry, but he needs you to protect us so he can finish this."

"No!" Beatrice cried out in anguish when she saw Tenzin's tears.

"Yes," she whispered.

Tenzin placed one hand on her shoulder, and she felt Carwyn's hand press against her back, holding her as she reined in her element. Beatrice finally nodded, and the water rushed over her skin, comforting her and washing away her tears. Then she called the river over them. As soon as the vampires were enveloped in their watery sanctuary, the room around them erupted in fire, and Beatrice fell to her knees.

CHAPTER 32

The air was dry and crackled with energy as Giovanni stalked toward her. Livia was trying to call the water toward her, but the river that poured from the gash in the marble floor was pulled with ever greater ferocity toward the storm on the far end of the hall.

Livia was no match for his mate.

He flexed his arms, and the fire burst forth.

Livia turned furious eyes toward him. "Stop!"

Giovanni kept walking, and the guards that rushed toward him turned to ash as he threw out streams of fire that enveloped them as they ran.

More.

The dry air fed the flames. He stepped over the bodies that littered the intricate marble mosaics on the floor.

More.

The flames grew higher. He could still hear the sound of voices calling from the eye of the storm. Once they were silent, he knew they were safe. That *she* was safe.

More.

Livia's guards scurried and ran around him, trying to find an opening to attack, but his fire only burned hotter in an ever-widening perimeter of flames.

The water rushed into the wind, pulled by his mate's extraordinary power. The flames along his body grew brighter. The blue fire singed his hair and the smell of it caused a rush of memories. Her cries when Lorenzo had taken her. The punch of a bullet as he fought toward her in the belly of a ship. Her tears on a lonely riverbank.

A FALL OF WATER

"You are my balance in this life. In every life."

Giovanni felt the last scraps of his clothes burn away as he walked toward Livia. With each step, the fire grew. He could feel it, the slow, angry shiver underneath his skin, quivering in anticipation, begging to burst forth. And at the core of his being, Giovanni realized he was exhausted. He could imagine no greater release than to finally release the fire he had suppressed for over five hundred years. He closed his eyes and thought of Beatrice.

The feel of her mouth on his skin.

Her soft sigh as she curled into his body.

The curve of her lips just before she smiled.

"I love you, Jacopo."

He met Livia's angry glare, and he could see the moment she truly began to panic.

"Stop!" she cried, giving up the water and snatching a blade from one of her guards. "Go no farther or my men will kill you!"

Giovanni came to a halt, but her guards no longer tried to approach him. The flames churned out, swirling and pulsing along the ground, reaching up the steps and curling around the legs of each vampire who screamed and fell away.

Livia's eyes narrowed. "If you do this, you will kill everyone in this room. Including your precious wife and friends."

Just then, the sound of the wind grew still. The room was utterly silent, and Giovanni knew that Beatrice had pulled the water over them. They were protected.

His mouth turned up at the corner, and Livia's eyes widened in terror as she loosed a feral scream. Giovanni whispered, "Enough."

Then he lifted his burning arms and released the fire.

CHAPTER 33

Beatrice had no idea how long she screamed, or how long the fire raged around them. The barrier of water she had erected held against the flames, just like he knew it would. The angry, red glow lit up the room and pressed against them as they huddled in their watery cocoon.

Was it minutes? Hours? Suddenly, the room blacked out.

She rose from her knees, lifted her arms, and brought a fall of water. It fell over and around them, rushing along the floors, pulling black ash from the room as the river returned to its course. Beatrice walked forward and surveyed the room that had been burnt beyond recognition. Slowly the river receded and floating just along the edge of the room was the pale form of her mate.

"Gio!"

She screamed and pulled the water back before he could be swept away. The river answered her and brought his body to her hands. She clutched his naked form; it was cold and limp in her arms. There was a rush of energy, then Tenzin and Carwyn stood at her side.

"God in Heaven," Carwyn breathed out.

"He's alive," Tenzin said. "How could he be alive?"

"No," Beatrice shook her head and pressed her hands to his temples. Every hair on Giovanni's body had burned away. His skin was smooth and unmarred, but he was cold. Colder than she had ever felt. "I can't feel him. I can't feel his mind. What's wrong? I can't feel him!" Her voice rose in hysteria.

"Shhh," Tenzin soothed her. "He must be alive. He is here. He is unmarked. He must be—"

A FALL OF WATER

"*I can't feel him!*" she screamed again, clutching him to her chest. She bit her wrist and held it to his lifeless lips. "Please. Please, Gio, please."

A drop of red blood fell into his mouth, but he did not move to swallow it. She pressed on his throat, willing him to taste her blood. His blood. The blood that ran between them. But there was nothing.

Beatrice rocked him in her arms as the surviving vampires crowded around them. She felt Carwyn's hand on her shoulder and flinched.

"Darling girl—"

"Get away! All of you!" She pulled Giovanni's body toward the scorched stone steps and held him close, still rocking him back and forth and whispering in his ear.

"Come back to me, Jacopo," she said. "Remember, you said you would always find me. I'm here, love. Come back to me. I need you to find me now."

She could feel the eyes of the room on her. She could see the worried stares of her friends, but she ignored them and placed a hand over his heart. "They don't understand. They don't know. I can feel your blood in me. It *hasn't* cried out, so I know you're still there. You just need to come back to me. They don't know. But you do. *Ubi amo; ibi patria.* Hundreds of years. Thousands of miles." She choked back her tears. "Pain. Loss. It's so clear to me now. You are my home. You just need to come back to me, Jacopo."

He didn't open his eyes. He didn't make a single movement. He lay still and cold and lifeless in her arms. But a faint hum of energy sparked under Beatrice's hands, and Giovanni's heart gave a single thump.

"Anything yet?"

"She's stayed with him all day, but no."

BEATRICE COULD HEAR THE WHISPERS OUTSIDE HER ROOM, BUT SHE IGNORED them.

"No movement at all?"

"She says she can feel his mind, and his amnis is a little stronger, but he hasn't moved or opened his eyes."

The sun rose in the sky, she could feel the pull of the moon, but Beatrice lay still and silent next to her husband, willing him to return to her. Willing him to heal from whatever black void had taken over his mind.

"Blood?"

"She's tried, but it just lies on his lips. She keeps trying to force it down his throat, but nothing."

Beatrice and Giovanni lay in their bedroom of the house in Rome as the city continued its maddening march.

A day.

A week.

Emil Conti was slowly pulling the immortals of Rome back from the madness of Livia's rule. The immediate and vocal support of Terrance Ramsay in London, Jean Desmarais in Marseilles, Oleg in Russia, and many other prominent immortal courts helped to ease the transition. Even more unexpected was the public support of the fabled Elders of Penglai Island.

"Any change?"

"No, and she told us to stop asking."

Lorenzo had disappeared again. This time, no one claimed to support him. Whatever connections he might have held, whatever sneaking influence he'd clung to, had been severed by the knowledge that the devious vampire had willingly supported Livia's quest for an elixir that could render even an ancient immortal helpless.

"She needs to drink. She hasn't fed in over a week."

"I know."

Ziri, Arosh, and Kato had disappeared as if their presence had been a dream. Though rumors of the ancients' appearance ran wild through Rome, the whole saga of Livia's defeat, and all that had led up to it, was quickly becoming more vague speculation than actual knowledge. Wild tales rose up, but the Roman noblewoman was no more. Dwelling in the past was useless. Emil Conti was the power in Rome, and despite the loss of his wife, he had quickly gathered a strong group of allies around him. There was no question who had control of the city.

"Anything?"

"I think we need to stop asking."

It was two weeks after Livia's defeat that Beatrice found herself standing in the kitchen, looking around blankly. She couldn't remember why she had come downstairs until the smell of a human reached her nose. She turned around with bared fangs.

"Whoa, B." Ben held up his hands, quickly walked to the refrigerator, and pulled out a bag of blood. He tossed it to her, and she caught it, biting into the thick plastic and sucking the cold bag dry. Ben watched her, then reached in and pulled out another.

"Looks like someone's hungry." He tossed her the second bag.

She bit into it, ignoring the stale taste of the preserved blood. It was enough to take the edge off.

Beatrice asked in a hoarse voice, "Where is everyone?"

Ben took a deep breath. "Most of us are... around. Jean took off back to France for political stuff. Gavin and Carwyn cooked up something to do with the last of the elixir, so Gavin's gone, but Carwyn stayed. And Angela's here, of course. Tenzin's even been staying here. All the family except for Dez and Matt. They're back at the hospital." She looked up in panic, but Ben was quick to continue. "The baby's *fine*, but Dez had some bleeding again, so they think they're going to do a C-section in the next couple of days. She's a few weeks early, but the doctors think the baby's big enough."

"Lucien?" she asked.

Ben's face fell. "He's in his room. It's not good. He's mostly just sleeping. Though, I guess since we know that Kato survived... There's still hope, you know?"

She nodded. "Okay. Good. Uh... you okay?"

He gave her a crooked smile. "Yeah. I'm good. Just been worried about you guys. Is there any... never mind."

She just shook her head. "No. Nothing so far. Everything's the same with him."

Beatrice turned when she heard a thump in the hall. "Who..."

Ben started toward the door. "It's early, but the sun's up; I thought everyone was asleep except for you."

Her eyes narrowed and her senses went on alert, but she could detect no unfamiliar scent. In fact, she thought she smelled Lucien, but he wouldn't be awake.

Then, she smelled the smoke.

She rushed toward the courtyard and pulled open the door, but reared back at the low light of dawn. No sunlight touched her, but she could still feel the agonizing heat from its glow.

Ben was right behind her. "What are you doing, B?"

"I think Lucien's in the courtyard!"

Ben's eyes grew wide. "Oh shit! I don't know if I can—"

"You have to drag him in. You *have* to!"

Ben ran into the courtyard while Beatrice held the door open, aching with the proximity of the light. Her skin wasn't burned yet, but she could feel the heat building. She heard a scuffling sound along with quiet curses, then Ben pulled a charred Lucien into the house, and Beatrice slammed the door shut.

His skin was blistered and smoking, and he clutched a letter to his chest.

"Ben, grab some blood from the fridge!"

Beatrice cradled him in her lap and rocked him back and forth. "Please, Lucien. Not you, too. I can't handle this. It's too much."

She saw his lips move and put her ear down to his charred lips.

"Rada," he whispered. "She is dead, Beatrice. The letter…"

She pulled the letter from his hand and smoothed it out. It was written in Bulgarian, and she could only read the date. It had been written the week before. She didn't try to stop the tears that fell down her face.

"Too much," he whispered. "I'm tired, B. I'm so tired."

She pressed a kiss to his blistered forehead and closed her eyes. "Please, Lucien, don't make me lose you. I'm so tired of losing."

Ben held out the bag of blood and Beatrice held it to his lips, mouthing the word '*Please*' again. Lucien's eyes held hers for a moment; then he closed them and bit. She watched as he forced down the blood she knew he didn't want. Lucien's eyes closed after a few moments, and he fell into a deep sleep.

Beatrice was just stirring to lift and take him back to his room when she felt the pulse of energy coming from outside the house. The hairs on the back of her neck rose, and she crouched over Lucien, immediately on alert.

The sun may have been rising in the sky, but her instincts told her there was an immortal only steps away. It was the oldest amnis she had ever felt. She looked at Ben, and she could tell he felt the strange energy, too. It hummed as if the very dust in the air vibrated. The scent of dark earth came to her nose. The smell of green and living things. Of soil and leaves. Moss and flowers. Her ears pricked at the sound of a light step in the courtyard.

Ben placed his hand on the knife he wore at his waist and walked to the door, but before he reached it, the door opened and a tall figure wearing a heavy cloak stepped through. It closed behind her, as if moved by an invisible hand. The stranger lifted her hands and pushed back the hood of her cloak as Beatrice gasped.

She was Saba. Beatrice knew it without question. She was earth and life. Her dark brown eyes were round and thickly lashed. Her black skin pulsed with energy, and her wide lips spread in a gentle smile. She was the most beautiful woman Beatrice had ever seen.

Beatrice couldn't stop the rush of joyful tears that came to her eyes as she looked up and whispered, "Mother."

Ben stepped back, even his weak human senses telling him that this was a creature of immense power. Saba stepped farther into the room and knelt down, placing a hand on Lucien's forehead.

"My son," she said. "My lovely child, what have you done?"

Beatrice was frozen as Saba gently lifted Lucien from her arms. The vampire rose and spoke to Ben. "Boy, you will show me where he may rest."

A FALL OF WATER

Ben looked at Beatrice, then back to Saba in confusion. "Um... yeah, okay. His room is up the stairs and down the hall."

Saba turned her eyes to Beatrice. "Daughter, you will follow me."

Beatrice rose without question, following them to Lucien's room where she saw Saba lay Lucien down on the bed before she came back to the door.

"Daughter, you will wait."

She shut the door, and Beatrice sat down in the hall just outside. Ben slid down to the floor next to her and asked, "B, who is that?"

"Saba," she whispered.

"How can she be out during the day? She wasn't burned at all."

Beatrice only shook her head. "Because she's Saba."

Ben frowned at her, then turned back to stare at the wall. Beatrice relaxed. For the first time in months, she felt complete and utter peace.

An hour or two later, Ben was slumped against her shoulder, napping. She heard the crack of the door; then Saba entered the hall. Beatrice quickly stood. Ben roused when his pillow moved and looked around, blinking like an owl. Saba smiled at him in amusement.

"Boy, you are faithful. Few know such strength so young. Go to sleep. Your time is not now."

Ben blinked again and stood up, stretching his lanky frame. He sniffed and rubbed his eyes. "Okay. B, you need me?"

She shook her head and placed a hand on his cheek. "Not right now. Go to bed, Ben."

He rubbed his eyes again, then turned and walked down the hall. Beatrice looked back at Saba, who was watching her.

"Daughter, where is your mate?"

Beatrice felt tears come to her eyes again, but she was not ashamed. Saba held out her hand and Beatrice took it, climbing the stairs to the third floor where Giovanni rested, cold and motionless in their bed.

The ancient healer entered the room and walked to him as Beatrice sat at the foot of the bed.

"Do you know what's wrong with him?"

Saba stroked his face and placed a hand at his temple. "He is tired."

Beatrice choked back a sob. "Will he wake up?"

"Do not be uneasy. He has earned this healing, Daughter."

Beatrice blinked and wiped the tears from her eyes as Saba sat next to Giovanni. She bit her wrist and held it to his lips. Immediately, he latched on and began to drink. Beatrice had to stifle a joyful laugh.

"How—"

"I use my power to make him drink."

"You can do that?"

Amusement colored the ancient's eyes. "Oh yes."

Beatrice stretched out next to him and put an arm around his waist, watching in fascination as Giovanni's lips moved. "I didn't think I would ever see him move again."

Saba's other hand stroked along her forehead. "Of course you will. I can feel your blood in him. Do not worry; he will come back to you, Daughter."

Beatrice stared up into her beautiful face. "Am I your daughter?"

"Of course you are."

"I've never had a mother."

The ancient smiled. "Now you do."

Beatrice watched Giovanni as he continued to drink from Saba's wrist. "Are you really the oldest of us?"

"I think so."

"Where do we come from, Mother?"

"Does it matter?"

"Yes," Beatrice whispered as she watched her mate. "It matters. The past matters."

She heard Saba draw a deep breath. "I have spent thousands of years searching for wisdom. I know enough now to know that I will never know everything."

"Does that mean you'll stop looking?"

She chuckled. "Of course not. And neither will you."

For the first time in weeks, she felt Giovanni's heart give a quiet thump. Saba withdrew her wrist, then paused, looking at Beatrice. She held it out. "Daughter, do you need to be healed?"

Beatrice looked at her, then at Giovanni. His amnis was faint, but it was slowly creeping over his skin. She put her hand to his neck and felt the warmth return. His green eyes flickered open for a second, met hers, then shut as he gave a great sigh and fell into sleep again.

Beatrice smiled. "You've already healed me."

Saba nodded with a smile. "I will rest with Lucien today. Your mate will wake at nightfall."

"Thank you, Mother."

She heard the door shut quietly, but she kept staring at Giovanni as the life returned to him. The warmth continued to spread over his skin. His hair, which had been completely burned off, began to grow before her eyes. First his eyelashes. His eyebrows. A faint stubble covered his jaw.

She felt an odd sensation under her fingertips and looked down. She couldn't stop the smile when she realized that Giovanni had chest hair, probably for the first time in five hundred years. She bit her lip, then laughed and buried her face in his neck. His scent wasn't exactly right, but his skin was warm. His amnis hummed, and she could feel the lively energy when she put her hands to his temples.

Beatrice laughed more. Then she curled into his side to wait until he rose.

When his eyes flickered open hours later, they immediately sought her own. She sat next to him, grinning down at his confused face.

"Where am I?" His voice was hoarse.

"At the house in Rome."

He kept blinking, looking around. A curl of hair fell into his eyes, and he frowned in confusion.

"What happened, Tesoro?"

Beatrice leaned down and brushed the hair from his forehead, tangling her fingers in the curls. She traced the shell of his ear before she pressed her lips to his in a gentle kiss. His arms reached up and held her to his chest, and Beatrice could feel the slow, steady beat of his heart.

"You found your way back to me, Jacopo. That's what happened."

CHAPTER 34

Crotone
Spring 1509

"What is your name?"

He looked up from tightening the fastenings on his leather jerkin. His father was standing at the door observing him as he dressed in the fine traveling clothes he'd been given. Tonight, he would leave the cold stone fortress. He was no longer Andros's student. He was his son. He no longer wore the clothes of a servant or the scraps of cloth he'd scrounged during his training. His jacket was richly embroidered, and his boots were made of the finest leather. His immortal body was strong and healthy. He had conquered the fire that burned within.

Andros stepped into the room and smiled at him. He asked again, "What is your name?"

The young vampire smiled back, amused by the old game his sire played. "Whatever I want it to be."

"Why?"

"Because I am superior to mortals."

Andros smiled at the rote answer and asked another question.

"Where is your home?"

"'*Ubi bene, ibi patria.*' Where I prosper is my home."

"Do not forget." Andros stepped close to him and put a hand on his cheek, smiling up at the child who towered over him. "Nothing endures, save us and the elements."

The young vampire smiled, feeling a surge of warmth for his sire. "I remember, Father."

Andros patted his cheek fondly before he stepped back and walked to the desk, paging through the books piled near his trunk. He carefully placed a few inside.

"You do need a name, though. You'll be introduced as my son, but the name you choose is up to you. You need something other than your mortal name. It was a peasant name, and you are a prince."

He ignored the old ache and pushed it aside. "I may choose it?"

"Of course." His father shrugged. "Haven't I taught you this? Your name is whatever you want it to be. Keep in mind that you will be introduced into the Roman court, so make sure it is something appropriate."

Andros began listing names. Aristocratic names. Fine names that would be acceptable for a rich merchant's son. A faint, human memory rose to his mind. The sweet burst of an apricot and the sound of trickling water in a stone fountain. He heard the buzz of bees in a summer garden and a woman's tinkling laugh.

"Giovanni! My Giovanni, sing me a song."

He could hear the echo in his mind. His uncle's lover teasing in a laughing voice before she was joined by another, who sang a childish tune. A song about a cricket that made a small boy giggle.

"Giovanni!" She laughed out his name. *"My love..."*

The young vampire blinked and looked up. His father was staring at him with calculating eyes.

"My name will be Giovanni," he said.

Crotone
December 2012

No one visited the cold stone building that jutted into the sea. Old women who passed by made the sign of the cross, and small children peeked at it from behind their parents' legs. Daring boys climbed the rocks that surrounded it to impress their friends, but no one ventured inside except a lone caretaker who visited the old fortress every few months. He slipped in silently then left after a few hours. The heavy locks that hung in the door were always in good repair.

Giovanni walked down the rocky path leading to his birthplace. The sound of the sea filled his ears, and the salt spray tickled his nose. It was a clear night, and the black outline of Andros's fortress rose ominously from the waves that rose and fell under the full moon. He walked to the front door, noting the broken lock, and pushed it open. Then he tucked his hands into the pockets of his overcoat and walked in.

He could feel the faint energy trace as soon as he entered. Giovanni took a deep breath and closed his eyes, then he followed the energy down the stone stairs. Down. Down. Until the damp walls around him pressed in and the haunting memories filled his mind. Childish voices seemed to echo off the walls.

"Paulo, give me back that book!"

He followed the hallway toward the ancient classroom, and he heard the mischievous laugh echo off the walls along with his steady footsteps.

"Cook says that I look like an angel."
"Then I congratulate you on your deception."
"She gave me a cake, too."
"Perhaps I need to speak more sweetly to Cook."

Giovanni turned the corner and passed by the room where his son had slumbered. He pushed it open, but he was not there.

"Will I ever be as tall as you?"
"I do not know. How tall was your father?"
"I never knew my father. I only remember Andros."

He entered the cold classroom to see his son's blond head bent over. Lorenzo was sitting in the center of the room, reading a book as the waves crashed against the stone walls.

Giovanni leaned against a stone pillar and watched him.

"What are you reading?"

Lorenzo looked up. "Virgil. *The Aeneid.* Book Four." He straightened his shoulders and lifted the book. "'But the queen, wounded by serious love, cherished the wound in her veins, and she was consumed by the hidden fire.'"

Giovanni stared at him. Lorenzo's face was gaunt. The shining blond hair he had always been so proud of was limp and hung around his face. His clothes were torn and stained with blood.

"She was so bitter with hate," his son said. "Maybe even more than me. It was easy to convince her that you had plotted to murder Andros."

"So you told her that I used amnis on you? That I used you to kill him."

"You *did* use me."

"You wanted him dead, too."

"I did." Lorenzo nodded. "I did. And she always hated you. I saw it even when you didn't. The way she looked at you when your back was turned. I knew it would not be difficult to fool her." A loud wave smacked the rocks outside.

Giovanni asked, "Did she know about the book? Did she ever really know the truth about the elixir?"

"I don't really know. She said that she did. When I went to her—after I knew what it was—she said that Andros had told her about it, but she thought it had been destroyed. She could have been lying. She was a good liar."

"But you knew?"

"Not at first. I only knew that Andros valued that book. It was one of the reasons I took the library. I heard him questioning Ziri once when we were in Rome. I was young, but I remembered the old vampire. After he was gone, I looked for the book that Andros was asking about. I didn't understand it. Not then, anyway."

"But you took it. You took it all."

"None of it would have been mine. All those years with him, and he would have given it all to you, his precious son."

Giovanni ignored the ache in his heart. "But you convinced Livia that she was included in his plan."

Lorenzo shrugged. "It wasn't hard. I played to her vanity. Told her Andros wanted them to rule the world together. With a weapon like the elixir, they could have subdued their enemies. In a few years, after the effects had taken hold, every immortal leader would have been under their thumb. Even the ancients."

Giovanni pulled a chair over and sat across from Lorenzo as the waves crashed up the walls. "It sounds like a plan Andros would have concocted. Nicely done."

Lorenzo cocked an eyebrow. "She's dead, of course. If you are here, then she is dead. She really was consumed by fire, wasn't she?"

"Yes."

"Good. I suppose that is good." Lorenzo sighed. "So all the secrets have come to light."

"Not all."

Lorenzo looked at him in surprise. "Not all?" Then he nodded. "Ah, the books. Of course, Andros's library."

"Where is it?"

His son shook his head and a bitter smile touched the corners of his lips. "Does your woman live, Father?"

"Yes."

"How happy you must be. You have everything now. You always did."

Giovanni's heart twisted in pain. "I did not kill her, Paulo. I did not kill your woman."

"It doesn't matter," he hissed.

"Yes, it does."

"No, it—"

"I drank from her, yes. But it was Andros who snapped her neck. He heard she carried your child."

He saw Lorenzo blink once before he spoke. His mouth opened, then closed again and he looked off into the distance, staring into the past.

"I had an irritating moment of clarity when we were in China," Lorenzo said. "Do you know what it was?"

"No."

"That infuriating Elder Lan asked me how many children I had sired."

"I remember."

Lorenzo looked up with a glare. "Do you know what my first thought was? *One.*"

Giovanni's hands clenched in old anger. "Serafina's child."

"I sired one child. Her child."

"Andros never would have allowed her to—"

"She asked me—the night before she died—she asked me to run away with her. To leave this place. I told her I had to think about it. I had to weigh my options."

Giovanni took a deep breath of the salty air. He could hear the waves growing louder. "Would you have?"

Lorenzo shrugged again. "I like to think that I might have. In my sentimental moments, I think I would have run away. Started a new life. A normal one with her as a wife, raising our child."

"That's—"

"But I doubt it." A sneer lifted his lip. "I have no illusions about who I am, Giovanni. Mortal or immortal. I am who I am. But you and Andros took the one thing that was *mine*. And I wanted revenge."

"So you killed him, and I sired you. How long would you have waited to kill me?"

"I don't know."

"After I was dead, would that have been enough?"

The bitter smile spread. "No."

"If Livia's plan had worked? If you had ruled the world with her?"

"Not enough."

"If you had forced Beatrice to take the elixir so she was your puppet. If you could have taken my lover as yours was taken from you... Enough?"

Lorenzo yelled, "It was never enough! *Nothing* could be enough!"

Giovanni shook his head. "Then you have been consumed by the fire just as Livia was."

Lorenzo said, "I won't tell you where the books are, Giovanni Vecchio. You figured out where I would be, you'll be able to find them, too. Why—why did you keep this horrid place?"

"Why did you come back?"

"Because I want to die."

Giovanni looked into Lorenzo's vacant blue eyes, and his son spoke again. "Aren't you going to kill me now?"

"No," he whispered. "I am too much at fault for what you became."

Lorenzo rolled his eyes. "So dramatic. I am a creature of my own making, *Papà*. Don't overestimate your influence. Tell the truth, why aren't you going to kill me?"

He took a deep breath and lifted his eyes over Lorenzo's shoulder.

"Because she is."

Giovanni had felt Beatrice enter the castle. She'd waited longer than he'd asked her to. Her elemental energy had filled the fortress, drawing the angry waves as he and his son had spoken. He knew Lorenzo had felt it, too. The amnis of an immortal as strong as his wife was unmistakable.

Lorenzo smirked, then tossed the book he'd held and darted down to grab his sword, which was tucked under the chair. He spun toward Beatrice and their blades clashed together.

His son was good with a blade, Giovanni thought as he watched them from the corner, trying not to intervene. But his wife was better.

Beatrice spun and twisted; the *shuang gou* she carried moved as if they were part of her own body. Sparks lit the dark room as they battled. Lorenzo ducked and darted around her, but Beatrice moved at a languid tempo as she parried with him. The room was utterly silent except for the sound of colliding metal. The two exchanged no useless chatter as they dueled.

She slid one blade down and swung it toward his legs, leaving a deep gash in his thigh. Lorenzo hissed and parried. He swung his blade up toward her face, but she only ducked away.

She was playing with him.

Her tempo slowly built, and he could see Lorenzo struggle to keep up. Even without the benefit of her element, she controlled the fight, forcing him around the room, pushing him into the corner.

"Because I want to die."

Even if it was true, when faced with a mortal adversary, Lorenzo was battling as if he wanted to live. Giovanni wondered whether he had changed his mind.

It didn't matter. Beatrice would have her revenge.

She looped one of the hooks of the *shuang gou* around his long hair and pulled, jerking him toward her and opening a gash on his neck as a chunk of his hair fell to the floor. The blood sprayed across the room, and Giovanni could detect the moment Lorenzo knew he was going to die.

A strange calm fell over his son's angry face, even as his sword reached up to block Beatrice. Sparks scattered across the floor as she lifted her blade again. She brought it down against his, and the sword flew from Lorenzo's hand.

He fell to his knees, weaponless, as Beatrice circled him. The tears streamed down her face as her blades ran around his neck, slowly deepening the bloody cut. She came to a halt in front of Lorenzo, and he lifted his brilliant blue eyes to hers. She crossed her swords at his neck, the hooks of the blade curling around the softest, most vulnerable part of his neck.

Giovanni could hear his son whisper as he looked into the face of his killer.

"Let it be enough," Lorenzo said.

Beatrice pulled back her arms, and the curved blades caught his neck, slicing off Lorenzo's head in one smooth stroke. Giovanni felt the sharp ache pierce his heart as the son of his blood fell to the ground, crumbled into a lifeless heap. He was frozen for a moment until he heard her sobs.

His mate dropped her swords and stared at the body of her enemy. At her father's murderer. The vampire who had thrown her world into chaos. Then, Beatrice pulled her foot back and began to kick.

She sobbed as she struck him, screaming into the silent room and stomping on Lorenzo's body over and over again, mashing it to a bloody pulp. Giovanni ran from the corner of the room and pulled her away, so she turned on him, striking his chest as she continued to scream.

"Let it be enough!" he whispered, pulling her close so that her fists could not strike. She sobbed into his neck until—finally—she wrapped her arms around her mate and let out a deep breath, exhausted by her rage.

He closed his eyes and whispered again, "Let it be enough, Beatrice."

Her rasping breath echoed off the walls of the cold chamber. The waves still bashed against the rocks outside. But her racing heart slowed as her anger turned to grief, and she let him hold and comfort her as she wept.

Giovanni kept whispering as he stared at the broken body of the child he had sired five hundred years before. Lorenzo's eyes stared from the corner, and a bitter smile was frozen on his face.

"Let it be enough, Tesoro. It has to be enough."

CHAPTER 35

Outside Florence

Beatrice arched her back as she moved over him, and her eyes caught the skylight they'd uncovered at dusk. A thousand brilliant stars shone over her head as his warm hands stroked over her shoulders, cupped her breasts, then trailed down her body until he grasped her hips in his hands. He groaned in pleasure and rose up, kissing along her collar as her hands tangled in his hair. The amnis sparked between them wherever their skin touched, and their pleasure built as they slowly made love.

His hands trailed down her spine, teasing the small of her back as his mouth met hers and his tongue traced her lips. Then he flipped her over so she was under his body. Beatrice smiled as she wrapped her hands around his wrists, and they moved in ancient rhythm.

Rise and fall. Push and pull. When she felt the wave lift her, she looked into her husband's eyes. Her mouth opened, and a soft breath escaped her lips. Giovanni leaned down and captured the small exhalation of pleasure before he pulled back, rocking into her faster as his eyes darkened in desire.

The wave crested and she pulled him closer. He reached down to lift her up and press their bodies together in one, final thrust before his back arched and he cried out in release. Then he leaned down and pressed his lips to hers in a long, luxurious kiss.

She rolled them on their side, and his fingers reached up, tracing the line of her nose. Her chin. The curve of her eyebrow. She smiled and looked at him from the corner of her eye.

"You're staring at me," she whispered.

"Yes."

"Why?"

"Because you are beautiful, and I like to look at you."

She grinned and turned to face him. "Then I guess I can stare at you, too."

Giovanni smiled. "You are allowed."

"Bet your ass, I am."

They laughed quietly, enjoying the peace of the house. Giovanni's home in Florence reminded her of his home in Cochamó with a few major exceptions. One, it was huge. An estate more than a home. It was in the country and one wing of the house had no electricity, which made it easier for Beatrice to rest. She had even been sleeping a little more, which was nice.

It was surrounded by an olive grove, so it was private; she could see them spending many, many months there in the years ahead, enjoying the isolation and the quiet hills. She sighed in contentment, and Giovanni stroked her skin, tracing the small scars where he had marked her years before when she was still human. Her fangs dropped when she heard his low growl, and her hunger began to rise again.

Just then, a sharp cry pierced the silence of the room.

"What did you do?"

There was a clatter in the living room below them.

"Nothing!"

"Well, you must have done something. She wasn't crying before."

"Tenzin, I was just sitting here, and the baby started crying. I didn't do anything."

"Well, I didn't do anything, either. I was just looking at her. She's not a drooler. That's good."

"Well, how do we get her to stop crying? It's gonna wake Dez up."

More footsteps came from below them. "Oh there, precious girl. Let me have you." Carwyn's deep voice rose as the baby's cry grew desperate. "Why didn't one of you try picking her up instead of squawking about whose fault it is?"

"I don't know what to do with babies! I'd probably break her."

Tenzin's voice replied, "That is not my child."

"Shhh." The vampire soothed the baby, whose cries began to die off. "There you are, Carina. No more crying, love. Uncle Carwyn is here, and he isn't a bleeding idiot."

"Hey!"

Matt's voice came from a distance, whispering down the hall. "Hey, Carwyn, is the baby hungry?"

"I don't think so. Let Dez sleep. I think she just woke up and realized she wasn't by her *mam*."

Matt's voice drew nearer. "I appreciate you guys helping out, but should I—"

"No, no." Carwyn interrupted. "She's *fine*. See? She's falling right back to sleep. Let Dez rest a bit. I'll call you if she starts to fuss again."

The baby's cries had turned into pleasant gurgles, and Beatrice smiled when she heard the low hum of activity level out. Carwyn sang a lullaby to the baby. Matt returned to sleep. Tenzin and Ben wandered off to a different part of the house, probably to start another fight. She turned when she heard Giovanni's low laugh.

"What?"

He shook his head. "Our friend is singing a drinking song to that child."

Beatrice couldn't contain her smile. "Well, it's a very *soothing* drinking song. Besides, probably better that she gets used to him now."

He only closed his eyes as his shoulders shook with silent laughter.

"I mean," Beatrice continued, "that baby's going to have the most messed up sleep schedule in history with all these vampires doting on her."

"Carwyn does indulge the child."

"You're just as bad! I saw you reading her a book at two in the morning the other night. Isn't she supposed to be sleeping at that hour?"

"*The Runaway Bunny* is a classic of children's literature, and an allegory of unexpected depth."

"Sucker."

He couldn't hide the smile. "It's not a... conventional family."

"But it *is* ours." She grinned and tucked her head under his chin as he wrapped his arms around her. "And conventional is boring."

"It is. Though... perhaps we could use some boring."

"Maybe just a little."

By the time they'd returned from Crotone, Saba had disappeared, taking Lucien with her. If anyone could cure the vampire, it would be Saba. Giovanni appeared to hold no lingering effects from the strange coma that had held him for weeks, except a deeper sense of peace and contentment than Beatrice had ever seen from him. He no longer struggled to control the fire within him. It was always there, bubbling under the surface, but the tension, the ever-present stress of it no longer seemed to affect him.

He was finally at peace.

As was Beatrice... as much as she could be. The wound from the loss of her father, from the loss of their friends and allies could only heal in time. But they had time. And though the cost of the battle had taken its toll on all of them, when Matt and Dez brought home their tiny daughter, the whole household seemed to heave a collective sigh as they looked to the future instead of dwelling in the past.

Only one mystery remained.

Beatrice lifted a hand to stroke along Giovanni's cheek. "We should get ready."

"What time is our appointment?"

"Ten o'clock."

"Yes, we should leave soon. It's a bit of a drive."

Citta di Castello
Perugia, Italy

WHEN THEY PULLED THROUGH THE GATES OF THE ISOLATED COUNTRY HOUSE, Beatrice noticed the glowing lights that welcomed them. It was a large home, and when she had called the number listed, the curator did not seem surprised by her request for evening hours. The polite woman had simply asked for their names, put her on hold for a moment, then asked when they would like to make their appointment. She would be at their disposal.

The front door opened, and an attractive woman wearing long slacks and a blouse waited for them to exit the car. She had curling brown hair and a friendly expression. Her name, records indicated, was Serafina Rossi. She was thirty-six, and a graduate of the University of Ferrara. She had worked for Lorenzo for ten years.

"How long had he owned this?" Giovanni asked quietly.

"The house was built about two hundred years ago, but the renovations were done just before he hired the curator. So about ten years or so."

"A few hours from one of my own homes," he mused before he stepped out of the car. "A few hours..."

The curator stepped forward and greeted them in Italian. "Dottor Vecchio, Signora De Novo, it is a pleasure to meet you both. I am Signorina Fina Rossi, welcome to the collection."

"Thank you so much for meeting with us," Beatrice answered. "I know it's late."

"Oh," she waved a hand. "We are accustomed to unusual hours here."

"Signor Bianchi would visit frequently?" Giovanni asked.

"Not frequently. He often traveled out of the country." She smiled. "Occasionally. But I always enjoyed his visits."

"I see."

"Signor Bianchi gave me your name, Dottore." Her eyes flickered. "He said that if anything were to ever happen to him, that I should contact you. Were you a relative of some kind? Has something happened?"

Beatrice looked into the woman's eyes. She didn't appear to be under the influence of any kind of amnis, but at the same time, her cautious expression told Beatrice she knew her employer was something other than what he seemed.

Nevertheless, she appeared honest and forthright as she spoke with Giovanni about the collection. Her husband broke the news to Signorina Rossi that her employer was no longer living.

The single home belonging to Paulo Bianchi had been buried in Lorenzo's files. It wasn't particularly noteworthy. A large country home in the province of Perugia. A weekly caretaker and a single employee who lived in the cottage on the grounds and received a generous, but not extraordinary, salary. In their search for Lorenzo's more illicit investments, the mundane had simply escaped their notice.

A shout drew their attention to the small cottage at the side of the house.

"*Mama?*" A small boy of nine or ten appeared in pajamas. A cloud of light brown curls covered his head and he blinked as he looked up at them from the open doorway. "*Chi e qui?* Has Signor Paulo come to visit?"

Signorina Rossi gave him a sad smile. "No, Enzo, we have other visitors. Go back to sleep; I'll be with the books if you need me."

The boy waved once more, then turned and went back in the house, closing the door behind him. Signorina Rossi gave them a sad shrug. "I will have to tell him tomorrow. Signor Paulo was a favorite of his. He would usually visit with Enzo when he came to see the books."

Beatrice frowned, curious if there were more humans on the property. "His father?"

The woman gaped. "Oh! No, no. Paulo was just a friend. Enzo's father... well, when Signor Bianchi gave me this position after university, it was very unexpected. A godsend, really. Not many employers would be so understanding about a single mother bringing a baby to work."

Beatrice glanced over at Giovanni, whose face was carefully covered by a polite mask. "Signorina Rossi, we don't want to keep you any later than necessary. If you would only show us—"

"Of course. I'm sure your time is limited. Though you may stay in the collection as long as you like, of course. I'll show you how to lock up. If Signor Bianchi trusted you, you are most welcome."

She ushered them in the door and Beatrice breathed in the cool, dry air that was so familiar and welcome. The smell of old paper and ink assaulted her. Vellum and the faint must it always held. The curious vanilla smell of old books and dusty covers. She looked around in awe.

Though there was an entryway of sorts, and she could see a small office to one side, the house had been renovated into a vast library. The vaulted ceilings sheltered row after row of dark, wooden bookcases and the arched windows were covered in smoked glass to protect the room from the harsh light that would shine through during the day. Signorina Rossi guided them through the room.

"In my ten years, I've had the privilege of curating the collection here. We rarely have visitors, though I do coordinate the loan of some materials to private institutions and universities. Most of the collection is private. I will confess, I almost feel guilty that many of these items are not in a museum, but that is not my decision, of course."

She guided them among glass cases, which displayed pieces of the collection. Beatrice grabbed Giovanni's hand and felt him clutch her fingers tightly as they walked among the treasures.

A finely preserved Asian scroll with red lacquer finish. Papyrus leaves pressed between clear protective sheets. A vividly decorated manuscript of intricate Arabic script that glowed with gold-flecked illuminations. A collection of small clay tablets marked by tiny cuneiform writing.

"Most of my time is spent organizing the collection. It was not in any order when I was first hired, and I am still organizing parts of it. It keeps me very busy!" Dottor Rossi laughed before she turned. As if she could sense the waves of emotion around her, the librarian halted and fell silent. Her eyes widened and she took a deep breath. "I'm sure you would prefer to examine it at your leisure. I'll leave you here. If you have any questions, please feel free to knock on my office door, but I will allow you your privacy."

Giovanni was silent, but Beatrice stepped forward and took the woman's hand, shaking it and sending a subtle message for the woman to go to her home and leave the key on the desk near the door. The friendly curator smiled and nodded before she left, and Beatrice waited until the door swung shut to turn to her husband.

He was overcome, and Beatrice was rocked by conflicting emotions when he pulled her into his chest. Sorrow. Joy. Relief. Anguish. Even pride. Giovanni looked around at the books that had caused so many trials and so much pain. A mystery that had brought them both the greatest joy and the deepest suffering.

"Beatrice..." He could not seem to form the words, so he held her hand and wandered among the rows of bookcases, stopping occasionally to open a manuscript box or scan the stacks.

Beatrice said, "This collection... Gio, it's priceless."

"She's right," he mused. "Most of this needs to be put into larger libraries or museums."

"But not all at once."

"No, not all at once."

He looked around at the collected treasures of his sire. Of his grand-sire. Centuries of wisdom hidden away from sight. They strolled among the lost books, and she could see him breathing in their scents. They would donate the most valuable pieces so the world could share them. Slowly, over many years, Andros' collection would belong to the world again. They had time.

Just then, a familiar volume caught her eye. Sitting unobtrusively on a shelf across the room, it was tucked among the others, but the scent of her father's blood marked the worn leather cover. She dropped Giovanni's hand and walked toward it. Then she reached over, picked up Geber's manuscript, and clutched it to her chest. Giovanni approached her from behind and placed his arms around her waist as the tears fell.

"Do you want to destroy it, Tesoro?"

She shook her head and patted her eyes with the handkerchief he held out for her. "It's just a book, Gio. It's just a book. It's not a secret anymore. It can't hurt us."

He reached around and plucked the small book from her hands, placing it on the table before he turned her and enfolded her in an embrace.

"That one goes home with us."

"Yeah," she sighed and buried her face in his neck. "Good idea."

After a few minutes, they parted to continue exploring. The library was arranged around a central reading area containing sturdy wooden tables and chairs, which was lined with glass display cases. Leading away from the reading tables, there was a long corridor down the center of the room, and two rows of bookcases lined either side. Small benches were placed at intervals, but the corridor was cloaked in darkness.

Beatrice looked for a light switch and spotted one on the far wall. She flicked it on with a pencil that lay on one of the library tables, and her eyes darted toward the single glowing light that lit the back wall.

"What is it?" she asked, blinking into the brilliant glow.

Giovanni's voice was soft when he answered. "San Lorenzo protecting the Holy Chalice."

An enormous stained glass window covered the back wall. Large and intricate, the yellow light shone from behind as if the window was lit by the afternoon sun. The scattered rainbow of colors dripped down the center aisle and Beatrice walked toward the light as Giovanni followed behind her. On the far wall, under the vivid stained glass, was a brass plaque with a Latin inscription.

Beatrice stepped closer to read it. "There's a quote here."

Desine iam tandem precibusque inflectere nostris,
   Ne te tantus edit tacitam dolor et mihi curae
   Saepe tuo dulci tristes ex ore recursent.
   Uentum ad supremum est.

"What is it?" Giovanni asked.

"It's from Virgil. The last book of *The Aeneid*."

His voice was soft. "What passage?"

"It's when Juno and Jupiter are making peace in the end. 'Now cease, at last, and give way to my entreaties, lest such sadness consume you in silence, and your bitter woes stream back to me often from your sweet lips.'" She paused, blinking back the tears as she read the final line. "'It has reached its end.'"

Beatrice heard him gasp, and she spun around. Giovanni's jaw was clenched tightly, and he was staring up at the window. She could feel his energy reach out toward hers as he held out his hand. She walked over and his arms encircled her. She closed her eyes and held him tight.

"Has this reached its end, Gio? Even after all the evil, he did some good, too. So much lost, but so much gained. We found each other. The past is gone, and no one can take our future. You asked me once to let it be enough." She nodded and pressed her cheek against his chest. "It is. For me, it is enough."

Giovanni pulled back and cupped her face in his hands. His eyes searched hers before he nodded. Then he leaned down and pressed a kiss to her mouth. "Yes, Beatrice, it is enough," he whispered before he kissed her again. "It is enough."

The light behind the stained glass glowed brightly, a reminder of all they had searched for and all they had found. Beatrice pressed her cheek against Giovanni's as they embraced, and she could feel their hearts beat together in a slow, steady rhythm. The two lovers held each other as the light poured over them, and everything was illuminated.

Follow further adventures in the Elemental series in all new stories featuring Carwyn, Baojia, Murphy, and Lucien in the Elemental World series, now available at all major retailers in e-book, audiobook, and paperback!

FIVE YEARS LATER

It was late Saturday night when Ben strode through the kitchen door. He put his motorcycle helmet on the kitchen table and tossed his backpack on the floor. Then he opened the refrigerator to grab a beer before he listened for who was around.

The only sound of life was the television in the study. It sounded like someone was watching an old kung fu movie with the volume turned low. The corner of his mouth turned up, and he walked down the hallway toward the noise. Tenzin sat on the couch frowning as she watched the screen. She didn't even glance at him.

"These movies are horrible," she said.

"Then why do you keep watching them?"

"I don't know."

She fell silent for a few more minutes.

"Are you done with your tests at school?" she asked, still staring at the screen.

"Yep."

"So you are done with the human schools?"

"For now."

"Good."

Ben propped his feet on the coffee table and looked around at the familiar room. He took a drink and stared at the screen. Then he looked at the small woman sitting next to him on the couch.

"Tenzin?"

"Yes?"

FIVE YEARS LATER

"I'm bored."
She turned from the television, and he smiled at the gleam in her eyes.
"Me, too."

※

You can follow Ben and Tenzin's new adventures in the Elemental Legacy series, now available in e-book and paperback from all major retailers.

ACKNOWLEDGMENTS

This special edition is dedicated to the many readers who have made this fictional universe such a fun place to write.

Special thanks to the pre-readers who keep me accountable and coherent, who make me a better writer, and who listen to my whining when I'm feeling insecure. They also ply me with wine, avocados, and sometimes chocolate so I will keep writing. Since we all benefit from this bribery, I'll call them out by name. (And I'll probably miss someone, so if it's YOU, you'll get the next manuscript first before anyone else gets a chance to see it.)

And so, I offer my many thanks to the excellent Kristine M. Todd, Kelli Good, Lindsay Mason, Sarah Reeder, Sandra Tuleja, C. S. Starr, Genevieve Johnson, Paulette Melton, Nichole Chase, and Molly Wetta. All of you have contributed to all or some of the books in some way that has helped me so much. You all have different strengths, and I am a richer writer for having your eyes, your brains, and your hearts part of my first series of books. Thank you.

My editor for all four of the Elemental Mysteries was Amy Eye, of the Eyes for Editing. I cannot thank her enough for her professionalism, flexibility, and dedication. My books are better for her excellent touch and she and my proofreader, Cassie McCown taught me so much.

I want to thank the amazing artists at Damonza.com for their wonderful work on the new cover art. I am so pleased to be working with them. Their vision is exceptional.

And thanks, always, to my family. You are God's gift to me, and you keep me sane. Thank you.

ABOUT THE AUTHOR

ELIZABETH HUNTER is a *USA Today* and international best-selling author of romance, contemporary fantasy, and paranormal mystery. Based in Central California, she travels extensively to write fantasy fiction exploring world mythologies, history, and the universal bonds of love, friendship, and family. She has published over thirty works of fiction and sold over a million books worldwide. She is the author of Love Stories on 7th and Main, the Elemental Legacy series, the Irin Chronicles, the Cambio Springs Mysteries, and other works of fiction.

ElizabethHunterWrites.com

ALSO BY ELIZABETH HUNTER

<u>The Elemental Mysteries</u>
A Hidden Fire
This Same Earth
The Force of Wind
A Fall of Water
The Stars Afire

<u>The Elemental World</u>
Building From Ashes
Waterlocked
Blood and Sand
The Bronze Blade
The Scarlet Deep
A Very Proper Monster
A Stone-Kissed Sea
Valley of the Shadow

<u>The Elemental Legacy</u>
Shadows and Gold
Imitation and Alchemy
Omens and Artifacts
Obsidian's Edge
(*novella anthology*)
Midnight Labyrinth
Blood Apprentice
The Devil and the Dancer
Night's Reckoning
Dawn Caravan
The Bone Scroll

The Elemental Covenant
Saint's Passage

Martyr's Promise

Paladin's Kiss

(Summer 2022)

The Irin Chronicles

The Scribe

The Singer

The Secret

The Staff and the Blade

The Silent

The Storm

The Seeker

Glimmer Lake Series

Suddenly Psychic

Semi-Psychic Life

Psychic Dreams

The Cambio Springs Series

Long Ride Home

Shifting Dreams

Five Mornings

Desert Bound

Waking Hearts

Dust Born

(Newsletter Serial)

Contemporary Romance

The Genius and the Muse

7th and Main

INK

HOOKED

GRIT

Sweet

Linx & Bogie Mysteries

A Ghost in the Glamour

A Bogie in the Boat